THREE GREAT NOVELS
Liverpool Sagas

Also by Maureen Lee

The Pearl Street Series
Lights out Liverpool
Put out the Fires
Through the Storm

The Girl from Barefoot House
Laceys of Liverpool
The House by Princes Park
Lime Street Blues

Maureen Lee

Three Great Novels: Liverpool Sagas

Stepping Stones
Liverpool Annie
Dancing in the Dark

ORION

First published in Great Britain in 2003 by Orion,
an imprint of the Orion Publishing Group Ltd.

A CIP catalogue record for this book is available
from the British Library.

ISBN 0 75285 644 8

Typeset at The Spartan Press Ltd,
Lymington, Hants

Printed in Great Britain by
Clays Ltd, St Ives plc

The Orion Publishing Group Ltd
Orion House
5 Upper Saint Martin's Lane
London WC2H 9EA

Contents

Stepping Stones

For Richard

Chaucer Street

1

It was still and deathly quiet one April night in the year 1931 in a place called Bootle in Liverpool. Cramped terraced houses, row after regimented row, were bathed in the clear, unearthly glow of a brilliant moon. Windows gleamed dully, front doors were firmly closed.

Not a soul was to be seen.

The cobbled streets, which shone like ribbons of polished lead between each row of houses, had a virginal, untrodden look. There was an air of emptiness, desertion – no sign at all of the overflowing hordes of human beings who dwelt within these two-up, two-down homes. Parents, children, babies, sometimes all crowded into one small bedroom with perhaps a grandparent sharing a room with the older children and unmarried or widowed aunts and uncles, orphaned cousins, often spilling out into the parlour downstairs to sleep on made-up beds or overstuffed sofas.

None of these people knew of the vivid, almost startling moonlight which bathed their homes and their streets, and even if they had, they would not have cared. They were too preoccupied with sleeping off the exhaustion of the previous day and preparing themselves for the next.

The men, the ones who had jobs, put in ten or more gruelling, back-breaking hours on the docks or in blackened, evil-smelling factories where the noise of pounding machinery near split their eardrums, and sparks attacked their eyes and smoke their lungs. Some of the women worked in the same factories, just as hard, but for even less money than their menfolk.

The women had to be up earlier than the men. At the crack of dawn they'd come down to their cold kitchens and put a match to the rolled-up paper and firewood laid on last night's raked-out cinders and then carefully put the coal on, piece by piece, until the fire caught and was hot enough to take the kettle for the first cup of tea of the day and a pan of water for washing.

Just beyond the houses ran the River Mersey, and that night it gleamed a dull and blackish-silver over which the silhouettes of great tall cranes loomed, brooding, waiting like carrion-crows to pounce on any unsuspecting person who might emerge from the neat forest of stiff, silent houses.

Low and fat, tall and thin, the funnels of the ships stood sentinel, bellies half-empty or half-full, waiting for the weary men to come and on-load or off-load their cargoes, and now the hulls could be seen gently moving to and fro in rhythm with the lapping tide.

Suddenly, the air of Chaucer Street was rent by a fearful scream.

In Number 2, Kitty O'Brien was about to give birth to her ninth child.

Three of these children were dead, their births occurring at a late and dangerous stage of pregnancy – not because her once-healthy body had difficulty in bearing children but because her husband Tom had beaten her so severely he'd brought on a premature delivery. Kitty was twenty-eight years old.

She'd been trying to hold the scream back, thinking of the children asleep upstairs, feared of waking them, of frightening them. Kitty would have laid down her life for her children.

But the scream couldn't be contained. It burst forth from her throat like water through a broken dam.

'Oh dear God, the pain! Dear God in heaven, make it stop! Make the pain stop!' These words were not spoken aloud, just in Kitty's head. With an effort, she turned her head to see the crucifix hanging over the mantelpiece and the statue of Our Lady which stood underneath.

'Holy Mary, Mother of God, make the pain stop!' She screamed again as an agonising spasm of hurt engulfed her body.

'That's right, luv. Let it go. Yell all yer like.'

Theresa Garrett, stout and tall, grey hair in steely waves under a thick net, surveyed the torn mess of Kitty O'Brien's female organs. Mrs Garrett was not a trained nurse. She'd never been inside a hospital except as a visitor, but she was the acknowledged midwife for the area that included Chaucer Street. As long as there were no complications, she would come and deliver a baby for anyone who asked, at any time of day or night, as competently as any doctor.

She was not fit to deliver Kitty O'Brien and Mrs Garrett was only too well aware of it. Every time the poor woman gave birth, she ripped herself open again and the tears were never repaired. Mrs Garrett couldn't sew her up. Kitty refused to leave her children to go into hospital and that pig of a husband wouldn't part with a penny to pay for a doctor to come and see to his wife.

Tom was upstairs now, sleeping off his ale. It had been six-year-old Kevin who'd come to Mrs Garrett's Southey Street home to say his mother had begun having the pains.

There was no charge for Mrs Garrett's services, but afterwards, when they were able, people would come round with a small luxury – a home-baked bunloaf, ten good cigarettes or a bag of fruit. She knew Kitty O'Brien would never be able to give something which cost money, but one day she would appear with a crocheted collar, knitted gloves or an embroidered doily made from bits and pieces salvaged from the clothes and bedding given her by the Sisters of the Convent of St Anne. Indeed, in her pocket at that very moment was one of Kitty's handkerchiefs, neatly hemmed and with a rose embroidered in one corner. The material had probably come from an old worn bolster or pillowcase, the silk for the flower carefully unpicked. That was for bringing Rory into the world five years ago. The midwife valued these little gifts more than most others, in her mind's eye imagining Kitty in a rare quiet moment, stitching away, screwing up her eyes to see in the dim gaslight.

Her rather grim features softened as she knelt beside the small heaving body. There was no bed in the house free for Kitty to give birth in. She lay on coarse blankets on the floor in front of the dying kitchen fire.

Mrs Garrett's experienced eye told her it was time for the woman to push. 'Come along, luv. A good shove now and it'll all be over.'

A neighbour, Mary Plunkett, hovered in the back kitchen doorway, waiting for something to do. Pots of steaming water stood on the hearth ready for use.

The baby's head appeared. Dark hair – that was a change. So far, all Kitty's babies had been blond like their father.

Kitty screamed again. 'Dear Jesus, help me,' she whispered.

Upstairs, several childish voices shouted in alarm: 'Mam? Mam?' And twelve-month-old Jimmie began to cry.

Glad to be useful, Mary Plunkett went up to quieten them.

'Nearly done now, luv, just one more shove.'

Mrs Garrett could see the baby's face. Oh yes, a dark one this. Suddenly, the entire body was expelled, taking the midwife by surprise. 'Lord, you're in a hurry,' she said in alarm. There was a slight pause before she added, 'It's a girl, Kitty, a lovely dark lass.'

She shouted upstairs, 'Mary, tell the boys they've got a little sister and then come down and give me a hand.'

Minutes later, Mrs Plunkett put an arm round Kitty's shoulders, lifting her slightly onto a second pillow, so that the mother could glimpse her first-born daughter.

Through a blur of thankfully-receding pain, Kitty saw the long smooth body of her new baby, the sleek hair. She heard the first cry, a sound she'd always found ominous. It seemed to her a signal of suffering to come, rather than an amen for suffering just ended; a heralding of broken nights, teething pains and colic.

She saw Mrs Garrett cut the cord with her large silver scissors and hand the baby to Mary to wash. But what Kitty was expecting to happen, didn't. She thought the colour of the baby's skin would change with the washing. Wasn't it the blood or the afterbirth that made the satiny skin look so dark? But no, the faint fawnish colour remained.

Kitty's heart began to beat so loud and so strong it seemed the very floor took up the sound and made the entire house throb. She felt herself go dizzy. A prayer, even more fervent than the unspoken pleas made during the excruciating birth, pounded through her brain: '*Please God, make me die. Holy Mary, make me die this minute.*'

'Here, what's the matter with her?' Alarmed, Mary Plunkett placed the baby in the laundry basket which had served as a cot for all the O'Brien children, and came over to mop Kitty's brow with a wet cloth. 'I think she's got a fever or somethin'. She's sweatin' like a pig.'

Mrs Garrett, gently cleaning Kitty with disinfectant, felt her pulse. 'It's racing,' she said worriedly.

'Should we get the doctor?'

'No, he'll expect to be paid.'

'The ambulance, then?'

'Give her ten minutes. Perhaps she'd like a cup of tea.'

A cup of tea! Kitty heard the words from far away. A cup of tea would cure everything. A cup of tea would turn the baby's skin white. Anyway, it seemed she wasn't going to die. Neither God nor Our Lady were going to answer her prayers. She wondered why neither of the other women were shocked by the baby's colour. 'A lovely dark lass,' Theresa Garrett had said calmly, even admiringly.

Almost as if she'd been reading Kitty's thoughts, Mary Plunkett, who was pouring tea into three chipped cups, glanced towards the baby and remarked, 'Isn't she just the colour of Eileen Donaghue's Marian? Wasn't she one o' yours, Mrs Garrett?'

'That's right,' said the midwife, carefully patting Kitty dry with the torn remnants of an old sheet, brought with her. 'Marian must be twelve or more by now. And d'you know Molly Doyle of Byron Street? All her little ones are dark like that. It's the Celtic streak, you know. Like a tribe of little Indians they are.'

'Well, it'll make a change,' mused Mary. 'A small dark sister for five big blond brothers.'

Kitty relaxed. Her body literally sagged with relief. So it was all right. It was quite normal for an Irish baby to be so dark-skinned . . .

The old armchair was brought over – Tom's chair – and Kitty was lifted and tucked up inside it, then Mary handed her a cup of tea. Despite the nagging ache in her gut and her feeling of total exhaustion, the new mother felt warm and comfortable basking in the rarely-afforded attention to her sole comfort.

It was only when a new baby was born that there was a day or two's respite from never-ending housework. Tomorrow, Mary Plunkett would come in again to help and her other neighbours would see the older boys, Kevin and Rory, got to school and they'd look after Tony and Chris and the baby, Jimmie – though he was no longer the baby now she had this new one, this little dark daughter.

The neighbours would also make Tom's tea and his butties for work, but they had their own families to care for and in a few days Kitty would have to look after her ever-increasing family by herself. Jimmie had only just been weaned. Now there was another one to feed and it meant three of her children were under the age of two.

She looked across at the new arrival. Such a pretty baby, sleeping peacefully, long sooty lashes resting on unwrinkled olive cheeks. Celtic streak? Oh, no! Kitty knew, though she would never be able to prove it – not that she would ever, in her whole life, *want* to prove it, it would be her secret forever and ever, amen – but Kitty knew this baby's father was not the beast upstairs. It was not Tom O'Brien, whom she could hear snoring away in the great soft bed where he used and abused her nightly.

No, this baby's father was someone else altogether.

Kitty remembered the night, almost exactly nine months ago. It had been a Thursday and there was no money left, not a penny, and nothing due till the next night when Tom came home with his wages. He was out at the pub, enough in his own pocket for a drink or two, whilst at home his children went hungry and the larder was empty, not even a stale crust left.

'I'm hungry, Mam.'

'What's for tea, Mam?'

Little desperate voices. Her children, asking their mam for food, and the baby whingeing away at her empty, sagging breast. No milk, for she'd had nothing herself that day but water. Four little faces looking up at her accusingly. A crying baby, chewing at her. She was their mam and she couldn't feed them and there was no prospect of feeding them till the next night.

Everything fit to be pawned had long since gone. All the wedding presents. The clock from her family in Ireland, the teaset from Tom's. She'd never had the money to redeem them. The tatty bedding was worthless, the furniture junk. Nothing left to pawn or sell.

Of course she could call on her neighbours – throw herself on their mercy. And they would rally round. They always did. Someone would go from house to house till they'd collected enough food to see the family through the night. No matter how short they were themselves, they wouldn't see her starve. She'd given food herself before, raided the contents of her meagre larder when another family was in need. They shared each other's bad fortune and good fortune, though the latter was rare, but when Joey Mahon won money on the football pools, he'd thrown a street party for the children and they'd had jelly with hundreds and thousands on it and real tinned cream.

But it seemed to Kitty – in fact she knew it was the case – that she had to seek her neighbours' help more often than anybody else. She didn't know another woman whose husband kept his family as short of money as Tom did his. Why, she thought with shame, should these other women's men have to work to keep *her* children fed? They had enough troubles of their own.

So, late on that hot moist evening, with her children wanting food and no money in the house and nothing left to sell or pawn, Kitty O'Brien, absolutely desperate for cash or food and leaving her young family behind with strict instructions to behave themselves and take good care of the baby, wrapped her black shawl around her shoulders, slammed the back door behind her and walked along the Dock Road to sell herself.

For there wasn't a thing in the world Kitty O'Brien wouldn't have done for her children.

A fine clinging sea mist had hung over the Dock Road that night nine months ago, making the sky darken sooner than it should have done. There were fewer people about than usual, though the pubs were crowded and the sounds of breaking glass and drunken voices, laughing and shouting, drifted out from time to time. One of those voices belonged to Tom, Kitty thought bitterly, in there drinking whilst his children and his wife starved.

Foghorns sounded, dull and ghostly, and Kitty hurried even faster along the road to the place where the prostitutes plied their trade. She knew this because once, before she was married, not long over from Ireland and on her way into town on the tram, her best friend Lily had pointed out the street where women hung round waiting for paying customers. From then on, every time they passed it, they giggled, freshfaced, bright-eyed and virtuously shocked.

Could that really have been only ten years ago? It seemed more like a hundred. She hadn't been into town since she'd married Tom and doubted if she ever would again.

The overpowering smell of spices mingled with the mist, tickling Kitty's nose as she came to the street where she had to wait. She didn't know its name but recognised the large brass sailing ship sign above an office on the corner.

Several women were already there, huddled in doorways, and she was worried they might come and shout at her, a stranger, taking away their custom, but in this fog, and they, like her, hidden by black shawls, they all looked the same.

There were no men to be seen, though. Panicking, Kitty wondered how long she'd have to wait, worried for her family, but then a dark figure loomed out of the dimness, approached a woman, and they disappeared together. Kitty strained to hear what was being said. Did you ask for sixpence or a shilling? It might even be half-a-crown. As long as she got enough to buy something for the children to eat, she didn't care. On the other hand, it was silly to ask for less than the going rate. Curiously, she felt no shame, no fear. Yet here she was, a good Catholic woman, intending to sell her body for money.

Kitty had no intention of being choosy. The first man who came along – assuming that he would want a poor worn-out housewife – would do. She had to get home as quickly as possible. Kevin, who was only six himself, was looking after a small baby . . .

But a foreigner! Not exactly dark-skinned but not light-skinned, either, with glowing, intense eyes and hair as black as night and very shiny, so shiny the yellow light was reflected on his thick waves.

By now, two other women had gone off with customers and this man, this foreigner, stood expectantly in front of her. Kitty's heart sank. At the same time she realised it was foolish to expect a tall blond Irishman, a young Tom, to proposition her. This was the docks – most of the men looking for women would be from abroad.

Was she prepared to do it with this man who was gabbling at her in a strange tongue, making exaggerated gestures with his long slender hands? She wondered if he was asking how much. 'Five shillings,' she said faintly, thinking that if it was too much he might go away. He didn't. Instead, he gestured again and Kitty's heart sank still further. He was signalling that they should leave. Together!

She followed him to the end of the street and round the corner. This particular area was notorious – full of criminals or so she'd heard. The man paused and Kitty realised he was waiting for her to lead the way, take him somewhere. Oh, God! Did he expect to go to her house? A hysterical laugh almost choked her, as she imagined turning up at Number 2 Chaucer Street with him, taking him upstairs, the children watching . . .

'This way,' she whispered nervously, turning the corner. There was bound to be a back alley behind the row of shops they'd just passed.

He was surprisingly gentle. No one but Tom had ever touched her there before. She still hurt from having Jimmie, but this dark-haired stranger was not vicious or rough like her husband, and after he had come – a soft, shedding release – he pressed her to him briefly, as though they had shared something remarkable together, and a strange feeling swept over Kitty and she found herself trembling.

She looked up at him, seeing him properly for the first time. His eyes were a lovely golden-brown, a colour she'd never seen before. From a window somewhere in front, a light came on and shone on his face. He was younger than she'd first thought, perhaps only twenty. His expression puzzled her until she realised it was pity, total, all-consuming pity – and she remembered with a shock that Tom had punched her in the jaw last night and it was black and blue and swollen, and she thought how repulsive she must look. If only she could speak his language, she'd tell him it didn't matter about being paid, she probably wasn't worth anything, but then she remembered the children and their hunger . . .

'T'ank you,' the young man whispered. 'T'ank you ver' much.' He pressed something into her hand and was gone.

Kitty pulled her knickers up, straightened her skirt and shawl and held what she'd been given up to the light.

It was a ten-shilling note!

'What's the baby to be called, luv?'

Kitty smiled, transforming her once-pretty, now caved-in face. Her blue eyes, usually so watery as if loaded with unshed tears, brightened, and for a few seconds at least they looked clear and healthy.

A name for the baby? She'd only been thinking of boys' names. So far, even the dead babies had been boys and all along she'd been expecting another.

'Elizabeth,' she said. She'd wanted to be Elizabeth herself when she was a little girl because it could be shortened to many other names.

Mary Plunkett changed it immediately to the only form she knew. Bending over the still-sleeping baby, she placed her finger in the tiny clutching hand. The baby's brown fingers tightened over hers.

'Jesus, she's strong!' she gasped. She chucked the infant under the chin with her other hand. 'You're going to be a fighter when you grow up, aren't you, Lizzie, me gal?'

'Well, that's what you need to be in this life,' Theresa Garrett said dryly. 'Isn't it, Kitty luv?'

Kitty nodded, smiling no longer. A fighter. Yes, she hoped that's what her Elizabeth, her Lizzie, would become – unlike her mother, who'd become a victim, long ago beaten by life.

2

Kitty lost the baby she conceived soon after Lizzie was born and the next a few months later.

Theresa Garrett, summoned to help with these painful miscarriages, demanded that Tom O'Brien call in a doctor to examine the poor, worn-out body of his wife, but he refused, so Theresa decided she'd pay the fee herself.

She asked the doctor to come early one evening when she knew that Tom would be home. Unfortunately, it also meant he would be drunk. Tom always called in at the pub on the way home from work for a few quick ones, and would arrive mildly stewed. After tea, he went out again and usually returned violent and half-mad with drink.

He was in his mild state when Theresa arrived with the doctor, who took Kitty upstairs.

The midwife didn't sit down but stood in the doorway watching the man sprawled in the armchair in front of the kitchen fire. There was no sign of the children. Lizzie, the baby, who was now eight months old, was probably asleep somewhere and the rest of them had made themselves scarce, as they usually did the minute their dad appeared.

Tom O'Brien had lodged opposite Theresa Garrett's house when he'd first come over from Ireland twelve years before. She remembered his buoyant good looks and charm, the spring and the hope in his step as he walked along the street, eventually appearing with pretty fair-haired, blue-eyed Kitty on his arm. For a moment she felt pity, viewing the coarsened, brutal man slouched in the chair. His blond hair, once the colour of sunshine, was now greasy and lank, and had turned to a dirty grey. His mouth and chin had slackened, fallen back out of control and slobber ran down onto his swollen neck and jowls. The oil-stained working shirt was open to the waist exposing a belly swollen by beer, bulging over the rope holding up his trousers.

But the pity didn't last for long. Hundreds, thousands of men came over from Ireland expecting to find the streets of England paved with gold. Had not her own dear husband done so, ending up stoking the engines of trains for twelve or fourteen hours a day till he'd died of emphysema at the age of forty-five? But unlike Tom O'Brien, these men didn't take out their failure, their loss of hope and dreams, on the weak and puny bodies of their wives and children.

The man was a brute and there were no two ways about it.

When Dr Walker, a well-dressed, harassed-looking man who was continually being pressed by his nagging wife to give up this ill-paying practice and move somewhere where the patients could meet their bills, came downstairs after examining Kitty, he said to Tom bluntly, 'Your wife is worn out by all this childbearing. You must let her be, at least for a while. Give her body a rest.'

'Let me wife be?' snarled Tom. Normally impressed by authority, he was too drunk and too angry to care. 'Why d'ya think I married 'er?'

'You'll kill her,' warned the doctor. 'And what will happen to the children if she dies?'

Tom didn't give a damn about the children. If Kitty died, then the Sisters at the Convent could have every last one of them and he would return to County Cork where he would starve in dignity and peace.

'Fuck the children,' he yelled. 'Take yer fuckin' advice and shove it where the monkey shoved its nuts. And fuck yer too, yer interferin' auld hag,' he directed at Theresa Garrett, waiting in the hallway.

When they'd gone he punched Kevin, the first of his children to venture indoors, and then went to the pub, drowning his sorrows by drinking even more than usual. On his return home, he dragged his wife upstairs, taking her so violently that she shrieked in pain and he felt so aggrieved he hit her. Then he fell asleep, half-dressed, his stained, acrid-smelling working trousers twisted round his ankles, so when he got up next morning, he fell over and woke up half the street with his shouting.

During the long night, Kitty tried to turn her head away from the stinking armpit beside her and wondered how on earth she would have the strength to get up in a few hours' time and cope with the drudgery of the day. Her head ached from where Tom had hit her and the pit of her stomach felt as if it had been pierced with a knife. She longed to move to a more comfortable position but if she did, and if she woke Tom, he might have her again and the thought was unbearable. She'd sooner remain cramped and stiff than risk that. Kitty felt her eyes prickle with tears. It wasn't often she felt sorry for herself, mainly because it wasn't often she had the time.

In the single bed jammed in a corner, little Lizzie gave a long shuddering sigh and Kitty held her breath, dreading the child would wake and disturb Jimmie and Chris, asleep at the other end of the bed. She couldn't imagine being able to raise the energy to get up and see to a crying baby just then, apart from which, it might wake Tom, but Lizzie was a good baby, always had been, and she remained fast asleep.

At the age of five, Lizzie started in the Infants at St Anne's Convent School, where she was regarded with mixed feelings by the nuns.

Several of the sisters made pets of Mrs O'Brien's children because they admired their mother's courage. Although all her brood were painfully thin, they didn't smell, their clothes were clean and neatly mended, and their hair was free from nits. The sisters had told Kitty about the clinic where she could get her children injected against illnesses like diphtheria, and be given free orange juice and cod-liver oil, and she'd taken them all, so they were bright-eyed and clear-skinned and all in all far better turned out and healthier-looking than many of the children from far less poverty-stricken homes.

One or two of the nuns looked down on Kitty, feeling that a woman of whom a man had had so much carnal knowledge must be a bad lot. However, in the main the O'Briens were regarded as individuals, with their separate faults and virtues, but when it came to Lizzie, many of the sisters weren't sure if they approved of what they saw.

For a child so young, she had an almost exotic look; there was a foreignness about her, with her dark creamy skin and bitter-chocolate-coloured hair carefully woven into a great thick plait reaching almost to her waist. And such unusual-coloured eyes – golden-brown with shreds of lighter gold – wise, wise, knowing eyes that belonged to someone years older, not a child of five.

Sister Cecilia had read a book which said a whole tribe of people from India had landed in Wales a long time ago and it was from them this dark alien look had emanated, spreading to Scotland and Ireland too. But there was a different air to Lizzie O'Brien, one that was not apparent with the other dark-haired children. Wrong though it might be to use such a word about a child so young, there was a look of *wantonness* about her.

One who found this more disturbing than most was Sister Augustus, who, when licking her lips, would find moisture on her faint black moustache when she leaned over Lizzie's sums – and she seemed to lean over Lizzie's sums more than anybody else's – and because she took so much pleasure in stroking the little girl's smooth satin arm, a pleasure which she instinctively knew was wrong, she was inclined to blame Lizzie for this, rather than herself, and marked the sums wrong even when they were right as a sort of penance. Why Lizzie should have to pay the penance, Sister Augustus found difficult to explain, even to herself.

None of the other teachers were so prejudiced when it came to marking Lizzie's work, and all agreed she was an exceptionally bright child. All the O'Brien boys were intelligent, but Lizzie outshone her brothers in every subject.

By this time, Lizzie had acquired two younger sisters, Joan and Nellie, the latter almost as dark as Lizzie herself, and another brother, Paddy, who'd been born in between the two girls.

Mrs O'Brien had been forced to make more visits to the Dock Road and carrot-haired Joan, although she would never know it, had a French sailor for a father. Kitty hadn't realised he was a gingerhead until he took his round hat off to say goodbye, and when the flailing red-skinned, red-haired baby was born nine months later, she was past caring. She'd discovered Tom hadn't paid the rent for a fortnight and the landlord was threatening eviction.

The rent arrears required several trips, for the ten shillings she'd earned that first time had turned out to be far above the normal going rate. Apart from being less profitable, none of these subsequent encounters were as pleasant – though Kitty hesitated to let herself even *think* about it in those terms – as her first trip, yet neither were they as unpleasant as what she had to put up with from her husband.

Tom not paying the rent worried her deeply at first, for what he could do once, he could do again. There was no conceivable way she could pay twelve shillings and sixpence a week to Mr Woods, the landlord – her entire housekeeping was less than that. Fortunately, she discovered that Mr Woods waited outside the dock gates to collect rent off his bad payers on the day they emerged triumphant with their wages. Kitty asked for Tom to be included in this arrangement, relying, quite rightly, on him being too proud to refuse with his mates looking on.

This was a relief. The idea of dragging her poor tired body down the Dock Road on a regular basis seemed more than she could bear, though Kitty would have done it – for the children.

So they struggled along, Mrs O'Brien and her children, as did everyone else in Chaucer Street, in Bootle, Liverpool . . . as indeed did the poor throughout the country, hoping, dreaming, yearning for change, for an improvement in their lot.

When change came, in September 1939, in the shape of World War Two, everybody's world, both rich and poor alike, was turned completely upside down.

3

Thanks to its proximity to the docks, Bootle became one of the first targets of Hitler's bombs.

Night after night they rained down on the areas alongside the River Mersey, killing its people and destroying their homes.

Along with her brothers and sisters, Lizzie scarcely knew what war meant until it came. The brief amount of history they'd learnt at school had made them think war was something which happened long ago, between men who wore resplendent red uniforms decorated with gold braid, and took place in strange foreign countries. It didn't happen in modern times, and certainly not in England.

But nightly visits to the communal air-raid shelter which stank of sweat and urine and excreta, where babies cried and old men and women spat and coughed and people did the most intimate, private things in front of other people and from which you emerged to find your house demolished or your street flattened or some of your family dead . . . all of these things taught the children that war was something very real that could happen to anybody at any time in any place.

Young men went off to fight, proud in their uniforms, and Kitty O'Brien prayed, oh how she prayed, night and morning, and whenever she had a moment throughout the day, that the war would be over, well over, in four years' time, when Kevin reached eighteen.

War made Tom a little happier, but this had no effect on his relationship with his family. He was deemed an 'essential worker', which made him feel important. He earned more money too and was employed on a regular basis, no longer having to suffer the indignity of waiting at the dock gates to be examined and picked out on a day-to-day basis by some uppity foreman. Tom was needed as much as any soldier in the fight against Hitler.

And how they hated Hitler! Hitler didn't care who he killed with his bombs. His pilots dropped them carelessly, or perhaps even deliberately, any old where, killing women and children, patients in hospitals, demolishing orphanages, old people's homes, even churches, whereas everyone knew that the brave young men in the Royal Air Force only bombed military targets like arms factories or barracks. German civilians were not being killed like British ones.

One night, the air-raid siren went much earlier than usual. A wave of fear gripped Kitty O'Brien's stomach when the awful whining noise sounded. It was only six o'clock and she was frantically gathering the children together to go to the shelter when the bombs began to drop. Normally she had them all prepared. She pushed the smaller ones into the cupboard under the stairs which some people used as a shelter rather than go to the communal one with the common people. There was an explosion close by and the house shook.

Suddenly, the bombardment ceased and at that precise moment, Tom knocked on the front door.

None of the family came in that way. Any other, safer time and Tom would have come in the back as usual. He didn't carry a front-door key.

A second sooner, a second later, they wouldn't have heard his knock.

Tony opened the door to let his dad in and Tom lumbered down the hall into the kitchen. He'd been frightened by the raid and, half-drunk, was ready to lash out at his wife if she so much as looked at him in a way he didn't like, when suddenly the bombs began falling all around like confetti. One fell right outside the house and the front door was torn off its hinges and flung down the hall where it smashed to bits on the stairs.

The children looked at the shattered door and tried to imagine it was their dad. He'd escaped death by a miracle.

Tom boasted about it for weeks afterwards. 'Surely the Good Lord looks after His own,' he bragged and went to two masses the following Sunday morning and Benediction in the evening to convey his fervent thanks to Jesus for saving him.

His children, remembering their mother's nightly plea in their joint prayers to keep their dad on a straight and narrow path, wondered if their prayers had therefore been answered and many times in the years to come wished they'd not prayed so hard or that God hadn't listened and it hadn't just been the front door which had been flung down the hall and smashed to pieces, but their dad as well.

In the mornings, bewildered parents, their crying children clutching at their legs, sat on the smoking wreckage of their homes. Many old people refused to leave the bricks and mortar they felt were just as much a part of them as their flesh and their bones. They rooted through the acrid-smelling dust, unearthing broken mementos of their lives, wedding presents, wrecked furniture and scorched photographs.

Looters hunted through the debris if they thought they could get away with it, though they were chased when spotted. In Birkenhead, a young woman was stoned to death by angry residents, her pockets full of bone-handled Sheffield steel cutlery, somebody's Silver Wedding gift.

Children still went to school, but the O'Briens' school, dangerously close to the docks, was closed down so they went for only half a day, sharing a school with the pupils of another one some miles inland. They whooped and laughed their way to the gate then dawdled outside, hoping the air-raid siren would go because the authorities said that when that happened, they must go to the place which was nearest, school or home. Wherever they happened to be, they went home, whooping and laughing even louder.

Many children had been evacuated to safe areas like Southport or Rochdale, but Kitty O'Brien saw little chance of someone willing to take on nine, soon to be ten – she was pregnant again – and she didn't want the family to be split up. She had visions of being killed herself and her orphaned children left scattered all over Lancashire, never to find each other again.

'If anyone's going to be killed,' she said to herself, 'then let us all be killed together.'

How happy the children were. Not just hers, but all children, in the midst of so much misery. Despite the war and the bombs, the poverty and the hunger, their worn-out mothers and drunken fathers, they seemed possessed by an almost unnatural energy which overcame the wretchedness of their lives and their surroundings.

They sang on their way to school and on the way back. '*Oranges and Lemons, said the bells of St Clement's,*' they chanted in the playground. '*One, two, three, four, five, once I caught a fish alive,*' they sang as they ran up and down the street like demons, and '*The big ship sails down the Ally, Ally, O,*' skipping through dark, dank entries or on their way to the grey, soulless air-raid shelters.

Tom O'Brien found a pub where the landlord ignored the legal 'last orders' and looked on the All Clear as his signal to close, no matter how late this was, so Tom never went to the public shelter with his family.

His wife and children were therefore without him when they returned to Number 2 Chaucer Street in the early hours of Christmas Eve, the second Christmas of the war, thankful to find the house still standing and themselves all in one piece. There was a united sigh of relief as Kitty unlocked the door and the family trooped into the back kitchen of their home.

That night a crowd of drunks had descended on the shelter and kept everyone awake with their raucous singing. Had the children been asleep, Kitty would have stayed there till morning, but she was glad to hear the sound of the All Clear so they could leave. There'd been no chance of rest that night, not only because of the drunks, but they'd never known so many bombs to drop. They'd rained down like hailstones and the shelter had rocked and shuddered for hours.

'Shush, now,' Kitty had cuddled this child and that, stroking the older ones' heads, comforting them. She was worried a bomb might drop, a dead hit, and one of her children would not have had the touch of her loving hands before death. Careworn hands they were, the skin wrinkled, silvery and transparent, the prominent veins a dark and vivid blue and they fluttered over her nine beautiful children, soothing, patting, comforting.

The previous week, Kevin had started work as a milkman's assistant. Tom kept back the five shillings Kevin was going to give her, so Kitty would be no better off. She willed her eldest son to sleep for he had to be up at half-past four.

A bomb dropped yards away and the shelter made an odd grinding noise as if it were about to collapse. Layers of concrete dust fell from the ceiling into their eyes, making them water.

So it was with an even greater sense of relief than usual that people heard the All Clear, and Kitty thankfully shepherded her wide-awake family out of the shelter, stepping over the drunken revellers who'd already begun to celebrate Christmas.

When the family entered the kitchen of their home, Kitty turned up the gaslight and they stopped, aghast at the sight which met their eyes.

Everywhere, absolutely everywhere was black. The dishes which had been left on the table, the furniture, every inch of lino was covered with a blanket of smooth, velvet blackness. Even the coloured paper chains which the children had made at school and which hung from corner to corner of the room were discoloured.

'Jesus, Mary and Joseph!' whispered Kitty O'Brien. 'What's happened to our house? It looks like the divil himself's been here.'

Lizzie bent and rubbed her finger in the blackness. It was powdery and had a sour, pungent smell.

'All the soot's come down the chimney,' she said. 'The bombs shook it down.'

And so they had. Vibration had loosened every particle of soot from every chimney, and investigation of the parlour and bedrooms showed that the same thing had happened there, though the effect was not so drastic as fires were rarely lit in these rooms.

Thankfully, all the children except Kevin were on holiday from school, and after a few hours' sleep, they set to and on Christmas Eve the house was scrubbed from top to bottom. Kitty was grateful for the blackout curtains supplied by the Government, for they didn't need washing, only a good shake to get rid of the soot.

For some inexplicable reason, when Kitty was an old woman she always remembered that day, that Christmas Eve, above all other days, for it seemed to contain all the misery and all the happiness and all the pride which made up her life.

She didn't expect Christmas presents from anyone and as usual had nothing to give her children, yet somehow the day still had a special, excited atmosphere.

At school, the children had been learning carols and as they scrubbed and brushed and dusted, the words of *Silent Night* and *Noël, Noël* filled the sooty, smelly house. The older ones put silly words to some, like 'While shepherds wash their socks at night' and Kitty tut-tutted and said it was sacrilegious, but at the same time hid a smile.

Then there was a knock on the front door and her heart thudded, for more often than not this meant trouble. Immediately, she felt convinced that the horse which pulled Kevin's milk-cart had kicked him to death, but instead it was a lady from a charity who'd been directed to the O'Briens by the sisters of the convent. She'd brought a package of groceries – a Christmas pudding, a cake with icing on, some crackers and a tin of meat.

'And how many children have you here?' she enquired brightly, blinking owlishly behind thick, wire-rimmed glasses.

'Eight,' said Kitty proudly. 'And me eldest Kevin's out at work and I've another on the way.'

'My! What a lovely big happy family,' said the charity lady and handed round presents to them all, only little things – celluloid dolls for Lizzie and Joan, yo-yos and rubber balls for the boys and a rattle, far too young for Nellie but which she loved.

Such a happy day, till Tom came home and said he didn't want charity, and threw the dolls onto the fire where they flared up in sizzling blue flames and melted to nothing and he would have burnt the other toys too if the boys hadn't immediately vanished with them, though he managed to stamp on the rattle.

Joan and Nellie set up such a screaming and yelling at this wanton destruction, that Tom felt bound to express his anger at the row on the person nearest, which happened to be his wife. He slapped her across the face with his open hand. The other side of Kitty's head slammed against the kitchen wall with a thud. Tom had his hand raised, ready to strike again, when suddenly he froze in astonishment. He was being thumped vigorously from behind. The blows had no force, they didn't hurt in the slightest, but their unexpectedness saved Kitty from a further slap. He turned, ready to strike, ready to knock whichever child this was from here to Kingdom Come.

'Leave 'er alone! Leave our mam alone!'

Lizzie, brown eyes afire, small fists clenched, stood daring him to strike. Her thick plait had swung over one shoulder and began to come loose, brown hair spurting out like strands of wild brown silk.

Tom knocked her sprawling. She could have been a flower on a stem for all the resistance she had to his great strength. Her dad was not so much angry as dumbfounded, for none of the boys had ever tried to defend their mam. This was not cowardice on their part, but knowing it upset their mam even more when he turned on them.

But Lizzie was beside herself with rage – a rage far greater than anything ever felt by Tom. A natural rage, not provoked by drink. She felt as if there was a fire inside her head and at any minute, flames would shoot out of her mouth and her eyes and her ears. She saw the breadknife on the kitchen table, a knife mam regularly sharpened on the back step. The blade gleamed dully in the orange gaslight. Picking it up, she approached her dad slowly, the handle in both hands, the point directed at his overhanging belly.

'I hate yer,' she said in a quiet, expressionless voice, a voice her astonished family had never heard before. 'I hate yer and I wish ye'd been bombed that night. I wish ye'd been here when the soot came down and it'd choked yer. *I wish yer were dead!*'

There was silence. Kitty felt as if she would faint. Surely Tom would kill them all.

Tom's drunken brain clicked over, trying to put a name to this hellcat of a child. Then he remembered. This was Lizzie, the eldest girl. The darkest one of the family. He always found it difficult to remember the children's names and sometimes was hard put to recall how many he had. Yes, he was sure this one was Lizzie and she was eight or nine, something like that.

Christ! She was a beauty. He'd never noticed before. Never given her a second glance. And what nerve! She was still approaching him, slowly, fearlessly, the knife pointed at him.

The rest of the family were frozen like statues in a park.

Unexpectedly, quite out of the blue, Tom felt a surge, a throbbing between his legs, but this time it was accompanied by something new, something different. Desire tinged with excitement. There was a flavour, a sensual tingling in this quivering, palpitating need.

But she was his daughter!

Without a word, and to the intense surprise of everyone, Tom turned on his heel and left the house, even forgetting to slam the door.

4

By the time Lizzie was twelve, her mother's miscarriages were on the increase. A baby due the first Christmas of the war was born dead, and two more were lost before 1942, when Kitty surprisingly gave birth to twin boys – Sean and Dougal. The following year she had to go into hospital to have a dead baby removed from her womb.

As he operated, the surgeon was horrified by what he saw. The uterus had been stretched in and out like a concertina. Innumerable, repeated tears had never been stitched.

When Kitty came out of the anaesthetic, he was standing by the bed sternly demanding details of her childbearing history. He was horrified to discover she had eleven live children but had lost the same number, born dead or miscarried.

'You can't possibly have any more children,' the doctor told her brutally. The woman was only forty but looked sixty. 'It's too dangerous, both for you and for them.'

'But my husband—' Kitty stopped, feeling embarrassed.

'He must take precautions, or if you like, I'll sterilise you.' The doctor wished he'd taken that step during the operation. She would never have known.

'What's that?'

'Removal of the ovaries so you can't conceive again,' he explained, thinking to himself how ignorant the poor were. He couldn't wait to finish his training and move to a hospital where he could treat patients of his own class.

'But that's a sin,' replied Kitty, deeply shocked. 'The Pope himself has forbidden birth control and Monsignor Kelly has spoken out against it from the pulpit.'

'Neither the Pope nor Monsignor Kelly have to bear your children or look after them. Nor do they contribute to the running of this hospital which deals with the consequences of such irresponsible behaviour.'

Kitty was even more shocked at this apparent criticism of the Holy Father and Monsignor Kelly.

The surgeon said he would send for Tom, and because when he was sober her husband was impressed and in fear of anybody in authority, whether it be doctors, nurses, policemen or members of the priesthood, when a letter arrived demanding his immediate presence at the hospital, Tom meekly went along.

'Your wife may well die if she has another baby,' the doctor said bluntly and superciliously to the hulking unshaven figure across the desk. Tom had come in his dinner-hour so as not to lose money and was in his working clothes. 'And if she does die, you will be guilty of murder. Do you understand?'

Tom nodded numbly.

'Murder!' the other man emphasised, relishing the sound of the word. 'Not the sort of murder you can be taken to court and tried for, but it would still be regarded as a mortal sin in your religion.'

Not knowing how to answer, Tom stared at his feet. The medical geezer must be right because he wore a white coat – a clear sign of superior knowledge.

'The Pope would consider it a mortal sin, as would your Monsignor Kelly,' the doctor assured him, privately thinking what a lot of hokum pokum this was, though this big oaf of a man seemed to be taking it seriously.

'If you wish,' he went on patronisingly, 'I could give you something to use which would prevent your wife becoming pregnant again.'

'Oh, I couldn't possibly use anything, doctor,' whined Tom. ''Tis a sin, worse p'raps than murder.'

'So your wife implied,' remarked the doctor dryly. 'What strange notions of sin you Catholics have.' He felt as if he was dealing with another race of people altogether. Many of the patients in this hospital, the Catholics in particular, were quite beyond his experience and his understanding.

Tom felt he couldn't tell this educated geezer in the stiff white coat, this God-like being who spoke as if he had a plum in his gob and probably put his prick through a hole so's he wouldn't see himself piss, that sex without knowing a woman took your seed to turn into a baby, was not sex at all. All his life, he and his brothers back in County Cork, and his friends who were Catholic, all of them felt this. That's why whores weren't satisfactory. Everybody knew they took precautions.

Having to pull it out or cover it up or knowing the woman had been messed about with or had something stuffed up her, that wasn't real sex. Basically, it was all about putting buns in ovens, even if you didn't want the damned kids when they arrived. It was a sign of virility to have a big family. Everyone at the docks, everyone in Chaucer Street knew Tom O'Brien was a real man because he made lots of babies.

But it sounded as if this medical ponce knew what he was talking about. It sounded like he'd even discussed it with Monsignor Kelly, and if he got Kitty in the club again and if she died, then the Monsignor would reckon Tom had murdered her. Even worse, God would know and when Tom himself died he would go to hell.

A week later, Kitty came home from hospital and a bed, provided by the sisters, was set up in the little-used front parlour.

'And not before time,' said the nuns, nodding at each other knowingly. 'Let's hope the poor woman gets a rest, for she surely deserves one,' and they made the sign of the Cross to endorse this hope.

*

Thus did life improve for Kitty O'Brien.

The bombing of Liverpool had virtually ceased and instead the people of London became the target of the Luftwaffe.

Kevin, Rory and Tony were all working and because of the shortage of manpower, their wages were higher than they would have been in peacetime. They bought Kitty several pieces of furniture, only second-hand, but a vast improvement on the battered old stuff she'd had before.

Tom must have felt inhibited by so many teenaged boys in the house growing taller and broader by the day, because he hardly knocked her about at all these days.

And Lizzie was such a good girl, taking a lot of the housekeeping off her mother's hands when she came home from school, and with only the twins to share her downstairs bedroom, Kitty enjoyed the luxury of night after night of undisturbed sleep for the first time since her wedding.

But in the course of time, Kitty's misery was to be transferred onto a pair of shoulders younger and even narrower than her own.

Tom O'Brien felt he was losing his grip on his family. That his power had gone.

He was lost and bewildered. His world of hard work and hard drinking needed an outlet. There had to be someone on whom he could vent his frustrations and his anger at the raw deal he felt he'd had from life. Now, with Kitty forbidden to him by God Himself and the boys growing bigger, becoming men, he began to feel a stranger in his own home, at odds with his entire family. Not that he'd given a fig for his family before, but suddenly they mattered. He wanted their respect.

The other day the older boys, the ones working, had talked about getting some distemper to decorate the parlour. The whole family had joined in the discussion about what colour to have, but no one consulted Tom, their dad, who should have had the last word on the subject. And this furniture which kept appearing – his permission hadn't been sought. He hadn't been asked for money towards it – not that he would have given any. Kevin just kept turning up with the borrowed milk-cart bearing a couple of armchairs or a new sideboard. It frightened Tom to think that his family could exist without his support, that they didn't need him any more.

But the worst thing of all was night after night, month after month, lying alone in the soft creaking bed, one thing on his mind, just one thing. Fucking. He missed it. He was lonely without it, nothing without it and until that bleedin' doctor shoved his oar in, had hardly ever gone without it since the day he'd married Kitty, nineteen years ago. How could a man be expected to make do with nothing when he'd been used to it once, twice, three times almost every night? There was no one to talk to about it. He was too ashamed to tell his mates. He had to suffer alone.

Tarts hung out in the pubs Tom used. One night at closing time, aching, burning with need, he asked one how much she charged. He'd given them all a good look over and this was the best of a bad bunch. Her name was Phoebe and she had a vast, bulging chest which strained against a tight hand-knitted red jumper. Her jet-black hair was permed to a frizz and maroon-painted lips gave her a clownish air.

'Five bob,' she answered in a squeaky querulous voice.

Christ! Tom thought of all the ale five bob could buy. Five bob for what he should be having at home for free every night.

'OK.' He had no choice. Otherwise, he'd go mad. 'Where'll it be?'

She'd noticed his face fall and said, 'Yer can have it fer half-a-crown if we just go outside. Five bob's back in me room.'

'Half-a-crown, then.' He arranged for her to go out first as he didn't want his mates to see him leaving with her.

She was waiting for him outside where a light drizzle fell. 'Come on.' She was in a hurry to get it over with so she could return to the pub before closing time and with luck, pick up another customer.

Tom shambled along a few feet behind, trying not to look as if they were together, though few people were about.

''Ere, this'll do.' She pushed open a heavy wooden gate that creaked and went along a short path which led to a deep, dark porch.

'This is a church,' said Tom, shocked.

''S'not Catholic.'

'Yeah, but even so.'

'Oh, come on. Do yer want it or not? And gimme the money first.' Tom fished in his pocket for half-a-crown and handed it over. 'Ta.'

He could dimly see Phoebe struggling to pull her skirt up and felt the full thrust of an erection. He couldn't wait to get inside her. As he began to fumble with the buttons on his trousers, he became conscious that she was holding something out for him.

''Ere, put this on.'

'Eh? What'cha talkin' about? What is it?'

'A French letter. It's a decent one – I got it off a Yank.'

'Fuck off, I'm not wearing that!'

'Well, you fuck off then. I don't want no kids and I don't want no VD neither.'

All desire had gone. He was limp. Empty. This is what happened when you went with a whore. Nothing but money, precautions and disease. It weren't natural.

''Ere, take yer money.' The half-crown was shoved back in his hand. She would have liked to keep it, but Tom was too big and strong to try that on. There wasn't anything to be gained from staying. She'd come across this situation before with the Irish Catholics and despised them for it. They wanted sex, they were desperate for it, 'cos their wives were frigid or dead or overloaded with kids, but show them a French letter and they ran a mile.

Tom was doubled up in agony, alone in the marriage bed. That woman, that bloody Phoebe. Got him all excited, made him feel worse than ever. He felt like going down and giving it to Kitty like she'd never had it before. He half-sat up, then remembered. She might get pregnant. She might die. And it would all be Tom's fault. He'd be a murderer. Monsignor Kelly might even denounce him from the pulpit and he'd be damned to the everlasting flames of hell.

He was about to lie down again when his eyes rested on the single bed alongside his where Lizzie, Joan and Nellie slept, the youngest girls at one end, Lizzie at the other.

Tom licked his lips. Sly little bitch. Every time he clapped eyes on her, ever since that night years ago when she'd come at him with the breadknife, he'd been watching her, desiring her. In his drink-sodden mind he put the fault for this on Lizzie herself. He saw her flaunting herself in front of him, brushing against him as she placed his tea on the table. And oh, those sly, tantalising glances, lowering those great long lashes when she caught his eye and twisting her lips provocatively.

Yes, it was all on her side, not his. Cunning bitch. It was *her* that wanted *him*.

He couldn't contain his pounding, feverish need any longer. He'd been without for nearly a year and if he didn't get it soon, he'd go mad. Reaching over, he lifted the sleeping girl, putting one hand under her neck, the other supporting her knees. Her skin felt slippery beneath the thin nightdress and as he laid her down beside him, his breathing became hoarse and he found himself gasping with desire.

Lizzie opened her eyes and was about to cry out in fear when her dad clapped his great clammy hand over her mouth. She knew what he was going to do. He was going to do what he'd done to her mam every night for as long as she could remember until Kitty had come out of hospital and begun to sleep downstairs. He was going to put his thing inside her and she knew it would hurt because Mam always moaned when he did it to her and cried when it was over and Dad had gone to sleep.

Now he snarled in her ear: 'Don't yer tell anyone about this. Not *anyone*, or I'll kill yer and then I'll kill yer mam too. Understand?'

Lizzie tried to turn her head away from the foul stink of his breath. Her eyes glowed like a cat's in the darkness. Tom was about to hit her for not answering when he realised his hand was covering her mouth. When he removed it, she took a deep, shuddering breath. Christ! He'd nearly suffocated her.

'D'yer understand?' he hissed again. Lizzie nodded. He felt rather than saw the gesture. 'I'll kill yer if yer tell,' he repeated, and, unable to control himself any longer, he forced himself on the unwilling body of his eldest daughter. At first, Lizzie wanted to scream out loud from the pain, but fortunately for her a few seconds later she fainted.

His power over his family restored, in his own mind at least, Tom felt in full control when a letter arrived in a thick white envelope on which his name and address were actually *typed*. It told him that his daughter Elizabeth had passed the scholarship and could go to a good school where she could stay until she was eighteen, and then, according to Kitty, who hovered anxiously in the background, on to university like Mrs Cooper's son from Dryden Street. Tom bellowed an emphatic and confident, 'No!'

Kitty pleaded, the boys pleaded. Even the little ones, sensing the honour involved, pleaded. Lizzie said nothing, regarding her dad with contempt.

'No,' he repeated. 'This letter's addressed ter me. It's *me* they're asking and I say no. It's me'd have to pay fer the bleedin' expensive uniform and books and things.'

'We'll pay,' said Kevin, Tony and Chris together.

'Yer don't have ter pay fer things anyway, Dad,' said Jimmie, who'd failed the scholarship, as had all the older boys. 'That's what a scholarship means, gettin' things fer free.'

'This sorta fancy education's not fer girls, anyways. Lizzie's the eldest girl and she has to help her mam.'

'I can manage, Tom. Joan and Nellie can always lend a hand. 'Sides which, it doesn't mean she'll go away, does it?'

Kitty was desperate. She wanted him to agree mainly for Lizzie's sake, but also the idea of an O'Brien child leaving the house for school dressed in a velour hat with a badge on and a satchel over her shoulder made her heart swell with pride. She could scarcely believe it. Fancy Lizzie turning out so much cleverer than the boys, particularly with a foreigner . . .

She stopped *that* thought dead in its tracks.

'See, the nearest grammar school's in Waterloo – Seafield Convent.' Kevin picked the letter up. 'She'd only have ter get a bus down the road. It'd take quarter of an hour at most.'

Tom snatched the letter back. 'Look what it sez 'ere,' he snorted. 'What yer need ter buy for this bleedin' convent. A hockey stick! A bleedin' hockey stick!'

Lizzie had crept into the hallway and sat on the stairs listening. Like lots of children, her education had been badly affected by the war, attending school only half a day for several years and missing lots of classes altogether when there were air raids. She should have started senior school a year ago. Now she was twelve and had sat the scholarship late as a special concession. She was too old to sit it again.

It was now or never. With all her heart she wanted to go to a school where she'd learn foreign languages and sciences, subjects not taught in the senior school she was about to go to with Jimmie.

She wasn't keen on having a hockey stick as she hated team games, but she prayed and prayed her dad would give in and let her go. Why had the scholarship people written to him anyway? He'd never been the slightest bit interested in any of them. They should have written to Mam. It was Mam who asked questions about what they'd been doing at school, and even went to the library to get books out on things they didn't understand, like caterpillars or Roundheads or long division, but the library staff always made her leave because the little O'Briens made so much noise and anyway, poor Mam couldn't understand what headings to look under.

Seafield Convent was probably just like *The Fourth Form at St Monica's*, a book Lizzie had borrowed from the school library, or the schools in the *Girls' Crystal*, a magazine which her friend Tessa loaned her every week.

What she would have liked best of all was to go to a boarding school where she could get away from the awful thing her dad did every night. Perhaps all dads did that to their daughters when their mams were ill, though nobody at school ever mentioned it happening to them. Perhaps they'd been sworn to secrecy, like her. Flora Steward's mam had died when she was a baby and she'd been brought up by her dad. Lizzie wondered if she could ask her. She wanted to know if it would always hurt so much, but was scared that if she confided in someone and her dad found out, he would kill her and Mam as he'd threatened to.

Lizzie rarely cried. It was weak to cry, but right now she felt the tears sting her eyes because she wanted to go to the posh school and she wanted her dad to leave her alone at night. She felt so tired.

Suddenly, there was a crash from the kitchen. Tom had pushed the table back and sent the chairs flying.

'Sod the lottya yis,' he screamed. 'She's not goin'. Me mind's made up.'

And with that, he left the house for the pub and although Kitty tried to raise the matter again several times, he flatly refused to discuss it and on one of the occasions, the boys being out, he managed to give her a black eye.

The letter from the Education Department remained unanswered, and one day Kitty put it away in a drawer. In years to come, she would often take it out and re-read it, although she knew the words by heart. She used to wonder . . . if Lizzie *had* gone to the grammar school, how differently would her life have turned out?

5

Tom was scared of losing Lizzie. A posh school – even if it was only down the road and she came home each day – could well give his daughter high and mighty airs and put her out of his reach.

Having Lizzie put new meaning into Tom's life, and fire returned to his belly. He looked forward to getting home at night and would even have left the pub early, but of course he had to wait till everyone was fast asleep.

So Lizzie went to the ordinary senior school, where she didn't do nearly as well as expected.

'Well, if this is a scholarship girl,' exclaimed a teacher, 'then all I can say is, it must have been a fluke. She couldn't have coped at grammar school.'

Although Lizzie grew taller and her body began to fill out and her dark creamy skin moulded itself like smooth soft silk over her high, almost Oriental cheekbones, at the same time her brown-gold eyes seemed to be sinking deeper and deeper into their sockets. Purple shadows, so startling they could have been drawn by a crayon, appeared beneath them. She was always tired, always listless. One day, a teacher found her fast asleep in a history lesson and woke her with a sharp slap, which he regretted when the girl came to with a hunted, frantic look on her face.

Perhaps all was not well at home, thought her teacher, but then he shrugged the problem off. After all, it was none of his business.

At home, Kitty was sick with worry.

'When will this awful war end?' she wailed. It was 1944. Kevin had been in the forces a year and now Rory had got his call-up papers.

'Don't worry, Mam,' he laughed. 'It'll soon be over. ''Sides, it'll be fun going ter France and Belgium and foreign places like that.'

'I hope it lasts long enough fer me ter fight,' said Tony wistfully.

'Me, too,' echoed Chris, and at this Kitty shrieked hysterically.

The only consolation she had was that Kevin had been accepted into the Fleet Air Arm. He wore a peaked cap and a uniform like a suit, not a battledress: he looked just like an officer.

Kitty was so proud. She had no favourite child – she loved each and every one as much as any mother could – but on the day Kevin appeared in his uniform, she overflowed with love for her oldest boy.

Except for the fortunate few who obtained supplies on the black market, rationing was a great equaliser. Nowadays, rich and poor ate the same, so the

O'Brien children were no longer painfully thin. The older boys' shoulders had broadened and Kitty was sure she was not being prejudiced when she judged her sons to be handsome, outstanding young men.

Kevin's once-flaxen hair had turned dark blond and beneath his cap, his blue eyes twinkled with excitement.

'I'll not be leaving the country, Mam,' he said. 'Least, not for a while,' but shortly after he'd gone, Kitty received a letter to say he was on an aircraft carrier whose whereabouts he couldn't disclose.

Then, before she knew where she was, Rory was getting ready to leave. He'd joined the Royal Air Force.

'It'll be over next year, won't it?' cried his mother, turning to her eldest daughter for comfort, but to Kitty's surprise, Lizzie twisted away and soon afterwards left the house without a word.

'It'll be the periods,' thought Kitty, remembering how a few months ago Lizzie told her she was bleeding between the legs and she'd provided her with a pile of clean rags. It struck her that she hadn't washed any rags for Lizzie for some time, but she supposed that at thirteen, the girl wouldn't be regular for a while.

Lizzie felt sick. She had been vomiting every morning in the lavatory at the bottom of the yard and the periods which had started four months ago had stopped after two. She knew as much about the symptoms of pregnancy as any grown woman, having slept in the same room as her mam all her life and helped with the births of Dougal and Sean.

She was expecting a baby. She was also desperate and knew no one she could turn to for help. Once or twice she'd walked along Linacre Lane where Dr Walker had his surgery, but she'd never summoned the courage to go in. One drizzly November evening she loitered outside, the rain penetrating her thin coat and shoes. She shivered, knowing if she hung around all night she wouldn't raise the nerve to call on him.

Anyway, Dr Walker charged a fee. Lizzie wasn't sure what it was, but even sixpence would be too much as she didn't possess a penny.

In the past her mam had taken the children to the doctor only as a very last resort and had called him out on one single, solitary occasion when Chris caught scarlet fever. The ambulance was sent for and her brother was carried out in a fluffy red blanket and a crowd gathered to see what was going on.

Right now, Lizzie earnestly wished someone would wrap her up in a blanket and carry her off somewhere safe and warm.

'Hallo, Lizzie.' It was her friend Tessa from school.

Lizzie wanted to be alone. She'd left the house for that reason. 'I'm on a message fer me mam,' she lied. 'She wants it in a hurry.'

'D'yer want me *Girls' Crystal?*' Tessa offered generously. 'I've just finished it. Come to our 'ouse and I'll give it yer now.'

Normally, Lizzie would have been off like a shot to Tessa's. She loved to creep in a corner with her favourite magazine and get lost in the world of boarding schools and mysteries and juvenile romances, but right now all her mind had room for was her horrifying predicament.

'Termorrer,' she told Tessa shortly. 'I'll come termorrer. I've got ter rush now fer me mam.'

She walked away without even saying tarra and Tessa felt hurt and decided to call on Cissy Smythe to see if she wanted the *Girls' Crystal* instead, and Lizzie O'Brien, who'd become proper stuck-up lately, could go without in future.

A third period missed.

Something else Lizzie knew was that the longer you had a baby in your belly, the more dangerous it was to get rid of. Not that her mam had ever even contemplated such a terrible thing, but a few girls at school had mams who'd had abortions even though they were Catholic. There was a woman in Wordsworth Street who did them and she charged a whole five pounds.

It was a sin, a mortal sin to murder a baby, even when it wasn't yet born. It was even more of a sin, though, and much more dreadful, to have a baby when you weren't married.

In fact, it was the worst thing in the world that could happen. The disgrace of having to tell her mam, and the whole street knowing, and having to go to school with a swollen belly. Though maybe she'd be sent away. That would be better, otherwise the baby might arrive in the middle of a lesson or even worse, school prayers, and everyone would stand around gaping, including the boys.

Lizzie lay in bed one icy December morning. Her dad had long ago left for work and she was in the small bed, her feet all tangled up with those of Joan and Nellie. They were both asleep. In the dim light Joan's copper curls were just visible on the pillow she shared with her sister.

Pulling up her nightdress, Lizzie stroked her normally flat belly. There was no doubt about it. It was beginning to swell.

'Dear Jesus. Oh, sweet Jesus,' Lizzie prayed. 'Please help me.'

In actual fact, Lizzie didn't have much faith in prayers. She remembered how hard the family pleaded to God to end the war before Kevin was eighteen, but He hadn't listened and now Rory was gone as well. She'd beseeched Him to make Dad let her go to grammar school, but He hadn't answered that prayer either.

She couldn't go on like this. Someone had to know, though once she'd heard of a girl who lived in a convent home who'd gone the whole way with a baby and the nuns just thought she was getting fat and the girl had given birth to the child in a lavatory and put it in a dustbin where it died. Someone found it and the police were called in.

Lizzie couldn't have done that even if she'd wanted to. When Mam was expecting, she puffed out like a great balloon and probably Lizzie would do the same and there was no way she could keep it secret.

If only she didn't feel so full of sin, so guilty. She hadn't confessed her sin either. If she told Monsignor Kelly or any of the other priests at Our Lady of Lourdes they'd recognise her voice and tell Mam and Father Steele always asked funny questions like, 'Have you been doing naughty things with boys?' or 'Has a boy touched you between the legs?' even when you only went to confess little things like telling a silly lie or saying bad things about the teachers. So if she got Father Steele when she went to confess she was carrying a sinful baby, he was sure to ask who'd done it to her and there was no way she could tell him about the horrible things Dad did every night.

Aching with misery, she dragged herself out of bed, dressed and went downstairs, leaving her sisters sleeping in envied innocence.

'Yer up early, luv.'

Her mam was sitting in front of the kitchen range crocheting. The fire glowed red and Lizzie could smell bread baking.

'I woke up early an' couldn't get ter sleep again,' she said. Could she tell her mam? Looking into those trusting, watery blue eyes in the prematurely-aged face, Lizzie decided she couldn't.

With Kevin and Rory away, her mam was already beside herself with worry and it would be selfish to add to this. Besides which, she felt she'd betrayed Mam by letting Dad do those things to her. Most importantly, Mam would never, never help her get rid of the baby. Mam would insist she had it and if that happened, Lizzie would be a public disgrace like Norma Tutty from down Chaucer Street who had a little boy everyone said was a bastard and they wouldn't let their children play with him. Lizzie wouldn't want her child to be called names like that.

'D'yer feel all right, Lizzie luv?' asked Kitty anxiously, struck by the haggard, almost desperate look on her daughter's face.

'Yes, Mam. I'm a bit tired, that's all.'

'Yer working too hard at school, that's what it is.'

On reflection, though, Kitty couldn't remember Lizzie doing homework for weeks.

'No I'm not, Mam.'

'Oh well, you'll grow out of it,' said Kitty complacently. The boys had always been as good as gold but she knew several women whose daughters had gone through a sulky, sullen stage around the time their periods started. 'Fetch some water, there's a good girl and I'll make yer a cup of tea. It's time the little 'uns got up. Give 'em a shout, will yer?'

However, her worry returned when she noticed the laborious and awkward fashion in which Lizzie rose to her feet to get the water from the back kitchen. The awful dark suspicion that occasionally flashed through her mind resurfaced, but she immediately pushed it back, unwilling and unable to think the unthinkable.

Jimmie and Lizzie walked to school together. On that same miserable morning, Lizzie told her brother to go ahead, that she'd catch him up.

'Yer not going to scag again, are yer?' His blond hair was flecked with snow. It was freezing.

'Of course not,' she snapped.

'Stop kiddin', Liz. You've been scaggin' lots lately. I know, because Mrs Robinson asked fer yer the other day. I told 'er yer were ill,' Jimmie said.

'Ta, kid.' Lizzie softened towards her brother. She and Jimmie had always been close.

'Better be careful,' he warned. 'Our mam won't half be mad if the Schoolie comes round looking fer yer.'

'I know,' said Lizzie. That was the least of her worries. 'Would yer like me butty, Jim? I don't feel like it terday.'

'Ta, Liz,' said Jimmie, trudging off through the falling snow which was turning to slush as soon as it reached the ground.

Lizzie walked in the direction of North Park. At this time of year the gardens and playing fields were completely deserted, and spiky, half-dead bushes spattered with snow-flakes lined the lonely path along which Lizzie wandered.

Exhausted, she sank onto a bench, little caring that the saturated wood soaked through her dress and coat. Her shoes were already wet and leaking and she began to shiver violently. Not only that, her head throbbed as she tried to think of a way out of her predicament. She wondered what would happen if she just turned up at the hospital where they'd taken Chris when he had scarlet fever, but all she could imagine was angry nurses shaking their fists at her and shouting that she was a dirty girl.

She wanted to cry, but was scared, even in this deserted place, of drawing attention to herself. The Parkie might come and want to know why she wasn't at school. If only she could *tell* someone, thought Lizzie – someone sympathetic. As soon as her mam found herself 'in the club' again, as she put it, she'd tell the whole street, half-ashamed, half-proud, and she'd also tell Theresa Garrett, the midwife, to make sure she'd be free about the time the baby was due.

Mrs Garrett! Remembering her kindly manner when dealing with her mam and her gentle handling of all the newly-born children, Lizzie's heart lifted. Of course! She would go and see Mrs Garrett this very minute. She would listen and understand.

Mrs Garrett lived beside a butcher's in Southey Street. The houses opposite had been bombed and the site only roughly cleared. Stained and tattered wallpaper which had once covered people's bedrooms and parlours, black-leaded fire-places and even a crooked picture of Our Lady were exposed to the world at the end of the row of houses which remained. Jimmie said it looked as if a giant had cut away a portion of the street to eat.

By the time Lizzie reached the house, the snow was falling thick and fast in great wet dollops and had begun to form a slippery carpet.

'Please, oh please be in, Mrs Garrett.'

Lizzie didn't realise she'd spoken aloud until the butcher, who was brushing snow off his step, said, 'You're in luck, luv. She is in, 'cos she's just made me and me mate a cup of tea.'

Lizzie managed a weak smile and hurried to knock on Mrs Garrett's front door.

'Lizzie O'Brien!' exclaimed the midwife in surprise. 'It's not yer mam, is it? I mean, she's not—'

'No, Mrs Garrett,' interrupted Lizzie, agitatedly. 'It's not me mam. Can I speak with yer a minute, please?'

The midwife's house smelled of polish and disinfectant. Had Lizzie not felt so distressed, she might have noticed the bright curtains on the kitchen windows with blackout material on the outside and cushion covers to match, the heavy cream lace cloth on the table and pot plants and ornaments scattered about the room. In pride of place on the mantelpiece stood a photograph of the deceased Mr Garrett.

'What's the matter, luv?'

Mrs Garrett had already decided the girl had come about her periods. Either bleeding had started and she didn't know what it was, or it hadn't and she wanted to know why. Women of all ages consulted her with their female problems, their dropped wombs, their lumps and cysts, tumours and fibroids, and she advised them as best she could.

But when Lizzie began to speak, she couldn't believe her ears. Pregnant! She remembered the night she'd delivered the child quite vividly, the way she'd shot out in such a hurry and how she'd caught her in safe, secure arms.

'I think I've gotta baby in me,' the girl said.

Thirteen years old and been with a boy! Of course it happened. Mrs Garrett wasn't ignorant of the ways of the world, but it didn't mean she had to approve.

'Yer a bad, bad girl to have done that with a boy,' she said severely. 'Yer should be ashamed of yerself.' And so she should be, too. Kitty O'Brien had devoted herself to her children and until now they'd been a credit to her.

'This'll kill yer mam,' she went on, shaking her iron-grey curls disapprovingly. 'And as fer yer dad, what he'll say—' She broke off. Having sampled Tom O'Brien's language in the past, she couldn't very well put into words his likely reaction.

Lizzie became hysterical. 'Yer not to tell me dad,' she screamed and shrank back into the chair, eyes wide, mouth gaping.

'Quiet, girl. Don't yer dare take on so in my house.'

The more Teresa Garrett thought about it, the more shocked she became. Lizzie O'Brien had always been such a pretty thing, quiet and demure – hadn't she passed the scholarship too, though Tom wouldn't let her go to the grammar school, but it meant she ought to have more sense.

Children today! They had no morals. Well, if this was the way Lizzie behaved, despite being brought up in a decent home, then she could put up with the consequences. She spoke her mind, there and then.

'I can't help yer. Yer got yerself into this mess, so get yerself out of it!'

Lizzie fled out into the snow. The friendly butcher had gone back inside his shop. She paused outside, frantically wondering which way to go.

Before the war, the bloody torsos of animals had hung in rows on great metal hooks outside here, but only a few pathetic joints of meat now lay on the white marble slab inside the window for people to buy their allotted amount with ration coupons. Each joint had a skewer driven through it. In her misery, half-taking in the scene, Lizzie remembered how her brothers had found a skewer like that once, a rusty old thing which they kept amongst their few treasures, using it to make holes through the conkers they collected in North Park.

Lizzie gave a deep and desperate sigh. The butcher saw her gazing through the window, winked at her and smiled. This time Lizzie didn't smile back. He wouldn't be so friendly if he knew the truth about her.

Her brain felt as if it had frozen, not just with the cold and the snow and the ice, but with numb bewilderment. She wished with all her heart she could stand in the sleet outside this shop, her feet so cold she could scarcely feel them, her clothes soaking, staring at the bloody scraps of animals in the window. She would be happy to just stay until she froze to death. To die on this very spot would solve everything.

But it was not to be.

The good-natured butcher came to the door. 'Are yer all right, luv?'

Lizzie gaped at him and for a moment the man wondered if she was right in the head, for the look she gave him was quite wild. Then, without a word, she turned and fled.

When she reached home, Lizzie was grateful to find her mam had taken Dougal and Sean out shopping.

The house was empty.

At last she was able to release the awful, wracking sobs that had been building up all morning. She lay on the stairs in her wet clothes, her body heaving with pent-up misery.

Suddenly she thought of something. A solution!

There was no need to ask for anybody's help with the baby. She would deal with it herself.

Theresa Garrett felt irritated when there was another knock on her door only minutes after Lizzie O'Brien had left. If it was that girl again, she'd give her a piece of her mind.

Instead it was her neighbour returning the empty cups. Mrs Garrett and the butcher, Mr Shaw, had an agreement. He let her have a pound of his best pork sausages each week and she made him and his assistant a cup of strong tea with sugar every morning and afternoon.

'That was nice,' he remarked. 'A really nice cuppa.'

He always said that. Mrs Garrett took the cups and noticed he'd forgotten to get his assistant to wash them, which was most unusual.

'Did a girl just call on yer?' he asked. 'Thin, dark kid?'

'Yes, she did,' answered Mrs Garrett indignantly. 'And I sent her packing.' Of course, she didn't reveal the reason why. Never, never would she betray a confidence, whatever the circumstances. She'd no intention of telling Kitty and Tom O'Brien about Lizzie's visit, despite her threat.

'Oh!' Mr Shaw appeared a bit dismayed by her attitude. 'It's just that she seemed a nice girl and she looked a bit . . . well, a bit lost, yer might say, when she went off.'

'Did she now!'

'Isn't she one of the O'Briens? That's right!' He slapped his forehead triumphantly. 'I've been tryin' ter place 'er. I always think, whenever I sees them kids, how well they've turned out, considerin' what they've got fer a dad. An ignorant lout of a man is Tom O'Brien, in my humble opinion.'

Mr Shaw said goodbye and as she closed her door, an awful, sinking feeling came over Theresa Garrett and she began to tremble.

'Oh, dear God in heaven, what have I done?' she whispered aloud to her empty house. 'It's Tom, I know it is. It's Tom who's been at the girl.'

Kitty O'Brien hadn't been pregnant for over a year. She still slept in the parlour. That left Tom in the bedroom with his three daughters, of whom

Lizzie was the eldest. She wouldn't trust Tom O'Brien as far as she could throw him and she couldn't throw him an inch.

Grabbing her coat, she half-walked, half-ran to Chaucer Street.

Kitty had just come in and put the kettle on for a cup of tea. With Tony and Chris at work and Kevin and Rory regularly sending money home, care of a neighbour – an arrangement which Tom knew nothing about – she had more money to spend than she'd had in her life before. She'd secretly been buying Christmas presents for the children for weeks – nothing extravagant, else Tom might get suspicious.

She picked up the breadknife, sharpened only that morning on the icy back step, and began to make butties for the little 'uns, at the same time wondering if she dare buy coats for the girls through the club man, as the ones they had were awfully thin for this weather, when Theresa Garrett appeared in the yard and came through the back door and into the kitchen without so much as knocking.

'Why, Mrs Garrett—' Kitty began indignantly. No matter how much respect she had for the midwife, she should always knock before coming into someone else's home.

'Where's Lizzie?' the woman demanded abruptly.

'Why, at school, o'course.'

'No, she isn't. Has she come back here?'

'Back here? No. I mean . . . I don't know. Why should she? I've just this minute come in meself,' said Kitty, totally confused.

Douglas and Sean sucked their sweets contentedly and regarded the distraught visitor with wide, solemn eyes.

'Can I look upstairs?'

'Yes. Yes, o'course, but why?' Kitty was frightened by the midwife's behaviour. What on earth was going on?

Mrs Garrett climbed the stairs as fast as her heavy frame would allow. She had no idea what was urging her on, why she had such a sense of foreboding.

Lizzie lay on the bed. Her eyes were closed and the sockets had sunk so far back that her face was almost skeletal. She was so still, so silent, that at first Theresa thought she was dead and her own heart almost stopped beating at the thought, but as she approached, the girl's eyes opened.

Luminous pools of dark golden light stared up at the midwife and Lizzie whispered. 'I'm sorry I've been such a naughty girl. I'm praying to Baby Jesus right now ter fergive me. D'yer think He will?'

Mrs Garrett felt tears running down her cheeks and she laid her large gentle hand on the girl's stomach. To her astonishment, Lizzie screamed in agony.

The premonition that something was wrong, even more wrong than the evil perpetrated by Tom O'Brien against his eldest daughter, the premonition that had prompted her to rush through the snow-filled streets to this house, caused Mrs Garrett to draw the rough blankets away from Lizzie and what she saw made her stomach churn.

From the waist down, the girl's clothes and the bed were soaked in dark red blood and Kitty O'Brien, who was standing bewildered in the doorway, gave a scream of horror.

But all that Kitty could see was the bloodsoaked bed. She was not close enough to see what Mrs Garrett could.

The circular fingerhold of a rusty skewer which Lizzie had thrust inside to rid herself of the sinful baby.

6

A new doctor was on duty in the Casualty Department the morning they brought Lizzie in. He was not only very young, but idealistic, with a wish to heal and mend and care for the poor. He wanted nothing to do with the rich. In the Norfolk village where he was born and his father was a lord, he was known as Sir Rodney Hewitt-Grandby, but to the hospital staff and patients in Liverpool he was just Dr Grandby.

There'd been no cosy wrapping up in a red blanket for Lizzie. She couldn't bend her body an inch. The horrified ambulancemen had the greatest difficulty getting her onto a stretcher and the moment she'd reached hospital, she'd been rushed into the emergency operating theatre where she was swiftly anaesthetised.

So Lizzie didn't know her feet were placed in cold stirrups whilst the metal skewer was removed followed by the dead foetus, a boy, whom the surgeon reckoned was a good three months old. Then Lizzie was disinfected, sewn and mended.

'You're her mother, I take it?' Dr Grandby came into the corridor where Theresa Garrett waited impatiently. Kitty had been persuaded to stay at home with the twins.

'No, Doctor, I've no children of me own. I'm a friend of the family. Will she be all right?'

'Well, her internal injuries are terrible,' replied the doctor gravely. He'd been horribly shaken by Lizzie's self-inflicted wound. 'There's always the chance she'll never have another baby.'

'Oh, my God!' Mrs Garrett knew she'd have this on her conscience for the rest of her life.

'The injuries are not just from the skewer, either . . .' The young man paused, not sure how much he could divulge to someone who was not a relative.

'I'm a close friend, Doctor, and I delivered her and all her brothers and sisters.'

'Well, Nurse, someone's been abusing her for a long time.'

Mrs Garrett didn't choose to correct the doctor's assumption of her profession. She put her hand on his arm in an unconscious, fervent gesture of assurance.

'I know who it was, Doctor. God help me, but I didn't realise it was going on. Perhaps I should've done, but I swear on the Almighty it won't happen again.'

She'd never meant anything so much in her entire life. If need be, she'd stand over Lizzie and her sisters day and night to protect them from that monster Tom O'Brien. He'd have to throw her out of the house, physically pick her up and throw her out, if he wanted her to leave, and if he did, she'd shout the truth to the whole of Chaucer Street.

Dr Grandby looked doubtful. 'This is really a matter for the police.'

Theresa Garrett shook her head fiercely. 'No, Doctor. Yer don't bring the police into private family matters like this, not round here. Would yer like me to ask Monsignor Kelly to come and see yer?' That would be the ideal solution – let him tell the priest what had happened.

'I'll think about it,' he said, unconvinced. 'She won't be going home for a while and I'll have a chat with the girl herself, see what she thinks.'

They had been talking directly outside the double swing doors which led to the ward where Lizzie lay, and through the windows, Mrs Garrett could see her lying, still and pale, her olive-skinned arms limp on the covers. A nurse had swept her great swathe of brown hair to one side and it hung like a silk curtain over the edge of the bed.

Dr Grandby's gaze followed hers and he commented, 'Unusual-looking girl, isn't she? Which side of the family is the foreign blood on?'

'Oh, no, Doctor! Why, she's as Irish as the pigs of Trogheady. It's the Celtic streak that comes out now'n again and makes them dark like that.'

'Oh, I see,' said the doctor noncommittally.

Dr Grandby was engaged to be married. His fiancée Suzanne was a clerk in the Admiralty in London.

The day after Lizzie's admission to hospital, the doctor was due for two days' well-earned leave and he drove down south in the small Ford car which he'd changed to at the beginning of the war as his big Rover used up too many precious petrol coupons. He was longing to meet Suzanne again. They hadn't seen each other for over two months.

That was the day a tramcar overturned in Stanley Road, and although no one was killed, several passengers and pedestrians were injured and a fleet of ambulances carried them to the hospital.

There was already a shortage of beds. An entire wing of the building had been demolished by a landmine the previous year. The senior doctor in charge did a tour of the wards to decide which patients were fit to return home and make room for the new arrivals.

'What's wrong with her?' he asked from the foot of Lizzie's bed.

The Matron who was deferentially accompanying him leapt forward to grab Lizzie's chart.

'An abortion, Doctor,' she said disapprovingly.

'Send her home,' he ordered. 'There's people here with injuries which are no fault of their own who need these beds.'

So, that afternoon, an ambulance took Lizzie back to Chaucer Street.

Kitty was flustered when the official vehicle drew up. Despite the cold, half a dozen neighbours turned out again to see what was going on. She helped her daughter in and hugged her, though she was still unsure what had happened.

Mrs Garrett had muttered something about a haemorrhage, and had promised to come and see Kitty 'before Lizzie gets home', expecting her to be in hospital a good week, which she should have been, for the poor girl could hardly walk and was clearly in great pain.

The terrible thought which had been trying to wriggle its way into Kitty's brain tried to break through again, but she pushed it away. She couldn't think that. *She couldn't.* She couldn't even bring herself to ask what had happened. Theresa Garrett would tell her later.

What she needed to concentrate on now was making Lizzie comfortable. She was so pale and weak, unable to sit down and right now was holding on to the banisters for dear life.

'I can't manage the stairs, Mam. Me legs won't lift up.' She was staring at the floor, unwilling to meet Kitty's eyes.

'Sleep with me ternight, Lizzie luv. Till yer better, eh?'

'Yes, Mam.'

'D'yer want ter lie down now, girl?'

'All right, Mam.'

Dear God! The girl could scarcely move. She shuffled into the parlour, where Kitty helped lower her onto the bed, lifted her legs and placed them gently on the covers, and all the time, Lizzie winced in agony, though she never cried out, not once.

Tom O'Brien lumbered into the house, his clothes soaked with the sweat of a day's toil. He carried with him a strong aroma of olive oil which he'd been unloading all afternoon.

As the years passed, Tom's gut had become even more bloated. Now it bulged out so far that the top of his trousers had disappeared behind a shelf of fat. His features had coarsened to the extent that sometimes Kitty thought he bore no resemblance at all to the mischievous charmer from County Cork who'd asked for her hand in marriage twenty years before – although it seemed more like a hundred and twenty.

As soon as he entered, the usual air of gloom fell over the house and everyone in it; it would not lighten till he left for the pub after tea. Not one of his children spoke to him. They never did. They faded away to sit on their beds or see their friends. Tony and Chris went to the pictures.

After he'd eaten his scouse, Kitty placed a mug of tea before him and said, 'Lizzie's home.'

Tom started. 'Where is she then?'

He'd missed Lizzie badly the night before and couldn't get out of his stupid wife what was wrong and why she'd had to go to the hospital.

'She's in the parlour. They sent her home early. There was a tram accident in Stanley Road and they needed the beds emptying.'

Kitty didn't mention Theresa Garrett was coming to see her about Lizzie because Tom couldn't stand the woman and it would only set him in a rage. She'd cross that bridge when she came to it.

Lizzie! Downstairs! All night long the thought haunted Tom as he sat in the pub drinking pint after pint of foaming beer. Was she going to stay down there forever, like Kitty? The twin boys, Tom couldn't remember their names, had been upstairs in the back bedroom ever since the eldest two had been called up. Kitty had been sleeping alone for months now, so there was plenty of room for Lizzie.

His brain, already half-rotten from the thousands of pints of beer consumed over the years, simmered in crazy confusion. His little Lizzie was being taken from him, moved out of his reach – the only one of his children whom he loved. Then the unimaginable happened. He actually felt tears prick his eyes and all night long remained so morose and silent that his mates wondered what on earth was wrong with Tom O'Brien. He was usually the life and soul of the party, with an endless fund of dirty jokes and patriotic Irish songs.

At closing time he staggered home alone. The streets were covered in black slush which had started to freeze, and swaying round a corner he slipped and fell full-length. He cursed loudly and fiercely. But although his body was cold and his clothes wet, inside he burnt with a feverish rage.

What a situation to come home to after a hard day's work and a hard night's drinking! All the other men had wives to poke. Why not him? He was a man, a real, vital man and he needed a woman. All men needed a woman, but he more than most. It was his right.

But now there was no Kitty, no Lizzie.

The house was silent when he entered. He made no attempt to keep quiet, but the family were used to his noise and usually slept right through it.

Tom threw himself half-dressed onto the bed. That familiar ache crept over him, as if the mere act of lying down, the feel of the mattress, the creak of the springs, meant that there should be a woman there, legs apart, waiting to satisfy his needs.

But there was no one.

That night, one member of the family was awake to hear Tom come in. Lizzie lay in the parlour, the pain in her lower abdomen so sharp and violent, there was no chance of sleep. After Dad settled down, she'd wake Mam and ask for more aspirin, which dulled the ache a little.

She heard Dad throw himself into bed, then the springs squeaked rustily, the headboard banged against the wall, and the floorboards creaked. It sounded so loud downstairs in the parlour, directly below.

An awful suspicion entered her mind.

She lay there for several minutes, trying to stop the suspicion from expanding and developing, when from upstairs there came a stifled cry, a frightened, fearful moan.

Lizzie sat up in bed so suddenly, that the pain inside her enveloped her entire body like fire.

'Lizzie! What is it?'

'It's Joan, Mam. Me dad's got our Joan. And I can hear it, Mam. I can hear it clear as anything so yer must've known, all this time. Yer must've known what he was doing ter me, 'cos I know, the very first night sleeping here, that me dad's got our Joan.'

Lizzie struggled to get up, gritting her teeth, willing the pain not to explode as she staggered to the door. About to go up the stairs, she remembered the breadknife. That had stopped Dad years ago when he was going to hit Mam.

It lay gleaming on the kitchen table ready to cut butties next morning.

Kitty appeared in the parlour doorway. In the dim gaslight left burning at the top of the stairs, her pale eyes looked desperate in her thin haggard face.

'Lizzie, girl, I didn't know,' she wailed. 'Gracious Christ, I didn't. Yer dad, he's always so restless, tossing this way and that, making the bed creak all night long.'

'Yer must've known, Mam,' said Lizzie coldly.

It was agony climbing the stairs. It was as if her legs were scissors, cutting away at her insides every time she took a step.

In the bedroom she could just about see the great half-naked figure of her dad kneeling over a struggling, snuffling Joan. He had his hand over her face, just as he'd done with Lizzie.

'*Gerroff!*' she screamed. '*Gerroff 'er!*' And she pointed the razor-sharp knife in the direction of the drunken man.

'Come fer a bit too, have yer?' snarled Tom. He'd have the two of them, he would – Lizzie first, then the red-haired bint. He tried to reach across the bed, difficult on the soft mattress and in his wild drunken state. Joan gasped aloud, retching for air when he moved his hand away and she began to push him off, bewildered, not quite sure what was going on.

Scrambling across the bed on his knees, Tom lost his balance and fell full-length, kicking Joan in the mouth when his feet jerked backwards. Intent on reaching Lizzie, he raised himself and lunged foward, unaware that a knife was pointing right at him, threatening him.

He fell off the side of the bed right onto it.

Right through his chest it went, and even though his body was covered with a thick layer of muscle and fat, the long sharp knife plunged in, right up to its handle, piercing his heart virtually right through. He breathed his last choking breath at Lizzie's feet.

Poor Joan, thinking she was waking up from one nightmare to another, crawled to the foot of the bed to see what had happened. Nellie woke and then the boys, all six of them, came into the room, rubbing their eyes. Jimmie carried a nightlight and this illuminated only too clearly the dead and bleeding body of their dad.

But before they saw anything, Kitty had crept into the room and was kneeling by the body, her hand on the knife, trying to remove it.

So only Lizzie knew it was she, not Mam, who'd plunged the knife into the hated heart.

Or so she and Kitty thought. It was many, many years before Lizzie was to discover that one other person had witnessed the true version of events.

7

'Going down Central Station ternight, Lizzie?' Marie Gordon shouted from the doorway of the newsagent's where she worked and which Lizzie passed on her way to school.

'You bet!' answered Lizzie, her best American accent emphasised by the fact that she was vigorously chewing gum. 'Got a date with Hank at half-past seven.'

'See yer then. I'll call fer yer about six, okay?'

' 'Kay,' agreed Lizzie and hands in pockets, hips swinging, she swaggered on her way.

In a few weeks' time she would be fourteen, and she was already taller than everyone in her class except for one boy. Her breasts, which Lizzie regretfully suspected were as big as they would ever be, were small but firm, high and pointed, the nipples prominent through her sparkling white though frayed school blouse. Those swinging hips were as lean as a young boy's, but curved up to an eighteen-inch waist, giving the impression of voluptuousness unusual in someone so slim.

Lizzie tossed her waist-length chocolate-coloured hair as a gesture of rejection at the boys who whistled and catcalled in her direction when she entered the school gates.

The girls mostly ignored her. Tessa was no longer her friend and Lizzie wouldn't have read the *Girls' Crystal* to save her life. *Secrets* and *Miracle* and *Red Star* were now her favourite magazines.

It was said at school that Lizzie O'Brien 'went' with boys, and that was the real reason why they whistled and stared and crowded round her at break-time, vying with each other to walk her home. It wasn't that they found her attractive. They'd pay just as much attention to other girls if they allowed the liberties Lizzie O'Brien did.

No one had any proof of this. Lizzie had never been seen *out* with a boy from school, but surely, the other girls told each other, being so free with her favours could be the only possible reason for her popularity.

It was nothing to do with her erotic looks, they said cattily. Yet those starry golden-brown eyes seemed to issue an invitation to anyone who wished to see an invitation there . . . and there was not another girl in school, nor in the whole of Bootle, with such high, exaggerated cheekbones or with a mouth that, without a touch of lipstick, was such a pretty pink colour. Well, more of a peach colour really. No one had seen a peach since the war began but, thought the boys, if that's what peaches looked like, then they wanted to get their mouths around one.

Lizzie was the cleverest of the O'Brien children by far, the teachers decided as they gossiped in the staffroom, but what a pity she'd waited until her last half-year to prove it. Of course, they'd never met Paddy who'd passed the scholarship and gone to a boy's grammar school in Waterloo, just along the road from the convent where Lizzie would have gone if her dad had let her.

Yes, she'd certainly blossomed since that awful tragedy at home last December when her mother had stabbed her father to death. No more sunken, shadowy eyes and falling asleep in class – but although she turned in more than adequate work without any apparent effort, and appeared to have a quick and lively brain which could grasp facts in a flash, the general consensus was that Lizzie O'Brien was a cheeky little madam with a provocative manner who had an unsettling effect on the boys, not to mention several of the male staff, and all in all, they'd be glad to see the back of her when she left at the end of the summer term.

In class Lizzie yawned. Not through tiredness, but boredom. They'd been doing square roots for nearly a week now and she'd got the hang of it straight away but some stupes kept on asking questions, then more questions, and it was all very tedious.

She stared out of the window and thought about the night ahead.

Marie Gordon, Lizzie's new friend, was a bold and brassy girl. She worked in the newsagent's on the corner of Chaucer Street and Marsh Lane and a few months earlier, when Lizzie went to buy her favourite magazines, Marie had confided they were her favourites too and saw in Lizzie a spirit equal to her own.

It wasn't long after Christmas and she'd asked Lizzie if she'd like to come with her to Central Station to meet the Yanks who arrived there nightly, entire battalions – or detachments or whatever you called it – of them, searching desperately for girls on whom to shower presents of cigarettes or cookies or gum or, best of all, nylons.

'All yer have ter do,' explained Marie, 'is ter let them take yer out, go to the flicks, or a pub or caff, then afterwards, let them have a little feel – yer know!' She winked at Lizzie knowingly.

'I know,' said Lizzie, who didn't know at all at the time, but since then the two of them had been going to Central Station every night.

With pearl earrings from Woolworths, nylons kept up with garters and high-heeled shoes borrowed off Marie's mother, Lizzie looked three or four years older than her age.

In pubs and dance-hall bars, she sipped gin and It and rum and orange, or funny drinks with slices of lemon and cherries on sticks. She took the cherries home to Sean and Dougal. One Yank, a Captain, had taken her to the Adelphi, the poshest hotel in Liverpool. That was the night Lizzie had inadvertently let slip she was still at school and he demanded her age. When she confessed she was only thirteen, the Captain had given her a stern talking to and told her to go home. Then he almost ran out of the hotel. 'Jailbait,' he'd said she was, which Lizzie didn't quite understand, but to avoid future embarrassment she invented a job. From then on, she said she worked in a florist's.

She gave the cigarettes she got to Mam. Kitty found smoking a great comfort since Tom's death. The rest of the family enjoyed the cookies, sweets and gum. One day Joan was sent home from school for wearing nylons.

'Where do they come from, luv?' Kitty asked querulously. She was a shaky, nervous figure nowadays and scarcely left the house.

'Off some fella,' replied Lizzie casually, not caring what her mam, or anybody, thought. No one was going to stop her from doing anything that took her fancy.

Poor Kitty. Her neighbours felt even more sorry for her than ever. As far as that brute of a husband was concerned, it was good riddance to bad rubbish, but trust Tom to depart the world in such a violent way, leaving his long-suffering wife to cope with the consequences. Kitty felt as if she'd never be able to face Chaucer Street again.

It seemed to Kitty, from the very moment it happened, that it really *was* she who'd plunged the knife into Tom. When she relived the events of that terrible night, she could actually recall the feel of the thick bone handle in her hand and the sensation, the crunching, squashing sensation, of the blade entering her husband's gross, beer-swelled body.

Oh, that awful night!

She'd ordered the boys back to bed, all but Tony who was sent to fetch a bobby. Then she'd helped Lizzie, who seemed to have gone into a trance, down to the parlour and told Joan and Nellie to stay with her.

Once they were all out of the way, she'd struggled to turn Tom's body over. He was lying face down on the bedroom floor. She knew he was dead, yet at the same time she expected an involuntary arm to reach out and hit her as one final gesture of hate.

She knelt over him and tugged at the knife until it came out of the body with an ugly, squelching sound. Then, gritting her teeth and saying a prayer, 'Hail Mary, full of grace,' she turned the weapon on herself, slashing her arms and chest. Her thin nightdress was soon soaked with blood and it wasn't until it ran down her arms and began to mingle with her husband's that she stopped and put the knife back in his heart.

Then Kitty began to weep. For Lizzie, for all of her children, for herself and even for Tom.

She was still weeping when the bobbies arrived.

There were two of them, one as big and gross as Tom had been, the other small and weedy with a narrow, suspicious face. On several occasions in the past when Kevin or Rory had gone to the police station to complain that their mam was being beaten by their dad, the bobbies, including these two, had just laughed and said, 'Good luck ter him. Get on home, lad, it's none of our business.' And now that the victim had fought back, they remained unsympathetic, both towards her and her injuries.

Not so the nurses at the hospital where Kitty was taken, though, nor the Detective Inspector who came to see her early the next day.

A sister whispered, 'Good for you, girl. I bet he deserved it,' and Kitty replied shakily, 'Oh, he did. Believe me, he did.'

It was the least she could do for her Lizzie whom she'd let lie with that beast for all that time.

Of course she'd known!

She, Kitty O'Brien, who thought herself such a wonderful mother, had lain in the parlour, comfortable and alone, whilst at the back of her mind lurked the suspicion, no, the *knowledge* of the awful thing going on upstairs. She'd hidden her head under the clothes when she'd heard the bed creak in that all-too-familiar way, telling herself it was too horrific to be true, that Tom was having a restless night after drinking too much. Never, never would she admit to herself that the unbelievable was really happening, because if she did, then she would have to stop it and because Tom *had* to have a woman, it would be Kitty who'd be upstairs again in the big soft bed subjected to his animal desires.

Yet there'd been only one time, one single time Lizzie had heard him at Joan, her little sister, and she'd been up there like an avenging angel despite the pain of the abortion which Theresa Garrett told her about afterwards.

So, when the Detective Inspector came into the hospital, Kitty was ready to confess, confidently and believably, to the murder of Tom.

'He'd always been violent,' she whispered, 'ever since we was married.'

The Inspector nodded. His men had already told him about the boys coming to the station, pleading for help, and the neighbours confirmed that the dead man had conducted a reign of terror over his family for years. Dr Walker had informed him of Kitty's numerous miscarriages, many caused by kicks and blows.

'Ternight, though,' Kitty said, 'I mean, last night, he came at me with a knife. He'd never used a knife before.'

'Upstairs?' queried the policeman. 'You mean, he brought the knife upstairs?'

'Y . . . yes,' stammered the woman. Her self-inflicted wounds were smarting from the iodine. She was worried sick about Lizzie and to a lesser degree about Joan. As yet, the fact she was a widow hadn't quite registered.

'He . . . he came in drunk, like he allus did,' she went on hesitantly. 'I was already in bed and he woke me slamming the door. He went out ter the lav then came upstairs, swearing and cursing. I thought ter meself, "He's in a worse mood than usual." Alluva sudden, he was in the room, slashing at me with the breadknife. I fell outta bed,' she continued visualising the scene as if it had really happened. 'And Tom, he tripped over me legs and dropped the knife, so I picked it up, in case he came at me again, like.' She paused, close to tears.

'Go on,' said the Inspector gently. He was a tall, ungainly man who'd interviewed half a dozen women like Kitty since he'd come to Liverpool. Women who'd spent their married lives as punchbags for vicious, brutish husbands. Women who took the beatings, took the violence, year after miserable year, for the sake of their children, of their marriage, or even, God help them, because they actually loved the men who made their lives a nightmare, but suddenly the worm would turn and the men got a taste of their own medicine. It was not until that happened that the Inspector became involved. Ironic, wasn't it, he thought to himself, that a woman can be nearly murdered for a lifetime and no one cared, but let her strike back . . .

Kitty drew a deep breath, forcing the tears back. 'I was lying there holding it, and he did no more than fling himself atop o' me, not knowing I had it like. He probably couldn't see it was pointing up at him, and he landed right on it.'

'I see,' said the Detective Inspector, genuinely believing he did.

'Can I go home now, mister?' pleaded Kitty. 'I've little 'uns there who need their mam. I won't have ter go ter prison, will I?'

The policeman smiled kindly. 'You can go as soon as the doctor says you're fit,' he said. Kitty's lawyer had arranged bail. 'As for going to prison, it's not up to me, but I shouldn't think so.'

There was a trial, though little publicity. The war took up all the headlines in the *Liverpool Echo*, what with Allied landings in Europe and victory in sight, even if only on the distant horizon.

Kitty was accused of manslaughter.

Kevin and Rory, smart in their uniforms, the rough edges of their Liverpool accents already fined down, testified to the continual beatings suffered by their mother at the hands of Tom O'Brien, Lizzie and Joan weren't even mentioned. Kitty was found Not Guilty and only a small paragraph about the case appeared in the *Echo* and this was ringed in pencil and passed round Chaucer Street, where the unanimous judgement was that Tom had only got what he deserved and it was surprising that Kitty hadn't done it long ago.

It was the least Kitty could do for Lizzie, but even so, she sensed her daughter never completely forgave her.

From then on, all Kitty could do was let Lizzie go her own way. Since that awful December night, she'd become a different girl altogether, going out most nights and not coming home till very late. Kitty said nothing. How could she, when it was all her fault?

On Saturday mornings, her eldest daughter lay in bed till midday when the other children were up and about by eight or nine o'clock helping with the housework. What was she doing to get these stockings and sweets and cigarettes and things? Kitty dared not ask.

The two girls waited on Central Station. Marie wore a second-hand green Moygashel frock which she'd bought the Saturday before from Paddy's Market where good quality second-hand clothes could be got without coupons. It was two sizes too big, which meant the shoulders drooped halfway down her elbows. There was nothing she could do about that, but she'd taken up the hem and buckled the stiffbacked belt as tightly as it would go. In fact, she could scarcely breathe.

The Yanks seemed to have so much money that they didn't know what to do with it, and sometimes they'd hand over as much as five pounds at the end of an evening out, so Lizzie went to Paddy's Market as well and she'd also bought a new second-hand frock. That meant she had three frocks and a camel coat. The latest dress was tangerine silk – a wraparound style which seemed in perfect condition until it was ironed, when Lizzie found that the inside seams were flame red, showing that the dress had faded with so much washing, but she didn't mind a bit. It was a hand-made dress and therefore unique, and Lizzie wondered if the previous owner would ever approach her one day and say, 'You're wearing my dress!' It had a wide, separate sash which wound round her waist twice, making it look so tiny that Marie, suffocating in her tight petersham belt, was green with envy.

Lizzie liked the way the tissue-thin material rested on her lean hips. There wasn't a long mirror at home so she had to examine her full reflection in the Ladies Waiting Room on Central Station. The first time Lizzie had done this she got a shock. Of course she'd seen herself full-length before, blurred and distorted, in shop windows, but to see herself properly for the first time was a revelation.

For one thing, behind her in the mirror were scores of other girls painting their faces, combing their hair and generally making themselves as attractive as possible for the Yanks about to arrive from Burtonwood, and Lizzie couldn't help but notice that a lot of the girls had lumpy bodies or stringy hair or faces full of spots. Of course there were *some* pretty ones, but Lizzie, trying not to be conceited, knowing vanity was a sin, couldn't see another pair of legs as slim and smooth as hers or eyes as large or glowing. And without a doubt – and this was not vain – there was definitely no one with such a cascade of silky shining hair flowing right down to their waist, and such a narrow waist at that.

That was the day, the day she saw herself full-length in a proper mirror for the first time, that Lizzie noticed lots of the girls glancing in her direction, some in admiration, but mainly with expressions of unconcealed jealousy on their faces.

'Hey, shove over!' A fat girl nudged her out of the way. 'Let other people have a go in the mirror,' she said nastily.

'Sorry,' stammered Lizzie, who'd just realised she was beautiful. Uncommonly and strangely beautiful.

Several weeks after that first visit to Central Station, a scraggy scarecrow of a woman, much older than the others, approached Lizzie. 'Does yer mam know yer come here, girl?' she asked.

'O' course,' lied Lizzie.

The woman's face was dead white and powdery as if she'd dipped it in a bag of flour, and her lips were a gash of crimson. Several teeth were missing. Her name was Georgie and she was always the last to leave on a Yank's arm – that is, if she left at all. It was reckoned a Yank would have to be really desperate before he would take on Georgie.

'Yer shouldn't be 'ere,' said the woman. One of her legs was shorter than the other and she would skip along in a fast, lopsided manner. 'Yer mam shouldn't letcha come.'

'She doesn't mind.' Lizzie tossed her head and wished Georgie would go away. For one thing, a train was due any minute and she didn't want to be seen in her company.

But Georgie wasn't to be put off. 'Listen, luv,' she said confidentially, 'in that case, yer should go up ter the Adelphi fer yer trade. Yer'd make a fortune there, a girl with your looks.'

'D'yer think so?' Lizzie answered, wondering what the woman was on about. Then Georgie was forgotten as the train steamed to a halt and Hank came bounding towards her, first through the barrier as usual.

'Hi, y'all,' he drawled in that lovely, lazy Texan accent, and picking Lizzie up he swung her round so high that her skirt swirled into the air and her long legs nearly knocked poor Georgie off her feet.

Like Lizzie and Marie, a few girls waited for definite dates, but in the main, the women were waiting for a Yank, any Yank, to pick them up, take them out and give them a good time.

Not only had Yanks got money and all sorts of goodies unobtainable in war-starved Britain, but they were incredibly generous and good-humoured. Most were young and handsome, but even the older ones and those who were downright ugly had a smart and glamorous air in their neat, well-cut expensive uniforms, and their film-star accents invested them with a charm the English lads couldn't match.

Hank, Lizzie's date, was a Corporal in the Pay Corps. He could only get to Liverpool three or four times a week and when he did, Lizzie was his girl, or 'gal' as he put it. His hair, bleached by the sun, was almost white-blond and his lifelong golden-tanned skin was just beginning to fade after a cheerless English winter. He was barely as tall as Lizzie when she wore her high heels, which she found strange, used as she was to rubbing shoulders with big brothers all over six feet. Back in the States, Hank's pa was a farmer and right from when he was little, Hank had ridden a horse and herded cattle, just like a real cowboy. He showed Lizzie a photo of himself with a spotted scarf around his neck, wearing a stetson hat and mounted on his favourite horse, Gyp. He looked just like Roy Rogers, only younger.

Lizzie, having only seen broken-down, weary cart-horses dragging coal merchants' or rag and bone men's carts round Bootle, was very impressed – by Gyp, by Hank and by Americans in general.

One night, Hank proposed marriage. Lizzie accepted. She thought it a huge joke. Of course, he said, he'd have to get his Captain's permission. The Captain might want to interview Lizzie and her parents, seeing how young she was and all, not yet seventeen.

Lizzie suggested they wait awhile. 'Let's see how we feel in six months' time,' she said, thinking how very mature and responsible this sounded, and much better than saying there was no question of marriage as she was only thirteen years old!

Lots of girls had received proposals, some as many as four or five. More often than not, they never heard from their prospective husbands again once the men were transferred or had 'got their way', as some girls put it bitterly, knowing their erstwhile suitors were off to Manchester instead to pick up and offer marriage to other innocent young women.

So Lizzie was not so naive as to take Hank's proposal seriously and anyway, she wasn't the least bit faithful to him. The nights he was on duty she still went to Central Station with Marie and joined up with other servicemen. Lizzie was a very popular girl and Marie was glad to be her friend, because it meant that with the boys nearly always in pairs she and Lizzie were always the first to be picked up.

Some nights they went dancing, to the Rialto or Reece's, and Hank or another soldier or airman Lizzie happened to be with would dance very, very close, so close you couldn't have stuck a matchstick between them.

It was so romantic, thought Lizzie, mooning about in class most days, staring out of the window, driving the teachers mad, particularly when they tried to catch her out and sharply asked a question, to discover that although she looked as if her mind was anywhere but in school, she'd understood more than most other pupils.

Hank was really taken with her new tangerine dress. He said she looked 'real cute' and they left Central Station arm in arm, ignoring poor old Georgie waiting awkwardly outside the gents' toilet, winking grotesquely at every man who entered.

Lizzie and Hank, Marie and Clifford – Yanks had such funny names – went to the Trocadero to see *Gone with the Wind* which they'd already seen twice. It made Hank feel homesick, but Lizzie loved every single minute, particularly the ending. It didn't seem possible that the Deep South of America and Chaucer Street actually existed on the same planet.

She made a strict rule and stuck to it: 'No necking during the performance'. She didn't want to miss a part of any picture, and particularly not *Gone with the Wind*.

Hank spoke about the American Civil War as if it had just taken place. It seemed more real to him than the war he was taking part in. He said Lizzie was the spitting image of Vivien Leigh, except their eyes were a different colour.

'Damn Northerners!' he'd mutter. 'Niggers are scum. Take it from me, they don't get treated like equals on my pa's spread.'

Lizzie had already noticed how the black Yanks stuck together and never mixed with their white comrades. The latter had even been known to beat the black boys up if they saw them in the company of white girls.

After the pictures, they went to Lyon's for a cup of coffee. Despite the blackout, the centre of Liverpool was teeming with people. Nowadays, the air-raid siren rarely sounded.

The café was almost full of Yanks and their girls. The few Englishmen there watched them enviously. A soldier in coarse battledress sitting at an adjoining table, fingered Clifford's smart tailored uniform in admiration.

'You a Captain, mate?' he asked.

'No, pal, I'm a Corporal, just like you,' Clifford told him.

The Yanks all seemed to know each other and they carried on conversations in loud voices across several tables. They were so brash and confident, so wealthy and generous.

After half an hour, Lizzie and Hank got up to leave.

'See yer half-eleven at the tram stop,' hissed Marie as they passed.

'Okay,' said Lizzie.

Hank put his arm around her shoulders as they wandered up Skelhorne Street, turning into a dark cobbled passage where they began to search for an empty doorway. Several they passed already contained couples locked in heaving, panting embraces.

Eventually they came to the back entrance of a laundry – dark, empty and inviting. Hank pushed Lizzie against the double doors and began to kiss her – long, wet, childish kisses. Sometimes Lizzie suspected she was the first girl he'd ever dated.

After a while, he began to breathe heavily and his hands groped her body. He kneaded her breasts with his thumbs, then moved his hands down to her waist, twisting and turning as if he wanted to break her in two.

'Lizzie, oh Lizzie,' he whispered hoarsely. 'I love you.'

'I love you, too,' Lizzie replied dutifully. She liked Hank a lot but didn't love him. The lovemaking she found bewildering. The kissing meant nothing, though she pretended to respond. Sometimes, when he touched her nipples, she felt a slight, pleasant thrill. But it was when he smoothed his hands over her hips, stroking, caressing, pressing his knuckles against the crevice between the top of her legs and her belly, his thumbs creeping closer, closer to the point where the moistness was swelling and throbbing inside that she would pray Hank would go further so that the moistness could be released and she knew, she could tell that when this happened the moment would be joyous. At the same time there was a feeling of disgust, with herself, with her body, with Hank, which she couldn't explain. Anyway, Marie's warning always came to mind in good time: 'Never let them up yer skirt, otherwise they can't control themselves and ye've got a fight on yer hands.'

So, half-sorry, half-relieved, Lizzie pushed Hank away and said, 'I'm going ter miss me tram.'

'Godammit, honey,' Hank gasped, 'I can't even get to first base with you.'

Lizzie didn't answer. She began to walk down the road and Hank ran after her. He put his arm around her, his hand cupping her breast and he kept squeezing it gently as they strolled towards the tram stop.

'When am I going to get to screw you, Lizzie honey? After all, we're practically engaged.'

Lizzie wanted to say 'never', but this might put Hank off and she quite liked having a regular boyfriend. She couldn't very well tell him that good Catholic girls didn't sleep with boys before marriage, even if they wanted to, and she wasn't sure whether she wanted to or not.

'Ye've never gone all the way with Hank, have yer, Liz?' Marie asked on their way home on the tram.

'Oh, no!' Lizzie replied, shocked. 'Not with him. Not with nobody.'

'Me neither,' said Marie. 'I'm still a virgin too, though the way Clifford behaved ternight, it was all I could do ter keep him off me. I'm going ter have to give in or give Clifford up.'

'Then give him up,' advised Lizzie virtuously.

That stuff with her dad couldn't have been real. It was just a nightmare she'd had. Those things he'd done, the things she'd dreamt he'd done . . . it wasn't possible, not with Mam downstairs in the parlour. And that day in North Park, so cold, so wet, so desperately unhappy. Mrs Garrett being horrid. Why, Mrs Garrett made such a fuss of her nowadays, coming round to the house specially to see her, taking her hand and asking how she was.

She'd imagined it. It hadn't happened. Lizzie couldn't live with the idea that it was true. Lying on the bed, the rusty old skewer, piercing herself. The pain, the doctor, the hospital.

Lizzie O'Brien, sitting on the tram, so pretty and smart in her tangerine dress and camel coat, could never have inflicted such a horrific injury upon herself.

Joan! Her dad and the bed creaking. The bread-knife always kept so sharp. 'Gerroff 'er.' A scream. Then blackness.

That was where the nightmare ended.

It hadn't happened, Lizzie told herself. It was merely a bad dream that kept returning in the darkness of the night, making her shudder and moan, even when she was awake.

It hadn't happened!

8

At the same time as Lizzie was being fondled by her American boyfriend, another US serviceman was coaxing his limping single-seater Mustang down onto the runway of an air base in Suffolk. He'd been as far as Berlin, trying to crack those bloody Germans who wouldn't give in. Jeez, you'd think they'd know they didn't stand a chance, surrounded on every side, with Russians, Americans, English and French, all closing in.

He'd dropped his bombs on a railway terminal. Trucks full of arms exploded like a giant firework, but he'd been hit from the ground. Gone in too low, trying to make sure the bombs were spot on.

Talk about coming back on a wing and a prayer! The engine faltered and spluttered all the way, but here he was, above base, and now the fucking undercarriage was stuck! So they'd got him there too. But he'd land the plane on its belly. It took skill, but he'd done it before.

He pushed the joystick forward delicately, trying to transmit his terror and his wish to live to the aircraft through its instruments. '*Don't explode. Don't crash. Smoothly does it.*'

The plane touched the ground, shrieking like a thousand madmen.

Christ! It veered crazily from side to side and he frantically moved the joystick left, then right, trying to steady course, and as the plane careered towards the side of the runway, one wing demolished a flimsy wooden hut where the mechanics sometimes went for their tea to save the long walk back to the mess.

The collision seemed to help the plane back on its right course. The pilot breathed a sigh of relief and saw an ambulance racing towards him. Report in, a cup of coffee, then bed and forget all about planes till tomorrow night. In fact, by the time he jumped out of the cockpit, he felt quite cheerful.

On the tram, Lizzie said to Marie, 'D'yer want ter come to Southport on Easter Monday, the week after next? Hank's taking me.'

'I wouldn't want ter be a gooseberry.' Marie had her pride.

'He's bringing a crowd of mates,' Lizzie told her. 'It's me birthday, yer see. We're having a day out ter celebrate.'

'Gee, Lizzie, I'd love ter come, but the shop'll be open Easter Monday and I've got ter go ter work.'

'Never mind,' said Lizzie, who didn't care if Marie came or not.

In Suffolk, where the young pilot of the damaged plane was having a welcome cup of coffee and comparing notes with his fellow aircrew who'd also survived the night, another young man in overalls was crawling out from beneath the splintered remains of the hut the plane had demolished.

He ran as fast as he could back to base, but every now and then his legs gave way and he fell and every time he fell, he cried like a baby.

Soon he was stammering incoherently at his Sergeant who strained to make sense of him.

'Pull yeself together, man,' commanded the Sergeant roughly. He was a Scot, a regular serviceman who considered all wartime recruits were yellow-bellied cowards. If they weren't there'd have been no need to call them up: they'd have volunteered. 'Speak up, Rogers. What the bleedin' hell are ye on aboot?'

Rogers started gabbling again and the Sergeant had to restrain himself from hitting the lad. Then he thought he caught a name. 'O'Brien, did ye say? What about O'Brien?'

'We were in the hut, Sarge, having a cuppa, when we heard this plane coming in. It was in trouble, we could tell, and Rory, I mean O'Brien, he stood up and looked out the window in case we could help, like, and one of the wings went right into us and it knocked O'Brien's head clean off, Sarge.'

There was something wrong.

When Lizzie arrived home, she just knew there was something wrong. The house looked exactly the same. Not a thing had changed. Everywhere was silent, but it was an electric, quivering silence, as if there were voices gabbling away in some far-off place, wanting to break through with an unwelcome message. The nape of Lizzie's neck prickled.

She crept upstairs. Her mam, Joan and Nellie were fast asleep in the front bedroom, whilst in the back the boys snored contentedly. She counted them. Tony, Chris, Jimmie, Paddy, Sean and Dougal. Three apiece in two double beds. All alive and breathing.

Yet the feeling of unease persisted.

Downstairs again, she put the kettle on for a cup of tea. Mam had a proper gas-stove in the back kitchen now.

Lizzie sank into one of the new armchairs. The fire was almost out, though the grey embers still gave off considerable heat. She often sat here by herself when she came home from town and thought about Hank and what it would be like to live in Texas. Then she'd imagine having enough money to buy lots of frocks and shoes and handbags from proper shops, not Paddy's Market. Sometimes she would even design the clothes in her mind, but tonight she couldn't concentrate. No matter how hard she tried to dismiss it, the feeling of foreboding persisted, so she drank her tea quickly and went to bed, deciding she'd be better off asleep.

The war was about to end – in a week, a month, two months . . . Everybody had a different opinion.

Each day, Kitty O'Brien listened avidly to the wireless. It was Kevin she worried about, stuck on an aircraft carrier on some far-off ocean. Rory was all right, safe in England. After the war they'd be able to get good jobs. They had trades now, both of them. When Rory had last been home, he'd said,

'We could move away from Bootle, if you liked, Mam. Get a house in the country – Formby or Ormskirk, like.'

But Kitty wasn't sure if she'd ever want to leave Chaucer Street.

After the older children had gone and she was left with just Sean and Dougal quietly drawing at the kitchen table, Kitty turned on the nine o'clock news. Nothing new, Hitler hadn't surrendered. He was still hanging on in his bunker somewhere in Berlin, refusing to accept the possibility of defeat even though it stared him in the face.

She turned the wireless off and went upstairs to make the beds, picking up clothes to wash, dusting. She'd be glad when these awful blackout curtains could come down. Tony had promised to buy new ones for the parlour so she was saving the coupons and had her eye on some green brocade in a shop in Strand Road.

Kitty sighed. Strange, but when she'd had a crowd of little 'uns, she'd longed for peace and quiet, yet now she had it, perversely, she yearned for a baby to nurse or a tiny hand to drag at her skirt. Sean and Dougal were such self-contained children, absorbed in each other, playing quietly all day long. They were no trouble, didn't need their mam like the others had.

She carried the washing downstairs and put it in a bucket to steep, and decided to have a cup of tea before starting on the baking. As she filled the kettle, she recalled with disquiet the funny question Lizzie had asked that morning before she went to school.

'Did anything happen last night, Mam?'

Kitty assured her that nothing out of the way had occurred and pressed Lizzie to explain why she'd asked, but her daughter just shrugged and wouldn't say any more.

She was just about to ask the little 'uns if they'd like a cup of tea when there was a knock on the front door and Kitty began to shake because she knew, she just knew, it was bad news.

'Oh, no!' she wailed, running down the hall to open the door. 'Oh, dear God, no!'

Sean and Dougal looked up from the table, alarmed by her cries, and they both began to sob as well.

Outside was a boy with a telegram informing her that Rory was dead.

Some people said, 'But you've ten more lovely children, Kitty. Imagine if he'd been the only one,' but Kitty felt as much sorrow for the loss of Rory as a mother who'd had just one child. After all, she reasoned defiantly, if you had a finger cut off, you wouldn't comfort yourself by saying, 'Never mind, I've got nine left.'

Unlike many mothers with large families, Kitty never got her children confused as they grew older. She remembered Rory's birth as clearly as if it were yesterday.

He'd been one of the few to arrive in the daylight hours. Theresa Garrett had been there, of course, and Rory was an easy birth, being only her second baby, and he turned out to be quicker at walking than Kevin but slower with his teeth which had given a lot of trouble. But apart from those restless, painful months, he'd been a sunny child, always good-humoured.

Of course his teething hadn't been nearly so bad as Nellie's. She'd screamed blue murder night after night, so much so that Tom had threatened to throw her out of the window. Rory had insisted on chewing the ring of his dummy instead of the teat and that helped to keep him quiet. Indeed, his first word was 'dum dum', though he hadn't managed that till he was eighteen months old.

Lizzie had been best for talking, though Jimmie hadn't been far behind and he hadn't stopped talking since. Paddy was the cleverest of the boys so far and was at grammar school, going off every day looking ever so smart in a white shirt and tie and blazer, though he kept his cap hidden in his pocket till he got on the bus.

Such lovely, lovely children, all of them.

You gave birth to your children, thought Kitty bitterly, went through hell to deliver them into the world, guarded them, cared for them. You shielded them from violent fathers, took the blows on your own back. Kept them warm in winter, knitted gloves, scarves, patched the soles of their shoes with bits of lino to keep their feet dry, then you scrabbled in the road for vegetable scraps after the outdoor market closed and begged the baker for yesterday's bread to feed them.

You even sold your body to stem their hunger.

Then you walked with them to school on their first day, even if it meant trailing three or four little 'uns along with you and you bathed their bruises, bandaged their cuts, wiped their noses and their tears.

Oh, how you cherished your children. You raised them to be fine young men and women and then in a freak accident, a moment of carelessness, or because a lunatic invades Poland or some country you've never even heard of before, despite all your love, all your care, your child, your lovely son, is taken from you.

For the first time in her life, Kitty found it hard to get comfort from the church. She wanted Rory here. She wanted to see him, laughing, straight and tall. She wanted to touch and hear him.

Monsignor Kelly said Kitty should be grateful that Rory was in heaven now, but instead of being grateful, she was angry. She couldn't understand how his death was part of God's great plan.

She was so upset at Monsignor Kelly's complacency, his insistence that she should be happy instead of sad, that in a gesture of defiance, she told the Air Force Captain who came to see her a few days later, that she wanted her son buried in Suffolk, near the base. She couldn't stomach the idea of a priest who didn't care, presiding over the Requiem Mass, chanting prayers he didn't mean.

Poor Kitty was nothing without her children. No one ever knew, but she often mourned her lost babies. The ones born dead or murdered in her womb by Tom. The little 'uns who hadn't got as far as this great cruel world. She'd given them all names and never forgot them. There were Peter and Brendan who'd be well into their teens by now, Clare and Kathleen . . . Kitty's heart often bled for her eleven dead babies, just as it bled now for her tall and handsome Rory.

The only good thing to come out of his death, not that Kitty noticed it, was that with so many people calling to express their condolences, and with them being so sincere and sympathetic, promising to remember Rory in their prayers or have special masses said, Kitty began to go out and mix with her neighbours once again.

Lizzie felt numb about Rory's death. Her brothers and sisters and her mam and even people like Mrs Garrett and Mary Plunkett cried openly. Lizzie couldn't cry, couldn't feel sad, and it worried her, watching her family weep as they knelt round Rory's photo at night, saying the rosary out loud, yet she felt nothing.

The Air Force people sent train tickets and Kitty and Jimmie went down to Suffolk for the funeral. Rory was to be burried in a tiny cemetery in a country churchyard a long way from the base.

'The nearest Catholic church, I'm afraid,' explained the priest, Father Watts, the first non-Irish priest Kitty had met. 'This isn't Roman Catholic territory, you see, Mrs O'Brien – not like Liverpool.'

Kitty asked to see the body but the Captain explained to the grieving woman that it was too late. The casket had been sealed. They'd made sure it would be, knowing the condition of O'Brien's head.

Really, Kitty thought unhappily, it should be Lizzie with her. It was a daughter's place to be by her mother's side in such circumstances. But Lizzie had refused, made some lame excuse about important work at school. As if anything could be more important than your own brother's funeral. And Lizzie hadn't seemed upset either, not like the other children. Perhaps she had used all her emotions up after that terrible time with Tom and the hospital and the stabbing.

Kitty and Jimmie were driven through fairytale Suffolk lanes, where the trees drooped and met overhead to form leafy tunnels, and they passed by thatched cottages with daffodils dancing on the lawns and long narrow paths which led to great mansion houses, past where sheep and cows grazed on rolling green fields . . .

But neither of them noticed the spectacular countryside. All they could think of was Rory.

9

On Easter Monday 1945, Lizzie's fourteenth birthday, Kitty was making a pathetic attempt to organise a special tea. Just back from Suffolk, she was finding it difficult to pull herself together, but she'd managed to buy a present for Lizzie, a nice leather purse, and Tony and Chris had clubbed together and got a real silver locket on a chain. Kevin sent a manicure set from abroad, very smart in a crocodile-leather case.

'Ta, Mam,' Lizzie accepted the purse ungraciously. She knew she was about to hurt Kitty's feelings and felt uncomfortable.

'We'll have a really nice tea, luv. Josie O'Connor's icing a bit of bunloaf fer us and I managed ter get a tin of salmon in the grocer's the other day and some tomatoes and I'll make a jelly later on.'

'Don't bother, Mam,' Lizzie said offhandedly. 'I'm going out.'

'Where to, luv?' Kitty's face fell.

'Ter Southport with Marie.'

So off she went in her tangerine dress and her high-heeled shoes, feeling very grown up because she was fourteen and soon to start work in the dye factory, the biggest employer in Bootle, though her mam didn't know that; she thought Lizzie was staying on at school till summer.

The other children persuaded Kitty to make the special tea anyway, if only because it was Easter Monday, but Kitty was miserable all day long thinking Lizzie would soon be as lost to her as Rory, but in her daughter's case, it was Kitty herself who was to blame. She felt particularly bad when Paddy came home and said he'd seen Marie Gordon serving behind the counter in the paper shop.

Anticipating an entire day out on the arm of a generous American led to an ever greater crowd of women than usual waiting at Central Station that Easter Monday morning.

Georgie, limping and white-faced, waited with them, though she knew it was unlikely she'd be picked up so early. It wouldn't be until a late, late hour she'd get a man, and even then it wasn't certain.

As ever, it was Hank who was first through the ticket barrier and with his usual enthusiasm, he picked Lizzie up and swung her round and round until a shoe flew off.

A crowd of GIs gathered round. One of them picked the shoe up and, bending on one knee, replaced it on Lizzie's foot with a flourish.

'It fits! It fits!' he shouted. '*This* is Cinderella and now she must marry her prince.'

'Honey,' said Hank, 'this is my greatest pal, Tex, who, as you might guess, comes from Texas same as yours truly.' He turned to the rest of the group. 'And this here is my greatest pal, Junior T. And another greatest pal, Duke.'

Tex was thin, lean and blond and could have been Hank's twin they were so alike. Both were dwarfed by Duke, broad-shouldered, flat-nosed and the squad's boxing champion, and also by Junior T, a leathery beanpole of a boy with strange silvery-coloured hair.

One by one Lizzie was introduced to Hank's greatest pals. Fred, dapper and neat, whose real name no one knew. They called him Fred because he danced all the time, just like Fred Astaire. Nero was dark-skinned, dark-eyed and Nero was his surname not his Christian name, and he was Italian and therefore a bit inferior to a real, red-blooded American like himself, Hank explained later, but because he was very, very rich and his paternal uncle was a 'godfather' in the New York mafia, he was considered acceptable as one of the greatest pals. Then came Buzz, with his horn-rimmed glasses and grave expression, who only looked about sixteen.

'He's going to be a great writer some day,' said Hank. 'Always scribbling. And last, but not least, my greatest pal, Beefy. And you can see where he gets the name from.'

'Shut yo mouth, yo Southern trash,' kidded Beefy, who was almost as wide as he was tall. He shook hands in a real gentlemanly fashion. They all did, and Lizzie felt like a queen amidst her adoring courtiers as they crowded round, looking at her appreciatively.

'You sho' was right, Hank boy. You picked a little beauty here,' drawled Junior T, breathing on Buzz's glasses so he couldn't see.

'Hank said you was as pretty as Scarlett O'Hara in that film,' whispered Duke from behind, right in her ear. 'But I reckon he was wrong. You're a whole lot prettier than that there actress.'

What wholesome, healthy and well-mannered boys they were. Not one of them over twenty. Bright-eyed, excited, not making any attempt to pick up other girls, but all set to spend the day with Lizzie to celebrate her birthday.

Most of the still-waiting girls cast covetous eyes as she left with her eight young men, all that is except Georgie, who shouted, 'Good luck, Lizzie, luv.'

To get to Southport meant walking through the centre of Liverpool to Exchange Station. As it was a Bank Holiday, all the shops and offices were closed. Not yet midday, a still-watery sun gave promise of a fine afternoon.

Hank draped his arm possessively round Lizzie's shoulders and as they walked through the deserted streets, the other boys danced around them, paying Lizzie extravagant compliments, walking backwards in front of her and blowing kisses, bowing, laughing, joking. Fred tapdanced on the kerb and invented a special step in her honour.

'C'mon, fellas, she's mine,' Hank protested, kissing her left ear.

'No, she isn't, she's ours. She belongs to all of us,' someone shouted and Lizzie wanted to cry with happiness.

The train was crowded with day-trippers going to Southport or the beaches on the way – Formby, Ainsdale or Birkdale. Despite the general resentment many English people felt towards the Americans on their soil, the unabashed exuberance of the eight young men soon charmed the long carriage full of people.

Beefy produced a mouth organ and in no time, fifty or sixty people were joined together in singing *Run Rabbit Run*, *The White Cliffs of Dover* and *Yankee Doodle Dandy*.

There was a chorus of goodbyes when they parted at Southport Station.

This was the furthest Lizzie had been away from Bootle. She was overwhelmed by the beauty of Lord Street with its central, tree-lined reservation, gracious and expensive shops and ornate Victorian arcades. She had never realised that such an elegant and lovely town existed so close to home. Perhaps Mam would like to come here one day.

'Gee, this sure is a stylish place,' said Hank admiringly.

By now the sun shone, bright and warm for an April day.

'How's about some chow?' suggested Junior T.

They went into the first café they came to, not bothering as Lizzie and everyone else she knew would have done, to check the prices on the menu outside. What did they care about money?

A sour-faced elderly waitress joined two tables together and Lizzie was placed at the head, Hank at the foot. She ordered turkey and stuffing, roast potatoes and peas.

Turkey! What with rationing and poverty, a turkey had never made an appearance on the table in Number 2 Chaucer Street, but now here were two thick white slices, which were tough and took a lot of chewing, but Lizzie convinced herself it tasted delectable.

For pudding there was fruit salad and ice cream, and in the salad there was a grape, a genuine grape! So, that was what a grape looked like. Purplish-red, the skin thick and difficult to cut and the inside juicy and green. It tasted tart and sweet at the same time and there were pips which she didn't like to spit out, not with eight pairs of eyes on her, so she ate them as well.

Even the bad-tempered waitress in her rusty black dress and lace cap and apron soon succumbed to the young soldiers' charm, particularly when Nero said she was the spitting image of his mother. She ended up smiling and nodding, and even brought extra milk and sugar for their tea without them having to ask. Then they toasted Lizzie's birthday, holding up their cups, and Hank reminded them they might be getting hitched pretty soon. Lizzie didn't disillusion them. If they learnt she was only fourteen they might disappear, like the Captain in the Adelphi.

'Hey, how many brothers and sisters you got, Liz?' Duke asked. He was sitting on her left and kept pressing his knee against hers.

'Eight brothers and two sisters,' she replied, entirely forgetting Rory was dead, but when she remembered, she didn't mention he'd just died for fear it would cast a gloom over the occasion and anyway, just thinking of home reminded her of the stuff Mam had bought for the special tea and made her feel real bad.

She didn't feel bad for long because Nero, who was on her right, leaned over – she felt his warm sweet breath on her cheek – and said, 'Y'know, Lizzie honey, you got the sweetest mouth and the cutest nose and the most beautiful eyes I ever seen on a gal. As for your hair—'

'Hey, you two, cut that out!' yelled Hank from the end of the table. 'That's *my* gal you've got there.'

'No, it isn't,' replied Nero, and along with the others, chorused, 'She's *ours!*'

Flushed, eyes like stars, Lizzie basked in their united regard.

Lizzie shrieked. She'd never been so frightened in all her life. Every ounce of breath had drained from her body and she was convinced she was going to suffocate and die.

'Gee, honey,' said Hank, on whom the roller coaster was having no apparent effect, 'calm down now.'

But Lizzie couldn't calm down and she didn't stop screaming until the ride stopped, when she adamantly refused to have another go, much to the regret of the other boys who'd been looking forward to riding with her.

'I'll never go on anything like that again as long as I live,' she vowed.

She did agree to ride the Bobby horses, though, and found the gentle up and down motion enjoyable, especially with a pair of strong arms around her. She lost count of the turns she had, at least one with each of the boys, two turns with some.

Buzz, looking so young and wise in his horn-rimmed glasses, was the only one who didn't kid her along or keep touching her. Lizzie wondered if he didn't like her, but found him watching her intently with a solemn, gentle expression on his face and decided he was just shy.

As the day wore on, she became more and more exhilarated. There'd never been a day like this in all her life and there might never be another, not with so many young men hanging onto her every word and rushing to do her bidding.

'Lizzie, honey, look at this!'

'C'mon, Lizzie, let's go on these dodgem cars.'

They were all so anxious to please. If this was what being pretty meant, then she was glad she'd been so blessed. Perhaps all the rest of her life would be like this; men forever on hand wanting to look after her, asking her opinion, needing her approval for everything they did.

'For you, sweetheart.' Fred bounded up with a furry rabbit and thrust it into her arms.

'Another prize!' she exclaimed delightedly. She'd already got a teddy bear and a golliwog, a comb in a leather case, a doll and a gold glass sugar basin which her mam would love.

Junior T, Tex and Hank were at the shooting gallery driving the stallholder wild. Such good shots, they won every time. He was considering refusing them any more turns, but a crowd had gathered to watch and applaud and he didn't dare turn them away, particularly when they began to give the prizes away.

Every now and again, groups of children would besiege them with cries of 'Got'ny gum, chum?' and the boys would hand out strips of chewing gum to eager, grasping little hands. Nero swopped a pack of cigarettes for an old shopping bag to put the prizes in.

Beefy tried to teach Lizzie how to use a rifle, putting his hefty arms around her from behind, pressing himself close against her. She felt his hand momentarily, accidentally, caress her breast.

'Hold it this way, cutie. That's it. I think you've got it now.'

But Lizzie couldn't stop giggling and missed every time, much to the stallholder's relief.

The fairground eventually lost its interest and together they began to wander towards the Southport sands and the far-off strip of silvery sea.

Beefy began to play a sad lament on his mouth organ whilst Fred did what he called a soft-shoe-shuffle on the sand.

'C'mon, old buddy,' yelled Duke to Buzz who was lagging behind, his hands stuffed morosely in his pockets.

Her boys! Lizzie almost felt like a mother to them all. Hank linked one of her arms and Tex the other. Duke, Nero and Junior T began to play football with an old can.

The late afternoon sun began to dip into the sea, turning the thin line of water into a strip of vivid orange, and the beach shone gold. Behind them were the dunes which the sea never reached, the sand pale and powdery and dotted with clumps of blackened reed, broken and bent by the wind.

The few people about appeared to be making their way back to the town for it was starting to get chilly. The sun was visibly sinking further into the sea and it began to get dark.

Lizzie shivered in her thin silk dress. In her hurry to leave that morning, she'd come out without a coat. Earlier she'd taken off her shoes as the high heels kept sinking into the sand and by now her feet were wet. She turned and began to walk in the direction of the dunes where the sand was dry.

'Let's go back,' she said. The boys stopped dead at the sound of her voice. 'I'm starving and I'm cold.'

'We'll warm y'up, honey chile,' said Tex, and there was something in the tone of his voice that Lizzie didn't like.

She looked from one to the other of her boys and what she saw made her heart begin to pound so loudly and so fiercely that she was sure her body must be shaking too.

They'd become different people, different boys altogether, with hard faces and narrowed eyes and they'd lost their smiles and their gaiety and their good humour. Suddenly they were menacing and didn't look as if they liked Lizzie one bit.

A sixth sense made Lizzie look up and down the beach for signs of life but the only people visible were tiny figures, way out of earshot.

Hank was the nearest to her. He was her boyfriend and would protect her. She moved over to him and took his arm. 'Hank?' She wanted him to explain what was happening and was thankful when he put his arms around her.

'Oh, Hank!' Everything was all right. Hank loved her. Hadn't he told her so dozens and dozens of times?

But she soon realised that Hank's arms weren't protective at all. His fingers dug into her shoulders with such force she yelped in pain. 'C'mon now, honey,' he said in a strange, harsh voice. 'You've bin asking for this all day.'

Asking for what? What was he talking about?

Hank dragged her towards the sandhills out of sight of the beach. She could hear the others following, their footsteps muffled on the sand, and she stumbled on a stunted, brittle bush, dropping her shoes.

She fell forward, full-length, and felt Hank straddle her and push at her dress. With her face buried in the soft, suffocating sand, she couldn't shout, could scarcely breathe. She coughed and choked as Hank tore away her clothes and shouted, 'Just look at that ass, fellas,' and there was a jeering laugh from his friends.

'Turn her over,' one of them said, so Hank did, and as she hoarsely gulped in air, she saw him looking down at her, eyes blazing and a wild cruel smile on his face. His trousers were undone and he held his bulging pink penis in one hand and was trying to force her legs apart with the other. When he couldn't manage it, Junior T and Beefy came over and each took one of her legs and held them apart whilst Hank entered her. Then he yelled to his pals, 'She sho' done this before, I can tell,' and when he'd reached a climax he moved away for Junior T, then Beefy, Nero . . .

Lizzie lost track. Her marvellous boys who'd made this the most wonderful day of her life now took their fill of her and instead of paying her compliments, they called her a 'little whore' and 'fucking English bitch'.

Duke thrust his tongue down her throat so hard it made her retch and he hit her. 'Slut!' he rasped. 'Don't make that noise when I kiss you.' He raised his hand to strike her again but someone stopped him.

When they'd finished and left her lying there, exposed, lifeless, numb, she began to cry. She could hear them on the beach, giggling like naughty schoolboys, sounding almost their old happy selves again. They were discussing what to do with her.

'Leave her,' someone said contemptuously. It sounded like Nero. 'We've shown her a good time.'

'Well . . .' that was Hank's voice. He sounded embarrassed. 'Don't you think we should take her back? I mean, we can't just leave her.'

'I was last,' that was Fred speaking, 'an' she seemed okay to me.'

'C'mon, fellas,' someone called from a distance, as if they were already walking away. 'Won't the English bars be open by now?'

'Duke's right. Come on, don't know 'bout you, but I could really do with a drink.'

And so they went.

The sky had darkened, turned to grey. Lizzie began to tremble uncontrollably. She wondered if she should stay, embedded in the sand until someone found and rescued her. But no, she had to get home, back to Mam, to her family and Chaucer Street.

But how? She had no money. The small amount she'd brought had been spent on postcards and a lavender bag for Mam which had *Welcome To Southport* embroidered on it. Hank had her return ticket.

A voice said hesitantly, 'Lizzie!'

Inside, Lizzie screamed. She thought they'd all gone. Not again. Please, God! Not again.

Buzz was crouched on top of a dune looking down at her, blinking through his glasses. He looked as if he'd been crying.

'Are you okay, Lizzie?'

She nodded dully and attempted to stand. Buzz leapt to his feet and came down and helped her up. He fetched her clothes and turned away as she put them back on and he collected her things together. The postcards were bent and the lavender bag covered with sand. Soft toys were scattered everywhere. Buzz stuffed them in the bag Nero had so charmingly exchanged for cigarettes an hour or so before. Could it really be only an hour? How could the world change so much in such a short time?

'I think you'd be better off without your shoes,' said Buzz, and he carried them as well as all the other things.

Lizzie feld cold and her thighs throbbed with pain. Buzz must have noticed her shivering, because he removed his jacket and wrapped it round her shoulders.

'I never . . . you know, Lizzie,' he said.

Lizzie nodded, though she hadn't realised at the time.

'I'm sorry, Lizzie,' Buzz was saying. 'I could just tell the way things were going.'

Her voice was locked in her throat. She wanted to ask, 'Why didn't you warn me?' but nothing would come. Even so, Buzz answered as if she'd spoken aloud.

'If I'd told you, you wouldn't have taken any notice. You wouldn't have believed me.'

Of course he was right. She would never in a million years have believed dear Tex and good old Junior T and courteous Nero and Duke and Beefy and Fred, felt so badly about her, considered her a whore and a bitch.

Hank was different. He was her fella and it was only to be expected that he'd want to make love to her. But not like that! It should never have been like that, thought Lizzie, stifling a sob.

Buzz coughed awkwardly. When they reached hard ground he returned her shoes and walked with her to the station where he bought her a ticket. Once on the train they sat opposite each other in complete silence till it reached Marsh Lane and Lizzie got off, too miserable to even say goodbye.

'You forgot this.'

She was on the platform and Buzz was standing by the open doors of the carriage holding out the bag of prizes. Lizzie didn't want them, but he looked so pathetic and young and had helped her, trying to make up for what his friends had done, that despite her wretchedness, she couldn't bring herself to refuse.

She took the proffered bag and whispered, 'Thank you. Goodbye, Buzz.'

His face lit up when she spoke to him.

'Goodbye, Lizzie,' he said as the door closed in his face.

Lots of people got off at the same time. Some small children were crying, tired after the long day out, but in the main, everyone was cheerful and happy and they jostled Lizzie as she sluggishly made her way to the exit carrying the bag full of mementos of her day out in Southport.

Queen's Gate

10

'Good luck, Lisa,' sobbed Jackie, who'd had too much to drink as usual. She emptied the remainder of the confetti over Lisa's head. 'Good luck.'

Lisa laughed, crossed her eyes and blew upwards at the bits that had attached themselves to the veil of her hat. Everybody applauded, even the landlord of the pub who'd have to clear up the mess. Brian's hand tightened on her elbow involuntarily, as if warning her not to be silly, to behave. At the same time, he glanced in the direction of his mother to see if she was watching.

She was.

Mrs Smith was the only person from their group sitting down. She didn't drink, disapproved of a reception in a public house, and had tried to insist on a church wedding, but her new daughter-in-law had a mind of her own and refused. She eyed her balefully over her glass of orange squash.

Of course she'd always wanted Brian, her only child, to marry someone pretty. After all, he deserved to. Such a handsome boy with his pale, almost translucent skin, flushed now with the excitement of the day. Baby blue eyes – the same blue he'd been born with – and silky fawn-coloured hair flopping on his forehead. She'd nagged him to get it cut, but for once he'd refused to do her bidding. Apparently Lisa preferred it long.

Lisa!

The girl was lovely, there was no doubt about that. Tall and slim to the point of skinniness, her height accentuated by her pink leather shoes with heels at least three inches high. Her suit was pink too – grosgrain, a tight-fitting calf-length skirt showing off every curve, and a short shaped jacket accentuating her small breasts. Today, her chocolate-brown hair was drawn back into a bun, the severity of the style countered by a pink pillbox hat with matching veil reaching over the eyes then gathered into a big flaring bow at the back. Not too much make-up, Mrs Smith conceded that much – just a touch of eye-shadow and shell-pink lipstick. Yet despite that she looked like a film star, a strange, exotic film star – Hedy Lamarr or Gene Tierney. Not quite English, with those huge brown-gold eyes and high cheekbones.

Mrs Smith had marriage planned for Brian at twenty-six, when he would wed a nice ordinarily-pretty girl – one perhaps not quite so intelligent as himself. A girl she could train to be a real wife, teach how to darn and cook, look after the house and take care of her boy Brian in the way he was accustomed, but most importantly, to provide her with a grandson. Another Brian. Another child to devote her life to. She sighed, impatiently waving away the cigarette smoke when it floated in her direction.

She'd designed her outfit for her son's wedding years ago, had imagined inviting all the old aunts and uncles, her brother and sister-in-law and their children, one or two friends. But Miss Lisa O'Brien had refused to be married in church and didn't want a proper reception, not even in her mother-in-law's home; Mrs Smith had had the menu worked out too. Instead, they were in this rowdy pub with someone playing a piano in one corner and crowds of strangers toasting Lisa and Brian in Guinness and pints of shandy.

In the end, the only guests invited were her brother George and his wife Margery, and there was George, enjoying himself no end, joining in the singing, unable to take his eyes off the bride. But then who could? She was radiant, the cynosure of all eyes, the recipient of dozens of congratulatory kisses.

When Brian told her about Lisa who worked in the bookshop on the ground floor of his office building, she'd built up a picture in her mind of a studious-looking girl and hoped she wasn't too mousy for her son. But when she'd met her – why, the girl didn't look as if she could read a comic, let alone a book! Then there was talk of marriage, and with Brian only twenty-two. She'd tried to make him see sense but he was besotted, so she'd shrugged, started to make arrangements and found just the right wedding dress in Dickins & Jones, but when she told Lisa, the girl just laughed.

'I don't want that sort of wedding,' she said dismissively.

Then Mrs Smith went to see the vicar and had a long talk with him, and despite the fact he hadn't even met the girl, he agreed to conduct the wedding in his church. She'd informed Brian and a few days later he told her Lisa wanted the wedding in a registry office.

As a wedding present, for their honeymoon, Mrs Smith had booked the bed and breakfast hotel in Hastings where she and Brian had spent all their holidays since he was a baby. She had photographs. Such a picture he made, toddling along the beach with his bucket and spade, then older and playing cricket on the sand, but Lisa was indignant when she discovered this. She'd decided on Paris. Paris! Well, she'd fit in there better than Hastings, Mrs Smith told herself spitefully.

She sipped her orange squash and thought with satisfaction, 'Once she's back and living in my house, I'll soon sort out Miss Lisa O'Brien. Or I should say, Mrs Lisa Smith.'

Eyes brimming with tears, Jackie said, 'I'll miss you heaps.'

'No, you won't,' Lisa laughed. 'I'll still be working for dear Mr Greenbaum and I can see you every single day, except Sundays.'

'Sunday is the day I'll miss you most of all,' sniffed her friend, getting ready to cry again. 'I never see Gordon on Sundays, either.'

Gordon put his arm around her shoulders and gave her a clumsy hug. 'Come on, old girl. Stiff upper lip, eh?'

Lisa felt like pouring her glass of wine over him. She hated Gordon with his ridiculous moustache. Forty, married with children, he'd been stringing Jackie along for years. Ex-RAF officer – or so he said. There was something phoney about his wartime slang, as phoney as his love for Jackie. She'd thought that even before he'd made a pass at her that day he'd called when

Jackie was away . . . Yet Jackie was so much in love with him and believed everything he told her, about his wife not understanding him and how he'd leave like a shot if it wasn't for the children.

'I won't sell a single book for two whole weeks till she gets back from Paris,' groaned Mr Greenbaum, his eighty-year-old face exaggeratedly mournful. 'The books I've shifted since she came to work for me! I've sold books on mathematics to people who can't add up, novels by Proust to customers who came in for an Ethel M. Dell, and do you know, she once sold an entire set of Dickens to a man who only entered my shop to ask the way to the nearest tube!'

'He'll be bereft without you, Lisa dear,' said Miriam, his wife, looking elegant in her best mauve silk dress and astrakhan coat.

'We all will,' said Ralph. 'Saturday nights will never be the same again, will they, Piers?'

Piers shook his head and gave an impish smile.

Beside her Lisa felt Brian stiffen. He had always resented her friendship with these two men.

'Lisa.' She felt a hand on her arm and turned to see Brian's Aunt Margery. Her heart sank, expecting some sort of lecture. The woman was probably in her late forties, quite smartly dressed. Her face was plain, but her expression friendly.

'Dorothy says you're going to live with her in Chiswick.'

'Only for a while,' said Lisa. 'Till we've saved enough for a place of our own.'

'Well, save quickly, dear. I know this is out of order and I couldn't have brought myself to say it if I hadn't had three gin and tonics, but get Brian out of his mother's clutches as soon as you can.'

'Where is his father?' asked Lisa, out of interest. 'Brian won't speak about him and I don't like to ask Mrs Smith.'

'Did a bunk, dear, when Brian was one. She, Dorothy that is,' Margery lowered her voice and spoke in a stage whisper, 'didn't like *It*. You know – sex. Once Brian was born he was the only male she wanted, so Peter either had to go without forever or find someone else.' She shrugged. 'Poor Brian has had a God-awful picture of his father painted for him all his life.'

'I see,' Lisa nodded sagely. 'Well, thanks for the advice.'

Aunt Margery squeezed her hand. 'All the luck in the world, dear. I wish we lived nearer than Bristol so I could be on hand if ever you need a friendly face.'

'Lisa! Another hour and the train leaves,' yelled Brian. Across the room, Mrs Smith winced.

'Time for one last drink,' announced Mr Greenbaum. 'Champagne, I think.'

Mrs Smith grudgingly accepted a glass and actually came and joined the small circle as they drank a toast to the young married couple.

'To Lisa and Brian,' said Mr Greenbaum, holding his glass high, his wrinkled face wreathed in smiles.

'Lisa and Brian,' everybody chorused.

The ferry swayed and seemed to perch at an acute angle for a long, long time, though it was probably no more than a few seconds before it righted itself. Then it swung the other way, like a giant shuddering seesaw.

Brian, along with at least half the other passengers in the lounge, was sick again. Lisa would have felt fine if it hadn't been for the pools of vomit which turned her stomach. The ship's motion didn't affect her at all. She decided to go up on deck. Brian was oblivious to her presence, too ill to notice her attempts to soothe him.

There were a few hardy souls on top holding firmly to the handrail.

'You'd best not walk on deck in those heels, miss,' said an elderly man clad in a waterproof cape and hat. 'A sudden dip and you'll lose your balance and be over the side. There's an observation lounge up front, you'll be safe in there.'

The small glass lounge was empty. Lisa sat in the front seat. Spray showered against the windows, obscuring the angry, foam-tipped sea outside. She took her hat off – the wind had nearly blown it away and the pins were hurting. Then she leaned back against the hard wooden bench and thought about the last long journey she'd made, from Liverpool to London.

They say – Kitty was always saying it – that time heals everything, but it didn't heal Lizzie. No matter how many months passed since that day in Southport, the horror remained as fresh as if it had happened yesterday.

Nightmarish memories haunted her. If it wasn't Hank and his greatest pals, then Tom entered her dreams. A night rarely passed that she didn't wake up in a suffocating sweat, arms thrashing, tossing and turning and disturbing Mam who shared the bed with her.

Poor Mam! Lizzie knew she was the only one of the children who worried her. The older ones were working, all in good jobs. Kevin had got married the year before and Tony and Chris were courting. All the little 'uns got good reports from school. It was only Lizzie who went around with a long face, some days scarcely bothering to comb her hair, throwing on the first clothes that came to hand before she went to work in the dye factory, a job she loathed. She'd started soon after her fourteenth birthday, but scarcely ever spoke to anyone there and after a while, no one spoke to her.

One day, she slashed the tangerine dress to ribbons and threw it in the bin.

Secretly, or so they thought, Nellie and Joan referred to her as 'old Sourpuss' and Jimmie kept saying, 'You're a real wet blanket nowadays, our Liz,' and he would hug her, try to cheer her up, then become hurt when Lizzie flinched. She couldn't stand anyone touching her, particularly a man, even if it was her favourite brother.

There was such warmth in the house, such love and demonstrative affection, but Lizzie was excluded – not from the getting but from the giving. She felt like a stranger, an alien who didn't belong in Chaucer Street amidst all these happy, outgoing people.

When Lizzie entered the house, people became quiet, just like they'd done when Tom came in, scared to laugh or joke in case they upset her.

On her sixteenth birthday, two years to the day she'd gone to Southport so full of anticipation of a nice day out, Lizzie left home.

She was always the first to wake. Mam was snoring beside her. Lizzie glanced across at her sisters, still sharing the same single bed, one at each end. Their faces were peaceful. Neither had a care in the world. She envied their innocence, their uncomplicated lives.

Mam had a party planned for tonight when Lizzie got home. It was supposed to be a surprise, but Lizzie had seen the birthday cake on the pantry shelf and noticed the jellies left to set on the back kitchen doorstep before she came to bed. Tonight, everyone would kiss her and wish her Happy Birthday and expect her to look cheerful and she couldn't, she just couldn't. Once again, she'd let them down and leave them wondering what had happened to their Lizzie, whom they loved so much, but who couldn't love them back in return. In fact, it was even difficult to raise a smile most of the time, particularly if it was expected of her.

She'd become a blight on her family, like Dad had been. They'd be better off without her.

Stealthily she climbed out of bed and took her clothes downstairs to get dressed. Then she put her Post Office savings book in her bag and was about to leave when she remembered she'd need her ration book too. She took it off the mantelpiece where Kitty kept them stacked in a neat row. The act of removing the book from all the others pierced through her like a knife, as if by this single action she was severing herself from the O'Brien family forever. Yet despite the pain, she felt a stir of excitement as she closed the door of Number 2 Chaucer Street behind her, and as she ran towards the tram stop, actually found herself smiling.

Where did you go when you ran away from home? London seemed the obvious place, the only place really.

Lizzie had to wait outside the Post Office by Lime Street Station for nearly an hour until it opened so she could draw the money out for her fare, which only left her with five pounds.

Buying a single ticket to London was almost as bad as taking her ration book – such a final, separating act. She sat on the train, oblivious to the varying countryside, the towns where the train stopped to pick up more passengers, scarcely aware it was a bright, warm April day, that people were dressed in their summer clothes. All she was conscious of was the noisy rhythm of the train's wheels as it ate up the miles on its way to London, and the enormity of what she had done. She'd left home. She was embarking on The Unknown, all alone.

So this was London. A big, dirty station, little different from Lime Street. Lizzie didn't even know what it was called. She stood outside the ticket barrier, unsure which way to go and feeling slightly panic-stricken. A lot of people were making their way down some stairs marked 'Underground', so she followed and to her surprise found herself in another station. Beneath her feet she felt the rumble of trains. She bought the cheapest ticket, went down an escalator and got on the first train that came storming out of the narrow tunnel. Inside, she studied a map on the wall opposite. The names of the stations meant nothing. Where had she got on? She'd never even met anybody who'd been to London, and she experienced a further bout of panic. Where on earth was she going?

The carriage was only half-full. Opposite her, a young negro sat reading a newspaper, a student's scarf thrown casually round his neck. He had a friendly approachable face and Lizzie tried to pluck up the courage to ask his advice.

The train stopped at several stations and she kept glancing at him nervously when suddenly, he closed his paper and her heart sank. He was going to get off. But no, he was merely turning to another page.

She took a deep breath. 'Excuse me.'

'Hello.' He lowered his paper and gave her a friendly grin.

'I'm looking for somewhere to live.'

'Well, you could move in with me, but my wife might complain.' His grin widened further.

'I mean, I've never been to London before. Where's the best place to look?'

'You want a hostel or a flat?' He noted her shabby clothes and untidy hair.

Lizzie thought a moment. Not a hostel. She wanted to be by herself, not with a crowd of other girls. Surely she had enough money for a place of her own.

'A flat,' she said.

'Try Earl's Court. *Everybody* lives in Earl's Court.'

'How do I get there?'

'Well, you're on the Circle line . . .'

'Am I?'

He looked amused and pointed to the map above his head. 'See the yellow line? That's the Circle. When you get to Gloucester Road, get off and it's just one stop on the District line to Earl's Court.'

'Thank you.'

'Any time,' he said, grinning.

She didn't say anything for a few minutes, then, 'Excuse me.'

'Hello again.'

'I'm sorry to appear so stupid, but when I get to Earl's Court, what do I do? Just knock on doors?'

'Christ, you're a greenhorn. No, you'll find dozens of little shops with cards outside advertising accommodation to let. Want me to come with you? Of course, my wife might divorce me if she finds out, and we've only been married a month . . .'

'No, no,' said Lizzie hastily. 'But thanks for offering.'

'You're very welcome.' He returned to his paper and got off a few stations later. 'Good luck,' he said.

After he'd gone and the space opposite became empty, she caught sight of her blurred reflection in the dark window and was horrified. Wild strands of hair had escaped from the bun into which it had been hastily scraped that morning and the black coat she'd bought from Paddy's Market nearly two years before was about three sizes too big for her. She'd bought it big deliberately, wanting to hide her body from the world and look as un-attractive as possible, but now, glancing round the compartment, she saw that most of the women, the young ones particularly, were smartly dressed. She felt like a tramp and searched through her bag for a comb, but there was none so she redid the bun as best she could with her hands.

Earl's Court bustled with people, mainly young, mainly foreign. Even those speaking English had strange accents. It was an exciting, cosmopolitan atmosphere. The afternoon sun beamed down on the crowded pavements.

Right outside the station, a sweet and tobacconist's shop had a window full of postcards, mainly rooms to let. Her heart lifted. This was going to be easier than she'd thought, though rents were higher than she'd expected. Some were as much as five pounds a week, though others were ten shillings or a pound less. There was one for only two pounds ten shillings: '*A girl to share two-roomed flat*', but Lizzie dismissed that one, determined to live alone. She made a list of numbers then went into the shop and bought a bar of chocolate, asking for the change in coppers for the phone box.

Lizzie had never used a telephone before and with her first call, she pressed the wrong button and her money came back. Some rooms were already gone. She made appointments to see two within the next hour and set off immediately.

The roads were like caverns with tall, four-storeyed houses looming up each side. She found the first street she wanted almost straight away. A grim-faced woman dressed in a flowered overall answered her knock.

'Yes?'

'I rang about the room.'

The woman looked her up and down contemptuously and said, 'Sorry, it's gone,' and slammed the door.

What little confidence Lizzie had completely ebbed away. For an hour she wandered the streets forlornly before plucking up the courage to keep the second appointment.

This time it was a man who opened the door. His trousers were sagging at the waist exposing a belly swelled by beer, and his shirt-sleeves were rolled up revealing hairy arms covered in tattoos.

'I've come about the room.'

'C'min.' He gestured with his cigarette and ash fell on the lino-covered floor.

The room was on the third floor. It was filthy, the corners covered in mould. Of course she could clean it herself. Wash the bedding. Scrub those walls.

'You share a kitchen and bathroom. They're along here.'

The bathroom contained a toilet and the room stank of urine. Food droppings littered the kitchen floor and the cooker was encrusted with dirt.

Four pounds a week for this!

'I'd like to think about it,' Lizzie said. 'I've got other rooms to look at.'

'Suit yourself,' the man said, shrugging carelessly.

She fled. Round the corner was a square, the centre a delicate garden of pink-flowered trees and bulging shrubs. She sat down on one of the wooden benches and wondered what to do next.

11

It was peaceful in the square. The sun glinted on the windows of the tall gracious houses. She wondered what time it was. It must be four or five o'clock by now and she had to find somewhere to live by tonight or waste money on a hotel. But you were supposed to have luggage for a hotel – she read that somewhere, and she had nothing except her handbag.

Pangs of hunger assailed her and she realised she'd had nothing to eat since last night's tea. Then she remembered the bar of chocolate in her pocket and took it out and unwrapped it. As soon as she'd finished eating it, she'd go back to the shop by the station and take down some more numbers.

Two women were approaching, leading a strange-looking dog. The back half of its body was shaven and the front was as fluffy as a powder puff. When they reached her, one of the women said in a hostile voice, 'Do you live in this square?'

'No,' said Lizzie.

'Well, this is private property. You're trespassing. This square is for residents only. They took the iron railings away for the war effort, otherwise it would be locked.'

Lizzie stared at her. What harm was she doing? Perhaps her bewilderment showed, for the woman looked a little ashamed.

'Finish your chocolate. There's no hurry,' she added, but Lizzie was already on her feet. As she walked away, the woman shouted, 'It *is* private property.'

Back at the shop, she peered at the cards again. A lot of them were no good – they wanted someone for an 'all-male household', or 'middle-aged lady to act as companion', or the rents were too high. She made a note of the only suitable numbers which remained and again noticed the card asking for '*A girl to share two-roomed flat*'. It was a pink card, neatly typed. Only two pounds, ten shillings! This time, Lizzie wrote the number at the bottom of her list and went into the telephone box for the second time.

The first number was answered by a foreigner whose accent was so thick, Lizzie couldn't understand a word. When she'd asked for the directions to be repeated a third time, the receiver at the other end was slammed down angrily. The second room had gone. The third had someone coming to view tomorrow. Would she ring back then and see if it was still available? Lizzie promised she would and then dialled the next-to-last number. A frosty voice asked if she had references.

'References for what?' she asked.

'Your character, from a previous landlady or an employer.'

Lizzie confessed she hadn't.

'Sorry, but I only take people with references.'

The only number left was the '*Girl to share*'. Lizzie hesitated. She could go around looking for another shop with a noticeboard, but it was getting late. Hundreds of people were pouring out of the Underground, coming home from work, the shops were closing and the sun beginning to dip behind the houses opposite. If this flat were still available, she could stay there for a few weeks until she found her feet – that's if the girl was prepared to share with someone who looked like a tramp . . .

Someone rapped sharply on the window of the telephone box. Lizzie had been ages just staring at the telephone, trying to make up her mind. She took a deep breath, picked up the instrument and dialled. The dialling tone sounded just once before the receiver was lifted and a cheerful, breathless voice said, 'Hallo!' and half-sang the number.

Lizzie swallowed. The girl sounded very confident. 'Hallo,' she whispered. 'It's about the flat. You want a girl to share.'

Of course it might have gone. It *was* awfully cheap.

'Ooh, of course I do. Can you come round now? That would be frightfully convenient, because I'm out at work all day. In fact, you're lucky catching me. I don't usually get home till eight.'

Lizzie assured her she could come immediately.

'Do you know Queen's Gate? It's in South Kensington. Where are you ringing from? I put cards in several shops.'

'Earl's Court,' Lizzie told her.

'That's not too far to walk. Of course, you could get the tube but it means changing.'

Lizzie assured her she'd prefer to walk, and took down the instructions carefully. Once there, she was to give three long rings and three short ones on the doorbell. Each flat had its code, the girl explained.

The houses in Queen's Gate were really grand, with tall white pillars and wrought-iron balconies. In one, the first-floor French windows were open and people were standing on the balcony wearing evening clothes. She could hear laughter and the clink of glass. Perhaps this was a cocktail party. Just like a novel, thought Lizzie, hugely impressed. Some of the houses were embassies. She couldn't imagine that anyone living in a road like this would want her, looking like she did, as a flatmate.

She reached Number 5 which was on the corner, rang the bell and waited so long for it to be answered that she began to wonder if the girl had seen her from the window and decided not to let her in.

At last the big stained-glass door opened and Lizzie's mouth dropped. The girl was actually wearing *pyjamas*! Pink satin pyjamas. Her milky blonde hair fell in soft waves and curls around her pretty, over-made-up face. She gave Lizzie a welcoming smile which lit up her wide, smoky-grey eyes and deepened the dimples in her creamy cheeks. She was as tall as Lizzie, but two or three stones heavier, the extra weight laid seductively on wide curved hips and a large firm bust. The backs of her plump hands were as dimpled as her face.

'Christ Almighty, don't you look a mess! Come in. It's a long trek upstairs,

I'm afraid. I'm on the fourth floor so take a deep breath. You're frightfully thin, aren't you? That's not a criticism, I'm green with envy.'

Lizzie was taken aback by the garrulous welcome. Although the girl's words could be construed as insulting, they were made in such a friendly way, she didn't take offence. The hallway was impressive, very big with a mosaic floor and a wide marble staircase. The girl began to run up the stairs, her fluffy pink slippers flopping on each step.

'It's two pounds ten shillings a week, by the way. Is that okay?'

'Fine,' said Lizzie, panting to keep up. With each floor, the stairs got narrower and steeper. By the time they reached the fourth, they were concrete and carpetless. The girl bounded ahead, her blonde curls bouncing. Lizzie's heart began to pound.

'Of course, I could afford all the rent, but then I think to myself – fifty-two lots of two pounds ten shillings! All the clothes I could buy with that. Does that sound horribly greedy?'

'No,' gasped Lizzie.

'Oh, you poor thing. You'll soon get used to the stairs. The exercise is good for you.' They'd reached the top landing. She turned towards the back of the house and opened a door. 'This is it.'

The slope-ceilinged room was painted white and the walls were covered with travel posters advertising holidays in foreign countries – Italy, Greece, France. There were two armchairs and a sofa scattered with brightly coloured cushions; a vivid silk shawl was draped over the sideboard which was littered with the petals from a bunch of fading flowers crammed into a glass vase. Beside the flowers, a cream-shaded lamp gave off a cosy, homely look. There was another, smaller lamp on a low table which also held a gramophone. A heap of records was stuffed underneath.

But the mess! The carpet was almost completely hidden by a layer of magazines, newspapers, books and clothes, even dishes.

Following Lizzie's gaze, the girl looked down. 'Gosh! It's in a God-awful state, isn't it? The bedroom's even worse. I'll tidy up tomorrow, though I say that every day. I'm Jackie, by the way, Jackie Rawlinson. Who are you?'

Lizzie was about to answer, 'Lizzie O'Brien', when something prevented her. Lizzie O'Brien belonged to the past. Lizzie O'Brien was not the person about to move, or so she hoped, into this exciting flat with a girl called Jackie who opened the door wearing pink satin pyjamas.

'Lisa,' she said. 'Lisa O'Brien.' She'd always wanted to be Lisa instead of Lizzie, it sounded more sophisticated.

'What a pretty name. Well, Lisa, I must tell you here and now, that I'm murder to live with. Flatmates come and go by the minute. Most girls take one look, make some excuse and run. Two came yesterday and did just that. I drive the ones that stay quite mad. I never put anything away. My mother says I'm a pig who'd be better off in a sty than a flat. Would you like a cup of tea or coffee?'

'I'd love either.'

'There's a kitchen along the corridor, but I only use it to get water. That's another thing – I never wash dishes. It's not that I mean to leave them on the floor, but somehow I always do. I keep an electric kettle here. I boiled it a few minutes ago. Usually I eat out. My boyfriend takes me to dinner after

work. Tonight he had to stay late else I wouldn't have been in when you
phoned.'

She knelt down, switched on the kettle and picked up two mugs. 'These
are *almost* clean. Do you take milk and sugar?'

'Just milk, please.'

After a short search, Jackie found the milk bottle on the mantelpiece.

'Sit down, you poor soul, you look worn out. Where's your things?'

'Things?'

'Clothes, luggage.'

'I haven't got any,' confessed Lisa, adding quickly in case the lack of
'things' deterred Jackie from taking her as a roommate: 'I ran away.' Since
she'd arrived, the doubts she'd had about sharing with someone else had
completely gone and she desperately wanted to move in. She accepted the
proffered cup of coffee, holding the handle in her left hand so as to avoid the
bright pink lipstick smear on the other side. Despite the milk being faintly
sour, the drink tasted good and at that moment she didn't particularly mind
a dirty cup.

'How incredibly exciting. I always wanted to run away, but my parents
were so glad to see the back of me there wasn't any need.'

Lisa leaned back in the chair, suddenly exhausted. It had been a long,
tiring day.

Jackie looked at her with concern. 'Have you eaten today, Lisa?'

'Well, no, apart from a bar of chocolate.'

'Then let's go out for a meal,' she cried enthusiastically. 'I'm bored out of
my mind without Gordon – that's my boyfriend.' A fleeting shadow passed
over her lively face. 'We can go to that new restaurant in Gloucester Road.'

Lisa said uncomfortably. 'I'd love to, but will it be expensive? I haven't got
much money and by the time I've paid you . . .'

'Oh, blow that. You can pay me next week. As to dinner, it's my treat.' She
paused. 'That is, if you want to stay? Do you want to live with a pig, Lisa?
You haven't seen the bedroom yet, have you?'

'I'd love to stay,' said Lisa, not caring a fig about the bedroom.

'Goody. I'm sure we'll get along – you look the patient type. But we can't
go out like this. You look as if you've been sleeping in a ditch. Is that coat
Army surplus? They'll chuck you out of the restaurant. What size are you?'

'I'm not sure. I'm a thirty-two-inch hip.'

'You horrible thing, sometimes my waist's that big! Everything of mine
will swim on you. Wait a minute, I've got a dirndl skirt with an elastic waist
– and my peasant blouse. Now, I wonder where they are?'

She disappeared into the bedroom and emerged with a flowered skirt and
a white embroidered top.

'Shoes! Those lace-up flats look hideous. I suppose you take a three or
something?'

'No, a seven.' The shoes had been bought in Paddy's Market at the same
time as the unfashionable coat.

'Really! I'm a six. You can have my open-toed sandals – *if* I can find them.
I'll get dressed again.' As she left the room she began to remove her pyjama
top, revealing full white breasts. Through the open bedroom door, she
shouted, 'I suppose you'll be looking for a job?'

'Yes.' Lisa pulled her jumper off and tried on the blouse. It had a gathered neck and full puffed sleeves.

Jackie appeared fastening her stockings onto a thin black lace suspender belt. She wore matching pants and brassière. 'Do you have shorthand?'

Lisa looked down at her hands in wonder.

Jackie gave a hearty laugh. 'Bloody hell, Lisa. *Shorthand*, can you write it? You know, little squiggly signs for words.'

'No,' Lisa had never heard of shorthand.

'Can you type?'

'No.'

'What can you do?'

'Nothing,' said Lisa.

'Then you'll have to get a job in a shop.'

'I'd quite like that.'

'If you worked in a fashion shop we could get clothes cheap. I love clothes. I've got two old aunts who send me all their coupons. I'll give you some if you like. Sometimes I buy things I don't really want, just to use the coupons up.' She disappeared into the bedroom again.

'Thank you,' Lisa called, though she couldn't imagine ever having enough money to use all her own coupons.

Jackie appeared brushing her corn-coloured hair and dressed in a white linen skirt with black buttons down the front and a short-sleeved black sweater.

Whilst she'd been gone, Lisa had hastily removed her skirt and stepped into the flowered dirndl, ashamed to let Jackie see her petticoat which was grey and shrivelled with so much washing.

'I say, that skirt looks lovely on you. It always made me look fat. You're beginning to look human, though I bet you haven't got any make-up.'

'I'm afraid not. All I've got is what I stand up in.'

'Well, help yourself to mine. There's a ghastly maroon-coloured lipstick somewhere that I've never used. I must have bought it when I was drunk – but it should suit your colouring. Come and sit by the mirror.'

Lisa followed her into the bedroom.

She saw twin beds with white candlewick bedspreads striped with blue, more posters and a pretty pink lamp on the table between the beds. The wardrobe door was open and bulged with clothes. Yet more clothes, dirty sheets and newspapers, covered the floor. The dressing table was loaded with bottles, creams, lotions, perfume, two half-empty cups of coffee and several dirty glasses. In the midst of the chaos stood a dusty black telephone.

Lisa's fingers itched with the urge to tidy up. She would enjoy achieving order out of this chaos.

Jackie pushed her down onto the stool in front of the dressing-table mirror. Despite the mess, she knew exactly where to find everything, and immediately handed Lisa a jar of foundation cream. As she rubbed it into her skin, Lisa was shocked to notice how much weight she'd lost over the last few years. She scarcely ever looked in the mirror at home. No wonder Kitty was forever urging her to eat more. And those purple shadows under her eyes made her face look drawn and skull-like. Her hair had not lost its shine, though. When she undid the tight bun on her neck, it flowed down to her waist, a shimmering, silken curtain, and Jackie gasped: 'Oh, you must borrow my velvet Alice band. It was made for someone with hair like yours.'

Lisa applied the maroon lipstick carefully. Jackie was right – she *was* beginning to look human. The gathered, fine cotton blouse suited her, accentuating her long neck and slim brown arms, and the full skirt flared out from her slender waist. Suddenly, she began to enjoy the feeling of being feminine again.

Behind her, Jackie was applying her own lipstick, her mouth contorted grotesquely. 'I can't be bothered washing my face,' she said. 'I'll just apply another layer.' She spat on her mascara and began to brush her eyelashes. 'Want some?' She offered the case to Lisa.

'No thanks,' said Lisa quickly. Dirty cups she could stand, but not mascara covered with Jackie's spit.

'God!' Jackie said admiringly. 'I'd kill for those cheekbones. I've no bones in my face, it's just fat.'

Lisa laughed. With a sudden rush of confidence, she said, 'You're very, very pretty.'

Jackie stepped back, a look of surprise on her face. Lisa watched through the mirror, wondering if what she'd said had been presumptuous.

'Why, Lisa, when you laughed and your eyes lit up, you looked – well, quite beautiful! Isn't this great? I'm pretty and you're beautiful. We're going to get on fine. I'm so glad you saw my card. Gordon will love you and you're sure to love him, he's a pussycat. Come on, let's go and eat, else we won't get a table. It's nearly half-past seven.'

12

A pink bath. Pink! And the bathroom walls were tiled, right up to the ceiling, in the same colour.

Lisa lay immersed in rose-scented bubbles, feeling like a Hollywood film star. This was the first real bath she'd ever had. At home they'd bathed in a tin tub in front of the kitchen fire, the girls on a Tuesday, all using the same water.

This room, like the kitchen, was shared by the residents of the other flats on the top floor. Jackie told her that the caretaker who lived in the basement took care of the maintenance of the house, whilst his wife did the cleaning, so everywhere was spotless.

They'd got back from the restaurant an hour ago. Lisa had eaten something called spaghetti bolognese which was delicious and very filling, and Jackie had ordered a whole bottle of red wine, drinking most of it herself. Lisa still felt pleasantly fuzzy after two small glasses.

Back in the flat, Jackie had said, 'I'm just off to have my bath,' as if she had one every single day, so Lisa, not to be outdone, asked: 'Can I go after you?'

So, here she was lying in luxury with Jackie's bubble bath, soap and shampoo at her disposal as well as her thick, fluffy but rather grubby towel and crimson silk dressing gown. It seemed unreal, like a dream. In less than twenty-four hours she had left one life and entered another, so totally different that the enormity of the change was difficult to grasp.

Tomorrow they were going to Knightsbridge where Jackie worked as a secretary in an office right opposite Harrods. She'd paused after saying this, as if waiting for some comment from her companion.

'Harrods?' Lisa said dutifully.

'Haven't you heard of Harrods? Gosh, you're an ignoramus. Harrods is the most famous shop in the world. It's where the very richest people go. I can see the front entrance from my window and almost every day famous people go in and out. Why, on Friday, I saw Herbert Lom outside waiting for a taxi.'

'Really!' said Lisa, impressed. She'd heard of Herbert Lom.

'There's an employment agency on the ground floor of my building. You must go there and see about a job.'

Lisa felt nervous at the idea of looking for work. The interview she attended at the dye factory had been in the company of half a dozen other girls, some from the same school as herself, and had not been in any way intimidating. Still, she had to get a job. There were clothes to buy, make-up, jewellery, and things like her own towel, soap, toothbrush and of course food. Unlike Jackie, she would make her meals in the kitchen.

She soaped her body, nothing how her ribs and hip-bones felt sharp and were covered only with the thinnest layer of flesh. 'I'll soon put weight back on again,' she thought contentedly. After she'd dried herself, she dressed in Jackie's dressing gown. The material felt cool and slippery against her body.

Jackie was back in pyjamas, boiling the kettle for cocoa. 'I'll have a head in the morning,' she groaned. 'All that wine!'

The clothes she'd worn were thrown over the back of a chair. Lisa picked them up, folded them neatly and put them on the sofa alongside the clothes she'd worn herself, then she sat on the chair and leaned back. Immediately her head began to swim and she felt an overwhelming desire to sleep.

'I'm so tired, I don't think I want a drink.'

Jackie, unsteady on her feet and searching for the cocoa tin, said, 'I'll find you a nightdress then. There'll be a clean one somewhere.'

Lisa protested. 'I'll sleep in my underclothes.'

'You'll do no such thing. You'll sleep like a civilised human being in a pretty nightdress.' She disappeared into the bedroom and emerged a few minutes later with a red cotton Victorian-style nightgown trimmed with white lace.

'I told a lie. It's not pretty, but grotesque, but at least I know it's clean because I've never worn it. My mother gave it me for Christmas.'

'It's very nice,' said Lisa, who would have gone to bed in a sack, she was so weary.

A few minutes later she climbed into bed. Jackie was sitting in front of the dressing table removing her make-up with cream. Lisa muttered, half-asleep. 'You've been awfully kind. I don't know why.'

'Because I like you. You're different from all the other girls I've shared with. And anyway . . .'

Lisa didn't catch the rest. She was fast asleep.

They walked to Knightsbridge under a pale sun in a pale sky. Tiny wisps of clouds were moving swiftly to nowhere. It was like being in a foreign country, Lisa mused, and you'd never think a war had not long ended. There were no bomb sites, no derelict buildings with every window smashed, no craters. Not like Liverpool, where signs of war were everywhere. And the women they passed, even the older ones, were exquisitely dressed. Their make-up and hair were so perfect, they looked as if they'd just stepped out of a beauty parlour. Even Jackie, considering the chaos at home, looked surprisingly smart in a cream Moygashel suit, frilly white blouse and black patent-leather court shoes with a matching bag tucked underneath her arm. Lisa wore the same dirndl skirt and blouse as yesterday and a borrowed cardigan.

She'd never seen such traffic: non-stop cars, tooting impatiently, big red buses stopping and starting as they crawled along the busy roads. The aroma of coffee, rich and strong, came from tiny restaurants, already open. Outside one, people were sitting at pavement tables drinking out of thick brown cups and eating crescent-shaped rolls. A delicious smell of baking bread came from a small corner shop called a 'pâtisserie', and the women who emerged, some carrying long thin loaves, were not dressed like the others she'd seen so far. They wore print overalls and one had a scarf wrapped round her head, turban-style, the way her mam used to. From one large, magnificent house a woman came out wearing a green gaberdine coat and a velour hat, just like a school uniform. She carefully levered a massive pram down the wide steps. As she passed, Lisa looked inside and saw a tiny baby clad in a lace-trimmed bonnet, fast asleep under a rich silk eiderdown.

'Come on, Lisa,' urged Jackie. 'Else I'll be late and I'm *never* late.'

Hard though it was to believe, Jackie was not an ordinary secretary, but Personal Assistant to the Managing Director of a travel company.

'You see,' she explained to Lisa in the restaurant the night before, 'I know how inefficient and scatterbrained I am, so I make a supreme effort at work. I write everything down; when I send letters, when I get them, when somebody rings up. I do the things I have to do straight away so I won't forget. If I'm asked to book plane tickets, I do it there and then, else I know it will slip my mind. You wouldn't believe my filing system, Lisa. I never lose a piece of paper. I'm the perfect secretary. Does that surprise you?'

Lisa conceded it did and Jackie looked pleased, as if she'd been paid a compliment.

'And because of this,' she went on, 'I've got promoted and promoted, till now I'm Mr Ireton's Personal Assistant and I earn twelve pounds a week. That's much more than an ordinary secretary.'

Jackie was a lot older than Lisa had thought – twenty-three.

'That's my office.' She pointed across the road. Lisa only half-heard. She was gaping at the fur coats in a shop window which had price tickets of over a thousand pounds.

'There's the agency. It won't be open for a few minutes yet. Good luck with the job, and see you back at home tonight. Got your key safe?'

Lisa nodded and Jackie dodged through the almost stationary traffic to the other side of the road.

The employment agency had a wide, floor-length window, just like a shop. As she watched, a woman unlocked the door and went in. Her hair was black and carefully waved, and she wore a severe tweed suit. She looked very unapproachable. What if she also asked for references like one of the landladies had? The last thing Lisa wanted was the dye factory being approached for a character reference. It would be all round the building within an hour and someone would be bound to tell her mam. Anyway, the woman over the road didn't look the sort who was used to dealing with people from factories.

She wondered if there was a Labour Exchange in Knightsbridge. That's where people in Bootle went when they were looking for work. Or she could look under *Situations Vacant* in a newspaper. Perhaps if she walked round for a bit, she might gain enough courage to enter the agency, though she doubted it.

If that was Jackie's building, then this shop with the fur coats for over a thousand pounds must be Harrods. She wandered along the pavement marvelling at the window displays. One in particular appealed to her: a wedding scene with six bridesmaids and two pageboys, all in dark-blue satin and velvet. The bride's dress was cream watermarked taffeta, an Edwardian style with a bustle extending to a long, fan-shaped train. The mannequin, gazing expressionlessly at her new husband, carried a bouquet of what looked like orchids, the leaves trailing to the floor. Lisa smiled, imagining Sean and Dougal in those pageboy outfits!

As she passed the main entrance, a man in uniform was opening the doors and almost immediately a woman in a sleek fur jacket swept past him regally without even a glance in his direction. The man caught Lisa's eye and winked. She winked back.

At the end of Harrods, she turned into a side street. By now the sun was shining brightly and she could feel its warmth on her back. Here there were smaller shops; lingerie, then shoes, one with nothing but leather luggage, a sweet-shop – though the elaborate displays of confectionery were unlike anything she'd ever seen before – and a tobacconist's exhibiting rows of strange-looking pipes. There was an art gallery on the corner and Lisa stopped and stared at the paintings hung on the white walls. After a while, she decided they must be a joke. They were nothing but smears and blobs of paint and made no sense at all. Nellie, who was top in art at school, could do better than that.

She came to a row of private houses and peeped through the windows. Such furniture! Brocade chairs and tall antique sideboards which almost reached the ornate, moulded ceilings. Displays of flowers that must have taken hours to arrange. In some of the basements, women in white overalls were preparing food, cutting vegetables or kneading pastry. In one, four small children were sitting around a large scrubbed table, whilst a woman in a grey cotton dress bustled about pouring milk into beakers. Lizzie smiled at the box of cornflakes on the table – it was just like Chaucer Street! As she passed one house, a postman knocked on the glossy red door which was opened by a maid, a real-life maid in a black dress and a small white cap and apron.

She glanced at her watch – well, Jackie's watch. This morning, when Jackie was telling her about the agency, she'd stressed the importance of keeping any appointments made for her on time.

'I bet you haven't got a watch, you poor impoverished thing.'

Lisa shook her head. 'I've never had one.'

'Well, I got three for my twenty-first. I'll lend you one,' and she'd fished in a drawer and brought out an expensive gold model with an expanding bracelet.

It was already nearly ten o'clock and she felt guilty, wandering about, nosily peering into people's houses when she hadn't been near the agency and doubted if she ever would.

She turned into another street – more shops, though not nearly so posh as the ones she'd already passed. There was a grocer's and a florist's, then a bookshop. She looked through the rather grimy window. Books were crammed onto the shelves, which extended from floor to ceiling all around the walls. They seemed to be second-hand books, many very old and bound in leather. Three more high, double-sided shelves took up almost all the floorspace. Behind a desk squeezed in a corner, an elderly man with a long grey wispy beard and wearing a small embroidered skullcap sat reading.

Lisa stood entranced. The scene was like something out of the nineteenth century. She'd seen *David Copperfield* with Freddie Bartholomew, she'd read *Pickwick Papers*, and this could be a set for a Dickens' film. It was a warm and welcoming oasis in the midst of smart and wealthy Knightsbridge.

She sighed and was about to move on when she noticed a dusty card in the window, '*Shop Assistant Required*' it said in sloping, old-fashioned script. Her spirits rose, but only momentarily. Someone well-educated would be wanted – someone who knew a lot about books. Well, she loved reading, always had, but apart from *Pickwick Papers* and *Treasure Island*, she'd read nothing they'd sell here. Nevertheless, it wouldn't hurt to try. The man could only say no and she'd be no worse off than she was now.

She took a deep breath and opened the door.

The old man looked up. She liked the friendly smile he gave her. At least he wouldn't be rude, she thought.

'Is it something specific you need, or do you just want to browse?' he asked in a deep voice with a faintly guttural accent.

Lisa swallowed. 'I've come about the job.'

For a moment, the man looked puzzled. 'The job? My goodness, I'd forgotten about the card. Is it still there?'

'Yes.' That probably meant the job had gone ages ago.

'You are the first person to apply. Come, sit down. Let's talk.'

The shop smelt of a mixture of dust and leather. Lisa sat down in front of the desk.

'What do you know of books?' The man's face was like a book itself, parchment-coloured and etched with wrinkles as fine as an old manuscript. His thick wiry eyebrows were like grey butterfly's wings above his brown eyes. He wore a flannel shirt and knitted cardigan, worn thin at the elbows.

'I only know I like reading them,' said Lisa.

'What have you read?'

She stood up suddenly. This was a waste of time. She had no answers to give him. 'I'm sorry. I shouldn't have come in. It's just that I'm looking for a job. I'm on my way to an agency now. Well, I'm supposed to be, but I'm going the wrong way. I saw your shop, then your card . . . I've only read *Pickwick Papers* and *Treasure Island*. I shouldn't have come in. I'm sorry.' She turned to leave.

'What did you think of them?'

She stopped. 'I liked the first but not the second. I think *Treasure Island* is a boy's book.'

'If you liked *Pickwick Papers* then you are a good girl to have working in a bookshop. Sit down, sit down. I am not conducting an examination here. When I was your age – what is it, sixteen, seventeen? – I had not read even those books. If you want to work here, let's talk about it.' He was standing, bowing and gesturing towards the chair Lisa had vacated. 'What is your name?'

'Lisa O'Brien and I'm sixteen.'

'And you come from Liverpool?'

'Yes.' Lisa had been doing her best to imitate Jackie's well-modulated speech. Obviously she hadn't been very successful.

'The Liverpool accent is my favourite. I was a mimic on the music hall, oh, a long, long time ago, but I still practise. I can do Winston Churchill, just listen. "Rise up ye peasants, throw down your chains and sit at the table of thy masters." '

Lisa burst out laughing. He'd got the voice just right, but it was delivered in a broad Liverpool accent. 'Did Churchill really say that?'

'No, but sometimes I amuse myself by imagining he did.' He slapped his forehead dramatically. 'Ach, there I go, showing off again. It is one of my weaknesses. Behave yourself, Harry,' he told himself sharply. 'This is serious. You want a job, Miss Lisa O'Brien, and I have a job to offer. The pay is not so bad – eight pounds a week. You would not get more in Harrods, though the atmosphere may appeal to some more than my old bookshop. Can you add up?'

'Yes, I was good at arithmetic at school.'

'Congratulations, I was not. My books are a mess. My legs are a mess. Rheumatism is my enemy and although I fight, I think the enemy is winning. My heart is not what it was. It goes too fast – or is it too slow? I forget which. One fine day it will stop going altogether. Until then, I need assistance to run my shop. My wife, Miriam, says I should ask for references. She thought people would be queuing up for this job.' He spread his hands, palms upwards, and shrugged. For a moment Lisa's heart sank. 'But you have an honest face. I take for granted you are not on the run from the police, or you didn't abscond from your last job with the petty cash?'

'Of course not!' Lisa said indignantly.

'I joke, I joke. Another weakness. I joke all the time. Tell me, Miss Lisa O'Brien, when can you start?'

'Tomorrow?'

'Fine, fine. My name is Harry Greenbaum, by the way. I am a Jew. Orthodox. You like my hat?'

'It's pretty,' said Lisa, smiling.

'It keeps my head together. Sometimes I get so angry with the world I think it will explode. You like a drink? Some coffee, tea? I ask from selfishness because I long for one myself and the back stairs to the kitchen are like Mount Everest so early in the morning. In other words, Miss Lisa, will you do your new employer a favour and make him a cup of coffee? Very black, very strong.'

13

Eight pounds a week! Eight pounds all to herself for working for a dear old man who made jokes all the time, in a shop like a film set.

She almost skipped back to Queen's Gate, stopping only to buy some groceries. As soon as she got in, she went into the kitchen and made herself a sandwich, although she felt a bit uneasy when she came to spread the butter. In Chaucer Street, even now they were better off, they ate margarine during the week and only had butter on Sundays. She eased her conscience by not smearing it as thickly as she would have liked.

After she'd eaten, she began to tidy the flat.

She discovered thirty-eight women's magazines and Sunday papers going back for months, ten blouses, eight skirts, three nightdresses, eighteen pairs of stockings and five odd ones, three pairs of shoes and a blue slipper without a mate. She didn't bother to count the underclothes, just stuffed everything in a bag for Jackie to take to a place called a 'launderette' – apparently there was one just around the corner. Underneath the mess, she found an assortment of mugs, some empty and covered in green mould, and others in which what had once been coffee or tea had turned into a revolting sort of jelly, and three bottles containing varying amounts of whisky. She poured the contents of two of the bottles into the third and fullest one, then put all the letters and pieces of paper together on the sideboard, stacking an assortment of books, nearly all romantic novels, at the back. Her proximity disturbed the drooping flowers and petals scattered onto the carpet, now revealed as plain green wool. She lifted the vase carefully and took it to where she'd spread newspapers to contain the rubbish and threw the flowers away.

She hung the clothes in Jackie's wardrobe, which was so packed, she wondered where she would put her own things when she bought them, took the dishes along to the kitchen and washed them, then collected the rubbish and carried it downstairs. There was a row of dustbins at the back of the house and she deposited her parcel in one of them with a sense of satisfaction.

Back upstairs she dusted, flicking cobwebs out of corners and off the low, sloping ceiling. She'd noticed a carpet-sweeper in the kitchen and used it to clean the floors in both rooms. Finally, she moved a small table into a corner for the clean cups and the kettle, adding the bottle of milk and packet of tea she'd just bought.

Finished!

From the bedroom doorway, she regarded both rooms with pride. They looked much bigger now with the floorspace cleared. The carpet in the bedroom was blue and matched the pattern on the candlewick bedspreads. Then suddenly, she felt worried in case Jackie would be annoyed. Perhaps she liked untidiness, and might be offended that Lisa had cleared up so ruthlessly . . .

After a few seconds of agonising over whether to throw some clothes about to make the place look less spick and span, Lisa decided that as she was paying half the rent, she had the right not to live in a pigsty. As long as she was prepared to do the work, that was all that mattered.

She made herself a cup of tea and looked through the *Guide To London*, one of the books she'd found on the floor. If she turned right outside the house, she could walk to a place called Fulham. Perhaps Fulham was not quite so posh as South Kensington and Knightsbridge, and she could do some much-needed shopping. Although Jackie appeared willing to lend her anything she needed, Lisa didn't want to sponge off her flatmate longer than could be avoided.

Fulham, it turned out, was a working-class area. Lisa felt quite homesick mingling with the harassed-looking women laden with shopping baskets, their shabbily-dressed children clutching at their coats as they trailed behind.

She was relieved to see several familiar shops – a big Woolworths opposite a Boots. In the High Street there was a market where things were even cheaper than in Bootle. She bought a pair of black court shoes, almost identical to those Jackie had worn that morning, for nineteen shillings and elevenpence, and a black pleated skirt for the same amount. A white blouse with a lace Peter Pan collar was seventeen and six. After two pairs of stockings and pants, a bar of soap and a cheap hand-towel, she still had a little money left. It would be nice to buy a jacket or a cardigan, but she'd need to get food during the week.

She reached the end of the market. The last stall was piled high with second-hand clothing and several women were rooting through it. Lisa joined them. There were lots of men's collarless shirts, trousers with frayed hems, children's jumpers and shorts without buttons. The women were picking at the clothes with an almost savage energy, turning the piles over, throwing them to one side and clutching at a garment they'd revealed, examining it briefly, then discarding it contemptuously.

''Ere, 'ere,' said the woman behind the stall in an aggrieved tone. 'Be careful with what's not your own.'

The woman beside Lisa ignored the warning and heaved a pile of clothes upside down. Lisa snatched at the corner of something which caught her eye and dragged it out. It was a Chinese jacket made from royal-blue quilted satin with a mandarin collar and elaborate cord fastenings, crumpled but quite whole. 'Not a break in it', as Kitty used to say when she got a second-hand bargain. She put her purchases on the ground and tried it on.

'That looks nice, darlin',' said the woman who had up-turned the clothes and revealed the precious item.

'Are you sure?' asked Lisa, who would have liked to look at herself in a mirror. The jacket was hip-length and felt all right, except for the sleeves being a bit too long, though she could easily take them up.

'Eh, Vera, don't that look nice?' The woman nudged the person beside her.

'Cor! Not much. Looks a treat,' Vera confirmed.

'How much is it, please?' Lisa asked the stallholder.

'One and six.'

'Come off it, Doris,' Vera snorted. 'This ain't 'arrods, it's Fulham 'igh Street.' She turned to Lisa. 'Offer her ninepence, darlin'.'

'Will you take ninepence?' Lisa wouldn't have dared make such a low offer without the backing of the women alongside her.

Doris pursed her lips and her weatherbeaten face took on a stubborn look. 'I'm not runnin' a charity 'ere. A shillin's the least I'll take.'

The women began to argue again, but Lisa had already taken a shilling out of her purse and handed it over, worried that Doris might refuse to sell the coveted jacket at all if she were pushed too hard.

She left, the women still arguing with Doris, and on her way home bought some stewing steak and vegetables to make scouse for that night's dinner, then called in at Woolworths for needles and cotton to alter the sleeves of the jacket.

Finally, she bought a bunch of flowers to replace the ones that had been thrown away.

Back in the flat, she prepared the scouse and left it on the stove to simmer. Afterwards, she tried on her new clothes.

She looked like a normal young woman again instead of the grim, frumpy person she'd been these last two years. The fine stockings shimmered on legs made slimmer and more shapely by the high-heeled shoes. The wide waistband of the skirt fitted tight around her slim body, the pleats flaring out to just below her knees, whilst the white blouse with its rounded collar and long full sleeves gave her rather a demure look.

It was the jacket she liked best, though. It added an air of chic to the rather ordinary outfit. Of course, she would never have dared wear it in Bootle, everybody would have laughed, but this morning she'd seen a woman dressed just like a Russian Cossack, with a big fur hat and a muff. A muff! And another woman wearing a collar and a man's tie. Down here, you could get away with outrageous outfits. Everyone would think she wore this satin quilted coat because she'd chosen to, picked it out of a dozen others, and not because it only cost a shilling in a market. At least, she hoped so.

She sat in front of the newly-polished dressing table. The telephone gleamed – just think, when she met people she could give them her number! Tomorrow she'd tell Mr Greenbaum in case he wanted to contact her out of shop hours. She sighed happily and began to comb her hair, experimenting with Jackie's wide collection of slides and combs and bows. Thank goodness she hadn't cut her hair short during the time she'd been trying to make herself look as unattractive as possible. She'd nearly done so several times. It was only the thought of upsetting Mam that had prevented her . . .

Mam!

She'd forgotten all about Kitty. Since she'd walked out of Number 2 Chaucer Street yesterday morning she'd scarcely given her family a second thought. Everything that had happened since had been so exciting and absorbing. But Mam would be distraught with grief, once she realised her Lizzie wasn't coming home again.

At first, she'd probably thought Lizzie had got up early to go to mass, then gone straight to work. She wouldn't have known that she'd left for good till she didn't come home that night. The whole family had probably been sent out to look for her.

What a cruel and thoughtless girl she was, walking out like that!

Lisa got up and began to walk restlessly around the two rooms. The traffic outside was never-ending, but up here the sound was muted and the large house was silent. Presumably everyone was at work.

She couldn't go back to Chaucer Street now, not ever. It held too many bad memories. Every time she looked at the mantelpiece she saw the gold sugar basin Hank had won, a prize for his lovely girl. Since she'd arrived in London, she hadn't thought about Southport, not once, and now she no longer had to sleep in that big double bed, there were no reminders of her dad.

In fact, in the space of less than two days, she felt a different person altogether, as if a part of her that had been dead for years had come alive again. And she *was* a different person, because Lizzie O'Brien no longer existed. Now she was Lisa, with a good job and nice clothes, and the world suddenly seemed a wonderful place.

She slipped into her new coat and went out to buy a postcard for Kitty. On it, she wrote she was fine and not to worry, but she didn't include her address, though she wasn't sure why. Perhaps she couldn't stand the thought of Kitty's sad, demanding letters wanting to know why she had deserted them, her loving, laughing family, or that one of the boys might be despatched to persuade her to go back . . .

She hadn't been home for more than five minutes when she heard footsteps on the stairs. A door slammed, dishes rattled in the kitchen and from downstairs came the sound of music. People were arriving back from work and the house was coming alive.

Tomorrow morning Mam would get the card and know she was all right. 'Anyway,' Lisa thought defensively, 'they'll be happier without me. They're probably glad I've gone.'

Jackie wouldn't be home until eight o'clock. She was having an affair with a married man, she'd told Lisa confidentially in the restaurant the night before. He was thirty-five, had been an officer in the Royal Air Force and his wife didn't understand him. As soon as his children were older, he would get a divorce and marry Jackie. In the meantime, they went for dinner together every night after work. They could never meet at weekends.

'Trust me to fall for someone unavailable,' Jackie said mournfully, her round grey eyes for once sad. 'I mean, I get asked out on loads of dates, but young men seem so callow compared to Gordon. Honestly, Lisa, wait till you meet him, he's gorgeous.'

Lisa was reading when Jackie came in. She'd gone through the books in the flat and rejected most of them, deterred by the description of the plots on the inside covers. Girls married men who turned out to be millionaires; men married girls who had a sordid past; two men loved the same girl, or two girls loved the same man. Then she found a book by the strangely-named Richmal

Crompton about a boy called William Brown. It was so funny that from time to time she laughed out loud. She became so absorbed that she lost track of time and was surprised when Jackie came into the room like a whirlwind.

'I've brought Gordon home to meet you!'

Lisa laid down her book and stood up to meet the gorgeous Gordon. She couldn't believe her eyes when he followed Jackie into the room. He looked older than thirty-five, at least ten years older. He was about five feet ten, of portly build, wearing a loud checked sports jacket, camel-coloured trousers and a military tie. His face was smooth, the skin on his cheeks red and mottled, and his lips were full and fleshy – what you could see of them, that is, for his top lip was almost hidden by a wide moustache parted in the middle with the ends twisted into stiff points.

What on earth did Jackie see in this ridiculous-looking man? Perhaps Lisa should have read one of the romances, rather than the William Brown book, she thought, for it might have given her some insight into why people were attracted to each other. Then she told herself to stop being so critical. Perhaps he had a lovely nature. But she soon decided this wasn't the case, for when she was introduced and took Gordon's limp, sweaty hand, he appraised her quite openly, looking her up and down while Jackie bounced around the flat, in and out of the bedroom, marvelling at the transformation that had taken place.

'I *told* you she was the most amazing person, didn't I, Gordon?' she said excitedly. 'I'm so lucky getting Lisa for a flatmate, I just don't deserve someone so perfect.'

Lisa felt embarrassed. 'Would you like some tea?' she muttered.

She felt Gordon's eyes on her legs when she went to pour the tea out and wished she'd changed back into Jackie's old clothes, but she'd wanted to show her new outfit off to her friend.

Jackie sat beside Gordon on the sofa, cuddling close and smiling up at him adoringly. She'd put a record on the gramophone. It was one of the few bands Lisa recognised, Glenn Miller. Smooth, romantic dance-music filled the room.

Lisa felt uncomfortable and wondered how long Gordon would stay. No wonder his wife didn't understand him! She probably didn't understand why he didn't get home from work till nine or ten o'clock each night.

After a while, he whispered something to Jackie and they stood up.

'We're just going into the bedroom for a while,' Jackie said with an embarrassed smile.

They disappeared and Lisa felt the urge to giggle. How long would they be? Collecting the mugs, she took them down to the kitchen and washed them slowly. She was taking even longer to dry them when a young man came in carrying a tray of dirty dishes.

'Ho, ho!' he said. 'Are you Jackie's new flatmate?'

'I am,' confirmed Lisa.

'Given in your notice yet?' he asked with a grin.

'Not yet,' she replied. 'I quite like it here.'

The young man's features were almost startlingly perfect. His face was tanned a rich gold, slightly darker than his long, curly hair.

'I suppose you're the one who used my pan.'

'Did I? I'm sorry. I thought they were for everybody,' she said contritely.

'No, we buy our own utensils and of course Jackie never cooks. What is that revolting mixture you've got in there, anyway?'

Lisa had made enough for two days. 'Scouse,' she said.

'Scouse? I suppose that's what you are, a Scouse. I'm Piers, by the way, Piers de Villiers.'

Piers! She'd never heard that name before. And de Villiers!

'Lisa O'Brien.'

He put his tray down and they shook hands.

'Pleased to meet you, Lisa. Your scouse may look frightful, but it smells delicious. You must show me how to make it some time.'

'It's just stew, really. I won't use your pan again, I promise. Is there something else I can put this in? A basin? I'll buy a pan of my own as soon as I get paid.'

'Don't be an idiot, there's a good girl. I've heaps of pans. It's just that that one's my favourite. Here, take this one as a gift. It's yours – your very own scouse pan.' He rooted through a cupboard and brought out a pan that was slightly bigger than the one Lisa had used.

'Thanks,' she said. 'You're very kind.'

'Any time,' he said cheerfully. 'New here, are you – I mean to London?'

'It's only my second day.'

'Well, Lisa, my friend's an actor. If you ever want theatre tickets, he gets them free.'

'I'd love some! I've never been to the theatre, but I'm sure I'd like it.'

Piers began to pile his dishes in the sink so Lisa said goodbye and returned to the flat, glad to have been detained and hoping that Jackie and Gordon had come out of the bedroom.

They had. Jackie was in her pink pyjamas, tying the belt of her dressing gown and Gordon, a complacent smirk on his face, was straightening his tie when she entered the room. He winked at her.

'I'm ready for take-off,' he said.

Lisa hoped they wouldn't embrace in front of her. Thankfully, they left the room together and a minute later Jackie returned.

'Did you like him?' she asked, and without waiting for an answer: 'Did you mind? I mean, us going into the bedroom like that? That's another reason my flatmates leave. They think I'm immoral. Well, I suppose I am. Are you terribly moral, Lisa?'

'No, I don't think so.'

'Thank God for that.'

'I met a nice young man in the kitchen – Piers. He's given me a saucepan and he's going to get me theatre tickets.'

'Oh, Piers!' Jackie wrinkled her nose.

'Don't you like him?' Lisa was surprised. She couldn't imagine Jackie disliking anyone.

'He's okay, though Gordon hates him – and his friend Ralph. He doesn't like me to have anything to do with them. They're queer, you see.'

'Queer?' Piers had seemed excessively normal to Lisa.

'Queer – homosexual. They're lovers, Piers and Ralph.'

Lisa was trying to digest this piece of information when Jackie asked if she'd got a job. She told her about Mr Greenbaum and the bookshop.

'A bookshop! Oh Lisa, couldn't you have got something more interesting? Clothes, perfume . . . is that all the agency had?'

Ignoring the reference to the agency, Lisa said defiantly, 'I think books are interesting. And it's eight pounds a week, and Mr Greenbaum, he's interesting too and very funny.'

'Oh, God! What an interfering body I am. I'm sorry, Lisa, you've done incredibly well. And the flat – you've worked miracles! You've even bought some clothes. That waist! I'd kill for it. You look truly elegant.'

Lisa showed her the quilted jacket. She put it on and twirled round. 'What do you think, Jackie?'

'That must have cost a fortune. I thought you hadn't got much money. How on earth did you manage to buy all this stuff?'

Jackie didn't look the least bit suspicious, just puzzled. She was so naive and innocent. Lisa felt a sudden surge of anger against Gordon, who probably told her all sorts of lies which Jackie believed.

'I went to a place called Fulham and things there were so cheap. The jacket was only a shilling on a second-hand stall.'

Apparently Jackie had only vaguely heard of Fulham and had no idea it was only ten minutes' walk away. Impressed with Lisa's purchases, she resolved to go the very next Saturday.

Lisa was waiting outside the shop when Mr Greenbaum arrived the following morning. When he saw her he began to hurry, shuffling along in his ankle-length black overcoat.

'I'll give you a key,' he panted, 'so in future you can let yourself in. Now I feel guilty because I have a prompt employee.'

Once inside, he lowered himself onto the chair behind his desk. 'Ach, Lisa,' he sighed. 'Why does my body grow old, but inside my head stay young? Tell me.'

'I have no idea,' she confessed. 'Perhaps some people have old heads and young bodies.'

'You sound like one of them,' he said accusingly. 'Now, when I get my breath back, I'll show you where things are.'

The books were in sections, marked alphabetically, *Aerodynamics, Anthropology* in the far corner by the window, followed by *Biography, Biology*, right through to *Zoology* on the opposite wall.

'Here is *Fiction* at the back.' His breath was ragged. Just the short walk round his shop had exhausted him. 'I keep a few modern authors, like Graham Greene, Evelyn Waugh and Somerset Maugham. Mainly they are old, pre-nineteen-twenty – Flaubert, Proust, Bennett, Hardy . . . Have you read *The Way Of All Flesh*, Miss Lisa O'Brien?'

'No, I've only read—'

'Of course, *Pickwick Papers* and *Treasure Island*. I forgot. Samuel Butler is my favourite. I will lend you *The Way of All Flesh*. And *Erehwon*. Do you know what that is?'

'A place?'

'Yes, a place – a mythical country. It is nowhere. "Erehwon" is "nowhere" back to front. A brilliant, brilliant book.'

Beside the desk there was a small section containing office supplies: reams of paper, typewriter ribbons, spiral notebooks, bottles of ink. Mr Greenbaum explained that there were several offices in the area which sometimes ran out of stationery and bought small amounts from him.

At this point, the letterbox suddenly rattled and a heap of envelopes landed on the mat. Lisa went over and picked them up. The old man chuckled: 'You have earned today's wages already. Picking up the post has become an ordeal lately. Perhaps you could help me open some but first, Miss Lisa, a cup of coffee would be more than welcome. If you want it white, there is a dairy just around the corner.' He laughed again, this time a trifle ruefully. 'Oh, what bliss this is, to be waited on. I'm ashamed of myself, a good socialist like me, sitting back and letting a fellow comrade labour on my behalf.'

'What's a socialist?' asked Lisa.

The old man's jaw dropped. He stared at her with shocked, rheumy eyes. She felt as if he might sack her on the spot.

'I'm sorry,' she stammered. 'I've never . . .'

'Oh, Miss Lisa! Make that coffee and I'll tell you.'

Five minutes later, when she came out of the kitchen with the drinks, he was opening the post, slitting the envelopes with a silver letter-opener. He stopped when she put the coffee in front of him.

'Who is the Prime Minister?' he demanded sternly.

'Mr Attlee,' she replied promptly.

'Thank God, you know that much.'

'Of course I do.' She remembered how just after the war, Kitty had proudly gone to vote and when she'd come back the little ones had been aghast to learn she hadn't put her cross by Mr Churchill's party, though the older boys seemed to understand why she had voted Labour.

'Do you know what Clause Four is?'

She wriggled uncomfortably. 'I left school at fourteen. We never did politics, at least not after Charles the First. I mean, I know they executed him for doing something against Parliament.'

'Forget about Charles the First. Clause Four of the Labour Party Constitution says that we must secure for the workers by hand or by brain the full fruits of their industry. Does that sound right to you?'

Lisa thought for a while. 'It sounds fair. Yes, I agree.'

'There, then! You are a socialist too.'

'Am I?'

'Of course you are. Very soon, Lisa O'Brien, dear Mr Aneurin Bevan will bring in the National Health Service. Free healthcare for all – free spectacles, medicine, deaf-aids. No more people will die because they can't afford a doctor. Britain will become the envy of the world. Oh, it is a good thing to be a socialist.'

'Is it?' Lisa felt bewildered.

'Of course it is. You'll realise that some day. Come, now we've sorted that out, let's finish opening these letters.'

There were at least twenty, several containing cheques.

'These people have already written or telephoned and I have the book they want put away,' Mr Greenbaum explained. 'Others are writing to ask if I have a certain book in stock.' He laid a letter in front of her. 'Now, this person wants Halsey's *Butterflies*. That is extremely rare. I will ring some friends, booksellers, to see if they have it, but it isn't likely.'

'Gosh! This one's from Australia!' gasped Lisa, carefully slitting open an envelope with an airmail stamp. 'He wants *The Road To Wigan Pier* by George Orwell, published by the Left Wing Book Club. Have we got that?'

'We most certainly have. Is that from a Peter Prynne?'

Lisa looked at the scrawled signature. 'Yes.'

'Then I'll send it off this afternoon with an invoice. I know he will pay.'

Just then the door opened and Lisa sprang to her feet. A middle-aged woman entered the shop. Remembering Mr Greenbaum's words when she'd come in herself the day before, she asked, 'Is it something specific you need, or do you just want to browse?'

The woman wanted a Latin dictionary for her son. 'I know I can get a new one, but he said if I do, everyone at school will know he's lost it. Something battered-looking, please.'

Lisa was about to take her to the *Languages* shelf when she recalled that on her quick tour round the shop, she'd noticed a section headed *Reference*. Sure enough, the dictionaries were there, including several Latin ones. A maroon leather-covered one was considered the most shabby.

'How much is it?'

The price was scrawled in pencil on the flyleaf. 'Five shillings,' Lisa said faintly, thinking the woman would make an excuse, leave and buy a new, cheap edition for half the price from somewhere else. Instead, she handed over two half-crowns.

She felt Mr Greenbaum's eyes on her as she faced the till and pressed the *Sale* and 5/- buttons. The drawer sprang open and she put the coins in the correct tray, took a medium-sized paper bag from the shelf under the desk and handed the book over.

'My first customer!' she exclaimed excitedly after the door had closed. 'Did I do it right?'

'Perfectly. If you go on like this, you will make me feel redundant.'

'Oh, I don't want to do that,' she said, alarmed.

'I joke, I joke. Take no notice of me ninety per cent of the time. I will make a signal when I'm serious. See, I'm wiggling my eyebrows. That means I'm serious.'

Lisa laughed. 'You'd better think of something else.' It looked as if a butterfly was frantically flapping its wings just above his eyes.

'Then I shall speak in a deep, grave voice, just like Mr Churchill. Can you type, Miss Lisa O'Brien?'

She laughed again. His imitation, as before, was perfect. 'I'm sorry, no.'

He sighed. 'Never mind. I can't type either, but I bet your young fingers are better at not typing than mine. Later on, whilst I wrap the parcels, you can reply to these letters.'

The shop door was opened with a quick rush and slammed violently shut. An elderly woman in a black astrakhan coat strode towards the desk. Lisa approached her.

'Is it something—'

'Don't speak to her, Miss Lisa. Ignore her. You horrible woman, go away!'

Lisa stepped back in alarm.

'See, you've frightened her! Coming in looking like Joan Crawford as if you owned the place. Get back to where you came from.'

The woman had once been beautiful. She was still striking. Snow-white hair, thick and shiny, was brushed smoothly back into a coil on the nape of her neck, though the cosmetics she wore accentuated her age rather than reducing it. Bright blue eye-shadow drew attention to the sagging lids, and the residue of rouge in the wrinkles of her cheeks gave them a raddled look. Scarlet lipstick, carefully applied, could not cover the spidery lines in the corners of her mouth and when she spoke, tiny cracks appeared in her lips.

'Shut up, you silly old man.'

Harry Greenbaum sighed deeply. 'Lisa, this is my wife, Miriam. Miriam, Lisa.'

Lisa swallowed in amazement. She'd thought they were sworn enemies about to attack each other.

Miriam removed her leather gloves and shook hands firmly. 'Is he treating you all right? Oh, he's a slave-driver is that man. I'm surprised you're still here.' She sat down opposite the desk.

'She's only come in to inspect you, Lisa. To warn you off. To confirm I'm spoken for. She thinks every woman is out to seduce me, steal me away. Oh, if only they would.' He raised his eyes to heaven and shook his head longingly. 'If only Minnie Kopek was still around, I should have gone off with her. She pleaded. How she pleaded!'

Miriam hit him over the head with her gloves. 'Stop going on about Minnie Kopek.' She turned to Lisa. 'For fifty years this man taunts me with Minnie Kopek. I never met her. Did she exist, I ask myself?'

Harry gave an enigmatic smile and didn't answer.

'Listen, Greenbaum, I'm going to the dentist which is right by the bank so I thought I'd put the cheques in,' Miriam said.

'That's right, woman, take my money as fast as I earn it. Here! Here's your damn cheques.' He secured them with a paper clip and flung them across the desk in front of her. She reached out for them and as she did so, the old man's hand went out and covered hers. At first Lisa thought he was about to snatch them back, but instead, Miriam turned her own hand upwards and clasped his. For a few seconds they stared into each other's eyes and Lisa saw an exchange of pure, explicit love. They adored each other. This was all a game. She felt a lump in her throat.

She'd brought sandwiches for dinner, though in London everybody had lunch at midday and dinner at night. Mr Greenbaum wandered off at twelve o'clock announcing in his Churchillian voice that he considered her perfectly able to look after the shop alone.

Whilst she munched her sandwiches, she got on with typing replies to the letters which had come that morning. It had been difficult with Mr Greenbaum present, as he chatted away distractingly as he wrapped and addressed the parcels. She was making a slightly better job of it than he had, judging by the carbon copies of letters she'd been given to show how they should be set out. The old letters were full of overtyping and words joined together. Already she could manage two-finger typing, though the main difficulty was remembering to press the shift key when she wanted a capital.

A customer came in to browse and eventually bought a book on magic by someone called Aleister Crowley. Lisa made a mental note of the name. Magic, Aleister Crowley. Then a girl no older than herself entered the shop and asked if they had the collected works of Byron.

Lisa bit her lip. She had no idea where to look. Who on earth was Byron? 'I'm not sure.'

The girl was chatty. 'It's this ghastly English exam. I've already done Chaucer and quite frankly, that old English script or whatever you call it, may as well be double Dutch for all the sense it makes.'

Chaucer! She'd lived in Chaucer Street and someone at school once told her he was a poet. Close by was Byron Street and Wordsworth, Southey and Dryden Streets. Perhaps they were all poets.

She looked under the *Poetry* section and there was Byron! Relieved, for she would have hated to make a fool of herself, she pointed out several collected editions.

Mr Greenbaum returned just after one. He looked mournful. His beard dripped amber liquid. 'One double brandy, Lisa. Just one and I feel like I drank a bottle. Oh, the trials of old age.'

'Surely that's a good thing,' she said. 'It means you can get drunk cheaper.'

He brightened. 'That's a very positive way of looking at things. I shall present you with all my problems in future and you can make them disappear with your words of wisdom.'

'Have you had anything to eat?' she asked severely.

He put his hands over his ears defensively. 'Quiet! You sound like Miriam. No, I had a liquid lunch. Now, get out of my shop. Have your lunch-hour. Wander around Harrods. If you, a working girl from Liverpool, were not a socialist when you went in, you will surely be one when you come out.'

One Christmas just after the war, Lisa had taken Dougal and Sean along Strand Road to a shop which had a grotto. Inside, it was just like a fairy tale, with frosted glistening walls strung with coloured lights. It was unreal, out of this world. She'd had trouble getting her little brothers out of the magic place.

Harrods reminded her of a grotto. Sparkling chandeliers shed brilliant light over the rich merchandise. Jewellery such as she'd never seen before, necklaces thick with rubies, emeralds and sapphires, twinkled beneath glass counters, next to rings containing stones as big as a shilling piece, and even tiaras.

The scarf counter was like a stall in an Arabian bazaar. Brilliant silks and satins cascaded like streams of coloured rain from their stands. As for the perfume section, it smelt like heaven. In front of one display of expensive scent stood a half-full bottle labelled 'sample'. She dabbed some behind her ears.

'Can I help, modom?' A sleek salesgirl approached.

'How much is it?' Lisa asked.

'Five pounds,' the girl answered.

Trying not to let her astonishment show, Lisa said airily, 'I'll think about it.'

She wandered upstairs. The clothes took her breath away. Voluminous sequinned ballgowns, embroidered cocktail dresses, filmy summer frocks, linen suits exquisitely cut. She looked askance at the price tags. The cost of just one ballgown would have kept the entire O'Brien family for a year!

There were plenty of customers, mainly women, nearly all beautifully dressed in clothes which could have been, and probably were, bought on this very floor. Lisa was struck by how few of them looked happy, though. It seemed to her that to be let loose to look through these lovely clothes with the intent of buying would be paradise itself. Why, then, did they all appear so discontented? They sorted through the racks of garments with no more care and far less enthusiasm than the woman Vera and her friend had done at the stall in Fulham market!

She heard phrases that until then she'd only read in magazine stories.

'I simply *must* get something for Freddy's ghastly preview on Friday.'

'What a frightful bore, darling. As for me, I haven't got a thing to wear for *Aïda*.'

'We're off to Paris on Saturday and if I don't get something today, I'll go in rags.'

All said so petulantly, so loudly, as if they didn't give a damn what other people thought. And they spoke to the assistants rudely, as if they were servants and didn't merit a 'please' or 'thank you'. Lisa felt anger rise in her breast. Did this mean she was a socialist?

It was such a warm day that she'd left her quilted jacket in the shop. Perhaps in her white blouse and skirt she looked like a shop assistant, because a man approached her – a vision, dressed from head to toe in dove grey: shoes, suit, overcoat. His shadow-striped grey tie was held with a pearl clip, and a soft felt hat was clasped in one white hand, on which the fingernails were polished to perfection. Even the slim rolled umbrella over his arm had been bought to match his outfit. A tall man with an authoritative face and pencil-thin moustache, his aquiline nose quivered as if the shop, the entire world, smelt somewhat unsavoury.

'I say,' he barked at Lisa, 'fetch my wife the blue dress, the one she decided against. She'd like to have another try.'

Lisa stared at him. It was an order, not a request.

'Come on, my girl, come on!' His eyes flashed with impatience.

'I am not your girl,' she said icily. 'And it wouldn't exactly kill you to fetch the dress yourself.' Resisting the urge to flee, for there was nothing he could do as she didn't work here, she stared at him, seeing the impatience turn to amazement. Then, to her astonishment, he began to laugh – a high, hysterical, unnatural shriek.

'Ginger,' called a voice from a cubicle nearby. 'Ginger, where is the girl with the blue dress?'

The laughter stopped abruptly.

Lisa haughtily threw back her head and without another glance at Ginger, who was clearly unhinged, she left the shop.

14

The afternoon passed swiftly. There were few customers. Mr Greenbaum said sales over the counter just about paid the rent for the shop. He did most of his business by post.

'But,' he added with his expressive shrug, 'I have to keep my books somewhere, so why not a shop?'

'Why not?' agreed Lisa.

When she got back to the flat that evening, she found an envelope pushed under their door. It contained two tickets to see a play called *Blithe Spirit* a week on Saturday, and a note which read: '*Why don't you come and have a drink with us when you get back?*' It was signed '*Piers*'.

She showed the note to Jackie later, after Gordon had left. 'Will you come with me to the theatre?' she asked eagerly.

'I don't think Gordon would like it,' Jackie said doubtfully.

'Not using tickets off Ralph, and as for going for a drink with them afterwards . . .' She wrinkled her nose.

'What right has Gordon to dictate what you do at weekends?' reasoned Lisa. 'If he can't see you, it's none of his business.'

The girl looked uncomfortable for a moment, then her face lit up. 'It wouldn't hurt, would it? You're right – I mean, he can't expect me to act like a nun. Anyway, it's not as if I'm going with another man.'

They were good seats in the rear stalls. Many of the theatregoers wore evening dress. Out of her wages, Lisa had paid her rent and bought herself a gold-braid Alice band and a black silk blouse. In her blue quilted jacket and new blouse, she didn't feel too out of place among the elegantly dressed audience.

At first Jackie was on edge, worried that Gordon might miraculously turn up with his wife and see her.

'What if he does?' said Lisa, trying not to sound impatient. 'You're not doing anything wrong.'

It was the first play she had ever seen. She sat entranced, glued to her seat, disconsolate when it finished.

'Oh, I wish there'd been more,' she moaned as they waited for a bus near Piccadilly Circus.

Jackie had livened up and seemed to have forgotten all about Gordon. 'It's been a super evening,' she enthused. 'I hope Ralph can get more tickets and we can do this often.'

The main room in Piers' and Ralph's flat stretched across the entire front of the house.

Lisa stopped in the doorway, taken aback by the decoration. The walls were painted dark red, the ceiling black. A tall black lacquered Chinese cabinet decorated with red and gold flowers dominated one wall. Against another wall stood a matching sideboard and a black enamelled bookcase. Above the marble fireplace hung a huge mirror with a thick gold frame. The chairs were upholstered in dark red velvet, and white fur rugs were scattered on the polished floor. Two red-shaded lamps provided the only illumination.

'Gosh!' was all she could say. Despite the forbidding colour scheme, the room looked warm and welcoming, though Lisa couldn't have lived in it. The style was too dominant and overwhelming.

'Like it?' said Piers. He wore black velvet trousers and a loose white silk shirt, and seemed pleased by her surprised reaction.

'It's very exotic,' she said. 'And foreign.'

'That's just the effect I wanted – exotic and foreign. It's my job, you see. I'm an interior decorator. I come back here and forget I'm in London, in England. It's like walking into a room in some strange country with an entirely different culture. Oh, I forgot, you haven't met Ralph. He's only just got in himself.'

Lisa hadn't noticed the person sitting reading at the black table at the opposite end of the room. Statue-still and silent, he hadn't even glanced up when they arrived.

He looked nothing like an actor. About thirty, plainly dressed in brown slacks and a fawn shirt, he was more like a comfortable family doctor or bank clerk. At Piers' words he got to his feet and came over to shake hands. He was almost excessively ordinary – neither good- nor bad-looking, of average height, with mouse-coloured hair cut very short. He was polite, but Lisa sensed he resented their presence.

'You already know Jackie,' Piers said and Ralph nodded.

They sat in armchairs around a black octagonal coffee table whilst Piers poured the wine. 'Did you like the play?'

'I could have stayed there all night,' said Lisa enthusiastically, 'I wish there'd been ten acts.'

'Are you a regular theatregoer?' Ralph asked in his subdued, rather colourless voice.

'It's the first play I've ever been to and I want to see every one in London. I didn't just like it, I *loved* it.'

'What did you think of Noël?' asked Piers.

'Who's Noël?' she enquired innocently.

'Christ Almighty, Lisa.' Piers exploded into laughter. 'I'm talking about Noël Coward. He wrote the play and starred in it. Didn't you realise that? Didn't you buy a programme?'

'Are they the leaflets they were selling when we went in?' She turned to Jackie. 'Why didn't you tell me? I didn't know you were supposed to buy a programme.'

Jackie had already demolished her wine. 'Sorry, I was so worried about Gordon I just didn't think.'

Piers refilled her glass. 'More wine, Lisa?'

'Not yet, thanks.' She felt uncomfortable, displaying her ignorance so shamefully. But the person she least expected to, boosted her self-confidence.

'I think Lisa has the makings of a genuine theatre-lover,' said Ralph quietly. Piers had not returned to his seat after pouring Jackie's wine. Instead, he sat on the floor, leaning against Ralph's chair companionably. Lisa wondered if Ralph had been so unwelcoming because he was jealous that Piers had asked her and Jackie in for a drink, and whether this gesture on his friend's part, this move towards him, had shown that his fears were unwarranted.

'Can you get tickets for the play you're in?' she asked. 'I'd love to see you on stage.'

'Would you really?' He looked surprised and flattered.

'Ralph's rehearsing *Pygmalion*,' Piers said proudly. 'He's got a leading part, Alfred Doolittle. It opens next week.'

'Who wrote *Pygmalion*?' asked Lisa.

'George Bernard Shaw,' said Ralph, adding with a smile, 'and he isn't in it.'

Jackie finished her second glass of wine. Lisa had already noticed in the short while they had lived together that she drank a lot. As soon as she came home from work she poured herself a glass of whisky, and the glass was regularly refilled until she went to bed. Lisa decided it was all Gordon's fault. He made her unhappy, deserting her at weekends, stringing her along with lies about his wife – at least Lisa was convinced they were lies and there was no way he would ever get divorced. He was just having a good time at Jackie's expense and didn't give a damn about the consequences. Right now the girl looked uncomfortable, simply because dear Gordon didn't like homosexuals. He'd gone on about them only the other night because he'd met Ralph coming out of the lavatory as he was about to go in.

'Had a narrow escape there,' he'd crowed when he came back. 'Scared the bugger was about to proposition me on the spot.' As if Ralph would fancy horrible, ugly Gordon when he had Piers!

Halfway into her third glass, Jackie suddenly came to life. Spurred on by the wine, her real, sunny nature surfaced. She began to talk about *Blithe Spirit* and the parts which had amused her most.

Piers opened another bottle. Lisa, on her second glass, began to feel faintly tipsy. The conversation turned to the cinema, something she could talk about without making a fool of herself. Going to the pictures by herself had been her only source of entertainment over the past two years, and she had a good memory for everything she'd seen.

Piers rested his head against Ralph's knee. It looked so gentle, so normal. Once Marie Gordon had told her about men who fancied other men, and there were even women who went with each other, apparently. At first she hadn't believed it, but Marie convinced her it was true, and she'd thought, 'Anyone who behaves like that must be a monster and if I ever meet one, I'll know straight away.' But watching Piers and Ralph together was not the slightest bit disgusting. It was just two people in love.

They stayed until three in the morning and only left after Jackie fell asleep in her chair.

When Lisa awoke, it was midday. She lay there, relaxed and happy, before realising it was Sunday and she'd missed mass – again! She'd forgotten all about it last Sunday until it was too late.

She jumped out of bed and grabbed some clothes. Jackie slept on, dead to the world. Perhaps she could find a one o'clock service somewhere, though she had no idea where the nearest Catholic church was. Then she remembered about Westminster Cathedral. Perhaps the underground train went there.

She was almost dressed when she stopped in the act of buttoning up her blouse. Going to mass seemed part of her past life, the life she'd abandoned, and would only bring back memories she was trying to forget. Some day she'd have to go to Confession and tell some unfamiliar priest that she'd run away from home – and what would she answer if he asked why?

Best not to go then, she decided, and put the kettle on instead.

She was amazed at how little it seemed to matter. After making herself a cup of tea and some toast, she sat on the sofa reading and the fact she hadn't been to church slipped to the back of her mind and it was almost as if she'd never been at all, ever.

The book she was reading was *Pride and Prejudice* by Jane Austen. When she'd finished *The Way of All Flesh*, Mr Greenbaum had eagerly asked for her reaction. She said she was amazed and delighted to find it so enjoyable. *Pride And Prejudice* was even better. It was just like the stories in the *Red Star* and *Miracle* – full of unspoken sex and frustration. Passions seethed beneath the sedate surface of the writing. Mr Greenbaum said Jane Austen had written a lot of books, and if Lisa liked them she should read Charlotte and Emily Brontë too.

'*Jane Eyre, Wuthering Heights* . . . Ach, Miss Lisa, you will adore them. Such love stories. And let's not forget *Madame Bovary* and *Anna Karenina*. My friend, you have a lot of reading to do.'

Lisa looked forward to it. In fact, she looked forward to everything these days. Sitting on the sofa, she glanced up when she heard Jackie stir. In a minute, she'd take her friend in a cup of tea.

She looked forward to going to the theatre every week, particularly to seeing Ralph in that play *Pygmalion* by – she wracked her brains – George Bernard Shaw. She loved her job. When she'd worked in the dye factory, Sundays were spoilt by the thought of tedious, smelly work next morning, whereas the prospect of Mr Greenbaum's bookshop tomorrow held only pleasure. Once there she would contemplate the evening ahead with quiet satisfaction; a period spent reading whilst she ate her meal and listened to the radio until Jackie came home. It was only when she brought Gordon with her that things were not perfect.

It was nice making friends with Piers and Ralph. In fact, life was nicer than it had ever been!

The time spent in London, living with Jackie and working for Mr Greenbaum, was perhaps the most carefree period of Lisa's life. 'The years of innocence', she called them, whenever she looked back . . .

On stage, Ralph was a revelation. At first Lisa didn't recognise him, but hadn't Piers said he played Alfred Doolittle, and wasn't that Alfred Doolittle on stage now? That meant it must be Ralph. This coarse, loud-mouthed, unshaven man, his sagging trousers held up by braces, the sleeves of his collarless shirt rolled up to reveal hairy, muscular arms, this really was the quietly-spoken refined man she'd met last week. The voice, the stance, the manner, were those of a Cockney born in the gutter. It was as if the spirit of some totally different person had taken over Ralph's body.

In the first act, the hilarious speech claiming he was one of the undeserving poor almost brought the house down. Some people even stood up to applaud.

Lisa enjoyed the play more than *Blithe Spirit* – at least, she thought she did. It was difficult to decide.

This Saturday night, Ralph and Piers were coming to the girls' flat for a drink after the performance. Lisa had bought fresh flowers and, allowing for the fact that Jackie would probably drink twice or even three times as much as everybody else, three bottles of wine.

When the two friends arrived, Lisa found she couldn't take her eyes off Ralph. She handed him a glass of wine and when he thanked her, found it incredible to believe that this quietly-modulated voice had so recently filled an entire theatre with its grating power.

Jackie had lost all her inhibitions and was chatting away to Piers about restaurants they both frequented.

'You're quiet, Lisa,' Ralph remarked eventually. 'Didn't you like the play? Were you disappointed by my performance?'

'Oh no!' she said passionately. 'I'm struck dumb with admiration. You were wonderful. I couldn't believe it was really you at first.'

'It's a good part,' he said modestly.

'I think I'd like to be an actor. It must be wonderful to lose yourself like that. I mean, you *were* Alfred Doolittle.'

'You could go to drama classes,' Ralph said.

'How could I do that?' she asked eagerly.

'Well, full-time schools like RADA are difficult to get into and the fees are horrendous – and you have to keep yourself.'

Lisa shook her head ruefully. 'Out of the question, I'm afraid.'

'Then you could go to night-school. I know someone who runs a course in Hackney. He charges half-a-crown a lesson.'

Lisa brightened. 'I could afford that much.'

'I'll find out for you,' he promised.

Lisa's life fell into a comfortable pattern. Work, a visit to the theatre every Saturday, then back for drinks with Piers and Ralph, and on Wednesdays her drama class run by a wild-eyed elderly actor, Godfrey Perrick, and his wife, Rosa. She felt like Eliza Doolittle, her Liverpool accent gradually fading as Rosa taught her to speak properly and throw her voice, how to walk and sit gracefully.

Godfrey concentrated on acting itself. They sat in a circle reading from a play and the words came alive when he spoke them. He never criticised, never praised, as they read their lines, just patiently pointed out how a particular phrase could be expressed, to bring out a meaning that they hadn't noticed.

Summer came. The London pavements were hot beneath her feet as Lisa walked to and from Mr Greenbaum's, though once inside the shop it was cool. On Sundays she dragged a sleepy, reluctant Jackie out of bed and they walked to Kensington Gardens at the end of Queen's Gate where they would have coffee in the outdoor restaurant, watch the model boats on the lake and the uniformed nannies wheeling giant prams, with small children in their stiff Sunday clothes following miserably behind.

Autumn. The leaves in the park turned gold and fell from the trees, crunching beneath their feet as they strolled down the narrow concrete paths. It was too cold to sit outside and Jackie suggested they go to a pub for a drink instead.

Lisa bought a winter coat – a real film star's coat in heavy tweed with a wide belt she pulled tight around her narrow waist. Many admiring looks were cast in their direction; at tall voluptuous Jackie with her creamy hair and skin and Lisa, the same height but slim as a model, her dark hair cut shoulder length – she'd had to keep her eyes shut tight whilst Jackie cut whole sheaths off – and arranged in her favourite style – combed low over one eye, like Veronica Lake.

She'd been asked out on lots of dates since she'd come to London. Customers in the shop had approached her, two of the boys in the acting class kept pleading for her to go out with them, and a young man in the flat below had asked her to dinner twice.

Lisa turned them all down. She wanted nothing to do with boyfriends, not yet anyway. Maybe some day she'd feel differently, but in the meantime the men already in her life were quite enough. Harry Greenbaum, Piers and Ralph: they were all she wanted.

15

Jackie was going home to Bournemouth for Christmas and she invited Lisa to come with her.

The invitation was tactfully refused. Jackie constantly complained about her parents, particularly her mother.

'You wouldn't believe it, Lisa,' she grumbled. 'My mother's maxim is "a place for everything and everything in its place". The house looks unlived-in, like a museum. You can't put a thing down before it's whisked away and put in a drawer where no one can find it. It drives my father wild. He sits in his surgery, even at night – I've told you he's a dentist, haven't I? It's the only way he can get some peace. The reason why I'm such a slob is probably a reaction against my upbringing.'

Staying with Jackie's parents for two days – the elderly aunts who supplied the clothing coupons would be there too – didn't seem to Lisa the ideal way of spending Christmas. Anyway, as she pointed out, Mr Greenbaum and Miriam had asked her for dinner on Christmas Day.

'I thought Orthodox Jews didn't celebrate Christmas,' said Jackie primly. She usually adopted a rather disapproving manner whenever the Greenbaums were mentioned. Lisa suspected Gordon was an anti-Semite.

'They don't, but they still have to eat,' she answered. 'It'll just be an ordinary Jewish meal. Kosher,' she finished knowledgeably.

She got enormous pleasure buying presents for her family: wooden toys for the little ones, scarves and gloves for her other brothers, brooches for Nellie and Joan and a three-strand pearl necklace with a diamanté clasp for Mam. She wrapped each present individually in holly-patterned paper, tied it with red ribbon and attached little labels to each and imagined the large package arriving in Chaucer Street and the youngsters pouncing, tearing it open and handing the presents round, or perhaps it might come whilst Mam was there alone and she'd put the things on the tree.

She sent a card separately, *'From your own Lizzie with lots and lots of love'* she wrote, but still didn't give her address.

There were heaps of parties to go to. The drama class had a special end-of-term celebration and some students were holding parties of their own. Ralph and Piers had asked her and Jackie in for drinks on the Sunday before Christmas. Piers was also going home for Christmas and Lisa sensed tension between the pair when this was mentioned.

Mr Greenbaum kept his shop open all day Christmas Eve. Lisa said goodbye to Jackie in the morning as she was finishing work at lunch-time and going straight to the station.

'I hope you have a nice Christmas,' Jackie said mournfully when they parted outside Harrods. 'I know I won't.'

'You do not mind, Miss Lisa O'Brien, working on this special day?' Mr Greenbaum asked. 'But you see, all the shops stay open and I might do lots of business this afternoon. Last-minute presents, you know.'

'I mind terribly,' she told him severely. 'But you're such a slave-driver you might sack me if I refused.'

'That's right, taunt an old man, an old man who can't hit back.'

'Whilst you've still got a tongue in your head you'll be able to hit back,' said Lisa. She enjoyed their day-long banter. When they were not talking about books, they traded good-humoured insults.

He sighed. 'Ah, Minnie Kopek! Why did I not listen? You pleaded and pleaded. If only I'd given in, I'd be with you in some heaven and not subjected to the slings and arrows of a wicked wife and a slip of a girl who has no respect for me.'

'Don't give me Minnie Kopek. Who on earth was she anyway?'

'A fat lady. She did a striptease – it was obscene. But I could have rested my head in her ample, ample bosom and had some peace, instead of this . . .' He spread his arms, looked around the shop, at Lisa, and shrugged.

She burst out laughing. 'Come off it, Greenbaum. You love your life, you love Miriam and you love your books.'

'Stop being so clever and so damn right. A Jew enjoys being miserable from time to time. You're spoiling my fun.'

The shop door opened and a boy entered.

'Brian – I haven't seen you in ages. What have you run out of this time? Ink – a typewriter ribbon?' Mr Greenbaum turned to his stationery shelf.

'A ream of foolscap copy paper, please.'

The boy approached the counter, caught sight of Lisa and stopped dead. He stared at her for several seconds, then dropped his eyes in confusion and his baby-smooth cheeks flushed pink. He was good-looking in a rather insipid way, with blond, silky hair and light-blue eyes framed with stubby, almost-white lashes which gave him a short-sighted, frightened look. He looked like a cherubic choirboy. She was amused by the way he kept glancing so furtively in her direction.

Mr Greenbaum also noticed. He said jovially, 'Brian, have you met Lisa? I don't think you've been in since she started. Brian works upstairs,' he explained. 'What sort of office is it? I forget, my old brain . . .'

'Imports and exports,' Brian said. His voice, masculine and deep, belied his youthful looks.

'You've made a conquest,' Mr Greenbaum laughed when he'd gone.

Lisa screwed her face into what Mr Greenbaum called her 'Harrods' expression, a mixture of disgust and disdain. 'A mere child,' she said dismissively.

'He is no child,' said Mr Greenbaum seriously. 'Twenty at least – much older than you. His mother calls for him sometimes and waits outside. She is a dragon. Once she came in and bought a cookery book.'

Someone else entered the shop and Lisa forgot all about Brian.

*

That evening she walked home along Old Brompton Road. Harrods was closed, though inside, it was still brightly lit, and exhausted assistants were emptying tills and tidying counters. She stopped entranced before each window, as she'd been doing for weeks. After Christmas, these exquisite displays would be dismantled ready for the Sales.

In the first window was a bridal scene, all white and red velvet, in another a larger-than-life dummy Santa Claus, with elves and fairies clustered at his feet amidst a carpet of real leaves – gold, red, rust. Then the toy window! Even now, at sixteen, Lisa coveted the beautifully dressed dolls with their uncannily-lifelike faces, and wished she could have bought the twins the train-set which chuffed around the floor, in and out of green-painted tunnels, stopping at miniature stations and moving off when the signal fell.

The centrepiece took her breath away. It was a three-storeyed Victorian doll's house, each room furnished with perfect replicas. The chandelier and wall-lights actually worked! A tiny woman stood in the kitchen, hands forever motionless on top of a half-kneaded loaf no bigger than a farthing. In front of the drawing-room fireplace a man in black stood puffing on a pipe whilst his wife sat in a blue brocade armchair sewing, her arm poised in mid-air. Lisa could even see the glint of a minuscule needle. Children played in the nursery, and in the attic a white-clad woman leaned over a cradle containing a baby.

Lisa sighed. Tomorrow morning some children would be waking up to presents like this, whilst others, through no fault of their own, would get nothing.

The night was balmy, the sky clouded, with a reluctant moon peeping out from time to time to float away almost immediately behind a mass of black. Stars twinkled brightly in the few clear patches of dark blue. It was so different from Liverpool where, right now, icy winds were probably blowing in from the Irish Sea and whipping down the streets.

Shops were emptying, doors were locked, assistants poured out onto the pavements, chattering excitedly, the fatigue of the busy Christmas season falling away as they began their journey home to commence their two-day holiday. Last-minute shoppers, laden with parcels, stood on the kerb, vainly yelling for a taxi.

Outside Brompton Oratory a circle of carol singers stood, their silvery voices scarcely audible against the roar of traffic. As Lisa passed, the faint strains of *The Holly and the Ivy* could just be heard above the noise.

Houses, their doors hung with holly wreaths, had trees glittering in front windows, rooms laden with decorations.

The atmosphere was almost heady, filled with a sense of delicious anticipation. Lisa felt an excited thrill run through her. Tonight, she was going to yet another party. Tomorrow, to the Greenbaums for dinner, though on Boxing Day she would be alone. Not that she minded. In fact, she was looking forward to a quiet day spent reading.

Tonight's party was in Lambeth, where Barbara from the drama class lived. Someone was calling for her at eight o'clock. She'd wear her green taffeta dress with the heart-shaped neckline and three-quarter-length sleeves. The skirt was an entire circle of material and she loved the feel of it swirling against her legs when she moved. The only problem would be fighting off John and Barry, who'd both been pestering her to go out with them for months. At every party one of them attempted to capture her for a 'snogging session' as they called it, where couples sat for hours and hours in darkened rooms, clutched in what seemed like an endless, suffocating and rather boring embrace.

'Never mind,' thought Lisa serenely. 'I'll get rid of them somehow. I always do.'

The Greenbaums lived on the ground floor of a rather gloomy block of flats in Chelsea. Lisa had already been there several times. The inside of the flat matched the facade of the building and was filled with dark, heavy furniture lavishly decorated with carvings and scrolls. Miriam had covered every surface with ornaments and photographs of long-dead relatives from Austria.

She'd gone to great trouble with the meal.

To start with there was barley soup, followed, to Lisa's surprise, by chicken in wine sauce served with giblet stuffing, fried potatoes and mixed vegetables.

'I don't usually cook in wine, but seeing as it's Christmas . . .' Miriam winked.

Lisa declared the food delicious but said she'd expected something entirely different. 'I thought kosher food would be more . . . well, foreign. Things I'd never eaten before.'

Miriam and her husband exchanged amused glances.

'Kosher food is the same as your food, but prepared in a different way, that's all. The animals are killed—'

'Don't tell her, not while she's eating!' choked Mr Greenbaum. 'Have some tact, woman. You'll be describing your operations next.'

Pudding was an unusual apple tart. Miriam said it was called 'strudel'.

'That's the nicest meal I've ever eaten,' Lisa said when they'd finished.

Miriam looked gratified. 'It's pleasant to have some appreciation for a change,' she said sarcastically. 'This man here! Never a word of thanks he gives me, even though I slave over a hot stove all day to fill his guts with decent food.'

Mr Greenbaum winked at Lisa.

Over the afternoon and evening, a good-natured argument raged. It appeared Miriam wanted her husband to work part-time in the shop.

'You're a stubborn old goat, Greenbaum, staggering off every day, putting in eight hours. For what? We have enough money. Lisa can look after the place on her own. You're lucky to have her.'

'My shop is my life,' the old man said simply.

'Are you saying I'm not?' Miriam countered furiously.

'Of course you're not! You're a boil on my bum. You think I'd stay at home with you when I can spend my time with a lovely young woman like this?' He gestured towards Lisa.

'I could compete with Lisa once.' Miriam nodded with satisfaction. 'Some day, she will be old too.'

'When Lisa's old, I'll give up the shop.'

'Tch! What do you think, Lisa?'

'I'm not taking sides,' said Lisa with alacrity. She sat contentedly sipping blackberry wine and nibbling frosted coffee biscuits. Privately she thought Mr Greenbaum should work as long as he wanted.

The argument continued and Minnie Kopek was not mentioned once.

On Boxing Day, Lisa had intended to sleep in but she woke at seven and found it impossible to drift off again. After a while, she got up. She dressed in slacks and a white blouse, made a pot of tea and picked up her latest book, *Vanity Fair*. She loved the character of Becky Sharpe – such a scheming minx and terribly hard-hearted.

Later on, she walked to Kensington Gardens, which to her surprise was crowded. Several little girls were pushing their new dolls' prams and looking very self-important, and a little boy careered wildly along the path, his small feet straining on the pedals of a bright red racing car. By the pond, fathers hovered anxiously as their sons sailed their new model yachts, advising them how to adjust the rigging, some watching in despair as the boats fell sideways and the sails filled with water.

A young couple came towards her, the man in soldier's uniform, his arm round the waist of a girl not much older than herself. With one hand each, they pushed a well-used pram and as they passed she saw a baby girl inside about nine months old playing happily with a rattle.

A sudden feeling of homesickness overcame her. Last January, Kevin had proudly announced that his wife Colette was expecting a baby. Kitty had been thrilled to bits – her first grandchild! In Liverpool, there was a niece or nephew Lisa had never seen and was never likely to see.

Her family! Would they be thinking about her too?

Blinking furiously to keep back the tears, she rushed home.

Not a sound came from behind the closed doors of the flats in Number 5 Queen's Gate as Lisa ran upstairs, not a single voice or note of music. Nearly everyone had gone away, though Ralph had stayed behind. Perhaps he had no family to go to. Later on, she heard dishes rattling in the kitchen and contemplated taking her own along to wash, pretending to meet him by accident, but although Ralph was friendly, it was a reserved sort of friendliness, as though he was just being nice to please Piers and would far sooner have nothing to do with her or Jackie.

It was impossible to get back into her novel. No matter how hard she tried, she couldn't stop thinking about home. She mended some stockings and tidied the flat. As she dusted the dressing table she noticed Jackie's bottle of whisky and stared at it thoughtfully. It seemed to help Jackie cope with her problems. She fetched a glass and poured out an inch, sipping it cautiously. Almost immediately her body was flooded with warmth. She sipped more and her head began to swim. It was a pleasant sensation and coupled with it came the feeling that things were not so bad after all. She drank some more. In fact, life was rather good. As if the sun had risen inside her head, everything turned rosy and she sat on the sofa, contented and sleepy.

There was a knock on the door. It must be Ralph. Too lazy to get up, she shouted, 'Come in.'

To her utter astonishment, Gordon entered the room. Jackie must have given him a front-door key.

'What on earth do you want?' It sounded rude, but she didn't care. 'Jackie's away. Didn't she tell you?'

'It's not Jackie I've come to see,' he said with an unpleasant leer.

'Well, I don't want to see you,' she said firmly.

She might just as well have not spoken. He sat down beside her and she glared at him, wishing now she didn't feel so dizzy and could get to her feet, open the door and order him out. What on earth did the man want? She was dumbfounded by his next words.

'C'mon, Lisa – I've seen you looking at me. You're really turned on, aren't you?'

She regarded him contemptuously. 'Turned on – by *you*!'

The scorn in her voice seemed to reach him. He looked angry. His blotchy cheeks flushed blood-red and his eyes narrowed. The ends of his silly, oversized moustache literally quivered with fury.

'You're a sexy little bitch. Don't think I haven't noticed the way you flaunt yourself around when I'm here.'

'When you're here, all I want to do is be sick.' The whisky seemed to have banished all her inhibitions. She said the first thing that came into her head. 'The thought of you and Jackie together turns my stomach. She's a million times too good for you.'

'Jackie likes a good poke and that's what I give her. Don't you want a good poke, Lisa? Lisa the sexy bitch.'

'If you don't get out immediately, I'll tell Jackie,' she spat.

'Fuck Jackie, I'd sooner have something going with you.'

He clumsily dragged her towards him and she felt his unsavoury breath on her cheek. Then he began to kiss her, his hands fumbling with her breasts. She struggled and screamed, 'Get off me, you bastard.'

'C'mon, Lisa, you're driving me mad. You want it, I know you do.'

She screamed again, but his arms were strong and although she fought, she could not escape his embrace. He tore at her blouse and bent his head to her throat.

Suddenly, she felt him being lifted off her.

Ralph! Ralph had him by the scruff of the neck and threw him onto the floor where he crouched on all fours like an animal, saliva dripping from his mouth.

'Get out,' said Ralph quietly. 'Get out, before I kick you down the stairs, all four flights of them.'

'Bloody pansy,' croaked Gordon, crawling out of reach.

Ralph took a step towards him. '*Out*, I said.'

He crawled along the floor until he reached a chair and pulled himself to his feet. One half of his moustache drooped down over his mouth like an untidy tassle.

At the door, he turned and his expression was obsequious.

'You won't tell Jackie?' he asked in a fawning voice.

Lisa didn't answer.

'*OUT*,' said Ralph.

16

They listened to his descending footsteps until they faded and soon afterwards came a faint thud as the front door was slammed shut. Lisa glanced at Ralph and they both burst out laughing.

'What a slimy character!' said Ralph eventually. 'What on earth does Jackie see in him?'

Lisa shook her head in perplexity. 'I don't know. She's in love and love's blind, so they say.' She attempted to stand, but her head swam and she fell back onto the sofa.

'Are you all right? Do you want something?'

'I'm drunk, Ralph. I've never been drunk before. I've been drinking Jackie's whisky. I felt so depressed. I think I'd better make some tea to sober myself up.'

'You should have come to see me – I feel depressed too. In fact, I've been contemplating knocking on your door all day but thought you might prefer to be alone.' He got up, a sturdy, comfortable figure, his usually withdrawn features animated by the recent excitement. 'I'll put the kettle on.'

'There's water already in it,' she said, adding quickly, 'I forgot to thank you. You saved my life, you're not half tough.'

'Not half tough!' He smiled. 'I doubt if it was your life I saved, just your virtue.'

'Oh, that's long gone,' she answered dismissively and could have bitten off her tongue, though he didn't seem to notice.

'What's making you so miserable, Lisa?'

'Just missing my family, that's all. I went to Kensington Gardens and there was a baby. I remembered I have a niece or nephew I've never seen. And you?'

He echoed her words. 'Just missing my family, that's all.'

'Couldn't you go home and visit them?'

'My wife and children, you mean?'

She gaped. 'You're married.'

'She's divorcing me – quite rightly. My parents have disowned me. Piers has gone, temporarily. I realised I was completely alone. It was getting to me more and more. Fortunately for me, unfortunately for you, you screamed and broke the spell, the bad spell.'

He poured two mugs of tea and brought them over. 'Can you hold this?'

'I'm not that bad. It's my legs and head mainly, they're all swimmy.' She began to sip the tea eagerly. 'I'll never drink so much so quickly again,' she swore.

'An excellent idea. I'll drink to that.' He held up his mug.

'I just wanted to blot things out, stop thoughts coming.'

'Ah, if only we could!' he said sadly. 'I've been thinking about my kids all day. Imagining how Christmas could be, how it used to be, you know, the few years we were together.'

'What happened? I don't want to seem nosy. Don't answer if I am, but why did you get married?' She glanced at him and wondered how she could ever have thought he looked anonymous. There was anguish in his eyes and his mouth was twisted bitterly.

'I got married because it was the thing to do. All men – well, most men – did it. And I thought I was in love. I can't have been, but I genuinely thought I was. How are you supposed to know what love is? My marriage wasn't perfect, sex was nothing like it was cracked up to be, but maybe it wasn't for anybody.'

He sighed. Lisa watched but said nothing.

'Then I was called up,' he went on. 'I'd never lived with men before. Suddenly it all seemed more natural. I felt more at ease, more myself, my real self. Then I was captured, went in a prisoner-of-war camp and . . . well, you can guess the rest.' He shrugged. 'Once home, I wrote to my wife and told her everything. I knew she'd be shocked, but the letter I got back! Full of filthy insults. The children have been told I'm dead.'

'That's awful.' Lisa laid her hand on his arm. He turned and made an effort to smile.

'Sorry. I'm heaping all my problems on you and making you even more depressed. I've been drinking too, you know. Wine, one bottle, two . . . I can't remember.'

'Don't be sorry, go on,' she urged. 'A trouble shared is a trouble halved.' That was one of Kitty's favourite sayings.

'In the camp I got involved in dramatics. To my amazement, I found I was good at acting. It seemed the logical thing to do when I got home.' He was holding the mug tightly in both hands and she saw the knuckles turn white.

'You know what I want more than anything, Lisa?'

'What?' she murmured.

'To become a famous star. For Ralph Layton to become a household name, like Charles Laughton or Laurence Olivier, then one day my wife might tell the kids who I am, that I'm not dead after all. Maybe things will have changed by then. They won't care that I'm a pansy, a faggot, a queer or any other insulting word you can think of which describes what God made me. Do you think I'll become a star, Lisa?'

'I hope so,' she whispered. 'I sincerely hope so. Anyway, Piers will be back tomorrow and—'

He interrupted harshly. 'Not tomorrow – next week. It's not just a two-day break at the old de Villiers ancestral home, you know. Piers will be having a whale of a time. Of course, he can't take me, as they don't know about . . . He'll be flirting with some girl, softening her up for tonight.'

'You mean Piers—?'

'Oh, yes. He likes women, though not so much as men. That's why, when he brought you along, I thought . . .' He stopped and shook his head. 'Enough!' he cried in a deep stentorian voice which made Lisa jump. 'You know, you're right – I *do* feel better. Now I've bared my soul, it's your turn. Where's that bloody whisky?'

He half-filled a glass and gestured towards Lisa. 'C'mon, have some more. Help get things off your chest.'

'Do you think I should? Drink, I mean.'

'On second thoughts, no, though you're quite safe with me.'

'I've told you what's wrong. I'm missing my family, that's all.'

'No it isn't, you're holding something back. I could tell when we first met. You're a very deep and mysterious woman for only sixteen. You've lived life far more than Jackie. I can see it in your eyes.'

There was something inherently appealing about confiding in someone, someone as warm and understanding as Ralph, the things she had told no one. Not a single person in the world knew about that day in Southport.

So she told him. Everything, including Tom and his bloody death.

The day grew dark. Neither bothered to switch on the light and by the time she'd finished, the room was illuminated only by the dim, shadowy moon.

He didn't speak for a long, long time. Eventually he sighed and said softly, 'My dear girl, I admire you more than words can say. What a fight you've had. Let's hope you'll always be on the winning side.'

She began to cry softly and he took her hand. They sat together, silently, companionably, until she fell asleep. When she woke, his head had fallen on her shoulder and he was snoring and she quickly dozed off again, grateful for the proximity of his warm, comforting body.

It was daylight when an astonished Jackie came home and found them.

'Sorry, I can't. I have a drama class tonight.'

'Well, what about tomorrow?'

'I wash my hair on Thursdays.'

Brian blinked, obviously considering whether to suggest another day.

Lisa prayed he wouldn't. She didn't want to go out with him and wished he'd take the hint and stop asking. Ever since Christmas Eve, he'd been coming into the shop once or twice a week. Mr Greenbaum had rubbed his hands and ordered more stationery because, as he said with a grin, Brian was rapidly emptying the shelves.

'I wonder if it gets used in the office or does he take it home?' he mused one day. 'Have pity on the boy, Lisa, persuade him to buy books instead. At least he can read them. He must have a dozen bottles of red ink and there is a limit to what a man can do with red ink, other than pretend he is Dracula and drink it!'

Today he'd come for a box of HB pencils. Lisa put them in a paper bag and gave them to him, smiling kindly.

He left the shop looking disconsolate, his head bent to guard against the torrential rain.

The weather this April was actually colder than it had been in December. Rain had fallen relentlessly for days. Jackie and Lisa had been forced to catch a bus to work and Mr Greenbaum had been coming and going in a taxi. Now, Lisa went into the kitchen to check that the hem of her fawn trench-coat had dried. It had got soaked in the scurry from the bus stop to the shop.

The hem was dry but crumpled. She'd iron it when she got home. Lisa was proud of her trenchcoat and wore it with the collar up and her hands stuffed in the pockets, just like Barbara Stanwyck. She was folding the umbrella which had been left standing in the sink to drip, when the shop door opened.

She hurried back. A middle-aged man had entered and was shaking himself on the mat. She blinked at his attire: a loud black chalk-striped suit, patent-leather shoes, topped by a massive sheepskin coat with a fur collar. He removed his hat, a soft suede fedora sporting a bright feather, and began to blow the raindrops off with loud puffs. Lisa wanted to laugh.

'Morry Sopel,' said Mr Greenbaum disapprovingly. This customer, she sensed, was not welcome. 'What can I do for you?'

'Exchange a few words, Harry, that's all. I was in the area on business, I saw your shop and thought to myself, "I've not seen Harry Greenbaum in a long, long time." ' He pulled off his suede gloves to reveal dark, hairy hands.

'I have shed no tears over that,' the old man said frostily.

'Harry, boy, don't hurt my feelings.' The man waved his hands. His fingers were covered in rings and a wide gold bracelet gleamed on his thick wrist. He had dark, good-natured eyes and had once been very handsome, though now his chin was slack and deep lines ran down from his nose to the corner of his wide mouth.

He looked up and saw Lisa standing at the top of the stairs.

'Well!' he said, whistling appreciatively. 'I didn't know you had help, Harry. And what help!'

Lisa wore a pale blue polo-necked jumper and a cream skirt with matching high-heeled court shoes. Her hair was parted in the middle and smoothed back behind her pearl-studded ears. She wore little make-up, just shell-pink lipstick and a touch of brown shadow above the eyes. Each morning, she smeared a little vaseline on her long black lashes to give them a silky look.

For some reason she couldn't fathom, Lisa found it difficult to take offence at the newcomer's open admiration. To please Mr Greenbaum, she didn't smile, but came down the stairs into the shop without a word.

'This is Miss Lisa O'Brien.' The old man introduced her reluctantly. 'Morry Sopel is an old . . . acquaintance.'

'How do you do, Miss Lisa O'Brien.' He shook hands, his grip warm and friendly. Mr Greenbaum glowered in their direction. 'Tell me,' said Morry. 'Is it nearly time for this lovely young lady to take lunch? If so, will she do me the honour—'

Mr Greenbaum interrupted, his voice gritty with anger. 'No, she will not.'

'Can't Lisa answer for herself?' said the visitor, his eyes crinkling with amusement.

'I am answering for her. She works for me. She is my responsibility and what's more, she is almost engaged to be married.'

Lisa glanced at him in astonishment.

The visitor was persistent. 'But lunch won't hurt, surely?'

'He works upstairs, her boyfriend, the almost-fiancé. He will be angry if he sees Lisa leave with another man. Won't he, my dear?'

'Why, er . . . yes,' she stammered.

Morry Sopel shrugged philosophically. 'Never mind. It isn't often I come across such a vision. I would have enjoyed treating Lisa to a slap-up lunch in Harrods.'

Lisa would have quite enjoyed it too. She rather liked this garishly dressed visitor and felt slightly irritated by her employer's proprietorial attitude, though she said nothing.

After the man had gone, she was quiet. Mr Greenbaum kept glancing in her direction and eventually he said, 'You're angry with me.'

'No, no,' she protested.

'Yes, you are, I can tell. But Lisa, he is a bad man, that Morry Sopel. A bad, bad man.'

'He seemed all right to me.'

'Oh, he has charm, I grant you that. Women fall for him. His poor wife left him many years ago, broken-hearted. So many other women she had to put up with.'

'But as he said, lunch wouldn't hurt,' she muttered defensively.

'Ach, Lisa! Forgive me. I was wrong to interfere, but believe me, Morry Sopel is not a man to eat with. Not lunch. Not anything. He mixes with evil people.'

She smiled, convinced the old man was exaggerating. He saw her smile and when he spoke again, his voice trembled with emotion. 'I cannot put it too strongly, my child. Now he has seen you, he may come back. Promise me you will have nothing to do with that gangster.'

'Gangster!' she gasped.

'Yes. That's what Morry Sopel is – a gangster, involved with thieves and murderers. How he has escaped prison, I do not know. Now, promise me, Lisa.'

'I promise,' she said, and shuddered.

The following week, Brian bought her flowers – deep red roses wrapped in silver foil. Mr Greenbaum was just about to leave for lunch as he came in.

'A visitor for you, Lisa,' he said with a mischievous grin.

She was embarrassed and angry. Why on earth wouldn't this boy leave her alone? It wasn't fair to keep pressurising her.

'I wondered what you were doing on Saturday,' he asked boldly after she had thanked him, trying to keep the irritation out of her voice.

'I'm going to the theatre,' she said. 'With a friend.'

'Sunday, then?'

'I'm sorry.' She tried to make it sound final, to deter him from asking again.

A woman customer entered and Lisa left Brian to attend to her. She was wrapping up the purchase when Morry Sopel came in. He wore the same clothes as before, though this time, his expensive coat hung open to reveal a diamond flashing on his bright blue and green tie. Over the head of the customer, he gave her a massive wink. She regarded him coolly and when the woman left, he came over.

'I waited till I saw old Harry go. Thought I'd ask you out to lunch without the presence of a chaperone who wouldn't even let you speak.'

She felt her insides quiver. This man was a gangster – a real-life gangster like Humphrey Bogart or Edward G. Robinson.

'The answer's the same – no,' she said shortly.

He looked unabashed. 'Dinner, then? The Savoy, Claridges? Ever been there?'

'No,' she said. 'And I've no wish to.'

'Come off it,' he said. 'Every girl likes dinner in a top hotel. Five courses, the best wine.'

Privately, Lisa agreed. She would have loved to go to Claridges or the Savoy. 'This girl doesn't,' she lied. 'Anyway, as Harry said, I've got a boy-friend.'

'Don't believe it!' he said flatly and his dark eyes flashed with fun. 'He was lying, was old Harry. He's too honest a man to lie. It doesn't work.'

'He wasn't lying.'

Brian! Lisa had forgotten he was there. He emerged from behind a row of shelves looking and sounding remarkably self-assured. 'I'm Lisa's boyfriend and tonight we're going out to dinner.'

Morry looked disappointed. 'Ah, well. No harm in trying. Goodbye, Lisa. And goodbye to you, young man. You are a lucky fellow. Tell me when you get engaged and I'll send a present.'

That Sunday, Brian took her out to tea then to the pictures.

It had been impossible to refuse his invitation after he had rescued her from Morry. In fact, he turned out to be surprisingly good company. Clearly infatuated, he was attentive, opening doors, pulling back her chair in the restaurant, paying for the best seats in the cinema where they saw *Anchors Away*. It was such a happy film and Gene Kelly's dancing was sheer magic.

Brian didn't say much himself, but he was a good, almost avid listener. She told him about going to see plays every week and getting the tickets off a real-life actor who lived in a flat on the same floor as her own and who was in *Pygmalion* at a theatre not far from where they were now, about her acting classes and Jackie and her awful boyfriend.

'And Piers, he also lives on our floor, is an interior decorator and presently is working for some duchess, I forget her name.'

'Really!'

When they came out of the cinema he spoiled things a bit by saying, 'It would be nice to go for coffee, but I promised Mother I'd be home before ten.'

At the door of Number 5 Queen's Gate, she said, 'I won't ask you in, else you might be late for your mother.'

He was aware of the touch of sarcasm in her voice and muttered something about his mother wanting help with filling in a form.

'Then you'd better hurry,' said Lisa in a chilly voice, thus firing the first shots in the battle which would one day commence between herself and Mrs Dorothy Smith.

When Lisa got in, Jackie was already bathed and ready for bed, clad in lemon silk pyjamas and a short matching dressing gown. She was lounging on the sofa drinking whisky.

'What was he like?' she asked in a blurred voice which told that this drink was not her first.

Lisa wrinkled her nose and said, 'A bit impressionable.'

Jackie giggled. 'You make it sound like he's a little boy.'

'In some ways he is.' Then she recalled the uncompromising manner in which he had dealt with Morry Sopel. 'And in other ways he's very manly and grown up. All in all, I quite enjoyed myself.'

'I suppose you'll be going out with him again?' said Jackie.

'Next Sunday.' He'd pleaded to see her earlier, but she'd been firm, not wanting the relationship to become serious.

'Oh dear, I hate you going out on Sundays. I've got used to you being here.'

'I'll make it another day,' Lisa said quickly. 'Brian won't mind.'

'I wouldn't hear of it.' Jackie was vehement. 'I shouldn't have complained. After all, I leave you alone most nights till gone eight.'

'We could make up a foursome,' suggested Lisa tentatively. Jackie looked so pretty with her damp curls sticking to her fresh peachy skin and it seemed a waste for her to sit alone in the flat saving herself for that awful man she loved. 'What about this chap in the office who keeps asking you out?'

Predictably, her friend answered: 'Oh, I couldn't possibly do that! I would be betraying Gordon.'

'But he's with his wife all weekend. Isn't that betraying you?'

'Oh no, Lisa. That's a different thing altogether.'

Although Lisa wished they could continue the conversation, she said no more. She hadn't told Jackie about Gordon's visit on Boxing Day, though she agonised over whether this was the right decision. Her main worry was that even if her friend knew, she wouldn't love the man any less, but just be more miserable with the knowledge – and she would make excuses for him, like he'd had too much to drink or he'd thought Jackie would be home sooner. She'd feel guilty about Lisa, too.

So she said nothing, but noticed that ever since Christmas, Gordon's manner with Jackie had been increasingly offhand, almost cruel. At times the poor girl was thoroughly wretched.

Lisa sighed. 'I'll make us a cup of tea,' she said.

17

The following Saturday, Lisa woke Jackie before she went to work. 'We're having a party tonight,' she said.

Jackie struggled to sit up, blinking. 'A party! Why?'

'It was my birthday the other day – I'm seventeen.'

'Lisa! You should have told me – I haven't bought you a present. Who's coming to this party?'

'You don't mind, do you? After all, it's your flat.'

'Of course I don't mind. I love parties.'

Lisa had deliberately not told Jackie before, in case she invited Gordon. Although he was supposed to be unavailable at weekends, on odd occasions he had appeared on the scene. Now it was too late for him to be contacted.

'Piers is coming, of course, and Ralph, though he'll be late. I invited the drama class, too, though not all of them can come. And poor Mr Greenbaum can't manage the stairs, I'm afraid.'

'What about food?'

'Sandwiches and biscuits, that's all. And of course, wine. I'll buy it on my way home from the shop.' Lisa finished at one o'clock on Saturdays.

'Oh, Lisa! I'm glad you came into my life. You've made it so much more interesting – something always seems to be happening.'

For her birthday present, Mr Greenbaum gave her a set of Jane Austen novels bound in dark green, gold-tooled leather inside their own special case.

She was so delighted that she spontaneously kissed his yellow wrinkled cheek.

'Thank you, thank you,' she breathed. 'I loved the books so much, I know I shall want to read them over and over again.'

'There's two there you haven't read,' he said. 'And I shan't tell Miriam about the kiss for fear she'll come in here and kill you.'

'Give her a kiss from me.'

'What, kiss that awful woman? Never!' Suddenly, his old face crumpled into an expression she couldn't at first identify. Was it fear? He leaned on the desk to steady himself then sank into his chair.

'What is it?' she asked, alarmed.

'Nothing, nothing. An old man being stupid.'

'Tell me,' she insisted. 'You look as if you're frightened.'

'I am frightened. A thought crossed my mind that when next you read *Pride and Prejudice*, I will be dead.'

'Don't be silly! Of course you won't.'

'Lisa, Lisa, don't patronise. I'm nearly eighty. Inside my head I feel eighteen. How I would have liked to go to your party with my lovely Miriam.'

She began to wish she'd held the party somewhere else, so that he could have come without difficulty.

He saw her concern and gave a disgusted grunt. 'Ach! What a neurotic old man I am, behaving like this on your birthday. Harry Greenbaum, pull yourself together.' He began to sing *Look for the Silver Lining* in guttural bass tones that made her giggle.

'There,' he said after a few lines, 'That's as much as I know and in cheering you up I've cheered myself.'

'Are you sure?'

'Sure I'm sure. Tonight at eight o'clock, when your party starts, Miriam and I shall drink your health. I hope you have as full and as happy a life as I've had, Lisa.'

'So do I,' she said fervently.

She remembered Kitty when the crowd sang 'Happy Birthday'. Jackie put out the lights and came in with a large cake she'd bought that afternoon: seventeen flickering candles, each set in a white rose and LISA written in pink on the smooth white icing surface. As Lisa laughingly blew out the candles, the guests began to sing and she immediately thought of her mam. Even when they were little and there was no money for presents or special food, they still sang 'Happy Birthday' when they sat down to their scouse or bread and jam or whatever Kitty could afford.

She was crying when the lights came on but everyone thought it was just the emotion of the moment. Except Ralph. As Jackie began to cut the cake he came and sat by Lisa.

'Sad?'

'A bit.'

'I thought you might be.' He squeezed her hand and Piers glanced at them curiously. Since Boxing Day a bond had been forged between Lisa and Ralph. Jackie had noticed it too.

'You are my greatest friend,' she whispered.

'I'm honoured.' He smiled.

'We'll always be friends, even if we don't see much of each other in the future.'

'Always. You can count on me if you're ever in trouble.'

Decades were to pass before Ralph had to keep this promise.

Brian was annoyed to learn that she'd had a party and not invited him.

'It went on till two o'clock this morning,' said Lisa mischievously. 'And I thought your mother might not like you being out so late.' In truth, it hadn't crossed her mind to ask him.

'Do you like my watch?' She pulled back her sleeve and revealed a tiny gold watch on an expanding bracelet. 'It's from Jackie.'

The one Jackie had lent her originally had been returned a long time ago, and Lisa had bought herself a cheap chrome model, which her friend declared looked like a boy's which indeed it was.

'And I got lots of perfume and jewellery, a set of Jane Austen's novels from Mr Greenbaum and a lovely doll off Ralph.'

'A doll?'

On Boxing Day she must have told Ralph about looking at the dolls in Harrods' window, for he'd bought her a two-foot high Victorian doll with real hair set in ringlets. Only that morning she and Jackie had sat on the floor staring in admiration at the doll, carefully placed on the sofa. It stared back at them with wide blue expressionless eyes.

'What will you call her?' Jackie had asked.

'Victoria – or does that lack imagination?'

'No, Victoria's just right. Just look at those buttons! I mean – they're real, you can undo them.'

'I know,' gloated Lisa. 'I undressed her earlier on. You should see her pantaloons. 'They're trimmed with lace – and so are her petticoats.'

'Really? Can I play with her this afternoon when you're out?'

'As long as you're careful.'

Then they had both collapsed on the floor in giggles.

'Yes, a doll,' said Lisa to Brian. 'She's lovely. I've called her Victoria.'

Brian looked mystified. Later on, he bought the largest box of chocolates in the cinema kiosk.

'Happy birthday,' he said stiffly. Lisa felt guilty. His feelings were obviously hurt so she was especially nice.

They saw a film called *Rope* with James Stewart. Brian said it was based on a true murder which had happened in America in the nineteen-thirties. It was so gripping that for two hours Lisa forgot where she was.

'That was marvellous,' she whispered when they stood up for the National Anthem.

'Alfred Hitchcock's films always are.'

'Alfred Hitchcock? What part did he play?'

'He was the director. Mother and I see all his films.'

Although he mentioned his mother several times during the evening, Brian didn't say he had to be home early, and suggested they go for coffee. When Lisa invited him back to Queen's Gate instead, he jumped at the idea.

At the flat, Jackie was wafting round clad only in pyjamas and clutching the inevitable glass of whisky. Brian looked embarrassed and Lisa smiled. He was such a baby sometimes.

After she'd seen him out, Jackie said, 'He couldn't take his eyes off you. He's definitely smitten.'

'Is he? I hadn't really noticed,' Lisa said dismissively.

'He's very good-looking, too.'

Lisa grinned. 'I hadn't noticed that, either.'

'I reckon Alan Ladd might have looked a little bit like Brian when he was very young.'

Lisa's opinion of Brian suddenly improved by leaps and bounds, and for the first time she felt flattered to be going out with him. After all, not many girls could claim a youthful Alan Ladd as a boyfriend.

This year, summer was not so fine as last year. The days were misty and damp with just occasional periods of fine hot weather, though autumn was as lovely as ever.

'This is my favourite season,' Lisa said to Jackie as they tramped through Kensington Gardens one bracing October day. A shower of leaves fell from a tree in front and Lisa ran forward, hands outstretched. 'Come on,' she shouted. 'Catch a leaf and make a wish, it's sure to come true.'

'My wishes never come true,' Jackie said bitterly.

'Oh dear!' Lisa came back and took her friend's hand. 'What are we going to do with you?'

Jackie gave a wistful smile. 'Make Gordon love me as much as Brian loves you,' she said. 'Catch a leaf, Lisa, and wish that for me.'

Lisa was seeing Brian twice a week, on Sundays and Thursdays. They nearly always went to the cinema. He searched through the newspapers to find where Hitchcock films were showing and sometimes they travelled out into the suburbs where they saw *Notorious* with Cary Grant and Ingrid Bergman, who was too lovely for words and also starred in the next film they saw, *Spellbound*, with Gregory Peck. Lisa fell in love instantly.

She enthused when they got outside, 'If I was younger, I'd send for his photograph.'

Brian looked annoyed. 'I didn't think he was all *that* handsome,' he said disparagingly.

'Oh Brian, he's *gorgeous*.'

Spurred on perhaps by jealousy, that was the night Brian proposed for the first time. Flattered, Lisa turned him down gently. He was a nice boy, but too immature. Most of the time she felt years older than him, though one day he would make a fine man.

Undaunted, he invited her to tea next Sunday to meet his mother.

Lisa remembered Mr Greenbaum's description of Mrs Smith. She was a dragon, he'd said. She told him about the anticipated visit next day, knowing he would have some awful tale to tell about Miriam's mother. True to form, he shuddered and said, 'Ach! Mothers-in-law.'

Lisa laughed. 'Was Miriam's mother a dragon?'

'Worse than a dragon, a Brontosaurus Rex. My own mother, she was a reasonable woman, a lovely mother, but as a mother-in-law she was a different person. A monster. Mothers become schizophrenic when their children get married. They show an entirely different face to the poor new son- or daughter-in-law.' He wagged his finger cautiously. 'Put your armour on this Sunday, Lisa. Be prepared for war.'

Lisa wore her new tweed suit – Jackie had advised her to buy one. 'They're useful whenever you're stuck for something to wear, and a suit always looks smart.'

The two-piece was fawn tweed, with a brown velvet collar. Lisa wore it with a frilly cream blouse and brown court shoes.

Brian's mother lived in Chiswick in a road of identical semi-detached houses, each front door containing a panel of stained glass.

'Mother loves her house, it's her pride and joy,' Brian said once.

Lisa couldn't understand why. Once inside, she thought the house unremarkable. There were few ornaments and no pictures, the carpets were faded and the curtains didn't match the wallpaper. It was scrupulously clean, but that was all. It entirely lacked imagination or originality. Although it was Christmas next week, there were no decorations up.

Mrs Smith was a reflection of her house. A tall bulky woman, she used no make-up and her dull, mouse-coloured hair was cut short and permed almost to a frizz. She wore a beige rayon dress with a V-shaped neck and long, ill-fitting sleeves which did absolutely nothing for her. Around the place where her waist had once been, a matching belt strained in the final hole. Lisa noticed the seams were rucked and badly pressed, and realised the woman had made the dress herself. Her only jewellery was a wedding ring which bit into the flesh of her finger. Brian had once said that his mother had had him when she was twenty-one. That meant this woman was only forty-two. She looked well into her fifties! It was as if she was determined on middle age and made no attempt to halt it – indeed, encouraged it.

Mrs Smith was looking Lisa up and down quite openly as if her son had brought home a piece of meat that needed to be examined, then accepted or rejected if found wanting. It seemed that at any minute, she might squeeze her wrists to check her bones. Lisa felt annoyed.

'How do you do?' she said boldly, and stuck out her hand.

Almost grudgingly Mrs Smith shook it. She smelled strongly of mothballs. 'Sit down,' she said gruffly.

Lisa sat on the rust-coloured armchair, dislodging one of the lace-trimmed linen arm-covers. Mrs Smith sprang over and straightened it. There was silence. Lisa glanced around for a photograph of Mr Smith, for surely that must be who Brian took after. Delicately-boned and fine-featured, he was nothing like his mother. There was none.

Brian sat on the edge of the settee and coughed nervously. 'Lisa works in a bookshop, Mother. On the ground floor of our company.'

'You told me,' said Mrs Smith. 'What does your father do, Lisa?'

Lisa was taken aback. It was the last question she'd expected. 'He's dead,' she answered.

'I'm sorry to hear that. What did he die of?'

I murdered him. She felt an almost hysterical desire to tell the truth, just to see Mrs Smith and Brian's reactions.

'He had an accident at work,' she lied. 'He was on the docks, you see.'

'A docker?' said Mrs Smith, making no attempt to disguise her contempt. Lisa felt annoyed again and rather to her dismay, found herself disliking the woman intensely. Despite Harry Greenbaum's warnings, she'd come with an open mind, hoping to become friends with Brian's mother.

'He was a foreman. A ton of rice fell on him one day when he was supervising the unloading.'

'Ah, a foreman.' Mrs Smith nodded her head less critically and Lisa wanted to shout, '*It's me that matters, not what my father did. I'm the one Brian's going out with.*'

'And your mother?'

'She's dead too. I'm an orphan.' Lisa felt her heart twist as she told the lie, but it seemed the best way to stop Mrs Smith from prying.

The woman's next words dumbfounded her. Turning to her son, she said, 'You didn't tell me she was an orphan,' as if Lisa wasn't there.

'I didn't know,' mumbled Brian.

'Have you been submitting a report on me?' She smiled at him, unconsciously separating him from the disagreeable relationship established with his mother.

He blushed and hung his head. Another silence. Then he looked up and said apologetically. 'We mainly talk about films, Mother, and all the interesting people in the house where Lisa lives.'

'Do you now?' She sniffed and added petulantly, 'We haven't been to the pictures together in weeks.'

Brian looked uncomfortable. 'Perhaps we could go on Monday night?'

'Oh, don't mind me.' The air was heavy with resentment.

Brian coughed again. 'Is tea ready?'

'It's been ready since two o'clock,' his mother said unpleasantly, as though they'd arrived late.

Tea comprised watercress sandwiches, a sponge cake and plain biscuits. Lisa, who'd been looking forward to something seasonal like mince pies or shortbread, hated the bitter taste of the vegetable and remembered the teas Kitty made when the boys brought their girlfriends to Chaucer Street. Despite rationing, she always prepared a feast – cold ham and tomatoes, trifle and at least three different sorts of cake.

'Mother does all her own baking,' said Brian proudly. 'She made the cake and biscuits herself.'

'I don't believe in shop-bought confectionery,' said Mrs Smith as grimly as if she was making a statement about religion.

'That's a pity,' thought Lisa, sipping the pale weak tea, 'for the sponge is crisp and the biscuits are soggy.'

'Do you cook?' Mrs Smith smiled as if the question was a silly one and the answer bound to be no.

'Oh yes,' Lisa replied brightly. 'I do all my own cooking. I make cakes all the time.' Another lie. She hadn't made a cake since she'd left home, though if she came again she would bake and bring a sponge, just so Mrs Smith could discover what they *should* taste like.

After tea, she offered to help with the dishes, but the offer was churlishly refused. Lisa sighed and returned to Brian sitting stiffly in the lounge.

'She likes you,' he whispered.

Lisa tried not to let her astonishment show. 'Does she?' she answered noncommittally, then with an effort she added, 'I like her, too.'

18

'How did you get on with the dragon?' Mr Greenbaum asked on Monday.

Lisa wrinkled her nose. 'Not very well. I got the third degree and a lecture on home-cooking. I can't imagine us becoming friends, though I'd far prefer it that way.' Kitty treated Colette, Kevin's wife, like another daughter.

He grimaced. 'You didn't get off to a very good start then?'

'No. In fact, she really got my back up. I feel like marrying Brian, just out of spite.'

He proposed nearly every week. He was besotted, so Jackie and Mr Greenbaum said.

'He adores you,' Jackie told her wistfully. 'It must be nice to have a man so much in love with you.'

Nowadays she looked miserable most of the time and drank non-stop when she came home from work, waking every morning with a hangover.

'You'll lose your job,' warned Lisa as they walked to work and Jackie stumbled along beside her complaining of a splitting headache.

'I'm all right once I get there.'

Then, at Easter, something happened that made Lisa review her life and accept Brian's offer of marriage.

There was a note stuck to the stove. '*Hope the sponge had the desired effect. Piers.*'

Lisa grinned. She'd borrowed two baking tins from him on the Saturday to make a cake for Mrs Smith. It had risen well, the surface golden and smooth. Piers said to use his icing sugar to sprinkle on top.

'Mother, this is delicious!' Brian had enthused. 'You must ask Lisa what her secret is.'

That morning, Mr Greenbaum nearly had convulsions when she imitated Mrs Smith's reaction. 'Do it again, Lisa,' he pleaded over and over again, so she pursed her lips and made her nose quiver, then sniffed, took three deep breaths, flashed her eyes angrily and drew up her shoulders till they nearly touched her ears.

'What's so funny,' she laughed, 'is that Brian thinks his mother is taken with me. "She likes you so much," he keeps saying, but I'm sure she loathes me. She'd loathe anyone who tried to take Brian away.'

She finished reading *Madame Bovary* that night. By the time she reached the last page, she felt close to tears. Poor Emma Bovary, her life was so sad.

Glancing at her watch, she was amazed to find it was half-past eight and she'd been reading solidly for nearly three hours. Jackie was late. With any luck, this meant Gordon wouldn't be with her when she eventually arrived.

Her hope was in vain. Not long afterwards, the door opened and a red-faced, angry Jackie marched in, followed by an equally angry Gordon.

'We've been to the pictures,' Jackie said immediately in a loud voice. 'They had an advertisement for people to emigrate to Australia and I've decided to apply. Gordon can't make up his mind whether to come with me.'

'That's not true,' Gordon blustered. 'I've no intention of emigrating, at least not until the children are much older.'

'Then you'll just have to get yourself another mistress, won't you?' Jackie poured a glass of whisky and swallowed it in one gulp.

'It looks as if I might,' Gordon sneered.

They'd forgotten Lisa was there. She slipped out of the room and went down to the kitchen.

Australia! Suddenly, alarmingly, she felt as if the world she loved so much was gradually falling apart. Ralph was leaving soon to make a film in Rome. Only last week, Mr Greenbaum, whose legs were now so bad he could scarcely move from his chair, announced he would only be coming into the shop a few days a week, so the rest of the time she would be alone. The shop wouldn't be the same without him, and the flat would be lonely without Ralph just along the corridor. There'd be no theatre tickets for ages. Now Jackie was leaving, going to the other side of the earth. Everything was changing. Changing for the worse.

And what was to become of her, Lisa? Where did she fit in this changing world?

'*Nothing lasts forever.*' Mam used to say that.

It was silly to expect this lovely life just to continue on and on. People were bound to move away, die, get married. So, where did she go from here? For one thing, she doubted if she would ever become an actress. Whenever the group performed a play, she was given the smallest part or no part at all. She was prompt or a stage-hand. Godfrey Perrick never criticised but she knew, just knew, that he thought her hopeless, though Ralph said she must keep on, keep trying.

Some day, Mr Greenbaum would stop coming to the shop altogether. Some day, he would die and it would be sold. She'd have to look for another job. In another shop? She couldn't go back to Chaucer Street, not after all this time. She'd never go home again.

Then, in a flash, she saw her place: it was at Brian's side. She would become a wife – a wife and mother. Hadn't she nursed her little brothers and sisters, cradled them in her arms and loved them as if they were her own? They would buy a house, she and Brian. He had enough money saved – he'd told her, nearly five hundred pounds. She'd have her own kitchen. She'd paint it . . . yellow! Yes, yellow, so the room would always look as if the sun was shining outside. Brian had prospects, too. By the time he was thirty, he assured her, he would be head of his section. Yes, next time he proposed, she would accept.

'*You don't love him,*' said a little warning voice in her head.

'It doesn't matter,' Lisa argued with herself. 'I respect and like him. I enjoy his company and he loves me. I'll grow to love him in time, I know I will. Anyway, being in love isn't so special. I never want to be like Jackie.' She remembered Kitty telling the girls how much she'd once loved Tom and look how *that* had turned out!

'*What about his mother?*' came the same cautionary voice. Lisa frowned. 'It's time Brian broke away and asserted himself. She's much too protective and selfish. She'll probably come round once we're married.'

There was the sound of shouting in the corridor and a door banged shut. Lisa peeped outside. Gordon was leaving in a temper, his broad face more purple than ever, his silly moustache quivering.

Back in the flat, Jackie was lying on the sofa in tears. Lisa knelt on the floor and stroked her soft, blonde hair. 'Is it all over?' she asked gently.

Jackie didn't answer and began to cry more violently.

'I think Australia is a good idea,' Lisa said. Presumably Gordon had refused to go and Jackie could start afresh without him.

'Oh Lisa, I've no intention of emigrating! I only said it on the spur of the moment to make him jealous. Instead, he didn't appear to give a damn. That's when I got angry and demanded he come too – either that or we get married.' She sniffed, sat up and added incredibly, 'Poor thing, I've never been angry with him before. I bet he's terribly upset.'

It was Lisa's turn not to answer. She went over and plugged the kettle in, feeling confused.

Jackie wiped the tears off her cheeks with the sleeve of her blouse. Suddenly she smiled. 'So you won't be rid of me after all, Lisa. I'll still be around for a long time yet.'

'As if I'd want to be rid of you!' Lisa said hotly. She paused. It would be wrong to change her mind over her recent decision. 'You'll be rid of *me*, though, but not for a while. I'm going to marry Brian.'

The boat lurched violently and Lisa slid along the wooden seat. She clutched her hat and bag to stop them falling on the wet floor. Although she longed for a cup of tea. She didn't fancy making her unsteady way back along the deck to look for a restaurant, possibly having to pass through the lounge where Brian and lots of passengers were being sick. She'd stick it out here in the observation room till the boat docked. Clutching the back of the bench to steady herself, she stood and peered through the spray-soaked window. Thank goodness land was in sight – a dark line on the horizon. She'd be glad when this journey was over, though not half as glad as Brian would be.

Just married! She fingered her new wedding ring through the pink suede gloves. A gold engraved band, just the sort, said Jackie sadly when she saw it, she'd always wanted herself. Next to it, her engagement ring. Lisa remembered the day she and Brian had chosen the diamond solitaire. It was a Saturday afternoon and he'd met her from work. She'd only agreed to marry him a few days before, but as soon as she'd said yes, he couldn't wait to get a ring and put it on her finger, as if this proclaimed to the world that she belonged to him. They were going to get married in twelve months' time when Lisa would be nearly nineteen. He'd wanted them to be married sooner, but she'd insisted on waiting a year.

After buying the ring, they'd gone straight to Mrs Smith's house to tell her the news.

'We're engaged,' Brian cried on entering, and his mother looked at them and said in an icy voice, 'You didn't tell me.'

Brian looked deflated. 'We only decided the other day, Mother.'

'You might have discussed it with me first.'

'Sorry, I just didn't think.'

She came to accept the engagement eventually, though with obvious reluctance, and started to make plans for the wedding. One day she called in at the shop. Mr Greenbaum buried his head in a book and pretended he wasn't there.

'I've seen a wedding dress in Dickins & Jones. It's your size, I should imagine, just slightly shop-soiled and reduced to half-price.'

'I don't want that sort of wedding,' Lisa said gently, trying to smile, knowing the woman would be disappointed.

White was for purity. She hadn't been pure for a long time, but she wasn't going to tell her future mother-in-law that. Mrs Smith had just glared at her and left without a word.

One day, Brian brought up the subject of the church.

'Mother knows the vicar of our parish church very well. She asked him and he'd be pleased to marry us.'

'No thanks,' she said. 'I'm a Catholic, though I don't go to mass.'

'A Catholic!' His pale eyes popped and he said in a complaining voice, 'You should have told me before.'

'Why?' she asked. 'What difference does it make?'

'Well, none, I suppose. But if you don't go to church, why does it matter where we get married?'

She wrinkled her nose. 'I don't know. It just wouldn't seem right, getting married by a vicar in a Protestant church. You know the saying, "Once a Catholic, always a Catholic". Sorry, Brian. It'll have to be a registry office.'

Of course, she wouldn't be married in the eyes of God, but neither would she in a Protestant church. A registry office seemed less sacrilegious.

He gave in, as usual. He would have got married in the middle of the street to please her, though he said awkwardly, 'Don't tell Mother you're a Catholic, will you? She's funny about religion.'

One day when they were at Mrs Smith's house, she threw an envelope on the table, saying, 'That's your wedding present from me.'

Brian opened it. 'Mother's booked us two weeks' bed and breakfast in Hastings for our honeymoon, Lisa. We've stayed in this hotel every year since I was a baby. It's very clean and the breakfasts are so big you don't need to eat again till tea-time.'

'Seeing as it's not far away, I might come down by coach the middle Saturday, just for the day,' his mother said.

'I thought we'd decided on Paris,' said Lisa, trying to keep the irritation out of her voice.

'Had we?' Brian glanced at his mother worriedly.

'Yes.' This was a slight exaggeration. They'd only discussed it so far. Ralph said it was an ideal place for a honeymoon and Lisa had some brochures in her bag to show Brian later, along with two passport application forms.

'I forgot.' Brian looked uncomfortable. 'I'm sorry, Mother, I'd forgotten about Paris.' Much as he wanted to please his mother, he wanted to please Lisa more. If Lisa wanted to go to Paris, then she would go.

'Can you get the money back?' he asked contritely.

'Well, does it matter whether I can or I can't?'

Lisa sighed inwardly. She doubted if she would ever be on amicable terms with this woman. 'Perhaps,' she thought hopefully, 'when Brian and I have children, she'll be nicer. She goes on enough about how much she wants a grandson.' Lisa jumped as the boat juddered and made an odd grinding noise as it slowed to a halt. Chains clanked and she could hear voices shouting in a foreign language. They were in France! She jumped to her feet and went to find Brian.

They were going to live with Mrs Smith until they'd saved enough to buy a house of their own. Brian said there was a thing called a mortgage you could get, but it meant borrowing a lot of money on which a high rate of interest had to be paid.

'We only need to save about another two hundred pounds. Mother will let us stay with her rent-free, so we can save up quickly with both of us working,' he said.

'I thought you told me you had enough to buy a little house?'

He definitely had. He'd used it as a ploy to persuade her to marry him, and only revealed this latest news a few weeks before the wedding.

Brian frowned. 'I talked it over with Mother and she said a cheap house wouldn't have a garden, perhaps not even a bathroom. It's best to start off with a decent house, Lisa, one like Mother's.'

Lisa hated the idea of living with her mother-in-law but she couldn't very well tell Brian that. She said crossly, 'It's me you should be talking it over with, not your mother.'

It was the only time she had doubts, but soon dismissed them. After all, his argument made sense. A flat would cost five or six pounds a week in rent and although she wouldn't have minded a cheap house, perhaps something big and modern would be better, particularly if they had children soon. Somewhat reluctantly she agreed. She didn't tell him, but she had more than fifty pounds saved in a Post Office account. She was keeping it as a surprise to buy furniture when the time came.

They arrived back from Paris late on a Saturday night. Fortunately, the weather on the return journey had been fine and the motion of the boat steady. No one was sick.

'Did you have a nice time?' asked Mrs Smith rather grudgingly. She was ready for bed in a thick plaid dressing gown over a washed-out nightdress. Her hair was screwed tight in metal curlers.

'Marvellous,' enthused Lisa. 'Paris is enchanting. I want to go there again and again. We've bought you a present. Brian, where's your mother's present?'

'In this bag, I think.' He rooted through the leather holdall, part of the set of luggage Jackie had given them for a wedding present. 'Here you are, Mother.' He handed her the velvet box which contained a tiny gold locket.

'It's real gold,' said Lisa excitedly. 'And the little stone is a real ruby.'

Mrs Smith stared down at the locket for several seconds. 'Oh God,' thought Lisa, 'she's going to say something rude like "I never wear jewellery", and poor Brian will feel mortified.'

To her relief, the woman said politely, 'It's very nice. Thank you.' Tucking the box inside her pocket, she added, 'I'm going to bed now.'

After she'd gone, Lisa said, 'Let's make some tea. I'm dying of thirst.' She thought Mrs Smith might have offered them a cup.

'You mean make one ourselves – in Mother's kitchen?'

'Where else?'

Brian looked worried. 'I'm not sure she'd like that.'

'Come off it, Brian, we live here now. It's our kitchen too, even if we're not paying rent.'

'I'm not sure.'

'Darling.' She sat on his knee and kissed his cheek. To her surprise, he stiffened and said quickly, 'Don't! Mother might come down for something.'

'Well, we're married, aren't we? Don't married people kiss?'

He wriggled uncomfortably. 'Make some tea then, but put everything back where you found it.'

They were using Mrs Smith's bedroom and she was sleeping in Brian's, which only had a single bed. Her room was large and crammed with heavy furniture; two tall wardrobes, each with several cardboard boxes on top, two matching chests of drawers and a dressing table in the bay window. All were polished to glassy perfection, as was the wooden headboard on the bed. A low-wattage bulb in a parchment shade hung low over the high bed with its chocolate-coloured eiderdown and matching coverlet, folded back. The wallpaper, a shade of putty, had a pattern of fawn trailing leaves. Curtains the same as in the parlour – navy-blue velvet with the reverse of the material turned inwards so only neighbours and passers-by saw the best side, hung at the windows.

'When we have a house, I'm going to have the curtains the other way round,' Lisa said, 'so we see—'

'Shush,' said Brian hoarsely. 'Mother might hear.'

He was already in his pyjamas, the striped jacket buttoned tightly up to the neck. Lisa slipped out of her clothes. She'd been allocated one of the wardrobes, but when she opened the door to hang her honeymoon suit up, the smell of mothballs nearly choked her. There were dozens of them. 'I'll throw them away tomorrow,' she decided, 'and splash some perfume around.' For tonight, she hung the suit outside. Naked, she slipped into bed beside Brian.

She urgently wanted to make love. On their honeymoon, they'd made love every night and morning and sometimes even in the afternoon. Lisa had been almost dreading this side of marriage. During their courtship, Brian had done no more than kiss her, sometimes passionately, but she'd been fearful to respond in case it encouraged him to go further and she wasn't sure if she wanted him to or not. Her experience of sex had been so unpleasant, so violent. But once in Paris, after some initial nervousness, even embarrassment, on both their parts, Brian soon took command of her body and to her utter relief, Lisa found making love was wonderful, more wonderful than she'd ever thought possible. Brian became a different person altogether, a real man, yet supremely tender, forever gentle and he would enter her, deep and satisfyingly, sighing in ecstasy when his climax came.

But tonight he bitterly disappointed her.

'Lisa!' he said when she cuddled close. 'Put your nightdress on.'

'Why?' she demanded. 'Has your mother got X-ray eyes? Can she see through the wall, through the bedclothes?'

'She might come in.'

'Now?' Lisa giggled.

'Of course not, but in the morning maybe.'

She slid her hand down his body and untied the cord of his pyjama trousers.

'Oh, Lisa,' he said in a faint voice. 'Lisa.' He turned to face her, his hands on her body, then raised himself to mount her.

The bed creaked.

'Shush,' he said.

'It can't hear you.'

Cautiously he moved on top of her. The bed creaked again. He stopped. She pulled him down, but he was tense, too scared to make another move lest the bed creaked again.

He lay back beside her. 'I'm sorry,' he said.

'Is it always going to be like this?' she whispered angrily. 'After all, your mother must have done it, else she wouldn't have had you.'

'Don't talk like that. My father—' He stopped.

'What about your father?'

'Nothing.'

Sulkily, she slipped out of bed and put a nightdress on and they went to sleep, for the first time with their backs to each other.

19

Sunlight filtered through the dark-blue curtains when Lisa woke, casting an unnatural ghostly light over the room. She held up her hand to see the time. Only seven o'clock. She'd hoped she might sleep in after the long, tiring journey yesterday. Beside her Brian was dead to the world. The clink of dishes came from downstairs. Her mother-in-law was up. She considered going down herself, but decided against it. On the few occasions she'd been alone with her mother-in-law, conversation had been forced and difficult. For a moment, Lisa desperately wished she was back in the flat and could wander round in her nightdress making endless cups of tea and later on she and Jackie would stroll along to Kensington Gardens, but she sternly told herself to stop thinking like that. She was married and Brian was fun to be with. He'd make a good husband and she would be a good wife, though his behaviour last night was alarming. Did this mean they wouldn't make love again till they left his mother's house in a year's time? In which case, how were they to have the grandchild Mrs Smith kept on about?

She smiled to herself, then sighed. Perhaps coming here wasn't such a good idea. If things hadn't altered in a few weeks' time, she'd suggest they bought a place of their own. The meanest little house would be better than this.

Feeling bored, she closed her eyes and designed some dresses. A few months ago she'd started making her own clothes. A woollen suit would be useful – she'd get coupons for the material off Jackie. Royal blue, with a long fitted jacket . . .

Suddenly, there was a knock on the door and without waiting for an answer, Mrs Smith came in.

Lisa felt a surge of irritation. All right, so it was her house, but what right had she to just barge in? She sat up, half-expecting, half-hoping, a cup of tea was being brought, in which case she'd forgive the infringement of their privacy.

But no, Mrs Smith was standing in the doorway, a bitter, disapproving expression on her face, as if seeing her son in bed with his wife was like coming face to face with the citizens of Sodom and Gomorrah.

'It's nearly half-past seven. You'll both be late for church.'

Brian groaned. He sat up, blinking and rubbing his eyes. Lisa saw him redden with embarrassment.

'Sorry, Mother.'

'I'm not going to church,' said Lisa.

Her hair, so thick and straight, became only slightly ruffled when she slept.

From its natural centre parting, it hung down, almost covering her wide, gold-flecked eyes. The strap of her black nightdress had fallen off one shoulder. Brian glanced at her. She saw desire flash in his eyes. Now was her opportunity. She reached beneath the bedclothes for the gap in his pyjama trousers and felt him quiver.

'Brian?' said Mrs Smith. There was a challenge in her voice. She was in her beige rayon dress. Fat bulged above and below the tight belt. Her thick legs were encased in flesh-coloured lisle stockings, wrinkled at the ankles. Brian looked from her to his new wife, sitting so innocently beside him, playing havoc with his body.

He gulped and said in a cracked voice, 'I think I'll give church a miss today, Mother.'

She glared at him. Lisa felt a surge of pity for the woman, but it soon died.

After she'd gone, they lay in silence, touching each other, until half an hour later, the door slammed and he fell upon her.

But it was the last time they were to make love.

Mr Greenbaum was thankful to see her back. Miriam had been helping out and driving him wild.

'She has been moving books round. Every day, she finds one, two, three books which she declares are in the wrong category. "This is a biography," she tells me, as if I did not know, "so what is it doing under *Art*?". "It's under *Art*," I say, "because it's a biography of Vincent Van Gogh and that's where my customers will look for it." ' He sighed. 'Still, she's a good woman.'

'And you love her,' grinned Lisa. Behind the grin, she was worried. Her employer looked ill. His shoulders were more stooped than ever and his face was gaunt. Seeing him after a gap of two weeks brought home how rapidly he was deteriorating. When it was time for lunch, she had to help him to his feet, and she felt tears prick her eyes.

Lisa was meeting Jackie at one. They'd decided to lunch together every day, though Brian was annoyed by this. He thought Lisa should have lunch with him. His mother would make sandwiches for her too, he said, and they could eat them in the park. She had refused.

'Jackie is my best friend,' she said. 'Lunch is the only time we can see each other.'

'How is the dragon lady?' Jackie asked after Lisa had described Paris in all its glory and given her a present of expensive perfume which would have cost a small fortune in London.

Lisa laughed. 'Being a dragon. Honestly, even St George would have had his work cut out with her. Yesterday, Sunday, was so tedious. I've never known the hours drag so much. We just sat there, Brian and I, like guests, whilst she had the radio on – non-stop hymns. I wasn't allowed to help with the meals, though I offered.'

She recalled the Sunday dinner. Knotty lamb, the cheapest cut, with boiled potatoes, cabbage and lumpy gravy. Nothing for dessert.

'It's horrible not being able to make a cup of tea whenever you like,' she complained.

'Never mind,' soothed Jackie. 'It won't be for long.'

'Not if I can help it,' vowed Lisa stoutly.

*

They had the same meal that night, except this time the lamb was cold. Lumps of white congealed fat stared up from the plate and Lisa felt her stomach churn. What real meat there was, was tough and no amount of chewing made it edible. She forced herself to swallow the stringy mess in her mouth. Another 363 days to go, she thought and giggled.

'Lisa!' said Brian reprovingly.

'Sorry, I'm not hungry.' She jumped to her feet. 'Excuse me.'

In the bedroom, she found that Mrs Smith had remade their bed. Although Lisa had made it carefully that morning, folding the sheets back to below the pillows the way Kitty liked it done, now the sheets and blankets were drawn right up to the headboard. Victoria, who'd been left on a pillow, had disappeared and was found stuffed in a suitcase. Lisa picked her up and smoothed her ruffled dress. 'I'll sit you in the wardrobe,' she whispered, 'So every time I open it I'll think of Ralph.'

That morning, she'd moved the mothballs to the other wardrobe which still contained some of Mrs Smith's clothes. When she went to put Victoria away, she found the mothballs had been replaced. Angrily, she put them in a paper bag to throw away. There was a key in her wardrobe door, so she locked it and put the tiny key in her purse.

'What stage is the battle at now?' asked Mr Greenbaum. Lisa and Brian had been married six weeks.

'Well, the goodies – that's my side,' she said, 'are in an advantageous position. The baddies haven't taken any ground at all.' Then she thought about the nights and Brian lying stiffly beside her, too scared to move no matter how hard she tried to seduce him. Under his mother's roof, his desire for Lisa had fled. Of course she couldn't tell Mr Greenbaum that. In actual fact, the baddies, slowly, stealthily, under cover of darkness, were making considerable progress.

'We'd be much happier, Brian, in a place of our own,' Lisa said one night on their way home from work. The tube was packed and they hung onto straps, buffeted to and fro as people pushed their way on and off. It wasn't the ideal place for a conversation, but they were so seldom alone together. Even in bed, he was reluctant to have a discussion.

'Oh, don't start that again, Lisa,' he complained petulantly. She stared at him, surprised by his tone of voice.

'I've only brought it up once before.'

He looked disinterested. Sometimes she thought she was losing him: now she felt convinced. She *had* to get him away from his mother's influence, or their marriage would die. She said, 'Brian, I don't feel as if we're married. I don't feel a bit like a wife.'

'Shush,' he said, looking round. 'People might hear.'

'Where can we talk when people can't hear?' she demanded. 'We can't talk in your mother's house, not even in bed.'

'We could talk at lunch-time,' he said, spitefully, 'but apparently you have to have lunch with Jackie. Mother thinks that's disloyal.'

Lisa's eyes flashed in annoyance. 'It's even more disloyal to discuss me with your mother,' she snapped. He looked shifty. 'Oh, Brian,' she went on in a rush. 'Your mother doesn't recognise that you've *got* a wife. She acts like I'm an intruder. I mean, in nearly three months I've never cooked a meal. She still darns your socks and mends your clothes.'

'Most girls would be grateful for that,' he sniffed.

'But I'm not a girl, I'm a *wife*,' she insisted. 'We have no privacy, no place to call our own. Whatever way I make the bed, she unmakes it and does it some other way. When I leave the dressing table tidy, she moves everything round. She takes the dirty clothes which I'm keeping to do at the weekend, even if I've put them in a drawer – she goes through our drawers, Brian.'

'But it's her house, her furniture,' he protested.

A seat became vacant and Lisa sat down, too weary to argue any longer. A few weeks ago, she'd suggested they go to the pictures and when Brian mentioned this to his mother, Mrs Smith had declared she'd like to come too, so now, each Wednesday, all three went together and somehow, Mrs Smith always managed to sit between them. Instead of enjoying the film, Lisa sat burning with resentment. On the last occasion, she'd declined to go, declaring she had a headache, so Brian had gone with his mother. 'Just like old times,' Mrs Smith had chuckled.

Lisa remembered when one of her brothers, Jimmie it was, had desperately wanted a bow and arrow. He'd saved his pennies for weeks until he had enough and returned from Woolworths, eyes shining with the pride of possession. After playing with the toy for a few hours, it had been left in the back yard until Kitty had found one of the little ones using it and had hidden it away. Jimmie never even noticed. That's how she felt with Brian – as if she was a toy he'd first seen, appropriately enough, on Christmas Eve, a toy he desperately wanted, had pursued with diligence, but which, once possessed, held no further interest.

The passengers on the train began to thin out and Brian sat beside her. 'I realise it's difficult for you,' he said awkwardly. 'But I promised Mother we'd stay a year. She'd be hurt if we left before. Just nine more months and we'll have enough for a house of our own.'

Lisa didn't answer but inwardly vowed that, whenever it was bought, the house wouldn't be within easy reach of her mother-in-law. Just before they reached their station, she ventured, 'Perhaps we could go away on a little holiday, just for the weekend?'

He frowned. 'Can we afford it?'

'Two nights' bed and breakfast wouldn't cost much. We could go to Brighton, that's not far away.' Mr Greenbaum said Brighton was the most cosmopolitan town in England with all sorts of exciting things to do. Years ago, he and Miriam used to go there every Sunday till the journey got too much for him.

'That's not such a bad idea,' Brian mused. 'A break would do us good.'

She felt so elated, she kissed his cheek and he blinked and looked at her, slightly surprised. 'He doesn't realise what he's missing,' she thought excitedly. 'He's entirely forgotten what it was like on our honeymoon.' She'd pack her black lace nightie and buy some sexy underwear and show him that making love was the most marvellous thing in the world so when they came back he wouldn't care if the bedsprings creaked all night. Either that, or he'd insist on them living in their own house.

Mr Greenbaum had a friend who owned a small hotel right on the Esplanade in Brighton.

'Give him a ring,' he said the next morning. 'Tell him old Harry Greenbaum recommended you and he might give you a discount.'

Lisa telephoned immediately and booked a double room for the weekend after next. They would travel straight after she finished work on Saturday and return Monday morning.

She told Brian on their way home.

'Our room's got a little balcony and looks right over the pier. Oh Brian, I'm really looking forward to it!' It was going to be a turning point in their marriage.

'What sort of room did you book for Mother?' he asked. 'I hope it isn't some little boxroom at the back.'

Mr Greenbaum wasn't in the shop when Lisa telephoned the hotel to cancel the booking. When he brought the subject up a few days later, she said brightly, 'We decided we couldn't afford it, after all.'

He looked at her, a sad, knowing expression on his dear, wise face, but said nothing.

Lisa hadn't bothered to argue with her husband, reckoning it was a waste of time. She'd just said later that perhaps Brighton wasn't such a good idea, adding pointedly, 'We'd be better saving the money for our house.'

On the Saturday morning when Lisa would have gone to Brighton, she was in the shop alone, burning with resentment, wondering what on earth she had to do to save her marriage.

'Perhaps I could move out,' she mused. 'Then Brian would *have* to leave.' But would he? She had the alarming thought he might not, that his mother's grip on him was too strong. She was grateful when the telephone rang to interrupt this depressing chain of thought. It was Jackie.

'Can you come round?' she asked in a despairing voice. 'I'm in awful trouble, Lisa.'

'I'll come as soon as I've closed the shop,' Lisa promised. Brian didn't work on Saturdays which meant she couldn't tell him she'd be late and there wasn't a telephone in Mrs Smith's house. Lisa didn't care. Her friend needed her and that was all that mattered.

She still had her key to Number 5 Queen's Gate and, puffed from climbing the unaccustomed four flights of stairs, arrived in the flat to find Jackie lying on the bed. Lisa had been declared irreplaceable, so no new roommate had appeared to tidy up, and both rooms were littered with clothes and other paraphernalia.

'I'm pregnant,' Jackie cried, bursting into tears. Her face was puffed and red, her eyes raw from weeping. She'd put on a lot of weight since Lisa left. The dimples in her cheeks had disappeared into a morass of fat.

'I suspected as much,' said Lisa. 'What did Gordon say?'

'He's ditched me! I thought to myself, he loves children – that's why he wouldn't leave his wife, because of the children. But they're growing up and if I had a baby, his baby, he'd leave and come to me, but when I told him . . . Oh, Lisa! He said I was a whore, tried to make out I'd slept with other men. As if I would, I love him so much.'

'There, there.' Lisa stroked her friend's head gently. 'You're better off without him.'

'No, no! I can't live without Gordon.'

It seemed to Lisa she had no choice, but now was not the time to say so. 'What about the baby?' she asked. 'Are you going to have it?'

'I've done the most stupid thing. I let myself go four months. I had, well, a suspicion that if I told him straight away he might insist on an abortion, so I left it until it was too late. I've *got* to have the baby, Lisa.'

Oh, God! What a mess. Lisa did the thing she did in every emergency. 'I'll make us a cup of tea,' she said.

As the afternoon wore on, Jackie became even more distraught. She would have to give up her job soon – some of the women at work already suspected she was pregnant. 'I can't go home,' she wailed. 'Mother wouldn't have me. How will I live with a baby I don't want? I got pregnant for Gordon, that's all. I'll never be able to work again.'

'Don't you get money from the State or something?' asked Lisa. 'They won't let you starve.'

'I've no idea,' cried Jackie frantically. 'I don't want money off the State. I want to work, not sit in this flat all day looking after a baby. And the stairs, Lisa, I can't carry a baby and a pram up and down those stairs. I'd have to find another place to live.'

Lisa shuddered, remembering her first day in London looking for a flat. Imagine doing that with a baby. Then suddenly she had an idea that was so audacious that it almost took her breath away.

'I'll have your baby,' she said, then put her hand over her mouth. Had she really said it?

'What d'you mean?' Jackie was so taken aback her hysteria disappeared instantly.

Lisa gulped. 'I'll have the baby. I'll pretend I'm pregnant. Mrs Smith's longing for a grandchild. You stay here for five months and when the baby's born, I'll say it's mine.'

'That's a mad idea, Lisa,' but Jackie's protest was half-hearted. 'D'you think it would work?'

'Of course it would.' She and Brian never made love. He never even saw her undressed. This was the solution she'd been wracking her brains for that morning. Once they had a family, he would *have* to buy a house, and as soon as they were alone together everything would be fine. 'It just fits in with our honeymoon. I'll say I'm three months' gone, not four, in case you're late. I'll pad myself out a bit. Oh, Jackie, it'll be fun. A real joke, fooling everyone.' She giggled and after a while her friend perked up and began to laugh too.

'But what about Brian?' Jackie looked puzzled. 'You can't expect to get away with something like that, not with your husband!'

Lisa laughed ruefully. 'I can with mine,' she said and Jackie looked at her curiously.

Later on, she asked, 'What about the actual birth, Lisa? Brian will expect to come with you to the hospital.'

'Oh, we'll cross that bridge when we come to it,' said Lisa airily. 'We'll think of something.' She got to her feet and danced around the room. 'I'm pregnant, I'm pregnant,' she sang.

'I'm pregnant,' she said.

Brian had come to the door to let her in – she'd never been given a key. He looked more cross than worried. Behind him, Mrs Smith stood with a sly grin on her face. There was an air of togetherness about them. They were the family, she the outsider.

'Where on earth have you been?' her husband demanded. 'It's nearly midnight. We've been worried sick.'

'Well, I've been properly sick. If you were on the phone, I'd have let you know.' Lisa decided the best method of defence was attack. 'I nearly fainted in the shop, so I went to Jackie's and she called the doctor. I didn't feel fit to come home till now.'

'What's wrong with you?' her mother-in-law asked.

So she told them she was pregnant.

Brian was overjoyed. He rushed forward to hug her, but she pushed him away.

'I'm tired,' she said. 'I'm going straight to bed.'

As she climbed the stairs, Mrs Smith said, 'Would you like a cup of tea?' Her eyes were bright and joyful. Lisa had never seen her look happy before.

'No, thank you,' she replied churlishly.

In bed, Brian said, 'Mother's absolutely thrilled. You know she's always wanted a grandchild.'

'Shush,' snapped Lisa. 'She might hear.'

They couldn't do enough for her, Brian and his mother. The following day they fussed around, fetching her endless cups of tea.

'Lisa loves her tea, Mother,' joked Brian, and she wondered why he'd never said so before.

'Of course, you'll have to leave work,' said Mrs Smith. 'You can't spend the day on your feet, not in your condition.'

With a jolt, Lisa realised she would indeed have to leave. If she really had been pregnant, she would have ignored the advice and stayed at the shop for as long as possible, but she couldn't fool Mr Greenbaum, not for six whole months. He was too canny, too wise, to be taken in, besides which, she liked him too much to deceive him. She didn't want to let him in on the lie, either, it might distress him.

This meant that without her salary, she and Brian would be longer saving up for a house of their own.

She was woken from her reverie by Brian.

'What do you think, Lisa?'

'About what?'

'Whether the baby will be a boy or a girl?'

'How on earth should I know?' she said crossly.

20

Suddenly, she could do no wrong. At last she was part of the family, though she realised it wasn't *her* they cared about but the baby they thought she carried – Brian's son and his mother's longed-for grandchild.

Mr Greenbaum was stunned when she gave in her notice, and she found it difficult to meet his eyes. 'I'm expecting a baby,' she told him, regretting for the moment at least that she'd become involved in such deception.

'Why, this is marvellous news,' he said when he recovered from the shock. 'Forgive me, Lisa, I am a selfish old man. My first thought was for myself and for my shop. You must be so happy, you and Brian.'

'Well, Brian is,' she thought, 'and so is Mrs Smith. I'm glad to be helping Jackie and the atmosphere's better at home, that's all.'

The months passed slowly. Mrs Smith bought yards of white winceyette and pounds of wool to make baby clothes, and announced she was going to teach her daughter-in-law to knit and sew, though Lisa needed no tuition. Kitty had been an expert needlewoman and taught her daughter all she knew. Her would-be teacher watched in wonder as Lisa sewed the seams of baby gowns with tiny, symmetrical stitches and knitted cardigans, six of each size to cover the baby's first year, and had no difficulty with the lacy panels or crocheted trim, whilst Mrs Smith struggled to make sense of the patterns, clearly chagrined at Lisa's expertise.

Twice a week, Lisa went into town for the day. She was having lunch with Jackie, she lied unblushingly to her husband, then she liked to wander around the shops, sometimes visiting her doctor. In fact, she spent the whole day in the flat.

'You should be resting,' Brian protested. 'And I wish you'd sign on with our local doctor, then Mother could go with you.'

Lisa didn't bother to argue with him. She went her own way. By now she was theoretically six months pregnant, so she stuffed a folded towel in her pants, jutting her stomach out to heighten the effect. The maternity gowns she made for herself contained a yard more material than the pattern called for, in order to add to her bulk.

Jackie was in the throes of deep depression. She'd left work and spent her days in bed drinking whisky and eating chocolates.

'You should get more exercise,' Lisa told her every time she came. 'You're not doing the baby any good, lying around like this.'

She said it again when she came one day in late September. Autumn, her

137

favourite season. A faint mist hung in the air and the leaves were damp beneath her feet.

'Who cares about the baby?' her friend said sulkily. 'I can't manage those stairs, not in my condition.'

Lisa looked down at her. Jackie was scarcely recognisable nowadays. She must have weighed thirteen stone, if not more. Her fresh complexion had turned grey and her uncombed hair was a mass of knots. Through the creamy curls, Lisa saw her scalp was dirty. Worst of all, she smelt! Jackie, so vivacious, so scrupulous about her appearance, had been reduced to this by Gordon.

'You're still not eating properly, are you?' Lisa said sternly. The only food she could see was the stale remains of a loaf and some cheese she herself had brought on her last visit. 'Where's your ration book and I'll get you something.'

'I don't know,' sniffed Jackie. 'It's wherever you left it on Tuesday.'

'While I'm shopping you can have a bath. I'll go and run it. Come on, out of bed!' Lisa clapped her hands and to her relief saw her friend grin.

'You're a worse dragon than your mother-in-law,' she complained.

An hour later, a freshly bathed and fed Jackie sat on the chair whilst Lisa tried to comb the tangles out of her wet hair.

'Ouch!'

'Well, if you combed it every day, it wouldn't get in this state.'

'Sorry, ma'am.' Jackie saluted and they both laughed.

'Why don't you go to the hairdresser's every week? Have you got enough money?'

'Stacks. My aunts send me cash from time to time and my boss gave me three months' wages. He felt sorry for me. He knew about Gordon.'

'In that case, I'll make an appointment for a shampoo and set next Tuesday – I'll get you down those stairs if I have to carry you myself. Don't forget, the week after next you're due at the ante-natal clinic.'

'I don't know why you put up with me.'

'Because you're my best friend, that's why. There, that's finished. You're completely unknotted.' Lisa sat opposite and asked. 'What will you do after the baby's born?'

'God knows.' Jackie shrugged. 'I thought I might emigrate to Australia – I mean it this time.' She burst into tears. 'Oh, Lisa, isn't life hell? I can't stop thinking about Gordon.'

'Try not to cry,' said Lisa softly. 'He's not worth it.'

'So I keep telling myself.' She wiped her nose on the sleeve of her dressing gown. 'You look lovely,' she said suddenly.

Lisa's maternity gown was red and white gingham with a high neck and long gathered sleeves. A wide frill went from a V between her breasts to the shoulders and the hem was similarly trimmed. Her hair was smoothed back and tied at the nape of her neck with a red ribbon.

'I feel as if I'm wearing a tent,' she said. Glancing at her watch she saw it was time to leave. 'Don't forget your orange juice and vitamin tablets,' she commanded.

'No, Lisa.'

'And I've brought you some fruit – you must eat some every day.'

'Yes, Lisa.'

They smiled at each other. 'See you Tuesday,' said Lisa.

Before leaving, she slipped a note under Ralph's door, hoping and praying that no one would hear and open it. '*Look after Jackie for me*,' the note said. She had deliberately kept away from Ralph these last months. When this was all over, she would tell him the truth, but not yet.

Brian was home before her. She unlocked the front door – her pregnancy had qualified her for a key – and could hear him upstairs with his mother. They were talking in animated voices.

'Lisa, is that you?'

'Who else could it be,' she thought. 'No one else has been in this house since I came to live here.' She found them in the small spare room standing each side of a chipped wooden cot.

'Look! Mother got this from a second-hand shop.'

'It was only five shillings,' Mrs Smith said proudly.

'I'll rub it down and re-paint it, and Mother'll make a new cover for the mattress.'

'Do we really need to buy second-hand things for our baby?'

Brian and his mother glanced at each other and for a second both looked shamefaced. 'Well no, but it's silly wasting money. Once finished, it'll be as good as new. But Lisa,' Brian went on enthusiastically, 'see, the cot fits in this alcove nicely and if we put these odds and ends in the attic, it'll make a fine nursery.'

'Nursery!' said Lisa. 'I thought we planned to move into a place of our own?'

His mother made no attempt to leave the room and let them have their argument in private. In fact, she edged closer to support her son.

'Lisa, you haven't worked for months. We haven't saved nearly enough for a decent house.' Brian spoke slowly and patiently as if addressing a child. 'You wouldn't want to bring our baby up in a flat, would you? Or a scruffy little house? Besides which, if we stay here, Mother can help out. Why, you can even go back to work if you want.'

She stared at him accusingly, her great brown eyes filled with sorrow. After a while, he dropped his gaze and she turned and silently left the room. He didn't follow.

Time dragged interminably by. She rose with Brian and sat with him whilst he ate his breakfast – a boiled egg in his Humpty Dumpty egg cup with bread soldiers to dip in the yolk. Mrs Smith assured her there was no need to get up, but Lisa couldn't stay in bed once she'd woken. If she wasn't going to see Jackie, an empty day stretched ahead. All the baby clothes had long since been made: dozens of gowns, cardigans and vests, bonnets and bootees. Lisa had crocheted two shawls. There was nothing else needed. Mrs Smith spent most of her time in the kitchen, though what she did there mystified Lisa, as the meals she produced were barely edible. The woman considered herself a perfect housewife, yet could neither cook nor sew.

'If I were in my own house,' thought Lisa, 'I would be really busy instead of sitting here with absolutely nothing to do – at least, nothing I'm allowed to do. I'd go shopping, there'd be housework and I'd make curtains and cushion covers and arrange my books and buy flowers.' Once she'd left her Jane Austen set on the sideboard but when she came home it had disappeared. She searched everywhere until eventually she had to ask her mother-in-law where the books were. 'Under your bed,' she'd been told. 'Out of the way.'

'There's nothing of me here,' she thought sadly as she sat in the dull, colourless room. 'Even poor Victoria is shut in the wardrobe. I'm not part of this family and I don't belong in this house. Brian and his mother don't really want me. We should never have come here to live.'

'Now, don't forget,' said Lisa sternly. 'As soon as the baby's born, get someone in the hospital to send a telegram addressed to Mrs Lisa Smith, else the dragon will open it. Just say something like "*Eureka*" and I'll know what it means. I'll be with you in an hour. Understand?'

'I understand,' said Jackie. Strangely, as her time approached, Jackie's physical and mental condition improved. She'd begun to eat better and drink less, and she'd lost some of the flabby flesh on her body as if she was already preparing to face the world after the baby's birth.

'Have you got the wedding ring I bought from Woolworths?'

'Of course. I'll not forget to say my husband's abroad, either.'

'Good. Ring for the ambulance the minute you get contractions and they'll help you downstairs.'

'Stop fussing! I may be pregnant, but I'm not an idiot.'

'Of course you are, that's why I like you so much,' said Lisa affectionately.

The baby was due on 14 December. Lisa prayed it wouldn't be late. If it arrived over Christmas it would make things awkward. By now, she'd begun to feel she really *was* pregnant. She'd taken a cushion from the flat and tied it round her middle and when at home, she made a great show of lumbering clumsily around, straining to get up from the chair. 'If Godfrey Perrick saw me now,' she thought dryly, 'he wouldn't think me a rotten actress any more. I'm doing this part perfectly!'

Two days before expected, on a dark wet afternoon, the telegram arrived. The bell rang and she heard her mother-in-law's heavy tread down the hall.

'Any answer?' a man's voice asked.

Lisa leapt to her feet and ran across the room, slowing when she reached the hallway, just in time to see Mrs Smith about to open the envelope. She blushed when she saw Lisa.

'It's for you,' she said.

'*Eureka*' was the message. 'No answer,' she told the delivery man. After he'd gone, she said to her mother-in-law, 'I have to go to Liverpool. My sister's very ill.'

She hadn't expected the woman to be pleased, but even so she was taken aback by Mrs Smith's violent reaction.

'Sister! You've never mentioned a sister. Why didn't she come to the wedding? I thought you said you were an orphan.' The woman's voice was hoarse with pent-up anger.

'She couldn't afford to come and orphans do have brothers and sisters. I'll go and pack a case.'

As Lisa was going up the stairs, her mother-in-law shouted, 'You can't travel to Liverpool in your condition. What will I tell Brian?'

'The truth, that my sister's ill. And I feel perfectly well. The baby's not due for a month.'

Lisa swiftly packed a small case of clothes – she couldn't wait to get back into her old things again. When she went back downstairs, Mrs Smith was still standing in the hall.

'I don't think I should let you go,' she said aggressively.

Lisa looked amused. 'Are you going to keep me prisoner?'

The woman's eyes were filled with hatred as she stepped to one side.

'I'll be back as soon as I can,' said Lisa. On the step, she turned, trying to think of something kind to say, not wanting to leave with such ill-feeling between them, but even as she opened her mouth to speak, the door was slammed in her face.

21

Jackie was sitting up in bed clutching the baby in her arms and looking surprisingly pleased with herself. She was in a small room at the end of the ward. The sister, a cheerful middle-aged woman with rosy, weatherbeaten cheeks rarely seen in the city, said, 'It's not visiting time till half-past six, but as her hubby's abroad and you're her only relative, I'll make an exception. We've put her by herself, so she won't get upset when the other hubbies appear. If you hear Matron, duck under the bed, there's a love, else I'll be for it.'

'How was it?' asked Lisa, sitting beside the bed.

'Easier than I thought,' Jackie said complacently. 'The nurses said I'm made for having children. You know, broad hips and I've got stacks of milk too, so won't have any trouble breastfeeding. Some women do.'

'Is it a boy or a girl?'

'A boy. I've called him Noël, because it's nearly Christmas. He's so beautiful, I just can't believe it.' She looked down at the baby in starry-eyed wonder.

Lisa felt worried. The last thing she had expected was to find Jackie overcome with maternal feeling.

'Let's see him.'

'You can hold him for a while if you like – isn't he lovely?' She handed the tiny bundle to Lisa.

The baby's beetroot-red face was crumpled like that of an old, old man and down the centre of his scalp a tuft of reddish-blond hair stuck up like a cockscomb. The rest of him was hidden, tightly wrapped in a white hospital shawl. Lisa watched with fascination as his tiny mouth opened and closed repeatedly.

'He looks like a goldfish,' she said, noting with increasing alarm Jackie's air of proprietorial pride. 'I've brought some baby clothes with me,' she added.

'You're an angel,' said Jackie gratefully. 'What would I have done without you these last five months?'

'You would have managed.'

'No, I wouldn't. I'd have gone to pieces without you.' She was silent for a moment, then looking faintly embarrassed, she said, 'Lisa, I've done more thinking in the few hours since Noël was born than I've done for months. You wouldn't be doing this if you loved Brian. You wouldn't fool someone you really cared about, no matter how much you wanted to help me.'

Lisa opened her mouth to reply but Jackie shook her head. 'No, for once I'm giving you an order. Shut up a minute. I've been so selfish and wrapped up in myself, that I've hardly thought about you and Brian. You don't love him, do you, Lisa, not like I loved Gordon?'

Burying her head in the baby's shawl, Lisa felt an unexpected flush of tears. 'No,' she whispered.

'Did you ever?'

'Not really. He seemed so immature, but I thought that once he had a wife and family, a house of our own, he'd grow up. There were glimpses, now and then, of what he could be, what he was struggling inside to be. Like on our honeymoon, for instance. I expected I'd grow to love him, but at home he's stuck firmly under his mother's thumb.' She sniffed. 'Oh dear, this is no way to talk. I should be comforting you.'

'No, no,' urged Jackie. 'Go on.' There was an unexpected tinge of sternness in her voice that Lisa had never heard before.

'Well, there's nothing much to go on about,' she said sadly. 'Mrs Smith resents me. In fact, I think she hates me.' She recalled the way the woman had acted less than an hour ago. 'Brian is so used to doing her bidding, so used to them being a couple and doing things together, that he doesn't realise it's *us* that's the couple now and I just get pushed to one side.'

'Will Mrs Smith hate the baby?'

'Oh no,' Lisa said emphatically. 'She can't wait for a grandchild, a grandson, "Little Brian", she wants to call him. It's all she's talked about for months. Brian thinks I should go back to work and she can look after him during the day. They've made the spare bedroom into a nursery. Why, only the other day, she was talking about putting the cot in her bedroom for the first few weeks so she can see to him during the night.' She smiled grimly. 'There's going to be some battles when—'

'Lisa,' Jackie interrupted harshly. 'That's no place for a baby, for Noël.'

'What?' Lisa's jaw dropped, the suspicions that had arisen since she entered the room confirmed.

Now Jackie looked close to tears herself. 'Oh, gosh! This is an awful thing to do. I can't let you take Noël back to a house with so much hate – you used that word yourself.'

Lisa didn't answer. The baby smacked his lips and wriggled gently. She felt his arms pushing, as if he was attempting to struggle free from his tight wrapping, and her insides began to churn as she realised the implication of her friend's words.

'When I was expecting him,' Jackie said quietly, 'I never imagined I carried a tiny human being. I know that sounds stupid. Even when he began to kick, he never seemed real. But when he was born and they handed him to me, it seemed like a miracle.' She shook her head in wonder and involuntarily stretched out her arms. Lisa placed the baby in them and Jackie bent her head and stroked his face with the back of her finger. 'I can't describe the feeling. It was so unexpected and I began to think, "How on earth can I give him away, even to Lisa, who I'd trust him with more than anyone in the world?" ' She smiled at Lisa warmly. 'At first, I felt really terrible. I desperately wanted to keep him but knew I couldn't possibly let you down. Then I began to think about you and Brian and realised how unhappy you were – you are, aren't you?'

Lisa nodded numbly.

'You're a wonderful friend, Lisa, but when you said those things about Mrs Smith! It wouldn't be right for her to get her hands on *any* baby, let alone mine. She'd suffocate him, like she's suffocated Brian. You know that's true, don't you?'

'Yes,' whispered Lisa. 'And I've just realised something else. If he really *was* my baby, I'd feel the same as you.'

'There!' Jackie relaxed back in the pillow, smiling. 'You don't think badly of me then?'

Lisa didn't answer. She was appalled to discover what a second-class mother she would have been to Noël. If she really *had* been pregnant, she would have insisted on their own place, would have known instinctively that the unhealthy atmosphere in that house was unfit for a baby. And if Brian had refused to leave? Why, she would have left all by herself.

She sighed. Jackie was watching her with concern.

'I've really landed you in trouble, haven't I?'

'At least I don't need to go to Liverpool, that's something,' said Lisa resignedly.

'What do you mean?'

'That's where they think I've gone, and as telegrams show the post office they're sent from, I was going to send one from Liverpool in a few days' time saying I'd had the baby early – I could have got there and back the same day. Then I would have gone to our flat and next week, I'd have just turned up at the house with Noël in a taxi and—' she paused. 'Oh, my God!'

'What's the matter?' asked Jackie in alarm.

'I didn't know how much I dreaded going back with the baby. I suddenly feel an enormous sense of relief, but more than that, I realise *I needn't go back at all!*' She stared at her friend, eyes shining with excitement, her body tingling. She was free!

'But that means I've broken up your marriage,' said Jackie tragically. 'This is all my fault.'

Lisa shook her head vigorously. 'No, it's Brian's fault and his mother's – and mine for not being firm enough. Anyway, it's not a proper marriage, not a proper marriage at all.'

Her heart lifted as she unlocked the door to the flat and switched on the lamp. She breathed a sigh of relief. It all looked so warm and cheerful compared to where she'd been living. There was a letter addressed to her propped up on the sideboard. It was from Ralph.

'*Reckon you'll read this just as quickly if I leave it here rather than post it,*' he'd written. '*I'm off to Hollywood. Hollywood! Just a smallish part, someone's dropped out, so I'm wanted straight away. Catching the plane tonight. Wish me luck!*'

'Good luck, Ralph,' she murmured aloud.

'*Jackie seems much better lately,*' he continued. '*I've been popping in every day. What have you two been up to? There's something funny going on!*

'*Hope you're happy, my good friend, Lisa. God bless, Ralph.*'

Lisa folded the letter and put it away in her bag. She was glad for Ralph, but sorry he wouldn't be there for Christmas. It reminded her that Victoria was locked in the wardrobe at home – no, not home now – in Mrs Smith's house in Chiswick. Somehow she'd have to get Victoria and her Jane Austen books and her clothes. In a few days, she'd write to Brian and tell him the truth, the whole truth – that it had been Jackie's baby all the time. Much as she despised him – and she hadn't realised until she'd spoken to her friend in the hospital just how much she did – she couldn't just disappear into thin air and let him go on thinking for the rest of his life that he had a child he'd never seen. 'If he had been a real man,' she thought contemptuously, 'there's no way I could have fooled him into thinking I was pregnant all those months. In all that time, he didn't touch me, didn't see me without my clothes on, not once.'

After unpacking her bag, she went out and did some shopping, made a meal and returned to the hospital to see Jackie, who by now was almost bubbling over with happiness.

'I want lots more children,' she said the minute Lisa walked into the room. 'Three more, at least. Another boy and two girls.'

Lisa laughed. 'Who is to father this ideal family?' she asked.

'Lord knows – I'll advertise! It won't be Gordon, though, I can tell you that. I've finished with him.'

'That's a relief,' said Lisa thankfully.

'And I've decided what to do. I'll have to leave the flat – it's too small for a baby and the stairs are dangerous. I'll go and live with my aunts. They're not the slightest bit stuffy. Both of them were suffragettes and they'll think having a baby outside marriage is very avant-garde. My mother will come round eventually.'

'I'm so happy you're happy,' said Lisa, and meant it with all her heart.

That Saturday morning, Lisa went to see Mr Greenbaum. She would have gone earlier, but was worried that she might encounter Brian. Every week since she'd left the shop, she'd written the old man a letter, making a variety of excuses for not coming to see him, and he had replied within a few days, often with a long message from Miriam at the end. He hadn't answered her last two letters and she was worried.

She made the familiar journey along Old Brompton Road, past Harrods, its windows ablaze with Christmas lights and decorations, and began to hurry as she neared the shop, longing to see her old employer again.

There it was, the windows thick with dust. She saw the Closed sign written in Mr Greenbaum's old-fashioned script as she approached the door and she thought fondly, 'He's forgotten to turn it round. He's always doing that.' To her surprise the door was locked, but still she peered inside, expecting to see his stooped form bent over a pile of books on his desk; the shop was empty, however. He'd only been coming in half a day since she'd left, but Saturday mornings were one of his busiest times. He must be ill, she thought with alarm, to miss a Saturday, right before Christmas too. She'd go round to his flat straight away.

She turned and bumped into a man who was vaguely familiar, a middle-aged man in a loud tweed suit and a grey overcoat with a velvet collar. His soft felt hat was pulled rakishly down over one eye.

'I've been following you,' he said. 'I came out of Harrods just as you were passing. Lisa, isn't it?'

'That's right. And who . . . oh, I remember, Morry Sopel!'

'Himself,' he said with a grin.

She also remembered he was a criminal and tried to look offhand, but it was difficult with his warm brown eyes smiling into hers.

'Where are you off to?' he asked.

'I came to see Mr Greenbaum,' she said. 'I left months ago to . . . well, I got married.'

'To the little boy I met?' he asked mischievously.

'Yes,' she said stiffly. 'Anyway, the shop's closed. I was just going round to the flat to make sure everything's all right. Goodbye.' She turned to leave but to her dismay he began to walk along beside her.

'Think a lot of old Harry, do you?'

'Of course I do.'

'And he thought a lot of you. I could tell by the way he hovered over you like a guardian angel when I asked you out to lunch.'

'I love him,' she said simply. 'He's been like a father to me.'

Suddenly, he put his hand on her arm. She was about to shrug him away indignantly, when he said in a gentle voice, 'I'm afraid there's bad news, my dear. Old Harry's dead.'

'What!'

'He'd been ill for ages, though you probably knew that. Two weeks ago, he had a heart attack and died a few days later.'

'Oh, no!' She felt an ache in her throat.

'Come on, let's get you a drink.' She numbly allowed herself to be led into the pub on the corner of the street, the one where Mr Greenbaum used to have his liquid lunch.

'What about Miriam?' she asked when they'd sat down.

'Miriam took it very badly. She's gone into a home.'

Lisa began to cry softly.

'He was an old man, Lisa. He'd had more than his share of time.'

'That doesn't make it any easier,' she sobbed.

On Christmas Eve Lisa stood by the window watching the traffic as it crawled along Brompton Road. Cars were bumper to bumper and drivers sounded their horns in frustration. The shops had just closed and people were making their way home along the crowded pavements.

Inside, the house was silent as the grave. Two days ago Jackie had come home from hospital with a thriving Noël. They'd spent one night in the flat before leaving for Bournemouth. Jackie had pleaded with Lisa to come back with her for Christmas.

'You can't stay here on your own,' she said impatiently. 'Ralph's in America and Piers is going home. And with the Greenbaums gone . . .'

'I'll be all right,' Lisa insisted stubbornly. 'I've got to learn to live by myself some time.'

Jackie shook her head in resignation. 'There's no arguing with you, Lisa. I'll telephone on Christmas Day.' She chucked the baby under the chin. His wide blue eyes seemed to stare right into hers. 'Say goodbye to Auntie Lisa, there's a darling,' then she was gone in a flurry of suitcases and carrier bags, Noël clutched to her breast as if she never intended letting him go. Lisa stood on the pavement waving until the taxi disappeared.

She sighed. As soon as Christmas was over she'd have to look for a job and decide whether to keep the flat on. The five pounds rent was more than half her anticipated wages, yet she couldn't bear the idea of advertising for a flatmate and sharing with a total stranger.

The telephone rang. Before picking up the receiver, she took a deep breath. Jackie wasn't expected to ring until tomorrow, so this could be Brian. She'd written to him a week ago and half-expected he might call.

It was Morry Sopel. 'What are you doing tonight?' he demanded.

'There's a good play on the radio,' she replied.

'Beautiful girls like you don't stay in listening to the radio on Christmas Eve,' he said in a shocked voice. 'How about dinner, the Savoy. Come on,' he coaxed.

Despite all she knew about Morry, she was tempted but remembered old Harry Greenbaum. He'd turn in his recently-dug grave if he knew.

'I'm sorry, no,' she said, trying to keep the regret out of her voice.

He rang off, sounding slightly annoyed, and Lisa hoped she'd never hear from him again.

As expected, Jackie telephoned on Christmas Day. Her aunts adored Noël who, in the space of a few days, had learnt to smile.

'Has Brian called?' she asked eventually.

'No,' said Lisa.

'He must be crazy to prefer his mother to you.'

That was the conclusion Lisa herself had reached. She imagined them sitting together in that cold cheerless room and felt enormously relieved that she wasn't there with them.

'How are you getting on? I keep thinking of you, all by yourself.'

'I'm fine,' Lisa said cheerfully. 'I went to Kensington Gardens this morning and I was just about to put some of your records on.'

Later on, she said to herself, 'I *am* fine, I really am. It's only natural to be upset over Mr Greenbaum and the fact my marriage turned out so badly, and it would be lovely if Ralph was here to talk to . . . But apart from all those things, I'm fine.'

A few days later, early on a dismal, grey Sunday morning, she took a taxi to Chiswick and asked the driver to park some distance down the road from Mrs Smith's house. She sat in the back of the cab, chatting to the driver, a gregarious Cockney, waiting for her mother-in-law to leave for church.

'Hope you're not intending to make away with the family silver, darlin',' the cabbie joked. 'Don't want no stolen goods in my vehicle.'

'No, it's just my personal possessions.' Somehow, she'd found herself spilling out the story of her marriage to this total stranger.

As she spoke, the front door opened and Mrs Smith emerged in her brown Sunday coat with Brian behind her. He sprang forward to open the gate and they walked down the road in the opposite direction, as Lisa knew they would. Mrs Smith linked her son's arm and Lisa thought there was something terribly pathetic about the pair, locked in their arid affection. They disappeared into the half-darkness.

'That's them.' She opened the door to alight.

The driver must have thought the same as she did. 'Poor sods,' he muttered.

The house smelled of stale cabbage. She went upstairs and unlocked the wardrobe. Victoria could just be seen, sitting comfortably on top of the set of Jane Austen novels, staring at Lisa in pained surprise.

'You poor thing, have you been lonely?' Lisa gave her a quick hug before laying her on the bed and dragging the suitcases out from beneath it. She quickly packed her clothes, leaving the coats to carry over her arm, and was about to remove her wedding and engagement rings and leave them on the dressing table when she changed her mind and, carrying her burdens downstairs, went into the kitchen. On the draining board stood Brian's Humpty Dumpty mug beside the matching egg cup. She dropped her rings in it and put the front-door key on the table.

When she went outside, the taxi was in front of the house and the driver got out and helped with the luggage.

'That the lot?' he asked, when everything was stowed away.

She nodded wordlessly.

'Goodbye, Brian,' she whispered, blinking back unexpected tears as they drove away. 'I would have made a good wife,' she thought sadly, 'if only you'd let me.'

22

On New Year's Day Lisa went to see Miriam. The home was in a small village on the edge of Epping Forest, a large pleasant house in its own spacious, tree-filled grounds.

'She's much better than she was,' the Matron said, 'but every now and then her mind completely goes and she's living in the past.' She took Lisa upstairs to Miriam's room. 'She won't sit in the lounge with the other residents, though she might come round to that in time.'

Without her garish make-up, Miriam looked terrible. At last she was the old woman she'd fought against becoming. She sat crouched and wizened in her chair, her silver hair combed loose.

She recognised her visitor immediately. 'Lisa! Oh Lisa, what am I to do without my Harry?' she cried.

Lisa took her liver-spotted hand. She had no idea what to reply. Eventually she said, 'I don't know, dear, but you're lucky to have such wonderful memories. Not many women are so fortunate.'

Miriam seemed anxious to know what he'd said about her in the shop. 'Was he miserable, Lisa? I used to nag him terribly. Did he complain about me much?'

'Never,' Lisa lied stoutly. 'He was one of the happiest men I've ever known.'

'Really?' Her eyes became moist. 'I loved him dearly, you know.'

'He knew that and he worshipped you.'

Miriam suddenly frowned. 'Are you looking after the shop properly?' She seemed to have forgotten Lisa was supposed to have a baby.

'The shop is closed,' Lisa said gently. Presumably, with Harry gone, it would be sold.

'Closed?' The woman's eyes flashed fire and for a few seconds the years fell away. 'Harry's shop closed! That's very presumptuous of you, Lisa. You must re-open it immediately.'

'But . . .'

'There are no buts about it,' said Miriam angrily. 'There's no way that shop will close while I'm alive. Harry lived for his shop. In fact,' she added bitterly, 'sometimes I think he thought more about it than he did me.'

Lisa was about to argue but the fire in Miriam's eyes suddenly faded and she turned away and began to rock to and fro and speak of things long past. 'Sarah has borrowed my blue satin shoes, Mama,' she said in a little girlish voice. 'And she didn't ask. Sometimes I hate her.'

'Oh, Miriam!' Lisa leaned over, kissed her raddled cheek and left.

She still had her key to the shop. Next morning, she opened it up for business again. The place smelt mustier than usual and there was dust everywhere. She cleaned up quickly and began to attend to the pile of letters that had arrived. A few customers came in and the familiar ones expressed surprise and pleasure to see her again. Most of them knew Harry was dead and offered their condolences.

The atmosphere was strange, uncanny without the old man. Although she'd worked alone before on numerous occasions, it was different now, knowing there was no chance the door would open and Mr Greenbaum would come shuffling in, mumbling something philosophic through his beard. 'At least,' she thought sadly, 'it solves the problem of me getting a job.'

All morning long, every time someone came in, Lisa looked up quickly, half-expecting Brian to walk in wanting stationery. But perhaps someone had told him she was back, because in the three years she remained in the shop they never once came face to face. Occasionally she saw him at lunch-time, clutching his sandwiches on his way to the park, or in the evening, a stooped young-old man going home to his mother.

At times, it seemed to Lisa as if nothing had changed. Then, just as quickly, she'd think everything had changed irrevocably. She re-adopted the old familiar routine, leaving Queen's Gate at half-past eight and walking the same route to work. Yet Harry wasn't there and she returned home to an empty flat which felt as lonely as the shop without Jackie.

'I'm only leading half the life I used to,' she thought sometimes, 'and it's the best half that's gone.'

After she'd worked in the shop for six weeks, Lisa began to get worried. Her salary hadn't been paid and the money in her savings account was almost gone. She didn't like to help herself to the takings and anyway, most of it was in cheques. Much as she loved Miriam, she couldn't work for nothing – the rent had to be paid and she had to eat. She was mulling over the problem one morning, wondering how to approach Miriam and sort out the matter of her wages, when the door opened and a young man came in. He wore a bowler hat and a dark formal suit and carried a briefcase and a rolled umbrella.

'Is it something specific you want or would you just like to browse?'

'Is this Mrs Lisa Smith I am addressing?' He removed his hat.

She couldn't help but grin; his stilted speech was quite funny. 'It is and you are,' she said.

He handed her a white card. 'I represent Harwich Cooper, the solicitors handling the late Mr Harold Greenbaum's affairs. I have a letter for you which he requested be handed to you personally.'

Her heart twisted as she took the crisp white envelope addressed to her in old Harry's lovely curved script. 'Should I open it now?' she asked, preferring to read it later when the visitor had gone.

'Read it whenever you wish,' said the young man stiffly. Lisa wondered if this was the first time he'd been sent on such a mission. 'I have another letter from my principal, explaining a detail of our client's will.' He coughed nervously. 'I understand from Mrs Greenbaum, wife of the deceased, that you have undertaken to look after this shop.'

'Your understanding is correct,' said Lisa, trying not to laugh. 'I hope that means you're going to pay me some wages.'

'A cheque will be sent monthly,' he confirmed.

'Thank goodness, I can eat tonight.'

'I shall instruct the bank to set up an account in your name so you can deposit the takings and draw cheques. I take it you know how to obtain new stock?'

'Harry mainly got it off people bringing books in, though sometimes he went to book-sales in a hotel near Victoria Station. I'll carry on doing the same.' She felt thrilled at the idea of so much responsibility.

'Good. Well, I think that's all.' His body sagged with relief. 'It's been nice meeting you, Mrs Smith.' He went over to the door. 'I say, I don't suppose you fancy coming for a drink?'

Lisa looked up in surprise. Now the formal business was over, he looked quite cheerful.

'Or lunch?' he added hopefully.

'Not likely,' she said indignantly. 'You seem to forget I'm a married woman.'

'My dear Miss Lisa,

'I asked for this to be hand-delivered in case the dragon opened it. I am leaving you a little something in my Will. It is to buy a house, dear Lisa. It is important that you escape soon, otherwise you will remain in the dragon's lair forever and eventually she will consume you with her fire and you will become ash, like Brian. You can call the house after me, "Harry's Haven", or "Greenbaum's Folly". My hand trembles because I know I will be dead when you get this. Still, death might bring some consolation. Who knows, as you read my letter, I might be having uproarious fun with Minnie Kopek!

'Your dear, good friend, Harry.'

'You silly old man,' whispered Lisa, smiling through her tears. Even in death, he was capable of making her laugh.

The solicitors' letter stated that their client, Mr Harold Greenbaum, had left her a thousand pounds in his Will. When the money came, Lisa put it in her Post Office account. She didn't need a house, but one day she'd spend it on something old Harry would have approved of.

Nowadays, Lisa saw little of Piers. He had a new partner, a surly middle-aged man called William who could scarcely bring himself to say hallo when Lisa met him on the stairs. Ralph had never returned from Hollywood, where he was acquiring a reputation as a solid, reliable supporting actor, though his parts were gradually getting bigger and more important. He wrote frequently.

'You MUST *start your acting classes again. Godfrey Perrick was an old ham, completely over the top. If he didn't think much of your acting ability, it probably means you're good! Anyway, hardly anyone in Hollywood can act, so why worry? You have no ties in England, why not come and live here? Your life sounds very dull, in the shop alone all day and no one to keep you company at home. Lisa, you're only twenty and too young and lovely to hide yourself away.*

'*And what about boyfriends – you never mention any? I have another "companion" by the way, Michael . . .*'

'*I never mention boyfriends because there aren't any,*' she replied. '*I'm still too numb over the breakdown of my marriage to start a new relationship. My life seemed to change course completely in the matter of a few days; I left Brian, old Harry died and Jackie went away. For the moment, I'm quite content with this quiet, rather boring life. I have to work* SOMEWHERE, *and the shop is where I most want to be – anyway, they've increased my wages by fifty per cent which means I can afford to keep the flat on. I couldn't do that working anywhere else.*

'*Your latest film sounds a joke – I can't see you as John the Baptist and hope they don't cut your head off for real!*

'*Jackie sends her love, Noël is thriving – I go down to Bournemouth to see them every month on a Sunday.*

'*Your dear, dear friend, Lisa.*

P.S. I kept thinking of Harry when Mr Attlee lost power and Churchill became Prime Minister again – that would have killed him if his poor old heart hadn't.'

She'd been back in the shop for over a year and was struggling with the typewriter one morning when a striking-looking middle-aged man came in. He was tall, well over six feet, with a shock of prematurely-grey hair and the face of a Greek god. His clothes were casual, though well-cut and clearly expensive. Lisa felt as if she'd seen him before, very recently.

'Is it something specific you've—'

'My God! What on earth are you doing here?'

His look of amazement was so disconcerting she began to stammer, 'I'm sorry, we must have met before, but I'm afraid I can't . . .'

He interrupted her again. 'Last time I came in here, there was an old man serving.'

'That was Harry Greenbaum, the owner. I'm afraid he died last year.'

'But why are you here? You're the last sort of person I expected to meet in a bookshop.'

Lisa wore a yellow jersey dress with a high neck and long gathered sleeves. The tan leather belt which encircled her narrow waist was the same colour as her high-heeled boots. She'd combed her hair into a pony tail and tied it with a yellow ribbon.

She felt too embarrassed to answer. She also felt slightly annoyed by the man's intense stare, his wide-eyed look of surprise.

'I don't know what you mean,' she muttered eventually.

'You should be on a catwalk modelling clothes or posing for a fashion photographer. You should be a society hostess or an actress.'

Her annoyance grew. 'Well, I'm not,' she snapped. 'I manage a bookshop.' She felt like sticking out her tongue and adding, 'So there!'

He burst out laughing. 'Sorry,' he said abjectly. 'I'm a writer and I continually see drama in the most innocuous situations. You look so out of place in this little drab bookshop. My immediate reaction was to wonder what you're doing here. I suppose I expected someone quite different. Sorry,' he repeated.

'You're forgiven – for the most part,' she said. 'I would describe this shop as interesting, not drab.'

She remembered now where she'd seen him before – though not in person. His photograph was in the window of a bookshop in Old Brompton Road, along with a display of his latest novel. She recalled thinking how attractive he looked. His name was Clive Randolph and she'd tried to read one of his books once, but took it back to the library in disgust. It was full of self-conscious preening, a selfish intellectual exercise unintelligible to the ordinary man or woman in the street.

Because she hadn't liked his book, she began to get irritated again. 'How can I help you?' she asked coldly.

'I'm looking for something on cannibalism for the background of my next novel.'

He stayed for over an hour and purchased three books. After promising to bring her a copy of his latest novel, he left.

'What did you think of him, Harry?' Lisa asked aloud. 'Good-looking but too clever by half, in my opinion. Needs taking down a peg or two, as my mam used to say.'

She rather hoped he'd forget to bring his novel. Apart from not wishing to read it, she wasn't sure if she wanted to see him again, but in less than two weeks' time, Lisa was sleeping with Clive Randolph.

He telephoned the shop the following day. 'Why don't I give you my novel over dinner?'

She said promptly, 'I'm busy this week.'

'Next week then.'

Lisa was about to turn him down again, when she hesitated. Lately, she'd begun to dread going home to an empty flat.

'All right,' she said grudgingly. 'How about Saturday?'

Saturdays seemed even more lonely than other nights. She was conscious that all over London people were out having a good time.

'Saturday it is,' he said cheerfully.

He spent most of the evening lecturing her on various aspects of modern literature, using his own work as an example of how things should be done. Lisa found him interesting but would have liked to get a word in edgewise now and then.

Outside the restaurant, he hailed a taxi. 'I really enjoyed myself tonight,' he said on the way home. 'We must do this again soon.'

When they reached Queen's Gate, he alighted from the taxi with her. 'There's no need,' she protested. 'You keep it to go home in.'

'I only live a short walk from here,' he said.

She had no intention of asking him in and was trying to think how he could be put off when Piers appeared looking gloomily tipsy.

'I'm in for a wigging off the horrible William,' he groaned. 'I promised to be back hours ago. Shelter me Lisa, please. I'm not in the mood to be told off. I need another stiff drink before I face him.'

'All I've got is wine,' she said.

'I suppose that'll do. What a pity you're not Jackie, then we could have got plastered together.' He sighed mournfully. 'I suppose I should get rid of the awful beast, but I don't know how to tell him his presence is no longer welcome.'

He unlocked the front door and it seemed only natural for Clive to come in too, up to Lisa's flat, where Piers tearfully told them of the ordeal of living with the horrible William. An hour later, fortified by an entire bottle of wine, he left to face the beast.

After he'd gone, Lisa smiled sadly. 'He's missing Ralph,' she said. 'Ralph is—'

Without a word, Clive Randolph fell upon her, crushing her in his arms and pressing his lips against hers. For a second, she was outraged but before she could raise her arms to push him away, her body responded to his kiss and she felt herself sinking, sinking . . .

He half-carried, half-dragged her towards the bedroom and once inside began to tear off his clothes. With equal enthusiasm, she removed her own and they sank on the bed together in a wild, naked embrace.

His hands were all over her, touching, caressing, driving her wild with desire. 'Please, please,' she whispered urgently. 'I can't wait any longer.'

Making love with Brian had been pale compared to this. She'd never dreamed it could be so glorious.

'Christ Almighty!' he groaned when it was over and they lay glued together by perspiration on the single bed. 'You were made for this. How much will you take to lie there for the rest of your life, waiting just for me?'

She ran her finger down his chest and he shivered. 'Nothing,' she said. 'In fact, I'm going to get up in a minute and make a cup of tea.'

He was married but lived apart from his wife, he told her a few weeks later. Divorce was pending – though, he added quickly, he couldn't make any promises.

'Then don't make them,' Lisa said, just as quickly. She'd grown to like him, but all she wanted was his presence in her bed once or twice a week. He made her feel like a schoolgirl as he continued to lecture her on modern literature and other esoteric subjects.

'You seem to think I'm a complete ignoramus,' she complained one night when they were in bed together.

'I'm not interested in your brain, only your body.' He began to caress her breasts and her insides turned to liquid. Nevertheless, she persisted.

'Wouldn't you like to know what *I* think about Jane Austen or George Eliot?'

'Shut up.' He began to touch her nipples with his tongue, little soft flickers that made her want to shout with pleasure and she didn't wait for an answer, just let herself be carried away by the passion of the moment.

Gradually he began to bore her. He was too taken up with the sound of his own voice, never asking for her opinion on anything. Nevertheless, she continued to see him.

'I'm not interested in his brain, only his body,' she thought with a grin. 'He'd have a fit if he knew.'

Just before Christmas, Jackie came to London to do some shopping and stayed with Lisa overnight. Noël, who was two, was quite happy to be left with his grandparents, who adored him. Jackie's mother had 'come round', as she put it, a long time ago.

'This is just like old times,' she said, 'except I'm drinking milk instead of whisky.' They were sitting in the flat and the floor was already strewn with paper bags and parcels.

'Not really,' Lisa thought sadly, and it wasn't just the milk. She vividly recalled the fresh-faced sparkling girl in pink satin pyjamas who'd let her into this very flat nearly six years ago. Jackie had aged considerably since she'd left London and had begun to acquire a matronly look. She wore a paisley-patterned, long-sleeved shirtdress, buttoned severely to the neck – the sort of dress that once upon a time she wouldn't have been seen dead in! Her blonde curls were brushed smooth, her only make-up a touch of pale pink lipstick. For some reason she couldn't fathom, Lisa felt a lump in her throat, remembering the spiky black lashes of the old Jackie.

Noël had sent a portrait of his Auntie Lisa – a wild, crayonned scribble. 'It's better than some of the stuff in that art gallery by the shop,' Lisa said dryly. 'The child is undoubtedly a genius. It's hard to imagine he was nearly mine.'

'I wonder if we would have got away with it,' mused Jackie. 'It seems a mad idea now.'

They were both silent for a while, then Lisa said ruefully, 'We've made a rare old mess of our lives, haven't we, Jackie? A few years ago, I was married and you were madly in love and now look at us!'

'Oh, I don't know,' said Jackie in a strange voice and Lisa looked at her quickly. Her friend was blushing.

'You've met someone,' Lisa said gleefully. 'Tell me all about him.'

'You must promise not to laugh.'

'As if I would!'

'It's the vicar. His name is Laurence Murray and he's a widower. His wife couldn't have children and he's longing for a family – he thinks the world of Noël.'

'Do you love him?' Lisa asked cautiously.

'I'm not sure, but I think so.'

'I hope you'll be very happy.' Lisa reached out and clasped Jackie's plump white hand.

'Oh, I will,' she replied serenely. 'I've discovered my vocation, you see. I want to be the mother of lots of children.'

*

Lisa went down to Bournemouth for Jackie's wedding in March.

Laurence was a tall, lanky man with a gentle face and eyes only for his new bride. Jackie, in a rather severe blue tweed suit and a white taffeta blouse, was starry-eyed.

'You only *thought* you loved him a few months ago,' Lisa said with a smile. 'It looks as if you're quite sure now.'

'I am, I am.' Jackie kissed her on the cheek. 'And it's so much better than with Gordon. In fact, it's magic!'

After the church ceremony they went back to the old shabby vicarage for refreshments. Lisa felt strangely alone, despite the friendliness of the other guests. 'I've got no one,' she thought bitterly. 'This thing with Clive won't last, I don't want it to. In a few weeks' time I'll be twenty-two. What on earth's to become of me?'

23

In the autumn of 1954, Miriam died. The Matron rang Lisa who'd been her only visitor. 'It was very peaceful,' she said. 'She was dead when we went to wake her this morning.'

Despite her sorrow, Lisa felt a sense of relief. Over the last twelve months, the shop had become a burden. She'd longed to leave and start afresh but knew Miriam's time on earth was limited, so waited. Now the shop would be closed and she could get on with her life.

She knew exactly what she wanted to do.

Ralph had sent a list of drama schools in London. The most prestigious ones she crossed off – she hadn't the nerve to approach a place like RADA – and wrote to the remainder for their brochure. In the end she settled on The Bryn Ayres Acting Academy in Sloane Square, mainly because they didn't demand an audition. The fees were horrendous and took half of Harry Greenbaum's legacy, though the remainder would be more than enough to live on during the year's course.

Most of the students at Bryn Ayres came from wealthy families. As long as they could afford to pay, they were taken on. Lisa's expectations were low when she started, so she wasn't disappointed.

The Principal was an American, Harvey Roots, a failed actor. Lisa could remember him in bit parts in old Hollywood films. He took himself very seriously, continually talked about his 'art' and was more interested in name-dropping than in teaching his students how to act.

'As I said to Clark during *It Happened One Night*,' he would drawl, or, 'When Greta and I were making *Ninotchka*.' Sometimes, it was all Lisa could do not to giggle out loud.

Still, it was an acting school, albeit not a very good one, and she was bound to learn *something* there – and it had one advantage over all the others. Every summer, Harvey Roots arranged for his students to spend a season acting in a holiday camp he part-owned in Wales.

'You'll be paid a pittance,' Ralph wrote, when she let him know what she'd done, 'and the plays are abominable, usually farces, though they amuse the campers no end. The good news is you'll get your Equity card, which means you'll be a professional actress!'

Clive Randolph was impressed by Lisa's decision to become an actress, convinced that his influence had steered her towards a more artistic career.

Lisa couldn't be bothered to disillusion him. One night as he was leaving, he said casually. 'I won't be around for a week or so. I'm going away.'

A few days later, she saw his photograph in the paper. He'd got married. The bride was another writer – a grim-looking woman wearing heavy horn-rimmed glasses. Lisa felt annoyed and hurt that he'd just walked out of her life without an explanation. After all, they'd shared some high emotion together. To her surprise, the following week he rang up. 'Same time as usual tonight?' he said breezily.

'But you're just married!' Lisa gasped.

'Oh, you saw that. I rather hoped you wouldn't. It doesn't mean we have to break up, Lisa.'

'Yes, it does,' she replied indignantly. 'I'll not be a party to you two-timing your new wife.'

'I married Patricia for her intellectual ability. She's not terribly interested in sex.'

'In other words, you want a woman for your head and another for your bed,' said Lisa. 'Well, too bad, Clive. Find someone else.'

She slammed the receiver down. Clive's services were no longer required, anyway. At Bryn Ayres there were half a dozen young men clamouring to take her out.

In the little holiday-camp theatre, Lisa was the despair of the producer. As Ralph had prophesied, the plays were mainly farces, requiring the actors to leap about the stage, shrieking their lines at the tops of their voices. Lisa could neither leap nor shriek. She had an almost deadpan delivery and an innate stillness on stage, quite unsuited to the parts she was given. She was almost in despair herself, when a young stagehand approached one night after the performance. He wasn't part of Harvey Roots' group, but was gaining backstage experience and hoped to become a producer himself one day.

'Have you been to a method-acting school?' he asked.

'Why, no,' she replied, somewhat surprised. 'Why do you ask?'

'Because of the way you act, so still and understated. You should be in serious drama, not shit like this.'

Lisa was so pleased, she kissed him. 'Thanks, I really needed that,' she said. After the way she'd been yelled at during rehearsals she was beginning to think the year at Bryn Ayres had been a waste of time and money.

When she got back from Wales, Lisa found a letter from a firm of solicitors to say that their client, Brian Smith, was suing for divorce on the grounds of desertion. She'd almost forgotten they'd been married. She wrote back and said she had no objections. When the Final Decree came through a few months later she felt sad and wondered if she'd still be married to Brian if they'd got their own place right after the wedding. Why, they might even have had several children by now and she and Jackie could compare notes. Her friend had already had another son, Robert, and was pregnant again. If it was a girl this time, she was going to call her Elizabeth. 'Though in fact she'll be Lisa, like you,' Jackie said, the last time Lisa went to stay in the big noisy vicarage.

*

Over the next year, Lisa, her Equity card tucked in her purse, got three non-speaking parts in films and a walk-on rôle in a West End play which ran for three months. She felt her career had got off to a healthy start and earned what seemed a lot of money for relatively little work.

However, her most important part was played in Bournemouth when she became Godmother to Lisa, a little creamy baby girl, the spitting image of her mother.

'One more and I've finished,' Jackie said as they walked down the path towards the church. Noël, his face unnaturally clean, trotted dutifully behind, holding Robert's hand.

Lisa glanced at the pretty baby in her arms, marvelling at how fast her eyes were turning from blue to Jackie's smokey grey. 'You should have an extra one for me,' she laughed. 'After all, you owe me a baby.'

Jackie squeezed her arm. 'You'll have your own some day,' she said. 'Don't forget, I was twenty-eight before I had Noël.'

'I suppose so.'

'You're happy, aren't you, Lisa? I mean, everything's turned out well for us both, hasn't it?'

'Of course it has,' Lisa said confidently. 'I love being an actress. After all, it's what I've always wanted.'

Afterwards, she wondered if she'd said that to convince herself, rather than Jackie.

She was sitting learning lines one night – next morning she was going for an audition – when the doorbell went, three long rings, three short, which meant it was for her. Glancing at her watch, she saw it was half-past ten and wondered who on earth it could be. She prayed it wasn't Clive Randolph, for every now and then he called or telephoned, pleading to renew their relationship. She always refused.

The man on the step was a stranger – or so she thought at first. 'Hi, Lisa,' he said with a grin.

'Ralph!' She flung herself at him and dragged him inside into the light. 'You look years younger and your hair's different! I didn't recognise you.'

'They made me grow it for my latest movie,' he said shamefacedly. 'Then they dyed it blond.'

'And permed it!' She collapsed giggling on the stairs. 'You don't half look funny.'

'Thanks!' he said dryly. 'The studio would have a fit if they could hear you. They think it makes me look outrageously attractive.'

In fact he did look attractive, though not a bit like the Ralph she used to know. He wore a leather jacket over a black shirt and tight jeans.

'You look gorgeous,' she soothed, linking his arm as they climbed the stairs together. 'So gorgeous, I might not be able to restrain myself once I get you in my flat – so beware!'

Ralph Layton was not yet as famous as Laurence Olivier or Charles Laughton, as he'd once hoped, but in his latest film, a thriller called *Raging Fury*, he had the starring role.

'The studio insisted I come over for the British première,' he told Lisa after he'd sat down. 'And I want you to come with me. Would you mind? It's next Tuesday.'

'Mind? Try keeping me away,' she said, eyes shining.

'You'll need an evening dress. I'll buy one for you.'

She bustled around him solicitously. He'd professed himself tired after the long flight from California.

'Would you like some wine or food?' she asked.

'No, but I'd love a cup of tea.' He settled himself comfortably in the chair. 'You know, it's an odd compliment to offer such a lovely young woman, but you make the best cup of tea in the world, Lisa. I've really missed it in Hollywood.'

On Tuesday afternoon, Lisa went to a beauty parlour for the first time in her life. Then she took her new dress and shoes with heels as fine as a pencil, together with a hired mink stole, along to Ralph's suite in Claridges to get dressed. A limousine would pick them up at half-past seven to take them to the cinema in Leicester Square.

When she emerged from the bedroom ready to go, Ralph gasped. 'My God, you're beautiful!'

Lisa already knew. The radiant woman who'd stared back at her from the mirror in Ralph's bedroom had started her. She literally glowed, seemed almost unreal. Was that really Lizzie O'Brien from Chaucer Street? Her eyes looked huge, bigger than ever now they were emphasised by black liner, the lids touched with gold shadow which brought out the golden shreds in the brown pupils. And what on earth had they done to her hair, to make it ripple and shimmer whenever she moved her head the slightest fraction?

The dress was vivid red chiffon, strapless, exposing her breasts to a degree she found embarrassing and clinging to her body down to the hips, where it flared out in a multitude of frothy layers of material. She was sure she looked indecent, but to her surprise, found she didn't mind a bit. In fact, she rather enjoyed the feeling.

'You're a tart, Lizzie O'Brien,' she told herself with a grin. 'If Mam could see you now, she'd have a fit!'

Ralph came over and touched her arm. 'Oh Lisa, when I look at you, how I wish, I wish . . .' He frowned and shook his head.

Lisa stroked his cheek. 'I wish too, Ralph, I really do.'

There was a crowd outside the cinema, mainly consisting of women. They screamed hysterically at Ralph when he and Lisa alighted from the car onto the red-carpeted pavement. Before entering the foyer, he turned and waved and they screamed again.

'That was frightening,' Lisa said when they were inside. 'They'd have torn you to bits if they'd got their hands on you.'

'You get used to it,' Ralph said easily.

She nudged him, almost beside herself with excitement. 'Ralph! Jill Ireland's over there with David McCallum and there's Diana Dors. Jesus, Mary and Joseph, Dirk Bogarde's actually *looking* at me!'

Ralph squeezed her shoulders. '*Everyone's* looking at you,' he said proudly. 'It's as if you're the star, not me.'

Raging Fury wasn't a very good film. Remembering Ralph's outstanding performance in *Pygmalion,* Lisa felt he was wasted in the part. It required only a mere fraction of his talent, though she began to wonder if there was something about the film which had escaped her, because when it was over, he was showered with congratulations.

'Marvellous!' people said. 'First class, Ralph. Best thriller I've ever seen.'

'Liars!' said Ralph in a quiet moment. 'They all hate it.'

'How can you tell?' she asked, amazed.

'Because even *I* know it's a lousy film,' he said with a grin. 'The only good thing about it was the money I got paid.'

It was gone midnight before the cinema began to empty. 'There's a crowd going back to Donnelly's place,' Ralph told her. 'Want to come?'

'Of course I do! I never want tonight to end.'

Donnelly Westover had written the novel from which *Raging Fury* was adapted. He was a slight, cheerful-looking man nearing sixty. Ralph and Lisa shared a taxi with him and his wife back to their top-floor West Kensington apartment. The long, low-ceilinged room was already full of people when they arrived.

'This lot weren't invited to the première,' Donnelly explained. 'They've been at it for hours.'

'It' appeared to be drinking. The twenty or thirty guests were in a state of advanced merriment and the shout of welcome which greeted Ralph and Donnelly as they entered almost lifted the roof off its black-painted rafters.

Lisa was besieged by people asking what films she'd been in, and had to confess that her appearances so far had been brief. 'If you blink, you'll miss them,' she said. 'I'm only here as a friend of Ralph's.'

She got separated from Ralph almost immediately, but was accepted without question by Donnelly's friends, men and women alike. Most of them seemed to be writers of one sort or another. One man had written a play with a part in it that was apparently perfect for Lisa. 'You must let me know where you live,' he said, 'and if I ever get it on, I'll contact you.'

The woman beside him laughed. 'Don't take any notice of him, Lisa. It's a lousy play. This is my husband's sneaky way of getting your address.' They began a good-natured argument about the merits of the play.

The rest of the group were involved in a heated debate over the Suez crisis.

'Churchill would never have got us into this mess,' someone said. 'Anthony Eden needs his behind kicking.'

'What! Churchill would have atom-bombed the lot of them,' a young woman cried. 'If a Labour government was in, we would have minded our own business. After all, the Suez Canal doesn't belong to us.'

Lisa hastily moved on, worried she might be asked for her opinion. She was only vaguely aware of the Suez crisis and wasn't even sure if it was over yet.

She joined another group where space flight was the topic of conversation. Donnelly Westover was waving his arms about excitedly.

'Come on, who'll take me on? A hundred quid that the Russians'll have a man in space by the end of the year.'

'I'd give a thousand,' a young man beside Lisa said fervently, 'to be at the launch with my camera.'

She turned to look at him at precisely the same time he became aware of her. He was well-built and tall, over six feet, with a mop of blond hair curling onto his neck. Bright, clear blue eyes, full of laughter, were set wide in his handsome, sensitive face. He wore jeans and a loose brown sweater over an open-necked check shirt, and he looked vaguely familiar.

He was staring at her, frowning. 'Have we met before?'

'I was just wondering the same thing,' she said, though she felt sure she would have remembered if they had.

'We can't have,' he said seriously, 'else I'd have remembered.'

'I was thinking that too.'

They were staring at each other with a mixture of curiosity and wonder when someone pushed between them to join their circle. Then Ralph touched her arm. 'There's a man I'd like you to meet,' he said. Hiding her reluctance, Lisa followed him to the corner of the room where he introduced her to a producer who was planning to stage a musical version of *Pride And Prejudice* in the New Year.

'I'm not auditioning yet, but ring my office in a few months' time and we'll arrange something.' He gave her his card and after tucking it inside her evening bag, Lisa glanced across the room, searching for the young blond man. She caught his eye immediately and wondered if he had been watching since Ralph had taken her away. The young man smiled across the crowded room. Lisa caught her breath as she smiled back.

'Eric was impressed with you,' Ralph whispered. 'I think you stand a good chance there.'

'Eric?' she replied vaguely.

'The producer who just gave you his card,' said Ralph patiently. He followed her gaze. The young man was still watching. 'Ah, I see you have more important things on your mind.' He squeezed her hand. 'Good luck.'

She smiled at him brilliantly. 'Oh, Ralph! I feel very strange. I don't even know his name, we only exchanged a few words, but I feel as if I've known him all my life.'

'That's a good omen.'

'Is it? Do people *really* fall in love at first sight?'

'They do in books and songs. I expect they do it in real life too.' He kissed her cheek affectionately. 'You make a remarkably handsome couple.'

A woman came and dragged Ralph away and Lisa suddenly found herself involved in an argument over foreign food.

'Believe me, one day pizzas will take over the world. What do you think?' a man demanded.

Conscious only of a blond head which seemed to be getting closer, Lisa confessed, 'It's not something I've given much thought to.'

'Pizza, pizza, pizza. Everywhere I go nowadays, I get pizza,' the man complained.

'Personally, I find ravioli a curse. You get given it as an hors d'oeuvre – and then there's no room for anything else. You're full before—'

'Hi, I'm Patrick.'

She turned, her eyes like stars. He'd come for her as she knew he would. His face held an expression of sheer joy mixed with something else – perhaps it was incredulity, she wasn't sure.

'I'm Lisa.'

He took her hand; it was a completely natural gesture. 'I know this sounds foolish, you can call me an idiot if you like, but I think I've fallen in love with you, Lisa.'

'Then I must be an idiot, too,' she said softly.

She felt him shiver. 'This is really weird,' he said. 'Do you feel weird?'

'Weird and wonderful.'

Perhaps they'd been made for each other. Perhaps this was the man she'd been waiting for all her life, just as he'd been waiting for her. That's why he seemed familiar. He'd always existed in a remote corner of her mind, and she in his, so that when they met they'd be bound to recognise each other instantly.

'Let's find a seat.' He put his arm around her and the touch of his large warm hand on her naked shoulder sent a delicious thrill through her body.

They would make love later on. Of that she was sure. They would make love every night for the rest of their lives. She was sure of that too. She had met Patrick. She had come home.

He lived in a flat below Donnelly Westover. 'Though it's less than half the size,' he explained. 'In fact, it's a bit of a hovel.' He was a freelance photographer and until recently only earned money sporadically when he sold a picture. 'Though lately, I've had a couple of commissions. I'm beginning to get known.'

Lisa felt a surge of pride. His career was already important to her.

'What about you?' he asked. They managed to find a space on the edge of the settee and sat close together. Lisa's body moulded into his, the skirt of her dress spilling onto his knee. 'What do you do?'

'I'm an actress, though please don't ask what I've been in because it hasn't been much – yet.'

'Okay, I won't.'

They said no more until the party broke up, both silently marvelling at the fact they'd found each other.

After she had said goodbye to Ralph and collected her coat, she took his hand and they went down to his flat, her whole being tense with anticipation of what was to come and conscious of Patrick trembling beside her.

It was even better than she could have imagined in all her wildest dreams. He didn't switch on the light. The open curtains allowed the bright moon to flood the room with a heavenly golden glow and as he removed her dress, his hands sliding down her slippery, satin shoulders, he gasped when her small pointed breasts were fully revealed to him and groaning, he buried his head between them. When his mouth touched her nipples, Lisa could scarcely stop herself from screaming aloud as an inexpressible sensation of sheer ecstasy tore through her. She pulled the dress away, throwing it to the floor where it lay like a pool of spilt blood. When Patrick removed his own clothes, Lisa reached up and with both hands began to touch him with featherlight fingers. As she travelled down his body, he began to groan again and she felt him, rock hard against her.

Now it was time for their union and as he entered her, Lisa felt as if she had left her body altogether and was somewhere on a higher plane where ordinary feelings were left behind and she was experiencing a joy which was beyond life itself.

When she woke, daylight was just beginning to struggle through the small window. Patrick's hand was flat on her abdomen. She watched him sleeping. He looked young and vulnerable and she had to resist kissing him awake. There was so much she wanted to ask him. About his family, for instance, and where did he come from?

Lisa glanced around the gradually lightening room. The furniture was shabby, nothing matched. The walls were a patchy cream and needed painting. He could come and live in Queen's Gate, she decided, and they'd push the twin beds together to make a double. They'd spend a lot of time in bed. Her swift intake of breath at the thought of them together for the rest of their lives was audible. She glanced at Patrick, half-hoping it had woken him. As she watched, a shaft of pale lemony sun lit up a small section of the room, enveloping him in its soft beam. Lisa marvelled at the way it caught strands of his blond hair and his long thick lashes and turned them gold. A sensation of déjà vu overcame her. How familiar it seemed, watching a fair-haired young man lost in sleep.

The warm touch of the sun must have disturbed him. He blinked and looked at her. 'So, it wasn't a dream.'

She shook her head. 'No,' she said softly.

He began to move the flat of his hand up and down her body and she felt her insides turn to liquid.

'Jesus,' he whispered hoarsely. 'I feel as if I should wait a few minutes, out of decency or something.'

'Don't wait, don't wait,' she pleaded. 'Now!'

'What are we going to do today?' he asked later.

Lisa looked at him coyly. 'What do you want to do most?'

He laughed. 'Okay, we'll stay in bed.'

She sat up and looked around the sun-filled room. 'I spy a kettle. I'm longing for a cup of tea.' She got out of bed. The linoleum under her bare feet was freezing so she slipped her feet into her red high-heeled shoes.

'Christ, you're beautiful.'

Patrick was staring at her nakedness, adoration on his face. She laughed and briefly posed for him before slipping into his check shirt. 'Where's the water?'

'In the kitchen down the hall, but you can't go like that, I'll have a riot on my hands. Anyway, I've only got one mug.'

'I can't hear a soul about and we'll share the tea, though bags I have the first half.'

When the tea was made and she was sitting up in bed drinking out of the large cracked mug, she said, 'Don't think I'm setting a precedent. In future, we'll take turns making the first cup of the day.'

'Yes, ma'am. Any other rules you'd like to set for the next fifty years?' She could sense deep emotion behind his joking words.

'Oh, Patrick!' She touched his shoulder. 'Isn't this wonderful?' He didn't answer but began to caress her underneath the sheets until she was forced to say, 'I'll spill my tea, please stop.' He took no notice and moved his head until it was against the hollow of her waist and began to kiss her. She groaned, put down her tea and slid down the bed into his arms.

She fell asleep. When she woke, Patrick was fully dressed and sitting at a small plastic table, writing. The atmosphere inside the small room was so intense, so highly charged, that she had a strong feeling that she and Patrick were the only two people left in the world. 'If I look outside the window,' she thought, 'it will be a wasteland. Everything and everyone will have disappeared except him and me.' She felt a surge of pure love that took her breath away as she watched him, his brow puckered in concentration as he wrote swiftly, the pen clutched in his hand in an awkward, schoolboyish way.

'How old are you?'

He jumped. 'You're awake! You've been spying on me. I was going to wake you soon. I've made more tea – I borrowed a mug off Donnelly.'

'You didn't answer my question. I don't usually sleep with strange men. I hardly know anything about you.'

'I'm twenty-two.'

'Is that all?' Lisa was dismayed. 'I'm years older than you, twenty-five and a half, to be precise.'

'I like older women,' he said contentedly.

'What are you writing? A report on me? What do I get out of ten?'

He laughed. 'No, I write to my mother regularly. She gets worried if she doesn't hear. If I gave you marks, you'd get eleven out of ten.' He tore two pages out of the pad, folded them and stuck them in an envelope. 'I must go out and post this later,' he said, propping the letter up against the wall. 'Now, about that tea . . .'

'Are you an only child?' asked Lisa as he handed her a mug, a pretty china one this time.

'No, I come from a large family, with lots of brothers and sisters. That's a strange thing to ask.'

'I just wondered why you wrote home regularly.' She'd immediately thought of Mrs Smith and Brian, though Patrick didn't give the impression of being a mother's boy. He put his left hand on her neck and began to stroke her cheek with his thumb. She closed her eyes briefly, dipping her head against his palm, little realising that the next words were to be the most devastating she would hear in all her life.

'Because my mother frets – it seems odd calling her "Mother". At home we call her Mam.' He smiled ruefully. 'You see, one of my sisters ran away from home when she was sixteen – just walked out without a word and never came back. She wrote to us from London, but never gave her address. It broke Mam's – my mother's – heart.'

Lisa felt herself grow cold. 'What was your sister called?'

'Elizabeth, but we called her Lizzie. Hey, don't get up! I was going to join you in a minute.'

'I've just remembered something – I have to go.' She began to struggle into her dress. '*Don't panic,*' she told herself. '*Stay calm or he'll guess something's wrong and he might even guess what it is.*' She tried to smile. 'I have an audition this afternoon, Patrick. I'd forgotten all about it.'

'I'll come with you.'

'No!' She spoke too sharply. He looked at her, surprised and hurt. *Paddy, my dear little brother.* Ah! She felt her eyes fill with tears.

'What's wrong, darling?' He hadn't called her that before.

'Why, nothing,' she said lightly. 'What a fool I am to have forgotten. It's something quite important.'

'Will you come back afterwards?'

'Yes, I promise. About five o'clock.' That was an awful thing to do, make a promise. He'd be waiting and waiting, but how else could she get out of here?

She couldn't manage the zip on her dress. He came to help, burying his head in her shoulder. 'There *is* something wrong,' he said, his voice muffled.

She turned to face him, clasped his dear, handsome face in her hands. 'I love you, Patrick,' she said softly, and kissed him full on the lips. Then, picking up her stole, she glanced briefly at the letter on the table just to make sure, to make absolutely sure.

Mrs K. O'Brien, 2 Chaucer Street, Bootle, Liverpool.

Poor Kitty, what a curse your Lizzie has turned out to be!

Then she left.

24

Somehow, she must have hailed a taxi, though she could never recall the journey home. It wasn't until she entered the flat in Queen's Gate that she realised where she was and found herself trembling. She ran a bath and lay in the steaming, scented water for an hour trying to make sense of things.

No wonder Patrick had seemed so familiar. No wonder she'd felt as if she'd known him all her life . . . In her mind, she went back to the party, re-living, re-writing the night's events, meeting him. What had he said: 'Have we met before?'

'No,' she'd answered. 'Else I'd have remembered.' She'd responded with her heart instead of her head. She should have been more curious. Instead, she'd thought it an aspect of love, that a man you'd been waiting to meet all your life would be *bound* to have a certain familiarity about him. She imagined herself answering his first question differently. 'I can't remember for the moment, but let's try and think where we *could* have met,' and one by one they would have crossed off Bryn Ayres, the film sets, the theatres, until it came down to, 'Where do you come from?' and the inevitable discovery that they were related. The attraction would almost certainly have died immediately – and if it hadn't, they would have pretended it didn't exist and would never, never . . . not when they knew they were brother and sister! She cursed herself for her lack of caution. Why, they hadn't even asked each other's surname!

Then she began to think about him, about Patrick. At five o'clock he would be waiting for her to return, but his wait would be in vain. Oh my God, he might even come looking for her! In fact, the more Lisa thought about it, the more certain it seemed. She would search for him, under the same circumstances. He'd ask Donnelly Westover where she lived, and she remembered telling Donnelly in the taxi from the cinema, 'On the corner of Queen's Gate and Old Brompton Road,' she'd said.

There was nothing else for it. She had to get away.

The water in the bath began to cool and she shivered, then shivered again as the memory of the glorious night she'd spent with her brother returned and for a brief, mad moment she considered going back and saying nothing. She could invent a new past, a new name, say she came from somewhere else. He could still come and live here, just as she'd planned. But the thought fled as swiftly as it had come. It could never be the same again, not for her. Not only that, he couldn't keep her hidden from his family forever and Kitty would know who she was straight away, even from a photograph.

'Oh, God!' she groaned aloud. She would remember their hours together for her entire life. There would never be another night like it, but it could never happen again. She must expunge it from her mind, try not to think about it, forget it happened. If she could.

'My brother, my lover, but for one night only,' she whispered softly.

Later on, when she was dressed, she made some tea and sat wondering what to do. In a few hours, it would be five o'clock. Despite everything, she had a strong feeling that if Patrick came through the door some time tonight, she would allow herself to be swept up in his arms and . . .

Yes, she had to get away this very afternoon.

But where?

'I'm doing it again,' she thought sadly. 'Jumping out of one life into another totally alien one.' One minute she had a family, then suddenly she had none. She'd come to London a stranger completely alone in the world. Now she was about to depart, equally alone, an empty broken marriage behind her. No ties, no possessions worth speaking of. Not even anyone close to wish her goodbye.

Most people's lives seemed to run smoothly. They stayed on the same path throughout, just changing course slightly from time to time. 'Mine is more like a series of stepping stones,' she thought ruefully, 'and I hop from one stone to another whenever things go wrong . . .

'Where do I go from here?' she asked herself again.

Suddenly, she knew exactly what she would do. She'd go to California, to Hollywood. Ralph had suggested it dozens of times.

But she wouldn't tell Ralph. She didn't want him getting parts for her. She knew the contempt other actors reserved for those who'd got a part, not through merit, but through connections. She'd make it on her own!

Lisa packed her bags swiftly, collecting her favourite clothes, the Jane Austen set, and Victoria, then she wrote a letter to the landlord enclosing a fortnight's rent and apologising for leaving so many possessions behind. 'Perhaps they could go to charity,' she suggested. On her way out, she'd push the note under Piers' door.

When she'd finished, she stood back and looked at the two rooms for the very last time. She'd left once before, but it hadn't seemed so final then and she'd been looking forward to getting married.

This time it was for good.

What wonderful times they'd had here, she and Jackie. So much laughter, so many bright-eyed, confident hopes expressed for the future, though there'd been sadness too. She remembered all the tears shed for Gordon.

Thunder rumbled in the distance and rain began to splatter against the windows, swiftly turning into a deluge. Lisa looked outside. People were running for shelter and the cars already had their windscreen wipers on.

'Where are they going, what are they thinking?' she whispered. 'How strange life is. No one knows I'm behind this window making one of the biggest decisions of my life.' What was going on behind all those other windows opposite? In some of those rooms, people might be dying or sunk in indescribable misery or having a furious row. On the other hand, they could be making love or happily reading a book. People's emotions were hidden away, behind their windows and their closed doors. In a minute she'd leave this house, walk round to Gloucester Road Air Terminal and ask for a ticket to California – and no one in a million years would be able to tell that last night she'd slept with her brother, and now she was running away to another continent.

The ringing of the telephone made her jump. It sounded extra loud, as if the rooms were stripped bare of everything. She went across to the bedroom door and stared at it, as if just by looking she'd be able to tell who was at the other end.

She didn't pick it up. It might be the last person in the world she wanted to talk to right now – or was he the person she wanted to talk to most?

'God help me,' she said aloud as she picked up her bag and left the flat. When she opened the big front door, she could still hear the phone ringing four floors above her.

South of Sunset Boulevard

25

Another sunny day. Ever since Lisa had come to California seven months ago, the sun had never seemed to stop shining. Day after day after day, from early morning until dusk, the world was blessed with glorious golden sunlight. She sat up in bed, nudged the white curtain aside and looked out onto the wide road of Spanish-style stucco houses painted in delicate pastel colours – shell-pink, cream, pale green, lilac . . .

Though it must have rained some time; how else could the long lawns be such an unnatural bright green, or the luscious, bulging flowers that filled every garden, grow and bloom so extravagantly? Lally had told her the names. The purple bell-shaped ones were jacaranda and already, a mere two or three weeks since bursting so ostentatiously into bloom, their petals were beginning to fall like confetti. And there were bougainvilleas, azaleas, gardenias – outrageous, brilliantly-coloured flowers, the likes of which she'd never seen before.

The telephone rang in the hall and Roma shouted, 'I'll get it.' Lisa slipped out of bed and went to the door to listen. Roma called, 'Gloria, it's for you,' and Lisa relaxed. She didn't trust Roma, not since the day Dick Broadbent had called Lisa to say Paramount were testing for slave girls for *Desert Princess* and she should get to the studios immediately. In her excitement, Lisa had told her flatmates, Gloria, Lally and Roma, as she ran to get ready. When she arrived at Paramount, however, she was told, 'Sorry, doll, we got all we need.' Two days later, she discovered Roma had taken a taxi before her and been hired.

Now she was out of bed, she might as well stay up. In just over an hour's time she had a singing lesson, and her shift at the coffee shop commenced at midday. After a quick shower, Lisa pulled on a pair of jeans and a yellow sleeveless tee shirt. She twisted and turned in front of the mirror, trying to decide if the tee shirt looked best loose, or tucked inside her jeans. She left it tucked in, inserted a tan leather belt through the loops of the waistband and slipped her feet into a pair of yellow canvas loafers. Sorting through her earrings, she selected a pair of gypsy hoops.

It was important to look her best for work. You never knew who might drop in for a coffee; a producer or director, even a famous star on the lookout for a new face for his or her latest film.

Dick, her agent, advised her not to wear make-up. 'You don't need it,' he said. 'A nice, fresh complexion makes you stand out.' Dick also said to take a few years off her age. '*I* know you're just starting out, but others don't. When you say you're twenty-five, folks'll think you've been hanging round for years.' In April, when her birthday came around, she told her flatmates she was twenty-two and was astounded when Gloria said, 'I didn't think you were *that* old.'

When she first arrived in Hollywood, Lisa stayed in Rollo's, a cheap hotel off Franklin Avenue. The taxi driver who'd brought her from the airport recommended it. 'It's pretty basic,' he warned, 'but you said you wanted somewhere cheap. Well, it's that all right, but clean. An' you'll be safe there. Rollo's particular who he takes in – no dopers, no prostitutes.' Rollo was his wife's cousin.

On her first day, after a dark-haired silent woman had brought her breakfast, she ventured out, but only for a short distance before returning to the safety of the mean, sparsely furnished room, where she lay on her bed and thought about the enormity of what she had done. She was alone in a strange country and not quite sure which way to turn.

On the second morning, she sat up in bed listening for the chink of dishes which heralded breakfast, anxious for her first cup of coffee. To her surprise, it wasn't the dark-haired woman, but a curly-haired, impish-looking young man who came in holding the tray.

'It's Adriana's day off,' he said, 'so I get the honour of bringing the breakfast.' He put the tray down on the cheap plastic table. 'I'm Brett Charwood, scriptwriter extraordinaire and you're Lisa O'Brien – I looked it up in the register. Hi.'

'Hi,' said Lisa. His relaxed, friendly manner made her feel at ease. 'What is an extraordinary scriptwriter doing working in a cheap hotel?' she asked.

The young man grinned. He wore shabby jeans and a tee shirt with a Mickey Mouse face on the front. 'Earning a crust,' he answered. 'Gotta eat, need a roof. Unfortunately, I don't get either from writing – yet. I'm the nightclerk here. Gives me plenty of time to scribble.' He looked at her, his head on one side. 'Understand you're English. Gee, Hollywood must seem strange. Took me a while to get used to it and I'm only from the next state!'

'Well, I haven't plucked up the courage to go far yet,' Lisa confessed. 'I've only been here a couple of days.'

'Expect you've come to take the place by storm?' he said cheerfully. 'What are you – an actress, dancer, singer?'

'Actress.'

'Tell you what, Lisa, I finish in half an hour. Wanna walk with me? I'm going to see my agent about a script idea I got.'

'I'd love to,' she replied.

'Brett!' a voice yelled. 'There's breakfasts down here waiting.'

'A man's work is never done!' He rolled his eyes. 'I'll give you a call when I'm leaving.'

Sunset Boulevard!

She was actually on Sunset Boulevard! It was so incredible that she wanted to shout, loud enough for it to reach Number 2 Chaucer Street: '*Look, Mam, your Lizzie is on Sunset Boulevard!*'

The atmosphere was exhilarating, vibrant, and the air spun with vitality and optimism. Everyone looked busy, their faces full of hope, their eyes almost manically bright as they pushed and shoved their way through the crowded pavements.

'Feel it?' asked Brett.

She'd forgotten he was there. 'Feel what?'

'The greed, the ambition, the will to succeed. Listen, Lisa, these people'd kill for fame. The actors'd sell their own mother for a bit-part in a B movie.'

'Would you?'

He looked at her, a half-smile on his face. 'Well, I kinda like my mom, but I'd seriously consider trading Grandma for a screen credit on a low budget no-hoper.'

Lisa laughed. 'I don't believe you.'

Brett shrugged. 'Don't bet on it.' He glanced around. 'It's all getting to look rather tawdry, isn't it? Gee, I would have loved to have been here ten, twenty years ago when Hollywood was in its heyday.'

'Isn't it now?'

'Nope – movies are on the way out, for sure.' He laughed at her crestfallen face. 'Don't worry, honey, television's taking over. That means there'll be even more work for us. After all, why should folks pay to see a movie, when they've got a screen of their own, right in their living room?'

She felt relieved. 'I was beginning to think I'd come too late!'

'Nah, don't worry,' he said dismissively. 'My agent's on the next block. Do you wanna hang around or can you find your own way back?'

'I'll look around a bit, thanks, and I can remember the way back.'

'While you're here, why not fix yourself up with an agent? Guess you'll want to start work pretty soon.'

'Can I use yours?'

'No, idiot, mine's literary, though I think there's an actors' agent in the same building. Take a look at the board outside.'

Shortly afterwards, Brett said goodbye and darted into a narrow doorway between a little cinema and a dress shop. After he'd gone, Lisa looked at the list of names beside the door. Quite a lot of agents worked in the building – insurance, literary, employment. On the fourth floor she saw what she was hoping for: *Dick Broadbent, Actors' Agent.*

Lisa took a deep breath, threw her shoulders back and marched up the stairs. 'Dick Broadbent, here I come,' she said out loud.

Later on, when Lally found Lisa was represented by Dick Broadbent, she urged her to change. 'He's eighty if he's a day, and likely to drop dead any minute.'

'I like him,' Lisa said stubbornly. 'He's nice.'

In fact, Dick wasn't quite that old, more like seventy. He worked entirely alone, without even a secretary. A tiny hunchback, no more than four and a half feet tall, much to his regret and chagrin he'd never had a star on his books. When Lisa walked in, nervous and prepared for rejection, he'd welcomed her with open arms. 'Star material!' he crowed. 'I recognise it straight away.'

Lally cautioned that he said this to everyone. 'The little creep has got a jinx on him. Sign with him and you're guaranteed to fail.'

Lisa said she was willing to take a chance, if only to prove Lally wrong.

Not only had Dick taken years off her age, but he'd changed her surname, too.

'Sure you ain't got some Latin blood?' he asked first time they met, staring at her with his rather crooked eyes.

'Positive,' she said firmly. 'I'm pure Irish-Liverpudlian. It's the Celtic streak makes me so dark.' Kitty had told her that.

'Well, you look Latin. Lisa O'Brien gives the wrong impression. You need something more romantic. You can keep the Lisa . . .'

'Thanks,' said Lisa dryly.

He didn't notice the interruption. 'How about Rosa? Lisa Rosa.'

'There's already a singer almost called that, Lita Rosa. She comes from Liverpool, too.'

'Hmm.' He put his gnomelike head on one side and stared at her intently. 'Lisa Gomez?'

Lisa shook her head firmly. 'I don't like that much.'

'Lisa La Plante?'

'No.' It had to be something she felt comfortable with. After all, she'd be living with it for a long time, perhaps all her life.

There was silence for a while in the dusty, over-furnished office. Both of them were deep in thought.

'How about Angelis?' Lisa suggested. 'No, An*gel*is, with the emphasis on the second syllable. Lisa An*gel*is.' She couldn't remember where she'd heard the name before but it sounded pretty.

'Perfect,' said Dick.

A week later she got her first movie work in Hollywood.

The film was a big-budget thriller and Lisa spent a whole day on set as one of the throng of passengers on a mocked-up station. The director, a hysterical, overbearing man, demanded the big chase by the two male stars through the crowds to be shot again and again; daylight was beginning to fail before he pronounced himself satisfied, to the relief of everyone including Lisa, who had a headache.

The clash of several overweening temperaments was nerve-wracking, and there'd almost been a real fight at one point. The hatred of the two male stars for each other was exceeded only by their joint hatred for the director – and he appeared to loathe everyone, extras included.

As for the language! Lisa heard more four-letter words that day than she'd heard in her entire life. Filming in England had been mild compared to this. She'd be glad to get back to Rollo's for some peace and quiet.

She was about to leave the set when a young man came up. 'Can you come back tomorrow, Miss er . . . ?'

'O'Bri . . . Angelis, Lisa Angelis. Yes, I can come back.'

'Right, see you at seven o'clock then.'

Her headache disappeared as if by magic.

She spent half the next day with three other extras, two men and a woman about her own age, in the tiny, claustrophobic setting of a lift. Lisa was dressed as a nun, feeling suffocated in the heavy costume. The four extras were instructed to remain impassive and disinterested throughout.

The thirty-second scene, in which the female star entered the lift, examined her face in a compact, and got out again, took all morning to shoot. According to the director, she wasn't casual enough.

'How can I be fuckin' casual, when you're screaming at me like a fuckin' maniac?' the actress demanded furiously. The woman extra beside Lisa whispered, 'And how are we supposed to keep a straight face with all this shit going on?'

Lisa didn't answer – her face felt as if it would never move again, and if she had to wear these clothes much longer she'd melt to nothing.

In the end, the director grudgingly conceded, 'That'll do,' and someone yelled, 'Break for lunch.'

Lisa made her way to the dressing room to rid herself of the nun's habit. Apart from feeling uncomfortably hot, wearing the heavy crucifix around her neck made her feel uneasy and vaguely sinful.

To her surprise, when she came out, the other woman extra was waiting for her. She was the first actress Lisa had come across since she'd arrived in Hollywood who wasn't beautiful. Indeed, she bordered on plain, but there was something appealing about her round, chubby face with its wide mobile mouth, snub nose and sparkling blue eyes. Lisa took to her straight away.

'Hi, I'm Lally Cooper. You're British, aren't you?'

'That's right. My name's Lisa Angelis.'

'I just love your accent.'

'Everyone says that, it's rather flattering.'

'Been here long?' They began to walk towards the canteen.

'Just over a week,' Lisa answered. 'This is my first job, though I did theatre and film work in England.'

'You're lucky getting a part with so much exposure straight away,' Lally said enviously.

'Am I?' Lisa wasn't quite sure what she meant.

'Yeh. I expect you were in the big station scene yesterday.'

'That's right. The director asked me to come back again today.'

'That's a really good sign. It means you've got a noticeable face.' Lally took Lisa's arm and steered her into a self-service restaurant, a tall, bright room with cream plastic tables and chairs. It was already crowded and there was a long queue of people waiting to be served.

While they stood in line, Lally showered Lisa with questions. What had she been in? Where was she living? Who was her agent?

Lisa didn't mind the third degree. It was nice having someone interested. Lally delivered her blunt opinion on Dick Broadbent. 'If you ever decide to ditch him, I'll recommend you to Elmer. He's a Grade-A swine, but a really good agent.'

They carried their food over to a table with two vacant seats.

'You ain't planning on staying in that hotel, are you?' Lally asked.

'Oh no,' said Lisa. 'I want a place of my own. Although it's cheap at Rollo's, I have to eat out except for breakfast, and my money's fast disappearing.'

'Hey, ain't that a coincidence? We'll have a room vacant in a week's time. Why don't you move in with us, Lisa? It'll be real nice, having a Britisher staying.' Lally's blue eyes lit up.

'Who's "we"?' Lisa asked.

'Gloria Grenville, Roma Novatora and me. Pam Redman, that's the fourth, is moving in with some guy. Come round tonight and take a look.'

Lally's apartment comprised the top floor of a pink stone house in a little road off La Brea Avenue, south of Sunset Boulevard. The entrance was up a black iron staircase at the back. Lally ushered Lisa into a narrow hallway which led to a big pleasant room with white, roughcast walls decorated with film posters. Two sofas and several armchairs were covered in coarse red linen and colourful woven rugs were scattered over the black tiled floor. In front of a large wide window was a pine table, a bowl of yellow flowers in its centre.

'It's really pretty,' she said.

Lally smiled. 'No one's ever called it that before. Come and see the room that's gonna be empty. Pam's out somewhere.'

The room was small, about ten feet square. One entire wall was taken up with a built-in wardrobe. Opposite was a single bed and on another wall, a small dressing table with a long mirror. The walls here were white too, as were the thin muslin curtains, and the bed was covered with a multicoloured patterned blanket.

Lisa said she'd definitely like to move in when Pam left. 'It's five hundred dollars a month,' Lally said. 'We pay a quarter each, plus twenty dollars for extras. Okay?'

'Fine,' agreed Lisa.

'Would you like a coffee?' Lally asked. 'Or do you Britishers only drink tea?'

'Coffee's fine.'

Back in the big lounge, Lisa sat down as Lally disappeared into the kitchen. 'You gotta job yet?' she shouted.

That seemed a strange question. 'Why do I need a job, when I'm going to work in films like you?' Lisa shouted back.

Lally appeared in the doorway, a kettle in one hand, a jar of coffee in the other. She looked astounded.

'You gotta get a job, kid, if you wanna pay your rent and eat. Today was my first movie work in weeks. I've been in Hollywood four years now and I ain't ever made enough from movies to live on. Some day I will. Some day.' She nodded fiercely, as if to convince herself more than Lisa. She disappeared again and emerged shortly with two cups of coffee. 'I work nights as an usherette at the Plaza – that's a movie house, case you didn't know. Roma's in an office, though she's going to get dumped any minute, the way she just disappears at a moment's notice for an audition or takes whole days off if she gets a part.'

'What about Gloria, what does she do?'

Lally's blue eyes twinkled. 'Well, you look the innocent sort, Lisa. I won't say what Gloria does to earn a buck or two, just that she lies down a lot.'

It had come as a shock to Lisa to discover that she was no longer an outstanding beauty. It wasn't that she'd changed, just that Hollywood was filled with women every bit as lovely as herself. Every time she went out, she saw dozens of women as pretty, if not prettier than she was. Tall girls, petite girls, all gliding gracefully along like models, their golden limbs gleaming, their blonde, brunette or red hair floating proudly behind.

She began to feel very ordinary, and understood Dick's advice not to wear make-up. At least this made her different from the others, who all looked as if they'd spent hours in front of the mirror.

When she met Roma Novatora, she understood what it must feel like to be plain.

The day Lisa moved into the apartment, Lally gave her a key before rushing off to work, so Lisa was left alone and had just finished unpacking when she heard the door slam and went out to say hello. She hadn't met Gloria or Roma yet.

A tall, statuesque girl had come in and was standing disconsolately in the centre of the room. Lisa gasped. She had never seen anyone so incredibly lovely. At least six feet tall, her figure was remarkable: large, high breasts, the nipples prominent through her fluffy white angora sweater, above an unbelievably narrow waist. Smooth, long hips arched outwards under a short red pleated skirt and her long bare legs were as smooth and glossy as marble. She jumped when she saw the newcomer. Lisa approached smiling, extending her hand.

'Hello, I'm Lisa Angelis. It's nice to meet you.'

'Hi, Roma Novatora.' The handshake was surprisingly limp and she didn't return Lisa's smile. Her face was as perfect as her figure, with wide, deep violet eyes surrounded by a thick tangle of lashes and a fine straight nose. Her glossy black hair was cut short and lay on the nape of her long white neck like feathers. Lisa felt overshadowed, small and insignificant beside this extravagant and glorious-looking woman. She also felt depressed. What chance had she of making good in films beside someone like Roma Novatura?

'You settled in yet?' She had a surprisingly dull, low-pitched voice.

'Just about. Would you like some coffee? I just put the kettle on.'

'No, thanks. I'd prefer something stronger. I just got dumped, lost my job.' She took a bottle of spirits and a glass from out of a pine cupboard and poured herself a drink.

'I'm sorry to hear that.'

'It happens!' Roma shrugged her perfect shoulders. 'It's not the first time. Tomorrow, I'll find something else.'

'I hope so,' said Lisa sympathetically. Roma threw herself into a chair and stared into space, her lovely violet eyes strangely expressionless. She didn't speak and after a while, Lisa said, 'Where are you going to find another job? I need one myself.'

'What sort?'

Now it was Lisa's turn to shrug. 'Any sort,' she said.

'Waitressing's best if you need time off. You can always get someone to cover. That's what I'm going to look for next. Office work's a drag, even though the pay's better. Too much hassle.' She returned to staring into space for a full five minutes. Suddenly she looked up and said, 'I've got an idea. If we could get a job in the same place, we could cover for each other.'

'That'd be great,' Lisa said enthusiastically.

'Right. First thing tomorrow, we'll go job-hunting.'

Finding a job was surprisingly easy. Roma, with an air of ruthless determination which Lisa found embarrassing, just went into half a dozen places, from greasy burger bars to expensive-looking restaurants, and asked if they wanted a couple of waitresses. They struck lucky with the sixth – a big, dimly-lit basement coffee shop situated on Hollywood Boulevard and called Dominic's, after the proprietor.

'I don't really need two waitresses,' Dominic said, 'but I've been going through a real bad patch with girls leaving every other week. If I take you both, I'll be overstaffed, but with my luck, someone's bound to take off soon, which means I'll be back to normal.'

A portly, dark-skinned man with a black moustache, he couldn't take his eyes off Roma. Before they left, he introduced them to his mother who was working in the kitchen.

'This is Momma,' he said proudly. 'The best pastry cook in all Hollywood.' Momma looked up from the table where her arms were buried deep in a bowl of flour and smiled at them broadly. 'She don't speak English much,' he went on. 'Here, have one of her chocolate éclairs. But be careful, you could get addicted.'

'It's sheer heaven,' said Lisa through a mouthful of featherlight pastry and fresh cream. Roma had rather churlishly refused, muttering something about them being fattening.

Momma had understood the word 'heaven' and beamed at Lisa.

'I'd appreciate one of you starting tonight,' said Dominic. 'Don't care who it is.'

'I'd like the evening shift,' said Roma with alacrity.

'I don't mind when I work,' Lisa said easily.

She soon regretted being so easygoing. Whilst Roma frequently asked her to take over the evening shift, she never seemed free to help Lisa out in the afternoons. Twice she missed work as an extra because she had to be at Dominic's and Roma couldn't fill in. One day, Lally said, 'Why weren't you there this afternoon?'

'Where?' asked Lisa.

'Warner Brothers. I thought Dick Broadbent called you this morning. They were taking people on for an eight-hour TV epic about the *Titanic*. I got a few days' work, Roma too.'

'I had to be at Dominic's,' said Lisa abjectly.

'You *what*?'

'I had to be at Dominic's,' she repeated. 'My shift's twelve till eight.'

Lally took a deep breath and said in a voice like setting concrete, 'Listen, kid, you don't ever, *ever* miss out on a job in the movies.'

'But I couldn't let Dominic down. He'd have been short-staffed if I hadn't turned up,' Lisa protested.

'Look, kid,' Lally was angry. 'Roma shoulda told you this. Dick, too. If something comes up again, you go. Don't mind who you let down. If it means getting dumped, then okay, you get dumped and you look for another job. Shit, Lisa, you're too soft-hearted by a mile. In this town you look after numero uno. Number one. You gotta be hard, real hard – understand?'

'I suppose so,' Lisa said reluctantly.

The thin-faced, sharply-dressed man had been staring at Lisa for nearly an hour, ever since she'd served him with coffee. From the corner of her eye, she saw his head turn every time she passed. It was three o'clock and customers were thin on the ground.

The trouble with Hollywood was that you couldn't get annoyed when people stared. He might be a famous producer wanting someone for his next film.

When the man gestured for the bill, she took it over to his table.

'Bet you're an actress,' he said, fishing in his pocket for change.

'Every woman here's an actress,' she replied pleasantly. 'Except for Momma in the kitchen.'

'Yeah, but you're special. You got star quality, I can tell. You walk good and you got class.' He looked her up and down openly. 'And a real good body, too.'

Lisa smiled nervously, undecided whether to be flattered or to tell him to go to hell.

'My name's Charlie Gruber. I got my own production company. Art movies is what I do. Like to try out for my next project? It's gonna be a real big number. See, here's my card – *Gruber Productions*.'

As she examined the card, a flicker of excitement ran through her. She'd been discovered!

'How about coming along tomorrow for a screen test?' he asked. 'What's your name, by the way?'

'Lisa Angelis.' She told herself to calm down; he might be testing dozens of girls. 'And I can come tomorrow morning.'

'Fine. Ten o'clock, then. The address is on the card. It ain't far from Paramount. Know where that is?'

'Sure.'

'See ya tomorrow then, Lisa. Ten o'clock.'

When Lisa finished work, she walked slowly back down Hollywood Boulevard to Grauman's Chinese Theatre, the ostentatious pagoda-like building where the stars left their hand- and footprints in the cement-covered courtyard. The brightly-lit streets were as busy as if it were midday; the bars and restaurants were crowded, and several shops were still open and full of customers. Lisa stared down at the hollowed-out prints. Tomorrow she was going for her first real screen test! Some day her name might be as famous as those immortalised here . . .

'I'm going to be a star too,' she vowed. 'I'm already on the first rung of the ladder.'

To her surprise, Gruber Productions was a small, rickety wooden house in a rundown road on the edge of Hollywood, nowhere near Paramount. Her excitement began to ebb as she stared at the blacked-out windows and the shabby door with its peeling paint. Charlie Gruber must have been watching for her, because the door opened and he greeted her jovially. He still wore the same suit, but in the daylight it looked worn and the collar of his shirt was frayed.

'Come in, Lisa. We're all set.'

Who 'we' were, she never discovered, because Charlie seemed to be alone in the house.

He led her into a large room at the front where a camera was set up in one corner, focused on a threadbare brocade-covered Regency sofa opposite. A dusty, unshaded lightbulb hung from the cracked ceiling. Charlie said, 'There's a rack of clothes over there. If you'd like to get changed, we'll begin.'

A row of flimsy, diaphanous garments, mainly black and red and full of pulled threads and ladders, hung off a crooked wooden rail. Lisa didn't know whether to laugh or cry. She stood in the doorway and made no move towards the clothes. 'What's your new film to be called?' she asked.

Charlie Gruber was fiddling with the camera. He looked up innocently and said, 'I haven't decided on a title yet.'

'Can I see the script?'

'I'm still working on it.'

'Where's my dialogue then?'

'I ain't testing for sound.' They stared at each other for several seconds without speaking. Charlie said, 'You getting changed or not?'

'Not.'

'I'll give you a hundred bucks. It'll only take fifteen minutes.'

'Get stuffed.'

Lisa walked down the dusty corridor and out the front door. She didn't bother saying goodbye.

'Do girls ever fall for it?' Lisa asked Lally in a whisper.

They were sitting on two little pull-down seats at the back of the cinema where Lally worked. The house had just filled up for the eight o'clock show and Lally only had to get up and show the occasional latecomers to their seats. Lisa had come straight from Dominic's, anxious to talk about her 'screen test'.

'Yeh,' said Lally. 'Some do – I suppose about one in ten. I wish I'd known, Lisa, I would've told you not to go. Charlie Gruber's famous as a con-artist.'

Lally had still been in bed when Lisa left that morning so there hadn't been any opportunity to tell her.

'Oh well,' sighed Lisa. 'I really thought he was genuine. But then, you only learn from experience, as my mother used to say.'

'My mom used to say something like that too,' grinned Lally.

Lisa looked in the mirror a final time. As she pulled her belt a notch tighter, her heart lifted, as it did every morning. After all, today might be the day when fate would smile. She picked up Victoria and kissed her, before laying her carefully back on the pillow. 'I've been here seven months,' she told the doll. 'And the longer I'm here, the closer that day comes.'

26

Roma's long lovely body was draped disconsolately over an armchair. From time to time she took a deep, shuddering sigh which everyone affected to ignore.

On the floor, Gloria lay with her face covered in a mudpack, a towel wrapped round her head, turbanwise, and her legs resting on a chair. 'The blood rushes to the head,' she declared. 'It's good for the brain.'

'What brain?' demanded Lally, looking up from the Sunday paper. She watched as Gloria gingerly placed a slice of cucumber on each eye. 'My God – if your customers could see you now, they'd pay you to go away.'

'Zip it, Cooper,' Gloria replied good-naturedly.

Despite living in the same house, Lisa never saw much of Gloria. In her early thirties, she was a tiny, fragile woman with a frail, waif-like beauty. Her enormous pale-blue eyes and pearly skin were in startling contrast to her autumn-leaf red hair which she wore in a bouffant style, cut just below the ears. However, the slight and delicate figure which Gloria presented hid a tough, fighting spirit and a wisecracking, cheerful personality which took people by surprise when they first met her.

Gloria made no secret of the fact she was a call girl. 'I make more in a day than you three make together in a whole week,' she boasted to Lisa on one of the few occasions they were alone together.

'Yes, but—' Lisa didn't go on, not wishing to be offensive.

'Yes, but what?' Gloria had laughed. 'You sell your labour, I sell my body and in this wicked world my body's worth more.'

'Yes, but—' Lisa began again.

'Wasn't it some famous Englishwoman who said, "I just lie back and think of England"? Well, I do the same but think of money. And if you say "Yes, but" again, I'll scream.'

'Yes, but—' said Lisa.

Gloria screamed.

'I'm sorry, Gloria. It's just that – oh, I don't know. It seems sort of, well . . .'

'Debauched?' offered Gloria.

Lisa laughed. 'I give up. Anyway, it's none of my business.'

'Y'know, Lisa, I've been in Hollywood ten whole years. Came here all bright-eyed and bushy-tailed and did well my first coupla years.' Gloria gave a rueful smile. 'Musicals – I started out a dancer and got a whole heapa parts, each one bigger and better. I was making fairly good money when – wham, bang! Suddenly, no one wants musicals no more. No one wants *me* no more, along with Howard Keel, Kathryn Grayson, Betty Grable – folks like that.' She stopped and lit a cigarette from the one she'd nearly finished.

Lisa murmured, 'Gee, I'm sorry.'

Gloria waved the cigarette furiously. 'Don't be. I can't stand people being sorry for me. After all, I was in good company. Anyway, I contemplated going home, back to Pittsburgh, but only for about sixty seconds. I thought, "Hell, no. I came here to make my fortune, and by Jeez, I'll make it." By then, I'd got used to the dough and didn't fancy going back to being a waitress or working in some crummy shop with the proprietor breathing down my neck. I had a friend, married, who told me about this agency, an escort agency, really high-class. She only worked one afternoon a week – Wednesdays – to pad the housekeeping out. Her husband never seemed to notice they were eating best steak all of a sudden.' Gloria smiled sardonically. 'Or perhaps he did and kept mum. After all, they say the way to a man's heart's through his stomach. When she told me, I kept saying "yes, but", just like you . . .'

'But you gave in,' said Lisa.

'Saw sense, more like. It was easier than I'd thought. The agency only sends us girls along to clients in first-class hotels, never to private addresses, like some do.' Gloria looked at Lisa, a half-smile on her face. 'If you're interested, I'll introduce you.'

Lisa shuddered. 'No thanks,' she said quickly. 'I'll stick to waitressing.' Afterwards, she felt ashamed of the shudder. She would never have admitted it to anyone, but sometimes, when she thought about what Gloria did, she found her imagination running away with her in a manner that was not altogether unpleasant.

Lally said, 'Are you gonna eat that cucumber when you've finished?'

'Yeah,' said Gloria. 'It's good for the bowels.'

'Oh, shut up you two,' Roma said petulantly.

'Why?' demanded Lally. 'You don't need to listen.'

'I can't help but listen.'

'What d'you wanna talk about then?' asked Lally.

Roma shrugged. 'Nothing.'

'You expect us to just sit here all quiet and talk about nothing – on a Sunday morning, too?'

Roma glowered at Lally and didn't answer. Her lovely pink mouth was sulky. Whatever mechanism in the brain caused people to laugh or smile was deficient in Roma. Her magnificent good looks brought no happiness. She was eternally sour, as if a crabby, twisted old woman existed inside the body of an angel.

'Any of you got movie work on tomorrow?' she asked suddenly.

'No,' the three other women chorused quickly. Lisa wouldn't have told her if she had, not after that time she'd pre-empted her with Paramount. She guessed Gloria and Lally felt the same. Roma had no shame when it came to pushing for work.

'I haven't had movie work in weeks,' she complained. 'And my last two jobs were as a corpse.'

'You'd be good at that,' said Lally. 'You'd make a perfect corpse.'

Roma stared at her, frowning slightly. Devoid of humour herself, she was never sure when people were joking. Suddenly, she unfolded herself out of the chair and left the room.

'Has she gone?' Gloria lifted the cucumber off her right eye.

'Lally really hurt her feelings,' said Lisa.

'She ain't got any feelings, 'cept nasty ones,' said Lally indignantly. 'I don't mind hurting nasty feelings. If she had nice feelings, I wouldn't dream of hurting them. What Roma needs is a live firework stuffing up her ass, then she might find she's got feelings.'

'Yeah, but they'd be even nastier,' said Gloria. 'Hey, someone, light me a smoke quick. I'm gasping down here.'

'Lally!' Lisa remonstrated. 'That's an awful thing to say.'

'Awful but true,' Lally answered. She poked a cigarette in Gloria's mouth and lit it.

'If you drop that match on me, I'll sue,' warned Gloria. 'This mud could be highly flammable.'

'Actually, I feel sorry for Roma,' Lally said. 'I mean, she's got that fantastic face and figure, yet she'll never get anywhere in the movies.'

'Why not?' Lisa asked curiously.

'She ain't got no screen presence, that's why,' Lally answered crossly, as though poor Roma had done something terribly wrong. She went on, 'Look at Judy Garland, f'r instance, or Shelley Winters, or Marilyn Monroe – shit, I could reel off a hundred names. All o' them got screen presence in abundance. They glow, radiate, though they're nowhere near as good-looking as Roma. She's got nothing inside, nothing to give. I wasn't joking when I said she'd make a perfect corpse, 'cos on screen, she looks dead.'

'It's come to the pitch,' said Gloria from the floor, 'that she's even finding it hard to get work as an extra. In a crowd, she stands out as looking downright glum.'

'Gee, that's really awful,' Lisa said.

'I mean, there's a limit to the times you can be a corpse,' said Lally with a wicked grin. 'Folks'd start laughing in the most serious movies if every time some woman got murdered it turned out to be Roma.'

Gloria began to giggle. 'Don't make me laugh. I'll crack my mask.'

'Why are you lying down there, anyway?' demanded Lally. 'You lie down so much in your job, I'd've thought you'd prefer sitting when you had the opportunity.'

Apart from Gloria, the women led a remarkably chaste existence, considering they lived in what was probably the most explicitly sensual town in the world. Lally had a serious boyfriend back home in New Jersey and once a month, he flew over to spend the weekend with her and sometimes she went back to see him and her parents.

'Frank's really worried I'll two-time him,' she told Lisa. 'He thinks Hollywood's a den of iniquity. I said not to worry. I told him I didn't have the energy to get laid. Lots of guys come onto me in the Plaza, but by 2 a.m. all I want to do is sleep. Alone.'

'I'm sure that put Frank's mind at rest,' said Lisa dryly, though she understood what Lally meant. Her own days were full, from morning until night. Each morning she took some sort of class in a studio along with anything from ten to a hundred other men and women. a dollar an hour learning how to dance – both ballet and tap – or how to develop her singing voice. Wednesdays she went to a gymnasium to work out. After her shift finished, some nights she went straight to a writing and acting group Brett Charwood had introduced her to, where aspiring writers brought scripts for aspiring actors to read, and other nights she went to the cinema. It was important to keep abreast of the current movie scene.

Every few weeks there was movie or television work. Clad in a skimpy tunic and wearing a silver wig, she'd spent two days frolicking over plastic grass hills as an inhabitant of Utopia, and half a day as a squaw fleeing from a burning wigwam. Her voice was hoarse after a day screaming, 'Off with their heads!' in a film about the French Revolution. So far, it had all been crowd work, though on two other occasions she'd been asked to stay behind, along with some other extras, because a few faces were needed in the background of the next shot.

Lally called this being a first-class extra as opposed to being second-class. 'There's a whole heapa difference between being one in a thousand and one in ten,' she claimed. 'Like that day we were in the lift. It's how you get noticed.' On filming days, the classes and the coffee shop were forgotten and Lisa was up at the crack of dawn and at the studio for seven o'clock when the cameras would, hopefully, roll.

One morning in June, Dick Broadbent telephoned, his voice squeaky with excitement. 'I got two lots of good news. Y'know that movie, *Black Corner*?'

'Never heard of it,' said Lisa.

'Christ, Lisa, you were in it! The one with the lift.'

'I remember, but it wasn't called that. It was called—'

'Don't matter,' he interrupted impatiently. 'They must've changed the name. Anyway, it ain't been released yet, but someone must have seen the rushes and Disney want you for their next production. It ain't a speaking part, but you'll get billing.'

'*Disney!* Gee, Dick, that's incredible. *Disney!*' Lisa sat down in the nearest chair, her legs weak. 'What sort of part is it?'

'A fairy o' some sort. The woman from their casting office said you suited your name, 'cos you looked like an angel. Lisa Angelis, the angel,' Dick said with a giggle. 'Anyway, they're gonna fix up a meeting pretty soon.'

'Oh, Dick! I could die with happiness.'

'I ain't finished yet,' Dick said. 'You heard of a writer, Cahil O'Daly? He's Irish,' he added, somewhat unnecessarily.

She remembered that Harry Greenbaum had stocked some of his books, though she'd never read any. 'Didn't he get the Nobel Prize for Literature a long time ago?' she asked.

'The very one! He's about a hundred and fifty now and in town 'cos they're making a movie from one of his books, *The Opportunist*. Thing is, angel, guess where the beginning part of this book is set?'

'I've no idea,' confessed Lisa.

'Liverpool, England!' cried Dick triumphantly. 'And there's a really plum part for an actress, only short, but lot's of women'll be after it. You've got a headstart, coming from Liverpool. In fact, I got you priority. Tomorrow afternoon, the Cascade Hotel in the Hollywood Hills, we're seeing this O'Daly guy. He got casting approval and wants to look everybody over.'

'What should I wear, Dick?' Lisa suddenly felt nervous.

'Something plain and simple. This woman was a servant, dead poor, so there's no use going all jazzed up in diamonds and stuff. You got anything black?'

'If I haven't, I'll buy something,' promised Lisa.

'Pick you up at one o'clock. Best to have your agent on hand, in case they want to sign you up on the spot.'

Gloria loaned her a simple black dress with a cowl neck and a soft flared skirt.

'I look like a waif and stray,' she decided when she was ready. Lally had woven her hair into a long loose plait. Even Roma proved cooperative for once and let her borrow a pair of flat black shoes. All she carried was a small purse and her portrait folio.

Dick called for her in his car. He'd had the pedals built up so his short legs could reach them, beneath a specially-adapted high seat.

'Do I look all right?' she asked when she climbed in beside him.

'Fine. You don't look poor, but then he can't expect you to turn up in rags.' He looked excited. 'There's a copy of the book in the glove compartment – I bought it yesterday. Seems a bit boring to me. In fact, I only read the beginning, but then I don't expect anyone ever got the Nobel Prize for writing something really interesting.'

'I've already read it,' said Lisa. 'I went to the library straight after you phoned. I quite liked it, though it got a bit wordy towards the end. I think he philosophised too much.'

'You prob'ly gotta do that,' Dick mused. 'To getta prize.'

As he drove out of Hollywood, they discussed the novel. It was clearly autobiographical. Cahil O'Daly had been a seaman as a young man, rising to become ship's captain. The book was a saga of his travels and the women he'd loved, the first being Mary, a poor worn-out woman, older than himself, who'd worked in the seamen's hostel where he'd stayed in Liverpool at the turn of the century. The writer had spread his favours far and wide, but his first love affair was the most tragic and moving. As Dick said, although small, it was a plum part.

Last night Lisa had felt homesick, reading about her home town. 'I used to play on the Dock Road when I was a child,' she told Dick. 'It was strange to think he'd been down the same streets as I have.'

She'd gone asleep thinking about Kitty and Chaucer Street. Dick squeezed her hand. 'Keep that sad look, kiddo, and he'll hire you on the spot.'

True to its name, the Cascade Hotel had bright blue water cascading down the steep, rocky gardens that fronted it. In a corner of the plush reception area a tinkling fountain was surrounded by several palm trees.

'He's in the penthouse,' said Dick. 'There's a special elevator at the end of the row.'

'Which studio is doing the movie?' Lisa asked as they rode up in the spacious lift.

'It's a small independent company,' explained Dick, 'set up a few years back by Busby Van Dolen, the writer, to produce and direct his own movies. He's only made three so far and they didn't earn much dough – they ain't commercial enough – though they got a really great reception from the critics. They call him another Orson Welles.'

The lift stopped and the door opened on a small square lobby with a peach-coloured carpet and half a dozen chairs. There was a six-foot display of imitation grasses in one corner.

Dick pressed the buzzer on the white-painted door twice. He was clearly enjoying himself. On the way he'd told Lisa it was a long time since he'd accompanied one of his clients to an appointment.

An elderly man opened the door. Dick coughed importantly. 'Hi, Mr O'Daly. I'm Dick Broadbent and this is—'

'Mr O'Daly is not feeling very well at the moment. I'm afraid you'll have to wait.'

They were still waiting an hour later and Dick began to get angry. 'He shouldn't ask for casting approval if he's not up to it,' he complained.

Lisa patted his tiny, gnarled hand. 'Calm down,' she soothed, though she was getting worried herself. She'd told Dominic she'd only be a couple of hours late. At this rate, the tea-time rush would be on by the time she got there.

At two o'clock, the lift doors opened and two girls came in. They knocked on the door and Dick stiffened, ready to leap off his chair if they were admitted. 'You'll have to wait,' the girls were told.

Half an hour later, the old man reappeared and motioned to Dick and Lisa to enter.

'Mr O'Daly is in the bedroom.'

They were led through a sitting room crammed with flowers and into a large bedroom. The Venetian blinds on the windows were closed and the room was in semi-darkness. Lisa could just about see an elderly man sitting in a wheelchair beside one of the windows, his eyes shut. He seemed unaware of the visitors. The room smelt like a hospital and she noticed the table beside the bed was full of medicine bottles.

Dick nudged her forward. Lisa took a deep breath and went over and stood in front of the old man, looking down at him. She'd never seen anyone so old. His face was criss-crossed with deep, jagged wrinkles.

She turned and cast a questioning look at Dick. What was she supposed to do? Dick loudly cleared his throat and to her relief the old man opened his eyes. It was clearly an effort; the lids were creased and heavy. He looked her up and down briefly, then the lids sank down again, as if it had all been too much. He mumbled something in a voice that seemed to come from a long way away.

'I'm sorry?' she stammered. His words made no sense.

'He said you're the wrong physical type,' declared a voice.

She turned, startled, unaware that there was anyone else in the room. A tall, bearded man wearing thick horn-rimmed glasses rose from a chair in the far corner.

'Busby Van Dolen.' He strolled over and shook Lisa's hand firmly.

'Gee, Mr Van Dolen, I didn't realise you were there,' said Dick. 'I'm really pleased to meet you.'

'And I'm pleased to meet you, too. Dick Broadbent, isn't it? I've heard your name mentioned a lot round Hollywood.'

Dick flushed with pleasure as the two shook hands. Cahil O'Daly began to speak again. Busby Van Dolen listened, then said to Lisa, 'He says the part calls for a small, fair woman and you are a tall, dark woman. You're too young, as well.'

'She could always wear a wig,' said Dick eagerly. 'And she's older than she looks.'

The writer shook his head firmly. 'Sorry, she looks far too exotic, I can see that for myself.' He began to usher them out of the room. Lisa turned to say goodbye, but Cahil O'Daly seemed fast asleep.

In the sitting room, Busby Van Dolen shouted, 'Rudy, are there any more girls waiting?'

'Half a dozen.' Rudy appeared out of the kitchen. Seeing him again, Lisa thought he looked almost youthful compared to his employer.

'Show them in, two at a time. Stay there, will you? Make sure he keeps awake.'

'Sure thing, Mr Van Dolen.' The man opened the main door and ushered two girls into the bedroom.

'Why's he doin' this?' demanded Dick. 'I mean, wanting to approve the cast when he can hardly see.'

'It's very important to him. The people in the book were real; he wants them to look right.' Busby Van Dolen gestured towards a group of armchairs. 'Sit down, I'd like a word with you both.' Dick took a sidelong look at Lisa and winked excitedly.

'So, you're Lisa Angelis.' The director regarded her keenly. 'May I have a look at your portfolio?'

'Of course.' She handed over the brown envelope. As he glanced through the large, glossy photographs, she watched him. He was probably in his early to mid-thirties and anything but handsome. His nose was too long for one thing and his black eyebrows were almost as bushy as Mr Greenbaum's, yet he had an agreeable, lazy charm she found immensely attractive.

'Hmm, very nice,' he said, pushing the photos back in the envelope. 'You done much work in Hollywood?'

'She just got a big part in the next Disney production,' Dick butted in eagerly.

The writer's eyes danced with humour. 'Does that mean when I've got the backing together for *The Opportunist*, Lisa won't be free?'

'Well, it's not all *that* big a part,' Dick said hurriedly.

'Good, because I'm seriously considering her. Have you read the book?' He turned to Lisa. She nodded. 'Good. There's two or three parts I can see you in.' He stood up. 'I better go back to Cahil.' He shook hands with them both again. 'I'll definitely be in touch.'

'Lisa, we've made it! You're gonna be a star, I feel it in my bones.' Dick virtually danced back to the car. Despite his age and his infirmity, he was as sprightly as a teenager. 'I knew it the minute you came into my office. You've got a sort of aura. Jesus! A Busby Van Dolen movie! Y'know, the biggest stars fall over themselves to act for him, even though it means a big drop in pay.'

He chatted all the way home, pointing out the homes of the stars, great colonnaded mansions with vast lawns and shining limousines standing outside. Lisa hardly listened. She was mentally going through *The Opportunist*, trying to think which parts Busby Van Dolen could see her in. It wasn't until Dick said, 'And that's where Ralph Layton lives,' that she looked up and saw a small grey turreted castle. The edge of a tennis court was just visible round the back and someone in white ran over and picked up a ball. The person disappeared before she could make out if it was Ralph.

There was no one in when Dick dropped Lisa off at her apartment. She pirouetted across the living room and fell giggling onto a chair. 'I'm so happy, I could *cry!*' If only there was someone in to share her news with. The coffee shop would be a real anti-climax. She felt more like going to a dance class or a workout where she could put all this bubbling happiness into sheer, physical hard work.

She went into her room and changed into a white silk blouse, a short denim skirt and tennis shoes. A few months ago, she'd stopped wearing a bra and, turning sideways, felt a pleasant thrill, seeing her nipples stand out through the thin material. It was like walking round half-naked. Unplaiting her hair, she combed it loose, parting it in the middle so that it hung in thick brown swathes framing her face.

'Cripes, Lisa mate,' she said in a broad Cockney accent. 'You don't 'arf look a treat, darlin'.' She cocked her head sideways. 'You've definitely got that glow Lally talked about.' Her mirrored reflection glowed back. It was as if a candle were lit inside her head, illuminating the brown-gold eyes, the skin, the whole being of the woman who stared back at her.

Reluctantly, she picked up her bag. She'd better go into work or Dominic would think she wasn't coming.

Suddenly she heard a noise. There was water running in the bathroom. Someone was home, after all. She knocked on the bathroom door. 'Hi, it's Lisa. Who goes there?'

There was a pause before Gloria answered in a scarcely audible voice, 'It's me.'

It wasn't like Gloria to sound so subdued. 'You okay?' asked Lisa.

The door of the bathroom opened and Gloria came out, clasping the collar of a towelling robe to her throat, her head bound in a towel. She had an angry purple bruise on her chin.

'What happened?' Lisa gasped.

'I don't want to talk about it,' said Gloria abruptly. She walked into the sitting room and lit a cigarette. 'No I've changed my mind – I do.'

'What happened?' Lisa asked again, gently.

'Pour me a drink, will you? Something strong and neat.'

Lisa poured out two brandies and handed one to the older woman, who swallowed hers in one go.

'Gee, that feels good!' She sank back in the chair. Without make-up, her face looked drawn and haggard, her white skin waxen. 'I had a client last night. He seemed a nice guy – at first. We had dinner in the hotel restaurant and went up to his room, only to find his friend was there too. I told them, I never do two guys. Never! Some girls don't mind, but I do.' She held out her glass. 'Fill me up, kid.'

As Lisa went to get the bottle, Gloria went on, 'By then, the door was locked and I didn't have much say in the matter.'

'You mean – they both . . . ?'

'Yeah.' Gloria managed a weak smile. 'I got this bruise – and a couple of others – somewhere in the middle of the argument.' She let the collar of her robe fall back to reveal purple marks on her neck. 'Reckon they both would have been at it all night if I hadn't gone into the bathroom and locked myself in. They kept hammering on the door, but I stayed there till the maid came this morning.'

'Gee, Gloria, what an awful thing to happen.'

'Isn't it just?' She grinned suddenly. 'Still, it's one of the hazards of the job. Serves me right, don't it, Goody Two-Shoes?'

Lisa didn't answer. She was staring at Gloria, frowning. She'd suddenly had the most amazing idea.

'You know the part I went for this morning? The one I borrowed your black dress for?'

'Gee, Lisa, I forgot to ask how you got on. How *did* you get on?'

'I didn't get it, but it'd be perfect for you.'

'Y'think so?' Gloria's eyes widened.

'Are you up to an interview?'

'I'd get up from my deathbed for a part. Who wouldn't?'

'It calls for a little drab woman in her late twenties, early thirties.'

'Gee thanks, Lisa, you've made my day.'

'Shut up. Don't put any make-up on, not even on the bruises, and wear the black dress you lent me.' Lisa bit her lip. 'The only problem is your hair, It looks too bright and glamorous.'

'No problem,' said Gloria. She pulled the towel off her head to reveal short mouse-coloured curls.

Lisa watched the taxi draw away. Gloria, looking even more fragile without her red wig, glanced out of the rear window and gave the thumbs up sign. There was no doubt about it, thought Lisa. In Hollywood, every cloud really *did* have a silver lining!

The telephone rang and for a moment, she considered not answering in case it was Dominic wanting to know where she was. It would be easier to make excuses once she got there. On the other hand, it might be Dick with another part. Who knows who else might have seen the rushes for *Black Corner*? Billy Wilder or John Huston.

The caller was a woman whose voice was familiar. She often rang and always asked for Gloria. Lisa said she'd be gone at least two hours.

'Would you mind leaving her a message? Tell her Mr Baptiste is in town. He's staying at the Belltower.' The woman phrased her words carefully. 'They've been the greatest friends for a long time and he'd like very much to see her again.'

'I'll leave the message by the phone,' Lisa promised. 'I'm going out myself right now.'

After she'd replaced the receiver, she stared down at the paper in her hand. Mr Baptiste, the Belltower. He sounded more in tune with her present mood than the coffee shop. Her mouth curved into a smile as she crumpled the paper up and pushed it in her bag.

She knocked on the door and a deep voice said, 'Come in.'

A slim, silver-haired man was sitting at a desk writing. He looked up as she entered and gave a start. 'I wasn't expecting anyone just yet. The agency said Gloria—'

'She's not well,' Lisa said softly.

He stood up, slowly, gracefully. Lisa closed the door behind her and leaned against it. The man was watching her intently. His face flushed and she saw desire leap into his eyes. His long thin hands tightened at his side. He took a step forward.

'Stay,' she ordered and he stopped as she threw her bag onto the floor and began to undo the buttons of her white blouse, slowly, tantalizingly, until her small, perfect breasts were revealed in full.

'Jesus!' he moaned, though he still didn't move. Lisa's eyes never left his as she unzipped her skirt, easing it gradually, lazily over her narrow hips. The man began to shake as she languorously reached for her panties and pulled them off. She stood before him naked and dizzy with desire.

She walked over to the bed and lay down, her body stretched out, ready, eager, waiting for him.

'Now,' she said.

Next morning, she found an envelope pushed under her bedroom door containing two one-hundred dollar bills. The scribbled note with it read:

'I got your part. You got mine. I reckon we're quits. Love, Gloria.'

27

'Hi Dick, it's Lisa. Any news yet?'

'You know I would've called if there was,' he said.

'It's months since we saw him,' Lisa complained. 'He promised he'd get in touch – perhaps he told all the girls the same thing.'

'It's only four weeks, angel, and you've called every day since. He said he had to raise the dough. Busby Van Dolen's not the sort to say things he don't mean. Anyone else and I'd take what they said with a whole shovelful of salt, but not Busby. He's a really decent guy.'

'I suppose so,' she said reluctantly.

'You still practising your accents?'

'Sure thing.' There were several parts in *The Opportunist* she might be asked to play and she was being taught how to speak with various foreign accents; French, Italian, Arabic.

'Can I ring off now, angel, and get on with some work?' said Dick, 'You ain't my only client, y'know. I got hundreds on my books.'

'Liar!' she retorted good-naturedly. Nevertheless, she said goodbye and put the receiver down, resolving to stop giving Dick a hard time over Busby Van Dolen. If he was going to call, he'd call, and there was nothing Dick could do about it.

On the wide screen, the dust-covered Cadillac screeched to a halt in front of an isolated roadside café. The two bank robbers got out and looked furtively around. One of them slipped over on the muddy forecourt and the audience burst out laughing. Once inside, the men sat in a corner and began whispering to each other.

Lally approached them, looking pert and pretty, a white apron over her gingham dress and a cap perched precariously on her long blonde wig.

'You wanna order?' she enquired.

The two men looked up, startled.

'What?' one of them demanded.

'You're in a restaurant. We serve food here. You wanna order some?' The audience tittered.

The two men looked at each other. 'I guess so,' one said.

'Huh! Don' do me no favours,' Lally replied sarcastically. 'It's just that it sez FOOD outside, and generally that's why folks come in here. To eat!'

'I'll have a coffee. Black.'

'Me, too.'

Lally made a face. 'Huh! Jack'll be able to sell his truck and buy a bicycle if we get more customers like you.'

'That's it,' hissed Lally as the audience laughed again.

'You were fantastic,' whispered Lisa.

'Y'really think so?' said Lally modestly.

'Shush!' A woman in the row in front turned on them irritably.

'Let's go outside and celebrate,' said Gloria. 'We can always see the rest of the movie some other time.'

It was Lally's first-ever speaking part. The film had been made last year and only just released. She'd already been offered two other parts on the strength of this movie, but was disappointed that they were almost identical to the character she'd just played.

'They've sent me scripts for both,' she complained a few minutes later when they were sitting in a bar, 'and I wear almost the same clothes and speak almost the same dialogue. I wish I had enough courage to turn 'em down.'

'Why?' asked Lisa incredulously.

'Because she'll get typecast, that's why,' said Gloria. 'And after a while, nobody will be able to see her in a different part. She'll be a tough, wisecracking waitress for the rest of her movie life.'

Lally shrugged. 'Oh well, if that happens I suppose I can always go home, get married and have a heap o' kids instead.'

It was a Saturday night and as usual the coffee house was packed. Every table was full and Momma's pastries were being eaten faster than she could make them. Lisa felt as if her feet had swollen to twice their size. She hadn't sat down for a minute since midday. Fortunately, it was nearly eight o'clock and almost time for her shift to end. Tonight, she'd be more glad than usual to get away. There was a man on one of her tables who'd been ordering coffee for nearly two hours now, and every time she took his order, he stroked her hand and insisted he take her to dinner when she finished. Why couldn't some men take no for an answer? she thought irritably. Roma had come in to work a couple of hours ago and looked unusually animated – for Roma.

'I got this really good job,' she said to Lisa as they walked back to the coffee station together. 'On a TV games show.'

It was nearly half an hour before they had an opportunity to speak again. 'What sort of job?' Lisa asked.

'I have to present the prizes. The programme's called *Beautiful Dreams*. There's a new series starting in a couple of months' time.'

'I don't think I've seen it.' Lisa rushed off to take more orders.

Later, Roma said, 'If I go down well, they're going to sign me up for a year. The pay's really good. It means I can quit this job. Jesus, I won't be sorry. My feet are killing me.'

'Best of luck,' said Lisa. 'I wish I could quit, too. *My* feet are already dead.'

Five more minutes to go. She signalled to another waitress that it was time to take over her tables. The girl made an agonised face. Lisa served her final order, putting the coffees down with visible relief. The man who'd been pestering her caught her skirt as she walked past. 'Another coffee, miss.'

'I'm off-duty,' she snapped. 'You'll have to ask someone else.'

'In that case, how about dinner?'

She ignored him and dodged back through the crowded tables.

'Excuse me.' A man stood up to bar her way.

'I'm sorry . . .' she began. 'Why, Mr Van Dolen!'

He stood looking down at her, smiling through his thick horn-rimmed spectacles. He wore a shabby corduroy suit and a check shirt. 'I've been waiting for you to serve me for nearly half an hour,' he groaned.

'That's not my table.' It was Roma's and she was notoriously slow.

'What time do you finish?'

'I already have. As of this minute, I'm gone.'

To her surprise, he followed her back to the counter and waited whilst she collected her bag.

'Fancy something to eat?' he asked.

Even more surprised, she said, 'I wouldn't mind a hamburger, but somewhere close, please, else you'll have to carry me.'

Smiling, he said, 'I wouldn't mind that.'

Lisa felt a pleasant warmth run through her body.

He was holding the door open for her to leave, when a middle-aged couple entered. 'Why, BD!' the woman cried. 'How are you, darling?' She kissed him on the cheek. The man patted him on the shoulder and said jovially, 'How's things, BD?'

'Stella! Mike! Things are coming along fine.'

'Why BD?' Lisa asked when they were outside.

'My initials, minus the V,' he said. 'You can call me that or Busby. No more Mr Van Dolen, if you please. After all, we're going to be working together pretty soon.'

'Are we?' That must mean he'd raised the money and was ready to start on *The Opportunist*. Suddenly, she didn't feel tired any more.

He ushered her into a nearby hamburger bar. 'Two burgers,' he told the waitress who came up for their order. 'Do you want a coffee?' He turned to Lisa.

She shuddered. 'I never want to see a cup of coffee again,' she said. 'I'll have a beer, please.'

'I like women who drink beer,' he said approvingly after the waitress had left.

'How did you know where I worked?' she asked, adding hastily, 'Assuming you weren't there by accident.'

'Dick Broadbent told me. Unfortunately, he didn't tell me where to sit.' His crooked, easygoing features relaxed into a smile. Smiling came easily to him. Behind the thick glasses, his brown eyes shone with an amused twinkle, as if he found the world and everything in it a never ending source of enjoyment. Even if he hadn't been BD, the famous writer and producer-director of highly regarded movies, Lisa would still have felt thrilled to be with him. He probably charmed everyone like this. As if to prove her point and emphasise his popularity, the door opened and a man shouted, 'Hi, BD. I was just passing and thought it was you. How's things?'

'Coming along fine, Doug,' Busby shouted back.

After the waitress had brought their food, Lisa asked, 'How soon are we going to be working together?'

'Keen, are you?' he asked, grinning.

'You bet!' she said enthusiastically.

'In about a month, I reckon. I booked the studio for two months' time, the outdoor shooting's first. How about your Disney job?'

'That'll only take a couple of days,' she replied. 'Next week I'm a nurse in a Civil War movie. I'll be on screen about half a second.'

'Seems like I got hold of you just in time,' he smiled. 'Another few months and you'd have been snapped up by some big studio.'

She didn't answer, but wondered if he was seeing everyone in *The Opportunist*, or just her. She desperately hoped it was just her. Gloria, who had a far more important part, hadn't mentioned him. Which reminded her, she didn't know what part she was going to play. As if reading her thoughts, he said, 'I've got a script roughed out. I think you'd be perfect for the Italian girl, Catarina. Perhaps we could meet tomorrow and I'll give you a copy?'

She looked at him directly. He stared back, a challenging expression on his face. She could meet the challenge or back away. He wasn't the sort to withdraw the part if she turned him down. It was up to her. She felt her heart quicken with excitement as she said, 'What time?'

To her surprise, he closed his eyes briefly and she thought she heard him give a soft sigh of relief. 'Midday,' he answered, 'I'll pick you up and we'll make a day of it. Go to the beach, have lunch.'

She gave him her address and said, 'I'm looking forward to it.'

'So am I.'

He was the best company she'd ever known. They went to Little Venice and ate lunch in a ramshackle wooden restaurant overlooking the crowded beach. They watched a group of well-muscled, suntanned men working out and pretending to ignore the onlookers, mainly women who surrounded them and cheered and whistled their every move. Teenagers sat clustered around radios listening to pop music and there was a serious-looking football match going on over to the left. In the midst of all this noise and activity, dozens of people lay prone on the sand sunbathing, oblivious to everything except the need to get a tan. Far beyond, where the pale blue cloudless sky touched the sea, tiny, whitemasted yachts were dotted, apparently stranded on the still turquoise water, and the faint drone of motor boats could be heard as they ploughed through the water, dragging water-skiers in their cream foamy wake.

Lisa stared at the sun-worshippers enviously. 'I'd love a tan,' she said, 'but I can't get into sunbathing. I get bored in five minutes.'

'So do I,' said Busby.

That was about the tenth thing they'd agreed on. In fact, they hadn't disagreed on anything yet. They liked the same authors, the same actors and the same movies. Lisa went along with Busby that *The Maltese Falcon* was the best thriller ever made and they'd both seen *Casablanca* half a dozen times.

They left the restaurant and strolled along the sea front. Busby took her hand companionably. It seemed the natural thing to do.

'Gee, I'd like muscles like that,' he said, pointing to a couple of weight-lifters on the beach, their wide powerful shoulders gleaming with oil, strained and knotted, as they hoisted the heavy weights.

Lisa shook her head. 'You wouldn't suit them,' she said. He wore a short-sleeved white tee shirt, revealing arms that were well proportioned though decidedly unmuscled.

A voice yelled, 'Hi, BD. How'ya doin'?'

In the middle of the crowded beach, a man was waving his arms furiously in their direction.

Busby waved back. 'Hi, Joe. I'm doing fine.'

'You know a lot of people,' Lisa remarked. That was the third time today someone had greeted him.

'He was in a movie I wrote a couple of years back,' Busby said. 'Hollywood's a great place for getting to know folk.' Lisa reckoned it was his warm, outgoing personality that made people speak to him. They knew they'd get a friendly response and always looked gratified when he remembered their names.

'Fancy a beer?' He stopped by an open-fronted bar with wooden trestle tables in the forecourt.

'I wouldn't say no. I never drank beer at home,' she said as she sipped the ice-cold drink. 'It was always warm.'

He shuddered. 'Warm beer! I remember that only too well.'

'You've been to England?' she asked, surprised.

'Just for a couple of months during the war.'

As if a cloud had suddenly appeared covering the sun, Lisa felt cold. Dark memories flooded in and she shivered. 'Where were you stationed?' she asked.

'Some little village near London. I can't remember the name.' He looked at her with concern. 'Are you okay? You've gone quite pale.'

'I'm fine. A goose walked over my grave, as my mother used to say.'

'Hey, look at that guy on roller skates!' She knew he said it to distract her and he succeeded. An elderly man with a flowing white beard skated past, his wispy, shoulder-length hair streaming out behind like a sail. He wore nothing but a pair of cutdown jeans and carried a basket full of shopping. Lisa couldn't help but laugh.

They finished their beer and carried on along the promenade. Loud music could be heard some way ahead and suddenly they came upon its source, a little funfair on the corner of the next street.

To be reminded twice in the space of a few minutes of that Easter Monday in Southport was devastating. Lisa had never been near a funfair since. She'd thought the memory of that day was deeply buried in her mind, though not forgotten. It just showed how close to the surface it was, that Busby's casual words and the sound of a funfair could bring it back with such a sense of shock.

Inhuman screams were coming from across the road and she saw a girl on the roller coaster, her face terrified, clasped in the arms of a young man and she winced, remembering.

'You'll never guess what I can see,' said Busby.

'What?' She tried to sound casual.

He was pointing down the street towards a tiny cinema. 'See what's on – *Casablanca!*'

*

He bought a tub of popcorn and two cans of drink, and they sat in the back row of the virtually empty cinema, his arm round her shoulders. She rested her head against him, feeling comfortable and safe. At the end of the film, she began to cry. 'It's so sad,' she sobbed. 'I keep hoping that one day they'll have changed the ending.'

When they came out, to her surprise, it had gone dark. The day seemed to be passing unnaturally fast. She remarked as much to Busby.

'It's the company you're keeping,' he said, grinning. 'It shows you're not bored.'

Later, as they drove back towards Hollywood, he asked, 'Are you interested in politics?'

'Not much,' she replied and tried to remember the name of the current American president, without success.

'I wanted to go into politics when I was a kid,' Busby said. 'In a background role, speech-writing, public relations, that sort of stuff.'

'You'd have been good at that,' she said.

'Somehow I got sidetracked into movies, though I never regretted it.' He explained that in America, the Democrats were the left-wing party and the Republicans the right. 'Just like Labour and Conservative in your country,' he said. He was a Democrat, an activist, deeply involved in the local party machine. 'When President Eisenhower – he's a Republican – bows out in 1960, there's a good chance we'll get in. You ever heard of Jack Kennedy?'

'I'm afraid not.'

'You will do soon. He's the Senator for Massachusetts. There's a group of us in California rooting for him to get nominated as our presidential candidate. I met him once. He's the most decent guy I've ever known. If Jack gets elected . . .' He didn't finish. She saw his hands tighten on the wheel of the car. Turning towards her, he grinned. 'Sorry. Have I managed to bore you after all?'

Lisa assured him she hadn't been bored at all. 'I should know something about the country I'm living in.'

'Let's stop here for dinner.'

He drove into the forecourt of a roadhouse and as he got out of the car, he took a briefcase off the back seat. After they'd eaten, he handed her a manuscript. 'The screenplay for *The Opportunist*,' he said.

'I'd forgotten all about it,' Lisa confessed guiltily. After all, this was supposed to be the reason for their day out together.

'So had I until we were on our way home. Your part starts on page forty-three.'

'Who's taking the main role?' she asked. 'The Cahil O'Daly character?'

'I got really lucky,' Busby answered, looking pleased. 'Ralph Layton asked if I'd consider him. I took him like a shot.'

'Ralph?' she remarked in delight. 'He'd be perfect!'

'You sound as if you know him.'

'I do. Gee, it'll be really great to see him again.'

Busby stopped the car outside her apartment and said, 'I'd like to see you again, Lisa, but I've got to tell you something first.'

She turned to gaze at him. He looked grave for once. Behind the thick glasses, his eyes were solemn. 'What is it?' she asked curiously.

'I'm married.' Before she could say anything, he went on quickly, 'My wife has left me for another guy and she's suing for divorce, so I suppose you could say I'm married going on single.'

Lisa couldn't imagine any woman in her right mind leaving Busby for someone else. She was stuck for a reply and remained silent for so long that eventually he asked anxiously, 'It's all right, isn't it?'

'Of course.' She put her hand over his and said, 'It's been a lovely day. I'd like to do it again some time.'

He leaned over and took her in his arms. His lips were moist and soft against hers. Immediately she began to kiss him back passionately, praying he'd suggest going back to his place so they could make love properly. Instead, he suddenly broke away and began to stroke her cheek. 'My God! You're beautiful!' he said hoarsely.

She felt let down, almost rejected. Perhaps he sensed this because he whispered, 'Let's leave the first time until it's just right.'

'Okay,' she said, smiling, though still disappointed.

As she stood on the pavement watching him drive away, she thought it had been an almost perfect day, marred only by those painful reminders of the past.

Later on, when she was in bed, she thought about Busby. He was so easygoing and laid-back, she couldn't visualise him having the authority or the downright bloody-minded imperiousness needed to direct a film.

'Lisa, Lisa, *Lisa!*' Busby screamed. Then, '*Cut.*'

He sprang nimbly over the rocky beach and grasped her by the shoulders. She shrank back. His hands hurt; the fingers dug into the flesh of her upper arms, though he didn't seem to notice.

'Christ, woman,' he yelled. 'Your lover has gone. GONE! Geddit? You're watching his boat sail away, knowing you'll never see him again. You're heartbroken. You think your life has finished.' He let go of her contemptuously. 'You look more like you've dropped a blob of ice cream down your dress.'

There was a titter from one of the crew. Lisa wished the sand would open up and swallow her. Perhaps she could have managed the look of heartbreak required if the scenes were being shot in sequence, but although this was her first day of shooting, it was her final scene in the film. She had to grieve over the loss of a man with whom she'd just had a passionate affair, yet that part wasn't due to be shot for another two weeks, when they moved into the studio for the indoor work. The isolated beach twenty miles from Hollywood where they were shooting today was supposed to be the coast of Italy; it was the farthest Busby could afford to go on location. He'd planned on finishing the scene by midday, when the company would move on somewhere else. The morning had mostly gone, wasted on Lisa, who by now felt convinced that if she stayed here forever, she would never get the expression Busby wanted. Perhaps, she thought vainly, if the boat she was supposed to be staring at was really sailing past, she could fix her feelings on that. But the ocean was an empty expanse of blue. The boat would be added later.

She stood there, miserable and close to tears, but Busby showed no mercy. 'Let's do it again,' he ordered. 'Take twenty-two, *roll it*.'

The wind machine started up again and Lisa pushed the hair out of her eyes. She felt the skirt of her long black dress wrap itself around her legs and the tears that had been threatening began to well and she swallowed hard, trying to hold them back. The cameraman moved in for a close-up. The tears refused to be held and she felt them coursing down her cheeks. 'I wish I was anywhere in the world but here,' she thought tragically. She wiped the tears away with the back of her hand, ashamed of crying in front of so many people. 'Any minute now, Busby will yell at me again and people will laugh.' Her bottom lip trembled as more tears began to fall and it was all she could do not to bury her face in her hands and weep quite openly.

'*Cut!*' Busby shouted. 'That'll do. Thanks, Lisa.'

Open-mouthed, she watched him come back over the rocks towards her. He passed without a second glance. She could have been invisible.

It was nearly midnight when he turned up in the bar where cast and crew had gathered hours ago. He slipped into the seat beside her and said, 'Sorry I'm late, I've been watching the rushes. You were great.'

'You know what you are?' she said accusingly.

'What?' He raised his eyebrows.

'A bloody Jekyll and Hyde, that's what.'

He looked genuinely astonished. 'Why, what have I done?'

'If you don't know, it only goes to prove my point.'

Lisa sat in a dark corner of the studio watching Busby as he examined the set of her next scene. His tall thin body stooped and intense, he prowled around the old-fashioned drawing room. Suddenly, he paused in front of a sideboard crammed with ornaments and framed photographs, frowning and scratching his beard. Then his face went black as he reached out and grabbed something from the back.

'Who put this photograph here?' he asked in a voice like thunder. 'The clothes are all wrong. Women weren't wearing hats like that in the nineteen-twenties!'

Chas, his assistant, snapped his fingers and a girl in jeans and a man's shirt scurried onto the set, took the photograph, and scurried off again. Busby was a perfectionist. The chances of someone noticing that photo in the few short seconds the sideboard was on screen, were millions to one, but his concentration would have been spoiled by knowing it was there. He opened the door of the set, closed it, came back in, sat down at the table and began to talk to himself. Several people had stopped work and were observing him, fascinated. Busby knew the script by heart and he was acting out the parts, matching movement with dialogue, so he would know exactly what directions to give when shooting began. As far as Busby was concerned, once in the studio, the world outside ceased to exist. Nothing mattered except the film he was making. A bomb could drop yards away and he wouldn't notice, and if someone told him, he wouldn't care.

High up above, somebody started hammering loudly and the sound echoed through the vast building. Everybody jumped, except Busby, who went on talking to himself, saying the lines under his breath.

Lisa opened her script and began to read. She knew her part backwards but was worried that she would forget everything once the cameras began to roll, particularly if Busby was horrible again, though from now on, Ralph would be there to support her.

Ralph! She remembered that first day in the studio. She'd gone in and there he was, sitting in a canvas chair next to Busby. His name was printed on the reverse. He had his back to her and so she crept up and put her hands over his eyes.

'Guess who?' she whispered.

He sat stock-still for several seconds, then 'Lisa!' he shouted in astonishment. He sprang to his feet and clasped her in his arms. 'My dear, dear girl, how on earth did you get here?' He turned to Busby. 'Last time I saw my lovely friend she was in hot pursuit of a handsome young blond gentleman – or was he in hot pursuit of you? What happened?' he demanded.

'We caught each other – but it didn't work out,' she said swiftly.

Busby was glowering at them jealously.

'Where have you been all this time?' Ralph asked. 'I rang the flat and wrote to you, but Piers said you had just disappeared into thin air.'

'I came to Hollywood,' said Lisa. 'After all, you invited me enough times.'

'But you didn't get in touch!' He looked dumbfounded and slightly hurt.

She took his hands and pressed them against her cheeks. 'I knew we'd meet up eventually. In the meantime, I wanted to make it on my own.'

'Well, that's Lisa O'Brien in a nutshell,' he said, laughing. 'The most independent-minded young woman I've ever known.'

'It's Lisa Angelis now,' she said. 'My agent thought O'Brien was too ordinary.'

Later on, when they broke for coffee, he asked, 'What do you think of our magic town?'

'It's like you said, magic,' she replied simply.

And it was. As she watched Busby discussing costumes with Maggie Nestor from the wardrobe department, she thought, 'If I stayed here too long, I'd get confused between real life and celluloid life.' So much more effort was put into the creation of a fictional, ninety-minute or so movie than into ordinary living, that eventually the imagery and myth became more important than reality.

Even more magically, in a few weeks' time Busby the wizard would take the thousands of feet of film shot so haphazardly, a few seconds here, a few seconds there, away to the editor in the cutting room. One day he would emerge, the patchwork complete, the beginning in its proper place, the ending duly at the end. To the eyes of the innocent audience, Lisa would be weeping at the sight of a real ship sailing away from the coast of Naples. In the dark cinema, a miracle would occur. The audience, reality suspended and their imaginations set free, would travel the world. Yet every foot of film had been shot within a few square miles of California.

Hollywood! The dream-maker. The story-teller par excellence.

*

Lisa tried not to be envious of Gloria, but she couldn't help it. Gloria seemed to get right inside the part of the little Liverpool servant woman, Mary, and Busby never had to raise his voice when she was on set. She understood what he wanted instantly.

'A touch more emotion there,' Busby would say, or 'Make that expression a little harder,' and in the next shot Gloria would do it just the way he wanted.

'Perfect!' he'd crow. 'Absolutely perfect.'

How had she done it? Lisa was lost in admiration. Busby had never said 'perfect' to her once. 'That'll do,' was the most she got.

On the second day of shooting Gloria's part, Busby declared her 'better than perfect', and Lisa decided she couldn't stand it any longer. In between takes, she left the studio, depressed at watching Gloria turn in such an impeccable performance, when she had to be bullied into expressing the most basic emotion.

She emerged at the back of the lot amongst a ramshackle collection of buildings which housed the wardrobe and make-up departments, and came face to face with Ralph, who was just emerging from make-up, his hair back to its original brown, curling onto the collar of his navy pea-jacket.

'What's wrong?' he asked. 'You look upset.'

Lisa said, 'I am. I've just been watching Gloria and according to Busby, she's better than perfect. I'll never be able to act like that.'

'Don't be silly,' said Ralph. 'Those scenes we did together were really good. Anyway, Gloria's had years more experience than you.' He looked down at her sternly. 'Busby Van Dolen's one of the best directors in Hollywood. He wouldn't have picked you if he thought you'd spoil his movie.'

She made a face and for the first time she could remember, Ralph looked annoyed. 'I don't think you realise what a great movie we're making here, Lisa. It's a real work of art and the best part I've ever had. You should be in there watching and learning from Gloria – and me, come to that, instead of sulking out here.'

'In that case, I'll go back,' she said contritely. She linked his arm and they strolled towards the main entrance. 'How's Michael?' she asked. There hadn't been much time to talk since they'd met again.

Ralph grinned and said, 'Apart from being a two-timing son of a bitch, he's fine.'

Lisa glanced at him. 'You don't mind?'

'Not as long as he comes back to me each night,' he answered. 'You must come and have a drink with us some time. Give *him* something to get jealous about for a change.'

'*Cut,*' shouted Busby. 'that's it – finito! All wrapped up. Thanks, everybody. Goodnight and goodbye.'

The crew and cast cheered and began hugging each other. Some of the crew began packing up their equipment.

'You got real Oscar material there, Busby,' someone shouted and there was a chorus of 'Hear, hear.'

Lisa felt a lump in her throat. What was she to do with herself now *The*

Opportunist was finished? What were all of them going to do? These last eight weeks, the film had completely dominated her life, all their lives. To her surprise, she heard someone say, 'Thank God that's over. I'm having a few days' holiday, then I'm off to Spain for eight weeks to do a thriller.' 'I've got a couple of weeks in a soap,' someone else said. To them, the movie was already part of their past. They would never forget it, but what mattered was the future and getting on with the rest of their lives.

Busby touched her on her shoulder. 'How about foregoing the wrap party and coming and taking a look at my etchings?' he whispered.

'How dare you, sir,' she answered primly. 'What sort of a girl do you think I am?'

'My sort.' He put his arm around her shoulders and they began to walk towards the exit. A couple of people watched them curiously. This was the first time he'd treated her differently from the other actresses and it made her feel very special.

They'd driven in companionable silence for ten minutes before Lisa asked, 'Where are we going?'

'Beverly Hills,' he replied. 'My place.'

She caught her breath. At last Busby had decided the 'right' time had come. For nearly three months she had been aching for this moment. His brusque, apparently uncaring attitude had hurt and she found herself longing for a kind word, yet the more he ignored her, the more she fell in love. Tonight, he seemed like the old Busby again, the man who had sought her out in the coffee bar and swept her along to Little Venice and other places, content with a kiss when he took her home. Tonight, a kiss wouldn't be enough. Tonight, they would make love.

He lay beside her, fast asleep. Without his glasses, he looked younger. She'd never noticed how long his lashes were before. As he breathed, they quivered gently. He looked contented and satisfied.

Lisa slipped naked out of the giant, oval-shaped bed. There was a dressing gown thrown over a chair and she put it on and padded towards the kitchen where she searched around until she found a box of teabags.

Why didn't she share Busby's contentment? Instead, she felt edgy and unfulfilled. He had brought her to the very brink of passion, but left her there, dissatisfied and frustrated. It had all been over so quickly. There had been no doubt of his love, his longing to possess her, his urgent need, yet . . .

'Perhaps it's my fault,' thought Lisa, 'I expect too much, particularly after Patrick—' She stopped *that* thought before it could get any further. It had been better with Clive Randolph, even Brian. Yet in every other way she and Busby were perfect together. She thought about the man she'd met in the Belltower – Carl Baptiste – and shivered, remembering the unbridled, savage passion of that afternoon.

'So there you are!'

She jumped. Busby had come into the kitchen. He wore a pair of pyjama trousers. 'I wondered where my robe had gone,' he added.

'Would you like a cup of tea?'

He came up behind her, pulled the robe away and began to fondle her

203

breasts. 'No, I want you.' He buried his head in her neck and whispered, 'That was wonderful before. Was it good for you too?'

'Yes,' Lisa lied. 'The best ever.'

28

They'd made love three times and Lisa's body was slippy with perspiration. Then he began to caress her once more, his fingers exploring her most intimate parts. She groaned in delight as he entered her yet again and brought her to the very peak of rapture, keeping her there, poised in a state of almost unbearable, quivering anticipation. Lisa cried aloud. Suddenly, inevitably, her body erupted in a gush of sheer ecstasy. They lay in each other's arms for several minutes, neither speaking. Then he lay back with a deep sigh and said reluctantly, 'I have to go soon.'

'So have I,' said Lisa. With a determined movement, she pushed the clammy sheets away and got out of bed. As she stooped to pick up her underclothes, he reached out and began to stroke her buttocks, first with one hand, then two. 'Your flesh is like silk,' he murmured and pressed his lips in the hollow of her waist. She began to moan softly and he pulled her back onto the bed.

'If I miss my plane, there'll be hell to pay,' he complained a quarter of an hour later.

'I refuse to get out of bed again until you're dressed,' said Lisa. 'It's a waste of time.'

'I refuse to get dressed until you're out of bed,' said Carl Baptiste.

Lisa lay still and after a while, he gave an exaggerated sigh and threw back the clothes. She watched under lowered lids as he pulled on his fine silk clothes, tightening a lizard-skin belt around his narrow, almost feminine waist with thin, brown hands and marvelled at the incredible things those hands had done to her over the last three years.

As he brushed his silver hair, he noticed her watching him and smiled. 'I'll be back in six weeks,' he said. 'Shall I give you a call?'

'If you feel so inclined,' said Lisa.

'I always feel so inclined, you know that.'

'And you know I always want you to call.'

'Asking is all part of the game,' he said. His voice was deep, with the merest trace of an accent. 'You know, I nearly bought you a present this time.'

'Why?' asked Lisa in surprise.

'Our third anniversary. I changed my mind. I thought it might spoil things.' He was having trouble inserting a cuff link into his right-hand sleeve. 'My wife always . . .' He stopped suddenly. 'Sorry, I forgot our pact. No personal details.'

'And no presents,' said Lisa.

He picked up his cashmere jacket and she noticed the designer label inside. After he'd put it on, he took a wallet out of the inside pocket, and pulled out a note and put it on the desk.

'A dollar, as usual,' he said. He stared down at her curiously. 'Why just one?'

'It makes it more exciting to be paid.' She sat up, pushed the clothes back and stretched extravagantly. He looked down at her hungrily, his eyes narrowing.

'You're doing that on purpose,' he said in a cracked voice.

'What?' she asked innocently, adding, 'You'd better hurry, or you'll miss your plane.'

'I can always get a later one.' He began to drag at his tie.

'No.' She shook her head vigorously. 'That's against the rules.'

He said angrily, 'There should be a rule against your flaunting your body at me once I am dressed.'

'I'm sorry,' she said mischievously, and pulled the sheet up to her neck. 'Is that better?'

He didn't answer and began to throw his belongings into a soft suede bag. When he had finished, he looked at her coldly and said, 'Goodbye.'

'Goodbye, Carl.'

The door closed behind him. She didn't care that he had gone in a bad temper. He'd done it before, riled at her shameless attempts to seduce him when she knew he had to go. She sank back onto the bed. It hadn't been a lie, saying she had to leave soon. In an hour she was due at the studio for a costume-fitting with Maggie Nestor, but she felt too limp and languorous to move. Carl always left her feeling like this, drained and satiated after two or three hours of lovemaking.

It was a perfect arrangement. She hadn't been married to Busby for long before she realised that he could never satisfy her needs – yet she loved him so much! There hadn't been a moment's hesitation in accepting his proposal. He'd asked her soon after *The Opportunist* had been completed and she'd said yes straight away.

'My divorce comes through in the New Year. What say we get married, Lisa?'

It was Christmas Day and they were sitting by his pool. There must have been a hundred people there who'd just turned up to wish him well, all happening to have a bottle of Scotch or wine with them and all free to spend the day at his place.

Busby didn't mind. He loved company. It was rare that at least half a dozen people weren't gathered in his big modern single-storey home for some reason or another. If it wasn't movies, then it was politics. This was why his wife, Sharon, had left. A quiet, timid girl he'd met at college, she couldn't get used to sharing her house with his numerous friends. Worst of all, she hated the film industry. Sharon had gone off with a bank manager, a man as quiet and unsociable as herself.

Lisa was lying on a lounger, her thoughts miles away. It was hard to get used to the idea of wearing a bikini on Christmas Day. Over and over again as she stretched out in the hot sun, she found her thoughts turning to

Chaucer Street. It would be evening there, the family would have got together and be gathered round the kitchen fire – or would they? she thought lazily. She tended to think of her brothers and sisters as they were when she left, but that was eleven long years ago; she hadn't recognised Patrick. Most of them would be married and have homes of their own. Wherever they were, the biting Mersey wind would be whipping across the city.

'What did you say?' She opened her eyes, aware that someone had spoken and found Busby, clad only in a pair of baggy khaki shorts, kneeling beside her.

'I said my divorce comes through in the New Year. What say we get married?'

Close by, someone dived into the pool and water splashed them both. Lisa shrieked and Busby took his glasses off and wiped them dry.

'Yes.'

'Yes?' He looked surprised, as if there was a chance she'd refuse! They got on so well, it would be madness to say no. There was that one thing, but as Kitty always used to say, 'practice makes perfect'. After a while, making love would be sure to turn out well.

But it didn't!

They got married by the pool late in January 1958. Lisa hadn't bothered to count the guests who turned up. Two hundred had been invited, and at least as many again gate-crashed.

Married life turned out to be a hectic round of socialising. Except for breakfast, they rarely ate at home, driving into Hollywood for lunch and dinner to eat Chinese or Greek or Italian food, two or three carloads of them, as folk began to drop in from early on. Wherever they ate, Busby was greeted with delight, and even more people were squeezed onto their crowded table and came back to the house. Often when Lisa got up, she found someone already in the kitchen making coffee or folks asleep on the couch or by the pool. She didn't mind. In fact, she loved the friendly, club-like atmosphere and helped Jacob, Busby's black helper, keep the giant-sized refrigerator stocked with beer and the cupboards full of snacks and cigarettes. Several times, they flew to New York to spend a week theatregoing, looking up yet more of Busby's old friends. Somehow, in the midst of this chaos, he managed to tuck himself away in his study to write the scripts by which he earned his regular money. After an exhausting day, they'd go to bed and always made love – but practice did not make perfect. Each time, Lisa was left feeling let down and disappointed, though Busby was more than satisfied. She came to the inevitable conclusion that for all his magnetism and charisma, his warmth and charm, Busby Van Dolen was a lousy lover.

One morning, after they'd been married three months, she woke up feeling irritated and on edge. Busby was still asleep. Last night, she'd tried to pour herself into him, stir him into the extra effort which would bring her to the state of joy for which she yearned, but it had been useless. As always, she pretended enjoyment she hadn't had.

She got out of bed, pulled on a bikini and went outside.

The pool was warm, despite the early hour. She swam a few lengths, forging through the water as if she were in a race, trying to rid herself of the feeling of frustration. After a while she climbed out, wrapped herself in a towelling robe and went into the kitchen to make a drink. She still felt as if live wires were rubbing against each other in the pit of her stomach.

As she plugged the kettle in, she noticed the wall phone had a message under it from Gloria. She wanted Lisa to ring back. Gloria! Seeing her name gave Lisa an idea – an utterly audacious idea that sent the live wires into a state of high-speed agitation. She flipped through the telephone directory until she found the number she wanted, then dialled it, her fingers, her entire body trembling with excitement.

'Good morning, Belltower,' a man's voice answered.

'I have a package for Mr Baptiste. Is he staying with you now?'

'Hold on, ma'am, and I'll check.' The man was gone less than a minute. 'No, ma'am, Mr Baptiste isn't due till next week, Thursday.'

'Thank you,' said Lisa.

She'd just turned up, knocked on his door and gone in as she'd done that first time. She'd been going every six or eight weeks since. They knew nothing about each other. He was not an American. He had a passport, but for which country she had no idea. Baptiste wasn't his real name, she knew that much. They rarely talked. There wasn't time. Each satisfied a need in the other. Outside that Belltower bedroom, she might not like him. It didn't matter. All he knew of Lisa was her telephone number and when he arrived in Los Angeles he'd call.

'Your dry cleaning is ready,' was the code. Sometimes it was Busby who took the call and Lisa was ashamed that she never felt guilty when he passed the message on. Indeed, it seemed to add an extra frisson to the whole thing.

She was going to be late for the fitting. Reluctantly, she got out of bed and went into the shower to wash all trace of Carl Baptiste off her body.

As she stood under the cool water, she seemed to wash the memory of him away too. These enchanting few hours were always difficult to emerge from. As he faded from her mind, she began to think about the new movie and her first starring role.

The last three and a half years, she'd turned down dozens of parts, preferring to stick to Busby's own movies.

'Your heart ain't in acting,' Dick Broadbent said accusingly when he rang to tell her about a part she'd been offered and which she refused, as usual. 'The minute you get married you give up.'

'I do Busby's movies,' she said defensively.

'Huh! Once a year and if Busby wasn't the director, you wouldn't even do them.'

'I quite like being just a wife,' she said meekly. She didn't add that she was desperately hoping to become a mother, too. 'I'm sorry, Dick. Come round to dinner on Friday. It's my thirtieth birthday and Busby'd love to see you.'

He grudgingly agreed. 'I still think you're star material,' he said quickly before he rang off.

That phone call had been nearly a year ago. Lisa stepped out of the shower and began to dry herself with unnecessary roughness.

Her thirtieth birthday!

She remembered that occasion with horror. She remembered staring at herself in the mirror, looking for age lines, seeing none, thinking 'What have I achieved?' The mirror held no answers, so Lisa answered herself.

'You've achieved a lot. You've had parts in three of the most highly regarded films made in America in the last few years.' *The Opportunist* had been greeted with critical acclaim and won prizes in several foreign film festivals. Ralph only just lost out on an Academy Award to Burt Lancaster's *Elmer Gantry* and Gloria Grenville was now a major star, though as usual Busby's film had gone out on limited release. It wasn't commercial enough to appeal to a wider audience, the distributors said, so it was only screened in small 'art' cinemas throughout America.

The same thing happened to Busby's next two projects: *The Lilac Tree* and *Beneath Contempt.* The critics had showered both films with plaudits and Lisa had been picked out for special praise. '*A sparkling, sensitive perform-ance,*' one reviewer wrote. '*Lisa Angelis is a real find.*' As usual, only the same small art cinemas showed them.

'You've done well for a girl coming from Chaucer Street.' She was rich beyond her wildest dreams. Although Busby didn't earn nearly as much as other successful producers, Lisa had more than enough money.

Why then, did she stare at herself, anxiously demanding answers? 'Because compared to other girls coming from Chaucer Street, Lisa, you've never done anything *really* worthwhile!' There was nothing to show for thirty years of existence except a few feet of celluloid film.

'That's not my fault. You know how much I want a baby.'

She'd been married to Busby for nearly three years and it wasn't his fault she hadn't conceived. He already had two daughters from his first marriage – pretty, outgoing little girls who came to see him once a month. Lately, Lisa found herself watching and wishing they were hers.

Staring numbly in the mirror on her birthday, she'd decided it was time to see a gynaecologist. Perhaps she had some blocked tubes, or whatever it was that prevented women from conceiving. She was totally ignorant on medical matters.

She had a feeling, a suspicion at the back of her mind of what the result of the tests would be, and her suspicions were confirmed. A long time ago, the doctor said, she'd had a badly injured womb, followed by serious inflamma-tion. Unfortunately, the damage was irreparable.

'You can't expect to get away with having this sort of thing done to your body,' he said angrily. 'Isn't this the result of what you call in England a back-street abortion?'

Despite her premonition, Lisa felt herself go faint. 'So there's no chance, no chance at all of conceiving?' she whispered.

'It would be a miracle if you did,' he said, his face cold and unsympa-thetic. 'Which is a pity, because otherwise you're an exceptionally healthy woman.'

The shock of that day never paled. Lisa finished drying herself and began to get dressed. Once again, she felt a surge of cold anger at her father for what he had done to her. She'd told no one of her visit to the doctor, not even Busby.

After she'd slipped into her cream silk shift, she sat down at the dressing table and began to draw a thin line above and below her eyes with a black kohl pencil, smearing the lids with gold shadow and brushing her long lashes, curling them upwards. She still didn't use powder or pancake, but finished off by painting her lips scarlet, building the shape outwards with a stiff lipbrush. Pulling a cream band over her hair, she combed forward the recently-cut fringe, then stood up to examine herself full-length.

There was no doubt about it: despite the absence of lines, she had acquired an air of maturity which added an extra dimension to her beauty. There was a sadness in her eyes which she was sure had only been there since she'd learned she could never have a child. Only the other day, Busby had said to her, 'You're like a rose, in its most perfect moment of blooming.'

She'd replied indignantly, 'I don't want to be like a rose, thank you very much. It means at any minute my petals will fall off and I'll just be a nasty twig with thorns on. I'd sooner be a sturdy old nettle which never dies. Least, I don't think it does.'

'I was just trying to be nice,' Busby said in a little-boy voice.

'Well, don't.' Lisa threw a cushion at him and he threw it back, then came over and dragged her onto his knee.

'I'll never be nice to you again,' he threatened.

'Yes, you will.' She snuggled into his arms. 'You can't help but be nice to everybody. Except when you're making a movie,' she added as an afterthought. 'Then Genghis Khan could take lessons in being mean.'

After a few minutes, he said seriously, 'You know, I've never been so happy. I've got you, I've got the finance together for *Easy Dreams* and I've got Jack Kennedy in the White House. The world is perfect.' Busby acted as if President Kennedy had been elected entirely due to his own efforts.

'Let's pause and remember this moment all our lives,' said Lisa. 'The moment when the world was perfect for Busby Van Dolen.'

He looked down at her quickly. 'Isn't it perfect for Lisa Angelis?'

She kissed him. 'Almost,' she said softly. 'Almost perfect.'

Before quitting the hotel room, Lisa checked that nothing had been left behind. Carl had departed in such a hurry. The room was clear. If she caught a taxi, she would just get to the studio in time.

Easy Dreams was set in the 1930s. Maggie Nestor had got hold of top fashion magazines for the period and Lisa's wardrobe consisted of slinky, tight-fitting suits and evening dresses that showed off her slender, curved figure to perfection.

'I've put a zip in this when it should be hooks and eyes. D'you think he'll notice?' Maggie asked. Lisa was struggling into a black lace spangled gown lined with fine, flesh-coloured silk.

Maggie was a homely, plump woman who bought her own ill-fitting clothes through a chain-store catalogue.

'He' was Busby, the monster. 'I wouldn't like to say,' said Lisa cautiously, remembering the way he'd exploded with rage on the set of *The Lilac Tree* when he found a newspaper with an out-of-date headline. 'I'll try and keep my left side away from him, just in case.' She walked to the mirror with difficulty. 'I'll have to learn to walk again in these narrow skirts.'

'You need to mince, not walk,' said Maggie, adding thankfully, 'I'm glad it's not me wearing them.'

'Wow!' said Lisa. 'I look as if I've got nothing on underneath this.'

'That's the whole point,' Maggie said. 'She wears that for the Mayor's ball. Causes a consternation – I read the script. At home, she wears even less. Have you seen these night-dresses and stuff?'

'Wow!' said Lisa again as Maggie pointed to half a dozen sheer garments hanging from the wall. 'They look like nylon. Did they have nylon then?'

'They're all crêpe or silk. I had a helluva job tracking the stuff down. Look at this one.' Maggie unhooked a black diaphanous negligée. 'I managed to buy this from an antiques market. Most of the trimming had gone, so I replaced it with feathers. If it tickles, blame me.'

'I might as well be wearing a sheet of glass,' said Lisa.

'You certainly won't be hiding any of your charms,' agreed Maggie. 'This movie's gonna give the censors a big headache. I've certainly never seen one yet with so much nudity. Busby's taking a real big chance.'

'He always takes chances with his movies,' said Lisa, holding the negligée in front of her.

Maggie was staring at her, looking puzzled. 'How you actresses can wear stuff like that in front of an all-male crew beats me,' she said. Then she grinned and added, 'But then, if I had a figure like yours, perhaps I'd be willing to flaunt it round a bit.'

Shooting of *Easy Dreams* went, appropriately, like a dream. Busby said it was the smoothest, least troublesome movie he'd ever made.

Lisa played a beautiful, shallow woman who causes havoc in the lives of four powerful men who are her lovers. Her lines were few.

'You don't need to say anything, you speak with your body,' Busby told her.

For the first time, Lisa seemed to sense what Busby wanted of her without him asking. The part had been written with her in mind and the entire movie centred around Cassie Royale.

'You are everything a man wants in a woman,' Busby said, 'and everything a woman wants to be.' So, oblivious to everyone else in the studio, Cassie Royale enticed her lovers into her bed, standing in the doorway, naked under the sheer black robe, hands resting provocatively on her lean hips.

'Perfect,' said Busby, peering through the viewfinder. 'Perfect . . . Just look at him and lick your lips, slowly. Your eyes hold a promise – you can fulfil his wildest, most impossible dreams. If he gives you money, you'll give him heaven in return.'

The film was a paean to his wife, to Lisa, into which he poured his very soul. On set, he was like a madman, pushing himself beyond exhaustion, expecting miracles from the cast and crew, driving them mad with his impossible demands. Yet no one complained. No one refused to stay late.

Everybody seemed to understand they were working with a genius who deserved, was entitled to, their total cooperation and commitment.

The movie was an allegory of the American Dream. It showed that what people were being encouraged to strive for was ultimately rotten and corrupt. Lisa said she didn't think anyone would notice. Busby pointed out Cassie Royale's address – 49 Republic Avenue. 'Americans will notice,' he said.

Unfortunately, they didn't have an opportunity. In the spring of 1963 when *Easy Dreams* was previewed, it was almost universally slammed by the critics.

'*A pornographic nightmare.*'

'*Too avant-garde for its own good.*'

'*Busby Van Dolen should never be allowed inside a studio again. The film is trashy, boring and wastes the talents of its excellent actors.*'

'*An abstract mish-mash of images which drives its message home with a sledgehammer.*'

'How can it be abstract *and* drive its message home?' groaned Busby. 'That's a contradiction in terms.' He was sitting up in bed reading the reviews. A couple of friends had already arrived to commiserate and were on the floor drinking beer. 'They like you, though, Lisa. Listen to this: "*The dazzlingly lovely Lisa Angelis is enchanting as Cassie Royale. Perhaps it is only because she is married to the wretched director that she agreed to take the part.*" ' He threw the paper down. 'I expect the Sundays will be just as bad.'

They were. There was just one favourable review. The critic in a little Greenwich Village magazine wrote, '*Some will call* Easy Dreams *pornographic. Some will say it is unpatriotic. It is neither. It is a movie made before its time. The day will come when every movie will not have to be a glorification of the American way of life. When that glad day comes,* Easy Dreams *will be regarded as a classic.*'

Easy Dreams won prizes at the Berlin and Cannes film festivals, though it was never released in America. Busby said he didn't know whether to laugh or cry when he learnt that a copy had been acquired by a pornographic film club and was now included in their library.

It was not in Busby's nature to stay downhearted for long. Anyway, his beloved President Kennedy was involved in confrontation with right-wing whites as he tried to enforce civil liberties for black people in the southern states. Busby went to Birmingham, Alabama, to march with those fighting for desegregation of schools. Lisa asked to go too.

'No, it's too dangerous. You could get hurt and I just don't want you to see how much Americans can hate each other.'

He was gone a week and Lisa was sick with worry. When Carl Baptiste called, she made an excuse. She couldn't have been unfaithful to Busby then. Night after night, she watched the violence of the marches on the television screen. The vicious hatred, the anger and prejudice were unbelievable. The demonstrators were showered with rocks, spat at, hit with sticks and iron bars. Where did they get their courage from?

Busby came home safe but appalled. 'Some day I'm going to make a movie about it,' he said. 'But not just yet. With my present reputation, it'd be sure to bomb.'

He had, however, made up his mind what to do next. 'I'm going to rehabilitate myself with a nice-as-apple-pie movie with Mom and Pop and a coupla kids and a scruffy dog and scatty neighbours.'

'It's not like you to fall in line so easily,' said Lisa. 'I thought you'd go in for something even more daring than *Easy Dreams.*

He shrugged. 'No point,' he said. 'It'd just be like a red rag to a bull. I'll stick to something safe.'

Inevitably, he threw himself heart and soul into the making of *Mr & Mrs Jones*, but there wasn't the usual excitement on the set. Cast and crew knew they were making just another humdrum movie, not, as they usualy did with Busby, sharing in a passionate adventure to produce a work of art. Lisa was cast as a vampish neighbour, a small, unimportant part. She'd hoped for the main female role, but Busby said she didn't look right and she accepted his judgement without a murmur. Once, when raising finance for a film, a businessman had offered half a million dollars provided his daughter was given a starring part. Busby turned him down. He wouldn't cast someone unless they were perfect for the part, not even Lisa.

Shooting reached its closing stages in November. Busby had never worked with children before and found them difficult to direct. The fact that the pair – a boy of twelve and a girl aged ten – disliked each other and squabbled incessantly off the set didn't help. Even the dog was proving difficult. 'W.C. Fields was right,' Busby groaned to Lisa one night. 'Never work with children or animals. I'm taking his advice in future.'

Today, on the set, the family Christmas dinner was turning out to be a nightmare. The children were tetchy and Grandfather was drunk. They were into the twenty-first take when suddenly, it all began to fall into place. At long last, everything was going perfectly, until a door opened and someone rushed into the studio and right onto the set.

'*Cut!*' screamed Busby. 'What the hell—?'

It was Maggie Nestor. Tears were streaming down her face. 'The President's been shot! I was watching TV. I think he's dead.'

A pall descended over America. Even Lisa felt heartbroken. Jack Kennedy had seemed so young and offered so much hope. The country had become a better place to live in since he had arrived at the White House.

With cool professionalism, Busby returned to the studio next day and finished filming. At home he was distraught. 'Such a fuckin' *waste*,' he railed. 'He made us feel good about ourselves. He shared our dreams. Ah, shit!' He poured himself a tumbler of Jack Daniel's.

Lisa could think of nothing to say that would soothe him.

One night she went to bed at midnight leaving him with his friends. They were sitting moodily, drinking, not saying much, each preoccupied with his grief. When eventually Busby came to bed, she could smell the liquor on his breath. His voice was slurred. 'Come here, I need you.' He reached out and took her savagely and she felt ashamed. It was the first time he'd ever left her satisfied. 'Oh, my dear, darling Lizzie,' he murmured softly before he went to sleep.

Lisa froze. She lay there for what must have been an hour, her head swimming. Eventually, she eased herself from his grasp, threw on a robe and made her way to his study. Voices came from the kitchen – music, the radio was on. There were still people in the house.

Busby's study was lined on all four walls with books: paperbacks packed tightly together on the narrow top shelves, larger hardbacks below. Beside his desk was a shelf of encyclopaedias and reference books. Lisa bit her lip. She was looking for a photograph album. Busby's parents were dead and he'd been an only child. If there'd been albums, they would have come to him and he'd have kept them. No one threw old photos away. Eventually she found what she was looking for – three blue, leather-bound albums tucked in a corner along with a College Yearbook and school reports.

She knelt on the floor and began to leaf through the books, trying to keep back her sense of rising panic.

The first contained pictures of his parents as children, growing up, getting married, then with Busby as a baby. The second was mainly Busby at school; grade school, high school, college. Towards the end, she found what she was looking for – Busby in his army uniform: a grave and serious-looking Busby, bespectacled, clean-shaven and horribly familiar.

No, it wasn't what she was looking for! Of course not. It was what she'd hoped she wouldn't find. *Busby. Buzz.* The two names chased each other round her brain. Buzz, the only soldier who hadn't raped her that day in Southport. Busby, her husband, who must have known who she was when she came into the Cascade Hotel bedroom years ago. He knew she was from Liverpool. Why had he married her? *Why?*

'So you noticed?' He was standing at the door, looking down. Without his glasses, he always looked so much younger.

'You've never called me Lizzie before,' she said.

'I tried not to.'

'Why didn't you tell me right from the start?' she asked in an agonised voice.

He sighed deeply, came into the room and helped himself to a glass of Scotch. Then he sat down, reached out and touched Lisa's hair. She flinched and his face twisted with grief. He looked close to tears.

'I didn't think you'd want to be reminded of that day,' he said eventually. 'I knew it for certain when we went to Little Venice. I saw how you reacted when I said I'd been in England during the war. That's why I lied and said I'd been stationed near London.'

She remembered the occasion perfectly. 'Why did you marry me? You went out of your way to get to know me.'

'Because I love you,' he said simply. 'I always have, I always will.'

They were silent. Lisa said, 'Can I have a drink?'

He handed her a half-full tumbler. She sat back on her haunches and leaned against the shelves. He watched her. The love in his eyes made her want to weep. She wanted to take him in her arms but she couldn't bear to touch him.

He said softly, 'The day you came into that hotel room I knew my wildest dream had come true. You'd been my first love, my only real love, but I never imagined we would meet again. Oh, that day! If only you knew how innocent you were. How lovely. And so trusting! I could have killed those others.' The knuckles on his hands tightened around his glass, so tight that Lisa feared it would break. 'I could have killed them,' he repeated.

'What happened to them? Do you know?' she asked curiously.

He shook his head. 'All I know is that Hank and Tex were killed in a plane crash just before we were demobbed. I never heard from any of the others – not that I expected to.'

They were silent again. Busby said, 'What are we going to do now?'

'I don't know,' said Lisa. 'Try and carry on, I suppose.'

She slept in the guestroom for several weeks. Eventually, she returned to his bed, but it was no use. Each time he touched her, memories flooded back and she relived that brutal day all over again.

'I'm sorry,' she told him tearfully. 'But I keep thinking that now, nearly twenty years later, you're having your turn.'

'Lisa!' He was shocked. 'Oh, Lisa!'

Although he denied it vehemently, to himself most of all, Lisa felt that she was almost certainly right.

She waited until Christmas had passed before telling him she was leaving. 'Do you love me?' he asked, his voice hoarse with emotion.

'More than I can say,' she answered truthfully.

'And I love you. If two people who love each other so much can't stay together, what hope is there for the world?'

'I don't know.' She began to cry and longed to bury her head against him, feel the warm comfort of his arms around her. 'We'll stay friends, won't we?' she sobbed. 'I'll always want to know you're there.'

'I'll always be there for you, Lisa,' he vowed. 'Always.'

29

Despite her protests, Busby insisted she keep his house. 'I've got a heap of friends who can put me up until I buy another place,' he said.

The house was strange and silent without him, without Jacob and the endless, noisy guests. It dawned on her that in all the years she'd lived here, she'd never really looked at it properly before. It seemed half-furnished with rather ugly, featureless modern pieces she didn't like. The white painted walls were bare and discoloured. Perhaps Sharon, Busby's ex-wife, had taken all the pictures and the ornaments and Lisa had never noticed before. She smiled wanly. If she *had* noticed, she probably wouldn't have cared.

As the days dragged by, a few of Busby's friends dropped in to see him, unaware he'd gone. They stayed a while out of politeness, making awkward conversation before leaving. She never saw them again. She hadn't realised how much she had relied on Busby for company, for work, for everything. Suddenly the world seemed bleak and empty. She was alone again and she had no one.

Lally had left Hollywood to marry Frank a long time ago after a string of identical parts. The last Lisa had heard, she was expecting her second baby.

The Opportunist had turned Gloria into a star and nowadays Lisa saw little of her. She was making up for those long years out of work and was always busy, always working, often abroad.

As for Roma, well she'd never been friendly with her, but Roma had just disappeared, no one knew where. Lisa had watched the programme *Beautiful Dreams*, for which Roma had been going to audition, but she wasn't in it.

Ralph only lived a few miles away, but she had gone to dinner there once and it had turned out disastrously. Perhaps foolishly, Ralph had been over-attentive, deliberately trying to stir his consistently unfaithful lover into jealousy. He'd done it too successfully. Michael, an excitable, brown-skinned Adonis, had reacted violently, seizing a knife and shutting himself in his room, threatening to hurt himself.

'I didn't realise he loved me so much,' Ralph had said. 'I'm sorry, Lisa. Let me call you a taxi.'

She had left sad and worried, and hesitated to contact him now, much though she wanted to.

Busby had been gone a week when Jacob came in a van to take his books away.

'How is he?' Lisa asked.

'Bearing up,' said Jacob, shrugging. 'He's got plenty of company, though he's drinking too much.'

After he'd left, Lisa picked up the telephone and dialled Busby's new number. He'd come back like a shot if she asked, but when the receiver was picked up at the other end and she heard his voice, she immediately rang off. Although it broke her heart to acknowledge it, their marriage was irrevocably over.

It was, however, time she got back to work. She picked up the phone again and called Dick Broadbent. It was months since she'd heard from him.

To her surprise – she had expected an enthusiastic greeting – Dick sounded subdued. His normally chirpy voice was flat and tired.

'Got anything for me?' she asked.

'Nothing,' he said. 'Folks got fed up offering parts and you turning them down. Nobody's enquired about you for ages. Of course, it didn't help, *Easy Dreams* having bombed. I know *you* got good notices, but even so, in folks' minds, you're connected with a failure. You know what they say – an actor is only as good as their last movie.'

'So there's nothing,' she said disappointedly.

'All I got is a bit-part in some crummy TV movie.'

'That'll do,' said Lisa. 'Give me the details.'

Dick reacted impatiently. 'Don't be stupid, Lisa. You can't do stuff like that! You gotta reputation to consider.'

'Sorry, Dick.' He didn't answer. 'Are you all right?' she asked tentatively. 'You don't sound yourself.'

'I keep getting these pains in my chest and they make me feel nauseous. Also, I got a splitting headache.' He laughed and added, 'Otherwise, I feel fine.'

Lisa told him firmly to see a doctor and he promised he would. Before ringing off, he assured her he would ask around and call back immediately he found her some work.

He didn't call. A few days later, she rang his office and there was no reply. Such a thing had never happened before. Dick seemed to be at the end of his telephone day and night. There was no reply the next day either, so she went to see him. His office door was locked and there was no sign to say where he was. She had no idea where he lived – sometimes, she used to wonder if he lived and slept in the office. A few days later, she saw in *Variety* that Dick had died at his desk from a massive heart attack. He was seventy-nine. By the time she read the news, he'd already been buried.

Lisa put the paper down and began to cry for Dick. He'd been such a kind, naive little man, full of life and enthusiasm. She smiled through the tears, remembering what Kitty used to say when someone elderly died: 'Oh well, he had a good innings.' Her mam had been so wise, so knowing with an inner strength that brought her through the most dire adversity. Lisa did what Kitty would have done on hearing bad news. She went into the kitchen and made a cup of tea.

She put Cole Porter on the record player and carried the tea out to the pool, together with a pack of cigarettes. Not long after Busby left, she'd started smoking. Every time she opened a cupboard or a drawer, there was a packet of Marlboros and in the end she couldn't resist trying one in an effort to lessen her loneliness; by now, she was already smoking ten a day.

It was a beautiful evening, but then, evenings were always beautiful in California. Dusk was just beginning to settle and between the tall trees bordering the garden, the last of that day's sun was sinking, leaving a strip of shimmering gold on the horizon. The sky, a lurid mish-mash of deep orange and purple, was zebra-striped with black. Coloured poolside lights, festooned from tree to tree, were reflected, wobbling gently in the pale, almost still water, and the faint scent of flowers hung on the warm air.

Lisa sat in one of the padded chairs outside the open French windows and watched the sun as it sank further, the gold strip narrowing until it became no more than a pencilled line separating land and sky. Then it disappeared altogether and darkness took over. Lisa shivered, overwhelmed by the beauty of the night. She wished someone was here to share that beauty with her. If she stayed in this house for the rest of her life, Lisa knew she would never get used to it being empty. It was Busby's house. His spirit, the spirit of his multitude of friends was everywhere. One day, she'd move, let him have his house back. But not yet. She had to get her life sorted out, get used to living without him. She had to make it on her own, yet again.

The telephone beside her rang and she picked up the white receiver.

'Your dry cleaning is ready,' said a familiar voice.

Carl! She made an instant decision which she hoped she wouldn't regret. 'I'm sorry, I won't be needing dry cleaning any more,' she said.

Dick's list of clients was transferred to a big reputable agency on Vine Street. Lisa received a letter saying a Karen Zorro would be looking after her from now on and to call if she had any queries.

She rang the firm immediately. It was a month since Busby had gone and she was becoming desperate for work, though her pride wouldn't let her tell this Karen Zorro how anxious she was.

The extension number rang just once before a brusque, efficient voice said, 'Zorro here.'

Lisa had scarcely managed to introduce herself before the woman interrupted. 'I was just about to call you, Lisa. There's a real emergency cropped up on *The Matchstick Man*.'

'Another one?' said Lisa. She'd read all about this movie, a comedy thriller which had been plagued with difficulties. Both male and female stars had withdrawn before shooting had even begun, and so far there'd been three directors, a score of writers and reports of endless trouble on the set.

'I'm afraid so,' said Karen Zorro with a touch of impatience. 'Now the second female lead has walked out in high dudgeon and they're desperate. I know it's asking a lot at such short notice, but could you possibly fill in?'

'I'd be willing to help out,' said Lisa. The calmness in her voice belied her inner excitement.

'Good. I'll call the studio immediately. They might even want you there this afternoon, if that's all right.'

'I had a few things planned for later today, but I'll cancel them,' lied Lisa.

The studio called and wanted her straight away. Lisa said midday would be fine and they promised to send a car.

She showered, scrubbing her body with a loofah until it tingled, then made up her face with extra care. Sorting through her wardrobe, she decided on a clinging cinnamon jersey dress with a deep V neck – one of Busby's favourites. She held her breath as she pulled the zip up at the back. It passed her waist smoothly and she sighed in relief. She'd been worried that the past month of inactivity, lazing round the house, drinking too much tea and Jack Daniel's and not doing any exercises, had made her put on weight. But she was as slim as ever. She pulled on a pair of black lace tights and slipped her feet into a pair of stiletto-heeled black court shoes. Brushing her fringe forward, she combed the rest back and coiled it into a bun on her neck. Finally, she clipped on a pair of gold drop earrings and stood back several feet to examine her full-length reflection in the mirror.

She felt her stomach turn. She had lost her glow, her radiance. Her eyes were lustreless and dull, her face flaccid. Busby going had affected her even more than she had realised.

But she was an actress! No matter how bad she felt inside, it was important not to let it show. She closed her eyes and took several deep breaths. The car would be arriving soon. She was at a crossroads in her career. The movie she was about to make could decide her entire future in films. It was vital to look right. She *would* look right! Straightening her shoulders, she stepped back and opened her eyes. They sparkled back at her. Her pink lips curved into an enticing smile. She was herself again!

A car horn sounded and she picked up her bag and ran outside, dazzling the driver with her beauty.

It would have been easy to lose her short-lived confidence not long after arriving on the almost empty set during the lunch-break. As soon as she went in, the assistant director rushed over to introduce himself.

'Hi, I'm Ben Shadley. I can't thank you enough for stepping in at such short notice. You've really got us out of a hole. We're close on reaching our budget and not a quarter of a way through the movie yet.' He was a plump, anxious-looking man. Lisa soon discovered he had good reason to look anxious. 'Come and meet our new director, Mr Dent. I hope you're thick-skinned. Please don't take any notice of his rudeness,' he said pathetically. 'It's never personal – he's rude to everyone.'

Joseph Dent was famous for his histrionics. Over the years, every film he'd made had been cursed with trouble because of his wild, uncontrolled temperament. He could reduce grown men and women to tears and once ended up in hospital when an actor, driven to the end of his tether by his insults, had thrown a table at him. Dent, who specialised in thrillers, hadn't worked for some time. With the contract system ended and actors no longer tied to a particular studio and forced to take parts whether they wanted them or not, big names refused to work with him, despite the fact that his movies were highly regarded and one or two were often included in critics' lists of the ten best thrillers ever made. The company behind *The Matchstick Man* must have been really desperate to put him in charge of a project already in deep trouble.

Lisa had never met the man, but he was a Hollywood legend and everyone had heard of him. Ben Shadley took her arm and ushered her cautiously towards a small figure stooped over a script, one arm draped over the camera.

'Mr Dent,' he said obsequiously. 'This is Lisa Angelis, who's agreed to take over the part of Honey.'

If ever the devil was needed for a movie, Joseph Dent could have done the part without make-up. Although he must have been nearing sixty, he had the demeanour and build of a man half his age. Thin and wiry, his heart-shaped face was brought to an exact point by a small goatee beard. His black-as-night hair was combed forward into little pikelets on his broad, flat forehead, and black eyebrows turned sharply upwards like the tails of two dark birds. Coal-black eyes flashed fire as he looked Lisa up and down with sharp intelligence.

'She's too old,' he said flatly.

'She's twenty-seven,' said Ben Shadley. 'The script calls for Honey to be twenty-two, but it's not important. Another five years—' He held his arms out, palms upward, and shrugged.

Joseph Dent looked Lisa straight in the eyes. 'Another *five* years?' he said disparagingly. 'Looks more like ten to me.'

Ben became flustered. 'But she looks the part, Mr Dent. She's the right type – classy, yet innocent-looking.'

'She's too tall for that idiot Gary whatever-his-name-is.'

'He can wear platforms,' Ben said desperately.

Lisa began to feel annoyed. Joseph Dent acted as if she were invisible.

'Does he always do this?' She ignored the director and spoke directly to Ben Shadley.

'What . . . what?' the man stammered.

'Talk about people so insultingly and pretend they're not there?'

'Well, um . . . I don't know.'

'It's frightfully juvenile,' said Lisa in her best upper-class English accent. 'I faintly remember doing it at school. Most people grow out of it. Oh, well.' She turned to go. 'Nice meeting you, Ben.'

'Don't!' Ben caught her arm. Lisa glanced at Joseph Dent and saw he was grinning. The charade she was performing was only hurting poor Ben Shadley.

'But I'm too old and too tall,' she protested.

'I suppose you'll do,' Dent said nastily. 'Beggars can't be choosers.'

'I expect that's what they said when they took *you* on,' said Lisa.

Making *The Matchstick Man* was one of the worst experiences of her life. Busby Van Dolen was regarded as a bit of a tyrant on set, but compared to Joseph Dent he was mildness personified. She had never encountered so much unpleasantness and venomous, unnecessary criticism.

The male star, Gary Maddox, was the latest juvenile heart-throb. With his suntanned muscular body and bleached hair falling into his blue eyes with a casualness that was anything but genuine, he was used to teeny-boppers screaming in adoration at the mere raising of a well-plucked eyebrow. Expecting to charm everybody and be charmed in return, instead he found his inadequate acting ability cruelly exposed. Joseph Dent tore him apart, taunted him. 'Mr Beefcake', he called him.

'If Mr Beefcake could bring himself to look intelligent for ten minutes, we might get this scene in the can.' The actor, driven beyond endurance, began to show the dark side of his nature. His arrogant, though easygoing manner turned into ugly aggression. Lisa found it difficult to act naturally, particularly in romantic scenes, with a man who'd just cursed the director, using the foulest language imaginable.

Ruth George, the female lead, coped by becoming mildly drunk as soon as she arrived on set and staying that way all day; the bit players, men and women alike, were constantly in tears, stripped of all pride and faith in themselves by Dent's caustic tongue.

He tried it with Lisa too. 'Christ Almighty, woman,' he screamed. 'You're opening and closing your mouth like a fuckin' fish.' He aped a fish, puckering his lips, pushing them forward, making smacking sounds.

Lisa put her hands on her hips and looked at him intently. 'Very good, Joseph,' she said admiringly – she called him Joseph deliberately to annoy him, knowing he preferred Mr Dent. 'If ever they make *Moby Dick* again, I'll nominate you for the title role.'

Some of the crew laughed and Ben Shadley looked as if he might have a fit, but Lisa had decided that the best way to deal with Joseph Dent was to make fun of him. Strange as it might seem, he was never annoyed and indeed often the first to smile. 'He just needs taking down a peg or two,' she'd thought to herself right from the beginning.

A day rarely passed without there being a row, perhaps two or three. One day, the set had to be rebuilt when Gary Maddox, driven to the end of his tether by the director's ridicule, kicked down a wall.

Despite these traumas, Joseph Dent worked a minor miracle. The movie was brought to its miserable end within the time limit, and only slightly over budget. There was no wrap party when it was finished. No one felt like celebrating. As the last scene was shot, there wasn't a single cheer. Instead, everyone gave a loud sigh of relief.

To the astonishment of everyone, when *The Matchstick Man* was released six months later, it was greeted with universal acclaim. During the course of shooting, it had lost all trace of comedy and ended up a genuine *film noir*. Lisa cut out her favourite review and pinned it to the kitchen wall.

'*Joseph Dent, back in top form, has teased top-rate performances out of the cast of this dark, psychological thriller. In particular, Gary Maddox, who so far has shown only a lightweight ability, gives his role a power and strength of which this critic had not thought him capable. Unshaven and unkempt, he attacks his part with raw, cynical savagery that shows great promise for the future. As the tragic, unbalanced heroine, Ruth George is also unexpectedly superb, wafting gently in and out of her scenes with an almost dreamlike quality. Making a welcome return to the screen as the downstairs neighbour is the lovely Lisa Angelis, who brings an air of appealing vulnerability to her part . . .*'

*

Over the next few years, Lisa took every part she was offered and acquired a reputation as someone reliable and entirely lacking in temperament. The 'Un-primadonna', one gossip columnist called her.

Budgets began to expand and movies took longer to shoot. Stars were paid phenomenal salaries – Elizabeth Taylor received over a million dollars for *Cleopatra*, which went way over time and budget. Lisa's latest statement from her bank showed a balance of nearly half a million dollars. Several times she went abroad on location as the film industry in Hollywood began to shrink, television took over, and Europe became the movie capital of the world. She always hated leaving Busby's house and was glad to return to the comfort and shelter of its four walls.

Between filming, she had the house completely redecorated, buying paintings, new carpets and curtains, never forgetting that one day it would be Busby's again, so choosing things she knew he would like. Inevitably, she began to make friends. The Beatles were all the rage and she acquired celebrity status just because she came from Liverpool. Several times she was asked to parties on that account alone, though she always refused. 'The Cavern opened long after I left Liverpool,' she told people honestly. 'I've never met The Beatles and I'm not accepting invitations just because we come from the same city!'

Busby telephoned often and sometimes they talked for hours. Two years after their divorce, he remarried, a young dark-haired actress caled Lulu, but it failed after only a few months.

'She was a substitute for you,' he said, the last time he called. It was midnight and Lisa was asleep. As soon as she heard the telephone she knew it would be him. 'Though I should have known it wouldn't work out. Poor kid! I expected too much of her. I expected her to act all day like Lisa Angelis and she just wasn't up to it.'

'Poor Busby,' Lisa said.

'Poor Busby,' he echoed. 'I've given up on my own company, you know. Now I just make movies, full stop.'

'I know,' she said. 'You told me last time.' Who could blame him? He'd put his heart and soul into his eight films and hardly anybody in America had seen them.

'Now the men in suits have control. They cut my work to shreds, leave out the bits I thought were my best work.'

'I know,' she said again, adding tenderly, 'but one day you'll make your own movies again, I feel it in my bones.'

'Do you? Do you, Lisa?' His voice became hoarse. 'Christ, I miss you. Why do we have to be apart?' Without waiting for an answer, he went on, 'The other day, I was wondering, if we hadn't met, you know, all those years ago in Liverpool, would I still have fallen in love when you walked into that damned hotel?'

'I don't know, darling,' said Lisa truthfully. She dragged a pillow up and propped it behind her back. Busby sounded as if he was in for one of his marathon chats.

'Is there anyone else?' he demanded suddenly.

'No,' she said truthfully. 'There's been no one since you.' She hadn't felt the slightest desire to become romantically involved since he went. In a recent magazine, it said she led a 'hermit-like' existence in Beverly Hills.

'I thought you had something going with Gary Maddox? I keep seeing pictures of you together at premières and stuff.'

This wasn't the time to remind him that it was none of his business, that they were no longer man and wife. 'Gary and I have the same agent,' she explained gently. 'And it suits us to be seen together. In fact, I don't like him much.'

'I see,' said Busby, sounding mollified. He stayed on for another hour telling her about the anti-Vietnam War movement he was involved in. 'Kennedy would never have let us get in this deep,' he said moodily. Now he was campaigning for Robert Kennedy to be elected as Democratic candidate for the presidential elections later in the year.

Compared to his, her own news was prosaic. She'd bought more pictures for the house – Impressionist reproductions. 'Very conventional,' she said. 'Monet, Cézanne, Renoir – and I've learnt to drive. I've got a Chevrolet estate.'

'A Chevy,' corrected Busby. 'No one says Chevrolet.'

He rang off later, still sounding depressed. Lisa got up, made herself a cup of tea and lit a cigarette. His call had disturbed her. She felt guilty for making Busby, of all people, so unhappy.

'Oh, my dear,' she whispered. 'If only we could be together.' But it could never happen. Only a few weeks ago she had seen him across a restaurant where she was lunching with Karen Zorro and immediately his stance, the movement of his shoulders, the glint of light falling on his thick glasses, had brought back the horror of that distant day in a rush of nausea. She stubbed her cigarette out and immediately lit another.

'You're a bloody hypocrite, Lizzie O'Brien,' she said angrily. 'Mooning over a man you two-timed right from the start. *You* might be the right woman for Busby, but *he* certainly isn't the right man for you, and it's about time you realised it.'

A few days later, one Sunday morning, she had an unexpected caller. The record player was on loud, and Lisa was humming along to Charlie Parker's *Laura* when the doorbell chimed. The windows were open to the pale blue March sky. During the night it had rained and the shrubs and trees were moist, glistening under the weak, lemony sun.

She jumped in alarm at the figure standing on her doorstep: a short man, wearing an enormous leather flying-jacket and helmet, with thick goggles pulled up over his forehead. It took several seconds for her to realise that it was Joseph Dent, which made her feel even more alarmed. Lisa stared at him, too taken aback to speak. Eventually she said, 'Where did you land the plane?'

'I came on Bessie.' She looked past him expecting to see a horse tethered outside. Instead, an old motorbike was propped up in the drive.

'Aren't you going to ask me in?' He had the gall to sound hurt.

'When I've got over the shock,' said Lisa. She took a deep breath. 'You can come in now.'

'Thanks.' He came in quickly and looked around with interest. 'Nice place you've got here.'

'Your small talk's not very original,' she said.

'I'm working on it,' he replied. He began to undo the strap of his helmet. 'Is that Renoir real?'

'Well, I can see it too, so it must be.' He was struggling out of the leather jacket with swift, jerky movements, then he put it on the floor where it stood as if the top half of him was still in it. His devilish appearance was emphasised by his clothes, all black, a polo-necked sweater under an old shiny suit.

'You know what I mean,' he said tetchily. 'Is it genuine or fake?'

'It's a copy.' Feeling she'd got the better of the exchange, she took him out to the pool and sat him down. 'Drink?' she asked. 'Coffee, tea or something stronger?'

'Something stronger,' he said. 'Anything'll do.'

She poured two Jack Daniel's. She needed one herself to get over the shock of having Joseph Dent in the house. When she took them outside, he'd got out of his chair and was walking up and down the edge of the pool, snapping his fingers. The sounds were so sharp and explosive that Lisa wouldn't have been surprised to see sparks fly.

'I'll come straight to the point,' he said when she sat down. 'I want you for my next movie.'

Lisa's mouth dropped. 'You must be joking. I wouldn't be in one of your movies again if I was dead broke and starving.'

He grinned. His teeth were surprisingly white and even. 'You always spoke your mind.'

'Didn't you?' she asked pointedly. 'Rather, didn't you always yell or scream your mind?'

'Point well taken,' he said. 'However, I didn't come to exchange insults.' He fished in his pocket and took out a pile of newspaper cuttings secured with a rusty paperclip. 'These are your reviews,' he said. 'All of them. You got good notices for the work you did with Busby Van Dolen, but since then, the only good review you got was for *Matchstick Man*. These last three years, you've made a load of junk. That movie you did in Rome, I can't remember the title . . .'

'*April Flowers*,' she said.

'. . . was one of the worst I have ever seen in my life. What did it cost? One million, two? Whatever it was, they wasted their dough.'

'It wasn't very good,' she conceded.

'It was abominable.' Suddenly, he came over and leaned on the table, his black eyes alight with enthusiasm. He looked like a giant blackbird which had just alighted on a worm. 'This book I got the rights to, *Attrition*, it's a futuristic thriller with a really neat twist ending.' He took a well-worn paperback novel out of another pocket. Lisa fully expected a camera next and he'd start shooting. 'I've brought you a copy. Read it and let me know what you think.'

'Even if it's the best thriller ever written, I don't want to make another movie with you, Joseph,' Lisa said emphatically. 'To be blunt, doing

Matchstick Man was a truly horrible experience which I never want to repeat.'

She knew she was being rude, but didn't care. He'd never given a damn about other people's feelings, so why should she give a damn about his? 'Any minute now,' she thought, 'he'll fly into a rage and if he does, I'll push him in the pool.' However, instead of looking mad, he grinned again. She'd never been alone with him before and was surprised to find him so calm and so, well, almost *charming*!

'Before you say no—'

'I've already said no,' she said quickly.

He ignored her '—read your cuttings and think about why you're in Hollywood – to turn out bland junk, or good movies? If it's the first, then you're not the woman I thought you were. If it's good movies, then do this with me. Okay, so we'll have a hard time . . .'

'*You* don't have a hard time,' Lisa said sarcastically. 'It's everybody else who has the hard time.'

'But it's the end result that matters, don't you see?' To her surprise, he sat down beside her and grasped her arm. She looked down at the taut, wiry hand and could feel the throbbing of his fingers through her thin blouse. It was almost like getting an electric shock. 'Two of my movies are part of the Film Studies course at several universities. One day, they might include *Matchstick Man*.'

The warmth, the throbbing of his hand spread upwards, to her shoulders, her chest, her entire body. Of course he was right. Not only that, his enthusiasm was catching. She looked up. His ugly little face was close to hers. His broad forehead was moist with perspiration and strips of black hair clung to his skin. Their eyes caught and they shared a moment of understanding. Lisa dropped her lashes, feeling shaken. She moved back in her chair, dislodging his hand.

'Who'll be putting up the cash?' she asked eventually. This might be a ploy to get her financial backing.

'Gary Maddox has got someone to back us.'

'Gary!' She laughed out loud, glad to have the opportunity of being offensive again. That moment their eyes had met she'd found strangely disturbing. 'You mean you've met Gary Maddox and he didn't kill you?'

'*He* approached *me*. Gary's on the skids. His last two movies bombed, not surprisingly, they were brainless fluff. But he really liked the notices he got from *Matchstick Man*. He knows he's got it in him to act – with the right director. In other words, me.' He smirked. God, he was a nauseating little man.

'Fancy yourself, don't you?' she said disparagingly.

'With good reason,' he said, standing up. 'I've got to leave now.'

Lisa felt strangely disappointed and wondered why. He was so unpleasant and obnoxious – why should she care if he stayed or went?

Six weeks later, Busby telephoned. 'Lisa, I just heard the most fantastic rumour.' He laughed nervously. 'You'll die when I tell you what it is.'

'Tell me,' said Lisa.

'Someone said you were going to marry Joseph Dent. I told them not to be ridiculous. It couldn't possibly be true.'

'It is,' said Lisa.

'What?' his voice squeaked.

'I *am* going to marry Joseph Dent,' she giggled. 'It's true.'

30

Soon after Joseph Dent's visit, he invited Lisa and Gary Maddox to his home on the edge of the Hollywood Hills for the weekend. The house, which had once belonged to the silent star Vita Reese, was a three-storeyed, oak-beamed, genuine Tudor mansion which had been dismantled, brought over from Suffolk, England, piece by piece, and then put together again with careful precision.

Lisa got out of her car on the Saturday and looked up in admiration. At first-floor level, a stone was set into the white plaster and on it was engraved *Tymperleys* and underneath, 1551. The writing, lashed by centuries of wind and rain, was scarcely readable. She thought wryly how odd it was that the first time she should set eyes on an olde English building like this was thousands of miles away in Hollywood. The white-painted, black-studded front door was wide open.

'Come in,' shouted Joseph Dent. She stepped down into the large, low-ceilinged hallway-cum-lounge with whitewashed walls, furnished with big, comfortable-looking chairs covered in subdued chintz. The wooden floors and the wide stairs, worn away to a curve, were uncarpeted. Four gnarled oak columns riddled with woodworm went from floor to ceiling and the broad brick fireplace was stuffed with bright yellow daisies. Gary was already there. Both men had a drink and Joseph was rocking restlessly from foot to foot.

'I love your house, Joseph,' she said. 'It's full of atmosphere.'

'And woodworm,' he replied, 'though it's static. In spring, you can hear the deathwatch beetles courting. They rub their legs together with a loud grating sound.'

Gary came over and kissed Lisa on the cheek. He'd changed a lot since their first meeting, three years ago. Gone was the bleached hair and carefully casual style. Back to his natural brown, he was already thinning on top. He had a slightly haggard look and needed a shave. Lisa perversely thought he looked immensely more attractive now, more rugged and manly. His stardom had been brief and he'd fallen fast. Last time they'd met, he told her he'd been offered a small though regular part in a TV soap. 'If I sign the contract, it's like signing my death warrant as a screen actor,' he said bitterly.

Dent rubbed his hands. 'Lunch is ready,' he said. 'I got caterers in for the weekend. My cook's speciality is soggy meatloaf so I gave her a couple of days off.'

Lisa shuddered – imagine working for Joseph Dent and being under the same roof all day long!

He led them into a long charming room where a French window opened onto an Elizabethan garden criss-crossed with hedges. Wide stone steps led down to a water-lily-covered lake. A smiling waiter was standing by the table ready to serve them.

The meal was delicious, but halfway through it Dent flew into a rage. 'This meat is tough,' he snarled at the waiter who stepped back, eyes filled with alarm.

'No it's not, Joseph,' Lisa demurred. 'It's just right.'

The director stood up and hurled his plate at the wall. 'Such a simple fucking thing to ask someone to do – to *pay* someone to do.' The waiter rushed across and began to wipe the food off the white-painted wall with a napkin. Lisa put down her knife and fork and went to help pick up the pieces of the smashed plate.

'Don't take any notice,' she said to the man. 'The meat was fine.'

She wasn't surprised to see that Joseph Dent was grinning. 'I get mad when people don't do their job properly,' he said.

'Do anything like that again, Joseph, and I'm going home,' she said.

After lunch they went down into the basement viewing room. 'Vita Reese had this put in first, then the house built on top,' said Joseph.

It was a perfect miniature reproduction of a 1920s cinema with gold and brown painted walls, five narrow rows of velvet-covered tip-up seats, and, covering the screen, matching velvet curtains which drew back at the touch of a button.

'I thought I'd show the movies in reverse order. Shall we begin with *Matchstick Man?*' asked Dent from the doorway of the projection room. Row after row of film was stacked on the shelves behind him.

'Yes, please,' Gary said quickly. He sat down, shoulders hunched, at the end of a row. Lisa sat a couple of rows behind just as the lights went out and the titles came onto the screen.

This was the reason for the weekend – to see all of Joseph Dent's movies and decide if she wanted to appear in his next one. Her first inclination had been to turn the invitation down, but Gary had telephoned the night of the producer's visit to ask what she thought of his proposition.

'I don't quite know what to think, Gary,' she'd replied. 'I suppose he talked a lot of sense, but working with him again . . .' She didn't finish. Gary would know what she meant.

'Have you read the book yet, *Attrition?*'

'Yes, I started it after he left and I just this minute finished. I couldn't put it down.'

'I can just see it as a movie. I can see myself in that part. Just the two of us on screen for most of the time. Shit, Lisa, it could turn out really sensational.' Gary's voice was raw, pleading. She lit a cigarette and wondered why.

Between puffs, she asked, 'Why does it matter if *I* say yes or no? He can always get someone else. Okay, so no big name will work with him, but there's scores of actresses who've probably never heard—'

Gary interrupted, his voice harsh. 'Because he refuses to do it with anyone else but you,' he said.

'Does he?' She was astonished.

'He's a real bastard, Lisa. As soon as he saw how desperate I was, as soon as he knew he had the power, he started laying down conditions, even though I told him I got the backing . . .'

So, when Joseph Dent called the following day and asked if she'd spend the weekend at his house, she had reluctantly agreed for Gary's sake, even though she'd never cared for him much. Anyway, she thought grudgingly, it was a good book and, as Gary said, would make a really sensational movie.

On screen, Gary's face was twisted in an awful rage as the camera moved slowly in for a close-up. Then his expression began to change, to melt into despair. There was no sound, no music. Without a single word he conveyed the suffering in his soul. It was brilliant acting.

Lisa glanced across the tiny cinema. The real Gary was staring at himself as if entranced. Incredibly she saw a tear run down his cheek, and thought how strange ambition was.

Gary's family were wealthy. She knew he could go home tomorrow and never need to work again, but this third-rate actor, by a freak of chance, had got the lead in *Matchstick Man,* a movie written off almost before it had begun. Joseph Dent had tormented him into giving a great performance and now Gary was desperate to give another. Those good notices had acted like a drug and he was willing to abase himself before the man he hated in order to read again that he was a good actor.

Suddenly the lights went on; the film had reached its end. As the curtains swung together, a gaudily-painted organ rose out of the tiny orchestra pit and raucous music blasted from the speakers each side of the screen. Joseph Dent appeared, grinning, went across to the organ and lifted the lid to reveal a fully-stocked bar.

'What's it to be?' he asked.

They watched two more movies that afternoon. Lisa's head began to ache, though she had to concede that Dent was a great director. His work had a dark undercurrent of fear, gripping the audience, right from the very first startling shot. She'd already made up her mind to agree to his proposition. A real actor should consider that the ends justified the means. She wouldn't let Dent know yet, let him hang on tenterhooks for a while longer; it would do him good – though she still wondered why he was so insistent on having her.

Dinner was served on the terrace. The waiter, no longer smiling, hovered over them anxiously. Lisa felt angry with the director for reducing the man to such a state. As the light began to fail Dent said, 'Watch this.' He went inside the French windows and suddenly the hedges and trees were lit by a thousand candle-shaped lights. 'Some sight, eh?'

The spangled garden seemed to stretch for miles. An old-fashioned street lamp shed its soft glow over the lake right into the faces of the creamy-white water lilies, so perfect and so still. Rustling, scrabbling sounds came from the nearby hedges and bushes as though small animals had been disturbed by the sudden intrusion of light on their slumber, and startled birds rose, squawking angrily as they flew haphazardly for a few seconds before settling back into their nests.

'It's breathtaking,' said Lisa.

Before going to bed they watched another movie – an eerie, haunted piece of work with an unexpectedly savage twist at the end that turned Lisa's stomach. She went to bed, having drunk too much whisky and seen too many frightening films. As she lay in the large four-poster, she felt strangely on edge. It had been an unusually weird day. Her feeling of unease was not helped when she half-woke during the night, convinced she could hear a child sobbing. She pulled the covers over her head, wondering if the sound had been made hundreds of years ago and she was only hearing it now.

Next morning, everything was back to normal. The sun was shining through the mullioned windows, dancing on the pink flowered carpet. Lisa was about to get up and have a shower when she froze in fright as the sound of wild, tumultuous music suddenly filled the room – she later learnt it was Wagner. Terrified, she leapt out of bed and could feel the floor throbbing beneath her. She searched for a radio and identified that the sound was coming from a speaker above the bed. There was a switch underneath. She clicked it down and the music ceased, but only in her room. The sound could still be heard outside.

Still shaking, she showered in the modern adjoining bathroom and dressed in white jeans and a bluebell-coloured blouse with wide gathered sleeves, pulling a white band over her long gleaming hair. She didn't bother with make-up. She still looked good without it, and doubted whether Gary or Joseph would notice if she wore it or not.

Downstairs, Joseph Dent said gleefully, 'Wagner woke you up, then?'

'I was already awake, thanks,' she said sarcastically. He explained that he'd fitted up a loud-speaker system throughout the house.

'Like to keep everyone on their toes,' he said. Lisa gave him a filthy look. The music had been changed to New Orleans jazz, which was more relaxing though still too loud.

The caterers had already arrived to prepare breakfast. Lisa said all she wanted was coffee. Gary, looking even more haggard this morning, said just coffee would do him fine, too. 'I'd like to get back to watching movies straight away,' he said. 'I learnt a lot yesterday.'

'Suits me.' Joseph Dent told the waiter to take the food away. 'You and the cook eat it,' he said curtly. Today he wore jeans and an open-necked black shirt. Lisa wondered if he was aware of his similarity to Old Nick and emphasised it by always wearing black.

'Do you mind if I give the first one a miss?' she said. 'I've still got a bit of a headache.'

'In that case,' said Dent, 'I'll set Gary up in the basement and show you around the house.'

When he came back a quarter of an hour later, he said, 'Maddox has turned out different from what I thought he would. He's not so empty-headed after all.' His black eyes glittered and he seemed to be gripped by an energy that threatened to explode.

'This way.' He darted over to the door and was about to forge through, then remembered his manners and held it open for Lisa to go first. As he walked alongside her, he snapped his fingers impatiently in time to the music. 'This is, was, a sewing room.'

'It's lovely!' A tapestry-covered window seat in front of a tiny bow window, a silk-cushioned rocking chair, a carved sewing-box.

'Vita had the original furniture brought over too.'

After a while she ran out of adjectives, though Joseph Dent didn't seem to notice. He didn't linger, just opened a door, let her look, then closed it abruptly. She felt as if he was leading up to something and had to go through the motions of showing her round beforehand.

'And this,' he said eventually, pausing before a door at the end of a corridor, 'is my studio.'

'And this is what you *really* wanted me to see,' thought Lisa, 'though I can't think why.' For some reason, Dent seemed set on impressing her.

The large room looked as if it might once have been a chapel or a schoolroom. Two storeys high, the walls were white and heavily beamed – what you could see of them, because they were hidden by hundreds of unframed paintings. At first Lisa thought he was a collector until she noticed an easel holding a half-done painting at the end of the room.

'Did you do all these?'

'Yes,' he said proudly, pulling at his beard. 'What do you think?'

Lisa walked slowly around the room. Some were paintings of the garden and the house, barely recognisable, just suggestions here and there of a window, a door, a lake, the water lilies. There were numerous portraits of women and children with names scrawled on their foreheads in black. The oil paint was laid on thick in smears as much as an inch deep.

'I like the colours,' she said cautiously – lots of deep mustardy yellow, purple, dark reds, bottle green.

'You fucking moron,' said Joseph Dent, behind her.

She spun round, almost choking with anger. 'You arrogant, insufferable pig of a man,' she spat.

To her utter astonishment, he was smiling. 'I was interested in seeing your reaction.'

She said nothing for several seconds. Then she returned his smile. 'Do you have a favourite?'

'This one.' He pointed to a large painting of what looked like a church at night, yellow light shining out of the half-open door.

Lisa picked the canvas off the wall, threw it on the floor and stamped on it. The stiff cloth split several ways and the interior framework splintered.

'I was interested in seeing your reaction,' she said, edging towards the door so she could escape if Dent decided to attack her.

Instead he looked quite indifferent. 'Actually,' he said, 'I hated that one most. Seriously though,' he went on calmly as if nothing had happened, 'what *do* you think?'

Lisa was outwardly as calm as he was. Inwardly she felt exhilarated by a sense of almost perverted satisfaction. She stepped over the broken painting and stared at the walls. 'I could grow to like them,' she said slowly. 'Who are the portraits of?'

'My wives and children. To save you counting, I had five of the first and sixteen of the second.'

'Where are they?'

'Who knows?' he shrugged. 'Who cares?'

Lisa drove home that night feeling exhausted. It was as if she'd switched off her own life for twenty-four hours and become immersed in a totally different world. When she went in, Busby's house seemed curiously bare and lifeless, and much too quiet. She immediately made a pot of tea – she hadn't been offered one all weekend and felt deprived. As she drank it, she thought about Joseph Dent. He was the most unusual man she'd ever met. There was something fascinatingly awful about him; he was a charming monster, mercurial and unpredictable. Yet so interesting. You never knew what he was going to do or say next. When she told him she would do his movie, his reaction was the opposite of what she'd expected. Instead of being pleased and grateful, he said in an offhand manner, 'You'd be crazy not to.'

'When will we start?' asked Gary. He'd said little over the weekend and his eyes were red-rimmed and weary. Instead of having lunch, he'd watched *Matchstick Man* again, as if he was trying to cram as much as possible into his stay.

'In a couple of months,' said Dent. 'Soon as I'm back from Cannes. I'm on the jury at the film festival there. Like to come with me?'

'You bet!' said Gary with alacrity.

'I didn't mean you, I meant her,' Dent said rudely, nodding at Lisa.

Gary blushed and Lisa felt angry at the director's lack of tact. Sometimes he was barely civilised.

'I'll go if Gary goes,' she said quickly, and Joseph Dent, confounding her as usual, actually laughed and said, 'Good, I'll book the hotel and tickets.'

But before Cannes, in a weak moment – or so she told herself – she'd promised to spend another weekend at his house, this time to see the movies Busby had made before they met. She'd long wanted to see them.

'But this time, no caterers,' she said firmly. 'Soggy meatloaf suits me fine.'

Joseph Dent's cook and maid-of-all-work, a plump black woman called Millie, treated him with utter contempt. With insults flying thick and fast, Dent was at his most charming. It was as if he could only be nice to people who didn't treat him with respect. Anyone who fawned, who was sycophantic, even good-mannered, was at the mercy of his cruel, lashing tongue. Inefficiency drove him crazy. Lack of intelligence goaded him into wild, uncontrollable anger, though Millie soon put him in his place if he shouted at her for not grasping what he meant instantly.

Just before dinner Lisa heard screaming and the sound of breaking crockery coming from the kitchen. Alarmed, she ran down the corridor and found Dent and Millie throwing plates at each other with gusto. With Wagner thundering in the background, it was like a scene from an operatic farce.

'That was one of Vita's,' hissed Dent as a plate narrowly missed him and shattered on the wall behind. 'It came from England and was a hundred years old.'

'I don't care if it came from the table of the Lord Jesus Christ,' snarled Millie. She stood beside the stove, her dark eyes sparking hate. 'You call me a stupid black bitch again and I'll throw *you* the length of my kitchen. Oh, hallo Lisa.' The change in tone was so abrupt that Lisa had to smile.

'We were just having a little argument,' explained Joseph. 'She put the Burgundy in the fridge.'

'What's wrong with that?' asked Lisa.

'See!' said Millie triumphantly. '*She* don't know it's supposed to be warm, either. I'll put it in some hot water, thaw it out.'

And as if it had never been any other way, the pair were suddenly on perfectly amicable terms again and later Joseph even praised Millie for her meatloaf.

Busby Van Dolen was one of the few people for whom Joseph seemed to have any respect. 'He never compromised,' he said after they'd watched the first movie. 'Never gave into commercial pressure.'

'He has now,' said Lisa sadly. 'Though I can't say I blame him.'

Surprisingly enough, neither did Joseph. 'You can't keep banging your head against a brick wall forever.' Afterwards, Lisa thought it was probably the kindest remark she'd ever heard him make.

She'd been given the same room as before and began to wonder why she needed an entire weekend to watch three films. A single afternoon would have sufficed.

In the middle of the night she woke to find the moon shining through the small windows, sharply illuminating the heavy oak wardrobe. There'd been a noise, a creaking of a hinge, the sound of a door closing. Nervously she peeped from under the bedclothes and shrieked.

Joseph Dent was standing beside her bed holding a tray on which stood a bottle of wine and two glasses. He was totally naked.

She struggled to sit up. He looked so ridiculous that she burst out laughing. 'What do you want?' she managed to say between the laughter.

'What do you think?'

She looked him up and down. 'Well, I suppose it's obvious.'

He came over and put the tray down beside the bed. 'Move over.'

Still giggling, she shuffled along and he climbed in beside her. By now tears were streaming down her cheeks. 'You,' she said with difficulty, 'are the most outrageous man I've ever met in my life.'

'I know,' he said complacently. 'Want a drink?'

'Has it been warmed?'

'It's champagne.'

The bubbly wine combined with the giggles gave her hiccups. 'Drink from the opposite side of the glass,' advised Joseph.

'You do that with water, not champagne, silly.'

'I'll come straight to the point,' he said. 'I want to marry you.'

Lisa hiccuped.

'Is that a yes?'

She hiccuped again and slid down the bed, convulsed with uncontrollable laughter.

Joseph slid down and reached for her. His arms were hard and he took her fiercely and swiftly and silently. No gentle words, no compliments, no avowals of love. Not even a kiss. Despite this, his lovemaking was surprisingly satisfying. When they'd finished he lay with his head propped on one hand, looking down at her. 'Wanna know something?'

'What?'

'When you walked onto the set of *Matchstick Man*, I made up my mind to marry you some day.'

'You could have fooled me. If you said you'd made up your mind to murder me I wouldn't be surprised. What took you so long to ask?'

'I was already married at the time.'

'A genuine enough reason,' said Lisa dryly.

'Then I was casting around for an excuse to call on you, like a movie, for instance.'

'I wouldn't have thought *you'd* need an excuse, Joseph.'

'Call me Joe, all my wives do.'

'In that case, I'll call you Dent. I'd like to keep our relationship formal.'

'I take it you've accepted my proposal. Was that hiccup a yes?'

'Yes,' she said, wondering if she'd taken leave of her senses.

'Tell me what you want most in the world and I'll give it you as a wedding present.'

'An ocean liner.'

'Which one, the *Elizabeth* or the *Mary*?'

'A desert.'

'Will the Sahara do?'

She laughed and then thought of what she wanted most in the world and felt sad. In the bright light of the moon Joseph must have noticed her expression change. 'What is it?'

'Nothing.' She turned away.

'You've thought of something I can't give you. What?'

'A baby,' she said softly.

'I can give you a baby.'

She shook her head impatiently. 'No one can.'

'I can give you a baby,' he repeated. He got out of bed and went over to the door.

'Dent,' she called. 'You've got nothing on. Millie might see you.'

'Wouldn't be the first time,' he said airily. Nevertheless, he came back and picked up her white cotton dressing gown. 'How does this look?' He twirled around in the frilly garment.

'Ridiculous,' she said, feeling laughter begin to well up again.

He was gone for ten minutes. She wondered what he'd bring her. A doll? A puppy or a kitten? To her utter astonishment he came back with a small child fast asleep in his arms.

He laid the sleeping child on the bed beside her. 'This is Sabina,' he said. 'She's yours.'

The girl was no more than a toddler. Snuggling into the pillow, she put her thumb in her mouth and began to suck audibly.

'She's beautiful,' gasped Lisa. The child was dressed in cotton pyjamas which were too small, exposing her plump legs to the knees. There was a red mark around her waist where the elastic was too tight. Long black lashes quivered gently on her chubby, butter-smooth cheeks.

'Who put her to bed like this?' she hissed angrily. 'You?'

'The nanny did. Why, what's wrong?'

'Her hair hasn't been unplaited; it must be awfully uncomfortable.' The child's thick, waist-length hair was woven tight, drawn hard back at the base of her skull.

'How old is she?'

'Two, three, four – I can't remember.'

'Dent, you monster! Is she yours?'

He grinned. 'I already said, she's *yours*.'

'She's not an article to be handed out as a gift, she's a living child. Let's put it another way, did you father her?'

'I did. Her mother was a full-blooded Cherokee called Koko.'

'And where is Koko?'

'Gone!' he said dramatically, throwing out his hands wide. 'Left directly her papoose was born. The divorce came through a year ago.'

Lisa was gently undoing the tight plait. When she'd finished, Sabina, still asleep, seemed to breathe a sigh of relief and nestled deeper into the pillow.

'You can keep her there all night if you want,' he said generously.

'Don't be silly,' snapped Lisa. 'She'd be terrified, waking up in a strange room with a strange woman. Take her back this minute.'

'If you say so,' he replied obediently.

Busby said, 'You *can't* marry Joseph Dent. He's a devil.'

'I know,' she said sympathetically, thankful he couldn't see her smile. 'That's what I've thought ever since I met him.'

'And a misogynist. He hates women.'

'Not just women, darling. He hates everyone.'

'Oh Lisa,' said Busby despairingly. 'Then why marry him?'

'I don't know,' she confessed. 'I think it's because he brings out the worst in me.'

'Your little girl is the image of you,' said a woman at the next table. 'I saw you on deck together this morning.'

'Do you really think so?' said Lisa delightedly. She could think of little in her life that had given her so much pleasure as that remark. Sabina's eyes were much darker than hers, but apart from that they could indeed have been mother and daughter with their long, thick chocolate-coloured hair and deep creamy skin. Even Dent had remarked on it that Sunday morning when he took Lisa up to the nursery.

The room, on the top floor of the house, spanned its entire width and could have looked pretty if the white flowered curtains and matching covers on the junior-sized bed had not been tinged with grey, and the floor not littered with so many toys, most of them broken and looking as if they'd been there for weeks, if not months. With the help of a twice-weekly cleaner,

Millie kept the rest of the house spotless. Presumably this part was the responsibility of the nanny.

Sabina, still in her pyjamas at ten o'clock, was leaning over a toy crib draped with soiled broderie anglaise, softly talking to a doll. As she leaned forward, her pyjama pants pulled away to reveal the same angry, red serrated mark Lisa had noticed before, and her hair had been replaited.

As they entered, a woman sitting in the corner reading a paperback book jumped to her feet in alarm. She wore a stained maroon dressing gown and her feet were bare.

'Why, Mr Dent,' she stuttered. 'I wasn't expecting . . .' She didn't finish, obviously petrified of Dent.

Sabina looked up at them gravely without speaking. You'd think she'd come running over to her father, thought Lisa sadly.

'Hallo, Sabina.' She knelt beside the child. 'What's your dolly called, sweetheart?'

The little girl's grave expression did not alter. She thought awhile then frowned. 'Dolly,' she said.

'I've got a dolly at home called Victoria. Do you think she'd like to meet yours?'

Sabina shrugged. 'Don't know.'

Dent, his usual uncivil self, had not thought to introduce the nurse. Lisa forced herself to smile at the woman. 'Hi, I'm Lisa Angelis,' she said. 'Will you get Sabina dressed so she can play outside, please.'

'Outside! What about the lake?' The woman was about fifty, pale, with a thin, unhealthy face. Her mouth was rimmed with cold sores and her hair hadn't been combed that day.

'She'll be quite safe if she's watched. Do I take it she never goes out to play, Mrs—?'

'Wright. Mrs Wright. Well, I do worry about that lake.' The woman glanced nervously at Dent who was twiddling his thumbs and staring at the floor, clearly bored with the whole proceedings.

'Do you, Mrs Wright?' said Lisa brightly. 'Well, the reason we've come to see you is to say that Mr Dent and I are getting married and then going abroad for a while, and we're taking Sabina with us, so I'm afraid your services won't be required any longer. Dent will give you a cheque for three months' salary in lieu of notice. So, if you could pack your things, please . . .'

'Now?' said the woman.

'Now,' said Lisa.

'Why did you do that?' asked Dent curiously as they went downstairs ten minutes later, Lisa holding Sabina's hand. She'd dressed the child herself in a pair of yellow overalls and a tee shirt, the only clothes she could find which still fitted. Everything else was too small.

'Because she plaits Sabina's hair too tight and hasn't got the sense to realise how much it hurts, particularly in bed,' Lisa replied angrily. 'God knows what time she dressed her in the mornings. Her doll hasn't got a name which means she probably doesn't talk to her. She doesn't go out to play and none of her clothes fit.'

'She only had to ask for money,' said Dent reasonably.

'Couldn't you see, she was terrified of you!' snapped Lisa. 'She was too scared to ask.'

*

It wasn't that Dent was cruel. As far as he was concerned, his responsibility ended when he engaged a nanny for his child. Then he had virtually forgotten she existed. It never occurred to him to play with her, or check whether she was being looked after properly, or if she was happy – and Sabina clearly was neither.

Her speech was limited to a handful of words and she had no idea how to play except with her doll. Once they were downstairs she regarded Lisa solemnly, her great brown eyes bright as if she was about to cry, an impression strengthened when her small mouth quivered. Lisa longed to hug the tiny, pathetic body, but felt that too much demonstrative affection from a complete stranger might upset the child even more.

Instead she said, 'I'm Lisa and we're going to be great friends. Do you know what friends are?'

Sabina nodded and said seriously, 'Dolly fwend.'

Lisa took her into the garden and taught her how to throw a ball and catch it. Dent came out and to Lisa's surprise he joined in and it was actually he who brought the first smile to the child's face when he threw himself dramatically onto the grass to catch her throw.

Later, when Lisa went inside to the kitchen to see about the little girl's lunch, Millie said, 'I'm sure glad to see the back of that Mrs Wright. I kept telling his lordship she was a no-good lazy bitch, but he didn't take no notice.'

'I'm going to marry him,' said Lisa.

Millie burst out laughing. 'Sooner you than me,' she snorted.

Suddenly the roar of a motorbike could be heard and Lisa rushed outside. Sabina had disappeared. Half an hour later Dent returned, his daughter clutching his hand, her cheeks pink, her long hair wild.

'Took her for a ride on Bessie,' he said. 'I think she enjoyed it.'

Lisa groaned. The man was impossible.

'Be a funny sort of honeymoon,' said Dent. 'With Sabina and Gary.'

'You don't mind, do you?' asked Lisa.

'Suits me,' he shrugged.

They were in the silver Duesenberg which had belonged to Vita Reese, on the way back from their wedding. It had been a spur-of-the-moment decision to bring the ceremony forward a few weeks and dodge the reporters who seemed to find it newsworthy.

No guests were invited. Two women from an office next door agreed to be witnesses and Dent had given them a hundred dollars each.

Lisa glanced at him. He had on the same shiny black suit he'd worn the day he'd called on her – could it really be a mere five weeks ago? It seemed an age. This small, virile man, bursting with energy – he was a stranger, really. She wasn't even sure she liked him. Yet, somewhat to her astonishment, she'd married him! Perhaps it was because there were no boundaries with Dent. She could be herself. There was never any need to worry about hurting his feelings, saying or doing the wrong thing. True, he might explode into a rage. But then, she could explode right back. She'd really enjoyed stamping on his painting that day.

'What are you thinking about?' he asked.

'You.'

'That's a coincidence – so was I.'

Dent was terrified of flying. He excused this weakness by declaring that anyone willing to trust themselves to a pressed steel tube thousands of feet up in the air was beyond his understanding. 'They must be stark, raving mad,' he said wonderingly. 'When you think of the things that can go wrong!'

'Trouble with you, Dent, is you think too much,' scolded Lisa. Nevertheless, she looked forward to the trip to Cannes by sea.

Sabina loved the water. With Lisa hovering anxiously behind, the child stood for hours at the stern of the ship, fascinated by the sight of the muddy grey ocean being churned into dirty foam. She held up her doll to watch the V-shaped wake, her brow creased in concentration. Lisa knew she wanted to ask questions but hadn't yet the words to form them. When she told Dent, he treated his three-year-old daughter to a lecture on propellers and velocity and water strength, of which neither of them could understand a word.

Meal-times in the luxury-class dining room turned out to be torture. Dent looked upon the rest of the passengers as morons, particularly the Texas oil millionaire and his wife who shared their table, along with another couple – working-class New Yorkers using their lottery winnings for the trip of a lifetime. The Texan was admittedly loudmouthed, voicing his opinions with a certainty that brooked no argument. Dent either ignored him or demolished the man with stinging rudeness.

'Perhaps we should set up concentration camps,' he said one night when the Texan had been sounding off on the stupidity of paying welfare to the unemployed. 'Feather-bedding the scroungers', he'd called it.

'Eh?' The man stared at Dent. He wore rimless glasses and behind them his small eyes were puzzled.

'Put the unemployed, the blacks, the sick and the old in concentration camps,' said Dent in a friendly voice. Lisa's heart sank. She knew he was leading up to a whopping insult. She also knew he didn't give a damn about the unemployed. If the Texan had declared the sky was blue, Dent would have demolished his premise with equal nastiness just because he didn't like the man. 'Put the able-bodied to work building ovens, then gas the lot.'

Even then the Texan wasn't sure if Dent was being serious or not, 'Well, perhaps that's a bit extreme.'

'That's a preposterous idea,' gasped the woman from New York. Dent ignored her.

'Not too extreme for a fascist like you, surely?' he said.

The Texan, aware by now he was being mocked, exploded in anger. On Lisa's right, Gary gave a little snigger and she felt doubly irritated. Gary's feelings about Dent had done a hundred and eighty degree turn. Now he almost worshipped the man and the longer the two were together, the more like Dent he became. His admittedly superficial charm had gone, along with the bleached hair, and day by day he became more caustic and offensive.

'Please excuse me.' She stood up. 'I think I'll skip dessert.'

On deck she lit a cigarette and stood by the rail watching the smoke disappear into the night air. Suddenly she found herself smiling. Serve that Texan right, expecting everyone to agree with his nauseous opinions. Dent had certainly taken him down a peg.

There was a loud crash from the dining room behind. It sounded as if someone was throwing dishes. Gary told her later that in the process of trying to strangle her husband, the Texan had dragged the tablecloth and everything on it onto the floor. It had taken three waiters to pull him away. Throughout the proceedings, said Gary with a giggle, Dent had adopted an air of injured innocence, saying wonderingly, 'The man just flipped, I can't think why.' The New Yorkers, not sure whose side they were on, asked to be seated elsewhere and the Texan remained out of sight for the rest of the trip so the Dent entourage had a table to itself – to Lisa's heartfelt relief.

31

It was truly a glittering event. Lisa had never seen so many women wearing so many precious jewels. The occasion was a reception for the judges, officials and stars of the Cannes Film Festival. The three pink-tinted crystal chandeliers which hung down the centre of the room added yet more sparkle to the big hotel ballroom, its walls hung with richly-coloured oil paintings depicting heroic scenes from the French Revolution.

Lisa wasn't sure if she felt underdressed or overdressed. That afternoon, Dent, who usually didn't give a damn what she wore, had bought her a silver lamé trouser suit. The legs were gathered, harem-style, into wide, multi-coloured jewelled bands; the top was full with a halter neck, the strap a delicate silver chain, and finally, a two-inch-wide belt which matched the ankle-trimming.

'Don't you think it's rather vulgar?' she asked Dent when she came out of the changing room in the tiny, exclusive boutique. He was dancing impatiently about, waiting for her to appear.

'Yeah, but everyone should look vulgar once in a while,' he said.

She agreed to bow to his awesome wisdom and let him pay, though once outside, she gasped, 'Christ Almighty, Dent! Wasn't that the equivalent of three thousand dollars?'

'Something like that,' he said flippantly.

'I doubt if I'll think I'll look as gorgeous as when I paid a couple of shillings for a frock in Paddy's Market,' she remarked wryly.

'Lisa! Someone told me you were here,' cried a familiar voice.

Ralph grasped her shoulder and she threw her arms around his neck in delight.

'Ralph! Have you met my husband, Joseph Dent? And this is our friend Gary Maddox.'

'We've met before,' grunted Gary, and moved rudely away.

Dent said accusingly, 'You wasted your talent in Hollywood. You could've been a truly great actor if you'd picked your parts more carefully.'

'No need to rub it in, old man,' Ralph replied courteously. Later, when Dent was out of earshot, he asked 'Is he always so blunt?'

'Always,' said Lisa.

'It doesn't seem to worry you, though. I've never seen you look so contented.'

'I've never been so contented,' she said. Afterwards, she thought with astonishment, 'That's true! Who would have thought I'd find such happiness with a man like Joseph Dent?'

Back in Hollywood, Dent and Gary were working together on the script of *Attrition*. It was a bitter, uncompromising story, virtually a two-hander, with Gary and Lisa's characters locked in a frightening game of cat and mouse. The studio was booked, the crew hired. To Lisa's disgust, she discovered Dent had been stringing the novelist along for years with repeated options on his book.

'You are a bastard, Dent,' she told him when she learnt that the poor man had been waiting to give up his job to write full-time for ages. 'I hope you pay him an extra large fee. And by the way, how did Gary come to raise the finance?' *Attrition* had a budget of over a million dollars. She knew there was animosity between Gary and his father, who didn't approve of his son's Hollywood career, so the money wouldn't have been forthcoming from that quarter.

'Don't know, don't care,' Dent replied brusquely. 'As long as he's got it, that's all that matters.'

Sabina had been registered at a nursery school. At first, Lisa let her go just two days a week, then, when the child showed every sign of enjoying it, she went full-time. Her vocabulary improved enormously and she mixed well. Those first isolated, friendless years didn't appear to have had any long-term detrimental effect. On her fourth birthday, Lisa invited the entire class to a party, a noisy, chaotic affair. None of the games which Lisa had planned so carefully were played. Instead, Dent led the children on an adventure trip around the vast garden. There were ogres under one tree and witches living up another. Fairy fish, invisible to the human eye, inhabited the lily pond and one little boy fell in, determined to catch one. After the guests had been collected and it was all over, Dent said, 'I enjoyed that.'

'That's because you're little more than a child yourself – at times,' said Lisa.

Marriage had not mellowed Joseph Dent. When they began work on *Attrition*, he was as vicious and cruel as ever. Lisa ignored his rages and, to her surprise, so did Gary Maddox. As if he had taken a vow not to lose his temper, the actor listened patiently to every criticism, responding with almost pathetic obedience.

One night, when they were at home, Dent said, 'I'm not getting the full works out of Maddox.'

'What do you mean?' Lisa asked.

'He's too damned submissive. I need to get under his skin to bring out the best in him. He's *acting* angry and frightened and it shows. I want him to *be* angry and frightened. I'll have to rile him more.'

Next day on set, they were on the ninth take of a scene where Gary thinks he has been betrayed by Lisa and the camera rests on his face as the reality of supposed betrayal sinks in and he is possessed with inward, overpowering rage. Gary just wasn't managing it so Dent managed it for him. Flinging his script onto the floor, he screamed. 'You fucking, lily-livered faggot! What's the matter with you? Ain't you got no balls at all? Too ladylike to lose your temper, is that it?'

Lisa heard gasps from the technicians. This was over the top even for Dent. She watched as Gary's face turned red and ugly. He leapt at the director, fists raised ready to strike. She screamed and Gary stopped, only a yard away from Dent. 'Don't you *ever* call me a faggot again,' he grated.

Dent faced him fearlessly. 'Get back on set,' he ordered. 'We're trying to make a movie here.'

Gary returned sullenly. Passing Lisa, he said viciously, 'One of these days, I'll kill that bastard.'

Attrition was more than three-quarters finished. All that remained to be done were the outdoor scenes, for which Dent had rented an empty house. 'It's real spooky,' he'd told Lisa a few weeks before. 'A little grey castle, thoroughly tasteless.'

To her surprise, the house turned out to be Ralph Layton's. It had a *For Sale* board outside.

'You didn't say it was Ralph's,' she said to Dent accusingly.

'I didn't think you'd be interested,' he replied.

That night, she called the operator and got Ralph's new number.

'Why didn't you tell me you'd moved?' she said straight off. 'Are you somewhere bigger and grander?'

'No,' said Ralph with a laugh. 'I'm somewhere smaller and meaner.'

'Why?' she demanded.

'As they say in England, I was short of a few bob. I needed money for something important and in case you haven't noticed, Lisa, I haven't worked much recently.'

Ralph had appeared in too many lousy films. People had forgotten what a good actor he was. Now in his fifties, he'd been relegated to minor supporting parts. 'I'd half-noticed,' she said apologetically. 'I've been so busy. I have Sabina now and Dent is very demanding.'

'For Chrissakes, Lisa, it's not your fault.' He laughed again, this time somewhat bitterly. 'I went to Cannes in the hope of making some foreign contacts, but no luck. I've shot my bolt as far as Hollywood goes. I was thinking of going back to the stage.'

'How's Michael?' she asked tentatively.

'Long gone. As the money shrank, so did his affection. But there's someone else – someone very special.'

On the final day of shooting, something odd happened.

'All I need now,' said Dent, 'Is a shot of the handyman coming out of the garage.'

'We did that last night,' said the actor who played the part.

Dent stared at the man. 'Last night?' he said, his face creased in a frown. Lisa could see he was struggling to remember. 'Last night,' he repeated to himself. He turned to Lisa for confirmation. To her consternation, he looked frightened and for the first time since she'd known him, unsure of himself.

'That's right,' she assured him. 'You were probaby tired. It'll come to mind eventually.'

Beside her, Gary Maddox sniggered at Dent's discomfiture. Relations between the two had hit rock bottom. Dent had kept the actor on the brink of savage, furious rage for weeks. Several times it had exploded into violence and the two men had come to blows. Gary only spoke to the director when he had to and then he was barely civil.

Lisa was thankful it was all over. She took another vow never to appear in one of Joseph Dent's movies again.

Dent had begun a painting – a massive canvas, ten foot by six. He laid it on the floor and began to throw paint on, smearing it with his hands into shapes that meant nothing to Lisa.

'What is it?' she asked.

'Life,' he snapped.

'Whose life? Yours?'

He shrugged. 'Anybody's.'

Gary Maddox turned up one day a few weeks after *Attrition* was finished. To Lisa's astonishment he was completely back to his normal self. After kissing her cheek, he asked, 'Is Dent about?'

'He's in his studio.'

She expected an explosion of anger when Gary went in, and was even considering getting Dent's gun from the kitchen in case they needed separating. Instead, she heard nothing until two hours later when they emerged together, laughing.

'Gary's had this script sent to him,' Dent said. 'It'll make a really sensational movie.'

Lisa groaned.

Millie came out into the garden looking angry. It was Saturday and Sabina was home from school. Dent was teaching her to climb trees and like a great black bird of prey, he was perched halfway up an elderly elm, reaching down to pull her up to the next branch. Lisa, wishing he would teach her something more useful and ladylike, watched anxiously.

'Are you staying in for dinner tonight or not?' demanded Millie.

'Going out,' said Lisa. 'Didn't Dent tell you?'

'Sure, he told me,' Millie said crossly. 'Then half an hour later he says you're staying in.'

'He must have forgotten,' soothed Lisa. 'We're going out.' After Millie had gone, she looked at Dent with troubled eyes. It wasn't like him to get confused. On the other hand, he seemed to be forgetting a lot of things lately. Perhaps he had something on his mind, she decided.

Sabina was growing fast. 'My jeans hurt,' she complained one day. 'They dig into my bottom.'

Lisa immediately felt guilty. 'We'll go shopping after school tomorrow,' she promised. It seemed no time since she'd bought the child a whole new wardrobe of clothes.

Dent was having one of his bored days and decided to come with them. As they walked along Sunset Boulevard, Sabina danced between them, holding their hands. 'That's a pretty dress,' she shouted, darting towards a window. Lisa followed and they stood discussing whether to try the dress on. On closer inspection, Sabina decided it was too fancy. 'Too many bows and frills,' she said. When they turned, Dent had disappeared.

Lisa looked up and down and saw him some distance ahead. He had his hands in his pockets and was staring down into the gutter. She caught up with him and said, 'Why didn't you wait for us?'

He looked at her, his black eyes puzzled. 'Oh, it's you,' he said eventually. 'What goes on down there?' He nodded towards a grid in the gutter.

'It's all muddy and dirty down there, Daddy,' Sabina explained patiently. 'It's called . . .' she paused. 'What's it called, Lisa?'

'A sewer.'

'Really?' said Dent in a surprised, almost childish way, as if it was something he hadn't known.

'Come along, Dent,' said Lisa gently. 'Let's go home.'

'But we haven't bought—' began Sabina in an outraged voice. Lisa quickly squeezed her arm and she fell silent.

Aware something was wrong, something she couldn't understand, on the way home in the car, the little girl put her arms around Dent's neck and rested her head on his shoulder.

When Lisa tucked her up in bed that night, she said anxiously. 'Daddy's all right, isn't he, Lisa?'

'Of course he is,' Lisa said comfortingly, but as she closed the bedroom door behind her, she wished there was someone who would say the same comforting words to her.

Dent's painting was turning into an eye. The giant pupil was black and oily, the iris muddy brown. One day, Lisa went in and found him walking around the edge of his canvas in his bare feet. When he saw her, he grinned. 'You get a really good effect doing this.'

'Sabina turns out better stuff than that at nursery school,' she said disparagingly.

'Who's Sabina?' asked Dent.

'Perhaps he's always been like this,' thought Lisa. 'After all, I haven't known him all that long. Perhaps he's always been vague,' but in her heart of hearts she knew it wasn't true.

'What's he up to?' asked Millie.

Lisa had gone into the kitchen for Sabina's bedtime milk. Millie nodded towards the window where Dent could be seen directly outside. He seemed to be digging. Lisa crossed over to the window and looked down and saw he was levering away at the grid into which the sink waste drained. She watched as he loosened, then lifted, the slatted square of metal. Then he stood, both arms outstretched leaning against the windowsill, staring deep into the black, murky depths. For a long time he remained stock-still and in the kitchen the two women stood silently watching. His sudden sigh was audible and made both of them jump. He looked from right to left, as if wondering why he was there and, frowning, replaced the grid.

Lisa looked at Millie and saw two solitary tears running down her black cheeks. She poured a glass of milk for Sabina and left without a word.

Dent and Lisa were driving home one night in the Duesenberg having been to dinner with some of his old friends, an elderly producer and his wife. Dent was trying to raise the backing for Gary's script and was halfway to talking the man into it when they'd had an argument over a movie they'd both been involved in. Dent flew into a towering rage. Lisa had never known him so angry. She sat with bent head as everyone in the restaurant listened to his blistering, raised voice. Eventually, he leapt up, spilling his coffee over the white tablecloth. Lisa, after apologising on his behalf, followed him out.

For most of the journey back, they didn't speak. Not far from home, Dent said: 'He was right.'

'What are you talking about?' said Lisa stiffly, still angry over the way he'd behaved.

'It *was* Vince Hobart who took over as assistant director when Bert Kent died.'

'Then when we get home, why not call and apologise?' she said coldly. 'For once, consider saying you're sorry.'

Dent chuckled. 'There's a lot hanging on it, so I just might, Maxine. I just might.'

They got in close to midnight. Except for the orange lantern outside, the house was in darkness. As she drew the bolt on the front door, she asked, 'Would you like a drink?'

Dent was standing at the foot of the stairs, his arms clasped behind him, rocking backwards and forwards on the balls of his feet. He jumped at the sound of her voice.

'No thanks,' he muttered. He stared at her thoughtfully. 'You're very beautiful.'

'Why Dent, you say the nicest things.' Her joking tone belied the anxiety she was feeling.

He turned abruptly and leapt up the stairs two at a time. Lisa went into the kitchen and made a cup of tea. To her surprise, the speaker in the corner crackled and Ella Fitzgerald began to sing *Every Time We Say Goodbye*, her favourite. She smiled. Sometimes Dent could be very thoughtful.

She was sitting drinking the tea when he came in dressed in his leather flying jacket, helmet and goggles. 'I'm going for a ride on Bessie,' he said.

'Dent! Not at this time of night, surely?'

'My dear, don't be so conventional. What on earth does it matter what time I go out?' He came over and kissed her full on the lips. 'Goodbye,' he said.

'Goodnight, Dent. I'll probably be in bed by the time you get back.'

He didn't answer. She hadn't expected him to. The front door slammed and soon after, Bessie roared and she listened whilst the sound faded into the distance. Leaving her tea half-drunk, she went along to his studio and looked at the portraits: Jennifer, Koko, *Maxine*! Maxine was one of his ex-wives.

Dent had propped his new painting up against the wall. In the pupil of the eye was another eye, and inside that another, until the final eye appeared, so tiny it could scarcely be made out. The painting had a reverse three-dimensional effect, the pupils like a tunnel reaching back into infinity. In the top left-hand corner he'd scrawled in red IT'S ALL MY EYE! Life, he'd called it initially. Life is all my eye!

Ella Fitzgerald was still crooning softly in the background. Lisa returned to finish her tea, but the drink had gone cold. She made more, knowing she was delaying going to bed for some reason she couldn't quite define. Or perhaps she just didn't want to define it. Not yet.

She looked through the window, at the hedges smudged black against the electric-blue, star-freckled sky, vaguely aware of the grandfather clock ticking loudly, cranking and grinding as it worked up to striking the quarter hour.

'Lisa.'

She jumped. Sabina was standing in the doorway clutching Dolly.

'Sweetheart! Can't you sleep?'

'Bessie makes an awful loud noise.'

'Come and sit on my knee a while. Would you like a story?'

'Yes, please. Goldilocks.' She padded over and climbed onto Lisa's knee. Lisa hugged the child close and wondered why her eyes felt moist as she pressed the small body to hers.

It was difficult to concentrate on the story whilst her ears were straining to hear the sound of Bessie returning. She'd stumbled halfway through when Sabina fell asleep, her thumb stuck firmly in her mouth.

The clock began to work up to striking a quarter to two. Lisa wondered how many hundreds, if not thousands, of people had listened to it striking away each fifteen minutes of their lives as they waited for sleep, waited to get up or go out, or for a loved one to come home. Waited for good news. Or bad.

Sabina's body was warm and her head nestled in the curve of Lisa's throat. She stroked the smooth soft cheek with her finger. A floorboard creaked and she jumped, disturbing the child, who began to suck furiously on her thumb. After a while Lisa carried the little girl up to her room and tucked her in. It would be best if she was out of the way when the news came.

Downstairs she switched on the television and sat unthinkingly watching the screen for a long time before she realised the presidential results were coming in and it looked as if Richard Nixon had been elected and Hubert Humphrey had lost. Busby would be heartbroken. She remembered his anguish earlier in the year when Robert Kennedy had been assassinated. 'America is a cursed country,' he had wailed. Dear, sweet Busby, so emotional and easily hurt, entirely different from Dent, who was the ultimate cynic. Dent hadn't voted. 'Politicians are scum,' he said flatly. 'All they want is power and none of 'em ever use their power to do any good.'

Lisa turned the set off, made another pot of tea and sat in the dark, waiting.

It was the headlights she saw first, the beam fanning out over the dark trees, turning the leaves into gleaming satin.

She opened the door as the car drew up. It was a police car, the men in uniforms looking grim and uncomfortable.

'What's happened?' she asked, as if she didn't know.

'I'm afraid we have some bad news. Your husband—'

'Is he dead?'

'I'm sorry . . . yes.'

He had driven off the road at speed, straight into a tree. Even then, Dent's iron constitution had held out. He was still alive when a passing motorist noticed the upturned bike and stopped to help. Still alive when the ambulance arrived and took him to hospital. He had finally died on the operating table, less than an hour before, of multiple injuries. Because he had no identification on him, it was the police who had discovered his name and address through Bessie's registration number.

The police had gone. She assured them there were other people in the house who would take care of her – not that she felt like sympathy. She felt cold and shivery, and almost indifferent to Dent's death. She wandered round the downstairs of the house, made more tea, drank several glasses of whisky and smoked endless cigarettes. Suddenly, a glimmer of light appeared above the green hedges outside and at the same time a bird sang, then another until the air was alive with the dawn chorus and Lisa watched as one by one they appeared briefly, appeared to shake themselves, then settled back into the leaves. She found herself smiling at this innocent hive of activity, when a loud hammering sounded on the front door.

'Lisa! Oh, my dear Lisa!' Gary Maddox, tearful and distraught, took her in his arms. 'I heard it on the radio,' he groaned, his voice muffled as he rested his face in her hair.

'Why, Gary!' she exclaimed, pulling away, holding him by the shoulders. 'You really care!'

'I never thought it was possible to love and hate the same person so much. That bastard! Jesus, the times I came close to killing him.'

'Don't get too upset,' she soothed. 'Remember, Dent wouldn't cry for you. Or me, come to that.'

She woke Millie and told her the news. The old woman burst into tears but soon recovered. 'The old devil's probably watching,' she muttered. 'I'll not give him the pleasure of seeing me shed tears.'

Downstairs again, Lisa said to Gary, 'I think I'll try and snatch a few hours' sleep. You're welcome to stay if you want.'

'Do you mind if I go down and see a few of his movies?'

'Well,' said Lisa, 'if he's watching as Millie says, I think that's what he'd like us to do most of all.'

She sat up in bed, lit a final cigarette and reached behind for a pillow to rest against her back. A note fluttered to the floor. As she reached for it, Lisa recognised Dent's wild scrawling handwriting.

'Lisa, My mind is going – rapidly. Early dementia. There's no cure, I've checked. You know, I can see it in your eyes. It can only get worse and I refuse to live with it. I decided if I ever forgot your name it was time to go. I've had a fucking good life and you were the best part of it. Don't show this to anyone. Have a good life, Dent.'

*

'I knew it,' whispered Lisa as she put her lighter to the corner of the note and laid it in the ashtray to burn. 'I just knew it.'

She watched the paper brown and curl as the flickering flame swiftly consumed it. In no time, all that remained were some scraps of burnt paper and a heap of grey ash.

32

Dent was buried early on a hot, fogbound morning in November. Strange to think how much he'd been loathed, yet at least two hundred people turned up for his funeral. So many that the edge of the crowd was shrouded in white mist.

'They've come to mourn the director, not the man,' whispered Gary. Lisa squeezed his arm affectionately. He'd been a tower of strength since Dent died. Not that she needed much comforting. Dent had come into her life like a whirlwind, stayed briefly, then departed violently by his own hand – though no one knew that but her. Occasionally she felt sad, but it soon passed; she knew Dent would have despised her for being maudlin. No one truly mourned the death of Joseph Dent.

Except Sabina. Deprived of a father for most of her young life, she had come to adore him. Since Dent's death, she had been inconsolable and slept in Lisa's bed, crying herself to sleep every night.

'She'll get over it in time,' said Millie. 'Everybody gets over everything in time.'

Sabina would need a lot of love, thought Lisa, and no one was more willing and anxious to give it than she was. Dent's daughter was his greatest legacy. He'd left Lisa his house and his fortune, two million dollars, but it was Sabina she valued most, her longed-for child.

There were no flowers or prayers at Dent's funeral. They played Wagner in the small chapel and Gary and two old friends spoke a few words, but that was all. Lisa was careful nothing should be done her husband would have sneered at.

When it was over, Gary said, 'A few folk would like to come back to the house. We could watch a couple of his movies, if that's all right?'

'Of course. I asked Millie to get some refreshments ready.'

The sun had appeared, brilliant in a pale-blue sky when a dozen cars drove in procession back to Tymperleys, Lisa and Gary in the first one.

'I'll be glad when today's over,' she said with a sigh as they turned into the drive. 'There's nothing worse than a funeral.'

Later that night, she was to remember those words.

Lisa knew something was wrong the minute she stepped into the hall. Millie was standing there, a tea-towel in her hands, and a look of horror mixed with grief on her plump good-natured face.

'What's the matter?' asked Lisa immediately, then, with mounting panic: 'Where's Sabina?'

'She's gone,' said Millie in a flat, toneless voice.

'Gone!'

Gary went over and took Millie's arm. 'Where?' he demanded.

'Her momma came and took her.'

Outside car doors slammed and footsteps sounded on the gravel path.

'You two go in the kitchen,' Gary said urgently. 'I'll see to the guests.'

'The food's already laid out in the dining room,' said Millie in the same dull voice.

'What happened?' cried Lisa when the two women were alone. Millie started to cry.

'I was laying out the table when I heard voices in the hall,' she sobbed. 'I didn't take too much notice at first. The front door was open and there's been folks in an' out of here like it was Woolworths all week. When eventually I go to see, there's Koko sitting on the sofa with Sabina. "I've come to take her back with me," she sez. There was this big car outside with the motor running.'

'Oh Millie, and you just *let* her!'

Millie stared at her reproachfully. 'What d'you take me for, Lisa? 'Course I argued with her. I told her there was no way she could just walk out with the child like that. I said you'd be home in an hour and to wait, but she sez, "Sabina's my child and I wants her back." She'd read about Dent dying in some paper in Canada.'

'Canada!'

'That's where she's living now. God help me, Lisa, I would have stopped her, I'm bigger than she is, but—' she paused, the expression of grief on her face turning to embarrassment.

'But what?'

'Well, Sabina, she *wanted* to go. She said, "I want to be with my mummy." She took to Koko straight away, like she'd always known her. I don't like telling you this, Miss Lisa, but she looked really happy.'

According to Dent's lawyer, if Sabina was traced and the case went to court, Lisa didn't stand a chance of keeping her.

'The mother is always given preference,' he said. 'Always.'

'But she just walked out when Sabina was born!'

'She may be able to give a good reason for that. Anyway, the child was left with her father. Now the father's dead . . .' He shrugged. 'I understand you called the police when the child was removed, but they refused to take action?'

'They said a mother couldn't be accused of kidnapping her own child,' Lisa said tiredly.

'That's right. It isn't as if your husband had been given custody. Sabina wasn't even mentioned in the divorce proceedings.'

Damn Dent! He'd probably forgotten Sabina existed.

The lawyer went on, 'It might have been different if you'd looked after her since she was a baby, but you'd only known her eight months.'

'Yes, but I grew to love her as if she was my own.'

'It must be upsetting for you,' the lawyer said sympathetically.

'It's rather more than that,' she said bitterly.

She never saw Sabina again, though she hired a private detective to find her and make sure she was all right.

Lisa put a tape of Wagner in the loud-speaker system and the sound crashed through the house for an hour, but when it finished the place seemed more like a morgue than ever.

Millie came in almost straight away. 'Want me to put another tape in, honey?'

'Stop treating me like a baby,' said Lisa shortly.

The old woman stood looking down at her with concern. 'Koko's a nice person. She'll take care of Sabina real fine.'

'You've been telling me that every day for two months.'

'Just trying to stop you worrying, Lisa, that's all I'm doin'. She probably wouldn't have left in the first place if Dent hadn't bullied her so much. You know what a shit he could be.'

'Only too well,' said Lisa dryly.

'That dick you hired come up with anything yet?'

'No.'

'Would you like a cup of tea?'

'Yes, please. Anything to get you off my back.'

'I'll bring it in a coupla minutes,' Millie said solicitously.

After she'd gone, Lisa smiled wanly. Millie, everybody, had been really sympathetic. One morning, she'd come down and found every single reminder of the little girl removed from the house.

She leant back and lit a cigarette. Sometimes it felt as if she'd only dreamt about Sabina, that she'd never been real. Now the lovely, long dream was over, she was awake again, and the memory was submerged, only rarely coming to the surface of her mind, as dreams do.

The basement door slammed. That must be Gary coming up for air after watching Dent's movies again. The other day she'd given him his own key. 'Saves me getting up every five minutes to let you in,' she said, though she was glad of his company and it was a good excuse for putting Busby off when he rang – he'd called a lot since Dent died.

'How're ya doing?' He came in and flung himself into a chair.

'As well as can be expected. I fancy throwing myself into work but there's nothing to throw myself into yet.' The movie Dent had been planning next wasn't due to go into production till spring – if it did at all. Matters were still up in the air.

'I've been thinking, Lisa. Y'know, no one will ever get me to act like Dent did. I'm going into direction.'

She looked at him. Lately, Gary had begun to look and act more like her husband. He'd grown a little goatee beard and combed his thinning hair onto his forehead. He wore black a lot. She'd had Bessie repaired and gave it to him as a memento of Dent, and Gary rode everywhere on it. Now he wanted to become a director. Maybe one day he might ask her to marry him, make yet a further gesture to take over Dent's life.

'I think that's wise,' said Lisa. No one would ever drag a great performance out of him as Dent had.

'Y'really think so?' He looked at her anxiously.

'It's a great idea, but who'll take you on, Gary?' Who'd trust someone so inexperienced with a seven-figure-budget movie?

He grinned. '*I'll* take me on. I'm going to start my own production company. *Attrition* is doing really well at the box office. I'm going to put two million bucks into a company of my own.'

Attrition had been released two weeks before on New Year's Day. Lisa had requested the words '*This film is dedicated to the memory of Joseph Dent*' to appear at the end of the credits. The movie had received even better reviews than *Matchstick Man*. '*Joseph Dent's posthumous work is perhaps the ultimate thriller*,' one critic wrote. '*A nervewracking two hours of nailbiting tension with superb performances from the two stars.*'

'That's a big step, Gary, and I admire you for taking it.' She smiled at him. 'Dent would have been proud of you.'

'I wondered if you'd like to be a partner,' he said shyly.

'Me!' she said, astonished.

'You could go into the production side for a change. You'd be good at that, you're very organised and you hardly ever blow your top.'

'Gee, thanks! I'd like to think about it a while. I'll let you know in a couple of days,' she said.

The more Lisa thought about it, the more she was drawn to the idea of becoming involved in the business side of making films, raising the finance, reading scripts, identifying locations. In other words, she would become a producer. Lots of actors turned to direction or production. John Derek, who'd been a youthful heart-throb like Gary, had recently directed a well-regarded movie called *Childish Things* with another actor, Don Murray, producing and writing the script. Kirk Douglas had produced *Paths of Glory* and *Spartacus*, which won four Oscars, and Mai Zetterling had started directing her own films.

'I'll do it,' she told Gary the following week. 'I'll put in a million.'

They decided to use Tymperleys as a headquarters until they found an office. The new movie, as yet untitled, would begin shooting in April as Dent had planned.

Suddenly, the house was full of people – set designers, script consultants, actors. Millie was delighted. 'It's nice to see some happy faces around for a change,' she said, looking happy herself for the first time in ages.

Gary was there from early morning till late at night. One day, Lisa asked if he'd like to move in. After all, she reasoned, he had Dent's hairstyle and Dent's beard and was gradually acquiring Dent's crusty manner. He dressed like Dent and was going to make the same sort of movies. It seemed only natural to move into the man's house.

'I'd like that,' he said and paused. 'There's a friend I'd like to bring with me,' he added in a strange, tight voice.

'Well, it's a big house,' Lisa said lightly.

That night in bed she began to feel worried. She shouldn't have been so impulsive. What if she and Gary's girlfriend didn't get along?

The friend was Ralph! She stared at him, stunned, when he arrived with Gary a few days later, their luggage piled in the back of a big station wagon. So that's why he'd sold his house – to finance *Attrition*.

'You don't mind?' he asked shyly. 'I'm a partner in this new company too.' Ralph hadn't aged well. No chance of him playing the role of a hero or a romantic lead nowadays, with his comfortable, portly figure, thinning hair and half-moon spectacles. He looked more like a grandfatherly bank manager than an actor.

'Mind! If there was one person in the world I'd choose to share my house with, it'd be you.' She danced around, showering him with kisses. 'To think, after – what is it, twenty years? – we're both under the same roof again!'

Ralph turned to Gary. 'I told you it would be all right.'

The younger man shuffled his feet and avoided Lisa's eyes. 'Not everyone understands,' he muttered.

'He's still in the closet,' laughed Ralph. 'Except where you and I are concerned.' By now, everyone in Hollywood knew Ralph was gay. The stars didn't bother to keep their sexual preferences from each other. 'Remember the way he pretended to be rude when we met in Cannes?'

That night when she and Gary were alone, he asked, 'What d'you think Dent would have said if he'd known?'

'Dent wouldn't have given a damn,' said Lisa dismissively.

They decided to call themselves O'Brien Productions after a long, heated discussion that went on into the early hours. A hundred names were suggested and rejected as too grand or too pretentious until, the three of them tired and tetchy, Ralph said, 'Why not O'Brien? It's Lisa's maiden name. O'Brien Productions. It's solid and respectable, trustworthy even. Investors will have confidence in a name like that, rather than Titan, for example.' He glowered at Gary who'd been arguing for Titan all night.

O'Brien Productions! Lisa got a real kick out of seeing that name up on screen at the beginning of their first movie, even more than Lisa Angelis. The critics had been generous, describing the new company's début as *'efficient and entertaining – a good first effort'*.

Six months after Dent's death, Lisa heard from the private detective she'd hired to find Sabina.

'She's living in an apartment block in Ottawa,' he wrote. *'It's not exactly luxurious, but pretty respectable. Koko Lecoustre has two other children, boys aged one and three. She's now married to a building worker; regular income, hard-working, a decent sort of chap. I observed the child going to grade school and she looks happy.'*

He enclosed a snapshot of Sabina looking strange, all wrapped up in a thick coat and boots, with a muffler around her neck and a woollen hat. She was smiling as she carried her lunchbox to school.

Lisa stared at the photograph for a long, long time, wondering if Sabina ever thought about the stepmother she'd had for eight short months. Then Millie came in and Lisa silently handed her the report.

After she'd read it, the old woman said gently, 'She's better off, honey, with two little brothers and a regular mom and pop.'

'I suppose so,' Lisa said dully. 'Though I'll miss her all my life. Do you think I should send some money?'

Millie shook her head firmly. 'Koko knew Dent was a rich bastard, but she never asked him for a penny. I reckon she'd sooner live like the rest of the folks on the block.'

'He gave her to me, you know. He brought her into the bedroom, laid her on my bed and said, "She's yours!" '

'You don't give children away like presents,' Millie squeezed Lisa's hand. 'Come on, honey, cheer up. The Good Lord's blessed you in lots of other ways. Why, this house has really bin jumpin' these last three months!'

Lisa liked having Ralph and Gary living in her house. They were almost like a family. People assumed Gary was *her* partner, not Ralph's, and she made no effort to disabuse them, not even Busby, who called regularly. Folks could think what they liked. She loved her rather unconventional household, though on Christmas Day, there was another, entirely unexpected arrival.

'We're going to have a real old-fashioned Christmas this year,' she declared. 'Our first one together.' Last year it had passed by almost unnoticed, caught up in the trauma of Dent's death and Sabina leaving.

She threw herself into the preparations, spending hours in the shops buying presents, holly, mistletoe and a giant tree. Much to Millie's disgust, she commandeered the kitchen nearly every day to make mince pies or a Christmas cake or puddings.

'How many folk are you baking for?' the old woman demanded. 'The whole of California? There's only three of you gonna be here.'

'There's a heap of people coming round Christmas night,' said Lisa, slapping pastry around with gusto.

Millie snorted.

Lisa bought a pile of seasonal tapes for the loud-speaker system, so the house echoed with *White Christmas* or *Sleigh Ride* or choirboys singing carols.

'Isn't this a bit relentless?' Gary complained. 'Dent would never have approved.'

'You're probably right,' agreed Lisa. 'I never got to spend a Christmas with him. He probably didn't even acknowledge its existence, but I'm not leading the rest of my life according to Joseph Dent.'

On Christmas Day, after they'd eaten dinner and Millie had gone off to spend the day with her daughter, the three of them sprawled on the patio, too full and too lazy to move. The table was laden with their dirty dishes and several half-drunk bottles of wine.

'We'll have to wash the dishes,' Lisa yawned. 'We can't leave them for Millie when she gets back.'

'Later,' groaned Gary. 'Much, much later.'

Lisa lit a cigarette and thought how incongruous it all was, the decorations, the tree, the Christmas dinner, yet here they were sitting outdoors in the brilliant afternoon sun. It was an aspect of Californian life to which she would never get used. Over to the left of the garden, a digger was waiting beside a half-excavated pool. *That* was something she *had* got used to – she'd really missed having a pool since she'd left Busby's. The workmen would finish in a couple of weeks' time.

The doorbell chimed and Ralph said weakly, 'I'm immovable. You go, Lisa, you ate the least.'

Lisa cursed them both and staggered inside to open the door.

A tiny old lady was standing on the step rooting through her handbag. She looked up and her pretty violet eyes danced with laughter. 'Shit! I lost my key again.'

Before Lisa could reply, the old lady pushed past, trotted over to an armchair and sat down.

'Get me a drink, Bobby. Rum and orange and go easy on the orange.'

'I think you've got the wrong house!' It was difficult not to laugh. She was such a dear little thing, dressed all in black – a cotton dress with long sleeves, a little straw hat with a veil and cuban-heeled, lace-up shoes.

The old lady didn't seem to have heard. Lisa sat down opposite. 'I think you've got the wrong house,' she repeated. The old lady had certainly been a beauty once, judging from those lovely eyes, long dark lashes and little rosebud mouth. Curly silvery hair fluffed out from under her cloche hat. 'And I'm not Bobby, either,' she added.

'Don't be silly, dear. You're having another one of your turns. Fetch me that drink and make it snappy. I'm as parched as a rhinoceros on heat.'

'This is Tymperleys . . .'

'Of course it's Tymperleys, idiot. Now where's that fuckin' drink?'

'Just a minute.'

Lisa scurried out onto the patio, convulsed with laughter. Ralph and Gary looked up in astonishment. 'What's the matter?'

Scarcely able to speak for laughing, she managed to say, 'There's a little old lady in the hall with the sweetest face and the foulest tongue, who seems to think she lives here!'

The three of them went back to the hall where the old lady sat tapping her foot impatiently. Lisa poured her a Jack Daniel's with ice.

'I'm afraid we're all out of rum,' she apologised, handing over the drink.

'Tut, tut,' said the woman, knocking the drink back in one gulp and holding out her glass for more.

Ralph knelt beside her and said gently, 'You've come to the wrong house—'

The old lady interrupted him. 'You think I don't know my own fuckin' house,' she snorted, 'when I had it brought over brick by brick from England!'

'Vita Reese!' they cried in unison.

'Who else? Though I don't usually need to identify myself when I get home.' She turned to Lisa. 'Who are these guys, Bobby?'

'Friends of mine,' gulped Lisa. 'Give her another drink, someone, I'm going to ring Millie.'

'I was just having an after-dinner nap,' Millie complained. 'Whassa matter, can't you live without me or something?'

Lisa ignored the sarcasm. 'Did you ever meet Vita Reese?'

'What a thing to ask a body on Christmas Day! No, I didn't. That old devil Dent was already there when I came.'

'So you don't know what she looks like?'

'No, but she left a heap of her own movies behind – Dent used to watch them sometimes. I expect I thought she was dead.'

'I expect I did, too,' said Lisa. 'Except she's down the hall, claiming she still lives here.'

'What! Well, hold on to her a while, I'm coming over.'

The old lady was already on her fourth glass of whisky when Millie appeared, looking tough and ready to rout the intruder.

'Delilah!' The violet eyes sparkled. 'Am I glad to see you! There's some confusion here. Tell these people who I am.'

Millie's face collapsed into tenderness. She laid her large black hand on the tiny, birdlike shoulder. 'Why, you're Vita Reese,' she said comfortingly. 'Of course you are.'

'I've no idea who she is,' Millie confessed later. After finishing off the whisky, the visitor had fallen asleep in the chair. 'I just felt sorry for her, that's all. What are you going to do with her?' she added sharply.

'I don't know,' said Lisa helplessly. Everyone she'd rung to ask about Vita Reese had replied, 'She's dead,' but no one knew when or how she'd died. Ralph had looked her up in one of Dent's anthologies where it said she was born in 1894; as it was now 1967, this would make the old lady in the hall seventy-three. 'I suppose people just assumed she'd died,' he said.

Gary put one of her silent movies on and they went down to watch it. The woman on the screen looked nothing like the one in the hall, but over forty years had passed, so that wasn't much help.

'She's lovely, though,' said Ralph. There was no doubt about that. They watched Vita Reese kneeling at an altar, sunlight streaming onto her fair curly hair, as she mouthed a prayer, her cupid mouth twisted tragically whilst her enormous dark eyes held an expression of deep despair. The background music soared majestically and violins quivered on their topmost note as Vita threw herself full-length on the altar steps.

'They don't make eyes like that any more,' said Millie. 'I think it's her.'

'What did the police say?' asked Ralph. Gary had forgotten why they were there and become immersed in the movie.

'There are no five-feet-tall, seventy-three-year-old ladies missing from anywhere,' replied Lisa. 'They're going to check on all the old people's homes and ring back. They asked if I wanted her taken away.'

'And what did you say?' demanded Millie.

'I said I'd think about it. I don't suppose it'd do any harm if she stayed on for a couple of days, except we'd soon be out of liquor.'

Three years later, Vita Reese was still at Tymperleys. Nobody ever found out where she'd been in the twenty years since she'd sold the house to Joseph Dent. As far as Vita was concerned, she'd never left. Lisa suspected she wasn't quite as vague as she pretended, that she was *acting* and dressing the part of a sweet old lady. If so, she did it very well and Lisa was the only one to have doubts. The others took Vita Reese at face value and listened avidly whilst she regaled them with tales and gossip from the 1920s. She spent a lot of time in the basement cinema with Gary watching her old movies.

In fact, everybody loved Vita. She was no trouble – unless you counted the drinks bill doubling.

Lisa was worried that things might change. She remembered when she lived in Queen's Gate and life was perfect, then gradually people left or died and she ended up alone. Now life was almost perfect again with her makeshift family all around her.

She tried to take things one year at a time. Christmas, 1971. They'd all be there as usual. Most of the presents were bought and she'd ordered the tree. This year they were going to Busby's after lunch.

As fate would have it, however, it turned out to be Lisa herself who deserted Tymperleys and its disparate residents that Christmas . . .

33

The first-class section of the plane was only half-full, and most of the passengers were asleep, though one or two overhead lights were still on.

Lisa looked out of the window. There was nothing to be seen except blackness, not even a glimmer of light. They must be over the Atlantic. The sky was inky, the horizon difficult to make out, just black ocean merging indistinctly with the dark sky.

The engines droned interminably on. Every now and then the aircraft seemed to pause and shudder as if it was stopping to take a breath, and Lisa's heart would miss a beat, convinced they were about to crash, but the engine just changed tone and they forged onwards.

If only she could sleep. She really envied those who'd just tipped back their seats and fallen into a deep slumber. Perhaps a drink would help relax her. She rang the bell and knocked Nellie's letter, read a dozen times since it came that afternoon, off her knee. She was reaching down, trying to locate it, when the stewardess appeared.

'I'll get that.' The girl bent down. 'You must have kicked it back with your heel.'

'Thanks,' smiled Lisa. 'Can I have a whisky, please? With ice.'

'Straight away.' The girl looked no more than eighteen, pretty and slim with white-blonde hair drawn back in a French pleat. What a responsible job for someone so young.

'You're Lisa Angelis, aren't you?' The girl was already back, the drink on a tray.

'That's right.'

'I hope you don't mind me saying this, but I saw *Attrition* a few weeks ago in Hong Kong. You were really wonderful.'

'Why should I mind you saying that?' smiled Lisa. 'I'm flattered, though I think Gary Maddox stole the acting honours.'

'You were every bit as good. Well, enjoy your drink.'

So *Attrition* was still being shown four years after its release. Not surprising, really. Like *Psycho*, it would go down in cinema history. None of O'Brien Productions' movies had come close to getting the same ecstatic reviews. Lately, she'd come to think that thrillers weren't Gary's forte and tried to suggest they try something else, but he was determined on becoming another Joseph Dent. Still, the company showed a healthy profit.

She put the whisky down – she was drinking it too quickly – and Nellie's letter nearly fell again. She folded it up and put it in her bag. She knew the contents almost off by heart. What a bombshell, though, to hear from her family after all these years!

Lisa rarely read her fan letters. Usually the studio or her agent took care of them, though occasionally, a particularly sensitive or sweet letter was directed on to her and she would write a short note and send a signed photograph.

When Nellie's letter arrived at the O'Brien Productions offices in Beverly Hills, the blue air-mail envelope was passed on to Lisa opened but with a little slip attached, saying '*This looks personal.*' She'd found it on her desk when she went in the next morning.

The sender's name on the reverse was: *Mrs Helen Clarke, 30 South Park Road, Crosby, nr Liverpool, England.*

'Oh, no!' she said aloud.

The writing was neat and clear. She unfolded the letter and looked at the signature. It finished, '*Your loving sister, Nellie.*'

Lisa groaned and began to read.

'*Are you OUR Lizzie?*' the letter began. '*If not, throw this away immediately. I'm sorry to have bothered you. If you ARE our Lizzie, read on, please.*

'*How did I find you? (If I have!) Well, five years ago on Mam's birthday, Joan and I took her into town to the pictures and we saw a film called* April Flowers. *As soon as you appeared Mam said, "That's our Lizzie!" As you can imagine everyone turned round and either laughed or told her to shut up, including Joan and I. Nevertheless, she insisted throughout it was you. In fact, she ruined the whole evening! Next night, she badgered Joan into taking her again and on Saturday she tagged along with Jimmie and his girlfriend after persuading them to go and confirm the discovery of her long-lost Lizzie.*'

Lisa groaned again. It was rare nowadays she thought about her family, and she wasn't sure if she wanted to be reminded of them now. She briefly considered tearing the letter up before she read another word, but that would be irresponsible. She sighed and continued reading.

'*Ever since, the family have scoured the* Liverpool Echo *every night to see if a Lisa Angelis film is on, and have taken Mam far and wide to see it. We even went over to the Continentale in Seacombe once to see a beautiful film called* The Opportunist. *Mam was even more convinced by that because you were younger, though none of us recognised you. You seemed far too elegant and lovely to be our sister! I think she even wrote a couple of letters, though Joan never posted them.*

'*Anyway, no one took much notice of Mam, though we tried to humour her and she fretted, not getting any reply to her letters. (Would they have reached you, I wonder? Would you have answered if they had? If you ARE our Lizzie, that is.)*

'*Why am I writing now? Well, last week Stan (my husband) took me to the pictures. I can't remember what we saw because I got just as excited as Mam did all those years before. I didn't think twice at "O'Brien Productions", but when "Producer, Lisa Angelis" came up a minute later, I thought, "That's too much of a coincidence!" and I decided to write myself.*'

'I'll come to the reason for my letter – you must be getting impatient. It's a sad, sad reason. Our mam is dying. Lung cancer. All those cigarettes! Sixty a day by the end. She's in Walton Hospital and has a week left, possibly two. If you really ARE *our Lizzie, please come. Please. It would make Mam's end so happy. She mourned as much over losing you as she did Rory, you know. It broke her heart when you left. Mam loved you so much, Lizzie – Lisa. She loved us all so much.*

'I'm getting emotional. Before finishing, in case you can't come or won't come, I'll just say we're all fine. I've been married fourteen years and Stan is a great husband. I'm assistant headmistress at a primary school in Waterloo and have two lovely children, Natalie, 12, and Luke, 8. (Mam had a fit at the names. Natalie isn't a saint and Luke is a PROTESTANT *saint!) Kevin's oldest, Sarah, is 24 and married, so our Kevin is a grandfather twice over. (He has two more daughters.) Tony and Chris are both married, both happy, two kids each. Jimmie got divorced (much shock horror from Mam, as you can imagine) and went to live back home for a while, but his new marriage is working out fine.*

'Where are we? Paddy . . .' Lisa's heart missed a beat *'. . . has done really well. He's a press photographer and gets sent all over the world. We hardly ever see him. Mam worries because it can be dangerous. At the moment, he's in Vietnam, so I suppose she's right to worry. Next Joan. I'm afraid Joan has turned out – well, I won't use Natalie's description – let's say, she's a not very happy spinster. Somehow she felt obliged to stay at home with Mam, though there was no need, and now feels she has sacrificed her life. Stan calls her a "self-made martyr". Last but not least, Sean and Dougal, our baby brothers. They both went to the same university, where Sean took Physics and Dougal Chemistry. Now they work together in a research establishment just outside Chester. They got married on the same day – my, what a do we had! The whole of Chaucer Street went to the church to watch. (Mam still lives in the same house, by the way.)*

'I'll finish, my dear Lizzie, I hope this letter doesn't upset you.

'Your loving sister, Nellie.'

'Fasten your safety belts, please.'

Lisa woke up with a start. Trust her to fall asleep just as the plane was about to land. Outside, grey clouds were massed above and below; the plane seemed to stall briefly and the engine coughed as it began to descend out of the skies. They passed through a bank of cloud and she saw houses, rows and rows of them, and green fields and the silver glint of a river. Then cars became visible and tiny people, no bigger than the head of a pin.

England! Home – or was it? Where exactly *was* home?

As soon as she'd read the letter she rang the airline and booked a seat. There were none available until the ten o'clock flight that night. On the way over, she would gain eight hours and arrive in London the next afternoon. She drove home to Tymperleys to pack.

Ralph came out to see who'd arrived. 'I'm going home,' she cried.

'What's the matter?' Dear Ralph, his face was full of concern.

'My mother is dying. I must go back.' She couldn't live with herself if she didn't try to reach Kitty before she died.

'Of course you must, I'll drive you to the airport.'

That evening, when they were on their way, he asked, 'Will you be back for Christmas? It won't be the same without you.'

'I'll do my best. The letter took a week to come, so poor Mam might already be dead by now,' though she was praying Mam would stay alive to see her Lizzie.

'Mam! I've never heard you say that before.'

'Make sure Vita eats, won't you?' And give Millie a surreptitious hand. Everything's getting a bit too much for her lately.'

'You don't have to worry about anything here,' promised Ralph.

It was freezing at the airport, which meant it was bound to be even colder in Liverpool. She'd decided against packing her sable, her only warm coat. She would have felt a fool turning up at Walton Hospital in a three-thousand-dollar fur. A swank, that's what they used to call people who wore too-posh clothes. Lizzie O'Brien, the swank, coming all done up in expensive fur to see her mam die. The next warmest coat she had was a fine, biscuit-coloured jersey. As she waited for a taxi at Heathrow, she felt the wind whipping through the thin material. The temperature here must be forty or fifty degrees down on California. She sat shivering on the back seat of the cab and when they reached London, wondered if she could spare a couple of hours and ask the driver to take her to Oxford Street where she could buy something heavier, but decided against it. In those few hours, Kitty might die and the journey would have been in vain. She'd get something in Liverpool tomorrow.

The sky was steely grey and sleet slashed against the taxi windows. The change in time, together with the cold, made her feel disorientated as she stared out at the shops, heavy with Christmas decorations.

At Euston Station, she just had time for a cup of tea before the next train to Liverpool. Inside the restaurant, loud with carols, everyone was wrapped up warmly; even a tattered tramp, sitting in a corner seat surrounded by his life's belongings in torn carrier bags, wore a thick tweed overcoat. A few people stared at her and she felt conspicuously underdressed. It was ridiculous, she thought wryly. She had millions of dollars in the bank, yet at this moment in time, an old tramp was more appropriately dressed than she was!

The journey to Liverpool seemed to take forever. The train kept stopping in the middle of nowhere or it slowed down to a snail's pace for mile after mile. At least the heating system was efficient. Too efficient, in fact; the air blowing out from under the seat burnt the back of her legs.

It was after midnight when they finally drew into Lime Street Station. The sudden change in temperature when she stepped off the overheated train was breathtaking. The drivers of the waiting taxis stood in a circle, stamping their feet, their breath white clouds in the dark, cold air.

A middle-aged man came over and took her bag. 'Where to, luv?' His adenoidal Liverpool accent came as a shock.

'Walton Hospital.' She could hardly speak, she felt so cold.

The man looked at her with concern as he took her suitcase, ' 'Ere, luv, get in quick,' he said. 'I've gorra rug in the front. Wrap this round yer. Jesus Christ, yer teeth are rattling so loud people'll think I've gorra rumba band in the back.'

He was leaning over, tucking a tartan rug around her legs. Lisa felt tears sting her eyes. Liverpool people, they were truly the salt of the earth.

'C'mon, luv, have a sup'a this.' He handed her a bottle of whisky. 'That'll warm the cockles of yer heart.' Lisa took the bottle. Her mouth felt numb and whisky dribbled down her chin as she took a gulp. The driver got in his cab and steered the car out of the station.

He chatted all the way to the hospital. Where had she come from? California! Jesus Christ, had she forgotten the world had different temperatures? Didn't she know Liverpool got cold in the winter?

'I should do, I was born here,' she said.

'Yer've lost yer accent then?'

'I've been away a long time.'

Why had she come back then, he enquired. Oh, her mam was dying. How sad. But what a lovely girl she was then, coming all the way from California for her mam. 'She won't half be pleased to see yer. What ward is she in?'

'I've no idea,' confessed Lisa. 'No one's expecting me.'

'When we get ter the hospital in a minute, you stay in the back and I'll find out for yer, then I can take yer right ter the door. Save yer wanderin' round, like. What's her name, luv?'

'O'Brien. Kitty O'Brien. And thanks, you're an angel.'

He laughed. 'Wait till I tell the missus I had a lady from California in my cab tonight and she called me an angel.'

When they reached the hospital, he leapt out and was gone for several minutes. He came back and said, 'She's in F2,' and drove right to the door.

After she had paid him, he said, 'Look, luv, I'm on duty till eight o'clock this morning. Here's the company telephone number. If yer want ter leave before then, ring and ask for Sam and if I'm there I'll come and get yer. Okay?'

She could hear the lights buzzing on the Christmas tree in the foyer. Apart from that, the hospital was eerily quiet and her footsteps echoed sharply on the tiled floor as she walked down the deserted corridors following the signs for F2. She passed a lighted office where a nurse was sitting at a desk writing and the woman looked up, startled. Feeling guilty, Lisa began to tread on tiptoe until she came to her mother's ward.

She put her hand up to push the swing doors open when her courage failed. After coming thousands of miles, the last few yards were beyond her. What would Mam look like now? It was almost a quarter of a century since she'd seen her.

The door opened and a young nurse jumped back with a startled cry. 'Sorry, you gave me a fright. Who are you looking for?'

'My mother, Mrs O'Brien.'

'She's in the first bed.' The nurse looked bright and cheerful, considering the hour. 'Her other daughter's been here every night for weeks. I just persuaded her to go and have a sleep.'

'Which daughter – Nellie?'

'Sorry, I don't know her name. She's got red hair.'

'That'll be Joan.'

'Mrs O'Brien must have been a lovely mother. She has more visitors than all the other patients put together.'

'She was,' said Lisa.

The ward was long, at least ten beds to a side, each one filled with a sleeping, silent woman. Decorations were strung along the putty-coloured walls and a dim red central light gave the room a sinister look. 'Hell might look like this,' thought Lisa.

Kitty was beside a dimly-lit, glass-walled office where another, older nurse could be seen looking through a filing cabinet. The curtains round her bed were the only ones drawn.

'She's asleep.' The nurse drew the curtain back a few inches and motioned her to enter. Lisa took a deep breath and stepped inside and heard the swish of the curtain being closed behind her.

They'd propped Mam up against three pillows so she was almost sitting up in her sleep. She wore a pink brushed-nylon nightdress, the bones on her neck showing sharp through the thin material. Her arms rested on the white sheet, which was drawn tight across and tucked under the mattress. There was so little of Kitty left that the sheet scarcely seemed to curve over the wasted body.

Lisa stood staring down at her and felt the years fall away. *Mam, oh, Mam.*

She sat down beside the bed and took Mam's thin hand. The waxen skin looked and felt like soft silk and the veins stood up as if the hand had been threaded with bright blue string.

'Mam,' breathed Lisa. She bent down and pressed her cheek against the shrunken, caved-in face. They'd taken her teeth out and Mam's jaw had fallen back so far she looked as if she had no chin. Her pale eyelids fluttered, though her eyes didn't open. Mam said, 'Lizzie?'

How did she know?

'Yes, Mam?'

'You're really there?' Her slurred voice was barely discernible.

'Yes I am, Mam. I'm holding your hand.'

Mam's eyes blinked as if the effort of opening them was too great. Eventually, her effort was rewarded and her eyes opened. She was staring at the empty chair on the opposite side of the bed.

'Where are you, Lizzie, luv?'

'I'm here, love.' Lisa reached out and turned Mam's face towards her. The blue eyes were covered with a milky glaze.

'I knew you'd come.' She dragged her other hand over and put it on top of Lisa's. 'There's something I want ter tell you.'

'No, Mam, there's no need to tell me anything.'

'There is, luv.' Lisa bent her head. She could scarcely hear what Mam was saying. 'I'm sorry about what happened, luv. Yer were right, I did know. I'm sorry, Lizzie, luv.'

'It doesn't matter, Mam. It never did me any harm.' The lies you tell at a deathbed, thought Lisa.

Kitty shook her head and began to cry. The tears were huge and they wobbled slowly down her wizened, lined face. Lisa fished in her pocket for a handkerchief but there was none so she wiped the tears away with the back of her hand.

'Please don't cry, Mam. I'm fine. You can't imagine how fine I am.'

'Terrible thing . . .'

'Mam, don't exert yourself. Let's sit together quiet now.'

'. . . fer a mam ter do . . .' Her voice faded and her eyes fell closed. It had clearly been an effort to get those words out. ' 'Nother thing.' It came out like a soft sigh. 'Tom, he wasn't yer dad, luv. Someone else, a foreigner . . .'

Christ! What had she just said? She must be rambling, out of her mind. Lisa clutched the thin hands in her own and could feel the pulse throbbing faintly against her palms. She laid her head briefly on the breast that had succoured her, then sat staring at the ravaged face. Somewhere in the ward, a woman cried out and the nurse's brisk footsteps sounded as she went to attend to her.

Lisa had no idea how long she sat there. One hour, two. At one point she glanced at the big white clock at the end of the ward and it had just passed midnight. Memories chased each other through her mind, memories of her mam during the war when they were in the shelter, the way she kept touching them all, hands fluttering from one to the other, her lovely children. Her mam covered in bruises after a beating from Tom, or sick with worry when Kevin, then Rory, had gone off to war. That party she'd got ready for Lizzie's fourteenth birthday . . . the jelly, the purse she'd bought for a present – and Lizzie had just walked out. Lizzie had better things planned for her birthday – a day out in Southport with her Yank boyfriend.

'I won't cry,' vowed Lisa. 'I won't. It might wake her up, she'd be upset and I don't want to upset her, I've done that enough.'

She looked down at the frail form which made so little impression on the bed and thought how remarkable it was that this tiny body had produced eleven children, eight big healthy boys and three daughters.

Suddenly, Kitty's breathing began to get hoarse, became louder. Lisa felt the pulse begin to race. She stood up in alarm and knocked on the window of the office. The older nurse came out immediately. She took hold of Mam's wrist almost roughly, her fingers pressing, moving, pressing again.

'I'm sorry, love. I'm afraid she's gone.'

Lisa sat down on the chair and began to cry softly.

'*You bloody hypocrite!*'

She looked up. A raw-boned, red-haired woman was looking at her, eyes burning with hatred. Joan! This couldn't be Joan, two years younger than her yet looking fifty, sallow skin, thin mouth tight and drawn back like a cat in anger.

'Joan, it's Lizzie.' Joan hadn't realised who she was. Lisa darted towards her eagerly.

'I know bloody well who it is. Turning up now and crying like the bloody hypocrite you are. Being with our mam when she died, when I've sat here, day after day, night after night . . .'

Lisa reached for Joan's hand, but she snatched it away. 'Don't *touch* me!'

'I'm sorry, I'm sorry.' She felt like an intruder, a stranger who'd forced her presence on a poor dying woman.

'It's too late to be sorry. Why don't you get out – go away from here. Get back to your posh house in America and leave our mam alone.' Joan began to sob, great wracking sobs that shook her blade-thin shoulders, and threw herself on top of Mam's dead body. As the nurse began gently to pull her away, Lisa looked at them both helplessly, then, picking up her suitcase, she ran out of the ward, conscious of the terrible clatter of her heels in the empty corridors. There was a telephone in the foyer. She fumbled in her bag for Sam's number. 'I'm sorry, Sam's gone to Speke Airport,' said the woman who answered. 'Shall we send someone else?'

'Please, straight away.'

She went outside into the black hospital grounds, oblivious to the icy wind which penetrated her thin coat. Joan was right, she *was* a hypocrite. For all Lisa knew, Kitty could have been dead for years and she'd rarely given her a second thought. Now here she was, pretending to be upset – no, not pretending, she *was* upset, yet . . . it didn't make sense.

Up and down the concrete path she walked, arguing with herself, struggling with her emotions, whilst the wind whistled through the tall, bare trees. She stumbled against a bush and felt thorns tear at her leg just as there was a screech of brakes and a car turned into the drive.

Her taxi! She ran back towards the entrance, but the car turned out to be an ordinary saloon. Two men got out – tall, fair-haired men. They slammed the doors and half-ran into the building. Her brothers, though she wasn't sure which.

She longed to call out to them, identify herself, 'I'm Lizzie,' but hadn't the courage. It was as if she was no longer Lisa Angelis, the Hollywood star who had more money in the bank than her family would earn together in their lifetime. Suddenly, she was little Lizzie O'Brien again, nervous and scared. Her brothers might turn on her the way Joan had done and she couldn't have borne it.

Shrinking back into the dark shadows, she waited for her taxi.

She had to sit in the waiting room for hours until the first train left at six o'clock, and she felt as if life had turned full circle. Throughout the long wait, and later on, during the journey from Lime Street to Euston, she was oblivious to everything except her own emotional upheaval and the realisation that, yet again, she was running away from her family.

34

The return journey was fast and there were no hold-ups, though Lisa scarcely noticed. The night's events churned over and over in her mind. Mam dying, Joan's hatred. Her sister's reaction was understandable, though Lisa should have stood her ground, insisted Nellie had asked her to come. At least *she* would have been pleased to see her.

She got Nellie's letter out and read it again. Guilt rose up in her throat, choking her, and she remembered Mam saying, oh, lots of times, 'It's no good being sorry after the event.' If only Lisa had written from time to time to say how she was. She remembered when Kevin joined the Fleet Air Arm and Paddy went to grammar school and how proud Mam had been. Imagine her knowing Lizzie was a film star! Lisa couldn't help but smile. Mam would have been unbearable.

And that incredible thing she'd said about Tom! The idea of her weary, broken mother having an affair was too ridiculous for words.

When she reached London, she wandered down a road beside Euston Station looking for a hotel and found a small, four-star establishment a few hundred yards away. She could have gone straight to Heathrow, but felt too weary to face the long flight home just yet. There'd only been that snatched half-hour of sleep on the plane the night before last. She'd fly back tomorrow after a good night's rest.

The hotel foyer was welcoming with a log fire burning in the wide, old-fashioned fireplace and red-shaded brass lamps on the oak-panel-lined walls. A tall Christmas tree stood in one corner, its jewel-coloured lights snapping on and off.

'I'd like a room, please,' said Lisa.

The receptionist, a sour-faced, middle-aged woman, asked churlishly, 'For how long?'

'Just one night, and I'd like to go to bed immediately.'

The woman sniffed and looked Lisa up and down almost contemptuously. 'That's ten pounds, in advance.'

Lisa didn't bother to argue though the woman's request was insulting. The sudden warmth inside the hotel made her feel faint and she swayed on her feet. She paid and was directed to her room on the first floor. In the corridor a young girl was wheeling a trolley full of sheets and towels. She smiled and said in a broad Irish accent, 'I've just done that room.'

With an effort, Lisa smiled back. The thought of bed and sleep had brought on a feeling of total exhaustion. Once inside the room, she was about to throw herself on the bed fully dressed when she caught sight of herself in the mirror. No wonder the receptionist had been suspicious. She looked an absolute fright! Her coat was crumpled, the lapels stained with whisky, and the right leg of her tights was torn and bloodstained where she'd caught it outside the hospital. The make-up she had put on nearly two days ago had worn away, except for the mascara, reduced to black smudges underneath her eyes making her look faintly ghoulish. Her hair had escaped its bun and hung wildly about her face.

'I don't care,' she muttered as she threw herself on the bed. Within seconds, she was fast asleep.

When she woke, it was daylight. At first she thought she'd slept through the night and it was morning, but the clock beside the bed showed half-past three.

It was the dream that had woken her. She was at Mam's funeral wearing her sable coat and hiding behind a tree whilst her family stood shoulder to shoulder around the grave. Paddy was there, so incredibly handsome, a camera strung around his neck. Then a voice yelled, 'She's here, she's here,' and Joan was up the tree, laughing and pointing down. Her brothers and sisters had picked up soil to throw onto the coffin. At Joan's words they looked up and began to march towards Lisa, their faces twisted with hatred, hands full of clumps of earth, ready to throw it at her. Paddy, Patrick, had recognised her and his eyes were filled with sick horror. Somehow, Joan had got down from the tree and was at their head. 'You bloody hypocrite,' they all screamed.

Her body was soaked with perspiration, yet she was freezing cold. For a while, she lay there shivering, almost lightheaded, trying to remember where she was.

When she got out of bed her legs felt like jelly. She gritted her teeth and forced herself to walk. Perhaps a hot bath might help. As she lay in the water, she realised she'd eaten nothing since she'd landed in England, though right now the idea of food seemed repugnant.

Later she dressed in one of the two outfits she'd brought with her, a lilac-ribbed jersey suit. She was beginning to feel human again – or was she? Out of the mirror, a stranger stared back – a hollow-eyed, gaunt-looking woman with a pinched mouth. This wasn't Lisa Angelis! This wasn't her! Who was she, this unpleasant, mean-faced person looking grimly into her eyes?

'*I don't feel real. I don't exist. Who am I?*'

The questions hammered at her brain, so hard, so loud, she put her hands up to her head to try and stop them. '*Who am I?*' The woman in the mirror merely asked the same question.

Lisa turned away and a wave of dizziness hit her. She willed herself to stay upright, and picked up her coat. There was something wrong with the coat but she couldn't remember what it was. She left the bedroom and walked along the corridor and down the stairs to the hotel foyer, gaining confidence as she went. Why, she could walk fine!

As she went by reception, a woman shouted, 'Miss O'Brien!'

Lisa ignored her – she didn't know a Miss O'Brien. Outside, a taxi was passing and she hailed it. 'Where to?' the cabbie asked.

'Queen's Gate and Brompton Road corner.'

'Right you are, darlin'.'

The window of the flat was dark. Jackie must be having dinner with Gordon. Lisa felt angry. She'd been relying on Jackie to tell her who she was.

'We're 'ere, darlin'.'

The cabbie had turned around and was looking at her impatiently. Lisa shrank into the seat. 'I don't want to get out.'

'Whatcha wanna do then, ducks, stay there all night?'

'No, take me to Kneale Street, down the side of Harrods.'

There was no sign of Mr Greenbaum's shop. Lisa couldn't understand it. The shop had been there only yesterday, surely? There was a chemist's, a sandwich bar, a dry cleaner's, but no bookshop.

The taxi edged down the street. 'I don't suppose you're gonna get out here, either?' the cabbie said resignedly when she made no move.

'Just drive slowly, I'm looking for something.'

'No chance of going fast, darlin', not in this traffic.'

She couldn't remember where the shop should be. Two men came out of a door beside the sandwich bar. 'Goodnight, Brian,' called one. The other man, the one called Brian, muttered something and shuffled off down the road, his shoulders stooped and weary as if he carried the cares of the world. Lisa frowned, wondering why the man looked so familiar. Then she remembered. This man was her husband, yet he looked so old, so hunched. She was about to open the door when the taxi suddenly shot forward and somehow it didn't seem to matter that she'd not spoken to Brian.

'Where next?' asked the driver.

'Back to the hotel,' she said, hoping he remembered where it was because she couldn't.

That night in bed, between fits of shivering, she remembered Harry Greenbaum was dead. What a fool she'd been, riding around London looking for a dead person. And what a fool Brian would have thought her, if she'd leapt out of the taxi and confronted him as if she'd only seen him yesterday. In fact, it was really very funny and she began to laugh hysterically, imagining his astounded reaction. She laughed long and hard and the bed began to shake and after a while someone knocked on her door and called, 'Are you all right?'

'Yes,' she shouted and pulled the clothes over her head and began to cry instead. Then she remembered Jackie. It had been silly looking in Queen's Gate. Jackie had got married and moved to Bournemouth.

'I'll go and see her,' she thought triumphantly. 'I'll go to Bournemouth tomorrow and maybe Jackie will tell me who I am.'

In the mirror next morning she decided she looked much better. Her eyes were star-bright, her cheeks flushed deep red. She got dressed and went downstairs where the disagreeable receptionist was already on duty. Lisa asked her which station the trains to Bournemouth went from.

'Waterloo,' the woman answered. Lisa turned to leave when the woman asked surprisingly, 'Are you all right?'

'I'm fine,' cried Lisa. 'I've never felt so well.' She had a lovely, slightly tipsy feeling.

'Have you had breakfast?'

Lisa frowned, wondering why this strange woman should care. She couldn't remember whether she'd eaten or not. 'Probably,' she replied.

Outside, a light snow had begun to fall and as soon as the white flakes touched the ground they were transformed into grey slush by the heavy traffic. Lisa drew in a sharp breath. Breathing in was like swallowing ice, and another wave of dizziness swept over her. She grabbed the metal railings to prevent herself from falling. The dizziness soon passed and she hailed a taxi to take her to Waterloo.

By the time she reached Bournemouth, the snow was falling thick and fast and the ground was covered with a lethal carpet of slippery ice. The grey leaden clouds seemed low enough to touch and the day was dark, more like dusk than mid-morning. In the taxi, she prayed Jackie would still be living in the same house. It was years since she'd last had a letter and vicars got moved to other parishes. Jackie might be living somewhere else by now. She should have checked before she left London, but these last few days she hadn't been thinking straight.

When they drew up outside the old rambling house she asked the driver to wait a while. 'Let me make sure my friend still lives here.'

The vicarage was exactly as she remembered it: mellow, russet-coloured bricks, the curtains shabby, the windows and doors in need of painting. A car was parked in the drive, an old Morris Minor, full of rust and minus a wheel. A stack of bricks was propped where the wheel should have been. Despite the weather, someone lay underneath the car and she could see a teenaged boy standing in the open garage. The person beneath the car yelled, 'Hand me that spanner, Rob.'

The boy in the garage ran out and crawled under the car. Lisa smiled and put her hand on the gate to enter. There was a light on in every room of the house. It *must* be Jackie's, she thought. Jackie never turned a light off, ever. The gate creaked and a cat ran across the frozen grass and began to scratch at the front door. A Christmas tree stood in the corner of the room where the wedding reception had been held and two young girls were dancing a minuet, their faces grim with concentration, yet at the same time you could tell they were on the verge of giggling. Lisa felt strangely reluctant to enter. She looked down at her hand poised on top of the gate, watching the snow fall, and soon her hand was covered in white. What was holding her back? The house looked warm and inviting, yet she remained outside. In the stillness, she could hear music, a jazzed-up version of *Silent Night*.

A woman appeared in an upstairs window and glanced down at the car, an anxious expression on her face. Jackie! A plump, matronly Jackie with a cloud of almost-white hair. Raising the window a few inches, she shouted, 'Noël! Robert! Get indoors this minute. You'll catch your death of cold out there!' She slammed the window shut and almost immediately opened it again, calling, 'There's coffee made.' The watcher at the gate went unnoticed; covered in snow, she had become part of the wintry landscape. Seconds later,

Jackie came into the room where the two girls were still dancing and all three of them began to laugh. She put an arm around each girl's shoulder and they left the room just as the two boys crawled from underneath the car and ran down the side of the house. They were probably all in the kitchen at the back sitting round that big chipped wooden table drinking their coffee, joking together, chaffing each other, a loving caring family.

Lisa felt rooted to the spot, unable to move, as the knowledge, the sure and certain knowledge swept over her that she would give up everything she owned, every cent she had, for a husband like Laurence and children of her own. It was all she had ever wanted from life, all she cared about. She felt a rush of raw, naked envy for Jackie who had everything, whilst she, Lisa, had nothing except a house full of misfits, a pretend family who meant nothing to her or to each other. Even Sabina, her only chance of a child, had been taken from her.

She had never felt so alone in all her life. Part of her wanted to escape the searing cold, knock on the door and be welcomed, kissed, fussed over, but the other part knew that this would only make her feel worse, more isolated than ever.

Turning to the taxi driver, she said, 'Take me to the station, please. It was the wrong house, after all.'

The journey on the virtually empty train back to London was a nightmare. Her body was so chilled she felt as if her blood had turned to ice yet when she touched her cheeks they were burning. The ticket inspector looked at her with alarm. 'Are you all right, miss?'

'I'm fine,' she insisted through chattering teeth.

After he'd gone, she felt tears slipping down her cheeks though she had no idea why she should cry. The sky had turned so black it could be night and by now a blizzard blew and large clumps of snow were being hurled at the train windows. Suddenly, Mam appeared outside the window in her pink nightdress. She flew alongside the train, holding out her arms beseechingly. Lisa cried out and tried to open the window so she could bring Mam in from the cold, but it was jammed shut.

A wave of nausea swept over her and she fell back on the seat. Everything was too much effort. Even sitting up was hard. She struggled to keep her body upright on the seat, but it was impossible. Slowly, unable to help herself, she crumpled sideways.

Later, she learnt that it was the ticket inspector who found her, unconscious and rambling, when the train stopped in London.

35

'Where am I?'

The room was empty. She was in bed and outside the open door she could hear loud, cheerful voices and the sound of laughter. She looked around; tall green-painted walls, white flowered curtains, an easy chair, a small table holding a bunch of pink carnations in a chipped vase and lots more flowers on the windowsill. Her handbag stood on a cabinet beside the bed, along with an unlit metal lamp. It was definitely not the hotel. She couldn't remember much about it, but she was sure it had been more luxurious than this.

'Ah, awake at last!' A young man wearing a white coat came in.

'Where am I?'

'You're in St Brigid's Hospital.' He came over and sat on the corner of her bed with a sigh of relief. Despite his reassuring smile, his eyes were blinking with tiredness. 'How do you feel?'

'I don't know.' Her body felt like cotton wool. 'I feel as if somebody's turned on a tap and drained off all my energy. What's wrong with me?' She could vaguely remember passing out on a train.

'You've had pneumonia, a pretty severe case. If you hadn't got the constitution of an ox you might have died.' He reached for her pulse. 'Yes, you're definitely alive.'

'Are you sure?'

He grinned. 'Pretty sure. Ah, here's Sister Rolands.'

A tall bulky woman bristling with authority entered the room, her nurse's uniform starched and ironed to perfection.

'Our star patient is back in the land of the living, Sister.'

'And about time too,' boomed the nurse. 'Well, Doctor, you can get on with your rounds now, I'll see to this patient.'

The doctor went obediently to the door. 'I'll see you again in the morning,' he said to Lisa.

'Why am I your star patient?' she asked when the doctor had gone.

Sister Rolands chuckled as she smoothed the bed where the doctor had sat. 'I hope that isn't a sign you've lost your memory, Lisa Angelis, the famous film star, in a National Health Service ward along with all the common people! I hasten to add I'd never heard of you, but my nurses tell me you're quite famous.'

'How did you know who I was?'

'We went through your bag, of course – how else could we locate your relatives? We found a bill for the Columbine Hotel. They said you'd been staying there but under a false name – O'Brien, I think it was.'

'That's my real name. Angelis is false,' protested Lisa. 'I felt so lousy when I registered that I must have used it by mistake.'

Sister Rolands gave a royally dismissive gesture. 'Doesn't matter. We also found an airmail letter with a Liverpool name and address on the back, which turned out to be your sister. Mrs Clarke has rung every day and said to tell you that as soon as the funeral's over she'll be down to see you. In other words, she'll be here tomorrow. You woke up just in time.'

'Oh dear!'

'I don't allow "Oh dears" on my ward,' the nurse said sternly. 'Just be grateful you've got a family who cares – look at all the flowers they've sent!' She pointed to the windowsill. 'Oh, and we despatched a telegram to the Los Angeles address, by the way. We would have telephoned there too, but according to the American operator your number wasn't listed.'

'It's under my married name, Dent.'

'Three names!' The Sister's shoulders heaved with laughter and her stiff uniform crackled. 'One real, one false, one married. Anyway, a gentleman called Ralph also calls every day. He said everyone sends their love and he'll be over after Christmas to take you home.'

'I won't be staying in England for Christmas,' Lisa said quickly.

Sister Rolands gave a grim smile. 'I'm afraid you will,' she said in a voice that brooked no argument. 'It's Christmas in four days' time and you won't even be fit to get out of bed by then.'

'Four days! How long have I been here?'

'Let's see.' She unhooked the chart off the end of the bed. 'You came in last Saturday and now it's Wednesday.'

'Shit!'

'Tut, tut. Language!' Sister Rolands frowned and wagged a broad finger, though her mouth twitched. 'Wait till I tell my girls our star patient uttered a four-letter word. They're all after your autograph, by the way, but I said to wait until you leave.'

'Why am I in a room by myself?'

'Because you kept us all awake with your shouting, that's why. I think you were re-enacting all your pictures. It was all highly dramatic. You can go in the general ward if you like, but let's wait a while till you've got some strength back.'

Lisa sighed. 'I'm starving. I could eat a horse!'

'The NHS is so hard up you may well have to. Tea will be ready in half an hour. I'll tell them to bring yours first.' She marched out, her uniform crackling.

Lamb chops with mint sauce, mashed potatoes and peas, followed by trifle, all delicious but not nearly enough, were duly served. Lisa ate ravenously, scraping the gravy up with a piece of bread and butter. Afterwards, she still felt famished. The young nurse who had shyly brought her meal came in to collect the tray.

'I'm still hungry,' Lisa said hopefully.

'Sister said you might be, but we're not to give you any more in case it makes you sick.'

'Bitch!'

The nurse giggled. 'Isn't she! But her bark's worse than her bite. Would you like me to sit you up so you can comb your hair for visitors?'

'I'm not expecting anybody, but I'd like to make myself respectable. I can manage on my own.' She struggled to raise herself but after a while fell back exhausted. 'No, I can't. You'll have to help, I'm afraid.'

After lifting her upright, the nurse laid her handbag on her knee. When she'd gone, Lisa took her compact out. With a sense of relief she found that although her face was much thinner, her eyes enormous and surrounded by deep purple shadows, it was once again *her* face. The horrible-looking woman encountered in the hotel had gone. She looked like Lisa Angelis again.

A bell sounded and a stampede of visitors clutching flowers and parcels passed the open door of Lisa's room on their way to the main ward. She lay and watched, feeling unreasonably envious of the other patients. After all, people had been telephoning every day about her, and Nellie would be down soon.

Sister Rolands marched in with a bundle of magazines and newspapers. 'Thought you might like something to keep you occupied,' she barked. 'According to one of my nurses who reads such rubbish, there's an article about one of your pictures in this.'

She threw a paper on Lisa's knee. 'Don't tire yourself now, or there'll be trouble,' she said threateningly as she marched out.

'I wouldn't be so tired if I was fed properly,' Lisa called and heard an answering 'Humph!' from the corridor.

She turned the pages of the paper eagerly. The article was on a centre page, accompanied by a photograph of Gloria Grenville in *The Opportunist*. It was called HOW TO TURN A CLASSIC INTO A FLOP – *Throw Money At It*!

She knew *The Opportunist* was being re-made. Busby had called more than a year ago with the news that Cahil O'Daly's heirs had sold the rights of his novel to another company, this time for a colossal sum. 'They've got a ten-million-dollar budget,' he said gloomily, 'a host of star names, and they're going on location all over the world.'

'It won't be half as good as yours,' she said soothingly, though this made him even more gloomy. Whether good or bad, the new movie would probably be shown throughout America and the world, whereas his, made on a shoestring and acknowledged by critics as a work of genius, had long ago sunk without trace, scarcely shown except in a few small cinemas.

According to the article, the new movie was a flop, a dismal failure. The script was poor, the acting terrible and the direction barely noticeable. Numerous critical comparisons were made between the first version, made fourteen years ago, and the current one – all to the advantage of the original.

'Fourteen years!' said Lisa aloud. 'It seems like only yesterday.'

'*Van Dolen's feeling for the novel was inspired, as was his direction, and his casting was perfect,*' she read, her excitement increasing. She must keep this and send it to Busby! The critic then mounted his very high horse and declared it sinful that such a perfect movie, a gem, a work of art, had been so cruelly neglected. '*Busby Van Dolen must be persuaded to re-release his version instantly,*' the writer thundered, '*so the world can see it isn't cash that makes a good film, but talent.*'

'Persuaded?' laughed Lisa. 'Busby won't need much persuading!'

There was a postscript to the article: in view of the renewed interest in Busby Van Dolen's work, a season of his films would be shown on BBC 2 later in the year.

'Shit!' said Lisa. 'I'm so happy, I could cry.'

Later on, Sister Rolands came in, took one glance at Lisa and clapped her hands disapprovingly. 'Just look at you!' she cried, 'You're over-excited.' She touched Lisa's cheek with the back of her hand. 'Burning!' she announced. 'I bet your pulse is racing.'

'How can anybody get over-excited reading the paper?'

'I don't know, but you seem to have managed it,' Sister barked.

'I feel wonderful. I'd feel even more wonderful if I had something to eat. Do you always starve your patients?'

'Only the famous ones.' She looked at Lisa critically. 'A tablet for you tonight, madam. You don't look in the mood for sleep.'

'Can I telephone my husband?' asked Lisa hopefully. She longed to talk to Busby.

'One of my nurses said you're a widow. One piece of equipment we *don't* have is a paranormal telephone.'

'I'd like to ring another husband, a live one. This one's an ex.'

'Well you can't, so there.' She bustled out, grumbling, 'These temperamental film stars, they'll be the death of me,' and Lisa grinned.

Shortly after Sister left, another young nurse came in with a plate of sandwiches. 'Sister said to say you're a bloody nuisance.' She giggled. 'I've never heard her swear before.'

'Gee, thanks.' Lisa grabbed the plate. Bread and cheese had never tasted so good.

'I'll be back in ten minutes with your tablet.'

She must have gone to sleep the second her head touched the pillow. If she had dreams, she couldn't remember them when she awoke to the rattle of a trolley being pushed down the corridor. Through the drawn curtains she could see it was still pitch-dark outside. The trolley stopped outside her room and a young girl in a green overall came in with a cup of tea.

'Good morning,' the girl sang cheerfully.

Lisa groaned. 'What time is it?'

'Five o'clock.'

'Jesus Christ, why do I have to be awake so early?'

'Don't ask me, darlin', I only work here. Up you come and drink this.' The girl hauled her into a sitting position and put the tea on the bedside table.

'What time's breakfast?'

'Half-past six. Tara for now.'

Another hour and a half before she ate. Lisa doubted if she could live that long. As she sipped her tea she remembered that Nellie was coming today and felt apprehensive. How would they greet each other? Would Nellie be cross with her for running away from the hospital? They might be really awkward with each other after all this time.

'Lizzie! Oh, my dear, dear Lizzie!'

Lisa had been half-asleep and woke to find herself being scooped up in a pair of strong arms and showered with kisses.

'Nellie! I wasn't expecting you for ages.'

'I got the first train out of Lime Street. Let me look at you! Christ, you look thin, thin but lovely.' She hugged her again and began to cry. Unable to help herself, Lisa too felt tears coursing down her cheeks. The two sisters stayed wrapped in each other's arms for several minutes, until, sniffing, they disentangled themselves. And she'd been worried Nellie might be cross, thought Lisa shamefully. Her sister was sitting on the bed, wiping her eyes. 'Oh, dear. I put mascara on specially for you. I don't usually wear it and now it's smudged.'

Nellie had only been twelve when Lisa left. She'd grown into a fine-looking woman with a rosy-cheeked, healthy beauty. Her thick brown hair, only a shade lighter than Lisa's, was cut in short curls in which the occasional silver strand shone and her brown eyes danced with merriment. 'I can't remember you having a nose like that,' said Lisa. It was short and snub.

'Stan punched it that shape,' Nellie giggled, adding hastily, 'That's a joke. He's a super bloke. I'd like you to meet him and the kids some time.' Then her face became serious and she said, 'We were all really angry with Joan for driving you away. You poor dear, coming all that way to see Mam die, then her turning on you. When she told us, so virtuously, as if she expected our approval, we could have killed her! Of course, no one could say much. Poor Joan, she was more upset over Mam dying than anybody.'

'I deserved it,' said Lisa.

'Nonsense,' said Nellie stoutly. 'Next day, we rang the airlines, trying to find out if you'd flown back, then all the posh London hotels. I was almost thankful when the hospital got in touch to say you were ill.' She gasped. 'Christ, Lizzie. I've been here all this time and haven't asked how you feel!'

'Strange as it may seem, I feel marvellous. I'm terribly weak, I can't even sit up by myself, but it's very relaxing just lying here being waited on and everybody's very nice, Sister Rolands especially.'

'Good,' Nellie looked at her fondly then began to tell her about the burial. 'It was a typical Liverpool funeral – a couple of flaming rows, mainly with Joan, lots of tears at the cemetery, then back to Chaucer Street where everybody got drunk and we ended up singing all Mam's favourite Irish songs.'

'I wish I'd been there,' said Lisa sadly. It was strange, but since she'd woken up in the hospital, she'd scarcely thought about Mam. It was as if those terrible, delirious hours between leaving Liverpool and collapsing on the train had expurgated her feelings of guilt.

'So do I.'

They talked all morning. Nellie told her about the wives – her sisters-in-law – and her multitude of nieces and nephews. Kevin was the only one so far with grandchildren, but Tony was about to achieve this status any minute. 'Everyone wants to come and see you,' she said, 'but I told them you mightn't be up to it yet.'

'I'm not,' said Lisa quickly. 'I feel far too emotional at the moment. What with Mam dying, then Joan . . . seeing you is enough for now.' She'd break down, she knew she would, if her brothers came. 'Next time there's a wedding I'll come over, I promise.'

'That's a wonderful idea – providing you mean it.'

'I mean it,' Lisa said sincerely, adding casually, 'Did Patrick come home for the funeral?'

'Patrick? Oh, you mean Paddy. No. We sent a telegram to his last-known address but there's been no reply. Naturally, we're all worried about him, but then we always are.'

Thank goodness! She had visions of Patrick living in London and dropping in to see her. Hopefully he wouldn't recognise her after all this time, but even so, Lisa preferred to put off the reunion as long as possible.

Sister Roland came in and clapped her hands imperiously. 'Time for the patient to have a little nap.'

'I don't feel the least bit tired,' protested Lisa.

'Do as you're told.' Nellie jumped to her feet. 'I'll do some last-minute Christmas shopping in Oxford Street and come back later.'

On Christmas Eve, Nellie returned to Liverpool. 'Don't let it be another quarter of a century before we meet again,' she whispered as she hugged Lisa close. 'I know I've promised to come again after Christmas but I'm worried you might disappear before I get here.'

'Sister Rolands says I'm going to be here another ten days. I'd be too frightened to disobey.'

'Lisa, my darling,' Ralph cried, 'How are you?'

'I'm fine, completely better. Which phone are you on?'

'The outside one. I'm on the patio, why?'

'I'm trying to visualise the scene.'

'It's a beautiful morning. I can just see Vita, fast asleep and pissed as a lord already. When she's sober, she keeps asking after Bobby.'

It was New Year's Day and Lisa was in Sister Rolands' office having been pronounced fit to take a telephone call. Ralph had arranged to phone in the evening, six o'clock British time.

'We missed you at Christmas,' Ralph added.

'And I missed all of you terribly.'

'When are you coming home?'

'I'm being discharged the day after tomorrow and I'll fly home immediately. I'm longing to see sunshine again.' She glanced out of the window which overlooked the hospital car park. A solitary orange lamp lit up the few vehicles which were parked there, their windscreens covered in thick frost. She shivered.

'I'll come over and bring you back.'

Lisa laughed. 'Darling, I'm as fit as a fiddle, a bit weak, that's all. I can manage perfectly well by myself.'

*

On the morning she was due to be discharged, Lisa was packing her few possessions in the suitcase which had been brought over from the Columbine Hotel when one of the nurses approached her. 'Are you taking your Get Well cards with you?'

'I hadn't thought about it,' Lisa replied. The top of her bedside cabinet was bulging with cards and there were more stuck to the metal headboard of the bed with sellotape – the latter concession only allowed because of Christmas. 'Why, do you want them?'

'Would you mind?'

'Of course not, help yourself.'

'We're going to share them out,' the nurse said. 'Why, there must be a card from every star in Hollywood here.'

Word must have got around that she was ill. Not only did she hear from friends, but actors she scarcely knew sent messages and flowers. Sister Rolands said disapprovingly, 'This ward is beginning to look like the Chelsea Flower Show,' as yet another extravagant bouquet arrived.

And it hadn't just been the Hollywood set who'd thought of her. She'd even heard from friends of her mam who'd gone to the funeral, where Nellie had told them Lizzie had been coming all the way from America but had fallen ill in London. One particularly poignant message, the most touching of all, had been from Mrs Garrett, the midwife who'd delivered her over forty years ago. Now nearly ninety, she sent a little round crocheted doily. *'This was given to me by your mam for delivering Chris and it's been on my sideboard ever since. I'd like you to have it now.'*

She was packed and ready to leave when a familiar figure came through the swing doors of the ward.

'Ralph, you idiot!' she cried. 'I said there was no need to come.'

He threw his arms around her. 'I *had* to. When I said I wasn't, Gary decided he'd better fly across and I swear to God Millie and Vita were threatening to come together.'

'How come I love you so much?' she whispered.

'Beats me,' he said warmly. 'I'm just glad you do.'

She felt so ashamed now of the awful thoughts she'd had in the snow outside Jackie's house, when she'd felt so lonely and isolated, and had mentally spurned her strange, unconventional family.

'Haven't you left yet?' Sister Rolands marched into the ward and glared at Lisa. Then she transferred her frown to Ralph. 'My poor nurses are all of a twitter. I understand this is another film star causing chaos on my ward. You look vaguely familiar.' I think I might have seen you in my youth.'

'I'm not sure whether I should feel flattered or not,' responded Ralph with a grin.

Turning to Lisa, Sister said, 'Well, I suppose it'll be a long time before we get another such distinguished patient.'

'I hope so for their sakes,' laughed Lisa. 'After a few weeks of being bullied by you they won't feel all that distinguished.'

'The National Health Service treats all patients equally. There's no special treatment for film stars,' the nurse said tartly. 'Even so, despite the fact you reduced my nurses to a flutter – after all, not many people can boast they gave a bedpan to Lisa Angelis – I'm sorry to see you go.'

'And I'm sorry to be going,' said Lisa quietly. 'I never thought I would enjoy a stay in hospital. As for your nurses, they're worth their weight in gold.'

Sister Rolands shook her hand firmly. After she had gone, Lisa turned to wave goodbye to the other patients and saw some eyes reflecting her own unshed tears. Several of these women were dying. Before Christmas as many patients as possible had been allowed home, some permanently, others to return after the holiday, so there had been only six left in the main ward – those too ill to be moved, and Lisa. She had been deeply affected and surprised by the strong emotional bond that had almost miraculously been forged between them, despite their differing ages and backgrounds. They had exchanged the most intimate, the most private confidences and by Boxing Day, she felt as if she had known them all her life. Those who were dying, three of them, spoke openly of their fear of death, yet incredibly, found the courage to laugh away these fears, and it was more often than not the three who still had life to live who cried and needed comfort. In that short time, a time of great joy and great sadness, Lisa learnt more about the real meaning of life than she had done in all the years that had gone before. From now on she would treat each new day as a blessing and feel lucky to be alive and well.

36

Gary had been offered what he called a really hot property and was raring to go, subject to Ralph and Lisa's approval.

'Another thriller?' said Lisa after she had read the script. 'I think we should diversify.'

'After we've made this movie,' Gary promised.

'That's what you said last time.'

'There's a really good part in it for you,' he coaxed.

The story involved a mother and daughter living in a New York apartment block, being terrorised by an anonymous phone-caller.

'You'd be perfect as Zoe,' Gary added.

Lisa said idly, 'I'll think about it.' Zoe was the mother. She had initially thought Gary meant the daughter.

Later on she went upstairs and examined herself closely in the mirror. It was a month since she'd got back from England and not only had she regained the weight lost, but long hours lazing by the pool meant she had at last acquired the tan she'd always wanted. Her dark golden limbs, smooth and silky, were shown off to perfection by her white shorts and halter top. She bent forward so her face was only inches away from the glass. Underneath her eyes she could see fine, barely discernible lines, though there were none around her mouth or on her forehead. She blinked. The close inspection had strained her eyes and she remembered the difficulty she'd had in reading Gary's script; she'd blamed it on a worn typewriter ribbon, though the depressing fact was that she probably needed glasses. Sighing, Lisa stepped back in order to see her full reflection. There was no doubt about it – she was still a beautiful woman, but there was equally no doubt that she was a beautiful *forty-year-old* woman.

'I'll look better with some make-up on,' she thought, grabbing a jar of cream. She was smoothing it into her cheeks when she stopped, aware of the slightly frantic expression on her face as she tried to rub away the years. She put the jar down and smiled at herself. Everybody grew old and there was no reason to expect the Almighty to excuse her from the aging process. What did a few wrinkles matter anyway? In hospital she'd exchanged addresses with the other women in her ward, and yesterday had received a letter to say that two of them had died. One, Donna, had been only twenty-five; she hadn't been given the opportunity to grow old and wrinkled.

Lisa marched downstairs and told Gary she'd be happy to play the part of

Zoe. 'I've been thinking,' he said. 'You look too young to be the mother. Perhaps we could turn them into sisters.'

'Please yourself,' said Lisa. 'I don't mind.'

She did mind, though. After an inward struggle she decided she was only human after all and couldn't deny that she felt immensely flattered.

Later that year she worked with Busby Van Dolen again. His first eight movies had been re-released and at last reached the audiences they deserved. Even his final independent production, the lighthearted *Mr & Mrs Jones*, was declared to have qualities unnoticed at first – much to his amusement – though it was *Easy Dreams* and *The Opportunist* which received particular acclaim. Lisa suddenly found herself in great demand. After making Gary's thriller, she went straight to Busby's set.

Her ex-husband had lost none of his old enthusiasm. Apart from the fact that his bushy hair and beard had turned grey, it could have been the old Busby again, urging, cajoling and bullying them into giving their finest performances. With finance no longer a problem – nowadays he was *approached* by investors eager to sink money into his films – he could afford the very best sets, or go on location wherever he wanted. Busby being Busby, he sought out all the old technicians, the cameramen, the set-designers with whom he used to work. Even Maggie Nestor, who'd long ago taken reluctant early retirement, was unearthed to provide the costumes for the new production. When they all met again, not a few tears were shed as they recalled old times. Again, Busby being Busby, he got impatient with them all and told them sternly to pull themselves together and concentrate on what they had to do now.

The leading man was an actor of some repute – a tall, rakish Welshman called Hugo Swann, a notorious womaniser with a penchant for the bottle. Lisa came prepared to dislike him, but like everyone else on set was quickly bowled over by his lazy, irresistible charm.

'I always sleep with my leading ladies,' he drawled when they met.

'I thought you always married them.' He'd just gone through a messy, very public divorce from his fifth wife.

'Is that a proposal?' He smiled down at her, his blue eyes twinkling.

Lisa felt her stomach give a pleasant quiver. 'Definitely not. I'm too old, anyway. You only seem to marry teenagers.'

'Ouch!' He pretended to wince. 'How about mothering me, then? Take me out to dinner tonight, then come back to my hotel and tuck me in.'

Lisa was tempted. Her bed had felt lonely since she'd got back from England, but with Busby around it could prove embarrassing.

'I'm sorry, but no,' she said regretfully.

If only things had been different, thought Lisa later, watching Busby prowl around the studio. If he hadn't called her Lizzie that night, they might still be together, though that would mean she wouldn't have met Dent, wouldn't have been living in Tymperleys.

Perhaps Busby was thinking along the same lines, for on the final day of shooting he said casually, 'Like to come back to my place and talk about old times?' and Lisa, nostalgic for the past, agreed.

But nothing had changed. He made love briefly and inadequately, then fell asleep whilst she lay beside him aching with the passion he had the ability to arouse but which he could never satisfy. Even if he hadn't called her Lizzie, in the long run their marriage would never have worked, she thought sadly.

Stealthily, she crept out of bed and went into the kitchen where she put on her glasses and looked through the directory for the number of Hugo Swann's hotel.

'Are you alone?' she asked immediately he answered.

'Sad to say, yes,' he replied morosely.

'In that case, would you like me to come round and tuck you in?'

It was well over a year before Lisa returned to Liverpool.

'*I've been nagging someone to get married so you can come,*' wrote Nellie. '*But all of a sudden young people feel it's all right to live in sin. Can you imagine the reaction if one of us had just gone off to live openly with someone of the opposite sex! Remember the endless gossip when a girl had an illegitimate baby? Nowadays no one gives a damn. I'm not sure whether I feel censorious or envious! Anyway, Chris's son Stephen is getting spliced in April . . .*'

Lisa bought a moderately-priced plain grey flannel suit, not wanting to stand out in something outrageously fashionable and expensive.

'What do you think?' she asked Millie when she got home.

Millie looked her up and down and asked what prison she intended working at. 'They'll be disappointed, you turning up like that,' she said flatly. 'They expect you to look like a film star, not like you've come to arrest them. Take it back and get something different.'

Vita came in carrying the inevitable glass of whisky. 'Hi, Bobby. You joined up or something?' She saluted.

'I like folks who speak their mind,' said Lisa. 'Both of you have given my confidence a really big boost.'

'Don't be so damn sarcastic. If you don't want a body to give an honest opinion, you shouldn't come asking for it,' Millie said. 'Now get out of my kitchen before I throw a plate at you.'

'Have these houses always been here?' Lisa asked.

'No, they built them because you were coming, Liz,' Jimmie grinned.

She jammed her elbow into his ribs and remembered doing the same thing when they were children. 'You know what I mean,' she giggled. 'The only part of Liverpool I'm familiar with is Bootle. I never knew houses like this existed.'

The girl Stephen was marrying came from Calderstones. 'Where the really well-off people live,' Nellie said. As they drove to the church, Lisa was surprised to see big detached houses which wouldn't have been out of place in Hollywood.

'Stephen's father-in-law is a solicitor,' explained Jimmie, adding with a wicked grin, 'I never thought the day would come when an O'Brien would marry into a family that votes Conservative.'

'Now don't you start an argument at the reception,' warned Nellie. She was sitting with her husband, Stan, in the pull-down seats opposite. 'Heath isn't such a bad chap. He doesn't get under the skin the way Macmillan did.'

'Who's Heath?' asked Lisa.

'Edward Heath, the Prime Minister.' Jimmie regarded her with mock astonishment. 'Christ, you've grown up ignorant, Liz!'

'Don't take any notice of him,' said Stan mildly. 'If you could make a living getting up people's noses, he'd be a millionaire.' Stan was a bespectacled bookish-looking man who worked for a transport company. On the other side of Jimmie, his new young wife, who had so far remained tongue-tied, murmured heartfelt agreement.

Lisa turned to look out of the window. It was a fresh and sparkling morning, though the brilliant sunshine was deceptive; there'd been a chill in the air when they left Nellie's house. The trees, full of young green leaves, swayed gently and dappled shadows danced on the grass verges. Even from inside the car, she could smell the freshness, the vibrant tang of spring.

'We're here,' someone said and the limousine drew to a smooth stop outside the church.

As they walked up the path, Lisa felt glad she'd taken Millie's advice and bought another outfit – a vivid scarlet linen suit with tan leather inserts on the shoulders, a wide leather belt and a red straw picture hat – when she noticed the bride's parents and relatives were far more expensively and showily dressed than the O'Briens. 'They're rotten with money,' Nellie whispered.

Chris came over and took Lisa's hand. She'd met him, along with all her brothers – except Paddy – the night before at Nellie's. 'C'mon, I'm going to enjoy introducing you to the in-laws. This guy was Lord Mayor of Liverpool once and never stops telling you.'

He took her up to a stout couple, oozing self-importance and wealth. The woman wore an emerald-green brocade coat and dress, and a pillbox hat decorated with billowing green ostrich feathers. She had a five-strand row of pink pearls around her reddening neck.

Tony introduced them. 'Charles and Rita Slattery. This is Stephen's auntie, my sister, Lisa Angelis.'

'Not *the* Lisa Angelis?' The woman blanched as they shook hands and looked Lisa up and down, her eyes narrowing in surprise.

The man plucked at his striped waistcoat uncomfortably. 'Stephen mentioned it once. We didn't . . . well, we thought . . .'

'That he was having you on?' Chris said gleefully. 'Well, he wasn't. This is Lisa – our Lizzie – in the flesh.'

The rest of the occasion passed in a daze. They went from the church to the reception in a large hotel in Woolton. As time went on, Lisa felt the gap of years away from her family dwindle until it seemed as though they'd never been apart. Her older brothers were their normal demonstrative selves – she remembered vividly the amount of hugging and kissing that used to go on in Chaucer Street. Every now and then she noticed one of the twins, Sean and Dougal, who'd grown into quiet, serious-looking young men, staring at her curiously. They'd only been four when she left. To them she was little more than a stranger. Paddy was away again; the best man read a telegram from Syria.

In the middle of the afternoon, Lisa suddenly noticed that most of the men had disappeared. 'Where's Stan?' she asked Nellie. 'And all the boys?'

'Where do you think?' her sister said sarcastically. 'They've gone to the match. Liverpool are playing at home. Even the bride had a job making Stephen stay behind.'

Lisa said quietly, 'I see Joan isn't here.'

Nellie looked uncomfortable. 'I hoped you wouldn't notice.'

'I noticed the minute we got to church.' She'd looked for Joan straight away, hoping to make up with her.

'Once she knew you'd be here she refused to come. Poor Joan,' said Nellie with a sigh. 'She's spent her whole life cutting off her nose to spite her face.' She looked at Lisa anxiously. 'It hasn't spoilt your day though, has it?'

'Of course not,' Lisa assured her. 'It's great seeing my family again – and my new family. All these nieces and nephews and sisters-in-law I never knew I had, not forgetting my sole brother-in-law, Stan. He's a lovely chap, Nellie. You're very lucky.'

'I know I am.' Nellie nodded then looked at her sister keenly. 'But what about you, Liz? Have you got anybody?'

'I have a lover,' Lisa said bluntly. 'Though we don't see each other very often, just between movies.'

'Is it someone we know?'

'Hugo Swann.'

Nellie's jaw dropped. 'Hugo Swann! Jesus, Mary and Joseph, d'you mean to say I've got a sister who's sleeping with Hugo Swann?'

Lisa grinned. 'You have.'

Just then, Nellie's son Luke came rushing over and grabbed Lisa's hand. 'Auntie Lisa, come with me a minute.'

'Not now, love,' said Nellie.

'I'll go,' Lisa said quickly. 'You know I can't resist him.'

She'd fallen in love with Luke the night before. A happy outgoing nine-year-old with wide, innocent eyes and a shock of blond curly hair, he was a typical O'Brien. 'He's exactly the son I would have wanted myself,' thought Lisa wistfully, the minute she set eyes on him.

'Surely you shouldn't be in here,' she said. Luke had dragged her into the bar, full of strangers who were nothing to do with the wedding.

'This man won't believe you're my auntie.'

He stopped in front of a stout man clutching a pint of beer and swaying backwards and forwards, very much the worse for drink.

'Tell him you're my auntie,' demanded Luke.

'I'm his auntie,' Lisa said.

The stout man peered blearily at her. Gradually, recognition dawned in his glazed eyes. He carefully put his glass down on the nearest table and fainted dead away.

'One last toast,' said Kevin, 'and one last song. The toast is "Mam", to our mam, the best mother anyone could ever have, and the song is *When Irish Eyes Are Smiling*, to be sung by our Lizzie, the prodigal returned.'

'I couldn't possibly,' Lisa gasped. 'I'm far too drunk.'

'Sing, sing,' everybody chanted. It was nearly half-past ten and the new in-laws and their assorted relatives had long ago broken up their staid circle and come to join the O'Briens. Charles Slattery was playing a rowdy piano when

Lisa found herself being picked up, carried over to the piano and placed on top. Charles stood up and gave her a wet kiss. 'What key do you want?'

'Any key?'

'Good, that's the only one I know.'

She began to sing. All those lessons years ago, yet this was the first time she'd sung in public. Halfway through her début, she thought of Mam and broke down, but by then the song had already been taken up by the crowd. The wedding party ended in tears and laughter. 'As all good weddings should,' said Nellie with a satisfied smile when they were on their way home to Crosby.

37

Ralph had been threatening to return to the theatre for years. His film career had long been over, though Lisa and Gary always tried to create a part for him in their current movie. Sometimes this was almost too obvious and Ralph smilingly turned the part down. Lisa wondered if the smile hid a sense of hurt.

In the summer, he gathered together a group of actors – old hands like himself and half a dozen youngsters waiting for their big break. 'I'm not going to tout around for parts any longer,' he announced. 'I'll start with my own little touring company.' His name was still big enough to attract audiences in small-town theatres. 'Would you like to join us?' he asked Lisa hopefully.

She recalled how it was seeing him in *Pygmalion* that had inspired her to become an actress. Nothing she had seen since, either on stage or screen, had impressed her so much as his powerful performance in that play. Nevertheless, she made a face, saying, 'A live audience would frighten me to death. I might forget my lines!' Anyway, she was deeply involved with O'Brien Productions, acting in some movies, producing others, and sometimes even doing both.

She and Gary flew over to Maine for the opening night of Ralph's first stop on his tour of the eastern states. The play was *Uncle Vanya* and Ralph's acting was poor; he kept stumbling over his lines and lacked the power and presence of his younger days. When they went backstage, Lisa was trying to think of a tactful way of criticising his performance, but to her relief he seemed well aware of his shortcomings.

'I'll grow into the part,' he said confidently.

A rosy-cheeked young actor who had a minor role came up and put his hand on Ralph's shoulder. 'The press would like a word,' he said. There was something familiar about the gesture and beside her Lisa felt Gary stiffen.

Ralph groaned. 'I can just imagine the notices: "*A crowd of old has-beens and would-be hopefuls inflicting their negligible talents on us iggerant out-of-towners.*" Instead, when he posted the reviews to them a few days later they were quite flattering. The reviewer wrote that although there'd been a few hitches on the first night, he'd felt privileged to have seen the great Ralph Layton in the flesh.

Nellie and Stan came over with the children the following Christmas.

285

Natalie, a typical bored teenager, was determined not to be impressed by anything, but Luke was bowled over by everything he saw, particularly the pool.

'Can you teach me to swim, please, Auntie Lisa?' he pleaded.

Lisa promised and took the family on a tour of Tymperleys, Vita trotting behind pointing out things she missed. 'To think of an O'Brien owning a property like this!' said Nellie in amazement. 'And we thought we'd moved up in the world when we bought a semi-detached.'

Lisa showed Gary a script she said she'd been sent by a writer called Mary Smith about six women spending Christmas together in a hospital ward. 'It's both funny and sad,' she said. 'I think we should do it.'

After he'd read it, Gary said he liked the basic idea but the dialogue was appalling, too contrived and unnatural. 'We could get an experienced scriptwriter to work on it, but the main characters should be cut down to four. Six is too many to give much depth to in ninety minutes. The title is a definite no-no, too. *Christmas at St Elspeth's* is too clumsy by a mile. Write to the author and get his opinion.'

'Her opinion,' corrected Lisa. 'I've already spoken to her on the phone and I know she won't mind.'

The script was handed to one of their writers, and when a revised version arrived a few months later with a new title, *Hearts and Flowers*, Gary began to get enthusiastic. 'I suppose you see yourself as the actress?' he said to Lisa.

'I'd feel at home in the part,' she replied. She'd no intention of telling anyone she'd written it. It was too private and intimate.

Work began on *Hearts and Flowers* at the end of the year and Lisa threw herself, as she'd never done before, into the part of the wealthy actress who finds herself in a charity hospital over the Christmas holiday.

With an almost feminine intuition, Gary seemed to recognise how women would feel in this situation, and Lisa was impressed by the sensitivity with which he directed them. Sometimes the four actresses found themselves shedding real tears which did not cease when the cameras stopped rolling, though on the other hand, there were times when they couldn't stop laughing either.

When the film was complete, Gary claimed it was his best work to date. 'Do you think Mary Smith will come to the opening?' he asked.

'No,' Lisa replied. 'She's too shy.'

Gary gave one of his rare smiles. 'Gee, that's a shame,' he said innocently. 'Y'know, I feel as if I know Mary already. Isn't that strange? Maybe she'll write something else one day.'

'I doubt it. Mary Smith only had the one script in her.'

'Well, I'm glad I was the guy who got it.' He rubbed his hands together with a mixture of anxiety and nervousness. 'I've never felt quite *this* uptight before an opening. I didn't realise till now, but I've never put so much of myself into a movie before.'

Remembering how cruel the critics had been to Busby, Lisa found herself equally on edge as the June opening drew close. She too felt she had given her finest performance, the best of which she was capable. 'I'll never act so well again,' she thought. If the critics slammed her, she decided she'd give up acting altogether.

'*I didn't know whether to laugh or cry.*'

'*This heart-warming, heart-rending movie had me leaving the theatre emotionally drained.*'

'*Plucks at the heart-strings.*'

'*Oscar-winning performances from all four women.*'

'*Gary Maddox has proved himself one of our finest directors.*'

They'd been standing on the corner of Hollywood and Vine for half an hour, waiting for the early-morning editions of the newspapers to arrive. There were a dozen people there – most of the small cast of *Hearts and Flowers* and Hugo Swann, Ralph and Vita – all drunk, more with excitement than alcohol. When the van drew up with a screech of brakes and several bundles of newspapers were thrown at their feet, they pounced and tore the bundles apart with eager, desperate hands. 'If the reaction of the audience is anything to go by, the notices are bound to be good,' someone said hoarsely.

Then they began to read the reviews to each other, all yelling at once. 'Listen to what Maurice Edelman says!' 'Hey, we even got Pauline Kael to cry!'

They stood staring at each other, lightheaded with relief, voices tremulous with excitement.

'What do we do now?' asked Gary. 'We can't go home, I'm on a high.'

'This calls for a slap-up dinner,' drawled Hugo. 'Come on, folks, let's find a restaurant. The meal's on me.'

'*Dinner?*' Vita's face was a mixture of disgust and disdain. 'After *my* premières, we used to have a fuckin' orgy.'

For three years, Ralph had been doggedly touring the country with his small band of actors. When he came home in the summer to rehearse a new programme of plays, a mixture of the classics and comedy, Lisa was thrilled to find *Pygmalion* had been included. She suggested he use Dent's studio as a rehearsal room, and for two months the house was loud with the laughter and noise of actors, young and old, as they rehearsed from early morning, often until midnight.

'You're certainly working me hard my last month,' complained Millie. 'I made more meatloaf these last few weeks than I made in my whole doggone life.' Millie had decided the time had come to retire. At the end of the month she was going to move in permanently with her daughter. 'I'm too old to be on my feet all day long.'

'I don't want to let you go,' whispered Lisa. She stood behind the old black woman and put her arms around her neck. 'The house won't be the same without you. Why don't you stay and I'll hire another cook?'

'For Chrissakes, Lisa! You can't go round filling your house up with everybody you sets your eyes on. You gotta learn to live by yourself someday. Now, out of my kitchen and let me get on with some work.' Millie banged a saucepan down on the stove – a clear indication she was moved.

The rosy-cheeked boy Lisa had seen in Maine was still with the company and she wondered if Gary minded. One day when they'd both been sitting in on a rehearsal, she noticed the youth lean against Ralph affectionately when the play had finished, and she turned to look at Gary curiously. To her surprise he gave a wan smile. 'He's old and easily flattered,' he said gently – Ralph had passed his sixtieth birthday earlier in the year. 'I don't mind as long as he comes home to me.'

'I remember him saying that once about Michael.' Lisa felt bemused. She would have expected Ralph to be the one to remain steadfast and loyal, but instead it was Gary, the one-time blond and handsome heart-throb whom she'd once considered superficial and shallow.

Nellie wrote to say that Patrick had got married in Saudi Arabia. '*He sent a photo of Pita, she's half-Indian, really beautiful – a bit like you in looks. He's forty-one, you know. I wonder why he waited so long? Still, better late than never, as Mam always said.*'

She finished, '*Things have been exciting here politically. The Conservatives have elected a woman leader, Margaret Thatcher. She'll be no match for Harold Wilson, but imagine the country led by a woman! If they get in again, it'll feel strange. What do you think?*'

Lisa sat staring at the letter for a long time. She didn't know what to think – about anything.

Gary was nominated for an Oscar for *Hearts and Flowers* along with one of the actresses, Dorothy West, who'd played the part of a woman twice her age. Lisa felt a twinge of jealousy when she first heard the news but brushed it aside. Their good news was equalled by Ralph's when he rang to say the off-Broadway production of *Pygmalion* had reached the attention of national critics and he'd had an offer to go to England to play King Lear. When he came home a few weeks later she heard him arguing angrily with Gary.

'Doesn't he want you to go?' she asked Ralph later.

'It's not that at all. I'm scared to go and he insists I should.'

'I think you should too,' she said, doing her best to sound convincing. Millie had left a few months ago and if Ralph went he could be gone a whole year. Secretly she hoped he'd stay.

'I'm worried I'm past it.'

'They wouldn't have asked you if they thought that.' She patted his shoulder. 'Dent was right, you know. You wasted your talents in Hollywood. There's still time to be a great actor, though I'd lose some weight if I were you. I'm sure King Lear isn't supposed to be a fatty.'

Gary came back to Tymperleys from seeing Ralph off on the plane to England. Lisa expressed surprise. 'I thought you'd go straight to the set,' she said. 'I only stayed at home to make a heap of telephone calls.' O'Brien Productions had just started on a political thriller loosely based on the Watergate affair. Lisa's part wasn't due to be shot for another two weeks.

'I've been feeling really lousy for a while.' Gary rubbed his forehead. He looked flushed, as if he had a chill. 'I think I'll go and lie down for the rest of the day. I would have done before, but I didn't want Ralph to know I felt bad in case he didn't go.'

He went upstairs. When Lisa looked in on him during the evening he was fast asleep. It must be really serious for Gary to take a day off when he was making a movie. Next morning he said he felt better and went off early to the studio. When Lisa arrived later Les Norman, the assistant director, said, 'Gary had to go home. He kept going dizzy.'

'Perhaps he's run-down or something,' Lisa said worriedly. That night, after finding Gary in bed with a raging temperature, she said, 'I think I'd better call a doctor.'

Dr Myerson had been a friend of Dent's. He came within the hour – a stocky middle-aged man who rarely smiled.

'You should be up and running within a week,' he said to the patient, though seven days later Gary's condition was unchanged. The doctor came back and pronounced himself mystified. 'I think you'd better come into hospital straight away and have some tests.'

'He can't,' said Lisa, who was hovering in the background.

'Absolutely not,' Gary concurred. 'Tomorrow night's the Oscars and I'll be there if they have to carry me.'

'I wonder if Dent is watching.' Gary looked up as if he half-expected to see Joseph Dent hanging like a big black bat from the roof of the large theatre where the Oscars ceremony was being held.

'I doubt it,' said Lisa. 'If he's in a position to watch anything, it'll be one of his own movies.'

Hearts and Flowers didn't win any awards, but the next best thing happened: Busby Van Dolen won the Oscar for Best Director. The night out seemed to do Gary good and next day he returned to work, apparently recovered.

'I think Gary's driving himself too hard. He looks like death.' Les Norman came over and spoke to Lisa between takes. She glanced across the studio. Even from here, she could see perspiration glistening on Gary's forehead and his face was drawn, his cheeks hollow.

'He's lost a lot of weight, too,' Les added. Gary's clothes were hanging loosely on his suddenly gaunt body. 'I guess he must be really run-down or something.'

'I've only just realised how bad he looks,' said Lisa. Last night she'd joked with Gary, 'You missing Millie's meatloaf?' when he'd pushed his plate away, the food scarcely touched, yet Chloe, the woman hired to take Millie's place, was a good cook. It dawned on Lisa that he'd done that a lot lately.

'I think you should go into hospital and have those tests the doctor suggested,' she said gently to Gary that night.

He looked up, his eyes drawn and tired. 'I'm too scared,' he confessed in a shaky voice. She began to argue with him, but he just pushed his untouched dinner away, saying mutinously, 'I'm going to bed.' Seconds later there was a crash, and she found that Gary had passed out on the stairs.

When Lisa went to collect him from the hospital a few days later, Gary was still in bed and he looked terrible. 'What's wrong?' She felt frightened.

'I've got PGL,' he said with a weak smile.

'What on earth's that?'

'Persistent generalised enlargement of the lymph nodes. In other words, I got lumps all over me that shouldn't be there. I should have told the doctor before.'

'You mean you've had these lumps a long time?' she asked angrily.

'A few months. I was worried it was cancer.'

A young woman came into the room. 'Hi, I'm Dr Evans. Your friend's pretty sick. We can keep him here longer if you like.'

'What do you mean, if I like?'

'Well, there's nothing we can do for him. Once he gets over his viral infection, the swellings will go and he'll be fine. He just needs looking after in the meantime.'

'Can't I look after him at home?' asked Lisa.

'If you're willing.'

'Of *course* I'm willing! He's family.'

Gary made a half-hearted protest. 'I can't expect you to—'

'Shut up,' she told him. 'You're coming back with me this minute.'

'It'll have to be by ambulance,' said the doctor. 'I doubt if he can make it to the car.'

'I can't understand it,' said Dr Myerson to Lisa. 'No matter what I give him, he gets worse instead of better.' He'd come downstairs from seeing Gary, looking both mystified and worried. 'I keep in touch with Dr Evans from the hospital and, quite frankly, we've run out of ideas. It's really peculiar, to put it mildly.'

'The lumps haven't gone?'

'No, and that rash is really bad.'

'He didn't say he had a rash,' said Lisa, pulling a face.

'That's because he doesn't want to worry you. It's all over his body.' The doctor sighed. 'I wonder if you should contact his family.'

'Is it *that* serious?' Lisa was horrified. Was he suggesting that someone as apparently healthy as Gary could die from a chill?

Dr Myerson fiddled with the handle of his black bag. 'He's gay, isn't he?'

'Yes,' she replied bluntly.

Looking uncomfortable, the doctor continued, 'One of my colleagues told me about a patient he'd heard of with the same prognosis as Gary and – well, I'm afraid he died. He was gay too.' He shrugged. 'It's probably just a coincidence.'

'I'll get in touch with his father. His mother died a few years back.'

The doctor's words still ringing in her ears, Lisa went upstairs. Gary was asleep and she looked at him as a stranger would and was shocked at the deterioration. He was like a skeleton, the skin on his face a strange ivory colour and tissue-thin. Vita was sitting beside him, completely sober. She'd taken his illness really hard. 'He's not gonna get better,' she whispered.

'Don't say that!' said Lisa angrily, but Vita ignored her.

'I hate people dying. It's bad enough when old people go, but when young people die, I hate it.' She picked up Gary's hand and stroked it gently. 'He's a really nice kid. I like him and he's a truly great director. He's the only one here who treated me like a fuckin' actress and not an eccentric old woman.'

'You're a fuckin' eccentric old actress.' Gary had opened his eyes and was looking at Vita blearily. 'Y'know what I'd like, Lisa?'

'What, darling?'

'I'd like my bed moved downstairs into the cinema so's I can watch movies.'

'I'll get someone in to do it in the morning,' she promised.

Les Norman called in to see Gary, 'My God, Lisa,' he said afterwards, 'he looks terrible! What's the matter with him?'

'I don't know,' Lisa answered. 'No one does. They took him back into hospital for more tests last week. All they can think of is his immune system has gone.'

'What does that mean?'

'It means he can't recover from anything he happens to catch. He was going in for radiotherapy for his rash but the side-effects made him feel so bad he refuses to go again. Anyway, that wasn't doing him any good, either.'

Les said casually, 'What's going to happen with O'Brien Productions, Lisa? We're scheduled to start on *Central Park* in two weeks' time.'

The Watergate movie had been completed under Les's direction and was due to be released soon. He'd done a competent job but lacked Gary's flair. 'I've got most of the production side sorted out,' said Lisa, 'though I'll be in each day to check how things are going. Should we hire a guest director, or can you manage?'

'I can manage,' Les said with alacrity.

'Good,' she replied, cynically noting the way his eyes lit up with greedy excitement.

'You haven't told Ralph I'm ill?'

'I promised I wouldn't,' said Lisa.

'And under no circumstances tell my father.'

'I won't.' In fact she had telephoned Gary's father weeks ago and he'd said, 'As far as I'm concerned he's been sick ever since he moved in with that old actor, so don't bother me again,' and slammed the receiver down.

Vita cut down on her drinking and spent all day with Gary in the cinema, where the middle rows of seats had been removed to take the big bed. The pair of them sat hour after hour watching films.

'It's not good for either of you. You're getting no fresh air,' Lisa complained.

'Fresh air ain't half as healthy as the air inside a movie-house,' said Vita. 'Watchin' that screen is a far better tonic for Gary than sitting under a fuckin' tree or something.'

The two of them burst into giggles and Lisa smiled. Sometimes there was almost a party atmosphere in the cinema as the old woman regaled Gary with her fund of dirty jokes and a string of lurid tales from her days in silent movies. The other day Lisa had come in while they were watching one of Vita's old films and found him almost falling out of bed from laughing.

'See this bit?' Vita was saying, pointing to a love-scene with a male star who'd become a household name. 'I'm supposed to be saying I'll love him till death do us part and all that crap. 'Stead, I told him his breath was worse than a goat's fart and if he stuck his tongue down my throat again I'd bite it off and stuff it you know where!'

At other times she found them singing together, Vita's voice surprisingly youthful, Gary's cracked and hoarse. No doubt this was an unconventional way to tend a sick, possibly dying man, but he seemed as happy as anyone could be under the circumstances. In fact she was surprised at the equanimity, the stoicism with which Gary had accepted changing from a healthy, vigorous man into a virtually bed-bound invalid in the course of three or four months. Only occasionally did his remarkable control give way and he would cry, 'What's happening to me? When am I going to get better?'

Vita excused herself. 'I'm just going to the ladies' room.'

After she'd gone, Gary clasped Lisa's hand. 'I'm not gonna make it, am I?'

'Don't be silly,' she began, but he squeezed her fingers with a strength that surprised her.

'Shush,' he whispered. 'Don't lie to me.'

She stroked his face with her other hand and thought how terrible he looked. What was left of his hair grew in little tufts out of his shining skull – she'd shaved his beard off weeks ago – and his sunken eyes seemed to stare out from the back of his head. At the same time there was a strange beauty in the gritty heroism of his expression. His next words surprised her. 'You never liked me much, did you?'

'Not at first,' she said honestly.

'I never liked you much, either.'

She smiled. 'Then what are we doing here like this?'

He looked puzzled. 'I ask myself that sometimes. I suppose people just get thrown together and . . .' He sighed and didn't finish.

'And what?'

'I dunno.' He began to cough and she could hear the raw grating noise inside his chest. She took a paper handkerchief and wiped his mouth. 'Thanks,' he muttered. Neither spoke for a few minutes, then Gary took a deep breath. 'I gotta tell you this now before it gets too late, but I love you, Lisa, far more than I ever loved Ralph, but it's not sex. It's just . . .' He licked his dry lips. Finding the right words was an effort. 'Pure love, I guess.'

Lisa felt a rush of tears. 'Oh Gary, I don't want you to die.' She pressed her cheek against his and began to cry. 'You see, I've grown to love you too,' she sobbed.

When Gary could no longer get out of bed, she hired a night nurse to sit with him, but after two nights the woman declared she wasn't coming any more. 'I don't like what's wrong with him. I never seen anything like it before. Whatever it is, I don't wanna catch it.' So Lisa gave up going into the office and took turns with Vita sitting with the patient, though for all the old woman's cheerfulness, she was beginning to look exhausted and sometimes when Lisa went into the cinema she found both of them asleep, Vita's head resting on Gary's sharp jutting knees, a bright blank screen in front of them and the noise of the projector whirring behind.

'This is a perfect way to die,' said Gary. At least, that's what Lisa thought he said. These last few days his words had become slurred and difficult to understand. 'Watching movies.' He blinked. His sunken eyes were red-raw from viewing the vivid, flickering images only twenty feet away. 'Next best thing to makin' them. Thanks, Lisa. Thanks for everything.'

'I think you should rest your eyes,' she said softly. 'How about some music for a change?'

'Music? Dent's music? That'd be nice.'

'I'll put the loud-speaker system on. What would you like?'

'That stuff he played the first morning we were here.'

'Wagner?'

'Yeah, I liked that.'

Lisa went upstairs. Over the past week the weather in Los Angeles had been strange. Through the lattice windows she could see dark threatening clouds drifting across the livid angry sky, and thunder rumbled in the distance. Another storm was on the way. She inserted the tape and vibrant, turbulent music filled the old, dark rooms, together with the equally restless spirit of Joseph Dent. Lisa shivered. The house seemed to be crackling with an almost palpable tension. She decided that before going back to Gary, she'd make a cup of tea and a sandwich.

The kitchen was spotless. There was no sign of Chloe, who went home each evening. Lisa glanced at the clock on the stove. Just before six – though whether that was morning or night, she didn't know. She'd been with Gary for so long she'd lost track of time. Thunder growled, closer now, and she heard rain splatter against the windows. She jumped when Vita came into the kitchen, still in her dressing gown, her eyes blinking with tiredness. Lisa had never seen her look so old.

'I overslept, dammit,' she complained. 'These storms, they seem to sap all my energy.'

'Go back to bed, dear. I'm just making some tea. Would you like to take a cup back with you?'

'No, but I'll go and sit with Gary while you get some rest.' Vita turned and swayed, clutching at the door for support. Lisa leapt over and helped her back upstairs, Vita complaining all the time, 'I want to sit with Gary.'

'After you've had a sleep. The storm might be over by then.'

'I like that music.'

'Is it too loud? Shall I turn it down?'

'No, we used that for one of my movies. I can't remember which.'

Lisa pulled the bedclothes up. 'Goodnight, or perhaps it's good morning!'

Vita managed to smile. 'You're a good sort, y'know that Lisa?'

As Lisa ran down the stairs, she realised it was the first time Vita had called her by her real name.

In the cinema, Gary's eyes were closed. Lisa sat beside him, touching his hand to indicate she was there. He lifted a finger to acknowledge her presence and mumbled, 'Is Dent with you?'

'No, darling.' For some reason she felt the hairs on her neck stiffen.

'He's somewhere about. He's in the music.'

Down here the sound seemed to be crashing against the walls, as if they were within a swiftly-moving ball of music that would never stop.

'There were an awful lot of movies I still had to make.'

'I know.' She'd long ago stopped pretending there was hope. 'Someone will make them.'

He began to cry silently. Lisa held his hand, too full of sadness to speak. After a while, unable to help herself, she began to doze and was woken by a crash of thunder that rocked the room. Terrified, without thinking, she clutched at Gary's hand, more for her own comfort than his and was shocked to find it icy cold. Frantically she began to rub it warm. Then she noticed that Gary's head had fallen to one side, and his mouth hung open. She stood up and straightened his head, closed his mouth and picked up his other hand to tuck under the quilt, but that was frozen too and finally, reluctantly, her tired brain told her Gary was dead.

She telephoned Dr Myerson, who promised to come immediately, then she went upstairs to tell Vita. But perhaps Vita already knew. Something had told her that she'd played her last part. She lay, curled on her side, exactly as Lisa had left her, with the smile still on her face, and she was as cold as Gary.

38

The big house had never been so quiet or felt so cold. Lisa was convinced she could hear the whispering of age-old ghosts behind the closed doors of the empty rooms as she wandered around the corridors of Tymperleys.

'Why, oh why do things have to change?' she moaned aloud, as if God would stop people dying to please her! Vita had been over eighty and not long for this world, anyway.

She went out to the pool; outside seemed warmer than in. The recent spate of thunderstorms had ceased about a week ago and there was a tangy freshness to the mid-morning air as if it had been cleansed and renewed, though by midday it would be baking out here. The pool-boy had arrived earlier and was scrubbing the rim of the bright-blue mosaic basin. He wore trunks and his body had been burnt nutmeg brown by the sun.

When he saw her the boy waved. 'Hi, Miss Angelis.'

Lisa tried to remember his name. Daniel, that was it. 'Hello, there,' she shouted. 'Would you like some lemonade and cookies when you've finished, Daniel?'

'Gee, thanks, but no, I've got another two jobs later,' he shouted back.

She sighed and sank down on a lounger to watch the boy. He was no more than thirteen or fourteen. The budding muscles in his young back rippled as he worked and she wondered dispassionately if the baby she'd carried those few short months when she was his age had been a boy. What joy it would have been to have had her own family – children conceived and carried in her womb, though the time would have come when they too would have left to live their own lives. By now, all might have gone and she could still be alone, though there might have been a husband. She backtracked over her life: if this had happened or if that *hadn't* happened, how would things have turned out?

The telephone began to ring and she ignored it. Chloe was out shopping so it would stay unanswered. Busby had called a lot lately. 'Darling, you can't stay in that big house all on your own.' He implored her to move in with him, but she refused. No point in starting *that* all over again, yet she was moved by his reliability, the dogged persistence of his love for her. Hugo Swann had taken flight when Gary first became sick, frightened by the mere mention of illness. A few months ago he'd married a model thirty years his junior.

Lisa knew she was being awkward. Several folk from O'Brien Productions kept demanding to know when she'd be back, though as she pointed out, the still-expanding company was quite capable of functioning without its three founders. Les Norman said there was a part in the next movie which would be perfect for her.

'I don't want to rush out and bury myself in work. I want to sort my mind out in my own time in my own home,' she said to herself.

Ralph tried to persuade her to come back to London with him. He'd arrived, numb with shock, for Gary's funeral. 'Why didn't you tell me he was ill?' he demanded angrily.

'He was adamant I shouldn't,' Lisa replied. 'He said your career was at a point where it shouldn't be interrupted.'

Ralph said nothing for a long time and after a while Lisa asked, '*Would you have interrupted it? I don't mean for a quick visit, I mean for all the months it took him to die?*'

'I was wondering that myself,' he said in a tight voice.

'After all, the show must go on,' she said lightly.

He looked uncomfortable and said, '*You* didn't think so.'

'Perhaps we have different priorities. Looking after someone dying seemed more important than making a movie.'

'Gary wouldn't have agreed with that,' he argued.

She managed to laugh. 'I did what was right for me.'

Next morning, when she drove him to the airport, he said, 'Think about coming to London for a while, a holiday.'

'I will,' she promised, and meant it.

At the ticket barrier, he kissed her and she felt him trembling. 'What's the matter?' she asked with concern.

'You know the saying "death goes in threes"? I keep thinking I'm to be the next. It seems only right. Vita, Gary, then me.'

'It might be me.' She remembered this was one of Kitty's more ghoulish sayings – and often she'd been right.

'Don't be silly, Lisa, you'll go on forever.' He turned swiftly and went through the barrier.

Frightened, she shouted, 'Call me as soon as you get back.'

It was midnight and she was in bed when the telephone rang. He had arrived safely. 'Thank God! For a minute there you had me thinking your plane would crash.'

She replaced the receiver and remained sitting up in bed listening to the creaks and groans of the old house. '*Somebody else is going to die,*' said a voice. She jumped and felt herself go cold, but the voice had been inside her head. Even so, she tossed and turned for hours, unable to sleep. At one point she opened her eyes and Dent was standing by the bed. He held a tray of champagne and was entirely naked. Lisa began to laugh and suddenly the room was drenched in sunshine. She'd fallen asleep, after all.

The boy had only one more side to clean. His movements grew slower as his strength began to ebb. Lisa felt admiration for his initiative. Cleaning three pools in one day for a few dollars' return showed great strength of character. She recalled how one of her brothers, she couldn't remember which, had done a paper round, going out early in all weathers for a few pennies a week to give Mam, though he'd had to wait till Dad left for work else the money would have been taken off the housekeeping.

Lately, she'd found herself thinking a lot about Chaucer Street. Perhaps it was because Nellie had told her it was about to be demolished and Joan was being moved into a council flat. Lisa had always imagined that one day she'd go back, but perhaps that would have raked up too many bad memories. Anyway, Nellie said she'd never recognise the place. 'It was all modernised years ago, with a proper kitchen and central heating . . .'

Busby said she shouldn't grieve alone; she should mix with people. 'I'm not grieving,' she protested and she wasn't, though the loss of two good friends was hard to take. It was watching a relatively young man die before her eyes that shocked her. What had Gary done to deserve such a cruel fate when other, lesser men lived? Gary, who had so much to give, so much to do – a good, decent man who harmed no one?

'God moves in a mysterious way,' Millie said at the funeral and Lisa felt annoyed with God. What right had He to be so mysterious? Why couldn't He be a little more forthcoming?

Most nights she went down to the little cinema and watched movies, usually Gary's, marvelling at him, young, blond and good-looking, acting his heart out in *Matchstick Man*, recalling the terrible animosity he'd felt towards Dent and the way they'd ended up the greatest friends. It was their obsessive love of movies that had brought them together. By the end of the night she was always in tears for what had been, for what might have been, and knew she was being maudlin again and over-sentimental.

'But I don't care,' she thought rebelliously. 'That's how I am, that's how I'll always be. I cling to memories, they haunt me. I can't forget the past, and after all, it's the past that shapes the future.'

After the funeral, Lisa received a letter from Gary's lawyers. As she read, she felt her eyes fill with yet more tears. He'd left her the bulk of his considerable fortune, as well as his share in O'Brien Productions. She took off her glasses and lay back in the chair, touched to the heart.

Something would have to be done with this money – she wasn't sure what, but one day it would be put to good use.

'Phew! I'm all done, Miss Angelis.'

The boy was standing beside her. She'd been so lost in her thoughts that she'd forgotten all about him. By now the heat outside was intense. It was far too hot. She'd better go indoors once he'd gone.

She sat up and said, 'Thanks, Daniel, you've done a fine job. Is Daniel right or should I call you Dan?'

'My ma calls me Daniel, everybody else says Dan.' Close up, she noticed his knees were grazed and there was a bright bruise on his shin.

'How much do I owe you?'

'Ten dollars.' Lisa picked up her purse and gave him twenty. 'Gee, thanks!' His eyes lit up.

'What are you going to buy with that, Daniel?'

'My folks are taking me and my brothers on a camping holiday this fall. I'm getting my spending money together.' The telephone began to ring again and he said, 'Your phone's been going all morning.'

'I know,' she smiled. 'I forgot to bring the extension out and I'm too lazy to go indoors. *What's more, I don't want to*,' she added inwardly.

'Want me to answer it for you?'

The telephone stopped and immediately began again. Lisa groaned and started to get up. You never knew, it might be important.

'I'll get it.' The boy darted through the open windows and the ringing stopped. He re-appeared, clutching the receiver to his chest. 'It's all the way from Liverpool, England,' he said in an awed voice. 'And they said it's urgent.'

Lisa felt a terrible premonition. *A third person was going to die!* Jesus Christ, who was it?

She ran into the house and snatched the receiver out of the astonished boy's hands. He mumbled, 'Well, I'll be off now, Miss Angelis,' as she screamed, 'Hallo, hallo!'

'Lisa, it's Stan. I've been trying to phone all night.' He was scarcely audible.

'Stan, what's happened? Is it Nellie?'

'No, Lisa, it's Luke.' He began to cry. 'Our Luke is dead.'

Lisa was aware of the atmosphere of death as soon as she entered the house: a gloom, the soft murmur of sad spirits chanting a requiem.

'Thanks for coming,' Stan said dully when he opened the door. He made a brave attempt to be polite and welcoming. 'Nellie asked specially for you. She's in a bit of a state, I'm afraid. Natalie's shut in her room, she won't answer to anyone.' He led her into the big living room, usually so bright and cheerful.

Nellie was hunched in an armchair, her eyes red-rimmed and bloodshot. When she saw Lisa, she stretched out her arms. 'Oh, Lizzie, Luke's gone.'

'I know, love.' Lisa knelt and embraced her sister. 'How did it happen? Do you want to talk about it?'

'He drowned. He was with some boys in New Brighton and they went swimming. Luke swam too far out – he was probably showing off. When they reached him, it was too late. Oh, my lovely Luke,' she wailed. 'He was only thirteen. I can't believe he's dead.'

Lisa listened for a long time, saying little. When she looked across at Stan, he was sitting in the corner, his head buried in his hands.

'I'll make some tea,' she thought. 'That's what we need, a cup of tea.'

To her surprise, there was already someone in the kitchen – a scraggy, raw-boned woman with faded red hair. She was bent over the sink washing dishes with a furious, intense energy.

Joan!

Lisa said nothing but just watched, noticing the scrawny neck, the freckled, yellowing skin, the wrinkled elbows. Unexpectedly, she felt conscious of her own beauty and wondered how on earth this plain woman could be her sister, could be Nellie's sister? She thought of the boys, all fair, handsome and well-built, nothing like this unpleasant-looking scarecrow of a woman. Yet Joan had been pretty as a child. What had made her turn out like this?

Joan suddenly became conscious of her presence. She looked up and her face flushed. 'So *you're* here,' she said in a flat voice.

'I am,' said Lisa lightly.

Her sister shook her wet hands in the sink and began to dry the dishes.

'You'll rub the pattern off,' said Lisa. The muscles in Joan's neck were rigid cords and the plates squeaked from the pressure of the cloth. She didn't answer.

'Joan, why can't we be friends?'

'Huh!'

'What does that mean?'

'It means no. I don't want to be your friend. You've caused nothing but misery for this family.'

Lisa thought of Tom. 'Perhaps this family caused nothing but misery for me, at least when I was a child.'

Joan looked at her contemptuously, her green eyes full of hate. 'I don't know what you're on about. All I know is Mam seemed to think the sun shone out of your arse. It was "our Lizzie" this, "our Lizzie" that, "I wonder what our Lizzie is doing now?" she'd say whenever it was your birthday. She never seemed to realise it was me, me who stayed at home and looked after her. Never a thought for our Joan.'

'There was no need to stay,' Lisa said gently.

'How would *you* know?' asked Joan sharply. She began to stack the plates carelessly, angrily, each one landing on top of the other with a sharp crack. 'You were away having a good time. I could have got married, you know. There was this chap—'

'Perhaps you should have. I'm sure Mam would have preferred it.'

Joan turned and looked at her, a strange, bitter expression on her plain features. 'Are you saying I wasted my life?'

'Of course not,' said Lisa hastily. 'I just meant Mam would have liked to see you happy, that's all.'

'You seem to know more about our mam than me, despite the fact you never saw her most of your life.'

Lisa said despairingly, 'You twist everything. I don't know what else to say.'

'Then don't say anything, just go away. If you hadn't taught Luke to swim, he wouldn't be dead. It's all your fault!' The words were spat out with such viciousness that Lisa stepped back, appalled.

'I only came because Nellie asked,' she stammered. 'She wouldn't want me if she thought I was to blame.'

Joan seemed to freeze. 'Oh, God!' thought Lisa. 'Now I've hurt her even more.' Nellie already had a sister close at hand, yet it was Lisa she'd wanted by her side in her misery.

That night, when everybody else was in bed, Lisa went for a walk on the sands close to Nellie's house.

It was a brilliant night, the sky a coverlet of shimmering, blinking stars, the moon a curve of gold. Was that a new moon or old? Lisa stared, but couldn't remember which side was which. Dent had explained it to Sabina on the boat on their way to Cannes.

Sabina! Her nearly-child, her dream. Which was worse, to have longed for a child all your life as she had done, or to lose one, like Nellie? Right now, she decided, it was worse for Nellie, much worse.

The beach was deserted – not surprisingly, as it must be midnight. All that could be heard was the soft sound of the River Mersey lapping against the sands. She went down and stared into the black water. What was it all about? What was it all for? Why had Luke been chosen as a sacrifice by some capricious God?

Questions, questions, always questions, but never any answers. The water began to lick her feet, but she didn't notice until a clump of seaweed wrapped itself around her ankle and she leapt back. Her shoes were soaked.

She thought of Joan, her sister. It hadn't taken much to turn her into a shrew, eaten through with bitterness. Yet far worse things had happened to Lizzie – the abortion, the stabbing, and that awful time in Southport, but Lizzie had come through. Things hadn't gone the way she wanted, but she was Lisa Angelis, successful, admired and, most of the time, happy. Yes, she'd overcome adversity and come through with honours.

True, life was a struggle, but she was forty-five and still on the winning side. Nothing was going to get her down, ever. For the next few weeks, she'd stay with Nellie, then she'd continue with the struggle on her own, as usual.

She shook her fist at the stars. 'I don't care what you've got in store for us, you bastards,' she yelled. 'But you've got a fight on your hands with Lizzie O'Brien, that I can promise.'

Ferris Hall

39

'Lisa, this is Tony Molyneux. He's been nagging something awful to be introduced.' Barbara Heany pushed a tall, silver-haired man wearing evening dress in the general direction of Lisa.

'How do you do?' She shook hands and someone knocked against her, thrusting her forward into the man's arms.

'Whoops!' he said as he caught her.

'Sorry, I think I've spilt some wine on your tie.' Lisa began to dab at the stain with a paper napkin.

'Don't bother, I never liked it anyway.' He smiled, showing white, even teeth. His eyes were an unusual colour, dark grey with flecks of blue, and he had a delicate, gentle face.

'If you can't get the mark out, I'll buy you another,' she promised.

'In that case I definitely won't get the mark out.'

Lisa looked at him; there was slightly more than a flirtatious tone to his words. He was watching her with a quirky smile on his fine, thin lips, though his dark eyes were grave.

'What's this party for, anyway?' he asked suddenly.

'If you don't know, you must be a gate-crasher,' she said accusingly. 'No wonder it's so crowded.'

'Let's go and pretend we're watching a play.' He took her arm and guided her off the stage and into the fifth row of seats. Quite a few people had already escaped the crowd and were sitting in the front stalls. She could see Ralph with his new friend, Adam.

'You didn't tell me what the party was for.'

'You didn't admit to being a gate-crasher,' she said sternly.

He looked faintly bemused. 'I'm not, at least I don't think so. I came with Carter Stevenson and his wife. They assured me they'd been invited back-stage after the show.'

'Carter Stevenson? That name sounds vaguely familiar,' said Lisa.

'I should hope so, he's the Home Secretary.'

'There's no need to sound so shocked,' she said indignantly. 'Not every-one's interested in politics.'

'Whoops again,' he said. He spoke in the slightly strangulated manner of the English upper classes, with long, exaggerated vowels. 'This party,' he insisted in mock exasperation, 'is the reason for it secret?'

'It's a highly confidential state secret but I'll tell you because you're with the Home Secretary. Tonight was the last performance of *The Curtained Window* starring Ralph Layton and me. Also, it's my birthday.'

'Many happy returns,' he said warmly, raising his glass. 'Is your age a secret too, or shouldn't a gentleman ask?'

'You know what a gentleman should ask better than me,' she answered tartly. 'In Hollywood they took four years off my age but it seems silly to keep pretending. I am what I am – in other words, I'm fifty.'

'Fifty!' He looked astonished. 'I would never have believed it.'

'People have been saying that all day, and it really bugs me that I feel so flattered.'

'You're the most beautiful fifty-year-old woman I've ever met,' he said sincerely. 'Mind you, I'd say that if you were twenty, thirty, forty.' He smiled into her eyes and she found herself smiling back. As if embarrassed, he dropped his gaze and jumped to his feet. 'I'm going for a refill, how about you?'

'I've had enough, thanks.'

She watched him climb the stairs at the side of the stage, a tall, slender, rather aristocratic figure in expensive, well-cut clothes. Within seconds he was lost in the crowd. Idly she began to speculate on what it was that attracted people to each other; was it looks, temperament or just sheer sex appeal?

Why had he been nagging to be introduced? She hoped he hadn't heard about that wild, furious time when she'd left Nellie in Liverpool, pale and sad-eyed, but fit to go back to her teaching job, and arrived in London, with her own grief still bottled up.

For nearly a year she'd gone from party to party, sleeping with anyone who took her fancy, and occasionally with someone who didn't. By the time she woke mid-morning in the bed of some stranger, her head thumping from a hangover, it was time to prepare for the night ahead. Another party, another stranger, no time for the aching frustration of wondering why, why, why?

Of course she'd come to her senses eventually, bought herself a little house in Pimlico, not wanting to move too far away from Nellie just yet. There was plenty of time to go back to Hollywood.

'Penny for them,' said a voice.

Lisa looked up, startled. Tony was back, looking down at her with a quizzical smile on his mild, good-humoured face. 'They weren't worth that much,' she said.

'That lovely head can't possible have cheap thoughts.'

'You'd be surprised,' she said. 'I was wondering, why did you ask Barbara Heany to introduce us?'

He looked puzzled. 'I just wanted to shake your hand, that's all. It's not often one has the opportunity to meet a famous actress, particularly one as beautiful as you.'

Lisa suddenly tired of compliments and silly conversation. 'What do you do?' she asked in a matter-of-fact voice.

He seemed to sense her change of mood and answered, equally matter-of-factly, 'I'm an MP.'

'Military Police, or Member of Parliament?'

'The latter.' He sounded slightly hurt and she hid a smile. 'What party?'

'Conservative, of course,' he replied with a pained expression, as if the idea he could be anything else was offensive.

Lisa laughed. 'Oh dear, what would my family say if they knew I was talking to you!'

'Are they Labour?'

'Emphatically so . . . well, most of them.' In the 1979 election two years before, Stan had voted Conservative, according to Nellie. 'In a way, I don't blame him,' Nellie had said. 'When his mother died last winter they had to keep her body in the morgue for weeks, as the gravediggers had gone on strike in Liverpool. How would we have felt, Liz, if we couldn't have buried Mam?' Now, every time an O'Brien lost his job in the recession, they blamed Stan.

'How about you?' He was looking at her with real interest.

'I didn't vote. I'm apolitical.'

He raised his fine, rather startlingly black eyebrows. 'Ah, fruitful ground. I'll have to get to work on you.'

'Tony, do you want a lift to the station?' A small plump man had come to the front of the stage and gestured in their direction with his glass. 'You'll miss the midnight train if you don't leave soon.'

'I'll be right with you, Carter.' Tony turned to Lisa and said, 'I have to be in my Yorkshire constituency tomorrow. May I see you again? How about coming up next weekend? I'm having a few people to stay.'

Lisa wrinkled her nose. 'It's not hunting, shooting and fishing?'

'Absolutely not. It'll just be wining and dining and general chat.' He kissed the back of her hand. 'Say you'll come, please.'

'You've talked me into it,' said Lisa.

After he'd gone, she remained in her seat and watched the revellers on stage. She saw Barbara Heany, their producer, catch the arm of the author of *The Curtained Window*, Matthew Jenks, a middle-aged, strikingly handsome man with a fine head of black wavy hair, and felt her lip curl. He was a good playwright, brilliant even, but she felt nothing but contempt for the way he'd gone about achieving his success.

It wasn't long after she'd moved to Pimlico four years ago that Ralph had called to say he'd come across a play, a two-hander that was perfect for them both. 'I met this guy, Matthew, on the train coming back from the Edinburgh Festival,' Ralph said. 'We got talking and – well, he moved in with me – you know there's been no one since Gary died. It turns out he's a playwright. Why don't you come over one night and we'll read it together?'

Lisa had gone, just to humour him, and had to agree *Dead Wood* was excellent. 'But I'm a screen actor, Ralph,' she protested. 'I'm far too nervous to go on the stage.'

'Matthew thinks you're ideal for Sarah Wood,' insisted Ralph. 'When I told him we were friends, he suggested I approach you,' and Matthew, hovering behind in his tight jeans and threadbare sweater, concurred.

'I didn't know when I was writing the play, of course, but as soon as Ralph mentioned your name I knew I'd had someone like you in mind.'

'I'd be petrified,' she said weakly. 'Even if I knew my lines backwards, I'd be worried I'd dry up.'

'Just give it a try,' coaxed Ralph. 'To please me, to please Matthew. We'll go into rehearsal, quietly, without publicity, then if you still feel the same, you can drop out and we'll get someone else.'

So Lisa reluctantly agreed and somehow, despite Ralph's promise, there was a great deal of publicity. *'Hollywood Star to Appear on West End Stage'*, she read in the theatre pages a few weeks later, though Ralph swore he knew nothing about it and she was inclined to believe him.

The rehearsals were murder. She was stiff and self-conscious, and although word-perfect off stage, as she had predicted, once on, nerves took over and she forgot everything. But for the fact everybody knew the play was in production, she would have withdrawn. The producer, Barbara Heany, an untidy ragbag of a woman with a growing reputation, was in despair and Lisa's understudy was visibly licking her lips, hoping to get a few nights' stardom during the preliminary tour of the provinces before another major actress was hired.

But something happened on the first night, Lisa was never sure what. They started off in Norwich and the theatre was packed. Her nerves were completely on edge so she sought Ralph out in his dressing room, hoping for some words of comfort, but found him looking ill, his face as white as chalk.

'Are you all right?' she asked, filled with alarm.

'No, I'm terrified. My stomach's where my mouth should be, but I always feel like this before the show first goes on.'

'Oh God!' she groaned. 'I think I'll kill myself.'

The house-lights dimmed, the curtain went up and Ralph sauntered onto the stage. There was a burst of applause. Lisa stared at him in amazement. He looked calm and perfectly in control.

'You're on, Lisa.' Someone gave her a push and she burst on stage, waving her arms like the half-mad woman she was supposed to be. The applause took her breath away, she hadn't been expecting it. Ralph came towards her and suddenly everything fell into place. She was conscious of the audience hanging onto every word, and felt they were behind her, urging her on. The lines, the movements became effortless and as time passed she sank deeper and deeper into the character she was playing until, by the end, she *was* Sarah Wood, the schoolteacher's wife.

'I never in my wildest dreams thought I'd *enjoy* it,' she said to Ralph later. 'I was really sorry when it ended. I have never felt like that making a movie.'

Stage-acting was like a drug, far more potent than the cinema. During the year-long run of *Dead Wood*, Lisa found herself aching for the evening to come when she would go on stage and lose herself in her part. She knew precisely when the audience would laugh or gasp, and the sound would urge her on to please and captivate them more. After she and Ralph had taken their curtain calls she still felt exhilarated, and some nights it took quite a while to return to being Lisa Angelis.

'Why didn't you persuade me to do this before?' she teased Ralph. 'I feel as if it was what I was born for.'

As soon as *Dead Wood* was established as a hit, Matthew Jenks went back to his wife and children.

'I didn't know he was married,' Lisa said in astonishment.

'Neither did I,' said Ralph bitterly.

'You're not gay at all, are you?'

'No,' said Matthew flatly.

'You just used Ralph. I think you're despicable!' He'd come into her dressing room with a new script. 'I'd like you to read it,' he'd said on entering.

He didn't appear the least bit perturbed by her insult. 'It was a means to an end, that's all.' He shrugged.

'Did you really meet him accidentally?' she asked curiously.

'No. I'd been in Edinburgh trying to make contacts, unsuccessfully, I might add. I was on my way home when I saw Ralph getting out of a taxi by the station so I spent the last of my cash on a first-class ticket and sat opposite him. The fact that he's gay is no secret. I made the right noises and he asked me to come home with him.'

'And later you revealed that by strange coincidence you happened to be a playwright,' she said scornfully.

'You got it in one,' he said unashamedly.

'Didn't you have enough faith in your plays to get them on in the normal way?'

He laughed sarcastically. 'What's the normal way?' he demanded. '*Dead Wood* had been rejected by eighteen theatres; some directors kept it a year and sent it back unread. I've half a dozen other plays, all as good, at home. Shakespeare would have a job getting *Hamlet* on in London now – it's all sewn up. I'm just an ordinary guy who'd come to realise talent is worthless without contacts. When I saw my opportunity, I grabbed it with both hands.'

'I still think you're despicable,' she said coldly.

'You're entitled to your opinion. I'd call it ambitious, myself.' He went over to the door. 'If I recall rightly, you married two directors in Hollywood. I wonder how far you'd have got without them.'

'But I loved them both,' she protested.

'Well, I quite like Ralph,' he said. 'That's why I'm giving him first option on my new play.' He nodded towards the script. 'That's the best thing I've ever done. I hope you won't be influenced by what's happened, you'd be cutting off your nose to spite your face. Ralph's keen and this time I *did* write the part specially for you.'

Matthew had noticed Lisa sitting in the stalls. He gave her a sardonic smile and raised his glass. She ignored him, though she conceded that it was thanks to him the last few years had been so productive and rewarding. She'd never expected to get so much satisfaction out of acting.

Barbara Heany was saying her goodbyes. Lisa went on stage and caught up with her in the wings. 'Let's share a taxi home and you can tell me all about Tony Molyneux,' she suggested.

For a woman who appeared totally incurious about people's lives, Barbara seemed to know everything about everyone important, mainly because she devoured *The Guardian* every day from cover to cover.

'I only know what I read in the paper,' she told Lisa on their way home. 'Did he tell you he was a Baronet? It's *Sir* Anthony Molyneux.'

'A Sir!' Lisa said, impressed.

'The title's been in the family for centuries. Tony inherited it when his father died a few years back and he became MP for Broxley in 1979, but I haven't a clue what he did before. He's divorced, no children, and lives in a run-down stately home, Ferris Hall.' She grinned suddenly. 'He was awfully anxious to meet you. I said it was your fiftieth birthday party, I hope you don't mind.'

'You told him? He acted as if he didn't know,' said Lisa.

'He was probably looking for an excuse to flatter you,' said Barbara. 'Looks as if he was successful, you seem interested enough.'

'Only vaguely,' Lisa said airily.

40

On Saturday morning, she and Tony travelled together on the train to Yorkshire. 'I hope you don't mind – I don't like driving long distances,' he said when he called to make arrangements for the journey.

She assured him she felt the same. 'I hate motorways, the lorries frighten me to death.'

He led her to a first-class compartment. He wore a British warm and cavalry twill trousers. 'Thank you for the flowers,' she said when they were seated. 'They were lovely.'

'I spent ages in the florists trying to decide which flower most suited you. In the end I decided it was a tiger lily but they didn't have any so I had to plump for roses, though they don't do you justice.'

He was a charming and attentive companion, though as the train sped through the diverse countryside, she began to tire of the never-ending compliments and sensed he indulged in flattery to cover his rather surprising lack of confidence. He seemed unsure of himself, slightly ill at ease in her company. Gently, she probed him on his work and he launched into a description of life in the House of Commons which was not only a relief, but fascinating too.

When the train drew into York Station in the early afternoon, he said, 'We get off here. There's a branch line to Broxley, but the trains seem to run when they please. Someone will be here to meet us.'

A somewhat ancient Mercedes was waiting outside the station and the driver, a stooped man in his sixties, approached them. 'Good afternoon, Sir Anthony,' he said courteously.

'Afternoon, Mason.' Tony nodded briefly and ushered Lisa into the back of the car, leaving their cases for Mason to stow in the boot. He made no attempt to introduce her and she thought how different the employer–employee relationship was in England compared to America, where the hired help often became friends, part of the family, like Millie.

'It's lovely here,' she said. They'd left the environs of York some time ago and were driving through narrow lanes lined with grey, moss-covered walls. Beyond, the fields rolled gently by, a patchwork of green and brown and yellow. An occasional stone house could be seen, nestling comfortably at the foot of a hill or perched proudly at its top. The area had a craggy, breathtaking beauty.

They turned into an even narrower road edged with hawthorn thick with red and white spring blossom. The hedge finished abruptly, to be replaced by a high, stout wall and shortly afterwards the car turned through a wide entrance bordered by two granite pillars. The word *Ferris* was worked into one of the open wrought-iron gates, and *Hall* in the other. Ahead of them was a solid-looking three-storey mansion of buff-coloured stone. On one side scaffolding had been erected, though there was no sign of workmen.

'This is it,' Tony said proudly.'Ferris Hall.'

'It's lovely,' she said dutifully. Privately she thought it probably had been once, though now it looked run-down and decrepit. The frames on the tall, arched windows were eaten away with rot and the stonework was pitted and crumbling.

Inside, the house was pretty much the same. The high-ceilinged hall had patches of damp in the corners and she could hear the floorboards creak as they walked. The furniture was old but, unlike that in Tymperleys, had been neglected and was in urgent need of repair.

'Mason will show you to your room,' said Tony. 'Then perhaps you'd like to come down and have a drink.'

When she came downstairs, Tony was in a long, gracious though sparsely-furnished room, talking to a red-cheeked man with a shock of brown curly hair. 'Lisa, my dear.' His eyes lit up with pleasure, as if surprised to find her there. It was these unconscious, boyish actions that attracted her to him. He came over and took her hand, 'This is Christy Costello, my agent.'

'How do you do?' The agent's handshake was firm, almost painful. He was tall, in his early forties and had an open-air, healthy look.

'Is that an Irish accent I hear?' she asked.

'Most definitely – Belfast through and through. Don't tell me you're Irish too. I refuse to believe it, not with those looks.' There was something slightly familiar about the way he looked at her.

'Then I'm afraid I'm going to confound you: both my parents were Irish, though I've never been there.'

'I'll be damned! You've got the most un-Irish eyes I've ever seen.'

The weekend guests turned up later – two couples in their forties, the husbands full of plans to further their joint construction company for which they sought Tony's help, the wives shy and tongue-tied, not speaking even to each other.

Christy Costello joined them for dinner and during the meal the men would have monopolised the conversation with their business talk if Lisa hadn't decided to draw the wives into the discussion. After all, Tony had sat her at the head of the table, so presumably he expected her to act as hostess.

In fact the women turned out to be far more interesting than their husbands. One was a part-time social worker, the other ran her own boutique. With Lisa's gentle encouragement, they began to talk about their jobs, their lives, their children.

'Have you any children, Lisa?' one asked.

'No, I'm afraid I've been too tied up in my career,' she lied.

'And what career is that?'

She smiled. There'd been no sign of recognition when Tony introduced them. 'I'm an actress,' she said.

One of the men burst out with, 'Does that mean you're *the* Lisa Angelis, the film star?'

'Didn't you recognise me?' Lisa laughed.

'Well, I haven't seen you in twenty years or more. Christ, woman, I was madly in love with you once.' He stared at Lisa, eyes wide with admiration. 'You're even better-looking close up than on screen.'

'Bob!' said his wife warningly. 'You'll embarrass her.'

They began to ask the inevitable questions. 'Have you met John Wayne? James Stewart? Did you ever know Marilyn Monroe? What's it like living in Hollywood?' She handled the inquisition easily, fending off some questions, answering others, at the same time signalling to Tony to refill the glasses.

The evening ended on a note of hilarity when Bob went down on one knee and proposed to Lisa. 'I used to dream of doing this,' he said. 'It's the only dream I've ever had that's come true.'

After the two couples had gone to bed Christy said, 'That's the best evening I've had in a long time. You're the perfect hostess, Lisa.' He turned to Tony and said jokingly, 'Snap her up quick if she's free. She's worth her weight in gold to an ambitious politician.'

The two couples left after Sunday lunch, the men looking highly satisfied with themselves. 'I can't promise anything,' she heard Tony say as they shook hands in the hall, 'but rest assured I'll get the motorway idea planted in the mind of the appropriate department head.'

'That's all we ask, Sir Anthony,' one of the men replied.

Afterwards, Tony took her for a walk on the fells surrounding the house. When they reached the top she looked back. Ferris Hall, in its wall-lined enclosure, looked like a doll's house from this distance, and its grey slate roof shone in the bright spring sunshine. The house had a look of permanence about it, an impression of having grown from the rich brown earth as had the massive oak trees surrounding it.

'It's very *Wuthering Heights*,' she said. 'Romantic and wild.'

'I'm pleased you like it so much,' he said almost bashfully. 'I desperately hoped you would.'

That night they went out to dinner in a small public house in Broxley. Lisa wore a plain shirtwaister dress of scarlet cotton topped with a black bolero. She brushed her hair back smoothly, securing it Spanish-style with an ornate red comb.

Tony was waiting at the bottom of the wide staircase and his eyes widened in admiration as she came towards him. 'You look lovely,' he said in an awed voice. He tucked her arm in his and led her outside to where the Mercedes was parked. 'I can't believe my luck, having you here. In fact, I'm scared to close my eyes lest you disappear.'

Lisa laughed. 'I've no intention of disappearing, believe me.'

Tony drove into town. He was a hesitant, nervous driver and she found herself pressing an imaginary accelerator to make the car go faster along the narrow, leafy lanes. They entered Broxley through a sprawling red-brick housing estate where children played on the pavements, though the town centre was old and well-preserved, and there were a lot of stone cottages, which, like Ferris Hall, looked as if they'd been there forever. At the end of the High Street stood a large sooty factory with the name *Spring Engineering* on a board attached to the padlocked iron gates.

'That's a real eyesore,' said Tony as they drove past. 'I'd like to get rid of it.'

'Why?' she asked. 'It's where people earn their living. I don't suppose they care if it's an eyesore.'

He was too busy manoeuvring the Mercedes into the car park of a public house to reply. As they entered the low-beamed building, the landlord came over and shook hands heartily. 'Good to see you, Sir Anthony. It's been a while since you were in town.'

'Pressure of work, Clough. There's a lot to do in Westminister.'

'Fergus seemed to find time for us.' The landlord's friendly expression didn't change, but Lisa sensed criticism in his words. 'Always on hand when you needed him, was Fergus.'

Tony muttered something unintelligible and when they were seated, he said, 'We shouldn't have come here. Clough was a crony of Fergus Lomax. I don't think he likes me.'

'He might do if you called him by his first name or put "Mr" in front of Clough,' Lisa commented. 'It's almost medieval addressing a person by his surname. Do you expect him to touch his forelock?'

Tony looked at her blankly. 'But he's only a publican.'

'Well, you're only an MP.'

He frowned and she could see he was struggling to make sense of her words. 'I think I see what you mean,' he said eventually. 'Come down to their level, in other words.'

'That's not the way I'd put it,' she said crisply. 'Just treat everyone as an equal, that's all.'

He smiled suddenly. 'You're good with people, aren't you? In future, I shall heed your advice.'

'In that case, when we leave, shake Mr Clough's hand, say the meal was delicious and ask if he has any problems you can sort out.' As Tony nodded thoughtfully, she asked, 'Who's Fergus, by the way?'

'Fergus Lomax represented the constituency for over thirty years. When he retired at the last election he took a large personal vote with him, I'm afraid. My majority's less than half his.'

'Then Sir Anthony Molyneux must work hard to get a personal vote for himself,' said Lisa. 'So at the next election your majority increases.'

Before leaving on Monday morning, Lisa sought out Mrs Mason who had prepared the excellent meals over the weekend. She and her husband occupied a small flat over the garage. A small stick of a woman, her forehead was furrowed in what looked like a perpetual frown, and her iron-grey hair was encased in a thick black net. She looked up in surprise when Lisa walked into the old-fashioned kitchen, with its scrubbed wooden worktops, deep white sink and stone tiled floors. Even the fridge and chipped cooker looked as if they were antiques and the room was cold and draughty. Plaster crumbled in all four corners.

'I've just come to thank you for the food. It was lovely! I never realised Yorkshire pudding could be so tasty.' Considering the conditions in here, the woman worked wonders.

'Why, thank you, madam,' Mrs Mason muttered, as if being thanked was not something she was used to.

'Please don't call me madam, I hate it. If we're going to be friends, I'd prefer Lisa – or Miss Angelis, if you can't bring yourself to use my first name.'

'Does that mean you're coming back?' the woman asked curiously.

'So it would seem,' smiled Lisa.

Tony courted her assiduously. Almost every day an exquisite bouquet of flowers arrived at Lisa's Pimlico house, often accompanied by a small gift – perfume, a silk scarf, expensive chocolates. Early one morning he turned up with a Harrods food hamper. 'It's a beautiful morning,' he cried. 'I think breakfast *al fresco* in Hyde Park is in order.' On another occasion a miniature portrait was delivered, oval-shaped in a heavy gold frame. It was of Lisa and she recognised the pose from a photograph outside the theatre where *The Curtained Window* had been staged. '*Even Rembrandt would have found your beauty difficult to transfer onto canvas*' said the accompanying note.

Every few weeks she went to Ferris Hall and began to get fond of the bleak, cold house. She was rehearsing a new play and Tony came so frequently to watch, then take her out to dinner, that she remonstrated with him. 'Surely you should be in the House of Commons? After all, it's what you're paid for.'

He seemed to like her reprimanding him and would smile coyly like a little boy. 'It's boring. I'd sooner be with you.'

He took her to the House on several occasions. She sat in the visitors' gallery and found the proceedings fascinating, particularly the way the elected representatives behaved, like spoilt, fractious children. Margaret Thatcher, the Prime Minister, was in her element at the despatch box, a formidable, commanding figure, though Lisa nursed considerable affection for the leader of the opposition, Michael Foot, a courteous, gentlemanly figure with a gift for heartstopping oratory.

She knew Tony was leading up to a proposal of marriage and sometimes wondered if she should discourage him. It would be cruel to string him along then turn him down, though she found herself unwilling to end the relationship. He made her feel precious and wanted, a very special person. When inevitably he asked her to marry him, she said, 'I'm fond of you, Tony, but I'm not in love with you.'

'But I adore you,' he said passionately. 'I have enough love for both of us. Say yes, please! We get on so well together, everything is right between us.'

'I know it is, but I'd still like to think about it first.'

Marriage was a lottery – she'd realised that a long time ago. Two people could be madly in love and end up hating each other because there was nothing behind the love; no liking, no friendship. Anyway, perhaps it was too much to expect, to fall in love at fifty, though Tony had managed it. Fondness, a need for companionship, were probably a better basis for marriage at their age.

When she was invited to Chester in August for a christening – Dougal's wife had just given birth to twin boys – she thought to herself, 'I always go up north alone. I've never once taken a partner.'

She asked Tony to come with her and he agreed with alacrity. He bought gold watches for the babies and Lisa exclaimed, 'They're only two weeks old!'

He said bashfully, 'I'd no idea what to buy. I suppose they'll grow into them.'

During the short visit, Tony was nervous and on edge.

'They're all sizing me up,' he whispered when they came out of the church. 'Trying to make up their minds if I'm good enough for you.'

'What do you think of him?' she asked Nellie later.

'He seems very nice, rather shy, but incredibly generous. Those watches must have cost a small fortune. Remember what Mam used to say? "Generosity covers a multitude of sins".'

'I remember, but I was never sure if that was a good or a bad thing,' Lisa said dryly.

Nellie squeezed her hand affectionately. 'I think it's good. He's madly in love – the way he looks at you! But if you're wondering whether to marry him, Liz, only your own heart can answer that question. All I'll say is I worry about you all the time, living on your own.'

That evening, she and Tony caught the train back to London.

'Whew!' He sank back in his seat with a heartfelt sigh. 'That was an ordeal. Do you think they liked me?' he added anxiously.

She laughed. Considering his position in life, his lack of confidence and wish to please were quite endearing. 'They loved you,' she said soothingly.

He gave his little boy grin. 'That's something, I suppose. Even if *you* don't love me, your family does! Perhaps I should ask them to marry me.'

Lisa didn't answer. It had been nice having someone of her own at the christening. People were made to go in pairs and she'd had no one for a long time. Even if she never grew to love Tony, it didn't matter. As he said, they got on so well. She looked out of the dark window and could see Tony's reflection, sitting opposite. He was watching her, an eager expression on his gentle face.

'I suppose I'd be an idiot to turn you down,' she said eventually and he leaned across, caught her hands in his and began to shower them with kisses.

They decided on a small registry office wedding. Lisa invited Ralph and Adam, Barbara Heany, Nellie and Stan.

'A Conservative MP! It's a good job you didn't mention that at the christening. Jimmie might have lynched him,' Nellie said after the ceremony. 'As for Mam, she's probably turning in her grave. On the other hand, Chaucer Street would never have heard the last of it, her Lizzie becoming Lady Lisa Molyneux. She was a terrible snob was our mam, in her own quiet way.'

'Lady Lisa! It sounds like a brand of cosmetics. I'll never use the title if I can avoid it, but when I do, it'll be Lady Elizabeth.'

'Married again, eh? This is the third wedding of yours I've been to.' Ralph kissed her. 'Let's hope this one's for keeps.'

They honeymooned in America, at Tymperleys. Lisa had only been back a few times since Luke died. Chloe and her husband Albert had moved into the nursery flat and between them kept the old house in immaculate condition.

When she arrived with Tony, Lisa made a particular point of kissing Chloe and Albert before presenting them both as her good friends. She was pleased when Tony showed no obvious sign of embarrassment at being introduced to servants. She'd yank her new husband up into the late twentieth century by his bootstraps if necessary.

'This furniture must be worth a fortune,' he said as she showed him round, his jaw dropping further with each room they entered. She took him into the studio and felt a sudden twinge of nostalgia, remembering Dent's outrageous behaviour when he'd brought her in here on that memorable weekend. The man beside her was so totally different from Dent – from Busby too, come to that. She had always been drawn to eccentric, exciting men with over-the-top personalities. How could she expect to live the rest of her life with this shy, diffident man who, now she thought about it, had few interests and only limited conversation? Her feeling of nostalgia turned to fear. Had she made a monstrous mistake? She turned to him blindly, close to tears, needing comfort, but Tony was walking around the studio, examining the paintings, and he didn't notice her distress.

'I suppose these could be valuable one day,' he said.

She composed herself. 'I'd never sell Dent's pictures,' she said quietly. 'Though I might take a couple back with me.'

'You know,' he said later, 'you could get quite an income by renting out Tymperleys, or you could sell it. What do you think it would fetch?'

'I've no idea. I've no intention of renting or selling.' She laughed to hide her annoyance. 'I didn't realise you were so interested in money, darling. I feel as if I've married my bank manager.'

He was instantly contrite. 'It's just that I'm so impressed,' he said apologetically. 'Tymperleys is a positive treasure trove.'

'I'm sorry,' Tony muttered. 'Really sorry. This has never happened before. I don't know what's wrong.'

'You're probably nervous,' said Lisa, kissing him softly. Was it her imagination, or did she sense him stiffen at the touch of her lips. 'Shall I help you?' She slid her hand down his body. This time she knew it wasn't her imagination when he jerked abruptly away.

'It'll come right soon,' she said gently. 'Don't worry.' She would have liked to talk about it but he lay there, stiff and unspeaking, so she turned over and tried to sleep. Over the months she'd known him, his only attempt at intimacy had been a kiss on her cheek, but she'd put his reticence down to gentlemanly old-world courtesy rather than lack of desire. There had been enough desire in his eyes and his words to convince her that he was aching to make love. Perhaps that was still the case. Perhaps he hadn't made love to a woman for so long that gentle wooing on her part was needed to restore his confidence.

After a long time he said softly, 'Lisa?' She could tell from the tone of his voice that he wasn't trying to attract her attention, but checking if she was asleep. She didn't answer. Seconds later, she felt the covers move and he slid furtively out of bed and left the room.

After he'd gone, she turned on her back and lay staring at the ceiling. 'Shit!' she said in a loud voice. 'Why do I always have such lousy luck with men?'

41

'You mean you've *never* made love?' said Nellie in an astonished voice. 'In eighteen months of marriage?'

'Never!' said Lisa dramatically.

'Gosh, Liz, that's terrible! Why don't you get divorced?'

Lisa was stretched out on the floor with her back against a chair. She looked up at her sister with amusement. 'That's a fine question – coming from a Catholic!'

Nellie blushed and said defensively, 'You've already been divorced twice. I didn't think another one would matter.'

'That's probably why I've never considered it,' said Lisa. 'I didn't want to admit failure again. Anyway, it hasn't failed really – in every other way we get on perfectly. Tony still acts like a devoted lover and sends me heaps of flowers and arranges little treats. He makes me feel very wanted and special.'

It was almost midnight, a Sunday. Nellie was going to a head-teachers' conference in the morning and staying with Lisa overnight. They'd been out to dinner earlier and when they got back to the house in Pimlico Lisa opened a bottle of wine, then another, and by now both sisters were slightly tipsy and in the mood for confidences. Nellie had kicked off her shoes, undone her skirt and half-sat, half-lay on the settee.

The women were silent for a while, deep in their own thoughts. Lisa picked up the wine and refilled the glasses.

'Are you happy, though?' Nellie asked suddenly.

Lisa didn't answer straight away. 'Yes,' she said eventually. 'I'm really enjoying life at the moment. The fact that Tony and I haven't got – what would you call it? – a *proper* relationship, means I don't feel obliged to stay by his side, so I go to America whenever I please. As you know, I made a movie there last year. During the run of my plays I live here, though Tony thinks I should sell this house and move into his Westminster flat when I'm in London. Most weekends I'm up in Yorkshire being an MP's wife and find myself getting more and more interested in politics. In fact, I know more about it than Tony does now. I've never been so busy. There's only ten or fifteen minutes each day I feel lonely.'

'When's that?'

'When I get into bed at night,' said Lisa.

'Oh, Liz!' Nellie reached out and touched Lisa's shoulder briefly. 'Did Tony manage it with his first wife, I wonder?'

'I've no idea.' Lisa shrugged. 'All I know is he didn't have any children. He won't talk about his ex-wife, though I suppose that's understandable.'

Nellie was looking at her with a worried expression. Lisa said quickly, 'I wish I hadn't told you. It's the wine, it always loosens my tongue. Honestly, Nell, I'm very happy, please don't worry about me.' She managed a brilliant smile to reassure her sister all was well, adding, 'Let's change the subject. Earlier on, you said Jimmie had been made redundant again. I wish they'd let me help out financially.' All her older brothers had refused her offer of money to help them through the recession.

'They look upon it as charity, I'm afraid, though I don't know if their wives would agree,' Nellie ran her fingers through her almost white hair leaving it standing up around her head like a wiry halo. 'I know *I'd* take it, but I bet Stan wouldn't let me.'

Lisa shook her head impatiently. 'I think families should stick together in emergencies. I've got millions in the bank doing nothing.'

'I'll have a word with the wives,' Nellie promised. 'See if they can bang a few heads together.' She reached down for her glass and her wedding ring fell off. 'One of these days I'll lose this.'

'You should get it altered, made smaller,' said Lisa.

'Stan won't let me. He says it's me who's got to get bigger.'

Lisa glanced at her sister. Since Luke died, Nellie had shrunk to a shadow of her former self. Noting the peaked, sad face, Lisa said softly, 'How are you, Nell? Have you gotten over . . .'

Nellie interrupted, her voice bleak: 'I'll *never* get over Luke dying, Liz. Never. Even on my deathbed, I'll be wishing he was there to see me off. I doubt if a day, an hour, goes by without me thinking about him. He would have been twenty now and at university – he wanted to study Economics. In my mind he's still alive and leading the life he would have led. I try to imagine what he would look like, how tall would he have grown, what size shoes would he take, would he have let his hair grow long and become a typical, scruffy student? When I see mothers with their grown-up sons, I feel so angry and so jealous, I want to scream, "It's not fair, it's not fair!" '

Nellie's voice became harsh but she didn't cry. Perhaps there were no tears left, thought Lisa.

'I'm sorry, Nell, I shouldn't have asked.'

Nellie shook her head vigorously. 'I'm glad you did. I feel better for talking about it. Stan and I never do and nobody ever mentions Luke in case they upset me, though I'd far prefer they did. I begin to wonder if Luke existed when his name is never spoken.'

She got off the sofa with a sigh. 'I'd better get to bed, I need to be up early in the morning.' Catching sight of her reflection in the mirror, she grimaced. 'I look like something the cat's dragged in, as Mam used to say.' She glanced down at Lisa curiously. 'I wonder why we're all so different?'

'What do you mean?'

'The O'Briens. The boys are so alike, there's no getting away from the fact they're brothers, but us girls! Joan's pale-skinned and red-haired, and we're both dark.' She frowned. 'Dad had blue eyes, didn't he?'

'I think so.'

'And Mam did too. I'm sure I read once that blue-eyed people couldn't have brown-eyed children, something to do with genes.' She laughed, 'D'you think Mam had a bit on the side?'

Lisa remembered the strange thing Mam said just before she died. She'd scarcely thought about it again, putting it down to the ramblings of a sick old woman. Despite what Nellie had just said, that was what she preferred to go on thinking.

'What – Mam?' she scoffed. ' "Pigs might fly", as she was also fond of saying!'

After Nellie had gone to bed, Lisa remained sitting on the floor and poured the last of the wine into her glass, 'Waste not, want not,' she said to the empty room. She thought about her conversation with Nellie. 'I *am* happy,' she told herself. 'I lead a deeply fulfilling life and Tony is a charming companion, attentive and caring. In his own way, he thinks the world of me,' though she wondered sadly why he'd never attempted to come into her bed again after that first night. Perhaps he was too ashamed, worried he'd fail again. By now she was used to separate rooms, though it still seemed strange at Ferris Hall to say goodnight to your husband and go through different doors to bed. How could he adore her, as he claimed, yet never want to touch her? Once or twice she'd tried to talk about it, but he changed the subject impatiently, just as he did when she asked about his first wife.

Upstairs the bed creaked as Nellie turned over, the sound as clear as if it had been made in the same room. The small house was part of a row of terraced properties built for artisans at the end of the last century and the partitions were paper-thin.

Lisa glanced around the room affectionately. She'd fallen in love with the place as soon as she stepped off the busy Pimlico pavement into the narrow hall and felt a strange sense of familiarity, as if she'd been there before. The estate agent had been surprised when she offered to buy. 'I thought you'd prefer something grander,' he said, though the price was grand enough to make her jaw drop in surprise.

The previous owners had modernised it tastefully. The downstairs rooms had been knocked into one, a brick arch the only reminder that a wall had ever been there. What had been a wash-house was now a bathroom, covered to the ceiling with magnolia tiles flecked with gold, and by dint of clever planning, the small kitchen had been fitted with every conceivable labour-saving device. Sometimes Lisa wondered what the original tenants would have thought if they could see the luxurious fittings in what had been their working-class home – the lantern-style wall-lights, the plush carpets, the candy-striped covered chairs. She'd put one of Dent's paintings up, a brilliant oil of Tymperleys, though no one ever guessed it was supposed to be a house.

She turned off the lights; the room remained semi-lit, illuminated through the rear window by the night-long floodlit patio – in other words, the old backyard. Suddenly, she realised why the house had seemed so familiar when she first entered it. Its basic geography was identical to Chaucer Street! She walked around the room. This part would have been the parlour with its flowered lino and Mam's bed when she slept downstairs, and over there the big black grate which had Tom's chair at an angle in front.

Perhaps she'd drunk too much wine, because she strongly felt that if she closed her eyes and opened them again, she'd be back in Chaucer Street and everything that had happened since she left would dissolve into nothing and she'd be fifteen again, her whole life yet to live.

No, she'd never get rid of this house, no matter how much Tony persisted. The flat in Westminster was usually full of his cronies playing cards. She'd never be able to learn her lines and there wasn't room to put people up. Why, she thought, did he keep on about selling? Not only here, but Tymperleys, too – even her share in O'Brien Productions.

Because he only married you for your money, that's why.

There, she'd acknowledged it at last! She'd been unwilling to admit it, even to herself, for months.

She sank into a chair, longing for a cigarette. She'd given up when Mam died from lung cancer twelve years ago, but there were still times she ached for one. At the start he'd just dropped gentle hints; the roof of Ferris Hall needed overhauling, slates were broken and rain poured into the attics. She offered to pay, estimates were called for and she'd written a cheque for over five thousand pounds, yet rain still seeped through the cracked slates and Tony was vague as to when the workmen would arrive.

The same thing had happened with the central heating. 'What a boon it would be,' he kept saying and his grey eyes lit up in delight when she joked, 'I'll buy central heating for your Christmas present!' But although she'd given him a cheque, wrapped in gift paper on the tree, the house remained cold and unheated. 'I'm still not sure which system is the best,' he'd said last time she mentioned it.

When it came to re-wiring – he claimed the existing installation was dangerous – she'd arranged for electricians to do the work herself. Although he accepted this in his genial, good-natured way, she had a feeling that deep down he was annoyed. She tried not to think he was getting money out of her, his wife, under false pretences.

A few months ago he had approached her with, 'Darling, would you mind terribly settling a few bills?' He was so charming about it, looking at her uncertainly, unsure of himself, a boyish smile on his face.

'Of course,' she said unhesitatingly, taking the bunch of invoices. After all, she lived in Ferris Hall and it was only right she should share in the running costs. The bills were for electricity, car tax, half a year's rates and other household expenses. Although she paid them willingly she felt slightly resentful when, the following month, she found another pile on her dressing table, alongside a beautiful bouquet of red roses. 'He might at least ask,' she thought to herself. It was almost as if the flowers were a bribe.

From what she'd gleaned from Mrs Mason, Sir Cameron Molyneux, Tony's father, had left a tidy sum together with a healthy portfolio of Blue Chip stocks and shares. What had Tony done with all this money, so that only five years later he had to ask his wife to pay basic expenses?

Nellie's bed creaked again and Lisa hoped she wasn't finding it difficult to sleep after all the wine. Suddenly, she felt an overwhelming desire to go upstairs and say, 'Nell, I was lying. I'm not happy at all, at least not with certain aspects of my life, in other words, my marriage.'

She didn't though. Tomorrow, in the daylight, everything would be all right again.

The sound of the telephone woke her. She picked up the extension beside the bed and gave the number, her voice husky with sleep.

'Lisa, did you watch the television last night?' It was Ralph and he sounded agitated.

'No, Nellie's here and we—'

'Dear God, Lisa, this is an awful thing . . .' He gave a hoarse sob.

She sat up quickly, wide awake. 'Darling, what's happened?'

'I saw a programme on TV last night about this new illness, AIDS. Have you heard about it?'

'Yes, I read an article in the paper.' Jesus, had Ralph got it?

'It must be what Gary died of, the symptoms are identical.'

'I wondered about that too,' she said, also wondering why Ralph should be so upset after all this time.

'Don't you see, Lisa?' he said despairingly. *'It was me that gave it to him!'*

'Oh Ralph, you can't possibly know that!'

'I do. They referred to it as the gay plague. I was Gary's only lover – I'm the only person he could have caught it off. I killed him, Lisa. If it wasn't for me, he'd be alive now. What am I going to do?' he wailed.

Lisa drew a deep breath and said crisply, 'There's nothing in this world you can do to help Gary. You know in your heart you wouldn't have hurt him deliberately.'

He groaned. 'But if I hadn't been unfaithful!'

'He didn't mind, he told me.'

'Did he really? What did he say?'

'I can't remember, it was a long time ago. Ralph, dear, it's all over now, in the past, but I'll tell you what you *can* do.'

'What?' he demanded eagerly.

'Help people who've got it now. I've still got the money Gary left me. I'm going to send a huge donation towards AIDS research. I think he would have liked that, don't you?'

She managed to calm him and he rang off sounding almost his normal self. Lisa sat staring at the telephone, thinking that if that article was right, Ralph must have AIDS in his blood – what was the condition called? HIV positive – which meant that one day he would die like Gary! She shuddered. Perhaps it was her age, but sometimes she felt that as each day passed, the world became a more frightening place in which to live.

Christy Costello said, 'Tony's very lucky. If he hangs onto his seat next time, it'll be entirely thanks to you.'

'I enjoy helping people,' Lisa said simply.

They were in Tony's 'surgery', a converted shop in the centre of Broxley which was open every Saturday morning for his constituents to bring problems which he might, or might not, be able to solve. Tony hadn't turned up yet. He frequently didn't, always seeming to find something more interesting to do in London. Usually Christy sat in on his behalf and when Lisa was free she took her husband's place.

That morning there'd been a string of people with complaints of one sort or another, some trite, some heartrending, like the old lady being browbeaten out of her lifelong rented cottage by a developer who wanted to modernise and re-sell. Lisa had a list of letters to write and telephone calls to make, though Christy would attend to these.

By one o'clock the surgery was empty and she felt satisfied that she'd done a good job of work.

'He's a lazy sod, our Tony,' Christy said with a grin. 'Wants his arse kicking, if you'll pardon my language.'

'I've heard worse than that in my time,' she replied.

'Fancy a drink?' he said. 'The Red Lion's just across the road.'

Lisa did fancy a drink, but wasn't sure if she should take one with Christy. She found her feelings for him confusing. Sometimes she liked his bluff, hearty manner, but there was a streak of hardness in him that warned her not to get on his wrong side. Occasionally she found him looking at her, a hungry expression on his broad red face, though what disturbed her most was the answering flicker in her own body which she always tried to shrug away. Still, a drink wouldn't hurt.

'Okay, I'll have a beer.'

'Lady Elizabeth Molyneux can't be seen quaffing a pint of best bitter!' He pretended shock. 'It's got to be sherry, dry at that.'

'If I can't have beer, I'm not coming,' she said stubbornly. 'I'm not changing my drinking habits just because I've got a title.'

He brought the beer in a half-pint glass. 'Looks better this way,' he hissed.

After he sat down Lisa said, 'Christy, you know these businessmen who ask Tony for help to get contracts for roads and stuff, is he allowed to do that?'

Christy's eyes grew blank and he stared down into his drink. 'What do you mean?' he asked.

'I think he's using his influence as an MP to fatten people's wallets and it doesn't seem right.'

He said vaguely, 'It's nothing to worry about,' and changed the subject, which she perversely took to mean there was.

When she got back to Ferris Hall she was surprised to hear raised voices coming from the kitchen. Tony and Mrs Mason were having a row. Lisa crept along the passage, curious to know what it was about.

'You can't expect me and Mason to work for nothing and we haven't been paid in weeks,' Mrs Mason shouted angrily.

'You know it'll be forthcoming eventually,' snarled Tony. 'And don't forget you live here rent-free.' Lisa felt her mouth drop open in surprise. She'd never heard him use that tone of voice before; in fact, she hadn't thought him capable of sounding so fierce. Usually he was so gentle and courteous.

'Eventually's no good, sir,' Mrs Mason said stubbornly. 'We need money to spend, like other people. As for rent-free, the accommodation's part of the job. Another thing – the butcher won't give any more credit till his bill's paid and the off-licence refuses to give credit at all – to anyone, not just you. Now you've used up all Sir Cameron's cellar, you need to start buying wine.'

'If you're going to make trouble,' Tony said coldly, 'I might consider looking round for new staff.'

Mrs Mason laughed sarcastically. 'Not when you find out what you'd have to pay them, you won't.'

'I'll have to see what I can do,' Tony said abruptly.

'You'll make it soon, won't you, sir?' Mrs Mason spoke with a mixture of contempt and pleading.

Lisa hurried back along the hall and when Tony emerged she leaned back against the door as if she had just come in.

'Darling!' His face broke into a warm smile of welcome. 'I didn't realise you'd arrived.' He came over, took her hands and rubbed his cheek against hers. Could this be the same man who'd just threatened Mrs Mason? Lisa began to doubt her hearing. He put his arm around her shoulders, led her into the drawing room and seemed so genuinely pleased to see her that all her misgivings about him faded. No one could be such a good actor as this.

'Sit down, my dear,' he said solicitously. 'I'll fetch you a drink. Where have you been? Mason said you arrived early this morning.'

'Where *you* should have been,' Lisa answered reprovingly. 'Taking care of your surgery.'

'You should let Christy do that, it's what he's paid for.'

'No, Tony, it's what *you're* paid for. Christy's only paid to be your agent.'

'I doubt if people notice who's sitting behind the desk whilst they pour out their silly worries,' he said disparagingly as he brought her a whisky. 'Anyway, last night I went out with some chaps and didn't notice the time. When I did, I'd missed the midnight train.'

She shook her head, smiling. 'Honestly, Tony, you're incorrigible.'

Later on she went to see Mrs Mason and asked how much Tony owed. When the woman told her, Lisa was shocked to discover how little it was, virtually slave wages.

'I'll pay you from now on,' she promised. 'And it's about time you had a raise. I reckon a fair rate would be more than double that.'

That night, when she went to change for dinner, she found a single orchid in a slender cut-glass vase on her dressing table beside a clutch of bills. They included final demands for the telephone and electricity and a long overdue invoice from a local garage for repairs to the Mercedes. The butcher's bill she'd heard all about, so she'd better settle that before she left Broxley if they wanted to eat next week. She felt indignant when she saw one from a Savile Row tailor for over a thousand pounds. Tony could smile and charm her all he liked, but she wasn't going to buy his clothes. Picking up her chequebook and the bills she marched along the corridor to his room, pausing outside, wondering whether to knock or just walk in. After all, he was her husband. In the end she knocked and he shouted, 'Enter.'

He'd changed into a dinner jacket and was sitting on the bed tying his shoelaces.

'I'm not prepared to pay this,' she said bluntly, handing him the tailor's invoice.

He made a horrified face. 'Darling, did I slip that in with the others? I'm so sorry.'

Despite his show of sincerity, she had an uneasy feeling that he was lying, that he'd put the bill there deliberately, hoping she'd settle it without question. 'I'll write cheques for the others now, else the phone and electricity might be cut off – you should have given me those before – and the garage are probably waiting for their money. It's six weeks since they fixed the car.'

'I could do with a new car,' he said hopefully.

'You can always borrow mine,' she said absently. She'd bought a Cavalier to use in Yorkshire. She sat on the bed beside him and opened her cheque-book. Suddenly she heard him gasp. What's the matter?' she asked.

'The top stub!' His voice was hoarse. 'It's for half a million pounds!'

'That's right, it was for charity.'

He was trying to read her scribbled record. 'The Challenger Trust, is that it?'

'Yes, it's an AIDS charity. A close friend died a few years ago; this is just a gesture in his memory.'

'A gesture!' His face was working furiously and his breath was raw. 'You mean you can just sit down and write a cheque for half a million?'

There was something almost frightening about his stupefaction. His face was like that of a starving man being taunted with food he couldn't reach. She cursed herself for letting him see the chequebook. 'It was his money,' she said eventually. 'He left it to me.'

'And you gave it all away? When I—' He broke off.

'I felt obliged to,' she said. She went over to the door, anxious to get away. In fact, half a million pounds was only a fraction of Gary's money but she wasn't going to let Tony know that. She'd been waiting for a just cause and now she'd found it. If necessary, the whole lot would go towards AIDS research. There was no way she'd spend the revenue from *Hearts and Flowers* and the other movies Gary made on her husband's tailor's bills.

At dinner, Tony was back to his normal self, as gracious and affectionate as ever, though he seemed to look at her with new respect and Lisa thought ruefully, 'It's only because I'm even richer than he'd first imagined.' Her misgivings returned in force. It was a really miserable situation. After all, at the wedding ceremony they'd promised each other all their worldly goods. If, at the beginning of their marriage, he'd told her he needed money, she would have given it to him. 'What's mine's yours,' she might have said, and even suggested a joint bank account. But Tony seemed incapable of being straightforward and she resented the way he dropped hints, wheedling money out of her so insidiously and telling lies. Anyway, what did he need all this cash for? Their lifestyle was modest and an MP's salary was not exactly a pittance, so what on earth did he spend it all on?

A general election was called in the spring of 1983. Suddenly Tony was alerted to the fact that he might lose his seat. The local newspaper published his poor voting record and his abysmal attendance in the House of Commons – both of which came as a shock to his unsuspecting wife – together with an article claiming he lacked commitment to ordinary voters.

'*Sir Anthony seems far more concerned with management than with workers,*' the reporter wrote. '*He fails to realise that he was elected to represent the entire constituency, not just the élite few. Broxley's large and expanding council estate has been gradually filling up with Labour voters over the last few years and this could well tip the balance against him when Polling Day comes.*'

Lisa had a trip to Hollywood planned but cancelled it so she could remain at Tony's side as he frantically began to canvass support for re-election. Despite the fact that he had neglected them, the people he met on the doorstep were clearly susceptible to his eager, boyish charm.

'This is what you should have been doing all along,' Christy Costello said irritably. 'Not waiting until three weeks before an election.'

Lisa went into the Party office and threw herself into a chair. Kicking off her shoes, she exclaimed, 'Phew, I'm beat.' That morning she had attended a press conference with Tony, visited a hospital and canvassed several streets.

She looked over at Christy, who was on the telephone. She expected a smile of recognition, but he ignored her. She could hear a faint voice on the other end of the line which seemed to be arguing fiercely. When the voice stopped, Christy said, 'I've already told you, freedom of the press can go fuck itself. Sir Anthony's taken out an injunction, so you repeat a word and you're breaking the law and I'll see your rag closed down if it's the last thing I do.' His face was even redder than usual and he practically spat his words into the receiver.

She listened with alarm. He was glaring at a magazine open on the desk in front of him. Lisa reached for it and he suddenly became aware of her presence. His hand slammed down, just missing the paper as she pulled it away. It was the satirical magazine *Private Eye*, and a section had been marked with a red felt pen. She began to read, conscious that Christy had transferred his glare in her direction.

'*Sir Anthony "Cardsharp" Molyneux, laid-back Tory MP for Broxley in South Yorkshire, has managed to reduce this once-solid Conservative seat to a marginal. Cardsharp, who took over from the well-loved and highly-respected Fergus Lomax at the last election, finds the atmosphere in Grundy's Casino more to his liking than the House of Commons, and only rarely graces the latter with his presence. Those with a suspicious turn of mind might wonder if Cardsharp's spectacular losses at Grundy's, where the minimum bet is four figures, together with the even more spectacular collapse of BrixCo, the offshore investment company in which he had a major share (currently being investigated by the Fraud Squad) is in any way connected with the sudden flurry of planned new roads and buildings in Broxley, where the old library, a fine example of late Victorian architecture, will be demolished to make way for a new modern eyesore, together with the cottage hospital. Locals claim themselves satisfied with the old buildings, and say that the motorway which will cut through the beautiful dales is unwanted and unnecessary. Is it just coincidence that the contractors for the new building works are regular guests at Cardsharp's ancestral home, Ferris Hall?'*

Christy slammed the telephone down. 'That was the editor of the *Broxley Gazette*. I frightened the shit out of him. He won't publish.'

'Is this true?' she asked, indicating the article.

He seemed resigned to the fact that she'd read it. 'Well, there's no smoke without fire, as they say.'

'So it is then.' She laid the paper on her knee with a sigh. 'I suppose that's where the money for the roof and the central heating went.' She felt numb, though not surprised. In her heart of hearts she'd suspected something was going on. If the magazine was right, Tony was a fanatical and committed gambler. That's where his salary went, his father's money and the thousands he'd tricked out of her.

'Has he really taken out an injunction?'

'He's thinking about it, just to keep the local press off our backs till after the election. Once it's over, the fire will go out in the editor's belly and he'll return to heel. Normally, no one takes much notice of *Private Eye*. You're never sure whether what they print is the God's honest truth or a load of cobblers.' He sighed. 'We never had a whiff of scandal with Fergus, he was as straight as a die.'

'Were you his agent, too?'

'Yes.' His rather hard features softened. 'Elections were fun in those days; even his opponents loved Fergus. Everyone called him by his first name, they still do. It was more like a three-week carnival than a campaign. But with Tony!' He gave a disgusted shrug. 'All these photo opportunities. I mean, Tony visiting schools, Tony walking around hospital wards, shaking people's hands. Makes you want to puke when he only does it every four years. Fergus did it all the time.'

'Why do you stay?' she asked.

He looked at her quizzically. 'I could ask you the same question. As for me, I think I'll review my position when the election's over.'

'After reading this,' said Lisa, 'I might do the same thing myself.'

The atmosphere at the count in Broxley Town Hall was tense with excitement. Lisa walked along the long trestle tables and watched the votes pile up in what looked like equal quantities for the three candidates, for Tony, Liberal and Labour. Christy, who was standing behind her, muttered, 'Broxley has deserted us, but the vote from the villages still looks solidly in our favour. He might just scrape home.'

Despite the qualms she felt over her husband, Lisa hoped the three weeks of hard campaigning she'd done on his behalf wouldn't be in vain. As the night wore on and the thousands of votes were being counted, Tony began to bite his fingernails nervously. 'I'm getting worried,' he said.

'It's a bit late for that,' Lisa said caustically and he looked at her, a hurt expression on his face. She hadn't discussed the *Private Eye* article with him and didn't know if Christy had told him she'd read it.

Suddenly, as if by magic, the tables were empty and there were no voting slips left to count. Instead, they were stacked in the centre of the room, in bundles of one hundred before each candidates' name, and a Town Hall official was slipping through them counting the bundles. Christy and the other agents were hovering anxiously around. From where she stood, Lisa felt sure the row in front of Tony's name stretched slightly further than the other two. There was a whoop of joy followed by loud cheers and suddenly Tony was back at her side. 'We've won,' he cried.

His majority had gone down yet again to less than a thousand votes. Labour and Liberal had virtually tied for second place.

Lisa went on stage with Tony for the official declaration, along with the other candidates and their wives. After it was over, he was swept away by his supporters for a celebration party. 'Come on, Lisa,' she heard him shout before he was almost carried out of the door.

'Won't it be a bit subdued?' she said to Christy as she followed him out. 'Under the circumstances?'

'Winning is all that counts, at least tonight,' he replied. 'If it had been by just one vote they'd be equally happy.'

When they got outside she went over to her car. 'Where are you going?' he said in surprise. 'The party's only across the road.'

'I'm not in the mood to celebrate. I'm going home.'

Back in Ferris Hall she telephoned Heathrow and booked a flight to California for the next day. O'Brien Productions had been making a lot of dud movies over the past few years and she urgently wanted to rap a few knuckles. She'd cancelled the visit arranged for the previous month in order to campaign for Tony. It was early evening in California, so somebody would still be in the office. She got through and arranged a meeting of senior staff for the following Monday.

After she'd removed the jacket of the blue suit she'd bought to campaign in, she poured herself a whisky and turned on the television. According to the election results already received, it looked as though Mrs Thatcher was heading for a landslide. After a while she turned the set off with a sigh. She felt a sense of anti-climax. The last few weeks had been hectic, emotional even. People got so passionate over politics. It was the same when you finished a movie, or a play ended its run. Life seemed to stop and you felt convinced nothing would ever be exciting again. She knew what would lessen this feeling of emptiness, but there was no chance of that with Tony! Not that she would have welcomed it now, it was too late. Maybe she should have gone to the party to pass the time.

Feeling irritated with herself, she went over to the window. There was no moon and the dales were muffled in blackness. In the far distance, the street lights of Broxley glowed orange and the town looked as if it was on fire.

Headlights swept up the drive and her heart sank. She didn't feel like talking to Tony just now. The front door closed quietly, footsteps sounded in the hall and she wished she'd had the forethought to rush up to bed. A man's reflection appeared behind her as she remained staring out of the dark window and she started in alarm. It wasn't Tony, but Christy. There was a soft thudding feeling in her stomach as he came towards her, his large frame swallowing up her own reflection, and she felt his hands on her waist, warm through the thin material of her blouse. A voice told her to move away, to stop him, but the words remained locked in her throat and by now she had hesitated too long. His hands moved up and began to caress her breasts and his lips were on the nape of her neck and the hunger she had suppressed for so long was aching to be satisfied. She gave a groan of supplication as she turned towards him and he picked her up in his broad strong arms and carried her upstairs.

42

Could she bring herself to sell Tymperleys, a house with so many rich memories, where she'd lived with Dent and Sabina, where Gary and Vita had died, where once she'd been so happy?

The meeting yesterday had been heated and passions flared. 'The company should go public. We need a massive injection of cash before we can make the sort of movies you're talking about,' she'd been told. 'Nowadays, any movie worth its salt costs thirty, forty million dollars. Our yearly budget is less than half that.'

'But just because our movies are cheap, they don't have to be crap,' she raged. 'And crap is all you've been making these last few years.'

She scarcely knew the people she was addressing, accountants all of them, young men with anonymous faces who cared more about money than quality and knew nothing about making movies. They made her feel old, as if her values were out of date, no longer relevant in today's climate, where making a quick buck was more important than making a good movie. It was her own fault. She'd neglected the company shamefully for years. It had moved on without her and she couldn't expect these people to reverse direction just because she'd suddenly noticed they were on the wrong course – or at least a course of which she disapproved.

Lisa said threateningly, 'Perhaps I should sell my two-thirds share,' and was saddened by the alacrity with which they fell on her suggestion. Ralph had sold out several years ago.

They didn't give her a chance to change her mind, not that she wanted to. Contracts were produced so swiftly she realised they must have had them ready, and she signed, to the tune of five million dollars, although she knew she could have got double if she'd bothered to argue. But there was one thing on which she did insist – that they change the company name.

'O'Brien is *my* name,' she said forcibly. 'Quite frankly, I don't want it associated with the rubbish you're turning out.' She thought this might make them feel ashamed, but it didn't.

'That's an idea we've been toying with ourselves,' one of them said smugly.

Tymperleys was so quiet, so peaceful, so welcoming. In the early evening sunlight the house had a warm, tranquil air. Chloe had been expecting her and there were flowers everywhere and the smell of lavender polish, the sort Millie used to use. Lisa sat on the patio and as dusk fell, she switched the garden lights on and put Wagner on the loud-speaker system. If she closed her eyes, it might be possible to imagine things as they used to be, before everything changed. She closed them, but snapped them open almost immediately. This was not the time for reminiscing, for raking over things past. She was too fond of doing that. This was time to think about the future.

No, of course she couldn't sell Tymperleys! It would be selling memories. After all, Dent's ghost was here and by now Vita and Gary's spirits would be hovering in the rafters. She smiled to herself. No they wouldn't; if Vita and Gary's spirits were anywhere they'd be down in the little cinema and in the middle of the night, when Chloe and Albert were asleep, the two of them would be sitting in front of the flickering screen watching movies. She thought about those movies; some were works of art, others great majestic films that left you choked with emotion and a few were just ordinary, competent works. All had been made without much money, though with much love and with the blood, sweat and tears of everyone involved.

As if she could draw a line under that! There was no way this would be the end of her Hollywood career. One day, she'd start another company with Gary's money and her own. That's what he would have liked most for her to do – make the sort of movies of which he would have been proud.

The old house creaked – perhaps it was giving a sigh of relief, knowing it wasn't going to be sold and that one day she would be coming back.

She'd only been back in Pimlico half an hour when the doorbell rang. As she went to answer it Lisa prayed that it wasn't Tony, for she hadn't yet worked out what she wanted to say to him. To her relief, it was her neighbour, Florence Dale, an elderly widow who'd lived next door for over fifty years. In her hands she held a square cardboard box filled with holes.

Lisa invited her in. Every time she entered the house the old lady marvelled at the alterations. 'It's difficult to believe this house was once the same as mine,' she said for the umpteenth time. 'I just came to tell you half a dozen bunches of flowers arrived while you were away. I've put them in water so they're still quite fresh.'

'Please keep them,' said Lisa. 'If they're not in the way.'

'Are you sure? They brighten up the parlour no end. This came for you too.' She opened the box and Lisa gasped. A tiny blue-grey Persian kitten stared up at her with round frightened blue eyes.

'Isn't she sweet!' she cried.

'He – it's a boy. I've christened him Omar, though you can change it. We've had some interesting conversations these last few days. He's a good listener.' The old lady smiled. 'I'll be sad to see him go.'

'Would you mind keeping him too? He's adorable, but I'm away so much he'd be cruelly neglected.' She couldn't resist picking the kitten up and putting him on her shoulder. His little heart was pounding, but as she stroked his fluffy back he started to purr and she felt his soft paw against her neck as he began to play with her earrings.

'You're a handsome young man, Omar, and I'd love you to be mine, but Florence has more time for you.' Reluctantly she handed the kitten back.

'There's a card inside the box. Omar did a little job on it but I washed it off.' Florence produced a stained piece of cardboard as Lisa giggled. '*To my wonderful, dedicated wife in gratitude for all your hard work during the election,*' Tony had written.

After Florence had gone, taking Omar with her, Lisa rather regretted giving the kitten away so hastily. Perhaps she could have arranged joint ownership and looked after him whilst she was home. Right now she too needed a good listener. She had to rehearse what to say to Tony when she told him she wanted a divorce.

It hadn't been a hard decision. In fact, she thought ironically, it showed how empty and shallow the marriage was that she could so easily rid herself of a husband, yet cling to a house. This weekend she'd go to Ferris Hall and have things out with him. In a few weeks, rehearsals would begin for a new play and it would be nice to make a fresh start, unencumbered by a husband whose behaviour worried her deeply. One day the revelations in *Private Eye* might reach a wider readership and she didn't want her name mixed up with his dubious activities.

Lisa travelled to Ferris Hall on the Saturday. Tony must have seen her drive up in the Cavalier which she'd left at the station, for he came running out to meet her. 'Darling, where on earth have you been?' he cried. 'I've been trying to contact you for the past fortnight.'

'I've been in the States,' she said shortly.

'You didn't come to our post-election party. I missed you terribly – if it hadn't been for you I mightn't have won.' He kissed her cheek and as they walked into the house he threw his arm around her shoulders, squeezing her tenderly. As ever, his welcome was so warm and he seemed so pleased to see her that she began to feel guilty for doubting him.

'I've a few friends here,' he said. 'They're staying the night.'

She groaned inwardly. That ruled out the heart-to-heart talk she'd planned for tonight and by tomorrow, if Tony kept this charm offensive up, she might even have changed her mind about divorce!

The friends were three middle-aged businessmen, new members of the moneyed classes, still with their bluff Yorkshire accents, oozing that noisy bright-eyed confidence that often seems to come with quickly acquired wealth. There was a certain sameness about them and even after Tony introduced them, she found it difficult to tell them apart.

Christy was there, but Lisa didn't meet his eyes. It was embarrassing to recall the almost animal-like vigour of her responses when they'd made love.

After dinner, one man, perhaps the most voluble, said, 'Right, then, let's get down to brass tacks, shall we?'

Tony raised his eyebrows at Lisa. So, he wanted her to leave! She ignored the signal and the man who had spoken glanced from one to the other. When Lisa remained seated, he said, 'You don't want to bother your pretty head with rather dull business matters, Lady Elizabeth.'

Christy burst out laughing. 'According to the *Financial Times*, that pretty head has just sold her share in a film company for five million dollars.'

There was a gasp from the guests and Tony's cup crashed in his saucer. Christy laughed again and Lisa glared at him. Tony had frequently urged her to sell out from O'Brien Productions and she would have preferred him not to know about the hefty rise in her bank balance.

'Well, I never!' The man who seemed to have appointed himself spokesman shrugged. 'I'll bring you up to date on what we discussed last week. I've done a bit of spadework, at least my solicitor has, and found that the property Spring Engineering occupies is covered by two leases, one for the ground, the other for the buildings themselves. The former is a nominal yearly charge that hasn't been changed since before the war, of two hundred and fifty pounds.'

One of the other men said contemptuously, 'That's chickenfeed in this day and age. Is it up for sale?'

'It could be. The owner is an old chap, a pensioner, who hasn't the faintest idea what it's worth. Offer him a couple of thousand quid and he'd be a knockover.'

'What about the buildings?' Tony asked.

'That's a bit more difficult. The rent is two and a half thousand a year and the owners, a London-based property company, are well aware of its value, but I reckon six figures would see them right.'

'So we could get the entire thing for just over a hundred thou?'

'Is this the factory in Broxley High Street you're talking about?' asked Lisa.

'That's right, Lady Elizabeth.'

'What on earth use is that to you?'

One of the men answered, 'Once we own the leases, we raise the rents.'

'But it would take forever to get your money back,' she said.

'Darling, don't you see?' Tony leaned towards her eagerly. 'That site is ideal for a hotel, right in the heart of town.'

'You mean you'd close the factory down?'

'The factory would have to close itself down when it couldn't meet its new rents,' the self-appointed spokesman said.

'And nearly two thousand men and women would be put on the dole! Why, that's a terrible thing to do,' she said angrily.

'I knew you wouldn't understand, Lisa,' Tony said stiffly. 'Anyway, there'd be loads of jobs available in the hotel.'

'That wouldn't be for years and anyway, skilled engineering workers can't be expected to become bottle-washers and wait on tables.'

There was an awkward silence. Someone said slyly, 'Think what the return would be if you invested some of your own capital.'

Lisa didn't answer. She sat staring down at the table, fuming inwardly at the idea of people's livelihoods being in the hands of such greedy, grasping men. Suddenly she got up, pushing her chair away with such force that a leg caught on the fraying carpet and it flew back, landing on the floor with a thud. Everybody jumped as she left the room without a word.

She wondered if Christy would come to her room tonight. But how could he, with Tony in the house? It was gone midnight when she heard the visitors go to bed, their voices loud and angry as they argued about something in the corridor outside. Then a car drove away, it could only be Christy's, and Tony's soft footsteps passed her room and the door of his bedroom opened and closed.

Sleep was a long time coming and she tossed and turned, still angry when she thought about the night's conversation. She had almost drifted into sleep when she was abruptly brought awake by someone slipping into bed beside her. Christy!

'I thought I heard you drive away,' she whispered. His hands were all over her body and she shivered in delight.

'I left it on the road and walked back.'

He began to kiss her and she felt herself melt into nothingness. It didn't matter that her husband was just across the corridor. All that mattered was this man thrusting against her, with his hard, demanding lips, his seeking hands. She gave herself up to him and just lay there, supine and willing, whilst he took her again and again.

His body was huge and she felt tiny and vulnerable as he crouched over her. Once again she experienced a dizzy, delicious pressure mounting inside her that ached to be released. She was poised, feverishly anticipating the glorious culmination of their lovemaking, when somewhere beyond, in a corner of her brain that must have remained alert to other things, she heard a noise, a soft clicking sound. Christy, his eyes closed, lost in passion, heard nothing. Lisa turned her head and saw the door to her bedroom was open a crack. Perhaps he'd not closed it properly when he came in. Then the door moved and she could see the white of a hand on the knob outside.

She said urgently, 'Christy! There's someone watching.' The door closed swiftly and silently.

He collapsed beside her, groaning, 'You must have imagined it.'

'I didn't. The door just closed, I saw it quite clearly.'

'Shit,' he said.

'Who could it be?' She wasn't sure why she felt so frightened.

'Who do you think?'

'Tony?' She was horrified.

Christy laughed coarsely. 'That's about the limit of his sex-drive I should imagine, a peeping Tom, a voyeur.'

'You can't know that,' she muttered.

'My dear Lisa, you acted with me like a person who'd been stranded in a desert without water. It's obvious you haven't been made love to in years, yet you're a lovely, passionate woman and I feel flattered you drank from me.'

'What are we going to do?' she asked.

'I'm going to continue what I'm already doing, looking for another job.' He propped his elbow on the pillow and looked down at her. 'Will you come with me when I find one?'

She shook her head. 'Now it's my turn to be flattered, Christy, but no. I've finished with men forever.' She was trying to be tactful. A person in a desert dying of thirst would accept a drink from anyone. Almost any man who'd looked at her as Christy had might have ended up as he was now, beside her in bed. In certain ways he wasn't much better than Tony when it came to integrity.

In the dim moonlight she could see that he didn't look the least bit upset. In fact he smiled. 'What were we then – two ships that pass in the night? A tugboat and a luxury liner, both Irish registered.'

'I suppose so,' she said. 'And now we must signal goodbye.'

He began to dress swiftly, stuffing his tie in his pocket. When he'd finished, he sat on the edge of the bed and looked at her, his normally hard features softening.

'I take it you're going to divorce Tony?' he said.

'Yes. I'd intended bringing the subject up last night, but those men . . .'

'Be careful, won't you, Lisa? I don't want you ending up like Rhoda.'

'Who's Rhoda?'

'Tony's first wife. He cleaned her out of every penny and as soon as her money had gone, he divorced her. Afterwards, she killed herself.'

The pale, early morning sun rose like a quickly blossoming flower out of a bank of snow-white clouds, and droplets of dew glistened like jewels on the rough, uneven grass. As Lisa jogged up and down the hills she could see the dew spurting underneath her feet like sparks from a Roman candle and the ankles of her tracksuit were soaking wet.

This was the part of the weekend she enjoyed most, running over the dales in the early morning.

The fresh air had cleared her mind and as usual the problems of the night assumed their true proportion in daylight. Although it was nauseous to think of Tony spying on her, what did it matter now she had decided to divorce him? There was no way she'd end up like his poor first wife. She'd continue paying the household bills, but apart from that Tony wasn't getting another penny out of her.

Her breath was hoarse as she virtually staggered up a hill. This was her first exercise in weeks. When she reached the top, she stared at the magnificent view, the rolling green dales, lost in admiration. This was what she would miss most of all when she no longer came to Ferris Hall.

After she got her breath back, she turned and began to run home, though by the time she arrived the run had become a walk.

Mrs Mason was waiting for her in the hall. 'There's been a phone call for you from Fergus Lomax. I've written the number on the pad. He wants to see you. It's urgent.'

'Thank you for coming so quickly.' Fergus Lomax was sitting in a high-backed chair in front of the open window, his legs wrapped in a woollen blanket. The house was unpretentious – a moderately-sized Victorian villa surrounded by a sweet-smelling garden. The window opened onto a figure-of-eight-shaped fishpond and she could see a frog sitting amidst the bordering plants, its gullet throbbing violently.

Fergus's wife had let her in – a tall, commanding woman who looked Lisa up and down disapprovingly. 'Don't tire him now,' she said sternly. 'He's not up to visitors.'

'He invited me,' said Lisa indignantly.

'I know that, but what I say still goes. He's not up to visitors and he shouldn't be tired.' She showed Lisa in and disappeared.

'I apologise for Gertie,' Fergus Lomax said as she entered the room. 'I'd never see a soul if it was up to her. I also apologise for not getting up. I'm afraid my legs have forgotten what they were put there for and no longer support me. Sit down, my dear, here, beside me, and let me look at you. Yes, you're every bit as lovely as people say and even nicer in the flesh than in your photographs.'

'Why, thank you!' He was flirting with her. She could tell he'd been a devil in his day. No wonder his wife was so protective! His bushy hair was still mainly black, gradually turning to silver on his lush, curly beard. He looked like a jovial Long John Silver.

'Why haven't we met before?' he demanded. 'I'd have thought Tony'd be in touch from time to time, but I never hear a word from him.'

'I'm afraid you'll have to ask Tony that.' She didn't say that Tony resented any mention of Fergus Lomax on the assumption it meant criticism of his own performance – which it usually did.

'One thing I'm famous for,' Fergus said, 'is coming straight to the point, so that's what I'll do now. What's your husband doing to my old constituency? Is he intent on bleeding it totally dry?'

The question was so unexpected that she felt her eyes widen in surprise. 'What do you mean?'

'I understand that after the fiasco of the new library and cottage hospital, and the motorway to nowhere which will desecrate our beautiful countryside, he now intends to close down Spring Engineering, Broxley's main employers. I also understand that you disapprove of this, which is why I don't feel it's an impertinence to raise the subject.'

Lisa felt even more surprised. 'How on earth do you know all that?' she demanded. 'They only talked about it in detail last night.'

He winked, looking more like Long John Silver than ever, and tapped his nose. 'I have my informant.'

'In Ferris Hall? It must be Christy.'

'I'm not telling, least not yet, not till I know you better. About Spring Engineering . . . ?'

'As you seem to know so much, I don't feel disloyal to Tony by telling you you're right, though he – and his friends – don't so much mean to close it down as raise the rents so high that the firm has no alternative but to close itself down.'

'And build a hotel?'

'That's right,' agreed Lisa. 'I think it's a terrible idea, putting all those people out of work.'

'Do you now!'

She began to feel angry again. 'It seems wrong. Surely people should have some control over their destiny.' A memory came to her of words spoken years, perhaps decades ago. She wracked her brain. 'It was explained to me once, I can't remember how it went, something about common ownership of the means of production. That's how it should be.' Of course, it was Harry Greenbaum who'd said it. Who else? she thought affectionately.

Fergus Lomax was staring at her, his face a mixture of disbelief and astonishment. As he stared his face turned bright red and he laughed. He roared until tears ran down his cheeks and he began to choke and gasp for breath and the laugh became more of a husky wheeze.

The door flew open and his wife came in. 'What have you done to him?' she demanded.

'I've no idea,' said Lisa nervously.

'You'd better take a tablet.' She grabbed her husband by the shoulder and tried to force a white capsule into his mouth.

'Get away, Gertie. No tablet can stop people laughing and I hope one's never invented. Leave me alone, there's a good girl.'

Gertie left reluctantly, throwing a murderous glance at Lisa as she went out of the door.

'What's so funny?' Lisa felt slightly annoyed.

'You know what you just quoted? Clause IV of the Labour Party constitution. Pure Marxism, my dear. Does Anthony know you're a dyed-in-the-wool socialist?'

'If I am it's unintentional. I've never really thought about it.'

'Then perhaps you should. I admire firm convictions, even when they are the opposite of my own. In fact, the best friend I have in the world is a socialist – Eric Heffer, the Liverpool MP.' He made an impatient gesture. 'I'm wasting your time. I asked you here to discuss the dismal future of the main source of employment in our town. What are we to do about it? The firm has been struggling to stay afloat as it is, with short-time working and redundancies, and the shareholders' dividends have been negligible, though I think things will start to pick up in a year or two. Until then, any increase in outgoings, rent for instance, would be a death blow and the company won't be there to be picked up when the time comes.'

'The obvious solution is for someone else to buy the leases first,' said Lisa.

'Yes, but where's the money to come from?' said Fergus glumly. 'It would take a fool to put up over a hundred thousand pounds without a hope in hell of a return on their investment for years, if ever. Mind you, I'm fool enough to do it, but all I could afford is the ground lease.'

'My mother used to say "a fool and his money are soon parted".' Lisa took a swift decision. If Fergus was willing to risk his money, she'd risk hers too. 'I'll buy the other lease, but I'd like to take a look around the place first. In the meantime, I'd appreciate you keeping my name out of things. I'll telephone tomorrow afternoon.'

Instead of going straight home, Lisa called in at the Red Lion and had a ploughman's lunch. If she missed the meal at Ferris Hall, Tony's visitors might have left by the time she got back. When she drove up to the house later, she was thankful to see their cars had gone.

Tony came out into the hall when he heard her come in and she regarded him warily, but there was nothing about him to indicate he'd recently seen his wife make love to another man. In fact he looked unusually happy and his normally pale cheeks glowed pink.

'I'm going back to London soon, darling. Like to come with me?'

'No, I've a few things to do in Broxley tomorrow,' she told him.

There was no one else in the house apart from the Masons. It was an ideal time to discuss divorce, but she found herself hesitating. It was important to be around Ferris Hall over the next few weeks whilst this business with Spring Engineering was so up in the air. The divorce could wait. She smiled at Tony and said, 'I think I'll go and lie down for a while. I hardly slept a wink last night.'

The words were scarcely out of her mouth before she realised how true they were! It was difficult to keep a straight face. Tony said something about being gone by the time she got up and she ran upstairs and collapsed on the bed, laughing. Better to laugh than cry, she thought when she calmed down, though it would be easy to cry when she thought what a mess she'd made of her life.

The smell and the heat in Spring Engineering were suffocating. As the young receptionist led her across the factory floor towards the manager's office, Lisa could scarcely breathe, though possibly the noise was even worse than the smell and the heat, a pounding monotonous hammering sound that seemed to echo off the dirty brick walls. Although she'd only been in the place a few minutes, she could already feel damp patches under her arms, and her neck was moist against the white collar of her blouse, fresh that morning.

It had taken a long time to choose the right outfit. She didn't want to appear to be slumming by wearing something too casual; on the other hand, it would be offensive to turn up in a designer outfit which had cost what these men could only hope to earn in months. In the end she'd decided on a plain black suit over a crisp white blouse, though the blouse no longer felt crisp. She'd left her hair loose for a change, drawing it back from her forehead under a black velvet Alice band.

The girl paused before the door of a glass-partitioned section in the corner of the building. 'This is Mr Oxton's office.'

Mr Oxton was the manager, and even though the receptionist had rung through to say Lisa was here, he jumped up nervously, knocking an empty cup over on the desk. There was no roof to the room so the smell here was as vile as in the factory, though there was an added odour which she couldn't identify.

'How do you do, Lady Elizabth. This is indeed an honour.' But he didn't look honoured, in fact he looked petrified.

'Please don't call me that,' she said pleasantly. 'It makes me feel uncomfortable.'

'Wh . . . what, then?' he stammered.

'What's your first name?'

'Arthur.'

'Well, if I call you Arthur, will you call me Lisa, please?'

They shook hands and she wondered why his palms were so clammy and why he still appeared so nervous and ill-at-ease. An elderly man with a stooped back and weak, flaccid features, he looked long past retirement age. He wore a khaki overall coat over stained, pin-striped trousers.

'What can I do for you, Lady . . . er, Lisa?'

'I've just come to have a look round,' she explained. 'That is, if it's convenient.'

He paused and she wondered if he was going to say it wasn't convenient and to get the hell out of his factory. Instead, he picked up the telephone and dialled two numbers. 'Can you come in here, Jim?'

Whilst they waited, he shuffled nervously from foot to foot without speaking. At one point he licked his lips and glanced longingly towards the top drawer of his desk and Lisa immediately understood the reason for his agitation when she recognised the extra smell in the office. Arthur Oxton had been drinking, even though it was not yet nine o'clock. Not only that, he was aching for another drink which was almost certainly kept in his desk.

There was a quick knock on the door and a man entered without waiting for a reply – a broad-shouldered, straight-backed man of about fifty with grizzled handsome features and steady brown eyes. His dark curly hair was slightly scattered with grey and cut short without any pretentions towards style. He wore a navy-blue overall coat over jeans and an open-necked shirt.

Arthur Oxton said with obvious relief, 'Jim, this is Lady Elizabeth Molyneux – Lisa – and she'd like to look around.' He made a hurried gesture towards the newcomer, muttered to Lisa, 'Jim Harrison, the foreman,' and ushered them out, clearly anxious to be rid of them.

'Have you come to do a valuation, see what we're worth?' the foreman said sarcastically. He spoke slowly, in a deep husky voice with a soft Yorkshire burr, and made no attempt to shake hands.

'I haven't the faintest notion what you're on about,' Lisa said indignantly, taken aback by the bitter tone in which he spoke and the expression, almost of hate, on his face. 'I've come to do precisely what I said, in other words, look around.'

'This way then.' He walked so quickly – she was sure he did it deliberately – that she had to run to keep up. Every now and again he muttered, 'The tool-room,' or, 'This is the stores.'

'It's very run-down,' she said at one point and he turned on her, eyes blazing. She shrank back.

'Shareholders are good at taking money out of firms, but not so keen on putting it back,' he said angrily. He stopped in front of a big machine, half-eaten away by rust. 'See this?' He pointed to a plaque screwed on the front. Lisa could see the name of the manufacturer and underneath the date 1925. 'That's when this lathe was made, nineteen-twenty-five. It's long past its usefulness. A modern machine would do the work required in less than half the time.'

'Why don't you buy some new machinery, then?' she asked innocently.

Even above the pounding noise, the man operating the lathe heard her question and she saw him exchange a grin with the foreman. She flushed, feeling ignorant and stupid, then thought defensively, 'They wouldn't know how to make a movie or act in a play. Why should I be expected to know all about their jobs?'

She wondered if her burning cheeks were obvious. If so, Jim Harrison showed no mercy. He led her to a large partitioned section where half a dozen machines stood empty. 'This is where we used to train apprentices,' he said coldly, 'in the days when the firm could afford it.' He showed her the canteen with row after row of chipped plastic-covered tables, crammed so close together there was little room to move between them, then the old-fashioned kitchen where several women in green overalls were already at work peeling potatoes and making pastry. They looked up and Jim Harrison said in a loud voice, 'This is Lady Elizabeth Molyneux, our MP's wife. She's come to have a look around,' and the women eyed Lisa curiously. She tried to smile but perhaps she didn't manage it because none of the women smiled back and after they left she heard shrieks of laughter.

He pushed through a pair of swing doors and suddenly they were outside.

She gulped in the fresh air. 'How do people breathe all day in that atmosphere?' she said, more to herself than her companion.

'In order to earn a living wage,' he said caustically. 'To pay their rents and their mortgages and feed their children, but you wouldn't know about that, would you?'

She stared at him angrily. She had come to help and this man had humiliated her, treated her with total contempt.

'You know nothing about me,' she said coldly. How dare he assume she didn't care if people lost their jobs?

'I know all I want to know,' he snapped.

They glared at each other. His brown eyes were the colour of tobacco and despite the dislike she felt, she had to concede that even in his working clothes, there was a dignity about his bearing that Tony, for all his aristocratic upbringing, didn't possess. In some strange, inexplicable way she found herself longing for his approval. She wanted to say, 'I come from a home as poor as any in Broxley, probably poorer, and I started work in a factory just like this when I was fourteen,' and then tell him the real reason for her visit. But why should she explain herself? He'd allowed her to be laughed at, and treated her so patronisingly, let him stick to his horrid assumptions!

She noticed her heel had speared a piece of thin metal and bent down to remove it, almost losing her balance. His hand came out involuntarily to prevent her falling, and she was conscious of his iron grip on her upper arm. Just as spontaneously, she smiled her thanks and for a second their eyes met and she knew, she could tell that behind the surly manner, the hard voice, he was attracted to her. Then he released her quickly and walked away, as if ashamed she had read the message in his eyes.

'What's it going to be then? Are you going to tell your husband this is the perfect place for a hotel?'

Another assumption, that she'd come to spy on Tony's behalf, 'Rumours fly round Broxley with amazing rapidity,' she said tartly.

'And so they should when people's livelihoods are at stake.'

If only he knew how much she agreed with him, but she wasn't going to disillusion him by saying so. He thought she'd come to spy and he could go on thinking it. She said bluntly, 'Yes, I am going to tell him that. As you say, it's the perfect place, absolutely perfect.'

Later, she telephoned Fergus Lomax and Gertie grudgingly allowed her to speak to him. 'I'll buy the buildings lease,' she said, 'though I don't know why. Arthur Oxton is a drunkard and the foreman, Jim Harrison, is the rudest man I've ever met.'

Fergus laughed. 'Jim's one of the most honourable men I know,' he said. 'We're the best of friends, though. I've never been able to persuade him to vote for me. He's a bit of an amateur poet is Jim, often gets published, so I understand. Once you get to know him, you'll like him very much.'

'A poet? You amaze me,' said Lisa. 'He didn't give the impression of knowing enough words to write a poem, let alone make one rhyme.'

'It shows how much you know about poetry. Anyway, that's no way to talk about a fellow socialist.'

'Sorry, that was awfully patronising,' she said apologetically. 'About the leases, can I leave matters in your hands? Do you need the money now? I haven't the faintest idea how you go about these things.'

'I'll see to everything,' he promised. 'Once I've got the details, I'll be in touch. You can give me the money later. Everyone knows Fergus Lomax's word is as good as his bond.'

Before she left, Lisa found twice the usual number of bills on her dressing table. Tony must have put them there last night and she hadn't noticed because this time there were no flowers, no 'bribe' as she called it. Angrily she stuffed them in her bag and wondered with a grim smile if there'd be an invoice for Omar amongst them. Florence Dale had told her that Persian kittens cost at least a hundred pounds.

43

Lisa was trying to learn the lines of a new play due to go into rehearsal later that week, but it was difficult. The dialogue of *Pacemaker* was trite, the words meant nothing. Matthew Jenks was right, she thought. The play had been written by a long-established playwright famous for his lightweight, entertaining comedies, but his latest offering was a vacuous hodge-podge of innuendo and plain bad taste. She reckoned there were probably thousands of plays lying around, immeasurably superior, yet this was getting a West End showing, just because the author was well-known. Fortunately, her part was small as the play had an all-star cast – eight big names in all – and the last she heard, the theatre was already booked solid for months ahead.

When she turned up for the first rehearsal, the other actors were already word-perfect. They sat in a semi-circle, Lisa the only one with a script on her knee, and she found her thoughts drifting away from the theatre to the world outside. She wondered if Fergus had managed to track down the leases for Spring Engineering. She thought about the workers in the factory, their livelihoods at the mercy of Tony's friends, rich uncaring men, their pockets already full of money yet greedy for more and willing to get it by stamping on their fellow men with no more thought than if they were stamping on an insect.

And that was the sort of man she'd married! Ironically, this stage was the very one where they'd met two and a half years ago. With a blinding flash of intuition she knew that although she'd long suspected Tony had married her for her money, she hadn't realised quite how unscrupulously he'd gone about it.

She remembered Barbara Heany saying, 'He's been nagging to meet you,' then later that she'd already told him it was Lisa's birthday, yet Tony had pretended not to know. Both had thought this an insignificant deception, an excuse to flatter. 'You're the most beautiful fifty-year-old woman I've ever met,' he'd said. And she'd been vulnerable to his flattery right from the start – she still was.

He'd sought her out, had Tony. There'd been a lot of articles about her in the newspapers since she'd come back to England, listing her most successful movies, the fact that she was Joseph Dent's widow, and mentioning her company, O'Brien Productions. He'd deliberately and coldly courted her, showering her with flowers and gifts, arranging those delightful surprises – the picnic in Hyde Park, the cosy little dinners. And he'd kept up the charm to keep her sweet so she would pay the bills whilst he poured away his inheritance and his MP's salary at the gaming tables and into shady investments.

Suddenly, she was conscious that everyone was looking at her.

'I know it's a lousy play, Lisa, but let's do our best with it, eh?' the producer said tiredly. 'Learning your lines would be a start.'

'I'm sorry,' she said in confusion. 'I was miles away.' She picked up her script. 'Where are we?'

When she arrived in Broxley that weekend, Tony was already home. As soon as she entered the house, he came out of the drawing room and looked at her coldly. 'What have you been up to?' he demanded, his voice as icy as his expression.

She cursed herself for being so weak; despite everything, she was so used to his affectionate, exuberant welcomes that his coldness upset her. Was he such a good actor that he'd been *pretending* all this time? Surely he felt *something* for her? Deep in her heart of hearts she felt a certain fondness, albeit reluctant, for him.

'I don't know what you're talking about,' she said coolly, praying that Fergus hadn't broken his promise to keep her name out of things.

'I'm talking about the leases for Spring Engineering. Who did you blab to?'

She looked at him indignantly. 'I didn't "blab", as you call it, to anyone.' She hadn't, either. There was undoubtedly a mole in Ferris Hall, but it wasn't her. 'Has something happened?' she asked, wide-eyed.

'It most certainly has.' He wasn't quite sure whether to believe her or not. 'Sowerby's just been on the phone, he's coming to dinner tonight.' Sowerby, if she remembered rightly, was one of the businessmen who'd been here a few weeks ago, the one with the most to say. 'When he approached the leaseholders, they'd already sold. Someone had got there before us.'

'I'm sorry to hear that,' she said virtuously, 'but I gave nothing away. It might have been one of those other men trying to get all the profit for himself.'

'You could be right,' he said eventually. 'I suppose it could have been Christy. A final gesture just to spite me.'

'Have you asked him, or should I say accused him, too?' she asked pointedly.

He flushed. 'Christy's left, gone to another constituency in Cornwall.' He came over, took her hands and crushed them against his lips. 'I'm sorry, darling. I felt convinced you'd betrayed me but I should have known you'd never do anything like that.'

Lisa didn't answer. Inwardly she felt delighted that Fergus Lomax had been successful. She'd call in over the weekend and give him a cheque.

Tony and Colin Sowerby were subdued throughout dinner and the conversation was forced. Despite Lisa's efforts to be a good hostess, brightly relaying theatre gossip, Tony only managed an occasional smile and Colin Sowerby was almost rude in his indifference. She was glad when the meal was over and Mrs Mason had cleared the dishes. Now they might get down to business. However, after an hour of desultory conversation, she realised they had no intention of discussing anything of importance whilst she was there. In the end she said, 'I think I'll have an early night, it's been a hectic week,' and they both gave such an obvious sigh of relief, she almost laughed.

Outside the door she paused and listened, but all she could hear was the sound of muffled voices, nothing distinct. She went down to the kitchen to get a glass of milk and was surprised to see the dinner dishes still piled in the sink waiting to be washed. Mrs Mason, with her back to the door, had her ear pressed against a rubber tube which hung from an old-fashioned communication system used to converse with the servants when the house was built two hundred years before. Lisa had assumed it no longer worked.

'What on earth are you doing?'

Mrs Mason nearly jumped out of her skin. She dropped the tube and turned to face Lisa, her face crimson with embarrassment. 'I thought you'd gone to bed,' she muttered.

Lisa went over, picked up the tube and put it to her ear. She could hear every word that was being said in the dining room!

'Can they hear us?' she whispered.

Mrs Mason shook her head. 'Only if they listened at the grille by the fireplace.'

'So *you're* the informant Fergus Lomax told me about?'

The woman nodded defiantly. 'My son works at Spring Engineering. I wasn't going to sit back and do nothing while they closed it down. I knew Fergus would help.'

'Do you often listen in?'

'Only when there's people like that man who came tonight,' she mumbled. 'That's how we found out he was taking bribes.'

'Who, Tony?' What a stupid question. Who else could it be?

'That's right,' Mrs Mason added proudly, 'It was my son who sent the information to that magazine.' She pointed to the tube. 'They'd started talking about Spring Engineering as soon as you left the room, something about approaching it from a different angle this time. Buying shares, I think that man said.'

Lisa put her ear to the tube and listened hard.

'I'm quite enjoying this,' she said to Fergus Lomax next morning. 'How do we foil them now?'

He regarded her with twinkling eyes. 'Thank God you're not the typical loyal Conservative wife,' he said.

'If this hadn't come up, I'd be well on my way to a divorce,' she replied ruefully. 'They're going to buy fifty-one per cent of the shares – what does that mean?'

'It means they'll have complete control of the company and can shut it down overnight. Before you can say Jack Robinson there'll be a hotel at the end of Broxley High Street and your husband will be a rich man, though if he runs true to form, it won't be for long.'

'But not if I buy the shares first?'

'Precisely, though it'll have to be done pretty damn quick.' He slapped his knee. 'You know, I'm quite enjoying this myself.'

'I'm just as ignorant about shares as I am about leases. Can you do it for me?'

'I'll get on to my stockbroker first thing tomorrow,' he promised. 'At the moment, the shares are at an all-time low, but even so, you realise this won't be cheap? That is why Tony and his friends didn't do it in the first place.'

'How much will it cost?'

'At least half a million pounds.'

'Oh, that's okay,' Lisa said lightly.

He looked impressed. 'I think I took up the wrong profession. I should have been an actor.'

'Errol Flynn would have had to look to his laurels,' she laughed.

'Do you still want to remain anonymous?'

Lisa nodded. 'Isn't life funny?' she mused. 'Who ever thought the day would come when I owned an engineering company? I don't even know what they make there.'

'Combustion engines,' said Fergus.

She groaned. 'I shouldn't have asked. What on earth are *they* for?'

The critics considered *Pacemaker* to be possibly the worst play ever seen in the West End. One wrote, '*This worm-eaten monster crawled onto the stage already half-dead. By the end of the first act, all life had gone from its mouldy body and we had to spend the second act watching the twitching of the corpse.*'

The actors had signed six-month contracts and as the box office reported healthy bookings on the strength of the eight star names, there was no alternative but to plod on and do their best. Lisa knew her performance was probably the worst of her career, though the play was so wretched nobody seemed to notice. She was never able to get into her role and even after several weeks' peformance, she still forgot her lines. By now it seemed unreasonable to blame it on the play. In fact, she seemed to be forgetting an awful lot of things lately – appointments, telephone numbers and, worst of all, names. Even more worryingly, sometimes her head seemed so fuzzy and she felt so vague and detached, that she began to worry for her sanity.

One night, in the middle of the second act, she felt herself go hot and without warning, her body was covered in perspiration. It occurred again a few days later when she was at home and looking in the mirror, she saw she'd turned an ugly dark red.

When it happened a third time she went to see her doctor. As soon as she explained her symptoms, he said abruptly, 'It's the menopause.'

'The menopause?' she repeated foolishly.

'It happens to all women, you know,' he said impatiently. 'It's not going to kill you.'

'Is there something I can take for these hot flushes?'

He shook his head. 'They'll go away eventually,' he said. 'In the meantime, you'll just have to grin and bear it.'

'I wonder if you'd be so flippant if it happened to men,' she said.

At least knowing helped; she wasn't going insane after all. She took herself in hand, determined to adopt a positive attitude, though felt angry when her body disobeyed her firm instructions and a hot flush seized her in the most embarrassing situations – on stage, out shopping, once on the train on her way to Broxley.

Fergus Lomax telephoned to say she was now the proud owner of Spring Engineering, but she found it difficult to get excited. He sent cuttings from the local paper. '*Mysterious Buyer Obtains Majority Shareholding in Local Company.*'

Nellie came to stay and was full of sympathy. 'You poor darling! What about HRT?'

'What's that?'

'Hormone Replacement Therapy. It works wonders for some women.'

'But my doctor said there was nothing I could take,' Lisa protested. 'He claims I must grin and bear it.'

'Then get another doctor,' Nellie said firmly. 'Preferably a woman.'

HRT didn't exactly work wonders for Lisa, but it helped. Within a few weeks she was almost back to her old self. She telephoned Nellie to thank her. 'I was getting really worried,' she confided. 'If I can't cope with the menopause, how on earth would I cope with a real illness?'

Nellie laughed. 'You're a real stalwart, Liz, you underestimate yourself. Anyway, there's no chance of *you* getting a real illness. You're one of the healthiest people I know.'

That was four days before Lisa discovered the lump in her breast.

She was having a shower and at first thought it was something in the soap and looked down, expecting to see a flaw, a bump, but it was as smooth as cream. She touched her breast again, the left one, on the outside, almost under her arm. The lump was no bigger than a pea, but it was definitely there, no doubt about it, and as hard as a pea too, those dried ones Mam used to buy and leave soaking in a bowl overnight. She felt her entire body tingle with goosepimples as she examined the breast in the mirror. Nothing! It looked as smooth and creamy as the soap. She pulled the flesh taut. Still nothing, yet when she let the flesh go the lump was there.

Cancer!

'Jesus Christ!' she wailed and began to cry. She looked at herself in the mirror again. She was so lovely, even at fifty-three. She felt proud of her lithe curves; although her skin no longer had the satin glow of youth there wasn't an inch of superfluous fat. She imagined the breast sliced off leaving a bloody, gaping hole and wept once more.

Her immediate reaction was to call someone. Nellie was the most obvious, but with her hand poised over the receiver she thought, 'I'll only worry her. There's nothing Nellie can do, there's nothing anyone can do.'

Except a doctor, who'd cut her breast off, deface her body and the beautiful Lisa Angelis would become an ugly, disfigured freak.

She went out and bought a book on cancer. The lump could possibly be benign or just a harmless cyst, she read. Only a small percentage were malignant. She breathed a sigh of relief and for a while her worries faded but as the day wore on she began to think, 'Somebody's got to have the small percentage of malignant lumps. Why not me?'

When she got to the theatre that night, Lisa tentatively brought up the subject of breast cancer with the actress who shared her dressing room. To her amazement the woman refused to discuss the matter, looking at Lisa with frightened eyes as if sensing the reason for her casual remark. At the end of the performance, she removed her make-up and left the room with almost unseemly haste.

'Perhaps if I changed my diet, ate more healthily, the lump might go,' thought Lisa, so she cut out meat and ate only salads and fruit. She began to go to a gymnasium each day and spent hours on a rowing machine or exercise bike, willing her body to return to perfect health.

Her life became dominated by the tiny, pea-sized lump in her breast. She was surprised when she discovered Christmas was only a few days away and went up to Ferris Hall for the first time in weeks. Tony was as effusive as ever. 'I've been worried about you, darling. Where on earth have you been?'

She looked at him. This man was her husband, yet he seemed like a stranger. Would she ever know what he was really like behind that bland, smiling mask? She'd still done nothing about a divorce but again this didn't seem the right time. As soon as the lump disappeared and life resumed normality, she would see her solicitor and commence proceedings.

Although she didn't tell him so, it wasn't for Tony she'd returned to Broxley. The place had come to feel like home. When she walked down the High Sreet, almost everyone said hallo. She felt as if she belonged. When she divorced Tony, she'd buy a house close to the dales so she could go jogging every morning.

She said coldly, 'You have my London number, Tony, you know where I live. If you've been worried you could have contacted me.'

He said nothing, but his face darkened as if he realised everything was over between them.

On Christmas morning she jogged over the dales, shivering at first as the icy wind cut through her tracksuit, but after a while she became accustomed to the temperature. She gulped the bracing, unpolluted air and thought it was probably doing a lot of good as it spread down to her lungs, her chest. All that exercise was proving its worth as already she'd run twice her usual limit and didn't feel the least bit tired. She slid her hand inside her tracksuit top to see if the lump was still there. It was.

It was exhilarating flying so effortlessly like this, her feet scarcely touching the wet lumpy grass. She must start coming to Ferris Hall every week again. Jogging in London, breathing in the poisonous fumes and smoke, was probably more dangerous than sitting at home.

She'd nearly reached Broxley. Fergus Lomax's house was on the other side of this hill. Would it be all right, she wondered, to call on Christmas Day? Surely it wouldn't hurt to drop in and wish him Merry Christmas – that's if Gertie would let her!

To her surprise, Gertie actually seemed pleased to see her, to the extent of planting a welcoming kiss on her cheek. 'All this cloak-and-dagger lease and share-buying business has really done Fergus good, made him feel important again. Would you like a drink?'

Lisa had stopped drinking alcohol. 'Just water,' she said.

When Gertie showed her into the room where Fergus sat in front of a roaring fire, she found he already had a visitor. At first she didn't recognise the man who got to his feet politely as she entered – a solid, broad-shouldered man with light brown eyes and a slow, dignified bearing, wearing dark trousers and a subdued-patterned sweater that looked as if it had been a gift that morning. Then Fergus said jovially, 'I think you've already met Jim Harrison.'

That pig of a foreman from Spring Engineering! Fergus had said he was a friend. Lisa managed a smile, though it was an effort. 'Nice to meet you again,' she murmured as he came over and shook hands. Better late than never, she thought. He hadn't condescended to the first time.

'I've just been congratulating Jim,' Fergus said. 'He's been made manager of Spring Engineering.' His eyes twinkled mischievously. 'You remember, don't you, Lisa? You took a look around the place once. Didn't think much of it, if I recall rightly.'

'The staff weren't very friendly,' Lisa replied. She thought Jim Harrison might look embarrassed, but instead he had the gall to smile as if she'd said something funny. 'How's the company doing?' she enquired innocently. 'I understand there were plans to close it down and build a hotel instead. Did nothing come of it?'

'A strange thing happened,' said Fergus with equal innocence. 'Some mysterious benefactor turned up and bought the leases and a majority of the shares right from under the noses of the would-be developers!'

'We can't be sure he's a benefactor yet,' warned Jim, 'We don't know what his plans are. Until he starts investing in new machinery, I'll be worried he hasn't got some trick up his sleeve.'

'Damn!' thought Lisa. 'It looks as though I've got to start buying lathes and stuff.'

After a while she said, 'It's time I went. Mrs Mason will be upset if I'm not back in time for lunch.' Not that Lisa intended eating much, but she'd better keep Tony company at the table.

'I'll be off too, Fergus. Annie's home, preparing her first Christmas dinner. I offered to help but she told me to get lost.' Jim Harrison stood up and came over to the door with Lisa.

When they got outside he asked, 'Where's your car?'

'I ran here,' she said.

'You can't run all the way back!' He looked shocked. 'You'll be lucky to be home for tea, let alone lunch. Let me give you a lift.'

'No, thanks,' she protested. 'I'd sooner run.' In fact, the idea of a lift home suddenly seemed welcome. Whilst she'd been in the house, a stiff, penetrating wind had sprung up. She shivered and Jim Harrison took her arm and led her to his car. After a half-hearted protest, she let herself be virtually pushed into the passenger seat.

Neither spoke for the first mile or so. Every now and then she glanced at him surreptitiously as he stared ahead, concentrating on his driving. These narrow roads could be tricky, particularly if someone came round a bend too fast on the wrong side. He had a firm, strong chin, already shadowed by a faint suspicion of stubble, as if he needed to shave more than once a day, and a long nose with wide, flaring nostrils. His lashes were long and straight and a darker brown than his eyes. As he drove his brow wrinkled in regular straight lines, like corrugated paper. Somewhat unwillingly, she had to concede he was attractive in a quiet, reassuring way. He was a man you would feel safe with, a man you could trust completely. 'Not like Tony,' a mean voice reminded her. He turned and found her looking at him and she felt herself blushing. If she had a hot flush now, she'd kill herself. Anyway, what was a woman in the middle of the menopause doing sizing up a member of the opposite sex!

'Who's Annie?' she asked suddenly to cover her embarrassment.

'My daughter. She's home from university for Christmas.'

She longed to ask where his wife was and found herself hoping he was widowed or divorced. Drat, she was doing it again! Becoming attracted to a man she didn't particularly like and who probably hated her.

'To save you asking, my wife and I divorced about fifteen years ago,' he said suddenly. 'She's in Canada with her new husband.'

'I had no intention of asking,' she lied, and felt half-glad and half-sorry when she noticed him wince.

'Look,' he said quickly. 'I want to apologise for the way I behaved when you came to the factory. It was inexcusable, and I'm truly ashamed.'

'Why apologise? What makes you think I didn't come for the reason you first thought, to size the place up on behalf of my husband?'

'Because I *know* you didn't – now.' At first she thought Fergus had confided in him, but then he said, 'Paul told me you were on our side.'

'Paul?'

'Paul Mason. His parents work at Ferris Hall.' He smiled. 'Am I forgiven?'

'I can't very well refuse an apology on Christmas Day,' she said stiffly. 'It would be un-Christian.'

'So I'm forgiven?'

'I suppose so.'

'Good.' He grinned broadly. 'That's made my day!'

'There's no reason why it should,' she snapped. She knew she was being deliberately rude because she found him so attractive. After Christy, she'd sworn to give up men altogether.

Without her realising it, they'd reached Ferris Hall. As they drove up to the door, she saw her husband outside. He and Mason were standing by the Mercedes having an argument and Tony was waving his arms about like a spoilt child.

Jim Harrison looked at him, then glanced back at Lisa, a puzzled expression on his kind, strong face. 'Why on earth did you marry him?' he seemed to be asking – a question Lisa increasingly asked herself.

44

Pacemaker closed at last. The mood of relief was so great that the actors put all they had into the final Saturday-night performance, so much so that the producer exclaimed indignantly, 'If you'd done that right from the start, we might have made something out of it!'

A party had been arranged for afterwards but Lisa took one look at the greasy sausage rolls and vol-au-vents laid out backstage and was sickened by the idea of stuffing herself with such unhealthy food, full of preservatives and chemicals. What she intended doing was catching the midnight train to Broxley and tomorrow she would run over the dales, breathing in the pure, unadulterated air. The fitter she got, the more likely it was that she would get rid of the lump which stubbornly persisted in her left breast despite all her efforts. Although it was no bigger it was still there every time she checked, several times a day.

She was alone in the dressing room and had just finished wiping off her make-up – the actress she shared with was keeping out of the way until Lisa finished, something she'd done ever since the dreaded word 'cancer' had been mentioned – when there was a knock on the door and a voice shouted, 'You've got a visitor, Miss Angelis.'

A woman entered. She was as big as a house, panting with the sheer effort of walking and bringing with her the salty smell of perspiration. Most of her long, pure-white hair had escaped from the bun on her neck and stuck up from her scalp like the bleached snakes of Medusa. She wore a silk dress with an unflattering V neck which hung on her overweight frame like a tent. Although she looked sixty, the skin on her face was as fresh and smooth as a young girl's.

She sank into a chair with a sigh and said, 'You don't recognise me, do you?'

'I'm terribly sorry, but no,' said Lisa, trying not to sound irritated. She wasn't in the mood for visitors.

'It's Jackie.'

'*Jackie!*' Jesus, how could that lovely curvacious girl she'd known all those years ago have turned into this . . . this freak! 'Why, how lovely to see you!' Lisa cried, conscious of how false and unenthusiastic the words sounded. 'How are Laurence and the children?'

'Laurence died four years ago,' said Jackie flatly. 'He was much older than me, you know, seventy when he went.'

Lisa made the appropriate soothing noises. 'I'm terribly sorry to hear it. How awful for you.'

349

'As for the kids, I had four in the end. Two boys followed by two girls. You knew about Noël, of course.' Jackie giggled. 'That was a rare old palaver, wasn't it? You met the middle two, Robert and Lisa, but by the time Constance arrived, you'd left the flat and my letters were returned marked Gone Away.' She paused for breath, as if the long speech had tired her.

'I'm sorry about that,' said Lisa, irritated again at being made to feel guilty after all this time. 'But I moved suddenly.'

'Anyway,' Jackie continued, 'the children are all married – Noël's in Australia and the others are scattered all over the country and I've already got three grandchildren. Of course, I don't see as much of any of them as I'd like, but I suppose all mothers feel that.'

'I expect so.' There was an awkward silence. 'Are you still living in Bournemouth?'

'I had to move out of the vicarage when Laurence died and there'd never been the money to save for a house of our own.' She giggled again but this time Lisa sensed a touch of desperation in her voice. 'You'll never guess where I am now! Earl's Court, no more than a stone's throw from our old flat. Quite a nice little bedsit, but a bit noisy.'

Oh, Jackie! All that loving and mothering and caring and you end up at sixty all alone in a bedsit in Earl's Court. 'Why on earth didn't you stay in Bournemouth?' Lisa asked curiously.

'I had to get a job, that's why I came to London, but in all this time, I've only had a couple of weeks' temping. The job market is virtually non-existent at the moment.'

That wasn't true, thought Lisa. The job market had long since begun to pick up again. The more likely explanation was that firms wouldn't want to employ someone looking like Jackie. She turned to the mirror and began to apply her ordinary make-up as Jackie chattered away. 'I passed the theatre the other day on my way to another agency and saw your picture outside. I recognised you immediately – you haven't changed a bit in all these years. You're still as lovely as ever,' she said admiringly.

Out of sight she sounded just like the old Jackie, as bright and cheerful as ever. There wasn't a hint of envy in her voice. She was pleased her old friend had remained slim and beautiful, despite her own appearance. Lisa half-expected to turn around and find her sitting there with her bright blue eye-shadow and spiky lashes, her creamy blonde hair cascading around her face. There was nobody in the world she would rather have met now than Jackie. She could tell her about the lump and Jackie would understand her fears and offer the warm, uninhibited sympathy Lisa remembered so vividly. But there was something inherently depressing about this woman with her ugly, obese body, deserted by her children, living in a London bedsit. Lisa gave an involuntary shudder and hoped Jackie wouldn't realise the reason for it.

'Laurence and I could never afford to go to the pictures,' Jackie was saying. 'Else I suppose I would have realised who you were years ago. I suppose it's living in London again, but recently I keep thinking about our old place. Gosh, we had some good times there, didn't we, Lisa?'

'We certainly did.' Wonderful times. Lots of laughter, lots of sadness too, but there'd been a freedom and a gaiety about those years that had never been recaptured. Why couldn't she bring herself to respond to Jackie, to kiss and hug her, welcome her back into her life?

There was another awkward silence. Lisa could think of nothing to say and Jackie seemed to become aware that she'd been doing all the talking, and suddenly dried up.

'Well,' with obvious effort she hoisted herself out of the chair, 'I'd better be getting along.'

With a feeling of relief, Lisa stood up and shook hands. 'Perhaps we could have lunch one day?' she said. 'Let me have your number and I'll be in touch.'

Jackie tore a page out of her diary and scribbled the number down. 'It's a communal telephone, so you'll have to ask for me, Jackie Murray.' Her eyes were sad and faintly accusing. '*I know darned well you'll never ring,*' they seemed to be saying.

Lisa had been turning down parts for months. She wanted nothing to do with the theatre, with anything, whilst she concentrated on getting rid of the lump. Surely you should have sufficient control over your body to *will* the bad parts away? She saw a television programme which claimed that fruit and vegetables were sprayed with so much fertilizer that they could actually *cause* cancer, so she changed to organically-grown produce. These and water comprised her daily diet. She ate nothing cooked, drank no tea, no coffee or alcohol.

'The water,' she thought frantically one day. 'It's full of fluoride and all sorts of chemicals. No wonder the lump hasn't gone!' She began to buy bottled water, gallons and gallons of it.

Nellie's daughter Natalie got married at Easter. Lisa travelled up to Liverpool and this time Patrick was there, as tall and handsome as all the O'Brien boys, though his tan and easygoing confident manner gave him a more glamorous air. He brought with him his beautiful Anglo-Indian wife, Pita.

'One of my main recollections is of you doing your homework at the kitchen table and complaining we were disturbing your concentration,' Lisa said, willing him to remember that and nothing more.

'Well, we were a noisy lot,' he said ruefully. 'Remember the argument when you passed the scholarship and Dad wouldn't let you go to secondary school?'

Lisa shuddered. 'Only too well!' She wondered if, at the back of his mind, he treasured the memory of the night he'd spent with Lisa, the girl who'd come into his life then vanished so mysteriously. Looking at him, his blond hair bleached almost white by the sun, his smiling blue eyes and long, sensitive hands, she told herself she felt nothing. How could she, when he was her brother?

At Ferris Hall, Mrs Mason said worriedly, 'Are you all right? I wouldn't have thought you could have got much thinner, but you have.'

'I don't look ill, do I?' asked Lisa, alarmed.

'No, that's the funny thing. You look as if you're brimming over with health, though if you keep on eating this rabbit food you'll fade away to nothing, particularly with all that jogging about you do.'

*

Tony probably wondered why she still came to his home. If he'd asked her, what would she have replied? 'Because I love it here and Broxley feels like home. Because I own an engineering company, and some day, when this bloody lump goes, I'm going to start investing in new machinery and you'll find out it was *me* who prevented you from making a fortune. Not only that, one day I'm going to buy a house here and settle down and I'm going to divorce you, Tony, before long.'

They scarcely spoke nowadays. In fact, she tried to avoid him, though she still found bills on her dressing table which she dutifully paid.

In the autumn Busby telephoned. She was so pleased to hear his voice that she burst into tears.

'Darling, what on earth's the matter?' He sounded so concerned that she cried even harder.

'Oh Busby, I think I'm going to die.' There, she'd told someone at last! It was a relief to get the words out.

'What's wrong?' he pressed. He sounded close, as if he was in the very next street not thousands of miles away in Los Angeles.

'I've got a lump in my breast,' she sobbed. 'And the damn thing won't go away, no matter what I do.'

'Shall I come over? I can catch the very next plane.'

'No, but I'd like to come to you. Do you mind – are you in the middle of something?' Busby's reputation had grown over the years. Nowadays he made big, stupendous films with fifty-million-dollar budgets. His latest was showing in London and had got rave reviews.

'No, I'm in between movies, but it wouldn't matter if I wasn't. You know I'd drop everything – for you. Dammit, Lisa, you should have told me about this before. When would you like to come?'

'Soon – in a few days.' She began to feel excited for the first time in months. 'Oh darling, I'm really looking forward to it.'

'Don't you want to know why I called? I'm having a house built and the builders haven't even started yet. I was wondering if I could rent Tymperleys for a while?'

'Of course you can.' She had a vision of him sitting round the pool with his friends. 'But I wouldn't want to go there, not just now.'

'How about New York – the same hotel where we spent our honeymoon? There's an Indian summer at the moment, so it'll be hot but exhilarating. Remember what Doctor Johnson said: "To be tired of New York is to be tired of life".'

'I think you've got your cities wrong, but I'm sure he would have said it anyway.'

'New York it is, then. I'm looking forward to it already.'

'Darling, there's just one thing,' Lisa said cautiously, hoping he wouldn't be offended. 'Could we be – what's the word – platonic? Celibate? I'm just not in the mood for that sort of thing right now.'

He laughed and didn't sound the least bit hurt. 'Can I quote you a little poem I read once? "A man is not old when his hair grows grey. A man is not old when his teeth decay. But a man is nearing his last long sleep, When his mind makes appointments his body can't keep." I think that just about describes Busby Van Dolen at the present time.'

It *was* hot in New York. The sun shone down with relentless, burning intensity on the ravine-like streets and was reflected back off the baking pavements so Lisa felt as if she was walking through an oven. She and Busby strolled round Central Park and ate in dark cool restaurants, where he bullied her into eating proper meals for the first time in months. They spent a small fortune in Macy's on silly, extravagant and useless presents for everyone they could think of, and at night went to the theatre – not the big expensive shows, but off-Broadway productions. 'I'm always on the lookout for new talent,' Busby said.

His hair and beard were completely grey now and the lenses in his glasses much thicker than she remembered, but for all that, he was the same old enthusiastic Busby, still fun to be with. Now he had a new enemy, President Ronald Reagan, to complain about. 'You wouldn't believe what he's doing to our country, Lisa,' he groaned. 'Welfare benefits slashed and families living in their cars or on the streets.'

'Wouldn't I?' she replied witheringly. 'I never thought I'd see kids sleeping on the streets of London, either. Nowadays, it seems everyone's out for himself.'

He put his hand over hers. 'We always agreed on things.'

At night they lay in the same bed, his arms around her, but just that, nothing more, though on the final night he kissed the lump in her breast. 'You know you are the love of my life,' he said softly. 'When your divorce comes through, couldn't we . . .'

Lisa laid her fingers on his lips. 'No, Busby, it's too late.'

'It's never too late,' he protested. 'We can spend the rest of our lives together.'

For a moment she was tempted. He was such a dear, sweet man and he'd been in love with her his entire adult life. It no longer mattered that he was Buzz, the young GI who'd come to Southport with her all that time ago – she scarcely thought about that episode in her life now – but it seemed wrong to go back to him after all this time.

When he came to the airport to see her off, he said, 'As soon as you get back, promise me you'll see a doctor about that lump.'

'I promise.'

She flew home feeling slightly more cheerful. Several times she picked up the telephone to call her doctor – after all, she'd promised Busby – but put it down again almost immediately, too scared to dial. After a few days she was gripped by a deep, dark depression. What if the lump was malignant and it had spread, was still spreading through her body like the dark and dirty roots of a tree? It was simply no use trying to cure herself.

Mrs Mason was right: if she kept on eating like this, she'd fade away to nothing.

There was nothing else for it. She picked up the telephone and dialled her doctor's number.

Margaret Ashleigh was a glamorous redhead who looked more like a model than a member of the medical profession. 'How long have you had this?' she asked after she'd examined Lisa's breast.

'Nearly a year.'

Lisa expected a stern lecture on her foolishness. Instead the woman said sympathetically, 'I suppose you've been too frightened to come?'

'You probably think I'm very silly.'

'Well if you are, you share it with an awful lot of women. All of us want to keep our bodies whole, though nowadays they can do wonders with cosmetic surgery. Anyway, let's hope such drastic measures won't be necessary.'

She arranged for Lisa to have a biopsy the following day.

That night, she thought, 'If it's serious, if I'm going to die, Tony will inherit all my money.'

She immediately wrote six-figure cheques to half a dozen charities and scribbled out a Will leaving everything to her family. Then she asked both her neighbours to witness it.

When Florence Dale was asked for the second signature, she looked at Lisa in alarm. 'What's all this in aid of?'

Lisa attempted to laugh. 'I just thought I'd like to put my affairs in order, that's all.'

'A bit sudden, isn't it? Is something wrong?'

She avoided the old lady's eyes. 'Nothing serious. I'm going for a test tomorrow, that's all.' She picked up Omar and kissed him. Although fully grown, he was still as playful as a kitten and began to jab at her pearl necklace with his paw. 'Omar, you are a very immature cat. It's about time you began to behave like an adult.'

Florence said, 'Tell me how you get on, won't you?'

'I won't know the result for a while, but I'll let you know, I promise.'

Benign!

When Margaret Ashleigh told her a few days later, Lisa fainted.

Mrs Mason said, 'I wasn't expecting you this weekend so I haven't got any salad stuff in.'

'I don't care,' Lisa sang. 'Just give me roast beef and potatoes, a double helping of Yorkshire pudding and drown the lot in a shovelful of your thick, lumpy gravy.'

'My gravy's never lumpy!' Mrs Mason replied indignantly. She looked at Lisa shrewdly. 'You're feeling better, aren't you? Not that you ever looked ill, you just acted it. I know something's been wrong.'

'There was,' said Lisa happily. 'But it's all over now.'

She ran across the misty dales and had never felt so happy. Exhilarated by her sense of newfound freedom, she laughed out loud and the sound was swallowed up by the white mist which surrounded her on all sides, ethereal, yet protective as a curtain. It was damp and cold, but Lisa felt as if she were running in heaven.

Suddenly, almost miraculously, when she reached the top of the hill, the mist disappeared and the sun came out and she could see for miles and miles. The view was glorious. As if lifelong blinkers had been stripped from her eyes, she saw the scene with a clarity never known before. The grass had never been such a vivid green or the fields such a rich brown, almost purple. Bare trees were stark, their branches crazy shapes against the now blue-grey sky and the roofs of the half a dozen scattered houses shimmered with a silvery glaze in the unnaturally bright sun. She had never felt so alive.

'When are you going back to London?' she asked Tony over lunch.

'Not till tomorrow morning,' he answered. 'Why?'

'I'd like a few words with you tonight.'

'What's wrong with now?'

Was it just her imagination, or had his face grown mean over the years since they'd met? Perhaps it was because he no longer looked at her in the same way, no longer smiled or showered her with those empty, meaningless compliments that had taken her in so convincingly. This was his *real* face, no longer gentle, but hard and empty of emotion.

'I can't now,' she said. 'It's Fergus Lomax's birthday and I've been invited for drinks at two o'clock.'

'They didn't ask me,' he said petulantly.

She dressed in a new white jersey frock, simply styled with a round neck and long straight sleeves. The fine material clung to her waist, which was slimmer than ever, falling in soft folds over her hips to the tops of her white leather high-heeled boots. After getting the result of the biopsy, she'd joyfully bought half a dozen new outfits – she seemed to have spent most of the previous year in a tracksuit. She brushed her hair thoroughly till it shone, parted it in the middle and left it loose. A final glance in the mirror told her she looked radiant. She'd never known her eyes shine back so brightly, so full of the delight of being alive. 'Anyone would look radiant if they felt as I do,' she thought. 'It's not peculiar to me.'

Fergus, so full of life and impishness, interested in everything that went on in Broxley and the wider world, was rapidly fading away.

'You're looking well,' she lied as she bent to kiss him.

'Don't tell fibs,' he snapped. 'I look awful.' Nevertheless, he managed a leery wink. 'Christ, I wish I'd known you twenty years ago. I would have shown you a good time.'

'Don't be foolish, dear.' Gertie came up behind him and slapped his hand. 'You're embarrassing her.' She smiled at Lisa over the chair but the smile didn't touch her eyes. 'I'm going to lose him soon and I can't bear it,' she seemed to be saying.

The room was crowded, full of his old friends from all the political parties, perhaps realising that this was the last birthday Fergus would have.

'Hallo, there.' Someone touched her shoulder and Lisa turned to find Jim Harrison standing behind her. He looked strange in a dark suit and tie and a white shirt, and she noticed the collar hadn't been ironed properly. 'It seems ages since I last saw you, so how come you've grown younger? You look wonderful.' There was a strange reluctance in his voice, as if he found compliments difficult and the words had been forced out against his will. His eyes held a similar expression – a grudging admiration.

Lisa understood how he felt. Despite the dislike they had for each other,

underneath there was an undeniable attraction. On this perfect day, however, she had no time for deep psychological theories.

'Why, thank you!' She licked her lips provocatively. 'Perhaps it's because I
feel wonderful inside.'

She'd never thought she'd flirt again. It was ridiculous, someone of her age
fluttering her eyelashes and looking coy. No doubt she was making an
exhibition of herself but she didn't care, not today. He seemed to sense her
mood. Although she could tell he wasn't used to it and probably felt
awkward, he couldn't resist responding in a like manner, and in no time at
all they were acting like a couple of teenagers who'd just met at their first
dance – there, that showed her age – nowadays it would be a disco. Glancing
around, she saw no one was taking a blind bit of notice – not that it would
have mattered anyway.

After a while he said, 'You haven't got a drink.'

'I've got wine somewhere. I think that's it on the mantelpiece.'

Through lowered lids she watched him cross the room to fetch her glass
and thought what a solid, reassuring figure he made, though at the same
time there was an air of recklessness about him that she'd never noticed
before, as if he was capable of great, unexpected passion – well, a poet would
be, surely! She felt that old quiver of desire in the pit of her stomach and
thought to herself, 'I hope they don't send a handsome priest to give me the
Last Sacraments, else I'm quite likely to grab him, even on my deathbed.'

'What are you grinning at?'

He was back with the wine. 'I daren't tell you,' she laughed. 'It was sacrilegious.'

'It sounds as if it might be interesting.'

By five o'clock, Fergus began to look tired and people started to leave. When
they were outside, Lisa went over to her car. 'I'm surprised you didn't run
over,' said Jim. Perhaps the fresh air had brought him back to earth, as he
sounded faintly sarcastic.

'Not in these boots,' she replied. 'Goodbye, perhaps I'll see you in another
year.' As she got into her car, she noticed he was walking down the drive and
wound down her window to shout, 'Can I offer you a lift this time?'

'But it would mean you going in the opposite direction,' he protested,
though coming hastily back. 'My car's in getting a new clutch,' he explained
and Lisa wondered why she felt so glad!

As she drove into Broxley, their conversation turned to more mundane
topics. 'Have you lived here long?' she asked.

'All my life,' he answered simply.

'That must be strange, to have lived in the same place forever.'

'It means you know where you are in the world,' he laughed. 'I don't mean
that literally. It's just I know where I belong. The town is as familiar to me as
the back of my hand.'

'I wonder why people say that?' she mused. 'The back of my hand isn't the
least bit familiar to me. I'm sure I wouldn't recognise it out of half a dozen
others.'

'That's because you've been too busy rushing around the world to stop
and look at it.'

They were passing Spring Engineering. 'I wonder if the new owner could be persuaded to give it a lick of paint,' he said, half to himself.

'I reckon so if you asked nicely.'

'I don't know who to ask. I'm sure Fergus does but he's keeping pretty tight-lipped about it.'

'He must have his reasons,' she said casually.

Jim told her to take the next right turn. 'Would you like to come in for a cup of coffee?' he asked when she stopped the car.

He lived down a narrow unmade road. His was the last house on a row of terraced properties with long front gardens. At the end of the road the moors sloped gently upwards.

'No, thanks. I'd better be getting home,' she said, trying to keep the regret out of her voice. There was no way she would agree to being alone with this man today – although it wasn't him she distrusted, but herself. He was holding the passenger door open, looking down at her, a half-smile on his face. 'Some other time, maybe,' she added.

'Some other time, then.'

He slammed the door and as she drove away, she tried to push him out of her mind. Over the next few hours she'd need all her wits about her. It was time for the showdown with Tony.

She'd never thought him capable of such rage. Astonished and afraid, she wondered how she could ever have thought him gentle, and almost hoped Mrs Mason was listening and would come to her rescue if he attacked her. She tried to contain her own anger and remain patient.

'You surely realised it was over between us a long time ago,' she said quietly. She'd tried to be reasonable from the start. 'I want a divorce,' she'd said and he reacted with instant, implacable virulence.

Now he was walking up and down the room, waving his arms like a child deprived of a favourite toy. At one point he even stamped his elegantly-shod foot in temper. 'I thought you liked the life I gave you,' he spat. 'A title, a stately home, a position in the community.'

'You forget I already had Tymperleys, my dear,' she said, trying not to sound sarcastic. 'And I've always been proud of my own status, not just in this community. As for the title, I never use it. I've never been entirely happy being called "Lady".'

'That's because you were born in the gutter,' he sneered. 'It takes a certain amount of breeding to carry a title.'

His insults weren't worth answering. After a while she said, 'I'm sorry you're taking it like this, Tony. Why can't we part friends?'

'Friends!' He stopped and looked down at her contemptuously. 'What sort of friend have you been to me, making me beg and grovel for every penny of your money, just like my father did?'

Lisa looked at him in amazement. 'That's a lie! I've been paying your bills for years at the rate of a couple of thousand pounds a month.' She couldn't be bothered adding that if he hadn't been so sneaky and dishonest right from the beginning, she would have been willing to share everything with him. All she wanted now was to get to her room and sleep in Ferris Hall for the last time, but perhaps if he got all this hate and resentment out of his system, the divorce would go ahead more amicably.

Suddenly his attitude changed. He sat opposite and gave a sly smile. 'I've been half-expecting this,' he said. 'And I've already been in touch with my solicitor. He thinks I should be entitled to a settlement from you, either that or alimony.'

'What!' Now it was her turn to be enraged. 'I'd give every penny away before I'd let you fritter my money away at Grundy's.'

His grey eyes narrowed. 'How did you find that out?'

'It doesn't matter. There's no chance of anything off me, Tony,' she said emphatically. 'No chance at all. Forget it.'

'One of my colleagues in Westminster got a massive amount off his ex-wife,' he said virtuously. 'In fact, she was almost thrown in prison for refusing to pay.'

'He sounds a nice type. I'm sure you're the greatest pals.' She stared down at the table. A cigarette! What she wouldn't have given for a cigarette right now to calm her shattered nerves. 'Tony,' she began with forced patience. 'I had intended the divorce to be on the grounds of marital breakdown . . .'

Before she could continue, he interrupted with, 'I've got a better idea. Why not adultery – with Christy Costello?'

'You saw and you said nothing?' She looked at him open-mouthed.

Her bewilderment must have made him feel uncomfortable. 'It didn't bother me,' he muttered. 'Why should it?'

'Because I'm your wife, that's why. What I was going to say before was, if you in any way attempt to get money off me, I'll forget all about a breakdown, but give non-consummation as my reason. I don't think we'd even need a divorce then – the marriage could be annulled. That would give your macho friends at Grundy's a good laugh.'

This time he said nothing. She stood up. 'I think I'll go to bed. Let's not quarrel any more, Tony. Let's sort this out like civilised human beings.'

'It's too late for that.'

His voice was so raw, so filled with hate, that she shivered. At the door, she turned. 'I don't want any unpleasantness, but if you insist on war then I'll use all the weapons at my command. What about your first wife? You used all her money and she killed herself after the divorce. That won't look good in court, Tony.'

The knuckles tightened on his long thin hands. He looked at her with an expression of utter loathing on his white face. 'I suppose Christy told you that, but you'll have a job proving it.'

She went upstairs feeling incredibly sad. This wasn't the way she'd expected the day which had started so gloriously to end. Halfway up the stairs a voice hissed, 'Lisa!'

Tony was standing in the hall looking up at her with burning eyes.

'What?'

'I'm going to get you for this – you just wait and see. This marriage never turned out the way I wanted it, but I'm going to make damn sure the divorce does.'

'What are you going to do?' she asked listlessly.

'Just wait and see!'

45

She ripped Tony's face into little pieces, separating his eyes, his nose, his mouth, and flung the pieces in the waste-paper basket. The portrait he'd had painted was already in the bin. Outside, Omar was sitting on the wall between her yard and Florence Dale's, watching with interest.

'It's a good job I gave you away,' she called out severely. 'Otherwise you'd be in here too.' She wanted no reminders of Tony left. Picking up the box-file which held all her favourite notices and photographs, she tipped the contents onto the floor – she'd been meaning to put them in albums for years – then put them back one by one into the file, removing all mementos of her husband. A leaflet from the last election with Tony smiling charmingly at the camera was screwed into a ball, a photo of their wedding torn to bits.

One by one, she put the cuttings and pictures back and as so often happened when the file was got out for some reason, began to reminisce . . . She re-read the review of *The Matchstick Man* which had taken everyone by surprise, then an article about Dent, cuttings from a Maine newspaper praising Ralph's lousy acting in *Uncle Vanya*, and she smiled at a snapshot of herself and Jackie in Kensington Gardens. A young man had asked if he could take it. They'd given him the Queen's Gate address and he'd sent them the photograph, along with a plea to take Jackie out to dinner. Although they'd laughed over it, Lisa had tried to talk her into going. The young man had seemed nice, a million times nicer than Gordon.

Jackie! The way she'd loved that horrible man! So trusting and childlike, she was too innocent for this scary, cruel world. Lisa remembered standing at the vicarage gate in the snow watching Jackie and her family. She'd known all she had to do was knock and be welcomed with open arms, drawn into that close family circle, made to feel part of it. Jackie would have been there when Lisa needed her, even after all those years. But Lisa had rebuffed her friend when *her* support was needed. God, how could she have been so cold and churlish? Of course there'd been the dreaded lump to worry about, but that was no excuse.

Had she kept Jackie's number, she wondered urgently, and began to search through the bureau – but there was no sign of it. She went upstairs and looked through her handbags, eventually finding it shoved carelessly in a pocket. The crumpled page from Jackie's diary showed a whole week in March, yet nothing, absolutely nothing was written on it except Jackie's number in her familiar untidy scrawl; this meant that during that week, Jackie had had no appointments – no lunch or dinner dates, nothing.

Lisa telephoned the number and a young man answered, his voice scarcely audible above the ear-shattering music in the background. She had to ask for Jackie Murray three times before he understood. 'Hold on a minute while I fetch her,' he said eventually.

It was a good five minutes before he came back. 'She's there all right, but she won't answer. I hope she's okay.'

'Give me your address and I'll come straight over.'

'Jackie, it's Lisa. If you don't open the door I'll fetch the landlord with the key.'

'You'll be lucky,' said the youth behind her, the one who had answered the phone. 'He's in Mexico.'

'What's he doing there?' asked Lisa, hammering on the door again.

'Spending the money he gets off this flea-pit, I guess.'

'*Jackie!*' Lisa thumped with both hands. 'She probably thinks this is part of the music, an extra dimension to the bases.'

'It's not all that loud,' he protested.

'Then I reckon you should get your hearing tested. You'll probably find you're almost deaf.'

Lisa pressed her ear against the door and was sure she could hear a shuffling from inside. 'JACKIE!' she yelled. 'Open this bloody door!'

The door opened a crack and no further. Lisa widened it gingerly. Jackie was walking away and threw herself face down onto the bed like a great floundering whale.

'She's all right then?' The young man looked relieved.

'Yes, thanks for your help. There's one more thing you can do.'

'What's that?'

He was quite a nice young man really. Lisa gave him a wide grin. '*You can turn that bloody music down!*'

'Turn over and look at me,' commanded Lisa. On the way over she'd decided to take control, just like she'd done when they were young. It would probably do Jackie more good than sympathy.

Jackie sniffed and sat up. She looked at Lisa miserably.

'What's the matter, you silly dollop? Why didn't you answer the door? You had that young man really worried, not to mention me.'

'Oh, Lisa!' She burst into tears. 'I feel so utterly wretched.'

'I'm not surprised, living in a dump like this. Just look at it!' The room was a reasonable size with a large window overlooking a pretty, tree-filled square, but Jackie had reduced it to a tip. Her clothes were everywhere, over the backs of chairs, on the floor amidst old newspapers and magazines, and the small round table was covered in dirty dishes. 'Honestly, Jackie, I feel as if I'm in a time warp. It's just like walking into Queen's Gate half a lifetime ago.'

'I'm sorry.'

'And so you should be! Get out of bed this minute and help tidy up.'

She noticed the difficulty Jackie had in hoisting her huge body upright. Jackie caught her look and said defensively, 'I keep intending to lose weight. I hate being fat like this.'

'It's bad for your heart,' said Lisa severely and Jackie suddenly smiled. Lisa almost gasped, as it took years off her age and she felt an ache, as if the old Jackie had miraculously appeared.

'I feel as if I'm in a time warp, too. It brings it all back, you bossing me about like this.'

Amidst the clothes Lisa found a pile of greasy fish and chip papers and bags from a confectioner's smeared with cream, and she remembered the way Jackie had overeaten when she was depressed and expecting Noël. She had turned to food for comfort, which meant she badly needed comforting right now.

Once the room had been tidied, the clothes put in the wardrobe and the rubbish in several plastic carrier bags, it began to look quite habitable. It was only then that Lisa noticed the music downstairs had been turned down considerably. She washed two mugs in a small corner sink and plugged in the electric kettle.

'I think we deserve a cup of tea after that,' she said with a sigh of satisfaction. 'What brought all this on, anyway? Locking yourself away and refusing to answer the phone?'

Jackie had found a dressing gown, a hideous flowered silk thing that hardly met across her stomach. 'Yesterday I was sent to a firm in Holborn,' she said, 'solicitors, and they gave me this awful electronic typewriter to work on. I'd only just got used to using an electric model. It was manuals when I left to have Noël. I've always been a good typist – I used to do Laurence's sermons and all his correspondence – so I never lost my speed, but this thing! It just ran away with me and my fingers turned into thumbs. At lunch-time they suddenly said they didn't need a temp any more, but it was just an excuse to get rid of me. I don't blame them, I was useless.'

'That was awful, no wonder you feel wretched,' Lisa said softly.

'It was the last straw. Sometimes I feel there's no point going on, what with Laurence dead and the kids so far away. I'm no good at being anything except a wife and mother.' She began to cry again. 'I can't get used to everyone being gone and being by myself after all this time. It was such a busy life at the vicarage, really hectic, but I loved it. There were kids everywhere, not just mine. Now everything's so empty.'

Lisa couldn't think of anything to say. After a while, she ventured, 'You could go to night-school and learn to use one of those new typewriters,' though it was a pretty lame suggestion.

'I've thought about that. Word processing would be even more useful, but who's going to employ me, Lisa? I'm sixty and I look a fright. I'm sure that's why the kids don't ask me up to stay more often,' she said despairingly. 'They're ashamed of me.'

'We're going to have to sort you out,' Lisa said briskly.

'How?' said Jackie hopefully.

'First thing is a diet. Join a club where you'll make friends with other people. Will you do that?'

'Yes, Lisa.' Jackie gave a half-smile.

'And remember when we first met and you gave me your clothes and lent me your gold watch and we shared the clothing coupons off your aunts?' Jackie nodded. 'Well, now it's my turn to do something for you. I'll buy you one of those word processor things – no, I insist.' Jackie had opened her mouth to argue. 'Once you've got the hang of it you could become a freelance temp or start your own agency – I know heaps of writers who need scripts typing.'

Jackie didn't say anything for a long time and Lisa began to wonder if she was offended. After all, what a cheek barging in like this, issuing orders on how Jackie should run her life . . .

'Thank you for the word processor, Lisa. I'm truly grateful and I'll do the things you suggest, but you know, I'll only be half-alive for the rest of my life without Laurence and my children.'

That night, as she returned home in a taxi, Lisa thought, 'I'll buy a proper flat, somewhere central where she can start an agency, and pretend it belongs to a friend who only wants a low rent. I can't leave her in that crummy bedsit.' She'd nearly asked Jackie back to Pimlico to live but the house was so small they might get on each other's nerves after all these years. It had been different when they were young, privacy didn't seem to matter, and anyway, there was a limit to how much charity a person could take. Jackie had her dignity to think about.

The day's events had taken Lisa's mind off her own problems, at least. Tomorrow morning she was going to see a solicitor about the divorce, and she dreaded the unpleasantness ahead.

'Of course you can't *prove* the marriage wasn't consummated,' said Alan Peel. He was a grave, portly man with an old-fashioned manner that made him appear older than his years – she guessed he was about her own age and she felt embarrassed discussing such intimate matters with him.

'He can't prove it was,' she replied.

'The question is, why stay? If you claimed non-consummation a week, a month, after the wedding, it would be more convincing. Four years and it becomes questionable. People will wonder why you didn't leave.'

'Don't *you* believe me?'

'Of course I do,' he said soothingly. 'But we have to look at this from the judge's point of view. Why *did* you stay?' he asked curiously.

She shrugged. 'At first, I thought one day he'd . . . well, manage it, though he never tried again. Then I'd got used to the life we led. I began to enjoy politics and I loved Ferris Hall – that's his home – and Broxley. I was fond of Tony, too, in a way. We got on famously for a long time though I gradually became disillusioned. Now there's nothing left except hate on his side and indifference on mine.'

'I see,' he said blandly. 'Now, about the settlement he mentioned. It's been done before, the man getting alimony or a lump-sum payment when the wife is the wealthier partner.' He gave a dry smile. 'When you think about it, it's only fair. You'd expect something off him if things were the other way round.'

'Fair!' she gasped. 'He only married me for my money.'

'And women never marry men for theirs?'

'If that's how you think, I'll get someone else,' she said angrily.

'My dear lady, I'm only pointing out the realities.' Did all solicitors look and sound so pompous, she wondered. 'I'm on your side in this, of course, that's what you're paying me for, but surely you prefer the facts to blandishments?'

'I suppose so,' she muttered. 'But it seems unfair in my case.'

'Well, I'll get things in motion and be in touch.'

Lisa stood up. As he accompanied her to the door, the solicitor said, 'We were at boarding school together, you know.'

Her doubts returned. 'You and Tony? But should you be acting for me, in that case?'

He raised a reassuring hand. 'Don't worry, I've never met him since. I wouldn't want to, to be perfectly frank. He was never a very popular chap. Had a thing about his father, always complaining he kept him short of cash. I remember he was a bit of a gambler, even then.'

Perhaps she should get involved in something, Lisa thought vaguely. A play, a movie, something to take her mind off the divorce rather than just sitting waiting for things to happen. A few weeks ago she'd been offered a role in a four-part television drama, though it was probably too late to take that up now. Nothing had come in since and there was no doubt about it, the older an actress became, the fewer parts she was offered. It was even worse in films, where the Robert Mitchums and John Waynes went on forever, playing romantic leads well into their sixties, usually opposite women less than half their age.

Maybe Tony had got over his rage by now and had come to see sense, and everything would go through without a hitch. After all, she knew so many awful things about him which could be brought up in court and make him seem unworthy of a settlement. There was little he could say about her – only that business with Christy . . .

Jackie was the first to telephone. 'Have you seen this morning's *Meteor*?' she asked.

'You know I'd never read a rag like that,' said Lisa indignantly. 'I'm surprised you do.'

'I only bought it because of the front-page headline. I think you'd better get a copy straight away, Lisa.'

'Why, what does it say?'

'It's best you read it for yourself.'

'*MP TO DIVORCE EX-PORN QUEEN WIFE.*'

The *Meteor* was stuffed in a wire rack outside the newsagent's shop along with all the other dailies, and when Lisa read the headline she didn't immediately connect it with herself and wondered what on earth Jackie was talking about. Then she looked more closely at the full-length photograph of a young, virtually naked woman beneath it and several seconds later, realised it was a still from *Easy Dreams*. The picture was of Cassie Royale – in other words, herself – wearing that black negligée with the feather border, and standing in front of a window, one arm stretched upwards holding the curtain, the other on her hips and looking the wanton, abandoned woman she was supposed to be.

'Oh bugger!' she said out loud.

'Sir Anthony Molyneux, Conservative MP for Broxley in South Yorkshire, yesterday instituted divorce proceedings against his wife, the aging beauty, Lisa Angelis. Sir Anthony claimed it had been brought to his notice that his wife had once starred in pornographic films.

' "Of course I never knew this when we married," Sir Anthony told our reporter yesterday. "But now I do, it leaves me with no alternative but to ask for a divorce. After all, I owe it to my constituents. A person in my position must have a wife who is above reproach . . ." '

Lisa took off her glasses and folded the paper in disgust. 'Aging!' she said to herself incredulously. 'AGING!'

Gertie Lomax telephoned later. 'We've had a couple of reporters round asking questions. Nearly everybody here is on your side, but Fergus said Tony's got a private detective digging into your past, so be prepared for more stuff like this.'

'Are you upset?' asked Nellie, calling from Liverpool.

'Not a bit,' said Lisa. 'I only took my clothes off in one movie. It was daring then, but not now, and *Easy Dreams* is regarded as a classic of its kind. It's even been on television a couple of times – they wouldn't do that if it was pornographic. All that bothers me is being called aging.'

Alan Peel said, 'This kind of publicity won't do any good, I'm afraid. Judges are very conservative and even if this newspaper report is totally exaggerated, it'll look bad if it's produced in court.'

Lisa had several more sympathetic calls that day and a few from newspapers asking for her opinion on the *Meteor*'s revelations.

'I wouldn't call them "revelations",' she told them. '*Easy Dreams* has always been available for anybody to see. One thing, though – would you refer to someone only fifty-four as "aging"?'

In fact, the publicity turned out to be advantageous. The following day, Lisa was offered three new parts – two stage plays and a movie – and she accepted the latter, an Edwardian comedy called *Barney's Castle*. It didn't matter that the pay was a tenth of what she would have got in Hollywood. The film was being made in London, which meant she wouldn't have to move away. She needed to be on hand in case Tony had any more tricks up his sleeve.

'TEN THINGS "LADY PORN" WOULDN'T WANT PEOPLE TO KNOW.'

It was several weeks later, and although this time the article wasn't on the front page of the *Meteor*, it still took up a lot of space on page eight. As she read it, Lisa felt a sense of real fright. How on earth had Tony's detective discovered some of this?

'Angelis walked out on her first husband after nine months of marriage. Brian Smith never remarried and his mother Dorothy claims he is a broken man.

'Angelis shared her Hollywood home with TWO men.

'Angelis' third husband, Joseph Dent, was the most hated man in Hollywood.

'*Angelis began an affair with fellow actor Hugo Swann during the making of a movie directed by her second husband, Busby Van Dolen.*'

. . . and so on.

Lisa felt sick. The rest of the article was lies, nasty gossip, claiming she'd had affairs with people she'd never met, caused scenes on set, slapped a director's face, but it was horrible to think of people delving into her past and inventing fictional stories to blacken her. Thank goodness Dorothy Smith hadn't told them about the baby Brian thought he'd fathered, that would have sounded really awful. Probably Brian was too ashamed to let people know.

'No comment,' she told other newspapers when they called.

'Aren't you going to fight back?' one reporter asked. 'Surely there's some dirt to be dug up on your husband?'

Alan Peel had advised her to say nothing to reporters. 'If they start printing stuff about him, it'll only make him more anxious to get at you. Keep your distance and your dignity, stay above the fray and people will get tired of a one-sided slanging match. Tony will start to look as if he's hounding you.'

Lisa told the reporter, 'No comment on that, either. However, I'd just refer you to *Private Eye*, the June 1983 edition. You might find something interesting there.'

No one on the set of *Barney's Castle* took any notice of the *Meteor*'s exposure. In their time several had been targets of the gutter press and to Lisa's relief they all regarded it as a bit of a joke.

Where was Ralph? It wasn't until Jackie asked about him that Lisa realised she hadn't seen him for ages – the older you got the faster time seemed to fly by and it was more than a year since they'd last met. She asked around, but nobody knew where he was. Adam, his friend, had disappeared too. Then out of the blue she learnt that Matthew Jenks, the playwright, had died of AIDS a few months before. Ralph had probably known Matthew was dying and she remembered how distraught he'd been, knowing he was the cause of Gary's death.

Lisa felt deeply hurt that he'd just disappeared without letting her know, but despite all her efforts to discover his whereabouts, there was no trace of Ralph anywhere.

The divorce proceedings seemed to take forever. A month would pass between each exchange of letters and when Lisa demanded the reason for the delay, Alan Peel said patiently, 'These matters can't be hurried.'

Tony was still seeking a settlement and she continued to refuse. 'He's not getting a penny,' she insisted.

'I feel bound to advise that if you agreed to pay him a large sum now, a million pounds say, this harassment in the press would cease,' her solicitor told her. 'He just wants to blacken your name so that when the case comes to court it will go in his favour. He'll demand a settlement and might get *more* than a million if it's left to the judge to decide.'

'If and when the case comes to court, there's a lot of things I can reveal about Tony,' said Lisa, thinking of the bribes and the gambling, and the attempt to close down Spring Engineering – not to mention his first wife's suicide.

'As you wish,' said Alan Peel with a sigh.

'Something's happened here,' said Nellie in a frightened voice. 'We've had a reporter sniffing round asking questions about you, and Joan's told him something.'

'What on earth could Joan have said?' laughed Lisa. 'There's nothing she knows that you and the boys don't.'

'I've no idea,' Nellie answered. 'But whatever it was, she said he'd paid a lot of money for it. She came round last night and I've never seen her so excited – she was really on a high. You know she's always hated you since Mam died.'

Lisa wondered why her stomach felt on edge when she woke up next morning. Then she remembered – *Joan.* Although she'd laughed off Nellie's warning, after she'd put down the phone a nagging sense of worry set in and last night she'd lain in bed thinking about things she hadn't thought of in years. Unpleasant, horrible things she'd deliberately pushed to the back of her mind. Had Joan known about the abortion, for instance? That awful time was suddenly so real again, so clear in her mind that she could remember the pain as acutely as if it had happened yesterday.

All of this was Tony's fault and she cursed out loud, calling him every foul name she could think of until she remembered how thin the walls were and that Florence Dale might be listening.

The telephone rang beside her bed. 'What have you got to say about the article in today's *Meteor*?' a voice demanded.

'No comment!' She slammed the receiver down, got out of bed and threw on some clothes. It seemed strange later that she actually noticed what a lovely day it was – brisk and sunny, the streets still deserted at this early hour. The newsagent's was open but it was too soon for the papers to be outside. She asked for the *Meteor* and folded it so she wouldn't see the headline until she got home. Perhaps it was just her imagination, but did the Pakistani man who ran the shop, usually so friendly, deliberately avoid her eyes?

'*PORN QUEEN KILLED FATHER.*'

'*In a sworn statement to our reporter, Joan O'Brien, sister of Lisa Angelis, the porno actress, revealed that in 1945, her sister stabbed their father to death.*

' "*I saw her,*" *claimed Joan, who lives in a council flat (Angelis is a million-airess several times over!), "and she let my mother take the blame." Joan went on to say that she has never forgotten that terrible night. "I don't know why Lizzie" (as Angelis was once known) "did it, but all I know is, as God is my witness, I saw her and I've never forgiven her for it."*

'*Joan O'Brien went on to say that whilst her father was not exactly the ideal parent, "He was a good, hard-working man who cared for his family in his own way and we were always well-fed and well-clothed."*

'In a final emotional outburst, Miss O'Brien claimed, "It's a relief to get this out of my system. It's been gnawing away at me for years but I could never bring myself to tell anyone – until the Meteor *came along!"' '*

Jackie came within the hour, though by then there were already two reporters banging on the front door, so she had to enter via Florence Dale's, and sneak in by the back door.

'Oh, you poor, poor thing!' She took Lisa in her arms and pressed her against her still-ample bosom. 'Here, let me make you some tea.' She took over answering the telephone. 'No comment!' she barked several times that morning. Sometimes it was friends calling to offer condolences, as if Lisa were dead, or one of the O'Briens to say they were right behind her. Even Busby had heard the news thousands of miles away in Los Angeles and offered to come over immediately but Jackie, in response to Lisa's mouthed 'no', told him there was no need.

It was midday; the telephone rang for the umpteenth time and Jackie picked it up. 'It's your solicitor,' she whispered. 'Do you want to speak to him?'

'I suppose I'd better.' Lisa got up listlessly.

'I've spoken to my partner who specialises in libel,' Alan Peel said brusquely. 'He thinks you should sue. This time Tony's gone too far.'

'It's no use,' said Lisa dully. 'What the *Meteor* says is true. I *did* kill my father.'

46

'My father was an animal who used my mother as a punch-bag for years,' said Kevin. On television he looked dignified, the salt of the earth, a working man, but getting old now. His face was more wrinkled than Lisa remembered. Unafraid of the camera, he spoke with the integrity of one confident that what he said was the complete and utter truth.

The news had actually reached television, had become a *cause célèbre*, far more interesting than politics or foreign affairs – a juicy item on a par with the Jeremy Thorpe case, the Profumo affair, Lord Lucan's disappearance.

'So your sister Joan is lying, then?' said the interviewer.

Kevin was standing outside his house, a modern semi-detached in Litherland. 'She probably doesn't remember much about Dad. He drank his wages and he didn't give a sh . . . a damn about us kids, except to give us a swipe when we went near him. It was our mother who kept the family together.'

'But what about this amazing accusation, that it was your other sister, Lisa Angelis, as she's now called, not your mother, who stabbed your father to death?'

Kevin began to look uneasy for the first time. 'I'm afraid I know nothing about that,' he said. 'It came as a total shock to me.'

'Your sister, Lisa, was invited to come on this programme, but she refused. What do you say to that?'

'I suspect she's in a state of shock. Wouldn't you be if something like this came up out of the blue after forty years?' demanded Kevin.

They'd even dug up a copy of the *Liverpool Echo* which reported that Kitty had been found Not Guilty of manslaughter. The newscaster concluded, 'Miss Angelis is in the middle of a bitter divorce battle with her husband, Sir Anthony Molyneux, MP for Broxley. Today, Sir Anthony said he was upset by the revelations. "Whatever my feelings for my wife, I think the *Meteor* has gone too far this time." '

'Bloody hypocrite,' seethed Jackie. 'What are we going to do?'

'I've no idea,' said Lisa.

'Oh my dear, you must come to. Stop acting like a zombie! We've got to fight this thing.'

'What would *you* do?'

Jackie paused. 'I've no idea,' she said eventually.

Somehow they managed to smile. 'What time is it?' asked Lisa.

'That was the ten o'clock news, love.'

'Mam used to call me love,' said Lisa. 'Poor Mam.' She lit a cigarette from the stub of her last one. Jackie had gone out and bought a hundred pack and there was hardly any whisky left in the bottle.

'Lisa,' Jackie said softly, 'I heard you tell your solicitor the newspaper story was true. Do you want to talk about it?'

So Lisa told her everything. When she'd finished, she told Jackie, 'You know, I'm almost pleased it's in the open. Like Joan said, it's been gnawing away inside me all my life. I've always had this restless, discontented feeling and could never identify the reason for it. Now I know what it was: guilt, a need to confess and make atonement for my sins.'

'Shall I open the post again this morning?' asked Jackie, coming in from the hall with a fat bundle of letters. Yesterday it had been mainly requests for interviews, a few anonymous letters which Jackie said there was no need to read, and messages of support from friends.

'Please,' said Lisa. After two nights of broken sleep she still felt unable to cope with the situation.

'More demands for a personal interview – this one offers five figures for your story. Oh, you'd better read this.' She handed over a letter typed on stiff white paper.

Alan Peel no longer wished to represent her. '*Under the circumstances arising over the past few days, I do not feel I am the right person to act on your behalf in the divorce proceedings instituted against your husband.*'

'Shit! said Lisa.

'That's good,' said Jackie.

'What's good?'

'You swearing. It means you're starting to feel your old self again.'

'I'll *never* feel my old self again.'

'You will,' Jackie said confidently. 'Hey, this looks interesting. Milo Hanna would like you to be a guest on his chat show.'

'Not likely!' said Lisa. Milo Hanna was a national institution, a puckish Irishman who hosted a chat show which went out at peak viewing time every Wednesday to an audience of millions. 'I wouldn't dream of going on television. I hate those programmes where people are persuaded to tell their all by some ghoulish interviewer – Milo Hanna being one of the worst – and everybody, including the audience, ends up in tears. All that false emotion makes me want to puke.'

'You're definitely getting better,' said Jackie firmly. 'If that's the case, it's time you started putting your side of the story about. If your lousy solicitor hadn't told you not to speak to the press, then your equally lousy husband mightn't have gone as far as he did.'

Lisa lit another cigarette. 'Honestly, Jackie, I haven't a clue which way to turn. I'd love to fight back, but how do you fight the truth? If I revealed that Tony ate newborn babies for lunch, so what? It has no bearing on this.'

'You could say *why* you did it,' Jackie said. 'Why you killed him.'

'Jesus, Jackie, I could never, *never* do that! I feel unclean just thinking about it. No, the best thing to do is hide out somewhere till it blows over. When the ratpack go away, I'll escape.'

'You know it'll never blow over. They'll track you down wherever you are.

I think you should come out fighting.' Jackie was opening another letter, a small square envelope containing a sheet of cheap lined paper. 'Here's another you'd better read.'

The writing was barely legible, a shaky childish scrawl.

'Dear God, Lizzie, what have I done? I'm sorry, I'll never forgive myself. That man was so persuasive and he asked so many questions. I keep thinking of Mam and how she would have hated me. I'm truly sorry for everything. Joan.'

'Poor Joan,' said Lisa. 'She probably feels worse than I do.'

Jackie nodded. 'Probably.'

'And Nellie and the boys are really angry with her. Perhaps I should go and see her.'

'Not now, Lisa, wait till things have simmered down. You're probably both too emotional just now.'

'Perhaps you're right.' Lisa grinned. 'You've been right an awful lot lately. I used to think I was the only one who was right and you were always wrong.'

'That's right,' giggled Jackie. 'Sorry, I shouldn't laugh.'

'Please do, it makes me feel better. After all, what's the saying – "Laugh and the world laughs with you . . ." '

' "Cry and you cry alone",' finished Jackie. 'Or what about, "laughter is the best medicine" – though it depends on what's wrong. It wouldn't do a burst appendix much good.'

'Damn it all, Jackie,' Lisa said suddenly, 'let's get thoroughly plastered like we used to. Where's that whisky bottle?'

'It was me that got plastered, you never did. Anyway, it's nearly empty,' Jackie said ruefully. 'I could buy another – sod my diet.'

'There's half a dozen under the sink. Busby sends them by the crate, best American bourbon.'

Milo Hanna himself telephoned that afternoon. By then Jackie was too hung over to answer and it was Lisa who managed a slurred 'Hallo.'

'I'd love to have you on my show next week,' he coaxed in his lilting Irish voice.

'Absolutely not,' said Lisa. To her surprise she couldn't help thinking how nice he sounded and almost felt mean for refusing.

'You know I was born in the same village as your mam?' he said. 'My auld mam remembers her distinctly. A pretty little Irish colleen, Mam says she was, blonde and blue-eyed with skin as soft as clover.'

He'd done his homework, finding out where Mam was born. Perhaps Kevin had told him. She found herself smiling and said accusingly, 'I know your sort, a silver-tongued Paddy who was born kissing the Blarney stone. I bet you could talk the hind leg off a donkey.'

'Only if he wanted to be three-legged,' laughed Milo Hanna. 'If you came on my show, I wouldn't ask questions you didn't want. We'll talk about your film career, your favourite plays, the people you knew in Hollywood. We'd work out a list of questions beforehand.'

Lisa imagined his impish leprechaun face grinning into the receiver. 'I don't like you much,' she said with a hiccup. 'In fact, I hardly ever watch your show.'

'Ah Lisa, I'll cry myself to sleep tonight. You are a cruel, cruel woman to be sure.'

'You'll get over it.'

'I never will, you've cut me to the quick,' he said sadly. 'Still, I suppose it was too much to ask. It would take a lot of courage to face several million viewers feeling as you must do now.'

'Are you suggesting I'm a coward?'

'Of course not! It's just that I understand your reluctance. Only a very special lady could raise the nerve to come on my show and be interviewed, even though the questions would be as gentle as the breath of a newborn lamb.'

Lisa burst out laughing. 'For Chrissakes, all right, I'll come on your show, but I don't know what good it will do me.'

'What have I done?' she said later in an appalled voice. 'I must have been mad to agree.'

'You weren't mad, you were pissed,' said Jackie. She rose to her feet unsteadily. 'I'm going back to Earl's Court for a bath.'

'But you can have a bath here,' protested Lisa.

'In a few months maybe, but not yet. Your bath's so narrow, last night I got stuck and had visions of the fire brigade hoisting me out. Anyway, I'm in the middle of packing. Don't forget I'm moving into my new flat next week. Will you be all right on your own? I'll be back first thing tomorrow.'

'Of course I will.' Lisa didn't feel nearly as confident as she sounded. 'You've been an absolute rock these last few days, I don't know what I would have done without you.'

'You would have managed,' said Jackie. 'People always manage. Even I did, in my own, muddled way.'

'I won't drink any more,' thought Lisa when Jackie left. 'In fact *I'll* soak in the bath for an hour and then make a cup of tea.'

She glanced out of the window. The reporters had disappeared. After two days of her refusing their noisy demands for an interview, they'd finally gone home disappointed.

It wasn't until she sank into the warm bath that Lisa realised how exhausted she was. Her body throbbed with tiredness and in no time she fell asleep and woke to find the water had gone cold. She put on a robe and combed her wet hair. The face that stared back from the dressing-table mirror was yellow with fatigue. She certainly looked an 'aging' beauty tonight, she thought dejectedly.

'How come you never change?' she demanded of Victoria, who was sitting on the bed, staring at her wide-eyed. 'You're as pretty now as the day Ralph gave you to me.'

She was putting the kettle on when there was a knock on the door. She glanced at the clock. It was nearly midnight, which meant it could only be Jackie, who'd had second thoughts and decided to come back, or possibly Nellie who'd been threatening to come for days.

It was neither Nellie nor Jackie but Jim Harrison who stood on the doorstep.

She took his coat, sat him down and offered him a cup of tea.

'You're the last person I expected to see,' she said as she sat opposite, conscious what a dismal picture she must make, compared with the last time they'd met, at Fergus's party the previous year.

'Fergus died yesterday,' he said abruptly.

She groaned. 'I'm so sorry, he was a lovely person. I'll write to Gertie tomorrow.'

'He was one of the finest men I've ever known,' Jim said simply. 'Though he always knew I never voted for him.'

'He'll be sadly missed in Broxley.' It was an effort to stop herself from bursting into tears.

'When I told Gertie I was coming to see you she let me into a secret.' He looked at Lisa accusingly. 'Why didn't you tell me you'd bought Spring Engineering?'

'I didn't see the need,' she said defensively. 'Have you come all the way from Yorkshire to be angry with me?'

'Of course not!'

'Then why have you come?'

He didn't answer immediately, then he said awkwardly, 'I'm probably making a fool of myself.'

'You're good at that. You made a fool of yourself when we first met and a fool of me at the same time.'

He managed a grin. 'Ouch! Don't rub it in. I thought you'd come to suss us out on behalf of your charming husband.'

'You shouldn't make such sweeping assumptions.'

'I never have since.'

'How do you intend making a fool of yourself tonight?' She had a feeling about what he was going to say and hoped she was right. He'd occupied her thoughts a lot since they'd met at Fergus's party and she felt safe with him there. Nothing could happen to her whilst he was here, so big and reassuring, looking uncomfortable in that silly little striped chair.

'We have a strange relationship, you and I. We seem to meet once a year, yet —' he paused.

'Yet what?' she pressed him.

He still hesitated. 'Yet I feel there's something between us,' he said eventually, the words coming out in a rush. '*Am* I making a fool of myself, Lisa? Is there some other man in the background waiting to marry you when your divorce comes through?'

'There's no one,' she said softly.

'What about us? Is it all a product of my overheated imagination?'

She laughed. 'You're far too steady and conventional to have an overheated imagination.'

He gave her a look that made her insides shiver. 'You'd be amazed at how unconventional my imagination can get at times, Lisa. Now it's you who's making assumptions.'

'I'm sorry.' She took a deep breath. 'You're right – there *is* something between us. Even on the day we met when I hated you, I liked you. Does that make sense?'

'Perfect sense.'

'What happens now?' She suddenly felt relaxed and happy for the first time in days.

'This,' he said and came over and sat beside her on the settee and took her in his arms. He didn't kiss her, just wrapped himself around her and put a big hand on her cheek and pressed her head against his shoulder. She could feel his strong chin against her still-wet hair and after a while she fell asleep. When she woke up it was still dark outside and her left arm was stiff. She moved it gently, so as not to disturb him, but he was still awake.

'I only came down to sort things out between us,' he whispered. 'I thought it might help while you're in this fix to know I'm always there if you need me.'

'It does,' she said happily and snuggled back into his arms.

When she woke up again a glimmer of daylight showed through the curtains. This time he was asleep and she moved her head and watched him. After a while she picked up his hand which lay heavily on her hip and moved it inside her robe onto her breast. He stirred, his eyes opened and she reached up and turned his face towards her own and kissed him softly on the lips.

Oh God, she had never been made love to like this before, so slowly, so passionately, so satisfyingly. She'd spent her entire life waiting for this, the ultimate, perfect giving between two people in love, the mutual respect, the adoration of each other's bodies.

When they had finished and she lay naked in his arms, he said softly, 'I have to get back, I've a factory to run.'

Lisa nodded sleepily. A few minutes later she felt her robe being tucked gently around her, then the door clicked and he was gone.

When Jackie let herself in, later in the morning, she found Lisa fast asleep on the settee. 'You idiot! Fancy dropping off down here. I bet you'll feel half-dead all day, you can't have slept properly.'

'I had the most perfect night's sleep ever.' Lisa sat up with a yawn. 'But I wouldn't say no to a cup of tea.'

'Where are the other guests?' asked Lisa.

The smartly dressed young woman who showed her into the hospitality room said, 'You're the only one.'

'But he usually has three.'

'Not always. If it's someone special, Milo gives them half an hour.'

'Why am I special? I didn't expect half an hour.'

The woman's eyes glazed over. 'You'd better take that up with Milo, darling. He'll be along in a minute. Help yourself to refreshments while you wait.'

She left and Lisa said to Jackie darkly, 'I'd only expected a ten-minute interview.'

Jackie had leapt on a plate of sandwiches and was rapidly devouring the lot. 'I'll be glad when this is all over, it's played havoc with my diet. Here, have some wine, calm your nerves.'

'It's a good job I don't want a sandwich to calm my nerves, they're nearly all gone.' She lit a cigarette and took some wine. 'Where's that bastard Milo Hanna?'

'Have you got your answers rehearsed?' said Jackie through a mouthful of bread.

'It's rude to speak with your mouth full. No, I haven't. We've agreed on a list of questions, but I haven't prepared the answers in case they sound forced.'

'Ah, my dear Lisa! Begorrah, you look lovely tonight.' Milo Hanna came in dressed in a velvet suit and a flowing black and white bow tie. With his dark wavy hair, he looked like a middle-aged Rupert Brooke.

'Why have I got a whole half hour?' she demanded immediately. 'You usually have three guests. Why —?'

He held up his hands defensively. 'Because we're showing a few sequences from your movies,' he said quickly. 'My darling girl, don't be so suspicious.'

'I've good reason to be suspicious, Milo. I hadn't agreed to do your show for five minutes before it was advertised on television.'

'That was so you couldn't back off, have second thoughts.'

'I did.'

'So, I did the right thing.' He gave a sly, mischievous grin. 'Have some more wine, my lovely one. We'll be on in ten minutes.'

'Y'know, I reckon that man's a bloody fake,' said Lisa when he'd gone. 'I bet he's been no nearer Ireland than those sandwiches. He was probably born in the Home Counties and talks like Noël Coward at home.'

'I think he's lovely,' said Jackie comfortably. 'How do you feel?'

'Terrified!' Lisa went over to the mirror. 'How do I look?'

'Lovely, brave, terrified.'

Lisa had agonised for hours over what to wear. It took days to settle on a calf-length strapless dress of soft turquoise crêpe and a dark green velvet jacket. Her hair was drawn severely back into a plump bun on the nape of her neck.

'Oh God, Jackie, I've got a grey hair – no two, three. What a time to find out!'

'You're lucky, I went grey before I was forty. And look at me now!'

'Three minutes, Miss Angelis.' The young woman had come back.

'Good luck, Lisa.'

'This is worse than any first night. Is everybody frightened?' She clasped the young woman's hand tightly as she was led to the side of the set. Milo Hanna was waiting, a script in his hand, unsmiling for once. The warm-up comedian was coming to the end of his spiel. Lisa glanced at the audience. Christ, the whole of Broxley was there: Jim and the Masons, Gertie Lomax, half a dozen other people she recognised . . . Nellie and Stan were there too, and all her brothers – some with their wives – though she'd known they were coming.

The familiar introductory music began and as soon as it faded, Milo Hanna ran on stage to a burst of enthusiastic applause. She couldn't quite hear what he was saying and was surprised when she was pushed out and suddenly she was walking towards him, her hand out in greeting and he kissed her fondly as if they were lifelong friends.

He began by asking about her Hollywood career, about Busby and Joseph Dent. He showed clips from several of her movies, beginning with *The Opportunist*, her first speaking part, then *Easy Dreams* – much to her relief she was fully clothed – followed by *The Matchstick Man*, *Attrition* and finally, *Hearts and Flowers*. Every time the short sequences ended the audience clapped.

'You've had a long and distinguished career,' said Milo Hanna. 'Several of those films are regarded as classics.'

'I've been very lucky,' she said modestly.

'Tell us about Joseph Dent. He had the reputation of being a bit of an ogre. What was it like being married to him?'

Lisa's eyes lit up as she described Dent's strange personality. 'I loved him dearly,' she said finally.

'What about Gary Maddox? If I remember rightly, your name was linked with his for a long time. He lived with you, didn't he?'

She shifted uneasily in her seat. Gary was down on the list of questions she'd agreed to answer, but only in the context of a fellow actor and director, co-founder of O'Brien Productions. Milo Hanna had departed from the script.

'Gary was one of my closest friends,' she said eventually. 'That was all we were, friends.'

'And what a good friend you turned out to be, Lisa,' he said warmly. 'I understand Gary was one of the first AIDS victims and you nursed him till he died.'

She looked up at him quickly, her eyes filling with unexpected tears. Who on earth had told him that? His researchers were better than Tony's. 'That's what friends are for,' she muttered.

To her amazement, the audience began to clap and she felt a surge of anger at such an intimate revelation being regarded as entertainment.

Milo, perfectly attuned to his guest's mood, changed the subject to the theatre. He asked her about Matthew Jenks' plays and how she liked acting with Ralph Layton. Then, 'You got married again, didn't you, and acquired a title, Lady Elizabeth Molyneux?'

'I did,' she said coldly. If he asked her questions about Tony or the divorce, she'd pour the jug of orange juice over him. That was also a subject she'd declared out of bounds.

'Not only a title, but an engineering company. That's a strange thing for an actress to buy. Why did you do that?'

She didn't answer for several seconds and someone in the audience shouted, 'Tell him, Lisa.'

'Someone was planning to build a hotel on the site. I thought it should remain a factory.'

There was another burst of applause and with an autocratic gesture Milo held up his hand and the clapping ceased. 'Was this someone your husband?' He was like a bloody magician the way he manipulated her – and the audience.

'It was my husband, yes,' she answered, wondering if Tony was watching.

Milo began to talk about Liverpool – 'City of the Stars' he called it – and ran through the famous names who had been born there.

'Do you miss it?'

'No,' she said, immediately regretting her honesty. If he asked why, all she could say was that it held too many bad memories and he might want to know what they were. She looked at the studio clock. Another ten minutes to go! Surely they'd reached the end of the agreed questions?

He was looking down at the script in his hand, biting his lip as if the next question was going to be difficult. Lisa could tell it was a deliberately staged gesture on his part.

'Did you kill your dad, Lisa?'

Oh, Jesus! The audience gasped then went silent and Lisa stared down at her hands. What good was there in denying it? she thought despairingly.

'I did,' she said eventually. 'Yes, I did. I killed him.'

There was a hissing sound as three hundred people drew in their breath simultaneously and Lisa felt her head begin to spin.

'And why should a thirteen-year-old girl stab her auld dad to death, now?' asked Milo Hanna gently.

She looked at him accusingly. 'You've betrayed me, you bastard,' her eyes said. He stared back at her unblinkingly, his face full of what looked like genuine concern.

The audience could have disappeared for all the sound they made. She could imagine them, Nellie, her brothers, Jim, all on tenterhooks waiting for her reply.

Milo Hanna reached out and took her hand. 'You'll feel better for the telling,' he whispered. It was another staged move; the whisper would have been perfectly audible to the viewers through his mike.

Suddenly, she began to speak, though she hadn't meant to. Words began to pour from her mouth in a rush she couldn't stop. She felt as if she no longer had control of her vocal chords. It was someone else, a stranger, who was babbling all this stuff.

'Becasue he had been abusing me for a long time,' the strange voice said. 'Because he made me pregnant when I was thirteen and I didn't know what to do. There was no one to turn to, no one. I was ashamed and terrified. What would Mam think? I tried to abort the baby myself with a metal skewer that belonged to my brothers and —' The voice stopped. Lisa looked at Milo Hanna in surprise. Had she really said all that?

Apparently she had because he asked, 'And what happened then, my love?'

'I can't remember much. They took me to hospital, but it wasn't until years later I found . . .' she paused.

'Found what?' he said encouragingly.

'I could never have any more children. I would have loved my own children.'

There were only the two of them in the entire world, her and Milo, under the bright lights together. He was looking at her protectively and quite out of the blue, her feelings for him changed and she felt an unexpected surge of love.

'About your auld dad,' he said softly. 'How did the stabbing come about? Did he come after you again, then?'

'He probably would have done, eventually. It was Joan he was after the night I killed him.'

'Joan!' Milo pulled his chair forward until their knees were touching. 'Why don't you tell us about it, Lisa?'

She felt as if she would do anything for him. 'It was the night I came home from hospital,' she said. 'I was in the downstairs bed with Mam. Dad came in. He was drunk – he was always drunk. After a while I heard the springs of the bed go and Joan cried out. I knew what he was going to do, I just knew, so I got the breadknife to warn him off and sure enough, when I got upstairs he was after her. I can't recall how it happened – but I killed him,' she finished simply.

There was another swift intake of breath from the audience and Lisa turned round, startled. She'd forgotten they were there.

Milo Hanna was asking another question in his soft, cajoling way. 'But my love, if *you* could hear your dad so clearly, couldn't your mam have heard him too?'

Lisa burst into tears. 'That's the worst part of all,' she sobbed. 'Realising that Mam knew *and she never did anything about it.* Perhaps that's why I didn't care when she took the blame for killing him.'

She wondered why there was music and why, although Milo was still holding her hand, he was talking to a point beyond her, his voice still thick with sympathy as he said goodnight and announced his guests for next week.

'There, I expect you'll feel a whole lot better now.' He patted her arm and got up. Lisa heard him say to someone, 'The whole country'll be in tears after that,' and she was left sitting alone feeling as if the world had turned upside down.

As the spotlights were turned off, the studio lights came on and there was a buzz of conversation. Lisa saw Nellie and her brothers coming towards her, tears streaming down their cheeks. For a minute she watched them numbly, then jumped to her feet and ran to the hospitality room where Jackie had been watching the programme on a monitor.

'Lisa, love!' she cried, but Lisa took no notice. She snatched up her bag and left the room, running out of the building as fast as her unsteady legs would carry her.

Epilogue

47

She'd been in the cottage less than a week when the dog appeared out of the wild, overgrown garden. He stood growling at her, a tatty, unkempt-looking animal, incredibly ugly with one eye half-closed and long ears caked with dirt. Bones jutted through his mangy knotted fur. Despite his aggression, he had a pathetic, desperate air, as if he wanted to be friendly but didn't know how.

Lisa had no experience of dogs. 'Here, boy.' She patted her knee but he refused to budge, though when she went in the house through the back door, he followed furtively, shambling awkwardly on his too-short legs, going straight for the gap between the sink and the old cooker. He sniffed and turned dejectedly away. She wondered if he'd belonged to the previous tenants and that's where his food had been left.

She looked through the fridge for something a dog might eat and found some ham.

'Here, boy.' He was standing outside, looking lost and lonely. When he saw the food, he bounded over and gobbled it up whilst his stub of a tail wagged briefly. 'Poor boy, are you hungry?' He growled again. 'You're not very friendly, are you?'

There wasn't much else to give him. She smeared jam on a few slices of bread and filled a dish with water. 'Your manners are atrocious,' she said as he demolished the food and drank the water with loud satisfied gulps.

He refused to come into the house that night, though in the morning he was waiting outside – to Lisa's surprise she found herself hoping he would be – still growling, but looking up expectantly. She put an old cushion in a cardboard box and left it in the kitchen with the back door open. A few days later she went out and found him in it, fast asleep, though when she approached his head came up and he growled. By then she'd bought dog food from the small supermarket in the village and was feeding him daily. He began to sleep regularly in the kitchen and one night when she was watching television, he nudged the door open with his black billiard-ball nose and slunk in, throwing himself in front of the fireplace with a deep, heartrending sigh.

'I've got to call you something,' she said thoughtfully. 'How about Rambo? You seem a very tough dog.' Later, she felt his nose snuggle against her feet. She reached down and gingerly patted him. His only response was to stretch his nose further across her slippers. The following week he allowed her to bath him, emerging from the filthy water like a drowned rat. When she tried to dry him, he ran around the kitchen like a mad thing, snatching at the towel. In the end, she gave up, and was astonished to find that when he had dried naturally, his fur had turned into a mass of dark brown fluff.

'Can I comb you?' she pleaded. She'd already bought a wicked-looking metal-toothed comb. He stood patiently as she pulled at the knots in his fur and by the time she'd finished, he bore little resemblance to the creature who'd emerged out of the long grass a month ago. She picked him up, cradling him in her arms like a baby. 'You're *still* ugly, Rambo, but you've got charm, there's no doubt about it. We're going to be the greatest friends because we need each other.'

For her, the cottage was a halfway house, a place where she could learn to live again. Once its exterior plaster walls had been painted pink, but the pink had faded to a washed-out sickly oatmeal. An old man had lived there until he died ten years ago and relatives were still embroiled in litigation over his Will so the cottage had been rented furnished to a variety of tenants. Only those desperate for a roof over their heads would want to live in such an isolated spot, the only house in a long narrow unmade road, which led from one village to another. The road was hardly ever used: years ago, a proper one had been built two miles away.

The house was full of the old man's furniture. 'Could this ever have been new!' thought Lisa when she first walked into the big living room which led directly off the front door. A leatherette three-piece, a chipped veneered sideboard, a scratched gate-legged table. The stone floor was covered with faded, rotten linoleum, eaten away at the edges.

She only bought a few things: new mattress and bedding, a fridge and television, a couple of table lamps – enough to sustain her, make life comfortable. The cottage had been rented sight unseen through a local estate agent. It bore little resemblance to the description she'd been sent but it didn't matter. She liked its quiet, lonely situation and no one in the village appeared to recognise her, at least if they did they said nothing, respecting her privacy.

It was a year now since she had moved in; she had come in the summer when the garden was abuzz with insects and filled with the vivid scent of flowers. In the garden shed, Lisa found a pair of rusty shears and an old-fashioned mower and she attacked the garden with vigour. She could have bought a modern mower and done the work in a fraction of the time, but stubbornly persisted with the old implements until the grass was cut and a relatively smooth lawn was revealed. Then she dug up the borders and pruned the shrubs, repairing the fence with odd pieces of wood.

As she stood at the top of the long garden early in the autumn throwing a ball for Rambo, she'd rarely felt so proud of her handiwork. He came galloping up the garden on his tiny legs and she held out her arms; he leapt right into them and began to lick her face. She rolled over, laughing, trying to escape his excited show of affection and he licked the back of her neck and behind her ears.

She'd never dreamt it was possible to love an animal so much. Perhaps it was because his love for her was so unreserved and spontaneous it was hard not to respond. His previous owners had treated him badly, she'd been told, leaving him to fend for himself whilst they went away, sometimes for weeks on end. Then they'd left for good without him.

Sometimes she put him in the back of the car and drove to Broxley dales where they ran till both were exhausted and his tongue hung out the side of his mouth like a moist pink tassel. Then she'd go home and spend the rest of the day replying to the letters which had arrived after the Milo Hanna programme.

Those letters! Those awful, tragic letters.

She'd rushed out of the studio onto the street without any idea of where she was, for she hadn't noticed the route the car which had collected them from home had taken. What time was it, what day, what year? What did it matter, anyway? The embarrassment and shame she felt left little room for anything else, though after a while she stopped running when she became conscious of the odd looks on the faces of the people she passed, some drawing back in alarm as she came rushing towards them. Her breath was ragged, her feet hurt in the spiky heeled shoes. Eventually, she stopped altogether and saw that she was in the Strand; the sun was dipping behind the buildings on her left, which meant it was late evening.

What was she to do now? Where was she to go? She could never appear in public again. Never! There was a large hotel opposite and she went in and booked a room, registering herself as Mary Smith. 'Could you send a bottle . . . no, a pot of tea up straight away, please.'

At midnight she rang home, hoping Jackie would be there. She was.

'I don't want to talk,' Lisa said in response to the demands to know where she was, how did she feel and to please, please come back straight away. 'I only called to say I'm all right and I'll be in touch again soon.' She replaced the receiver in the middle of Jackie's rush of questions.

The front page of next morning's *Meteor* was stark.

'*WHAT A PERFORMANCE!*'

'*Lisa Angelis, the actress, gave the greatest performance of her life on the Milo Hanna Show last night. In an emotional display that made the blood curdle, the ex-porno queen attempted (unsuccessfully) to present herself as a saviour of the working man, a friend of the dying and an abused child. Surely no one was taken in by this? Even if it were all true, the fact remains that this woman is a confessed murderess . . .*'

Lisa screwed up the paper and threw it in a bin in the hotel lobby. It had all been a waste of time. All she'd done was to make things worse – and she cursed Milo Hanna with all her heart.

She remembered Ralph saying a long, long time ago: 'I'll always be there if you need me.'

The television had been on all day and she had her meals served in the room, though she scarcely touched the food. Most of the news bulletins showed an excerpt from the Milo Hanna Show, always the same one, the last few minutes when she'd broken down, and she stared at herself curiously. She hadn't thought herself capable of such an agonised, painful expression.

On one subsequent programme, a child psychologist explained how child abuse could affect people over their entire lives and a lawyer was interviewed on the legal position. 'There's no way she would be prosecuted after all this time,' he said. Unlike the *Meteor*, the coverage was entirely sympathetic.

The late-night news had reached a halfway point and was about to break for adverts when the announcer said, 'In the second half we'll deal with the question "Why has this woman been persecuted?" – and there she was on screen again, sitting next to Milo Hanna.

The adverts had never taken so long. She sat, willing them to end and the bulletin to begin again. When it did, the same excerpt was shown, followed by the child psychologist, the lawyer, then, to her surprise, all the damning *Meteor* headlines. Then the announcer said, 'Miss Angelis is in the throes of a bitter divorce battle with her husband, the Member of Parliament for Broxley, Sir Anthony Molyneux. It was revealed today that the industrialist, Colin Sowerby, a close business associate of Sir Anthony, is a member of the *Meteor*'s board of directors. People may well ask the question, "Should the press be used to persecute people on behalf of their friends?" '

'Oh, my God!' said Lisa. 'Now it all makes sense.'

The newscaster hadn't finished. 'In a final, dramatic move, Ralph Layton, the distinguished actor of stage and screen, issued a statement from his remote Scottish home where he is suffering from AIDS. "*In response to the* Meteor *'s claim that Lisa Angelis made up the facts about her father, every word she spoke is true,*" he said, "*I know, because she told me those same facts more than thirty years ago.*" '

She felt better, but it didn't really make much difference. She still couldn't face people, not with them knowing what had been done to her, what she had done to herself and to her dad, even though he had deserved it and she would do it again under the same circumstances.

After the programme finished, she called Jackie again. 'I'm going away for a while. Will you look after the house?'

'Of course I will. I'll move in here instead of the flat,' Jackie said tearfully. 'But Lisa, love, there's no need to hide. You wouldn't believe the calls we've had, the letters and visitors. Jim Harrison – you kept *him* a tight secret – is going up the wall with worry. He stayed here last night waiting for you and the studio said they've been inundated with mail; they're going to send it over.'

'Then you'll just have to re-direct it,' Lisa said. 'I'll let you know when I've found a place to live.'

Where in the world did she most want to go? The answer came immediately. Broxley! Not the town itself, but one of the nearby villages where she wouldn't be recognised. There she would decide what to do with the rest of her life.

But first of all, she had to find Ralph. She was devastated by the news that he had AIDS, though she'd suspected something was wrong for months. She telephoned the television studio and asked for the location of his home in Scotland.

'Even if we had that information, we wouldn't release it,' a cold voice told her. 'We've already had half a dozen calls from the press, I think he deserves to die in peace, don't you?'

'I'm not the press,' Lisa said quietly. 'I'm Lisa Angelis.'

'Oh!' The voice changed tone, became friendly. 'I was telling the truth before. Someone called Adam phoned the message in. He wouldn't give the address, just said it was up in the wilds of Scotland, though I've got a number. We had to phone back and check, in case the call was just a ruse. You can have that if you like. We promised to keep it confidential, but I guess it's okay to make an exception with you.'

'Please, oh please,' breathed Lisa.

She called immediately, her hands shaking as she pressed the numbers. Adam answered.

'It's Lisa,' she cried. 'Can I speak to Ralph?'

Adam said ruefully, 'We thought you'd track us down.'

'I want to see him, Adam. I want to be with him when—'

'When he dies?' he finished for her.

'Yes,' she sobbed.

'He doesn't want to see you, Lisa. He doesn't want to see anyone.'

'But he can't refuse to see me, not *me*!'

Adam didn't say anything for a while and she could hear a whispered mumbling in the background.

'He has difficulty speaking,' Adam said eventually, his voice wracked with pain. 'He said you did enough for Gary and he wants you to remember him as he used to be.'

Lisa wanted to argue, insist she come, but how could you force yourself on a dying man who didn't want you? She could hardly speak for crying. 'Tell him I'll never forget *Pygmalion*.' Such magnificent acting, such presence and that voice, filling the theatre with its grating power.

She heard the same sound again, that slightly hoarse mumble and Adam came back, close to tears himself. 'He says he thinks about you all the time and you'll pull through your present difficulties, you always do.'

'Put the phone by his ear, let me say goodbye to him,' she demanded.

Adam said gently, 'No, Lisa. You know, sometimes there can be too much emotion.' He paused. 'I'm going to ring off now, he's getting distressed.'

'Goodbye, Ralph,' she shouted. 'Goodbye.'

The receiver at the other end was quietly replaced.

She'd only intended staying in the cottage a few months, but had reckoned without the letters. Letters often full of misery, of hopelessness and despair, mostly from women, though several were from men. They'd watched her tell her story on television and wrote to tell their own. She read them carefully. Not all were sad. Some wrote to say they had survived the terror of their childhood and married good men who understood what they'd gone through. '*You'll feel better for having told*,' they said – hadn't Milo Hanna said something like that too? Nearly all ended, '*Putting these words on paper makes me feel a great weight has been lifted.*'

Jackie opened the letters in London – she didn't read them, the contents were for Lisa alone – and sent a typed acknowledgment promising a personal reply in due course. Lisa rarely managed more than four or five handwritten replies each day and even as she wrote, more letters came from women who'd been waiting to pluck up the courage to write.

Other things were happening in the outside world, but she was disinterested, though some affected her personally. Even the fact that Tony was in serious trouble failed to stir her. The newspapers had followed up *Private Eye*'s revelations and now the police were investigating allegations of bribe-taking; the Fraud Squad were mounting a prosecution against his offshore company.

The divorce, with a new solicitor, went through without a hitch and Lisa didn't even have to appear in court.

The only thing to upset her was an item on the news one night. Ralph was dead. She cried all night at the loss of a true friend.

She had never been so popular as an actress. Play and movie offers poured in, and one in particular caused her to smile: Masthead Movies, once O'Brien Productions, wanted to make a film of her life!

Most of this went over Lisa's head. All that mattered was answering the letters. The long feverish hours daily spent holding a pen caused a painful lump to appear on the middle finger of her right hand where it remained for the rest of her life.

She tried to lift the spirits of the writers and offer hope for the future. Sometimes, with her head aching and her right hand taut with cramp, she thought about asking Jackie to type the replies, but always changed her mind. 'If it takes the rest of my life I shall answer each one personally.'

It took a year. Suddenly, it was July again, and she'd reached the end of her task and began to think about what to do next.

On one matter she'd already made up her mind. Months ago, a charitable organisation set up to help victims of abuse had asked her to become their president and she had accepted.

'*I can't take up the position immediately,*' she replied, '*but I would like to become an active president, not just a name on your letterhead.*' By then, she would be ready to face the world to which she had so publicly confessed her secret.

Only Jackie knew where Lisa was. As the months passed and her confidence increased, Lisa began to call her family and friends on the old-fashioned bakelite telephone in the lounge, though she made them promise not to come and see her. She had difficulty in stopping Busby from flying over immediately. 'Damn you, Lisa, I've been worried sick,' he said angrily.

'We'll meet soon,' she promised. 'Are you still in Tymperleys? I'm longing to see it again.'

'Are you all right?' demanded Nellie. 'Swear you're all right.'

'I'm fine,' Lisa assured her. 'I'll come to Liverpool in the New Year.' She'd already made up her mind that she'd stay in the cottage until New Year's Eve, then begin a new life.

Winter began to close in again. Last year had been mild, but suddenly Lisa became conscious of draughts sweeping across the rooms under the ill-fitting doors and through the windows. She had logs delivered for the big black fireplace and Rambo began to sleep on her bed. One morning, she found the dishes frozen to the wooden draining board.

'Bloody hell, Rambo, I wouldn't like to be here if it snowed. We could be stranded down this lane for weeks.'

He looked at her intelligently with his odd eyes – one still stubbornly remained half-closed – and gave a woof of agreement.

Perhaps she should move back to London immediately before the cold really set in, Lisa thought, but then decided against it. Her mind had been programmed like an alarm clock which would ring on New Year's Day. To leave the cottage now would be like getting up at five o'clock when the alarm had been set for seven and you hung about, feeling a bit lost and wondering what to do with the extra hours. She'd leave on the day originally planned.

She supposed it was inevitable that in time she'd meet someone she knew from Broxley.

It was a Sunday morning in November and she and Rambo had been for a run across the dales, only a short one as the air was damp and penetratingly cold. She shut him in the car and was about to climb in the front, looking forward to getting home where she'd left a roaring fire burning, when a car passed and she heard a screech of brakes.

She looked up and her heart sank. Jim Harrison was striding towards her, an expression of incredulity on his face.

'What on earth are you doing here?' he demanded.

'I've been for a run,' she said awkwardly. Rambo began a furious, possessive barking in the back of the car.

He moved to take her in his arms, but she shrank back, dropping her eyes to avoid his look of hurt. She'd scarcely thought about this man since they last met.

'You're not living at Ferris Hall, surely?'

'Of course not. I've rented a cottage.'

'Where?'

She considered refusing to answer, but it seemed childish. When she told him where it was, he said angrily, 'That place is a dump. All sorts of hoodlums have lived there. They might come back – it's dangerous.'

'I've been there for over a year and had no trouble,' she argued.

'A year! And you never let me know?' He said this in an uncomprehending voice, more to himself than Lisa.

'Hardly anyone knows where I am,' she said defensively.

He was looking at her curiously. 'Did that night mean nothing?'

Lisa blushed and looked down at her feet. She hated treating him like this. He was such a good man through and through, decent and sincere. She should feel flattered, a man like this being in love with her. Instead, she felt nothing, just a desire to escape, to get back home where there was only Rambo to talk to. 'It meant everything – when it happened.' Then she looked him full in the face. 'But not since.'

'I see.' He began to back away and the agonised, bitter look on his face made her feel physically sick.

'You don't understand!' she cried. 'You can't possibly understand.' She opened the car door and Rambo tried to scramble over the back of the seat to welcome her. Jim had almost reached his own car. His broad shoulders were bent and she felt a surge of tenderness mixed with pity. Despite this, she shouted, 'You won't come and see me, will you?'

He turned, looking at her coldly. 'As if I would,' he shouted back.

Rambo lay on his back in front of the roaring fire, his little legs stuck up like flagpoles. Lisa looked up from the child's exercise book she was scribbling in and regarded him affectionately. He'd been the best company she could have had these last eighteen months. She smiled and returned to her writing. It was Masthead Movies' offer to make a film out of her life that had inspired her to begin setting it down on paper. She'd started jotting down trivial things that had stuck in her mind, like that Christmas Day kosher dinner with the Greenbaums, the time Mam sent Jimmie out with a penny to light a candle to Our Lady to implore her to make the jelly set in time for a party, the day Vita arrived in Tymperleys. She already had two notebooks full of reminiscences. When she got back to London she'd start joining them together with the important events in her life, and Jackie had promised to type the manuscript out when it was finished.

After a while, the lump on her finger began to throb and she sucked it to ease the pain, then took a sip of bourbon. Busby had sent a crate for Christmas. It was already beginning to take effect and she felt pleasantly tipsy. She would have liked a cigarette, but had given up – for the second time – when she came to the cottage.

'Cheers, Busby,' she said aloud and imagined him sitting by the pool at Tymperleys, surrounded by his friends who'd 'just dropped in'. She closed the exercise book, lay down on the settee and stared into the fire, watching with fascination as vivid blue flames ran up and down the logs and deep orange, ash-framed grottoes appeared in the gaps between them. The fire and the little capiz-shell-shaded lamp were the only illumination in the room and the ugly furniture was lost in dark shadows. In fact, thought Lisa, the room had never looked so lovely as it did now, on her last night.

It was New Year's Eve and her things were packed, ready to leave first thing in the morning. Rambo would hate the Pimlico house with its little backyard. She'd look around Broxley for a place to buy and spend a lot of time here. In last week's local paper, she'd read that Ferris Hall was up for sale. Could she live there, she wondered, after all that had happened with Tony?

Snuggling into a cushion, she decided not to think about it just now. Tomorrow, next week, next month, would do. There were lots of decisions to make, not just about where to live, but how to continue with her career. There was a play script she really liked and the movie company she'd vowed to start, another O'Brien Productions.

She picked up the remote control for the television and began to flick from channel to channel – typical New Year's Eve programmes, a games show with celebrities as panelists, a Victorian Music Hall, but on Channel 4, a movie which looked vaguely familiar. She left it on and suddenly a face from the past appeared on screen. Lally Cooper! Lally, in her blonde wig and waitress's uniform, saying, 'It's just that it sez FOOD outside, and generally that's why folks come in here. To eat!' This was the film that was going to launch her to stardom, though the last she'd heard, Lally had five kids and was probably a grandmother ten times over by now. Lisa raised her glass. 'Cheers, Lally.' When she disappeared from the screen, Lisa turned the sound down.

The logs spat and the sound disturbed Rambo. He began to scramble up and she leaned down and stroked him. 'Go back to sleep,' she ordered and he looked up at her adoringly before closing his eyes.

This was the second year she'd spent Christmas and New Year entirely alone, but she didn't care. She'd turned down invitations to Liverpool, London, California. It seemed like a test of strength to stay in this lonely, isolated house with only Rambo for company.

She listened; the silence was so complete it could be felt, though a few minutes later the faint drone of a plane could be heard, muted and distant, but when it had gone the silence became even more total.

Rambo got unsteadily to his feet and staggered towards the door. Obviously nature called. Lisa sighed and swung her legs off the settee. She needed to get up anyway to put more logs on the fire.

'You're such a good little dog,' she said lovingly as she opened the door and he shuddered at the icy blast of air which met him before padding reluctantly down the path with his awkward clumsy gait.

Shuddering herself, Lisa closed the door and drew the collar of her velvet dressing gown up to her throat. Away from the fire the room was freezing, but she was well prepared for this in her thick woollen slipper socks and warm nightdress. She threw some logs in the grate, picked up her glass and went to get more ice out of the fridge. The kitchen itself was as cold as the fridge and she hurried back to stand in front of the fire, watching the flames begin to take hold of the fresh wood. A chrome mirror, spotted with age, hung above the fireplace and she looked at her blurred reflection.

'At least I've gone grey glamorously.' Two symmetrical wings of silver had appeared just over her ears. It would be good to start buying some new clothes, wearing make-up again, going to a beauty parlour. She bet she could still turn a few heads, even though she'd be fifty-six in a few months. In the half-dark room, the face that stared back at her from the dim, cloudy glass was unlined and beautiful. This was the Lisa Angelis of *Easy Dreams* and *Matchstick Man*. She moved back and Lizzie O'Brien of Bootle was suddenly in the room with her.

No! She quickly turned away. It was too ghostly, particularly on New Year's Eve.

She sat on the edge of the settee, reluctant to get comfortable again until Rambo came back. He'd probably got used to the cold by now and was chasing a rat or some other poor unsuspecting creature.

Glancing at the television, she saw the programme had changed and a familiar face was mouthing words she couldn't hear. Milo Hanna! 'Cheers, Milo.' She toasted him, hoping there wouldn't be many more faces she recognised, else she'd be paralytic by morning. She still wasn't sure whether he was a fake or not, but he'd helped sort out her life. 'Not completely,' a little voice reminded her. 'What about Jim?'

Jim Harrison! She'd forgotten all about him during the year spent answering those tragic letters, but then she'd forgotten about everybody.

Could they get together again? Did she want to? More importantly, did he, after that disastrous meeting? She thought about the night they'd spent together. It had been so good, so perfect, yet the memory meant nothing. Why? she wondered.

It was nearly midnight. She turned the television up; it would be nice to have someone, particularly Milo Hanna, wish her a Happy New Year, though people would begin telephoning soon. She especially wanted to talk to Kevin. When she began her book she wanted his advice on the background. There were things about Chaucer Street he could help with. Maybe he could remember the night she was born . . .

Only a minute to go before the New Year came in. In the distance, above Milo's soft Irish voice, came the roar of a car engine, gradually getting louder as it approached the cottage. It wasn't often anything came this way and it must have been doing a hundred, the noise it made. She winced as it passed, then heard the shriek of brakes and a bumping sound and she screamed, 'RAMBO!'

The car was just red tail-lights in the distance and Rambo was lying on his side, completely still. Lisa screamed again, scooped him up in her dressing gown and ran into the house. His body was limp, a dead weight, but there was no blood. She sat down, buried her face in his warm fur and began to cry, rocking back and forth and clutching his sturdy little body.

She cried all night, great wracking sobs that grated her ribs, threatening to tear out her insides. After a while, she stopped crying for Rambo and cried instead for her mam, for Ralph, for Nellie and her dead son, for Jackie and Sabina, for everyone she could think of, even, at one point, her dad. Vaguely she heard the telephone ring and it never seemed to stop. Beyond the ringing, the television blared and people laughed and sang and cheered. Then a movie began and she wondered if it was one of hers because the music was familiar: passionate, haunting music that made her weep harder. Finally, she cried for herself. Nothing would ever go right for her. Nothing.

'I'm going to die tonight,' she whispered. It was only right that she should die in this lonely spot with Rambo still warm on her knee. 'I don't want to go on living, anyway.'

Closing her eyes, she leant back in the chair. She was drowning, drowning, and as if a film was being fast-forwarded, Lisa saw her life pass before her eyes, from its raw, uncompromising beginning to now, its bitter end. She was a child again in Chaucer Street where there was so much hate and so much love. A young girl in her best dress going to Southport on her birthday, then Jackie appeared in her pink satin pyjamas, dimpled, creamy-skinned and smiling and she saw Harry Greenbaum in his bookshop, a misty figure, so wise and good. Patrick! Oh, Jesus, Patrick, my lovely brother. Hollywood, Busby, there'd been some glorious times making movies together. Then Dent, Dent the monster, carrying Sabina into the bedroom, grinning his wicked grin. Ralph, dear Ralph. Gary dying, a sad time, yet the memory strangely uplifting. Tony Molyneux, you bastard, Tony. Milo Hanna, the letters, the letters . . .

She was eight years old and bombs were falling all over Bootle and Dad was banging on the door demanding to be let in. 'Leave him,' Mam said in a hard voice and the children chorused gleefully, 'Leave him, leave him.' Then a bomb dropped outside and the front door flew down the hall, followed by Dad. When he reached the stairs, he exploded, and lay there, split open, oozing blood. The children started jumping up and down, shouting, 'He's dead! He's dead!' Their footsteps thumped on the lino-covered floor and Mam began to jump too and the noise was so tremendous it drowned out the sound of the bombs.

Lisa opened her eyes. What a weird dream. Oh God, it was cold in here. She shivered and was about to get up and stir the mountain of grey ash in the fireplace, trying to revive a hopefully hidden flame, when she noticed Rambo on her knee and moaned aloud. The thumping sound in her dream still persisted and she realised the noise was real. Someone was banging on the front door.

She got up, still clutching Rambo, and opened it. It was snowing outside and Jim Harrison was standing with his hand poised, ready to knock again. He wore an old duffel coat and urgently needed a shave. She walked away, leaving the door open, and returned to her seat. He came in and stood looking down at her.

'Are you all right?'

Lisa stared at the floor and didn't answer.

'That was a stupid question,' he said gently. 'You look terrible. Let's do something with this fire then I'll make a drink. Here, have a sip of this first.'

He poured out an inch of bourbon and sat beside her, holding the glass against her lips as if she was an invalid. The drink burned her raw, aching throat. She blinked and found her eyes were sticky with crying.

There were still some logs smouldering underneath the ash and he coaxed them back into life and soon a small fire was burning.

'Why are you here?' she asked.

He looked at her quickly, as if relieved to hear the sound of her voice. 'Jackie telephoned. She was worried. Apparently she'd been calling all night and you didn't answer.'

'I fell asleep,' she lied. 'I didn't hear anything.'

She could tell he didn't believe her. 'New Year's Eve isn't a good time to be alone. I would have come over if—' He didn't finish. 'If I'd thought you wanted me to,' he was probably going to say.

'It wasn't that,' she tried to explain. 'Just thoughts, memories, getting out of hand, that's all.' She wasn't going to tell him about Rambo. He'd think her too emotional and stupid, wanting to die because her dog had been killed. She moved Rambo's still-warm body onto the settee, settling his head carefully on a cushion. He'd grow cold now, away from her. After Jim had gone, she'd bury him in the garden.

'That's exactly what I meant. You've been by yourself too long. It's time to return to the land of the living again,' he said seriously.

'Things are easy for you, aren't they? Everything's black or white. With me, life has been all shades in between.'

'You're making assumptions again.' He smiled. 'I learnt a long time ago to take each day as it comes. I've had my ups and downs too, you know. Some day I might tell you about them.'

'I'm sorry.' She plucked at her dressing gown as the telephone rang.

Jim answered it. 'Yes, she's fine. Fit and well, just drank a bit too much, I reckon, and fell asleep.' Lisa heard Jackie laugh. 'Yes, I'll tell her that, goodbye.'

'She said she's been inundated with calls, people trying to get through and worried when you didn't answer.' He paused. 'You're very lucky, having so many people care about you. Some people'd give anything to be in your shoes.'

He was right, she thought. So right. It had been selfish to cut herself off all this time and refuse to let people who loved her come and visit. She smiled at him wryly. 'I needed that advice, thanks.'

'Are you feeling better? Got over your bad thoughts?'

She glanced down at Rambo. 'Most of them,' she said.

'Do you want me to leave? I don't want to be in your way. Jackie said you were going back to London today.' Lisa looked at him. He would have hated to know how much his eyes were pleading, desperately pleading for her to answer, 'Stay, please stay.'

'I don't know,' she said eventually.

'Lisa, can't we begin again?' he said urgently. 'Let's pretend we met this morning . . .'

She knew she would be happy with this man, this safe, secure man who loved her so passionately, but . . . 'I suppose we could – begin again, that is,' she said slowly. 'But I can't promise anything and I'd hate to let you down again.'

'I'll take that risk,' he said quickly.

'And I have loads of things to do. I'm writing a book and I want to start making movies again and I'm involved in a charity.'

'Well, I have a factory to run,' he laughed.

'I'm even thinking of buying Ferris Hall.'

'I could stand that.'

He made no attempt to touch her, for which she was grateful. There would be time for that in the future – possibly.

'You know, you should get out of here straight away. Would you like me to load your things in the car while you get dressed? In fact,' he added hopefully, 'I could drive you down if you want.'

'Well . . .' She rather liked the idea, but what about Rambo? 'I'd appreciate that, but can you come back for me in an hour?'

He looked puzzled. 'Why?' he demanded. 'I can see you're packed. What's wrong with now?'

She couldn't think of a reason to give, except the true one. She burst into tears. 'Because Rambo's dead and I've got to bury him, that's why. A car came racing down the lane last night and ran him over.'

'Oh Lisa, my love. Why didn't you tell me?'

My God! There were tears in his own eyes. He knelt by Rambo and touched his chest with the flat of his hand. 'He's still warm.'

'That's because I've been holding him all night.'

'There's the barest flicker of a heartbeat. He's still alive, you stupid woman. He's concussed, that's all – look at this bump on his head. The car must have glanced off him.' He stood up and said peremptorily, 'Get dressed and we'll take him to a vet immediately.'

*

She sat beside Jim in the car with Rambo wrapped in a blanket on her knee. The snow had thickened and was beginning to stick to the bare hedges and the fields were peppered with white. It was a desolate lonely scene, but Lisa thought the world had never looked so beautiful.

She felt as if she was waking up after a long, stifling dream and suddenly her blood began to race and her body tingled with excitement at the thought of the future. 'It's going to be wonderful, I know it is,' she whispered. Of course, there were bound to be more ups and downs, but so what? Everybody had them. After these last eighteen months, she was convinced she'd learnt to cope with life, but it only took Rambo's supposed death for her to completely go to pieces. She'd give up learning to cope, and vowed to do what Jim did and take each day as it came. Well, she'd try! She remembered taking that vow before on more than one occasion.

Jim touched her arm. 'How are you feeling?'

'Fine,' she said. 'Absolutely fine.'

She turned and watched his lovely broad, handsome face, his strong hands firm on the wheel and thought again about the night they'd spent together and suddenly there was that old familiar tingle in her stomach. She laughed.

'What's so funny?'

'Nothing,' she said happily.

A New Year.
    A new man.
    A new life.
    Another stepping stone . . .

Liverpool Annie

For all the Margarets I have known,
not forgetting Audrey and Evelyn

Orlando Street

1

Annie stopped running. Her breath was raw within her pounding chest, and her legs felt as if they were about to give way. She'd come to the stretch of sand where Auntie Dot used to bring them in the summer when they were little, and where she and Sylvia came on warm evenings to talk. Now, at half past ten on a bitter March night, Annie found herself drawn towards the dark isolation offered by the litter-strewn beach.

What had she done? What had possessed her to say those terrible things? She wandered, stiff-legged, towards the water. The texture of the sand beneath her feet changed from fine to moist and the heels of her flat school shoes sank into the mushy surface. The horror of what she'd just witnessed couldn't be true: she'd imagined it, or she'd wake up any minute and find it had been a bad dream, a nightmare.

'Please God, make it not be true!' she prayed aloud in a strange, cracked, high-pitched whisper.

Before her, the black, oily waters of the River Mersey glinted, rippling, reflecting the distant lights of Wallasey and New Brighton and a segment of orange moon which appeared from behind a veil of cloud.

Annie stared into the water which lapped busily at her feet, at the black seaweed which wrapped itself around her shoe, to be swept away when the tide rustled forward in a frill of dirty froth to reclaim it as its own. She was fifteen, nearly a woman, yet felt as if, from this night on, her life was over. She knelt on the sand and began to pray, but soon the prayers gave way to recollections: of her mam and dad, her sister Marie, of Sylvia, and of course, Auntie Dot . . .

She searched for her first memory, but could think of nothing in particular. Those early years living with the Gallaghers had been happy, full of fun, despite the fact the war was on. She remembered it was the day Dot threw the cup at the wall that caused things to change. The cup had been a catalyst. Afterwards nothing was ever the same again.

Auntie Dot was still in the same house in Bootle: small and terraced, outwardly the same as the one in Orlando Street where the Harrisons had lived for over ten years, but inside so very different – full of ornaments and pictures, warm with the smell of baking, and the grate piled high with glowing coals. In 1945, Dot put a big picture of Mr Attlee, the new Prime

Minister, over the mantelpiece and kept a little candle burning before it, as if he were a saint.

When Annie and her family were there, there was so much furniture you could scarcely move, because stuff from the parlour had been moved out to make room for a double bed for Mam and Dad. Annie and her sister slept upstairs with Auntie Dot. Then the war ended and Uncle Bert came home and, somewhat unreasonably Annie thought, expected to sleep with his wife. She was indignant when another bed was acquired from a secondhand shop and put in the boxroom for her and Marie. This meant the settee from the parlour had to be placed precariously on its side, and they had to climb over an armchair to get in and out of bed – which was too small, anyway, even for two little girls.

Still, Annie loved the crowded house, swarming with people, though it was irritating to have to stand in a queue for the lavatory at the bottom of the yard, or compete for food with three growing, hungry boys. The boys were older than Annie, having been born before the war, and she thought Dot was sensible not to have more whilst Bert was away, because they were a handful. Not that Marie was much better. Despite being only three, she was as 'mischievous as a sackful of monkeys', as Dot put it.

'I don't know what I'd do without you, Annie,' Dot said frequently. 'You're the only one who knows how to behave proper, like. You'd never think you were only four.' Annie helped make the beds and dry the dishes. Her favourite job was dusting the ornaments on the sideboard: souvenirs from Blackpool and Rhyl and Morecambe, places where Dot and Bert had gone when they were courting.

'Poor little mite,' Dot said sometimes, ruffling Annie's mop of copper curls. 'What's to become of you, eh?'

Annie had no idea what she was on about. She didn't feel the least bit poor, but warm and secure in the shambolic house where, as far as she knew, the Harrisons would stay for ever. In September she would start school, the one the boys went to, and life would be even better. She loved Auntie Dot with all her heart, and Uncle Bert, once she forgave him for taking over the bed. A tall man with a halo of sandy hair, red cheeks and a bushy moustache, he reminded her of a teddy bear, and bought little presents for the children on pay day: sweets or magic painting books or crayons. Bert was an engine driver who worked shifts, and they had to be quiet when he was on nights and slept during the day.

But gradually, Auntie Dot, who laughed a lot and was always in a good mood, began to get bad-tempered. Perhaps it was because she was getting fat, thought Annie, noting the way her auntie's belly was swelling, getting bigger and bigger by the day. She snapped at the boys and told Annie and Marie to get out of the bloody way, though her bark was worse than her bite. If anyone at the receiving end of her temper got upset, she was instantly and extravagantly remorseful. Once, when Marie began to cry, her auntie cried, too.

'I'm sorry, luv,' she sobbed, gathering Marie in her arms. 'It's just . . . oh, hell, I dunno, I suppose everything's getting on top of me.'

It was a blustery rainy day in April when Dot threw the cup. Annie and Marie were in their best frocks, having been to nine o'clock Mass with their aunt and uncle and the boys. The pegs in the hall were full of damp clothes, with a neat row of Wellingtons underneath. After Mass, Uncle Bert had gone to bed, with a stern warning to the boys to keep the noise down. Dot knotted a scarf turbanwise around her ginger hair, pulled a flowered pinny over her head and tied it around her nonexistent waist, making her belly look even bigger. She began to iron on the back room table. As each item was finished, she placed it in a pile, until there were two neat folded heaps of clothes and bedding.

'Can't put this lot away till Bert gets up or I can get in the parlour,' she muttered to herself. Every now and then, she changed the iron for the one left on a low gas ring to re-heat. As the fresh iron was brought in, she spat on it with gusto.

The boys, restless at being kept indoors by the rain, disappeared upstairs. After a while, they began to fight, and there was a series of muffled howls and bumps. Dot went into the hall and hissed. 'Tommy, Mike, Alan! Shurrup, or ye'll wake your dad.'

She smiled at the girls, who were squashed together in the other armchair from the parlour. 'Oh, don't you look a picture! The royal princesses don't hold a candle to you pair. What are you drawing? Do your Auntie Dot a nice picture for the kitchen, there's good girls.'

Their best drawings were pinned to the larder door, but now Annie abandoned hers to watch Dot at work. Her aunt's movements always fascinated her, they were so quick and efficient. She would have offered to help, but Dot didn't like anyone under her feet when she was ironing.

The ironing finished, Dot put both irons on the back step to cool and went into the kitchen to prepare dinner, deftly peeling a stack of potatoes and chopping up a cabbage. There was already a pan boiling on the stove, a corner of muslin sticking out under the lid. Annie licked her lips. Suet pudding! She hoped it was syrup, her favourite.

Dot lit the oven and placed a big iron casserole dish of steak and kidney on the middle shelf. To Annie's surprise, she remained stooping for several seconds, wincing. She grasped the draining board, panting, before lighting another ring on the stove and pouring almost a whole pint of milk into a pan. Then she took a big tin of custard out of the cupboard, mixed the remainder of the milk with two tablespoons of powder, poured the whole lot into the pan and began to stir vigorously, her face creased in a scowl. Making custard was a hazardous business: if you didn't remove the pan at just the right time, it burned.

Sitting watching, listening to the spoon scraping the side of the pan, the spit of water on the hot stove, the muffled voices of the boys upstairs, Annie, in the warm, comfortable chair pressed close to her sister, felt a sense of perfect happiness. In about an hour – and although an hour seemed an age away, it would pass eventually – Dot would ask her to set the table, then nine plates would be spread on every conceivable surface in the kitchen and the food would be served, with Dot moving bits of potato and spoonsful of steak and kidney from one plate to another, 'to be fair, like', as she put it. In the middle of this, Dot would say 'Tell your dad the dinner's ready, luv', and Annie would knock on the parlour door and her dad would emerge and collect two meals, one with only minute portions for Mam, and take them back with him. Uncle Bert's dinner would be kept warm for later.

The boys began shouting and there was a crash, as if they'd knocked something over. Uncle Bert thumped on the floor and yelled, 'Keep the noise down!' just as there was a sharp rap on the front door.

Dot groaned. 'See who that is, Annie.'

Annie trotted to the door. Father Maloney stood outside. He gave Annie a brief nod, and, without waiting for an invitation, pushed past and walked down the hall, straight into the room full of ironing and thick with the smell of cooking dinner – boiling cabbage predominated.

'Why, Father!' Dot's pretty, good-natured face flushed as bright red as her hair with embarrassment. She pulled the turban off and dragged the pinny over her head, dislodging one of her pearl earrings. It fell on the lino-covered floor with a little clatter and, as she rushed forward to greet the priest, she stood on it, 'I wasn't expecting you today. Annie, Marie, get up and let Father have the armchair.'

She closed the kitchen door and called the boys. They came down and stood meekly against the wall, hands behind their backs, whilst Dot carried out a quick inspection, straightening their collars and smoothing down the tousled ginger heads they had inherited from their mam and dad. Father Maloney gave them a cursory glance. As soon as his back was turned, Mike pulled a face and Marie stifled a giggle.

'Who is it?' Uncle Bert shouted.

'It's Father Maloney, Dad,' Tommy shouted back. Uncle Bert said something incomprehensible and the bed creaked.

The priest didn't stay long. He asked the children if they'd been good, and they assured him they had in their most convincing voices. When he turned to Dot, Mike stuck out his tongue as far as it would go. Annie did her best to keep a straight face. Mike was the favourite of her cousins. His hair was redder than his brothers', he had twice as many freckles, and his blue-green eyes danced with merriment.

'And how are you, Dorothy?' Father Maloney asked gravely.

'I'm fine, Father,' Dot replied with a glassy smile and a killing look in the direction of Mike, whose tongue was performing contortions.

'You look tired, child.' He frowned at the stack of ironing. 'You should treat Sunday as a day of rest, someone in your condition.'

'It's a bit difficult, Father, y'see . . .'

But Father Maloney wasn't interested. He blessed them quickly and departed. Annie and Marie immediately reclaimed the armchair.

The front door had scarcely closed, when Uncle Bert appeared, fully dressed. He'd even managed his tie, though the knot was crooked.

'You're too late, Dad. He's gone,' said Mike.

'Bloody hell!' Uncle Bert swore, and stumped back upstairs. The bed creaked again. He must have thrown himself on it fully clothed.

Dot was scraping her earring off the floor when Alan said, 'What's that smell?'

'Jaysus, the custard!' She opened the kitchen door and a cloud of smoke billowed out. The top and front of the stove were covered with a brown, blistering mess.

'I like it burnt,' said Mike.

'I don't,' Tommy countered.

As if this were a signal for another fight, the boys fell upon each other and began to wrestle.

And that was when Dot threw the cup.

It shattered against the wall and the pieces fell onto the sideboard. 'I can't stand it!' she screamed. 'I can't stand it another sodding minute!' She stood in the kitchen door, her hands on her hips, looking madder than anyone had ever seen her look before.

Marie burst into tears, and the boys stopped wrestling and looked at their mother in alarm. Something terrible must have happened, something far worse than burnt custard.

'Is Mr Attlee dead, Mam?' Tommy asked nervously.

Dot glared. Upstairs, the bed creaked and Uncle Bert's weary footsteps could be heard descending. The parlour door opened and the tall gaunt frame of Annie's dad appeared. His hair, paler than Dot's, almost salmon-coloured, was plastered close to his narrow head, and his face wore an expression of unrelieved gloom. He looked at everyone nervously, but didn't speak.

Uncle Bert came in and, to Annie's surprise, he sat down and clumsily dragged Dot onto his knee. 'What's the matter, luv?'

Dot buried her head in his shoulder and gave a deep, heartrending sigh. 'I can't stand it another minute. This morning was the last straw.'

'Here, youse lot, buy your mam a bar of Cadbury's milk chocolate and get something for yourselves and the girls while you're at it.' Bert handed Tommy half a crown. 'Take a ration book off the mantelpiece.'

Dot lifted her head. 'Put your coats on, it's still raining.'

Marie's sobs ceased at the prospect of the chocolate, and as soon as the boys had gone, Annie's dad crept into the room and sat down.

'Come on, luv, spit it out.' Bert stroked his wife's arm.

'It's just there's so much to do, Bert, looking after nine people; all the washing and ironing and the cooking. And when Father Maloney came, walked right in and there I was in the middle of the dinner and washing everywhere, I just wished I had me parlour back, that's all.'

There was something significant about this last remark which Annie didn't understand, because everyone fell silent.

It was Dot who spoke first. She looked at Annie's dad directly. 'I'm sorry, Ken, but it was only supposed to be temporary, and it's been over four years. Now, what with Bert back, and another baby on the way – well, the house just isn't big enough.'

There was another silence, and once again it was Dot who broke it. 'If only Rose could give a hand, that'd help a bit.'

Uncle Bert said awkwardly, 'Dot said the corporation came up with a house in Huyton, a nice modern one with three bedrooms.'

Annie's dad spoke at last, and the words came out in a breathless rush. 'It's too far away. Me work's on this side of town, Litherland and Waterloo. I couldn't ride me bike to and from Huyton every day, it must be fifteen or twenty mile.'

Dot took a deep breath. She was still sitting on Bert's knee, clinging to him as if it gave her the courage to speak out. 'Ken, you're me little brother, and I know you've been through a lot with Rose. If this was a bigger house, you could stay for ever, but . . .' She broke off and began to cry quietly. 'Oh, soddit! I hate saying this.'

'It's not right, y'know, Ken,' Uncle Bert said gently. 'Rose'll never get better as long as you and Dot wait on her hand and foot. If you had a place of your own, the responsibility might do her good.'

Annie's dad stared at his shoes. 'I'll see what I can do tomorrer. Bootle lost so many houses in the Blitz, there's not much going . . .'

'Good lad!' Bert said heartily as Annie's dad got up and left the room without another word.

Dot looked worried when the parlour door slammed shut more loudly than it need have. 'Now he's got the hump!'

'Never mind, luv. It had to be said.'

'I could kill that sodding Hitler for what he did to Rose.'

Annie, listening avidly, wondered what her auntie was on about.

'She weren't the only one, Dot,' said Uncle Bert. 'Other folks had as bad – and some had worse.'

Dot sighed. 'I know. Even so . . .' Her voice trailed away and they sat together companionably on the chair. 'I suppose I'd better see to the dinner before something else burns.'

'I'll give you a hand, luv.'

Dot giggled. 'You know what our Tommy said when I threw that cup? He asked if Mr Attlee had died. Jaysus, if anything had happened to ould Clement, I'd've thrown the whole bloody tea service.'

Three weeks later, the Harrisons went to live in Orlando Street, Seaforth, and life changed so completely that Annie felt as if they'd moved to the other side of the world.

2

Orlando Street seemed to stretch for miles and miles. More than one hundred polished red brick houses were on either side, built directly onto the pavement, identical, and as seamless as a river. The paintwork was severe: bottle green, maroon or brown doors and window frames, a few black. Once a year, Annie's dad repainted the outside woodwork the same bitter-chocolate colour.

When Annie was older, she would remark disdainfully: 'The world would end if someone painted a door blue or pink. *I'm* going to have the front door of *my* house bright yellow!'

In all the years she lived there, she always had to check the number to make sure it was the right house, and her heart sank when she turned the corner into Orlando Street. The awful day the Harrisons moved to Number thirty-eight remained for ever etched in her mind.

Uncle Bert turned up with a lorry and the beds were loaded in the back, along with their possessions, which Dot had carefully packed in cardboard boxes. Dad's bike was fetched from the backyard.

Dad looked bewildered and angry when he emerged with Mam. She wore her best coat made of funny, curly fur, and blinked at the daylight, as if she rarely saw it, her face all tight and pale.

'The girls'd better go in the back, they can sit on one of the beds,' Dad said curtly as he helped his wife into the cab.

Dot pursed her lips and yelled, 'One of you lads, come here.' When Mike appeared, she said, 'Go with them, luv. Poor little mites, they'll be scared out of their wits stuck in there all on their own.'

Mike evidently thought this a treat. His face lit up, and he leapt into the lorry and threw himself onto the bedsprings with a whoop.

When Uncle Bert picked up Marie, Dot burst into wild tears. 'There's no need to take the girls, Ken. Why not leave them with us?'

Annie, unsure what was going on, had a feeling this would be preferable, and grabbed her auntie's hand, but Dad shook his head.

'No,' he said in a thin, stubborn voice. 'It's about time Rose took some responsibility, like Bert said.'

'Jaysus!' Dot sobbed. 'He didn't mean the girls. Oh, if only I'd kept me big mouth shut!'

An hour later, Annie and her sister watched Uncle Bert drive away, Mike hanging out of the passenger window, waving. They waved back until the lorry turned the corner, then looked at each other nervously and went back into their new house.

Annie hated it as much as she hated the street. She hated the dark, faded wallpaper and the furniture left by the previous tenant, which Dad told Dot he'd got at a knock-down price.

The parlour was scary. There was something sinister about the tall cupboard with its leaded glass doors, the panes like a hundred eyes, glaring at her, unwelcoming and unfriendly, and the big black sideboard, full of whirls and curls, was something the devil himself might have.

She went upstairs and gasped in amazement. A bathroom! She climbed onto the lavatory with some difficulty, and stayed perched on the wooden seat for several minutes to get the feel of it, then pulled the chain. It was odd using a lavatory indoors, and rather exciting, though she'd prefer to be with Dot and Bert and the lavvy at the bottom of the yard.

She tiptoed into the rear bedroom which overlooked the backyard. 'Strewth!' she gasped, in exactly the same tone as Auntie Dot used. Like the parlour, the room was full of dark, gloomy furniture. A dressing table in front of the window shut out most of the light. Another single bed was already there, as well as their own, which meant they could have one each. Their clothes were in a box on the floor.

One by one, Annie gingerly opened the drawers in case anything interesting had been left behind. 'Strewth!' she said again, when the smell of mothballs made her sneeze. Apart from their lining of yellow newspapers, the drawers were empty, as was the wardrobe, except for three coathangers which she couldn't reach.

She unpacked their clothes and put most away, leaving the frocks for Dad to hang up. As she gravely carried out this task, she felt grown up and responsible, though she knew she was only delaying the time she dreaded: the time when she would have to go downstairs and face her mam.

Eventually, when she could put it off no longer, Annie crept down into the living room. Mam was in the armchair by the window, her head turned towards the wall.

Annie stared at her curiously. This pretty lady with the sad grey eyes and cascade of dark cloudy hair was supposed to be her mam, yet she seemed like a stranger. It was Auntie Dot who'd brought them up, taken them to the clinic and to Mass. It was into Dot's warm, rough arms they snuggled when they needed love, whilst their mam remained in the parlour, emerging occasionally on Sundays or at Christmas or if Dot had arranged a birthday tea, when she would sit, wan and pale and silent. Sometimes, at Dot's urging, the girls went in to see her. Mam would be in bed or in a chair, staring vacantly out of the window. The girls never stayed long, because Mam never spoke, hardly looked at them, and a few times she hadn't even opened her eyes.

'It's not her body that's sick, it's her mind,' Dot had told them only a few days ago, and Annie imagined inside Mam's head being full of sores. 'It's that sodding Hitler what done it!' Dot, angry, slammed the iron down onto the collar of Bert's working shirt. 'Poor girl, such a pretty thing she was, well, still is, but the life's been squeezed out of her.'

'What did Hitler do to me mam?' Annie asked, imagining the monster personally squeezing the life out of her mother.

Dot sighed as she steered the iron around a row of buttons. 'Oh, I suppose you've got to know some time, and now's as good a time as any. It's just that you and Marie would have had an older brother if he hadn't been taken to heaven at eighteen months.' She made the sign of the cross. 'Johnny. Lovely little lad he was, dark, like your mam and Marie. He was born the first month of the war, just after our Alan.' She folded the shirt and reached for another. 'One night, after the siren went, your mam left him by himself for a minute, just a minute, mind, when the house was bombed and Johnny was killed. Poor Rose, she's never got over it.' Dot paused over a cuff. 'Mind you,' she said thoughtfully, 'she should be better by now, it's six years. Lots of terrible things happened to people during the war, but they pulled through.'

Standing by her mam, Annie felt overcome with misery. She didn't want to be in this dark, quiet house, away from Dot and Bert and her boisterous cousins. She badly wanted to be kissed and cuddled and told everything was going to be all right. Marie was in the kitchen, chattering away. Dad just grunted in reply. Mam didn't appear to have noticed Annie was there; her face was still turned away. Annie climbed onto her knee and lay there, waiting for an arm to curl around her neck. But her mother remained as still as a statue. After a while, Annie slid off and went upstairs to sit on the bed and wonder what was going to happen to them.

A few minutes later, Marie crept in, her impish little face downcast. 'Don't like it here,' she said tearfully. 'Want Auntie Dot.'

'Sit on me knee,' commanded Annie, 'and pretend I'm your auntie.'

So Marie climbed on her sister's knee, and they sat there, sniffing miserably, until Dad called to say tea was ready.

A month later, Dot appeared with a black pram containing a tiny baby with bright red hair and bright blue eyes. Her belly was back to its normal size, and she looked lean and pretty, in a white cardigan over a green skirt and blouse, and with a green ribbon around her carroty curls.

'This is Pete,' she said proudly. 'Your new cousin.'

She left the pram outside and carried the baby indoors. The girls were so pleased to see her they clung to her skirt, hugging her legs. They'd feared they might never see Dot again.

'Where did he come from?' Marie demanded.

'Can I hold him?' asked Annie.

'I found him under a gooseberry bush,' Dot twinkled. 'Sit down, Annie, and you can nurse him for a while. Careful, now. I'd have come before, but as you can see, I've been rather busy.' As soon as the baby was deposited in Annie's arms, Marie climbed onto her aunt's knee.

Dot turned to Mam, who was in her usual chair by the window. 'How are you, Rose? Have you settled in, like?' she asked brightly.

Annie looked up from examining the baby's face, his short ginger lashes, his petal pink ears, curious to see Mam's reaction. She scarcely moved from the chair all day except to make the tea, when she would waft in and out of the kitchen like a ghost to peel potatoes laboriously and mince meat in the curious rusty machine left by the previous tenant. Often, the potatoes hadn't boiled long enough and were hard inside, and Dad had to do them again. He brought the meat home in his saddlebag, and at weekends did the washing, hanging their frocks and petticoats and knickers on the line. When Mrs Flaherty, the widow next door, offered to help, 'Your poor wife being ill, like,' he churlishly refused.

Mam rarely spoke. Even if the girls asked a question, she mostly didn't answer, just looked at them in a vacant way, as if they were invisible and she wondered where the voice had come from.

'I think so,' Mam whispered in response to Dot's enquiry.

'And how are you coping with the girls, Rose? Don't forget, I'd be happy to have them if they're too much for you. We've missed them a lot. In fact, Alan cried every night for a week after they'd gone.'

Not to be outdone, Marie said quickly, 'We cry too, Auntie Dot. Me and Annie cry every single night.'

'Do you now!' Dot said in a tight voice. 'And what do you do with yourselves all day?'

Annie and Marie looked at each other.

'We draw.'

'And play with our dolls.'

'Have you been to the park yet? And there's sands not far away.'

'No, Auntie, we haven't been anywhere, 'cept to the shop for a loaf sometimes,' Annie said importantly. 'Our dad leaves the money.'

'I see!' Dot's voice was still tight. 'Shall we go to the sands now?'

'Yes, please!' they chorused.

'Get your coats, then. There's a chill in the air for June.'

Dot didn't say another word until they were outside. As they walked along Orlando Street with Pete tucked up in his pram and the girls skipping along each side clutching the handle, she asked casually, 'Are you eating proper? What do you have for breakfast?'

'Cornflakes,' replied Annie, 'and we have bread and jam for dinner.' She didn't add, because she felt Dot wouldn't approve, that it was she who got the cornflakes because Mam usually forgot, and by the time they were hungry again and there was no sign of food on the horizon, she would cut four thick slices of bread and smear them with margarine and jam. Twice she'd cut her finger as well as the bread, but the blood merged with the jam and was hardly noticeable.

'Bread and jam? Jaysus, that's no meal for two growing girls,' Dot said caustically. 'You got better than that in our house.'

'Bread and jam's me favourite,' Marie piped, so Dot said no more, though later, as she steered the pram across the busy main road, she said firmly, 'From now on, your Auntie Dot'll come as often as she can.' Then she muttered, half to herself, 'As for your mam, I'm not sure whether to feel sorry for her, or give her a good kick up the arse!'

Annie started school in September. On her first day, Dad went into work late and took her on the crossbar of his bike.

St Joan of Arc's was in Bootle. Her cousins were already there and could 'keep an eye on her', Dot promised. It was a long walk, but Annie was glad to return to the familiar bombscarred streets, where women sat on their doorsteps on sunny days, and children played hopscotch on the pavements or whizzed around the lampposts on home-made swings. No-one played out in Orlando Street. Most residents were old, and if a child dared so much as kick a ball, they were told to play elsewhere.

One of the best things about school was the dinners. Dinners were almost as nice as lessons. Because she wanted the nuns to like her, Annie paid close attention during class. She was one of the first to learn to read and do sums, but her favourite lesson was drawing. The nuns called it 'Art', and were impressed with her pictures of 'pretty ladies in nice dresses'. One, Sister Finbar, wrote a note to Annie's mam to say she must be 'encouraged with her artwork', but Mam merely held the unopened envelope on her knee till Dad came home and read it.

'Good,' he mumbled tiredly.

Annie's dad was an insurance collector. He went into the office each morning to 'bring the books up', and spent the rest of the day riding round on his bike collecting payments, a penny here, twopence there. He came home at seven, exhausted. This was because he had a gammy leg, Dot told them. He'd broken it when he was little and it hadn't set properly.

'That's why he didn't fight in the war like your Uncle Bert. Poor Ken, he should have a sitting-down job, not be riding round on that sodding bike eight hours a day,' Dot sighed. 'Who'd have thought our Ken would end up like this, eh? Your gran, God rest her soul,' she crossed herself, 'thought the sun shone out his arse. She hoped he'd go to university, him being a scholarship boy an' all, but he met your mam, and . . . Oh, well, it's no use crying over spilt milk, is it?'

Annie hadn't been at school long when Colette Reilly asked her to tea. She enjoyed being made a fuss of by Mrs Reilly.

'Our Colette's little friend!' she cooed. They sat down to jelly and cream and fairy cakes with cherries on top. Then Mrs Reilly cleared the table and they played Ludo and Snakes and Ladders and Snap.

'When can I come to yours?' Colette demanded as Annie was leaving.

'Don't be rude,' Mrs Reilly laughed. 'Wait till you're invited.'

'I'll have to ask me mam,' said Annie. She pondered over the matter for days. If she could go to Colette's, it seemed fair Colette should come to hers, but she couldn't imagine Mam making jelly or fairy cakes, and she felt uneasy asking someone to the dark, gloomy house which was exactly the same as the day they'd moved in. Although Uncle Bert had offered to decorate – 'A bit of distemper'd go over that wallpaper a treat, Ken, brighten the place up no end' – her dad had turned him down as churlishly as he'd done Mrs Flaherty when she'd offered to help with the washing. 'I like it the way it is,' he said stubbornly.

Eventually, Annie plucked up the courage to approach her mam. 'Colette wants to come to tea,' she said nervously.

Mam was in her dressing gown, the blue one with silk flowers round the neck and cuffs. The red one with the velvet collar had gone to the dry cleaner's on Saturday. Mam wore her dressing gowns a lot. She looked at Annie, her lovely grey eyes vacant, empty. 'No,' she said. 'No.'

That night when Annie was in bed, Dad came in. 'You must never ask children to this house,' he said in his faint, tired voice. 'Never.'

So Annie never did. In a way, she felt relieved. She didn't want anyone to know her mam couldn't make jelly and wore a dressing gown all day and didn't know how to play Snakes and Ladders.

If the nuns expected another star pupil when Marie Harrison started school, they were to be sadly disappointed. Marie was in trouble from the first day, when she stole another new girl's ball and threw it on the roof where it lodged in the gutter. Annie had been looking forward to her sister's company, but at going-home time, Marie was nowhere to be seen. She was off to play on a bomb site or down a crater or in North Park with a crowd of boys, and came home hours late with grazed shins and torn clothes, though Mam didn't seem to notice.

Not to be outdone, Annie began to wander the streets of Bootle and Seaforth, staring in shop windows or through the gates of the docks, where dockers unloaded cargoes from all over the world. Her imagination soared, visualising the boxes of fruit and exotic-smelling spices being packed in sunny foreign climes. As the nights grew dark, though, and the cruel Mersey winds whipped inland, her adventurous spirit wilted, and she wished she were at home in front of the fire with someone to talk to and something to eat. Since both girls started having school dinners, Mam didn't make a meal till Dad came home.

One day in November, when it was bitterly cold and raining hard, she went down the entry and in the back way, and was surprised to be met by

Auntie Dot, looking extremely fierce. 'Where the hell have you been?' she demanded. 'It's gone five. And where's Marie?'

Dot was growing fat again, but this time Annie knew it was because she was having another baby. She jealously hoped it wouldn't be a girl. Dot mightn't love them so much if she had a daughter of her own.

Her aunt grabbed her arm, full of angry concern. 'Look at the state of you! You'll catch your death of cold. Get changed this minute and put your coat in the airing cupboard while I make a cup of tea.'

When Annie came down in a clean frock, she found Pete, now eighteen months, playing happily with wooden blocks. She glanced at her mam, and was surprised to see her cheeks were pink and she was twiddling with the belt of her dressing gown. Dot came in with a cup of steaming tea.

'Get those wet shoes off and put them on the hearth,' she barked. 'And I'd like an answer, madam. Where have you been till this hour, and where's your sister?'

'I went for a walk and Marie's gone to North Park.' Annie thought it wise not to mention the bomb sites and craters.

'Really!' said Dot caustically. 'It's not what I'd call walking weather, meself. As for the park . . .' She shook her head as if the situation was beyond her comprehension. Annie fidgeted uncomfortably.

'Do you know what day it is?' Dot demanded.

'Tuesday,' Annie replied, adding, 'the seventeenth of November.' She remembered thinking when Sister Clement wrote the date on the blackboard that it had a familiar ring.

'That's right, Marie's birthday! Nice way for a five-year-old to spend her birthday, in the park in the rain – isn't it, Rose?' She turned on the hunched woman in the corner. 'I come round with a cake and presents from us all, thinking there'd be a birthday tea, and what do I find? You've *forgotten*! Forgotten your own daughter's birthday! Not only that, there's no food in the offing of any description.'

This was said with such derision that Annie winced. For some reason she felt guilty. Her own birthday had fallen on a Sunday in October and they'd gone to Dot's for tea. Mam didn't answer, but began to shake her head from side to side. Dot, well into her stride, continued, 'Even worse, the girls aren't even in, and you're sitting here in your sodding dressing gown and don't give a shit, you selfish cow!'

Annie gasped. Her mam's head turned faster and faster and her eyes rolled upwards. She started to moan, and Dot leaned across and slapped her face, hard. 'Don't put on your little act with me, Rose,' she said in a low, grating, never-heard-before voice. 'You've had me fooled for years, but no longer. You're taking our Ken for a ride. If he's idiot enough to be taken in, that's his concern, but you're not getting away with it with these two girls. They're little treasures, the pair of them. I love them as if they were me own and you'll look after them proper or I'll have them taken off you. Do you hear?'

To Annie's surprise, Mam stopped moving her head and nodded. For a while, her mouth worked as if she were trying to speak, and perhaps she would have if Marie hadn't come bouncing in. Her shoes squelched and she was soaked to the skin and covered in mud, though she gave Dot a cocky smile. The smile vanished when Dot removed the shoes none too gently, and ordered her upstairs to change.

Then Dot turned to Mam, and in a gentler voice said, 'This can't go on, Rose. Two little girls wandering the streets, it's just not right. God knows what sort of trouble they could get into. In future, I'll get our Alan to stand by the gate and make sure they go home.'

Poor Alan, thought Annie, he'd have a fit. Dot dropped to her knees, somewhat clumsily due to her big belly, and grasped Mam's hands. 'I know what our Ken was up to that night, luv, but it's time to forgive and forget, if only for the sake of your girls.'

At this, Mam's face grew tight and she turned away, just as Marie came running downstairs.

Dot sighed and got awkwardly to her feet. 'Where's the ration books? Keep an eye on Pete for me while I get some cold meat, a few tomaters and half a pound of biscuits from the corner shop. There'll be a birthday tea in this house today or my name's not Dot Gallagher.'

Dot stayed till Dad came home, and after the girls had gone to bed there came the sound of a big argument. Annie crept onto the stairs to listen.

'I've told you before, Ken,' her aunt said loudly. 'If you can't cope with the girls, Bert and me will have them.'

'They're my girls, Dot,' Dad said in the quiet, mutinous voice he often used with his sister. 'They're my girls, and I love them.'

Things improved, but only slightly. There was a meal waiting when they got in – beans on toast, or boiled eggs – and Mam was dressed properly. Their normally curt and reticent dad gave them each a front-door key, as well as a stern lecture on coming straight home, describing the bloodcurdling things that could happen if they didn't. A girl had been murdered during the war, he told them, strangled with a piece of string in a back entry a mile away. Marie, easily frightened, rushed home panic-stricken, clutching Annie's hand.

But Mam stayed enclosed in her own private, grief-stricken world, hushed and uncommunicative. She only showed signs of life in the minutes before her husband was due home, when her head would be cocked like a bird's, waiting for the sound of the latch to be lifted on the backyard door, the signal of his arrival. During the meal, she sat watching, noting his every move, her listless eyes lifting and falling as he ate.

The meal finished, Dad would turn his chair towards the meagre coke fire and read the newspaper, the *Daily Express*, his wife still watching with the same hungry, melting expression on her face. No-one spoke. After a while, Annie and her sister would go upstairs and play in the chilly bedroom, and later on they'd go to bed of their own accord, and Dad might put his head in to say goodnight if he remembered.

Except for the occasions when Dot and Bert came round, this was how every evening passed; there was never any variation.

As the years went by, Annie became protective of her mother. She lied when Dot asked questions. Although her aunt only had their best interests at heart, she'd hated seeing Mam slapped and bullied.

'Mam made a cake for tea the other day.'

'We play Snakes and Ladders nearly every night.'

Anyroad, Dot didn't come round much nowadays. As soon as she'd had the new baby, another boy called Bobby, she'd fallen pregnant again and Joe was born a year later. Now she had six boys, 'Three little 'uns and three big 'uns', as she cheerfully put it. 'By the time afternoon comes, all I want to do is put me feet up.' It meant it was Dad who took Annie to the shops to buy a white dress and a veil for her First Holy Communion. The same outfit did Marie the following year.

Auntie Dot insisted the girls visit on Sundays. They did for a while, until Annie, conscience-stricken, decided she should stay at home and help her dad. Despite the long hours he worked, he spent all weekend doing housework. At eight, Annie was doing the week's shopping and even wrote the list herself. 'Poor little mite,' Dot said sorrowfully. 'She's old before her time.' Annie learnt to iron, and, as she knelt on the chair in front of the table, she couldn't help but wonder what the hunched, helpless woman in the chair by the window was thinking. About Johnny, her brother? Did she know she had two daughters? Once, Dot said Mam should be in hospital, but that was silly, thought Annie. Where would they put the bandages?

On the Sundays her mother could be persuaded to go to Mass, Annie felt proud as they walked along Orlando Street, just like a normal family. Mam looked so pretty in her curly fur coat, her long hair tied back with a ribbon, though Annie couldn't help but notice curtains twitching in the windows of some houses as they passed; curious neighbours watching 'the funny woman from number thirty-eight' on her way to church – which was how she'd once heard her mam described whilst she waited, unnoticed, at the back of the corner shop.

It would be nice to have a mam who wasn't 'funny', Annie thought wistfully, and a cheerful dad like Uncle Bert. One day, she found a wedding photo in the drawer of the big black sideboard. She stared at it for quite a while, wondering who the handsome couple were; the bright-eyed, smiling girl in the lacy dress clutching the hand of a young man with dashing good looks. The pair stared at each other with a strange, intense expression, almost sly, as if they shared a tremendous secret. It wasn't until Annie recognised a younger Dot, and Uncle Bert before he'd grown his moustache, that she realised it was her parents' wedding.

She showed the photograph to Marie, who looked at it for a long time before her face crumpled up, as if she were about to cry. Then she turned on her heel and left the parlour without a word.

Annie put the photo back in the drawer and resolved never to look at it again.

3

When Annie was eleven, she sat the scholarship. The entire class were to take the exam, but she was one of the few expected to pass. Passing the scholarship meant attending a grammar school instead of an ordinary secondary modern.

Marie was contemptuous. 'Seafield Convent! You'll never catch me at an all-girls' school. When *I* sit the scholarship, I'll answer every question wrong for fear I pass.'

The exam was set for nine o'clock one Saturday morning early in June. Annie's dad, who rarely became animated, was concerned she wouldn't arrive on time.

'I'll wake you when I leave,' he said in his flat, tired voice.

'Don't worry, Dad,' Annie said cheerfully. 'It's like any other day, except it's Saturday. I'm never late for school, am I?'

When the morning came, she was woken by the pressure of his hand on her shoulder. 'It's seven o'clock,' he whispered. 'There's tea made. Mam's still asleep,' he added somewhat superfluously, as if Mam were likely to be of use if she were awake.

'Rightio.' Annie snuggled under the clothes. She heard him manoeuvre his bike into the back entry and the wheels creak as he rode away. Sunlight filtered through the thick brown curtains. She lay, dazzled by the long bright vertical strip where the curtains didn't meet. She didn't feel at all nervous. She liked exams and was looking forward to the scholarship. They'd been doing special homework for weeks.

But after a while, she began to feel uneasy. Something was wrong. The bed felt sticky and her nightie was glued to her legs at the back. Annie stayed there for a good five minutes trying to work out what it was, then, gingerly, she got up. She gasped in horror. The sheet was stained with blood! Terrified, she twisted her nightdress round, and found it even bloodier.

She was going to die!

There was a dull, tugging ache in the pit of her stomach, as if heavy weights were suspended there about to pull everything out. Annie shook with fright and uttered a thin, high-pitched wail. The sound disturbed Marie, who turned restlessly and pulled the eiderdown over her head.

'Marie!' Annie shook her sister awake. She had to talk to someone.

'Whassa matter?' Marie sat up, pushing her dark hair from her eyes.

'Look!' Annie pointed to the bed, then to her nightdress.

'Jaysus!' said Marie in a startled voice. 'It must be that thing.' Despite being younger, Marie was better versed in the ways of the world than her sister. Months ago, she'd described how babies were born.

'What thing?' Annie cried piteously.

'I can't remember what it's called, but it happens to everyone – women, that is.'

'Why didn't you tell me!'

Marie shrugged. 'I thought you already knew.'

Her sister's lack of concern calmed Annie somewhat, though she still felt frightened. So, she wasn't going to die, but would she bleed like this for the rest of her life? The thought was infinitely depressing.

'What shall I do?' It didn't cross her mind to approach her mam.

'Tell Dot,' Marie said promptly, which was what Annie had already decided as soon as the words were out of her mouth.

The questions in the scholarship paper didn't make sense. Annie read and re-read them, but all she could think of was the lump of old petticoat between her legs and the fact that blood might come rushing forth and drown the whole class. She forgot entirely how to do decimals, and couldn't remember what an adjective was.

The two and a half hours dragged by interminably. When the time was up, she left the paper on the desk, knowing she had failed miserably.

Tommy opened the door to Annie's knock. The eldest of Dot's boys, at seventeen he was as tall as Bert, though as thin as a rake like his mam. He wore a blue shirt under his best suit, and his ginger hair was cut Tony Curtis style. If he hadn't been her cousin and she hadn't felt so wretched, Annie would have thought him immensely attractive.

'I'm just off into town to the pictures,' he said vaguely as she entered the house. Music came from a wireless upstairs; Alma Cogan sang 'How much is that Doggie in the Window?' In the kitchen Dot was singing along at the top of her voice. There was no sign of Bert, and Annie had already noticed the younger boys playing in the street.

'Hallo, luv,' Dot smiled, but the smile faltered when she noticed Annie's tragic expression. 'What's the matter?'

'I've failed the scholarship!'

Dot's face fell, but only slightly. 'It's not the end of the world, luv, I don't believe in grammar schools, anyroad. Most kids pay to go and they're just a crowd of snobs. You'll be far better off in an ordinary secondary modern like the boys.'

'It's not only that,' said Annie tearfully, 'it's . . .'

Mike came banging down the stairs, pushed Annie to one side, and began to clean his teeth in the sink. Alan had taken up the singing where Dot left off, and he was trying to mimic Alma Cogan's gutsy tones in a way which, at any other time, would have made Annie smile.

'What, luv?' urged Dot, then seeing Annie's eyes flicker to her cousin, she said, 'Come on, let's go in the parlour.'

The parlour had long been returned to its former glory. The three-piece suite was in its proper place and the polished gatelegged table in the centre took up an inordinate amount of space considering it was only used on special occasions. In the corner, in pride of place, stood a new addition, a television, covered with a brocade cloth and a statue of Our Lady. A few days ago, at least twenty people had crowded into the room to watch the coronation of Queen Elizabeth and listen to Richard Dimbleby's commentary, almost drowned out at times by Dot's vigorous condemnation of royalty and all it stood for.

As she sat in the grey moquette armchair, Annie began to weep the tears she'd longed to weep all day. 'When I woke up this morning, the bed and me nightdress were covered in blood . . .'

'Oh, you poor love!' Dot dropped on her knees and stroked Annie's face with her chapped hand. 'And you weren't expecting it?'

Annie shook her head dolefully. 'That bloody Rose, I could strangle her!' Dot raged. 'I should have told you, shouldn't I? It's just that having boys, it didn't cross me mind.' She began to cry, her emotions seeming to swing wildly from sympathy for Annie, anger with Rose, and recriminations against herself. After a while, she wiped her face with her pinny. 'Tell you what, let's have a treat! A little drop of whisky each, eh? Do your tummy good and calm your nerves.'

She opened the sideboard, took out a half full bottle, and poured an inch of liquid into two glasses. 'I often have a tot meself,' she said, cheerful again. 'But only one, mind; more, and I'm not responsible for me actions. Bert'll kill me when he finds it half gone.'

Annie choked on the whisky at first, but it seemed to warm her insides and she began to relax.

One of the boys suddenly yelled, 'Mam, where's me blue shirt?'

'Jaysus!' gasped Dot. 'I'm sure that's what our Tommy went out wearing. It's in the wash!' she screamed.

'Oh, Mam!' the voice said mournfully.

Dot grinned. 'Do you feel better now, luv?'

Annie nodded. She felt pleasantly light-headed.

'I'll fit you up with something before you go,' Dot promised, 'and tell you what to buy each month.'

'You mean it's not for ever? It stops sometimes?'

'It's just a few days once a month, that's all. You'll soon get used to it,' Dot said comfortably. 'Some women look forward to the curse.'

'The curse!' Annie smiled for the first time that day. 'You won't tell me dad, will you?'

'No, luv, but what about your mam? Are you going to tell her?'

Annie avoided Dot's eyes and shook her head.

Dot gave a disgusted, 'Humph! You've been having me on, haven't you, Annie? Rose playing Snakes and Ladders! You must think I was born yesterday. I never said anything, because Bert told me to mind me own business. He said as long as you and Marie seemed all right, I shouldn't interfere.' She absent-mindedly poured herself another glass of whisky.

Annie fidgeted with a loose thread of grey moquette on the arm of the chair. She noticed faint smudges of crayon in the rough loops of the material. It must be from the kitchen, where she and Marie used to draw.

'Will me mam ever get better?' she asked Dot directly. It was something she'd wanted to know for a long time.

As if it had provoked a chain of thought, instead of answering, Dot said, 'Oh, your dad! He was a real ladykiller in his day, just like our Tommy. He'd got more girls in tow than a sheikh with a harem.'

Annie resisted the urge to laugh. Dad, her stooped, weary father with his peaked face, the man who brought meat home in his saddlebag and spent the weekends doing housework – a ladykiller!

Dot noticed her incredulous expression. 'He was, Annie,' she said indignantly. 'He attracted women like a flypaper attracts flies. Out with a different girl every night he was, until he met your mam. Then, wham, bang! It was love at first sight.'

Annie recalled the wedding photograph in the sideboard drawer, the couple sharing a great secret.

'I'm glad I didn't fall in love like that!' Dot said primly. 'I love Bert with all me heart, but with our Ken and Rose, it was too hungry, too . . .' she searched for another word, 'too overwhelming,' she finished.

'Dot,' Annie said cautiously, knowing her aunt was slightly drunk and might reveal things that ordinarily she wouldn't, 'what was me dad up to the night Johnny was killed? You said something about it once . . .'

'I remember,' Dot said darkly. She leaned back in the chair and finished off the whisky. Suddenly, the wireless was switched off and Mike and Alan came stamping down the stairs like a pair of elephants.

'Tara, Mam,' they shouted. The front door slammed, then there was a clatter, and 'Tara, Annie', came through the letterbox.

Dot smiled and looked as if she might cry again. 'Aren't they lovely lads? I'm a lucky woman, what with Bert an' all.' She didn't speak for a while, and Annie thought she'd forgotten her question, until she leaned over and took her niece's hand. 'I suppose you've a right to know, luv. You're nearly grown up, specially with what happened today.' She took a deep breath. 'Your mam and dad had their own house off Chestnut Grove in those days. The night Johnny died, your dad was late; he should have been home long before the siren went. The shelter was only at the bottom of the street and Rose got all the things together you need for a baby. She took them to the shelter, meaning to come straight back for Johnny, and . . . well, you know the rest. She'd only set foot inside when the bomb fell. If your dad was there, they'd have taken Johnny with them.' Dot paused and eyed the whisky bottle, but made no move to touch it.

'And what was me dad up to?' whispered Annie.

Dot stared into her empty glass. 'He was an awful weak man, your dad. He couldn't resist a pretty face, even if Rose was the only woman he wanted. It came out he was with someone else, and no, Annie, I don't think your mam will ever get better, because she's too eaten up with jealousy and hatred, all mixed up with terrible love, and in my opinion, it's nowt to do with Johnny dying, but because your dad betrayed her.'

'I see,' said Annie, wondering if she did. Her aunt was still clutching her hand, and now her grip tightened, so hard that Annie winced.

'He's me little brother, and he did an awful thing, but no man has paid more thoroughly for his sins than our Ken.' Dot's voice began to rise and became grating, almost hysterical. 'Sometimes I wonder if it's all a sham with Rose, if she's putting it on, trying to squeeze every last drop of remorse out of him. But no-one could put on an act like that for so long, surely? No-one could be so twisted as to wreck so many lives, including their own, could they, Annie?'

Annie wished she'd never raised the subject. Dot frightened her. Her eyes glinted strangely and she looked almost unhinged. She tried to extricate her hand, but her aunt's grip was too strong.

'She was already expecting you when it happened,' Dot said hoarsely. 'We thought another baby'd do the trick, bring her back to her senses, but it made no difference. As for Marie, she was an accident.' She laughed bitterly and eyed the whisky bottle again.

Annie managed to drag her hand away. She returned the bottle to the sideboard and said brightly, 'Shall we have a cup of tea, Auntie Dot?'

Later, when they were having the tea, Dot recovered her good humour. 'I'm sorry, luv, for letting off steam just now. I should never have had that second glass of whisky.'

Annie was relieved her aunt was back to her amiable, good-natured self.

She was glad she'd come, after all. She'd learnt a lot about Mam and Dad, though she doubted if it would help to understand them better.

When the letter arrived to say she'd failed the scholarship, Dad merely shrugged his shoulders wearily and didn't say a word.

Grenville Lucas Secondary Modern school had been built after the war. It was a light, airy two-storey building with modern desks and equipment. The walls were covered with drawings, the work of the pupils themselves, done in the art room overlooking the tree-lined playing fields.

Annie went into the top stream, though soon discovered she was no longer a star pupil. There were many boys and girls cleverer than she would ever be. After a while, being clever didn't matter. What mattered was making friends, being one of the 'in-crowd'. The worst thing that could happen was not being invited to join a clique, being an outsider.

To her surprise, she found herself quite popular, and eventually attached herself to Ruby Livesey, leader of a nameless sisterhood of about a dozen girls. Ruby was stout, with the gait of a heavyweight boxer and the reputation of being a bully. It seemed wise to be in her good books, though Annie was to regret this decision in the years to come.

Also, she was flattered to be asked. The other girls in Ruby's gang were all in their second year. When she asked why they'd chosen her, the reply was astonishing. 'Because you're so pretty.'

Pretty! That night, Annie studied herself in the misty, scarred wardrobe mirror. 'Do you think I'm good-looking?' she asked her sister.

Marie was lying on the bed reading *Silver Star*. 'You're okay,' she shrugged. 'Your face is quite a nice shape, though I couldn't stand having red hair meself.' She tossed her own brown tresses. 'What are the boys like at Grenville Lucas? Have you been asked out yet?'

'Of course not!' Annie hooted. 'I'm not quite twelve.'

'I've been going out with boys since I was five.'

'If me dad knew, he'd kill you.'

'He wouldn't give a shit!'

'Don't swear!' The reproof was automatic. Marie swore like a trooper.

'Dot swears,' countered Marie.

Annie couldn't be bothered arguing. She continued examining her face. It *was* a nice shape, sort of oval, rather pale and slightly freckled between the eyes. Her hair was more copper than red, darker than the Gallaghers', and thicker, a mass of natural waves and curls.

'You've got nice eyes.' Marie put down her magazine and regarded Annie speculatively. 'Sometimes they're blue and sometimes they're grey, and your lashes are a lovely gold. I'd advise you not to use mascara when you're older.'

'Thanks!' Annie said sarcastically. 'Do you think we'll grow tall, like Dad and Auntie Dot?'

Marie frowned at the ceiling, as if her height were something she often put her mind to. She was remarkably adult, though in a different way from her sister. Whilst Annie ran the house as confidently as a woman, Marie did nothing to help at home, but *thought* like a woman. She read adult magazines and spent hours in front of the mirror combing her hair and posing like a film star. The effect of the lecture Dad had given all those years ago had long since worn off. Annie knew her sister went to North Park with boys after school. When she tried to reason with her, Marie laughed in her face. Last term she'd been caught smoking, and the nuns had written to Dad, though nothing had been said. He was increasingly tired nowadays, as if everything were too much for him.

'I reckon I'll be the same height as our mam,' Marie said after serious consideration. 'Dot always says I'm the spitting image of her. You'll probably end up tall. Fortunately, you've already got more curves than Dot, who's as skinny as a scarecrow, so I reckon you'll look okay.'

Annie went to bed that night feeling unusually happy. It was nice to discover at such a late age that you were pretty!

One good thing about Grenville Lucas was that, although Annie was asked to some girls' houses, they didn't automatically expect to come to hers. It was taken for granted that not all parents welcomed their daughters' friends. After school, Ruby Livesey and the gang went to the shops in Waterloo, where they hung around Woolworth's and Boots. A few girls shoplifted. When this happened, Annie edged into another aisle so she wouldn't appear to be with them if they were caught.

Other days, they went to a café for a cup of tea, where they often met up with boys from Merchant Taylors, and Annie was amazed at the change which occurred in Ruby. Normally overbearing and bossy, she collapsed into simpering giggles and her gruff voice went up an octave. No-one else seemed to find this transformation in any way remarkable; indeed, they were too busy simpering themselves.

It was at this time Annie realised she needed money of her own. It was embarrassing when someone else had to pay for her tea, and she was never able to buy anything from Woolworth's. When the girls went to the pictures on Saturdays, she had to refuse.

'Ask your dad for some pocket money,' Dot urged when Annie explained her predicament. 'He can afford it.'

'Can he?' Annie felt bewildered, having assumed they were poor.

'Of course he can. One thing our Ken's always been is a good insurance salesman. His wages aren't up to much, but he earns as much again in commission.'

So Annie approached her dad for pocket money, and was surprised when he offered five shillings a week, much more than the other girls.

The incident was a revelation. Since they'd moved to Orlando Street, nothing new of any description had been bought for the house. Their food was basic, almost meagre. The only expensive item on the weekly shopping list was fresh fruit for Mam, which Annie had never seen her eat, but she must have done some time, because the fruit had always gone by Saturday when she went shopping again. Even at Christmas nothing extra was bought, because they always went to Dot's on Christmas Day.

Annie wasn't sure whether to be angry or pleased at the discovery they weren't poverty-stricken. Emboldened, she approached her dad for new clothes. In December, the gang were planning a day in town to go Christmas shopping, and she didn't fancy wearing her school uniform.

Her dad's expression was one of sheer bewilderment when she asked for a coat, as if it had never crossed his mind his daughters might want anything other than the barest essentials. Annie stared at his drawn, white face. She hadn't noticed before, but his features seemed to be collapsing in on themselves as the years took their toll, smudging and blurring, and she felt scared that the day might come when he'd have no face at all. His light blue eyes were sinking back into his narrow skull, and there were little silvery channels glistening underneath where the eyes had watered. They looked like eternal tears.

Annie felt a pang of guilt for having bothered him. She touched his sleeve. 'It doesn't matter, Dad, honest.'

He glanced down at her hand with a look of faint surprise, as if he were unused to human contact. She could feel the sharp bones in his wrist. 'It doesn't matter, Dad,' she said again.

To her astonishment, he smiled, and the change was so enormous it almost took her breath away. His thin, almost invisible mouth quivered upwards and his face took shape again. For a brief, magical moment, Annie glimpsed the ladykiller in him.

'I suppose you want to look nice for the boys,' he said in a jokey voice which Annie had never heard before and would never hear again.

'That's right, Dad.' She didn't disillusion him, but it wasn't the boys she wanted to look nice for, but herself.

'Well, my girl must look as good as the others,' he said simply.

Straight after work the following Saturday, he took her to Stanley Road in Bootle, and bought her an emerald green winter coat, two jumpers and a skirt, and a pair of black patent leather shoes.

'Oh, Dad, it's lovely,' she breathed as she twirled in front of the mirror. The green was a perfect contrast to her bright copper curls.

But Dad was no longer interested. He nodded briefly and paid the assistant. They walked home without saying a word, and so fast that Annie could scarcely keep up.

4

Pupils who hadn't been at Grenville Lucas from year one, who appeared in class suddenly and without warning, were regarded with the deepest suspicion. The suspicion was even greater if they had a strange accent. It took Ian Robertson from Glasgow a whole term to make friends.

So when Sylvia Delgado arrived during Annie's third year, she was looked upon with loathing – but only by the girls. When Mr Parrish, the headmaster, ushered the new girl into class halfway through a Geography lesson in November, several boys risked a cheeky wolfwhistle.

Annie was in the process of colouring a map showing the wheat-growing areas of Canada. She looked up to see a tall, slender girl beaming at them with a heroic and slightly aggressive self-confidence, as if she expected everyone to like her on the spot.

The wolfwhistles weren't surprising. The girl was the first genuinely beautiful person Annie had ever seen, with fine, delicately-formed features and ivory, almost translucent skin. Her long blonde hair was dead straight, cut in a jagged fringe on her forehead. Even from the back of the room, it was possible to see the startling azure blue of her eyes, the thick dark lashes under equally dark, perfectly shaped brows.

'This is Sylvia Delgado,' Mr Parrish said brusquely. 'She's from Italy, and I hope you'll make her very welcome.'

Italy! There was an excited buzz. There'd never been a foreigner at school before. The girl nodded at the class and smiled again.

'It is so very nice to be here,' she said, in perfect English with just the faintest suggestion of an accent.

The headmaster exchanged a few words with the teacher, Mrs Wayne. After he'd gone, Mrs Wayne looked around for an empty seat. As usual, there were vacant desks near the front. She indicated to the girl where to sit and told the class sharply to settle down.

The agricultural map of Canada forgotten, Annie glanced covertly at the new girl, who was on the next row to her, several desks in front. Her long slim legs, clad in honeycoloured stockings and crossed elegantly at the ankles, protruded into the aisle, as if the desk were too small, and the heel of one black suede ballerina shoe was dangling from her toes. She wore a uniform of sorts: a gymslip made from fine serge material, more like a pinafore frock, with a scooped neck instead of square. The folds of the full flared skirt fell in a half circle beneath the seat. Annie felt convinced that the white blouse underneath this remarkably fashionable garment was pure silk from the way it shimmered when the girl bent her elbow and began to write.

She would love Sylvia Delgado to be her friend, Annie thought longingly, not just because she was beautiful and wore expensive clothes, but because there was something appealing about her demeanour. She felt sure that, if they got to know each other, they would have lots in common – though probably every other girl felt the same. New pupils weren't usually accepted for ages, but it was bound to be different with this girl. Everyone would be clamouring to be her friend.

But Annie couldn't possibly have been more wrong.

She had no idea where the new girl sat at dinner time, but when they emerged from the dining room, Annie saw her standing alone in the playground, looking rather deflated.

'Who's that?' demanded Ruby Livesey.

'Her name's Sylvia Delgado, she's Italian,' Annie said importantly. 'She only started this morning.'

'Italian!' Ruby expostulated rudely. 'Why's she blonde, then? I thought Italians were dark.'

'I've no idea.' Annie had wondered the same. 'Shall we talk to her?'

'Not bloody likely,' Ruby snorted. 'Being Italian's almost as bad as being German. We fought them bloody Eyeties during the war.'

Even Sally Baker, Ruby's trusted first lieutenant, felt bound to remark, 'But the war ended ten years ago, Ruby.'

'Yeah, but even so!' Ruby stared belligerently at the new girl. 'I've changed me mind. I *will* have a word with her, after all. Tell her what I think of bloody foreigners.'

'No!' cried Annie, but she was ignored. As the girls, Ruby at their head, marched across the playground, Annie trailed miserably behind. She couldn't wait for the summer term when Ruby Livesey, who was already fifteen, would leave. She was sick of belonging to her gang, fed up going to the pictures and seeing only Ruby's choice of film, and hanging around in cafés talking to stupid boys. She would have broken off relations long ago, but lacked the courage, having witnessed what Ruby did to those who got on her wrong side. She didn't fancy being dragged into a back entry and beaten up on the way home from school.

Two boys were already chatting to the new girl when they arrived. 'Sod off!' Ruby barked. The boys looked at her in surprise. They laughed, but readily departed. She plonked herself squarely in front of the girl and sneered, 'So, you're a bloody Eyetie!'

The girl's lovely dark blue eyes grew puzzled. She threw back her head. 'I am Italian, yes,' she said with dignity.

'Me Uncle Bill was killed by your lot during the war.'

This was a lie. Uncle Bill's ship had been sunk by a German U-boat, but it was more than Annie's life was worth to point this out.

The girl replied with the same quiet dignity, 'I'm sorry about your uncle. But my father is a communist who hated Hitler and spent the war fighting the Germans in Yugoslavia.'

Annie gasped. Although Russia had been an ally of Britain during the war, for some reason she couldn't quite understand it was now her greatest enemy, ready to atom bomb the country any minute. Russia was made up entirely of communists. Fortunately, Ruby seemed ignorant of this fact and appeared momentarily confused. She swiftly recovered her composure, 'What the hell are you doing in our country, anyroad?' she demanded.

'My father has bought a hotel in Waterloo. My mother is English, she was born in Formby. We have decided to make England our home.' The girl tossed her long blonde hair defiantly and Annie admired her spirit. Although clearly shaken, her manner was proud, almost queenly.

'You got any brothers or sisters?' one of the girls asked curiously.

'No. I am a lone child.'

The gang tittered, and Ruby said threateningly, 'We don't like foreigners in this country, particularly Eyeties, so keep out of our way in future. Understand?'

Sylvia Delgado nodded stiffly. 'I understand.' Her dark eyes swept slowly over the group, as if she were memorising them. Annie dropped her own eyes and wished she could crawl under a stone.

To emphasise that her threat was real, Ruby gave the girl a vicious shove, grabbed her leather satchel and flung it across the concrete yard where it slithered to a halt in a cloud of dust.

As if taking their cue from Ruby, not one of the girls spoke to Sylvia Delgado, apart from Ruby's own frequent verbal, and sometimes physical, assaults. Wherever Sylvia was, she would be tracked down and given the sharp edge of Ruby's tongue, along with a blow if her tormentor happened to be in a particularly foul mood. Sylvia became the sole topic of conversation, and Annie was shocked by the sheer spite of the comments.

'Me dad said columnists are a load of shit. He reckons Sylvia's dad should be shot.'

'He's a communist, not a columnist,' Annie said hotly. 'When I told me Auntie Dot, she said he was a hero.' But no-one was willing to listen to a word in Sylvia Delgado's favour.

'Have you seen where she lives? It's that big hotel opposite the Odeon. S'not fair, a foreigner living in a dead posh place like that.'

'What gets me is she don't half fancy herself. She walks around as if she owns the place. You'd think she was Marilyn Monroe or something.'

'Not Marilyn Monroe, she's nice. I wouldn't mind being her meself. No, Grace Kelly. She always looks as if there's a bad smell under her nose, and she's living in a palace with that French prince, isn't she?'

'It's that cruddy gymslip that gets me,' complained Sally Baker. 'If any of us wore one like that, Mr Parrish'd have a fit.'

'We should rip it off her back and tear it to pieces,' Ruby said balefully. 'Tell her to get one the same as ours.'

The girls glanced at each other nervously. 'Perhaps that's going a bit far, Ruby.'

'Y'reckon!' Ruby sneered. 'Well, something's got to be done to take the bitch down a peg or two.'

'But she hasn't done anything,' Annie protested. She felt angry. Although Sylvia Delgado still walked with her head held high, she looked slightly desperate, as if she were gradually being worn down. Annie wished she were brave enough to ignore Ruby, because she liked Sylvia Delgado more than ever and longed to be her friend. She didn't care if she came from Italy or Timbuctoo.

Ruby turned on her and began to list all the terrible, imaginary things Sylvia had done to justify her treatment. Intimidated, Annie didn't say another word.

As the autumn term drew to a close, the subject of Sylvia Delgado was put aside temporarily as plans were made for Christmas. The gang were going to the pictures on Christmas Eve, but Ruby hadn't yet made up her mind what to see. On the Saturday after school finished, a shopping trip to Liverpool was planned. Several girls were having parties.

Annie had asked for more housekeeping and had been buying extra groceries for weeks: a tin of assorted biscuits, a plum pudding and a fruit cake she intended icing herself, several tins of fruit. She was determined the Harrisons would enjoy the occasion for once, and had even bought decorations and a little imitation tree.

The sisters put the decorations up one day after school. Throughout the entire operation, their mam sat in her usual chair, her head turned away, her long dark hair falling like a curtain over her incredibly girlish face. She seemed oblivious to everything, even when Marie climbed on the table and banged a nail directly above her head. The girls would have been astonished if she'd acted any differently.

'What do you think, Mam?' Annie nevertheless asked when the decorations were up and the room actually looked quite cheerful. She saw Mam's hands were clasped tensely on her lap, the knuckles white and strained. 'Perhaps she's frightened,' Annie thought with compunction.

Mam didn't answer, and Marie said contemptuously, 'It's no use asking her, is it? You'd only drop dead if she answered.'

'Shush!' Marie frequently made horrible, insensitive comments in Mam's hearing – at least, Annie assumed she could hear.

'Why should I?' Marie demanded. 'She's way out of it, drugged to high heaven.'

'What on earth are you talking about?'

Marie looked at her sister impatiently. 'Honestly, Annie, you're not half thick. You haven't a clue what's going on. Mam's got all sorts of tablets in the cupboard. She takes pills all day long.'

'You mean aspirin?' Aspirin were the only pills Annie knew of.

'I've no idea what they're called, but they're different shapes and colours. They deaden your brain so you don't have to think. I pinched one once when she went to the lavvy. It was a nice feeling, nothing seemed to matter, but I fell asleep in the pictures and it was *Singin' in the Rain.*' She pouted. 'I missed most of it.'

With that, Marie flounced upstairs to get ready for a date. She spent all her pocket money on clothes and cosmetics. In a while, she'd come down dressed to the nines, her face plastered with Max Factor pancake, burgundy lipstick, and far too much shadow and mascara on her lovely grey eyes, looking as glamorous and pretty as a film star, and more like eighteen than thirteen.

Annie knew it was a waste of time saying anything, and neither Mam nor Dad seemed to care. She sighed as she went to get the tea ready – Mam had given up the ghost ages ago when it came to preparing meals.

Grenville Lucas held their customary party on the day school broke up. Lessons finished at mid-day. After a turkey dinner, festivities would transfer to the gym. It was the only day in the year when the pupils could dispense with school uniform and wear their own clothes. Marie even got up early as she couldn't make up her mind what to put on.

Annie wore a new plaid skirt and her favourite jumper, pale blue cable knit with a polo neck. The two girls set off at half past eight full of excited anticipation, Annie little realising the day would turn out to be one of the most momentous of her life.

In class the girls were eyeing each other with interest, assessing the various fashions, when Sylvia Delgado came in wearing the most beautiful frock Annie had ever seen. Made of fine, soft jersey, it was turquoise, with a high buttoned neck and full bishop sleeves gathered into long, tight cuffs. A wide, tan leather belt accentuated her incredibly slender waist.

A girl behind gasped involuntarily, 'Doesn't she look lovely!'

Sylvia's long blonde hair was tucked behind a gold velvet Alice band decorated with tiny pearls. When she sat down, Annie saw she was wearing tan leather boots with *high heels*! Annie's skirt and jumper suddenly seemed very drab, and her feeling of envy was mixed with alarm. The outfit would drive Ruby Livesey *mad*!

'Who the hell does she think she is, coming to school tarted up like a bloody mannequin!' said Ruby for the fifth, possibly the sixth, time.

Christmas dinner was over and they were in the gym watching the dancing; Mr Parrish was playing his Frank Sinatra records. Sylvia Delgado had been up for every dance, but not a single boy had approached Ruby or her gang, though some girls danced with each other. Annie felt a stirring of interest in the opposite sex. She hated dancing with girls, particularly Ruby, who insisted on being the woman and it was like pushing a carthorse round. It was particularly irritating to see Marie floating past, always in the arms of a different boy.

'I hate her!' Ruby spat. 'If it wasn't for her, those boys'd be dancing with us.'

The logic of this escaped Annie, as there was only one Sylvia Delgado and eleven of them. As far as she was concerned, the party had turned out to be a wash-out. She couldn't wait for it to be half past three when she could throw away her paper hat and leave – not that she intended going home. They were going shopping; Ruby might well get on her nerves, but was infinitely preferable to her silent mam.

It was almost dark by the time they reached Waterloo, and freezing – the road led straight down to the River Mersey. Little icy spots of rain were blowing on the biting wind which gusted under their skirts and up their sleeves, penetrating the thickest clothes.

Despite the cold, they were happy. Every now and then, they would burst into song, 'White Christmas', or 'I saw Mommy kissing Santa Claus', though it ended in a giggle after a few bars when their jaws froze.

Annie had recovered her good humour. It was difficult not to when there were decorations everywhere, and coloured lights, and the shops were packed with happy people. There was a lovely atmosphere, and she felt heady with excitement.

Carols could be heard along the road, and they came to a churchyard, where five black-cloaked nuns were standing around a large crib with almost life-sized figures, singing 'Away in a Manger' at the top of their glorious soprano voices. A large crowd had stopped to sing with them.

Annie paused, entranced. The scene was like a Christmas card. The churchyard was surrounded by frost-tipped holly trees strung with sparkling lanterns, and the vivid colours were reflected over and over in the gleaming, thorny leaves. The white starched headdresses of the women were like giant butterflies, quivering slightly as if about to soar away. Above it all, icy drops of rain could be seen against the navy-blue sky, blowing this way and that like tiny, dancing stars. As Annie watched, a real star appeared, which seemed to be winking and blinking especially at her. The other girls were already some distance ahead. 'Let's sing some carols,' she called.

They stopped. 'It's bloody freezing,' Ruby complained.

'Just one,' pleaded Annie. 'After all, it's Christmas.'

'Oh, all right, just one.'

The nuns began 'Silent Night', and everyone joined in. Annie was singing away when Sally Baker nudged her. 'See who's over there!'

Sylvia Delgado was standing at the back of the crowd, staring wide-eyed, as if as entranced as Annie by it all. She wore a thick suede coat with a fur collar which looked incredibly smart.

Annie only half heard the message being passed along the line of girls. 'See who's over there!' She felt annoyed when her arm was grabbed and someone hissed, 'Come on, quick! Let's get out of here.'

'Why?' she asked. 'The carol hasn't finished.'

A man's voice shouted angrily. 'Look what someone's done to this poor girl!'

Ruby and the gang were nowhere to be seen. Puzzled, Annie left the church and saw them running down the road, laughing. They disappeared into Woolworth's and were still laughing when she caught up with them.

'What happened?' she demanded.

'Ruby pushed Sylvia Delgado right into the middle of a holly tree. You should have seen her face! One minute she was there, then, "whoosh", she'd completely disappeared!'

Annie said nothing. She thought of Sylvia innocently watching the lovely Christmas scene, little realising she was about to be attacked.

The girls were at the jewellery counter discussing what presents to buy each other. 'What would you like, Annie?' Sally Barker called.

'I wouldn't be seen dead with anything off youse lot,' Annie said coldly.

They stared at her in surprise. One or two had the grace to look ashamed, as if they knew the reason for the normally easy-going Annie Harrison's strange behaviour.

'Merry Christmas,' she said sarcastically. Turning on her heel, she marched out of Woolworth's to cries of, 'But Annie . . .'

The nuns were still in the churchyard, but there was no sign of Sylvia Delgado. Minutes later, Annie stood by the Odeon opposite the hotel where Sylvia lived. The traffic was heavy, and every now and then her view was blocked when a doubledecker bus or a lorry crawled by. The hotel was called the Grand, an appropriate name, she thought, because it was very grand indeed. Three storeys high, it was painted white and had little black wrought-iron balconies outside the windows of the first and second floors, and a red-and-black striped awning across the entire front at ground level. The doors were closed, and she wondered if it was more a posh sort of pub, rather than a hotel where people stayed.

She wasn't sure how long she stood there, hopping from one foot to the other, and swinging her arms to try and keep warm. Time was getting on, and if she didn't take her courage in both hands soon, she would be late with Dad's tea. She didn't want him coming home on such a bitter night to find there was no hot meal waiting.

Eventually, she took a deep breath and dodged through the traffic across the road. She peeped through the downstairs window of the hotel. Apart from a string of coloured lights across the bar, the big room was in darkness. She went around the side and found a small door, where she rang the bell and waited, her stomach knotted with nervousness.

After a while, the door was opened by a slim woman whom Annie recognised immediately as Sylvia's mother. Not quite so beautiful, eyes a slightly lighter blue, and several inches shorter than her daughter, but lovely all the same. Her blonde hair was cut urchin style, in feathery wisps around her face. She wore black slacks and a pink satin shirt blouse, and smiled kindly at the visitor.

'Is Sylvia in?' Annie gulped.

'I heard her come home a minute ago. Are you a friend from school?' The woman looked delighted. 'Come in, dear. Quickly, out of the cold.'

'Thank you.' Annie stepped into the neat lobby and the change from numbing cold to instant heat was almost suffocating. She noticed a metal radiator fixed to the wall, which explained why Sylvia's mother could walk round in a satin blouse in the middle of the winter!

'And who are you? You must call me Cecy, which is short for Cecilia. It's pronounced, "Si Si" – "yes" in Italian. I can't stand being called Mrs Delgado by my daughter's friends. It makes me feel very old.'

'I'm Annie. Annie Harrison.'

'Come along, Annie. I'll show you up to Sylvia's room.'

Annie felt uncomfortable when Mrs Delgado – Cecy – linked her arm companionably and they went upstairs together. Would the welcome be quite so warm if Sylvia's mother knew she hadn't exchanged a single word with her daughter since she'd started school?

When they reached the first-floor landing, Cecy shouted, 'Sylvia, darling, one of your friends is here.' She pointed up the second flight of stairs. 'First door on the right. I'll bring coffee in a minute.'

'Thank you, Mrs . . . I mean, Cecy.'

The knot in Annie's stomach tightened. What sort of reception would she get? It would be quite understandable if Sylvia ordered her off the premises. As far as she was concerned, Annie was an acolyte of Ruby Livesey, someone who'd made her life a misery for weeks.

She was about to knock on the door when it opened, and Sylvia regarded her haughtily. There was an ugly red scratch on her creamy cheek. The two girls stared at each other.

'Hello,' Annie said awkwardly.

'Hello. I was wondering if you'd come. I've been watching you across the road for ages.' Sylvia gestured towards the window.

Annie took a deep breath. 'I came to say it wasn't me. I knew nothing about it till afterwards. Are you badly hurt?'

'Did they send you to find out?' Sylvia looked angry. 'I wouldn't have thought they cared.'

'No!' Annie said quickly. 'I came of me own accord. They don't know I'm here – not that it'd worry me if they did.'

'If you must know, there are tiny scratches all over my head. It's a good thing I went in backwards or I could have been blinded.' She shuddered. 'The scratch on my cheek happened when I was being pulled out. Cecy will have a fit. I've managed to avoid her so far.'

'I'm awful sorry,' Annie mumbled.

'Are you truly?' Sylvia looked at her keenly.

Annie nodded her head. 'I'm sorry about everything.'

Sylvia's lovely face broke into a smile. 'In that case, why don't you come in and sit down, Annie – it is Annie, isn't it?'

'That's right.' Annie entered the room and sat in an armchair. The suede coat Sylvia had been wearing lay over the arm.

'I think my coat's ruined,' Sylvia said sadly. 'Bruno bought it for me because he said England would be cold.'

Annie saw the coat was scored with little jagged marks. 'Bruno?'

'My father. It cost two hundred thousand lire.'

'Jaysus!'

Sylvia laughed. It was an attractive laugh, like everything else about her, deep and faintly musical. 'That's not as expensive as it sounds, about a hundred pounds in English money.'

'Jaysus!' Annie said again. Her coat had cost £8.9s.11d. 'If you use a wire brush, the marks won't show so much.'

'Perhaps,' Sylvia shrugged. 'It's my own fault. I was only showing off. I wore my most elegant dress and Cecy's boots as a way of thumbing my nose at those awful girls. Why should I look drab to please them?'

It was Annie's turn to laugh. She forgot that until very recently she'd been one of the awful girls herself, albeit unwillingly. 'You couldn't look drab if you tried!'

Sylvia tossed her head conceitedly and looked pleased. Her eyes met Annie's for a long moment, and in that moment, Annie knew the ice had been broken. There was no need for more explanations and apologies. Sylvia had forgiven her and from now on they would be friends.

'Is this room all yours?' Annie had only just noticed the bed tucked underneath the white sloping ceiling. The room was large, almost twenty feet square, thickly carpeted from wall to wall in cream. Somewhat incredibly, because Annie was unaware such a thing was possible, the fresh daisy-sprigged wallpaper was exactly the same pattern as the frilly curtains and the cover on the bed. There were a wardrobe and dressing table in pale creamy wood, a desk and two armchairs.

'It's what's called a bedsitting room,' explained Sylvia.

'It's dead gorgeous!' Annie breathed. 'It's like a film star's.' Sylvia even had her own gramophone with a stack of records underneath. Amidst the paraphernalia on the dressing table, the silver-backed mirror and hairbrush, several bottles of perfume and pretty glass ornaments, stood a pearl crucifix with a gold figure of Jesus. Sylvia was Catholic. It meant they had something in common.

'What's that?' She pointed to a small wooden shield on the wall.

'Our family coat of arms,' Sylvia explained. 'Please don't tell anyone at school, but my father is a Count. He has another, much larger shield in the bar, and thinks it a great joke to tell everyone he's a Count, then tell them he's a communist. Bruno is very gregarious; he loves arguing, particularly about politics. That's why he bought the Grand, so he would have an audience for his views. He's not interested in money. We already have pans.'

'Pots,' said Annie. 'You have pots of money, not pans.'

There was silence for a while, then Sylvia said shyly, 'What are you doing on Saturday, Annie?'

'Nothing.' Annie had decided to have no more to do with Ruby Livesey. The decision would cause unpleasantness when she returned to school, but she didn't care. She and Sylvia would face it together.

'I haven't bought a single present yet. I wondered if you'd like to go shopping in Liverpool? We could have lunch and go to the cinema.'

'I'd love to!' cried Annie. 'Having lunch' sounded dead posh. If she did the washing on Friday, she'd have Saturday to do as she pleased.

Cecy came in with coffee and a plate of chocolate biscuits. She yelped in horror when she saw her daughter's scratched face, and immediately fetched disinfectant and cotton wool.

'I caught it on a tree,' Sylvia explained.

'You silly girl!' Cecy said fondly as she dabbed the wound.

Annie would have loved a room like Sylvia's, and a two-hundred-thousand lire coat, but what she would have loved most of all was a mam who cared if she came in hurt. 'Mam wouldn't notice if I came home carrying me head underneath me arm,' she thought drily.

5

At ten o'clock on Saturday morning, Annie waited on Seaforth station for the Liverpool train. Sylvia was catching the five past ten from Waterloo and they would meet in the front compartment. It was colder than ever. A pale lemony sun shone, crisp and bright, in a cloudless blue sky.

Annie thought of the rack in the kitchen which was crammed with clothes she'd washed the night before, the larder full of groceries, and the beef casserole slowly cooking in the oven. There was nothing for Dad to do when he came home from work. He could read the paper or watch sport on the recently acquired television which had been bought at Annie's insistence. Even Marie stayed in one night to watch a play.

She stared at the signal, willing it to fall and indicate the train was coming, and did a little dance because she had never felt so happy. Next week, it would be Christmas and today she was going into town with her friend! On the platform opposite, a porter watched with amusement.

'Someone's full of the joys of spring, even if it is December,' he shouted.

The silver lines began to hum, the signal fell, and a few minutes later the train drew in, and there was Sylvia, exactly where she'd said she'd be! She wore a red mohair coat and a white fur hat and looked every bit as happy as Annie.

Liverpool was glorious in its Christmas splendour. Carols poured out relentlessly from every shop and the pavements were crammed with people laden with parcels struggling to make their way along.

The first thing they did was buy a copy of the *Echo*. In the Kardomah over coffee, they excitedly scanned the list of films. They had to finish shopping in time for the afternoon performance.

'Which one do you fancy?' asked Sylvia.

'You say first.'

'I'd love to see *Three Coins in a Fountain*. It's set in Rome and I miss Italy awfully.'

'Then that's what we'll see.'

'Are you sure?'

'Positive,' Annie said firmly. 'I saw Rossano Brazzi in *Little Women* and I thought he was dead smashing.'

'Next time, you can have first choice. Now, as soon as we've finished our coffee, you must take me to George Henry Lee's. According to Cecy, it's the finest shop in Liverpool.'

On her few excursions into town, Annie had never ventured inside George Henry Lee's, deterred by the mind-boggling prices in the window. Once there, Sylvia began to spend at a rate that took Annie's breath away; a black suede handbag for Cecy, a silk scarf for Bruno, a fluffy white shawl for her grandmother.

'My grandparents are flying over for Christmas,' she explained. 'Now, what shall I get for Grandpapa?'

They went to the menswear department, where, after much deliberation, she chose a long-sleeved cashmere pullover. 'Aren't you going to buy any presents?' she asked Annie after a while.

'Not here,' Annie said, embarrassed. She'd managed to save nearly five pounds by assiduously putting aside a shilling a week from her pocket-money for a whole year. 'I'll get mine in a less expensive shop.'

Sylvia was profusely apologetic. 'I'm so tactless! Shall we go somewhere else? You lead the way.'

They linked arms as they made their way towards the exit. At the jewellery counter, Sylvia paused. 'Are we going to exchange presents? Those bracelets are very elegant. I'd like to buy one for you.'

The bracelets were diamanté, huge dazzling stones in a chunky dark gold setting. They were very elegant indeed, but they were also £4.19s.6d!

'No, ta,' Annie said quickly. 'They're lovely, but your present must cost the same as mine. I couldn't afford that much.'

Sylvia nodded understandingly. 'What about these pretty little pendants? Nine and elevenpence. Is that too much? I haven't got the hang of English money yet.'

'That's half an English pound.' Annie stared at the pendants on a display card on the counter. There were ten different designs, tiny enamelled flowers no bigger than a sixpence on a fine gold-plated chain.

'This one would suit you perfectly, an orchid.' Sylvia pointed to the second pendant down, a red and blue and gold flower. 'You are like an orchid, Annie, you seem to change colour all the time. One minute your hair is red, then the light changes and it's gold. Your eyes are different, too; blue, then grey, then blue again.'

Annie felt as if she could cry. No-one had ever paid her such a lovely compliment before. 'I'd like it very much,' she whispered.

'In fifty years' time,' Sylvia said sagely, 'you will see this little orchid in your jewellery box, tarnished, faded and old, and will always be reminded of Sylvia Delgado and the day she bought it for you.'

'That's a very profound remark from such a young lady!' the elderly assistant said, wrapping the orchid in tissue paper and tucking it inside a cardboard box.

'Thank you,' Sylvia said demurely.

Annie noticed one of the pendants was shaped like a rose. She'd never bought a present for her mam before, it seemed a waste of time. 'I'll have a pendant, too,' she said impulsively. A rose for a Rose!

Later, when they were having their lunch in Owen Owen's restaurant –

special Christmas fayre, roast chicken and plum pudding – Annie said, 'Why didn't you go to a private school, seeing as you're so well off?'

Sylvia made a face. 'Because Bruno doesn't believe in private education. He considers it a basic right which should be the same for everyone, rich and poor alike. No-one should be allowed to pay for better teachers, better schools. He's the same with most things. When Cecy had me, he insisted she use the local hospital, where they left her in labour for days because they were so backward. Then she was stuck in a ward with peasant women who hated her. That's why I am a lone child. She had such a terrible time, she swore she'd never have more children.'

'Bruno'd get on with me Auntie Dot and Uncle Bert. They're in the Labour Party.' Bert was chairman of the local branch.

'I doubt it,' Sylvia said darkly. 'He hates socialists almost as much as he hates fascists. Don't ask me why, it's something to do with state ownership and banks and shares and capitalism.' She glanced at her minute gold watch. 'We have half an hour before the film starts. Just time enough for you to show me St George's Hall.'

Annie gaped. 'What on earth do you want to see that for?'

'Bruno said it's one of the most beautiful buildings in Europe.'

'Is it really?' Annie had never noticed anything remarkable about it. 'I haven't bought you a present yet!' She'd got dad a tie, earrings for Marie, a box of handkerchiefs for Dot and tobacco for Uncle Bert.

'I told you, I'd like those red gloves.'

Annie screwed up her nose. 'But they'll wear out.'

'What else do you expect gloves to do?'

'It means one day you'll throw them away. I'd like to get you something permanent, like my pendant.'

'Maybe we'll see something on the way to St George's Hall.'

But by the time the curtains closed on *Three Coins in a Fountain*, and Frank Sinatra crooned the last notes of the haunting theme song, Annie still hadn't bought Sylvia a present.

Sylvia was in tears. The picture had made her feel homesick. 'The music is so beautiful,' she sniffed. 'I could listen to it for ever.'

Annie had a brainwave. 'I'll buy you the record for Christmas! In fifty years' time, when I look in my jewellery box and think of you, you can play *Three Coins in a Fountain*, and think of me!'

It was an anti-climax after the glorious day to walk into the house in Orlando Street: like entering a tomb, Annie thought miserably. The television was on without the sound and Dad looked up, but didn't utter a word of greeting. Mam's face was turned away. Annie wondered if they spoke to each other when they were alone.

Marie was out, as usual. Annie could go out later if she wished. She'd been invited to a party, but as Ruby Livesey would almost certainly be there, she decided to stay in and watch television.

She went upstairs to unpack the presents. She still had Sylvia's record, and had been invited to the Grand on Christmas Eve to get her pendant. She opened the box containing Mam's rose and touched the little petals with her finger. Downstairs, her father's footsteps sounded in the hall and the door slammed. He must be going to the corner shop.

Annie was never quite sure afterwards what prompted her to do what she did. In fact she could remember nothing between Dad slamming the door and finding herself standing in front of her mother, gazing down and marvelling at her girlish face. How incredibly pretty she was! She hadn't aged a bit, not like Dad. In fact, she looked much younger than Cecy, who, according to Sylvia, spent a small fortune on creams to keep the wrinkles at bay. Annie noticed the almost childish curve of her chin, the way her long dusky lashes rested on her smooth cheeks. It was such a shame, she thought sadly, such a waste.

'Mam,' she said loudly. 'I've got you a present.'

Mam didn't stir. It was as if Annie had never spoken.

'I've got you a present, Mam,' she said again, even louder, but still there was no reaction. She leant down and twisted the frozen face towards her. 'I've got you a present. It cost nine and elevenpence and you've got to take it off me,' she shouted.

Annie fell to her knees until the face was level with her own. It was of tremendous importance that she make her mother hear. 'Look, Mam, it's a pendant, a rose.' She took the pendant out of its box and dangled it by the chain. 'A rose for a Rose. I bought it specially because it's so pretty. Please, Mam, please take my present.'

Mam opened her eyes and looked directly at her daughter, and Annie stared deep into the pools of grey, seeing little shreds of silver and gold that she'd never known were there. Mam gave an almost audible gasp, as if she'd never seen Annie before.

'Let me put it on for you, Mam.' Annie's hands trembled as she reached behind and fastened the clasp. Mam's hands went up to her throat and she began to finger the little pink rose.

'There!' Annie said with satisfaction. 'It looks dead nice.'

'Thank you,' Mam whispered.

Annie felt the urge to weep. She stayed at her mother's feet and laid her head on her lap. Slowly, surreptitiously, she slid her arms around the slim legs until she was hugging them tightly.

They stayed that way for a long time. Then Annie felt her body tingle as there was a soft, almost imperceptible movement, and Mam was gently stroking her head.

'Oh, Mam!' she whispered.

There came the sound of Dad's key in the door, and the hand was abruptly removed. When Annie looked up, her mother's head was turned away and her eyes were closed.

She scrambled to her feet, heart thudding, and was in the kitchen by the time Dad came in. What did it mean? Had it been a charade all these years, a sham, as Dot suspected? Why did Mam stop when she'd heard the key?

Annie let the clothes rack down and began to feel the washing, removing the items that were dry, spreading the still damp clothes out so they'd be ready for ironing by tomorrow. Her hands were shaking as she pulled the rack up and wound the rope around the hook in the wall.

Could it be that Mam really was so full of a mixture of hate and love that she'd deliberately shut herself off from the world just to punish Dad? Or maybe it was herself she was punishing for leaving Johnny alone. Either way it wasn't fair, Annie thought bitterly.

In the end, she decided she'd probably imagined the whole thing. Mam hadn't been stroking her head, not really. It had merely been an involuntary action and she didn't know what she was doing.

Any other explanation didn't bear thinking about.

On Christmas Eve, Annie set off with Sylvia's record tucked under her arm and permission from Dad to stay out late – not that Marie, who came home at all hours, ever asked. After the Grand had closed they were all going to Midnight Mass, even Bruno, who, said Sylvia, had promised not to sneer. He'd offered to bring Annie home by car. Annie had been looking forward to the evening ever since Sylvia had suggested it.

'If you've nothing else to do on Christmas Eve, why don't you come and have supper? We could play records and talk.'

Supper! Annie hadn't realised you could ask someone to supper, and they were going to have *a glass of wine* with the meal!

Although it was only half seven, through the window she could see the Grand was already packed with customers. Every table was occupied and there were crowds massed around the bar. The noise was deafening.

She went round the side and rang the bell, and had to ring a second time before Sylvia answered. To Annie's surprise, she wore a plain black dress and a white apron. The scratch on her cheek had faded to pink.

'Oh, Annie!' she cried dramatically. 'How I wish you were on the telephone and I could have prevented you from coming!'

Annie's heart sank. 'What's wrong?' she asked, hoping her awful disappointment didn't show on her face.

'Two of the waitresses haven't turned up.' She dragged Annie into the lobby. 'We are all at sevens and eights at the moment.'

'Sixes and sevens.' Annie made an attempt at a smile.

'There's a dinner for thirty in the Regency Room and a party in the Snug. I'm so sorry, Annie, I was really looking forward to tonight, but I can't desert Cecy when she only has one helper.'

'I'll help,' offered Annie, praying the offer would be accepted. She would do anything rather than return to Orlando Street.

'Sylvia!' Cecy shouted impatiently. 'The soup's waiting.'

'Coming!' Sylvia shouted back. She turned to Annie, looking sceptical. 'Another pair of hands would be more than welcome, but it's not a very exciting way to spend Christmas Eve.'

'I don't mind a bit what I do.'

Sylvia still looked sceptical. 'Are you sure?'

Annie nodded with all the enthusiasm she could muster. 'Positive!'

'In that case, hang your coat up and come into the kitchen.'

'*Sylvia!*' Cecy screamed.

The kitchen was a long room at the back which ran the entire width of the hotel. Several pans, lids rattling, steamed on the eight-ringed stove. Wearing a white overall, a red and perspiring Cecy was carving a massive turkey. A middle-aged woman dressed like Sylvia was just leaving with a tray laden somewhat precariously with bowls of soup.

'Annie's come to help,' said Sylvia.

'Take those sandwiches to the Snug,' Cecy snapped.

'I'll show you.' Sylvia picked up a tray of soup. As they went upstairs, she said, 'My grandparents are asleep in all this chaos. Their plane was held up, the train was late and they're exhausted. That's the Snug.' She nodded towards a door on the left.

Annie knocked. There was a buzz of voices inside, but no-one answered, so she cautiously opened the door and went in. The room was thick with smoke. A dozen people in armchairs seemed to be engaged in a furious argument with everyone else. A dozen hands reached for the sandwiches and she found herself holding a magically empty plate.

A voice called, 'I say, miss, we'd like another round of drinks.' The man turned to the others. 'What are you having?'

'I'll have a beer.'

'Me, too.'

'Whisky and ginger for me.'

The orders came thick and fast and Annie did her best to memorise them; four beers, three ciders, a whisky and ginger, two gin and tonics, a Pimms No 1, an orange cordial.

Repeating the order under her breath, she raced back to the kitchen. 'Four beers, three ciders . . .' She searched wildly for paper and pencil and wrote it all down with a sigh of relief.

'Whew!' She mopped her brow. 'The people in the Snug want these,' she said, handing the list to Cecy.

'Take it to the master in the bar,' Cecy said cuttingly. 'Say it's for his bloody Marxist friends. Once you've done that, there's sausage rolls to take up. I daren't give them all the food at once, else they'd eat the lot and still ask for more.'

After trying several cupboards and a lavatory, Annie found the door to the bar. It was like walking into a wall of noise. She gave the order to a tall, incredibly handsome man with smooth jet-black hair and the face of a Greek god, whom she assumed was Bruno.

'It's for the people in the Snug,' she yelled.

'Who are you and why aren't you in uniform?' His dancing brown eyes belied the apparent curtness of the question.

'I'm Annie, Sylvia's friend,' Annie explained. 'I've got to rush, I've something else to do.'

She had 'something else to do' for the next three hours. It wasn't how she'd expected to spend Christmas Eve, but she enjoyed herself immensely. She made more sandwiches when the bloody Marxists declared themselves on the verge of starvation, and helped wash and dry the dishes when they appeared out of the Regency Room in great numbers, thirty of everything.

It was almost half ten by the time Cecy sank into a chair, crying. 'Why did I let Bruno buy this place? I've never worked so hard in my life.' Her eyes lighted on Annie. 'What are you doing here?'

'Who do you think looked after the bloody Marxists?' Sylvia laughed.

'Was that you, Annie, dear? I was too busy to notice.'

'Is it all right if I go now, Mrs Delgado?' The other waitress had removed her shoes and was wearily massaging her feet.

'Of course, Mrs Parsons. Would you like a lift home?' Cecy was gradually becoming her normal charming self.

'No, ta. It's only round the corner.'

'Now, what do I owe you? The master insists I pay double for anti-social hours, so five pounds should do nicely. Is there much in tips?'

'There's a pile of silver from the Regency Room.' Sylvia pointed to the plate of coins on the table. 'You take it, Mrs Parsons.'

'Oh, I couldn't, miss. You did half the work.' The waitress eyed the money longingly.

At Sylvia's insistence, Mrs Parsons emptied the coins into her bag. 'Happy Christmas!' she cried happily as she left.

'The bloody Marxists didn't leave a penny,' Sylvia snorted. 'I bet they'd say the workers should be better paid and not rely on tips.'

'They're just too mean to put their hands in their pockets.' Cecy looked disgusted. 'Annie! I seem to recall a red-haired young person dashing in and out all night and washing loads of dishes. I insist on paying for your hard work. You weren't here as long as Mrs Parsons, but you didn't get a single tip.' She handed Annie a five-pound note.

'But I didn't expect to be paid,' Annie said faintly.

'It would have cost twice that if the other waitresses had turned up.' Cecy adamantly refused to take the money back.

'Ta very much,' gulped Annie. *Five pounds!*

Bruno appeared at the door. 'How did things go, darling?'

'Don't darling me,' Cecy snapped. 'We've been worked off our feet whilst you've been in your element behind the bar.'

Bruno laughed and blew a kiss. Despite Cecy's cross words, she smiled and blew one back. Annie sighed, because it seemed terribly romantic. They obviously loved each other very much.

'I suppose I'd better wake the old folks ready for Mass,' Cecy said wearily, 'but how anybody can sleep in this din is beyond me. As for you pair, help yourselves to food. There's wine opened in the fridge.'

Sylvia piled sausage rolls and mince pies onto a plate. 'Come on, Annie. I'm dying to hear my record.'

Halfway upstairs, she paused. 'You can see everything going on from here. It's how Bruno keeps an eye on the bar when he's not there.'

Annie hadn't noticed the little oblong window in the wall before. The girls sat on the stairs and peered through. The bar was more crowded than ever and people were still coming in. A few customers were singing drunkenly and there was the sound of breaking glass.

'Normally, we'd be closed by now,' Sylvia explained, 'but there's an extension because it's Christmas Eve. It's not usually so crowded, either. Scarcely any of these are regulars and one or two are getting out of hand. Bruno will throw them out if they continue. He's very particular who he allows in his pub.' She pointed. 'See that lot over there! They look awfully common and are very much the worse for wear.'

Annie followed her gaze. Half a dozen men and two young women were at a table in the centre of the room. As she watched, one man knocked a glass onto the floor with his elbow, but was too engrossed in the woman next to him to notice. The woman said something and the man grinned and kissed her full on the lips.

Oh, Jaysus! Annie felt her blood run cold. The young woman was Marie! She wore a tight-fitting black jumper, emphasising her budding breasts. Annie gasped as the man on her other side angrily pushed the first away, and it looked as if there could actually be a fight. Marie appeared quite unconcerned. She seemed to be enjoying herself, and threw back her head, laughing uproariously, as the second man dragged her into his arms. The first got up and made his unsteady way towards the Gents.

'Is something the matter?' Sylvia asked.

Annie nodded numbly. 'The girl in the black jumper is me sister!'

Sylvia frowned. 'But you said your sister is at Grenville Lucas and she's younger than you!'

'That's her. That's our Marie. She's only thirteen.'

'But she looks years older,' Sylvia gasped. 'Shall I tell Bruno? He'll throw them out immediately. He's strict about that sort of thing.'

'I'd sooner you didn't.' Annie felt unable to watch another minute. What on earth was she going to do about Marie?

'Come on, Annie,' Sylvia said gently. 'I'll play my new record and you can tell me all about it.'

It was half one when Annie let herself in and she felt almost cheerful again. She'd told Sylvia everything, from living with Dot and moving to Orlando Street, to Mam stroking her head – or *possibly* stroking her head – the other day. It was a relief to share her worries with someone else.

She crept upstairs and felt in the dark for her nightdress so as not to disturb her sister, but as her eyes got used to the darkness, she realised Marie's bed was empty and her heart sank. Where was she?

Despite being so tired after all her hard work, she couldn't sleep. She tossed and turned, thinking about her sister. They weren't 'boys' she'd been with, but grown men. Did they know she was thirteen?

Eventually she began to doze, but was jerked awake by a sharp noise. She sat up, trying to work out what the noise had been when it came again. Stones were being thrown at the window. Marie!

Annie got out of bed. Her sister was in the yard about to throw another stone. She flew downstairs and let her in. 'Where the hell have you been?' she demanded.

'Out and about,' Marie said airily. 'Ta, sis. I forgot me key and I didn't want to wake the old fool up.'

'He's not old, and he's not a fool,' Annie hissed when they were in the bedroom. 'He's a poor helpless man trying to do his best for us.'

'Really!' Marie said sarcastically. She threw her clothes on the floor and pulled on her nightdress. 'Goodnight, Annie. Merry Christmas,' she said in the same sarcastic voice as she got into bed.

'I saw you in the Grand tonight,' Annie said accusingly.

Marie hiccuped. 'Did you now! And what were you doing in the Grand, Miss Goody Two-Shoes!'

'Me friend lives there. I was helping in the kitchen.'

'Honest!' Marie sat up. 'You're friendly with that Italian girl? What's she like?'

'I'm the one asking the questions,' Annie snapped. 'What were you doing with those horrible old men? They looked at least twenty-five.'

Marie snorted. 'Mind your own business!'

'No, I won't. I felt ashamed, seeing them paw me sister in public. Things aren't so bad at home that you have to do horrible things like that. You could have stayed in and watched television.'

'You didn't!'

'I was working,' Annie said virtuously.

'And what do you mean, things aren't so bad at home?' Marie guffawed incredulously. 'Are you blind or something? It's Christmas Eve, and if we hadn't put those decorations up, there'd be no sign of it here. There never has been, not even when we were little; no presents by our beds, nothing.' She leaned forward and said fiercely, 'As soon as I'm old enough, I'll be out this house like a shot, and I'm never coming back.'

Annie sighed. There seemed little she could say because Marie was right. She was drifting off to sleep again, when a small voice tinged with desperation and misery said, 'I've got to have someone to love me, Annie. That's what I was doing tonight, looking for someone to love me.'

'I love you, Marie,' Annie said quickly. They weren't as close as she would have liked, they were two such very different people, but she loved her sister dearly.

'It's *them*!' Marie began to cry. 'They make me feel invisible, as if I don't exist. It's all right for you, you do things. You make yourself useful so they know you're there, but if I disappeared tomorrow, neither of them would notice.'

Annie got out of bed and climbed in with her sister. 'Never mind, luv,' she said soothingly. 'Never mind.' She tried to think of some comforting words to cheer her sister, but there didn't seem to be any. 'Never mind,' she said again.

Minutes later, the two girls were fast asleep in each other's arms.

On the day they returned to school, Annie and Sylvia met outside so they could face the inevitable storm together. They linked arms, marched through the gates and waited for the fireworks, but there was no sign of Ruby Livesey and no-one else took the slightest bit of notice.

Feeling let down, they wandered around the playground, arm in arm. After a while, Sally Baker came up. 'Hello, Annie. Why didn't you come to my party?' She didn't wait for a reply, but went on, 'Hey, you'll never guess, Ruby's left. She's got a job in Jacob's Biscuit Factory. I'm dead glad, I never liked her.'

They were joined by another girl from Ruby's old gang. 'Our Brian went to the Grand on New Year's Eve. You never said your dad was a Count, Sylvia. Isn't it smashing news about Ruby? Who'd like a peppermint cream? I got a whole box in my Christmas stocking.'

6

Tommy Gallagher married Dawn O'Connell in the summer of 1956, soon after he had done his National Service. Dawn was a skinny, darkly dramatic girl who wore an enviable amount of eyeshadow and too much lipstick. As she had no sisters, she asked Annie and Marie to be her bridesmaids.

'Now, about the dresses,' Dot said, full of importance. 'Dawn fancies blue, which should suit both your colourings.'

'Blue's fine,' Annie said blissfully. She would have agreed to black, she was so thrilled.

'Don't worry about the money,' Dot assured them. 'I'll have a word with our Ken. I think I'm the only one who can get through to him. Bert says it's because I've got the most penetrating voice in the world.'

The dresses were bought at a discount from Owen Owen's, where Dawn worked in Ladies' Underwear. Pale blue slipper satin, they had a low neck, a gathered skirt and a dark blue sash. 'You can get them altered afterwards,' said Dot. 'They'll do to go dancing in when you're older.'

'You lucky thing!' Sylvia said enviously when she heard. 'I'd love to be a bridesmaid.'

'You can be mine,' Annie offered, though she couldn't visualise getting married.

'And you can be mine! Though that means one of us will be a matron of honour. I wonder who'll get married first?'

'You will,' Annie said with conviction.

Sylvia had been invited to the wedding, and spent an entire evening modelling her vast wardrobe in front of Annie. 'Which dress do you like best? Perhaps I should buy something new. Oh, dear!' Sylvia said distractedly. 'I don't know what to wear!'

Annie laughed. 'You've got too many clothes, that's the problem. The peachy coloured frock really suits you.'

'Does it? You don't think it's too old – or possibly too young?'

'It's just right,' Annie assured her. 'You're dead conceited, Sylvia. You don't half fancy yourself.' Their friendship had reached the stage where they could be critical of each other without causing offence. Sylvia stuck out her tongue, but otherwise ignored the comment.

Annie had never heard Mam and Dad argue before – well, not exactly argue, Mam wasn't saying a word, but Dad was going on and on in the voice that had turned husky of late and sounded like an old man's.

'But you've got to, you've got to,' he insisted. After a while, he came into the kitchen and said wearily to Annie. 'I'd like you to buy your mam a dress for Tommy's wedding. How much d'you think it'll be?'

So that was it! 'Okay, Dad,' Annie said, in the forced cheerful tone she used with her father. 'She'll need shoes and a hat as well – about fifteen pounds, I reckon. I'll go after school tomorrow. Don't worry, I'll get something nice.'

Dad sighed. 'You're a good girl, Annie.'

With Sylvia in tow, the following day Annie went to Waterloo in search of a dress. 'Pink,' she said firmly. 'It's got to be rose pink.'

She'd almost given up hope by the time they entered the final shop ten minutes before closing time. The assistant looked up impatiently when they came in and began to go through the rows of dresses.

'This one's perfect!' Annie had reached the last few frocks on the final rack when she took one out. 'And it's her size.'

The dress was deep pink grosgrain with a square neck and little puffed sleeves. The bodice was fitted and the panels widened into a full, almost circular skirt.

'It's pretty,' Sylvia said admiringly. 'I'm sure she'll love it.'

The assistant perked up and became co-operative when she realised she was about to make a sale without the garment being tried on. She helped Annie choose a hat from the small millinery selection.

'This could have been made to go with the dress.' She picked up a pink feather band with a tiny veil. 'It's exactly the same colour.'

Annie tried it on. 'What do you think?' she asked Sylvia.

'It looks ghastly with red hair, but the style is very flattering.'

'In that case, I'll take it,' Annie said thankfully.

'Shall we put some lipstick on her?'

'Leave her alone, Marie. She looks fine. She's lovely as she is,' Annie glared at her sister.

Marie had adopted a proprietorial air with their mother on the morning of the wedding, spending ages combing her hair into a variety of different styles until she settled on a big fat bun at the nape of her slender neck. Mam stood in the middle of the room, a lost, confused figure, whilst Marie prowled around, adjusting the sleeves of the dress, straightening the little rose pendant.

'A bit of lipstick'll finish her off.'

'She's not a doll,' Annie snapped. 'Anyroad, why the interest in what Mam looks like all of a sudden? You've never cared before.'

'I never realised she was so gorgeous. Just imagine, sis, if the girls at school knew we had a Mam who looks more like our big sister!'

'Hmm,' Annie sighed.

'You should have got her a pair of lace gloves.'

'I didn't think.' She was pleased the dress fitted so well, the material clinging to Mam's lean hips, the short sleeves revealing milky-white arms. The hat looked perfect on her dark hair.

'I wouldn't mind those shoes afterwards. I mean, she'll never wear them again.' Marie stared enviously at the black suede shoes with little narrow heels. 'They're too small for you.'

'You're like a bloody vulture. Would you like her nylons, too?'

'I wouldn't mind. Or that bag.'

'That's Cecy's, Sylvia bought it her for Christmas. I'd run out of money by the time I remembered a handbag.'

'Where's Dad?' Marie demanded.

'Outside, waiting for the taxi.'

'Doesn't he think the driver's capable of finding the house himself? Keep still, Mam. I think I'll comb her hair loose, after all.'

The taxi would drop Mam and Dad off at Dot's, then take the girls to Dawn's house where they would change into their bridesmaids' frocks.

'I wonder if she realises what's going on?' Marie combed their mother's hair loose and began to curl the ends under her finger.

'I hope not. She'll think she's turned into a tailor's dummy.'

'Did you see Dad's face when he saw her dressed?' Marie giggled. 'It went all gooey and stupid, as if he was about to cry.'

Annie didn't answer. She had also noticed Dad's incredulous expression, as if he were seeing his wife for the first time and had fallen in love all over again. Annie had looked away, feeling as if she were intruding on something intensely private. Unlike Marie, she didn't find it the least bit funny.

Annie stared at her reflection in Dawn's wardrobe mirror. 'Gosh, I look *strange.*' She was growing taller, as Marie had predicted, and filling out. She'd been wearing a brassiere for more than a year and took a thirty-four, though suspected she'd soon need a bigger size. Her hips were quite broad, but shapely, she told herself, because her waist was narrow, the narrowness accentuated by the wide sash of the dress. She placed the coronet of blue flowers on her hair.

'Do you want this straight?' she asked Dawn, who looked radiant in her white satin wedding gown, 'or tipped towards the back?'

Dawn pursed her lips as Annie placed the coronet in various positions on her red curls. 'Straight, I think, almost on your forehead. It looks sort of regal.'

Marie sidled up. 'Are you sure you've got the right frock? This one feels really tight.'

'Mine's bigger. If that feels tight, it wouldn't go near me.'

'I'd better not eat anything, else I'll bust the zip.' Marie mopped her brow. 'I wish it wasn't so hot. I'm sweating like a cob already.'

'Tara, Tommy, lad,' Dot screamed. 'Have a nice honeymoon. Don't do anything I wouldn't do!'

As the newly-married couple's car turned into the traffic, Dot and the bride's mother burst into tears and fell into each other's arms.

Everyone began to drift back into the big room above the pub where the reception was being held. The musical duo, pianist and drummer, started to play 'Jealousy', and seconds later Bert swept a still tearful Dot across the floor. In no time the wooden floor shook as more couples began to tango. The children played tick, darting in and out of the dancers, and the room rapidly turned into a steambath with the heat.

'Oh, Bert,' Dot sobbed when the dance had finished. 'One of these days, I'll have no boys left. The house'll be empty.'

'Never mind, luv, you'll still have me,' Bert said comfortingly.

At this, Dot began to cry even more. Bert grinned. 'She always gets maudlin when she's been at the whisky. Fetch us some of that fruit punch, Annie, luv. Least if she's got a glass in her hand she mightn't notice it's non-alcoholic.'

Annie helped herself to another glass at the same time. The punch was an invention of Alan's, who was at catering college training to be a chef. He came up and regarded the nearly empty bowl with satisfaction. 'Another lot gone! I'd better make some more.'

'It's delicious,' Annie said. 'I could drink gallons in this heat.'

'I bet our Mike'll be gone within the year,' Dot sniffed when Annie returned. 'He's dead serious about that Pamela girl.'

'He was until today,' said Bert. 'Pamela's been given her cards. Ever since our Mike laid eyes on Annie's friend, he's gone as soppy as a puppy. Look at them dancing together!'

Mike was staring at Sylvia fixedly, an expression of total adoration on his face. A girl of about seventeen glared at them from the side of the room. Sylvia caught Annie's eye and winked.

'Have you noticed our Ken?' Dot was saying. 'He looks like a skull and crossbones. I'll have a word later, make him get a tonic off the doctor. Give them some punch, Annie. Our Alan's brought a fresh lot.'

'Isn't she lovely?' Dad said brokenly when Annie appeared. 'Isn't my Rose a picture?'

'Jaysus, Dad, have you been drinking?' He looked slightly idiotic, his head poised in a peculiarly stiff, lopsided way as if he were scared it might fall off. Tears were trickling down his hollow cheeks.

'Only that punch. Your mam really likes it.'

'Everybody's crying,' Annie complained. 'Dot, Dawn's mam, now you!'

The evening wore on. Night brought no respite from the sticky, suffocating heat. The men forced open the old sash windows, to such an extent they would probably never close again, but there was still no breath of wind to relieve the perspiring guests, and Dawn's grandma fainted in the middle of the Hokey Cokey.

Annie was dancing with the best man, Colin Donnelly, when Sylvia tugged her shoulder. 'Come quickly. Your cousin is in a state!'

'Which cousin?' Annie asked irritably as she reluctantly detached herself from Colin's arms. She'd actually found herself flirting for the first time in her life.

'Mike. He wants to kill himself because I won't marry him,' Sylvia burst out laughing. 'I don't think he means it, but what are we to do?'

'I'll see to him,' Colin said manfully. 'Where is he?'

Mike, usually so cheerful and full of beans, was in the kitchen, beating the wall with his fist and sobbing hopelessly. 'I love her, Annie,' he cried when they arrived, 'but she won't marry me.'

'Is he drunk?'

Sylvia shook her head. 'He's only had the punch, like me.'

'Come on, old chap, pull yourself together.' Colin slapped Mike on the back. 'Act like a man!' He glanced covertly at the girls to see if they were impressed. Annie and Sylvia burst out laughing.

Colin looked hurt. 'What's so funny?'

'I've no idea,' Sylvia giggled. She and Annie ran back into the main room and watched the revellers, trying not to laugh. Mike joined them after a while. He sat beside Sylvia and watched her soulfully. Every now and then he gave a pathetic sniff and the girls tried not to laugh even more. The discarded Pamela had gone home in tears hours ago.

Colin returned and gave Annie and Sylvia a cold look before asking Marie to dance.

The lights darkened for the 'Anniversary Waltz', and Annie was amazed when her mam and dad danced past. Mam's eyes were closed, but she was smiling, her head cocked on one side, and holding the hem of her skirt in her right hand so that it fell like a fan. Dad was watching her, his mouth half open and a glazed, inane look on his face.

To Annie's horror, she felt an overwhelming urge to giggle! What on earth was wrong with her? She clapped a hand over her mouth and tried her best to keep a straight face. She became aware that, beside her, Sylvia was sobbing quietly. 'What's the matter with you?' she snapped.

'Your mother and father! She is so incredibly beautiful. It's so sad, Annie.' Mike slid his arm around her shoulders and she collapsed against him. Mike began to cry, too.

'Bloody hell!' Annie said disgustedly. She went into the kitchen, where she found Alan pouring a bottle of vodka into a bowl of punch. 'You bugger!' she cried. 'No wonder everyone's crying, they're drunk!'

Alan looked unperturbed. 'Seemed like a good joke. Those who don't drink are more pissed than those who do! I got the vodka off this mate at college, a whole crateful. It fell off the back of a lorry.'

'All of Bootle'll have a head in the morning, including me!' No wonder she'd flirted with Colin and laughed at poor Mam and Dad.

Marie came bursting into the kitchen, red-faced and perspiring. 'Eh, Annie, our dad's just had a nervous breakdown,' she panted.

'But he was dancing with me mam a few minutes ago!' Annie said dazedly. She wondered if the world had gone insane.

'I know, but he suddenly slid down on the floor and began crying his eyes out. Dot and Bert are seeing to him in one of the bedrooms.'

'I'd better go and look after Mam.'

'There's no need. She's doing the rumba with the best man, though she's got a face on her like a zombie.'

'Jaysus, Mary and Joseph! This is a madhouse, not a wedding. It's all your fault!' Annie turned accusingly on Alan. 'None of this would have happened if you hadn't spiked the bloody punch.'

'No-one was forced to drink it!' Alan departed with another bowl.

Marie turned her back to Annie. 'Undo the zip will you, sis, I can hardly breathe.' She wriggled uncomfortably as Annie struggled with the zip. 'I can't understand it. This dress fitted perfectly a few weeks ago. Even me breasts feel bigger, all swollen.'

'Oh, Marie!' A terrible suspicion swept over Annie. 'You're not, you're not . . .' She couldn't bring herself to finish.

'Pregnant?' Marie said calmly. Then her pretty face wrinkled in horror. 'Jaysus, Annie, that explains it!'

The sisters stared at each other without speaking for several seconds, then they both burst into tears.

*

'What are we to do?' asked Annie. It was the day after the wedding, Sunday; they were in the bedroom discussing Marie's predicament.

'I've no idea,' Marie said sullenly.

'How far gone are you?'

'I've no idea,' Marie said again. 'I've never been regular like you. That's why it didn't cross me mind.'

'Didn't you take – what are they called, precautions?' Annie was still in a daze of shock. Marie had been going out with boys since she was little, but even after seeing her with those awful men in the Grand last Christmas, she'd never imagined her doing that *thing* with them.

'Don't talk so stupid.' Marie's grey eyes blazed. 'If I'd taken precautions, I wouldn't be up the bloody stick, would I? Anyroad, where the hell was I supposed to get precautions from?'

'It's no good getting stroppy with me,' Annie said in a hurt voice. 'I only want to help.'

'I'm sorry,' Marie muttered.

If only it weren't such a horrible day! It was still hot, but the sky was black and heavy, as if there was going to be a storm. The light was on, but the dim bulb behind the dark yellow shade made the room look even more miserable and depressing.

As if Marie had read her thoughts, she said, 'I hate this room, I hate this house and I hate this street. I went into another girl's bedroom once, and it was full of pictures of film stars: Frank Sinatra and Gene Kelly and Montgomery Clift. This place stinks.'

Annie, sitting crosslegged on the bed, began to fiddle with the eiderdown, feeling at a loss. Marie's attitude was so belligerent, as if the whole thing were Annie's fault. Perhaps she should have done more to protect her sister, she thought guiltily.

Thunder rumbled in the distance, and seconds later the room was lit by a brilliant flash of lightning, followed by another and another.

'We've got to sort this out today, Marie,' Annie said firmly. 'I take it you don't intend to have the baby?' A child would be the last thing Marie wanted. She was little more than a child herself.

She was surprised when Marie's hard expression softened. 'I wish I could,' she said longingly. 'I'd love a baby of me own, someone to love and love me back. There's no way I'd be like *them*!' She gestured at the door as if their mam and dad were outside. 'But I'm only thirteen, I couldn't stand living in one of them homes for unmarried mothers.' Her voice became harsh. 'I suppose I'll just have to get rid of it, though apart from having hot baths and drinking loads of gin, which doesn't usually work, I haven't a clue how to go about it.'

An abortion! Annie hated the very word. It actually sounded cruel, and so very final. 'Neither have I,' she said. 'We could ask Dot?'

Marie shook her head. 'Once Dot's had a good yell and called me all the names under the sun, she'll be all right, but she won't help get rid of it. Some woman from down the street had an abortion and Dot hasn't spoken to her since. She'd offer to bring the baby up, that's all.'

'Perhaps that would be the best solution,' Annie said hopefully.

'No!' Marie said vehemently. 'I couldn't bear to see me own child being brought up by another woman.' Rain splattered against the window and within seconds became a downpour. The panes rattled in their frames.

Annie began to play with the eiderdown again, pleating and unpleating the shiny cotton between her fingers. Marie was so grown up at times, and seemed to have feelings and emotions she found alien. There was far more to her sister than the flighty, hard-hearted impression she usually gave. It made Annie feel rather inadequate, as if she herself were incapable of feeling strongly about anything.

'Abortion is against the law,' she said. 'You have to have it done in a back street or something.' Ruby Livesey had known a girl who'd known a girl who'd had one and she'd bled for days and ended up in hospital where the nurses treated her like dirt. 'Have you any money?'

'I've still got last week's pocket money, five bob.'

'I've three pounds saved for Christmas. I wonder what it costs?'

Marie shrugged. 'Search me!'

'I bet that's not enough. What about the father, would he help?'

'No, he wouldn't,' Marie snapped.

'Are you going to tell him?'

'No!'

'I think you should.'

'I think I shouldn't.'

'Why not?' Annie persisted.

'Because,' Marie breathed on her nails and polished them on the sleeve of her dress, 'it could be more than one person.'

'Oh, Marie!' Annie felt herself grow very hot. She stared at her sister, scandalised.

Marie said furiously. 'Don't look at me like that! Sometimes, Annie, you're so holier-than-thou it makes me sick.'

'You're taking it out on me again,' Annie said through gritted teeth. More than one person! She could easily be sick herself. She was about to say how utterly disgusted she was, but noticed Marie's jaw was trembling as if she were about to cry. All the nonchalance, the couldn't-care-less attitude was put on. Marie was hurting badly inside.

Annie got off the bed and reached inside the wardrobe for her best coat. She'd ask around at school as tactfully as she could to see if anyone knew about abortions – and how much they cost.

'Where are you going?' Marie demanded.

'To the Grand for tea. Afterwards, me and Sylvia are going to the pictures in Walton Vale.'

'Leaving me all by meself! Thanks, Annie. You're all heart.'

'I promised.' Earlier, she'd thought of ringing Sylvia from the phone box at the end of the street and cancelling the arrangement, but had changed her mind. It would be embarrassing, but she'd ask Sylvia for a loan. She'd bring the subject up on the way home.

They'd been to see *The Last Time I Saw Paris*, and were strolling arm in arm along the little stretch of sand where Dot had taken the girls when they'd first moved to Orlando Street. No-one brought their children to play on the sands these days. It was stained with oil and littered with debris from the sea, and with human debris; rusty cans and sodden mattresses, old clothes and scraps of paper. After the thunderstorms that afternoon, the air was refreshingly cool.

'Isn't Elizabeth Taylor too beautiful for words?' Sylvia breathed. 'As for Van Johnson!' She put her hand to her forehead and pretended to swoon. 'I think I'm in love.'

'Mmm,' muttered Annie.

'What's the matter, Annie? You've been awfully quiet all night. Didn't you enjoy the picture?'

'It was dead lovely,' Annie had scarcely taken it in.

'There's something wrong, I can tell.'

Annie took a deep breath. 'I want to borrow some money,' she said in a rush. 'I'll pay back every penny, I promise. I hate asking, but it's an emergency and I've no-one else to turn to.' She was glad it was dark so Sylvia couldn't see her shamed expression. She kicked violently at a tin can, suddenly angry that it was her who'd been put in the awkward position of having to get her sister out of the mess.

'You can have all the money you want,' Sylvia said instantly. 'How much: five pounds, ten, a hundred?'

'Oh, Sylvia!' Annie felt close to tears.

Sylvia squeezed Annie's hand. 'Don't be upset. What's it for? Don't tell me if you'd sooner not,' she added hastily.

'It's for Marie,' Annie sniffed. 'She's pregnant. I don't know how much, because I've no idea what an abortion costs.'

'*Pregnant!*' Sylvia stopped dead and her mouth fell open. 'Pregnant!' she said again.

'Isn't it terrible? It makes me go all funny, *thinking* about it.'

'I wonder where she did it?' Sylvia shuddered.

'I didn't ask.' Annie had visions of her sister under shadowy trees or in dark back alleys with men who had no faces.

'Where will she get the abortion done?'

'I don't know that, either.'

'Come on.' Sylvia veered them towards Crosby Road. 'Let's go back to the Grand and we'll discuss it over a cup of coffee.'

Annie paced nervously up and down the pale cream carpet. The coffee had long been drunk, and it was half an hour since Sylvia had gone downstairs promising, 'I won't be long.'

Cecy might regard Annie as a bad influence when she knew what her sister had done, and refuse to let Sylvia see her again. She'd think there was bad blood in the family and Annie could do the same thing.

The longplaying record finished, but she couldn't be bothered to turn it over. Anyroad, the music, the jazzy score of *Guys and Dolls*, had begun to get on her nerves.

Suddenly, Sylvia burst into the room. 'It's all settled,' she said breathlessly. 'Marie's booked into a nursing home in Southport this coming Saturday. She'll have to stay overnight.'

Annie sat down, overcome with relief. 'I can't thank Cecy enough,' she began, but Sylvia interrupted with a horrified, 'Don't mention a word of this to Cecy! She'd never approve. It's all Bruno's doing, with the help of the bloody Marxists.'

'I'll pay him back as soon as I can,' Annie vowed.

Sylvia shook her head. 'Bruno's only too pleased to help. It makes him feel good, doing something for the proletariat.'

Bruno Delgado picked Annie and Marie up from the corner of Orlando Street on Saturday morning. Sylvia was in the front of the big black Mercedes car.

Marie was subdued throughout the journey to Southport, overawed by the handsome, garrulous Bruno, who lectured them on politics the whole way. The law should be changed, he declared, so women could have an abortion legally. 'A woman's right to choose,' he called it.

'Your Parliament makes me sick,' he exploded at one point. 'All those middle-aged, middle-class men pontificating on what should happen to a woman's body. What the hell do they know about it? It's even worse in Italy, where the church makes all the rules.'

They were nearly there when he enquired, 'What excuse did you give at home to explain Marie's night away?'

'We didn't need an excuse,' Annie said carelessly. 'They won't notice she's gone.' She could have bitten off her tongue when she saw in the rear mirror Bruno's dark eyebrows draw together in astonishment. Marie stiffened at her side. 'I feel invisible,' she'd said once. In a moment of awareness, Annie knew why she'd let the men make use of her body. They'd made her feel wanted, though for all the wrong reasons. She pressed her sister's hand. 'It'll be over soon,' she whispered.

Sylvia's attitude didn't help. She completely ignored Marie, not once even glancing in her direction. Annie had known she disapproved since Christmas Eve, but she didn't realise the dislike was so intense.

'She's led a charmed life,' Annie thought wryly. 'She doesn't know the half of it.' Marie had only been trying to survive as best she could.

Bruno and Sylvia remained in the car when the sisters went into the nursing home, a gracious detached ivy-covered house in a wide tree-lined avenue. 'They're expecting you,' Bruno said. 'It's all arranged.'

A woman in a white starched overall came towards them, her face expressionless. 'Miss Harrison?' She looked from one to the other. Annie pushed Marie forward. 'Come with me, please.'

Marie turned, and Annie felt a fierce stab of pity at the sight of her stricken face. 'Do you want me to stay?' she said.

The woman in the overall said coldly, 'That's not allowed. You can pick her up at the same time tomorrow.'

Annie put her arms around her sister. As their cheeks touched, she said softly, 'Don't worry, Marie. We'll come through. One of these days, everything will be all right, you'll see.'

7

'I'm glad the summer holiday's nearly over,' Annie said with a sigh. 'School seems a nice change when you've been off six whole weeks.'

'I suppose it does.' Sylvia echoed Annie's sigh. They were bored, having done everything there seemed to be to do; gone to Southport and New Brighton numerous times, seen so many pictures that the plots had become muddled in their minds, and they were sick to death of Liverpool city centre. School offered variety to what had become tedium.

They were sitting on the sands, having removed rubbish to make a clear space, watching a small cargo boat sail towards a rippling green and purple sunset.

'Have you made up your mind what to do when you leave?' Sylvia enquired. 'You'll be fifteen in October.'

Annie frowned. 'Dot thinks I should stay at school till next July. After that . . .' she paused, picked up a handful of sand and let it fall through her fingers. 'The thing is,' she burst out, 'I can't imagine things ever being different. I've got to look after me mam and dad.'

'You can't look after them for ever, or you'll end up with no life of your own,' Sylvia said warningly.

'Dot said that. She suggested I go to Machin & Harpers – that's a commercial college,' she explained in response to Sylvia's puzzled look.

Sylvia nodded her smooth blonde head. 'Good idea, but it doesn't solve the problem of your parents. What happens when you fall in love?'

'In love?' Annie burst out laughing.

'All women fall in love,' Sylvia said wisely, 'even if all men don't. I can't wait. Bruno gets angry with me. He wants me to go to another school and get some qualifications, then go to university, when all I want to do is fall in love and get married.'

'You never told me that before!' Annie said in astonishment. Sylvia seemed too much in love with herself, her clothes, her hair, her figure. 'I thought you didn't like boys much. When we went on that double date, we decided afterwards it was more fun being with each other.'

They'd gone out in a foursome, their first dance and first date. The boys had them in stitches when they met on the New Brighton ferry, pretending to be Dean Martin and Jerry Lewis, but on the date, the spark had gone and everyone was stiff and formal. Annie and Sylvia kept going to the Ladies for a laugh.

'We won't always feel that way. One day we'll each meet a man who'll be far more important to us than anyone else in the world.'

Annie felt slightly hurt. 'Will we?'

'Yes, though we'll still meet. We can take our children for walks together and ask each other to dinner.'

But no matter how hard Annie tried, she couldn't visualise Sylvia's version of the future. It was impossible to imagine living anywhere other than Orlando Street, and leading a life different from the one she led now. She would merely go to work each day, instead of school.

'How's Marie?' Sylvia asked politely.

It was almost two months since Marie had had her 'termination', as the nursing home called it. 'Quiet. She stays in watching television.'

'She'll bounce back up again. She'll feel better at school.'

'As long as she doesn't bounce back up as high as she was before,' Annie said darkly.

There was a new teacher at Grenville Lucas when they returned. Mr Andrews didn't look much more than a schoolboy himself. The girls fell hopelessly in love, despite the fact he wore glasses and wasn't exactly good-looking. There was just something carefree and exhilarating about Mr Andrews that appealed to everyone, girls and boys alike. He had an enthusiasm for life that the other teachers lacked. Nor did he dress as they did, but wore corduroy trousers and a polo-necked sweater under his shabby tweed jacket.

'Good morning, class!' He'd burst into the room, eyes shining and rubbing his hands as if he were genuinely pleased to see them.

'Good morning, Mr Andrews,' they'd chorus – they'd been ordered not to call him 'sir'. English lessons were turning out to be fun. Shakespeare wasn't rubbish any more, and *The Mill on the Floss* and *A Tale of Two Cities* suddenly seemed quite interesting.

'If only we could study something written by a twentieth-century writer,' Mr Andrews grumbled one day, 'but the bloody education authorities won't let us.'

The class gasped. A teacher, swearing!

Mr Andrews decided a drama group was needed. 'Who'd like to join?' he cried. 'It's both educational and enjoyable at the same time.'

The entire class raised their hands. Annie and Sylvia were always on the look-out for something interesting to do.

'Perhaps I should have mentioned, but the drama group will meet *after* school.' Mr Andrews' eyes twinkled mischievously.

Half the hands went down. He laughed. 'Thought you were in for a skive, did you? Well, you've got another think coming. All you budding Thespians meet me in the gym at four o'clock. What is it, Derek?'

'What's a budding Thespian, sir? It sounds rude.'

'I told you not to call me sir. A budding Thespian, Derek, is someone who wants to be an actor, which you quite obviously don't.'

Mr Andrews thought the new group should cut their teeth on something simple like a pantomime. After a majority vote for *Cinderella*, he said he'd write the script himself.

'Why turn down a part?' Sylvia linked Annie's arm on the way home.

'I couldn't bear to go on stage with everybody looking at me!' Annie shuddered. 'He made me wardrobe mistress, though the men's costumes will be hired. Wardrobe mistress! Doesn't it sound grand? I'll borrow Dot's electric sewing machine. It can go in the parlour, no-one uses it. I'm dead excited! You'll make a marvellous principal boy, Syl.'

'I hope Bruno hasn't got some prejudice against them. He has some weird ideas sometimes. Shall we go for a coffee?'

'We're awfully late and there isn't time,' Annie said regretfully, 'I've got to make the tea.'

'If only I could help! I've become quite good at cooking since we moved to the Grand. I can peel potatoes like a whirlwind.'

Annie felt uncomfortable. 'You don't mind not coming, do you, Syl? I mean, I'm forever in the Grand, yet you've never set foot in our house. It's just that me dad's dead funny about letting people in.'

'Of course I don't mind,' said Sylvia.

'Anyroad, if you came once, you'd never want to come again. Me mam never opens her mouth. It's like a grave compared to yours.'

Sylvia looked sympathetic. 'It must get you down.'

Annie said nothing for a while. 'It's funny, but it doesn't get me down a bit,' she said eventually. 'I scarcely think about it.' She looked worriedly at her friend. 'Dot's always on about how ill me dad looks. It sounds awful, but I don't notice. I just make the tea and can't wait to meet you so we can go to the pictures or the youth club.'

They stopped in front of a small haberdashery shop. The window was piled high with packets of cellophane-covered wool, and half a dozen cheap cotton frocks hung crookedly from the partition at the back.

'Who on earth wears such ghastly rubbish?' Sylvia said scathingly.

'Women who can't afford anything else, I suppose.'

'Oh, God!' Sylvia clapped a hand to her forehead. 'What a terrible snob I am! Why do you bother with me, Annie?'

Annie laughed. 'Because I like you!'

Sylvia looked forlorn. 'I must tell Father MacBride what a snob I've been at my next confession.'

'Is snobbery a sin?'

'I'll confess it just in case.' Sylvia took confession very seriously. 'What do you tell at confession, Annie? I can't imagine you doing anything wrong.'

'I've never committed a mortal sin,' Annie said earnestly. 'Least I don't think so. I'm not sure how the church would regard helping Marie with the abortion – not that I confessed that. The priest can see you through the grille, that's if he hasn't already recognised your voice. I tell lies occasionally, but only white ones, and I'm a bit vain, though not nearly as vain as you. I just mumble I've had a few bad thoughts and get five Hail Marys and five Our Fathers as a penance.'

'But you don't really have bad thoughts, do you?'

They turned into Orlando Street. The long, red brick walls seemed to stretch for ever and ever. There wasn't a soul about. Annie shivered. Sometimes she wondered if her life might reflect the street: empty, dull, with every year exactly the same, like the houses.

She stopped, and Sylvia looked at her questioningly. 'What's wrong?'

'You asked if I had bad thoughts. I don't, but what worries me is that I don't have any thoughts at all,' she said tragically.

'Don't be silly,' Sylvia said warmly. 'We discuss all sorts of things and you always have an opinion.'

'It's hard to explain . . .' Annie paused as she struggled for words. 'I suppose I mean *deep* thoughts. The reason Marie went off the rails is because everything's so horrible at home. Why haven't I done something equally bad? Why am I always so calm and normal? Nothing seems to affect me. I never cry or make a scene or even lose my temper. It's as if I haven't any feelings underneath the surface.'

'Oh, Annie!'

'Most of the time I'm happy, least I think I am, but it doesn't seem right to be happy with things the way they are. Sometimes, I wonder if I'm completely dead inside because I'm always so bloody cheerful.'

'It's your defence mechanism,' Sylvia said knowledgeably.

'What's that?'

'You don't allow yourself to feel things, otherwise you'd go mad, but deep down at heart it's affecting you all the same.'

Annie managed to smile. 'Where did you get that from?'

'Bruno, who else! You should talk to him some time, Annie. He admires you tremendously.'

'Does he?' Annie gaped in astonishment.

'He calls you a "little brick". Compared to you I am no more than a useless flibbertigibbet. Oh, look, we've walked right past your house.'

'I usually do,' Annie said bitterly.

'You've done a wonderful job with Cinderella's ballgown, Annie,' Mr Andrews said, impressed. 'Where did the material come from?'

'Me and Sylvia . . .' Annie corrected herself; after all he was the English teacher. 'I mean, Sylvia and I went to a jumble sale in Southport. We bought heaps of stuff for just pennies. I made the gown out of an old frock and a curtain.'

The jumble sale had been Cecy's idea. The church hall had been like an Aladdin's cave, full of clothes, many as good as new. Even Cecy had been delighted to find an old-fashioned Persian lamb coat, which she was going to have remodelled.

Annie had removed the skirt from the blue-and-pink striped taffeta frock, and made another, full length, from one of the blue curtains, faded at the edges. She'd sewn little blue and pink rosettes around the hem, and turned the other curtain into a hooded cloak for Cinderella's entrance to the ball. There was enough material left over for a muff.

Mr Andrews shook his head admiringly. 'You have quite a talent for this sort of thing.'

'I used to love drawing dresses when I was little,' she said shyly.

'The Ugly Sisters' costumes are just as remarkable.'

'They're not quite finished. I brought them to see if they fitted.'

Mr Andrews looked at her keenly. 'What do you intend to do when you leave school?'

'I'm going to Machin & Harpers Commercial College next September.' Dot had had a serious talk with Dad, and it was all agreed.

He wrinkled his rather stubby little nose. 'That seems a waste. You should go to Art College, take a dress designing course. What does your mother think about these outfits? They're quite outstanding.'

'She liked them,' Annie lied. Only Marie had been interested enough to enquire why Annie was spending so much time in the parlour.

'I should hope so! Perhaps one of your parents could pop in and have a word with me some time,' Mr Andrews suggested. 'A talent like yours shouldn't be squandered at Machin & Harpers.'

'I'll ask them,' promised Annie. Two lies within as many minutes! At least she'd have something real to confess next time she went.

That night, she thought about Mr Andrews' words. She'd loved making the dresses. It was like painting a picture or writing a story, because she kept having fresh ideas what to do next, where to put a bow, how to shape a neckline, finish off a sleeve. As the material sped through the machine, she felt a thrill of excitement, because she couldn't wait to see what the finished garment would look like. When it was hanging on the picture rail in the parlour, she looked at it for ages, scarcely able to believe the beautiful gown had recently been odds and ends thrown out for jumble. Not only that, it was all her own work, a product of her industry and imagination.

But it would be too much effort explaining this to her dad, she thought tiredly. Bruno would be different. He'd move heaven and earth to ensure Sylvia went to Art College, but Annie's father would never understand. Anyroad, the course might take years, and Machin & Harpers only took nine months.

Annie woke up a few weeks later with butterflies in her stomach. Today was the dress rehearsal, and she was worried the costumes might clash on stage, or Cinderella would trip down the plywood steps into the ballroom and it would be her fault for making the dress too long.

She met Sylvia in their usual place on the way to school. 'I've forgotten my costume,' she announced crossly when she arrived. 'It's Cecy's fault. She insisted on ironing it and left it in the kitchen.'

'Honestly, Syl. You'd forget your head if it wasn't screwed on!'

'Only if someone left it in the kitchen instead of in my bedroom as they'd promised.'

'You should have ironed it yourself,' Annie sniffed. 'Cecy waits on you hand and foot. If me mam ironed something for me I'd drop dead.'

'Thanks for the lecture, Annie.' Sylvia grinned. 'Anyway, it means I'll have to rush home at dinner time.'

'I'll come with you.'

It was a glorious December day. The sun shone with almost startling intensity out of a luminous, clear blue sky.

Sylvia took deep breaths as they walked swiftly to the Grand. 'Isn't it exhilarating! Bruno says Liverpool air makes him feel quite drunk.'

'Sunny days in winter are much nicer than summer ones.' Annie pointed. 'Look at those people queuing outside the Odeon. Fancy going to the pictures on a lovely day like this!'

'What's on? *The King and I.* We must go one night. Apparently, Yul Brynner is completely bald.'

Cecy shrieked when they appeared. 'What are you doing here?' She made something to eat and offered to take them back in the car.

'No, thanks,' Sylvia said with a martyred air. 'We'll walk, but we'd better hurry.'

The queue outside the Odeon had begun to move. People were paying to go in at the glass cubicle in the foyer. A dark-haired woman with a bright scarf around her neck bought a ticket and disappeared into the darkness. Annie froze.

'Come on!' Sylvia dragged her arm impatiently.

Annie didn't move. She turned to her friend and opened her mouth to speak, but nothing would come.

Sylvia left her hand on Annie's arm. 'What's the matter?'

The power of speech had returned. 'I could have sworn that woman was me mam!' Her head swirled with the shock.

Sylvia gasped. 'Are you sure?'

'Yes. No. Not really.' Annie grimaced. 'I only saw her for a second, but it looked just like her.'

'What was she wearing?'

'All I noticed was her scarf. It had a swirly pattern, like that new blouse of Cecy's.'

'Paisley?'

'That's right, Paisley.'

'Why not go home and see if she's there? Who cares if we're late?'

'But say she isn't?' Annie stared at her friend in horror.

Sylvia rolled her eyes dramatically. 'Gosh, Annie, I don't know.'

'I don't know, either.' Perhaps some things were best left undiscovered, she thought dazedly, otherwise the entire world would be turned upside down. 'Oh, come on,' she said with an attempt at indifference. 'If we run, we might get back to school in time.'

'If that's what you want.'

'It's what I want,' Annie said firmly, though she couldn't get the incident out of her mind all afternoon. Perhaps she should have gone home – and if Mam hadn't been there . . . ?

Although Annie racked her brains and puzzled over the matter at the expense of the History and French lessons, she couldn't for the life of her visualise what would have happened then.

The dress rehearsal was a complete disaster. Everyone forgot their lines, the prompt couldn't be heard without shouting, and Cinderella fell headlong down the steps on top of Dandini and burst into tears.

Mr Andrews remained serene throughout. 'A lousy dress rehearsal is a sign of a good show,' he assured the petrified cast. 'Thank goodness you didn't do well. I would have been really worried.'

Annie arrived home, pleased to find Dot in the back kitchen where she'd already started on the tea. 'Have you been here long?' she asked.

'Since about four o'clock, luv. Why?'

'I just wondered.'

'It's no use coming before you two get here, is it? I'd only end up talking to meself.' Dot jerked her head angrily in the direction of the living room, where Annie's mother was in exactly the same position she'd been in when the girls left for school that morning.

'Oh, Dot!' Annie laid her cheek on her aunt's bony shoulder. If only she could tell Dot what she'd seen, or thought she'd seen, but it would only cause ructions. She smiled, imagining Dot pinning Mam down on the floor the way wrestlers did on television, and twisting her arm until she conceded she'd been to see *The King and I.*

'What's the matter, luv?' Dot laid down the sausages she was unwrapping and took Annie in her arms.

'Nothing.'

'Feel like a cuddle, eh?' Dot said tenderly. 'Pity you're not little any more, or you could sit on me knee the way you used to.'

Annie was now as tall as Dot, perhaps slightly taller. 'I wish we could have stayed with you and Uncle Bert in Bootle,' she sighed.

'So do I, luv! Oh, so do I!' Dot patted her niece's back. 'It was all Father Whotsit's fault, walking in when I was in the middle of the dinner. If only I hadn't burnt the custard and got in such a temper!'

'You threw a cup at the wall, remember?'

'I remember. It was out me next-to-best tea service, too. I said things I didn't mean to say, and it got your dad all stubborn.'

'Still, the house wasn't big enough – and you've had three more boys since.' Annie moved out of her auntie's arms to put the kettle on.

'We could have asked the landlord for a bigger house. In fact, that's what Bert and me intended,' Dot said surprisingly. 'I was going to approach our Ken as tactfully as I could and suggest he found somewhere for him and Rose and we'd keep you and Marie. I think he might have agreed.' Her mouth curled in an expression of disgust. ''Stead, I go and lose me flaming rag, don't I?' she finished bitterly.

Such a little thing, a few unguarded words, and the whole course of their lives had changed, Annie thought.

'Never mind!' Dot patted her arm. 'Deep down at heart, our Ken thinks the world of his lovely girls. Christ knows what you'd have turned out like if you'd stayed with Bert and me.' She cut a sliver of lard for the frying pan and lit the gas underneath. 'I'll leave these sausages for you to finish, Annie. I'd better be off. And oh, there's a Blackledge's cream sandwich in the larder.'

'Ta, Auntie Dot.'

Marie came in, saw the sausages sizzling in the pan, and said, 'Dad hardly ever eats his tea lately. He puts it in the dustbin.'

Annie glanced at her in surprise. 'I hadn't noticed!'

'You're never here, are you?' Marie said, with a hint of accusation in her voice. 'You just plonk his dinner down, then you're out the door like a shot.'

'Has he seen the doctor yet?' Dot demanded.

'I don't know,' Annie said guiltily.

Dot flushed angrily. 'It's not your job to mind your dad, Annie.' Her voice rose so it could have been heard out in the street, let alone the living room it was intended to reach. 'But we know whose job it is. Our Ken could die on his feet, but some people couldn't give a damn.'

'I'm going to the lavatory,' Annie said abruptly. It was too much; what with Dad ill, Marie moping around looking dead miserable, and Mam, or someone who looked very much like Mam, going to the pictures.

'Tara, Annie!' Dot shrieked after a while. 'I've left the spuds and sausages on a low light.'

When Annie emerged, she found Marie sitting on her bed, looking sulky. 'Did Dot tell you?' she said.

'Tell me what?'

'We can't go to their house for Christmas dinner this year, they're going to their Tommy's. What are we going to do all day, Annie?'

Annie's heart sank. The highlight of the festive season had always been the cheerful, chaotic meal at Dot's. Once Sylvia knew, she would be invited to the Grand, but she couldn't desert Marie on Christmas Day.

'What can we do,' she said patiently, 'except make our own Christmas dinner? We've got decorations – in fact, it's time we put them up.'

'That sounds fun!' Marie said scornfully. 'Like the most miserable Sunday you can think of with knobs on. I'd sooner stay in bed.'

'What do you expect?' Annie demanded. 'I can't pluck another auntie out of the air for us to have Christmas dinner with. Anyroad, unless you go to Midnight Mass, you've got to get up for church.'

'Sod church,' Marie pouted.

'Marie!'

Marie squirmed uncomfortably. 'I've felt really peculiar in church since . . . you know! I keep expecting the priest to point at me during his sermon and denounce me as a murderer.'

'Don't be silly,' Annie chided gently.

'I'm not being silly. Me baby would have been born in January if I hadn't had him murdered. It was a boy, they told me.'

'You must stop brooding.' Annie felt very inadequate. 'Why don't you go out with some of the girls from school?' she said cautiously, half expecting to have her head bitten off. It was.

'Because they're stupid!' Marie snapped. 'They watch *Muffin the Mule* on television, and some still play with dolls.'

'I'd better get the tea,' Annie paused in the doorway. 'By the way, have you ever seen our mam with a Paisley scarf?'

'No,' Marie said abruptly. She seemed too preoccupied to ask why Annie had asked such a funny question, and Annie was left wondering if she'd ever have the courage to look for the scarf herself.

According to Dot and Bert, the pantomime went down a treat. 'It was better than the ones you see at the Empire,' Dot claimed. She gave a sarcastic laugh. 'I see your mam and dad didn't come.'

'I didn't ask them,' said Annie.

'Our poor Mike nearly fainted when Sylvia walked on stage,' Bert said, smiling broadly. 'He only came to see her in tights. Now he's in love all over again. Not that I blame him. She's a real Bobby Dazzler, that Sylvia. If I wasn't already married to the best-looking woman in the world I could fancy her meself.' Dot dug him sharply in the ribs with her elbow, but at the same time looked girlishly pleased.

Mike had Sylvia, in white spangled tights and red frock coat, pinned against the wall, where he was talking to her earnestly. Later, she said to Annie. 'Your Mike wants to take me out. What should I do?'

'He's dead nice, but he'll never be able to keep you in the manner to which you're accustomed. He's only an apprentice toolmaker.'

'He asked me to the pictures, not for a lifelong commitment. I know, I'll suggest he brings a friend so we can make a foursome!'

'No!' cried Annie, but Sylvia departed, grinning, just as Mr Andrews came up holding a cardboard folder, looking strangely sheepish. To the chagrin of the girls, he'd brought his fiancée, a pretty girl with China-blue eyes and long straight hair who looked like Alice in Wonderland, and seemed entirely unaware she'd ruined several Christmases.

'This is a play I wrote at university,' he mumbled. 'I thought we'd do it next term. I wonder if you'd mind reading it over the holiday? I'd like to know what you think.'

Annie took the folder, flattered that he was interested in her opinion. *'Goldilocks!'* She looked at him, puzzled. 'Another pantomime?'

'It's a play.' He shuffled his feet awkwardly. 'Goldilocks is the nickname of the main character.'

'Do you want me to be wardrobe mistress again?'

'No, I want you to play Goldilocks.'

'Me!' Annie looked at him askance.

'You'd be perfect, Annie.' Suddenly, he was the old Mr Andrews again. His eyes sparkled with an enthusiasm which was catching. 'You've got the right air of authority – and the red hair! I didn't know it at the time, but the part could have been written specially for you!'

Goldilocks was an orphan. Having lost both parents in a car crash, she arrives at an orphanage where she sets about altering the strict, oppressive regime. By the end, it is the orphans who are in charge, ordering the staff around with the same unfeeling cruelty used on them.

'What's that you're reading?' Marie enquired. She was brushing her hair in front of the dressing-table mirror.

Annie threw the folder onto the bed. 'A play. Mr Andrews wrote it.'

'Honest! What's it like?'

'Dead good.' It was incredible that a play could be so sad and so funny at the same time.

'Can I read it?'

'If you like. Mr Andrews wants me to play the main part.'

'Are you going to?'

'I'm not sure.' She felt admiration for Goldilocks, who despite all her adversities was able to take control of her own life. Unlike me, she thought wryly, who just bumps along from day to day.

'We're going to see *The Ten Commandments* at the Forum on Saturday,' Sylvia announced gaily the next day. 'Mike's bringing his best friend, Cyril Quigley, for you.'

'Cyril! There's no way I'm going out with anyone called Cyril,' Annie said in a horrified voice.

'He's called Cy for short. That's not so bad, is it? In fact, it sounds a bit American.'

Annie looked grudging. 'I suppose so.'

Cy Quigley – Annie refused even to *think* of him as Cyril – had short, very black curly hair, and dark eyes which seemed to be laughing all the time. To her intense relief, she quite liked him. It was difficult not to. He had her in stitches in the cinema, making fun of Moses, particularly when he received the Ten Commandments from God.

'Not another one!' he groaned when number six was reached.

The people nearby kept demanding they be quiet, and even Sylvia got annoyed. 'Don't be sacrilegious,' she hissed.

'Fancy doing this again next Saturday, Annie?' Cy asked when they were in Lyons having coffee and he was rolling a cigarette. He'd already smoked twice as many ciggies as there were commandments.

'I don't mind,' Annie said casually. Inwardly, she was thrilled.

He held her hand on the way to Exchange Station. Annie stiffened when they arrived, hoping he wouldn't kiss her. She wasn't ready for her first kiss just yet. To her relief, he shook hands politely.

'See you next week, then.'

'Have a nice Christmas,' Annie said.

He grinned. 'Same to you.'

Annie watched him cross the road. He stopped and bent his head, cupping his hands around a cigarette as he lit it. She sighed happily.

'Where's Mike?' she asked in surprise when she turned to find Sylvia alone and looking rather glum. They walked onto the platform where the Southport train was waiting, doors open.

'Gone!' Sylvia said abruptly. 'Let's get in the last compartment so as to avoid him.'

The girls sat facing each other. The doors closed and the train started. 'I know he's your cousin, Annie,' Sylvia continued in a complaining voice, 'but he bores me silly. He asked me out again, but I refused. I think he's taken umbrage.'

'But I'm seeing Cy next week!' Annie said in consternation.

'I know, I heard,' Sylvia said stiffly.

'I thought we'd be going in a foursome again.'

'You'll just have to go in a twosome, won't you!'

Annie felt terrible. 'We always go out together on Saturdays.'

'Well, next Saturday I'll just have to stay in alone.' Sylvia turned to look out of the window, her face cold.

'Why didn't you say you didn't want to see Mike again?' Annie said reasonably. 'I wouldn't have made another date with Cy.'

'Why didn't you discuss it with me beforehand?'

'In the middle of Lyons! Don't be silly, Sylvia. It would look as if I was asking for your permission or something.'

Sylvia tossed her head and didn't answer. 'Anyroad,' Annie went on, 'the whole thing was your idea. I didn't want any part of it, did I?'

Neither girl spoke for several stations. The train reached Marsh Lane and Annie saw her cousin get off further down the platform. He looked as miserable as she felt as he went through the exit without a backward glance.

She'd never had a row with Sylvia before, and felt all shaky inside, particularly as she couldn't quite understand what she'd done that was so wrong. 'It was you who said we'd both meet a man one day who'd be more important to us than each other,' she said accusingly.

'I meant when we were really old, eighteen or nineteen,' Sylvia said accusingly back.

'I'm getting off in a minute, we're nearly at Seaforth.'

'So?'

'So, I'll see you tomorrow afternoon, shall I?'

Sylvia shrugged carelessly. 'If you like.'

The train drew into the station, the doors opened. 'Tara, Sylvia.'

'Goodbye, Annie.'

Annie's legs nearly gave way when she stepped onto the platform. Her friendship with Sylvia had come to an end, she thought tragically. There was no way she'd go to the Grand tomorrow, although it had come to feel like home and she was dead fond of Cecy and Bruno.

The guard had blown his whistle and the doors were whirring as if they were about to close, when a figure launched itself out of the train and half fell beside her.

'Oh, Annie!' Sylvia cried. 'What a truly horrible person I am! I'm jealous, that's all. You had such a lovely time with Cyril . . .'

'Cy!'

'Cy, and I was so miserable with Mike. Will you ever forgive me?'

'I thought we weren't going to be friends any more,' Annie said in a small voice.

'Just as if!' Sylvia linked Annie's arm affectionately.

'I'll ask Mike for Cy's address and cancel the date,' Annie offered.

But Sylvia pooh-poohed the offer vehemently. 'I wouldn't dream of such a thing. I hope you have a lovely time on Saturday. Just spare a thought for me occasionally, listening to records in my lonely room . . .'

8

'Well, Annie, what did you think?' Mr Andrews' eyes blinked nervously, as if he would be devastated if she hadn't liked his play. It was the first day back at school, and Annie had stayed after the English lesson.

She coughed importantly. 'I think it's very good. Me sister read it and she really liked it, too.' Marie had been so impressed, both with the play and the pantomime, that she couldn't wait to join the drama group when she reached her final year. She'd decided she would like to be a proper actress when she grew up.

Mr Andrews looked relieved. 'What about playing Goldilocks?'

'I dunno.' Annie wriggled uncomfortably.

'I'll be vastly disappointed if you don't give it a try. In fact, I might give up without you. You're the only one I can see in the part.'

He was so nice she didn't like to let him down. 'I mightn't be any good. I've never acted before.'

'All of us are acting all the time,' he said enigmatically.

'I'll give it a try, then.'

'Good girl!' he said delightedly. 'In that case, keep this copy and start learning your lines. I'll cast the rest of the parts on Monday.'

Perhaps she'd known deep down she would play Goldilocks, because, with Marie's help, Annie already knew the lines off by heart.

'I hardly ever see you,' Sylvia complained on the way home from school. 'You go out with Cyril – I mean Cy – every week, and tonight you're staying in again. We always go to the youth club on Wednesdays.'

'I've only been out with Cy three times, and I changed it to Friday last week, didn't I, so I could see you on Saturday.'

Sylvia said petulantly. 'You've been really funny all week, just because he kissed you.'

'It was only a peck on the cheek.' She felt a little thrill every time she thought about it.

'I think it's getting serious.'

'Don't be silly!'

'Promise you won't go to that club, the Cavern, with him. It's our own special place. I'd be upset if you shared it with Cyril.'

'Cy! I promise. I don't think it's his cup of tea.' The girls had gone to the new club last week, the night it opened. The queue snaked right round the block and they'd been almost the last to be allowed in. Down a narrow street of old warehouses in the centre of Liverpool, the rough basement with its bare brick walls and foot-tapping music had made them feel very cosmopolitan and sophisticated. Ever since, they'd sung 'When the Saints Go Marching In' as they went through the gates to school.

'Anyway,' said Sylvia, returning to the matter in hand, 'why can't you go to the club tonight?'

Annie sighed, 'I don't like leaving our Marie. She's dead upset over losing the baby.'

'It's taken her long enough to find out.'

'She's been upset all along. I didn't know how bad until recently.'

Sylvia snorted derisively. 'If I remember rightly, she didn't lose the baby. It was taken from her at great expense.'

'Oh, Sylvia! What a horrible thing to say!'

'It's not your job to act as a social worker to your sister, Annie,' Sylvia said with an irritating air of self-righteousness.

'Then whose job is it?' Annie asked simply. She was determined not to get annoyed, because she knew what would happen. Any minute, Sylvia would collapse like a pricked balloon and declare herself to be the most horrible person in the world.

'It's your mother's job, or your father's. What about Auntie Dot?'

'Don't be stupid! Me mam and dad live in a world of their own and Dot knows nothing about it. I'm the only one Marie's got to talk to.'

Sylvia stopped dead. 'Oh, Annie! What a dreadful person I am!' She stared at Annie soulfully. 'How do you put up with me?'

'I dunno, I must be daft.' Annie jerked her head. 'Come on, stop posing, else there won't be time for a coffee.'

'Posing?' Sylvia caught her up. 'Was I posing?'

'You pose all the time. You'd think you were Vivien Leigh.'

'Do I actually look like Vivien Leigh?' Sylvia tossed back her long blonde hair with a slender hand.

'Not in the least,' Annie said bluntly. 'You just pose and look dramatic, the way she did in *Gone with the Wind*.'

Sylvia looked puzzled. 'Was that a compliment?'

'It was a statement, that's all.'

When they were in the café, Sylvia said, 'Why don't you ask Marie to come with us to the youth club?'

'I did once, but she refused. She knows you don't like her.'

Sylvia looked hurt. 'I've never said I didn't like her.'

'You didn't have to, Syl. It's obvious. Still, it was generous of you to offer, under the circumstances,' Annie said kindly.

'I've got an idea!' Sylvia's lovely blue eyes brightened. 'Cecy's terribly short-handed. Two women left after Christmas. Would Marie like a job? She'd be so busy, she wouldn't have time to be upset.'

'A job? What sort of job?' Marie demanded.

'Working in the kitchen in the Grand. It's good fun. I did it once and I really enjoyed meself.'

Her sister looked dubious. 'I'm no good at that sort of thing.'

'How do you know?' Annie enquired. 'You've never tried. The pay's good, five shillings an hour, plus tips.'

'Why don't you do it, then?' Marie asked suspiciously.

'Because I don't like taking money off me best friend's mother.'

'Five bob an hour!' Marie pursed her lips thoughtfully. 'How many nights a week?'

'You'd have to sort that out with Cecy. As many as you want, I expect, though they don't do meals on Sunday and Monday.'

'Gosh! I could earn pounds. I could buy meself stacks of clothes.' Marie looked animated for the first time in months. Annie reminded herself her sister was only fourteen. She might have lost a baby, but she was still childish enough to be excited at the idea of buying clothes.

'You'd have to work really hard,' she said sternly.

Marie looked virtuous. 'I don't mind hard work.'

'You could have fooled me!'

'I really fancy one of those taffeta petticoats that make your skirt stick out,' Marie said longingly.

'We'll go to the Grand tonight and you can discuss it with Cecy.' Annie felt hopeful that the problem of Marie might be solved. 'By the way, she knows nothing about that business with the nursing home, so don't mention it whatever you do.'

Annie felt certain that everyone on the train was looking at her. It was as bad as – worse than – having nothing on. She caught the eye of an old woman, who quickly turned her head away.

'I feel dead stupid,' she whispered to Sylvia.

'For goodness' sake, Annie,' her friend snorted impatiently. 'You'd think you were the first woman in the world to wear slacks.'

'My bottom's *huge!*'

'No-one can see your bottom whilst you're sitting on it.'

'I wish I hadn't let you talk me into buying them.' It had seemed a good idea in Bon Marché. Lots of the girls in The Cavern wore slacks.

'Don't start putting the blame on me!' Sylvia said indignantly. She grinned. 'You'll soon get used to them.'

Annie wriggled. She felt as if she were being slowly cut in half. 'I suppose so,' she sighed.

'Where did you go last night with Cy?' Sylvia asked casually.

'For a Chinese meal. It was horrible, like eating roots.' Annie glanced slyly at her friend. 'I'm not seeing him again.'

Sylvia tried not to look glad. 'I hope it's nothing to do with me!'

'It's because he kissed me!'

'But he kissed you before and you said you liked it!'

'This time he kissed me on the lips and his breath *stinks*! Honestly, Syl, it was like being kissed by a sewer! Phew!' Annie waved her hand in front of her face. Between kisses, he'd whispered how much he loved her and how beautiful she was, but all she could think of was how to escape from the rotten smell coming from his mouth. In the end, she'd pulled away and run into the station, where she'd jumped on a train before there was time to make arrangements for another date.

Sylvia burst out laughing. 'It's all those cigarettes!'

'I know. He'll just have to find a girl who smokes as much as he does. Anyroad, I couldn't have gone out with him next Friday, could I? We're going to the theatre with Mr Andrews.'

After discovering that not a single member of the drama group had seen a real play in a real theatre, and, worse, they'd never heard of the Liverpool Playhouse, Mr Andrews decided it was time they paid a visit.

'It'll be my treat,' he said, 'though that's not as generous as it sounds. It's only a bob each at the back. That's where I used to sit in my hard-up student days.'

The play was *School for Wives*, a period piece which told the story of a disreputable old man in search of a young wife. Sylvia spent all week deciding what to wear and turned up in a long black coat and a Greta Garbo hat. She complained bitterly she was getting creased as more and more people squeezed into the next-to-back row until they were squashed together like sardines.

'What do you think so far?' Mr Andrews asked in the first interval.

'It's the dead gear, sir – I mean, Mr Andrews.'

'That old man's a marvellous actor,' one of the boys said.

Mr Andrews' eyes twinkled. 'That "old man" is called Richard Briers and he's only twenty-one! When he becomes famous, which he surely will, you can tell people you first saw him at the Liverpool Playhouse.'

'I wish I hadn't come,' Annie said miserably. 'It makes me realise how awful my Goldilocks is.'

'Don't be silly,' Sylvia chided. 'I think you're very good. I've been telling you so for weeks.'

'She's still a bit stiff,' Mr Andrews said easily. 'She needs to relax a bit, that's all.'

'Are Mam and Dad going to see *Goldilocks*?' Marie asked.

'I haven't mentioned it,' Annie replied. Her sister was helping to prepare the Sunday dinner. Since working at the Grand, she gave the occasional hand at home. 'I didn't ask them to the pantomime, did I?'

'That was different. This time you're the star. They went to Tommy's wedding, and they'll go to the christening when Dawn has her baby, so they should go and see their daughter in a play!' Dot and Bert would be grandparents at Easter. 'Cutting it fine,' Dot said darkly. 'Nine months to the day. I'll kill our Tommy if it's early. The whole street'll talk.'

'I suppose I could ask them,' Annie mused.

Later, on her way to see Sylvia, she thought, 'I've never made demands. In fact, it's *me* who's looked after *them*, rather than the other way round. When Mr Andrews asked what they'd thought of the pantomime, I had to lie again, say Mam was ill. It would look dead funny if they didn't turn up for *Goldilocks.*' People would wonder what sort of mam and dad she had.

She'd definitely ask them. 'It's time they did something for me.'

'That was brilliant, Annie,' Mr Andrews enthused when the dress rehearsal finished. 'Absolutely brilliant.'

'I got quite carried away,' Annie said modestly. It was Wednesday and the play was only two days off. Today, she'd actually managed to get *inside* Goldilocks, and feel her bitterness and frustration at the hand that fate had dealt her.

'That's as it should be.' Mr Andrews came onto the stage. 'Gather round, cast, I've some news.' They sat on the floor at his feet. 'We've nearly sold out of tickets for the main performance, and Mr Parrish wants us to do an extra one on Friday afternoon just for the school.'

Everyone groaned affectedly and pretended it would be a bore.

Mr Andrews wasn't fooled. 'I knew you'd be pleased. There's a reporter coming from the *Crosby Herald*, so you'll have your names in the paper next week. Now, who's brought money for tickets? You'd better be quick, there's only a few left.'

Annie supposed she'd better buy tickets for Mam and Dad before it was too late. She kept putting off asking them, but perhaps if she produced the tickets and waved them in their faces, it would be harder for them to refuse. The more she'd thought about it, the more important it seemed that they should come. It proved something, though she wasn't sure what. As soon as Dad finished his tea tonight, she'd bring it up.

Marie was about to leave for work when Annie got home. 'There's a big dinner tonight, Crosby Conservative Association. Bruno nearly hit the roof when he found out. Cecy said he was nothing but a bloody Marxist. They had an awful row.'

'They often row, but it doesn't mean anything,' Annie said.

'I know. They're terribly in love. It's dead romantic.' Marie sighed happily. 'It's smashing there, sis.' She kissed Annie's cheek. 'Ta!'

'Get away with you!' Annie flushed with pleasure. She couldn't remember her sister making a spontaneous show of affection before.

Marie left, and Annie began to prepare her father's tea. Since hearing he was throwing his dinner away, she'd been making appetising little treats. She smeared butter on a piece of plaice and slid it under the grill, peeled two small potatoes and opened a tin of peas.

She made herself a jam butty and ate it in the kitchen, staring through the window at the wall separating the house from Mrs Flaherty's. She felt restless and on edge, aware of the blue tickets in the breast pocket of her gymslip. She moved to the door where she could see her mam. The television was on without the sound. Once, when Mam was in the lavatory, Annie had looked in the cupboard, and there, as Marie had said, were several bottles of tablets with funny names she'd never heard of.

'God, it's *horrific*!' she thought. 'It's like a nightmare – Mr Andrews could write a play about it.'

The clock on the mantelpiece struck seven, and she saw her mother's body tense. Her head cocked slightly as if she were listening for something. She was waiting for the sound of the latch on the backyard door, the signal that her husband was home.

As soon as her father had cleared his plate, Annie fetched the tea. 'Would you like a pudding? I've got a Battenburg, your favourite.' He'd never said it was his favourite, but whenever she bought one it rapidly disappeared.

'No, ta,' he grunted. He turned his chair towards the fire, opened the *Daily Express* and began to read.

The clock struck half past seven. If she didn't leave soon, she'd be late meeting Sylvia – she realised she'd forgotten to change out of her uniform. She stood irresolutely in the middle of the room, wondering whether to go upstairs and change, but the tickets seemed to be burning a hole in her pocket. 'I'll ask now,' she decided. If she didn't, she wouldn't stop thinking about it all night.

She sat down, took a deep breath, and said in a voice that shook for some reason. 'I've got tickets for the school play. They're only ninepence each. I've got the main part. I'm the star. Please come, *please*!'

There was no answer and in the ensuing silence Annie felt as if her words were still there, hanging in the air full of urgent desperation. But Mam had heard, she could tell. Her mother's body shrank. She hunched her shoulders and folded her arms and stared down at her knees, which were clenched together like teeth. Dad looked up from his paper, but instead of looking at Annie, he looked at the television, at the characters talking soundlessly to each other. Then he shook his head, not at Annie, but at the screen, though she knew it was meant for her. There was a finality about the gesture. She knew straight away there was no point in trying to change his mind.

So that was it. They weren't coming.

Jaysus! With a feeling of reckless rage she'd never experienced before, Annie took the tickets from her pocket and threw them on the fire. She watched them curl, turn brown, catch alight, and as they were consumed by the blue, flickering flames, she felt a similar flame begin to kindle in her heart. She loathed them! She loathed them both, particularly her mother. You never knew, Dad might have come if it hadn't been for her.

The floodgates broke. 'Why didn't you leave us with Auntie Dot?' she cried in a voice raw with hate and anger. 'You're not fit to be parents, either of you.'

Her father was still staring at the screen. He didn't even glance in Annie's direction during her outburst. If he turns the sound up, I'll hit him, she vowed.

'*Why don't you listen to me?*' Suddenly she was screaming. 'I'm your daughter. I'm Annie. Don't you know I'm here?'

She had to get through to them! She had to say something that would touch a nerve, instigate a response. 'Marie had an abortion last year. Marie's your other daughter, in case you've forgotten. She had an abortion because she'd been looking for someone to love her, and when I started my periods I thought I was going to die! That's why I failed the scholarship.'

Annie remembered the mothers waiting outside school to collect their children when it was raining, the sportsdays and speechdays which she hadn't bothered to mention because she knew they wouldn't come, the pantomime. But what she'd missed more than anything was a knee to sit on and arms to embrace her when she'd needed them. She wanted to explain the aching misery of her childhood to her parents in words they would understand, but perhaps she wasn't clever enough or literate enough, because she couldn't think of a way of phrasing how much she'd missed their love. Instead, she got to her feet and began to walk back and forth, waving her arms furiously, and all that came pouring out was a stream of bitterness and despair that she'd never known, never dreamt, she'd been storing up for years, perhaps her entire life.

'I hate you. I hate you both!' she screamed finally.

Still silence. Oh, if only they would speak! If only they would answer back. Why didn't they at least make excuses, defend themselves?

Mam's eyes were closed, screwed tight, as if she were shutting everything out. Annie turned on her. 'I saw you going into the Odeon, Mam,' she said brutally. 'There's nothing wrong with you, is there? All this is a sham.' She gestured around the room. 'You're just getting back at me dad because he was out with another woman the night Johnny was killed. You've ruined his life, and you've ruined my and our Marie's lives, because you're so eaten up with sheer bloody spite!' She bent down and began to shake her mother by the shoulders. 'Are you listening to me, Mam?' she demanded shrilly.

'Don't,' said Dad. 'Don't.'

Annie glared at him, ready to continue with her invective, but the words choked in her throat. Jaysus, his face! Why hadn't she noticed how grey it had become, the skin like rubber, pitted and eaten away, his eyes almost invisible in dark, shrunken sockets? In a moment of blinding clarity, she realised he was very ill, that he was dying. She could actually smell the sickness, the sweet, rotten odour of decay that came from somewhere deep inside him.

Annie turned on her heel wordlessly and left the room. She snatched her gabardine mack off the rack in the hall, left the house and walked quickly to the youth club. A vicious wind had sprung up; she shoved her hands in her pockets because she'd forgotten her gloves.

'Where on earth have you been?' Sylvia demanded crossly when Annie came into the church hall where the youth club was held. 'We've lost our place on the table tennis rota.'

But Annie didn't care. 'Let's go for a walk,' she said abruptly.

'A walk?' Sylvia looked startled. 'Gosh, Annie, are you all right? You haven't changed and you're as white as a sheet.'

'Come on!' Annie marched towards the door.

'I'm coming!'

Annie was halfway down the street by the time Sylvia caught up with her, still struggling into her suede coat.

'Where are we going?'

'Nowhere. Anywhere.'

'Something awful's happened, hasn't it?'

Annie nodded. 'I can't tell you, not yet,' she replied in a flat, emotionless voice. 'I just want to walk.'

'All right, Annie, that's what we'll do.'

Sylvia linked Annie's arm and the two girls walked silently for a long time. After a while, the monotonous clatter of their shoes on the pavement began to get on Annie's nerves. The sound seemed to echo, magnified, in the near-empty streets.

'Talk to me,' she demanded.

'What about?'

'I don't know.'

Sylvia began to speak, hesitantly at first. She told Annie about Italy, about the little village in the south surrounded by misty lavender hills where she was born. They'd lived in a big house, 'Almost as big as a castle, Annie, with little turrets on each corner and acres and acres of vineyard at the back.' During the war, Cecy had been worried she'd be arrested because she was English, but no-one in the village informed on her and she'd been left alone. Bruno had gone away to fight with the Communists in Yugoslavia soon after Sylvia was born and she hadn't seen him till she was four. 'When the war ended and he came back, I was thrilled to discover this tall, magnificent man was my father. I wouldn't let him out of my sight. He had to take me with him everywhere. Then he decided he wasn't prepared to tolerate the Mafia any longer. They virtually ruled the village and demanded a huge share of the profits from our wine business.' And Sylvia had started school. 'All we did was say prayers, I learnt scarcely anything.' So they'd moved to Turin. 'Such an elegant city, Turin, Annie. It's where Bruno and Cecy met. He has a cousin there, and Cecy was on holiday with one of her aunts. I went to a proper school, but soon Cecy became homesick. She yearned for Liverpool. Now, you'll never guess, Bruno is quite gloriously happy, and Cecy occasionally feels homesick for Italy!'

Sylvia's voice trailed away. Annie saw they'd reached a crossroads and there was a pub on the opposite corner. 'Have you got any money?'

'Of course. How much do you want?'

'I'd like a drink, a whisky.' A whisky had helped once before, the day she'd failed the scholarship. Perhaps a drink would help calm her pounding heart and the turmoil in her stomach.

'You're still in uniform!' Sylvia bit her lip. 'Turn your collar up to hide your tie. Stay away from the bar so the landlord won't see you.'

The pub was packed. Annie found two stools and carried them to a corner. Sylvia was ages getting served at the crowded bar. She arrived looking flustered. 'I got you a double.'

'Ta.'

Two men approached. 'Mind if we join you, girls?'

'Yes,' Sylvia said crisply. 'Go away!'

'Toffee-nosed pair of bitches!' one man muttered audibly.

The whisky had the opposite effect from what Annie hoped for. It made her feel worse, as if a kettle was boiling inside her stomach, emitting clouds of steam, and her heart was pounding even louder.

'I think I'm going to be sick,' she said plaintively.

'Come on, you need some fresh air.'

Back outside, Sylvia said, 'Shall we go to the Grand? You can rest in my room and Cecy will make a nice cup of tea.'

The idea was tempting, but Annie shook her head. 'I should go home,' she said tiredly. Go home and apologise for saying such terrible things.

'What time is it?' she asked when they reached Orlando Street.

'Nearly ten o'clock. We've walked for miles, Annie. I'm surprised we found our way back.'

Annie had left her key in her satchel. She knocked on the door of number thirty-eight. 'Thanks, Sylvia,' she muttered.

'What for?'

'For putting up with me tonight.' Sylvia hadn't complained, not once. 'I'll never forget it.'

Sylvia laughed shyly. 'That's what friends are for. Whatever happens, I'll always be there for you, Annie.'

Sylvia had disappeared by the time Annie knocked a second time. She stepped back and looked up at the window of her parents' room; the curtains were open and the room was in darkness, which meant they were still up. Perhaps Dad was so angry he'd decided not to let her in. Annie rather hoped this was the case. She'd welcome anger, understand it. It was the mute, uncomplaining acceptance of her tirade that had driven her to say more and more wicked things.

She knocked a third time, then peered through the letterbox. Total blackness! Marie wasn't due home for half an hour, when Bruno or Cecy usually brought her in the car.

Perhaps the back door was open; it wasn't usually locked until they went to bed. Annie walked to the end of the street and turned down the narrow passage leading to the back entry which ran between the two rows of houses. The path was unlit. Dad had warned them never to use the entry in the dark, reminding them of the girl who'd been murdered in such an entry less than a mile away. Remembering, Annie started to run. She stumbled against a dustbin and nearly screamed when she saw two luminous eyes staring at her from on top of a wall. It was a cat, who spat and snarled as she passed. At last, she reached thirty-eight and almost fell into the yard. Her fingers shook as she fumbled with the latch on the back door. She sighed with relief when the door was safely closed behind her.

There was a light in the kitchen, but not the living room, which was odd. Annie squinted through the net curtains, but no-one was there. They must be out, but it was unheard of for her parents to go out unexpectedly. Perhaps one had been taken ill! If so, it was entirely her fault.

She tried the kitchen door, convinced it would be locked, and was surprised to find it open, and even more surprised when it jammed after a few inches. There was something preventing it from opening further. Annie pushed hard with her shoulder and the door gave way.

The smell hit her immediately. Gas, so powerful, that she instinctively put her hands to her face to prevent herself from retching. Then she screamed.

Mam was lying on the floor, her head on a pillow, rosary beads threaded through her still, white fingers. Dad's head was in the oven, his body half draped over his wife's. One of his hands lay protectively on her breast. His poor legs were twisted crookedly because Annie had pushed at them trying to get in.

Annie screamed again and couldn't stop screaming. She screamed so loudly she didn't hear windows opening and irritable voices demanding to know what the hell was going on, nor footsteps in the entry and the latch lifting on the back door. She was unaware that the back yard was suddenly full of people. It wasn't until she was roughly yanked aside that she came to.

'Jesus Christ!' a man's voice said hoarsely. 'Get the kid out of here. Someone call an ambulance, quick!'

'Come on, luv. Come indoors with me.' Mrs Flaherty from next door took hold of Annie's arm and tried to lead her away.

She stared at the old woman, eyes wild with terror. 'I killed them! I murdered me mam and dad.'

Shrugging off the restraining arm, she fought her way out of the yard. Her ankles struck the pedal of Dad's bike, which was propped against the wall. It slid to the ground with a crash.

There were more people in the entry outside. 'What's going on?' someone asked.

'It's the Harrisons. They've done themselves in.' The speaker's voice throbbed with excitement. 'Gas, I think it was.'

Annie emerged from the entry into Orlando Street. People were pouring out of the pub on the corner. Above the sound of the shouting and the laughter, she could hear a voice calling, 'Empty your glasses, *please*!' There was something strangely familiar about the desperate cry. 'Please come, *please*!'

She stood outside the pub for a long time, being jostled by the crowd and in everyone's way. Several men, unsteady on their feet, began to cross the road and she followed them blindly, then began to run again.

After a while, Annie stopped running. Her breath was raw within her pounding chest, and her legs felt as if they were about to give way. She'd come to the stretch of sand where Dot used to bring them in the summer when they were little, and where she and Sylvia came on warm evenings to talk.

Now, at half past ten on a bitter March night, she felt herself drawn towards the dark isolation offered by the litter-strewn beach . . .

Upper Parliament Street

1

Sylvia stuck her head round the office door. 'Lunch time!' she sang.

'Already?' replied Annie without looking up. Her eyes were glued to the paper in her typewriter. 'Are you sure?'

'You must be the only typist in Liverpool who doesn't watch the clock all day long,' Sylvia said as she came into the tiny room. She wore a knitted shawl with a long fringe over an ankle-length black jersey dress, boots, and a red scarf tied around her head like a gypsy. Gold hoops dangled from her ears. The outfit looked casual, as if it had been thrown on without a thought, yet she'd probably spent ages deciding what to wear that day for Art College.

'I'll just finish this letter,' Annie murmured. Sylvia stood behind and watched, impressed, as her friend's fingers flew over the keys.

'There!' Annie typed 'Yours faithfully', left five clear spaces, then 'J. Rupert', and withdrew the sheet with a flourish. 'I'll do the rest this afternoon.'

'I should think so!' Sylvia lounged against a filing cabinet and said with a twinkle, 'Where's your boss?'

'Now as he's seen you, likely to come in any minute, I reckon.'

The words were scarcely out of her mouth when, through the glazed wall separating her cubbyhole from Jeremy Rupert's luxurious office, they saw a bulky figure rise from the desk. Sylvia was as visible to him as he was to them. The girls grinned at each other.

Annie's door opened and a man entered. His roly-poly figure and noticeably short arms and legs must have presented a challenge to his tailor. Chubby red cheeks and round spectacles gave him a Billy Bunter look. He had tiny feet and walked in a curiously dainty manner for someone of his bulk. 'Can I have a copy of this please, Annie.' His eyes widened in surprise which both girls knew was entirely faked. 'Oh, hello, Sylvia, I didn't know you were here.'

'Hello, Jeremy.'

Annie could never get used to Sylvia addressing her boss as 'Jeremy'. 'I don't work for him, so if he calls me by my first name, I shall call him by his,' Sylvia argued.

'You look a sight for sore eyes, I must say,' Jeremy Rupert's mouth almost watered as he looked Sylvia up and down.

'Thank you,' Sylvia said prettily. 'I'm about to whisk your secretary off to lunch. She's already five minutes late.'

'Then she must take an extra five minutes for her lunch hour,' Annie's boss said expansively. 'No, another ten. In fact, Annie, I don't expect to see you back until two fifteen.'

As his own lunch hour was quite likely to stretch to three or even later, there was no likelihood of him seeing Annie at two fifteen. Nevertheless, she unhooked her coat from behind the door, and said demurely, 'Thank you, Mr Rupert.'

'Well, we're off,' smiled Sylvia. 'Nice seeing you, Jeremy.'

Jeremy Rupert opened the door with exaggerated courtesy. As the girls went through, he put a heavy arm around Sylvia's waist to usher her out. Sylvia paused deliberately, and with an expression of distaste, took his cuff between her thumb and forefinger and let the arm drop. No words were spoken, but the man smiled as if it were a great joke.

'Is he always like that?' Sylvia asked when they were outside.

'Like what?'

'Like a bloody octopus. He can't keep his hands to himself.'

'I do have a job fighting him off sometimes,' Annie conceded. She'd only worked for Jeremy Rupert for two months. At first, she thought the way he slipped his arm around her waist or shoulders was merely a paternal gesture on his part – he had two daughters slightly older than herself – but lately she'd noticed his hand brush her breasts. She hadn't said anything because she couldn't think of a way to put him off without risking her job. She acted as if the incidents hadn't occurred.

'You should slap his face,' Sylvia said indignantly.

'And get the sack?' Annie hooted.

'If Bruno knew, he'd give the creep a good punch on the nose.'

'In that case, I'd get the sack and Bruno would end up in jail.'

'Bruno wouldn't mind. He'd think it a cause worth fighting for.'

'But I would,' Annie argued. 'It's a good job. I get eight pounds ten a week, which is at least a pound more than in another solicitor's. Not only that, I really enjoy the work since I was promoted.'

Stickley & Plumm, solicitors, were situated in North John Street, in the business centre of Liverpool, where they occupied three floors above an exclusive gentlemen's outfitters and a travel agent. An old-established, highly reputable firm, Mr Stickley and Mr Plumm were old bones, and of the four partners, Jeremy Rupert was the most junior. There were nine other solicitors, ranging from very young to very old.

Annie had started in the typing pool two and a half years ago. She was sixteen and had just left Machin & Harpers with the next to highest speeds in her class; 120 words per minute shorthand, 60 typing.

Just as she had been a good pupil, Annie was an equally good worker. She was neat, both in her dress and in her work, conscientious and punctual. Only Annie herself was surprised when, despite her youth, she was offered the job of Jeremy Rupert's secretary when the current occupant retired. The other secretaries were more than twice her age.

Not only did it mean an increase in wages, but Mr Rupert was head of the Litigation Department, where the work was vastly more interesting than conveyancing or probate, involving simple but fascinating disputes from litigants squabbling over the situation of boundary walls and fences, to violent criminal activities including the occasional murder.

Annie loved the work. Lately, though, Mr Rupert's roving hands had become a problem.

Sylvia linked her arm. 'Let's have lunch in the New Court.'

'But it'll be nearly all men,' Annie protested.

Sylvia flung the corner of her shawl over her shoulder with a flourish. 'Why do you think I want to go?'

'You know what you are?' said Annie as they strolled along. The streets were packed with office workers. It was a crisp, sunny December day and the small shops were tastefully decorated for Christmas. 'You're a prickteaser. You enjoy flaunting yourself in front of men.'

Sylvia raised her fine eyebrows. 'That's a rather vulgar expression coming from the prim and proper Miss Annie Harrison!'

'That's how Mike described his new girlfriend. Mind you, Dot still gave him a clip round the ear, even though he's twenty-three.'

'Mike! Is he still so depressingly boring?'

'Mike isn't the least bit boring.' Annie sprang to the defence of her cousin. 'Anyroad, he considers you incredibly conceited.'

'That's because I've got plenty to be conceited about.' Sylvia glanced at her reflection in a shop window as if to confirm the truth of this remark: not that there was any need for confirmation, the admiring looks from passers-by, particularly the men, were enough to convince any girl she was outstanding.

The looks weren't just for Sylvia. The two girls were in stark contrast to each other: Sylvia in her flamboyant outfit, her straight creamy hair spread fanlike over her woollen shawl, and Annie, quietly dressed in a sensible coat, the frill of her white blouse spurting from under the collar, yet, in her own way, equally flamboyant with her russet curls, cheeks pinker than usual from the cold, and gold-lashed blue-grey eyes. Both were tall, though Sylvia was as slender as a model and two sizes smaller than her more voluptuous companion.

The men in the New Court were suitably impressed when the girls went in. Sylvia swept haughtily up to the bar and ordered shandy and cheese sandwiches, apparently oblivious to the stir they had created. She winked at Annie. 'If you ignore them, it drives them wild.'

'Do you like my shawl?' she asked when they were seated.

'It's very nice,' Annie said dutifully.

'Cecy had it made. She'll order one for you, if you like.'

'I don't want to hurt her feelings, but tell her no ta. I can't see meself in a shawl.'

'She misses you terribly, Annie,' Sylvia said, serious for once.

'I miss her, too – and Bruno.'

'You didn't have to leave. You can come back any time you want.'

'I know, Syl,' Annie said patiently. They had the same discussion at least once a week. 'But it was time me and Marie lived together.'

'But Marie will be moving to London once she finishes her drama course. You can't live in that horrible little flat all on your own!'

'It's not little and it's not horrible. I really like it there.'

'Better than the Grand?' Sylvia looked hurt.

'Of course not!'

The girls finished their meal and left the pub. Outside, they made arrangements to meet when Annie finished work at Saturday lunchtime. 'We'll go shopping, catch a movie, and finish off at the Cavern,' Sylvia announced.

Annie couldn't help but smile at the 'catch a movie'. Her friend had become very Americanised since she started College. She referred to men as 'guys' and said 'kinda' instead of 'kind of'.

Sylvia kissed her cheek and said, 'See ya, Annie', and waltzed off into the crowd. Annie submitted to the kiss, embarrassed. It was something else Sylvia had started to do. They must be a pretentious lot at Art College.

As she climbed the stairs to her office on the second floor, she passed Reception, where Miss Hunt, secretary to Mr Granger, the senior partner, was on the telephone. She put the receiver down and glanced pointedly at her watch.

Annie stuck her head inside. 'Mr Rupert said I could have an extra fifteen minutes. I was late leaving.'

Miss Hunt was the longest-serving female employee in the firm. A tall, painfully thin woman with a penchant for pastel twinsets and tight perms, she was the butt of cruel office jokes of which Annie hoped she was ignorant, or her permanent anguished frown might have grown deeper. Miss Hunt had spent most of her adult life attending to Arnold Grayson's every whim. She shopped for him, to the extent, it was rumoured, of buying his underwear. On his behalf, she sent birthday presents to his wife and children, arranged his holidays, paid his bills. More than once, she had been seen kneeling on the floor tying Arnold Grayson's shoelaces.

Outside his office, Miss Hunt was a different person. She was nominally in charge of female employees, who often felt the lash of her acerbic tongue if they were late or their work didn't come up to scratch, and woe betide them if they spent too much time gossiping in the Ladies.

Her narrow yellow face twisted into what might possibly be a smile when Annie spoke. 'I thought it wasn't like you to be late, Miss Harrison. Was that your friend who came for you earlier?'

'Yes, Sylvia. It's all right for her to come in, isn't it?'

'Of course. She looks rather Bohemian,' Miss Hunt said wistfully, as if she wouldn't have minded being a bit Bohemian herself.

'She's at Art College,' said Annie, as if that explained everything. She was never sure if Sylvia was a Bohemian, an Existentialist or a Beatnik. 'We only lunch on Thursdays, when she has a free period.'

Back at her desk, Annie flicked through her shorthand notebook and found only two more letters, both short. She typed them quickly, put them in the blotting folder on Mr Rupert's desk ready for him to sign along with those done that morning, and swept the leather top clear of cigarette ash. She then caught up with the filing. It wasn't yet half two and she had nothing else to do. In practice, she was supposed to collect work from the typing pool to fill in time before her boss appeared, but Annie wasn't in the mood to be a model secretary that afternoon.

She sank her chin onto her hands, laid palm downwards on the typewriter.

She'd hated leaving the Grand and upsetting Cecy, but there'd been Marie to consider. Marie was living next door to Auntie Dot with an increasingly ailing old lady, and Annie was left with the old, familiar sensation of guilt, of feeling responsible for her sister.

The telephone rang in Mr Rupert's office. Annie picked up her extension, which usually made her feel very important, and made an appointment for a client to see him the following week.

Downstairs, someone called, 'Rose, Ro-ose. Mr Bunyon and his client would like a cup of tea straight away.'

'I've only got one bloody pair of hands. I'll be as quick as I can,' a hoarse voice replied. Rose, the tealady, could be heard angrily banging dishes in the kitchen. Almost eighty, Rose was a breath of fresh air in the dull and stultifying atmosphere that prevailed in the offices of Stickley & Plumm. She never hesitated to speak her mind. If anyone didn't like it, all they had to do was sack her, she said challengingly.

Annie returned to her reverie. *Rose!*

'How are you getting on with the girls, Rose? Don't forget, I'd be happy to have them if they're too much for you.'

'Don't put on your little act with me, Rose.'

'It's time to forgive and forget, Rose.'

Dot's voice. Then another, throbbing with excitement. *'It's the Harrisons, they've done themselves in. Gas, I think it was.'*

Although she was sitting down, Annie's legs felt weak, as if she'd been running too fast and too far. Perspiration trickled down her armpits, despite the deodorant she'd rubbed on that morning, as she began to relive that terrible night. She'd relived it a thousand times already. Lately the memory returned less and less, but it took the smallest thing, like someone calling 'Rose', for it all to come flooding back.

She left the sands and ran towards the Grand, trying to keep a look-out for Bruno, but the cars that whizzed by all looked the same. Suppose he just dropped Marie off at the end of Orlando Street!

Bruno was about to leave when Annie came stumbling up. She threw herself onto the bonnet, and the Mercedes stopped with a screech of brakes. 'For goodness' sake, Annie!' came Bruno's irritable voice. 'Are you trying to commit suicide?'

She tried to explain, but the words refused to come. There seemed no words in the dictionary to describe what she'd just seen. 'Me mam, me dad' she croaked, but that was all. She stood, ice-cold and trembling. Even when Bruno shook her by the shoulders, she still couldn't speak.

Then Cecy and Sylvia came and took her inside. Bruno said crisply, 'Stay here, Marie.' He got into the car and drove away.

Cecy made a cup of tea and Annie drank it gratefully. 'Perhaps a drop of whisky?' Cecy suggested, but Sylvia said in a scared voice, 'She had whisky earlier and it made her sick.'

Marie looked terrified. 'What's happened, sis?'

Annie opened her arms and her sister fell into them. Words came at last. 'They're dead, Marie. Our mam and dad are dead.'

Cecy gasped. 'God rest their souls.' She crossed herself.

'The thing is,' Annie sobbed, 'it's all my fault. I killed them. They wouldn't come to see the play and I said the most terrible things.'

'You can't kill people with words, Annie,' Cecy said, puzzled.

'*I* did!'

'I don't understand, dear.'

But no matter how Annie tried, she couldn't even begin to describe the horrific sight she'd so recently witnessed.

After a while, Bruno returned with a weeping Auntie Dot. A neighbour had known she was a relative and the police arrived with the tragic news. Bruno found her and Bert in Orlando Street. Bert stayed behind to deal with all the questions that had to be answered.

'Oh, my poor little lambs!' Dot embraced Annie and Marie in her scrawny arms. 'Trust our Ken! Even at the very end, Rose is the only one he gives a toss for. Didn't care, did he, that one of you girls was bound to find them? Poor Annie!' She stroked Annie's curls. 'What a thing to happen, eh? I could strangle the bugger with me bare hands,' she added.

Bruno had been talking quietly to his wife and daughter, and Cecy began to cry. Sylvia stared at Annie unbelievingly.

'But Dot, none of it would have happened if it wasn't for me,' Annie cried hoarsely. 'It was my fault. I drove them to it. Oh, if only I'd kept me big mouth shut, they'd still be alive.'

'What are you talking about, luv?'

'I'm the wickedest person in the world.' Annie felt as if her head would burst. How was she going to live with this for the rest of her life? 'The things I said!'

'Hold on a minute.' Bruno grabbed Annie's arm. 'Your father killed your mother, then himself. It was nothing to do with you.'

'It was, it was,' Annie wept.

'He left a note,' Bruno said harshly. 'He was dying of cancer. There were only a few weeks left. He took your mother with him.'

Annie shook her head. 'That was just an excuse. He didn't want me to think I was responsible.'

'No, luv,' Dot broke in. 'The note was typed. Your dad must have done it in the office before he came home. Nothing you said would have made any difference. He had it all planned.'

It was long past midnight by the time Bruno took Dot home. Marie went with them. Cecy had offered to keep both girls, but Marie preferred to be with her aunt. 'She can sleep with me. Bert won't mind dossing down in the parlour for a night or two,' said Dot.

Annie went to bed in the spare room feeling light-headed with relief, but when she woke next morning she could smell gas and, every time she closed her eyes, she saw the bodies of Mam and Dad lying in the kitchen. I pushed his legs all crooked, she remembered.

When Cecy came in, she found Annie almost hysterical with guilt and grief. 'They were still terrible things to say when he felt so ill, when he was dying,' she said in a cracked voice.

Cecy stroked her forehead. 'He probably wasn't listening, dear. He almost certainly didn't take in a word you said.'

'But what if he did? And another thing, if I'd looked after them better, he wouldn't have felt the need to take Mam with him.'

'Annie, dear, you're only fifteen,' Cecy said softly. 'You've had far too much responsibility in your young life. Soon, you can put this all behind you and start having a nice time, like other young girls do.'

'I was already having a nice time. I neglected them. I should have stayed in more often. I should have stayed in all the time.' Annie began to cry. 'I'd never have gone out if I'd known me dad was dying.'

'Of course you wouldn't,' Cecy said gently. 'You know, your forehead's awfully hot. I think I'll call the doctor.'

The doctor came and prescribed tablets. For the next few days, Annie swam in and out of nightmarish sleep and periods awake when everything in the room seemed to be moving silently. The furniture would loom up as if it were about to fall on top of her, then recede just in time. The pictures on the wall detached themselves and floated around like leaves in a breeze. Dot came, and Marie. Sylvia and Cecy seemed to be there all the time. Heads were unnaturally large, voices slow and deep like a broken record on a gramophone.

'I'm a terrible nuisance,' Annie would say in moments of lucidity.

One morning, she woke up feeling better. She sat up. The furniture stayed in place and the pictures remained on the walls. Annie looked around with interest. She hadn't noticed what an elegant room this was, with its silver and grey wallpaper and dove-grey satin curtains that hung in smooth folds over the narrow windows. The eiderdown and coverlet were the same material, and even the furniture was a pale bleached grey. By contrast, the carpet was deep rippled pink.

Cecy came in. Her head was a normal size and she gave a delighted smile when she saw Annie sitting up. 'Ah, I think this is the old Annie. You're looking well, dear. The colour's already back in your cheeks.'

She rushed away to make a cup of tea. A few minutes later, Sylvia appeared in a white quilted dressing gown, her blonde hair mussed. She gave a sigh of relief. 'Jaysus, Annie, you had us worried.'

'You caught that from me Auntie Dot.'

Sylvia sat crosslegged on the plump eiderdown. 'Caught what?'

'The "Jaysus". She always says it.'

' "Jaysus" is such a lovely word!'

They grinned at each other. Sylvia reached for Annie's hand. 'Oh, it's good to see you your old self again.'

Annie sighed. 'I doubt if I'll ever be me old self, Syl.' She had memories, terrible memories, that she'd never had before.

Sylvia looked grave. 'In the long run, what happened was probably for the best. Your father was going to die, and Dot thinks your mother wouldn't have wanted to live without him.'

'How did he do it?' She wasn't too sure if she wanted to know.

'The police said he put sleeping tablets in her tea.'

'Then he carried her into the kitchen and lay down beside her . . . Jaysus!' Annie bit her lip and tried not to cry, just as Cecy swept into the room with a tray of tea things. She took one look at Annie's distraught face and said sharply to Sylvia, 'Is this your doing?'

'I was only telling her about the sleeping tablets.'

'It was me that asked,' Annie put in.

'Oh, well, I suppose you had to know some time.'

'What day is it?' Annie asked suddenly.

'Monday,' Sylvia replied.

'The play, *Goldilocks*. It should have gone on last Friday!' She'd let Mr Andrews down.

'Don't worry,' Sylvia assured her. '*Goldilocks* went ahead as planned. Mr Andrews managed to get a red wig, and according to all reports, Marie played Goldilocks to perfection.'

'Marie? *Our* Marie?'

'Who else? She knew the part as well as you did.'

Annie felt relieved. It was time her sister got some recognition.

'Now, get dressed the pair of you,' Cecy said impatiently. 'I'll make breakfast, and if Annie feels well enough, we'll all go into town. I feel in the mood to spend lots of money today.'

There was no question of the girls going back to Orlando Street. In fact, they never went back at all. Dot and Bert cleared the house of its contents, and brought Annie's few possessions to the Grand. To everyone's astonishment, it was discovered the house had been purchased, not rented, and the small mortgage had almost been paid off.

'He was always a secretive bugger, our Ken,' Dot said, shaking her head. They were in the Grand, in the vast private lounge which was big enough to hold two suites. Cecy and Bruno were working, and Sylvia was upstairs supposedly doing her homework, but probably playing with the hulahoop she'd just bought. 'What do you want to do with the money, Annie? Bert said the house is worth eight or nine hundred pounds. I suggest you and Marie put it in the bank and when you're a bit older, you can buy a little house between you.'

It was a month later. The Harrison girls were back at school. The news of their parents' deaths had been in the newspaper and everybody was treating them with a mixture of kid gloves and ghoulish curiosity.

Annie had remained with the Delgados, who had assured her that she could stay in the silver and grey room permanently, whilst Marie had moved into the house next door to Dot's which was occupied by an old lady, though she had all her meals with the Gallaghers, and still came to work in the Grand several nights a week. Marie appeared entirely unaffected by recent events. She actually seemed slightly more cheerful, as if she'd been freed from a great burden.

The girls had been shielded from the inquest – even the police understood that Annie had suffered enough – and weren't told about the funeral until it was over. Annie didn't ask, but she'd once read that suicides couldn't be buried in consecrated ground. She tried to stop herself from even formulating the thought that Dad wasn't just a suicide, but a murderer – unless, and she wasn't sure if this was worse, Mam had actually *wanted* to go with him!

'I think the money should go in the bank,' she said to Dot. 'I'll want the fees for Machin & Harpers – oh, and me and Marie will need pocket-money.'

She had no intention of sponging off Cecy and Bruno. She would help in the kitchen in return for her keep.

'Are you happy here, Annie?' Dot sniffed. 'That Cecy's all right, but she's a bit toffee-nosed if you ask me.'

'Cecy's anything but toffee-nosed,' Annie assured her. 'And Bruno is the nicest person in the world.' She had quite a crush on Bruno.

Dot winked. 'Oh, that Bruno. He's dead gorgeous, he is.'

'Auntie Dot!'

'Well, I'm not so old that I don't recognise a handsome-looking feller when I see one. Bruno's so good-looking I could bloody eat him.'

'I'll tell Cecy you've got designs on her husband,' Annie threatened. 'Not that she'd care. They're mad about each other.'

'There's no need to tell Cecy anything, luv,' Dot said comfortably. 'I'm happy with my Bert. He's no oil painting, but he's the only man I've ever wanted. Anyroad, you're wrong about those two. There's something funny about that marriage. It's not all it's cracked up to be.'

Annie had no intention of getting embroiled in an argument about the Delgados' marriage. She said cautiously, 'Dot?'

'Yes, luv?'

'When you sorted through me mam's things, did you happen to come across a Paisley scarf?'

Dot went over to the window. It was April, still daylight at eight o'clock. 'It must be nice to live right opposite the pictures – and on top of a pub,' she said. 'You've got all the entertainment you need close at hand.' Then she shook her head. 'A Paisley scarf, luv? No, I never found anything like that.'

'Are you sure?'

Dot turned and looked straight at Annie. 'Sure I'm sure. Most of your mam's things were only worth throwing away, except for that dress she had for our Tommy's wedding, and your Marie snapped that up. I would have remembered seeing a Paisley scarf.'

Annie was relieved to leave school in July. She felt she was cutting herself off from her childhood. The long summer holiday was spent as it had been the year before, in Southport and New Brighton, at the pictures. Now the Cavern had been added to their list of activities, and they regularly went dancing; to Reeces, the Rialto, the Locarno. Annie turned her blue bridesmaid's frock into a dance dress.

It wasn't until she was in bed that she thought about Mam and Dad. Some nights, she woke up in the darkness to the smell of escaping gas, but the smell always disappeared when she sat up.

Bruno insisted his daughter transfer to Seafield Convent where she could take O and A levels in readiness for university, whilst, shortly before her sixteenth birthday, Annie began a shorthand and typing course at Machin & Harpers Commercial College.

'It's such a shame,' Mr Andrews complained when told. He wrinkled his stubby little nose. 'You should take a course in fashion or design.'

'But it would be years and years before I could get a job,' said Annie. 'I need to support meself as quickly as possible.'

472

'Your sister doesn't think like that. Marie wants to take a drama course when she leaves next year.'

Annie smiled. 'Perhaps she's got more guts than me.'

'That's not true, Annie. You're too sensible for your own good.'

Machin & Harpers found employment for their students when they finished the nine-month course. Within a week of leaving, Annie started work in the typing pool at Stickley & Plumm.

Shortly afterwards, Sylvia got the results of her O levels. She'd failed the lot except Art, in which she achieved a B grade.

'Well, I suppose we should be thankful for small mercies,' Bruno said glumly. 'I didn't know you were good at Art.'

'Neither did I.' Sylvia had no desire to go to university and didn't care a jot. 'I've never done oil painting before. I quite enjoyed slapping the colours on. I felt sort of reckless. According to Sister Mary, my pictures had a message, though I don't understand what it was.'

'Well, you needn't think you're leaving Seafield,' Bruno snapped. 'You're going back for A levels.'

'Okay, Bruno.'

As Sylvia later explained to Annie. 'I don't mind it there. The nuns like me because I'm half Italian. They seem to think I've some connection to the Pope. And if I don't go to school, Bruno might make me get a job.' She shuddered. 'Having seen you leave at eight every morning and not get home till six, *and* work Saturday mornings, I'd sooner go to Seafield Convent any day. It's only a few minutes down the road.'

'You're dead lazy, Syl.'

Sylvia yawned. 'I know.'

Time passed pleasantly. She and Sylvia went dancing several times a week, and always to the Cavern on Saturdays to hear the Merseysippi Jazz Band. Sometimes they went on a Wednesday, Skiffle Night, when Lonnie Donnegan or the Gin Mill Skiffle band played.

Marie developed a passion for the theatre and dragged her sister to the Playhouse and the Royal Court, where they saw Margaret Lockwood, Jean Kent, Jack Hawkins and Alec Guinness. Marie insisted on waiting for almost an hour outside the stage door for Sam Wanamaker's autograph, only to discover he'd left by a different door. One night, they followed Michael Redgrave and Googie Withers along Lime Street as they made their way to the Adelphi.

'Just think,' Marie crowed as they trailed several feet behind. 'One day, there might be fans following *me* back to my hotel!'

'Only if they're idiots,' Annie snapped. 'Frankly, sis, I feel dead stupid. They might think we're private detectives.'

Marie left school and enrolled part-time at the Sheila Elliott Clarke Drama School in Bold Street. With a tenacity Annie never dreamed her sister possessed, she increased her hours at the Grand, and took a Saturday morning job as a waitress. She had no intention of spending her share of the money from Orlando Street on another house; apart from which, the sum was considerably depleted, what with school fees and other expenses. Anyroad, house prices were soaring. Someone Marie knew had actually paid an unbelievable three thousand pounds for a semi-detached in Child-wall.

'As soon as I've saved enough money, I'm off to London,' Marie declared. 'It's the only place if you want to become an actress.'

It all sounded terribly exciting. Annie felt very dull, particularly when, much to Sylvia's astonishment, her friend got an A level in Art, and managed to obtain a place at Art College.

It even seemed a tiny bit unfair. Annie would have loved to have taken a course in dress design as Mr Andrews had urged, but it had always seemed out of the question. Now Sylvia was about to take 'Art in Advertising', yet she wasn't the least bit interested. It was merely a way of passing a few years in an enjoyable way without going to work.

What future was there for her at Stickley & Plumm? If she stayed long enough, Miss Hunt would retire and she might become Mr Grayson's secretary, and it would be *her* turn to tie his shoelaces!

She supposed one day she might get married, but so far had rarely met someone she would go out with twice, let alone marry. Apart from Cyril Sewerbreath, most males seemed incredibly childish. They had spots, dirty fingernails, and giggled all the time. It would be nice to go out with someone of at least twenty-five. 'Perhaps I'll have to wait till I'm twenty-five meself.'

Mrs Lloyd, the old lady Marie lived with, was becoming more feeble by the day. Dot gave a hand when she could, but Marie had to get the woman out of bed each morning, and lately had felt obliged to help her dress.

'The other day, I found the chamber pot and it was full to overflowing,' Marie said when she turned up for work. 'I emptied it, but it didn't half pong. I nearly puked. I'll ring her son later. The thing is, he seems to think she's my responsibility, but I'm just the lodger. I'm quite fond of Mrs Lloyd, but it's horrible, sis. It reminds me of home.'

She didn't want to move elsewhere. 'I'm fed up being a lodger, and I don't earn enough for me own flat. Still, never mind, eh! In another nine months I'll be off to London. In the meantime, I'm terrified one morning I'll find poor Mrs Lloyd dead in her bed.'

It was then Annie decided it was time she left the Grand. She would be eighteen soon, and couldn't live with Cecy and Bruno for ever.

'But Marie's old enough to find herself a bedsit, surely,' Sylvia said crossly when Annie broke the news.

'You're older and you haven't,' Annie pointed out.

'And it wouldn't do her any harm to look after a sick old lady for a while,' Sylvia's voice was tart.

'She's looked after a sick old lady for more than a while, apart from which, you wouldn't look after a sick old lady for five minutes. Mrs Lloyd would be long dead if she'd had you for a lodger.'

Sylvia grinned. 'I'd probably have killed her – which reminds me, it'll kill Cecy when she hears you're going to leave.'

Cecy was devastated. 'But Annie, there's no need for you to go,' she cried. 'I hoped you'd stay till you got married. Bruno and I think of you as our daughter.'

'But Marie . . .'

'There's room for Marie! It would be lovely having you both.'

Cecy didn't know this was out of the question. Marie and Sylvia scarcely spoke. Although Annie felt wretched at the thought of leaving the people who had supported her through the worst time of her life, in her heart, she knew it wasn't solely to do with Marie. It was time she became independent. To her relief, she found Bruno on her side.

'You must allow Annie to make her own decisions, darling,' he told Cecy. 'Just as you must allow Sylvia to make hers – if she ever gets round to making one,' he added darkly.

Bruno helped Annie find the flat. It was on the top floor of a gracious four-storey house in Upper Parliament Street, a short bus ride from Stickley & Plumm – within walking distance, if she felt energetic. Thin partitions had been erected to form a small bedroom and kitchen on one side of what had once been a large attic, and a second bedroom and bathroom on the other, leaving the middle section as the lounge. The bath was full of rust stains and the kitchen had no ventilation, but the view from the pretty arched window was magnificent, encompassing the entire centre of Liverpool with the protestant cathedral protruding upwards like a candle and the River Mersey twinkling in the distance. Everywhere was very shabby and urgently in need of decoration, but it was cheap and Annie fell in love with it at first sight.

'Upper Parliament Street!' screeched Dot when she heard. 'Jaysus, girl, it's dead scruffy there. It's where the prostitutes hang out.'

'As long as no-one takes me for a prostitute . . .' She'd found the area very interesting. People of all shades and colours lived there.

Dot said scathingly. 'Upper Parliament Street was once the poshest part of Liverpool. All the shipping and cotton merchants lived there, but it's been going downhill for years.'

'I like it,' Annie said stubbornly. 'And the rent's not much. I'll be able to afford it when Marie goes to London.'

'I should bloody hope so,' Dot grumbled. 'I'm amazed they've got the cheek to *ask* rent, in an area like that.'

The sisters were excited as they settled into their new home. They covered the walls with posters to hide the dirty marks and did their best to polish the scratches out of the furniture. Annie made new curtains for the lounge.

Cecy and Dot came, breathless after climbing four flights of stairs, to make sure they'd settled in. They grudgingly agreed the place looked quite homely, but Dot swore she'd been propositioned on the way.

'This geezer asked how much I charged. I told him, "More than you're ever likely to earn in your bleedin' lifetime, mate".'

'What did he say?' asked Marie, fascinated.

'He said, "You look worth every penny, Missus".'

Annie didn't believe a word of it.

The door flew open and Rose hobbled in with a cup of tea. 'Here you are, darling. A nice hot cuppa to warm the cockles of your heart.'

Annie looked at the old woman vacantly. Rose snapped her fingers, 'Wake up, Annie. It's tea time.'

'Oh! Thanks, Rose.'

'You were miles away, darling. Your boss is on the way up.'

'Is he?' She began to shuffle papers around in order to look busy.

Jeremy Rupert appeared in the doorway. 'I've some letters I'd like to get rid of before my four o'clock appointment arrives, Annie. You can bring the tea with you.'

Groaning inwardly, Annie picked up her things and took them into his office. She was longing for her tea, but it would inevitably go cold while he reeled off the letters without pausing. She was about to sit beside the desk, when Mr Rupert pushed past and pinched her bottom.

Annie gritted her teeth and said nothing.

2

The Cavern was packed to capacity. Cigarette smoke mingled with the condensation on the walls, so they appeared to be shrouded in steam. On the small stage, a band was playing traditional jazz with pulsating exuberance. The rows of wooden chairs in front were packed with an equally exuberant audience, who tapped their feet and clapped their hands to the music and from time to time burst into spontaneous applause.

There were as many people standing as sitting. Almost all were in their teens or early twenties, and scarcely any were even mildly intoxicated. Alcohol was not on sale at the Cavern, though a few youngsters secretly brought their own, adding gin, rum or other spirits to their soft drinks when no-one was looking.

The atmosphere was friendly. Merely to be there meant that normal reservations had been dispensed with. Everybody talked to each other as if they all belonged to the same family, rather than just a club.

Annie and Sylvia were with a group of students from the Art College. Nearly all wore black, even the boys. Sylvia was dressed in tight black slacks and an over-long black sweater that came almost to her knees. With her black-rimmed eyes, lashes stiff with mascara and pale lipstick, she looked like a ghost. Annie didn't feel out of place in her red-and-blue striped slacks and white sweater. She'd tied her hair back with a white chiffon scarf and draped the ends over her shoulder.

She loved the Cavern. It was the only place in Liverpool where she felt unconventional. It was the sort of club you would find in London, perhaps even Paris!

One of the boys asked her to dance, and they went into the dark, arched section given over to dancing. They jigged to and fro, not touching – Annie never knew what to do with her hands. The noise was too great to talk, unless you yelled at the top of your voice.

After a few minutes, she and the boy smiled at each other and returned to the group. An older man had arrived who looked the longed-for twenty-five. Sylvia hung onto his arm and stared at him provocatively. Annie managed to discern his name was Ted and he was a lecturer at the college. He was attractive, with untidy brown hair and an engaging grin, and as shabbily dressed as the students.

As the night wore on, Annie felt she would melt in the heat. She made her way to the rather disgusting Ladies to powder her nose, in case it was shining like a beacon. It didn't look too bad when she examined it in the mirror attached crookedly to the wall. Even so, she gave it, and the freckles between her eyes, a dab of pancake, and freshened up her lashes with spit. The door flew open and Sylvia came whirling in.

'I saw you sneak off, Annie,' she shrilled excitedly. 'Oh, isn't Ted Deakin delicious? I'm sure he fancies me.'

'He's okay. He's a bit old.'

'You hypocrite, Annie Harrison! You're always on about preferring older men.'

Annie made a horrible face. 'For me, not you.'

'Anyway, we're going to Bold Street for a coffee. Are you coming?'

'And be a gooseberry! Not likely.'

'There's a crowd of us going, silly. Come on, Annie,' Sylvia said coaxingly. 'Live a little.'

Annie glanced at her watch. 'I'd better go home.' It was almost midnight, and she wanted to go to Holy Communion in the morning, which meant coffee was out as it would break her fast. Marie was staying at the Grand, not that Annie minded being alone. Although meals weren't usually served on Sundays, it was Cecy's uncle's Golden Wedding and she was providing lunch for forty. It wasn't worth Marie's while to come home and go back in the morning.

She collected her coat, said goodbye to Sylvia, who was sulking, and took her time walking home. As she neared the house where the flat was, she blinked in astonishment when a taxi skidded to a halt outside and Sylvia and Ted Deakin climbed out. Sylvia was flushed and no longer sulking. She gave Annie her most charming smile.

'Ted's missed the last train. Could he sleep on your sofa tonight?'

'Well . . .' Annie wasn't sure if she wanted to spend the night alone with a strange man.

'I thought I'd sleep in Marie's room, if you don't mind,' Sylvia went on coaxingly. 'She's staying at the Grand, isn't she?'

It would be churlish to refuse. Annie took them upstairs. In the flat, she spread the spare blankets on the worn tapestry sofa. 'I'm afraid there's only a cushion for a pillow.'

Ted grinned. 'It looks very comfortable. I'm sure I'll sleep well.'

She doubted it. He was about two foot longer than the sofa, which had several protruding springs. She went to bed herself and fell asleep as soon as her head touched the pillow. When she awoke, she was greeted by the sound of church bells. She sat up, stretched her arms, then leapt out of bed to go to the lavatory.

To her surprise, the blankets on the sofa hadn't been touched. To her even further surprise, she could hear voices coming from the other bedroom. Ted and Sylvia were in the room together.

Annie turned cold. *Sylvia had slept with Ted Deakin!*

She rushed into the kitchen, made a pot of tea, put everything on a tray, and carried it to her room. She returned to bed, fuming. It seemed an age, and she'd already drunk four cups, before the door to Marie's room opened.

There was a pause, then the front door banged. Sylvia had actually *slept* with a man. It made Annie feel dead funny. She was annoyed that her heart was beating so rapidly, as if something truly dreadful had happened.

There was a tap on her door. 'What?' she growled.

The door opened and Sylvia stuck her head round. 'Morning!' she cried. She was wearing Marie's flowered dressing gown, and looked bright-eyed and incredibly beautiful.

'Bitch!' Annie snorted.

Sylvia looked startled. 'What?'

'You're a bitch.'

'Now, look here, Annie . . .'

'No,' interrupted Annie. 'You look here. How dare you make a fool of me by pretending Ted had missed his train?'

'But he had missed his train.'

'Then how dare you make a fool of me by pretending he wanted to sleep on the sofa?'

Sylvia looked ever so slightly uncomfortable. 'We couldn't very well say what we really wanted, could we?'

'Why not? I'm no prude.'

'Huh! Are you sure about that? Anyway, I wasn't completely sure if he *did* want to sleep with me. Until he came into the bedroom, I thought he could well have intended to sleep on the sofa.'

'You make yourself very cheap, Sylvia,' Annie said haughtily.

'You're just jealous, that's all. I'm going to make myself a cup of tea.' She slammed the door.

'You'll have a job,' Annie shouted. 'I've got the teapot here.'

The door flew open. Sylvia strode in and picked up the tray. Her face was expressionless.

'Was it the first time?' asked Annie.

'Yes,' Sylvia said briefly. On the way out, she tripped over Annie's slippers and nearly fell headlong.

Annie got up for the second time that morning. 'What was it like?' she asked from the kitchen door.

'Okay.'

'Okay! Is that all? I thought it was supposed to be glorious, y'know, mind-boggling and world-shattering and all that sort of thing.'

'I read in a book once, women don't always like it straight away. The more you do it, the more likely you are to have an organism.'

'An orgasm, not an organism. An organism is a structure.'

'How on earth did you know that?'

'You're not the only one to read books,' sniffed Annie. 'Would you like bacon and eggs for breakfast?' She took it for granted Sylvia wasn't going to Holy Communion after spending the night with Ted Deakin, and it was entirely Sylvia's fault that she herself had unwittingly drunk a whole pot of tea, which meant Holy Communion was out for her as well.

'Only if you do the egg both sides,' Sylvia said as if she was granting a great favour.

Annie saluted. 'Yes, ma'am.'

Sylvia slammed into the bedroom. She emerged shortly in her black trousers and long sweater, just in time for breakfast. They ate in silence. Both seemed to find the view from the arched window of tremendous interest.

When they'd finished, Annie began to clear the table. 'Do you feel different?' she enquired.

Sylvia thought hard. 'Not terribly.'

'I'd feel incredibly different. Just the thought of a man seeing me with nothing on makes me go all funny.' Annie disappeared into her room to get dressed. 'Did it hurt?' she shouted.

'A little bit,' came the reply.

'A girl at school did it with a sailor. She said it hurt a lot.'

'Well, it only hurt a little bit with me,' Sylvia said crossly. 'I wish you'd stop going on about it, Annie.'

'It's just that I can't get over the fact that one of us has slept with a man.' Annie paused whilst fastening a suspender. 'I feel we should have done it at the same time – not that I feel the urge, mind.'

'Perhaps if you'd come into the bedroom, Ted might have managed the operation slightly better. He quite liked you, Annie.'

'What do you mean?' Annie hopped to the door with a stocking half on, and just managed to dodge out of the way as Sylvia came hurtling into the room and threw herself onto the bed. She burst into tears.

'He couldn't manage it. He said he was important or something.'

'Impotent. Do you mean to tell me you're still a virgin, after all?' She felt slightly let down.

'I'm not sure.' Sylvia's voice was muffled in the pillow. 'He did it with his finger. He called it finger pie.'

'Jaysus!' muttered Annie, shuddering and giggling at the same time.

'He tried to put a French letter on, but it just fell off.'

Annie turned away to hide her face as she finished fastening her suspenders. She felt her cheeks grow red as she tried to stifle the hilarity she felt at the idea of a French letter dropping off a tiny penis. She slapped her hand over her mouth, so hard it hurt. Her shoulders heaved. Eventually, the laughter bubbling up from her stomach refused to be contained another second, and she collapsed in a heap on the floor, shrieking hysterically.

'Annie!' Sylvia twisted round until she was leaning over the edge of the bed, watching her friend's contortions. Her long hair hung down like curtains. 'It's not the least bit amusing,' she said in a hurt voice. 'In fact, it's tragic. I had a terrible night. He kept wanting to try again and again. We had to watch it, like waiting for bread to rise.'

Which only sent Annie into shrieks of laughter all over again.

'You're terribly cruel, Annie Harrison.' Even as Sylvia spoke, her lips began to twitch. 'I suppose it *does* have its funny side.'

With an effort, Annie managed to bring her hilarity under control. 'What made you do it, Syl?'

'I'm not sure.' Sylvia rested her face in her hands. 'Lots of girls at college have been with guys. I thought it was time I did. Ted Deakin seemed perfect to start with. He's old, he's experienced. Trouble is, he's too experienced. He's never been able to do it since his wife divorced him. He thought I'd get him started again. Trust me to pick someone who's past it,' she added moodily.

Ted being divorced only added further piquancy to the night's events. It was as if Sylvia had stepped into the adult world.

'Poor Ted,' Annie said soberly. He'd seemed quite nice. She recalled his rather engaging grin. 'Are you going to try again?'

Sylvia grimaced. 'Not bloody likely! Last night did my ego no good at all. Mind you, I'm glad I'm a woman. We don't have to put on an act. If we're not in the mood, we can just lie back and think of England.'

After lunch on Christmas Eve, Stickley & Plumm held their customary office party. It was a formal affair, with everyone gathering in Mr Grayson's office for a glass of sherry and one of Miss Hunt's mince pies. The conversation was forced, the atmosphere drier than the sherry. Everyone breathed a sigh of relief when, at half past three, Mr Grayson said jovially, 'Happy Christmas to one and all,' which meant it was time to leave. They could go home or do last-minute Christmas shopping.

Annie scurried upstairs. She was buttoning her coat when the rotund figure of Mr Rupert appeared in the doorway. 'Going, Annie?' he said with mock incredulity. 'I haven't wished you Merry Christmas.'

'You wished it me downstairs,' she stammered.

'That was just a handshake.' Before she knew what was happening, he had pressed his plump face against hers and was kissing her wetly on the lips. 'Merry Christmas, Annie.' He tried to kiss her again, but she managed to duck underneath his arm. As she ran downstairs, she rubbed her mouth on her sleeve. She felt dirty. If he didn't keep his hands to himself, she'd leave, even if it did mean getting less money elsewhere.

'But why should *you* leave?' Marie said angrily. 'He's the one who should leave. Why don't you tell this crabby Miss Hunt what's going on?'

'I'll see what happens after Christmas.'

'Where are you going tonight?' Marie was getting ready for the Grand. She put her white apron in a bag, along with a pair of flat shoes. Her face was beautifully made up. She still wore plenty of make-up, but drama school had shown her how to use it with skill.

'There's a crowd of us going to the Cavern.'

'Think of me whilst you're enjoying yourselves. There's a big dinner tonight as well as a party in the Snug.' Marie smiled happily. 'We seem to have swopped places. It used to be me out on the town every night, and you were left to look after our parents.' Elocution lessons had ironed out Marie's Liverpool accent, and she no longer said mam and dad.

'I'm ever so proud of you, Marie,' Annie said quietly. Her sister was so busy working that she'd never been to the Cavern.

'I'm proud of you, sis.' Marie looked through the window at the dark streets, a far-away expression on her face. 'Remember the day Bruno took us to the nursing home in Southport? As you were leaving, you said, "Don't worry, Marie. We'll come through. One of these days, everything will be all right, you'll see." They were your exact words. I kept thinking about them after they'd taken the baby from me. At the time, I didn't believe them, but they've come true. We're okay, aren't we, sis?'

'Apart from the loathsome Jeremy Rupert, we're fine.'

*

It was bedlam at the Gallaghers' on New Year's Day. There were far too many decorations, for one thing, and they kept falling down. The parlour was out of bounds, being occupied by Alan and his fiancée, Norma. Tommy's girls, Marilyn and Debbie, had been left with Grandma whilst their mam and dad went to the pictures. The girls were playing with their dolls on the floor. Upstairs, Mike was listening to Elvis Presley's 'Blue Suede Shoes' on his new record player, whilst the three younger lads mooched about picking at food and generally making a nuisance of themselves. Uncle Bert had wisely taken himself to the pub.

Annie watched Pete help himself to Christmas cake. It seemed only yesterday that his mam had brought him round to Orlando Street, shortly after the Harrisons moved in. She remembered him sitting on her knee, a few weeks old, whilst she examined his tiny fingers and little pink ears. Now Pete was fourteen and his voice was already beginning to break. She was taken aback by how quickly time flew, and said as much to Auntie Dot.

'I know, luv,' Dot agreed, 'and the older you get, the quicker it flies. I'll be fifty this year, not that I feel it, but it seems like only yesterday I was twenty-one.'

She didn't look fifty, either. Although her ginger hair was streaked with silver, the skin on the sharp bones of her face was shiny and unlined. A few years ago she'd started wearing glasses and her latest pair had fancy blue and silver frames which Annie thought grotesque.

Uncle Bert walked in that very minute, accompanied by a man Annie had never seen before who was introduced as Lauri Menin.

'Lauri with no "e" at the end,' said Bert. 'He's a comrade from the Labour Party. This is me niece, Annie Harrison.'

'She's a secretary at one of those big posh solicitors in town,' bragged Dot.

'How do you do.' Annie shook hands amidst the chaos. Lauri Menin's grip was firm and hard. He was a tall man, well built, with broad shoulders and twinkling brown eyes. She rather liked his moustache, which suited him perfectly, being just the right size: not small enough to look like Hitler, not big enough to look ridiculous. After taking this much in, she never gave him another thought. He was really ancient, at least forty, and probably already had a wife and several children.

Bert said, wincing at the noise, 'I'll take Lauri into the parlour, luv. We want to talk politics for a while.'

'Unless you want to talk with our Alan and Norma canoodling on the sofa, I wouldn't if I were you,' Dot said tartly.

'Is there anywhere in this house I can get some privacy?' Bert demanded exasperatedly.

Tommy and a very pregnant Dawn arrived to take their daughters home, and the house quietened down a little. Annie helped Dot make a pile of brawn sarnies, and Mike took his upstairs to eat with Elvis Presley. Alan and Norma were allowed theirs in the parlour on the strict condition it was vacated as soon as they'd finished. 'Your dad's got political matters to discuss,' Dot said importantly.

'Did you say you worked for a solicitor?' Lauri Menin asked Annie.

'Well, Dot did. It's Stickley & Plumm in North John Street.'

'I'm thinking of buying a house. Do they do conveyancing?'

'Oh, yes. The conveyancing department is the biggest.'

His brown eyes twinkled. 'I've never done this sort of thing before, and I'm rather nervous. Are they a reputable company?'

'One of the most reputable in Liverpool – and one of the oldest.'

Not much escaped Dot's sharp ears. 'We'd never let our Annie work in a place that wasn't completely above board,' she said firmly, as though she'd personally inspected the office and interviewed the staff.

Annie gave him the telephone number, and enquired where the house was he was thinking of buying. She wasn't sure whether to call him Lauri or Mr Menin.

'It's not built yet,' he replied. 'It's on a small estate of just fourteen houses in Waterloo, very ordinary, but there will be a view of the Mersey from the upstairs window. I was born within sight of a river, so it will remind me of my childhood in Finland.'

'Finland!' exclaimed Annie. She'd never dreamt he was a foreigner. His English was perfect.

'He came over to fight in the war when he was only nineteen,' explained Dot. 'And he couldn't bring himself to go back after the Finns ended up on the side of the Germans.'

Bert was beginning to get impatient. The younger lads had disappeared, Alan and Norma had gone out, and the parlour was vacant. He wanted to get down to politics. 'C'mon, Lauri. See you later, Annie.'

'No you won't, Uncle Bert. As soon as I've helped Auntie Dot with the dishes, I'll be off.' She'd only come to wish everyone a Happy New Year. 'Sylvia and I are going to the pictures tonight to see *Marjorie Morningstar* with Gene Kelly.'

'Hang on a minute,' Dot waved her arms. 'We can't let our Annie go without making a toast.' She produced a bottle of sherry and quickly poured some into four glasses and handed them round. 'To 1960,' she cried merrily.

'To the sixties,' Lauri Menin murmured. 'Let's hope they bring happiness and good fortune to us all.'

The sixties! All the way back to the flat, Annie wondered what the sixties would bring for her.

In February, without telling a soul, Annie decided to look for another job. Jeremy Rupert's attentions were beginning to wear her down.

She searched the Vacancies in the Liverpool *Echo*, but the secretarial jobs invariably called for someone aged 'twenty-one plus', and the wages for ordinary shorthand typists were so low, she'd have to give up the flat. Of course, she could always return to the Grand – Cecy would welcome her with open arms – but that seemed a retrograde step to take.

If only she'd been more careful with the money from Orlando Street! Her share had nearly all gone. Apart from the fees for Machin & Harpers and three months advance rent, she had recklessly bought a refrigerator, because food in the unventilated kitchen went bad within a day. The rest of the money had disappeared in dribs and drabs, whilst Marie had carefully held onto hers, adding to it over the years.

In the end, she decided her only option was to put up with Jeremy Rupert a while longer until a suitable job came up, though it seemed degrading. 'I'm letting him maul me 'cos I won't give up the money,' Annie thought to herself. 'In a way, I'm a bit like one of them prostitutes Auntie Dot's always on about.'

On a grey, drizzly Good Friday morning, Marie Harrison left Liverpool for London. She had over six hundred pounds in her bank account. A room was waiting for her in a house with four other budding actresses.

After Mass, Annie went with her sister to Lime Street Station. Marie found a seat, then leaned out of the window.

'Look after yourself, Marie,' Annie pleaded. She had never felt so sad and was doing her utmost not to cry. It was a different feeling altogether from when Mam and Dad had died. The sight of Marie's happy, hopeful face tugged at her heart-strings. She prayed her sister wouldn't be hurt, wouldn't be lonely, that she'd quickly be successful.

'You look after yourself too, sis. Give that Jeremy creature a kick in the groin next time he tries something.'

'I will, don't worry.' Annie tried to laugh. The train began to move and she ran along the platform holding onto her sister's hand. 'Tara, Marie. Tara.'

'Goodbye, Annie. I'll write soon, I promise.'

Annie watched the dark-haired figure waving from the window and waved frantically back until the train curled round a bend and Marie could no longer be seen.

The centre of Liverpool was deserted on Good Friday. She hurried through the empty, wet streets, trying to hold back the tears. It wasn't until she arrived home that she felt able to let them flow. She cried for ages. Her sister was the only flesh and blood she had left. She remembered cuddling Marie the day they moved to Orlando Street, recalled her anguished face when they'd discussed what to do about the baby, and how upset she'd been when it had been taken away. Even now, all these years later, it still seemed unbearably sad; a thirteen-year-old girl longing for a baby, longing for someone to love.

Later, when the tears had finally stopped, she had a long soak in the brown-streaked bath, using the last of the pine bubble bath she'd got for Christmas. It seemed a more cheerful thing to do than make the Stations of the Cross, which she usually did on Good Fridays. She felt better when she emerged with crinkly skin and a face pack hardened to concrete.

It was nearly five o'clock. At half seven she was meeting Sylvia off the train at Exchange Station. They'd not made up their minds what to do, but in case they decided to go dancing, Annie used her best deodorant, put on a set of fresh underwear, her new green dress with the pleated skirt that she'd been saving for a special occasion, and her black ballerina shoes with buckles on the toes. She put her hair up for a change. The style looked rather flattering as little curls escaped from the enamelled slide onto her neck.

The whole operation made her feel even better. After all, it was unreasonable to be unhappy when her sister was embarking on a great adventure. As soon as Marie had settled in, Annie was going to stay for the weekend. She decided to make a list of which clothes to take. As she wrote, a weak sun appeared and the lounge was flooded with pale yellow light. By the time the list was finished, Annie was her old self again, and began to look forward to the evening ahead. She and Sylvia always ended up having a good time and a good laugh.

A pleasant smell seeped up through the floorboards from the flat below. The horrible man with the big buck teeth who lived there was making curry for his tea. The smell made her feel hungry and she realised she'd been too upset to have dinner. She'd just slid two slices of bread under the grill and put half a tin of beans in a pan to heat, when she heard light footsteps running up the stairs.

For a moment, her heart leapt at the thought it might be Marie who'd caught the same train back, having decided to stay in Liverpool after all. There wasn't time to decide whether this was good or bad before there was a knock on the door and Sylvia shouted, 'It's me.'

'You're miles early.' Annie felt annoyed when she saw Sylvia was wearing her black slacks and jumper, which meant a dance was out of the question. 'Here's me, dressed up like a dog's dinner.'

Sylvia walked into the room and sat down without a word.

'What's wrong?' Annie frowned.

'The most awful thing has happened,' Sylvia replied in a small voice. 'I've brought a bombshell.' It was rare for Sylvia to sound so subdued. 'Cecy and Bruno have had the most terrible row. They followed each other round the Grand all afternoon, shouting and screaming.'

'Is that all!' Annie said, relieved. Cecy and Bruno rowed all the time, though she had to concede their fights were usually over quickly. She'd never known one last for more than half an hour, after which they usually made up with extravagant hugs and kisses.

'You don't understand, Annie.' Sylvia's blue eyes were frightened. 'Bruno's been having an affair and Cecy's just found out. The woman's called Eve, a waitress who worked for us a short while last year.'

'An affair!' Annie was horrified. 'I don't believe it. Not Bruno!' Bruno Delgado epitomised everything true and honest in the world. He was perfect. She couldn't visualise him doing any wrong.

'The thing is, it isn't the first. He's had affairs before. He told Cecy all about them, confessed them one by one.'

Annie gaped. 'Did they know you were listening?'

Sylvia nodded bleakly. 'Every now and then one of them would say, "Keep your voice down, Sylvia will hear", and they'd be quiet for a while, then they'd get so mad, they'd start shouting all over again, sometimes in Italian, sometimes in English, as if they didn't care whether I heard or not.'

'Oh, Syl! Do you hate him?'

'I don't know. He said the oddest things. He said, "Everyone's entitled to a healthy sex life. I'm a normal man with normal needs. If you weren't so bloody religious, the situation wouldn't have arisen." '

Annie tried to make sense of this, but couldn't. 'What did he mean?'

'There's something burning,' Sylvia said.

Annie looked perplexed. 'I don't understand. What's religion and a healthy sex life got to do with burning?'

'I meant I can smell something burning.' Sylvia jumped to her feet. 'There's smoke coming from the kitchen.'

'Me beans on toast!'

The toast was cinders and the pan was ruined. The man with the buck teeth came stamping up to make sure Annie hadn't set the house on fire. He went away, disgusted, when she explained what had happened.

Sylvia opened the windows to let the smell out and Annie gave the cooker a superficial clean. She made a cup of tea to calm their nerves.

'That's a nice dress,' Sylvia said when they were sitting down again. 'Green's your best colour.'

'I got it from C & A. I thought we might have gone to a dance tonight. I prefer making me own frocks, but I can't manage pleats.'

'Your hair looks nice, too. It suits you up.'

Annie patted her curls. 'I was trying to cheer meself up. I felt dead miserable because our Marie had gone.'

'I forgot about Marie.' Sylvia made a face. 'She telephoned earlier. Cecy said to tell you she'd arrived safely.'

'There must be a phone in her new flat.'

A long silence followed. Sylvia stared into her cup. Annie didn't raise the subject of Cecy and Bruno until she was ready to talk again.

'They actually spoke about divorce, Annie,' Sylvia said suddenly. 'Least Bruno did. Cecy said she'd never divorce him. Never.'

'Oh, no!' Nothing was permanent. Nothing could be relied on to stay the same. Marie had gone, and now another part of her life was falling apart. She still didn't understand what had happened. Bruno had had an affair – affairs – but why, when he had always seemed so completely in love with Cecy? She said as much to her friend.

'He still loves her,' Sylvia explained carefully, 'he said so, but from what I could gather – and this is truly incredible, Annie – they haven't made love since I was born. Bruno yelled, "Do you think I'm made of stone? Eighteen years, Cecy, eighteen years." You see, Cecy had an awful time with me and she was too frightened to have another baby. I think I told you that once.'

'But you can use things.'

'Apparently she won't. The Catholic Church forbids it.'

'Me Auntie Dot's every bit as religious as Cecy,' Annie said, 'but she says that's a load of rubbish. It's all right for the Pope to lay down the law, but he hasn't got to look after the unwanted babies. Anyroad, there's something called the rhythm system . . .'

'It's not reliable. Even I know that.'

Annie sighed. 'Jaysus, Syl. It must have come as a terrible shock.'

To her surprise, Sylvia said thoughtfully, 'It did and it didn't. Over the years, I've had this funny feeling there was something wrong. Bruno used to look at Cecy with a strange expression on his face that I couldn't understand.' She smiled unexpectedly. 'I'm sick of talking about it. Let's go for a meal and the pictures. There's a new Alfred Hitchcock picture on at the Odeon, and I love all his films. *Rear Window* and *Vertigo* are two of my all-time favourites. It'll take our minds off things for a few hours.'

They went to a Chinese restaurant and had curried prawns and rice, not just because it was Good Friday and they couldn't eat meat, but because Annie had been longing for curry since the smell had drifted through the floorboards, though as she said to Sylvia over the tea that tasted like dishwater, 'I'll have to cut down on this sort of thing now that our Marie's not there to help with the rent.'

The new Hitchcock film was called *Psycho*. It was utterly terrifying, nothing like *Rear Window* or *Vertigo*. Annie kept her eyes shut most of the time, particularly during the last ten minutes.

'What happened?' she asked when the curtains thankfully closed and the stunned audience stood to leave. Instead of the usual buzz, everyone was strangely quiet.

'I've no idea. I didn't look,' Sylvia replied in a shaky voice. 'Thank God we haven't got a shower!'

A woman behind put her hand on Annie's arm and she yelped in terror. 'What happened at the end?' she asked. 'I was scared to watch.'

'So was I,' said Annie.

Outside, Lime Street appeared dimly lit and had a gloomy, sinister air. Every man who passed looked like a potential murderer.

'Oh, Lord,' Annie groaned. 'I left all the windows open. Someone might have climbed in.'

'No-one's likely to climb in a fourth-floor window.'

Annie shivered. 'I'll be on me own tonight and that chap downstairs gives me the creeps. Have you noticed his eyes? The lids are heavy and they move dead slow, like a lizard.'

'Would you like me to stay?' offered Sylvia.

'*Please*, Syl. I'm petrified at the thought of going back by meself. I wish we'd never seen that picture. It took me mind off things all right. I'm scared bloody stiff!'

They looked for a telephone box so Sylvia could call the Grand. When she emerged, she gave Annie a sardonic smile. 'Cecy thinks I'm staying away because of the row.'

'Did you tell her the real reason?'

'No,' Sylvia said in a hard voice. 'She can think what she likes. If things get any worse, I shall leave home.'

'You've changed your tune. You were upset before.'

'I'm still upset, but it's no good crying over spilt milk, is it?'

The table was propped against the door, the bedroom doors were open and the beds had been moved so they could see each other across the lounge and communicate in case of emergency. Every light was switched on.

They sat up in bed and chatted about clothes, as if nothing out of the ordinary had happened. Annie was seriously considering making herself a plain black costume.

Sylvia looked surprised. 'I thought you were going to be hard up?'

'Once I've made the costume, I won't buy another thing,' Annie said virtuously, 'though I'd love a pair of those stiletto-heeled shoes.'

'They snap easily. I've had mine mended twice and Cecy complains about dents in the carpet. And don't get those winklepickers. A girl at college bought a pair. We thought she had deformed toes.'

After a while, Sylvia said she was tired and ready for sleep. Her blonde hair disappeared beneath the bedclothes. 'Goodnight, Annie.'

' 'Night, Syl. Things'll probably seem better in the morning.'

There was an answering grunt. Annie's head was buzzing and she had rarely felt so wide awake. She lay down reluctantly and tossed and turned for ages. The traffic outside gradually faded to the occasional car and she began to drift off, but woke up seconds later with a painful jump. Eventually, she fell asleep and dreamt a buck-toothed man with an enormous knife was butchering Marie in the bathroom, and the brown stains on the bath had turned brilliant red. Marie was screaming, but to Annie's horror, she found herself glued to the bed, paralysed, unable to do anything but listen to her sister's agonised cries. She woke up again, heart pounding, bathed in perspiration, conscious of the pungent smell of escaping gas, but afterwards realised the smell was no more real than the dream.

It was a terrible Easter weekend. They went dancing on Saturday, but their gloomy faces must have put off any would-be partners. Not a soul asked either to dance. They left in the interval, more miserable than when they'd arrived. Sylvia telephoned an anxious Cecy to say she was spending another night with Annie.

The following morning they went to Mass, then caught the train to Southport, and had scarcely been there five minutes when the heavens opened and the rain poured down. As they sheltered in a doorway, Sylvia began to giggle. 'This has been the worst Easter of my life.'

'It's not over yet. We've got Monday to get through.'

'There'll probably be an earthquake.'

They laughed and the tension broke. They searched for a café and stumbled inside, drenched to the skin. Sylvia ordered a pot of tea, buttered scones and strawberry jam for four.

'I've led a charmed life up to now,' she said at one point. 'Bruno and Cecy have been magical parents. They always seemed superior to other people's. I'll just have to get used to the fact they're human like everybody else.'

It was still raining an hour later and there seemed little else to do but to return home. Sylvia thought it was about time she put in an appearance at the Grand, if only to change out of her wet clothes. They confessed they were sick of the sight of each other and wouldn't meet until the following weekend. Annie stayed on the train only as far as Marsh Lane Station. She was dying to see Auntie Dot.

Her shoulders immediately felt lighter when she went into the Gallaghers' noisy house. The rain lifted, the sun came out, and after dinner, she and Dot went for a walk to escape the din. She told her auntie about the Delgados.

'It's often the way when couples are all lovey-dovey,' Dot said soberly. 'It's only done to disguise the faults, from themselves as well as everyone else. I always suspected things weren't all they were cracked up to be between those two.' She nudged her niece sharply with her elbow. 'If it weren't for Bert, I wouldn't mind helping Bruno out!'

'Auntie Dot! You're terrible, you are.'

'I'm only joking, luv, but you must admit he's a bit of all right.'

Annie was about to climb the final flight of stairs to the flat when she nearly jumped out of her skin. On the shadowy landing, someone was sitting on a suitcase outside her door.

'Hello, Annie,' Sylvia beamed. 'Relations have completely broken down at home. They were using me to convey messages to each other. I'd like to move in, if you don't mind. I promise to be incredibly cheerful, do my share of housework and pay half the rent. We'll have a wonderful time. They say every cloud has a silver lining. I suppose this is it!'

3

She had lost her temper only once in her life, and Annie Harrison had vowed never to do so again. Occasionally, people would remark how calm she was, particularly for someone with red hair. But it was dangerous to lose your temper, dangerous to lose control and say terrible things you didn't really mean which you would regret until the day you died.

Despite her vow, the day came when Annie could easily have murdered Jeremy Rupert. Instead, she merely slapped his face.

By keeping a sharp eye on his movements, she managed to keep out of his way most of the time, but when summer arrived and along with it summer frocks and bare legs, he became more and more difficult to repel. His round eyes would devour her as she sat by his desk. Once again, she began to scan the paper for another job.

The days he was in court were best. He came into the office early, rattled off dozens of letters, and she was left to type them in peace.

He was due in court at eleven o'clock the day she slapped his face. She had already packed his briefcase with the files concerning the case he was defending, together with a lined pad and two freshly sharpened pencils, whilst he went for a quick confab with Mr Grayson. She fastened the case and put his wig in its white drawstring bag on top.

A few minutes later, he came in with Bill Potter, the junior solicitor who was accompanying him to court. He lit a cigarette and flung the lighter on the desk.

'Hallo there, Annie,' Bill smiled.

Annie smiled back. Bill was only twenty-three and quite attractive in a weedy sort of way, but unfortunately engaged to be married.

Mr Rupert picked up the briefcase. 'Everything here?' he puffed.

'Everything,' confirmed Annie.

'What about the Clivedon file, Jeremy?' Bill Potter said. 'Old Grayson thought it might prove useful.'

Jeremy Rupert clicked his fingers impatiently at his secretary. 'The Clivedon file, Annie. Quickly, there's a good girl.'

The Clivedon file was in the end cabinet, third drawer down. Annie disturbed the file behind as she hastily pulled it out. Mr Rupert shoved the folder in his briefcase and the two men left.

Before closing the drawer, Annie bent down to straighten the files. Suddenly, Jeremy Rupert was back in the office. He snatched the lighter off the desk and held it aloft. 'Nearly forgot this.'

Annie muttered something meaningless and returned to the filing. She

488

never felt his hand reach beneath her flared skirt until it was directly between her legs, squeezing.

'Hmm, nice,' he murmured.

She felt herself grow dizzy with hot, uncontrollable rage. She span round and slapped his face with such force that his head turned ninety degrees and his glasses flew off. *'How dare you!'* she gritted.

He went pale and retrieved the glasses, which were miraculously all in one piece. There was a bright scarlet patch on his right cheek. 'But . . . but, Annie,' he stammered. 'You've never said anything before.'

Annie didn't reply, but slammed into her own office without another word. She was shaking because she'd completely lost control. Had she been holding something heavy, she could have killed him.

For the remainder of the week, he appeared slightly shamefaced, but over the weekend must have decided he'd done nothing wrong. On Monday, he began a reign of terror. He found fault with her work where no fault existed, insisted he'd said one thing during dictation, when her notes proved he'd said another. They argued fiercely over the situation of commas and semi-colons, and Annie found herself with no alternative but to type letters a second time, usually long ones, when there was nothing wrong with the first. He insinuated she was incompetent, that she was slow, unintelligent. He claimed one of his clients had said she was rude on the telephone.

'Who was it?' Annie demanded. 'I'll ring up and apologise.'

'I've already apologised,' Mr Rupert snapped.

'Liar!' Annie muttered underneath her breath.

In the lunch hour, she remained at her desk and applied for *every* single secretarial vacancy in the *Echo*. She knew she was finished at Stickley & Plumm. Her lip curled when she thought about her boss. He was utterly despicable, using his little bit of power to harass a helpless young girl – she forgot, for the moment, that she'd nearly knocked his head off. He'd probably like to sack her, but was scared she'd make a fuss and he'd get into trouble. Instead, he was trying to drive her into leaving of her own accord, but Annie's blood was up. She was damned if she would leave before she found another job.

'What's up with you?' Sylvia asked one night when they were clearing the table after tea.

'What do you mean, what's up with me?' Annie snapped.

Sylvia pretended to back away in fright. 'I mean exactly that. You don't speak normally, you explode. Is everything all right at work?'

'Everything's wonderful at work. Jeremy Rupert is the perfect boss.'

'Are you being sarcastic?'

'Yes,' Annie said briefly, but refused to say what was wrong. 'I'm in the middle of a feud. I'll tell you about it when it's over.'

The crunch came one Thursday, nearly three weeks after she'd slapped Mr Rupert's face.

He dictated a long Writ that morning. The Litigant was called Graham Carr. 'How do you spell that?' Annie enquired.

'C-A-R-R.'

The document was complicated and full of legal jargon, it had to be done on very thick paper with two carbon copies, which meant the typing was slow, hard work. It was three pages long when finished, and had taken two hours, but there wasn't a single error. Mr Rupert had gone to lunch, so she put it on his desk, and quickly typed half a dozen letters applying for jobs advertised the night before. She'd already been rejected by five of the firms she had applied to; she was either over-qualified, under-qualified, or too young.

Jeremy Rupert returned at three. A few minutes later, he waddled into her office and threw the Writ on the desk. 'You've spelt the name wrong. It's Kerr, K-E-R-R. Same as Deborah,' he added with a sneer.

'But you spelt it the other way,' cried Annie. She produced her notebook and turned to the page. 'See!'

'You misheard. It's Kerr with a K. You'll have to type it again. I'd like the correct version by five o'clock, if you don't mind.'

He'd done it deliberately! Every shred of anger fled and she felt close to tears. She reached in her stationery drawer for a sheet of special paper, two flimsies, two carbons.

'C'mon, girl, c'mon.' Mr Rupert was watching her slow movements. Annie jutted out her jaw. She'd sooner die than let him see her cry. It was a ludicrous thing to think of, but she desperately wished she had a mam or dad to go home to, someone who would stroke her head and say her boss was the most evil man in the entire world and she wasn't to work for him another minute. She was fed up being on her own. Sylvia wasn't the same as a proper adult.

'I need to go to the cloakroom,' she said abruptly.

'Don't forget, I want that Writ by five o'clock,' Mr Rupert called after her. She could have sworn she heard him chuckle.

She would never get the Writ done in time. Her hands were already shaking and her fingers would turn to thumbs with nervousness. She sat on the lavatory for a good ten minutes and made up her mind what had to be done. She would hand in her notice and hope one of the jobs she'd applied for would turn up soon, though it went against the grain to be forced out by a bully.

After splashing her face, she went to see Miss Hunt and told her she was leaving.

'Leaving, Miss Harrison! But why?' Miss Hunt's long jaw dropped.

'I think I would be happier in another job.' Annie had no idea why she should feel uncomfortable, as if she were letting Miss Hunt down. It was she who had recommended Annie for promotion.

'Happier? But I thought you were happy in your present job. We have had glowing reports about your work from Mr Rupert. Even Mr Grayson has expressed his pleasure more than once at the way you have progressed.'

'I love the work, it's just . . .' Annie paused, wondering how she could explain to this prim and proper woman what her boss had done.

'It's just that what, Miss Harrison?' Miss Hunt's permanent frown deepened in annoyance.

'Me and Mr Rupert don't get on all that well.'

The frown turned to one of surprise. 'Have you been crying? Your eyes are all red.' She no longer seemed annoyed.

Annie felt her eyes fill up again. She nodded.

'Sit down, Miss Harrison, and tell me all about it.' The older woman pulled up a chair. 'Mr Grayson has a client, so we won't be disturbed.'

'It's awfully embarrassing.'

'Despite appearances to the contrary, I am not easily embarrassed.'

Annie explained about the Writ. 'He definitely spelt it Carr. I can show you my notebook. I'll never get it done by five o'clock.'

'In that case,' Miss Hunt said briskly. 'We'll get the typing pool to do it. The girls can type a page each. Now, why on earth should Mr Rupert do such a mean thing?'

Annie took a long breath. 'I slapped his face. He's been . . . well, too free with his hands. I couldn't stand it any longer. He . . . he did something awful, and I couldn't help myself, I hit him really hard.'

Miss Hunt's face emptied of expression. 'And how long has Mr Rupert been behaving like this?'

Annie shrugged. 'Since I started working for him. Oh, I know you're going to say I should have mentioned it before, I should have stopped him, but I was scared of getting the sack.'

'I see,' said Miss Hunt. She pursed her yellow lips.

In the next room Mr Grayson could be heard showing his client out, a woman with a loud, pleasant laugh. Annie felt envious; she was so miserable, she was convinced she would never laugh again.

Mr Grayson returned to his office and pressed the buzzer for his secretary. 'Come with me, Miss Harrison. I'd like you to repeat what you just told me to Mr Grayson.'

Annie gasped. 'But I couldn't *possibly* . . .'

'I'm afraid you must. Come along.'

Mr Grayson looked mildly surprised when they both appeared. 'Miss Harrison has something to tell you,' Miss Hunt announced.

Throughout her halting and muddled explanation, Mr Grayson stared grimly at his blotter and didn't look at her once. 'Thank you, Miss Harrison,' he said pleasantly when she'd finished.

Miss Hunt showed her to the door. 'Don't forget the Writ,' she said.

The Writ delivered, Annie returned to her office. A few minutes later Jeremy Rupert's internal telephone rang, and she heard him say, 'Yes, sir, right away.' He immediately went downstairs.

The only person he called 'Sir' was Mr Grayson. Annie tried to get on with her work, but kept making mistake after mistake, and the waste-paper basket became increasingly full of crumpled letterheads.

It was a good hour before her boss returned. Through the thick glass, she saw him sit at his desk and put his head in his hands.

Not long afterwards, a girl from the pool brought the Writ. Annie thanked her. 'I would never have got it done in time.' She read the document through. There were two spelling errors which hadn't been on the original, but she didn't care. She combed her hair in the mirror behind the door and briefly practised looking as if she didn't have a care in the world before taking the Writ into Mr Rupert's office.

He hadn't moved from the desk. His face was ghastly white and he was gazing into space, entirely unaware she had come in. She stared at him nervously. She hadn't planned on it going this far. If only she'd put a stop to things months ago!

She told Sylvia the whole story when she got home. As she expected, Sylvia howled with laughter. 'He's gross, Annie, gross in more ways than one. I hope he's got the boot, he deserves it.'

'I didn't want him to lose his job.'

'But you were quite willing to give up yours! When we get to the Grand, I think I shall ask Bruno to give you a little pep talk.'

'I'd sooner you didn't mention it. I feel dead ashamed.' She'd saved her own job, but at the cost of Mr Rupert's. It was an uneasy feeling.

The situation at the Grand had become bearable. Cecy and Bruno no longer rowed; instead they were scrupulously polite to each other. Bruno was openly consorting with Eve, the former waitress, and there was nothing his wife could do about it. Cecy looked worse each time they saw her. Although only forty-two, she could easily have been taken for fifty. Her blonde hair was thinning, her face was haggard and her blue eyes were glazed with sadness – whereas Bruno seemed younger. Annie found herself glancing at him surreptitiously from time to time. She'd always had a crush on him, but now, although it was shameful to admit, since she'd learnt about the affairs he was even more attractive. She felt a little shiver when she thought about him making love to Eve, a plump and comely woman with a jaunty walk, as dark-haired as he was.

Shortly after the girls arrived, Cecy announced she intended buying herself a little bungalow.

'You mean move out?' Sylvia said in astonishment. 'But what will Bruno do without you?'

'Bruno already does quite well without me.'

'You know what I mean, Cecy. I meant the food, that sort of thing.'

Cecy turned away with a sour twist of her lips. Eve had worked in the Grand. She could easily take over Cecy's role in the kitchen.

Mr Rupert had recovered slightly by next morning. His manner was bland, as was his voice. He asked Annie to come in with her notebook, but stumbled badly over the dictation, as if his mind was unable to grasp the intricacies of the work involved.

'That will do for now,' he said after a short while.

Annie remained in her chair, wondering if she should say something, perhaps express some regret. She was searching for the appropriate words when Mr Rupert said again, 'That will do, Miss Harrison.'

Pauline Bunting from Accounts came round with the wages at the usual time, directly after lunch. Annie's brown envelope was unusually thick.

'Hey! It feels like I've got a bonus!' she chortled.

Pauline gave her a strange look. She didn't stay for a chat as she often did, but mumbled she was in a hurry and quickly left.

The envelope contained twice the usual number of notes. Bemused, Annie searched for her wage slip. It was still in the envelope, along with a folded letter. She felt a flicker of alarm, followed by a sensation of dread. She knew exactly what the letter would say. Signed by Mr Grayson, it was short and to the point; he would be obliged if she would leave the offices of Stickley & Plumm when they closed for business that afternoon. A week's wages were enclosed in lieu of notice.

She'd been sacked!

Angry tears pricked her eyes, and she was simmering at the cruel injustice of it all when Miss Hunt came in. Her initials were beside those of Mr Grayson on the letter, AFG/DH, so she must have typed it.

'I'm sorry, Miss Harrison,' she said stiffly, her long, thin body poised clumsily, like that of a gauche young girl.

'Why on earth should I be dismissed when I've done nothing wrong?' Annie cried. She felt like throwing her typewriter through the window. Either that or bursting into tears.

'I'm afraid it's the way of the world, dear. Us little people are no more than pawns on a chessboard. When the powerful want us out of the way, we just get shoved aside.'

Annie blinked at this rather emotive response. 'If you hadn't made me tell Mr Grayson, this wouldn't have happened.'

Miss Hunt's yellow face grew bleak. She nodded. 'I know. The fact is, Miss Chase is emigrating to Australia at the end of the month and I felt sure Mr Grayson would allow you to take over as secretary to Mr Atkins. Unfortunately, he feels it would be better all round for the firm if you weren't here. Of course,' she went on caustically, 'the firm is all that matters where Arnold Grayson is concerned.'

Annie laughed contemptuously. She nodded towards Mr Rupert's empty room. 'What's happening to him?'

'Mr Rupert has been given a severe dressing-down. It would be difficult to get rid of a partner. Nevertheless, his behaviour falls far short of what is considered acceptable.'

'In other words, he's got off scot free!'

'He has been warned it must never happen again.'

'Did you say anything to Mr Grayson when he dictated the letter?' Annie asked curiously.

Miss Hunt averted her eyes. 'It would have been a waste of time.'

'I'd like to leave right now. I'm up to date with me work.' She couldn't stand the thought of seeing Jeremy Rupert again.

The older woman frowned briefly, then her face cleared. 'Perhaps that would be wise.' She went to the door. 'Good luck, Miss Harrison. I hope your next job turns out more happily than this one.'

She was about to go, when Annie called, 'Miss Hunt?'

'Yes, Miss Harrison?'

'How do you stand it?'

'I don't know,' Miss Hunt said as she closed the door.

Annie gathered together the belongings accumulated over the years; spare make-up, emergency sanitary towel, paper hankies, aspirins, soap and towel, toothbrush, and all the other odds and ends she had acquired. She had nothing to put them in, so helped herself to a stout envelope with plackets in the sides – the first thing she had ever stolen.

Throughout, her cheeks burned and her hands shook with anger. She glanced around the tiny office to make sure she'd got everything. It was important to get away quickly. Pauline Bunting might have passed on the news of her dismissal and the office would be agog. She didn't want to discuss why she'd been sacked with anyone, no matter how sympathetic they might be.

Feeling like an outcast, she slipped quietly downstairs with the envelope clutched to her chest, and was about to open the front door leading to North John Street when the enormity of what had happened sank in. For over three years, she had been coming in and out of this door regularly, without once being late. She had always given conscientiously of her best, yet where had it got her?

Annie sat on the bottom stair and sniffed hard several times. It had got her nowhere. She was brooding over the unfairness of it all when the door opened and the stairs flooded with sunlight. Annie cursed inwardly for not making herself scarce. If it was Jeremy Rupert . . . ! But the man who entered was a stranger, jacketless, with crumpled navy cotton trousers and a long-sleeved check shirt.

However, he turned out to be a stranger who knew her. 'Hello,' he said pleasantly. 'This is a coincidence. It's Annie, isn't it, Annie Harrison? I was going to come and see you today.'

Annie stared at him for several seconds. There was something familiar about his affable features and bright brown eyes, but it was the moustache that finally did it; a moustache that was not too big and not too small, but just the right size for his face, though she had to search for his name.

'Mr Menin,' she said eventually. 'We met at Auntie Dot's on New Year's Day.' He was buying a house in Waterloo and she'd recommended Stickley & Plumm. She had forgotten all about the incident.

'Lauri, please!' he protested. 'Mr Menin makes me feel very old. I have an appointment at three to sign the final contract for my house.'

'It's taken a long time!' she remarked.

'The building work has just finished. It'll be ready to move into soon.' He was still holding the door. 'Are you coming in or going out?'

'Going out,' Annie said brightly. She went past him into the street. 'Goodbye, Mr . . . Lauri.'

To her astonishment, he let the door go and began to walk along the pavement beside her.

'What about your appointment?' she stammered.

'That can wait,' he said gently. 'There are more important things at the moment, such as why does Miss Annie Harrison's face show so many different emotions? Her eyes say one thing, her lips another and her forehead is full of worried lines. None of the emotions are happy ones, and her voice tells the same story. What's wrong, Annie?'

'Oh!' She had rarely felt so moved. It was incredible that this virtual stranger was able to see through her so easily. She'd thought she'd put on a brave face when they just met. She stared up at him. Her head came to just above his shoulder and she didn't think she'd ever seen such a kind, concerned expression on a face before. His brown eyes smiled into hers. She noticed his eyebrows were like little thatches and his luxuriant brown hair curled onto his broad neck. Why hadn't she noticed how nice he was on New Year's Day?

'May I invite you for a coffee? Or would you prefer to tell me to get lost and mind my own business?' he twinkled.

'I'd love a coffee.'

The first place they came to was a long, narrow self-service snack bar which was virtually empty after the mid-day rush.

Lauri Menin brought two coffees over to the plastic table. 'The truth is,' Annie blurted as soon as he sat down, 'I've got the sack.'

'I thought as much. At least, I thought you were leaving.'

'How on earth could you possibly guess?'

He nodded towards the envelope. 'The contents told me the whole story. People don't usually walk round with stuff like that. Changing jobs is a bit like changing house, on a smaller scale.'

Annie felt glad the sanitary towel was hidden. To her astonishment, in a rush of scarcely stoppable words, she found herself explaining the reason she'd lost her job, yet she didn't feel a bit embarrassed. Lauri Menin listened to the whole sorry tale right up to the point where he'd found her on the stairs. He didn't interrupt once. When she finished, he said seriously. 'This Jeremy Rupert sounds a most disagreeable creature, but also rather tragic. How terrible to have to get your kicks out of forcing your attentions on a young girl. You must feel very sorry for him.'

Pity was the last thing Annie felt. 'I never looked at it that way.'

Lauri continued, 'Mr Grayson – who my appointment was with – is even more to be pitied. The man is totally unprincipled.'

'Why were you coming to see me?' she asked shyly.

He folded his broad arms on the table. 'To thank you,' he said. He had a soothing, slightly husky voice with only a trace of Liverpool accent. She couldn't imagine him sounding angry. 'For all their faults, Messrs Stickley & Plumm handled the purchase of my house efficiently.'

She murmured something about it being a highly reputable firm, and he said that under the circumstances, that was open to question and it was time to change the subject from Stickley & Plumm. 'What do you know about interior decoration?' he asked.

'Absolutely nothing!' Annie replied.

'According to your Uncle Bert, you're very artistic. The thing is, I'm in a quandary over what colours to have my house painted. The decorators are waiting on my instructions. If I don't let them know soon, they'll paint everywhere white, including the front door.'

'You must have the front door bright yellow,' Annie said quickly. She knew he was only being kind and trying to take her mind off things. 'Our front door used to be a horrible dark brown. I swore if I had a house of me own I'd have the front door yellow.'

Lauri Menin grinned. He had large, slightly crooked white teeth. 'Then yellow it shall be. It's lucky I spoke to you. I could well have chosen horrible dark brown. What about the lounge? My favourite colour is red, but I have a feeling that might not look so good.'

Annie cringed. 'Red would look dead awful. Pastel colours would be best, pale pink or lemon, with matching wallpaper on the breastwork. According to the women at work, that's the latest fashion.'

'No wallpaper, I'm afraid, until the building has settled. Pink or lemon sounds fine. I like the sound of it.'

'What about your wife? Isn't she allowed a say in the colours?'

He drained his cup, 'I haven't got a wife.'

'You don't look like a bachelor.' According to Sylvia, bachelors were either men of the world or mothers' boys. Lauri Menin appeared to be neither.

'I'm a widower,' he said lightly.

Annie clapped her hand to her mouth. 'Gosh, I'm awful sorry. I mean, I'm sorry about taking you for a bachelor and sorry about your wife.'

Lauri looked amused by her confusion. 'There's nothing to be sorry about. The bachelor thing I don't mind, and Meg died more than half a lifetime ago. Our time together was short but sweet. We were only twenty. She was killed in the Blitz.' He returned to the subject of his house. 'I would like a young person's opinion on furniture. Having lived in rooms for more than twenty years, I possess nothing of my own except clothes and books. I need to furnish the place from top to bottom.'

Annie thought he was the most splendid person she'd ever met. How fortunate she'd sat on the stairs those extra few minutes, or they wouldn't have run into each other! He seemed genuinely interested in her views. She suggested he describe the new house and she would offer advice, though warned that up to now the only household item she'd bought was a refrigerator.

'I'll do better than describe it. My car is parked just round the corner. As you appear free for the rest of the day, if you fancy a trip to Waterloo, I'll show it you.'

The tiny estate was shaped like a light bulb. There were fourteen identical creamy brick semi-detached houses. Two pairs, which already had people living in them, lined the narrow opening. Infant climbing plants had begun their long journey up the front walls. There was a half-built rockery in one garden, freshly dug flower beds and borders in the others, a tiny hedge. A bright new road sign said, 'Heather Close', with 'Cul-de-Sac' underneath in smaller letters.

'Heather is the name of the main contractor's daughter,' Lauri said.

Once past the opening, the houses flared out into an oval, with two pairs on either side, some of which were already inhabited, and one pair directly ahead completing the oval. Annie thought the top pair were in the best position. It was where the king and queen would live, with their subjects spread out either side and on guard at the entrance. She was pleased when Lauri drove his Ford Anglia car into the drive of one of the furthest houses, the left one, number seven.

'Oh, it's *lovely!*' she breathed when he unlocked the door and they went inside. The hallway was light and bright and airy, with bare pink plaster walls and glass panelled doors.

'This is nice.' She stroked a glossy wooden cupola-shaped knob on the bannisters.

'It's the only house to have that particular feature,' Lauri said.

'Why is that?'

'I was employed on the site as a carpenter. I took the opportunity to make a few additions to my own property.' They went into the lounge, which had a small curved bay at the front and French windows leading to the back garden. The long red-brick fireplace with little niches each side for ornaments and a rough slate hearth was a work of art. Lauri said it was something else unique to this house.

'It's super – and I love French windows!' Annie could scarcely contain herself. 'They're the sort of thing you see in films. I've never come across them in real life before. Can we go outside?'

'Of course, but I'm afraid it's a sea of mud and clay out there.'

The large newly-fenced back garden was almost triangular, like a slice of cake with the house at the narrow end. Wild new grass and a million dandelions had thrust through the upturned clods of earth, but what caused Annie to gasp with pleasure was the tree almost in the centre; a big willow tree with lacy branches trailing the ground.

The estate had been built in the grounds of an old house, Lauri told her. 'Unfortunately, the beautiful gardens were destroyed by the builders. Only a few trees escaped.' He went on to say he'd always wanted a garden. 'I keep my landlady's tidy, but it's very small.'

Everywhere was very quiet except for the subdued chirrup of invisible birds and the drone of a bee which had landed on a nearby dandelion. It dawned on Annie what a lovely day it was. She'd been too preoccupied to notice until now. The entire garden was flooded with dazzling June sunshine and the yellow dandelions shone and flickered like candles. Annie blurred her eyes and saw a smooth green lawn bordered by flowering shrubs, a vegetable patch, a garden shed, and small children dodging in and out of the delicate tendrils of the willow tree. She sighed.

'What's the matter?' asked Lauri Menin.

'Nothing. I was just thinking how beautiful it will be one day.'

They went back inside. Annie oohed and aahed over the little breakfast room and the kitchen, which had a double stainless steel sink, white units and a black and white tiled floor. She was equally impressed with upstairs, particularly the bathroom with its pale green suite. The main bedroom was at the back. Through the window, Lauri pointed out the River Mersey shining glassily in the distance.

She remembered him saying the river would remind him of his childhood in Finland, and asked if he missed his old country.

'Only that.' He nodded towards the view, and said he'd lived on the edge of a river and the beginning of a forest. 'It was enchanting, but after my mother died, I was very unhappy. My older brothers married and went away, my father was a taciturn man who rarely spoke. When war broke out in 'thirty-nine, I was glad of an excuse to leave.' He'd never felt any urge to return. 'I think of myself as a Liverpudlian.'

'It's the nicest house I've ever been in,' Annie declared once she'd seen everything there was to see. The Grand was – well, too grand in a way, and compared to Orlando Street, Heather Close was a palace.

Lauri smiled appreciatively at her breathless admiration and duly noted her suggestions of colour for the walls. 'Would it be too much trouble for you to come with me when I buy the furniture?' he asked.

Annie vowed it would be a pleasure. The next best thing to spending money was spending someone else's.

He murmured it was about time he took her home and she was startled to find it was nearly six o'clock. Sylvia, knowing how critically things hung at Stickley & Plumm, would be concerned.

When the Anglia drew up in Upper Parliament Street, she shyly invited him inside. 'For a coffee and to meet me friend, Sylvia.'

She was disappointed when he refused. 'Sorry, but I have a meeting at half past seven – in fact, I'm seeing your Uncle Bert.'

Of course, he belonged to the Labour Party. She gave him her phone number – Sylvia had declared she couldn't live without a telephone and had one installed shortly after she moved in.

His brown eyes twinkled down at her when he shook hands. 'Goodbye, Annie. Thank you for your help. I'll be in touch soon.'

'Tara, Lauri.'

'Annie! Where on earth have you been? I've been worried sick about you.' Sylvia stood with her hands on her hips like a fishwife.

'I met this lovely chap, Syl,' Annie said dreamily. 'His name's Lauri Menin. We went to see his new house in Waterloo.'

'What happened at Stickley & Plumm? I kept imagining Jeremy Rupert had got the push and attacked you with a knife, like that chap in *Psycho*.'

'It wasn't Mr Rupert who got the push, it was me. All he got was a thorough dressing-down or something.'

'Why aren't you upset?' Sylvia demanded.

'Because I feel sorry for him. It's tragic, getting your kicks out of forcing your attentions on a young girl. As for Mr Grayson, the man is totally unprincipled.'

'What the hell are you talking about?'

'I'm not sure. Is the kettle on?' Annie threw herself onto the sofa.

'There's tea made. Who's this Lauri chap?'

'Lauri Menin. We got on like a house on fire and I really liked him. The trouble is,' Annie said wistfully, 'he's ancient, nearly forty.'

'Jaysus, that's *old* old. Bruno's not much more than that. By the way, there's a pile of letters for you on the table.'

There were more rejection letters, and two inviting her to attend an interview. One was from the English Electric in Longmoor Lane, where Mike Gallagher worked as a toolmaker. It was a long bus ride to the outskirts of Liverpool, but according to Mike, working there was a laugh a minute. The company had tennis and badminton courts, a dramatic society, and all sorts of other leisure activities.

First thing on Monday morning, Annie telephoned and arranged an interview. She discovered the wages were twenty-five shillings a week more than at Stickley & Plumm, easily covering her bus fare. The following week she started work as secretary to the Sales Manager of the Switchgear Department.

4

The English Electric was as different from Stickley & Plumm as chalk from cheese. Annie's boss, Frank Burroughs, insisted she call him by his first name. He was a harassed man in his thirties with five children and a demanding wife who telephoned several times a day to tick him off for something he'd done or hadn't done, or to complain about the children. An engineer, Frank hated paperwork, and left his secretary to do everything that didn't involve technical detail. His first action was to show her how to forge his signature.

Annie immediately joined the tennis club. Members were free to invite their friends, so Sylvia bought a tennis frock which had no sleeves, no back and scarcely any skirt, and with Annie in her more demure white shorts they flaunted themselves on the courts all summer. They never went without male partners, though were hopeless at tennis.

When winter came, they played badminton. Sylvia had a mad, month-long fling with the star player, the English Electric dentist. A *proper* affair! She went to his house in Childwall two or three times a week and didn't return until the early hours. Annie lay in bed listening for her return, wishing she could bring herself to be more free with her favours. Kissing was as far as she'd gone, and she hated having a tongue thrust in her mouth. It seemed grossly unhygienic.

Sylvia broke off with the dentist when he wanted to photograph her with nothing on. Meanwhile, Annie had met a young man from the Fusegear Department who'd been in the same class at Grenville Lucas. She went out with him several times, but after they'd dredged up every single memory of their schooldays, there seemed to be nothing else to talk about.

She had lots of other dates, but rarely felt inclined to go out with the same boy twice. She preferred being with a crowd at parties or the Cavern, where the music and the musicians had suddenly changed. The groups had funny names, like Rory Storm & The Hurricanes and Cass & The Cassanovas. They played something called 'rock and roll' instead of jazz. Sylvia went out with a drummer called Thud.

Once every few months, Annie went down to London to see Marie. After taking part in numerous off-beat plays in suburban pubs and run-down theatres, Marie had managed to get an Equity card, which meant she could call herself a professional actress. Stardom was waiting just around the corner. In the meantime, her savings having run out, she'd taken up waitressing to keep the wolf from the door.

Cecy moved to a bungalow in Blundellsands. Bruno was devastated, but didn't ask her to stay. He loved Cecy, but the relationship was doomed. His affair with Eve came to an end and he remained in the big hotel, alone.

'It doesn't seem right, us having such a good time when so many people are dead miserable,' Annie commented.

'It's the best reason in the world,' Sylvia snorted. 'Considering the way our parents ended up, I think we should put everything we can into enjoying ourselves. After all, we're nineteen. We're getting on.'

*

Lauri Menin's house was gradually becoming a home. The walls were pretty pastel colours, the curtains up, carpets had been fitted throughout. He seemed content to do things slowly, and every now and then would ring Annie from the red telephone at the bottom of the stairs to ask for her advice. 'What do I need for the breakfast room?'

'A table and chairs, of course, and a dresser if there's space.'

'Will you help me choose?'

Annie would meet him in town the following Saturday and they would tour the furniture shops until they found something she considered just right. He seemed happy to leave the selection entirely to her.

'You must be made of money,' she said one day just before Christmas, when they were in George Henry Lee's and he'd just paid cash for the final major item, a burgundy moquette three-piece that would tone in perfectly with the pink walls and beige carpet in the lounge.

He shrugged his muscular shoulders. 'I've had nothing else to do with my money but save it all these years. I don't drink, apart from the occasional beer, I don't smoke. I have no expensive vices.'

Annie laughed. 'Do you have any inexpensive ones?'

'I bite my nails in times of stress,' he admitted.

She loved spending time with him, and wished she got on half as well with the boys she met. She would store up things to tell him because he was always interested in what she'd been up to. It was irritating that Sylvia judged him boring, which was the worst sin of all in her book.

'He's anything but boring,' Annie maintained hotly when the judgement was delivered. 'He's the most interesting man I've ever met. I could talk to him for ever.'

Two days after another hectic Christmas, Sylvia and Annie went to Lither-land Town Hall to see a group called The Beatles, four scruffy young men in desperate need of a haircut and decent clothes. They talked and smoked the whole time they played their instruments – one held his guitar in a most peculiar way, like a machine gun. But their music was raw, uninhibited, wild.

Perhaps it happened that night, no-one was quite sure, but from then on, the entire city of Liverpool began to reverberate to the urgent, pounding beat of rock and roll. The sound gradually spread around the world, but Liverpool was the place to be, particularly if you were young, unattached and had money to spend.

Annie and Sylvia joined the new clubs that had sprung up and travelled far and wide to the most unlikely venues: town halls, church halls, ballrooms, to hear Gerry & The Pacemakers, The Vegas Five, The Merseybeats . . . The Beatles began to play regularly at the Cavern, where Mike Gallagher could often be seen, always with a different girl. Dressed in black, with long red hair and a turned-up collar, Mike looked very much a part of the club scene. He studiously ignored Sylvia and she studiously ignored him back.

In August, the girls went on holiday to Butlin's in Pwllheli. They had a glorious time, but on the Wednesday Annie met Colin Shields from Manchester, a tall, thin young man, desperately shy, with a prominent Adam's apple which wobbled when he spoke. He regarded Annie with sheepish, adoring eyes which she found hard to resist. She willingly gave him her address, and a few days after they'd arrived home, she received a beautiful letter, as lyrical as a poem. The minute he'd set eyes on her, he'd fallen in love, he wrote. She was like a lovely exotic flower. He raved on about her perfect lips, her limpid eyes and peachlike skin. Please, *please* could he see her again? Manchester was no distance away. He could come on Saturday. If she refused, he didn't think he could go on living.

Annie didn't show the letter to Sylvia. She wasn't sure whether to be touched or amused. She wrote back and told him she'd meet him at Central Station.

Over the next few months, she enjoyed having such a nice young man hopelessly in love with her, hanging on to her every word and fetching chocolates and flowers all the way from Manchester. But Annie didn't want to take advantage. She genuinely tried to love Colin Shields back, particularly when he proposed and suggested they get engaged at Easter.

'What should I do?' she asked Lauri Menin. His house was furnished, though it looked bare without a single ornament or picture. He said he was too busy getting the garden into shape to think about such things; laying a lawn, planting shrubs, laying coloured slabs outside the French windows to make something called a patio. He'd even built a garden shed with a verandah. Every few weeks he asked Annie out to dinner, which Sylvia said was utterly sick considering his great age.

'You should follow your heart,' said Lauri.

'But I don't know where my heart wants to go,' Annie cried.

'What does your friend have to say?'

'Sylvia thinks I should turn him down, but only because she wants to get married before I do.'

Lauri gave his benign smile. 'That seems rather selfish.'

'Sylvia's as selfish as they come.' Annie sighed. 'The thing is, Colin and me get on, though not as well as I do with you. And he's got a good job in an insurance company – he's what Auntie Dot would call "a good catch". His mam and dad are nice, too. He took me to meet them the other week. They made ever such a fuss of me.'

'I'm not surprised. You're a catch, Annie Harrison. Whoever gets a nice old-fashioned girl like you will be a very lucky man.'

Annie blushed. It was the first time he'd made such a personal remark, though she couldn't understand the bit about being old-fashioned. She considered herself extremely modern and with it. 'I'm not in love,' she confessed, 'but is everyone in love when they first get married? Perhaps love comes after you've lived together a while.'

'What if it doesn't?' He raised the thick clumpy eyebrows that she always wanted to comb and regarded her kindly. 'I don't want to influence you,' he went on, 'but you asked what you should do. In my opinion, no-one should require advice on getting married.'

'I just thought if you said, "go ahead", or "definitely not", it might help me make up my mind.'

'Go ahead then, Annie.' His voice was rather brusque, and she wondered if she was getting on his nerves.

She thought for a long time. 'See!' she said eventually, 'I knew it would help. As soon as you said, "go ahead", I knew I couldn't possibly. I'll turn him down.'

There was the strangest expression on Lauri's face which she must have misunderstood. She could have sworn he looked relieved.

She told Colin gently that she could never marry him, but that one day he would meet a girl who would make a far better wife than she would, a wife who genuinely loved him.

Nineteen sixty-two dawned, by which time it seemed as if every young man in Liverpool belonged to a rock group. The Cavern gave up jazz altogether and every night was rock and roll. Mike Gallagher took up the guitar and drove his family insane.

Jerry Lee Lewis came to the Tower Ballroom in New Brighton, followed by Little Richard, with The Beatles on the supporting bill. Annie and Sylvia were there, of course. They went everywhere. At night, they fell into bed, exhausted. Annie was glad she was no longer at Stickley & Plumm because her work was suffering. She was tired and made endless mistakes, but as she signed most letters herself, Frank Burroughs didn't notice.

She knew one day it would end. It was bound to. She couldn't go on enjoying herself in this crazy way for ever. In June, Sylvia would finish college and begin her career in advertising. She was thinking about moving to London, which meant Annie would once again be left in the flat by herself. But when June came, Sylvia decided to stay put. 'Who in their right mind would leave Liverpool when it's the epicentre of the universe? I'll have a few months off, I don't need the money.'

The city was changing in other ways: new buildings were going up, bomb sites at last being cleared, the city centre looked different. There was a new *avant garde* theatre. Sculptors and poets blazed a cultural trail from Liverpool to the world outside. The narrow streets of homely little houses off Scotland Road, where everyone knew their neighbours, were ruthlessly razed to the ground and the people dumped in soulless new estates like Kirkby where they didn't know a soul, and the architects and town planners, despite their degrees and vast salaries, hadn't thought to provide shops and pubs beforehand.

Liverpool was changing all right: sometimes for the better, sometimes for the worse.

Annie would be twenty-one in October. She was lucky, her birthday fell on a Saturday. Cecy offered to provide a party at the Grand. She and Bruno were now on quite amicable terms, and she often turned up to help organise big functions.

'It's your twenty-first the month after,' Annie remarked to Sylvia. 'I'd have thought she'd have enough to do with one party.'

'I told her I don't want any fuss. I can't stand the thought of the pair of them drooling over me. I'd prefer to go to dinner with you.'

The dining room in the Grand held forty guests, fifty at a pinch. 'They can use the Snug if they want some quiet,' Cecy said excitedly when she went through the arrangements. It was pathetic, thought Annie; it wasn't even as if she were her daughter. However, the excitement was catching; she was looking forward to her party.

It was easy to find fifty guests. Annie made a list. The first person she put down was Lauri Menin. The Gallaghers made up fourteen, what with all the wives and children and Mike's current girlfriend, and there were loads of people she could ask from the English Electric and the Cavern. There was also Marie, though her sister had never been back to Liverpool, and Annie doubted if she'd come just for a party. She gave the list to Cecy, who was having proper invitations printed.

There was endless discussion on what to wear. Sylvia bought a daring white tube thing, more like a stocking than a frock, which showed off every single curve, but Annie could find nothing she liked. She ended up buying several yards of ivory taffeta, polka-dotted with black, and made herself a ballerina length, off-the-shoulder dress with a wide velvet sash which tied in a long trailing bow at the back.

When the day came, the woman from the ground floor flat came up with the cards which had just come through the letterbox. Sylvia was still in bed. 'You must be popular, Annie,' the woman said. 'There's dozens!'

There was a lovely one from Marie which had pressed flowers in the shape of a key – and a message; 'Sorry I won't be there, sis, but I've got an audition which is too good to miss. If I get the part, my name will be in lights by Christmas.'

Colin Shields hadn't forgotten it was her birthday; he couldn't forget her, he wrote, and never would. The 'never' was underlined. Nearly everyone in Switchgear had sent cards, even those who hadn't been invited to the party. There were cards from Dot and Bert, her cousins, Cecy, Bruno, and people she hadn't seen for years. One was particularly huge. To Annie's astonishment, it was signed by everyone at Stickley & Plumm. She searched for Mr Grayson and Jeremy Rupert's signatures and was annoyed to find them there. Hypocrites!

She'd opened the lot when a white envelope was slid under the door. The man with the buck teeth in the flat below wished her the happiest of birthdays.

Sylvia emerged, yawning, 'Happy birthday, Annie,' she grunted. She handed over yet another card, along with a box containing a pair of onyx and ivory pearl earrings and a necklace to match.

'They'll go perfectly with me dress,' Annie breathed.

'Which is precisely why I bought them, idiot.'

Annie indicated the cards covering the table. 'I never realised I had so many friends. Even the man downstairs sent one.'

Sylvia didn't appear the least impressed. 'That's because you're so nice,' she said in a bored voice. 'Everybody likes you. You never get on people's nerves or rub them up the wrong way. Me, now! On my birthday, I'll get half a dozen cards and certainly not one from the horrid man downstairs because I completely ignore him. That's one of the reasons I didn't want a party. I haven't got stacks of friends like you.'

'Don't talk silly,' Annie began, but Sylvia interrupted. 'Don't argue. I'm arrogant and conceited and, on the whole, I don't like people, unlike you who likes everybody.'

She disappeared to get dressed, leaving Annie, for some reason she couldn't quite define, offended. She wasn't sure if she wanted to be the sort of person who never rubbed people up the wrong way or got on their nerves.

It made her feel like . . . like an anonymous jelly, something that couldn't possibly be taken offence at.

Hurt, she went into the bedroom where Sylvia was rubbing body lotion on her thighs, announced she was offended and explained the reason why.

'An anonymous jelly!' Sylvia hooted. 'Seriously, Annie, you've got a sharp tongue on you. You can be sarcastic and funny, but no-one would believe me if I told them what the real Annie Harrison was like.'

'You mean I'm playing a part all the time?'

'No, you're too anxious for people to like you. It probably stems from looking after your parents; you were walking on eggshells, trying to please everybody.'

To Annie's irritation, the phone went before the rather interesting discussion could be taken further. It was Dot, who'd just had a telephone installed, ringing to wish her niece a happy birthday. After that, the phone didn't stop all day.

Bruno said his lungs would never be the same after blowing up fifty balloons of all shapes and sizes – the long sausage ones were the worst. They were pinned in bunches to the walls of the oak-panelled Regency Room. The tables had been removed and the chairs pushed back.

It was a wonderful party. To Annie's delight, Cecy had booked a group, Vince & The Volcanoes, who weren't quite as good as The Beatles, but nearly, though Dot said caustically she'd never really appreciated how well her Mike could play until she heard Vince erupting.

Annie felt loved and very precious as she was showered with gifts and kisses. She was always the first to be asked on the floor – everybody wanted to dance with the birthday girl.

Except Lauri Menin.

Where was he, Annie wondered, when they stopped for refreshments and there was still no sign. She hadn't heard from him in weeks, and she was looking forward to dancing with him more than anyone, though Bruno came a close second. Cecy had lost track of who'd replied to the invitations; some people had telephoned, others had written, and she had no idea if Lauri Menin was coming.

Everyone had gone down to the kitchen to collect the food that Cecy had been all week preparing. Annie went up to Sylvia's room to give her freckles a coat of pancake. Impulsively, she searched through the records until she found *Three Coins in a Fountain*, and put it on the gramophone. She sat in front of the dressing table and listened to Frank Sinatra's haunting, mellow voice whilst she powdered her nose. It was nearly six years since the record was bought – she still had the little orchid pendant, but it was too tarnished to wear.

How different things were now from then! Mam and Dad were dead, Marie was in London, too busy to come to her party. She recalled the Christmas Eve when she'd served the Bloody Marxists in the Snug, and Bruno and Cecy seemed so much in love. Now she was twenty-one, a proper grown-up, able to vote in the next election, with . . .

Annie stopped powdering her nose and stared at her reflection.

With what?

With a decent job, a shabby flat, but that was all. There was nothing exciting ahead of her, no dazzling career in advertising or on the stage like Sylvia and Marie. She had never met a single man she'd like to marry, except for . . .

Annie saw a pretty, red-headed young woman in a polka-dotted dress put a startled hand to her startled face.

Except for . . .

There was a knock on the door. 'Come in,' she shouted.

Lauri Menin entered the room. 'Dot told me you were here. I'm sorry I'm late. We had a rush job and didn't finish till seven.'

She'd never seen him in a formal suit before. Even when he took her to dinner, he wore a sports jacket. The suit was dark grey, with a blue shirt underneath and a light grey tie. His wavy hair was flattened with Brylcreem, his eyebrows were neatly combed. He looked so solid and reassuring. She knew she would be safe with Lauri, that she would trust him with her life.

She stared at him wide-eyed and unspeaking. It seemed a miracle that he should appear just when she'd been thinking about him so intensely.

'I've brought you a present.' He handed her a small box clumsily wrapped in brown paper.

Her voice returned. 'What is it?'

'Open it and see.'

The box contained a Yale key. She'd received dozens of keys that day. This was the first real one. She held it up and looked at it curiously. 'What's it for?'

'Number seven Heather Close.'

'I don't understand.' She understood completely and wanted to cry.

He knelt beside her. 'Annie, it's been murder, but I vowed I'd wait till you were twenty-one before I asked you to marry me. I hope I'm not making a fool of myself, but I love you, Annie. I want you to be my wife more than I've ever wanted anything.'

'Lauri!' She twisted round and fell into his arms. 'I love you, too. I've loved you ever since you found me sitting on the stairs at Stickley & Plumm.' She hadn't realised until just before he'd entered the room.

His brown eyes had lost their twinkle. Instead, they glistened darkly and she felt as if she was staring into his very soul. 'Then I'm not making a fool of myself, it's "yes"!'

'Oh, yes, Lauri. Oh yes, it's "yes"!'

Annie had a blazing row with Auntie Dot when she turned up at the flat next morning. Sylvia took one look at Dot's face and quickly made herself scarce. 'I'm off to Mass,' she declared, though they'd already been to the nine o'clock one.

It would have been too much to announce she was going to marry Lauri in front of everyone last night. She would have only burst into tears and made a show of herself. She merely whispered the news to Dot and Bert as they were leaving. Dot looked stunned and muttered something incomprehensible; Bert kissed her warmly, slapped Lauri on the shoulder, and shook his hand several times.

Dot had obviously been brooding overnight. 'The thing is, luv,' she began cautiously, 'he's twice your age.'

'Not for ever,' Annie said calmly. 'After a while, he'll just be twenty years older.' She'd have thought Dot would be thrilled at the idea of her settling down with a responsible man who had his own house.

'It's not as if he's like Bruno, full of life and with an eye for the girls. Lauri's already dead set in his ways.'

'Perhaps I should marry Bruno, then,' Annie said sarcastically. 'He'd be having affairs behind me back within a couple of months.'

'But you've hardly had any proper boyfriends, luv,' Dot persisted. 'You haven't "played the field", as we used to say.'

'That's because I didn't want to, Auntie Dot. I don't care if Lauri's dead set in his ways. I love him. He makes me feel all safe and comfortable.'

Which was the worst thing she could have said. Dot immediately lost her famous temper. 'Safe and comfortable!' she screeched. 'That's no way to begin a marriage. *Un*safe and *un*comfortable more like. Marriage is an adventure. It's not till your kids have grown up and you're growing old together that it's time to feel safe and comfortable.'

'I'd have thought you'd want me to be happy,' Annie said stiffly.

'Not with a man old enough to be your bleedin' father,' yelled Dot. 'That's it!' A look of dawning awareness came over her gaunt face, and she struck the arm of the sofa with her fist. 'That's it, isn't it? Our Ken was never much of a dad, was he? You're looking for a father figure, and Lauri Menin fits the bill perfectly.'

'You've read too many newspaper articles, Auntie Dot.' Annie did her best to keep her own temper. 'You'd think you were Dr Freud.'

Dot turned her anger on the absent Lauri, 'He had no right to ask an impressionable young girl to marry him. I'll bloody well tear him off a strip next time I see him.'

'If you do, I'll never speak to you again!'

'Oh, luv!' Dot's face twisted in anguish. 'I want you to be happy.'

'I *am* happy, happy with Lauri. And he waited over two years before asking me to marry him. Why do you think he let me pick everything for his house? It was because he always hoped one day I'd live there, that the things would be mine, yet all the while he just sat back and let me enjoy meself. Oh, Auntie Dot,' Annie sat beside her aunt and took her hand, 'I'm no longer an impressionable young girl. I'm a woman and I want to settle down with Lauri. Please be happy for me. You're the only person in the world whose opinion I care about.'

Dot looked mollified. 'I suppose you're old enough to know your own mind,' she sighed. 'But what about religion, luv? Lauri's an atheist.'

'Yes, but he's happy for our children to be brought up Catholic.' Annie blushed when she thought about what happened before you had children.

'What's Sylvia got to say about it?'

'She thinks I'm nuts. According to her, Lauri's smug and boring.'

'The nerve of the girl! He's a lovely chap. I've always liked him.'

Annie gaped at the sudden swing in Dot's position. Dot saw the look and grinned. 'I'm just an ould meddler, aren't I?' She gave Annie a warm hug and said tearfully, 'I hope you'll be very happy with Lauri. You have my blessing, girl.'

Heather Close

1

The lawn looked thick and smooth, shimmering like emerald velvet in the summer sunshine, although close up the grass was thin. The turfs took time to reach the earth beneath and flourish. Lauri cut the lawn at least once a week with the electric mower. He said the more it was cut, the quicker the grass would grow.

There was scarcely a breath of breeze, just enough to make the branches of the willow tree give off a whispery rustle. The leaves changed colour; light–dark, dark–light, when they moved.

From her deckchair on the patio, Annie could hear Gary Cunningham next door bawling his head off. He either had a dirty nappy, was hungry, or just plain fed up. Gary was three months old and a difficult baby. Valerie, his mother, found it hard to cope.

The Cunninghams had moved into number eight at the same time as Lauri had moved into number seven. Gary, their first child, had been born in April. Valerie Cunningham, an intense, wiry woman with dark fiery eyes behind heavy horn-rimmed glasses and short crisp hair, was in her mid-twenties. Her husband, Kevin, who worked in a bank, was just the opposite, with a round soft face, pale lips and pale eyes. His rimless spectacles seemed so much a part of him that Annie couldn't imagine him without them.

They fought a lot, the Cunninghams. It was rare that an evening passed when the Menins weren't forced to listen to a row. They yelled at each other, sometimes for hours, whilst Gary cried in the background.

On the other side, Mr and Mrs Travers were talking in subdued voices as they worked in their showpiece garden, full of glorious flowers, rustic seats and arches. The Travers were an unfriendly couple, who'd lived all their lives in India. Perhaps they thought they'd come down in the world, coming to live in Heather Close, with a building worker on one side and a comprehensive schoolteacher on the other.

Annie had been thrilled to find Chris Andrews, the teacher she'd liked so much, living by the Travers'. Chris was just as pleased to discover his favourite pupil, or so he said, had become a near neighbour. He had married Lottie, the Alice-in-Wonderland fiancée who had come to the pantomime. They had no children, and no matter how hard she tried, Annie found it difficult to take to Lottie. Despite her wide-apart blue eyes and butter-wouldn't-melt-in-the-mouth expression, there was something sly about her.

Gary gave an unearthly scream and Valerie screamed back, 'Give us a minute, you little bugger.' Annie might go round soon and give a hand; change his nappy or make a bottle. It would be good practice.

Her own baby rolled gently in her stomach. He or she never kicked, just made little gentle movements. Annie imagined a tiny figure shifting position, stretching and yawning inside her womb.

She loved being pregnant, loved the feel of her swelling body under her hands. She hadn't had a moment of sickness. According to the clinic, everything was going perfectly, as if she'd been born to be a mother.

The baby was due in September. Two weeks ago, she'd left the English Electric, and been presented with a Moses basket, which made her feel guilty: it was only six months since the wedding, when she'd been bought a set of saucepans.

Annie stretched comfortably. It was lovely being at home with nothing to do except make baby clothes and read and watch Wimbledon on television. She'd already had stacks of visitors. Bruno had bought Sylvia a car for her twenty-first and she'd got a job in something called 'public relations', which meant she was sent out on assignments and always managed a detour to Waterloo. Cecy was so thrilled you'd think Annie was bearing her first grand-child, and of course Dot came bearing stern advice nearly every day.

The patio, a suntrap, was becoming too hot. Annie struggled out of the deckchair and went through the French windows into the cool house.

There were pictures in the lounge, reproductions of Impressionist paint-ings; Monet, Degas, Pissarro, Van Gogh.

'Why didn't you buy them before?' Annie asked Lauri. He'd had bare walls for more than two years.

'I wasn't sure if you'd like them. I wanted your approval.'

'They're beautiful!' Sunsets, rippling trees, Parisian streets, water lilies.

Brilliant sunshine flooded through the open windows and made the pictures look as if they were alight. The pink walls glowed softly, the dark red suite looked brighter than usual. Annie sighed with pleasure. It looked equally lovely when it was dark, the curtains drawn and the cream-shaded lamps on each side of the fireplace switched on. She would sit with Lauri on the settee, discussing names for the baby, what pattern wallpaper to put in the room which would be a nursery, or watching *Steptoe & Son* on television. Occasionally, Annie would compare their blissful situation with the Cun-ninghams', and Lauri would say something like, 'They've got to learn to adjust to each other, else life will be one big fight.' There'd been no need for Annie and Lauri to adjust; they hadn't exchanged a cross word since the day they'd met.

Oh, she was so *lucky*!

There was a framed photo of their wedding on the mantelpiece. To most people's disappointment, Annie had decided she didn't want a big posh do, about twenty guests at the most: the Gallaghers, the Delgados, Marie, one or two friends from work.

'Is that your idea or Lauri's?' Dot snapped.

'Mine,' lied Annie. Cecy had offered to pay for the reception and Uncle Bert for the cars, but Lauri felt as if he would be accepting charity. The bride was supposed to pay for the wedding, but Annie hadn't got a penny saved. It seemed silly for Lauri to spend hundreds of pounds when there were still things to buy for the house: neither of the spare bedrooms was furnished, and he wanted a garage built on the side. Anyroad, Lauri said he would prefer a quiet affair. It made such sense that Annie gave up the idea of the wedding dress which she'd designed years ago – very regal, slightly Edwardian, with a tiny bustle – and made herself a simple calf-length frock in fine, off-white jersey, with a high neck and bishop sleeves. Cecy loaned her a white hat covered with frothy white roses.

Sylvia was the only bridesmaid, and considerably put out when told to wear something plain. She thought she was being awkward when she bought a scarlet costume, but it turned out just right for a December wedding.

Annie traced Lauri's features on the photo with her finger. He was smiling, the contented smile of someone entirely happy with his lot. He was always happy, Lauri. His only dour words were for the politicians on television. Otherwise, he exuded good humour all day long. It was impossible not to be happy when Lauri was around.

A loud crash sounded through the separating wall, followed by a scream. Gary was still crying. Annie hurried next door.

Valerie was in the kitchen, almost in tears, a baby's bottle in her hand. The room, identical to Annie's own kitchen in reverse, was in chaos. Every surface was covered with dishes, clean and dirty – Valerie never bothered to put them away. The fronts of the white units were streaked with coffee and tea. On the floor were two buckets full of dirty nappies soaking, and a basket of clean ones waiting to be hung out. Also on the floor, the reason for the crash, an upturned drawer and a scattered assortment of cutlery in urgent need of polishing.

'The whole bloody drawer came out when I pulled,' Valerie groaned.

'Never mind,' Annie bent down, scooped the cutlery into the drawer and shoved it back in. 'What's the matter with Gary?'

'Bloody little sod wants his dinner, that's what, and I can't find the brush to clean his bottle.' Valerie had been a nervous wreck since Gary was born; her milk had dried up so she couldn't breastfeed.

'I think I saw the bottle brush in the drawer.' Annie took the bottle out of Valerie's hand, cleaned it thoroughly, stuck a funnel in the neck, discovered the milk powder amidst the mess and measured out three spoonsful. 'Is there any boiled water?'

'In the kettle, I'm not sure if it's too hot or too cold.'

The water felt just right. Annie poured some over the back of her hand the way it said to do in her baby book. Then she filled the bottle up to eight ounces, found a teat soaking in a bowl on the window sill, and gave the bottle a good shake. 'Would you like me to give it him?'

'You'd better. My hands are trembling.'

The carrycot was in the lounge, which was as untidy as the kitchen. Gary's little screwed-up face was bright red with rage. Annie picked him up and shoved the bottle in his mouth just as he was preparing for another mighty yell.

'Whew!' Instead of tidying up whilst she had a few minute's peace, Valerie threw herself onto the black velvet settee and lit a cigarette. She wore jeans and pumps and one of Kevin's old shirts, covered in stains. Her short dark hair was uncombed and her face bare of make-up. 'Look at me!' she groaned. 'I'm a sight. You'd never think this time last year I was a career woman who wore tailored suits and wouldn't have been seen dead without lipstick. Don't have children, Annie. They ruin your life.' Valerie had been manageress of a travel agency.

'It's a bit late to tell me that,' Annie said drily.

'Of course, I forgot. In a few months, your lovely house will be just like mine.'

Never! There was no way she would have a kitchen like Valerie's. Not only that, she would feed her baby regularly, *breast*feed, and take it for long walks if it cried – Gary always calmed down in his pram, but Valerie was too disorganised to take him.

Gary finished his milk, so Annie laid him on her shoulder and began to rub his back.

'You should have let him suck it longer,' Valerie complained. 'At least it keeps him quiet.'

'But he'll only get more wind, sucking at an empty bottle.' Which was something else she'd read in the baby book.

'Aren't you already the perfect mother!'

There was a sarcastic edge to Valerie's remark that Annie resented. After all, she'd only come to help. She didn't have to be in this rather smelly house trying to raise a burp from an equally smelly baby. Hurt, she stared silently at the brick fireplace, almost identical to the one Lauri had built. The Cunninghams had taken the standard tile one out and had this installed as soon as they'd seen next door's.

'Sorry, Annie,' Valerie said stiffly. 'My nerves are at breaking point. I had a terrible row with my mother on the phone this morning, and last night Kevin and I had an even worse one.'

'I know, we heard.' It was something to do with Kevin wanting a clean shirt every day, which Valerie felt was unreasonable considering all the washing she had to do for their son.

'He seems to expect *his* life to go on exactly as it did before; his dinner on the table, shirts ironed and the house looking like something out of a magazine. He even had the nerve to suggest I weed the garden in my spare time. Spare time, I ask you!'

Annie and Lauri had listened to the subsequent row. Lauri smiled. 'If I'd known the Cunninghams were going to live next door, I would have asked for extra thick walls.'

Lauri was nothing like Kevin. He brought her a cup of tea in bed each morning, helped with the housework at weekends, and had no inhibitions about washing dishes just because he was a man. He laughed the time she burned the rice pudding, and didn't give two hoots when she made a terrible mess of her first omelette and they ended up with scrambled egg.

Gary burped and began to bawl. 'I'll change his nappy, if I can find a clean one, and take him for a walk,' Valerie said tiredly.

Annie offered to change the nappy whilst Valerie had another cigarette. It was difficult to get the terrycloth square around Gary's flailing legs and even harder to fasten the pin without piercing his tummy.

'One of these days I'll stab the little bugger, so help me,' his weary mother remarked.

Ten minutes later, she went marching off pushing the big expensive pram, her baby dressed only in his nappy and vest because she couldn't find clean clothes. Everywhere was still in a mess and there was no sign of a meal being prepared for Kevin.

Annie presumed there would be another row that night.

Sara Menin, weighing eight pounds, arrived without a single hitch on the last day of September.

'Isn't she beautiful!' Annie whispered the first night home. Sara was fast asleep in her cot beside their bed. She had pale fair hair with a touch of red and a tiny, almost grown-up face.

'Like her mother.' Lauri kissed Annie on the cheek. He stared at Sara as if he couldn't believe he was a father. 'It's like a dream come true,' he murmured softly. 'My wife, my child – my family.'

'Why didn't you get married again years ago?' Annie asked curiously, at the same time thinking how terrible it would have been if he had.

'What a strange question!' He looked amused. 'Because I was waiting for Annie Harrison to come along.' He kissed her other cheek.

'But you decided to buy a house.'

'I was fed up with lodgings, that's why. You appeared quite fortuitously right after I had made the decision.'

Sylvia always found the baby most peculiar. 'She's so *helpless*. Horses can walk the minute they're born. You've got to do everything for her.'

'Well, Cecy had to do everything for you. You didn't come leaping from her womb and go for a run.' Annie transferred two-month-old Sara to her other breast.

'I never thought the day would come when I'd see you breastfeed, Annie. Does it hurt when she sucks?'

'No. Actually, it's rather nice.'

'Ugh!' Sylvia shuddered. The Bohemian look had gone since she entered public relations, and she wore a short green shift dress with a thick gold chain slung around her slim hips. She looked incredibly elegant with her long blonde hair tied in a knot on top of her head and dangling jade earrings. Her white Mini was parked on the drive outside. 'I'm only joking. I half envy you, having Sara. She's lovely.'

'Only half envy me?' Annie raised her eyebrows.

'Well, you're missing everything, aren't you? Liverpool's the most famous city on the planet. The atmosphere in the clubs is terrific. You should hear the way girls scream at the Beatles nowadays.'

'Do you scream?'

'Jaysus, no, I'm too old. But,' she added wistfully, 'sometimes I wish we were still teenagers. I wouldn't mind a good scream.'

It seemed very juvenile to Annie. She listened to the old groups on the radio, but they seemed to belong to a world she'd left behind.

'Hey, you'll never guess who I saw the other day in the New Court,' Sylvia said. 'Jeremy Rupert.'

'I hope you spat in his eye for me.'

'I was contemplating doing that very thing, except he was with this gorgeous guy. I said "Hello" in the hope he'd introduce me, which he did. The gorgeous guy's a solicitor called Eric Church.' Sylvia smacked her lips. 'He's a Catholic and I'm going out with him on Saturday.'

Annie felt she'd been rather traitorous. 'I hope that doesn't mean Jeremy Rupert's likely to come to the wedding if you end up marrying this gorgeous Eric,' she grumbled.

After Sylvia had gone, Annie put Sara in her Moses basket and went to fetch the washing in; the gusty November wind had blown everything dry. Valerie was bringing in her own washing at the same time. After the initial turmoil, Gary had turned out to be a lovely baby. His nature had become quite sunny and he rarely cried. The Cunninghams were trying for another baby and Valerie was already a week late with her period.

They waved to each other and Valerie looked inclined to stop for a chat, but Annie explained she had to get Lauri's dinner ready.

'I thought he was working in Manchester at the moment?'

'He is, but it doesn't take long to get home. I'm about to make a cottage pie.'

Lauri Menin belonged to a co-operative with four other carpenters, skilled tradesmen like himself. Sometimes, all five might work together on the one site if a large estate was being built, or else they took on jobs which required just one or two men, jobs that could last for as little as a single day. Fred Quillen, the oldest and longest-standing member of the co-op, handled the bookings with scrupulous fairness, and the Quillens' address and telephone number was on the sign over the yard in Bootle where the materials and vans were kept. The men were often fully booked for months ahead. At the end of the month, their earnings were pooled so each man earned the same as the others, barring overtime which went to the individual himself.

At the moment, Lauri was the only one to be employed on the building of a luxury house on the outskirts of Manchester. It was dark by the time he arrived home. 'And how's our daughter been today?' he asked, after he'd kissed his wife affectionately.

'Fine. She couldn't possibly be finer.'

'The food smells nice, my love, I'm starving.'

Annie bustled round, making fresh tea before sitting down to the cottage pie. When they'd finished, Lauri went into the lounge whilst she washed the dishes. She removed her apron and went to join him. He was on the settee reading the paper and looked up, smiling briefly when she came in. Next door, the Cunninghams were having their nightly row, but in number seven everything was quiet. Sara slept peacefully upstairs. Lauri didn't approve of having the television on unless there was something they specifically wanted to watch.

Out of the blue, Annie had the strangest vision. Instead of Lauri, she saw her dad sitting in front of the fireplace of the silent house in Orlando Street. For a moment, she felt quite dizzy. What on earth had triggered off such an awful memory? Then Lauri patted the settee and said, 'Come on, love', and the vision went, but later she found herself thinking about Sylvia and the Cavern, the groups they'd travelled the length and breadth of Liverpool to see, the dances, the tennis club.

'Do you think we could go out one night?' she asked. Dot had already offered to babysit.

'Of course, my love. Where to, the pictures?'

'The pictures would be fine.' She'd look in the *Echo* to see what was on. 'And you know I couldn't think of anything to have for me birthday? Well, if we can afford it, I'd like a record player.'

'Then a record player it will be,' said Lauri.

There were three very good reasons for throwing a party: it was their second wedding anniversary, it was Christmas, and Labour had recently won a General Election. Dot's new heart-throb, Harold Wilson, was Prime Minister.

Sylvia said to ask twice the number of guests they could accommodate because half were bound not to come. The trouble was, everyone had come and there was scarcely room to stand. If it had been summer, they could have opened the French windows and let everyone spill out into the garden, but it was December and snowing outside and guests had spilled out into the hallway and the breakfast room instead. There were several people sitting on the stairs.

Still, everyone seemed to be enjoying themselves. Valerie and Chris Andrews were dancing to 'Good Golly, Miss Molly'. Lauri, the perfect genial host, beamed at everyone in sight.

'This is the gear, sis.' Marie came into the kitchen and helped herself to a sausage roll.

Annie was frantically cutting sandwiches. She hadn't done nearly enough food. 'I thought you didn't say things like "the gear" any more.'

'Scouse has become really fashionable in London. People are always asking me to say something in a Liverpool accent. When I tell them my sister was at the Cavern the night it opened, they're really impressed.'

Marie had arrived that morning and would stay for the next few months. She had a small part in the pantomime at the Empire. Pantomime wasn't what Marie had in mind when she'd gone to London in search of stardom, but, as she said with a shrug, it was better than nothing. She'd brought an actor friend who was staying just for Christmas, Clive Hoskins, a sunburnt Adonis with perfect features and a halo of golden curls. Annie couldn't very well object when they took it for granted they would occupy the twin beds in the spare room. Her sister's morals were her own affair. When Annie asked if it was serious, Marie merely said, 'Clive is a dear friend. I'm very fond of him.'

Marie grimaced. 'What possessed you to wear that dress, sis? It looks frumpy, particularly with those flat shoes. And why don't you do something with your hair? It's been like that since you were little.'

'Oh, do I look awful?' Annie put a distraught hand to her head. 'I intended putting me hair up, but people started arriving before I'd got me make-up on. I made the frock for me twenty-first. I thought it looked dead smart.'

'That length went out of fashion years ago.' Marie looked very smart indeed, in a black form-fitting tailored dress with a daring deep V neckline revealing an inch of black scalloped lace. The skirt finished just above her knees. Her dark hair was cut severely, the same length all round, level with her eyebrows and the tops of her ears. Dot remarked it looked like a plant pot.

'I'll ask Lauri if I can buy material for some new frocks.'

'Don't *ask*, sis. *Tell* him you need more clothes.'

Sylvia came floating into the kitchen, in a dazzling pink dress styled like a toga, which left one gleaming shoulder bare. The hem was edged with silver braid, and she wore spiky-heeled silver sandals. Marie immediately made an excuse to leave, and Annie wondered if they could still remember why they disliked each other.

'More wine,' Sylvia sang. 'White for me and red for Eric, and for goodness' sake, Annie, get out of the kitchen and enjoy yourself. We're all having far too good a time to want food. You look harassed.'

'Oh, Marie said I looked frumpy, now I look harassed. I'm not exactly the perfect hostess.'

'No-one expects you to be perfect.' She took hold of Annie's arm. 'Come on.'

'Will you finish the sandwiches?'

'No I bloody won't. Hang the sandwiches and have a glass of wine.'

'It'll only make me sick. Everything makes me sick at the moment.' She was not quite three months pregnant, but having this baby was already very different from the first time. She felt wretched every morning and almost everything she ate upset her stomach. If she'd known she would feel this bad, she wouldn't have suggested the party, but the invitations had gone out weeks ago.

Sylvia dragged her into the lounge, where Eric Church was leaning against the wall, smoking. Annie had taken an immediate dislike to Eric. Perhaps it was only natural not to like the man who was to marry your best friend; after all, Sylvia had been scathing about Lauri. So far, Annie had kept her thoughts to herself.

He reminded her of a Regency buck, and wasn't so much handsome as attractive, with a thin aquiline face and sleeked-back fair hair. Tall and rather dashing, she imagined him in a frock coat with a lacy cravat and a whip twitching in his long white hand.

The pair had been virtually living together in Upper Parliament Street since they met fifteen months ago, and were getting married at Easter, though how Sylvia had the nerve to wear white for virtue, Annie found hard to understand.

'Hi, Annie.' Eric looked bored. He took the glass off Sylvia and she draped herself over him and nuzzled his neck. Annie felt embarrassed. The pair could scarcely keep their hands off each other, even in public. Eric looked slightly less bored and licked his loved one's ear.

After a short conversation during which they had eyes for no-one but one another, Annie made her excuses, and was immediately captured by one of Lauri's colleagues from the co-op.

'Lauri told us about the baby, Annie,' Fred Quillen said in the high-pitched voice that always sounded odd coming from someone with the build of a heavyweight wrestler. 'Congratulations. When's it due?'

'The middle of July. Sara will be twenty-two months by then.'

'So, they'll be nicely spaced apart.'

'I would have liked them closer, but Lauri wanted to wait a while.'

It was difficult to hear above the din of the music and the buzz of animated conversation. Annie noticed Lauri, a wine bottle in each hand, had forgotten he was supposed to be refilling glasses, and was deep in discussion with Dot and Bert and the couple from the Labour Party whose names she couldn't remember. She excused herself for a second time, saying she'd like to take a peek at Sara in case she'd been awoken by the noise. She'd already taken several peeks, but an earthquake wouldn't have disturbed Sara once she was asleep.

'Smashing party, Annie,' Chris Andrews said as she pushed past. He was talking to her sister and Clive Hoskins and she briefly remembered his play, *Goldilocks*, had sparked off Marie's desire to be an actress.

Valerie came out of the bathroom as Annie went upstairs. She looked very glamorous in a sleek blue satin dress with a halter neck, her hair newly set that afternoon. Annie felt very drab, particularly as Valerie now had two small children, and she only had one. Kelly Cunningham had been born in June, and was now six months old.

'False alarm,' Valerie said.

'Sorry?'

'I told you I was a week late, didn't I? Well, I could have sworn I'd just started, but it was a false alarm. Looks like you and me will be going to the clinic together. By the way, have you seen Kevin?'

'No, but there could be a dozen Kevins down there and I wouldn't have noticed. I'm off to have a bit of peace and quiet with Sara.'

'Feeling rough, are you?' Valerie said sympathetically. 'I was like that with Gary. It makes you wonder why women keep on having babies, doesn't it?' With that, she ran downstairs.

Sara was in her own little room at the front of the house. The wallpaper was creamy yellow patterned with white lace. She was lying on her side, so still that Annie quickly checked she was still breathing, something she must have done a million times before. She stroked the pale curls which had just a touch of ginger. Sara didn't stir, despite the fact the floor throbbed in time to the music.

Annie felt her heart quicken. Did all mothers have this sense of overwhelming love, mixed with anxiety and all sorts of other emotions, when they looked at their small children? She wondered if it would stop when they grew older. Did Dot still feel the same about her lads? Tommy and Alan had families and mortgages and were anxious for their jobs. Mike had given up his perfectly good job at the English Electric to start a pop group which had failed, and now worked for an engineering firm that was little short of a sweatshop; the younger lads were only just starting out in the big wide world.

With a sigh, Annie went to the window and lifted the curtain to see if it was still snowing. It was, and the close looked like a Christmas card with its covering of white. Brightly decorated trees glittered in most windows. Some houses, including their own, had coach lamps outside.

She was about to drop the curtain, when two people came out of the Andrews' house and began to run towards her own. As they got closer, Annie felt herself grow cold. Kevin Cunningham and Lottie Andrews! Laughing, they hurried down the side path and went in the back way.

Perhaps there was an entirely innocent explanation. Annie hoped they could think of one if someone noticed the footprints going from one house to the other in the otherwise smooth snow. She let the curtain fall, took a final glance at Sara and opened the door to return to the party.

Sylvia and Eric were at the top of the stairs. They didn't notice Annie about to emerge from the bedroom. She took a step back and half closed the door, although she knew she shouldn't watch, but there was something odd about their posture, something still and wary, like animals about to pounce. They didn't touch, just stared at each other. There was a look on Sylvia's face Annie had never seen before. Her lovely eyes were half closed, her lips curved in a quivering smile. Then Eric clasped her face in his long white hands and kissed her, not an ordinary kiss, but savage. His jowls moved, his mouth was wide open, as if he was trying to devour her in front of Annie's startled eyes.

His hands moved down her body, rested fleetingly on her breasts, ever so slowly, almost teasingly. Sylvia said, 'Oh, *God*!' in a strange hoarse voice, and Eric opened the bathroom door and they went inside. The bolt clicked into place.

Annie remained transfixed, holding the half-open door. She had never looked at Lauri like that! Lauri didn't open his mouth when he kissed her – she would be horrified if he did. Making love with Lauri couldn't be nicer. He was gentle, always respectful. Even on the first night, he made sure it didn't hurt. She always felt content and satisfied, lying in his arms when it was over.

Sylvia and Eric had looked *disgusting*. For some reason, Annie felt extraordinarily disturbed.

She went downstairs, to find Kevin and Valerie dancing cheek to cheek. Lottie was in the kitchen making a sandwich. 'I hope you don't mind, Annie. I always feel hungry after . . .'

'After what?'

Lottie looked at her with wide, innocent blue eyes. 'After a few glasses of wine.' She giggled, as if at a private joke, but Annie understood only too well what she'd been about to say. After sex!

'That chap's a card, isn't he?'

'Which chap?' queried Annie. She hated this party and desperately wished it were over. Would anyone notice, she wondered, if she crawled underneath the coats on the bed and went to sleep?

'That Clive chap with your sister. I mean, it's obvious. I've never met a queer before. I thought it was against the law.'

Annie didn't answer. Lottie departed with a sandwich in each hand.

Marie was sleeping with a homosexual.

And if that wasn't enough, Sylvia and Eric were behaving like animals and Kevin Cunningham and Lottie Andrews were having an affair.

It was too much!

'I think that went very well, don't you?' said Lauri. 'Everybody seemed to have a good time.'

Annie nodded numbly. It was nearly three o'clock, the last guests had left, and Marie and Clive had gone to bed. She began to collect the dirty glasses, but Lauri took them off her. 'You look exhausted, love. I'll clear up in the morning. Go on up and I'll bring you some cocoa.'

She was sitting up in bed when he brought the drink. He put the mug on the bedside table and took both of her hands in his. He could read her like a book, and always knew when there was something wrong.

'What's the matter with my little girl?' he asked tenderly.

'I feel all peculiar, I don't know why,' she confessed.

'I expect it's the baby. Do you feel queasy?'

'A bit. But it's not just that . . .'

He ruffled her hair. 'What is it then?'

She told him what had happened over the evening, the things she'd seen and heard. Lauri smiled. 'And why should they make you feel peculiar?'

'I've no idea,' Annie sniffed.

'Do you think you're missing something?'

Oh, he was so astute. He'd guessed before she had herself. She bit her lip and said nothing.

'Does that mean you'd like an affair with Kevin Cunningham?'

'Of course not!' Annie was shocked.

Lauri wiggled his eyebrows. 'Do you want to sleep with a homosexual?'

She giggled. 'No.'

'Shall I bare my teeth and look at you like an animal then? What shall it be, an elephant maybe, or a squirrel?'

'Oh, Lauri!' She flung her arms around his neck. 'I'm a terrible person.'

'No you're not, my dearest Annie. It must be very boring stuck at home all day with Sara. Why don't you and Sylvia go to the Cavern one night? Or to the pictures?'

'As if I'd leave you all on your own!'

Lauri shrugged. 'But I leave you when I go to the Labour Party. I was out every night for weeks before the General Election.'

'Perhaps I could go to the Labour Party with you some time? Dot would always look after Sara. I'd feel a bit peculiar at the Cavern. I'm sure they don't get very many pregnant women there.'

To her surprise, because Lauri usually agreed to almost everything she asked, he shook his head. 'You'd find the meetings very dull, and anyway, you've never shown the least interest in politics.'

She thought she might if she went to a meeting and heard what people had to say, but didn't bother arguing. She felt much better. It was enough to know she could go out if she wanted. Maybe she and Valerie could go to the pictures. It was no good asking Sylvia because she went everywhere with Eric.

'I suppose the best marriages are slightly dull,' Lauri was saying. 'And I dread Valerie finding out that Kevin is up to no good with Lottie Andrews – we'll have to get sandbags for the walls.'

2

According to Dot, who joined the crowds outside St Edmund's church to watch, there had never been a more glorious, a more radiant bride than

Sylvia Delgado. She didn't like to hurt anyone's feelings, but it was the God's honest truth.

In her dress of paper-thin taffeta with several petticoats underneath, long fitted sleeves and a shawl collar thickly trimmed with lace, Sylvia looked almost unreal, out of this world, too beautiful to touch. Her filmy veil was waist length and a coronet of pearls encircled her gleaming blonde hair. Eric looked dazed as she came floating up the aisle towards him on Bruno's arm.

No expense had been spared for the wedding of the Delgados' only child. The men wore top hats and grey morning suits and the women's outfits came from the most exclusive shops. The hired cars were long and sleek, the flowers in the church had been flown from the Channel Islands, the organist was a professional hired for the occasion. Bruno didn't give a damn, but Cecy wanted to impress the family her daughter was marrying into.

There had been a Church & Son, Solicitors, in Liverpool for over a hundred years. The firm had been established by Eric's great-great-grand-father, and was more highly regarded than Stickley & Plumm, if such a thing were possible. Specialising in litigation, the name of Peter Church, Eric's father, was frequently mentioned in the national media when he defended infamous criminals in long, attention-grabbing trials. Eric was his only son and reputed to be as brilliant as his father. The family lived in a pala-tial house in Southport, where they employed a cook and a gardener. Peter Church drove a Rolls Royce.

They were an impressive couple, the Churches, Peter, with his prominent beak nose and piercing eyes, had the arrogant look of a man who wouldn't suffer fools gladly. His wife Mildred, in her oyster brocade suit and over-feathered hat, looked a pillar of the community, as indeed she was.

Cecy felt it was essential to prove, by spending as much as possible, that the Churches had met their financial match by marrying into the Delgados – Sylvia was the daughter of a Count, and she had the family coat of arms printed in silver on the invitations. She'd gone to London to buy her lilac chiffon dress and matching hat from Harrods.

The only thing to spoil what should have been a perfect wedding was the matron of honour. At least, so Annie thought.

'But, Syl,' she reasoned. 'The trouble Cecy's going to, the expense. It seems dead stupid to muck things up with a matron of honour who's six months pregnant.'

'I don't care if you're ten months pregnant,' Sylvia said flatly. 'You shall be my matron of honour, and that's that.'

'I won't half feel silly. I'll look a sight.'

'I don't care about that, either. We promised each other, we took a vow, that when we got married one of us would be bridesmaid and the other matron of honour.'

Annie couldn't remember taking a vow, but perhaps she had.

'If you refuse, I'll never forgive you!' Sylvia stared menacingly at her friend. 'I suppose I could delay it for six months until you've got your slim, svelte figure back?'

'Syl! You know darn well I've never been slim or svelte. As for delaying it, you're joking, because Cecy would die of shock. Oh, all right, I'll do it, but I'll look like a bloody house!'

In fact, she didn't look too bad. The blue lace frock with its long jacket discreetly disguised the bump in her stomach. She loaned Sylvia a handkerchief for something borrowed, and she wore a daring garter for something blue. The something old was the pearl coronet which had been Cecy's when she married Bruno all those years ago.

It seemed an odd thing to wear, mused Annie, standing behind her friend as she was betrothed to Eric Church, because Cecy and Bruno's marriage had turned out to be a disaster. Her musings were forgotten when the baby gave her stomach a series of vicious kicks. She turned and caught Lauri's eye. He was sitting at the end of a pew with Sara, in her new white broderie anglaise frock, on his knee. He smiled and Annie felt a shiver of sheer happiness run through her.

Then Sylvia lifted her veil. Annie caught her breath because she was so beautiful. Her eyes had never looked so huge and the irises were the dusky blue of an evening sky. They shone with unshed tears as Eric kissed her on the lips. Annie distinctly recalled the day Sylvia Delgado had come into the classroom at Grenville Lucas. She'd known straight away that they were going to become friends. They'd had some wonderful times together, but now both were married women.

An era had ended. A new one had begun.

Daniel Menin decided to arrive late, very late. Nine uncomfortable months elapsed, but still he showed no sign of being born. Annie was huge, absolutely massive, as she lumbered round. It was impossible to turn over in bed; she had to get out and in again. She virtually lived in the clinic. The baby's head wasn't in the right place.

'It's too busy kicking to know it should turn upside down,' she moaned. 'If it doesn't come soon, I'll have to have it induced.'

It was in the butcher's one sunny afternoon in late July that the baby gave the first hint of his arrival, a painful hint. She never went far these days in case this very thing happened. The shop was only a few minutes away from Heather Close. She screamed and bent double when a searing pain scorched through her stomach. There'd been no previous warning, nothing to indicate that today was to be the day.

The butcher looked scared. 'Jaysus, luv! What's wrong?'

A woman in the shop said cuttingly, 'The girl's about to have a baby. Don't stand there like a pill garlic, man, ring for an ambulance. Come on, luv,' she said kindly. 'Hang on to me. If you have another pain, squeeze as hard as you like.' The woman began to tell Annie in bloodthirsty detail about her own deliveries. 'With the first, I was torn to shreds. Twelve stitches I needed. Twelve! The second saw me two days in labour and in agony the whole time. The third, you wouldn't believe what happened with the third . . .'

Fortunately, Annie never found out what happened with the third. She was seized by an even worse pain, just as the butcher returned with a glass of water and announced an ambulance was on its way.

'But me little girl,' Annie gasped. 'I left her with a neighbour . . .'

The bloodthirsty woman said, 'Where d'you live, luv, and I'll go round and tell her.'

'Seven Heather Close, and if you could ask me neighbour to contact me husband? She knows where he's working.'

'All right, luv. Don't worry, everything's going to be all right,' which Annie thought an odd remark considering all she'd said before.

The ambulance arrived and with it more pains, terrible contractions that made her feel she was being ripped in two. The next eight hours were a nightmare, a tortured daze of piercing contractions and anguished screams. Lauri arrived, his face grave.

'Is there something wrong with the baby?' Annie yelled.

'Of course there's nothing wrong with the baby,' a nurse said. 'He's just an awkward little bugger, that's all.'

It was midnight when Daniel kicked and fought his way out of his mother's womb. Those last few minutes brought agony so fierce that Annie felt convinced she was going to die.

'You've got a lovely little boy, Mrs Menin.' There was a slap and Daniel Menin sent up a great howl. 'He's a whopper, too. Not far off nine pounds, I reckon. What are you going to call him?'

Annie, totally exhausted, could think of a dozen names to call her new son, none of them favourable. 'Daniel,' she said.

'He's a fine little chap,' Lauri said when he was allowed to see her. His eyes looked all puffy, as if he'd been crying. He stroked her damp brow. 'That was a terrible experience, my love. I felt every contraction with you.'

'Lauri?'

'Yes, my dear Annie?'

'Promise we'll never have another baby.' She couldn't go through that again.

'I promise. Frankly, I couldn't stand it, either. Two children are quite enough, and now we have a boy and a girl, the ideal family.'

There were two deckchairs on the Menins' patio. In one, Valerie Cunningham was suckling month-old Zachary. Valerie had given birth to four children in just over three years, a fact she never ceased to boast about. Eleven-month-old Tracy was crawling purposefully across the Menins' lawn, a dummy in her mouth.

'Just look at the birthday boy,' Valerie chuckled.

Annie watched as Daniel tried to drag a doll away from two-year-old Kelly. The chuckle was a warning to tell him to stop.

'Daniel,' she called. 'Leave Kelly's doll alone.'

Daniel ignored her. A wilful scowl appeared on his handsome little face. He tugged even harder, the doll's head came off and Kelly burst into tears.

Annie went over to where the children were playing. She knelt by her son, took him by his sturdy waist and said firmly, 'Look, you got loads of presents this morning. Why don't you play with them?'

'No,' said Daniel. He stared at his mother mutinously. It was the only word he knew. Lauri said it was typical; other children's first word was 'Mummy' or 'Daddy'. Daniel's was 'no'.

'What about that lovely big ball Auntie Dot sent?'

'No.'

'Or the telephone off your Uncle Mike?'

'No.'

She released him, and he immediately went for the broken doll. Annie grabbed it off him. Fortunately, the head clicked back on. She gave it to Kelly and Daniel tried to get it back, so she picked him up and carried him to the deckchair. He settled on her lap and watched Valerie feeding Zachary with genuine interest in his intelligent brown eyes.

Dark-haired, dark-eyed Daniel had been a handful since the day he was born. Unlike his sister, he scarcely slept and demanded constant attention. Annie was driven frantic, trying to keep the house nice, prepare Lauri's meals, and keep her small son occupied. He was far more advanced than Sara had been, sitting up unsupported at five months, walking at ten. Lauri had to build a gate at the bottom of the stairs after the day Annie couldn't find Daniel anywhere and he was discovered upstairs, trying to climb into the lavatory. Fortunately, Sara was no trouble and very self-contained. At the moment, she was playing house all by herself in the willow tree. Annie glimpsed her golden daughter crouched inside the leafy shade making an imaginary meal for a row of furry animals and dolls, a serious expression on her gentle little face.

Gary, Valerie's eldest, was playing with Daniel's new blue and white ball. He charged after it, without noticing his small sister crawling across the grass, and tripped and fell headlong. Tracy, more frightened than hurt, dropped her dummy and started to wail.

'*Gary!*' Valerie screamed. 'Come here.'

The child came across, dragging his feet. Valerie delivered a stinging slap to his bare leg. 'Look where you're going in future,' she snapped. Gary's bottom lip quivered, but he didn't cry.

'I think it was an accident,' Annie said mildly. Gary was a nice little boy and she hated to see him punished unfairly.

'Accident or not, he should look where he's going.'

Valerie never hesitated to lash out at her children, but Annie had sworn never to lay a hand on hers. She wanted, more than anything in the world, for them to be happy, for them not to know a single moment of the misery she had suffered in her own childhood.

She wished Auntie Dot and Sylvia would come soon so they could have their tea and Valerie and her brood could go home. It had seemed only proper to invite them, because the Menins were always invited to tea at the Cunninghams when there was a birthday.

Valerie began to complain in a loud voice about Kevin. 'He's off to London next week, the lucky bastard. Some sort of conference.' She laughed unpleasantly. 'If I didn't know him better, I'd swear he was having an affair, he gets home later and later. He hasn't got the guts, though. He knows I'd kill him if he went with another woman.'

Chris Andrews had mentioned the other day that Lottie was staying with a friend in Brighton next week. Annie was wondering if there was a connection, when Auntie Dot and Sylvia came round the side of the house.

Dot beamed. 'Where's my Danny Boy? Come on, you lovely little lad, and give your ould auntie a nice big kiss.'

Daniel slid off his mother's knee and trotted into her arms. There was something about Dot, with her rough voice and exaggerated manner, that attracted children like moths to a flame. The little Cunninghams gathered round. Gary often asked for his Auntie Dot.

Annie noticed her daughter hanging back, as if unwilling to join the throng. Sylvia, Sara's Godmother, had also noticed. She sat on the grass and pulled the little girl onto her knee and gave her a present, a blue leather shoulder bag. 'I didn't want her to feel left out,' she said. 'Daniel always seems to be the centre of attention.'

'It only seems like that. Lauri idolises Sara. Daniel isn't the centre of attention when Daddy's here.'

Sylvia looked casually elegant in jeans and a loose shell-pink blouse. She'd given up work when she got married and spent her leisurely days caring for her beautiful bungalow in Birkdale. She was learning to play bridge and spent a lot of time helping her mother-in-law with coffee mornings to raise money for charity. Almost every night, she and Eric went to a dinner party, usually with the same crowd of up-and-coming solicitors, accountants and businessmen. Once a week, they held a dinner of their own. Annie and Lauri had been invited, but declined. 'I wouldn't know which knife to hold,' Annie confessed. 'Anyroad, Syl, I'd feel out of place with those sort of people, and Lauri said if there's one profession he can't stand above all others, it's accountants.'

The birthday tea was served in the breakfast room. Instead of blowing out the single candle, Daniel made a grab for it and burnt his fingers. He didn't scream, but regarded the burnt fingers curiously, then looked to his mother for an explanation. Dot declared he was a marvel, a miracle of a child.

The Cunninghams left. 'I suppose I'd better tidy up a bit before Kevin comes home,' Valerie said sullenly.

'She's a mardy girl,' Dot remarked after Valerie had gone. 'She doesn't know which side her bread is buttered. Four lovely kids, yet she's always moaning. Mind you, I've never taken to women who leave their pegs on the line.'

Dot took the children into the garden and Annie cleared the table. Sylvia ran water into the sink. 'I'll wash, you dry.' This had been the pattern when they lived in Upper Parliament Street. Sylvia loathed drying dishes. She claimed it sent her into a trance.

'You'll get your lovely blouse all wet,' Annie warned.

Sylvia rolled up her sleeves before plunging her hands into the soapy water.

'What have you done to your arm?' Annie exclaimed. There was an ugly purple bruise on her left forearm, stretching from wrist to elbow.

'Oh!' Sylvia laughed and made a half-hearted attempt to pull the sleeve down. 'Oh, it looks much worse than it is. I fell upstairs! It doesn't hurt at all.' As soon as she'd finished, she rolled down her sleeves and buttoned the cuffs.

Annie put the kettle on so they could have a cup of tea in peace. 'I can't tell you how welcome silence is. Daniel's on the go all day.'

'But he's a super little boy, Annie.'

'Don't get me wrong,' Annie said quickly. 'I'm not complaining. Both my children are adorable and I'm entirely happy with my lot.' She looked sideways at her friend. 'Aren't you?' She wasn't quite sure why she asked the question that way, as if there was some doubt about it. Perhaps it was the bruise that made her feel uneasy.

'Eric and I are blissfully happy,' Sylvia gushed. 'Though we'd love a baby – the in-laws are for ever dropping hints. Eric is their only son, and there must always be a Church & Son in Liverpool.' She winked. 'Eric and I go at it hammer and tongs, but I don't seem able to conceive.'

'There's plenty of time. You've only been married fifteen months.'

'Yes, but I'll be twenty-five soon, we both will, and I want to be a young mother for my children when they grow up.'

Then Dot came in with Daniel wanting his potty, and the peace was shattered until he decided to go to sleep that night at half past ten.

Annie told Lauri about Sylvia's inability to conceive. 'Not like me. I must be very fertile.' It made her feel very feminine and fruitful.

'No, Annie,' Lauri said firmly. He knew straight away what she was leading up to, the same discussion they'd been having for months.

'Please, Lauri,' she implored. 'I'd love another baby. In fact, I'd like two. Four children is the perfect number, two boys and two girls.' She'd already chosen the names; Sophie and Joshua.

But Lauri's face had the stubborn expression that always came when she raised the subject. 'After Daniel, you made me promise that we'd never have another baby. How on earth can you have forgotten that time? It was sheer torture, love. I couldn't go through it again.'

'I haven't forgotten,' Annie said eagerly, 'but, looking back, I realise it was worth it. We ended up with Daniel, didn't we? I wouldn't care if it was twice that bad for another Daniel or Sara. It's what women do to have babies. Dot had an awful time with Alan, and Valerie did with Tracy, and the woman in the butcher's . . .'

Lauri broke in. 'I know all about Dot and Valerie and the woman in the butcher's, but it's *you* I'm married to, not them. I couldn't stand it, Annie. I'd be on tenterhooks – and what about the expense?'

'The expense?' Annie said, puzzled. 'We've already got a cot and a pram and all the things we need.'

'There'd be another mouth to feed – two, if you had your way.'

'I thought we had plenty of money.' They rarely talked about money. Lauri gave her housekeeping every Friday, and never protested if she asked for more if there was an extra expense that week.

'All my savings went on the house because I wanted it to be perfect. We're not short, but we're not flush either. Interest rates have gone up which means mortgages have gone up with them. Now, if you don't mind, Annie, I'd sooner not discuss it any further.' He rattled the newspaper and started to read.

After a long silence, Annie said, 'What would happen if I forgot to take my pill?' She'd threatened this before and the reply was always more or less the same.

Behind the paper, Lauri said, 'I would consider you very deceitful.'

There was another silence, then Lauri lowered the paper. His eyes were twinkling. 'Are you sure this isn't a bit of one-upmanship on your part,

Annie? The Cunninghams had a fireplace put in like the Menins. The Menins must have four children like the Cunninghams.'

She conceded he was probably right. She was jealous of Valerie.

'Come here,' Lauri lifted his arm and she cuddled beside him. 'Why risk our happiness by treading into the unknown? We already have two beautiful children. Be content, Annie. Be content.'

She was nearly asleep when she remembered the purple mark on Sylvia's arm. She'd done it falling upstairs! She also remembered that the Churches lived in a bungalow which had no stairs. She imagined Eric, a Regency buck with a cane twitching in his hand, and knew, as surely as she'd ever known anything, that incredible though it might seem, it was he who was responsible for the bruise on her friend's arm!

Sara looked tiny and lost in her yellow overalls and pink T-shirt, with her favourite Teddy clutched to her chest. She looked at Annie trustingly. 'It's all right, sweetheart,' Annie whispered and gave her a little push, though she felt like a torturer. More than anything, she wanted to snatch her daughter up and take her home.

Then a helper swooped on them. 'Hello, Sara.' The woman took Sara's hand. 'What a good little girl you are! I think you're the only new one who's not crying.' She turned to Annie. 'She'll be fine, Mrs Menin. Say bye bye to Mummy, Sara. I'm sure you're going to just love playgroup.'

There was a lump in Annie's throat when she got home. She played with Daniel for a while, but what she really needed was someone to talk to, someone who would understand how she felt. Valerie would be no good. Valerie would think her an idiot getting upset over Sara. She was always looking for ways to get her children off her hands and would consider Annie lucky to have got rid of Sara for three mornings a week.

Perhaps Sylvia would come round? She hadn't seen her since Daniel's birthday, nearly three months ago. Though they spoke on the telephone frequently, it always seemed to be she who called. Lauri laughed like a drain when she said she thought Eric was responsible for the bruise. 'She could have fallen up someone else's stairs, my love. Really, Annie, your imagination knows no bounds.'

But Annie *knew*, she just knew! Sylvia hadn't been round because she was black and blue all over and had to stay indoors.

She dialled Sylvia's number, and it rang out for a long time. She was just about to replace the receiver when it was picked up. Sylvia answered, her voice muffled.

'Are you all right?' Annie enquired. 'You sound dead funny. Oh, I do hope it's morning sickness.'

'It's not, I'm afraid. I'm just a bit off-colour, otherwise I'm fine.' Eric was also fine. Everything was fine. 'How are Lauri and the children?' she asked.

'Fine,' giggled Annie. 'I'd be fine, too, except I feel dead miserable. Sara started playgroup this morning.'

'I expect she'll love it there,' Sylvia said dully.

'Do you feel too off-colour to come and cheer me up?'

'Sorry, Annie, but I think I'll go back to bed.'

'I'd come and see you, except I've got to pick Sara up at twelve.' Anyroad, the few occasions she'd gone to Birkdale by train, Daniel had shown an unhealthy interest in the Churches' valuable ornaments.

'I'm not really in the mood for visitors.'

Why not? Annie was immediately suspicious. 'You sound peculiar!'

'So do you!' Sylvia rang off with a curt 'goodbye'.

Annie immediately took her son next door, where Valerie was vacuuming the lounge. Tracy and Kelly were on the settee, pretending to be terrified. 'D'you mind looking after Daniel for a couple of hours? Sylvia's not well and I'd like to go and see her.' Daniel wasn't clinging like Sara and Annie didn't feel uncomfortable asking, because Valerie often requested the same favour. 'I'll be back in time to collect Sara.'

'Of course, it's Sara's first morning at playgroup, isn't it? I suppose you're feeling rather sad,' Valerie said surprisingly. 'Don't rush back for Sara. I'll pick her up with Gary. You'll have a job getting to and from Birkdale in time.' She said to give Sylvia her love and hoped she'd soon be better.

Annie took a last glance at Daniel. He had already thrown himself on the settee and was trying to get a doll off Kelly.

The Churches' bungalow was in a quiet tree-lined road close to Birkdale golf course. It had a white pebble-dashed exterior and a distinctly Spanish look, with an arched porch and smaller arches each side leading to the rear. The Venetian blinds on the big front windows were closed so the sun wouldn't fade the expensive carpets. Sylvia's new car, another Mini, this time red, was visible behind the half-raised garage door.

Annie rang the bell, which sounded like Big Ben. No-one answered, so she went through the left arch and tried the side door, which was open. She went inside and called, 'Sylvia? It's me, Annie.'

The kitchen was spacious, nearly three times as big as her own, with marble-topped units and every conceivable modern device. There were a few dishes on the stainless steel draining board waiting to be washed.

Annie went into the hall, which was vast and thickly carpeted in eau-de-Nil. There were genuine oil paintings on the walls, but none were as attractive as the Impressionist prints in her own lounge.

'Sylvia,' she called again. Faced with an array of doors, eight altogether, she couldn't remember which led to the main bedroom. She opened one and found a study, opened another and a broom fell out. She jumped back, startled. 'Sylvia!' she yelled.

Music was coming from somewhere, the Beatles' 'We Can Work It Out'. Annie tried another door and peered inside. Sylvia, in a Victorian nightdress, all frills and lace and pleats, was leaning against a heap of pillows reading a magazine and on the point of popping a chocolate into her mouth. She looked up and said casually, 'Hi.' She appeared fit, healthy and entirely at ease.

'Why didn't you answer when I shouted?' Annie said indignantly.

'Because I knew the indefatigable Annie Harrison – sorry, Menin – was bound to track me down.'

Annie blinked, taken aback. Sylvia sounded cold, almost rude. 'I was worried about you,' she stammered. 'I thought I'd come and make sure you were all right.'

'I said I was a bit off-colour, that's all. Thank God I'm not ill, else you'd have hired a helicopter and landed on the lawn.'

'I'd have thought you'd be pleased someone cared enough to come all this way.'

Sylvia said haughtily. 'There's already several people who care, thanks; Cecy, Mrs Church and, of course, my husband.' She pointed to the chocolates. 'The bumpy one is ginger cream, your favourite.'

'No, ta. But I wouldn't mind a cup of tea.'

'You'll have to make it yourself – *I'm* a bit off-colour.'

Annie's hands shook as she got together the tea things. Had she made a terrible mistake? No, not terrible, a *welcome* mistake, but if that was so, why was Sylvia so aggressive, as if she knew Annie had guessed and was resentful. Why was she wearing such a concealing nightdress? Was it to hide all her scars and bruises? Perhaps the best thing would be to have it out with Sylvia, face to face, and see what happened.

She took the tray into the bedroom. 'I want you to do something for me,' she said slowly.

'Anything, Mrs Menin. Name it and it shall be done.'

'I want you to take your nightdress off.'

Sylvia's jaw dropped in astonishment. 'Whoa, Annie! You're showing tendencies I never suspected. Are you going to rape me? The press will love it. You can get Peter Church to defend you. It's his sort of case.'

'Oh, don't be stupid, Sylvia,' Annie said, blushing furiously. 'I want to see if there's any bruises, that's all.'

'Bruises! And why should I have bruises, dear friend?'

Annie didn't answer. Sylvia undid the buttons down the front of her nightgown and pulled it off. She slid the whole thing down to her hips. Annie blushed again. Although they'd lived together for years, she'd never seen Sylvia naked before. She was surprised at how small her breasts were. Sylvia turned round to show her back. The nobbles of her spine were like large white pearls. There wasn't a mark anywhere.

'Are you satisfied? I think you could say my skin is flawless. At least, that's what Eric says, "Sylvia, darling, your skin is flawless."' Annie recoiled at the anger in her eyes. 'I saw the look on your face on Daniel's birthday when you saw my arm. I hurt it in the Grand, by the way, but you immediately thought Eric had done it. I sensed it again in your voice this morning and as soon as I heard you shout I knew why you'd come. What a terribly, terribly wicked thought to have! Incredibly wicked. You've got too much ghoulish imagination. I feel sorry for you, having such wicked thoughts about entirely innocent people. Eric is the dearest husband in the world. We're desperately in love and he would never lay a finger on me.' She was so angry she was almost in tears.

Annie poured the tea and put Sylvia's on the bedside table. 'I only had your best interests at heart,' she said inadequately.

'I'd sooner you didn't in future.'

They drank the tea in silence, Sylvia still smouldering.

'I suppose I'd better go,' said Annie.

'It wouldn't be a bad idea. I'm harbouring the notion of throwing this cup at you once I've finished the tea. I might have thrown the lot, except it would have stained the carpet.'

Annie took the tray into the kitchen and returned to the bedroom. She had one last try. 'Are you sure everything's all right, Syl?'

'Everything is brilliant, Annie. I concede my social life is tedious compared to what it used to be, all the charity functions and dinner parties bore me shitless. I can't help recalling the fun we used to have at dances and the Cavern . . .'

'The Cavern's closed.'

'I know,' Sylvia said sharply, 'and The Beatles went to Buckingham Palace to collect their MBEs. The Mersey Sound is no more. Everything comes to an end eventually, including friendships.'

'I'll be off then.' Annie shuffled her feet uncomfortably. 'If you ever need . . . I mean, if there's ever any trouble, well, we've put Daniel in the spare bedroom, but there's an extra bed in Sara's room.'

'Why, thank you, Annie.' Sylvia's voice was gracious and edged with steel. 'And don't forget either, that there's always room for you and the children when Lauri threatens to bore you all to death.'

Annie gasped. 'That was a *horrible* thing to say!'

'Not quite as horrible as suggesting Eric is a wifebeater.'

'Tara, Sylvia.' Annie turned on her heel.

'Goodbye, Annie.'

Annie had opened the door, when Sylvia shouted, 'Don't call me, I'll call you.'

She waited on the path outside for a good ten minutes, half expecting Sylvia to come hurtling out, crying, 'Come back, Annie. Come back. You were right all the time.'

But she waited in vain. Her legs shook as she walked to the station. It was bad enough that a friendship of more than half a lifetime was over, but the thing was, she didn't believe a word Sylvia had said.

A few weeks later, Sylvia sent a card and a pretty dress on her god-daughter's birthday. Annie thought hard before replying. She wasn't sure if the dress was a peace offering and Sylvia wanted to make up. In the end, she wrote a polite letter of thanks, adding, 'If you're ever passing, do drop in. Sara often asks for Auntie Sylvia.' But Sylvia hadn't dropped in by Christmas, when more presents for the children arrived and an expensive card, signed just, 'Eric and Sylvia.'

The same thing happened next Christmas. The following year, Daniel started playgroup, and later Sara started school. Annie felt her heart contract at the sight of her daughter in her gymslip and too-big blazer.

Lauri, the most understanding husband in the world, took a rare day off on Sara's first day. He knew Annie would be upset, alone in the house for the first time in five years. 'Let's do something exciting,' he suggested. 'We have three hours before it's time to collect Daniel.'

'Such as?' Annie couldn't think of anything exciting you could do for three hours on a Tuesday morning.

Lauri put his hands on his hips and glanced thoughtfully around the room. 'I've been thinking, I'm fed up with pink walls. Let's buy some wallpaper! I fancy a geometric design, something ultra-fashionable that will drive the Cunninghams wild.'

'What a good idea,' said Annie. At that particular moment, nothing seemed less exciting than picking wallpaper.

Lauri went to get the car ready, and she glanced at the telephone. What she'd *really* like was a good laugh with Sylvia. It was two years to the day, to the minute, since she'd called and Sylvia said she felt a bit off-colour. She'd never told anyone, not even Lauri, how much she missed her friend.

Impulsively, she picked up the phone and dialled the Churches' number. She could still remember it by heart. No-one had answered by the time Lauri came back. She put the receiver down, feeling guilty for some reason.

'Who are you calling?' he asked.

'It rang,' she lied, 'but when I picked it up there was no-one there.' She supposed that was partially true.

They got in the car. Lauri was putting on weight. She was feeding him too well, he claimed when he couldn't fasten his trousers. 'I must adjust this seat one of these days.' He had trouble sliding behind the wheel. Annie leaned over and kissed him. 'What's that for?' he smiled.

'Because I love you,' she said. 'I love you with all my heart.'

Choosing wallpaper for the lounge was definitely not exciting, but the message, the reason, the meaning behind it, was. Loving someone, and that person loving you back, was the most exciting thing in the world.

3

Mike Gallagher got married on New Year's Day, 1969, but his poor mam was driven to despair beforehand. Dot wasn't sure which was worst: a register office ceremony which meant the union wouldn't be recognised in the eyes of God; the fact the bride, Glenda, was a widow, five years older than the groom, with two teenaged children; or the outfits the couple had planned.

'He's getting married in *cowboy* boots, Annie!' Dot fanned herself frantically with a newspaper. 'Cowboy boots and a leather jacket covered in fringes. I said, "At least you could get your hair cut, luv. You look like Diana Dors", but he told me, his own mother, to get stuffed.'

Mike had a glorious head of ginger hair which fell on his shoulders in lovely little ringlets and waves. Annie thought it very attractive, particularly with his gold earrings. Most young men had long hair, but Mike's was particularly outstanding. 'Lots of the girls at the English Electric had a crush on your Mike,' she said.

Dot patted her own hair self-consciously. It was more silver than ginger nowadays. 'Folks always said our Mike took after me. Mind you, I'm not sorry he's settling down. After all, he's nearly thirty-two. An unmarried man with earrings and hair like that might set tongues wagging, but not to that Glenda woman with two grown kids.'

'I quite like her.' Glenda had been a widow for ten years. She was small and plain, but had a lovely warm smile that made her look quite beauti-ful and you quickly realised why Mike had fallen in love. Her children, Kathy and Paul, were a credit to her.

'What are they going to live on, I'd like to know – fresh air?' Dot demanded aggressively, as if Annie could provide the answer. 'The kids are still at school, Glenda earns peanuts in that factory, and our Mike's job wasn't up to much, but at least there was a wage coming in.'

For the second time, Mike had thrown in his job to tread into the un-known. Along with a member of his failed pop group, Ray Walters, he had started Michael Ray Engineering & Electrical Services, with the intention of repairing vintage cars from a rundown shed on Kirkby Trading Estate. 'Never,' Dot said, in a flutter, 'did I envisage having a son with headed notepaper.'

She was in a worse flutter now. 'You should see Glenda's wedding dress. It's one of those mini things that hardly covers her arse. Oh,' she groaned tragically, 'I hope none of the neighbours come to that heathen register office. They'll think they're watching a circus, not a bloody wedding.'

'Actually, Auntie Dot, I'm making myself a mini dress for the wedding.'

'Where does it end?' Dot asked suspiciously.

Annie touched halfway down her thigh. 'There.'

'I hope it covers your suspenders.'

'Oh, Dot, I'll be wearing tights, won't I?' Tights were probably the greatest invention known to man – to woman. It was great to be able to do away with suspender belts and not have big red indentations on your legs when you got undressed.

'You'll never catch me in a pair of them tights,' Dot said, tight-lipped. 'I think they're disgusting.'

Lauri thought the red mini dress looked very nice when it was finished and Annie twirled around for his approval. The children were in bed and it was okay to use the sewing machine. Daniel watched, fascinated, as the needle flashed up and down, and it wasn't safe to use it when he was around.

'I'm not showing too much leg, am I?' she asked anxiously.

He regarded her thoughtfully. 'I reckon that's just enough. One inch higher and it would look indecent, an inch lower would be dowdy.'

'Are you making fun of me?'

'As if I would! I know hemlines are a very serious matter.'

'You don't think me legs are too fat?' She was fishing for compliments and he knew it. He grinned. 'You've got perfect legs, Annie.'

'You don't mind other men looking at them?'

'As long as they just look, why should I mind?'

Annie smiled with satisfaction. It was just the right answer. She looked in the mirror and said. 'I wouldn't mind having me hair cut very short.' She still wore it in the same style as she'd done all her life, which wasn't really a style at all.

Lauri murmured, 'You know I prefer it long.'

'It's *my* hair!' she pouted.

He looked at her, amused. 'No-one's arguing over the ownership of your hair, love. It's just that you asked my opinion on your frock, so I thought you'd like it on your hair.'

She threw herself onto his knee. 'Am I getting on your nerves?' Perhaps it was the frock, but at the moment, she felt more like a teenager than a woman of twenty-seven with two children.

He stroked her cheek. 'I like it when you act like a little girl.'

Annie fingered his moustache. 'Why don't you let it grow, Zapata style?' He'd already refused to grow his hair, saying he would look ridiculous at his age.

'I like my moustache the way it is.'

'Why is it I leave my hair long for you, but you won't grow your moustache for me?' She pretended to look hurt.

'For the same reason we have flowered wallpaper instead of geometric which I preferred. The wallpaper wasn't important, my moustache is. If it's important that you have your hair short, Annie, then get it cut.'

Lauri always talked the most astonishing common sense, which was probably one of the reasons they didn't have rows like the Cunninghams. In fact, they never rowed at all.

She decided to leave her hair alone.

Annie came hurrying home, having deposited Sara at school and Daniel at playgroup. Daniel was pleading to go five days a week instead of three. Perhaps next term . . .

She worked out her programme for the morning. The beds were already made, the breakfast dishes washed. Friday was the day she cleaned the fridge and vacuumed upstairs. After that, she'd make some gingerbread men and prepare a boiled fruitcake. One of the neighbours might pop in for coffee. She hoped it wouldn't be someone who'd stay long, as she wanted to get on with Sara's dressing gown. Sara was shooting up; that blazer was unlikely to last till she was seven.

It was March and appropriately windy. Old dried leaves whipped against her legs and skipped across the Close to become entangled in the tall hedge which bordered the Travers' front garden. The old couple were gradually being buried within a cultivated jungle of towering trees and shrubs. Later on, Mr Travers would emerge, remove the leaves and glare accusingly down the Close. Last autumn, he had swept up every single one of his leaves for his compost heap and resented those from less conscientious gardeners encroaching on his property.

Inside, the house was beautifully warm, since they'd had central heating installed. Annie checked the boiler in the kitchen for no other reason than she liked seeing the pilot light flickering behind the glass door. Daniel was convinced a fairy lived inside who lit the flame each morning to cook her breakfast, and put it out when she went to bed.

The fridge cleaned, Annie wiped the draining board with a sigh of satisfaction, and was about to take the vacuum cleaner upstairs when the doorbell rang.

She tut-tutted to herself and straightened her pinny before opening the door. Sylvia, startling in a short white fluffy coat over a brief black frock and thigh-length patent leather boots, stood posing on the doorstep like a model in a magazine. She wore sunglasses and a big black floppy hat with a white feather. 'Hi, Annie,' she sang, as if it were only yesterday they'd last met, not two and a half years ago.

'Come in,' Annie stammered.

Sylvia sailed into the lounge and parked herself on the settee. Annie stood awkwardly in the doorway. 'Would you like a coffee?'

'Please. No milk, no sugar,' she added, as if Annie didn't know.

When Annie returned with two mugs of coffee, Sylvia had removed her hat and sunglasses and was staring around the room with interest. 'I see you've got new wallpaper,' she remarked.

The wallpaper was misty pearly beige with a pattern of shadowy poppies. Annie still couldn't get over how different the room looked after plain pink walls for so many years. 'Lauri wanted something more regular, like squares or triangles, but I preferred flowers.'

'I bet that was a serious topic of conversation in the Menin household for at least a month.'

Annie plonked the mugs on the coffee table with such force that the liquid spurted out onto the varnished surface. 'Is that why you've come after all this time,' she snapped, 'to make nasty comments?'

Sylvia looked unabashed. 'I just came to see how you were.'

'I was fine until you arrived.'

'How are Lauri and the children?' Sylvia took an embroidered hankie out of her pocket and wiped the coffee up.

'Very well, ta.' Annie had been considering telling Sylvia to get lost, but felt slightly mollified by the gesture of concern for her coffee table. 'Sara loves school, and Daniel's settled in playgroup. They've both had mumps and German measles, but got over it all right. Lauri's put on a bit of weight, but otherwise he's fine. How's Eric?'

'Eric!' Sylvia's blue eyes shone brilliantly. 'Eric's doing ever so well. He has cases on his own nowadays. People say that he'll turn out to be even more successful than his father.'

'Good,' said Annie. 'And yourself?'

Sylvia tossed her blonde head proudly. 'Tip-top. Never felt better, but I can see it's a waste of time asking how *you* are, Annie. You look very much the contented *hausfrau* with your pinny and new wallpaper.'

'I think you'd better go,' said Annie.

'But I haven't finished my coffee!' Sylvia raised her perfect eyebrows and pretended to look outraged.

'Well, finish it, then go.'

'If you insist.' Sylvia sighed and began to sip the coffee slowly.

Annie ignored her own coffee. Her head was in a whirl. What had happened? Sylvia had been her greatest and closest friend. They had sworn to let nothing come between them. Perhaps it was she who'd pushed in the wedge by suggesting Eric . . . How would she have reacted if Sylvia had accused Lauri of doing something far worse than being merely boring?

She opened her mouth to speak, to say she was sorry for what she'd said about Eric, and dammit, Sylvia, we're friends. We promised to be friends for ever. I've missed you more than I can say over the last few years. There's no-one I can talk to the way I talked to you. You're the only person I can tell *really* intimate things, like I'd love to go to bed with Warren Beatty. Remember when we used to disappear into the Ladies for a laugh because we were the only ones who found a situation funny when everyone else thought it deadly serious?

Sylvia swallowed the coffee and reached for her hat and sunglasses. 'Thanks for the refreshments, Mrs Menin.'

The moment was lost. They went into the hallway. Sylvia put her hand on the latch and gave Annie a dazzling smile. 'It's cheerio, then, or "tara" as you would say.'

Annie nodded. 'Tara.'

But she couldn't let Sylvia walk out of her life, because this time she knew it would be final. She took a step forward, 'Syl!'

Sylvia didn't hear. She turned the latch, then suddenly her body seemed to crumple and she leant her forehead against the door and twisted her lovely face towards her friend. 'Jaysus, Annie,' she whispered, 'I'm so bloody miserable, I could easily *die*.'

Eric hated her because she hadn't given him a child. He wouldn't mind if it was a girl, because girls can become lawyers and everybody knew it was the father who influenced the sex of their children. By now, the whole family hated her because she'd let them down. And the more they hated her, the more ridiculously she behaved because it was the only way she knew to fight back, otherwise she would become cowed.

'I wear the most ludicrous outfits, Annie. Mrs Church winced when I turned up to Mass last Sunday in this hat. I get pissed and tell dirty jokes in a very loud voice at dinner parties and generally make a show of myself.' Sylvia gave a terse laugh. 'Actually, shocking people can be fun, but it only makes Eric hate me even more.'

'Oh, Syl!' Annie said sadly.

They had returned to the lounge and were sitting on the settee. Annie was holding her friend's hand. Sylvia hadn't cried, but her eyes were unnaturally bright, and there were tense lines around her jaw. Her grip on Annie's hand was so tight it hurt.

'Have you seen a doctor about why you can't conceive?'

'I've seen a specialist, no less, but he could find nothing wrong. He said I should relax, stop thinking about it all the time.' She gripped Annie's hand even harder. 'As if I could! Every time I start a period I feel physically sick.'

'It might be Eric's fault,' Annie suggested.

Sylvia pretended to look astonished. 'I hope you're not insinuating that a Church is not totally perfect!'

'Sorry, I didn't realise it was a crime.'

'Well, it is,' Sylvia said matter-of-factly. 'I once suggested that Eric see a doctor same as me. He was pouring tea out at the time and decided to pour it on my legs – it was the morning you came to see me. You didn't ask to see my legs, did you?' Sylvia released her hand. She got up and began to walk to and fro in front of the fireplace. 'You were right, Annie. Eric was responsible for the bruise on my arm. He doesn't hit me often and I give back as good as I get, but oh, God, if you knew how much I loathed you for guessing.' She glanced at Annie curiously. 'You never liked him, did you?'

'I thought he looked cruel.'

'The thing is, Annie, the terrible thing is, I love him.' She went over to the French windows and stared out. The fence between the Menins' and the Cunninghams' creaked in the wind and the willow tree shivered delicately. 'You'll never believe this, but Eric loves me back. He hates me and he loves me. Making love is heaven, but that's all that's left, making love. Everything else is shit.'

Annie found it all beyond her comprehension. 'If Lauri laid a finger on me, I'd walk out and never come back.'

'Perhaps you don't love him enough.'

'I think it's just a different sort of love.' She had no intention of getting cross. 'I understand why you were so angry when I came storming over to Birkdale. With me and Lauri getting on so famously, it must have made you feel lousy . . .'

'Oh, for Chrissakes, Annie!' Sylvia said savagely. 'I'd sooner be married to Eric any day than Lauri. I wouldn't marry Lauri Menin for a million pounds.'

Annie felt as if a fist had curled up in her stomach. 'That's stupid!' she said weakly. Rising from the settee, she went to the window at the front of the room. She noticed a gold Mini parked outside.

'Jaysus, these boots are killing me.' Sylvia undid the long zips and kicked the boots off. 'Is there anything to drink?'

'There's sherry in the kitchen from Christmas.'

'That'll do. A large one, treble or quadruple or bigger.'

Annie poured herself half a tumbler of sherry at the same time. She was anxious for Sylvia to continue, even though she wouldn't like what she had to say. 'That's stupid,' she repeated, returning to the lounge.

Sylvia had settled crosslegged on the hearth. 'Oh, Annie, as if I'd resent you being happy just because I wasn't! What a trite person you must think I am! I love you, in the way I'd love a sister.' She swallowed half the sherry in one go. 'No, what got up my nose was you feeling sorry for me, and at the same time thinking you and Lauri were blissfully happy, when you're not. Well, Lauri may be, but not you.'

'You're talking nonsense,' Annie said doggedly. 'We couldn't possibly get on better. We never fight. He lets me do anything I want.'

'*Lets* you!' Sylvia raised her eyebrows. 'Marriage is a partnership. One half doesn't give the other permission to do things.'

Annie frowned irritably. 'I didn't mean it to sound like that.'

'Why haven't you got four children, Annie? Four's what you planned.'

'Well, Lauri thought . . .'

Sylvia interrupted. 'And if I remember rightly, you wanted another baby straight after Sara, not to wait nearly two years.'

'Lauri . . .' Annie began, but Sylvia seemed determined not to let her finish a sentence.

'Remember when we used to plan our grand weddings?' she said reflectively. 'When I married Eric I wore the dress I'd always wanted, but I can't recall you wanting that ghastly thing you wore in front of about half a dozen guests. As for my red suit, I gave it away.'

'Grand weddings don't come cheap,' Annie said weakly.

'Cecy offered to do the reception. Uncle Bert wanted to help.'

'Lauri didn't want charity,' Annie muttered.

'It wouldn't have been charity. Cecy thinks of you as a daughter, but Lauri wanted a small wedding to his child-bride and Lauri got his way, just as he gets his way on all the really important things.'

Without realising, Annie had drunk all her sherry. She stumbled to the settee, feeling light-headed. 'Why are we discussing my marriage, when it's yours that's failed?' she enquired.

Sylvia leaned forward, her face screwed up with the effort of trying to explain. 'Because you're suffocating, Annie. It's time you snapped out of this eager-to-please, obedient-little-wife shit and became the sparkling, witty, intelligent Annie I used to know. I find it incredible you and Lauri have never had a fight. You must never talk about anything remotely controversial if you don't row from time to time.'

'Lauri . . .' Annie paused. 'I suppose it's me own fault. I give in too easily.' She resented the admission there could be something wrong.

'It's about time your husband knew he was married to someone with firm opinions and a temper.'

'I'm not sure what you mean,' Annie said faintly.

'I'm not sure myself. All I know is, since you married Lauri you've become a zombie.'

Annie giggled. 'I think you're exaggerating, Syl.'

'Is there any more sherry?'

'It's in the cupboard next to the fridge.'

Sylvia came back with the bottle and refilled their glasses.

'Why did you come?' asked Annie.

'Because Eric was particularly vile this morning and I desperately wanted to talk to someone.' She returned to her place on the rug. 'There was only one person. I've missed you awfully these last few years.'

'I've missed you.'

Sylvia smiled. 'But I wasn't prepared to have you dripping sympathy all over me. I thought it was time you knew the truth about yourself.'

'That's kind of you, I must say,' Annie said caustically. 'Your own marriage is up the creek, so you're trying to convince me mine is too!'

'It's not that. I was fed up watching you kowtow to Lauri all the time. You'd think he was your father, not your husband.'

Annie's head was swimming too much to get annoyed. She lay down on the settee and mumbled, 'Oh, bugger off, Syl.'

'Jaysus, Annie,' Sylvia sighed pleasurably. 'I'm pissed out of my mind.' She put down her glass and fell back full length on the rug.

'Where do we go from here?' Annie said carefully.

'From here? Once I'm sober, I'm going to Liverpool to buy a frock I saw in a boutique for tonight's dinner party, a truly cute little purple number made entirely of fringes. It's the sort they used to do some dance in during the 1920s. I can't remember what it's called, the dance, I mean.'

'The Charleston.'

'That's right.'

'Mike Gallagher got married on New Year's Day in a leather jacket covered with fringes.'

Sylvia raised her head, dismayed. 'Mike's married?'

'Auntie Dot nearly did her nut, but I thought he looked fab.'

'Wow! I never told you this, Annie, but when we saw Mike in the Cavern, I thought he looked fantastic with that gorgeous hair, like Henry the Fifth. I was sorry I dumped him all those years ago.'

Annie hiccuped. 'Well, it's too late now, you've lost him.'

'Shit!' Sylvia beat the rug with her fist in mock chagrin. 'I thought, if I ever left Eric, I could have Mike.'

'Are you likely to leave him?' Annie tried to look deadly serious.

'It's inevitable. One of these days, the sex will wear off and we'll hate each other completely. Of course we can't get divorced, his family would never stand for it.' She put her hands behind her neck, stared at the ceiling, and said reflectively, 'I might become a nun.'

'In your purple frock with fringes?' Annie laughed.

'I'll start a new order; the Little Sisters of Rock and Roll. We'll chant Beatles' songs and worship at the shrine of Paul McCartney.'

'Not John Lennon?'

'No. He was at Art College before me, but nobody liked him.' Sylvia suddenly sat up and cried, 'Oh, Annie! Why are we both so miserable?'

'Believe it or not, Syl,' Annie said slowly, 'I don't feel the least bit miserable, despite you saying I should be.'

'That's because your brain has turned to cotton wool.'

'Then perhaps everyone should have cotton wool for brains and the world would be a happier place.'

The back door opened and Valerie Cunningham called, 'Annie, are you there?' She came into the room with Daniel. 'You didn't turn up at play-group, so I thought I'd better bring him home.'

She'd actually forgotten to collect her son! Annie made a brave attempt to sit up, but fell back with a groan. 'Jaysus, me head!'

'Hello, Sylvia,' Valerie said brightly. 'It's ages since I've seen you.' She made them both black coffee. 'This is a turn-up for the books,' she remarked. 'I never thought I'd find Annie Menin as drunk as a lord at this time of the day.'

Annie still had a hangover when Lauri came home. He was amused and didn't mind there was no meal ready. She didn't mention she'd forgotten to pick up Daniel, an awfully negligent thing to do. She'd feel guilty when the hangover wore off. Sylvia had gone to Liverpool by taxi, because she was too drunk to drive. She was coming back for her car.

Lauri was peeling the potatoes, because his wife had forgotten how to use the peeler, when Sylvia came bursting through the back door. She pulled off her white fur coat and threw it on the floor.

'What d'you think?' she cried, wiggling her hips.

Annie blinked as the brief purple dress shimmered. She blinked again at the violent purple and black striped tights. Sylvia also had a black velvet band around her forehead with a jewel in the centre.

'You look . . .' Annie searched for words, ' . . . truly ghastly.'

'Good!' Sylvia smacked her lips.

'Are you going to a fancy dress?' Lauri asked innocently.

'No, I'm going to play charades with Eric.'

She only stayed long enough to re-introduce herself to Sara and remark how incredibly tall she'd grown. The little girl turned out to have never forgotten her Auntie Sylvia. Then she departed in a cloud of expensive perfume and a final shimmy of her purple frock.

Annie watched the gold Mini drive away. She returned to the kitchen, where Lauri said, 'I'm glad you two have made up, but is Sylvia all right? She looked rather manic to me.'

'She's desperately unhappy. I'll tell you about it later.' Daniel clung to her legs demanding a story. Sara was patiently waiting in the armchair, her favourite Noddy book on her knee.

'You read to them, love,' Lauri said. 'I'll do the sausages.'

'Are you sure you don't mind?' Annie asked anxiously. 'I've been a terrible housewife today.'

He kissed her. 'It does no harm to go off the rails occasionally.'

Annie squeezed into the armchair with the children. This was her favourite time of the day; her husband home and two little bodies snuggled against hers. Lauri was singing something tuneless in the kitchen. He was a husband in a million – Kevin Cunningham would raise the roof if he came home and found Valerie with a hangover. But was it enough to be married to someone prepared to cook sausages and let you pick the wallpaper, yet who put his foot down when it came to really vital things like having children? Kevin wouldn't make the dinner, but he and Valerie had a joint bank account and she could write cheques whenever she pleased. Annie had no idea how much money was in the bank and Lauri had laughed, as if it were a big joke, when she suggested *they* had a joint account, just as he'd laughed when she'd asked if, like Valerie, she could take driving lessons.

If it wasn't for him, they'd have four children, Joshua and Sophie, as well as Sara and Daniel. Sara mightn't be so withdrawn if she had a sister or brother close in age, but Lauri had insisted they wait. He claimed she would be 'overworked' with two small babies.

'If Valerie can manage, so can I,' Annie argued at the time.

'But Valerie doesn't manage, does she, love? I don't want to come home every night and find you exhausted.'

'But it's *me* who would have been exhausted,' Annie thought, several years too late. Could it be that Lauri was selfish, that he didn't want the smooth running of his home disrupted by too many children and an exhausted wife?

'You've lost your place, Mummy,' Sara said accusingly. 'You've missed out where Noddy crashes his car.' She knew the book off by heart.

'Sorry, sweetheart. I was miles away. Where am I up to?'

By the time she'd finished, Annie decided, because it seemed the safest thing to do, that Sylvia had been talking nonsense. Just because *her* marriage was a mess, she had no right to suggest there was something wrong with Annie's.

'Bloody cheek!' she murmured.

'You've gone wrong again, Mummy. That bit's not in.'

It was June, and something of vital importance was happening in the Labour Party. People kept ringing up to speak to Lauri. One night, several members, including Uncle Bert, came to the house. They stayed in the breakfast room all evening, arguing furiously. Lauri argued loudest, and it was strange to hear his normally pleasant voice raised in anger. At one point, he came into the lounge and asked Annie if she would kindly make them a cup of tea.

'I don't know how you stand living with this man, luv,' Uncle Bert said jocularly as he was leaving. 'I bet you're fed up having politics pushed down your throat the whole time.'

Annie smiled politely. People had said more or less the same thing before, but Lauri scarcely mentioned politics at home. 'What was the meeting about?' she asked when everyone had gone.

'Nothing, love,' he said absently.

It was a national issue, she'd gathered that much. Harold Wilson, the Prime Minister, had been mentioned. She started to watch 24 *Hours* on television when Lauri was out, and bought the *Daily Telegraph* several times. There were some weighty articles that gave her the facts.

She hadn't realised there was such high unemployment in the country – the highest since the war. Prices were rising, wage demands soaring out of control. The Employment Minister, a woman called Barbara Castle, was trying to push through a White Paper called *In Place of Strife*, to curb the power of the unions, but the Trades Union Congress and the left wing of the Labour Party were totally opposed.

A few days later, Uncle Bert and the same crowd turned up again just after Sara and Daniel had gone to bed. Annie left the lounge door open and listened. She gathered they were opposed to *In Place of Strife* and were drawing up a resolution to send to Transport House for the eyes of the Prime Minister himself. She was impressed.

'How does this sound?' said a voice, 'The Party is letting down the entire Trade Union movement with the proposed White Paper and . . .'

'Not letting down, betraying,' said Lauri. 'And point out the Labour Party grew out of the Trade Unions.'

Annie was innocently watching *The Avengers* when Lauri poked his head around the door and asked if she would make tea.

The tea served, they returned to their resolution. Annie hung round, wondering if she could bring herself to stick her oar in and ask what the Trade Unions intended doing about the really poor people; the ones who worked in very low-paid jobs and didn't have a union, or had no power to strike, like nurses. Did the unions care about the people who didn't have a job at all? And what about women? What had the transport union done to help the woman who'd become a bus driver and had been forced to quit by the other drivers, all men?

Lauri looked up and said, 'Did you want something, Annie?'

Her courage failed. 'I . . . er, would you like some biscuits?'

'Not for me, luv,' said Uncle Bert. The others were too involved with the resolution to notice that she'd spoken, just as they'd been too involved to thank her for the tea.

The meeting dispersed and everyone went home. Lauri came into the lounge rubbing his hands with satisfaction. 'Did you finish the resolution?' enquired Annie.

'Yes, love. Dan's having it typed.'

'Lauri,' she said eagerly. 'If I had a typewriter, a portable one, I could type things for you. Not only that,' she had an even more brilliant idea, 'if I went to meetings, I could take the minutes down in shorthand. I'm sure I'd get my speed back in no time.'

Lauri passed the back of the settee where she was sitting and ruffled her hair. 'No thank you, love. We don't want your pretty little head bothered with politics.'

Annie's brain must have turned to cotton wool. It took an age for the words and all that lay behind them to sink in. Her husband was deep in a newspaper when she said furiously, 'How *dare* you say that!'

He stared at her, mildly astonished, 'Say what, love?'

'How dare you suggest I'm too dim to be bothered with politics?'

'I never suggested any such thing. You've never shown the least interest, that's all.' He shrugged and returned to the paper.

Annie snatched the paper off him and flung it to the floor. 'That's because I haven't had the opportunity. All we talk about is wallpaper and children and what flowers to plant.'

Lauri was getting agitated. 'This isn't a bit like you, Annie. What's got into you tonight?'

Annie glared at him. 'Why couldn't *I* be at that meeting?'

'Because you're not a member of the Party,' he said easily. He tried to put an arm around her shoulders, but she moved out of his reach. 'Anyway, you hadn't the faintest idea what it was about.'

'I know exactly what it was about,' she said cuttingly. 'Barbara Castle's *In Place of Strife*, which I thoroughly approve of. The country will never get back on its feet if we give in to the unions.'

Lauri groaned. 'That, Annie, is a perfect example of why I have never wanted to bring politics into my home. Nothing is more divisive.' He looked at her beseechingly and for once there was no suggestion of a twinkle in his brown eyes. In fact, everything about him was different, not just his eyes, but the expression on his face, the way he spoke, his gestures. With a shock, she realised for the first time he was addressing her as an adult, not a young girl. He continued, 'I totally disagree with what you just said – people nearly came to blows over that very thing at the last ward meeting.'

'Why do you go, then, if it's so awful?' Annie sneered.

Lauri winced. 'It's not awful, I love it. But I like to leave it all behind when I close the front door. Here, this room, this house, is my sanctuary, the place where I expect peace and quiet, not violent arguments about politics.'

Then Annie understood what Sylvia always had, that behind his charming, easy-going persona, Lauri Menin was a very selfish man.

'In other words,' she said quietly, 'your wife must never bother her pretty little head over anything that might disturb your peace and quiet.' She resisted the urge to bring up the children she'd wanted, Joshua and Sophie, children who'd never been born for the sake of his peace and quiet. Perhaps some things were best left unsaid, otherwise the words would create a barrier that might never be breached. Suddenly, without warning, she resented he was so much older and settled in his ways. Dot said marriage was an adventure and Annie wondered what it would be like to be married to someone her own age, because nothing about her marriage had been adventurous. It had been safe, comfortable, secure, the things she'd wanted once, but wasn't sure if she wanted now.

The thought seemed so traitorous that it almost took her breath away. She was conscious there'd been silence for quite some time and she glanced across the room at her husband.

Lauri looked poleaxed. He had his hands on his stomach and his mouth slightly open as if someone had just delivered a terrible blow. Despite everything, Annie felt a pang of love that almost hurt, and with it came the awareness that things had changed; not massively, perhaps not even noticeably, but life would be slightly different from now on. Lauri might never be aware of it, but a barrier had been erected after all. Only a tiny one, but a barrier all the same.

Their eyes met. He said brokenly, 'I never dreamt you were unhappy.'

'I'm not unhappy.'

He held out his arms and she went to him. 'All I've ever wanted is for you to be happy.'

Annie knew that wasn't true, or there would be four children sleeping upstairs, but no doubt Lauri meant the words sincerely.

They never referred to the row again. A card came from the Labour Party. She was a member, though she never went to a meeting. Nor did she bring up the subject of more children. She'd wanted them close together, not years and years apart, so it was too late.

Two weeks later, men landed on the moon and Neil Armstrong took 'one small step for man, but one giant leap for mankind', and the whole affair of Lauri and the Labour Party seemed rather trite.

4

The August sun beat mercilessly down out of a lustrous blue and cloudless sky. The gardens of Heather Close were at their peak, bursting with flowers and bushes in full bloom. As the years passed, the creamy bricks were gradually turning golden brown. The children were on holiday; their voices could be heard, slightly muffled in the thick, humid air, as they played in the back gardens. A dog chased butterflies, barking in frustration, and birds sang joyfully in the trees.

On such a glorious day, no-one was prepared for the hearse, followed by a single black car, which drove slowly into the cul-de-sac and stopped at number six, the Travers'.

In Bootle, a crowd would have gathered. Here, there was an agitated twitch of net curtains. The Travers' had always kept very much to themselves. There was no coffin in the hearse, yet no-one was aware a coffin had been delivered, that death had visited Heather Close for the first time.

Annie made the Sign of the Cross when she saw a coffin carried by four pall-bearers emerge from behind the tall hedge that hid the old couple from the world. Then Mrs Travers followed, alone. She was dressed entirely in black and her face was hidden behind a heavy veil. The coffin with its single wreath was carefully stowed into the back of the hearse, and the miniature procession drove away.

'Did you see that, Annie?' Valerie Cunningham shouted.

Annie hurried into the back garden, relieved to have someone to talk to. There had been something inherently depressing about the scene: not so much the death of a very old person, but the fact it had occurred without anyone knowing. Mrs Travers must have been alone with the dead body of her husband for several days.

Valerie was leaning on the fence. She looked upset. 'They mustn't have any children.'

'Or relatives.'

'Or friends.'

'They didn't want friends,' Annie said. 'I tried talking to them over the years, but they always snubbed me.'

'I mean, I would have sent a wreath if I'd known.'

They stayed talking, anxious for company on a morning when death had cast its shadow over their comfortable and more or less contented lives.

'Just think, Annie,' Valerie said soberly. 'One of these days, we'll be as old as the Travers'. Either that, or we'll be dead.'

Annie shivered. 'I'm not sure which I'd prefer.'

They decided to call on Mrs Travers that night and offer their condolences. After a while, Valerie went indoors. She'd bought a new cookery book and wanted to make something nice for Kevin's tea.

The Cunninghams rarely rowed these days. They had sown their wild oats early and emerged unscathed, so Valerie claimed. Years ago, Kevin had confessed to an affair. 'It was when I was pregnant with Tracy,' she confided. 'He felt weighed down by the responsibility. It made him feel young again.' He refused to name the woman, said it was someone Valerie didn't know. 'I was so hopping mad, I had an affair myself with this nauseating chap from the TV rental shop. Kevin blew his top when he found out. But everything's all right now,' she added complacently. 'In fact, our marriage is stronger after all the ups and downs.'

When Valerie had gone, Annie sat on the patio and watched the children play. Sara was idly pushing herself to and fro on the swing Lauri had recently made, and Daniel was sitting in the plastic paddling pool playing with a blow-up boat, a bit half-heartedly, she thought. She hoped it was the heat and he wasn't coming down with something.

There'd been no ups and downs in the Menins' marriage, nothing to make it stronger. There was no way she could bring herself to be unfaithful to Lauri. It would show on her face, and she'd give the game away if she had to tell lies. She was no good at lies, apart from little white ones. Anyroad, not a single man had made anything remotely like a pass since she got married, so who would she have an affair with?

How could it be, she wondered, that you could love someone as thoroughly as she loved Lauri, yet be so . . . Annie searched in her mind for how she felt; not exactly fed up, not exactly bored, not really unhappy, maybe a bit of all these things. Last year, the Cunninghams had dumped their progeny on Valerie's mother and gone on holiday to Paris. Next month, they were off to Spain, this time taking the children with them. Other families in the close took holidays.

But when the children broke up last month and she suggested the Menins went away, Lauri protested they couldn't afford it. 'It could cost hundreds, love, and you know work's been dropping off.'

This was true. Inflation was soaring upwards in a dizzy spiral. With prices rising, people were reluctant to buy a new house and building firms were closing. Lauri had been working shorter and shorter hours.

'We could hire a tent and go camping,' she suggested hopefully. 'The Shepherds in number two go camping every year to this lovely site in North Wales. It wouldn't cost much more than staying at home.'

According to Connie Shepherd, it was really back to nature. The site was on a farm with only half a dozen tents. First thing each morning, they would cross the wet fields to buy fresh milk and eggs from the farmhouse. On fine days, they ate outdoors. The children loved exploring the Welsh woods and valleys, playing in streams and catching tadpoles.

'What happens when it's raining?' Lauri asked.

'You can still go walking in the rain.' Annie lifted her head and could almost feel the clean, invigorating rain falling on her face. 'Oh, it would be lovely! Sara and Daniel would have the time of their lives.'

'Quite honestly, love, it's not my cup of tea. When I'm off, we can go to New Brighton or Southport for the day, as we've always done.'

She couldn't very well put her foot down. You couldn't *force* someone to take a holiday they didn't want. She said, 'When Daniel starts school a year from now, I'll look for a part-time job. Then we can have a proper holiday.'

He shook his head emphatically. 'I don't want you working, Annie. You've enough to do, what with the house and the children.'

'*I'm* the one to judge what I can and can't do, Lauri,' she said sharply. 'I'm quite capable of doing a part-time job and looking after things. It won't inconvenience you at all.'

'I wasn't thinking of myself, love. I just don't want you taking on too much.' His voice was pleasant. He never lost his temper.

But Annie knew he was thinking solely of himself. There was nothing vindictive about it, not like with Eric. Without realising it, he wanted his wife to be dependent on him. Maybe it was why he'd refused to let her learn to drive, though when she threatened to use the housekeeping for lessons, he'd agreed. She was down to take the test in December.

She said no more, though was inwardly simmering, when Lauri redeemed himself completely. 'I've been thinking, why don't you go to London for a weekend with Marie?' he said. 'You haven't been since we got married and it's ages since you've seen her.'

'You mean, by meself?' Annie gasped.

'Well, it wouldn't be much good with the children! I can manage them on my own for a few days. Dot will lend a hand if necessary.'

'Oh, Lauri!' She didn't throw herself into his arms as she would have done once, because of the invisible barrier that had been erected. 'Oh, Lauri,' she said again, 'that would be the gear.'

From the Travers' garden, the sound of clippers could be heard.

She's back! God, she must feel terrible!

But Mrs Travers was dry-eyed when the women called that night to express their sympathy. She didn't even ask them in.

'Thank you,' she said coldly. Her parchment-coloured face was a cobweb of deeply etched wrinkles. Through the door, an umbrella stand made from an elephant's foot could be seen, and there were ugly wooden masks on the wall. She closed the door in their faces.

'Well, what do you make of that!' Valerie remarked indignantly.

'I don't know,' Annie said slowly. 'I really don't know.'

A week later, Chris Andrews called. He still taught at Grenville Lucas, and Annie found it incredible that she'd once regarded him as old. At thirty-four, he was only a few years older than herself. Lottie had left him the previous year, and for a while he was devastated, but pulled himself together with a vengeance. He lost weight, had contact lenses fitted and grew a pigtail – Annie showed him how to plait it. He wore flared trousers, embroidered waistcoats and Indian shirts. The current fashion of platform soles added to his height. The transformation was amply rewarded when a procession of glamorous young women started to descend upon his house, some quite brazenly staying the night.

'If Lottie could see you now, she'd be back like a shot,' Annie told him admiringly, but Chris said he didn't want her.

He hadn't come on a social visit. His house adjoined the Travers' and there'd been no sound, nothing, for the past two days. He'd knocked and there'd been no reply, but even when the old man was alive, the Travers' had not always answered. He wanted to know if Annie had seen Mrs Travers in the garden.

'You can't see much for the trees, but now I think about it, I haven't heard her, either.' Annie panicked. 'I hope she's all right.'

'Why don't you call the police?' Lauri suggested.

'I'll take a look around first.'

Lauri went with him. He told Annie afterwards that they looked through the windows and the letterbox, but could see nothing, so went round the back. Mrs Travers was sitting upright on a rustic bench in the garden. She had a pruner in one hand and a single red rose in the other. According to the doctor, she had been dead for two days.

An ambulance came and the body was removed. Nothing was heard about a funeral. Later, a van arrived and removed the foreign-looking furniture and a 'For Sale' sign went up. Rumour had it the Travers' had left their money to an orphanage in India.

The house was sold almost immediately to a middle-aged couple, the Barclays, from Smithdown Road. They had three teenage children, and the whole family spoke with a pronounced Liverpool accent and weren't the sort of people usually found in Heather Close. Sid Barclay ran a fruit and veg stall in various markets; Great Homer Street, Ormskirk and Birkenhead. His wife, Vera, was never seen without a cigarette hanging from her mouth. Their car, the latest Ford Granada, went in the garage, and a big shabby van was left on the drive for the whole world to see.

The first thing the Barclays did was to remove the hedge, lop the trees, and clear most of the plants out of the back garden so they could lay a lawn.

Soon, there was no indication the Travers' had ever lived there. Indeed, as far as anyone knew, there was no indication that the Travers' had ever lived at all.

'I don't know why you find it depressing,' said Sylvia. 'They probably led a gloriously exotic life in India. Think of the clothes they used to wear in those days; the women in pure silk, dripping lace and precious stones, the men in military uniforms, and everywhere smelling of spices and musky perfume. I bet she had an affair with an army colonel who drank champagne from her slipper and Mr Travers shot him to redeem his honour. Imagine white-clad servants with dark handsome faces oozing sex appeal, fanning them with bamboo leaves as they lay naked and perspiring sensuously in their net-covered beds.'

'Wow!' said Annie. 'And here's me thinking they were just a lonely old couple who died within a few days of each other.'

'They'll have lived on their memories, Annie. I'd like to think *my* husband would die quickly because he couldn't live without me. Eric's more likely to laugh uproariously and get married again within a week.'

'Are things no better?'

'Things will never get better. We had our nastiest row ever last night. I think he might have killed me if his mother hadn't turned up. It was my fault. He told me I wasn't a whole woman because I couldn't become a mother, so I said he wasn't man enough to father a child.'

'Why is that your fault? It sounds childish, but *he* started it.'

It was Monday, and Sylvia was following Annie around upstairs as she stripped the beds; dirty sheets and pillowcases were heaped on the landing ready for the wash. The children had returned to school and playgroup the week before.

'I know, but men can't stand slights on their sexual prowess. Tell them they've got BO, squinty eyes or warts on their bottom, and they don't give a damn, but insult their manhood, and they're likely to explode. Wouldn't Lauri?'

'I've no idea, Syl. I wouldn't dream of insulting his manhood.'

Annie went into the main bedroom and pulled the clothes off the double bed where, apart from when she had been in the maternity hospital, she'd spent every night with Lauri for the last eight – nearly nine – years. 'I wouldn't mind getting those duvet things,' she said. 'They're so much more convenient – you could make the bed in a jiffy.'

Sylvia said, 'You never talk about sex, do you, Annie?'

'I suppose it seems rather private.'

'I tell you everything that happens between Eric and me.'

'That's your choice,' Annie said primly. 'You tell me because you want to, not because I've asked.'

'You can be a proper Miss Goody Two-Shoes sometimes, Annie Menin.' Sylvia sat down at the dressing table, opened Annie's jewellery box and began to try on earrings.

'Our Marie used to call me that.' One occasion came back in a sharp memory; their dark bedroom on Christmas Eve after seeing her sister in the Grand pretending to be grown up when she was only thirteen.

She forgot the beds and opened the wardrobe door. 'What shall I take to wear in London? I'm going on Friday.' One of the women Marie shared a house with would be away and Annie could have her room.

'Don't ask me. I wouldn't be seen dead in anything you own.'

'Thanks very much,' Annie said tartly. She sorted through her frocks. They did seem rather drab.

'Hey, here's that orchid pendant I bought you in George Henry Lee's all those years ago. Poor little thing, it's all tarnished.'

'It was only nine and eleven.'

'What happened to the rose you bought your mother?'

'I've no idea. Perhaps it was left on when she was buried. She always wore it.' Annie abruptly sat down on the bed.

'I'm sorry, Annie.' Sylvia was instantly contrite. 'That was tactless. As you've nearly finished, shall I make us a cup of coffee?'

'Please.' Annie shuddered away the picture of Mam lying in her coffin wearing the little pink rose.

Sylvia sang at the top of her voice as she ran downstairs. Her relationship with Eric was a mixture of tragedy, comedy and farce, but she was deter-mined to keep her spirits up. 'I won't let him turn me into a victim. If I become a victim, I'm lost. Anyway, everything will be over soon. Either he'll murder me, or I'll murder him.'

It was like a film, Annie thought. Trust Sylvia to have a marriage that was like a highly dramatic film. She shook the cases off her pillow, then picked up Lauri's to do the same. There were two hairs on his, rich brown and wavy. She removed them, then sat staring at the hairs, held between the thumb and first finger of her right hand.

No, she never talked about sex. There wasn't much to talk about. Lately, they made love less and less, and then it was not exactly a chore, but just something she put up with. There must be more to it than she knew. Sometimes, with Lauri asleep beside her, she could hear little desperate, delighted cries coming from the Cunninghams' bedroom. Nothing she'd experienced had made her want to cry out loud like that.

'There's no real *intimacy* between us,' she whispered. 'I don't mean sex, just intimacy.'

Valerie used a cap as birth control. Once, she told Annie laughingly, she'd been unable to get the cap out that morning. 'Kevin had to get it out for me. He had a terrible job.'

Annie had flushed red with embarrassment. She could never, *never* have asked Lauri to do such a thing. Never!

'Coffee's ready, Annie.'

'Coming.' She hastily collected the sheets and pillowcases together and carried them downstairs.

On Friday, Fred Quillen arrived in the van. Lauri was about to leave, when he did one of the endearing things that made her love him so much.

'Have a nice time in London, love.' He kissed her cheek and put some-thing in her hand. 'It'll be your birthday soon. Buy yourself some new clothes while you're there. Don't worry about the children. Dot and me will manage between us.'

After he'd gone, Annie looked down to see what she'd been given. Twenty-five pounds!

'Oh!' She opened the door. He was just climbing into the van, looking rather stooped and dejected she thought. 'Lauri!' She ran down the path and threw her arms around his neck. 'I'll miss you,' she cried.

He patted her on the back. 'I'll miss you, love. We all will.'

'Perhaps I shouldn't go!'

'Don't be silly.' She was pleased to see the twinkle back in his eyes. 'You deserve a break. It'll do you good.'

'You're definitely coming back, aren't you, Mummy?' Sara asked gravely when Annie left her at the school gates.

'Sweetheart, as if I'd ever leave my little girl!'

Daniel seemed unconcerned that his mother was going away. Annie told the playgroup leader his auntie would collect him at mid-day. The woman looked dismayed. On the few occasions Dot had done this before, she was apt to arrive early and tell them how to run things.

5

If Liverpool had ceased to be the place where everything happened, then London had taken over. London was the swinging city, and the very air seemed to buzz with excitement. Annie could feel it the minute she stepped off the train at Euston Station and saw a pretty girl wearing flared brocade trousers, a tight maroon velvet jacket and a big velvet hat covered with cabbage roses. She felt over-conscious of her own neat navy-blue frock and white cardigan, and wished she'd brought her red mini dress, but always felt uncomfortable showing too much leg.

'Hallo, sis,' said the girl, and gave Annie an enormous hug.

'Marie! Oh. I didn't recognise you. You look so young and so . . . so way-out! You look terrific – and you've had your ears pierced!' Black stones dangled from Marie's ears. 'I've always wanted me ears pierced.'

'You don't look so bad yourself. You'd never guess you were an old married woman with two children.'

The sisters hadn't met for nearly five years. Sometimes, Annie worried they might never meet again, that Marie was one of those people who didn't need a family. It was a waste of time telephoning: Marie was never there and whoever answered the communal phone either didn't pass on the messages, or Marie ignored them, just as she ignored her sister's letters. It had taken a telegram to persuade her to ring up and arrange the weekend.

She linked Annie's arm. 'Let's go for a coffee.'

Annie was about to enter the station café, but Marie steered her outside. 'There's a nice little place along here.'

The coffee bar was in a dark basement, surprisingly full for the middle of the afternoon. They found an empty table next to two men playing chess. After ordering two cappuccinos, Marie said eagerly, 'How is everyone?'

'I've brought some photos,' Annie said shyly. 'We took most of them at Daniel's fourth birthday party in July. Just look at Sara. She'll be six next week. She's dead slim, like you, but I think she's going to be tall. She's got my eyes and almost my hair. And this is Daniel.'

'Shit, Annie! He's growing to look just like . . .' Marie bit her lip.

'I know, he's the image of our mam. No-one's noticed except me, not even Auntie Dot. I wondered if you'd see it.' The similarity was most marked when Daniel was asleep.

'He's incredibly good-looking, but then so was our mother.' Marie sighed. 'Lauri looks well. Who's this?'

'That's Valerie from next door with her children.'

'She's the one whose husband made a pass at me at that party!'

'Kevin. Did he really?'

'Jaysus, Dot looks old. Her hair's completely white.'

'She'll be sixty next year. She's been a bit down lately, all her lads are married except Joe, the littlest, and he's joined the Paras. There's only her and Uncle Bert left. He's retiring at Christmas.'

'I can't imagine Dot being down,' Marie smiled.

'She's already planning a huge do next August on her birthday. Uncle Bert's the same old Uncle Bert. He never seems to change. His hair's a bit thinner, that's all.'

'He lives in Dot's shadow, but he's like the Rock of Ages, Uncle Bert. Dot would be lost without him.'

'I think she realises that.'

A man on the next table shouted, 'Checkmate'. Marie sighed as she put the photos away. 'I'm missing everything, aren't I? Particularly Sara and Daniel growing up.'

'You don't have to, sis. Sara's making her First Holy Communion next month. Why don't you come? There's always room for you with us.'

'I know, sis, it's just that it's all so frenetic here. I hardly think about Liverpool most of the time.'

Annie felt hurt. Her sister was always at the back of her mind.

'I'm terrified of leaving for even a short while in case something comes up, in case my agent rings to say I've got a part or there's an audition that day, and if I'm not here, I'll miss out. Even hanging round in pubs, you hear useful gossip.'

'Not much has come up so far, has it, Marie?' Annie said gently. It was a decade since her sister had left Liverpool, and stardom was no nearer now than it was then.

'I didn't expect overnight success,' Marie said defensively, though Annie distinctly remembered she had. 'Don't forget *The Forsyte Saga*.'

Everyone at home had watched *The Forsyte Saga* to see Annie Menin's sister play a maid. Marie had done the non-speaking part adequately, but it wasn't exactly a platform for displaying her acting talent. Annie sometimes wondered if Marie *had* talent. Perhaps she was flogging a dead horse and would be better off getting married or pursuing a career with more chance of success.

Marie had guessed her chain of thought. 'I'll never give up you know, sis.' Her small pointed chin jutted out stubbornly in a way Annie remembered well. It used to drive the nuns wild when she was chastised for some very real misdemeanour. 'I'm not doing so bad. A repertory company in Portsmouth want me next spring, and I've another bloody pantomime at Christmas. When I'm "resting", I do office work. Did I tell you I'd learned to type?'

'Yes, years ago.'

'I'm not very good, not like you.' She pulled a face.

Annie squeezed her sister's hand. 'Never mind, sis. I've a feeling in me bones you'll take the world by storm one day.' Inwardly, though, she was worried her sister was wasting her life. Marie had her eyes set on a far distant star, possibly too distant. It wasn't worth the effort.

She had the same thought when she saw where her sister lived: 'Is it worth it?' Her heart sank when she entered the dark Victorian terraced house in Brixton. The kitchen had an old-fashioned sink which was badly chipped and without a plug, and the grubby floor had several tiles missing. There were no curtains on the window. It was a million times worse than the flat in Upper Parliament Street.

Marie's room was at the back, overlooking the yard. The situation of the window and the dismal view were exactly the same as the room they'd shared in Orlando Street, but there the similarity ended. The walls could hardly be seen for theatre posters, and a brightly checked blanket covered the single bed on which Annie sat, as there was only one chair.

'Welcome to my happy home,' cried Marie. She removed her hat. Her hair was a cloudy mass of little curls and waves.

'You've had a perm!' Annie wasn't sure if she altogether liked it.

'What d'you think?' Marie pirouetted. 'I hope you're impressed. It cost twenty quid in Knightsbridge.'

'Twenty quid, for a perm!'

'You could do with spending a few bob on your own hair. I don't know how you can stand having it always the same.'

Annie glanced at herself in the dressing-table mirror. The top was littered with pots of different shades of foundation, eye-shadow and lipsticks. 'I've been meaning to have it cut short for years.'

'Shall I cut it for you? I'm quite good at cutting hair.'

'I'm not sure. What's this?' Annie leaned over and poked her finger in a bright red pot. It looked too greasy for rouge.

'It's lipstick. You put it on with a brush.'

'Really! Can I try some?'

'If you let me cut your hair. Come on, sis,' Marie said coaxingly.

'Oh, I dunno. I've only been here five minutes.'

'What does that matter!' Marie picked a pair of scissors up off the dressing table and approached her sister, clicking them threateningly.

Because she was enjoying them being together and it was so much like old times, Annie gave in. 'Don't be too ruthless. I only want a trim.'

'But then you'll look no different than before.' Before Annie could say another word, Marie seized a lock of hair and snipped the lot off.

'Marie!'

'Shush. Don't look in the mirror. Close your eyes till I've done.'

Annie closed her eyes and gritted her teeth and prayed she wouldn't look a sight.

'You can look now,' Marie said after what seemed like an age.

'Jaysus! I look like Topsy.' Her hair was in tiny curls all over her head. It was a shock at first, but the more she stared, the more she liked it. It made her look rather sophisticated.

'You've got a lovely long neck, sis.' Marie stroked her sister's neck then left her hands on her shoulders. They stared at each other in the mirror. Marie rested her chin on Annie's curls. 'This is like old times. I almost feel like coming back to Liverpool with you.'

'Then why don't you?'

Marie turned away. 'I can't, sis. I can't ever. Come on, wash your hair and it will look even better.'

They had dinner in an inexpensive restaurant off the King's Road. As soon as they were back, Annie phoned home. Dot informed her that yes, the children were still alive, Annie wasn't to worry about a single thing, and if anything happened they would call her instantly, and of course she knew Annie would come home like a shot if it did.

Annie went to bed, feeling peculiar, in a room belonging to an actress called Shelley Montpelier whose real name was Brenda Smith. There was a life-size head and shoulders photograph of Shelley/Brenda on the dressing table. After a while, she had to get out of bed and turn the photo round because it felt as if Shelley/Brenda was watching the stranger in her bed with her slightly pop eyes.

Saturday was sunny and warm. Straight after breakfast, the sisters went to Carnaby Street, bustling with brisk activity, the very hub of the swinging city, though not nearly as exciting as the Cavern used to be. It was too commercial. There were too many people on the make rather than just enjoying themselves, and the clothes were expensive.

After a hamburger lunch, they caught the tube to Camden Market, where Annie bought a full-length skirt in flowered corduroy, and a skinny ribbed jumper which matched the green leaves perfectly. Marie insisted she must have a pair of clunky-heeled sandals because ordinary shoes would look silly with a long skirt, after which Annie only had five pounds left of the twenty-five. She bought Sara a rag doll and a brightly painted soldier wearing a real busby for Daniel.

She was wondering what to get for Lauri, all she could think of was a tie, when she found herself drawn towards a stall glittering with cheap jewellery. Unfortunately, the earrings were for pierced ears.

Marie pointed to a notice. EAR PIERCING, INCLUDING GOLD HOOPS – £2. 'How about it, sis? It can be your birthday present from me. I've a feeling I completely forgot about it last year.'

'All right,' said Annie recklessly. A few minutes later she was sitting on the sunny pavement of a strange street in Camden having her ears pierced by a bearded man with arms a mass of colourful tattoos.

They went to a pub for a drink so she could recover. 'Sylvia will be dead envious. It's not often I do things before she does. It's not just my ears, she hasn't got a long skirt, either.'

'How is the high and mighty Sylvia Delgado?' Marie asked acidly.

'Not so high and mighty at the moment.' Annie briefly described the situation between Sylvia and Eric. 'She puts on a brave face, but she's desperately unhappy.'

Marie pursed her lips. 'I'm sorry. I never liked her, though I think it was more a case of her not liking me. I'll never forget the way she completely ignored me when Bruno drove us to that clinic in Southport.'

The final stall was heaped higgledy-piggledy with dusty books. Annie passed by without a glance. 'I'll get a tie for Lauri somewhere else.'

'Just a minute.' Marie picked up a tatty paperback. 'Lauri collects these. I noticed them in your bookcase. They were published by the Left Wing Bookclub before the war. Has he got this one?'

The title meant nothing to Annie. 'I don't think so.'

'I bet Lauri would prefer this to a tie. How much is it?'

The old man behind the stall shrugged. 'A tanner.'

'Fancy you remembering such a thing,' Annie said as she paid. It seemed rather mean to have spent so much on herself and a mere sixpence on her husband, though as Marie said, it was the thought that counted.

Wearing her new clothes, it was a very different Annie Menin who stared back from the full-length mirror in Shelley Montpelier's room. The long skirt made her appear taller, slimmer, and it was true she had quite a nice neck which she'd never really noticed before. Her ears hurt like mad, but the pain was worth it because the gold hoops made her look like a gypsy. She'd always liked to be fashionable in the days when she was single and it seemed to matter more than when you were a housewife, but now she looked – what was the word Sylvia used? – *outré*!

Annie took a final satisfied glance in the mirror before going to show her sister. Marie said she looked terrific, and on no account to take the clothes off as she could wear them for the theatre that night.

There was something familiar about the man playing the villain. He had smooth black hair and a swarthy complexion, but it was his walk that convinced Annie she'd seen him before, and something about his voice.

The play was a highly enjoyable thriller and she wondered how Marie could have afforded such good seats, right at the front. In the interval, she checked the programme to see if the villain was someone she'd seen on television.

'Clive Hoskins!' she exclaimed. 'Why didn't you tell me?'

'I wondered if you'd recognise him,' Marie said smugly. 'Isn't he brilliant? He did his best to get me the part of Constance, but the producer wanted someone older. Clive got us the tickets for free.'

When the play was over, they went backstage and found Clive in his dressing room, in the process of wiping off the dark make-up. He beamed when he saw Marie. 'Hallo, darling. As soon as I've got this muck-up off, I'll give you and your gorgeous sister a nice big kiss.'

He asked after Lauri and insisted on seeing the photos of the children. Sara was going to be a very beautiful young lady. 'And is this the chap who was giving you so much trouble when I stayed? You were expecting him, remember?'

Along with several other members of the cast, they went to a club in Soho, where Annie drank only a single glass of wine, but innocently took a puff on a big fat cigarette which was being handed round, mainly because everyone else was doing it. Her head instantly left her body and still hadn't returned when it was time to leave. For some reason, Clive Hoskins was in tears and refused to be parted from Marie. They took a taxi back to Brixton and between them helped Clive indoors.

'Poor pet,' Marie crooned as they laid him on the bed. 'He's just been jilted.' She kissed his cheek. 'I love him so much.'

'Isn't that a waste of time?' said Annie. 'Being in love with him, I mean.' In the taxi, her head had returned to its proper place, but everywhere looked slightly askew. Marie had never mentioned a man in her life. Perhaps, as well as wasting herself on a futile career, she was wasting her affections on a futile relationship with a homosexual.

'I'm not *in* love with him, Annie. I said I loved him, which is a different thing.' She looked down at the sleeping figure. 'Me and Clive cling to each other like creatures drowning in this cruel world.'

'I see,' said Annie, though she didn't see at all. 'I think I'll make a cup of tea and go to bed. Do you want one?'

Marie had already started to remove her clothes. 'No thanks.'

'Would you like to sleep with me? We could sleep top to tail, the way we used to do when we were little.'

'It's all right, sis. I'll cuddle up beside Clive.'

Annie was careful only to use things out of the sparsely stocked wall cupboard marked, 'Marie', when she made the tea. There was no fridge, the milk was sour and little shreds of white floated to the mug's surface, but she didn't care. The other two cupboards were marked 'Shelley' and 'Tiffany'. Tiffany lived in the downstairs room and worked in a nightclub. There'd been no sign of her as yet.

She sat up in bed feeling exceptionally relaxed, staring at Shelley/Brenda's carefully posed portrait which she'd turned round again that morning. The face seemed almost real, almost alive. A street lamp shone through the thin curtains and everything in the room was unnaturally clear, the shadows sharply defined. A long woollen dressing gown hung behind the door like a headless monk.

It seemed odd, wearing earrings in bed, but the man had said to leave them in for six weeks and just turn the rings round from time to time. Her ears throbbed and her heels smarted where the strap of her new sandals had rubbed, yet neither seemed all that unpleasant, almost as if it was happening to someone else.

She'd actually smoked a drugged cigarette! Although she hadn't realised it at the time, she was quite glad she'd done it. Wait till she told Sylvia! It made her feel very much part of swinging London. How strange to think that on the nights she and Lauri were staidly watching television or fast asleep in bed, Marie was flitting round Soho smoking cannabis or whatever it was called. And what a peculiar set-up with Clive – how could you love a man, yet not be in love?

The front door opened and voices whispered in the hall, one male. Someone used the bathroom, then all was silence. An occasional car drove by, briefly illuminating the room with a flash of yellow light.

Annie sighed and wondered if Sara and Daniel were missing her, just as another car went by, and as the headlights swept the room, everything became clear. *She wasn't in love with Lauri, but she loved him!* It had been so right from the start. Dot's words after her twenty-first came back distinctly. 'Ken was never much of a dad, was he? You're looking for a father figure and Lauri Menin fits the bill perfectly.'

'Oh, God!' She put the mug on the bedside table and leaned forward with her arms around her knees.

After all those years of responsibility, how nice to be treated like a child and let Lauri take all the decisions. But she'd grown up without him realising, without realising herself, and he resented her becoming independent, just as she resented not being treated as an adult. It explained all those confused, mixed-up emotions she'd had recently.

Her head was spinning, but it had been an exhausting day and she quickly fell asleep. When she woke, her mind was as clear as crystal. It was early, not yet light outside. Everywhere was very quiet and she missed the sound of birdsong, usually the first thing heard in Heather Close. A radio was switched on next door and she could hear hymns and remembered it was Sunday.

She would never know what she'd missed by not falling in love. 'I've made me bed, and I'll have to lie on it.' She had the children, and it wasn't an uncomfortable bed to spend the rest of your life on.

Clive Hoskins was still asleep when they left for Mass at Westminster Cathedral – Marie admitted she rarely went nowadays. Afterwards, they lunched in Lyons Corner House then window-shopped, arm in arm, in the nearly deserted West End. The weather had changed dramatically and it was dull and overcast. A sharp breeze whipped the air.

'Have you enjoyed yourself?' Marie asked as they tore themselves away from Liberty's window.

'I've had a lovely time. What I like most is just being with you. Sometimes, I worry you've forgotten me.'

Marie laughed. 'Sis! You're like an arm or a leg. I don't think about them all the time, but I'd be devastated if I didn't have them.'

'It's funny,' Annie said thoughtfully, 'I've got a family, yet I miss you more than you do me. You've got no-one except Clive.'

'Ah, but I've got an obsession – acting. Everything pales into insignificance beside that.'

'That time you were pregnant, you wanted a baby to love.'

'That was then, sis, this is now.'

They walked in silence for a while. 'I want to tell you something I've never told another soul, not even Clive.' Marie released her arm and began to walk ahead so her face was hidden behind the velvet hat. 'I was offered a big part in a play once. It was to go on in the West End, but the leading man died and it came to nothing. I was ten weeks pregnant at the time. I had an abortion – the law's changed, it's legal now.'

'Oh, Marie!' Annie breathed.

Marie didn't turn around. It was as if she were talking to herself. 'When I first realised, y'know, I thought of giving up acting, perhaps coming back to

Liverpool. Till then, I was getting nowhere fast. Then came the play and I was presented with two choices. The baby didn't stand a chance.'

A bus trundled along Regent Street and Annie wondered if she should have bought Daniel a bus instead of a soldier. He loved buses. 'What about the father?' she asked.

Marie shrugged her shoulders carelessly. 'Roger? Oh, he never knew.'

'Was he an actor?'

'He *is* an actor. He was in *The Avengers* the other week, playing a good guy for a change.' She paused outside a shop which sold Indian ware. 'I quite like that carved box with mosaic round the edge.'

'Did you feel upset afterwards, like you did the other time?' Marie's face was reflected in the window. She looked quite calm, yet . . .

'It didn't affect me a bit.' Marie's voice was brittle. 'I had to have that part, you see. Even when it turned out to have been a waste of time, I didn't care. It had made me realise what my priorities were. Kids weren't on the agenda, acting was.'

'Marie!' Annie touched her sister gently on the shoulder.

'Ah, but I haven't forgotten the other, my little boy.' Marie spun round. Her eyes were unnaturally bright and Annie was shocked by the naked misery there. 'He'd be fourteen, a year older than I was then. If I try hard, I can see him. I've watched him grow up over the years. He's as tall as me and, for some reason, he's got straight fair hair and blue eyes.' Her face twisted bitterly. 'Oh, Annie, sometimes I don't half hate our mam and dad.'

A man and woman passed, tourists, with cameras slung around their necks. They stared curiously at Marie's impassioned face.

'Come on, luv.' Annie linked her arm. 'Let's have a cup of tea.' She felt she understood her sister better. Acting wasn't an obsession, but an escape from the past.

That night was Annie's last in London. Marie seemed to have recovered from her outburst and they went to a party in someone's attic. Annie might have enjoyed herself had she been able to stop thinking about her husband and her sister. There was little she could do about Marie, but she would look upon Lauri differently when she got home. Now she knew where she stood, perhaps they could get off to a fresh start.

It was dreadful, the thought of leaving Marie. Just as Annie was fastening her suitcase next morning, the phone rang.

'It's for you, Marie,' someone called, presumably Tiffany.

Annie wasn't sure whether to cringe or smile when she heard Marie's voice downstairs. It was loud, pretentious, false. 'Fantastic, darling,' she gushed, 'I'll be there in an hour.'

'Sorry, sis, I won't be able to come to Euston with you,' she said breathlessly when she returned, her face radiant. 'That was my agent. I went for an audition last week and they want to see me again.'

'That's all right, luv.'

Marie scarcely heard. She stared at herself in the mirror. 'I'd better get changed and do something with my hair.'

'I'll be off or I'll miss me train.' Annie felt in the way. Perhaps this was the real Marie, and the chummy, companionable sister was false.

'Right.' Marie said abstractedly. 'Oh, I'll come downstairs and see you off. Can you remember the way to the tube?'

'Yes, just round the corner.'

'Sorry about this, but it's an opportunity I can't miss.'

'I'm glad your agent called before we'd left,' Annie said politely. 'I hope you get the part.'

'So do I. Oh, so do I.'

They embraced briefly on the step. Annie hadn't taken a step when the door closed. She was about to turn the corner of the cheerless street, feeling indescribably sad, when she heard her name called. 'Annie! Annie!' There was a hint of desperation in the sound.

She turned. Marie was standing outside the house blowing kisses with both hands. She looked as if she were crying. 'Goodbye, sis. Goodbye.'

Annie backed around the corner blowing kisses in return.

Heather Close looked peaceful in the late September sunshine, and the yellow door of number seven shone welcomingly at the end. Annie sighed with relief. She'd enjoyed the short holiday, but it was good to be home.

Daniel had spied her from the window. He came running out, followed by Auntie Dot. 'We were just about to collect Sara. Oh, you've had your hair cut! It looks nice. I always said you'd suit it short, didn't I?'

Annie couldn't recall a single time, but readily agreed. 'I've had me ears pierced, too,' she said proudly. She scooped her son up in her arms. 'Did you miss Mummy, sweetheart?'

'A bit,' Daniel conceded, twisting her nose.

'I've just put the kettle on, least I think I have. You can never tell with them electric ones.' Dot looked slightly moidered. 'There's time for a quick cuppa and you can catch up on the news.'

'What news?' She quickly learned that in the space of four days Sara had lost a tooth, Lauri had cut his finger sharpening the lawnmower and had to get it stitched at the hospital, and Sylvia had left Eric and was living with Bruno at the Grand.

Sara's face lit up when she saw her mother waiting at the school gate. 'I missed you, Mummy,' she said gravely. 'Please don't go away again.'

'Next time you can come with me,' Annie promised. It meant visits to Soho clubs would be out, but that wouldn't be such a bad thing.

When Lauri came home, she made a big fuss of him. The first finger of his left hand was heavily bandaged.

'You should have taken a few days off,' she cried.

'We can't afford it, Annie.'

She thought he didn't seem at all well. His cheeks looked heavy and grey and he moved slowly, as if it was an effort. 'I think you should have an early night,' she insisted. 'Perhaps you're run down.' She felt guilty. It was he who should have had a holiday, not her. 'I'll get you a tonic from the chemist tomorrow.'

'I might turn in a bit sooner than usual.' He went upstairs at half nine and Annie took him up a cup of cocoa. He was sitting up in bed reading the book she'd bought and appeared slightly better.

'Your hair looks nice,' he said. 'And you suit the earrings.'

Annie sat on the bed. 'You always said you preferred it long.'

'I did, but as you reminded me, it's *your* hair.'

She felt guilty again, but only a little, for going against his wishes. 'So it is,' she said.

Their eyes met, and Annie saw fear in his. He'd always been able to read her mind. Perhaps he sensed their roles had changed.

She telephoned her sister to say she'd arrived safely home. Whoever answered, Tiffany, or possibly Shelley/Brenda was back, promised to pass the message on. If they did, Annie never heard. Marie didn't turn up for Sara's First Holy Communion in October.

Nor did she come when Auntie Dot threw the best party ever to celebrate her sixtieth birthday. As she was surrounded by her husband, her lads and their wives, her grandchildren, Dot said emotionally, 'I'm the luckiest woman in the world.'

'And I'm the luckiest man,' said Uncle Bert. Love for his flamboyant wife glowed as fresh in his eyes as the day they were married.

No-one allowed the fact that the Conservatives had won the recent General Election to ruin the great day, even though the new Prime Minister, Edward Heath, declared it was his intention to denationalise everything that moved and do something about the Trade Unions.

Annie received a little scribbled note to say her sister had a part in *Dr Who*, but no-one would recognise her because she played an alien and the make-up was really weird. Although reconciled to the fact that their paths had parted for ever, Annie couldn't help but wonder if there was *anything* that would fetch her sister back to Liverpool!

6

'Thirty!' Sylvia said gloomily. 'Thirty! It wouldn't feel so bad if my divorce hadn't come through the same day.'

Parliament must have had Sylvia and Eric Church in mind when they changed the law to allow divorce by mutual consent after two years' separation. The Decree Absolute had arrived that morning. Eric's family were horrified, but had to concede it was the only way out. If they stayed together, either Eric would kill Sylvia, or she would kill him, and divorce was more socially acceptable than murder.

'How does it feel?' Annie enquired.

'Being thirty or divorced?'

'I know how thirty feels, don't I?' It had been her own birthday the month before, and it hadn't exactly seemed a landmark, but things were different for her. 'I mean divorced.'

'Odd,' Sylvia said reflectively. 'Peculiar. Very sad.'

'If you'd had children it might have been all right.'

'I doubt it. We would have found something else to fight about, at least Eric would. He's a sadist. He likes hurting people. I feel sorry for that woman he's going to marry.' Eric was already sort of engaged to the daughter of a friend of the family.

'I think you've been dead brave,' Annie declared.

'Thanks,' Sylvia said briefly. 'I'm glad you were around.' She'd vowed never to fall in love again. She'd had enough of men to last a lifetime. 'Perhaps the worst thing is that the Beatles have broken up,' she said tragically. 'It's the end of a great era. There'll never be another decade like the sixties.' The Fab Four had gone their separate ways. When he wasn't studying mysticism with Paul McCartney and George Harrison in the Himalayas, John Lennon was in America with his new wife, Yoko Ono, making records of his own.

They were in Sylvia's bedroom in the Grand, still the same as when Annie had first come on that bitterly cold night when Ruby Livesey had pushed Sylvia into a holly bush. The two women were lost in youthful memories, until Sylvia said brightly. 'I won't be staying in Liverpool now that I'm a free woman again. I cramp Bruno's style. He's dying to screw that new barmaid.'

'Where will you go?' asked Annie.

'I might give London a try. There's more openings when it comes to work, and far more to do socially.'

Annie had suspected this would happen. There seemed little to keep a single woman of thirty in Liverpool. 'I'll miss you,' she sighed.

'It goes without saying I'll miss you too.' Sylvia rolled off the bed. 'Tell me seriously, Annie, do I *look* thirty?'

'You don't look a day over twenty-nine.' Annie stared at her friend's beautiful face. Sylvia looked no different from when she started at Grenville Lucas sixteen years ago.

'You're a great help.' Sylvia patted her cheeks worriedly. 'Say if I go like Cecy! She's beginning to resemble a wrinkled, dried-up prune.'

'You haven't changed, some people never do. Others grow old before your very eyes.'

'I hope I'm the first sort,' Sylvia said frantically. 'I hope I take after Bruno. He still rakes in the women at fifty-six.'

Annie supposed charming, flirtatious Bruno *must* have changed a bit since they first met, but she still nursed a secret yearning for him, with his dark laughing face. She thought about Lauri; he was one of the second sort. Of course, he wasn't changing before her eyes, that was ridiculous, but he was nothing like the man with the warm twinkling smile she'd met at Auntie Dot's. It wasn't just that he'd grown so bulky or his hair had thinned – after all, Uncle Bert no longer had the sandy halo she remembered – but Lauri's whole attitude had altered. He was always depressed, rarely smiling. He'd never been the same since he cut his finger on the lawnmower two years ago when she was in London. It was stupid to think someone's personality could alter because of a cut finger, but the finger had never regained its feeling. It remained numb, unbending. Then the numbness spread to the next finger, and the next, until Lauri could hardly move his left hand. Although he'd been to see a specialist and had a variety of different treatments, the hand remained the same, completely dead, yet the specialist could find nothing wrong.

There was a knock on the door and Bruno came in. He grinned at Annie. 'How much do I pay you to keep my daughter company?'

'I clocked off mentally at half past two.' She'd been working lunchtimes at the Grand since Daniel started school last year. Lauri had been totally opposed, but it was fortunate she'd gone ahead regardless, as her small earnings had helped to subsidise the housekeeping ever since. There'd been no holiday, as originally planned.

'I came to say Cecy's just telephoned,' Bruno said to Sylvia. 'As it's your birthday and my night off, she's invited us both to dinner. I promised to ring back. What shall I tell her?'

Sylvia pulled a face. 'Yes, I suppose, but fancy having nothing else to do on your thirtieth birthday than go to dinner with your parents!'

After several visits to the hospital over nearly a year, it was concluded the cause of Lauri's frozen hand was psychosomatic. Annie was with him in the specialist's office when the diagnosis was made.

'What does that mean?' she asked.

'It's all in the mind.' The specialist was a pleasant man, but rather distant, with a narrow white face and deep-set eyes.

'But I can't feel it,' Lauri said a touch impatiently. 'I can't bend my fingers. How on earth can it all be in my mind?'

'I'm afraid that is a mystery medical science has so far been unable to solve. Some people go blind or lose their power of speech for no apparent reason.'

Lauri's brow creased. 'You mean there's no cure?'

'The cure is within yourself. Only you can make your hand better.'

'Bloody ridiculous!' Lauri said when they were outside. He rarely swore. When they reached the Anglia, Annie said, 'Shall I drive?'

'Don't you trust me?' he snapped.

'Of course I do.' He managed to change the gears by pushing the lever with his wrist, though he couldn't use the handbrake. She was sorry she'd asked. She'd offered to help because he was upset, but he couldn't stand it when she drove. 'I don't want to be seen driven by a woman, even if she is my wife,' he had said soon after she'd passed her test.

As Annie made her way to school to collect the children, she recalled the journey back from the hospital. She kept trying to start a conversation, but Lauri merely answered with a grunt. It wasn't until they were going into the house, that he patted her arm and said, 'Sorry, love. I'm finding this business with my hand hard to take.'

That was the night Fred Quillen came, uninvited, and asked if he could speak to Lauri privately. Annie shooed Sara and Daniel into the garden and left the men in the lounge whilst she got on with the ironing. Fred didn't stay long. After about fifteen minutes, she heard the front door open and went to say goodbye. Fred was letting himself out, there was no sign of Lauri.

Puzzled, she went into the lounge. Lauri was sitting stock-still on the settee. His face was pale.

'What's the matter?' Intuition told her what the answer would be.

'They want me out of the co-op. They claim I'm not pulling my weight,' Lauri said dully.

'Oh, love!' Annie breathed. She felt as if her heart could easily split in two on his behalf. She sat down and laid her head on his shoulder. 'What are we going to do?'

She winced at the bitterness in his voice as he replied, 'They've given me a month to pull my socks up.'

But how could he? Lauri had always been the strongest and most conscientious of workers. She sensed how degraded he must feel. 'Why not tell Fred Quillen what to do with the co-op and find another job?'

Lauri looked at her as if she were mad. 'I'm fifty, Annie, and I've only got the use of one hand. What other job?'

The children came running in. Lauri reached for Sara. 'Come to Daddy, darling.' He adored his daughter. Sometimes, Annie wondered if Sara had taken her own place in Lauri's heart, to the detriment of boisterous Daniel who got on his father's nerves.

She ruffled Daniel's dark hair. 'Help me fetch the rest of the washing in, there's a good boy.'

Annie joined the mothers outside the school gates. Valerie Cunningham wasn't amongst them. As soon as Zachary started school, Valerie had taken a full-time job. Her children were what the newspapers referred to disparagingly as 'latchkey kids', though they spent the hours between school and their mother coming home at the Menins'.

It was a blowy November day and russet leaves danced across the playground. A bell went and suddenly the double doors flew open and children came bursting out like wild animals. Daniel was one of the first. He was a fine-looking boy, Annie thought tenderly, as her son raced another boy to the gate, a look of determination on his handsome face that reminded her of Marie. The shirt that had been clean on that morning was grubby and the buttons were undone, or possibly lost.

'Hi, Mum,' he grunted when he reached her.

'Hi, Daniel.' She chucked him playfully under the chin. It would have been more than her life was worth to kiss him in public.

Sara followed more sedately. Annie watched lovingly as she paused to catch a falling leaf. A slim, serious girl with gold blonde hair and light blue eyes, at eight years old, her head already came up to her mother's shoulder. 'I've lots of homework,' she said importantly. 'I shall go straight up to my room and get started.' Annie would have to make sure that neither Kelly nor Tracy invaded her room to play.

The Cunninghams gathered round. 'Have we got orange squash at home?' Gary demanded.

'Yes,' said Annie drily. They regarded number seven as home until their mother put in an appearance.

With the children settled in front of the television and Sara in her room, Annie began to make pastry for a steak and kidney pie. She used to feed her own two at four o'clock and she and Lauri would eat later, but since the advent of the Cunninghams, all four Menins ate late. Annie wasn't prepared to subsidise Valerie's wages by providing her children with a meal, and it didn't seem fair to feed just Sara and Daniel.

It must have been the conversation with Sylvia about people changing, but her mind kept going back to the day she'd gone to the hospital with Lauri and Fred Quillen had said he must pull his socks up.

The children had gone to bed and Lauri had still scarcely moved from the settee, when Annie said tentatively, 'Y'know, love, I could take a refresher course and get a job as a secretary. I wouldn't earn as much as you, but it would be enough to live on.'

'I don't understand,' said Lauri.

Annie could tell from the black look on his face that he understood only too well. She plunged deeper into the mire of his anger. It was important that she make the offer, then it was up to him. 'It's not a law that the man has to be the breadwinner. I'm perfectly willing . . .'

He broke in coldly. 'Do you think I would allow my wife to keep me?'

'I thought I'd mention it. It can be one of the options we discuss.'

'I don't intend to consider such an option, let alone discuss it.'

Annie was secretly relieved. The last thing she wanted was to return to secretarial work.

She said no more and neither did Lauri. He went to bed early with a curt 'Goodnight'. He was usually asleep by the time she went up. She tried to forget they hadn't made love since she'd returned from the weekend with Marie in London.

The 39 Steps with Robert Donat started on television. She'd been mad on Robert Donat for quite a while until she discovered he was dead. But good though the picture was, she was unable to concentrate. The specialist had said the matter of Lauri's hand was – she searched for the word – psychosomatic, all in the mind, and she was struck with the horrific thought, *'Perhaps it's all my fault.'*

It was essential she talk to someone; not Sylvia, who'd say tell Lauri to get stuffed. Tomorrow, she'd go and see Auntie Dot.

'I have never,' Dot scoffed, 'heard such a load of ould cobblers in me life. Lauri's hand's seized up just because you had your hair cut! Come off it, girl, talk sense.'

'You're exaggerating, Auntie,' Annie said stiffly. She was rather put out when Dot's face turned more and more incredulous as she came out with her tortured explanation for Lauri's hand. 'It's not just me hair. It's everything. I'm no longer the girl he married.'

'I should hope not,' Dot expostulated. 'You were only twenty-one. If Lauri didn't think you'd change, he needs his bumps feeling. People change all the time. It's only natural. What do you want me to say? Grow your hair long again like Samson and Lauri's hand will be all right?'

'I wish you wouldn't concentrate on me hair. I told you, he didn't like me learning to drive, either. And I don't automatically assume everything he says is right. I argue with him all the time – he can't stand it when I talk about politics . . .' Annie's voice faltered at the sight of Dot's outraged expression.

'In other words,' she said, 'he's not the lord of the manor any more! I've no time for these feminists who say men are crap, but women have a right to their own identity. Lauri doesn't *own* you. Be yourself, luv, and if he can't take it, that's his problem, not yours.'

'I thought, if I acted differently . . .'

'You're not to change a jot, Annie,' Dot said firmly. 'I think the whole thing's daft, but if it's true, your husband's not much of a man.'

She went into the kitchen to make a cup of tea. Annie sat in the same place from where she used to watch her aunt when the Harrisons had lived there, though the kitchen was very different now. Five years ago, the Gallaghers had bought the house off the landlord, and bamboo-patterned units lined the walls. Beside the freezer, a new door led to the former washhouse, now a bathroom and toilet.

Annie transferred her gaze to Dot's current pride and joy, the fireplace fitted last Christmas, along with a gas fire which glowed with imitation coals. Her aunt's taste was very different from her own, and she thought the wooden surround truly ghastly, with its two-tier mantelpiece, the top supported by brass pillars. She had to concede that the warm wood went well with the hessian wallpaper on the breastwork, which in turn toned beautifully with the coral-painted walls.

Dot came in with the tea. 'This business with Lauri's job, now that's something worth worrying about.' Her sharp nose twitched with pride. 'I wonder if our Mike's got a vacancy that would suit him.'

'Lauri's a carpenter, Auntie Dot. It's engineers and electricians that your Mike needs.'

Within the space of two and a half years, Mike's business had taken off and now employed eight people. The firm was still expanding and had recently taken over larger premises in Kirkby. They no longer dealt with vintage cars after getting several important long-term contracts from much larger firms. But Mike and Ray weren't satisfied. In the even longer term, the contracts offered no security; the firms, however big, might fold, cut back, take on staff of their own to do the work.

'It's a bit like singing someone else's songs, compared to singing your own,' Mike declared in reference to the group he and Ray had once belonged to. 'I always preferred our own.'

So they'd developed, of all things, a burglar alarm, much to Dot's dismay as she couldn't imagine anyone in their right mind sticking a burglar alarm outside their house. So far, only Mike and Ray worked on the prototype, but it would be ready for production and marketing soon when Michael Ray Security would be born. Glenda, Mike's wife, had prepared a brochure for the printers.

Dot was forced to concede her judgement of Glenda had been totally wrong. Glenda had turned out to be a wife in a million, working overtime to help get the business off the ground. Then she taught herself to type and did all the office work.

'Mike was talking the other day about taking on a salesman to go round with these alarm things,' Dot said. Her chest expanded with the magnitude of the fact she had a son who was an employer. 'Of course, he wouldn't be able to pay as much as Lauri's used to.'

'Mike'll want someone younger than Lauri.' Her husband was the opposite of her idea of a pushy salesman.

'I'll ring him later. I was going to, anyroad. Glenda, poor lamb, has been feeling a bit rough lately. I'd like to know how she is.'

It was Annie who answered the phone when Mike rang that night. 'How's Glenda?' she enquired.

Mike sounded worried. 'Not so well, Annie. She's tired all the time, which isn't a bit like her. I'm having a heck of a job persuading her to see the doctor.' He asked if he could speak to Lauri.

'What have you been saying to Dot?' Lauri demanded when the call finished. Annie had shut herself in the lounge so she wouldn't overhear.

'I'm not sure what you mean,' she said innocently.

'Did you tell her about me, about the co-op?'

'I think I did mention it this morning. Why?'

Lauri looked irritated. 'Mike's just offered me a job, that's why.'

'Doing what?'

'As a salesman.' He shook his head. 'I'd be no good at that sort of thing. What's more, I don't want charity.'

'Is that what you told him?' Annie asked sharply.

'I told him I'd think about it.'

'Honestly, Lauri,' she said, exasperated. 'Mike wouldn't offer a job out of charity. Anyroad, what's dole money if it's not charity?'

'He did say he'd interviewed a couple of chaps but they were too young, too brash,' Lauri conceded. 'He'd thought someone older might give a better impression.'

'Mike's an astute businessman. He must know best.'

'The basic wage isn't so hot, but I'll get commission on each sale, and there's a car, a secondhand Capri.'

'You're very lucky,' Annie said. 'Unemployment's going up, and last night you said you'd never get another job at your age. You've just been offered a soft job on a plate. If I were you, I'd be jumping for joy, but you look as if you'd just lost a pound and found a sixpence.' Personally, she couldn't have been persuaded to buy a baby's rattle, let alone a burglar alarm, off someone with such a miserable face.

The children were squabbling over the television. Daniel was almost certainly the cause. He probably wanted it changed to another station. Annie cursed Valerie Cunningham. She never offered a word of thanks for looking after her kids for two hours every day, yet seemed to consider herself superior because she had a full-time job and Annie hadn't. 'I'm getting as bad as Lauri,' she thought. 'Nothing but moans.'

It was strange, but over the last fifteen months Lauri had turned out to be a good salesman and Mike was very pleased. Perhaps potential customers felt sorry for him and bought an alarm to cheer him up. Far more likely, Lauri was his old self once outside the house and away from the wife who no longer hung onto his every word.

The steak and kidney pie smelt delicious. She felt her taste buds stir and looked at the calendar to remind herself where Lauri was today; Rochdale, which meant he might be late and she could eat with the children as soon as Valerie honked her horn to signal she was home.

The horn went when she was making the gravy and the Cunninghams came hurtling through the kitchen without a 'thank you' for Annie's pains. Valerie made no attempt to teach her brood good manners.

She was reading to the children when Lauri arrived. There was quite a gale blowing. The garden fence groaned and the willow tree swished wildly. She worried about him negotiating strange towns and unfamiliar roads in the dark, but he seemed to enjoy driving long distances and was adept at manoeuvring the gears with his numb hand.

To her astonishment, his face was beaming when he came in. He looked ten years younger. 'I sold eighteen alarms today,' he said immediately. 'Eighteen!' The usual total was two or three and some days he sold none.

She did a quick calculation. 'That's ninety pounds in commission!'

'I know, marvellous, isn't it!' The words tumbled over each other in his excitement as he tried to explain. A few weeks before he was due to arrive in a town, Michael Ray Security would advertise in the local press for leaflet distributors. Only business premises and wealthy homes were targeted. That morning, Lauri had arrived at an estate of mock-Tudor properties and discovered there'd been a spate of burglaries and the leaflet had sparked off a residents' meeting. 'Nearly every house wanted an alarm, fifteen in all. I nearly came home at that point, but decided to press on and sold another three. I'll give Mike a ring later. He'll have his work cut out fitting that lot.' His enthusiasm was catching. Annie couldn't possibly have been more pleased. He looked rejuvenated, like the Lauri of old. The children had been listening, wide-eyed. He pulled them down, one on each knee.

'Next year, you might earn that much every day when the business goes national,' she said. He would be selling in bulk to stores, not just to individual customers.'

'Listen to us!' he said, aghast. 'We sound like capitalists.'

'What's a capitalist, Dad?' Daniel enquired.

'A person who makes a lot of money off the backs of others,' his father explained. 'But Mike's okay, he pays fair wages, and the alarm is good value for money. It's not as if it's something essential that people have to buy to live. I don't mind exploiting the rich.'

'Can we have an alarm, Dad?' Daniel piped up. 'A yellow one to go with our front door?'

'No, son. We don't need protecting from burglars in Heather Close. But I tell you what you can have, a nice day out in town on Saturday. I'll buy you both a present. What would you like?'

'*Robinson Crusoe*,' Sara said instantly.

'The person or the book?' Lauri asked jovially. It was ages since he'd been heard to crack a joke.

'The book, of course, Daddy.'

'I'd like a toy burglar alarm for my room.'

'There's no such thing, son, but we'll find something else.'

'It's terrible to admit,' Lauri said later, 'but I got a real buzz today at the thought of making all that money.'

'Just because you're a socialist, it doesn't mean you're not human. Socialists still have to pay mortgages and feed their families.'

'I suppose so. On reflection, it wasn't just the money. It was the feeling of achievement, excitement almost, at the idea of belonging to a company that might become a great success. I realised how much I enjoyed being on the road. I'll be going further afield from January. I'll have to stay away overnight, perhaps several days. Will you mind, love?' He looked at her anxiously.

'No, Lauri. I'll miss you, but I won't mind as long as you're happy.' Annie felt as if they'd turned a corner.

He took her hand. 'I'm sorry, love. I've not been easy to live with over the last few years. I kept thinking of you on the way home, how pleased you'd be, and how lucky I was, having you and two lovely kids.' He sighed with satisfaction. 'I'll ring Mike now.'

He came back a few minutes later, his face grave. 'Wasn't Mike pleased?' said Annie.

'He wasn't much interested. Glenda's gone into hospital again. She's in a coma. Mike thinks this is it.'

'Oh, no!'

Mike had taken Glenda to the doctor's by force. She had leukaemia, and it was too late to do anything about it. Glenda got sicker and sicker. As the company thrived, Mike's wife began to die.

Lauri held up his left hand and stared at it with contempt. 'Pathetic, isn't it? Getting worked up over a hand, when a relatively young woman's about to die from something a hundred times worse.'

Annie didn't answer. That night, for the first time in years, she fell asleep in her husband's arms.

Glenda fought on until Christmas Eve, rarely coming out of her coma. She died with Mike and her children at her side.

Dot was inconsolable. She would never forgive herself for the things she had said when Mike got married. 'I'll never make judgements on people again. I couldn't have been more wrong with Glenda.'

The feeling in Lauri's hand gradually returned. 'It was awful while it lasted, but it's been a blessing in disguise. I wouldn't have left the co-op and got the job with Mike.'

Michael Ray Securities continued to expand. Lauri was provided with a new Cortina. Some weeks, with commission, he earned twice what he'd done as a carpenter. Despite this, he never suggested Annie give up her job at the Grand. He seemed to accept she was entitled to make her own decisions. Annie enjoyed her few hours with Bruno behind the bar; it broke up the day and gave her a few pounds of her own to spend as she liked. Now Valerie was at work and Sylvia had moved to London, she had fewer visitors and Lauri was sometimes away for an entire week.

She was happy. Her marriage was not as perfect as she'd once thought, but she and Lauri jogged along contentedly and she knew she would never stop loving him. Sara and Daniel were her main joy; watching them develop and grow. It wasn't often nowadays that she thought about Joshua and Sophie, the children who'd never been born.

'Tenth anniversary!' gasped Sylvia. 'Isn't the tenth special?'

'It's tin or aluminium, take your pick. We're having a party. It's weeks off yet, but do you think you'll be home?'

'Of course. I wouldn't miss it. I'll be home for Christmas, anyway. I'll come early.'

It was almost a year since Sylvia had gone to London, where she found herself a cushy job in an advertising agency. She telephoned Annie from work several times a week.

'Will your boss let you off?' Annie enquired.

'I've got him eating out of my hand. He's dying to get me to bed.'

'What's he like?'

'Hideous!' Sylvia giggled. 'I wouldn't sleep with him if my life depended on it. I'm happy with my handsome Arabian prince.'

'I still can't believe he's a proper prince,' Annie said doubtfully.

'He's as real as they come,' Sylvia assured her. 'We've fallen for each other like a ton of bricks, gold bricks! Ronnie's made of money.'

'I thought you swore never to fall in love again?'

'I don't expect anything to come of it. He's returning home next year. We're having a mad, bad fling whilst we have the chance.'

'Ronnie seems an odd name for an Arabian prince.'

Sylvia clucked impatiently. 'I can't pronounce his real name. He's happy with Ronnie. By the way, I saw your Marie the other day.'

'Really!' She was becoming increasingly fed up with her sister, who never answered a letter and only wrote to boast she'd got a part.

'Did she tell you she's in *Hair*?'

'*Hair*! Isn't that the show where they're all naked?'

'Yes! Poor Ronnie was terribly embarrassed.'

'She hadn't told me, no, but then I'm not surprised.'

The guest list was pretty much the same as the one for their second anniversary party, though she wouldn't be asking anyone from the co-op. They'd made new friends since then. The Barclays, who lived in the Travers' old house, were genuine salt-of-the-earth scousers. Some in the close still didn't like the idea of rubbing shoulders with market traders, but it would be hard to find a nicer couple than Sid and Vera Barclay. Having scarcely any education themselves, they were making sure things were different for their children. Ben, their eldest, was hoping to go to university next year, a fact that irritated Valerie Cunningham no end. She thought universities should be reserved for the middle and upper classes. The Cunninghams considered themselves very much middle.

For days beforehand, Annie baked trays of sausage rolls and mince pies. She was looking forward to Friday. Ten years! The fact that they were so happy together after all that time was a confirmation of their wedding vows, and it was only right to celebrate with a grand do.

Lauri was away, covering the Home Counties from his base in the London hotel where he always stayed. He promised faithfully to leave at mid-day on Friday so he'd be home in time.

Annie bought herself a new outfit; a black ribbed-jersey suit. The top had tight sleeves and a cowl neck, and the skirt was long and narrow. She'd have to remember to hold her stomach in all night.

On Friday, she fetched the decorations from the loft. It was earlier than she usually put them up, but it seemed appropriate with the party so close to Christmas. Bruno said there was no need to come to work that day, but she went to calm herself down because she was so excited.

The children came out of school, Cunninghams included, excited themselves because they'd broken up for the holidays. She gave stern instructions not to touch the food in the breakfast room, already set out for tonight. Sara had made a pretty centrepiece of cones glued to a small log, sprayed with gold, and finished off with a red ribbon.

At half five, Valerie sounded her horn and her children made their departure. Annie had hoped the horn was Lauri's. Glancing at the clock, she saw he was late. Maybe he'd found it difficult to leave at mid-day.

'Is there time for a story?' Sara asked. They could both read well, but it wasn't the same as squeezing in the armchair with their mother.

'Just a quick one.' She was about to turn the television off when the announcer said something about an accident on the M6; a lorry had overturned. No-one had been hurt, but there was already a tailback of traffic. 'That probably accounts for why your dad's not here.'

The children were still addicted to Noddy. Annie read the one about Father Christmas getting stuck in the chimney and Noddy coming to his rescue with a tow hook and a rope on his little red car.

When she finished, Sara said in an awed voice, 'Look, Mummy, it's almost snowing.'

Through the French windows, little particles of ice were floating like fireflies against the black night air, and the lights of the Christmas tree were reflected; blurred smudges of red and yellow, blue and green. They could see themselves, very far away, as if they were at the bottom of the garden in the cold, their bodies joined together, but three distinct heads, one copper, one golden, the other dark.

Annie had a sense of perfect happiness as she sat with her children and imagined Lauri waiting impatiently in a traffic jam, longing to get home to his family, to the party which was being held to celebrate the fact that they had been married for ten whole years. There was that special atmosphere in the house, the thrilling, anticipatory feeling there always was when something particularly nice was about to happen, as if the bricks and mortar were aware a party had been planned.

Sara and Daniel had felt it, too. They were silent, staring at themselves in the garden whilst tiny dazzling fireflies flew around.

'Well,' Annie broke the spell, 'I'm getting nowhere fast at this rate. People'll be here soon. I'll trust you two to get washed and changed on your own. I reckon your dad's going to be late.'

Cecy was the first to arrive, she always was. Annie sent her next door to remind Valerie to bring her wine glasses. Then Chris Andrews came and wanted to know if Marie would be there.

'Pigs might fly,' Annie said sarcastically.

'It's just that I've written a play. I wondered if she'd read it. I say, you look nice, Annie. I've never seen you in black before.'

'You don't look so bad yourself,' she said. He wore a brocade waistcoat over a long, loose shirt and floppy trousers. 'I'll give you Marie's address and you can send the play to her.' She put him in charge of the music. 'I'm afraid it's all sixties stuff; the Beatles and the Rolling Stones. I haven't bought a record in ages.'

More people came. The Barclays brought two bottles of best sherry. Sid gave Annie a smacking kiss on the cheek and wished her, 'Happy Anniversary, luv.' Everyone wanted to know where Lauri was. Dot hollered, 'I heard about the M6 being blocked. I said to Bert, didn't I, luv? I said, "I wonder if poor Lauri's bogged down in that." And you can't let people know, can you, when you're stuck in a car?'

Mike Gallagher arrived in the fringed jacket he'd got married in, his red hair in a pony tail, and wearing the round metal-framed glasses that had become fashionable. Despite his freckles and still-impish face, Mike had acquired an air of gravitas since becoming a successful businessman. Tonight he looked rather subdued. Annie remembered it would be a year next week that Glenda had died.

Every time she heard a car, she looked to see if it was her husband, but it was more guests; more cousins and their wives, people from the Labour Party. Then Sylvia in a taxi, even though the Grand was only ten minutes walk away.

Mike opened the door to let Sylvia in. They allowed each other a cold smile. Sylvia grabbed Annie's arm and began to drag her upstairs.

'Syl!' Annie protested. 'There's a party going on.'

Sylvia ignored her. She pushed her friend into the bedroom. 'I'm pregnant!' she sang. She threw herself on the bed. 'It's due in July – I'd give anything to see Eric's face when he finds out!'

'Oh!' Annie breathed. 'I couldn't possibly be more glad. When are you getting married?'

'Who's getting married? Ronnie's already got several wives. I've no intention of joining a harem.'

'But that means the baby will be illegitimate!'

Sylvia laughed merrily. 'Don't be so old-fashioned, Annie. This is the seventies, remember! Being illegitimate doesn't matter any more.'

'What's Ronnie got to say?'

'Oh, *him*!' Sylvia snorted. 'I've run away from Ronnie. I'm back in Liverpool for good. He had the nerve to suggest the baby was *his*!'

'Isn't it?' Annie said faintly.

'Yes, but he wanted me shut in a nursing home for the next six months, then the baby would be sent to his mother. Cheek!' She began to comb her hair in the mirror. 'I've chucked in my job. I suppose I'm a fugitive in a sort of way.'

'Bloody hell!'

Dot screeched, 'Annie, where's the corkscrew?' and she remembered the party and the fact there was still no Lauri at almost nine o'clock.

She wasn't quite sure when her feelings changed from worry to the almost certain knowledge something was wrong. Lauri's continued absence was beginning to concern everybody. People began to recall times when they had been stuck in a traffic jam for three hours, four hours, five. Dot said stoutly that if anything serious had happened, Annie would have heard hours ago. Chris Andrews suggested Lauri might have broken down.

'But he would have phoned,' Annie said, trying to sound sensible. 'They have telephones on the motorway, don't they?'

It was gone ten when the doorbell rang, and Gerry & The Pacemakers were singing, 'You'll Never Walk Alone'. Lauri wasn't very keen on music, but this was one of the few songs he liked.

Uncle Bert had opened the door. He held out an arm and Annie could feel it heavy on her shoulders when she saw the two policemen outside. She noticed how pretty the frost looked, glinting on the pavements, the blue light flashing on the car parked down the close.

'This is Mrs Menin,' Uncle Bert said. His arm tightened. The music came to a sudden halt and everyone gathered silently in the hall.

'I'm sorry, madam,' a policeman said. Annie thought dispassionately what a terrible job some people had. 'I'm afraid we have bad news . . .'

7

Lauri must have arrived at the hold-up on the M6 just before an exit. He left the motorway just past Manchester to take an alternative route home. Perhaps he got lost, perhaps he thought the country lane would take him home more quickly to his family and the party being held to celebrate the tenth anniversary of his marriage to Annie. No-one knew except Lauri himself, and Lauri was dead. His car skidded on the ice as he was about to drive over a little humpbacked bridge. Instead, the car had plunged into the stream below. The water wasn't deep enough to drown in, but the impact killed him instantly. He'd been there several hours before the headlights of a passing motorist revealed the Cortina, nose down in the stream.

Annie felt as if someone had removed a warm, comfortable blanket from her body. She was cold all the time. She couldn't stop shivering, and although she did her level best not to cry in front of the children, she wept when she lay in her cold bed at night and thought about the future without Lauri.

People couldn't have been kinder. Because they were there when the news arrived, they felt as if the tragedy was partly theirs. It helped to be surrounded by so much love, everyone saying what a fine man Lauri had been, such a devoted husband and father.

Fred Quillen came, looking uncomfortable, bringing condolences from the co-op. 'He was always on about you, Annie. He idolised his family.'

Mike Gallagher was the greatest help of all. 'You're thinking the world will never be the same again, but it won't last for ever, luv. Bit by bit, everything will return to normal. Lauri will always be part of you and the day will come when you'll be able to look into the future and it won't all be black. I know, it happened to me with Glenda.'

There was so much to do: the police came several times and she had to get confirmation of the death so a Death Certificate could be issued and she could arrange the funeral. Lauri had lodged a Will with the bank, leaving everything to her. The manager offered to release funds in the meantime to pay the undertakers.

Dot thought it terrible the coffin wasn't being brought back to Heather Close so everyone could say prayers around it.

'Lauri would hate that,' Annie said stubbornly. 'It would frighten the children, a dead body in the house, even if it is their dad.'

*

On the morning of the funeral, Annie woke up shivering, wondering how she would get through the day. It was still dark. She sat up, switched on the bedside lamp and pulled the duvet around her shoulders. Although she was used to Lauri being away, the empty space beside her seemed unbearable now she knew he would never sleep there again. She began to weep.

There were light footsteps outside, the door opened and Sara came in. Annie did her best to smile as her daughter crept into the bed.

'Sylvia's gone to make a cup of tea,' Sara whispered. Sylvia had scarcely left the house since the night of the party. She'd slept in the spare bed in Sara's room. 'Daniel's still asleep. I looked.'

It was odd, but Sara, Lauri's favourite, seemed far less affected by his loss than Daniel. Daniel wasn't upset. He was angry. 'Why won't Daddy be coming back?' he demanded when Annie tried to explain.

'Daddy's gone to heaven, sweetheart.' She couldn't bring herself to use the stark word 'dead', not to a seven-year-old child, though 'heaven' was a lie, because Lauri was an atheist and should by rights be burning in hell if everything she'd ever learnt about religion was true.

'How *dare* he go to heaven and leave us?' Daniel burst out furiously.

She felt totally inadequate. More than anything, she wanted the children to be upset as little as possible by Lauri's death. Christmas was only a few days off. Their presents had been bought. She would do all she could to make it happy for them.

'I hate him. I bloody hate him.' Daniel stomped up to his room and, before Annie could follow, the telephone rang for the umpteenth time.

Sara snuggled underneath her mother's arm. 'Why can't me and Daniel go to the funeral, Mummy?'

'Because young children don't normally go to funerals, luv. Cecy's coming to look after you.'

To Annie's relief, Sylvia came in with three cups of tea. She sat on the edge of the bed. 'How do you feel?' she asked.

'As well as can be expected.'

Sylvia was too happy within herself to look sombre all the time. Every now and then she would burst into song, then stop when she remembered what had happened. Annie didn't mind. In fact, it was far preferable to Dot, who collapsed into paroxysms of tears every time she came, upsetting the children no end. Even Valerie Cunningham was distraught. She'd always had a soft spot for Lauri, she confessed. Sylvia had never liked Lauri. Although it didn't make sense, it was almost a relief to be in the company of someone whose eyes didn't fill up with tears at the mere mention of his name.

'Auntie Sylvia's expecting a baby,' said Sara. 'The daddy is a prince. He wears a gold turban with a jewel in the middle, and lies on a couch while beautiful ladies feed him with purple grapes.'

'You're filling her head with nonsense,' Annie said mildly.

'I thought I'd turn it into a fairytale,' Sylvia patted her flat stomach. 'It *is* a fairytale in a sort of way.'

'Has Cecy got over the shock yet?'

'She'd got over it by next morning when she realised she could ring Mrs Church and tell her I was pregnant. I've no idea how she'll explain the lack of a husband. Eric's got a wife, but I'll have a baby, which means the Delgados have come out on top.' She grinned slyly. 'Talking of husbands, I really dig Mike Gallagher in those glasses.'

'Sylvia! You're to leave Mike alone. He's terribly vulnerable at the moment. It's only a year since Glenda . . . you know.'

'What was she like, this Glenda?'

'Very nice. Much nicer than you'll ever be.'

Daniel came into the room looking very grim and clutching the Teddy he'd discarded years ago. Annie patted the bed. 'Come on, luv.'

'I'd sooner sit the side Daddy used to sleep,' he said gruffly.

Sara obligingly climbed over her mother. Daniel got into bed and sat stiffly in Lauri's place. When Annie put her arm around him, he shrugged her off. 'I'm fed up Daddy's gone to heaven. Why couldn't he stay here?'

'Because heaven is a much nicer place than Heather Close, silly,' Sara admonished him.

Sylvia frowned and said, 'I think you should be a bit more honest with the children, don't you?'

Annie was about to explain she didn't want them hurt, when the doorbell rang and Sylvia went to answer it. She supposed she'd better get up. She glanced at Daniel. His brow was furrowed and his bottom lip trembled as if he were about to cry. She nudged him. 'Cheer up.'

'Don't want to,' he muttered.

'You've got a visitor, Annie,' Sylvia shouted.

It must be someone like Auntie Dot or Valerie, or Sylvia wouldn't have let the visitor come upstairs. Annie wasn't prepared for her sister to come into the bedroom. 'Marie!' she gasped.

'Dot rang yesterday wanting to know why I wasn't coming to the funeral. I told her I knew nothing about it. I'm terribly sorry to hear about Lauri.' Marie looked stricken. 'Oh, sis, why didn't you tell me?'

Annie's voice was very slow and deliberate when she answered. 'Because if I had, and you'd ignored it like you ignore everything, then I would never have forgiven you. I thought it best to say nothing.'

Marie looked deeply hurt. 'What sort of person do you take me for? I may not turn up for parties and stuff, but do you honestly think I'd turn a blind eye to the death of my sister's husband?'

Annie glanced sharply at the children, but the word 'death' didn't seem to have penetrated. Instead, they were staring, fascinated, at the strange young woman in the curly fur coat that Marie mustn't have realised was just like the one Mam used to have. 'This is your Auntie Marie,' she said. 'She was in *Dr Who*, remember?'

'You look different,' Sara remarked.

'I should hope so!' Marie made a funny face and the children giggled. 'I looked ghastly in that make-up.'

'Did you meet the Daleks?' Daniel asked eagerly.

'Every single one.'

'Would you like a cup of tea, Marie?' Sylvia called.

'Thanks.' Marie jerked her head. 'What's she doing here?'

'Keeping me company.'

'I'm your sister. I would have been prepared to do that.'

'Really!' Annie smiled sarcastically. 'What about *Hair*?'

Marie shrugged uncomfortably. 'Who told you?'

'Sylvia saw it a few weeks ago.'

'I'm only in the chorus. I'll easily be replaced.'

'Would you still be here if you were the star?'

'For goodness' sake, Annie,' Marie said wearily. 'You always expect things to be perfect. You have this rose-tinted picture in your mind of what sisters should be like, for ever in each other's pockets. Why can't you accept me for what I am? I'm an actress, a hopeless communicator, but I'll always be here for you when you really need me.'

Sara had slipped out of bed and was stroking the fur coat. Marie smiled. 'Try it on, darling.'

Sylvia came in with the tea. 'How long are you staying?' she asked.

'Till Boxing Day.'

'In that case, I'll take my stuff away and you can have the bed.'

'There's no need, Syl,' Annie put in. 'Marie can sleep with me.'

'I'd sooner go. Bruno will welcome the extra help over Christmas.'

Marie made a face at Sylvia's departing back. 'She still hates me.'

Downstairs, the doorbell went and the telephone rang, both at the same time. Annie threw back the duvet. 'I'd better get up. It's going to be one hell of a day and I'm not looking forward to it a bit.'

Daniel crawled across the bed and grabbed Marie's skirt. 'Will you tell us about the Daleks?'

Marie leant and clasped his face in both hands. 'Of course. You know, you remind me very much of someone I knew a long, long time ago.'

'Has he gone to heaven?'

'It was a lady and I've no idea if she went to heaven.' She glanced wryly at her sister. 'What do you think?'

Annie supposed it was no different from any other funeral. Sylvia loaned her a black coat to save buying one and she bought a black beret, because it seemed silly to spend a lot of money on a hat she'd never wear again. She looked a bit like a refugee, but what did it matter?

A cold wind blew across the cemetery and it was impossible to accept that Lauri lay inside the coffin when it was lowered into the grave. A lump came to her throat when she thought she would never see him again.

A small crowd came back to Heather Close, to the refreshments that Cecy had prepared. Most didn't stay long. Perhaps Sylvia felt in the way, because she left early, and by one o'clock only Marie, Dot and Bert remained. As Mike Gallagher was leaving he handed Annie an envelope. 'We'd just started a pension fund. That's due for Lauri.'

Annie knew nothing about a pension fund. She opened the envelope later and found a cheque for five hundred pounds. Like Lauri, she didn't want charity. Next time she saw Mike she'd give him the cheque back.

Christmas came and Christmas went. Marie got on well with the children. She seemed able to come down to their level without being patronising. Annie thought wistfully she would have made a wonderful mother. Daniel wanted to know everything about Dr Who and she promised to send a photo signed by Dr Who himself, Patrick Troughton.

On Boxing Day morning, it was Marie who came into the room and got into bed with Annie. They sat up, hugging the duvet around them.

'You won't forget that picture, will you?' Annie pleaded. 'Otherwise Daniel will be bitterly disappointed.'

Marie promised to post it as soon as she got home. 'I won't leave it so long before I come again,' she vowed.

'I've a feeling you said something like that before.'

'I'm sorry, sis, but everything's so frenetic down there.'

'You said that, too.' Annie smiled. 'It doesn't matter, luv. You came when I really needed you. That's all I care. How's the acting going, anyroad? We've scarcely had time to talk since you came.'

Marie paused before answering. 'Lousy, sis,' she sighed. 'I think I'm the oldest female in *Hair*. I'm thirty, and the others are at least ten years younger. I was surprised they took me on at my age.' Her face twisted bitterly. 'I'm *old*, Annie, and I've got nowhere.'

'I don't suppose you've thought of giving up?' Annie prayed the answer would be 'yes', but Marie shook her head.

'If I give up now, I'll have wasted thirteen years. No, sis, I'm keeping on. I'll be a success if it kills me.'

Chris Andrews came over later to see Marie. He blushed when she told him he looked adorable with his pigtail. 'I've written a play,' he said nervously. 'It's the first I've done since *Goldilocks*. I wondered if you'd read it and let me have your opinion.'

'Of course,' Marie said grandly, as if budding playwrights regularly pressed their work on her. She left that afternoon to return to the chorus of *Hair* and her dream of becoming a famous actress.

Marie had gone, Christmas was over. Tomorrow, things would be back to normal. People would get on with their lives, including Annie, though it wouldn't be normal for her. She had to learn to live without Lauri.

She'd never looked in the drawer containing Lauri's papers before. He'd taken care of everything; written cheques for the bills which he left on the windowsill beside the front door for her to post.

'Crikey!' she muttered when she sorted through the bank and building society statements, the bills for gas, electricity, rates, telephone, insurance. 'I never realised the central heating cost so much.' She'd never realised *anything* cost so much, and felt resentment that he'd kept her so much in the dark, not shared things the way other couples did. The resentment was immediately replaced by guilt, as it seemed awful to feel even mildly angry with someone who'd so recently died.

She immediately turned the central heating down. It was New Year's Day and snowing heavily, but Sara and Daniel were next door.

The papers were spread on the table and she saw that, according to the last statement from the building society, two thousand pounds was owed on the house, yet the initial loan hadn't been for much more. The monthly payments had been taken up in interest charges.

'Bloody hell!' She multiplied the quarterly bills by four, the mortgage payments by twelve, added the yearly bills, and divided the total by fifty-two.

'Bloody hell!' she said again. It came to nearly twice what she would get in widow's pension coupled with Family Allowance for Daniel. She might be allowed other benefit from the State, but it would never be enough to meet the bills – and there were food and clothes to buy on top. She searched for the latest bank statement. It was irritating that she had no idea how much money was in the bank.

'Well, *that* won't last long,' she thought when she found it was four hundred and eighty-two pounds, but the statement was dated the first of December and would be taken up by funeral costs. 'I think I'll keep that cheque from Mike, after all. It will last until I get a job. We should have taken out one of those insurance things me dad used to sell.' People paid coppers a week towards a lump sum when someone died. 'But it never crossed me mind one of us would die.' She screwed up her face, determined not to cry. 'Anyroad, funerals cost a fortune nowadays, it would have taken more than pennies to save four hundred pounds.'

As soon as the children were back at school, she'd look for a job. Bruno said she could return to the Grand, but the wages weren't nearly enough. Even so, the job would have to be part-time. There was no way she'd let Sara and Daniel become latchkey kids like Valerie's.

It was strange how life seemed to repeat itself. Annie found herself again searching through the Liverpool *Echo* for work. Chris Andrews let her borrow his typewriter to practise on, and after a few hesitant starts, she found her fingers as nimble as ever. It was the same with shorthand. Machin & Harpers were good teachers. If she were asked to take a test during an interview, she would pass with flying colours.

If she ever went for an interview! Only a few of the jobs advertised were part-time. Annie wrote after every single one, but by the time February arrived all she had received was letter after letter of rejection. In desperation, she discussed the matter with her neighbour. Valerie had found a job. What magic formula had *she* used?

'No-one will take you if you've got young children,' Valerie said flatly. 'They think you'll be off every five minutes if they've got a cold or something, that you'd always put the kids before the job.'

'I would,' said Annie.

Valerie shrugged, as if this proved her point.

'How did you manage it?' Annie asked curiously. 'You've got four.'

'I told them my mother lived with me.' Valerie had the grace to blush. Mrs Owen had been persuaded to stay in Heather Close during the holidays, but that was all. Tracy had suffered from a bad cold the whole of last term, but she'd still been sent to school.

School holidays were something Annie hadn't allowed herself to think about. She was concerned only with the immediate future. The money in the bank was shrinking alarmingly. If she wasn't fixed up by Easter, she had no idea what would happen.

That night, she walked round the house to see if there was anything to sell, but all she found was the children's old cot which might fetch enough to pay for half a week's groceries. Of course, she could sell the Anglia which was old, but it ran well and she wanted to keep it. It would save time hanging round for buses if she ever got a job, though that seemed more and more unlikely, and when Sara started at Grenville Lucas next year, she could give her a lift when it was raining.

'Oh, Lauri,' she whispered. She tried to imagine him, wherever he was; perhaps his spirit still existed, looking down on her, offering advice, telling her what she should do. They'd never talked about death, they'd never really talked about anything serious. No doubt he thought he'd always be there to look after her and the children.

Annie sighed. It was story-time. The hour spent together in the chair had become very precious lately. When she finished reading, Daniel always wanted to know about heaven, what was it like? Tonight, he twisted his face earnestly. 'Will Dad get on well with God?'

'Your dad got on well with everybody.' Except me, she thought.

She'd gone to see the headmistress, Mrs Dawson, and told her about Lauri the day the children returned to school. 'We'll keep an eye on them,' Mrs Dawson promised. 'The loss of a parent affects different children in different ways, but in my experience, they always pull through.'

The children went to bed. Marie had sent the signed picture of Dr Who, and it was stuck with a drawing pin to Daniel's wall.

Sylvia was coming round later. She was happily househunting, looking for somewhere with a garden for children to play in. 'I'm not stopping at one,' she said cheerfully. 'Once this is born, I shall look round for a suitably gorgeous man to sire the second. D'you think Mike would be interested?' she added teasingly. 'I'd quite like a red-haired baby.'

Lucky old Sylvia, Annie thought moodily. She's never had to worry about money.

She made tea ready for when Sylvia came, and was sitting in the breakfast room, thinking tearfully about Lauri, and wondering what the hell she was supposed to do, when the back door opened.

'It's only us,' Valerie Cunningham shouted. She came in followed by Kevin. 'We'd like a little word.'

'Sit down. I'm expecting Sylvia any minute.' Annie felt a moment of hope. Perhaps Valerie had told Kevin about her unsuccessful search for work, and he'd come to offer her a job in his bank!

They looked at each other expectantly, then, when her husband made no attempt to speak, Valerie began in a rush, 'I've been talking to Kevin about your little problem.'

It didn't exactly seem a *little* problem, Annie thought, and her expectations of a job offer soared slightly higher.

'The thing is, we wondered if you'd thought of selling the house?'

'Selling the house!' The idea had never crossed her mind.

Kevin was becoming jowly. His throat wobbled when he spoke. 'It's just that we've got these friends, it's a chap I work with, actually, and when I told him there was a possibility next door might become vacant, he was immediately interested.'

'No-one told me there was a possibility my house might become vacant.' Annie's head felt very hot, as if the blood were rushing through at top speed and becoming over-heated. She told herself they were only being kind in attempting to solve her 'little' problem.

'I don't know if you realise how much these houses are worth, Annie,' Valerie said eagerly.

'My friend is prepared to pay five thousand – cash, that is.' Kevin's pale eyes blinked behind his glasses. 'So you wouldn't have to wait until he got a mortgage. He wouldn't want a survey. There's nothing wrong with our house, so yours is bound to be all right.'

'Five thousand!' Annie gasped. 'But Lauri only paid . . .' What was it? She'd only looked at the building society papers a few weeks ago.

'Two thousand, seven-fifty,' Valerie said promptly. 'Property is the best investment you can have.'

'My friend is even prepared to pay the solicitor's costs,' Kevin went on. 'It would be over and done with in a few weeks, and you'd have a few thousand to play with once you've paid off the mortgage.'

'And where do me and the children live then, on the streets?'

Valerie laughed. 'You can get a nice little place for a couple of thou or less. Some of those terraced houses look quite cosy done up.' She glanced around the room. 'You have an eye for decoration, Annie. I've always thought your house looked far smarter than ours.'

A nice little place like Orlando Street, Annie thought bleakly. A place without a garden, so there'd be no willow tree, no shed with a verandah, no swing. If she'd stayed with Auntie Dot, that sort of house might hold no terror, but there was no way she'd return to somewhere like Orlando Street now.

'Heather Close is such a desirable place to live,' Valerie said.

'I know,' said Annie. 'Which is why I intend to stay.'

Next morning, Annie phoned an estate agent and said she was thinking of selling her house in Heather Close and how much was it worth?

'Whereabouts in Heather Close?'

'The far end, number seven.' She hoped he wouldn't ask to put a board up, as she had no intention of parting with Lauri's house.

'The best part!' the man said warmly. 'I can see it in my mind's eye. We handled next door, the old couple who died. You've got an exceptionally big garden. Are you the one with the willow tree?'

'That's right.'

The estate agent hummed a little tune. 'Well, I'd need to look round, but I'd say, roughly, mind, six and a half thou. You could ask a few hundred more, then wait and see how the cookie crumbles.'

'Thank you,' Annie said faintly. She assured him she'd be in touch immediately she'd made up her mind.

Six and a half thousand! She cast aside the suspicion that the Cunninghams had been trying to deceive her, because it scarcely bore thinking about. She supposed she *could* sell and buy somewhere cheaper and live on what was left, but although she didn't know much about this sort of thing, she had a feeling the building society would never give her, a widow without a job, another mortgage, which meant she'd have to buy the 'somewhere cheaper' for cash. By the time she'd repaid the two thousand pounds owing, the rest wouldn't last all *that* long. The cost of living was rising, despite the fact Edward Heath had promised to 'cut prices at a stroke', and the new Value

Added Tax didn't help. Food prices were set to rise even further now the country had joined the European Community. Lauri had always said joining the EEC was a terrible mistake. Nearly everyone in the Labour Party was dead against it.

Annie touched the smooth cupola-shaped knob at the bottom of the stairs which Lauri had made specially. She couldn't stand the idea of another family living here. It was intolerable to imagine a strange woman using *her* kitchen, strange children playing inside the willow tree, an entirely strange family sitting in front of the fireplace that Lauri had built. It may only be a rather ordinary semi-detached in a suburb of Liverpool, but the house was part of Lauri, part of her. It was the only home the children had ever known. The time might come when she'd have no option but to sell, but until that time came, Annie vowed she would do all she could to cling on to the home she loved.

She wasn't sure where to turn next. She typed out a dozen cards for shop windows offering typing at ten shillings an hour, and was thrilled when a girl, a medical student, brought a thesis to be typed. The writing was execrable and contained numerous Latin terms. Annie typed till past midnight for two nights in a row. The girl looked startled when asked for three pounds, although it should have been more.

Days later, an elderly man turned up with a novel he'd written in a neat, crabbed, though legible hand, but when she began to type, there were lines and circles everywhere, moving words, sentences or entire paragraphs from one place to another, and she'd be halfway down a page, only to discover she hadn't included something from the page before. It took two weeks of solid work to complete the nearly five hundred pages. Annie totalled up the hours; it came to over a hundred. She couldn't possibly ask for fifty pounds! She asked for thirty, and the man looked even more startled than the student.

'I hope I get it published after all this expense,' he grumbled.

She doubted it. It was the worst novel she'd ever read.

Although a very nice man from a garage brought several invoices and insisted on giving her a pound when she only asked for ten shillings, she realised she wasn't going to make a fortune as a typist. A few weeks later she gave Chris Andrews his typewriter back.

She economised on everything, kept the central heating turned down during the day, cancelled some of the insurances, bought the cheapest mincemeat and made pies and stews. The children remarked on how often they seemed to have jelly and custard for afters.

They had no idea how hard up she was. She still gave them dinner money for school, although they could have had free meals, because she didn't want them thinking they were different. No-one knew the difficulties she was having, except the Cunninghams. She would have had the telephone disconnected, but people might guess why. When Dot or Bert asked how she was coping, she assured them, 'Fine.' They had a few pounds put away, and would insist on helping if they knew she was in trouble. But it would be degrading to take money off two old people who enjoyed splashing their tiny amount of wealth on their grandchildren.

In May, the balance in the bank had shrunk to double figures, and the electricity bill was due any minute. 'I should have stayed at the Grand, there would have been a few pounds coming in.' But Bruno had hired someone else months ago. 'If only I had someone to *talk* to,' Annie fretted. 'If only our Marie would get in touch!' Marie was impossible to get hold of, never there when she phoned. Chris Andrews, though, had received a letter. Marie thought his play 'wonderful', and promised to show it to a director she knew.

One Sunday after Mass, she was in the garden, digging at the weeds in a desultory fashion, conscious of the sun warm on her back, when she heard Vera Barclay come into her garden. Vera helped on the fruit and veg stall all week and could only do her washing on Sundays. Annie straightened up, relieved to give the weeds a rest for the moment.

'Morning, Vera,' she shouted over the Travers' old shiplap fence.

Vera was hidden behind a sheet she was pegging on the line. Her rosy, weatherbeaten face appeared, the inevitable cigarette hanging from her mouth. She bade Annie a cheerful 'Morning, luv.' She was a small, outgoing woman with short curly brown hair. 'How's things?'

'Fine,' Annie said automatically.

After Vera had pegged out another sheet, she came over to the fence and looked at Annie searchingly with her bright blue eyes. 'You're always "fine",' she said.

'Well . . .' Annie shrugged.

'I wouldn't be fine if my Sid had passed away and I was left with two young kids to bring up on me own.'

'Well,' Annie said again. She'd always known that Vera and Sid were kindness itself. They were good neighbours, and had sent a lovely wreath for Lauri's funeral, but the two women had never become close. They talked mainly, as now, over the fence. Annie was more friendly with Valerie, whom she'd never particularly cared for, than with Vera.

Sara and Daniel came wandering into the garden, looking rather lost. 'Why don't you go and play next door?' Annie suggested. Shouts and screams could be heard from the Cunninghams.

Sara shook her head. Daniel took no notice and headed for the swing. They sat on it together, Sara pushing slightly with her foot.

'I've got something that'll cheer you two up.' Vera disappeared into the house and came back with two big Jaffa oranges. 'They're lovely and sweet and juicy – and there's no pips!'

To Annie's embarrassment, Daniel made no move to get the orange, but Sara came across and took them both. 'Thank you very much,' she said politely. 'It's ages since we had an orange.'

'Is it now!' Vera leant her brown, sunburnt arms on the fence. 'Finding things difficult, are you, Annie? And if you say "well" again, I'll fetch another orange and chuck it at you!'

It was awfully difficult not to cry with Vera regarding her so understandingly. Annie nodded without speaking.

'Look, luv, I've another load of washing to hang out, and there's dinner to cook, but I'll pop round to see you this avvy, about three. I think what you need is a shoulder to cry on.'

*

'I would have come before,' Vera said, 'but folks are dead snooty round here, and I didn't want to appear as if I was intruding. Back where we used to live in Smithdown Road, I wouldn't have hesitated. That's what I miss most since we left, me neighbours. Have you got an ashtray, luv?'

Annie shoved an ashtray in her direction, and described the pickle she was in, holding nothing back. Vera said she thought she'd be mad to sell the house. 'It's going back when you want to go forward.'

'But what else can I do?' Annie said desperately. 'I'm down to eighty pounds.'

Vera puffed furiously on her cigarette and thought hard. 'What about dressmaking?' she suggested. 'I could hardly believe it when you told me you made your own clothes. They look dead professional.'

Annie glanced at the sewing machine on the small table in the bay window. 'I don't know,' she said doubtfully. 'I've never had a lesson and I'm hopeless at turning collars.' She remembered the awful time she'd had with typing, but supposed dressmaking was different as you could give a firm quotation beforehand.

'Women are always on the look-out for a good dressmaker,' Vera said encouragingly. 'You could take a course, finish yourself off, as it were. I'd be only too happy to recommend you to me mates.' She tapped her teeth with a tobacco-stained fingernail. 'In the meantime, you need to get a few bob together, don't you?'

'The electricity bill's due any minute, and the mortgage has to be paid at the beginning of June.'

Vera snapped her fingers as if she'd had a brainwave. 'Look, why not have a good clear-out? Get rid of the kids' old toys, the odd dishes and cutlery you never use, tools, knick-knacks like ornaments you hate which have got shoved to the back of a cupboard, and I bet your wardrobe's stuffed with clothes you'll never wear again.'

'And what do I do with them?' asked Annie, mystified.

'You sell 'em,' Vera grinned.

'Who to?'

'Have you never been to Great Homer Street market, luv?' When Annie shook her head, Vera went on, 'Traders are always on the look-out for good stuff to sell; bric-a-brac and secondhand clothes, mainly. Once you've got the stuff ready, I'll take it and see what I can get.'

'There's no need for you to go to so much trouble. I'll take it meself.' There was still tax and insurance left on the Anglia.

'Lord Almighty, luv, when they see an innocent like you, they'll offer peanuts. No,' Vera said firmly, '*I'll* take it, and make sure you get a good price. There'll be enough for the electricity bill or my name's not Vera Barclay.'

After Vera had gone, Annie thought, 'Dressmaking!'

She'd do it. She'd do anything to keep the house and get herself out of the hole she was in, but she wasn't keen on making clothes for other people. Customers would want things made to a pattern, but she rarely used a pattern. She made things up out of her head, adding little imaginative touches, like a pleated bodice, an embroidered flower on a pocket. She actually got a little thrill when the garment was finished, though nothing had given her such pleasure as the costumes she'd made for the pantomime at Grenville Lucas. It wouldn't be possible to use your imagination on other women's clothes.

The children joined in the great sort-out, as if it was a game, delving in cupboards and drawers. Annie was pleased. Daniel loved going in the loft, though he wasn't willing to part with a single item of his own. He glared at her mutinously when she opened the cupboard in his room in search of baby toys.

'But you haven't played with it in years,' Annie cried, when he refused to give up the plastic telephone he'd got on his first birthday.

'Want to keep it,' he mumbled. 'It's mine.'

'All right, sweetheart. I wouldn't dream of taking anything you want to keep. Where did all these come from?' She pointed to the neat row of Matchbox cars at the back of the shelf.

'Dad gave them to me.' He burst into tears. 'Don't take the cars that Daddy bought.'

'Oh, Daniel!' Annie knelt and took him in her arms. He felt hot. He'd been very sullen since Lauri died, but she was at a loss what to do. All she could think of was to make as much fuss of him as possible. 'I didn't realise Dad had bought so many, that's all.' Lauri brought a Matchbox car for Daniel and a book for Sara each time he went away.

It was nice to have a good clear-out, she thought later, when the table was full of old cups and saucers she'd never use again and several Pyrex bowls that she'd never used at all. How on earth had she managed to acquire three tin-openers and so many pairs of scissors? She was glad to see the back of that hideous set of three monkeys which was a wedding present from she couldn't remember whom, and where on earth had the bronze lion which Daniel had found in the loft come from?

Uncle Bert had taken Lauri's clothes for a seamen's charity in town, though there was no way she would have sent them to a market. Annie found herself stopping from time to time, remembering, as she ruthlessly cleared her wardrobe. The ivory polka-dotted dress she'd made for her twenty-first, the night Lauri proposed. The brown coat she wore to Stickley & Plumm. Her wedding dress, which wasn't a proper wedding dress at all. In fact, it was a miserable garment which she'd never worn again. She paused over a green dress with a pleated skirt which she'd forgotten she had. The first time she'd worn it was when she'd gone to see *Psycho* with Sylvia. God, what an awful night! *Psycho* had been on television months ago, but she still couldn't bear to watch.

The bed was heaped with clothes when she finished, most in very good condition. She and Sylvia had been mad on clothes, and Annie had thrown little away. It was always in her mind to re-model things, though she rarely did. She recalled meaning to turn the green dress into a suit, and the ivory taffeta would look lovely as a skirt with a black top.

But there was no chance of that happening now. In a few days, the things would be gone, and what would she get? Enough to pay the electricity bill, along with the stuff downstairs. It wasn't that she cared about losing a few old clothes, but the manner of their going upset her.

'Damn you, Lauri!' she swore. It was terrible, but with the non-stop worry over money since he'd gone, the main emotion she felt for him was anger; anger that they'd never had a joint bank account, that he resented her having any responsibility so she didn't know how much electricity and gas cost, that they'd never talked about death. Valerie Cunningham boasted that Kevin had a massive insurance policy. 'Me and the kids will be better off with Kevin dead than alive.'

Annie burrowed under the clothes and began to cry. She cried until she felt as if her heart would break; for Lauri, for Sara and Daniel, a little for herself. She emerged what seemed like hours later, but a glance at the alarm clock showed it was only ten minutes. The telephone was ringing, but she ignored it and began to fold the clothes neatly.

She wasn't sure where the idea came from; it arrived quite out of the blue. If someone was prepared to pay for all these things, they must be planning to sell them at a profit.

In which case, *she would start a secondhand clothes stall herself*!

Great Homer Street

1

Vera Barclay said Great Homer Street market only operated on Saturdays which was a relief, as there would be no problem with the children.

However, Vera went on, getting a stall wasn't easy. There was a list of people waiting for a place. She tapped her nose and winked. 'Leave it to Sid. He'll put in a word on your behalf. His ould ma had a stall in Paddy's Market all her life, so he's quids in with the powers that be.'

All Annie could do was wait. She put her clothes back in the wardrobe, and Vera got just over seven pounds for the bric-a-brac.

Of course, she couldn't just sit and do nothing in the meantime. Money was needed to live on. Yet again, she returned to the jobs section of the *Echo*, but this time she didn't bother with office vacancies. With relative ease, she found employment as a cleaner-cum-kitchen worker in a residential hotel in Blundellsands, a short distance away. From Monday to Friday, she stripped and re-made beds, cleaned bathrooms, and vacuumed till one-thirty. Then she went down to the kitchen to wash dishes and mop floors. At half past three she went home, just in time to meet the children coming out of school.

She told no-one what she was doing, not because she was ashamed, but because she didn't want their comments. When anyone asked, she told them she was in Reception. 'It's only temporary. Soon, I'm going into business on me own.' On Saturdays, she left the children with Valerie and took herself in the Anglia to jumble sales in Southport to acquire stock. The garage was full of stuff which she had yet to wash and iron.

'What sort of business?' Dot demanded. Annie said she'd explain when she was ready.

She earned enough to keep her head above water until she started the market stall. Although she didn't expect to become rich, she hoped and prayed she'd earn enough to pay the mortgage and the bills and keep the children, if not in the manner to which they were accustomed, at least so they didn't go short of the things other children had.

Annie was almost asleep when the phone went. She glanced at the clock, just gone midnight. She threw back the bedclothes and ran downstairs, praying it wasn't bad news.

'Sylvia's had the baby.' Cecy was exultant. 'I'm a grandmother!'

'But it's two weeks early!' Annie gasped.

'I know, but the first contraction came at ten o'clock tonight. Bruno got her to hospital just in time. It's a little girl, Annie, a beautiful little girl with jet black hair.'

'Has she decided on a name yet?' Sylvia had thought of a hundred names over the last few months.

'Yasmin.'

'Yasmin!' Annie had never heard that mentioned before.

'Actually, Annie,' Cecy's voice sank to a whisper, 'I wouldn't say this to another soul, but I've a strong suspicion the baby is coloured. Has Sylvia ever discussed the father with you?'

'No, she hasn't,' Annie lied.

When she went to see her friend in hospital the next day, Sylvia was sitting up in bed wearing a frilly blue bedjacket over a matching nightie, her face made up and her blonde hair perfectly groomed. She looked unreasonably glowing and unbearably smug.

'Have you seen Yasmin?' she crowed the minute Annie appeared.

'Yes. Cecy pointed her out in the nursery. She's gorgeous.' Apart from Sara, Annie had never seen such a pretty baby. Yasmin's skin was a creamy coffee colour, and she had thick glossy hair.

'You know,' Sylvia hissed, glancing surreptitiously around the ward, 'some of the babies are actually *bald*!'

'They don't stay bald.'

'And some are hideously ugly.'

Annie made an impatient face. 'They don't stay ugly, either.'

'You know something else? I can't understand all the fuss you made over Daniel. Having a baby is as easy as pie.'

'It would be wise not to say that to the other women, Sylvia,' Annie snapped, 'else you won't be very popular in the ward. Daniel was three and a half pounds heavier than Yasmin.' Sylvia's air of self-satisfaction was irritating. 'I hope your next affair is with a man built like Mr Universe and the baby weighs at least twelve pounds.'

Annie could have a market stall in August, three weeks off. 'But if anyone asks,' Sid Barclay said, 'you've been waiting six months.'

'Oh, Sid. What can I do to thank you?'

He winked. Sid was a small man with unnaturally broad shoulders and muscled arms from hoisting thousands of boxes of fruit and veg over the years. 'If I wasn't married, luv, I could think of a hundred things.'

Annie blushed. The message had come just in time. She'd given her notice in at the hotel as the children were about to break up for the summer. If the stall failed, she'd look for another job in September. 'But it *won't* fail,' she vowed. 'I'll make it work if it kills me!'

That night, she washed the remainder of the clothes which had been stored in the garage. She wondered if Valerie was ever curious about the never-ending assortment of strange garments hanging on her neighbour's line, but Valerie was probably too busy to notice.

It was amazing what people threw out. Some things were virtually new. Perhaps they didn't fit, or the owner decided she didn't like the frock or blouse or skirt when she got home, and couldn't be bothered returning it.

There were items that seemed to have been thrown away merely because a seam was undone or the hem was coming down, which were easily repaired. There might be a button missing and, occasionally, there was actually a spare button inside. Otherwise, she sorted through her button box and could always find one that matched reasonably well.

The washing finished, she did some ironing. Fancy chucking out a white silk Marks & Spencer's shirt blouse that looked as if it had never been worn! It was the sort of thing that would never go out of fashion.

She hung everything in the garage when she'd finished. She'd made two clothes-racks out of broomhandles. They were rough and ready, but would do until she could afford the professional sort. The wire hangers she'd got a shilling a dozen in a shop in Bootle which was closing down.

The children were as thrilled as she was when she told them what she had planned. They'd come to the last few jumble sales. Sara had bought loads of books, and Daniel acquired the oddest things; an old toaster, a clock with no hands, and last week an ancient wireless that he was carefully taking to pieces in his room.

She could hardly wait for August. Mike Gallagher had said that the day would come when she would look forward to the future, and Annie was astonished that it had arrived so quickly.

'A *market* stall! Jaysus, girl, have you no shame? Your mam and dad'll turn in their graves.' Dot Gallagher's face had turned white with shock. 'What will people think?'

'Oh, you're a terrible snob, Auntie Dot,' Annie said crossly. 'I don't give a damn about what people think.'

Dot looked quite faint. '*Me*, a *snob!*'

'You're a working-class snob, which is the worst sort. Cecy thinks it's dead exciting, and she's got far more to be snobbish about than you.' After all, if Bruno was a Count, then Cecy was a Countess. 'She's given me loads of lovely things to sell.' She'd even offered to go to jumble sales on Saturdays when Annie was busy, or look after the stall if she preferred to go herself. Bruno too was full of admiration for Annie's entrepreneurial spirit.

Dot muttered there was no need for Lady Muck to put on her airs and graces now there was an illegitimate baby in the family. She offered to turn out her wardrobe. 'I'll let you have all me old things.'

'Thanks, Auntie Dot,' Annie said gratefully, though she couldn't imagine anyone wanting to buy the stiff, violently patterned Crimplene frocks her aunt usually wore.

For some mysterious reason, Sylvia had bought a thatched cottage down an isolated country lane just outside Ormskirk, miles away from Waterloo. Perhaps she'd been influenced by the big, wild garden with its mature trees that would be ideal for children to play in. It was awkward to get to and she complained bitterly that no-one came to see her.

'I'm not surprised,' said Annie the second time she went. 'Why didn't you buy somewhere nearer? Anyroad, Cecy comes every day.'

'I wish Cecy would stay away, she drives me mad!' Sylvia looked harassed. Yasmin had turned out to be a fractious child – Annie tried hard not to be glad. 'She keeps reminiscing about when I was a baby. If you must know, I find it distasteful to be reminded I was breastfed. She even had the nerve to suggest I give Yasmin a dummy!'

'What's wrong with that! A dummy dipped in Virol might stop the poor child crying so much.'

'And spoil the shape of her lips for ever, not likely!'

Yasmin started to cry, and her anxious mother raced upstairs to fetch her beautiful five-week-old daughter from the Victorian pine cradle draped with old Nottingham lace. Most of the furniture in the cottage was genuine antique pine. Even the lovely, floppy three-piece with its feather cushions was old, and had been re-upholstered in dusky pink velvet. Annie dreaded to think what would happen when Yasmin started walking and touched everything with her sticky fingers.

The early morning sky was black, threatening rain. Annie made sure she had the tarpaulin before she set off at six o'clock for her first day as a market trader. The boot had been packed the night before, the clothes neatly laid on top of each other until it would barely close. There were smaller things on the passenger seat and Sara and Daniel were in the back with more stuff piled on their knees.

'Ready for off!' she cried cheerfully, though she felt anything but cheerful. Now the moment had come, she was petrified. A market stall seemed a stupid idea. What on earth had made her think of it?

'Ready!' the children said gleefully.

What if it rained? What if she didn't sell a thing? Were her prices too high? Too low? Vera said she should mark each item with old and new currency because some folk hadn't got the hang of the new decimal currency yet.

'Neither have I!' Annie confessed, but it turned out Sara had. She'd written the labels attached to each garment.

She had to drive slowly because her legs felt like jelly, and the market site was crowded by the time she arrived. Scores of traders were already busy setting up their stalls. She stopped the car on the pavement and went in search of someone who knew which pitch was hers. After a long while, during which she began to feel quite frantic, she found a man who looked as if he might be in charge.

'Menin?' he said, as if the name meant nothing to him, '*Menin*? Oh, yes, you're over there. Looks like rain, don't it, luv,' he added conversationally. The sky was slightly brighter than when they had left, but the brightness was a fearsome yellow more ominous than black.

She managed to manoeuvre the car through the stalls. 'You're late,' grumbled the man who turned out to be her neighbour. He had to remove his tables to let her in. Incredibly, there were already several people wandering around with bags of vegetables and meat.

Her hands were shaking too much to fix the broomhandles together. Sara took them off her. 'We'll do it, Mummy. Which bit goes where?'

Her neighbour came to help. He was in his sixties, huge, with a bluff red face and mutton-chop whiskers which went perfectly with his old-fashioned collarless shirt and stained chalk-striped waistcoat. His blue jeans seemed rather out of place. 'These are a bit flimsy, luv. A breath of wind and your lovely clothes will be on the ground.'

'I'll get better ones if I make some money,' Annie said weakly. She was glad he'd turned out to be friendly, even though he'd had to move his tables to allow her in.

He extended a large red hand. 'Ivor Hughes, fine antiques.'

'Annie Menin, secondhand clothes.'

She actually sold a frock before she'd begun to fill the second rack. It was one of Dot's, a horrible purple and yellow thing she'd almost not brought with her.

Sara and Daniel's eyes glowed as the woman tucked the frock in her bag. 'We're in business,' whispered Sara.

Another two frocks and a blouse went before there seemed to be a lull, during which the early customers went home and more arrived, many with children, obviously come for a day out. She got angry when some women carelessly yanked her precious things off the rack. Some made offers which she firmly refused. After this had happened several times, Ivor said, 'You should mark your prices up a bit, luv, allow for bargaining. Some customers won't buy if they don't get a reduction.'

'But that's not fair on those who don't make offers!'

Ivor shrugged. 'It's the way of the world, luv. A market's not a market if you're not prepared to barter.'

From then on, Annie took offers if they seemed reasonable. She'd get Sara to price the tickets up for next week.

She'd sold a few more things when Cecy arrived with a plastic carrier bag, a pleased expression on her prematurely wizened face. 'See what I found in a rummage sale.' With an air of triumph, she pulled a long blue dress out of the bag and held it up by the shoulders. It was sleeveless, with a heavily jewelled bodice and a floating gauzy skirt lined with taffeta. 'Look at that label! It must have cost the earth.'

The label meant nothing to Annie. She was about to say she couldn't imagine anyone wanting to buy such a posh frock in a market, when a well-dressed woman approached. 'Is that dress for sale?'

'It certainly is.' Cecy winked at Annie. 'Five quid and it's yours!'

'I'll take it.'

'Cecy!' gasped Annie when the woman had gone, obviously delighted with her purchase. 'You missed your vocation. You should have been a market trader. I would never have dared to ask so much.'

'I'm enjoying the whole experience.' Cecy looked pleased, as if she'd been paid a great compliment. She began to go through the clothes. Despite Annie's protestations, she insisted on paying for the Marks & Spencer's silk blouse. 'It will go with all my suits,' she claimed.

She took Sara and Daniel for a drink and a bun, and Annie was left to herself. There being no customers to keep an eye on, she surveyed the nearby stalls. On her other side, an elderly woman was selling odds and ends of pretty china. The woman smiled and remarked she hoped the rain would keep off. Opposite, a bookstall was safe from the threatening rain beneath a striped awning. 'I wouldn't mind something like that,' Annie thought. 'And a van would be useful. If I make enough money . . .' There were watches and jewellery on one side of the bookstall, and secondhand radios and televisions on the other.

The things on Ivor Hughes' stall looked more like rubbish than fine antiques. Even so, he was doing brisk business. To her amazement, she recognised the bronze lion she'd found in her loft. 'How much is that?' she enquired.

'Eight quid,' Ivor said promptly. 'Very rare piece of work, that is. Got it off one of the landed gentry.'

'Really! I'll think about it.'

'Here's Grandma back with the kids,' Ivor remarked.

'He thinks you're my mother,' Annie said when Cecy came up, Sara and Daniel skipping happily beside her.

Cecy's blue eyes grew wistful. 'I sometimes wish that were so, dear. You're a far nicer person than my own daughter.'

Two women had begun to sort through the clothes. 'You've got a good assortment here, luv,' one said. 'Will you be here next week? There's lots of things me daughter might like.'

'I'll be here every week from now on,' Annie promised.

After the women had bought a blouse each, Cecy suggested Annie have a break. 'It's almost noon. I expect you've been up since dawn.'

She hadn't realised the market had an indoor section, and supposed you had to have been there for years to become entitled to such a choice pitch. The goods were a repetition of those outside. She waved at the Barclays when she saw them behind their fruit and veg stall.

Sid made the thumbs-up sign. 'How are you doing, luv?' he called.

'Not bad.' They looked too busy to stop and talk.

She came to a clothes stall where everything was piled on top of each other on two old tables, like jumble. The stuff didn't look very clean. Annie was about to walk past, when a gruff voice from behind the tables drawled, 'Well, if it isn't Annie Harrison!'

Annie tried to place the tall woman, almost six foot, with a hard, lined face and small eyes. Her brown hair was cut short like a man's, and she wore a shabby leather bomber jacket and jeans.

'Don't recognise me, do you?' she chortled. 'It's Ruby, Ruby Livesey, though it's Crowther now, I'm married with five kids. We knew each other at school.'

'Ruby!' Annie swallowed. She'd always dreaded coming across Ruby Livesey one day. 'What are you doing here?'

'Running this stall, obviously. Me and me sister inherited it from our mam. And what are you doing, slumming it?'

Annie bridled. 'I happen to have a stall meself,' she said shortly.

'Come down in the world, have we?'

'I never thought of meself as up. I only lived in Orlando Street and me dad collected insurance on his bike.'

'Maybe so,' Ruby sneered, 'but you always looked like you had a bad smell under your nose at school, as if you thought us all beneath you.'

'Well, it's been nice meeting you again, Ruby.' Annie made no attempt to keep the sarcasm out of her voice. 'I'd best be getting back.' She vowed never to enter the indoor section again.

When she returned, Dot had arrived and was talking stiffly to Cecy. Her face shone with relief when her niece turned up. 'I was just saying, I'll always lend a hand, luv, if you're stuck.'

'She won't ever be stuck whilst I'm around,' Cecy said pointedly. 'I took another couple of pounds whilst you were gone, Annie. I'll just go and see if I can buy one of those apron things you keep the money in. All the other traders seem to have one.'

The minute Cecy had gone, Dot pounced on a cream jacket. 'I didn't want her ladyship to see me buying secondhand. How much is this, luv?'

'For you, Auntie Dot, nothing.'

But Dot also insisted on paying. Annie didn't mention the jacket was Cecy's and hoped the women would never meet whilst Dot was wearing it.

Auntie Dot left. She was taking two of her grandchildren to the pictures. A few minutes later, Annie could have sworn she felt rain. 'Get that tarpaulin out,' she said to Daniel. A huge black cloud loomed menacingly overhead.

'So, this is where you are!' Ruby Livesey looked even bigger and more unpleasant close up. She was accompanied by a plain girl of about twelve. 'And you're selling clothes, too. Is this stuff new?' Ruby fingered Annie's polka-dotted dress.

'No, it's all secondhand.'

Ruby's small eyes glinted in disbelief. 'It *looks* new.'

'Well, it isn't.'

'Can I have this jersey, Mam?' The girl pulled a fluffy white sweater off the rack.

'How much is it?' Ruby growled.

'Fifty pee or ten bob, I'm not sure,' the girl said.

'Ten bob for an ould jersey, not fucking likely. C'mon,' Ruby jerked her head at her daughter. 'Let's sod off.'

As everyone had been predicting since early morning, the heavens opened and the rain came thundering down. Annie shoved the racks together and, with the help of the children, managed to get everything safely beneath the tarpaulin. They huddled in the car, listening to the rain beating on the roof. Sara and Daniel counted the money. 'Sixteen pounds, seventy-five pence, Mummy,' Sara cried triumphantly. 'We should be able to live on that for weeks.'

Annie shook her head. 'Not really, sweetheart. We need to make rather more.'

The rain didn't last long. The skies quickly lightened and a pale sun had appeared by the time they emerged from the car. A great pool of water had gathered in the middle of the tarpaulin. Annie gently lifted it by two corners so the rain would pour away without touching the clothes, but the weight was too much for the clumsily made racks. There was a crack as one rail snapped and collapsed, taking the clothes with it.

'Oh, no!' she cried. Half the things had fallen outwards, onto the dirty wet concrete. The others were precariously suspended on the broken pole, the end of which was caught in the sleeve of a coat.

Sara and Daniel seized the pole whilst Annie removed the clothes before they could join those on the ground – they'd all have to be washed and ironed again. She cursed herself for her lack of carpentry skills. Lauri could have made a couple of stout rails with perfect ease, but then, if Lauri were around, there would be no need for a market stall to keep a roof over their heads. If Lauri were around, they'd be at home, and he'd be pottering in the garden, or the garage if it was raining. But Lauri *wasn't* around, and she *did* have a market stall to run. Annie sighed and threw the dirty clothes into the boot. She managed to squeeze the rest onto the remaining rack. She'd just have to buy proper equipment for next week.

The rain seemed to have washed most of the customers away. It was a quarter to three, and a few traders began to pack up ready to leave.

'Will you be going soon?' she asked Ivor. He was puffing contentedly on a cheroot and didn't seem to care that his fine antiques were wet.

'No, luv. I always stay till the end. I often do good business at the last minute. If folks arrive late, they'll buy almost anything. No-one likes to leave a market empty-handed.'

'In that case, I'll stay, too.'

Cecy was shocked to find half of the stall had disappeared when she returned with a canvas apron. Annie explained she'd have proper racks by next week – Ivor had told her where they could be acquired secondhand. Cecy patted her arm affectionately. 'You're a brave girl, dear. Indomitable, that's what Bruno calls you.'

No-one bought a thing for the next hour. Even Ivor was gazing at his fine antiques as if wondering whether to pack them away, when a crowd of at least twenty coloured men appeared, chatting excitably amongst themselves in a foreign language.

'Lascar seamen,' Cecy hissed. 'You saw hundreds of them on the Dock Road before the war. I doubt if they'll be wanting women's clothes.'

But she couldn't possibly have been more wrong. Half a dozen of the men descended on the stall and began to pull the garments out. They showed them to each other, dark eyes flashing.

It didn't take long for them to make up their minds. Within the space of ten minutes, Annie was presented with a huge bundle. She carefully added up the total. 'Eighteen pounds, ten shillings,' she said weakly. 'But eighteen pounds will do.'

One of the men carefully counted the money out. 'Eighteen pound, ten shilling,' he said, grinning widely.

She tried to give the ten shillings back, but he refused. 'No, nice clothes for ladies back home. You take all.'

'Thank you.'

'Thank *you*, nice lady. Like her.' He tapped his head and winked.

'Like who?'

'He likes your hair,' Cecy whispered.

The men departed as quickly as they'd come. 'I told you it was worth while staying,' said Ivor. 'One of them bought that bloody brass lion. I thought I'd never get rid of the damned thing.'

'I gave you a brass lion like that when you first got married,' Cecy said. 'You said you needed a doorstop between the kitchen and breakfast room. Have you ever used it?'

Annie's exhausted brain searched in desperation for an answer; in other words, a lie. Assistance came from an unexpected quarter. 'We kept stubbing our toes on it,' Sara said sweetly.

'So it got put in the loft,' Daniel added.

'You should never normally tell lies,' Annie said seriously on the way home, 'but a white one doesn't matter occasionally if it saves hurting people's feelings. Thanks. You got me out of a hole. Cecy would be dead upset if she'd known I'd sold her lion.' She glanced at their bright faces through the rear mirror. 'Did you enjoy yourselves?'

'It was smashing, Mummy,' Sara enthused. 'You'll have to go to lots more jumble sales next week.'

'I hope I can find some on weekdays. How about you, Daniel?'

'It was okay,' Daniel said grudgingly.

As Daniel was not usually given to exaggeration, Annie assumed he'd had a good time. On the way home, she stopped at a fish and chip shop and bought three cod and chips for their tea. 'I'll open some fruit for afters, that's if I've got the strength to use the tin opener. I don't know about you two, but I could sleep for a week.'

She had never felt so weary. Her legs, her arms, her entire body throbbed with tiredness. It had been the longest day of her life, physically and emotionally draining. The children needed no persuading to go to bed. When Annie looked in a few minutes later, both were sound asleep. Despite her exhaustion, she made herself unpack the clothes before they got creased, then assembled the rail and hung them up. She carried the muddied garments into the kitchen and loaded the washables into the machine. The heavier things would have to be brushed when the dirt dried. It wasn't financially viable to have them dry-cleaned.

Financially viable! Annie grinned. Lauri would have been amused at the phrase. She sat down and began to count the takings, but her brain felt light-headed and refused to work. She put the money away, the children would enjoy counting it tomorrow.

Her mind slowly travelled through the day. It had been worse than starting a new job, but she'd get used to it. It was a pity about Ruby Livesey. Hopefully, she'd keep out of her way in future. Annie frowned. Where was the white sweater Ruby's daughter had tried to persuade her to buy? It wasn't in the garage or the washing machine, and it definitely hadn't been sold. Someone must have pinched it! She recalled Ruby had been the ringleader when the gang used to shoplift from Woolworth's.

'Bitch! I bet she took it. I'll appoint Daniel stall detective and he can keep an eye on things from now on.'

The phone went. It was Sylvia, full of apologies for not turning up on Annie's first day as a businesswoman. They were in the middle of making arrangements to see *The Godfather* next week, because Chris Andrews said it was the best film ever made, when Annie fell fast asleep, still clutching the receiver. Sylvia thought she'd died and nearly rang for an ambulance.

2

Annie began to recognise her regular customers. She gave them names: there was the Handknitted Lady, who would buy anything crocheted or knitted in a complicated pattern; the Lady with the Veins, always after a skirt or frock long enough to hide the bright purple veins in her legs. After a while, she began to keep a look-out at jumble sales for items that would suit particular women, like the Lacy Lady or the Velvet Lady.

The well-dressed woman who'd bought the evening dress off Cecy returned several times to look for another. 'My husband's a councillor,' she said, 'and we're always being invited to functions where we have to wear evening dress. I hate turning up in the same outfit, but I can't afford to buy evening frocks I'll only wear a few times.'

'I'll keep an eye out for you,' Annie promised. A few weeks later, she unearthed a long dress with a blue and green tartan skirt and a velvet bodice from beneath a heap of clothes in a jumble sale. She washed it carefully in Lux soapflakes and replaced the broken zip, which seemed to be the only reason it had been thrown away. She kept the dress in the car until the woman returned and felt a bit put out when she tried to beat her down to half the asking price.

'It's worth two pounds fifty,' Annie said stubbornly. 'I had to sew the new zip in by hand.'

'One pound fifty, then.'

'Two pounds.'

'All right, two pounds, but I hope it fits.'

The children, particularly Daniel, were beginning to get bored with spending all day in the market. Cecy was only too pleased to take them into town. She liked being taken for their grannie.

Annie thoroughly enjoyed running the stall. It was hard work, but gave her a tremendous sense of satisfaction. She'd never dreamt herself capable of making her living in such an unconventional way. Throughout the week, she travelled far and wide to jumble sales, and spent the evenings washing, ironing and mending. She found it helped to put two, or even three, items on the same hanger; a cardigan over a matching blouse, a sweater with a toning skirt, or a jacket, blouse and skirt altogether, which often persuaded customers to buy the lot. The money earned was enough to pay the bills and live reasonably. If she'd had more rails, she might have made more profit, but the Anglia was already packed to capacity, and she doubted if she'd earn enough to buy a van. Her heart had been in her mouth when the car had gone for its MOT, but apparently the rust was in places that didn't really matter. She'd had to buy two new tyres and the brakes needed tightening, or was it loosening? She wasn't quite sure.

A sense of camaraderie prevailed amongst the stallholders and Annie swiftly made friends. If business was bad one week, it was bad for them all. They would bemoan their misfortune and hope things would be better next Saturday. Ivor Hughes would look after Annie's pitch if she wanted a break, and she in turn looked after his.

Ruby Livesey turned up occasionally to make a nuisance of herself and Annie always kept a sharp eye open for her daughter in case something went missing. Clothes *did* go missing from time to time, but the culprit or culprits were never caught in the act.

When winter came, it was a touch less enjoyable being on her feet in the cold for nine or more hours, so she bought herself a pair of fur-lined boots and thick jeans and came across a well-worn sheepskin jacket for ten pence at a jumble sale, but it still took several hours to unfreeze when she got home. On the coldest days, she made the children stay in the car until Cecy arrived.

'I honestly don't know what I'd do without you,' she said one freezing day in December when Cecy came bustling up in her sable coat, cossack hat and smart suede boots, rather incongruously laden down with old clothes she'd acquired from a friend. Sara and Daniel immediately got out of the car, delighted to see her.

'I'm only too pleased to help, dear. It makes me feel needed. I always look forward to Saturdays, to seeing these two darling children.' She put an arm around each. Sara nestled her face in the expensive fur.

'Frankly Cecy, I think I need you far more than you need me.'

Cecy flushed with pleasure. 'That's what everybody craves, isn't it, to be needed? I've always felt rather superfluous since I've been on my own.' She beamed at the children. 'I think a shopping trip's in order. It's only two weeks off Christmas.'

Daniel's eyes shone. 'Can I have an army outfit for my Action Man?'

'Daniel!' Annie said, horrified. 'Don't be so greedy.'

Cecy smiled. 'I think it's only natural for little boys to be greedy. Ah, look! You've got a customer wanting to buy that lovely red coat. Such a bargain, isn't it?' she cried when the woman came up. 'I've seen coats like that in George Henry Lee's for fifty pounds.'

The woman paid the asking price without a murmur. Cecy would have made a fortune on a market stall.

It was a very different Christmas from the sort she'd grown used to since she married. All Lauri had wanted to do was watch television. He declined to leave the house, even though they were often invited to Christmas dinner, and there was always something happening on Boxing Day or New Year's Eve.

Annie still missed his reassuring presence, but after Mass on Christmas morning, it was a joy to drive through the frost-tipped countryside to Mike's new detached house in Melling, a village not far from Kirkby Trading Estate where Michael Ray Security had taken over even larger premises as the demand for burglar alarms grew and grew.

Every member of the Gallagher clan, thirty in all, had gathered for their Christmas dinner. Mike had engaged professional caterers to provide the food. The children ate first, and the sixteen adults just fitted around the long table, extended to its fullest. The meal was delicious and wine was liberally distributed throughout the meal.

When the tables had been cleared, Mike stood, a trifle unsteadily. He banged the table and everyone fell silent.

'I've never made a speech before, but I suppose there's a first time for everything.' He paused and took a deep breath. 'We've come a long way, us Gallaghers,' he said emotionally. 'There's our Tommy, a foreman in A C Delco; Alan, a chef at one of the poshest hotels in Liverpool. Our Pete's not doing bad with Bootle Corporation, and Bobby's coming to work for me in the New Year. Last, but not least, there's Joe. Who'd have thought our baby brother would end up a corporal in the Paras?'

Joe's heavily pregnant wife, Alison, leaned over and kissed his cheek. Dot glowed with pride at her six lovely lads.

Mike paused and sighed. 'I won't go on about meself, just to say I'd far sooner me pop group had taken off, rather than me business, and I'd give the whole lot up in a minute if I could have Glenda back.' His face grew sad and his eyes sought out Glenda's children, Kathy and Paul. 'But this is not the time for being maudlin. The reason I got up is to say "thanks" to our mam and dad. Thanks for having us, for bringing us up the way you did, for giving us so much love. I know things were hard when we were little, but we never went without. You've always done your best by us, and we'll always be grateful. I'd like you all to raise your glasses and drink a toast to Mam and Dad.'

There was a loud murmur of appreciation and shouts of 'Hear, Hear'. The company rose and drained their glasses willingly. Dot's daughters-in-law found her hard to take at times, but there was no denying her heart was made of solid gold, and if it wasn't for her, there wouldn't have been a Gallagher for them to marry.

Dot burst into tears. Bert patted her shoulder and stood up himself. His face was red with perspiration. He undid the top button of his shirt and loosened his tie. 'I'd like to say a few words if you don't mind, Mike. I won't mention me ould wife here, or she'll only cry even more, but I want to say you lads have done us proud, and you've done it on your own, without any help from those useless geezers in Westminster. I won't go on about politics, not at Christmas. You won't want to hear me ranting on about the mess the Tories are making, the three-day working week, the country plunged into darkness, all because the miners have banned overtime. Everyone, including the government, knows the miners deserve more money.' Dot recovered enough to nudge him sharply with her elbow and hiss that he wasn't at the Labour Party. 'No, no, I won't go on about politics,' Uncle Bert said hastily. 'I'd like to make a toast meself to another member of the family, your cousin, Annie.'

Annie looked up in surprise. Perhaps she'd drunk too much wine, because instead of Bert with his fading blue eyes and wispy hair, she saw the soldier who'd returned after fighting in the war, and recalled how much she and Marie had resented his presence in the little house in Bootle. She'd never dreamt how quickly she would grow to love him.

'Our Annie's had a hard time of it since Lauri went to meet his maker,' Bert was saying, 'but she's come through with flying colours. Annie's living proof of the resources we have within us, but fortunately not many of us have to call on.' Bert raised his glass. 'To Annie!'

The assembled Gallaghers chorused merrily, 'To Annie!'

Mike came out with her when it was time to go. The children climbed into the car, laden with presents and Christmas cake.

'How are you doing, luv?' Mike asked. 'I've been meaning to ask all day, but there never seemed to be a minute.'

'I'm fine,' Annie said happily. 'We all are.'

'Good,' he smiled.

She was fastening her safety belt when Mike knocked on the window. She rolled it down a few inches, which was as far as it would go.

'How's Sylvia?' he enquired. 'Me mam told us about the baby.'

'She's okay. Yasmin's five months old now. She's beautiful.'

Mike grinned. 'I've always fancied that girl!'

'You thought she was conceited.'

'I suppose she had plenty to be conceited about, with them knock-out looks. Mind you, she thought I was boring.'

Annie started up the engine. 'Actually, Mike,' she shouted, 'I think Sylvia quite fancies *you*!'

New Year's Eve was spent quietly with the children in Ormskirk. Sylvia's lounge was warm and cosy, with logs spitting in the inglenook fireplace and the peach-shaded wall lights glowing softly. Delicately patterned gold and silver decorations hung from the black beamed ceiling, shimmering gently in the draught. They played word games, watched TV, and Annie and Sylvia drank too much. Both were more than a little inebriated by the time Big Ben chimed in 1974 and Sara and Daniel went to bed. Yasmin, adorable in her long white nightie and lacy boots, lay asleep in her mother's arms. Cecy rang, then Bruno, followed by Auntie Dot, to wish them a Happy New Year.

'Well, that was nice!' Sylvia said tartly at half past twelve, the phone calls finished.

'I thought the evening very enjoyable.'

'Jaysus, Annie! It was as boring as hell. I kept wishing we were at some crazy party.'

'You can't expect life to be exciting when you've got kids, Syl,' Annie said practically.

'I don't see why not!' Sylvia looked down at her daughter's lovely face. 'I'm not sure if having Yasmin was such a good idea.'

When Annie looked horrified, she said irritably, 'I wouldn't be without her now she's here, but I get lonely, stuck on my own all day.'

'Why don't you get a job?'

Sylvia snorted. 'Oh yes, and take Yasmin in her carrycot!'

'No, make two people happy and leave her with Cecy.'

'I suppose I could.' Sylvia looked quite tearful. 'I love her so much it hurts, then I hate myself for not feeling happy. I suppose I only had her to spite Eric.' She stared moodily into the log fire. 'Did I tell you Eric came the other day?'

'No!' Annie gasped. 'You canny bugger! What did he want?'

'His second marriage didn't last five minutes, he's getting divorced. He wants us to get back together. He's prepared to accept Yasmin as his own.'

'Bloody hell! What did you say?'

'I was so desperately fed up, I nearly agreed. At least we'd be a proper family, and the sex between us is still as good.'

'Sylvia, you didn't . . . !'

'I did,' Sylvia said smugly. 'I've been feeling frustrated along with every-thing else. He said wife number two was tame in bed compared to me.' She wrinkled her nose. 'Oh, Annie, all those plans we had when we were single! Now we're thirty-two, you're a widow and I'm divorced, and we've got three kids between us. What's to become of us, eh?'

'I don't know,' Annie said slowly. 'I'm too busy coping with the present to worry about the future. I won't think about it until Sara and Daniel don't need me any more.'

Sylvia said curiously, 'Don't you ever get the itch, Annie?'

'The itch? Where?'

'Honestly, you're too naive for words! Don't you ever feel sexually frustrated?'

'I'm not sure. I miss things . . .' She missed a shoulder to cry on, the occasional unexpected kiss, someone warm in bed beside her. It would be heaven to be kissed by Robert Redford or Sean Connery or the man on television who advertised cigars, but her imagination stopped there. She couldn't visualise going the whole hog. 'I'd feel as if I was being unfaithful to Lauri if I slept with someone else,' she said. 'Perhaps I'm under-sexed, who knows?'

In February, faced with a miners' strike, Edward Heath called an election with the cry, 'Who rules Britain, unions or government?'

The voters were divided over the issue. Labour emerged as the largest party, but without a majority in the House of Commons. Harold Wilson was once again Prime Minister, and struggled on until October, when another election was called.

Annie had been attending Labour Party meetings since Lauri died. She was one of the few women there and rarely opened her mouth in case she said something stupid, though the men said stupid things all the time. She still felt uncomfortable when she remembered her first meeting. A resolution was put forward about the National Health Service which seemed a very good idea. Then someone proposed an amendment which sounded even better. When the time came to vote, Annie put her hand up straight away. For some reason, they had to vote a second time, so she raised her hand again. A man sitting behind roughly pushed her arm down.

'Idiot!' he hissed. 'You just voted for the amendment. You can't vote for the original resolution as well.' Since then, she'd sat in a corner and said nothing, though she had got the hang of things eventually.

In both elections, Annie delivered leaflets and addressed hundreds of envelopes. The children helped. Sara wrote addresses in her small, square writing, and Daniel folded the election address and stuffed it inside. When, in October, Labour won a working majority, the Menins had been politically blooded. 'Your dad would be proud of us,' Annie said contentedly. She had visions of Lauri happily waving a red flag.

To her surprise, Chris Andrews asked her out to dinner to celebrate, although he was a Liberal and his party had come nowhere. When they arrived home, he surprised her even more by kissing her cheek and confessing that he loved her. They were both unattached. Was there a chance she might feel the same about him one day?

Annie let him down gently. She liked him very much, but couldn't imagine falling in love. 'Anyroad,' she said to herself, 'it's too soon. I feel as if Lauri only died yesterday.'

On a bleak, stormy day the next January, with snow gusting against the windows, Sylvia triumphantly descended on Heather Close, and announced that she and Eric Church were getting married again.

'You must be mad,' gasped Annie. 'He's already proved he's a brute; once bitten, twice shy. Fancy getting involved with him again!'

'Thanks for the good wishes!' Sylvia said acidly. 'Eric's turned over a new leaf. He's utterly charming whenever he comes round, and he adores Yasmin. He's going to move into the cottage with us.'

Annie went into the kitchen to put the kettle on. 'But there's no need to get married,' she said when she came back. 'Why don't you just live together? Couples live together quite openly nowadays.'

'Oh, really! Cecy, of all people, said the same thing.'

'Why don't you?' Annie persisted. 'Then you can kick him out if things go wrong.'

'I'm surprised at you, Annie Menin!' Sylvia snorted. 'What a way to go into a relationship! We're getting married mainly to please Eric's parents. You know the Churches, everything must be official, though it'll be a register office this time.'

Annie shook her head despairingly. 'I don't understand you, Syl. You're continually getting involved with the most unsuitable men.' Ted Deakin, that weird dentist, the Arabian prince were just a few she could bring to mind. Eric Church was the worst of the lot.

Sylvia wrinkled her nose thoughtfully. 'I suppose everyone's in search of happiness – except you.'

'What d'you mean, except me?' Annie said, outraged. 'Are you suggesting I don't want to be happy?'

'No, but you sit back and wait for it to happen. When you get a proposal, it's from someone across the road. Me, I look for happiness. That's why I often end up in a mess. And we're different in other ways.' Sylvia warmed to her theme. 'You're content to go on in the same way, year after year. I can't stand one year being the same as the last.'

'Does that mean Eric will be swopped for a new model next January?'

Sylvia merely grinned. 'At least I'll have a decent social life for a change. I hate being a single woman at dinner parties – you wouldn't know, because you never go. I'll give up that loathsome job.'

'You said the job was brilliant!' For almost a year, Sylvia had been working as personal assistant to the manager of a stockbroking firm, whizzing around in tailored suits whilst Cecy looked after Yasmin.

'All I do is wait on this chap hand and foot.'

'That's what personal assistants are for.'

Sylvia looked at her slyly. 'There's something else, I'm pregnant.'

'Jaysus, Syl!' Annie gulped. 'Is it Eric's?'

'No, he's seen a doctor, he's sterile. It must be that Norwegian naval officer I met last November.'

Annie sighed. 'You make me feel extraordinarily ordinary.'

'Annie, dear friend,' Sylvia cried affectionately. 'Thank God there's people like you in the world. If everyone behaved as I did, anarchy would prevail.' Before Annie could ask, she said that Eric knew all about the baby. 'That's why he pleaded, implored me on his bended knee, Annie, to marry him, so everyone would think it was his.' Only Cecy and Annie knew the truth.

It seemed incredibly complicated, Annie thought when she went to make the tea. With luck, the wedding would be on a Saturday which meant she wouldn't be able to go because of the market. The last thing she wanted was to see her friend married to Eric Church a second time.

Chris Andrews' play was being put on in London. He came over to see Annie, his face red with excitement. 'A producer's just telephoned. Marie had given him my play. He wants to put it on at Easter.'

'I'm ever so pleased, Chris.' It wouldn't be the West End, merely over a pub in Camden, where it would run for three nights.

For the next few weeks, he kept her abreast of developments. The actor in the main role had once been in *Z Cars*. Marie had phoned her congratulations and promised to be there on the first night. He asked Annie's advice on what he should wear. Since becoming Assistant Head at Grenville Lucas, his pigtail had gone and he'd reverted to glasses, and was also growing plump again. 'Should I look formal or casual?' She advised casual.

He was a bag of nerves by the time Easter came. 'Give Marie my fondest love,' Annie said when she saw him off. She would have loved to see the play herself, but Easter Saturday was one of the busiest and most profitable market days of the year. She hadn't seen her sister since Lauri's funeral. There'd been a few postcards since to say she'd got parts – she'd appeared briefly in *Upstairs, Downstairs* – and there was mention of a film in Spain, but nothing so far this year. Annie had got used to her letters remaining unanswered, and, as usual, Marie was never there when she phoned.

Easter Saturday was warm and sunny. Crowds poured into the market and Annie had her best day ever. Her stock was hugely diminished by the time five o'clock arrived and it was time to pack up. Cecy had taken the children to a fête in Ormskirk and would be bringing them home later.

The trouble with the stall was, Annie mused as she drove home, although she loved it, you could never take time off or you lost a whole week's income – she hadn't missed a Saturday in nearly two years. During the week, she was for ever flying off to jumble sales, and although some people said she was too finicky and there was no need to wash and iron the clothes and do all the necessary repairs, it made her feel she was earning her money more honourably.

It left no time for other things, however. She'd not stopped thinking about Chris Andrews and his play. Tonight would be the final performance. She would have given anything to be there, and the children would have enjoyed a weekend in London. They'd never had a holiday in their lives. 'I'm missing out,' she thought. 'If I had a conventional job, even a conventional business, I would have had the weekend off.'

Sara and Daniel had enjoyed their day out. Sara had won a jar of home-made jam and a bottle of shampoo on the hoop-la, and Daniel had come first in the sack race. The first prize was a pound.

'A measly pound,' he said disgustedly. 'I mean, what the hell can I buy with a pound?'

Annie felt too tired to remonstrate. Daniel had become very aggressive lately. Dot said her boys had got too big for their boots when they went into long trousers. 'I just gave them a clock around the ear and it soon brought them to their senses.' Annie felt this was a bit extreme. She'd have a talk with Daniel tomorrow.

'Was Auntie Sylvia there?' she asked.

'Yes, and Yasmin,' Sara replied. 'Uncle Eric bought us ice-creams.'

Uncle Eric! Annie grinned. Eric had been nothing but sweetness and light since the wedding.

Chris Andrews arrived home on Sunday evening. He reported to Annie immediately. 'It went beautifully,' he beamed. 'The actors were superb. They put everything they had into it.' He babbled on breathlessly. A woman from the BBC had been there. She thought the play ideal for television and asked for a copy of the script. 'She warned me not to get my hopes too high. Even if it's accepted, these things can take years. She asked if she could read *Goldilocks*. As soon as I get home, I'll start typing it out afresh.' He gave Annie a copy of the duplicated programme with his name on the front as a memento.

'I'm so pleased for you, Chris.' She felt even more sorry she'd missed all the excitement. 'How's our Marie?'

'Well,' Chris paused and Annie felt a twinge of alarm. 'She seemed a bit low, rather depressed.'

As soon as he'd gone, Annie telephoned her sister. There was no reply. She called again an hour later. A man with a foreign accent answered and told her Marie wasn't in.

'How do you know?' Annie demanded.

'I saw her go out, that's how I know.' He slammed the receiver down.

Annie left it a further two hours before ringing a third time. The same man answered and said brusquely, 'She's still not in.'

'Do you mind slipping a note under her door saying to ring her sister? It's an emergency, a real emergency. I've got to speak to her.'

'I might,' he said, and rang off.

At ten o'clock when she called and the voice with the foreign accent answered, she put the receiver down herself.

It was past midnight when the phone rang. Annie was getting ready for bed. She raced downstairs. To her relief, it was Marie.

'Sis, what's wrong?' Her sister's voice was slightly slurred.

'Nothing. I just wanted to speak to you, that's all.'

'But there's a note under my door to ring my sister, there's been an emergency. I thought something had happened to one of the children.'

'The children are fine, except that the school doctor says Sara has to have glasses. She's at Grenville Lucas – I think I told you in a letter. Anyroad, it was a terrible blow. She's so pretty, and . . .'

Marie interrupted crossly. 'It's scarcely an emergency, sis.'

Annie decided to plunge straight in. 'Chris said you seemed depressed. I was worried . . . are you drunk? Your voice sounds odd.'

'Chris doesn't know what he's talking about,' Marie said listlessly. 'And no, I'm not drunk, I'm tired. I've just taken a sleeping tablet.'

'Why do you need a sleeping tablet if you're tired?'

'Oh, for Chrissakes, sis. I'm not in the mood for this.'

There was a pause and Annie said gently, 'What's the matter, Marie?'

An even longer pause followed, and Annie could hear a snuffling sound and realised her sister was crying. 'Oh, Annie,' she whispered. 'I had another abortion last year. There was this movie in Spain. I only had a small part, but you never know what may come of these things.' Her voice sank so low that Annie had to press the receiver against her ear. 'Afterwards, I had non-stop periods. I've just had a hysterectomy.'

'Marie, luv, why didn't you tell me? I can't stand the thought of you being in hospital all by yourself.'

The programme for Chris's play was on the windowsill in the hall. In a way, it was all his fault. If it hadn't been for *Goldilocks* Marie would never have caught the acting bug. She'd probably be married with a family by now. Annie imagined him feverishly re-typing the play that had caused so much havoc in their lives. *Goldilocks* had been the cause of the terrible scene the night Mam and Dad died.

Marie said, 'You've got enough to worry about, what with the children and this famous market stall.'

'Oh, so you read my letters?'

'I read them over and over, sis. One of these days I might reply.'

'In that case, I might drop dead.' Annie transferred the receiver to her other ear. 'Seriously, sis, why don't you come home?'

'I hope you don't mean for good,' Marie said coldly.

'Of course not,' Annie said hastily, though she had. 'I meant for a holiday. Are you working at the moment?'

Her sister sighed. 'I'm on the dole. I was told to rest for three months after the hysterectomy, but I've got a summer job in a holiday camp.'

'That's good.' There'd been a repertory company in the camp she'd gone on holiday to with Sylvia.

'I'll have to give my room up. I suppose I could stay with you then go straight to Skegness.'

Marie arrived a few weeks later with two suitcases containing the possessions of a lifetime. Annie was shocked by her appearance. She didn't look so bad with her make-up plastered on, but without it her skin was grey and she looked haggard. She had little patience with the children and spent a lot of the time in bed.

Mike had bought his mam and dad a car, so Dot and Bert came several times to see their errant niece. The first time, the conversation turned to reminiscing over the years they'd spent living together in Bootle.

'I used to think you were my mother.' Marie's expression was wistful. 'It was a terrible blow when we left for Orlando Street.'

'My main memory is of Dot throwing the cup against the wall after she'd burnt the custard,' Annie put in.

'I remember that day,' Uncle Bert said. 'It was raining cats and dogs. Father O'Reilly came and got me out of bed.'

'It was Father Heenan,' Dot corrected him.

'No it wasn't, luv, it was Father O'Reilly.'

'I distinctly remember it being Father Heenan.'

'Actually,' said Annie, 'it was Father Maloney. You didn't see him, Uncle

Bert. He'd gone by the time you came downstairs.' The morning had been a turning point in her young life, vividly etched on her mind.

Marie went upstairs to the bathroom and Dot hissed. 'Is she all right? She looks bloody terrible.'

'She's just a bit run down,' said Annie.

'Doesn't Dot look terrible!' Marie remarked when they went back into the house after waving goodbye.

'Dot! Why she looks exactly the same,' Annie said, astonished. 'Her face has scarcely changed, there isn't a wrinkle on it.'

'No, but she hobbles around like an old woman, and why was she waving her hands about all night?'

Annie laughed. 'She's got a touch of arthritis, that's all. She waves her hands to exercise them. You know Dot, she'll overcome it.'

'Can you overcome arthritis? I always thought it came to stay.'

Sylvia was seven months pregnant. She came lumbering along one afternoon with Cecy and Yasmin in tow. Cecy embraced Marie fondly. 'I still regard you as my third little girl.'

Behind her mother's back, Sylvia made a face which Annie ignored. Cecy's presence was only tolerated in Ormskirk because she looked after Yasmin whilst Sylvia rested. This pregnancy was more tiring than the first. Cecy would have both children when their mother found another job. Eric, graciousness itself, thoroughly approved.

Marie was fascinated by Yasmin. Almost two, she was a beautiful, exotic child with glossy black hair cut in a fringe and curling slightly under her ears. Her long-lashed velvet brown eyes glinted mysteriously. Annie was never sure whether it was mischief, or some secret knowledge that she found amusing. Marie sat on the grass and showed her how to make daisy chains until the little girl was covered with them.

'Sylvia's got everything, hasn't she?' Marie remarked after the visitors had gone.

Annie glanced at her sharply. There'd been a touch of envy in Marie's voice. 'What do you mean, everything?'

'A husband, a kid, a mum and dad. She's not hard up for a few bob, either, *and* she's pregnant.'

'You sound as if you're jealous.'

'I'm not jealous of the mum and dad or the husband, and I don't care about the money, but I'd give anything for a little girl like Yasmin.'

Annie was preparing a salad for the tea. She continued laying ham on each plate, took four tomatoes from the fridge and began to slice them neatly with the breadknife and lay them decoratively around the edges.

'Cat got your tongue?' Marie said lightly.

'Possibly.' Annie turned exasperatedly on her sister. 'I was thinking what a stupid remark that was! You've been pregnant three times. The first abortion was unavoidable, but no-one forced you to have the others.'

'You're all heart.' Marie tossed her head and went into the lounge.

Annie followed, waving the breadknife. 'You can't expect sympathy if you go all dewy-eyed over another woman's child, when you could have had two of your own.'

Marie flounced through the French window. Annie went after her. 'It was you, nobody else, who decided to put your career before a family.'

'Thanks for reminding me,' Marie snapped.

'You shouldn't need reminding. We're all authors of our own destiny.'

'What pretentious twaddle!' Marie disappeared into the willow tree.

Annie knelt on the grass outside. 'Another thing, have you never heard of birth control?'

'Of course, but the pill disagrees with me and nothing else works. I must be the most fertile woman in the world. Least I was. I'm not now.'

'Oh, Marie,' Annie sighed. 'I don't know what to say.'

'I think you've said enough already.'

Annie did her best to think of something encouraging. 'At least you've got a nice acting job lined up for the summer.'

'I don't know where you got that idea from.' Marie's voice was cutting. 'I'm working in the bar.'

'But I thought you were in the theatre!'

'Well, I'm not.'

Annie opened the curtain of leaves and crawled inside. 'Must I climb the tree to escape from you?' her sister groaned.

'Remember when we used to go to the Playhouse? Some of the actors were brilliant, but I've never heard of most of them again.'

'Is there a message hidden there, sis?'

'You're working in an over-crowded profession, luv. Even I know only a tiny percentage of actors become successful.'

Marie glared at her belligerently. 'Well, I've no intention of dropping out and making it less crowded.'

'In that case, stop bloody moaning and get on with it.'

To her relief, Marie smiled. 'I don't often moan, sis. It was the hysterectomy that did it. They took away my womb, and I felt as if I was no longer a proper woman. All I had left was acting. What had I given up two babies for? I've spent more than half my life trying to become an actress, and I'm no nearer now than the day I left Liverpool.'

'You *are* an actress, Marie,' Annie said comfortingly. There probably wasn't another person in the world who'd feel sorry for her sister, so ruthlessly pursuing this ephemeral success. 'Anyroad, something might come of the picture you made in Spain.'

'It isn't released until next year and it was a crap movie, sis. It was made on a shoestring, and the director was hardly out of nappies. He hadn't a clue what he was doing.'

Annie patted her hand, 'You'll make it, sis. I feel it in me bones.'

Sylvia's new daughter, Ingrid, was pale and fair, the absolute image of Eric, according to his parents. 'I feel a bit lousy about it,' Sylvia confessed when Annie went into the expensive nursing home to see her, 'but it was Eric's idea to fool them, not mine.'

'I'm glad I don't get into pickles the way you do. I'd give meself away in no time.' Annie played with Ingrid's tiny fingers as she lay sleeping in the frilled cot beside Sylvia's bed. She was like a little ice maiden, skin pure white and hair the colour of milk. 'I'd give anything for another baby.'

'There's nothing stopping you, Annie.'

Annie laughed. 'In case you haven't noticed, I've no husband.'

'Who needs husbands?' Sylvia said airily. 'Seduce Chris – he'd be a knockover. Then we could walk our babies in the park together the way we said we'd do. It'd be ten years later than planned, but so what!'

'I'm too old-fashioned.' Annie made a face. 'I'm not the type.'

3

She felt slightly despondent when winter approached, the hour went on the clocks and the nights grew darker. People began to talk about Christmas when it seemed scarcely any time since the last.

'What have I done with meself during 1975?' Annie asked herself one miserable grey day in November. She was surrounded by clothes which she was supposed to be mending. Instead, she leant on the sewing machine and stared gloomily out of the window at the damp pavements and limp gardens of Heather Close.

'Absolutely nothing,' she replied. 'Nothing of any significance.' Whilst Marie had got another small part in a film, Valerie Cunningham had been promoted to office manager, and Sylvia's life was once again a whirl of dinner parties, her own life was nothing but hard work followed by more hard work. She never went anywhere, not even the pictures. There wasn't the time, and anyroad, she had no-one to go with, apart from Chris Andrews. If the stall were more profitable, she could have taken on a partner and had every other Saturday off, but she didn't take enough to share with someone else. She'd had to ask the bank manager for a loan to get the Anglia through its last MOT. The garage had suggested it was time she bought something else, but the car seemed like a member of the family and she couldn't bear to part with it. Anyroad, she would have had to borrow even more for a replacement.

She sighed, told herself to stop wasting time, and picked up a skirt which had a button missing. 'I'm fed up washing and mending other women's cast-off clothes,' she said aloud. 'If Sara goes to university, as Chris thinks she should, I could be at this for the next decade.'

But what else could she do? By this time next year, Daniel would be at Grenville Lucas and Sara would be thirteen – a teenager! Perhaps she could have another stab at getting a job. Though the same problem still remained, young children: not as young as last time, but young all the same. She still wasn't prepared to leave them at a loose end during the holidays. Another thing, she didn't fancy taking orders after running her own business. It was nice being independent, your own boss.

It was a relief when the phone rang. She hoped it would be Sylvia, she felt like a good gossip, but it was Auntie Dot. 'Are you watching telly, luv?' Dot asked eagerly.

'No, I find it a distraction when I'm working.' She stared out of the window instead.

'The Conservatives have elected a woman leader, Margaret Thatcher. I'd never vote for them, but I think it's great. God forbid it should happen, but if they get in again, we'll have a woman Prime Minister.'

Annie agreed that a woman, Tory or otherwise, could only do the country good. 'How are your aches and pains?' she asked.

'Not so bad, girl, not so bad.' Dot chuckled. 'I got stuck on the lav this morning and Bert had to help me off. We've been married forty years, and it's the first time he's seen me on the lavvy.' The arthritis was spreading at a terrifying rate. Bert said she was often close to tears with the pain. She went on, 'The trick is not to give in or you're done for. One day, I'll wake up and the pain'll be gone.'

'I hope so, Auntie Dot.' Annie prayed nightly this would happen.

After Dot rang off, Annie phoned Sylvia. Cecy answered and said she was lunching with Eric. 'Sorry, dear, I can't stop, Ingrid's crying.'

Annie gloomily envisaged her friend, done up to the nines, driving into town in the new Volvo estate and lunching in an expensive restaurant, whilst she was stuck in this dead quiet house with heaps of clothes to mend. She switched the lamps on, hang the extravagance, and played a Freddy and the Dreamers record to cheer herself up. It would be today that both the children planned to be home late; Sara was having tea with her friend, Louise, and Daniel was playing snooker. One of the boys from school had a six-foot table in the garage. Daniel desperately wanted one himself. 'You could leave the car outside, Mum,' he pleaded.

'If I could afford it, son, you could have a table tomorrow,' Annie told him. Daniel had turned away, disgusted. He refused to believe they were hard up. 'We're not *really* hard up,' she thought. 'There's always enough food, the house is warm, and I've never had to buy their clothes secondhand – and Daniel's shoes cost a mint.' His feet were so broad, she had to get Clarks. 'It's just there's never enough for luxuries.'

'I'm getting nowhere at this rate.' She searched for a black button for the skirt, but could find none the right size. Determined not to use the lack of a button as an excuse to do nothing, she fetched the box of odds and ends in from the garage, stuff she'd bought because she liked the look of the material. She'd always meant to do something with them one day, she wasn't sure what.

She tipped the box upside down and the clothes spilled out onto the floor. Her eyes were searching for a garment that might have a black button, when she noticed an olive-green frock sprinkled with little dark roses had fallen on top of something made of glossy plum velvet.

'Oh, don't they look lovely together!'

She picked the velvet up. It was an old dressing gown, and the material ran through her fingers like silk. Underneath the arms was completely frayed and the collar was hanging off, but the rest was whole. Perhaps it was the years of wear that made it feel so soft. She examined the frock, which was crepe with square padded shoulders, and vaguely remembered thinking it too old-fashioned to sell. The roses were exactly the same colour as the velvet.

Annie laid the things side by side on the arm of the settee and stared at them for a long time. Then she closed her eyes and in her head she designed an outfit; a plain dirndl skirt with an elasticated waist from the dressing gown, a loose, shapeless top out of the dress with scalloped velvet trim on the sleeves and hem. Baggy sleeves, a low round neck that wouldn't need a fastener. Both garments already had their own tie belts. She would decide which one to use when she finished – no, she'd open up both belts and sew them together so they could be used either way.

Excitement mounting and mending forgotten, Annie picked up her scissors and got down to work. The skirt took no time, she already had several yards of wide elastic. Making the top took slightly longer. She had to face the neck and put a dart in the bust. The scalloped trim required the patience of Job. She ironed it lightly before attaching it to the top. She could hardly wait to see the whole thing finished, and impatiently began to pick at the stitches on a belt.

It was almost five o'clock and she'd forgotten all about Daniel's tea by the time she'd done. Her hands were shaking when she put the suit on a hanger and suspended it from the door. She tried the two-sided belt one way, then the other, before deciding to leave the green uppermost. The plum velvet was revealed when she tied the knot.

She took a step back and regarded her handiwork with a gasp of pleasure. It looked *beautiful*!

When Sara came home, Annie asked what she thought. 'You're not going to wear it, are you, Mummy? It's horrible.'

Dismayed, Annie took her precious suit next door to show to Valerie. 'It's certainly different,' Valerie said dubiously. 'It looks expensive – I can see you or Sylvia in it. How much will you ask for that?'

'I wasn't thinking of selling it.'

'Actually,' Valerie cocked her head sideways, 'it grows on you. I bet it's comfortable to wear, and stylish at the same time.'

Perhaps she could put it on the stall, Annie thought when she got home, but she wasn't prepared to take a penny less than ten pounds, and not many women came to Great Homer Street market prepared to pay that much for an outfit, despite the fact it was completely unique. If no-one bought it, she'd keep it herself.

When Saturday came, she put the two-piece at the front of a rack. Several women approached and looked at it longingly, but pulled a face when they saw the price. It was mid-day when the woman who was always on the look-out for evening wear came up. Annie was serving someone else. Out of the corner of her eye, she saw the woman pounce on the suit and hold it against herself. Then she looked at the price tag. 'Will you take six pounds for this?'

'Sorry, no.'

'How about eight?'

'I'll not take a penny less than ten,' Annie said stubbornly. 'It's an original. You'll never see another woman in the same thing.'

'All right, ten it is. Are you likely to have any more? We've been invited to all sorts of functions over Christmas.'

'I might have one next week.'

*

By the time next Saturday came, Annie had made another suit. She'd kept her eye open at jumble sales for things made from suitable material, regardless of the style, and had converted a cream Viyella frock and an old-gold silky bedspread, threadbare in places, into a thing of beauty, according to Chris Andrews who saw the finished outfit. Following the same pattern as last week, she made a skirt from the bedspread. This time, she attached big gold diamond shapes down the front of the baggy cream top, and cut the hem so it hung in points. Then she covered several tiny buttons with the gold material and attached one to each point. Once again, she made a reversible belt.

'This is the sort of thing you should have been doing years ago, Annie,' Chris said admiringly. 'It's a work of art.'

She was still setting up her stall when a customer bought the suit.

'I saw the one you had last week,' the woman said breathlessly. 'I only wandered off to make me mind up, but when I came back it was gone. I came early this time in case you had another. This one's even nicer. Will you be having more? I'd love to send one to me sister in Canada.'

Annie was pleased when she was able to tell her regular customer, whom she'd never much liked, that, yes, she'd had one of her 'unusual outfits', as the woman called it, but it had gone hours ago.

'I thought you'd have kept it for me.' The woman looked annoyed. 'I wore the other to a dinner dance on Wednesday and everyone asked where I'd got it. Of course, I didn't say it came from a market.'

'I'll have another for next week.' She thoroughly enjoyed creating her 'unusual outfits'; it was a pleasant and easy way of making money. If she managed to sell one a week until Christmas, there'd be enough to buy Daniel a snooker table.

It was New Year's Eve, no, New Year's Day. Annie held her watch up to the light which filtered through the white curtains of Sara's room. Ten past four and she hadn't slept a wink.

This year, the Cunninghams had thrown a party. Annie had taken Daniel but they hadn't stayed long as it began to get rather wild. Fortunately, the children were playing Monopoly in the breakfast room and didn't seem aware of what the adults were getting up to elsewhere – you daren't open a door lest you found a couple involved in some sort of hanky-panky. Kevin had pinched Annie's bottom and suggested they go out to the garage. Lord knows where Valerie was, she disappeared for ages.

Annie had a good excuse to leave at eleven because her daughter was due home. Sara had been to her first proper party. When the invitation arrived, Annie began to plan a party dress, but Sara insisted on a skimpy black skirt and a black polo-neck jumper.

'For a party, luv?' Annie said, dismayed.

'Yes, Mummy, and I know we can't afford it, but I'd love a pair of pixie boots.'

Annie had bought the pixie boots for Christmas and Daniel had got his longed-for snooker table. Bruno kept it in the Grand, then brought it round after the bar closed on Christmas Eve and helped to erect it in the lounge. As soon as Christmas was over it was going in the garage.

'Merry Christmas, Annie!' Bruno had kissed her warmly on the lips before leaving and her stomach gave a pleasant little lurch. He was sixty, but still gorgeous. Cecy must be stark raving mad!

She turned over for the umpteenth time. She hadn't been sleeping well for weeks, ever since she'd made that first outfit. Her mind buzzed with ideas and she had to keep a notebook by the bed to jot them down in case they'd been forgotten by morning. It wasn't exactly true to say her outfits had sold like hot cakes, because there hadn't been enough, the most she'd managed was three a week, but word seemed to have spread. On the last Saturday before Christmas, a woman had asked, 'Are you the lady who makes the patchwork frocks?' Annie had to tell her she'd sold out, but would have more in the New Year.

Then a terribly haughty woman, beautifully dressed, had offered to buy two suits a week on a regular basis at seven pounds fifty each.

'I'll think about it,' Annie said, dazed.

'What did she want?' Cecy asked.

'Do you know her?'

'I know who she is. She runs an expensive boutique in Chester. You can't buy anything there for less than fifty pounds.'

'Fifty pounds? She offered to buy two outfits off me every week for seven pounds fifty.'

'Cheek!' Later, Cecy said thoughtfully, 'You know, Annie, it wouldn't be a bad idea for you to start a shop yourself.'

A shop of her own! It was another reason for not sleeping. She'd seen a lot of Cecy over Christmas – Sylvia, Eric and the children had gone to Morocco for the holiday, so she was at a loose end. They talked all the time about opening a shop.

'The thing is,' said Annie, 'I couldn't possibly make enough clothes to fill a shop.'

Sylvia telephoned as Annie was about to go to the Cunninghams'. They'd just arrived home and had enjoyed themselves tremendously. 'We went to the Casbah every day. I bought heaps of lovely things.'

'What are you doing tonight?' Annie enquired.

'We're spending the evening quietly as a family. I'll be thinking of you, friend, when the clock strikes twelve.'

Annie remembered glancing at the Churches' Christmas card as she put the phone down. Only Sylvia could send something so ostentatious; a photo of the family taken in the cottage, Sylvia in the pink armchair looking queenly, with Ingrid on her knee, and Yasmin leaning against her mother, staring at the camera with her dark, mysterious eyes. Both girls wore frothy white dresses. Eric was sitting on the arm of the chair, his arm laid casually on his wife's shoulder. There was a Christmas tree, lights glowing, in the background. They must have put the tree up exceptionally early, as the card had been one of the first to arrive.

'I'm never going to sleep tonight.' Annie carefully eased herself to a sitting position, so as not to disturb Sara, though the house could fall down and Sara wouldn't wake up. Even when the doorbell rang about two hours ago, she'd slept right through.

The doorbell had rung on and on, as if someone were leaning against it.

Worried it might be a drunk come to the wrong house. Annie shouted 'Who's there?' before answering.

'It's me,' a voice said huskily.

Sylvia! Annie opened the door. 'Oh, Jaysus!' she exclaimed. Sylvia's jaw was swollen and there was blood trickling from her nose. She was in her nightclothes, as were the children. Ingrid was fast asleep in her arms. Yasmin, looking scared, clutched her mother's dressing gown.

'What happened, Syl?' Annie picked Yasmin up and carried her inside.

Sylvia sank onto the settee. 'Eric had one too many,' she said dully. 'We were just about to go to bed, when something seemed to snap. He said he loathed me more than ever because I'd been with other men. He particularly hates . . .' she nodded at Yasmin, 'because she's coloured. According to him, people snigger behind his back and regard him as a cuckold. I didn't think that word was used nowadays, Annie. Cuckold!'

'Oh, luv!'

'You were right, after all.' Sylvia closed her eyes briefly. 'I should never have got involved with him again. They say the leopard never changes its spots, don't they?'

After several cups of tea, Sylvia went to bed. Annie put all three in her room, emptying the wardrobe drawer for the baby.

'You're the only person in the world I could turn to,' Sylvia said gratefully as Annie tucked her in. 'Cecy would have had hysterics, and Bruno'd have driven to Ormskirk and slaughtered Eric in his bed.'

'You know I'll always be here for you, Syl.'

'And me for you, Annie.'

Annie slid back under the bedclothes, feeling envious of her daughter's regular breathing. Despite what had happened, her thoughts went back to the shop. Cecy had asked what she would call it, should the dream turn into reality. ' "Annie's" would be nice,' she mused.

But this was something Annie had already decided. 'No, I've already thought of a name. If me shop gets off the ground, I'll call it "Patchwork"!'

Patchwork

1

Uncle Bert bent on one knee beside Dot's wheelchair and began to sing 'If you were the only girl in the world . . .' in a surprisingly steady baritone, considering the amount of beer he'd drunk that night.

There was scarcely a dry eye in the room over the pub where Tommy and Dawn's reception had been held twenty-four years ago. The place was packed, the music loud, the August night stuffy. The windows were even more difficult to open than in 1956.

All the Gallagher lads were there with their families. There were eighteen grandchildren at the last count – twenty if you counted Mike's stepchildren, Kathy and Paul. Great-grandchildren had begun to arrive, two so far and two more on the way. Mike, elegantly handsome in a dark grey silk suit, his red hair cut short, had become a sort of grandfather when Kathy had a son the previous year. Kathy and her boyfriend were living together in Melling. It was, thought Annie, incredible how things had changed. Young people no longer required a piece of paper to formalise their relationship.

Bert wheeled Dot to the side of the room. He did everything for her nowadays; washed and dressed her, carried her to the lavatory, did the cooking, the cleaning. The lads, their wives, Annie, came to give him a break, to sit with Dot whilst he went for a pint or to the Labour Party. Otherwise, Bert dedicated his waking hours to the care of his beloved wife. 'He even wipes me botty for me, poor feller,' Dot told Annie with a chuckle that turned into a sigh. 'I can't reach round that far.'

Despite being severely crippled and wheelchair-bound, Dot had still insisted on a party on her seventieth birthday. Her infirmities did nothing to dampen her indomitable spirit.

Annie had never seen her aunt look beautiful before. Perhaps it was because she could no longer use her body that Dot's face appeared so wonderfully alive. Her skin glowed taut and silvery over the angular bones and her eyes glittered behind her new pearl-rimmed spectacles. Even the fact Bert had applied her lippy crookedly did nothing to detract from the brilliant radiance of the seventy-year-old woman with the cruelly twisted body. She wore a white gossamer knitted shawl, Annie's present, over a pale blue dress and pretty slippers with pom-poms on the toes, because Bert could no longer get shoes on her feet.

Her lads fussed over her all night, terrified their mam might not see another birthday. After all, there was a limit to what a body could stand. Steroids had given her diabetes and now she had angina, which meant awful pains in her chest, which, Dot said with a grin, was the only place the arthritis hadn't reached.

The pianist was playing all the old tunes; 'Amongst my Souvenirs', 'The Old Lamplighter', 'There's a Small Hotel' . . . He ran his fingers up and down the keys and began, 'Goodnight Sweetheart', as Mike came over and asked Sylvia to dance.

Annie had a strong feeling of *déjà vu*, as Mike's girlfriend, Delia, an attractive blonde in her thirties, glared at him from across the room. He hadn't been so rude as at Tommy's wedding with poor Pamela, but Annie noticed he'd had eyes for no-one but Sylvia all night. And as if a circle had taken twenty-four years to form, he was dancing with her again, holding her closely and scarcely moving to the music played on the same old piano as before.

Annie went into the kitchen in search of a cup of tea. The room was empty and a giant kettle steamed gently on the antique gas stove. She put a teabag in a cup, filled it with water, added powdered milk and drank it leaning against the sink. Wouldn't it be marvellous if Sylvia and Mike got together! It was about time Sylvia settled down; after all, they'd both be forty next year. Annie recalled the New Year's Eve when Eric had gone berserk and his wife and children had landed on her doorstep. Next morning, Eric turned up, having already been to Cecy's and roused Bruno from a hangover, utterly contrite, swearing he'd never do anything like that again. Annie refused to let him in.

Bruno's hangover was not so bad that he didn't begin to wonder why his son-in-law was searching for his family so early on New Year's Day. He came storming round to Heather Close to see if Annie had an explanation, and found Eric on the doorstep almost in tears.

'What's going on?' he demanded.

Sylvia came down in her bloodstained nightdress. A big purple bruise had appeared on her swollen chin. Bruno's horrified glance went from his daughter to her husband, then, with a growl, he took Eric by the scruff of the neck, dragged him down the path and threw him on the pavement. 'You're never to come near Sylvia or the girls again!'

Annie, though glad it was too early for the neighbours to witness, quite enjoyed the scene.

Eric disappeared. Cecy heard he'd been transferred to the Churches' new London office. Divorce proceedings commenced a second time.

Sylvia stayed a month with Annie, then she put the cottage on the market, bought a house in Waterloo and announced that, from now on, she was going to write poetry and devote her life to the children. She wore dirndl skirts and baggy sweaters and let her hair flow free and wild. She often turned up at Annie's to read her latest poem.

'What do you think?'

Annie's opinion was usually more or less the same. 'If you want the truth, I think it's awful. It doesn't rhyme and it doesn't make sense.'

'It's not supposed to make sense. Life doesn't make sense.'

'Anyone could write poetry that doesn't make sense. Even *I* could.'

'You haven't got a poetic bone in your body, Annie Menin.'

'No, but I've plenty of practical ones. I need to make a living.' Annie was in the throes of an inner debate; should she give up her small, regular income from the stall and take the risk of opening her own shop? It was the most difficult decision she'd ever had to make. Sylvia and her poetry were getting on her nerves.

'One day,' Sylvia said haughtily, 'my poems could make my fortune.'

'Huh!'

After a year, the dirndl skirts and baggy sweaters were thrown away and the poetry forgotten. Cecy was pressed into service to look after the girls whilst her daughter changed her image for the umpteenth time and went to work for an employment agency in Southport.

'It's not what I want, Annie,' Sylvia confessed. 'What I want more than anything is a happy marriage. I would have made a go of it with Eric, but I wasn't prepared to be a punchbag for the rest of my life.'

'I don't blame you,' Annie murmured.

'What do *you* want, Annie?' Sylvia asked seriously.

'I'm not sure.' Annie thought hard. 'Same as you, I suppose. I never planned on having a market stall or a shop. I still miss Lauri, but can't visualise marrying again, not that anyone but Chris has asked.'

Sylvia shuddered. 'One day the children will be married, and we'll be stuck with each other. We can go to whist drives and play bingo.'

'Oh, don't, Syl! That sounds too depressing for words.'

'Mummy, there you are! I've been searching for you everywhere.' Sara came into the kitchen. 'We're going into town to a disco.'

'Who's "we"?' demanded Annie.

'Becky, Emma and me.'

'Will you be all right, three girls on your own?' Becky and Emma were Alan Gallagher's daughters.

'Of course we will,' Sara assured her.

'Give Auntie Dot a nice big kiss before you go. Where's Daniel?'

'He's in the pub.' Sara wriggled her tall, slim frame uncomfortably. 'He's drinking an awful lot of cider. I think he's showing off.'

Annie made a face. 'All right, luv, I'll see to him.' She gave her daughter an affectionate shove. 'Enjoy yourself – don't be late home.'

'I've told Becky and Emma I have to be in by half eleven.'

Sara left. She was still a model child, awkward and gangling, and childishly innocent for seventeen, despite being so clever. Annie worried men would take advantage of her naivety. Her glasses emphasised the babyish curves of her face and the wide blue eyes that seemed incapable of seeing wrong. How on earth would she cope at university?

Annie sighed and transferred her thoughts to Daniel. He shouldn't be in the pub, but the landlord was unlikely to guess the handsome six-footer with the deep voice was only fifteen. If she yanked him out he'd claim she'd made a show of him in public, which apparently she'd done when she found him smoking behind the gym at Grenville Lucas last year.

'What will me mates think?' he said angrily as she marched him home. 'No-one else's mother turns up to spy on them.'

'I was there to see Mrs Peters about something to do with Sara,' Annie said defensively. 'I only came across you by accident.'

'I won't be able to hold me head up in class tomorrow.'

She recalled Marie had been found smoking when she was only nine or ten and supposed it was something most kids got up to, particularly boys. She made him promise never to smoke in the house and said no more.

Since then, Daniel had grown another six inches and took size ten shoes. Like Marie, he seemed adult before his time. He badly needed a father to keep him in line. How would Lauri have dealt with his over-sized son? Annie had a feeling he would have left everything to her.

She was rinsing the cup when Dawn Gallagher came into the kitchen. No longer thin and darkly dramatic, Dawn had grown stout and grey over the years. She looked Annie up and down enviously.

'I bet you could still wear that bridesmaid frock. My wedding dress wouldn't go near me.' She patted her wide hips. 'How's your Marie?'

'She's making a film in America.' According to the critics, the young director Marie had been so contemptuous of had turned out to be a youthful genius. He'd used her in his subsequent films, as he liked having the same actors in supporting roles. Unfortunately, the films were uncommercial and had never gone out on general release, so Annie had never managed to see one.

'America! You've both done well for yourselves; Marie in films and you with your shop. Dot said it's really taken off. What's it called? I keep meaning to come and buy something off you one day.'

'Patchwork, but I'm afraid things are rather expensive.' Nowadays, her dresses and suits cost upwards of thirty pounds.

Dawn sighed and glanced around the shabby room. 'I remember coming in here on me wedding day to take two aspirin, me head was splitting.'

'Everyone cried their eyes out at your wedding.'

'Perhaps they sensed how it would turn out,' Dawn said bitterly.

'What do you mean, luv?' Annie asked astonished. Dawn and Tommy had always seemed very happy.

'Don't say a word to Dot, I don't want her to know until it's absolutely necessary, but me and Tommy are getting divorced.'

'I don't believe it!'

'Annie, luv, he's had another woman for years. He promised to stay with me until the kids were off our hands. With Ian getting married at Christmas, he reckons it's time he went.' Dawn glanced at her reflection in the darkening window. 'They're a flighty lot, the Gallaghers. I'm being ex-changed for a younger version of meself.'

Annie sat with Dot and Bert during the last waltz. She had no-one to dance with. She could have brought Chris, but it seemed wrong to use him just because it was convenient. Anyroad, he might get ideas . . .

'I see our Mike's at Sylvia again.' Dot's eyes gleamed wickedly. 'He's a much better catch these days. He'll be a millionaire soon.' She gave a triumphant cackle. 'That Delia's gone home in a huff, I'm pleased to say. Never did like those peaches-and-cream, butter-wouldn't-melt-in-me-mouth women like Mrs Thatcher.'

'Now, luv!' Bert said warningly. 'Don't get yourself all worked up.'

'Not Mrs Thatcher again, Auntie Dot,' Annie groaned.

'Well, I can't stand the woman. Said she'd reduce taxes when she got in, and what did she do? Put that VAT thing up double. Going to tame the unions, is she? Well, let's see her do it.'

'She'll do it, luv.' Bert shook his head sadly. 'Unemployment's going through the roof. The unions'll be on their knees before long.'

'The whole country'll be on its knees if Mrs Thatcher has her way, apart from the nobs and the bosses.' Dot's voice rose.

'Auntie Dot, remember your heart!'

'Sod me bleedin' heart. If I can't pass an opinion on someone I loathe and detest, then I might as well be dead. Not that I've any intention of going before that woman. They're making such a cock-up, they'll never get in at the next election.'

Bert made a face at Annie behind his wife's back. In a bid to distract her attention, he said, 'Aren't Sylvia's kids a picture? One's as dark as the other's fair.'

The bid worked. 'Is the eldest one coloured, Annie?' Dot enquired. 'She looks as if she's got a touch of the tar brush in her blood.'

'I don't know,' said Annie. Seven-year-old Yasmin and Ingrid, two years younger, were as striking as their mother.

Dot lapsed into silence as she watched the dancers. Although Annie wouldn't have dreamt of saying so, she thought Labour deserved to lose last year's election. Over the winter, the unions had gone completely crazy – the gravediggers had gone on strike in Liverpool and ordinary people were unable to bury their dead. Of course, she'd canvassed and leafleted as usual, but felt it was in aid of a lost cause.

The last waltz ended. The pianist played a few final crashing chords. Tommy demanded three cheers for the birthday girl. 'Hip, hip . . .'

'Hooray!' roared the entire Gallagher clan.

And Dot burst into tears as her party came to an end.

Valerie Cunningham had spotted the empty premises in South Road, a few minutes' walk from Heather Close, four years ago. Annie had gone round straight away to peer through the double-fronted windows. It turned out to be where she'd bought Mam the pink dress for Tommy Gallagher's wedding. Empty, the place looked bigger. It needed decorating and the carpet was hideous, shades of green, squares within squares. She'd like a plain carpet so as not to detract from the clothes; a warm oatmeal.

After making enquiries, she found the rent was reasonable, though the agent wanted a year in advance. A ten-year fixed rate lease was available if she wanted. She dithered for another month, trying to make up her mind. What had she got to lose? She could always go back to the market. Actually, there was quite a lot to lose; the advance rent, the cost of decoration, the carpet . . .

Annie discussed it with the children. Daniel didn't care one way or the other, but Sara thought she should go ahead. 'You love making clothes, Mummy. You should do what you enjoy. You've only got one life.'

So Annie had taken the plunge. The bank manager was forthcoming when asked for another loan, 'Your own shop! What an enterprising lady you are, Mrs Menin,' he said, a trifle patronisingly she thought.

The problem of being unable to turn out sufficient stock was solved. She wouldn't just sell her own clothes, but other things with the same patchwork theme. Cecy knew a woman whose sister made beautiful patchwork quilts and cushion covers. When Annie approached Susan Hull, she was pleased to have an outlet for her work.

'I'd take twenty-five per cent,' Annie told her.

Susan pulled a face. 'Twenty-five!'

'You've got nothing to lose. I'll have all the outgoings; rent, rates, advertising, as well as the upkeep of the shop. It's costing the earth for a new carpet and the place is being decorated throughout.'

'I suppose that's fair,' the woman said reluctantly.

'If it doesn't suit you, I'll find someone else.' Annie wasn't keen on Susan Hull, with her thin rhubarb face and long red hands, but her quilts were glorious and she'd quite like them in her shop.

'There's no need for that,' Susan said hastily.

'Do you know anyone with a knitting machine?'

'Sorry, no.'

But Auntie Dot did. 'There's this ould feller in Frederick Street who turns out smashing jumpers.'

'A man!' Annie only imagined women having knitting machines.

'He took over his wife's machine after she died. He's far better at it than Minnie ever was.'

She'd gone to see Ernie West, a wizened little chap who looked at death's door. He lived in a tiny terraced house, furnished as it might have been in the last century. 'I can turn out a jumper in a night,' he said boastfully when she explained what she wanted.

'Yes, but as I said, I don't want them dead plain. I'd like at least two different colours.'

Ernie looked at her indignantly. 'I got you the first time, missus.'

'I'll take twenty-five per cent.'

'Take what you like, luv, I don't give a toss about the money. I just like knitting on ould Minnie's machine.'

She asked for a couple of samples. Two weeks later, Ernie turned up at the house with an old sack, bulging. Annie's heart was in her mouth, worried they'd be awful. Instead, she gasped. 'They're lovely!'

There was one black and white, the squares the exact size of a chess board, with a single red stitch in each centre. Another, red at the hem, gradually turning to blue, green, yellow at the neck; one maroon and navy, the sort of colours she would have chosen herself, though she'd never dream of combining lemon with mustard, but it looked really effective.

'I'm dead pleased with these,' she said.

'I knew you'd be.' Ernie preened himself. 'I'm an artist in me own way.'

'You certainly are,' Annie conceded.

She was sad at giving up the market stall which had seen her through the worst times after Lauri's death. On her final day, she reduced the remaining stock to half price and bought two crates of beer to share with her fellow traders when she said her goodbyes.

'You'll have us caught for drunk driving,' Ivor Hughes protested, downing his third bottle. 'Well, good luck with the shop, girl.'

Annie made a special point of going into the indoor section to say goodbye to the Barclays on their fruit and veg stall. Sid and Vera had recently sold the house next door and gone to live in Woolton.

'I don't know what it was, Annie,' Vera confessed, 'but I never felt right there. It was as if the place was haunted, which is a stupid thing to say about a place so newly built.' She shuddered. 'I always had the feeling the old couple who used to live there resented us.'

Number six had been bought by the Dunns, a childless couple in their forties. They were an unsociable pair, who complained about the noise from the children. Annie was glad her two no longer played in the garden. The Dunns had recently planted a tall hedge at the front.

There were shouts of, 'Good luck, Annie', as she began to pack up early. Ruby Livesey appeared. Annie gave her a beer and asked if she'd like the remaining clothes as she was giving up.

'I knew you'd never stick at it,' Ruby sneered. 'And you can keep your clothes. They're not the sort I sell.'

'Suit yourself,' said Annie.

On the Monday morning after Dot's party, Annie paused outside Patchwork. A signwriter had painted the name, each letter a different colour. Even after four years, she still got pleasure from looking at her shop.

A single outfit hung in the left-hand window, a white voile two-piece with a wide band of soft blue satin bordering the hem. Inserted between the blue and white was a strip of white lace threaded with blue ribbon. The top had a blue shawl collar tied in a knot. A handwritten card indicated the price was £35. In the other window, a brightly patterned quilt was draped over a pine box, and one of Ernie's jumpers lay casually on the floor.

Annie unlocked the door. Two rails of clothes, one following the other, were to her left, and a rail of jumpers and waistcoats to the right. A small cane settee was heaped with patchwork cushions. Three more quilts, folded on their special racks, hung from the wall. The place looked uncluttered without appearing bare, though the wall above the clothes bothered her. It needed pictures.

She sat down at the Regency desk at the rear of the shop and wrote out an order for Mr Patel in Bolton. Mr Patel owned a small mill that turned out exclusive cloth for the very best shops in London. Although Annie was one of his smallest customers, he always made a great fuss of her when she went to look at his latest designs; the silky velvets, the soft jerseys, coarse knobbly cottons, delicate voiles, all dyed the most unusual colours. It was the sort of stuff you never saw in shops like Lewis's or Owen Owen's. Once she'd turned professional, it was no good relying on jumble sales for material.

The order written, Annie stood the envelope on the desk ready to post. It was ten minutes before the shop was due to open, but she changed the sign from 'Closed' in case she forgot, and went into the minuscule kitchen to put the kettle on.

On the way, she paused in front of the fitting-room mirror. Dawn was wrong, that bridesmaid frock would never fit, she'd only been fourteen then. On the other hand, she'd get into her wedding dress, except it had been sold in the market. Her figure had scarcely changed since she got married. She was lucky to be uninterested in food. In times of stress, she ate less, whereas other women were inclined to gorge.

Annie peered closely in the mirror. Hardly any wrinkles. She didn't look so bad for a woman not far off forty. Her crimson and tan dress, one of her own creations, set off her red hair. She could do with more earrings – she could sell jewellery in the shop!

'I'd love to grow me hair long.' It was as short as the day Marie had taken the scissors to it all those years ago. She ruffled her curls. 'I don't half fancy one of those thick plaits that start at the scalp.'

She took a step back and regarded her full reflection thoughtfully. 'I wonder what Lauri would think of these gold sandals?' They consisted of merely a few straps with high, spindly heels, and were torture to wear. Her eyes went from her feet to her face. 'I still give Sylvia a good run for her money, but am I wasting me life like Cecy said?'

Two years ago, Cecy was convinced she had cancer. The day before she was due to see the specialist, she told Annie tearfully how much she regretted leaving Bruno all those years ago. 'You don't know the details, dear, but I should have stayed and made the sacrifice.'

Annie didn't let on she'd known the details from the start. Sacrifice! Sleeping with Bruno, a sacrifice! She clutched Cecy's hand, terrified she'd die. It would be like losing her mother.

'I'm only half alive. Women need men. Men don't need us, except for one thing,' Cecy blushed, 'but we're wasted without them. Marry again soon, dear, before you become a useless, dried-up old woman like me.'

'Frankly,' Annie said to her reflection, 'I feel more alive now than when I was married to Lauri. Am I useless just 'cos I'm a widow? And would I be less useless if I became Mrs Andrews instead of Mrs Menin?' Chris proposed on average once a month. 'He's a lovely chap, but not one I'd pick to spend the rest of me life with, and I'd definitely prefer the telly in bed!' She'd bought a colour portable for the bedroom and stayed up till all hours watching old films. She smiled at herself, 'Maybe I'm already a dried-up youngish woman!'

The specialist had diagnosed kidney stones, not cancer, and Cecy had been as fit as a fiddle since the operation, but it had given Sylvia a terrible fright. 'I didn't realise how much I loved her till I thought she could die. Bruno's the same. He visited the hospital every day.'

A woman opened the shop door and shouted, 'D'you sell tights, luv?'

'Sorry, no.' Annie hung up the clothes she'd made over the weekend. She put two suits behind the sign that said 'Maternity', to replace those sold last week. The skirts had narrow braces so they wouldn't slide below the bump, and were perfectly wearable after the baby had been born.

It had been twelve months before Patchwork had 'taken off' as Dawn put it, but nowadays it provided her with a more than respectable income. Lots of customers came recommended by others, some dropped in drawn by the window display. The white outfit, for instance, was very likely to sell before the day was out.

As if to prove the point, the door opened and a woman came in to ask if she could try on, 'That lovely white and blue thing in the window.'

She ended up buying an entirely different outfit. 'I've a friend who'd love a two-piece like this. Have you got a branch in town?'

'No, this is the only one.' People often suggested she open a branch in Liverpool or Southport – or both.

'I might one day,' she usually replied. Perhaps she wasn't very ambitious, because one shop seemed enough.

Annie returned the white suit to the window. Her fingers itched to get on with more sewing; she had some lovely stuff at home, but she'd have to wait until Barbara turned up at one o'clock. She'd been obliged to take on an assistant when it became impossible to be in two places at once – in Patchwork selling clothes, and at home making them. There'd been five replies to her advert, but she had only interviewed Barbara Eastleigh. She recognised the name immediately. She and Barbara had worked together in the English Electric and they'd got on well. She was a bubbly cheerful woman, ten years older than Annie, with two young children. Now the children were married and she was anxious for a part-time job. She was delighted to find Patchwork belonged to her old friend. Annie had no hesitation about leaving the shop in her capable hands every afternoon from one o'clock.

Barbara arrived early and Annie went home. The children were on holiday and Daniel would be wanting food. Sara was out for the day with her friend, Louise. They did the same things Sylvia and Annie used to do; wandered round the shops, caught the ferry to New Brighton, went to the pictures – though only a fraction of the cinemas remained.

As she walked unsteadily down Heather Close on her spiky heels, she saw the garage door was open. Daniel was playing snooker with a lad from school. Two girls lounged against the Anglia, which was parked outside. 'If you scratch me car, I'll kill you!' she said lightly when she passed. The Anglia had been thoroughly overhauled and re-sprayed turquoise. It looked like new.

The girls giggled. Daniel looked up. 'Hi, Mum. Is there grub going?'

She assumed he meant grub for four, so opened two tins of soup and buttered half a loaf of bread. She cut four wedges of boiled fruit cake and hid the rest in the bread bin – if she left it out, the whole lot would go, and it was Sara's favourite. They ate noisily – the girls seemed unable to stop giggling. Annie left them to themselves and was glad when they returned outside. She went into the kitchen to clean up, but to her surprise found it already done, though someone – it could only be Daniel – had taken the cake from the bread bin and every crumb had gone.

'Bloody hell!' she swore, and threw fruit, butter and sugar into a pan, and added half a cup of water to make another. The mixture was simmering nicely when the phone rang.

'This is it!' Sylvia's voice throbbed with excitement.

'Syl! I tried to call you yesterday, but there was no answer. What's "it"? What are you on about?'

'Me and Mike. This is it, Annie. I can't understand how you ever thought him boring.'

'*I* thought him boring! I did no such thing, you idiot. It was you.'

'He's the least boring man who ever lived. Me and the girls went back to his house from Dot's party and we've been here ever since. They love him, I love him, and he loves us.' Sylvia drew in a deep rapturous breath. 'I've moved in permanently, Annie. I've chucked in that lousy employment agency. We're getting married in September.'

'Isn't that a bit quick?' Annie sat down suddenly.

'Quick!' Sylvia snapped. 'Jaysus! It's a quarter of a century since we first went out. I think me and Mike have been in love all along.'

Annie didn't think it wise to point out that Sylvia would never have fallen in love with a mere toolmaker. As his mam had said, Mike was a far more attractive proposition nowadays.

'I see congratulations aren't forthcoming,' Sylvia said grumpily. 'Honestly, Annie, every time I get married you disapprove.'

'Oh, Syl, I couldn't possibly be more pleased. You took me by surprise, that's all. If Mike wasn't me cousin, I'd be green with envy. He's a super bloke.' As the news sank in, Annie felt quite emotional. Sylvia was happy at last! 'Are you getting married in church?'

'We can't. As far as the Catholic Church is concerned, I'm still married to Eric. It'll have to be a register office – you'll be my matron of honour, won't you?'

'Of course.'

'But,' Sylvia said crisply, 'you're not to wear a ghastly Patchwork creation. Something a bit more stylish, if you don't mind.'

'What do you mean, ghastly!' snorted Annie. 'I thought you liked them – you bought one the day I had me Grand Opening.'

'Yes, but have you ever seen me wear it? It's been hanging in the wardrobe ever since. In fact, you can have it back if you like.'

An unspoken truce was declared when Cecy Delgado's only daughter married Dot Gallagher's second son.

'It's awkward arguing with a woman in a wheelchair,' Cecy grumbled. 'I let her have her own way over all sorts of things, the guest list, for one. There's over forty of them Gallaghers, and she insists that every last one come. I hardly know anyone to ask.' Her aunts and uncles had long since died, and her only sister in Bath was fed up being invited to Sylvia's weddings and had refused to come.

'I let her take care of the flowers and the cars, Annie,' Dot said condescendingly, 'but I couldn't very well insist on the usual place for the reception when they've got the Grand.'

'That's very kind of you, Auntie Dot, but the bride's mother is supposed to make those sort of arrangements.'

In the past, Dot had driven the mothers of several Gallagher brides to the verge of gibbering insanity by the time the wedding arrived. 'I'll leave most of it to Cecy this time. She's got the dosh. If she wants to waste it on posh flowers, it's up to her.'

Sylvia wore a simply styled calf-length dress of the palest pink lace, and a coronet of matching roses on her gleaming blonde hair. Annie's dress was deeper pink, soft, slippery crushed velvet. The bridesmaids, Yasmin and Ingrid, wore darker pink still, a lovely warm rose.

'Gosh, I was pregnant last time I was Sylvia's matron of honour.' Annie turned round, half expecting Lauri to be there with Sara on his knee. Instead, Sara was sitting between Chris Andrews and Daniel. Her son looked bored and had threatened not to come. He wore the Grenville Lucas navy blazer and his grey school trousers. It had seemed extravagant to buy a suit which he might never have the opportunity to wear again.

When the time came for Mike to kiss his new bride, he put his finger under Sylvia's chin, tipped her face towards his and kissed her softly on the lips. Their eyes smiled at each other.

Behind them, Annie had a quite unexpected thought. 'I wish someone would look at me like that! I wish . . . I wish . . .'

She turned round again. Chris Andrews gave her an encouraging smile. 'No, not Chris, never Chris. Just someone. I don't know who, perhaps I'll never meet him, but oh, I do wish . . .'

2

Sylvia did a pirouette and threw herself onto the cane settee full of patchwork cushions, which Annie had taken ages to arrange and weren't there to be sat on. 'I shall feel far more cheerful on my fortieth birthday than I did at thirty,' she cried gleefully. She and Mike had been married six months and the doctor had just confirmed she was pregnant. She'd come straight to the shop to impart the good news. The baby was due two days before her birthday.

'Does Mike know?'

'He's over the moon. Twice he's married a woman with two children, but never had one of his own. We're going to try for another before I'm too old. The doctor wrote "Geriatric Mother" or something on my notes.'

They'd been a long time coming together, Mike and Sylvia, but now nothing could disguise their love for each other. 'I can actually see us growing old together, Annie,' Sylvia confided. 'I never thought about the future with Eric.' The urge to lead a frantic social life had gone. She and Mike stayed in, watched TV or talked. 'I've discovered I really enjoy cooking.' He liked old-fashioned food, like stew with dumplings, and Dot had shown her how to make treacle pudding and scouse. Lately she'd been in her element furnishing their new home, an eighteenth-century manor house set in wooded grounds in Ince Blundell. It had eighteen rooms, and an *oak-panelled banqueting hall*! She'd bought two of Susan Hull's quilts and four cushions.

'You'll be having your baby just as I'm losing one of mine,' Annie sighed. Sara had been accepted by the University of Essex in Colchester, and would be leaving in October.

'I'll be going on for sixty by the time this one gets itchy feet.' Sylvia patted her stomach.

'But you'll have Mike!'

'That's right, I'll have my darling Mike.'

There was silence, until Sylvia said softly, 'I hate you being unhappy, Annie.'

'It's your fault for telling me about the baby.' Annie smiled. 'I never visualised you having more children than me.'

'It's not too late. Why not marry Chris and start a second family?'

'That would be too easy.'

Sylvia shrugged. 'You shouldn't avoid things because they're easy.'

'It would be like giving up, taking the soft option. I mean,' Annie spread both hands, palms upwards, as if she were weighing something, 'when you compare Chris with Mike . . .'

'I get the picture.' Sylvia nodded understandingly.

On the first Sunday in October, a day she'd been dreading for months, Annie drove her daughter to Colchester. The car was packed with Sara's belongings; her record player, her favourite doll, text books – she was taking Sociology – and almost every item of clothing she possessed.

'I got you a nice new set of towels, twelve pairs of those bikini pants you wear, and there's enough tinned food to last for weeks.' Annie's list had been several pages long. She mentally ran through it; soap powder, plasters, coffee, deodorant, toothpaste, spare spectacles, needle and cotton . . . 'I don't think I've forgotten anything.'

'Okay, Mum.'

'If you feel like a weekend at home, phone and I'll come and fetch you. Barbara will look after the shop. I'll catch up with your washing.'

Sara nodded, white-faced. She hardly spoke during the journey. Annie chatted away about nothing, anxious to keep her mind busy so she wouldn't dwell on the parting which grew closer with each mile.

They reached the university, crowded with young people and their parents. It took ages to transfer Sara's things from the car to her bare, grey room on the fifth floor of a tower block on the campus.

'The view's nice,' said Annie from the window. All that could be seen was green parkland and fields. A river shone like ribbon. Colchester was out of sight on the other side of the building. Sara would have been better on that side. She was a city person, not used to a vast empty space devoid of people, no matter how pretty it might be. Annie prayed it wouldn't make her feel lonely.

Everything had been put in its place. The doll on the window sill, the books on the shelf. A fresh notebook, pens, and a matching stapler and punch were set neatly on the desk. The room still looked bare.

'You could do with some posters,' Annie said.

'I'll buy some,' Sara said in a thin voice. She was sitting on her hands on the narrow bed, shoulders hunched. She looked fourteen.

The thought of her daughter wandering around Smiths or Athena by herself looking for posters was too much. Annie felt her throat tighten.

Shouts could be heard from the corridor, 'Cheerio, darling. Look after yourself.'

'Bye, Mum.'

'Bye, son, stay cool.'

'Bye, Dad.'

'I think everyone's going,' said Annie. 'I suppose I'd better be on me way.' She sat on the bed and put her arm around Sara's shoulders. 'Tara, luv. Take care.'

'Mum!' Sara turned to her mother, her face stricken. 'I don't want to stay. I want to go home with you.'

There was nothing, absolutely nothing, that Annie wanted more than to return Sara's things to the car and whisk her back to Heather Close. She swallowed hard, but the tightness in her throat remained. 'You'll soon settle in, sweetheart. You'll make new friends in no time.'

Sara began to cry and threw her arms around her mother's neck. 'I'd sooner be home and get a job, like Louise.'

It was time to be hard, and being hard was something Annie had never been good at. She took hold of Sara's hands and firmly removed them from her neck. 'No, luv.'

'*Please*, Mum!'

Annie felt as if her heart would break. She gritted her teeth, determined not to cry. If she did, they'd both be lost. Sara would be back in Liverpool and would probably regret it for the rest of her life. 'No, luv,' she said sharply. 'You must stay. This is what you've always wanted. You'd never forgive me if I took you home.'

Sara removed her glasses and the sobs continued. 'Shall I make some tea?' Annie offered desperately. 'The kitchen's along the corridor.'

'No thanks, Mum.'

'Perhaps you can make one after I've gone. Don't forget, the food's in the top drawer – I made two of your favourite fruitcakes.'

'I won't forget.' Sara pulled a handkerchief from her sleeve, wiped her eyes and her glasses and blew her nose. The sobs subsided.

They both stood. Annie embraced her daughter one final time. She was conscious of Sara's heartbeat, and remembered how frequently she used to check her heart was beating when she was a baby just in case she'd died.

'Tara, Sara, luv.'

'Tara, Mum.'

Annie left her eldest child standing wanly in the middle of the bare, strange room, in a strange town she'd scarcely heard of before. She flew down the stairs. When she reached the second floor, a woman was sitting at the bottom, her body racked with sobs. Annie touched her arm. 'Are you all right, luv?'

'I will be. Oh, isn't it terrible! He looked so cheerful when I left, and all I wanted to do was die. Children! Why do we have them, eh?'

'Don't ask me,' said Annie. She managed to reach the car before dissolving into tears herself, but quickly drove away, just in case Sara came looking for her, wanting to come home. It was one of those days that provided a marker in her life, like the day Mam and Dad died, the day she met Lauri, got married, the times the children were born. Then there was the day Lauri died. Now Sara had left home and things would never be quite the same again. Annie had left part of herself in that miserable tower-block room.

*

'This is the first time,' Sylvia said proudly, 'that I've had a baby and the father's been around.'

'That's nothing to boast about,' Annie said scathingly. 'Most women'd be ashamed.'

Sylvia nuzzled her fine nose against the baby's little snub red one. 'Don't take any notice of your Auntie Annie, darling. She's quite nice when you get to know her.' She grinned. 'I'm calling her Dorothy.'

'Toad!'

'I know, but it's a way of getting in your Auntie Dot's good books for ever, and she's got Dot's ginger hair. Mike said the girls will look like liquorice all-sorts when they're together.'

'I bet he's thrilled.' Annie held out her arms for the baby.

'He's tickled pink. He's letting all his two hundred and fifty-eight workers home early today, and giving them ten pounds bonus each.'

Annie hadn't realised Mike employed so many people. 'Isn't that rather paternalistic?' she frowned as she traced Dorothy's pale gold eyebrows with her finger.

'Seems generous to me.'

'I mean, it implies *his* baby is more important than any of theirs.'

'No it doesn't.'

'Yes it does.'

'I'll have my baby back if you continue.'

Annie took no notice. 'She's got three chins.'

'As long as she hasn't got three eyes or three noses, I don't care.'

Sara was too busy to come home during her first term. Annie pored over her frequent letters, trying to read between the lines. *I think I've made a friend,* Sara wrote.

'She only "thinks",' fretted Annie. 'I thought she'd've made stacks of friends by now.'

Some people on my floor play loud music all night long.

'It must be deafening if it keeps our Sara awake,' Annie said to Daniel. 'Perhaps I should write to the university authorities?'

'She wouldn't thank you if you did.'

'I expect not,' Annie sighed.

'When's she coming home?'

'Not till Christmas, luv.'

Daniel missed his sister more than Annie had expected. They'd never seemed close, yet he moped about the house, lost, now she'd gone.

'How's the sixth form?' Annie asked him.

He pulled a face. 'Okay.'

'You know, you could always go to university like Sara. You'd need three good A levels, though.' His O level results had been abysmal. His teachers claimed he was intelligent, possibly more so than his sister, but he seemed determined not to do well.

'There's no chance of that, Mum.'

Annie stared worriedly at her son. He had no ambition, no aims. There was nothing he was good at except snooker. Physically, he was becoming more like a young Lauri every day, big, broad, handsome, but he had none of his father's commitment to hard work. She was constantly concerned about him. 'What are you going to do with yourself when you're eighteen?' she asked casually. She'd already asked several times before.

Daniel scowled impatiently. 'Shit knows.'

Barbara gave in her notice at the beginning of December. 'I'm dead sorry, Annie, but me husband's been made redundant. I need to work full-time.' She deeply regretted having to leave Patchwork for a factory. 'I love working here. It's a bit much, having to go on an assembly line at my age, but there you are. Stan's not the only one to lose his job. People are being made redundant like nobody's business.'

Unemployment had passed an incredible two million. There were riots in Toxteth, a few miles away. For the first time, CS gas was used on the citizens of Britain. A protester in a wheelchair died. Auntie Dot acted as if the world had ended. 'It's that woman's fault,' she croaked.

Annie regretfully advertised for another assistant. Instead of five replies, this time she received over fifty. She interviewed half a dozen, and decided on Chloe Banks, a small, plain girl with narrow, deep-set eyes and brown hair parted in the middle, giving her the look of a Victorian waif. She'd just finished a course in fashion design and showed an expert interest in Annie's clothes. Despite being only eighteen, she had an air of maturity unusual in one so young.

'I'd like it here so much, I'd work for nothing,' she said at the interview.

'I wouldn't dream of such a thing! It's three pounds an hour. I'll need you full time occasionally.'

Cecy and Valerie dropped in when Annie wasn't there and reported that Chloe managed perfectly well on her own. She didn't press the customers, but left them to browse as she'd been instructed to.

A week before Christmas, Sara came home by train with a haversack full of washing. She seemed more confident and self-assured than when she left. 'I'm glad you made me stay,' she said when Annie collected her from Lime Street station. 'I'm beginning to enjoy university.'

Annie squeezed her hand. 'If you only knew how much I wanted to bring you back! Now,' she said happily, 'let's get you home. Daniel can't wait to see his sister.'

After Mass on Christmas Day, they went to Mike and Sylvia's for dinner. It had become a tradition that the Gallaghers collect together on this one day of the year, and Sylvia was determined it should continue, particularly as they now had a room where everyone could eat in one sitting. Cecy and Bruno were there, and Tommy Gallagher brought his girlfriend, Trish, twenty years his junior. They were getting married as soon as his divorce from Dawn came through. Dawn had been invited but refused, saying she would feel uncomfortable.

After the meal, Dot nursed her latest grandchild. Cecy hovered anxiously nearby in case Dorothy might drop from the twisted arms.

'She's the spitting image of her gran,' Dot boasted loudly. 'Bert, where's that photo of me when I was two? I bet you forgot to bring it.'

'It's here, luv.' Bert fished a faded black and white photo out of his pocket. 'We were thinking of getting it coloured.'

There was no denying the resemblance between two-year-old Dot and Sylvia's new daughter. Dot's head swelled to monumental proportions.

'Never mind,' Annie whispered to Cecy. She was Dorothy's other grandmother, but was being kept very much in the shade. 'Ingrid's very much like you.'

'Do you think so, Annie?' Cecy said pathetically. 'I keep expecting Dot to lay some claim to Sylvia and I'll have had no part in this gathering at all.'

Annie hid her hurt when Sara refused a lift back to Colchester. 'I'm meeting some friends in London, Mum.' She'd been looking forward to the long drive with her daughter. The holiday had flashed by and there'd been little time to talk. She smiled. 'At least let me take you to the station.' Later, she watched, appalled, as Sara carelessly stuffed the freshly washed and ironed clothes into her haversack.

'I wonder if children ever feel the same about their parents?' she thought as Sara hauled her tall, slight form onto the train. She wore jeans and a scruffy anorak she'd acquired from an Oxfam shop. 'Would she have this same, sad feeling if it was me leaving her?'

Sara found a seat and opened the window. 'Look after yourself, Mum.'

She looked so happy to be going back! 'Don't worry, luv, I will.'

The train started. Annie hurried alongside. 'Eat properly, now.'

'Okay, Mum.'

'And keep warm. I put your vests in with your things.'

Sara laughed. 'Mum! I wouldn't be seen dead in a vest.'

Annie was almost running as the train picked up speed. 'There's Vick in your toilet bag. There's nothing like Vick for a cold.'

'Thanks, Mum.' Sara held out her hand, but the train was going too fast for Annie to reach it.

The police rang one afternoon when Annie was busy with a new design; a plain shift dress, no sleeves, no collar, just two pieces of material sewn together, but with a dazzling patchwork jacket to go over. She was only making a few and would see how they sold.

Outside, a gentle wind rustled the trees in Heather Close. She stopped for a moment, watching. 'They were only titchy when we first came. Now they're fully grown, just like the kids.' Except the trees couldn't leave!

To think it was March already! 'The year's flown by,' she thought. 'I can hardly believe it's twelve months since Sylvia came into the shop to say she was expecting Dorothy.'

When the phone went, she wondered if it was Sylvia and she was pregnant again. She and Mike were trying hard for another baby. Instead, it was the police. A male voice demanded that Annie come immediately to Seaforth police station.

Sara's been murdered, was her first thought, until she pulled herself together. Seaforth the man had said, not Colchester.

'What's happened?' she asked dazedly.

'We'd like you to collect your son.'

'Daniel? But he's at school.'

'No, Mrs Menin. He's at the station. Now, if you wouldn't mind . . .'

'I'll be there straight away.'

Daniel was lounging nonchalantly on a bench just inside the door. He looked up when his mother entered. His expression didn't change, but she sensed fear behind his eyes.

Annie ignored him. 'What's he done?' she asked the desk sergeant.

'As far as we can gather, nothing, but he was with a group of lads who mugged an old man for his wallet on Liverpool Road this afternoon.'

'*Daniel!*'

He got to his feet and stuffed his hands in his blazer pocket. Annie noticed the hands were shaking. 'I didn't know what they were up to, honest, Mum. One minute we were walking along, next they ran off and there was this old chap on the floor. I know I should have helped him, but as soon as we saw what had happened, the rest of us just scarpered.'

'He'd never do anything criminal,' Annie assured the policeman.

'That's what every parent says,' the man said drily.

'But he wouldn't!'

'Luckily, the attack was witnessed. Only three boys were involved. Take your son home, ma'am. He needs a lecture on the company he keeps.'

'Why aren't you at school?' Annie demanded as soon as they were in the car. Now that it was over, her heart was thumping with fright.

'What's the point? I'm not interested in A levels. I'm only wasting me time.' He was already his old arrogant self.

'And you feel your time is spent more usefully mugging an old man?'

'I had nothing to do with it. Even the police believed that.'

Annie believed it too. It had happened to her. She'd been with a gang of girls when Sylvia had been pushed into a holly bush. She hadn't known about it until after the act was done.

Daniel said, 'If you don't mind, I'd like to leave school, Mum.'

'But what's to become of you, son?' Annie said anguishedly. 'You'll never get a job in this climate. Unemployment's going up all the time.'

'I don't want a job.'

'But you've got to do *something*! How about a course?'

'On what?' Daniel asked sarcastically.

'Electronics!' Annie cried after a pause. 'You used to love taking clocks and radios to pieces when you were little. I'll ask Mike Gallagher. He'd find an opening for you. Your dad worked for Mike.'

'I told you, I don't want a job. I'm not working for some cruddy employer, even if it is Mike Gallagher. There's no point.'

'You can't see any point in school, either.'

'I don't see any point in anything.' Annie was taken aback by the unexpected despair in her son's voice. 'It's a fucking lousy world. No-one gives a sod for anybody else. The politicians, all politicians, not just the Tories, are only out for what they can get. It might be power, it might be money. It's not making things better for the people.'

'Where did you get all this from, luv?' Annie asked quietly. She'd never dreamt he felt like this.

'From inside me own head.'

As soon as they were home, Daniel went upstairs. Annie made tea and took a cup up to him. He was lying face down on the bed. The little cars Lauri had bought were arranged in their usual neat line on the window sill. 'You can leave school,' she said. It seemed wrong to let the teachers waste their time on someone who had no wish to be taught.

He didn't raise his head. 'Ta, Mum.'

'Perhaps you should talk to someone about . . . about all that stuff you were saying before.'

'Who?'

'What about Bruno?' Bruno seemed to have an answer for everything.

'He wouldn't understand,' Daniel said in a muffled voice. 'No-one understands.'

Annie twisted her hands together worriedly. 'I wish I did, son.'

'So do I, Mum.'

A few days later, Annie switched on the television to discover foreign troops had landed at Port Stanley, in the Falkland Islands. In no time, Great Britain was at war with Argentina.

Dot blamed it all on the British diplomats who'd let the Argentinians think we were no longer interested in maintaining control of the islands. Now, Mrs Thatcher was bent on war and it didn't matter how many lives were lost to save face. Dot was particularly concerned. Sergeant Joe Gallagher, thirty-four, still had two years to go in the army – and the Paras had been mobilised.

'I mean,' Dot argued, 'lads don't join the army expecting war.'

But Uncle Bert disagreed. 'They're fascists, them Argies. We can't let them get away with invading one of our possessions.'

A task force set sail, the Argentinians were routed. The British flag again flew over the Falkland Islands, though much blood was spilt in the campaign, including that of Joe Gallagher, husband of Alison and father of two, who lost his life at Wireless Ridge on 28 May 1982.

Dot's youngest lad was dead, but against all the predictions, she herself was still around a year later when the Conservatives were swept back to power with a majority of 144 seats. Unemployment had passed three million, but Labour was in disarray. The party had split and many MPs had switched to the new Social Democrats. The Labour leader, Michael Foot, was a sweet old man, but, Annie thought sadly, it was no longer a world in which a sweet old man became Prime Minister.

It was the afternoon after the election, a lovely sunny Friday. Annie was sewing and watching television at the same time. Experts were analysing the result as final figures came in for the far-flung seats in Scotland. Dot had telephoned earlier. 'It looks like my poor Bert's stuck with me for another five years,' she groaned. 'I'll see that woman out, I swear it.'

There was laughter from the garage. Daniel was playing snooker with a couple of old schoolmates, out of work like him, and totally uninterested in the election. They'd disenfranchised themselves.

'We're powerless,' Daniel said. No matter who got in, nothing would change. 'Politicians and multinationals have got the world sewn up. There's nothing people like you and me can do about it.'

'What's to become of him – of them?' Annie wondered aloud. She cheered herself up by remembering Sara was due home shortly for the long summer holiday. In October, she would return to university for her final year.

Annie abandoned her sewing and went upstairs to her daughter's room. It still had the same wallpaper as when she was a baby, which had faded badly over the years. She felt overcome with the urge to redecorate – it would be a lovely surprise for Sara.

She went into the garage to check if there was wallpaper paste and a decent brush. There was. 'I'm popping round to South Road for wallpaper,' she told Daniel. 'I'm going to decorate Sara's room.'

'I'll help,' he offered. He was anxious to have his sister home.

Annie chose a pattern of tangled golden flowers and ordered four yards of matching curtain material. She'd get new duvet covers at the weekend. Yellow, Sara's favourite colour.

Seeing as she was here, she supposed she might as well call in Patchwork and see how Chloe was getting on.

Her assistant was displaying a quilt to a woman customer. It was a startlingly beautiful thing; octagonal patches of black, red and green on a cream background. Annie tiptoed past, mouthing 'Hi'. She sat at the desk, waiting for Chloe to finish, and glanced around the shop.

Sadly, Ernie Ward had gone to meet his maker, God bless him. His replacement, Pearl Sims, didn't have his imagination, his way with colours, but her sweaters sold well. Annie had found two elderly sisters at a craft fair who made pretty silver jewellery. They were pleased to leave a selection with her. Pendants and earrings were pinned to a black velvet board inside the door. She must find an artist and have pictures for sale. The blank wall above the clothes still niggled her.

She wondered why Chloe was so jumpy. She kept glancing nervously in her direction, and had twice dropped the quilt. Annie turned away in case she was embarrassing the girl. It was then she noticed the thick spiral artist's pad on the desk. The pad was open, and her latest outfit, the blue and lilac twopiece she'd made the other day, was half drawn on the page. She flicked through the book. All her designs were there, going back for months. They were drawn well, in the elongated, unnatural style of fashion magazines, the colours filled in with crayon.

The customer decided not to buy the quilt after all. 'I'll think about it,' she said, which meant she'd never be seen again.

The door closed. 'What's this?' Annie asked, pointing to the pad.

Chloe no longer looked nervous. She laughed, 'Oh, I draw them for my mother. She'd love to come to the shop, but she's stuck at home, an invalid. I got fed up trying to describe your lovely clothes, so decided to draw them for her. I show her the book every night.'

'I didn't know your mam was an invalid.' She and Chloe never chatted the way she'd done with Barbara.

'She's got multiple sclerosis.'

'Oh, luv, I didn't realise.' Before leaving, Annie took one of the prettiest pendants off the wall. 'Give this to your mam with my love.'

624

Chloe's eyes shone with gratitude. 'Why, thank you, Mrs Menin.'

Walking home, Annie wasn't sure what she'd thought when she saw the drawing pad. It was unlikely some big London fashion house had bribed Chloe for her designs. 'I must have a suspicious mind,' she decided.

Six rolls of wallpaper was a fair weight. She was glad when the house came into view. After a cup of tea, she'd start stripping the old stuff.

Daniel's friends seemed to have gone. He was standing on the path, waiting for her, which wasn't a bit like him, and it was even less like him to come and meet her. 'Sara's just phoned,' he said breathlessly.

'Oh,' Annie cried delightedy. 'Is she coming home early?'

'No, Mum. She called to say she's just got married.'

3

Annie knew immediately that this was the man her daughter had married. Sara was sitting next to him for one thing, and he was in his late twenties, older than the dozen other students around the long wooden table outside the riverside pub.

Sara looked incredibly proud, as if she'd done something unique and remarkable. She wore a yellow dress that had been made a long time ago for somebody else's wedding. A gold ring glinted on the third finger of her left hand. The ring was proof, not that Annie needed proof by now, that it was true. Sara was married!

Her daughter's husband seemed to be the only one with anything to say. He was sounding forth confidently in a loud, harsh voice, and she could actually hear the occasional word, although it was noisy outside the pub and she was standing some distance away. He wore a too-big white shirt, like a cavalier, with the collar turned up, and heavy, horn-rimmed glasses. Every now and then, he would brush back the dark, untidy hair which fell onto his forehead. She could tell he thought very highly of himself. It was obvious, from his voice, his sharp confident gestures, the conceited way he tossed his head, that this man considered himself a cut above everybody else.

Annie hated him immediately.

Students were only allowed to live on campus in the first year. From then on, they found their own accommodation. During her second year, Sara had shared a small terraced cottage in Wivenhoe with three other girls. Although nominally a town, Wivenhoe was more like a large village. Within walking distance of the university, it stood on a river, the one visible from the tower-block room where Sara had first lived, and had a picturesque quay packed with sailing craft.

Annie had taken a walk to see the sights when she brought Sara down to help her settle in last October. On that occasion, the journey had taken roughly five and a half hours each way. Today, she'd done the same journey in just over four hours.

After numerous attempts to get through to the house where Sara lived, she'd given up. The pay phone at the other end must be out of order, somebody must have tried to use a foreign coin and it was blocked. It had happened before.

Annie tried to contact her daughter via the university, but after being transferred from department to department, apparently no-one had the faintest idea where Sara was.

'Is it an emergency?' one woman demanded.

'Well, yes,' Annie stammered.

'By an emergency, I mean has someone died?'

As she had no intention of explaining to the crisp, disembodied voice that her daughter had got married without telling her mother, Annie made up her mind to go to Colchester herself.

'Did she sound drunk?' she asked Daniel.

'No, she just sounded excited.' He looked sulky. Perhaps he, like Annie, felt deeply, horribly, hurt.

She kept her foot on the accelerator the whole way, dodging in and out of traffic, overtaking, things she wouldn't have dreamt of doing normally. The Anglia wasn't a high performance car; the engine was taxed as it had never been before. It rocked crazily at seventy.

The contents of Sara's letters flashed through her mind. 'We went to the debating society, Derek is a brilliant speaker.' 'Sam and I went to London to see the Boomtown Rats.' 'Nigel drove us to Norwich.' 'Joanna's in love for the umpteenth time.' Joanna had stayed in Heather Close last summer. Annie tried to think of other boys' names; Gareth, Jonathan, Paul – no, Paul had given up last term and gone home. Sam came from Australia, or was it Derek? Nigel was a post-graduate student. There'd never been any suggestion that one of the names was special.

It was half past nine when she stopped in the narrow street where Sara lived. The car groaned with relief when she turned the engine off.

Annie hammered on the door with her fist. When there was no reply, she hammered with both fists. Upstairs, a window opened and a girl's voice said crossly, 'Who's that? Have you forgotten your key again? There's some of us got revision to do.'

'I'm sorry to disturb you.' Annie stepped back. The window was open a few inches and she couldn't see whoever was there. 'Is that Joanna?'

'No, it's Sam. Joanna's out.'

The window moved to close. Annie said quickly, 'It's Sara I wanted.'

'Oh!' The voice changed, became kind. 'You're Mrs Menin, aren't you? Sara's down on the quay in the Rose and Crown.'

'Is she – I mean . . . ?' Perhaps, after all, it was a joke, or Daniel had got the wrong end of the stick. 'Is she married?' Annie blurted out.

'Yes.' The word was uttered in a clipped, disapproving way.

'This probably seems a stupid question, but who to?'

'Sara's completely flipped her lid and married Nigel James. He's a creep, Mrs Menin, a total creep, but then you'll soon find that out for yourself.' With that, the window shut and the girl disappeared.

Annie left the car where it was and walked the short distance to the quay. From memory, it was impossible to park there.

It was a beautiful evening. Dusk had fallen and the sky glowed pink and red. There were lots of people about. Several doors were wide open, the occupants sitting on the step, the way they had in Bootle when she was a child. She passed a house where a party was going on; laughter, music, the hum of conversation came through the open window.

'Of course, it's Friday. Friday always seemed special when me and Sylvia were young.' It was the start of the weekend, and who knew what sort of adventures they might have over the next two days!

She arrived at the quayside. Crowds were gathered outside the Rose and Crown, standing, or sitting at the wooden tables outside, only a few feet from the water. The boats moved gently in the lapping tide, and there was a faint jangling sound from the masts.

Annie shoved her way through the throng, searching for her daughter. She was at the door of the pub itself, when she saw her sitting at an outside table next to Nigel James. She stood stock still, in everybody's way, just staring, whilst the hurt ate away at her body like a cancer.

'I had such plans for you, Sara! I was going to make your wedding dress meself. We talked about it, remember? Organdie, you wanted. I said I didn't think you could still get organdie, but Mr Patel would have something just as nice. We'd have the reception in the Grand – where else? Uncle Bert would give you away because he's the nearest thing you've got to a dad. You said you weren't getting married for ages yet, and Daniel would be old enough to do the honours by then.'

A man stood on her foot and apologised profusely. 'It's all right,' Annie said. She began to edge closer. As soon as she felt calmer, more controlled, she'd let Sara know she was there. She didn't feel angry, just this deep, gnawing hurt.

A girl's voice said, 'Excuse me,' and Annie stood aside to let her past. Then the girl gasped. 'Mrs Menin!' It was Joanna, small, cheerful, friendly. She grabbed Annie's arm. 'Don't bawl Sara out, will you? It was all Nigel's idea. She's completely under his thumb.'

'Do you mind saying I'm here? I'd like a word in private.'

'Okay.' Joanna, obviously relishing her role, crept up behind Sara and whispered in her ear.

'Oh, God!' Annie murmured when her daughter's face lit up and her eyes searched happily for her mother in the crowds. It was almost dark by now. 'She doesn't think she's done anything wrong.'

Sara hurried towards her. 'Mum! You shouldn't have come all this way, we're coming to Liverpool on Monday. I tried to phone again, but the number was engaged. Oh, Mum!' She flung her arms around Annie's neck. 'You don't mind, do you? It seemed so romantic to get married on the spur of the moment. Anyroad, we didn't have that much time.'

'Surely you could have waited, luv, and got married from home?' Annie's voice was stiff. Was she being unreasonable? Sara was almost twenty. But didn't all mothers want to be there when their children got married? 'What do you mean, you didn't have that much time?'

'Nigel's finished his Doctorate, Mum, and he's already got a job. He's due back in Australia a week on Monday.'

Annie felt faint. Her daughter wasn't merely married, but was going to live on the other side of the world.

Nigel must have noticed his wife was missing. He arrived suddenly and put his arm protectively around her shoulders. This was no ordinary T-shirted, jean-clad student. As well as the oversized shirt, he wore baggy, pleated trousers and lace-up shoes. His eyes were shrewd and intelligent behind the heavy glasses, and he had a large bony nose and wide mobile lips. Annie resented the way he faced her, as if she were the enemy. Sara said, 'Darling, this is my mother,' just as Nigel muttered, 'We don't want any fuss.'

'No-one's making a fuss,' Annie said mildly. She didn't like his words, or his warning tone. She wished Lauri were there to punch his smug, arrogant face. He wasn't as tall as she thought he'd be, an inch or so shorter than Sara. 'Perhaps I could take him on meself,' she thought hysterically. 'I'd love to shove him in the water.' With luck, he wouldn't be able to swim.

She stayed another hour and refused the offer of Sara's room to sleep in – Sara, slightly embarrassed, explained she had moved in with Nigel. All Annie wanted was to get back to Heather Close. She made the return journey through dark, empty villages and along the deserted motorway, in even less time than it had taken to come.

Sara and Nigel arrived by car at tea-time on Monday. Chloe was looking after the shop until further notice, so Annie could spend every available minute with her daughter who was flying to Australia with her new husband on Friday. Over the weekend, the Gallaghers, the Delgados and the neighbours had been given the news.

'Isn't it marvellous!' Annie told them excitedly. 'Nigel James, his name is. He's twenty-nine, and has just got his Doctorate in Physics. Everyone says he's brilliant.' Even Joanna had conceded Dr Nigel James was exceptionally clever. 'I'm so pleased,' Annie trilled. 'There's so many opportunities in Australia – Nigel's already got a job in a top-class laboratory in Sydney. There's a lovely flat for them to move into.'

Only to Sylvia did she express her real thoughts. 'He's a prick, Syl,' she said flatly. 'I hated him on sight, but Sara's totally besotted. She doesn't realise how much she's hurt me, though he does, I can see it in his eyes. He persuaded her to get married straight away because he knows I might have talked her out of it.'

'Oh, Annie,' Sylvia breathed. 'I hope you're exaggerating.'

'I'm not,' Annie said savagely. 'See for yourself next week.'

Nigel was mainly boorish to everyone who came to congratulate Sara and wish the young couple luck. He clearly couldn't be bothered being polite to people he considered inferior, which, as far as Annie could see, comprised the entire human race. After the first day, Daniel swore he'd never speak to him again. He hurt Cecy's feelings and was rude to Valerie when she asked a quite reasonable question about his country.

'Of course we make our own cars,' he answered cuttingly. 'I'm from Australia, not the Third World.'

'I thought you imported most factory-made goods,' Valerie stammered.

'That was a long time ago.'

The Gallagher lads came in a bunch and weren't inclined to let Nigel put them in their place. When he made a sarcastic remark, they mocked him gently, whereupon he sulked and said no more until they'd gone.

Sylvia thought he was pathetic. 'Have you noticed he wears built-up shoes? He doesn't want people to think he's small.'

Annie nodded. 'I've noticed.'

'Doesn't Sara care he gets on everybody's nerves?' Sylvia asked. The young couple had gone into town for last-minute shopping.

'Sara thinks the sun shines out of his arse,' Annie said bitterly. 'The way she runs after him! "Fetch me this, Sara. Fetch me that."'

'Why not have a quiet word with her, Annie?'

'I've already tried.' It was impossible to get Sara on her own. Nigel never left her side. Only that morning Annie, unable to sleep, had been up at six, and taken her tea onto the patio. Sara appeared shortly afterwards, rubbing her eyes. Annie indicated a white plastic chair. 'Sit down, luv. I'll fetch another cuppa.'

She'd gone into the kitchen. At last, the chance to talk! Though what would she say? 'I'll try and make her realise what a giant step she's taking, going to a strange country with a chap she hardly knows.'

But Nigel was already in her chair when she returned. She could have sworn he looked at her triumphantly, as if Sara were a prize he'd managed to snatch from under her mother's nose.

To Annie's amazement, Auntie Dot quite liked him. The first thing she did when Uncle Bert trundled her into the house, was grab him by the collar and pull him down until their noses touched. 'Let's take a look at you, young feller,' she said in her piercing voice. 'I hope you're going to take good care of our Sara.'

'You can count on it,' Nigel said meekly. Perhaps even he realised he couldn't be rude to a sick old woman in a wheelchair.

Dot proceeded to question him closely about his job. 'You're not going to cut rats and mice up in that there laboratory, are you?'

Nigel actually laughed. 'No, it's a physics lab, no animals.'

Annie wondered guiltily if she should have tried harder to get on with her son-in-law, but remembered how he'd faced her when they met, as if she was an enemy. He didn't kiss her, shake her hand, apologise for stealing her daughter. 'We don't want any fuss,' was all he said.

'He seems a nice lad, Annie,' Dot whispered as she was leaving.

Nigel was equally impressed. 'What a feisty old lady!' He squeezed Sara's hand. 'Only one more day . . .'

Sara looked at him adoringly. 'I can't wait,' she said.

Four large, strapped suitcases stood in the hall when Annie went to bed on Thursday. They looked ominous, as if they contained terrible things like bloody, dismembered limbs, not Sara and Nigel's belongings.

She woke up next morning with a jolt, knowing something awful was about to happen. After several seconds she realised what it was – Sara was going to Australia! They were leaving at ten to drive to Heathrow. The plane took off at seven that evening. Someone from the university had bought Nigel's car and would collect it from the airport later.

'I'm not sure how I'll get through the day. It's worse than Lauri's funeral.' The house would seem dead quiet, for one thing. There'd been endless visitors all week who'd come to say goodbye to Sara.

Suddenly, there was a bump, a crash and a cry, followed by the sound of loud weeping. Annie leapt out of bed and onto the landing. The sounds came from Sara's room. She knocked on the door and went in.

Sara, in a brief, frilly nightdress, was lying face down on the bed, sobbing as if her heart would break. Nigel, clad only in white shorts, was kneeling on the floor beside her.

'Sara,' he was saying helplessly. 'Sara.'

'What's the matter?' Annie demanded.

At the sound of her voice, Sara raised her head. 'Mummy, oh, Mummy, I don't want to go to Australia. I want to stay with you.'

'Jaysus!' Annie muttered. 'Would you mind leaving us a minute,' she said to Nigel.

'But . . .' he protested.

Grasping his arm, Annie virtually flung him out. Daniel, in shorts and T-shirt, came out of his room. 'What's wrong?'

'It's your sister. She doesn't want to go.' Annie slammed the door and turned to her daughter. There was something she had to know first. 'Sara,' she said firmly. 'Did Nigel pressurise you into marrying him?' If he had, then as far as she was concerned, Sara could stay. She stared at the heaving back and prayed, willed the answer to be, 'Yes.'

It was a while before Sara replied. Eventually, she took in a long, shuddering breath and said, 'No.'

'I see,' Annie sighed.

Sara turned over. Her eyes were bloodshot and red-rimmed, her face blotchy. 'He proposed, but it was my idea to do it straight away. He wanted to wait till Liverpool. He was worried you'd be upset and make a fuss, but I said you wouldn't mind.'

'I've spawned an idiot,' Annie thought. It was worse than the first day at university. Then, Sara had only been a car ride away, but was Annie supposed to persuade her to go to the other side of the world?

'Do you love Nigel, sweetheart?' she asked awkwardly.

'I'm not sure,' Sara sniffed. She sat up and hugged her knees. 'I loved him until yesterday, but when I woke up I knew I didn't want to go.' She looked at her mother wretchedly, 'Oh, Mum! What shall I do?'

'I don't know, luv.' Annie shook her head. 'Y'know,' she said reluctantly, 'you've got a responsibility to Nigel. You shouldn't have married him if you felt like this.' The words stuck in her throat. 'It's not right, him going back and leaving his wife behind.'

Sara bent down and picked something up from the floor; Nigel's glasses. A sidepiece had come off. 'I broke them. They fell off when I pushed him. I'll fix them for him. You know, Mum, he's ever so sweet when you get to know him. Oh, Nigel!' She began to cry again.

Annie sat on the bed, took the shaking body in her arms and began to rock her daughter back and forth. 'Sara, only you can make the decision. I've no intention of saying you should go or stay.' She stroked the pale golden hair that still felt as soft as a baby's. 'Why not have a nice bath and I'll make some tea? Perhaps it'll help make up your mind.'

Sara nodded tiredly. 'Okay, Mum.'

Annie opened the door and found Daniel pacing the landing like a father expecting his first child. Nigel was sitting at the top of the stairs. He stood up when she appeared. Without his oversize clothes, built-up shoes and glasses, he looked extraordinarily small and very young. His features were much softer than she'd realised.

'How is she?' he asked hesitantly.

'She's about to have a bath. I'd let her alone if I were you. Daniel, lend Nigel your dressing gown.' He must feel uncomfortable half-dressed with Daniel towering over him. 'I'll make a cup of tea.'

Daniel took his tea into the lounge and switched the television on. Left with her son-in-law, Annie searched desperately for something to say. He'd lost all trace of his brash, confident manner, and huddled nervously within the towelling dressing gown. He was the first to break the uncomfortable silence.

'I'm sorry I was rude when we first met,' he said thinly. 'I thought you'd start a row, not that I would have blamed you.'

Annie made a face. She admired him for not putting the blame on Sara. 'I wanted to kill you. I contemplated pushing you in the water.'

He managed a weak smile. 'I'm a good swimmer.' He rubbed his eyes, as if they felt odd without his glasses. 'I love Sara, Mrs Menin. If she comes, I'll take good care of her, I promise.'

'You better had,' Annie said fiercely. Her intuition told her Sara would be leaving for Australia at ten o'clock. She put her hand over his slight one. 'If you don't, I'll be on the first plane to sort you out.'

Sara entered the room, already dressed in jeans and T-shirt. Her eyes caught Nigel's, and for the first time, Annie felt totally excluded from her daughter's life.

'I'm coming,' Sara said quietly.

Several people from the close came out to wave the couple off. Most had known Sara all her life. She hugged and kissed them all. Gary Cunningham seemed especially sad to see her go. They'd been babies together, gone to playgroup, then school. Valerie had always hoped they'd fall in love. But it was not to be. Gary was getting married in November to a girl from Knotty Ash, and Sara was off to Australia with Nigel James.

'Bye, Daniel.' Sara threw her arms around her brother.

'Tara, sis, take care.' Daniel's face was hard, as if he were doing his best not to cry.

Finally, Sara turned to Annie. 'Mum!'

'Sara!' Oh, what did you say at times like this! Look after yourself, take care, have a nice journey. Not, 'See you soon,' because she wouldn't be seeing Sara again in a long while.

'I've left our Daniel's eighteenth birthday present under my bed. I wish I could have been here, but never mind . . .'

'No, never mind,' said Annie. 'Tara, luv, look after yourself, have a nice journey.'

Then they were in the car, and Nigel had started up the engine, and the car was slowly moving down Heather Close. It paused at the end and everyone waved frantically, then the car turned the corner and was gone.

There was no sign of Daniel when Annie went back into the house. She called upstairs; no answer. Having just lost one child, she badly needed the other. She found him in the garden, moodily kicking an old football.

'That's that then,' she said with an attempt at cheeriness. It wouldn't do to let him see she felt as miserable as sin.

Daniel kicked the football savagely into the willow tree and the leaves swished wildly. 'Why did you let her go?'

Annie was taken aback by the accusing look on his face. 'It wasn't up to me, luv. It was Sara who decided to go.'

'No, it wasn't,' Daniel said in a grating voice. 'You talked her into it. I heard you. All that guff about "responsibility". If you'd played your cards right, she would have stayed with us. Instead, she's gone to the other side of the world with that . . . that utter wanker!'

'Nigel's not so bad. I think we misjudged him.'

'He's a wanker!'

Annie went back into the house. She'd expected comfort from her son – not words or actions, merely an unspoken awareness of how they both felt – but he seemed to think Sara's leaving was *her* fault.

'Don't you think I would have given anything on earth to keep Sara?' she asked when Daniel followed her in.

'You had the opportunity and you muffed it,' he said coldly. 'Most mothers would have leapt at the chance, but not you! You let our Sara go because you don't give a damn about anything.'

'Daniel!'

He threw himself into an armchair. Annie stared, horrified, at his dark brooding face. For a moment, he looked exactly like her mam, sullen and unforgiving. 'I'll not forget when Dad died,' he sneered. 'You didn't cry, not once. You told us he'd gone to heaven. For years, I thought he'd just walked out on us.'

'I'm sorry, perhaps that was wrong,' Annie said carefully. She felt confused and had difficulty putting the words together. 'I wanted to make it easier for you, that's all.' She was about to tell him that she'd cried for Lauri, secretly, in bed, that she still cried for him occasionally, but that she didn't want her children to know their mother was unhappy. Her own parents had caused too much unhappiness when she was a child. But Daniel didn't give her time to speak.

'When Sara left for university, you didn't give a toss,' he went on bitterly. 'Now it's Australia, and all you can say is, "That's that then!" in this stupid, cheerful voice, as if she'll be back tonight.'

Annie said slowly, 'I think it's you that's being stupid, luv. I'm tearing apart inside for Sara. I didn't want to make you feel worse by letting you see me cry.'

'For fuck's sake, Mum. I'm eighteen soon. How old do I have to be to see me mother cry? I've never seen you lose your cool, let alone cry.'

The phone went. It was Sylvia, wanting to know if the young couple had left and how did Annie feel? 'I'm not sure,' said Annie. She glanced at Daniel. He got out of the chair and left the room. 'Can I ring you back?' she asked her friend.

Minutes later, the roll and clip of snooker balls could be heard in the garage. Annie went into the kitchen and began to peel potatoes, though she'd never felt less like food. It was as if a hive of bees were buzzing angrily in her head, and her thoughts veered wildly from Sara to Daniel, Daniel to Sara. 'What have I done wrong?' she asked herself.

About mid-day, her son appeared in the kitchen doorway. 'That time the old man was mugged, Frank Wheeler's dad gave him a good leathering, yet Frank had no more to do with it than I did.'

'In that case, Mr Wheeler was unfair.' Annie said shortly.

Daniel gave a sardonic laugh. 'At least it showed he cared.'

'Are parents supposed to beat their children to show they care? Your dad would never have leathered you, and you're half a head taller than me, Daniel, so I couldn't if I wanted to.'

'And Frank's dad wouldn't let him leave school, either.'

Annie didn't answer, and after a few seconds he returned to his snooker. She fried a piece of cod and shouted that his dinner was ready.

'I'm not hungry,' he shouted back.

'Well, it's here whenever you feel like it,' she said tiredly. She made a cup of tea, took three aspirins and went to bed.

Surprisingly, she fell asleep straight away. It was five o'clock when she woke. There was activity in Daniel's room and she wondered if he'd had the meal. 'What I'd like,' she whispered, 'is for the door to open and Lauri to come in with a cup of tea and tell me everything's going to be all right.'

The door opened and Daniel came in. She'd never known her husband at eighteen, but this is surely what he would have looked like; the same easy walk, the same brown hair curling onto his neck, broad shoulders, but he had Mam's face. He would never have his father's twinkling eyes. She wondered why he had Sara's old haversack thrown over his shoulder.

'I'm off, Mum.'

Annie sat up so suddenly it hurt her head. 'What do you mean, son?'

'I'm off to find meself – or lose meself, I'm not sure.'

She scrambled out of bed and nearly fell. 'Where are you going?'

'I don't know. I might drop in on Sara.'

'*Daniel!*' She was conscious of the raw fear in her voice.

'Oh, you won't let my going bother you, Mum. You won't cry. You'll just say, "That's it, then", and get on with your life.'

He closed the door. Annie opened it and ran after him down the stairs. 'Daniel, please stay, and we'll talk.' She'd tell him about Mam and Dad and about how dangerous it was to lose your cool because you said things you regretted for the rest of your life.

'There's nothing to talk about,' Daniel said and slammed the front door.

Annie collapsed on the stairs. She didn't watch him go, because each step would have driven a nail into her heart. She felt tears stream down her cheeks, warm, salty when they touched her lips, and she lifted her arms towards the door. 'I'm crying now, son, I'm crying now.'

After a few minutes, or it might have been an hour, perhaps several hours, Annie got stiffly to her feet. She took the telephone off the hook, locked the doors, drew the curtains, and wondered what she was to do with the rest of her life now that both her children had gone.

4

It was a nightmare, a black nightmare. She wandered round the house, made tea, took aspirin, and then more aspirin, slept fitfully. The doorbell rang several times, but she ignored it. There was no-one she wanted to see except Sara and Daniel. She heard a baby cry one night and found herself in Daniel's room; it could only be him, because Sara never cried. Instead of a baby, she found an untidy, empty bed, and a neat row of Matchbox cars on the window sill. The nightmare enveloped her again and despair flooded the furthest depths of her spirit.

On Sunday afternoon, she heard laughter from next door's garden. She peered through the bedroom curtains; Valerie was in a deckchair and the children were lolling on the grass. Gary and his girlfriend whispered together. Kevin appeared with a tray of drinks. He put the tray down, threw himself at his wife's feet and began to read the paper.

'What a perfect scene!' she thought. Yet the Cunninghams had never seemed a contented family. Valerie and Kevin had been unfaithful to each other, and Valerie had lashed cruelly at her kids when they were little. It was Annie who'd looked after them when their mother went to work.

'Why are they so happy and I'm not?'

She was unable to find an answer. She stayed with her arms resting on the sill, remembering the day Lauri had first brought her to the house. It was the only time he'd ever talked about his childhood. She mostly forgot he wasn't from Liverpool. He'd pointed out the River Mersey from this very window. To her dismay, the river could no longer be seen. She'd never noticed before, but a new building blocked the view. Annie shuddered, drew the curtains together, and turned to face the dark, silent room. After a while, when she could stand the noise from next door no longer, she went downstairs and played all her favourite records at top blast. She sat on the floor with her eyes closed, whilst the Beatles sang, 'Penny Lane', 'Eleanor Rigby', 'Can't Buy Me Love', 'Yesterday' . . . When it came to 'The Long and Winding Road', the song she liked best of all, she sang along in a cracked, tuneless voice. Without too much effort, she transported herself back to the flat in Upper Parliament Street, the Cavern, the Locarno, the places where she and Sylvia had had such wonderful times. 'And I was mostly happy with Lauri. There was only a little patch when things went wrong.' Even after Lauri died, the market had been hard work but fun. Patchwork, her very own shop, would always be a source of pride.

But Annie knew that everything real, everything of worth, had already taken place. Nothing of significance would happen again. From now on, it would all be second best.

Sylvia came on Monday afternoon. Annie knew who it was when the doorbell rang and rang and didn't stop.

'I know you're there, Annie,' Sylvia shouted through the letterbox. 'If you don't come soon, I'll call the police.' Then, seconds later, 'Dorothy's about to wee-wee on your front garden.'

Annie opened the door. 'Jaysus, you look a sight!' Sylvia said briskly. She came in, rushed upstairs with Dorothy, returned, yanked the curtains back, and put the kettle on. Then she shoved Annie onto the settee and said, 'Now, what's up with you?'

'Nothing,' said Annie.

'In that case, why didn't you ring me back? Why has your phone been off the hook for days? And why do you look twice as old as you did last week?' She turned exasperatedly on her twenty-month-old daughter. 'Lord, Dorothy, do you *have* to crawl under your Auntie Annie's rug? I had to bring her,' she explained. 'I think I told you we're between au pairs.'

'I think you did.'

'Annie, friend,' Sylvia said gently. 'What's wrong?'

Annie sighed. She'd cried so much over the last few days that her body felt completely dry. In a dull, emotionless voice, she told Sylvia what had happened. Sara had gone, Daniel had gone, she was alone.

'Daniel might be home in a few days.'

'No.' Annie shook her head. 'I know my son. He'd consider it a sign of weakness if he came back too soon. He might not come back at all.'

'As for Sara,' Sylvia went on, 'she's been trying to ring since yesterday to say she's arrived safely in Sydney. She ended up calling me at six o'clock this morning, worried stiff because she couldn't get through to her mum. I've got her number in my bag.'

Annie leapt to her feet. 'I'll call this very minute.'

'It's three o'clock in the morning there. Why not wait until tonight?' Sylvia grasped Annie's shoulders and sat her down again. 'I'll make that tea.' On the way, she put the receiver back in its place.

Dorothy came crawling towards her Auntie Annie with the rug draped over her head. 'I'm a little bear,' she roared.

'You're a little madam!'

Dorothy Gallagher the second was a wearing child, hyperactive and intelligent beyond her years. Her bright blue eyes missed nothing and she was every bit as bossy and inquisitive as her paternal grandmother.

Annie said, 'You'll get all dirty from that mat.'

'Why you got a dirty mat?' Dorothy asked curiously.

'It's not exactly dirty, luv, more dusty.'

'Auntie Annie clean it so Dorothy can be a bear.'

'I'm not in the mood, luv. You'll just have to be a dirty bear.'

Sylvia came in with the tea and orange juice for her daughter. 'I know it's no comfort right now, Annie,' she said, 'but you should feel proud having two such independent-minded children. It shows how well you brought them up.'

'That's not what Daniel said,' Annie moaned. 'He thinks I'm a hopeless mother.'

'He'll see sense one day,' Sylvia said comfortingly. 'Now look, you must snap out of this. You've got a living to make and a shop to run. You're bound to feel down in the dumps, but open the shop and get down to making clothes again. It'll take your mind off things.'

There didn't seem much point, the money had been mainly to make life better for her children. 'The shop's still open,' Annie said. 'Though I suppose I'd better go in tomorrow and see how things are.'

'Cecy said Patchwork was closed when she passed on Saturday,' Sylvia exclaimed. 'She came to see you, but no-one answered the door.'

'But Chloe was looking after it,' Annie said, puzzled.

The phone rang and she went to answer it, just in case, you never know, it might be Sara. Instead, it was Susan Hull, who didn't waste time on formalities. 'I've been trying to get through to you for days,' she said angrily. 'What's happening with Patchwork? I had that girl, what's-her-name, on the phone on Friday, asking if she could take my quilts and cushions to new premises in St John's Precinct. Are you closing down, Annie? It would have been polite to let me know.'

'I'm not closing down,' Annie said, astonished. 'Was it Chloe?'

'The one with the narrow eyes,' Susan explained impatiently. 'The new shop's called Pasticcio, which sounds like an ice-cream to me. She said it's sited in a good position, right in the middle of town, the others were going with her and I'd do much better than with you.'

'Bitch!'

'That's what I thought. I told her she was a traitor, but when I tried to call you, the operator said your phone was off the hook.'

Annie bit her lip. 'Things have been a bit upside down here – my daughter went to Australia on Friday.'

'Really! I've got one girl who's a secretary in Japan, and the other's hitch-hiking across India with her boyfriend at the moment.'

They rang off on a friendly note, agreeing that children were a worry, and when they left home, you worried even more. Annie assured her Patchwork would open normally tomorrow.

She returned to the lounge, where Dorothy appeared to be taking a serious interest in last week's *Radio Times*. 'What does pasticcio mean?'

Sylvia wrinkled her nose. 'Isn't it a nut?'

'It can't be.' According to the dictionary, pasticcio was a medley of bits and pieces, rather like patchwork. Pistachio was a nut. She explained what had happened with the shop. 'The other week, I found Chloe had a notebook full of drawings of my clothes. She's opened her own shop with a similar name and *my designs!*'

'You should sue her, Annie,' Sylvia was outraged.

'I can't be bothered.' Annie was angry, very angry. At any other time, she would have at least come face to face with Chloe and told her what she thought, but in a way she was almost glad it had happened. For fifteen minutes, she'd thought about something other than the events of the last few days. The sense of muggy despair had lifted. Tomorrow, she'd assess the damage, get other people to supply knitwear and jewellery, build up the shop so it was better than before. She'd find an artist and sell paintings. And she'd need a new assistant, one she could trust this time.

Dawn Gallagher! Dawn had felt very low since her divorce from Tommy. She'd been on the look-out for a job for ages. 'But who wants a woman going on fifty, when able-bodied men are being thrown on the scrapheap,' she'd said despairingly last time they met. She'd ring Dawn later.

But, deep down, Annie wasn't much interested in Patchwork any more. 'Y'know,' she said slowly, 'I'd like to do something dead selfish.'

'Such as?'

'I'm not sure. Something absorbing, not sewing, when me mind's all over the place. I'd like to use me brain instead of me hands.'

Sylvia looked dubious. 'You'd never stop thinking about the kids.'

'I know,' Annie said soberly. She would never get over the suddenness of Sara leaving, or the brutality of how Daniel had gone. She would still cry for her children, but couldn't mope for ever. She was forty-two. For the very first time, she had no-one to consider but herself.

Sara was unhappy in Australia. The flat was small and poky and she was lonely. Nigel had no family, no friends. Unemployment was high and she couldn't get a job. She pleaded with her mother to come for Christmas.

Annie's first inclination was to rush out and buy a ticket, Dawn could look after the shop, but common-sense prevailed. It wouldn't do Sara's marriage any good if she knew she only had to pick up the phone and her mam would come running.

'Sorry, luv, I can't,' she said, hoping she didn't sound too harsh. 'Anyroad, your Auntie Marie's coming on Christmas Eve.'

Marie had spent eight years in America, but the young director who'd wanted her in his films was no longer all that young. Now Hollywood had wooed him away from the low-budget, critically-acclaimed movies that had become his trademark, and he was about to embark on a major project with a twenty-million-dollar budget. Casting control was no longer his. Marie Harrison had been shown the door.

To Annie's relief, her sister didn't seem to mind. 'It was good while it lasted, I did some TV work over there. The thing is, sis, I was getting nowhere.'

Annie felt she'd heard those words before. Marie smiled, as if she guessed her thoughts. 'I've no illusions any more. The penny dropped when I reached forty. I'm not sure what it is; no great acting ability, not exactly great good looks, no charisma, or a bit of all three, but I know I'll never see my name in lights. I'm not giving up. You can make a fairly good living in supporting roles. I earned enough in the States to buy my own place in London. My agent's got a small part lined up in a new TV comedy series. We start shooting in the New Year. I play the dizzy American next-door neighbour – I've got the accent off pat.'

'Chris will be pleased to see you. His plays came back from the BBC years ago. He was too disheartened to write more.'

'That's stupid!' Marie said contemptuously. 'If you want to succeed, you've got to keep on and on and on. Even then, you might not make it.'

There was something different about her. Her hair was just the same, thick and dark, curling up slightly at the ends and, as usual, she was perfectly made up. The difference was something to do with her remarkably unlined girlish face. After a while, she burst out laughing. 'You'll never guess what it is, sis!'

'Sorry, luv, I didn't realise I was staring.'

'I had a nose job a few years ago. See!' Marie turned sideways. 'It now tips up when it used to tip down.'

'It never did tip down,' Annie said indignantly. 'It was a perfectly good nose before.' She felt ill at ease with her sister. They'd drifted too far apart. She was reluctant to say how shattered she felt when the children left.

'I'm surprised Daniel isn't home for Christmas,' Marie remarked.

'He's travelling round with a group of youngsters the same age as himself. They wanted to stay together.'

'Will he telephone? I'd like to speak to my one and only nephew.'

'He called to wish me Merry Christmas yesterday,' Annie lied. She had no idea where Daniel was, or who he was with. There'd been one card which had arrived months ago, the day after his eighteenth birthday, with a smudged postmark which might have been Cardiff or Carlisle. 'Thinking of you, Mum. Daniel,' was all the card said. Since then, there'd been no more word.

'You haven't put the decorations up.'

'I thought the tree was enough, me being on me own.' Perhaps she should have brought at least a few decorations down from the loft, because it didn't seem remotely like Christmas Eve.

Marie glanced at her sharply. 'Are you all right, sis? It must have been a blow, both of them leaving about the same time.'

'It was a bit, but the shop keeps me busy.' She'd managed to get used to being alone – no, not used to it, to accept the fact that this would be her lot from now on – but the run-up to Christmas had been painful. To think of all the food she used to buy! She'd always got far too much, and some years there'd still be special biscuits or figs or nuts left in January. Now there was no need for mountains of groceries, little gifts for the tree, crackers, cans of fizzy drinks or Christmassy serviettes. She'd stopped going to the super-market, anyroad, because passing the cornflakes, the fish fingers and beefburgers she wouldn't have dreamt of buying for herself only made her want to weep. She felt uncomfortable at the checkout with her miserable basket of groceries, when there were women with trolleys packed to the gills. Nowadays, she bought everything from a little corner shop that was open all hours.

Marie yawned. 'What will this dinner be like at Sylvia and Mike's tomorrow?'

'It's bound to be more cheerful than last year. Joe had not long died and Mike left an empty chair at the table as a sign of respect. No-one could take their eyes off it all day.' This year, for the first time, Sara and Daniel wouldn't be there, but only their mother would regard that as a reason to be sad.

5

The miners sang defiantly as they marched back to work. As with Dunkirk, defeat was being celebrated in a carnival atmosphere, despite the cold rain of a dark March morning. A pit band led the triumphant procession and the streets were lined with onlookers, clapping and cheering. Annie felt a lump in her throat. These men were the salt of the earth, beaten by a government backed by multi-millionaires.

The newsreader appeared on the screen and introduced another topic. Annie switched the television off and turned to Auntie Dot.

Her aunt was in tears. 'Such stout lads, only fighting for their jobs, but you know what Thatcher called them, her own people? – "the enemy within".'

It was the end of one of the bitterest disputes in trade union history, as miner fought miner. For a year, TV screens had shown the ugly violence on the picket lines and vicious battles with the police.

Annie patted Dot's hand with its swollen knuckles and bulging wristbone. 'Don't upset yourself, luv.'

'I can't help it, Annie, when I see what that woman's doing to the country.' Dot made a move to dry her eyes. Annie dried them for her.

'Would you like me to put your make-up on?'

Dot sniffed. 'Would you mind, luv? Bert does the lippy all crooked. Go easy on the rouge, I don't want to look like a tart.'

It was heartbreaking to see such a once-vital, energetic woman so completely helpless. Dot rarely left the house these days. The parlour had once again been turned into a bedroom, and a double bed stood in the place where Annie's mam and dad had slept during the war. Dot lay propped against a heap of pillows, her stick-like arms and twisted hands resting on the eiderdown. A row of bottles were lined up on the bedside table; pills for this, pills for that, pills to maintain almost every bodily function, as well as a variety of other medical aids which kept her aunt alive. Despite the fact it was a sick room, the atmosphere was usually one of gaiety and fun, and Dot's hoarse, infectious laugh could be heard halfway down the street.

Annie dabbed powder and blusher on the wax-like cheeks and drew the lipstick outline carefully. 'Close your eyes,' she murmured. She smeared a suggestion of blue shadow on the almost transparent lids, then gently combed the silver hair, inserted pearl stud earrings and helped her aunt into a frilly pink nylon bedjacket. Then the final adornment, a pair of horrible zebra-striped spectacles.

'There, you're done! What scent are you in the mood for today?' Everyone seemed to think an appropriate present for a bedridden woman was perfume. Dot had an assortment worth several hundred pounds.

'Poison!' Dot cackled.

Annie sprayed her aunt and herself, then held up a mirror so Dot could see the finished result. 'You look dead beautiful!'

Dot turned her head from side to side. 'I don't look so bad, do I?' she said conceitedly. 'I've far fewer wrinkles than Cecy, and she's years younger than me. The Harrisons and the Gallaghers were at the front of the queue when the Lord handed out good looks.' She peered over the mirror at her niece. 'It's about time you got yourself another feller, Annie. You're a fine-looking woman, in the prime of life.'

Annie made a face. 'Chance'd be a fine thing.'

'How long is it since Lauri died?'

'Thirteen years.'

'And you've never met anyone over all that time?'

'No-one special. I was always too wrapped up in the children.'

'Sara's married and Daniel's on his travels, so you can get yourself a feller.' Her eyes narrowed. 'Have you heard from Daniel lately?'

'Yes, Auntie. He rings every week.' Annie began to pack the make-up away in its little zipped bag.

'You know, luv,' Dot said softly, 'I may be old, but I've got a dead good memory. You said that in exactly the same voice as you told me your mam played Snakes and Ladders and made cakes.'

Annie stood the mirror on the mantelpiece. 'You didn't cross-examine me then, Auntie Dot, and I'd sooner you didn't now.' Only Sylvia, and she'd had to tell Sara, knew the truth about her son. She couldn't stand the thought of people feeling sorry for her.

'If that's the way you want it, luv.' With an effort, she lifted her arms a few inches from the bed. 'Come and give your ould auntie a hug.'

'Oh, Dot!' Annie buried her face in the bony shoulder.

The parlour door opened and Uncle Bert came in with three cups of tea. For a man two years off eighty, he was the picture of rude health. 'It smells like a knocking shop in here.' He looked at his wife in amazement. 'Bloody hell! I left an ould woman in me bed, and I come back to find Rita Hayworth!'

'I'll have to go soon.' Annie took the tea. 'I've a lecture at eleven. I thought I'd drop in on the way. I knew you'd be upset when you saw the news.'

Bert nodded at the television. 'I couldn't bear to watch. The Government might have won the battle, but they didn't win many hearts. Most people were on the miners' side.'

Dot had perked up and her blue eyes shone as brightly as a young girl's. She said, 'Perhaps you'll click at university, Annie.'

Annie grinned. 'As I said, chance'd be a fine thing. Anyroad, all I'm interested in is getting me degree.'

'Your dad was a clever lad. He passed the scholarship. Me mam always thought he'd end up at university. 'Stead, he met Rose . . .' Dot shrugged. 'Your dad'd be proud of both his girls. It's a pity Marie's programme ended – what was it called? She was a scream in that part.'

'*His and Hers,*' supplied Uncle Bert.

'They're making another series,' Annie said. 'Next time, Marie's part will be bigger.'

She said goodbye. Every time she left, she was convinced she would never see her aunt again. Dot had lost her appetite completely. She hardly ate. Only willpower, and a determination to see the back of Mrs Thatcher, kept the scraggy, undernourished body alive.

After seeing the miners, it was equally depressing to drive into town along the Dock Road and witness another major industry laid to waste. When she was young, the Docky had been jammed end to end with traffic; lorries, horses and carts, handcarts. The funnels of great ships had once loomed over the high walls of the docks, whilst a noisy bustling mass of humanity thronged the busy pavements – you could hear a dozen languages being spoken in the space of a few minutes, as ships from all over the world came to the great port of Liverpool. The Germans had done their best to destroy the docks during the war, but since then 'progress' had done what Hitler had failed to do, and all that now remained was mile after mile of dereliction and neglect. Annie was glad to reach the Pier Head and see signs of life.

Sylvia had expressed herself astounded when one of Mike's employees gave in his notice. 'You should see him, Annie. He's thirty-five and is covered in tattoos, yet he's going to university to study Philosophy.'

'There's nothing wrong with that.'

'I thought that's what you'd say. In which case, why don't *you* go to university. You're always on about wanting to use your brain.'

'Me!' Annie burst out laughing. 'I'm totally ignorant, Syl. I left school at fifteen and I haven't got a single qualification.'

'Ignoramuses can take an Access Course at night school. It brings your brain up to condition. That's what Nick, the would-be philosopher, did.' Sylvia seemed to have everything worked out. 'You wouldn't have to go away, Liverpool University is one of the best in the country.'

'I dunno.' The idea appealed enormously, but she couldn't for the life of her imagine someone like her being accepted.

'It wouldn't hurt to try,' Sylvia said encouragingly. 'We're both awfully ignorant. We've known each other thirty years, yet we've never once talked about anything deep or intellectual. It used to be boys and clothes and the Beatles, now it's kids and food and general gossip. We're a very shallow pair.'

'You used to write poetry,' Annie reminded her.

'Yes, but it was crap poetry, nothing about it was profound.'

'I'm not even sure what "profound" means!'

'See! It's about time one of us had a decent education.'

'Why can't it be you?' Annie raised her eyebrows.

'Don't be silly, Annie, I'm pregnant, aren't I?'

'So you are!'

Annie parked the Anglia on Brownlow Hill and walked to the building where the lecture was to be held. Sylvia's fourth daughter had been born last July. Lucia had chestnut brown hair and Bruno's clever mind.

'That's my lot!' Sylvia announced when Annie went to see her. 'I've gone through all the hair colours, I don't want any more kids.'

'It seems odd, you having a baby when I'm about to become a grandmother,' Annie said. The older she got, the more peculiar life seemed.

The lecture room was already crowded. Annie waved to everyone she knew as she slid behind a desk. She put on her glasses and took a pen and notebook from her bag.

Sara's son, Harry, had arrived just before Christmas. Again, she pleaded with her mother to come and stay. She was still lonely. Things weren't going well between her and Nigel, even though they'd moved into a detached bungalow with a swimming pool in a nice part of Sydney.

'I've just started university, Sara, luv,' Annie said reasonably. 'It's hardly worth me while coming all that way for only a few weeks. Anyroad, I can't afford it.' Dawn Gallagher worked full-time at Patchwork, and two women machinists made the clothes to a few standard patterns. Annie did nothing, except somewhat guiltily take the profit, which wasn't much once the bills and wages were paid. She still had a mortgage and needed to support herself over the next three years. Nevertheless, she started to put money aside for Australia.

Annie knew she was being selfish, but not for obvious reasons. She'd got used to being without the children, the wound no longer festered, but still hurt. She didn't want to open up the wound by going to Australia, then returning, alone, to Heather Close, and the agonising worry over Daniel. There'd been another card, this time from London, just after his nineteenth birthday. The message was the same as the first; 'Thinking of you, Mum.'

Being accepted at university was easier than she'd thought. Mature students, particularly women, were especially welcome. After discussing it with Sylvia, she decided to take American Literature. On the Access Course, she learnt how to discipline her mind and assemble her thoughts, how to write a paper using other writers' work to support her thesis.

The lecturer had arrived, Euan Campbell. The students fell silent and directed their gaze towards his sad, beautiful face. Euan's dark hair was parted in the middle like a saint in a stained glass window, his velvety liquid eyes had the same blank stare. He'd come to Liverpool from Glasgow University at the same time as herself. The younger students made fun of his morose manner, but it was whispered that he'd left Glasgow after his wife and two young children had been killed in a car crash. Annie wasn't the only woman who felt the urge to take him in her arms and comfort him.

He began to speak in his gentle voice with its soft Scots burr. Gradually, enthusiasm for his subject – Ernest Hemingway – took over and his tone became firmer. 'On close scrutiny, Hemingway's work doesn't stand up to his reputation. He's overrated, a good writer, but not a great one. Much of his work was written in Paris, an advantage to any artist. Paris is the most beautiful and inspiring city in the world.'

'Have you ever been to Paris, Annie?'

The lecture was over and the class were shuffling out of the room for lunch. Annie turned to the questioner. Binnie Appleby was a divorcee with three grown-up children. It seemed sensible to attach themselves to each other when surrounded by students less than half their age.

'I've never been abroad,' Annie replied. 'We couldn't afford it when the children were young, and I was too busy when they got older.'

'That's always the way, isn't it?' Binnie giggled. She linked Annie's arm. 'Fancy a sarnie and a beer for lunch?'

'Perhaps you and me could go to Paris sometime,' Binnie suggested as they strolled along Hope Street towards the Philharmonic pub.

'That would be nice,' Annie said politely. She wasn't sure if she cared too much for Binnie. They'd been thrown together, and she felt about her as she did about Valerie Cunningham, someone she'd lived next door to for more than half her life, yet never truly liked. Binnie was pretty, flirtatious and man-mad. Annie had got used to going to places and being deserted the minute Binnie saw a man she only faintly knew, something she and Sylvia had never done to each other. Today, she was quite likely to end up eating her meal alone, not that she minded. She'd get on with the Hemingway novel they'd been set.

The ornate Victorian pub was crowded. They bought a sandwich and half a lager each and searched for a seat. Binnie eyed up the male customers with an expert eye. She was, she had confessed to Annie, desperate to get married again. It seemed any man would do.

They sat at the end of a long table of dark-suited businessmen who were far too preoccupied discussing office politics to notice two middle-aged women. Annie produced a photograph of her grandson which had arrived from Australia that morning. 'He's ever so like me son,' she said proudly. 'I shall send Sara a photo of Daniel at three months so she can compare them.'

Binnie shuddered. 'I don't know how you can stand being a grandmother, Annie. I shall keep it to meself if it happens to me. Oh, look!' She waved to a man who'd just entered. 'There's Richard Cross. I used to work with him. Richard!' she hollered. She picked up her bag. 'I'll be back in a minute.'

'Like hell you will!' Annie muttered. She took *The Sun also Rises* from her bag and began to read.

'Is anybody sitting here?'

Annie looked up and saw Euan Campbell standing politely in front of her, a plate in one hand and a glass in the other. 'No,' she said. He obviously didn't recognise her. She returned to the novel, only vaguely conscious of the young man settling beside her.

Some minutes later, he spoke. 'Were you at the Hemingway lecture this morning?' He nodded at the book.

When Annie confirmed she was, he continued, 'I'm afraid I haven't familiarised myself with all the faces yet, let alone the names.'

'I'm Annie Menin.' Close up, his skin was olive, smooth and clear, his eyes deep, dark wells of sadness. He had full, rather feminine lips. She searched for something to say that wouldn't rake up unpleasant memories. 'How are you settling in Liverpool?'

'Not so bad. It's a lively place, lots to do.' He finished off his sandwich. 'What do you think of the book?'

'It's lovely,' Annie said enthusiastically. She bit her lip. Perhaps 'lovely' wasn't the right word to use to a university lecturer. She should have said 'intellectually stimulating'. 'I never had much time to read in the past, what with the children. After me husband died and I became the breadwinner, I had less time than ever. I never dreamt that books by reputable authors could be so, so . . .' she searched for the word, 'so *enjoyable*! I thought they'd be beyond me,' she finished a trifle lamely.

Euan Campbell gave a sweet, gentle smile. 'That's good. Wait till we come to F. Scott Fitzgerald, you'll like him even more.'

Annie sighed with pleasure. 'I can't wait.' She actually found it exciting to read novels *properly*, not just skim the surface as she'd done the occasional books she'd read before, but search for nuances and hidden meanings, admire metaphors and clever turns of phrase, try and diagnose the author's own personality from his or her words. She found herself quite good at it and her marks so far had been high.

The businessmen had gone. Binnie Appleby returned, and winked when she saw Annie's companion. 'Tell us all about Paris,' she demanded.

Euan winced. 'That's impossible. You need to see it for yourself.'

'Annie and I thought we might go.'

'I hope you enjoy yourselves,' he said stiffly. He finished the remainder of his drink and left abruptly. Annie cursed Binnie inwardly as she'd been enjoying their talk.

Binnie looked hurt. 'I must have BO! You made a conquest there.'

'Don't be stupid,' Annie said irritably. 'Women are the furthest thing from his mind at the moment. Anyroad, I'll be forty-four this year, and he's what – twenty-nine, thirty?'

'Toy-boys are all the rage. I'd go for a twenty-nine-year-old, particularly one that looked like Euan.'

'Well, I wouldn't.' There was only one boy Annie wanted. Daniel.

The usual card arrived in July a few days after Daniel's birthday. He was twenty. 'Thinking of you, Mum. Daniel.' The card bore a Swedish stamp, Annie tore it in two in a rage. 'What the hell's he up to in Sweden! What did I do to deserve this? Doesn't he realise he's crucifying me, staying away all this time?'

A few days later, Sara phoned and implored her mother to spend the summer holiday in Australia.

Annie was implacable. 'I can't, luv. I'm going to the Isle of Wight with Sylvia and Cecy and the girls, then I'll be staying with your Auntie Marie in London for a while.'

'You don't *want* to see me, that's it,' Sara said sulkily. 'You've turned your back on your own daughter.'

'Sweetheart, as if I would! I'll come, I promise, as soon as I've finished me degree – I'll stay three whole months, six, if you like.'

'But that's two years off!' Sara wailed. There was a pause. 'I'm pregnant again. The baby's due in November.'

'Congratulations, luv,' Annie said warmly. 'That's marvellous news.'

Sara rang off and Annie went into the lounge clutching her head in both hands. Children! There were times when she wished she'd never had any – and to think she'd actually wanted four!

The hotel overlooked the cliffs in Ventnor. Sylvia, Cecy and the two youngest girls shared one room, whilst Yasmin and Ingrid slept in a three-bedded room with Annie. The weather was perfect. They woke every morning to find sunlight flooding through the windows and a cloudless blue sky. Most of the time was spent in a little sandy cove, where the children built castles and made channels to the water – Dorothy stared, entranced, as the tide came rushing into the little ditch she'd dug. 'Dorothy made a river,' she announced grandly.

Cecy rolled up her skirt and led Lucia, who'd just started walking, into the sea, where the tiny girl kicked and screamed in delight.

'I loved it when mine were that age,' Annie said wistfully. 'In the summer, I used to take them to the sands in Waterloo.'

'Yes, but they don't stay that age, do they, Annie?' Sylvia replied sagely. 'Time rolls on. See how those boys are eyeing Yasmin? She's only twelve and her breasts are almost as big as mine.'

Annie hadn't noticed the way Yasmin's young body curved enticingly in the skimpy swimsuit. Her black hair was in bunches, her mysterious, exotic face screwed up in concentration as she covered a sandcastle with shells, entirely unaware that half a dozen lads, fifteen-, sixteen-year-olds, were watching her every movement with considerable interest. Ingrid knelt on the other side of the castle, equally engrossed. Her face already held the promise of an icy beauty.

It was a lazy, relaxing holiday. Nights, they drank wine and watched television in the hotel lounge. On the final evening, Annie and Sylvia stumbled their way in the dark down to the little cove, where they sat on a rock beside the inky water and watched the reflection of the full moon dancing further out on the waves.

'Remember when we used to sit on that little scrap of sand in Seaforth and talk about the future?' Sylvia said. 'It was there you told me Marie was pregnant, she was only thirteen, a year older than Yasmin.' She picked up a handful of sand. 'Actually, Annie, I've been meaning to say this for ages. I was horrible to Marie. I pretended to be shocked, but really I was jealous. Oh, not because she was pregnant,' she said quickly in response to Annie's gasp of surprise. 'I was jealous of her being your sister. I wanted you all to myself. I couldn't bear the thought of Marie having so much of your attention.'

Annie picked up a handful of sand herself. It was moist, and she moulded it into a ball and threw it into the water where it landed with a loud plop.

'Are you shocked?' said Sylvia.

'No.'

'Then why don't you say something?'

'I've just said, "No", I'm not shocked.' Annie picked up more sand.

'Mind you, it was years before the penny dropped and I realised my true feelings. By then, it was too late and Marie hated me.'

'I don't think she hates you,' Annie said mildly. 'I think it's more a case of thinking you dislike her.'

'I'll try and make up with her next time we meet.' Sylvia slipped off her shoes and made for the water. 'I think I'll have a paddle.'

Annie watched her friend silhouetted against the moonlit sky. 'I've a feeling we should have a row about what you just told me,' she called.

'We'll have one if you like.' Sylvia kicked water in Annie's direction. Annie threw a ball of sand and missed.

'Why is it I never get angry with you?' she asked.

'Because you understand me, probably better than I understand myself.' Sylvia giggled. 'You've always known I'm not very nice.'

'You're too honest to be nice,' Annie said. 'You didn't have to come out with all that stuff about being jealous of Marie.'

'And you're too nice to be honest. Oh, this water's lovely and cool. Why don't you join me?'

'I'm not in the mood. Shall I be honest for once?'

Sylvia stopped paddling. 'I'm all ears.'

'Just then,' Annie said calmly, 'when you turned your head against the sky, I saw quite clearly that you're getting a double chin.'

'*No!* Is it really bad?' Sylvia frantically began to slap her chin.

Annie shook her head sorrowfully. 'It does sag quite a bit. I don't know about these things, but perhaps you can have plastic surgery. Whilst you're at it, you could get those bags done under your eyes.'

'Bags under my eyes! Oh, Annie, you're joking!' She was so relieved, she sat down in the water. 'You horrible thing!'

Later, they walked back arm in arm, Sylvia soaked to the waist.

'It's been a lovely week,' Annie said. 'I've really enjoyed it.'

'Me too, but I can't wait to see Mike.' Sylvia uttered a blissful sigh. 'I'm so lucky, Annie. I don't deserve such happiness.' Her face grew dark. 'It's too good to be true. I have nightmares that something will happen to Mike or one of the girls, and it will all be spoiled.'

Annie didn't say anything, because she knew how cruel fate could be. Nor did she say that she hadn't been joking about the double chin.

Marie's flat was on the top floor of a four-storey house in Primrose Hill. The lush greenery of Regent's Park was visible from the wrought-iron balcony that Annie was too scared to sit on. 'It looks too precarious,' she claimed.

The walls were white and the furniture new; plain bleached wood, and grey and white upholstery. It looked cold and unlived in. Annie's housewarming present, a red and blue vase, might have looked too bright in such colourless surroundings, if it hadn't been for Marie herself.

Her sister dazzled like a too-bright light bulb. Her eyes were brilliant, her face glowed. At last, her dreams were close to being realised: she was almost, nearly, a star.

A second series of *His and Hers* had already been recorded and would be on television that autumn. Audience research had shown that Marie Harrison had scored a hit as Lorelei, the wise-cracking American neighbour. Her part had been expanded – to the detriment of the two main characters, whose roles were inevitably reduced.

'They hate me,' Marie chuckled on Annie's first day there.

'Don't you care?' Annie enquired. 'I couldn't stand it meself.'

'I don't give a shit,' Marie said icily. 'Avril Paige was horrible at the start, really condescending. I'm glad she lost pages of script to me. There's talk of an entirely new programme, *Lorelei*, based on my character. Avril will spit tacks when she finds out.'

'I hope it comes off,' Annie murmured. 'Dot will be thrilled.'

Marie squeezed her palms together as if she were praying. 'Oh, so do I, sis, so do I. Guess what I did last week?' she boasted. 'I opened a supermarket in Birmingham. The mayor was there, and all the local dignitaries. I got paid two hundred and fifty quid.'

'Good for you,' said Annie. It was difficult to believe this was the same cheeky, frightened little girl she'd shared a room with in Orlando Street. They had nothing left in common except their roots. She began to dread the week ahead and longed for Saturday when she could go home.

'Can I have a bath?' she asked. She had to get away. Two babies had been sacrificed, for what? So another actress could spit tacks and her sister open a supermarket in Birmingham. It scarcely seemed worth it.

The strained week ended and Annie returned to Heather Close. To her astonishment, there was a For Sale board in the Cunninghams' front garden. Valerie came to see her that evening.

'I suppose you noticed the board?'

'Where are you off to?'

'Kevin's been offered early retirement,' Valerie said in a rush. 'We thought we'd buy something smaller now there's only Zachary at home.' Both Kelly and Tracy had got married the previous year. Gary and his wife already had a baby girl. 'Kevin fancies over the water, his brother lives in Greasby. He intends to take up golf.' Valerie paused, eyes gleaming. 'Guess how much the estate agent said we should ask for the house? Fifty-five thousand!'

'Jaysus!' gasped Annie.

'Incredible, isn't it, to be worth so much money?'

'It doesn't make much difference if you're buying another place. It just means estate agents and solicitors get a bigger cut.'

Valerie burst into peals of laughter. 'Oh, I'll miss living next door to you, Annie. I truly will.'

'And I'll miss you.' To Annie's surprise, she really meant it. You got used to people. You actually grew fond of them, even if you didn't like them all that much. The house would feel peculiar without the Cunninghams next door. 'I hope you'll be very happy over the water.'

Dawn Gallagher telephoned on Sunday. 'Can you come into the shop tomorrow, Annie? This chap from Yorkshire, Ben Wainwright, turned up the other day wanting us to sell his paintings. I told him it was up to you. He said he'd come back at nine o'clock on Monday.'

'What are they like?' Annie asked.

'Weird! I didn't care for them much, but then I'm totally ignorant about art. They could be works of genius for all I know.'

'I'm as knowledgeable about paintings as you are,' Annie said drily.

'The thing is, luv,' Dawn said in a husky low-pitched voice, 'he's drop-dead gorgeous. If I hadn't got another feller, I'd have bought the lot meself, despite them being weird.' Dawn was getting married again in a few weeks' time to a six-foot-six-inch Detective Sergeant in the police force who she'd met at a Divorced and Separated club. 'Another thing, Annie. Our Marilyn went into town on Saturday. She said Chloe Banks' shop in St John's Precinct has closed. According to one of the other shopkeepers, she left owing thousands of pounds.'

Annie grimaced. 'I'm trying me best to feel sympathetic.'

'Don't try too hard, luv. She deserved all she got.'

On Monday morning, Annie was about to get dressed up to the nines to impress the drop-dead gorgeous artist, but changed her mind. He might be married and she mightn't think him gorgeous. Anyroad, she was too busy with her studies to become entangled with a man, but then she'd always been too busy with something or other since Lauri died.

She put on jeans, a baggy blue T-shirt and a pair of espadrilles. It was years since she'd covered her freckles with pancake. Nowadays, she merely used powder and a touch of lipstick, though she still rubbed her lashes with spit. In front of the mirror, she inserted gold hoop earrings and ran her fingers through her short red curls. There was no doubt about it, she still looked youthful. She turned sideways to check if there was any sign of a double chin – it had come as a shock to notice Sylvia's sagging jawline. Her own chin looked just the same, but then she should tip it down, not up. She made a face. Perhaps it would be best not to find out, because there was nothing she could do about it.

At half past eight, she walked round to the shop. Patchwork no longer gave her a thrill, it was just another dress shop, more attractive and unusual than most. She cast an expert eye over the clothes. They were well made to her own designs, but several styles were duplicated which had never happened when she'd run the place herself. Susan Hull's quilts and cushion covers were as lovely as ever, and the knitwear was almost as good as Ernie Ward's. She paused in front of the glass jewellery, wondering if Sara would like an earring and necklace set for Christmas.

Annie contemplated the paintings on the wall; watercolours, done by an elderly lady, a friend of Cecy's. Each was a precise reproduction of a single flower; a staid iris, a curved rose, a frilly carnation . . . Framed in narrow pine, they sold well, usually two or three a week.

The door opened and a man about her own age came in. 'I know it says "Closed", but I saw someone inside,' he said in a strong Yorkshire accent. 'Are you the owner? I'm Ben Wainwright. You're expecting me.'

'Annie Menin.' She shook hands. Dawn must need glasses. There was nothing remotely handsome about Ben Wainwright. He was tall, lanky, with a very ordinary face. His skin was dark and rough, as if it had been chipped out of stone. 'His eyes are nice,' she conceded, dark blue, almost navy, with stubby lashes. His hair was black and curly like a gypsy's. He wore shabby jeans and a knitted sweater covered in snags.

'How did you hear about Patchwork?' she asked, easing her fingers apart. His grip had been exceptionally strong.

'Through the local Labour Party. I presented them with a painting at last week's meeting in appreciation of their support during the miners' strike. You weren't there!' he said accusingly.

'I was away.' She hadn't been to a meeting in months.

'Someone said you exhibited paintings. I'm always on the look-out for an outlet for my work.' He glanced contemptuously at the neat watercolours. 'When I saw these, I nearly didn't come back.'

'No-one made you.'

He grinned. It was nice the way the skin crinkled around his navy blue eyes. 'I hoped your taste mightn't be as execrable as it seemed.'

Annie hooted sarcastically. 'Ta very much! Where are these wonderful paintings, anyroad?'

'Outside in the car.'

'Well, you'd better bring them in, hadn't you?'

He grinned again. 'Right away, ma'am.'

She watched through the window as he walked towards an old Cortina estate. His walk was confident, as if he were very sure of his place in the world. He came back carrying three unframed canvases.

'What do you think?' He held up a painting for her to see.

The picture was almost wholly black, with just the suggestion of four miners in the bowels of the earth, bare to the waist, bent double as they hacked at walls of coal. The lamps on their heads glowed dully. The paint was laid on thick and oily, with broad strokes of the brush. Close up, she could see straining muscles, beads of perspiration, tired eyes. It was so real, she was conscious of the acrid smell of coal.

Ben Wainwright put the painting down and picked up another, a pit head at sundown, the black wheel stark against a dull red sky tinged with purple and green.

The final painting showed half a dozen miners leaving the pit at the end of their shift, eyes shining with unnatural brightness in their coal-smudged faces. There was something joyous and free about it, as if the men couldn't wait to get home to their families.

'They're beautiful, but I can't see my customers buying them.'

He looked at her, aghast. 'They're not supposed to be beautiful.'

'What do you expect me to say?' Annie snapped. 'That they're ugly?'

'I'd prefer ugly to beautiful.'

'In that case, I can't see my customers buying ugly paintings.'

'I suppose they prefer this shit!' He gestured at the walls.

'Quite frankly, yes. We sell several a week.'

'Huh! Sorry to have bothered you.' He picked up his paintings.

'Just a minute,' Annie called. 'I wouldn't mind the first one meself, as long as it's not too dear.'

He stopped and looked at her, an expression of amusement on his rugged face. 'You're just being tactful.'

'Tactful! You don't look the sort of chap who'd appreciate tact. No, I like it, but it depends on the price.'

'It's seventy-five pounds.' He regarded her challengingly. 'That's cheap for an original.'

'I know.' The watercolours were twenty-five. 'Will a cheque do?' She sat down at the desk and took her chequebook and glasses from her bag. 'Do you make your living as a painter?'

He lounged against the wall and shook his head. She was suddenly very aware of his powerful masculinity, and her fingers trembled slightly as she wrote his name. 'No,' he said. 'I give a lot of stuff away, to miners' clubs and unions. I can't abide artists who paint only for themselves. I've something to say about the working man's lot and I want to spread the word. I'm always searching for places to exhibit.'

'In that case, you must be a miner.'

'I was, but I watched my dad and two uncles die of fibrosis of the lungs and decided I didn't want my sons to see me go the same way. I gave up years ago. Now, I paint when I can and earn my living as a plumber.'

He was married! Annie felt slightly disappointed. She handed him the cheque. 'It won't bounce.'

'Ta.' To her astonishment, he tore the cheque in two and handed it back. 'Regard it as a gift, Mrs Menin.'

'But . . .' She realised it was no use arguing. 'Call me Annie.'

'I'd best be going, Annie.'

She followed him to the door. When he bent down for the paintings, she noticed how his black hair curled tightly on his weatherbeaten neck. His fingers, long and narrow, gripped the paintings, and he stood and faced her. Annie opened the door. He paused on the threshold.

'I don't suppose you're free for dinner tonight?'

'I'm sorry. I've promised to visit someone.' Dot was longing to hear all about Marie. 'I'm free tomorrow.'

'I'm going home in the morning, back to Yorkshire.'

'Oh, well, never mind.' A voice inside Annie's head urged, 'Take him to see Auntie Dot, then have dinner. She'd like him, and he'd like her. Men like

Ben Wainwright don't grow on trees.' The voice seemed to have forgotten he was married.

She'd opened her mouth to speak, when Dawn Gallagher arrived. She glanced curiously from one to the other.

'Bye, then,' said Ben Wainwright.

'Bye,' said Annie, closing the door.

Dawn looked at her eagerly. 'I've been stood across the road for ages, waiting for him to go. What d'you think, Annie?'

'You were right. He's drop-dead gorgeous.'

'He asked you out, I could tell. Oh, I had this really strong feeling in me water that he would. I just knew you two would get on.'

'I'm not in the habit of going out with married men.' Annie said primly, thinking what a hypocrite she was. If Dawn hadn't turned up, she would have gone out with Ben Wainwright like a shot.

'You bloody idiot!' Dawn's face twisted in disgust. 'He's divorced.' She gave Annie a shove. 'Catch him and say you've changed your mind.'

But another car was already backing into the space where Ben Wainwright had been. The Cortina had gone.

6

Annie pushed Ben Wainwright to the back of her mind and confidently returned for her second year at university. The course had become more difficult. It was no longer a matter of reading books and dissecting them; she had to work out why the novels of the great Theodore Dreiser, a communist, were so obsessed with capitalist tycoons and crooks; show where anti-semitism could be found in the poetry of Ezra Pound; what was the central theme behind the liberal works of William Faulkner.

Some nights she worked till the early hours, reading and making notes. Sylvia persuaded Mike to let her have an old electric typewriter when Michael Ray Security converted to computers. She became involved in some of the university's extra-mural activities, joining the debating society, the Fabians. If an old film was shown on television that related to the course, *Sister Carrie, The Sound and the Fury, The Great Gatsby,* Chris Andrews recorded it on his remarkable new video machine, and Binnie Appleby would come over and they would watch it at Chris's.

In the autumn, Bruno Delgado turned seventy and celebrated the fact in the Grand. He was still a magnificent-looking man, with a comfortably lined face that only added to his air of distinction and a fine head of jet black hair, which, Sylvia told Annie, he regularly dyed.

'Look at him, the old devil,' Sylvia said as she regarded her father fondly across the bar. Bruno was holding forth to an entranced audience consisting mainly of young women. He wore a red shirt, open at the neck, and black leather trousers. Dozens of cards were strung across the bar. 'He'll screw that blonde barmaid rotten when this is over.'

Annie glanced enviously at the fiftyish woman with dyed yellow hair and too much eyeshadow who was drawing pints of beer.

Later, someone took a photo of Bruno with Sylvia and Mike and his four beautiful granddaughters. 'Where's Cecy?' he called.

Cecy had been invited but hadn't come. The following morning, she rang Annie to ask how things had gone.

'We had a lovely time,' Annie enthused, 'but why weren't you there?'

'I would have felt in the way,' Cecy said with a sigh.

'Don't be silly – Bruno asked for you.'

'Did he? Did he really?'

'You're still his wife.' They'd never got divorced. Having a wife suited Bruno down to the ground. It was a good excuse for not letting other women get their claws into him.

'Yes, but in name only – just a minute, Annie, there's someone at the door.' Cecy returned, seconds later. 'It's Bruno,' she said happily, 'he's brought flowers. I'll speak to you another time, dear.'

Annie rang off thinking that Bruno needed two wives; Cecy, whom he loved with all his heart, and another he could go to bed with.

Nigel James telephoned early one Friday morning in November to say Sara had given birth to a little girl. 'She's seven pounds, six ounces, and she looks just like you. We're calling her Anne-Marie.'

'Oh, that's lovely!' Annie blinked back the tears. 'Congratulations, luv. Tell Sara to ring as soon as she can.'

Next day, the Cunninghams moved to Heswall and Valerie came to say goodbye. She made Annie promise to stay in touch. 'Even if it's only letters with our Christmas cards.' Annie duly promised and wished her good luck with the move.

Valerie pulled a face. 'We'll need it, Annie. I've had to give up my job, it's too far to travel. I'm not sure how me and Kevin will get on, under each other's feet all day.' She looked at Annie, perplexed. 'It's funny, the children used to drive me mad when they were little, but I've been thinking how much I'd love to have those days back.'

'Let's hope Kevin likes golf – or you find another job.'

'Let's hope, eh!'

They kissed for the first and only time. 'Kevin'll pop in and say goodbye once the van's loaded.'

Annie watched as the Cunninghams' furniture was carried out. She was surprised how shabby it looked in the cold light of day. The back of nearly everything was covered in cobwebs. Zachary, a tall, drooping lad, as anaemic as his father, stood miserably on the pavement.

Hours later, the van drove away and Valerie and Zachary climbed into the car. Annie opened the door when she saw Kevin approaching. She extended her hand. 'Cheerio, Kevin.'

'D'you mind if I wash my hands, Annie?' His pasty face was sweaty.

She stood aside to let him in. 'You know where the bathroom is.'

'The kitchen will do.'

He washed his hands, dried them, then, to her everlasting astonishment, grabbed her shoulders and began to kiss her passionately.

'Kevin!' she spluttered, struggling free.

'You've not changed, Annie. You're still as stunning as when you first moved in,' he said in a thick voice and tried to kiss her again.

'*Kevin*! Valerie might come in.'

'Sod Valerie. When can I see you again?' His eyes were wet with emotion. 'Please, Annie. We could meet in town one afternoon.'

'Absolutely not!'

Outside, a car door slammed and Valerie called, 'Kevin!'

Kevin adjusted his glasses with shaking hands. 'I'll phone, Annie. Some time when Valerie's out.' He backed out of the door.

Annie followed through the breakfast room. '*NO!*'

'We could book a room in a hotel.'

'No way, Kevin.' She pushed him into the hall. He stumbled backwards out of the front door and into the arms of his wife.

As the Cunninghams drove away, Annie dutifully waved goodbye. The minute the car disappeared, she collapsed in fits of laughter. 'Jaysus! I never thought that sort of thing would happen to me again at my age!' She staggered towards the phone. 'I must tell Sylvia.'

Her hilarity had subsided somewhat by the time she'd dialled and the ringing tone sounded in her ear. 'Poor Valerie,' she thought soberly.

The silence from number eight was ghostly over the weekend, but when Annie came home on Monday, she saw thick net curtains on the windows. She immediately called to introduce herself; Valerie had said an elderly widow, Mrs Vincent, and her unmarried daughter had bought the house.

A distracted, fiftyish-looking woman opened the door. She had short grey hair and round glasses that gave her an owlish look. Her clothes were twenty years out of date; a tailored woollen blouse, tweed skirt and flat shoes. She wore no make-up and her skin was finely lined, but flawless. Her only jewellery was a tiny gold locket on a chain.

'Hi, I'm Annie Menin from next door. I just came to say hallo.'

The woman blinked timidly behind her glasses. 'I'm Miss Vincent, I mean, Monica.' Her voice was faint and whispery.

'Who is it, Monica?' someone called.

'It's the lady from next door.'

'Well, ask her in, you silly girl.'

'Would you like to meet Mother?'

Annie stepped over the cardboard boxes in the hall and went into the lounge, which was already in some semblance of order. An expensive oak display cabinet, as yet empty, stood against the wall, and a matching dining-room suite with six chairs was in front of the French windows.

Mrs Vincent was sitting on a peach brocade settee watching television. She looked too young to be Monica's mother. Heavily made up, she wore a purple mohair sweater and a cream skirt. Her hair was a cloud of pure white. She greeted Annie effusively. 'Would you like tea or coffee, dear? Monica!' she snapped her fingers.

'Nothing, ta,' Annie said quickly, as Monica sprang to attention.

'Now, dear,' Mrs Vincent gushed. 'If we're going to be neighbours, we need to know all about each other. I can see you're married. What does your hubby do? Have you any children?'

Annie had never imparted so much information so quickly as during the intense interrogation she was subjected to. When she finished, Mrs Vincent told the story of her own life. Her hubby had died twenty years ago. 'So I was left a widow, like you. Fortunately, he had a pension so I was well provided for.' Monica was a nurse in those days, but Mrs Vincent's heart wasn't strong. 'I was terrified when she was on nights in case I had one of my attacks.' Her daughter had given up nursing and was now a Health Visitor, though there was no need for her to work. She glanced with contempt at Monica, who was twisting the gold locket nervously.

'Mother seems to think we can live on fresh air,' she said in her little-girl voice. 'Dad's pension hasn't gone up with inflation.'

'She's actually going back to work tomorrow and leaving me with this mess,' Mrs Vincent said fretfully.

Monica gave Annie an imploring look, as if seeking her support. 'I've got several families I don't like letting down. I should have this place more or less straight by tomorrow.'

'You've done wonders so far,' Annie remarked. She said goodbye and made for the door. Monica came with her.

'You don't remember me, do you?' she said breathlessly. 'I was in the class after you at Grenville Lucas. I knew I recognised you, but it wasn't until you were talking to Mother I remembered who you were.'

Annie would never have dreamt the woman was younger than herself. 'I'm afraid we didn't take any notice of the kids below us.'

'You were friendly with that lovely Italian girl, Sylvia.'

'I still am. She's married to my cousin and has four daughters.'

Monica looked wistful. 'I always wanted a family, but things never seem to work out the way you want, do they?'

'Not always,' said Annie. 'By the way, if you remember me, you'll remember the English teacher, Mr Andrews. He lives across the road.'

'I used to have a crush on him.' Monica blushed.

'I think we all did in those days.'

It was gone midnight by the time Annie finished the paper on Ezra Pound. She made a cup of cocoa and took it into the lounge. Noises were coming from next door; thumps and bangs, as if boxes were being humped around, drawers and cupboards opened and closed. Mrs Vincent's voice could be heard, shrill and complaining, 'Not there, you silly girl!'

There was a shattering of glass, something must have dropped, followed by Mrs Vincent shrieking, 'You're stupid, stupid, *stupid*! I've had that vase since before the war.'

Annie turned the television on to drown the noises out. She might feel low at times, but compared to some women, she was incredibly lucky.

The second series of *His and Hers* had come to an end, and no more would be made. It hadn't been a particularly good programme; the only attraction was the fizzy, extrovert Lorelei. Viewers were informed a new series, *Lorelei*, would be screened next year.

Marie was in seventh heaven when she called her sister. 'It's all happening, sis. My agent is besieged with offers of more work, and journalists are queuing up to interview me.'

'I couldn't possibly be more pleased, Marie,' Annie said warmly.

'Could you come for Christmas? I've been asked to tons of parties.'

Annie squirmed uncomfortably. 'I'd sooner not miss dinner with Mike and Sylvia, sis. Anyroad, you won't want me at the parties. They'll be full of your friends.'

'Yes, but . . .' Marie paused.

'But what?'

'Well, they're not really friends. I've been a rolling stone for too long. I haven't gathered any moss.'

'What about Clive Hoskins?' Marie hadn't mentioned him for ages.

'Clive died years ago, when I was in America. I thought I told you. I suppose,' Marie said slowly, 'I want my own flesh and blood.'

'I know the feeling.' There'd been numerous times when Annie had needed her sister, but Marie had been too embroiled in her career. Perversely, in her moment of triumph, Marie wanted *her*! 'Perhaps I could come for a few days in the New Year,' she suggested.

'It doesn't matter,' Marie said coldly. 'I'm sure you've got more important things to do.'

Mike Gallagher refused to entertain the notion of the ritual Christmas dinner without his mam and dad there. He hired a private ambulance to transport them from Bootle to Ince Blundell. Dot persuaded the driver to switch the siren on for most of the way.

'I felt really *urgent*!' she trumpeted gaily when she was carried out on a stretcher.

'What's that?' asked Annie, as Bert emerged with a complicated contraption of tubes and a cylinder.

'Oxygen, luv. Dot loves it. It makes her talk even more.'

All five of Dot's remaining lads were grandfathers, and fifteen of her grandchildren were married, most with children. The Delgados, Annie, and forty-two Gallaghers sat down to dinner, whilst Punch and Judy, the housekeeper and the Danish au pair entertained the children.

'I don't know what we're going to do next year,' Mike chuckled. 'Even the banqueting hall isn't big enough for us Gallaghers.'

It was incredible, thought Annie, that the womb of one frail old lady was responsible for too many people to fit a banqueting hall.

To Annie's surprise, early in January an air-mail letter arrived from Australia. She'd only spoken to Sara on New Year's Day.

Dear Mum, Sara wrote, *I felt it best to put this down on paper, rather than tell you on the phone – I know how upset you are over Daniel. The thing is, Mum, he stayed with us over Christmas . . .*

'Oh, God! Annie clapped her hand to her breast. She read on.

He had our old address, but fortunately the people there knew where we'd moved. I didn't recognise him at first. He looked strange, terribly grown up and very thin. His eyes are incredibly wise, as though he's seen and done everything – as if he understands everything. I found it hard to accept that this was my little brother, Daniel.

'Did he ask about me?' Annie breathed. 'Did he ask about his mam?'

He seems to have been everywhere in the world, even the places that are dangerous – Cambodia was one, Iran, Iraq. He and Nigel got on reasonably well. Nigel, being Nigel, knows all about the various religions and that was mostly what they talked about.

Of course, he wanted to know all about you, Mum. Annie sighed with relief. *He was chuffed when I told him about university, and said he'd always thought you were clever. I think he's sorry he walked out so suddenly. 'I had to do it,' he said. 'I had to sort out my life.'*

No, Mum (I know you'll be wondering), he didn't say anything about coming home. He'd only just arrived in Australia and was about to hitch-hike round the coast.

Don't ring straight away, Mum. Get used to the news before you get in touch. The truth is, I'm still all choked up, and I'll only cry if you do. Every time I close my eyes, I see my little brother, so different from the way I remembered, waving goodbye on the day I left.

I think that's all there is to say. This is not the sort of letter where you try to think of a nice cheerful ending.

Your loving daughter, Sara.

At Easter, the Anglia gave up completely. The engine had clocked up a hundred and twenty-eight thousand miles.

'I'm afraid it's a write-off, Mrs Menin,' she was told in the garage. 'The bodywork's more filler than metal, and last year I had to patch the patches underneath to get it through the MOT.'

Annie was forced to dip into her special account for Australia. She bought an ancient red Mini with low mileage and a long MOT. She was allowed ten pounds on the Anglia, which looked lonely and forlorn when she left it on the garage forecourt, fit only for scrap. Over the years she'd come to regard it as a friend.

She didn't go away that summer. Sylvia, Cecy and the children were going to Italy for six weeks – Bruno still had relatives there. He and Mike would join the party for the last fortnight. Annie was invited but declined. 'I've got to look after Patchwork when Dawn's on holiday, and there's a couple of projects to do for me degree.'

Out of a sense of duty, she telephoned Marie and offered to come and stay. Relations with her sister had been frosty since Christmas.

'I'm sorry, sis, but I've been invited to this private island in the Caribbean. It's owned by a lord.'

Chris Andrews was also away and she felt slightly neglected as July turned into August, then became September. There wasn't even someone she could ring for a chat, Auntie Dot tired quickly on the phone.

She decorated Sara's room with the wallpaper bought three years before, and tidied up the garden, which was as neglected as herself. Next door's French windows were usually open, and she often heard Mrs Vincent laughing as she played bridge with the friends who came several times a week. The situation reminded her slightly of Orlando Street, although Mrs Vincent was nothing like Mam, because Monica would come home in her navy blue uniform at six and prepare the evening meal. At weekends, Monica did the washing and cleaned the house from top to bottom. Annie suspected there was nothing much wrong with her mother and she was just taking advantage of her soft-hearted daughter.

To cheer herself up, she applied for a passport and went to a travel agent's to get details of flights to Australia. She would be free to visit Sara in less than a year; the final term at university finished early in June. She also picked up a brochure on holidays in Paris. Euan Campbell continued to mention it as a source of inspiration, and Binnie was for ever suggesting they should go. 'If it was good for so many writers, it might help us with our exams,' she said persuasively.

The cost of a few days' bed and breakfast was surprisingly cheap. Patchwork had done well lately and her bank balance was quite healthy – after all, she'd only need spending money in Australia.

'I'll show this to Binnie next time I see her,' she resolved.

'What shall we do when we've got our degree?' Sylvia demanded.

'Get a job,' said Annie.

'What as?'

'We could go to training college and become a teacher.'

Sylvia was lying on the rug in front of the fire. She sat up and poured herself more sherry. 'We might find that rather boring.'

'One of us might, the other wouldn't.' Annie wandered over to the window. What an awful day! February was a hateful month. She'd never liked it. The willow tree looked bedraggled. The sky was as black as night and rain was coming down in sheets – there'd been hailstones on the way home from Mass and she'd got soaked.

Sylvia had arrived at mid-day claiming she felt depressed. Mike was locked in his study with his accountant; Michael Ray Security was about to be floated on the stock exchange. The children were getting her down, so she'd left Sunday dinner to the housekeeper, the children to the au pair, collected a bottle of sherry and driven to Heather Close.

Annie wasn't all that pleased to see her. She'd had a horrible dream the night before in which an enraged Lauri stood at the foot of the bed demanding to know what she'd done with his children. The dream was still there; she was unable to get Lauri's angry face out of her mind. She was about to lose herself in a novel when Sylvia turned up.

'Couldn't we do something more exciting than teaching?'

Annie refilled her glass and returned to the settee. The collective 'we' was getting on her nerves. 'Such as?'

Sylvia rolled onto her stomach and groaned. 'I'm so stiff, I can't sit crosslegged any more.' Her body was becoming thick and heavy, particularly round the waist, but her face was as radiantly lovely as ever, despite her slightly sagging jawline. She leant her chin on her hands. 'We could write a novel.'

'Could we really?' Annie was conscious of the sarcasm in her voice. 'And how much effort will your half of the partnership put in?'

'You write, I'll read and give my opinion.'

'Oh, ta! If you're so anxious to see your name in print, why not write a book yourself?'

Sylvia burst out laughing. 'Don't be silly, Annie. I've got a husband, four children, and a big house to run.'

'You've also got a housekeeper and an au pair,' Annie snapped. The remark had touched a raw nerve. 'Anyroad, do you have to rub it in?'

'Rub what in?'

'The fact I haven't got a husband and children, and my house is rather small.'

'I didn't mean it like that, Annie.' She looked hurt.

'You're for ever emphasising how full your life is compared to mine.'

'No, I'm not. Least, I don't mean to.'

'You've always had to be on top, haven't you? You couldn't stand me being happy with Lauri. Your own marriage was shit, so you had to convince me mine was shitty, too.' Working backwards, Annie was able to put the blame for last night's dream on Sylvia. Lauri never got angry until his wife turned bolshie, and she didn't turn bolshie until Sylvia suggested it was time she did.

'But it *was* shitty, Annie,' Sylvia said reasonably. 'Lauri was a misogynist of the worst kind.'

'I didn't know what a misogynist was in those days.' Annie got up and began to walk round the room, waving her arms wildly. 'At least my husband didn't thump me like yours did.'

'What's Eric got to do with this?' Sylvia's cheeks flushed red.

'What's Lauri?'

'I've no idea. You brought him up, not me.'

They glared at each other angrily. 'Even now, you're not content with what you've got,' Annie said hotly. 'You're trying to take credit for my degree, that's if I get one. It's *me* that's done all the hard work, but apparently it's *our* degree.'

Sylvia's bones creaked as she got up. 'You must have got out of the wrong side of the bed this morning, Annie, and where's your sense of humour? I called it "our" degree as a way of encouraging you along.'

'I didn't need encouragement, thanks. I would, though, appreciate some time. What makes you think you can land on me without notice? I've stacks of work to do for *my* degree.'

'I didn't think you required notice,' Sylvia said coldly. 'I'll leave you to work and go and see another friend.'

'You haven't got another friend.'

Sylvia unexpectedly grinned. 'I know I haven't, Annie.' She spread her hands. 'Why are we rowing?'

The grin disconcerted Annie. She kicked the back of the settee. 'You started it by saying how empty my life was compared to yours.'

'No, you took offence at a perfectly innocent remark.' Sylvia looked amused. 'Shall we have another row over who started the first?'

They both jumped when hailstones rattled against the windows. The sound brought Annie to her senses. 'I'm sorry,' she mumbled.

'So am I.' Sylvia said warmly. 'I wouldn't crow over you for worlds. I won't deny I'm deliriously happy, but I do envy you sometimes.' She shook her head at Annie's incredulous face. 'I do, honest. I envy your freedom to do exactly what you want; Paris at Easter, Australia in June. I envy you being able to watch what you want on television, or read in bed until the early hours – Mike can't bear the light on. You're not beholden to any other person, your life is completely your own.'

'If you're not careful,' Annie warned, 'I'll get upset again.'

'But it's true, Annie,' Sylvia said earnestly. 'Being independent has its attractions.'

'I wonder why I flew off the handle like that?' Annie mused later.

'Perhaps you secretly resent me. Perhaps you always have.'

Annie thought about this for a while. 'Nah!' she said eventually. 'You were right the first time. I got out of bed the wrong side. Pass the sherry, Syl. We'll finish it off, then I'll make a cup of tea.'

Sylvia went home just as it was growing dark. The sherry had given her a terrible headache.

'But you never get headaches,' Annie said in surprise.

'I had one all last week. I wonder if it's the change of life?'

Sylvia phoned next evening. 'Guess what was on TV late last night? *Three Coins in a Fountain*.' She hummed a few notes. 'I recorded it. Shall I bring the video machine over sometime and we'll watch it? We'd never get any peace here and I'd hate the girls to spoil it.'

'I'd love to.' They'd been teenagers when they last saw it. 'I've no lectures on Wednesday, I was going to work at home.'

'Wednesday it is then, say early afternoon?'

'Great. How's your headache?'

'It's just returned with a vengeance,' Sylvia groaned.

'I hope it goes soon,' Annie said sympathetically.

'So do I!'

To Annie's surprise, Mike turned up just after lunch on Wednesday. 'I've brought a video and the film. Sylvia thinks you've just got to plug it in, she doesn't realise the TV has to be tuned.' He grinned. 'Women are no good with electronics.'

'I'm amazed a busy executive can spare the time to do such a mundane thing,' Annie said in mock surprise.

'I'm on me way back from a business lunch in town. Sylvia should be here any minute.' He knelt down beside the television and began to fiddle with the knobs. 'You can keep this machine, Annie. It's just one that was lying round the office.'

'Mike, I couldn't possibly!'

'Shurrup, luv, and take it. The richer you are, the harder it is to give things away. I'm for ever offering to move me mam and dad into a nice bungalow, but they refuse to leave that house in Bootle.' He inserted the video into the machine. 'I hope she recorded it on the right station. It's quite likely to be something different altogether.'

Minutes later, Frank Sinatra began to croon the theme song and *Three Coins in a Fountain* appeared on the screen. Annie closed her eyes briefly. She was fourteen, watching the same credits and feeling that excited little thrill that always came at the beginning of a film. 'We saw it the first time we went out together,' she said.

'I know, luv, Sylvia told me. If it hadn't been for you, we'd never have met. Look, here she is now!' He went over to the window. A dark brown BMW had drawn up and Sylvia got out. Her hair was loose and she wore a white padded fur-trimmed coat over a crimson dress. Her blue eyes danced when she saw Annie and Mike watching. She waved and Mike's gasp of admiration was audible. 'Isn't she a cracker, Annie? I thought that the minute I first set eyes on her at our Tommy's reception.'

'She's beautiful, Mike.'

Halfway down the path, Sylvia paused. She looked at them, a strange, puzzled expression on her lovely face. Her eyes glazed. Her hands lifted slowly to clutch her head and her blonde hair spilled through her fingers like strips of torn silk. Later, Annie supposed the whole thing took less than a minute, but watching, it seemed to last an age. Sylvia's body seemed to crumple, as if her bones had turned to jelly, and she collapsed into a distorted heap on the path.

'Why couldn't it be me?' Cecy wailed. 'No-one expects their children to die before them. Why did God take Sylvia when he could take me?'

'I've no idea,' Annie said calmly. She couldn't get her head around the fact Sylvia had gone, although she'd actually watched her die. She kept expecting the phone to ring and her friend to be at the other end, eager for a chat or to exchange a bit of gossip.

'You'll never guess what's happened, Annie!'

'Are you sitting down, Annie? I've got some incredible news.'

People didn't usually die unless they were very old or very ill or had an accident, like Lauri. For someone to be taken without warning, as Sylvia had been, from an unsuspected brain tumour, was unfair on those left behind; monstrously, stupefyingly unfair.

It wasn't fair of Mike, either, to have them play 'The Long and Winding Road' when everyone was filing out of the little chapel at Anfield Crematorium. It was enough to make you weep even if Sylvia hadn't been the best friend in the world. It was only then it hit Annie, forcefully and painfully, that she would never see Sylvia again. At this very second, her friend's body was being reduced to ashes. Sylvia was dead.

Everyone stood awkwardly in the fog outside, not knowing what to say, reading the cards on the wreaths which were spread on the damp grass. Mike stood alone, his eyes empty, his face expressionless; Uncle Bert and the Gallagher lads stood protectively nearby.

Cecy was inconsolable. Her sobs echoed like a banshee's wail around the rose bushes and the dark green trees. Bruno, oh, Bruno, he looked so old, old and shaken. He took Cecy in his arms and tried to comfort her. Then he led her away, though she could hardly walk in her distress.

Annie didn't go back to Mike's for refreshments. Instead, she drove to Auntie Dot's.

Dot was too ill to attend the funeral. Annie thanked the neighbour who'd kept her company and sat on the edge of the bed. Her auntie's body was nothing but skin and bone, yet her eyes still gleamed in her haggard face. 'How was it, luv?' she asked hoarsely.

'Terrible, auntie.'

'Our poor Mike,' Dot lamented. 'Two wives gone and he's only fifty. Christ, I wish it could have been me instead of Sylvia.'

'That's what Cecy kept saying.'

Dot's eyes clouded with sympathy. 'Poor lamb, she took it hard?'

Annie nodded. 'Really hard.'

'And you, luv? Sylvia was more like a sister than Marie.'

'I don't know how I'll live without her,' Annie said simply. 'We had some great times, me and Sylvia.'

'You were there the night the Cavern opened.'

'We saw the Beatles before anybody else.'

Dot squeezed her knee, though the pressure was so light you could scarcely feel it. 'You'll never lose that, luv. Memories, memories, they make your life so much richer. I don't know what I'd do without them, lying here night after night with Bert asleep beside me.' Her voice became fretful. 'I can hardly sleep at all, Annie, for the pain.'

'Oh, Dot!' Annie bent down and kissed her auntie's cheek. 'Would you like a tablet now? I'll make a cup of tea.'

'No, I'll wait till Bert comes. He sorts out me medicine. I take morphine for me aches and pains.' She cackled. 'I've become a drug addict. I haven't seen me arse in years, but I bet it looks like a Spotted Dick after all the injections.'

The phone was ringing when Annie got home. She picked up the receiver gingerly, half expecting it to be Sylvia calling from another world.

'Hi!' a man's voice said cheerfully. 'Remember me? It's Ben Wainwright. You've got one of my paintings.'

'I remember.'

'It's just that I'm in Manchester, and I wondered if I drove over if you'd be free for dinner tonight?'

'Sorry,' Annie said regretfully, 'but I'm just back from a funeral. Someone very dear to me died. I'd be terrible company at the moment.'

'I wouldn't mind terrible company, not if it was you.'

'I'd sooner not, but thanks for asking.'

She rang off. Maybe she should have gone. 'Not if it was you,' he'd said, as if he remembered her in a special way. Last time she had been sorry afterwards, but tonight she preferred to stay in and grieve for Sylvia. Until today, she'd been too stunned to take it in.

Three Coins in a Fountain was still in the video. Annie watched it from beginning to end. It wasn't nearly as good as she remembered. At fourteen, it had seemed deeply dramatic and romantic, but now it was rather trite. Rossano Brazzi, though, was still mournfully handsome.

Annie was dry-eyed when she turned the television off. What had been the beginning had become the end. As long as she lived, she would never have another friend like Sylvia.

A month after the funeral, Bruno and Cecy came to announce the Grand was to be sold and they were going to live in Italy.

'Together?' Annie said hopefully.

Bruno took Cecy's hand. 'Together.'

'I couldn't be more pleased, though I'll miss you terribly.' Annie smiled tremulously. 'What about the girls?' She was amazed they could bring themselves to leave their granddaughters.

Cecy's face grew troubled. 'That's what made us decide to go, Annie. Have you seen Mike since the funeral?'

'I've rung several times, but his secretary or the housekeeper always say he's unavailable. There was no sign of him each time I've been to see the girls.' They'd clung to Annie, four little lost souls. Dorothy wanted to know what she'd done with their mummy.

'We found the same,' Cecy nodded, 'till last time, when Bruno forced his way into the study. Mike's changed, Annie. His face was set like concrete. He made it obvious he doesn't want us around. Maybe we remind him too much of Sylvia. He promised to send the children over once a year – Yasmin and Ingrid are almost old enough to fly alone. They're already looking forward to staying with us during the summer holidays. We thought it best to leave now and prepare a second home.'

'You must come, too, Annie,' Bruno said emotionally. 'I feel as if we're losing our other daughter.'

Annie watched them walk away, two people who had played such a major part in her life. Bruno wasn't as stooped as he'd been at the funeral. He was the first man she'd fallen in love with, though he'd never known.

She gripped the windowsill with both hands. Pretty soon, there'd be no-one left to leave.

7

Paris stretched before her, a glittering carpet of twinkling lights. How many miles could she see? Ten? Twenty? Places looked so lovely in the dark. The neon lights on the tall buildings blazed on and off as if they were sending out mysterious messages, and the sky was navy, shot with deep, ruddy orange.

She'd climbed literally hundreds of steps to reach the basilica of Sacré-Coeur – throughout the day, she kept glimpsing the white stone monument shimmering above the city. After getting her breath back, she went inside, admired the statues and the stained glass windows, then lit three candles. She knelt in a pew and prayed for everyone she knew.

Outside again, she sat at the top of the stone steps and marvelled at the glorious view. So many windows! Thousands and thousands of them. It made you feel dead funny, trying to imagine what people were doing inside those thousands and thousands of rooms. It also made you feel very small and rather unimportant, as if you were merely the tiniest speck on God's universe.

A black man approached; his face ebony smooth, he wore an embroidered gown and a round beaded hat and offered her a lizard skin clutchbag to buy. She shook her head. 'No, ta.' She wouldn't dream of carrying a poor dead lizard under her arm.

On the terrace below, someone was juggling with fluorescent sticks. A guitarist strummed idly and sang 'Volare' in a soft, husky voice. The steps were crowded; old couples hand in hand, young ones arms entwined. In front of her, a man and woman sat, each with a small child on their knee. Two teenage boys on her right kept leaving to explore and returning to their mam, faces shining with excitement. On her other side, about a dozen youngsters lounged, drinking Coke and gabbling away in a tongue she couldn't understand. Their haversacks bore tiny flags of many countries, and she wondered if they'd been to every one.

She seemed to be the only person alone. Now she knew what it meant to be isolated in a crowd. She had never felt so lonely in her life. The loneliness welled up in her throat, a bitter, choking ball. She bit her lip, held back a sob, and smiled at nothing in particular.

Annie had come to Paris by herself. The holiday had been booked months ago, and when Sylvia died she'd considered backing out but hadn't liked to let Binnie down. The week before leaving, she and Binnie rang each other constantly.

'Shall we take jeans?'

'I'll take a hairdryer, you bring your travelling iron.'

They were travelling on a Tuesday. On the Monday, Binnie called, her voice thick with cold. 'I've got the flu,' she groaned. 'I feel lousy. I'll never make it. Do you know anyone who'd like a free holiday?'

Annie was filled with disappointment. 'No, but if you're sick, we could get a refund with a doctor's note and go to Paris another time.'

'The doctor's not coming till tonight. It's awfully short notice to cancel. You go by yourself, Annie,' Binnie urged. 'It's only five days.'

At the time, it hadn't seemed a bad idea. People often went on holiday alone. She called Binnie later to see what the doctor had said and was surprised at how chirpily she gave the number.

'It's Annie.'

There was a silence, then Binnie's voice, heavy with cold as it had been that morning. 'Oh, hallo. The doctor said I'll live.'

Annie knew the doctor had been nowhere near her so-called friend. There was nothing wrong with Binnie. Almost certainly a man had something to do with the change of heart, perhaps the one she'd spent a weekend with in Chester, the one who'd 'dumped' her as she put it, Roy. Roy had probably reappeared on the scene and she wanted Annie out of the way in case she came round to see how she was.

'I hope you're better soon,' she said shortly.

The first day was taken up with travel. It was late when the coach arrived and almost midnight by the time she was dropped off at the hotel and allocated her gloomy room with its tall, narrow window in the corner.

Until she'd come to Sacré-Coeur, the second day had gone reasonably well. She'd dutifully gone up the Eiffel Tower in the lift, visited the Louvre and Notre Dame, window-shopped in the Champs Elysées, though she felt rather like a sleepwalker, unable to appreciate anything she saw. It was difficult to believe that so many great artists had found inspiration here. Too nervous to use French restaurants in case she ordered the wrong thing, she bought frequent snacks in McDonald's.

But now! She wanted to shrivel up inside her anorak, hide herself, so no-one would notice she was alone. And there were two more days like this to get through! One of the youngsters produced a mouth organ and began to play. Of course, it had to be a Beatles' song, 'Yesterday', Sylvia's all-time favourite.

'Oh, no!' Annie moaned. She looked at her watch. It was only just after ten, and as she never went to bed at home before twelve, she had no intention of doing so in Paris. Was it safe for a woman to walk the streets late at night? Perhaps she could wander slowly back to her hotel in République and have a coffee on the way.

She was searching her bag for the map, when a surprised and vaguely familiar voice said, 'Mrs Menin, Annie!'

Almost any familiar voice would have been welcome. Her heart lifted as someone in jeans and a thick woollen sweater squeezed himself onto the steps beside her. Euan Campbell! They'd rarely spoken in Liverpool, but it was like meeting a long-lost and greatly loved friend. She grabbed his arm and gave a shaky laugh. 'Oh, am I pleased to see you!'

He was also alone, and Annie suspected he was as pleased to see her as she was him. There was relief and pleasure on his thin brown face. Two lost souls, she thought, brought together by accident in a strange city. He asked for her first impressions and she confessed she didn't know. 'I've felt a bit peculiar all day,' she said, 'as if I was seeing everything through dark glasses.'

After a while, they left the steps and began to stroll through the crowded Place du Tertre, where the trees were festooned with coloured lights. Artists, easels and charcoal ready, offered portraits at a hundred francs each. The pavement cafés were packed to capacity.

'I met my wife in this square,' Euan said in a dull voice. 'We were only eighteen, students. We came back year after year, including our honeymoon. I haven't been since the children were born.' He looked at Annie with his sad, dark eyes. 'I suppose everyone knows what happened?'

She nodded. 'Yes, luv.'

'I've been too scared to return by myself and there was no-one else I wanted to be with. I thought it was time to lay the ghost. I arrived yesterday . . .' He broke off and sighed.

'How's it working out?' Annie asked.

He gave the suggestion of a smile. 'Awful! Everywhere I go, I went with Eva. The memories are killing me. I was thinking of going home.'

'I'd toyed with the same idea meself. I was coming with a friend, but she took ill at the last minute.' Despite his obvious unhappiness, everything had changed since they met, although she knew it was only temporary. Her spirits had soared, for one thing, and Paris seemed an entirely different place; colourful, unusual, coursing with vitality. She wondered if he'd mind if she linked his arm. She did so, and he smiled, properly this time. 'I was never so glad to see a face I knew,' she said thankfully.

'Frankly, neither was I. I'm glad it was you and not your friend,' he added surprisingly. 'Have you eaten yet? Suddenly, I'm starving.'

'I've been in and out of McDonald's all day.'

His face brightened. 'Let's have dinner. Not here, it's too expensive. I know a little place not far away.'

'As long as you let me pay my share.'

They walked through the narrow, sloping streets, Sacré-Coeur behind them on the skyline. Euan turned into a cul-de-sac and they entered a café that was half as big as her lounge. The only illumination came from a flickering candle on each table.

Annie chose a herb omelette, Euan ordered coq au vin and a bottle of red wine. His French was good. The wine came first and tasted vinegary.

'Dilute it with water,' he advised when she pulled a face. 'That's a genuine Parisian working man's drink.'

The omelette was delicious and she soon got used to the wine. The bottle went quickly and he ordered another.

'Did you use to come in here with your wife?' she asked.

'Yes, I doubt if there's anywhere in Paris I haven't been with Eva.' He glanced around the dimly lit room. Only three of the six tables were occupied. 'We used to sit at that table by the window. We considered it *ours*. Eva used to get cross if it was occupied.'

'Have you got a photograph of Eva?'

He crumbled a piece of bread on the red and white checked cloth with long, lean fingers. 'I chucked them away after . . . after it happened, and those of Meg and Jenny – they were twins, mirror images of each other.'

Annie put her hand on his. She felt strangely light-headed. The wine must be very strong. Euan had drunk half the first bottle and was swiftly demolishing the second. 'Do you want to talk about it, luv?'

He looked at her, his face tragic. 'Do you mind? I've never spoken about it before, but it's all seemed unusually real today. The girls were conceived in Paris.'

'Then why don't you begin,' Annie said softly.

It came pouring out; the rage, the grief, the utter waste of three young lives. 'Eva was taking the girls to buy ballet shoes. We'd had a row over it. I thought they were too young, they were only three.' He'd wanted to kill the lorry driver who was responsible. Once, he'd actually gone round to the man's house with the express intention of doing that very thing. 'I don't know what stopped me – yes I do. I hadn't thought to take a weapon and he was considerably larger than me.' His eyes, no longer sad, burned into hers. 'You know what happened when it came to court? He was fined two hundred and fifty pounds, and his licence was suspended for six months. His lawyer pointed out he'd lose his job, as if that were a worse punishment than me losing my family.'

The wine was beginning to take effect. His speech became slurred and disjointed. Tears began to roll down his smooth, olive cheeks. Annie watched helplessly. After a while, she said, 'Come on, luv. I think we'd better get you back to your hotel.'

She sat up in bed, head spinning. 'Well, Syl. I've got meself into a fine old mess, haven't I?'

On the bed that should have been Binnie's lay the boyish figure of Euan Campbell, fully dressed except for his shoes. He was breathing heavily, but otherwise dead to the world.

There was no way she could have got him to a Metro station, even if she'd known where one was. The waiter had called a taxi, and as she hadn't liked to go through Euan's pockets looking for the name of his hotel, there seemed no alternative but to bring him back to hers. One good turn deserved another, anyroad; he'd rescued her from Sacré-Coeur.

'Jaysus, Annie!' Sylvia laughed. 'He'll feel embarrassed tomorrow.'

Annie slid under the clothes and continued her conversation with Sylvia. 'It's ever so strange, Syl. If we'd met in Lewis's or the Playhouse, we'd have just said "hallo". But abroad, it's different. I'd have been pleased to meet me worst enemy on those steps.'

'Such as Jeremy Rupert?' Sylvia said with a sly chuckle.

Annie shuddered. 'Well no, not him.'

'What about Kevin Cunningham?'

'Not Kevin, either.'

'Seems to me, Annie,' Sylvia said in an amused voice, 'that you quite fancy Euan Campbell.'

'He's too young to fancy, Syl. I mean, we'll be forty-six this year – we're old enough to be his mother.'

Sylvia giggled. 'That wouldn't stop me, friend.'

It was still dark when Annie woke. The window was open and the room smelt pleasantly of baking bread from the boulangerie opposite. The occasional car drove down the side street where the hotel was situated, and heavier traffic was audible, muted and distant, on the Boulevard de Magenta which ran along the top. Women's voices could be heard, penetratingly clear in the early morning air. Feeling wide awake, Annie slipped out of bed to see what was going on.

The boulangerie was brightly lit, the door wide open. Two women were outside, their bags crammed with sticks of bread. Their voices rose and fell in the lovely melodic way of the French. There was something fascinating about the scene. It looked so appropriately *foreign*!

A voice said, slightly incredulous, 'Annie?'

She turned. 'Sorry, luv, did I wake you?'

'No, it was those women. Oh, my head!' Euan Campbell groaned as he struggled to sit up.

'You drank a lot of wine.' Annie wished she'd brought a robe. They hardly knew each other, yet here they were, waking up together in a hotel bedroom in Paris. Still, her cotton nightie was quite chaste.

'I'm sorry. Did I make an exhibition of myself?'

'Not really. You could walk, but you couldn't tell me where you were staying, so I brought you back with me.'

He groaned again. 'I feel terribly embarrassed.'

'Sylvia said you would.'

'Sylvia?'

She could just about see his puzzled face. 'Me friend, Sylvia. She died two months ago, but we still have conversations in me head.' It must be Paris and their crazy situation, because she wouldn't have dreamt of telling anyone that under normal circumstances.

'I sometimes talk to Eva.' He stretched. 'Despite my head, I feel good this morning. I hope you didn't mind listening to all that stuff? I found it very cathartic.'

'Always glad to be of assistance,' she said lightly.

He sighed. 'I'd give my right arm for a cup of coffee.'

'I wouldn't mind a drink meself,' her mouth felt like the bottom of a birdcage, 'but breakfast's half seven and it's only just gone five.'

'Where exactly is this hotel?'

'République.'

'There's an all night café by the canal.' He swung his legs onto the floor. 'Gosh, you took my trainers off! Now I feel embarrassed again.'

'I've seen men's stockinged feet before,' Annie said drily.

He laughed for the first time since she'd known him. It was deep and rather attractive. He pushed his feet into his shoes. 'I won't be long.'

The door closed and she heard his quiet footsteps down the stairs. She wondered if the coffee was an excuse to escape and she wouldn't see him again until she returned to university. Would she mind? 'I'd be hurt him leaving so deceitfully. I'd sooner he told me to me face.'

She lay down. In a minute, she'd get dressed for when Euan came back – *if* he came back.

A shaft of yellow sunshine had penetrated the curtains by the time Euan returned, and Annie was fast asleep. She sat up, flustered.

'I meant to get dressed. I must be more tired than I realised.'

'It's lovely out!' His eyes were shining and his face was flushed. He was barely recognisable as the sad young man who'd lectured her on American literature. He sat on the edge of her bed quite naturally, as if they'd known each other for ever, and handed her a carton of coffee. 'The canal looks beautiful. We must go there later . . . if you want to, that is,' he added hurriedly. 'I'll make myself scarce if you prefer.'

'I'd love to spend the day with you, Euan,' Annie said gravely.

He looked relieved. 'That's good. I don't know what I'd have done if you'd told me to get lost.'

The coffee tasted lovely. Annie thought how envious Binnie Appleby would be if she could see her. How fortunate Binnie had been 'ill'!

She drained the carton and Euan threw it in the waste-paper bin, along with his own. 'I'll go back to my hotel shortly for breakfast and a change of clothes.'

'You can have breakfast here,' Annie said. 'It's been paid for.'

'Can I?'

'Yes.'

Their eyes met and the atmosphere in the room subtly changed. Suggesting he have breakfast seemed pretty innocuous, after all, they'd just spent the night together, but the words seemed to contain a double meaning she hadn't intended.

Euan said casually, 'Please tell me to stop if you find this offensive.' He leant down and kissed her softly on the lips.

The last thing in the world Annie had expected was for Euan Campbell to kiss her. At the same time, she wasn't the least bit surprised and not at all offended.

He kissed her harder. His hands slid round her waist and he pulled until she was lying flat on the bed. For the barest second, her body was stiff and unyielding, then, as if a brilliant flower was unfolding inside her, the inhibitions of a lifetime slipped away; her arms went round his neck and she began to kiss him back. She took her nightdress off, or perhaps Euan took it off for her, she wasn't sure. She only knew she was naked in his arms. With a gasp of delight, she felt his tongue on her breasts. Wild, ecstatic sensations swept through her, feelings she'd never experienced before. His mouth tore down her body to between her legs, and in the pit of Annie's stomach, something was building up, a swelling almost too delicious to stand.

Suddenly, he was no longer kissing her. 'Don't stop!' she screamed.

He tore off his clothes, knelt over her, then entered her, rock hard, and the swelling mounted sweetly to a point when she thought she must have died and gone to heaven. Despite his delicate build, he was surprisingly strong and at the back of it all, there was something urgent and desperate about the way their bodies tangled together. Annie knew she wasn't just making love, but attempting to purge herself of the misery of the last few years; of Sara's sudden marriage, Daniel leaving, Sylvia dying. The memories vanished as everything burst, and the explosion was gut-wrenchingly glorious and better than anything that had gone before.

'Aaahhh!' She gave a long, shuddering gasp of delight, followed by a brief sigh that she'd had to wait so long for her first orgasm.

Euan buried his head in the pillow and didn't speak. 'What's the matter?' she asked after several minutes of silence.

His voice was muffled when he replied. He didn't look at her. 'That's the first time since . . . I feel as if I've been unfaithful.'

Annie shook him impatiently. His tragedy was a million times worse than hers, but it wasn't right to let him think he had a monopoly on misery. 'Me own husband was killed in a car crash,' she said, although Lauri had been far from her mind when they were making love.

'Gosh, I'm sorry.' He raised his head and she felt a moment of unease when she thought how young he was. Was she taking advantage of his vulnerability? She remembered he'd made the first move. Perhaps it would help him, as it would help her, to indulge in two days of sheer madness in Paris. She stroked his arm, the skin smooth and unblemished, like satin.

'Don't be sorry,' she murmured. 'You know, luv, you can't grieve for ever. You've got the rest of your life to live. Eva wouldn't have wanted you to stay celibate, would she?'

To her relief, he gave the glimmer of a smile. 'I'm not so sure. She was very selfish. Even from beyond the grave, she'd hate the idea of me being with another woman. What about your husband, would he mind?'

'Lauri would wag his finger at me and look very disapproving, though if I'd gone first I'd've wanted him to get married again.'

'I would have wanted the same for Eva. It feels odd, criticising her. I haven't had a single bad thought since she died.'

'That's a good sign,' said Annie.

'I suppose it is.' He kissed her shoulder. 'I'm sorry. Before was wonderful. I hope I haven't spoiled it for you.' He ran his slim hand down her body, and within seconds they were making love again.

The trees that lined the Canal Saint Martin were bursting into pale green life. Numerous pretty bridges spanned the narrow width of rippling water, which was a glaring, dazzling yellow as it reflected the rising sun. The air was fresh and cool and smelt slightly salty. Some of the wrought-iron benches on the bank were already occupied: two very old men in deep conversation, a woman sketching, a couple of girls eating croissants and sharing a carton of milk.

'I would never have come to a place like this,' Annie said happily, as she strolled arm in arm with Euan. She breathed in the heady atmosphere. 'Paris seems entirely different today.'

Euan squeezed her arm. 'I nearly didn't go to Sacré-Coeur last night. I thought it would be too painful. At first it was, but then I saw you . . .' he skipped a few steps like a child and she had to hurry to keep up. 'You know, I've always liked you. I remember sitting by you in that pub, you were reading *The Sun also Rises*. I wanted to talk to you again, but you were always with your friend.'

He veered her off the bank of the canal when industrial buildings came into view. They stopped for coffee, then walked further and came to a wide boulevard full of shops. To Annie's pleased surprise, the clothes on the racks outside were cheap; everything she'd seen yesterday had been way beyond her means. She treated herself to a colourful Indian skirt, a blue embroidered T-shirt and a pair of gold-embossed sandals. The lot came to less than twelve pounds.

'I'll just look for something for me aunt and uncle,' she murmured. 'There's hardly anyone left to buy presents for nowadays.'

'What about your children?' Euan asked.

'Me daughter's in Australia. As for Daniel, I haven't a clue where he is. Oh, Lord!' To Annie's intense horror, she felt tears pour down her cheeks. 'It was terrible,' she sobbed. 'Sara got married and was gone within a week, then Daniel walked out on me the very same day. I still can't get over it, years later. I don't think I ever will.'

'Come on, Annie.' Euan took her gently in his arms in the middle of the crowded pavement. 'Let's go home.'

On the way, he bought a bottle of wine. Back at the hotel, Annie drank hers sitting by the open window. The boulangerie was still busy. In an apartment opposite, a family were eating their mid-day meal. A woman came down the street with a fluffy white poodle on a lead. As she passed a parked car, a black cat shot out and ran across the road and was narrowly missed by a van. Further down, where the street sloped towards the canal, purple roofs glinted in the April sunshine.

'It's lovely,' she said. 'There's nothing the least bit extraordinary about it. It's just lovely.'

'It gets under your skin, Paris.' Euan was sitting on her bed. He raised his glass, 'To Paris, the enchanted city!'

'To Paris!' She already felt slightly drunk. Perhaps it mightn't be a bad idea to stay that way until it was time to leave. She drained her glass and refilled it. 'I could get addicted to this wine.'

'Do you feel better now?'

'Much better. Thanks for listening.' She'd told him about Daniel and the fact he'd been gone for almost four years and all she'd received were a few postcards. It all seemed rather tame. At least Daniel was alive and there was every likelihood she'd see him again, whereas his girls were lost for ever.

'One good turn . . . ! Come here.' He patted the bed. Annie felt her stomach turn pleasurably when she sat beside him. He took her glass and laid it on the floor, then slid his hand beneath her T-shirt. Quickly, she succumbed to the touch of his fingers, the pressure of his lips, the final act of making love when he sank right into her and she felt he'd touched her very core. Her body was hot, as if the blood raged through her veins like burning oil. The shuddering, gushing climax was so exquisite that she screamed out loud.

Euan had been back to his hotel to fetch his clothes. Annie sat at the dressing table and watched through the mirror as he changed into a fresh pair of jeans and a clean sweater. His body was slim and lithe, without an ounce of surplus fat. His shoulders were neither narrow nor broad, and the planes on his back glistened when he pulled on the jeans.

He was so *young*! He was thirty-two, but looked less. Annie held up her arm and examined it closely. It didn't look a particularly *old* arm, but in the mirror she could see her elbow was wrinkled. She held up the other arm, which looked exactly the same. Still, so far no-one had looked at her and Euan peculiarly, as if wondering what such a handsome young man could see in an obviously middle-aged woman. Perhaps they thought she'd hired a gigolo for the week!

She patted her hair, inserted her earrings, and as an afterthought rubbed moisturiser on her elbows. 'Ready!' she sang. They were going to Montmartre for dinner.

Euan was still stripped to the waist. 'You look nice,' he said. She wore the clothes she'd bought that morning. The Indian skirt fell on either side to the floor, the gauzy material soft against her legs. He knelt behind her and put his arms around her breasts. Annie felt her body melt. 'Jaysus!' she groaned.

When eventually they left for dinner, it was very late.

He was the sort of young man Auntie Dot would call 'lovely'. Annie could find no fault with him, not that she looked for any. Despite the tragedy of his past, he was naive, unworldly, incredibly *nice*. He was also virile, with a healthy sexual appetite that had been suppressed for the last few years. She regarded it as lucky she'd been around when he snapped out of the long drawn-out mourning for his dead family. She assumed almost any woman in the right place at the right time, as she had been, would have done for Euan. And he was lucky to have found someone who'd make no claims when the perfect holiday was over.

She liked him. She liked listening to him, talking to him, laughing with him. She woke up in his arms on the second morning, their last full day, feeling as if the world had been touched by a magic wand. The room was golden with sunshine and the curtains lifted gently on the open window. Euan's hand stroked her belly then sank into the warmth between her legs. It wasn't just magic, it was heaven.

The outdoor market was full of tourists. Between the stalls it was packed and you could scarcely move. Annie clung to Euan's hand. It was a poor market, difficult to get near the stalls and once you did, the goods were new and expensive. 'Shall we go somewhere else?' she shouted, but he didn't hear. She tripped over someone's foot and her sandal fell off.

'Euan!' she called, releasing his hand. She bent down to look for her lost sandal. By the time she'd found it, Euan had disappeared.

Annie remained where she was, searching for his dark head in the crowds. She felt slightly panic-stricken as she was buffeted by eager bargain hunters. Perhaps she should go after him. Her panic rose as the minutes passed and he didn't reappear. She couldn't understand why she was getting in such a state; if he didn't come soon all she had to do was go back to the hotel.

It was twenty minutes before a voice called, 'Annie!' and she saw his arm raised several feet away. She was about to shove through the seething mass towards him when he shouted, 'Stay where you are.'

Suddenly he was there, his face flushed. 'I thought I'd lost you!'

Annie flung her arms around his neck. 'Euan, darling. I was dead frightened.' She was shaking and her stomach was knotted, but now he was back, she felt entirely at home in his arms.

He buried his face in her neck. 'Don't worry, Annie. I'm here. You'll never feel frightened again.'

Annie froze. She didn't just like him, she loved him. But it was a passing thing, a romantic interlude in an enchanted city. She had no wish to hurt this lovely young man, but she was going back to Liverpool tomorrow and that would be the end of her affair with Euan Campbell.

The wine had almost gone, as had the night. Pale yellow touched the grey sky, and one or two stars remained, blinking weakly. Annie poured the last of the wine and filled the glass to the brim with water. Her throat was sore. They'd talked for hours, argued bitterly most of the time.

'Can I have a sip?' said Euan.

She took the glass over to the bed and held it for him, as if he was a child. 'Finish it off, if you like.'

'No, thanks.' He put his arms behind his head and turned his face away from her.

Annie kissed his ear, let her mouth wander down to his chest . . . She'd learnt many things over the last two days.

'Don't do that!' he said hoarsely.

'I thought, just one more time. The coach will be here at eight o'clock to pick me up.'

'I couldn't stand it, knowing that it's all over.'

She finished off the wine and lay beside him, her arm loosely on his waist. 'Darling, it would be mad for us to see each other again.' She thanked God it was her last year at university. There would be no more lectures, only the final exams. 'We've got no future, you and I.'

'You've said that a hundred times.' His voice shook. 'The thing is, I love you and you love me. What future could be more perfect?'

'I don't think you do love me, Euan,' she said softly. 'It's Paris. It's been like a fairytale, with you my wonderful Prince Charming, except I feel a bit like the wicked Stepmother, rather than Cinderella.'

'Don't talk stupid!' he said angrily. 'And how dare you tell me I don't love you. Am I incapable of knowing my own mind?'

'No, luv. I think you're just fooling yourself. Once you're home, you'll soon see sense and realise I'm not the one for you. There's stacks of young women who'd jump at a handsome young man like you.'

He propped himself on an elbow and looked down at her. 'If you knew how pompous and ridiculous that sounds.' He laughed sarcastically. 'I don't want stacks of young women jumping at me, I want you.'

'Euan, I'm nearly old enough to be your mother.' Lauri had been old enough to be her father, but it seemed different when it was the man.

'You've said that a hundred times, as well,' he said coldly. 'I don't give a damn. What does age matter when two people are in love?'

Annie sighed. She was convinced he'd see things differently in the cold light of Liverpool. It was best to leave things on a high, rather than let it filter out with embarrassing excuses from him in a few months' time, when possibly she'd love him even more. 'I'd like to think you'll get married again and have a family one day.'

'Now you're beginning to *sound* like my mother. As for a family, there's no way I'd bring more children into the world.' He shuddered violently. 'I couldn't stand it!'

'Is that the attraction I hold, Euan?' Annie said gently. 'The fact I'm too old to have a baby?'

He groaned. 'The only attraction you hold is that you're *you*! Oh, Annie!' He took her in his arms. 'How can you be so cruel?'

'I'm not being cruel, luv. I'm being sensible.' He began to stroke her body and delicious sensations shivered through every nerve. In the midst of it all, Annie told herself he'd thank her one day when he met someone his own age. And she'd thank him. The memory of this holiday would stay with her until she was a very old woman.

The coach stopped at Victoria Coach Station for a twenty-minute respite. Annie got off to stretch her legs. She felt restless, unable to get Euan Campbell out of her mind. He wasn't due home until tomorrow, but had decided to leave today. 'What point is there staying without you?' he said bleakly. She dismissed the idea of going to Euston Station on the off chance that they'd meet. She'd said goodbye, and she meant it, though her heart contracted when she remembered closing the door on the dismal hotel room where she'd reached such dizzy heights of happiness, leaving behind the beautiful young man who claimed he loved her.

'Oh, Syl,' she whispered. 'I wish you were here to talk to.' There was no-one now, no-one. She noticed a row of telephones on the wall. 'I'll ring our Marie and say I'm in London! It's ages since we spoke.'

She dialled her sister's number. After three rings, the receiver was picked up, and a voice said, 'This is Marie Harrison.'

'Hallo, sis,' Annie began, but the voice continued as if she'd not spoken. 'I'm sorry I'm not in at the moment, but if you'd like to leave a message after the long tone, I'll get back to you as soon as I can.'

It was one of those weird answering machines. Annie waited for the long tone, then said, 'Sis, it's Annie. I was just passing through . . .'

'Annie!' Marie, the real Marie, broke in. 'Are you in London?'

'Only for a few minutes. I'm on me way home from Paris.'

'Oh, sis, why don't you come round? You can go home any time.'

'I'll see you in half an hour,' Annie said promptly.

Her sister was on the balcony when Annie turned the corner. She waved and disappeared. By the time she reached the house, Marie was waiting at the door. There was something different about her, but then there often was. Her face was smooth and serene. Perhaps she'd had it lifted!

'Hi, sis!' She kissed Annie warmly. 'You look wonderful. Your holiday in Paris did you good.'

'I had a lovely time.'

Marie took her bag as they walked upstairs. 'Who did you go with?'

'I went by meself. Me friend let me down at the last minute, but I met someone I knew, so it was all right.'

Fortunately, Marie didn't enquire into the identity of the someone; the memory was too precious to share just yet.

'Your flat looks nice,' Annie remarked as she went in. There were pictures on the walls and bright cushions scattered around.

'I made some tea. I knew you'd be gasping.' Marie went into the kitchen and returned with a tray. Annie settled herself onto the settee.

'I had no idea you were going to Paris,' Marie said. She looked slightly hurt, as if she felt she should be kept up to date with her sister's affairs.

'I didn't think you'd be interested.'

'I'd have invited you to stay over so you'd have an easier journey.'

'Would you?' Annie looked at her sister, eyebrows raised. 'The usual reaction when I tell you anything is no reaction at all.' Perhaps that was rather blunt, but she wasn't in the mood to be tactful.

Marie looked uncomfortable. 'I wouldn't say that.'

'Oh, luv! I'm not complaining, because you've had your career to think of, but over the years I've written and told you about all sorts of things, anniversaries, birthdays, weddings, and you've ignored them.'

'Oh, God!' Marie got up and went out onto the balcony. Annie poured herself more tea and waited for her to come back. A few minutes later, she returned, her expression sombre. 'I've been thinking about this sort of stuff a lot lately,' she said. 'It was when I heard Sylvia had died – you didn't write until a month after it happened!'

Annie sensed a slight accusation in the words. 'I didn't think you'd be much interested in that, either.'

'It meant it was too late to do anything about it. Cecy and Bruno would have appreciated a wreath.'

'You've never so much as sent a Christmas card before.' Annie wasn't quite sure how the conversation had so swiftly become acrimonious. 'Let's face it, sis. The Menins, the Gallaghers and the Delgados have played a pretty small part in your life since you left home.'

'I know,' said Marie.

The room was silent. Annie noticed the vase she'd brought as a house-warming present was on the hearth, full of dried bronze leaves. A clock shaped like a sunflower ticked loudly on the wall.

Marie threw herself into a chair. 'Oh, Annie, if you knew the way I clawed and fought and slept my way to recognition. Now I've achieved it. I'm a star.

We've just wrapped up a third series of *Lorelei*, and they're planning a fourth, and I've been asked to make a film in Hollywood.'

'Congratulations,' Annie murmured.

Marie grinned mischievously. 'I've turned everything down. I'm retiring from show business, sis. I'm getting married.'

Annie regarded her sister in astonishment. 'You've got a prospective husband tucked up your sleeve and you didn't let me know!'

'I've only known a few days myself. I phoned on Tuesday but you must have been in Paris.'

'What's his name?'

'Justin Taylor. He's a doctor in Tower Hamlets. I met him at an AIDS concert in January – that's what Clive Hoskins died of, AIDS. You'll see him tonight, he's coming to dinner.' Marie leaned forward, her face twisted with the effort to explain. 'It was when I got your letter saying Sylvia was dead, that the penny dropped. I thought about all the people who would miss her, then thought, "Who the hell would miss me?" ' She shook her head when Annie began to protest. 'Don't tell me not to be silly, sis. I know you miss Sylvia far more than you would me.'

Annie said slowly. 'I miss having someone to phone when there's no earthly reason for phoning.'

'That proves my point!' Marie nodded emphatically. 'When have you been able to ring me for a chat? I've always been too frantically involved in my career to return your phone calls. It paid off, the involvement, but only at the expense of the people who loved me; Dot and Bert, Bruno and Cecy, but most particularly you, my sister, not to mention my niece and nephew who I've never really got to know. The thing is, I was the one who lost out most.'

'Where does Justin Taylor fit into this?' Annie enquired curiously.

'Ah, Justin!' Marie's expression grew dreamy. 'I knew he was in love with me, but that he'd never ask the star of *Lorelei* to marry him. The other day, I decided to pop the question myself, and he graciously accepted. So, sis, I'm going to be a doctor's wife in Tower Hamlets, where there's an awful lot of very poor and very sick people.'

'When's the happy day?' asked Annie.

'The thirtieth of June. You'll be there, won't you?'

'I'm afraid not,' Annie said regretfully. 'I'll be in Australia, but my thoughts will be with you, you can be sure of that.'

She realised what was different about her sister. Marie hadn't had a face lift. She was truly happy for the first time in her life.

There was no sign of Euan Campbell during the examination period. Annie's nerves were ragged; worried that she'd fail, terrified he'd be the invigilator and she wouldn't be able to concentrate on the paper. Sometimes, it felt as if Paris had been a dream. Looking back, it seemed unreal, like an incident from one of the novels she'd been reading.

She managed to avoid Binnie Appleby, and concentrated on studying for next day's paper, then the next. She also avoided, though not deliberately, doing anything for the election which took place in the second week of June.

'We're stuck with that woman till the end of the world,' Dot moaned when Mrs Thatcher was elected for a third time. The Conservatives had lost seats, but still won a majority of over a hundred. 'I thought we'd do it this time, Annie, with that nice Kinnock lad.'

'Never mind, Auntie Dot. There's an awful lot of people as upset as you are. Nearly sixty per cent of the country voted for someone else.'

'I know, luv,' Dot sighed. 'Democracy can be a pain in the arse.'

Dot wanted to die and give Bert some peace. She'd been hanging on by the skin of her teeth waiting for the election. Now it meant her old painful bones, her threadbare body, would have to hang on even longer.

8

Before leaving for the other side of the world, Annie wrestled with the problem of what to get Marie and Justin for a wedding present. In the end, she had a brainwave and rang the Labour Party for Ben Wainwright's address. She wrote, enclosing a cheque, and asked if he would kindly send one of his paintings directly to her sister.

He telephoned next morning. 'What's this about "something bright and cheerful"?' he demanded. 'I paint real life, not happy images.'

'You know what I mean,' Annie said. 'I don't want a picture that will make our Marie feel depressed.'

'How about "Sunset over the Slag Heap"?'

'You must be joking! Have you still got that one of the miners finishing their shift?'

'No. I had an exhibition in York a few months ago and it was sold. Don't worry. I'll find one that won't send your sister into a decline.'

He said he'd be in Liverpool shortly and could he take her out to dinner? Annie told him she was going away for at least three months.

'We seem fated never to meet again, you and I,' he said ruefully.

'Perhaps when I get back.' She was finding it impossible to get Euan Campbell out of her mind. If she still felt the same when she returned from Australia, another man, one so completely different, might help her to forget her tender young lover of Paris.

Chris Andrews offered to cut the grass and keep the weeds at bay during the summer, and Monica Vincent would come in once a week to make sure everything was all right – last year, number two had been completely ransacked when the occupants were away, and an expensive bike had been taken in broad daylight from outside number eleven. Two houses had burglar alarms on the front wall.

Annie asked Chris if he'd open the letter which had the result of her degree and let her know what it was, even if she'd failed. 'I'll leave Sara's number by the phone. The results are due mid-August.'

'You won't fail, Annie,' he said staunchly.

She kissed him warmly before she left. He'd always been supportive of everything she'd done, even as far back as when she was at school.

Sara had warned her mother that it was winter in Australia. 'Bring warm clothes, not summer frocks,' she advised.

'Winter!' Annie expostulated after a few days, convinced she would melt in the heat. 'It's at least sixty degrees out there.' She put her thick coat in the wardrobe and never wore it again. She'd actually seen women walking round Sydney in fur coats and boots! Their blood must be awfully thick – or was it thin? She'd ask Nigel.

Since she'd last witnessed them together, the relationship between Sara and Nigel had completely reversed. It had been obvious from the moment they picked her up mid-morning from Kingsford-Smith Airport that things weren't merely rocky, there'd been a shipwreck.

Annie felt guilty when Sara threw herself into her arms, clinging to her, sobbing, 'Oh, Mum! I'm so pleased to see you. Oh, Mum!'

'There, luv.' Annie patted her daughter's shoulder. 'I should have come before,' she thought. 'I never realised she missed me this much.'

Nigel shook her hand. He'd grown a beard and his fringe was longer. There was little of his face to be seen behind the hair and heavy glasses. He didn't look as cocky as she remembered. 'Glad you could come,' he murmured.

She was introduced to Harry, three, a serious little boy with dark straight hair, and Anne-Marie, eighteen months, who had Annie's colouring, even down to the same blue-grey eyes. It wasn't until then that Annie herself felt tearful. These were her grandchildren, her own flesh and blood, they carried the same genes. She knelt down, not wanting to overwhelm them with hugs and kisses, something Sara and Daniel had hated from strangers when they were small.

'Hi,' she said. 'I'm your grandmother, but you can call me Annie.'

'Hello, Annie,' Harry said solemnly. Anne-Marie giggled and hid behind her father's legs.

'See to the luggage, Nigel,' Sara said sharply. 'Come on, Mum.' She picked up her daughter and made for the exit. Annie took Harry's hand and followed uncertainly. Nigel didn't look up to managing two large cases and a travelling bag on his own.

They reached the car, a long silver Peugeot estate with a red suede interior. Sara strapped the children in the back and climbed in with them. 'You sit in the front, Mum. It's a bit squashed here.'

Nigel turned up with the luggage in a trolley, and it was horrid the way Sara nagged him the whole way home. He drove too fast, he drove too slowly, and if he thought this was a short cut, then he was mistaken.

Annie felt too on edge to take in Sydney. She'd known Sara was unhappy, but hadn't realised things had sunk so low. She was thankful when, after about an hour, they turned into a large leafy drive. She had a photo of the bungalow, but it looked bigger than she had expected, a white stone square with floor-length sliding windows on every side.

'It's pretty,' she remarked. Everywhere was beautifully tended, with big exotic bushes and flowerbeds surrounding a vast lawn. A small, kidney swimming pool was covered with canvas at the far end.

Inside the house was light and airy, the rooms large. The oatmeal-coloured walls were bare. Annie couldn't abide a bare wall. She itched to put up pictures.

'I'll make some tea,' said Sara.

Annie followed into the kitchen. Nigel's job in the laboratory must bring in a pretty penny, she thought, impressed. The automatic washing machine looked more like a computer with its range of dials and knobs. There was a dishwasher, a drier, and one of those split-level cookers she'd always fancied herself. In front of the window overlooking the rear of the house, four wickerwork chairs stood around a glass-topped table with cane legs. Sara put the kettle on, then slid the windows open. The children rushed outside.

Annie admired the view, so green and fresh and pleasant. It was hard to believe this was part of a big, noisy city.

'I can't tell you how glad I am you're here, Mum,' Sara sighed.

'I'm glad to be here, sweetheart. I would have come before, but I had me degree, and the fare to Australia's not exactly cheap.'

Sara blinked tearfully. 'No-one's called me "sweetheart" in years.'

'I'll drop a hint to Nigel,' Annie smiled.

'If he called me sweetheart, I'd be sick,' Sara said, in such a harsh, cracked voice, that Annie felt her scalp prickle.

Harry came in and asked for a drink and Sara said no more. She poured her mother a cup of tea and Annie asked mildly, 'Where is Nigel?'

'Gone to work. He took the morning off to collect you.'

He hadn't said goodbye! Things were even worse than she'd thought.

After a few days, Annie recovered from the jetlag and the tiredness of the long journey. From then on, each morning after breakfast, she and Sara and the children set off on a sightseeing tour.

Sydney was a city in a desperate hurry. Cars, pedestrians, shoppers, seemed to be possessed with an urgent desire to be somewhere other than the street, the pavement or the shop where they currently happened to be. The city centre throbbed with brash and exuberant energy. Although Sara could drive and had a car of her own, they mostly used public transport, which was cheap and quick and far less nerve-racking than trying to manoeuvre yourself through the horrendous traffic.

They had tea in the Sydney Opera House, a building that looked more like a magnificent yacht about to break loose from its moorings and float into the glorious blueness of Sydney Harbour; explored The Rocks where the first fleet had dropped anchor in 1788; and saw the statue of Captain Bligh, which didn't look a bit like Charles Laughton. Everywhere she went, Annie collected postcards for Auntie Dot.

Sara said, 'I hate the thought of her dying and me not being there.'

They'd climbed to the top of Observatory Hill, with its breathtaking view of the harbour. Annie nursed Anne-Marie, tired after scrambling up so many steps. Harry was searching for stones for his collection.

'It's what happens, luv, when you move far away.'

'I made a terrible mistake, Mum. I should never have married Nigel.'

Annie had no idea what to say in reply. It was obvious that every single thing that Nigel did or said drove her daughter to distraction. Her husband, so assertive back in Liverpool, was a shadow of his former self, scared to speak lest Sara lash out contemptuously at the most innocent remark. Nothing he did was right. If he put something down, it was in the wrong place and he would be told sharply to put it elsewhere. When he put his dirty dishes in the sink, Sara would take them out again. If he left them, he should have put them in the sink. He crept round like a mouse, and spent most of his time either tending the garden or in the little room that purported to be his study.

Sara was short-tempered with the children, particularly Harry. He was an intelligent little boy, obviously aware of the tension between his parents. Annie noticed his reluctance to go to his father if his mother was around, as if he knew it would upset her.

It was disconcerting to see the sneering, discontented way her daughter's mouth turned down, her hot angry eyes. She looked ugly, unpleasant. There were lines of strain round her jaw and a permanent furrow in her brow. She'd lost all interest in her appearance and lived in jeans and T-shirts which she didn't bother to iron. When they went out, she wore a navy donkey jacket.

'You look as if you're a member of a road gang,' Annie said once.

'What's the point of getting dressed up?' Sara answered listlessly.

Annie had been looking forward to a relaxing, carefree holiday, but found herself struggling to come to terms with the fact that the fresh-faced innocent girl who was once her daughter had turned into a sharp-faced harridan.

Why? Was it Australia? Was it Nigel? Would Sara have changed whatever the circumstances? Annie loved her daughter, but she didn't *like* her all that much. If only Sylvia were alive, and she could sneak a phone call in the middle of the night. 'Honestly, Syl. It's dead embarrassing when she's having a go at poor Nigel. I don't know where to put meself sometimes.' Some days she woke up feeling physically sick at the thought of the day ahead. Sydney was beautiful, she adored her grandchildren, but the atmosphere in the house made her stomach knot.

The couple had no social life. 'Haven't you made friends?' Annie asked one day. Nigel was at work.

'There's one or two girls I have coffee with sometimes. One's from Devon. She's as homesick as me.'

'Why don't you go out in a foursome? I'll babysit,' Annie offered.

Sara snorted. 'You must be joking, Mum. Dinah's husband wouldn't be seen dead with Nigel. No-one can stand him.' She kissed her mother's cheek. 'Anyroad, I don't want to go out and leave you.'

Annie couldn't disappear into her bedroom for a minute before Sara would come and root her out, or sit on the bed and ask questions about the Gallaghers or Heather Close or something else to do with Liverpool.

Some mornings, they strolled through picturesque Rushcutters Park, a stone's throw from the bungalow, or went to the beach, which wasn't far away. The smooth golden sands, washed clean by the white frothy waters of the Pacific, were virginal and untrodden so early in the day. It might be winter, but the sky was blue and cloudless from horizon to horizon, and the sun was warm.

On one particularly glorious day, Harry ran ahead, stamping his feet, fascinated by the sight of his own footsteps. Anne-Marie followed, shrieking happily.

'It's beautiful!' Annie breathed. 'You're so lucky, Sara. You've got a lovely house, two lovely children and you're not short of money. You're living in one of the most interesting cities in the world. God must have been in a really good mood when he made this beach. There's millions of women who'd give anything to be in your shoes.'

Sara's mouth twisted discontentedly. 'I'd prefer Liverpool any day.'

'You haven't given Australia a chance, luv. You didn't like it from the start. I'd have thought a lovely place like this would grow on you.'

'There's not much chance of that, Mum.'

'Mummy,' Harry called. 'Come and see the lovely stone I've found.'

'In a minute,' Sara said abruptly.

Harry came running up, his eyes alight with triumph, holding up a blue mottled stone. 'Look, Mummy. It's terribly pretty.'

'I said *in a minute*!' Sara swung her arm and slapped his face.

The little boy dropped the stone and stared at his mother in bewilderment, his bottom lip trembling. Annie felt a rush of pure anger. She picked the child up and could feel his heart pounding wildly against her own. She said hoarsely, 'If you do that again, Sara, I'm catching the next plane home.' She was conscious of the rage trembling in her voice.

'Mum!' Sara looked as bewildered as her son.

'How *dare* you hit him! No-one ever laid a finger on you.'

Harry buried his head in Annie's shoulder and began to cry. 'There, sweetheart,' she murmured softly, stroking his back. 'Mummy didn't mean it. Did you?' she said in a steely voice to Sara.

'No, no.' Sara burst into tears and reached for her son. Annie handed him over and picked up Anne-Marie, who'd decided to cry in sympathy with everyone else.

Later, as they walked along the flat sands, Harry having recovered his good humour and off in search of more stones, Annie said, 'The mistake you made by marrying Nigel, it's scarcely his fault, is it?'

Sara kicked at the sand. 'I suppose not,' she said sulkily.

'And the fact you don't like Australia isn't his fault, either.'

'Yes, but you see, Mum,' Sara began, but Annie wasn't prepared to listen to any excuses.

'So why take your unhappiness out on him? You knew exactly what you were doing when you married him. You knew where you'd be living. To be frank, I wasn't over-thrilled being married to your dad some of the time, but I didn't make his life a misery.'

Sara gaped. 'But you and Dad had the perfect marriage!'

'That's what you think, and the fact you do shows I kept me feelings hidden. It's sheer bloody selfishness to radiate your discontent onto innocent people, particularly the children.'

'Oh, Mum, please don't get cross and spoil the holiday!'

'I'm not cross,' Annie snapped. 'I'm as mad as hell, and as for spoiling the holiday, it's already spoilt. I've been here a month and I haven't enjoyed meself a bit. In fact, it's made me sick, and I mean properly sick. I'll have to sit down for a while before I fall over.'

That night, she knocked on Nigel's study door. He was listening to a jazz record. It was disgraceful the way he was forced to isolate himself from his family. His face was pathetically pleased when she went in.

'That's nice,' Annie said, sitting down and nodding at the hi-fi. 'It's New Orleans, isn't it?'

He looked surprised. 'You know something about jazz?'

'Not a thing, only that's what they played when we first went to the Cavern. We only went for the atmosphere, not the music. It wasn't until they played rock and roll that we began to listen.'

'The Cavern?' he said, impressed.

'We were there on the opening night,' Annie said proudly, 'and me and Sylvia saw the Beatles before hardly anyone else.'

'I always thought the Beatles rather pedestrian. I far prefer the Rolling Stones.'

'I find them too raucous, but how you can find the Beatles pedestrian is beyond me. What about "Eleanor Rigby" and "She's Leaving Home"?'

'"Twist and Shout" and "I Wanna Hold Your Hand" could hardly be termed musical.' His tone was abrasive, and Annie was about to take umbrage when she recalled the thin little figure sitting at the top of the stairs the morning Sara had changed her mind about coming to Australia. Behind the beard and the glasses and the hair, she sensed a lonely man trying to get out. Nigel was unable to communicate like normal people, and Sara had made no attempt to get to know him better.

'I suppose it's all a matter of taste,' she said. 'All I know is, I cried for days when John Lennon was shot.'

They talked about music for a while. Nigel said, 'I go to this jazz club sometimes, Jock's Café. Perhaps you'd like to come one night?'

'If you don't mind being seen in public with your mother-in-law!' Nigel was thirty-three. It was strange to think she'd slept with a man younger than her daughter's husband.

Next morning Annie was woken by the sound of an argument. Nigel couldn't find a clean shirt. As she listened to the row, she felt nauseous. The situation was playing havoc with her insides.

'I told you, they're in your wardrobe where they always are.'

'I've looked, Sara, and they're not.'

The voices got angrier and angrier. Then the front door slammed, a car started and drove away. Had Nigel gone to work in a dirty shirt? Her heart was racing and she was bathed in perspiration. She wondered if it was the menopause. Her May and June periods had been unusually scanty and the July one was late. Dawn Gallagher had suffered terrible nerves and palpitations with the change.

She tried to coax Sara into hiring a babysitter so she could come with them to the jazz club, but she refused. On Saturday night, she looked at her mother accusingly when she was about to leave, as if she were a traitor. 'You'd think there was a war on,' Annie thought.

Nigel looked painfully casual in a check shirt with the collar daringly turned up, jeans with knife-edge creases and polished shoes. Annie got dressed up for a change, in a chocolate brown crushed velvet suit which had a long loose top and a long, gently gathered skirt. She wore boots for the first time, as it did get rather chilly in the evenings. It was awful, but she was glad to be getting out of the house without Sara. Her body felt thick and heavy with tension. She was desperately in need of a lighthearted break.

As they drove towards the centre of Sydney, Nigel kept clearing his throat as if he were about to speak. Eventually, he managed to bark, 'I love her, you know, Mrs Me- . . . An- . . .'

'Please call me Annie.'

'I love her, Annie. I don't know what's got into her since we came home. When we met, I thought she was the girl of my dreams.'

'You mean she was willing to run round doing everything you wanted?'

'No, no' he said, hurt. 'I didn't feel uncomfortable with Sara the way I did with other women. I felt I could be myself. Not many people understand me,' he added humbly.

'I was wondering – it's what I came to see you about the other night, but we got talking about music – perhaps it might help if Sara and the children came home for a holiday, Christmas, maybe.'

'Anything,' he said willingly. 'Anything's worth a try if it will sort this mess out.'

Jock's Café was beneath a camping equipment shop by St Mary's Cathedral, where Sara had taken Annie to Mass. The large cellar had tartan wallpaper and a tartan-shaded lamp on each table. It was like entering a Turkish bath; the air was thick with cigarette smoke and so warm she could scarcely breathe. The band were playing New Orleans jazz with a remarkable lack of enthusiasm.

To Annie's surprise, Nigel seemed to know quite a lot of people. They sat with a group from the laboratory where he worked.

'This is Rod, Mitch, Charles and Barbie. Barbie's Rod's wife.' He coughed awkwardly. 'This is . . . er, Annie, my mother-in-law.'

They shook hands. 'Mother-in-law!' Mitch said in astonishment. 'You lucky so-and-so, Nige. My ma-in-law resembles a rogue elephant.'

Charles was older than the others. He was English, an attractive man with deeply suntanned skin and prematurely silver hair. He bombarded Annie with questions about what it was like back home. 'I haven't been for years. You get all sorts of mixed stories in the press.'

'It's fine if you're in business,' she told him. 'There's a boom at the moment. The price of houses goes up every week and the estate agents are having a ball. If you're poor, it's another matter. I never thought I'd see beggars on the streets of Britain.' Her voice rose. 'There's what's called Cardboard City in London, whole acres of young people living in cardboard boxes. It makes you dead ashamed, yet we're told we should feel proud of our country.'

Charles looked slightly taken aback by her vehemence. Mitch leaned over and said, 'What's it like having a genius for a son-in-law, Annie?'

'I don't know,' she smiled. 'I've not seen all that much of him.' A genius! She knew Nigel was clever, but a genius!

Listening to the subsequent conversation, she understood he was head of the laboratory. Rod actually called him 'Boss'. There was respect in the voices of the other men when they spoke to him, and she realised they looked upon Nigel as a brilliant scientist. His personality was of no concern to them.

'You know,' she said to Charles, who was beside her, 'I've no idea what you lot actually do.'

'Have you heard of President Reagan's Star Wars Initiative?'

'Yes.' The US president had some mad idea about waging war in space.

Charles was only too pleased to expand. 'We have a contract from the States to develop high-energy lasers using crystals. The lasers will be mounted on satellites orbiting the earth, capable of destroying incoming intercontinental ballistic missiles.' He went on about death rays, the speed of light, weapons entering the outer atmosphere . . .

'It sounds fascinating,' she said, awestruck.

'It's the most interesting work I've done.' He looked embarrassed. 'Annie, you obviously don't realise, but your nose is bleeding.'

'Jaysus!' She jammed a hanky over her nose and made for the Ladies, where two girls glanced at her sympathetically as she mopped her nose with toilet paper. The bleeding wouldn't stop. 'Have you got something cold to put down your back?' one asked. 'It's what my mum always does.'

Annie ran her metal powder compact under water, and the girl slid it down the back of her velvet top. 'Hold it between your shoulder blades for a while,' she advised. They both left.

'I'm fed up!' Annie said aloud to her miserable reflection. She was rarely ill, but since coming to Australia, she felt lousier by the day. She wriggled uncomfortably. The compact was no longer cold and her arm felt dead. She let it go and managed to catch it with her other hand.

Barbie came in, her face full of concern. She was a lovely young woman, tall and well-built, with shining, healthy hair and rosy cheeks. Her teeth were very large and very white. 'Are you all right? Charles said you had a nose-bleed.'

'I'm fine,' Annie said automatically. 'It's more or less stopped.'

'I used to have terrible nose-bleeds when I was pregnant.'

'Did you really!' Annie mopped her brow with tissues; her face suddenly felt as if it was on fire. 'Would you mind telling Nigel I've gone for a walk? I'm desperate for some fresh air.'

'Have you got a coat?' Barbie frowned.

'No, I came as I am.'

'Your son-in-law may be clever, but he's totally impractical. He should have told you how hot it gets in here.' She shook her head in despair. 'I'll lend you my cardy, otherwise you'll catch cold.'

The four men were too engrossed in conversation to notice their return. Barbie handed Annie her thick cardigan. 'Keep it to go home in. I've got a coat as well.'

She was glad of the cardigan when she got outside. The change from the steamy atmosphere of the jazz club to the cool night air of Sydney was pleasant, but she definitely needed the extra clothes.

Annie walked slowly along the unfamiliar streets of the unfamiliar city and everything fell into place. She knew the reason for the nausea in the mornings, the meagre periods followed by no period at all, the thick, heavy body. She paused in front of a shop selling bicycles. She'd yearned for a bike when she was a child, but not as much as she'd wanted skates. Closing her eyes, she imagined herself skating down the middle of Orlando Street, which seemed an incredibly stupid thought to have when she'd just realised she was carrying Euan Campbell's child!

Next morning after Mass, she bearded Nigel in his den and asked if he'd look through the medical emergency section of her travel insurance policy – Australia wasn't blessed with a National Health Service like Great Britain. She knew he would appreciate being asked for his advice. 'It says it doesn't cover anything I had back home. The thing is, I didn't know I was pregnant.'

'Pregnant!' His eyes widened in shock and his mouth fell open. After a few seconds, a grin appeared on his face. 'Have you told Sara?'

'No. I thought I'd wait to see a doctor and get it confirmed.'

He looked flattered that they were sharing a secret. After glancing through the policy, he declared it to be ambiguous. 'The firm I work for has comprehensive medical insurance for employees and their families. I'll have you added temporarily.'

'Will it be expensive?' If so, she'd have to return home.

'There's no need to worry about the expense.'

'But, Nigel . . .' she began, but he dismissed her objection with a wave of the hand.

'We haven't seen much of each other in the four years since I married Sara, but you've been a great mother-in-law, Mrs . . . Annie.' The remark must have been an effort, because his face turned dark red.

The female doctor had a long, gaunt face and a thick East European accent. According to the tag on her white coat, her name was Nina Kowlowski. After an internal examination, she confirmed Annie was pregnant. 'What was the date of your last period?'

'April Fool's Day – I mean, the first of April,' Annie added quickly when the woman looked blank.

'That means you're carrying a sixteen-week-old foetus. You must make up your mind quickly if you want a termination.'

'You mean an abortion!' Annie gasped, horrified. 'I believe in abortion for other women, but not for meself. I've never been so delighted about anything in me life.'

'I merely thought, with your age.' The doctor shrugged. 'In that case, I'd like urine and blood samples, and you will require careful monitoring throughout.'

'Is everything all right?'

'Absolutely fine. You're a very healthy specimen, Mrs Menin, but way past the age when women normally bear children. Now, lie back and I'll listen to your heart and take your blood pressure.'

'What did you buy?' asked Sara.

'Nothing!'

'I thought you went out early with Nigel so you could do some shopping on your own?'

Annie grinned. 'I was lying. I've been to the doctor's. I didn't say anything, because I didn't want to worry you.'

Sara's hands flew to her cheeks and she cried frantically, 'Mum! Oh, Mum! Are you all right?'

'I'm absolutely tip-top,' Annie sang. She removed her daughter's hands from her face and held them tightly. 'I'm expecting a baby, Sara.'

Sara's expression was a mixture of disgust and shock. 'A baby! Mum, how could you?'

'Same way as everyone else does it, luv!' She wasn't ashamed. She didn't give a damn about what people thought.

With an anguished cry, Sara broke away and disappeared into the lounge, where Harry and Anne-Marie were watching television. Annie hummed a tune as she went into the kitchen and made herself a cup of tea. She took it into her own room, where she sat on the bed and thought about the entirely unexpected situation she found herself in. She'd always been ultra-conventional. For the first time in her life, she was doing something out of the run.

Of course, things weren't ideal. She'd be sixty when her child was fourteen, and it wasn't much of a world to bring children into, but it would never become a better world if women stopped having babies. And the baby would never have a father. Even if she and Euan Campbell had a future, which they hadn't, he'd made it clear he didn't want children, which she completely understood. Losing two was enough to put you off for ever. She'd make sure she never saw him again, which meant the degree ceremony in November was out, that's if she'd passed. She chuckled.

'What's so funny?' Sara snapped from the door.

'I was just thinking about turning up for me degree when I'm seven or eight months pregnant!'

'You find that amusing?'

'Yes.'

Sara sidled into the room. 'Who's the father?' she asked curiously.

Annie sighed. 'A lovely young man called Euan Campbell. He lectures at the university and I happened to meet him in Paris. He's thirty-two.'

'Oh, Mum!' She sat on the bed. 'Have you seen him since?'

'No, luv. He wanted to very much, and I did, too, but I refused. It didn't seem right, me being so much older.'

'Age doesn't matter, surely, if you love each other?'

It seemed strange to be discussing such matters with her daughter. 'Euan said much the same thing, but you see, luv, it's not long since he lost his entire family in a car crash. I didn't think he was ready for a serious relationship yet.'

Sara looked dubious. 'He's the one to decide that, not you.'

'You sound as if you want to get me married off,' Annie said.

'I want you to be happy, Mum.'

Annie opened her arms and Sara collapsed into them. 'And I want you to be happy, sweetheart. I can't stand seeing the way things are between you and Nigel.'

'I wonder what he'll think about his mother-in-law being pregnant,' Sara sniffed.

'He already knows. Now, don't be hurt,' she said quickly when she felt her daughter's body stiffen. 'I only told him because I wanted advice on me medical insurance. It was him who arranged for the doctor.' She stroked her daughter's hair. 'He's a nice chap, and he loves you. You should be proud of him. The other night, someone said he's a genius. You can't expect him to be like everyone else, luv. He's different. I mean, you can't nag a genius for not putting his dishes in the sink.'

'I've been horrible to Nigel,' Sara sobbed. 'It's Australia. It's a lovely place, but it isn't Liverpool. I miss the streets and the people. I miss everything. When I drive into Sydney, I get this awful lump in my throat, and I wish, like I've never wished for anything, that I was driving into town, that I'd end up in Lord Street or London Road.' Sara looked at her mother, her face anguished. 'Christmas is unbearable, they have dinner in the garden. Imagine, Mum, having turkey and Christmas pudding out of doors! I long for snow and hail and frost.'

'Have you never thought of coming home on holiday, Sara?'

'Loads of times, but I know this sounds stupid, I can't bear to leave Nigel. He adores the children and he'd miss them terribly. I hate to think of him being unhappy.'

Annie smiled wryly. 'And you think he's not unhappy now?'

Nina Kowlowski found Annie's blood pressure to be rather high. She returned fortnightly for a check-up and was told to rest and take things easy. Sightseeing stopped altogether, and most days they strolled to the beach or the park. Occasionally they went on gentle shopping trips and had lunch or tea in one of Sydney's lovely restaurants. The weather grew warmer as the Australian spring approached. She dreaded to think what it would be like in summer.

Barbie and Mitch came to see her several times, and Charles often arrived with flowers. 'Do you like Sydney enough to settle here?' he asked once.

'I love it, but me roots are in Liverpool. It would take an awful lot to make me leave.'

'That's a pity,' Charles sighed.

Annie felt totally content as her baby grew inside her, although she had several more nose-bleeds and if she walked too much her ankles swelled. Harry and Anne-Marie joined her in bed in the mornings and she told them tales about when their mam and Uncle Daniel had been little. Sara, buoyed up by the knowledge she was going home for Christmas, was being nicer to her husband. Nigel remained his boastful self, but Annie was aware of the decent, honourable man within and grew quite fond of her awkward son-in-law.

In the middle of August, Chris Andrews phoned. 'Congratulations, Annie. You got a Two-one. I always knew you had it in you.'

She hadn't thought about the degree for weeks. 'That's marvellous news,' she said excitedly. She asked how things were at his end.

'Good, in fact things are quite wonderful.' He sounded unusually cheerful and she wondered what had made her old friend so happy.

'Chris, I'll look a bit different when I get home.'

'Have you dyed your hair or something?'

'I've put on a bit of weight. I'm expecting a baby in January.' She hoped he wouldn't feel hurt – he still asked her to marry him occasionally – and was relieved when he laughed out loud. 'Trust you to do the unexpected, Annie!'

She thought that a rather odd remark, as she couldn't think of having done anything unexpected before. That night, she wrote to everyone she could think of and told them about the baby. She didn't want to encounter a series of incredulous faces when she got home.

Annie had been in Australia over three months, and September was drawing to an end, when she decided it was time to go home.

'Why not wait till Christmas and we'll go together?' Sara suggested.

'No, luv. I've got to book meself into hospital, and there's things to do, like get a cot, for instance. I sold the old one after your dad died and we were hard up. Anyroad, if I wait much longer, I'll never get on the plane. I'm already as big as a house.'

A few days before she was due to leave, she saw Nina Kowlowski for the final time. The two women had become friends. Annie lay on the examination table and could hardly see Nina for her bulging belly.

'You must promise to send me a card when the baby arrives.'

'I promise.'

Nina's head appeared. She was tapping Annie's stomach and listening hard. There was a puzzled look on her gaunt face.

Annie felt her blood run cold. 'Is something wrong?'

'No, nothing wrong,' Nina said absently. She continued to prod and listen, totally absorbed.

'Is there a radio in there and you can hear music?'

'No, no.'

'Then what the hell d'you find so interesting?'

Nina jerked upright. 'Are there twins in your or the father's family, Annie?'

'Twins! Why, yes, I told you about Euan, didn't I? The little girls who died were twins.'

'Well, Euan, bless his heart, has scored again. I don't know how you feel about this, Annie, but I can definitely hear a second heartbeat. You're expecting twins.'

9

Heather Close seemed narrow and cramped in the English autumn sunshine, the houses squashed too closely together. She noticed the paintwork was peeling on quite a few doors and windows, including her own. The Vincents had had a bright red burglar alarm fitted whilst she was away.

'Here you are, luv!' the taxi driver grunted. 'Bet'cha glad to get home after that long journey. Good job it's a nice day, else you'd feel dead miserable after Australia.' They'd had a long conversation during the drive from the station. He had a cousin in Darwin. He carried her cases into the house. 'Would you like me to take these upstairs?'

'No, ta, I'll unpack down here.' She paid him, closed the door and leaned against it, exhausted. As soon as she'd had a cup of tea, she'd go to bed. The house seemed dark and small and drained of colour. Beside the phone, she noticed a thick wad of post held together with an elastic band. She picked it up and took it into the breakfast room. It looked like mainly bills and circulars.

To her surprise, there were dirty dishes on the table. Annie felt a prickle of alarm. Had she acquired a squatter?

She crept into the lounge and saw records spread over the floor. The French windows were open. She went over and called, 'Who's there?'

The garden was neat and tidy and appeared to be empty. Then the branches of the willow tree parted and a young man with long plaited hair emerged. He was a bag of bones, thin to the point of emaciation, with hollow cheeks and deep-set, haunted eyes. He was either growing a beard or badly in need of a shave. The jeans he wore were filthy and full of tears, and his collarless shirt was little better.

They stared at each other for several seconds without speaking.

'Haven't you had a bath since you got home, Daniel?' said Annie.

'There's no hot water. The fairy in the boiler isn't working.'

'It should be switched on in the airing cupboard first.' It was a terrible anti-climax. She'd thought about him, prayed for him, worried, cried, longed for him for over four years, but now he was back and it was difficult to feel anything but mild irritation. 'Did you find yourself?' she asked.

'I'm not sure.' His voice was deep and mature and he'd lost some of his Liverpool accent.

'D'you want a cup of tea? I was just about to make one.'

'Please.' Inside, she could smell the dirt on him. She told him to go upstairs and switch on the water. 'I'd like a bath meself later.'

When he came down, he nodded at her stomach. 'The woman next door said you were in Australia, so I rang Sara. They'd just been to see you off, but she told me about the baby.'

'Babies,' said Annie.

'That's right, babies.' His smile was sweet and gentle. 'You don't do things by halves, Mum.'

Perhaps it was the smile, perhaps it was the 'Mum', but Annie felt a sudden rush of emotion. Daniel was back, her son was home. In two months, Sara would arrive and she would have all her family there. She patted his shoulder. 'It's nice to see you, son.'

'Same here, Mum.'

The post was mainly bills as expected, but there were a few personal letters, one from a solicitor informing her that the ten-year lease on Patchwork had expired. Annie blanched when she saw the cost of renewal. The sum had gone up fivefold. Patchwork would have to go.

Ben Wainwright had written to ask if he could borrow her painting. *I'm having an exhibition in London. If you're back before the end of October, please get in touch.* He added that she'd made a good investment. *They went for five hundred pounds each at the last show.*

Annie recognised her sister's writing on the next envelope. *Just thought I'd let you know, sis,* Marie wrote, *that I'm ecstatically happy. Being a doctor's wife makes you feel very NECESSARY! Of course, I'm chuffed to hear your news. A baby! It makes me realise I might have managed it myself. Still, I feel as if*

Justin's patients are my family. I've been asked to make another series of Lorelei and I might, just might, agree. The money would be useful, as Justin would like to start an AIDS clinic, but can't raise the cash . . .

She was relieved her sister was so happy and felt a lifetime's worry slip from her shoulders. 'I must write and tell her it's twins.'

The final letter bore a Turin postmark, so she knew it was from Cecy. *How delighted Sylvia would have been about the baby, Annie, dear. Her girls were over for the summer, Yasmin and Ingrid for three whole months, Dorothy and Lucia for just a fortnight with a nurse that Mike had hired. We hear nothing from him, but Bert wrote to say there's been a terrible row. Apparently Mike voted Conservative at the last election and Dot refuses to speak to him, so the Gallagher clan are split.*

'Jaysus' Annie gasped. 'I must get round to Dot's as soon as I can.' She turned to the final page of Cecy's letter.

I've left the worst news till last, my dear Annie. You'll be sorry to learn that my darling Bruno is dead. But trust him to go down with flying colours. You'll never believe this, but he got involved in a fight at some silly anti-Mafia demonstration. They're not sure if it was the blow to the head or the heart attack that killed him. It's curious, but I'm glad he went that way. Bruno hated growing old. He would sooner die upholding his beliefs than become a doddery old codger like me.

Annie had rarely seen her doctor since the children were young. Once contacted, he regarded her as a challenge. A twin pregnancy was risky at any age; with Annie, the risk was even greater. She was told to do nothing except lie on the settee and take things easy.

'If I'm lying on the settee, I won't have much choice, will I?' she said the first time he came to see her.

'I do hope you're not going to be an awkward patient, Mrs Menin.' He was a short, stout man with a friendly outgoing manner.

'Don't worry, doctor,' she said hastily. 'I'll do everything you say. There's no way I'll risk me babies by over-taxing meself.'

'I'd like you to attend the ante-natal clinic fortnightly. You mustn't hesitate to contact me if you have a problem.'

She felt rather like a precious object that had to be handled with extraordinary care. The Gallaghers came in their hordes, bearing gifts of babyclothes and toys, some new, some old, though there was no sign of Mike. He'd cut himself off from his family.

'It was losing Sylvia that did it,' Tommy claimed bitterly. He had a new, young family to support, but had just been made redundant by AC Delco. 'He's become as hard as nails, our Mike. He bought out Ray Walters, so now the whole lot's his. All he thinks of is the business. That's why he voted as he did. He doesn't give a damn about people any more, just business.'

Daniel took his mother in the car to see Dot and Bert regularly. Apart from the clinic, it was the only place she went. Dot's face twisted in pain the first time she spoke about her errant son. 'Me heart's shattered into a million little pieces, Annie,' she cried. She might be at death's door, but she'd not lost her taste for the dramatic. 'I never thought the day would come when a Gallagher would vote Tory.'

'Oh, Dot, you'd think he'd committed murder or something.'

'It's worse than murder,' Dot said chillingly. 'Anyroad, luv, how are you feeling? You look as if you're carrying a whole football team. Jaysus, the world's changed. Forty years ago, a woman would be ashamed to show her face if she was carrying a baby out of wedlock. Nowadays it's all the rage.'

Annie patted her stomach. 'I'm fine. Everyone's looking after me. People pop in all day long to ask if I want shopping done, or to make a cup of tea, and I don't know what I'd do without Daniel. He's a tremendous help, aren't you, luv?'

'I do my best,' said Daniel. 'I came home just in time.'

She would never have the same close, demonstrative relationship with her son as she had with Sara, but Annie and Daniel got on fine. They mostly kept out of each other's way. He more or less kept the house clean, ate like a horse, went for long walks by the river or sat in his room, reading. He never spoke about his travels and she never asked. He'd tell when he felt ready, if he ever did. Annie sensed that if she hadn't been pregnant, Daniel would have gone by now on another fruitless journey to find himself. She had no idea for what her wandering son was searching, perhaps he didn't know himself, but she desperately wished she could present him with the Holy Grail of his dreams. Daniel, alas, would have to find it for himself. He was part of a lost generation, completely disillusioned with the world and the way it was run. Still, he'd come back a better man than when he'd left. He was patient, even-tempered, and that sad, sweet smile was too mature for a man of twenty-two. It reminded her of Euan Campbell and made her want to weep.

Dot winked. 'Give your ould auntie a big kiss, lad. I live on kisses, they keep me going, otherwise I'd've been dead years ago.'

Daniel embraced her warmly, which he would have hated doing before.

Ben Wainwright looked flabbergasted when he arrived to collect his painting. 'I didn't realise you had a partner!'

'I haven't,' said Annie.

He nodded at her bulging frame. 'You did that on your own?'

She blushed. 'No, it was . . . well, the affair was lovely when it happened, but it's all over.'

'I don't know why, but that news gives me great pleasure.'

Annie blushed again. 'Where's your exhibition being held?'

'A gallery in Hackney. It's not exactly Bond Street, but every little helps. I'll return your painting in January when the show's over.'

He stayed for dinner; salad, which was all Annie could eat. Hot food gave her heartburn, coffee made her sick, the least sip of wine and she was dizzy. She lived on fruit, raw vegetables and de-caffeinated tea.

After Ben left, Daniel said, 'I thought that was the father at first, but Sara said he was only thirty-two. What's his name?'

'Euan Campbell,' Annie said uncomfortably. It was parents who asked their children questions like that, not the other way round.

'Does he know about the babies?'

'No, and I'm not telling him, either.'

'He has a right to know.'

'Since when have you been such an expert on people's rights?' Annie demanded crossly.

'It's only fair. I'd have a fit if some woman had my baby and I knew nothing about it.'

'Well, you're you, and I'm me, and we're both different.'

'I can't argue with that, Mum.'

Annie remained fit, the babies were growing nicely in her womb, but in November she was visited with terrible depression. Everything seemed dark and bleak and the future held no promise. What was she supposed to live on? Dawn had taken over the lease of Patchwork. Annie had received two and a half thousand pounds for the stock and goodwill and the rights to her designs. She'd finished off the mortgage, but what was left wouldn't keep her for more than a few months. She hated the thought of being a burden on the State.

Even worse, it was cruel and irresponsible for a woman of her age to have children. She could die at any time – look at Sylvia! In the blackness of the night she imagined two tiny waifs being thrust into uncaring hands and placed in a Dickensian orphanage. In a blinding panic, she stumbled downstairs and telephoned Australia.

'Mum, what on earth's wrong?' Sara cried.

'If anything happens to me, will you have my babies, Sara?'

'Oh, Mum, of course we will. In fact . . .' Sara paused. 'Nigel and me have already talked about it. But nothing will happen to you, Mum.'

'I'm terrified, Sara.' Annie shivered on the stairs.

'Don't worry. I'll be there in a few weeks to look after you.'

Monica Vincent called every evening and said it was perfectly normal to feel depressed. 'Lots of pregnant women have depression, Annie.'

'It's worse at night. Everything seems so dark and it plays havoc with me blood pressure.' The doctor had been quite stern the other day, and asked if she'd been climbing mountains.

'You could take sleeping tablets.'

'Oh, no! I haven't taken a single tablet, except iron. I'm too scared it'll do the babies harm.'

'It'll pass, Annie.' Monica squeezed her hand. 'You know, I'm envious. I wish I was in your position.'

'It's not too late, luv. You're younger than me.'

Monica's cheeks turned pink. Annie had found a little gold pendant down the side of the settee which she immediately recognised as her neighbour's. At the time, she looked from the pendant to the neat grass outside, thought about the way Chris Andrews went round whistling his head off since she came back, and the shy but rapturous look on Monica Vincent's face, and realised something had happened between them whilst they'd been looking after her house. When she returned the pendant, the woman had almost collapsed with embarrassment. 'I wondered where it had gone,' she muttered.

So far, the affair seemed to be a secret. Perhaps they were waiting for the right moment to tell Mrs Vincent.

November passed and so did the depression. It was a shame, with Christmas so close, that she was unable to go out and choose little presents for the tree for Harry and Anne-Marie. Sara would do the Christmas shopping when she came home.

Annie half-lay, half-sat, on the settee, dozing a lot of the time. She felt extraordinarily relaxed, her head thick and dreamy. Sometimes she woke and wondered why on earth she was asleep during the day, then remembered the babies moving gently inside her. In a detached sort of way she watched television, read, listened to records. With the Beatles playing softly in the background, she would nod off and dream she was in the Cavern with Sylvia. One dark afternoon, she woke up with a start to see Sylvia sitting in the armchair watching her anxiously.

'Syl!' Annie's heart turned a somersault.

'It's Ingrid, Auntie Annie,' a small voice said. 'We didn't like to wake you. Daniel let us in. It was Mummy's birthday last week, and we still feel miserable, so asked if we could come and see you.'

'Oh, luv. Hello, Yasmin.' She held out her arms and the two girls knelt and buried their faces against her. 'Now as you're getting bigger, you can come and see your Auntie Annie more often – in fact, you can help with the babies.'

'We'd like that,' Ingrid said eagerly. 'Do you know if they're boys or girls?'

'I preferred to wait and see.' She could have had a test to discover the sex and ensure the foetuses were perfect, but what if they weren't? She would still have felt unable to go through with an abortion.

The girls spent the next hour trying to think up names for the twins, and ended up in fits of giggles as they outdid each other with outrageous suggestions; Mutt and Jeff, Tom and Jerry, Gert and Daisy. 'Granny Gallagher was always on about Gert and Daisy, but we haven't seen her for ages.'

One of Mike's employees turned up at six o'clock to collect them. Annie felt sad as she watched them go. Sylvia would do her nut if she thought her darling girls were unhappy.

The days merged, became muddled. Sometimes Annie wasn't sure whether it was morning or night. Visiting the clinic was a shock to the system; the cold, different people, loud voices, white, clinical surroundings. She blinked, confused by the strangeness of it all, relieved to get back home. Things were proceeding nicely, but she *must* take it easy, otherwise she might bring on a premature birth. More twin than single babies, she was told, died within the first few hours due to being premature.

It was nice to be ensconced on the settee and have everybody wait on her. Daniel fetched the decorations from the loft and all she had to do was lie there and give orders as he put them up, ready for when Sara and the children arrived the next day.

He reminisced over every ornament as he hung them on the tree. 'I remember this! Ah, this was Sara's favourite! And this was mine!' He held up a golden ball covered with red stars. 'There should be another somewhere. There used to be four. One year, I took them off and broke two. You didn't get cross.' He looked at her curiously. 'You *never* got cross. Why was that, Mum?'

'I dunno, luv. I don't suppose you meant to break them, did you?'

'No, but you took everything so calmly. I thought you didn't care.

Sometimes, I wanted to do really shocking things, like draw on the walls, throw something at the television, just to see what you'd do, but I couldn't imagine anything that would make you lose your temper.'

'It doesn't do to lose your temper, luv,' Annie said. Her voice sounded odd, husky and far away, and it was an effort to speak. She felt dazed and lethargic, and made an effort to pull herself together. 'You say terrible things you don't mean. Afterwards, it might be too late to take them back.'

'I don't understand,' said Daniel.

'I lost me temper once and I've never stopped regretting it.'

'When was that, Mum?'

It all came back, as fresh as if it had happened yesterday. She watched the tickets for *Goldilocks* shrivel on the fire, heard her furious voice, shrieking at her parents that they were unfit to have children. She walked down the back entry, opened the door to the yard, tried to get in the kitchen, but couldn't because Dad's legs were in the way. The smell of gas was overpowering. She gagged . . .

'Mum, Mum, stop! Mum, it's all right!'

Annie opened her eyes. Daniel was shaking her by the shoulders. 'That was awful. Why have you never said anything before?'

'You mean I told you? I thought I was just reliving the whole thing.' Her heart was racing. She felt hot and could still smell gas. 'Now you see why I vowed never to lose me temper. I only did it one other time. This chap at work got fresh and I nearly laid him out.'

'I'd like to know more about my grandparents,' Daniel said, 'but not now. Lie back and rest and I'll make some tea. You're all worked up and it's my fault. I'll have the doctor after me.'

Christmas Day, and Sara and Daniel were in the kitchen preparing the dinner. It was just like old times, Annie thought dreamily as she listened to them arguing, except her grandchildren were playing with their new toys on the hearth.

'Do you sleep all right in your bunk beds?' she asked. The beds were secondhand, but good as new.

'Yes.' Harry looked up from the Junior Science Kit that Monica had bought on Annie's behalf. 'I like being on top.'

'Why can't me sleep on top?' Anne-Marie queried.

''Cos you're too little,' Harry told her brusquely. He turned to Annie. 'When's my new auntie coming?'

'Marie? Any minute, luv.' Marie and Justin were on their way from London. They'd booked into the Blundellsands Hotel for two nights, as Annie's house was too full to put them up.

'Mum,' Sara shouted, 'do you want wine with your dinner?'

'I do,' Annie shouted back, 'but me stomach doesn't. Just give me fresh orange juice. It's in the fridge.'

Sara came in with a cup of tea. 'I thought you'd like this to keep you going. Is there the usual big do at Mike's today?'

'No.' For the first time in many years, the Gallaghers wouldn't be gathering for their Christmas dinner. 'Some of the lads are going to their mam and dad's.'

'Can I have orange juice, Mummy?' Harry tugged his mother's sleeve.

'Of course, sweetheart. Come in the kitchen and I'll get you some.'

Sara began to sing 'Away in a Manger', and Annie thought that never had anyone changed so swiftly as Sara had since she came home. The lines of tension on her face had disappeared. Her voice was softer, her eyes shone, she sang a lot, and there was colour in her cheeks. Annie was relieved to have her real daughter back, but dreaded what would happen when she had to return to Australia.

Marie arrived in a mink coat, with a weary Justin trailing behind. 'He was called out twice in the middle of the night,' Marie said, pulling a face. 'A patient, an old man he was very fond of, died.'

'I'll never get used to death,' Justin said tiredly. He wasn't at all the sort of man Annie had expected her glamorous sister to marry. Approaching sixty, his face bore an expression of perpetual worry, as if he carried the weight of the world on his shoulders. But he was a good man, who cared for his patients to the detriment of his own health.

'Can this really be Daniel!' Marie smothered an embarrassed Daniel with kisses. 'And Sara! I would never have recognised you. Where are the children? Look, darlings, I've brought loads of presents.' She turned to Annie in her usual prone position on the settee. 'My God, sis! You're *massive*! When are the babies due?'

'In a fortnight. I feel as if I've been pregnant for ever.'

Dinner was a noisy, chaotic affair. Except for Annie, who remained resentfully sober, the adults drank too much and laughed too loud and the conversation geared dizzily to a peak of utter ludicrousness.

'I'm so happy,' Annie whispered to herself. 'So, so happy. I never thought I'd have me family back again.' There was only one person missing, the father of her babies. She rested her hands on her stomach and wondered what Euan Campbell was doing right now.

After dinner, she went upstairs for a nap. The laughter downstairs sounded muffled and muted. She dozed off and dreamt she was in the hotel in Paris with Euan. His lithe brown body was bent over hers. There were strange noises coming from the boulangerie. 'The bread's exploding,' said Euan. He kissed her lips, kissed her breasts, buried his head in her flat belly. Then a poodle came leaping through the window and Euan laughed and chased it away. He got up and closed the window, and Annie held out her arms, her body aching for the feel of him, his touch, the oneness when they were making love. Their eyes locked together and the feeling, the yearning, was so strong that she gasped. Then Euan disappeared, literally vanished before her eyes, and she was alone.

'Euan!' she shouted in alarm.

'Who's Euan?' a voice said.

Annie woke and saw Justin Taylor sitting on the bed. For a moment, she forgot he was a doctor and was annoyed to find him there.

'A friend,' she said.

'I see.' He nodded briefly. 'I came to see if you were all right. You've been asleep for quite a while. There are more guests downstairs.'

Chris Andrews and Monica Vincent! Monica had an engagement ring on the third finger of her left hand. 'Mother's flaming mad,' she grimaced.

Annie kissed them both. 'I couldn't be more happy for you. As for your mother, she'll get used to the idea.'

Annie felt increasingly as if she were drunk. Her head swam most of the time and she could hardly walk. She was asleep on the settee more often than she was awake. Marie and Justin returned to London, and on New Year's Eve, Daniel and Sara stayed in and watched television. She tried to persuade them to go for a drink. 'Why not try the Grand?' she suggested. 'See what it's like under new management.'

'The Grand wouldn't be the same without Bruno,' Sara said. 'Anyway, Mum, you're not fit to babysit. You'd fall asleep.'

Daniel woke her a few minutes before midnight. 'Come on, Mum. It'll be 1988 shortly.'

The telephone rang just as Big Ben finished chiming in the New Year. 'That'll probably be Sylvia,' Annie said groggily.

It was Marie, for the first time ever, ringing to wish Annie a Happy New Year.

She stayed in bed on New Year's Day, and the day after. On the third day, when she felt too exhausted to sit up, Sara called the doctor. He examined her thoroughly. 'Everything seems to be all right,' she heard him say. 'But I think we'd better get her to hospital.'

Annie was only vaguely aware of being helped downstairs and into the ambulance, where she promptly fell asleep. When she came to, she was lying in a high bright room and a dazzling neon tube on the ceiling above was hurting her eyes. She felt light-headed and her stomach hurt.

'Good, you're awake.' A nurse appeared, smiling, and mopped her brow. 'How do you feel?'

'Not so bad, but I'm dreading the labour,' Annie groaned. 'I know it's going to be much longer with twins.'

'What labour? It's all over, Mrs Menin. You've got two lovely little boys. One four pounds ten ounces, the other a whopping five pounds.'

The boys were small but much fitter than their mother. All Annie's health and strength had drained into them in the weeks prior to their birth. Too weak to withstand the protracted labour, the babies had been removed by Caesarean section. Some women felt disappointed if they missed the experience of delivery, but Annie didn't care. Nor did it bother her that she had no milk to breastfeed. All she wanted was to feel well again and get her babies home.

Within twenty-four hours, she managed to make her way to the incubators where Andrew and Robert had automatically been placed.

'They're mine!' she whispered as she stared through the glass at the tiny sleeping bodies. 'Oh, Syl, if only you were here!' And what would Euan think if he knew he had two sons with Scottish names that she'd chosen specially in his honour!

Andrew was the biggest, not that you'd ever notice. His hair was possibly a darker shade of red than his brother's, but otherwise they were identical. The flesh lay loosely on their stick-thin limbs and their tiny hands were curled in fists. They were beautiful. She longed to hold them.

Two days later, Annie did. She felt almost giddy with happiness as she looked down at her babies, one in each arm. At the same time, she felt fearful. Her other children weren't particularly happy. What did fate have in store for Andy and Rob?

Scores of visitors, cards and flowers arrived; roses from Cecy, chrysanthemums from Marie and Justin. A basket of dried flowers came with a little handpainted card, 'From Yasmin and Ingrid (and Mummy)'.

To Annie's astonishment, Ben Wainwright appeared at her bedside one afternoon. 'I returned your picture and your daughter told me the news. Congratulations! I've seen the boys and they're a grand little pair.' He glanced round the ward. 'This takes me back! I remember going to see my wife each time our sons were born. It felt as if a miracle had happened, but at the same time, the world seemed a more frightening place. You knew you had this heavy responsibility for the rest of your life.'

'Where are your boys now?' Annie enquired.

'Vincent's in Leeds, married with two kids and a big mortgage. Gavin wants nothing to do with such nonsense. He's living in a squat in London without a clue what he wants to do.'

'He sounds a bit like my Daniel.'

'Annie, I want to tell you about my marriage.'

She glanced at him, perplexed. 'But it's nothing to do with me!'

'It's just that Janice and I were childhood sweethearts. We married in our teens, but outgrew each other. There was nothing sordid about the divorce. We're still friends.' His dark blue eyes danced in his grizzled face. 'You can say it's nothing to do with you, but I'd like to think it might be some day.'

Once home, Rob and Andy thrived and their weight increased. Their bodies filled out and gradually different personalities began to emerge. Although one was rarely awake without the other, Rob cried and demanded more attention than his brother. Andy was patient, but his legs were never still. The second a sheet or blanket touched him, he would contemptuously kick it off.

Daniel was fascinated by the twins. Annie often found him in her bedroom where they slept, staring. 'I always wanted a brother,' he said.

'I always wanted four children.'

The operation had taken a lot out of her and she tired easily. She'd lost weight and could zip up her jeans without a struggle. Her face was bloodless, and she could see her cheekbones for the first time in her life. Strangely, her fragile appearance made her look younger, almost girlish, and her red hair looked even redder against her white skin.

Annie didn't know what she would have done without Sara. In the middle of the night, it was more often Sara who got up to prepare the bottles, and mother and daughter would sit up in bed, each with a desperately hungry child in their arms. If they weren't fed together, poor Andy would be left as Rob was fed first to shut him up.

At half past three one morning, Annie said, 'Isn't it about time you went home, luv? I love having you, but what about Nigel?'

'Liverpool's home, Mum. I'm not going back to Australia.'

Sara's tone was so implacable that Annie knew it was no use arguing. It was an undeniable fact that Australia, that young, vibrant country, disagreed with her daughter. To return was to condemn herself and her family to a life of misery. Annie wasn't sure which was worse for Nigel: an unhappy, nagging wife, or no wife at all.

As the weeks passed, Ben Wainwright seemed to discover frequent reasons for visiting Liverpool, until it became clear the only reason he came was for Annie. They got on well, he was the right age, he adored the twins, and Daniel and Sara liked him. Annie knew one day he would ask her to marry him, and thought it would be sensible to accept.

In March, Nigel James turned up. Annie answered the door, and there he was, looking slightly ridiculous in a wide-brimmed felt hat and wrapped in several scarves against the searing wind that had been shaking the house all day.

'Am I pleased to see you!' she cried, thinking mainly of her phone bill. Sara spent hours in urgent, whispered calls to Australia. She told him his wife was out shopping with the children and made him coffee and a sandwich. 'Nigel, luv,' she said when he'd thawed out and looked as human as he was ever likely to, 'I know it's none of me business, but I hope you don't intend persuading Sara to go back with you. You wouldn't believe the difference the last few months have made. I think you'll find she's the girl you married back in Wivenhoe.'

'Don't worry, Mrs . . . Annie,' he said harshly. 'I've got a job in a laboratory in Chester. The pay is poor, and the work's way below my intellectual capacity, but I'd do anything to keep Sara.'

She patted his arm, smiling. 'That's my Nigel! Now, if you've finished your coffee, you can give one of your brothers-in-law his bottle. I heard a cry, which means Rob's about to bawl the house down.'

It meant Sara would leave soon, and Daniel was getting restless. She could tell he was itching to take off, but this time she wouldn't be left alone. Her daughter wouldn't be far away and she had Rob and Andy. One day they too would go, but it was so far in the future it wasn't worth thinking about. All she hoped was that fate would be kind and it wouldn't be *her* leaving *them*. That wasn't all. Ben had decided to take up painting full time, something he could do anywhere, including Liverpool. He had asked her to marry him. All she had to do was make up her mind. She knew she would be safe and comfortable with Ben Wainwright.

Tomorrow

It was the sort of day she loved; late autumn, crisp and brilliantly sunny, though not particularly warm.

The twins were sitting on the hearth, the soles of their feet planted firmly against each other. In the diamond formed by their chubby legs stood a wooden garage, and they were pushing Daniel's Matchbox cars up the sloping ramp onto the roof. When the roof was full, they pushed them down again, making engine noises the whole while. Their faces were intent, as if what they were doing was more important than anything in the world. They had no idea that history was being made that day.

The television had been on since early morning. In a week of political turmoil, Michael Heseltine had challenged Margaret Thatcher for the Conservative leadership. To everyone's astonishment, the support for her from Tory MPs was much less than expected. The imposition of the Poll Tax had done it, so grossly unfair. The whole country had been up in arms. Annie had taken the twins in their double pushchair on several protest marches. The leadership election had gone into a second round and rather than risk losing and be humiliated, Mrs Thatcher had announced her resignation. Annie was waiting for her to arrive in the House of Commons for her final appearance as Prime Minister.

She jumped when the French windows slid open and a couple stepped into the lounge, wiping their feet carefully on the mat, the way strangers did in someone else's house. The events unfurling on the screen before her were so gripping that she'd forgotten Mr and Mrs Loftus were looking round.

'I love the tree,' Mrs Loftus said, 'and the estate agent failed to mention the summer house in his details.'

'The summer house? Oh, you mean the shed!' Annie was trying to keep one eye on them, and the other on the television.

'Do you mind if we have another look upstairs?'

'Not at all. Look anywhere you like. After all, buying a house . . .' her voice trailed away when Mrs Thatcher was shown leaving Downing Street. The cameras switched to the packed benches of the House of Commons, where the atmosphere sizzled with excitement.

The couple came back down. 'We like your house very much.' Mr Loftus rubbed his hands together. He looked pleased, as if they'd been searching for a long time. 'Have you been here long?'

'Nearly thirty years.'

Mrs Loftus was staring at the boys, as if she'd love to pick them up. 'What are they called?'

'This is Andy,' Annie pointed to the slightly darker red head, 'and that's Rob.'

'Their hair's your colour, but they're not particularly like you.'

'They're the image of their father. They're nearly three,' Annie added to save the woman asking.

Mr Loftus was walking round the room, hands in pockets, as if he already felt at home. 'I'm surprised you can bring yourself to leave a place like this. It's got such a happy, lived-in feel about it.'

'Thirty years is a long time to be in the same house. We're moving to Sefton Park to be near my daughter.' Two years ago, Sara had started a playgroup in her home. Now Anne-Marie was ready for school and Sara wanted to finish her degree at Liverpool University, Annie would take over the playgroup and look after her grandchildren when necessary. At some time in the future, she intended making use of her own degree.

Mrs Loftus had become aware of the events occurring on television. 'She's resigned, hasn't she? I suppose it's the end of an era.' They stood watching as Mrs Thatcher took her seat in the Commons, then Mr Loftus shrugged. 'We'd better be on our way, dear.' He turned to Annie. 'We'll go straight to the estate agents. We definitely want to buy.' He shook hands. 'Well, goodbye Mrs . . . sorry, I've forgotten your name.'

'Campbell,' said Annie. 'Mrs Campbell.'

It was a bravura performance, full of defiance and gritty pride. In the rows behind, the politicians who had betrayed their leader hung their heads in shame. Annie had never witnessed a scene so full of drama and emotion, not even in all the films and plays she'd seen.

Mrs Thatcher had left the Commons, and the first of the interviews which would probably go on all day had begun, when the phone rang. It was probably the estate agent to say the house was sold.

'Annie!' Dot sounded as if she were speaking from the bottom of the world. Her voice was thick and deep. Her voice and a smattering of hearing was all she had left. 'Did you see her, luv? Oh, what a grand ould girl she was at the end! She's worth twenty of those men who voted against her. Jaysus, if only she'd been born a socialist!'

The voice faded and Uncle Bert came on. 'She's happy now, luv. I'll have to ring off and see to her.'

Annie replaced the receiver slowly, knowing that was the last time she would ever speak to her Auntie Dot.

Dot Gallagher died one minute after midnight, her goal achieved. Despite the years of crippling pain and suffering, her indomitable spirit had kept her alive long enough to see the back of Margaret Thatcher.

The weather changed. The funeral was held on a bleak, cheerless November afternoon. The lads looked stunned, even though their mam had been on the verge of death for years – but this was no ordinary mam, this was Dot, interfering, opinionated, embarrassing, and much too loud. They were grown men in their forties and fifties, but almost to the end, their mam always had something to say, not always welcome, on almost every aspect of their daily lives. They had no idea how they would live without their best friend and closest confidante.

Mike Gallagher stood slightly apart, his body language such that no-one dared approach him. The effervescent young man with the long ginger curls whom Annie had seen in the Cavern, the man who'd married Sylvia, was no more. He had a new woman with him, as thin as a lath, with smooth black hair and a brittle face. Dot would never have taken to her. It was said the woman was an executive from an electronics firm that Michael Ray Security was about to take over.

Mike didn't come back to the house with the others and Annie didn't stay long. Dot would never have approved of such a miserable funeral. Perhaps, later, everyone would get drunk and sing her favourite songs. After a cup of tea, Annie approached Uncle Bert. 'I'll have to be going soon to catch the bus. Sara came over to look after Rob and Andy and she'll want to get home for Nigel's tea.' Daniel had the Mini. When she last heard, he was on his way to Dubrovnik. Although Euan had never said anything, she knew he hated the thought of her driving, particularly with the children. She apologised for his absence. 'He's in America for a month, on some sort of exchange visit with a university in Maine. He'll be back in December.'

Bert had aged a decade in the past week. Dot had been his wife for almost sixty years and his eyes were watery with grief. 'Just a minute, luv. There's something I want you to have.' Annie followed him into the front room, where he took a shoebox from under the bed. 'It's what Dot called her "things", just stuff she collected over the years. I can't bear to open it meself. The lads won't know what to do with it, and I don't fancy the wives rooting through. It probably just wants burning.'

'I'll see to it, Uncle Bert.'

He glanced at the bed, his old face bewildered. 'I can't get used to sleeping there without my Dot beside me.'

The box was falling to pieces and had been mended with Sellotape from time to time. Even that was coming off in places. According to the faded label at the end, the box had once contained 'Court Shoes, Black, size 6.' They'd cost seven and elevenpence halfpenny.

At first, it appeared to contain only papers. Dozens of letters from Bert to Dot posted during the war. Annie put them on the floor. She'd burn them later. There were postcards from all over the world, some dating back to the fifties. She found one she'd sent from the holiday camp in Pwllheli, one from her honeymoon with Lauri, cards from all the places where the Gallagher lads and various friends had gone on holiday over the years. She put them with the letters to burn.

Underneath the letters and the cards, she found the photo of her mam and dad's wedding, the pair of them looking so pleased with themselves, as if they shared a huge secret. 'Jaysus!' she muttered, and was about to rip it into shreds, when she remembered Daniel often asked about his grandparents. She'd show him what they looked like before Hitler put in an appearance and Johnny was killed.

A prayer book, well-used, the corners dog-eared; two pairs of rosary beads in worn leather purses. She used to love rosary beads when she was little, but although she still went to Mass, she hadn't said the rosary in years. Perhaps she could say one for Dot on Sunday.

Near the bottom of the box, she found a cameo brooch with the pin broken, and decided to get it fixed and wear it. There was more jewellery, none expensive; a few strings of beads and earrings. She'd give them to Yasmin and Ingrid next time they came to see the twins. They'd loved their Granny Gallagher.

Finally, she came to a brown paper bag with something flat inside. She pulled out the contents and found a Paisley scarf in her hand, a scarf identical to the one on the woman going into the pictures on a sunny December day a million years ago. What had the picture been? *The King and I*! She still hadn't seen it.

Annie sighed and thought of ringing Marie, but what did it matter after a million years? She took everything down to the compost heap at the bottom of the garden. It was bitterly cold and pitch dark, but the light from the lounge was enough to see by. She set fire to one letter, then another. The flames flickered eerily. One by one, she added the other letters and the cards. Finally, she put the scarf on top of the miniature inferno. The material melted to nothing in no time, and she thought she could see her mother's face in the red ash, which quickly turned grey, then black, until Annie could see nothing at all.

For a man of eighty-three, Bert Gallagher was in excellent health, but nine days after the death of his wife, he passed away peacefully in his sleep. There was no apparent cause, but everybody took it for granted that Bert had died of a broken heart.

That night, Annie telephoned Mike. His voice was stiff with grief and he sounded glad she'd rung. 'They won't talk to me, Annie,' he groaned. 'I found a note through the letterbox to say me dad was dead.'

Annie came straight to the point. 'I want you to do something, Mike. I want you to hold the usual dinner on Christmas Day.'

'But no-one will come, luv.' He was close to tears. 'No-one came near me at our mam's funeral.'

'Everyone was too scared. You looked very unapproachable. In fact,' she said bluntly, 'you've been unapproachable for a long while.'

'After Sylvia died, all I wanted to do was bury meself in work.'

'You shouldn't shut people out when they want to grieve with you,' she chided. 'The Gallaghers have always grieved together. If you hadn't cut yourself off, Dot wouldn't have got so worked up about you voting Tory.' He would just have been subjected to a non-stop earbashing.

'I suppose not,' he sighed. 'Mind you, Annie, a man's politics is his own affair.'

'I agree. Now about that dinner . . .'

'I'll do it, luv, though I can't see them being persuaded to come.'

'*I'll* persuade them,' she vowed. 'Every single Gallagher will be at your house on Christmas Day, or my name's not Annie Campbell.'

Mike actually chuckled. 'You sound just like our mam!'

Euan came home from America a week before Christmas. The tree stood in its old place in the corner, the lights reflected like little jewels in the dark windows behind. Number seven was sold, and Annie had brought the decorations down from the loft for the final time.

'Have you missed me?' he asked tenderly. The boys were clinging to his legs, demanding to be picked up. 'Not till I've kissed your mother,' he told them.

'Missed you!' Annie said shakily. 'It's been sheer torture.'

It was, as a character in Shakespeare said, the stuff that dreams are made of. A year after Paris, when Rob and Andy were three months old, Euan had arrived out of the blue. Sara, Nigel, and the children were out house-hunting, and the twins were taking their afternoon nap upstairs.

Annie had never ceased to think of Euan, to miss him, since their enchanted holiday, but had assumed she'd been right and things had seemed different in the cold light of Liverpool. Perhaps he'd taken her advice and found someone his own age. One glance at his thin dark face confirmed what she already knew. She loved him still. He was too young, she was too old, she didn't really know him all that well. Now there was something else, a family that he'd never wanted.

'Have you been ill?' was the first thing he said. 'You look much thinner and your face is pale.'

'I'm tired, that's all.' Annie already felt rejuvenated just seeing him. Quite unexpectedly, she felt a rush of desire and longed for him to take her in his arms.

'The last year's been hell,' he said slowly. 'Women haven't exactly jumped at me as you predicted, but I took out a few. I've just got back from Paris, but it was hopeless without you.' He looked at her defiantly. 'You were wrong, Annie, completely wrong. I wasn't fooling myself, I love you . . .' He paused, as if struggling for more words to emphasise the way he felt. Then he shrugged his shoulders and said simply, 'I love you and I want us to be married!'

'I know, luv.' Annie nodded. They were a mismatched pair, but so what? 'It's just that something's happened since Paris.'

'You've met someone else!' His face contorted with alarm.

'No, nothing like that.' She completely forgot that safe, comfortable Ben Wainwright was still waiting for an answer. 'It's . . .' At that moment, Rob set up a wail. She went upstairs without a word. How did you tell someone they'd acquired two sons since you last saw them?

She picked up Rob. 'You little tyrant,' she whispered. 'Look at your brother! There's not a word of complaint from him.' Andy was regarding her serenely whilst doing his utmost to kick away the blankets.

Suddenly, Euan was in the room, staring open-mouthed from one baby to the other, dazed incomprehension on his face. Andy gurgled in triumph when his legs broke free, and he regarded his toes with delight.

'I told you something had happened,' Annie said, hastily returning a still complaining Rob to his cot because Euan had burst into tears. She took him in her arms, feeling as if her heart was about to explode with happiness, and thanked her lucky stars that Binnie Appleby had decided not to go to Paris.

'Are you ready?' said Euan. 'The taxi will be here soon.'

'I think so.' She glanced round the lounge. The removal van had just left and their furniture was on its way to the big Victorian semi in Sefton Park in the road next to Sara and Nigel. The Gallagher lads would be arriving en masse tonight, including Mike, to help them get sorted. Annie had wheedled, bullied, yelled, and had managed to get the entire clan together on Christmas Day. 'Our mam will never be dead while you're alive, Annie,' Tommy said weakly. Cecy had flown over from Italy, and Marie and Justin had come. Only Daniel wasn't there, still wandering the face of the earth searching for a reason to be alive. The atmosphere had been frosty at first, but quickly mellowed, and the lads were again the best of friends. Of course it would never be like old times with Dot and Bert not there, but old times inevitably became new times. Mike had insisted Annie take Dot's place at the table.

'I'll keep an eye on the kids,' Euan said. 'Rob's upset because we can't take the willow tree.'

He blew a kiss and disappeared and Annie went upstairs. Much as she was looking forward to their spacious new house, it was a wrench leaving Heather Close, but she felt it was time to go.

The walls and carpets were full of pale patches where pictures used to hang and furniture had stood for nearly thirty years. She cleared her throat and the sound was ghostly in the empty rooms. She glanced briefly in Sara's room, Daniel's, then the bedroom she had shared with Lauri. Memories chased each other: Sylvia and Eric outside the bathroom at that Christmas party; Marie turning up when Lauri died; Lauri himself, so kind, so difficult – she was never quite sure whether they'd been mostly happy or not. Then there was the time Daniel left, when the house had seemed more like an enemy than a friend.

She sighed and returned downstairs, caressing briefly the smooth, cupola-shaped knob at the bottom, one of the first things she'd noticed when Lauri first brought her to the house. Through the front window, she saw a woman she didn't recognise coming out of number three. Apart from Mrs Vincent, there was hardly a soul in Heather Close she knew. She was the last of the original residents. Chris and Monica Andrews had moved to Crosby when Mrs Vincent refused to give them any peace.

The Close bristled with burglar alarms – no wonder Mike Gallagher had become a multi-millionaire. The red, blue, yellow boxes seemed to signal a warning, not just to prospective burglars, but to ordinary citizens, that the world was becoming a more evil and dangerous place. In fact now, at this very minute, in the first few days of 1991, Great Britain was poised on the brink of war in the Gulf. In a newspaper yesterday, it had been reported that eighteen-year-olds were to be mobilised ready for call-up. The report had later been denied on television as scaremongering, but she couldn't help but think that if Daniel was younger or Andy and Rob were older, they could be killed.

She rushed to the other end of the room to make sure the twins were safe. Ready for the journey in their anoraks, jeans and boots, they were dodging in and out of the willow tree. Euan was clapping his hands and they were singing, *Here we go round the mulberry bush, the mulberry bush, the mulberry bush. Here we go . . .*

It was a picture of pure innocence, the total opposite of what she'd just been thinking. Perhaps, in the end, Annie thought hopefully, innocence would prevail. She felt sure it was what most people wanted.

A horn sounded. Euan looked up and caught her eye. He signalled he was going round to the front. Annie watched as the deceptively fragile branches of the willow fell into place. They shuddered momentarily, then were still. She felt a lump in her throat; the tree was the hardest thing of all to leave.

She closed the front door for the final time. Euan was trying to persuade Rob and Andy into the taxi, but they refused until she came.

'Mummy!' they shouted together.

'Coming,' she called. Euan held out his hand and Annie thought she had never seen a sight more beautiful than her young, handsome husband waiting for her with their children.

Dancing in the Dark

For Yvette Goulden

Prologue

It always began with the sound of the footsteps, the soft, slithering footsteps on the stairs, the unshod feet in their well-darned socks lifting steadily from one step to the next. He wasn't the sort of man to wear slippers. Listening, I would picture him in my mind's eye, just his feet, coming up the narrow beige carpet with the red border, the cheapest you could buy, worn away to threads in the middle and secured to the stairs with triangular-shaped varnished rods that slid into bronze brackets at the side. I saw everything very, very clearly, in precise detail.

Even on the nights when there were no footsteps, I never went asleep before Mam came home from work at ten o'clock. Then I would feel relatively safe, but not completely. Mam had never been able to offer much protection. But even he must have realised that a child's screams at dead of night might have alerted someone; a neighbour, a passer-by.

I still dream about it frequently, always the footsteps, never the violence, the terror that was to come. Because in my dreams I am not there when he enters the room. My bed is empty. Yet I can see him, as though an invisible me is present, the tall figure of my father, an expression on his dark, handsome face and in his dark eyes that I could never quite fathom. Was it excitement? Anticipation? Behind the glitter of the main emotion, whatever it might have been, I sensed something else, mysterious, sad, as if deep within him he regretted what he was about to do. But he couldn't help it. The excitement, the anticipation, gripped him like a drug, stifling any other, kinder, feelings he might have had.

In my dream I would watch him slowly undo his belt buckle, hear its tiny click, the feathery smooth sound the leather made as he pulled it through the loops of his trousers until it dangled from his hand like a snake.

Then he would reach down to drag me out of bed, but this was a dream *and I wasn't there!*

Oh, the look on his face then! I savoured it. I felt triumphant.

At this point, I usually woke up bathed in perspiration, my heart beating fiercely, still triumphant, but at the same time slightly sick.

I'd escaped!

Sometimes, though, the dream continued, just as life had continued in the days when the dream wasn't a dream but real.

I knew that when he came back from the pub, always drunk, he would scratch around downstairs, poking here and there, in the dirty washing, through the toys, searching for something that would give him an excuse to

705

let rip with a thrashing. He liked to have an excuse. He'd find the mark of a felt-tipped pen on a tablecloth that Mam hadn't had time to wash, paint dropped on a frock at school, the arm off a doll, or toys not put away properly. Anything could trigger the sound of those slithering footsteps on the stairs.

There were other nights, the best ones, when he would fall asleep in the chair – according to Mam, he worked hard – or he might watch television. Looking back, my memory softened slightly by time, this probably happened more often than I used to think.

In the extended dream I still wasn't there, but now my little sister was in the other bed, and it was she who bore the brunt of our father's anger, or frustration, or excitement, or self-loathing, or whatever it was that made him want to beat the life out of his wife and children, so that his dark shadow lay heavily over our house, even when he wasn't there.

There would be no feeling of triumph when I woke up, just desolation and despair. Would the dreams never end? Would I ever forget? For the rest of my life, would I, Millie Cameron, never stop wishing that I was invisible?

Millie

1

The sun spilled under the curtains, seeping on to the polished window-sill like thick cream. The wine bottle that Trudy had painted and given me for Christmas dazzled, a brilliant flame of light.

Sunday!

I sat up and stretched my arms. I was free to do whatsoever I pleased. In the bed beside me, James grunted and turned over. I slid carefully from under the bedclothes so as not to disturb him, put on a towelling robe and went into the living room, closing the door quietly behind me.

With a sigh of satisfaction at the thought that it was all mine and mine alone, I surveyed the room, its dark pink walls and off-white upholstered sofa, old pine furniture and glass-shaded lamps. Then, I switched on the computer and the television and reversed the answering-machine. In the kitchen, I paused momentarily to admire the effect of the sun on the Aztec-patterned tiles before filling the kettle. Back in the living room, I opened the door to the balcony and stepped outside.

What a glorious day, unseasonably hot for late September. The roses bordering the communal garden were overblown red and yellow cabbages, the dew-drenched grass glistened like wet silk. In the furthest corner, the biggest tree had already begun to shed its tiny, almost white leaves, which scattered the lawn like snow.

I loved my flat, but the thing I loved most was the balcony. It was tiny, just big enough for two black wrought-iron chairs and a large plant-pot in between. I knew nothing about gardening and had been thrilled when the squiggly green things I'd been given last spring had turned out to be geraniums. I enjoyed sitting outside early in the morning with a cup of tea, savouring the salty Liverpool air; the River Mersey was less than a mile away. Occasionally, just before bed on warm evenings, I would sit with the light from the living room falling on to the darkness of the garden, reliving the day.

Most of the curtains in the three-storey block of flats that ran at right angles to my own were still drawn. I glanced at my watch – just gone seven. From the corner of my eye, I became aware of activity in a kitchen on the ground floor. The old lady who lived there was opening a window. I kept my head turned away. If she saw me looking she would wave, I would feel obliged to wave back, and one day I might find myself invited in for coffee,

707

which I would hate. I was glad I'd managed to get a top-floor corner flat. It meant I was cut off from the other residents.

The kettle clicked and I went to make the tea. There was a political programme on television, so I switched it off and turned up the sound on the answering-machine. I nearly turned it down again when I heard my mother's voice. A shadow fell over the day when I remembered it was the last Sunday of the month; my family would be expecting me for lunch.

'. . . this is the third time I've called, Millicent,' my mother was saying shrilly. 'Don't you ever listen to that machine of yours? Ring back straight away, there's bad news. And I don't see why I should always have to remind you about dinner . . .'

I groaned. I could tell from the tone of my mother's voice that the news wasn't seriously bad. Possibly Scotty had been on one of his regular sexual rampages and other dog owners had complained, or Declan, my brother, had lost his twentieth job.

Just as I was about to take my tea on to the balcony, the bedroom door opened and James came out. He wore a pair of dark blue boxer shorts and his straw blond hair was tousled. He grinned. 'Hi!'

'Hi, yourself.' I eyed his tanned body enviously and wished I could turn such a lovely golden brown in the sun.

'Been up long?'

'Fifteen, twenty minutes. It's a lovely day.'

'The best.' He enveloped me in his muscular arms and nuzzled my neck. 'Know what today is?'

'Sunday?'

'True, but it's also our anniversary. It's a year today since we met.' He kissed me softly on the lips. 'I went into a wine bar in Castle Street and there was this gorgeous leggy ash-blonde with the most amazing green eyes – who was that guy you were with? I knew him slightly – that's how I managed to get introduced.'

'I forget.' I felt uneasy. Remembering anniversaries seemed a sign of . . . well, that the relationship *meant* something, when we had always maintained stoutly that it didn't.

'Rodney!' he said triumphantly. 'Rod. I met him at a Young Conservatives' do.'

I moved out of his arms and went to the computer. 'I didn't think you were interested in politics.'

'I'm not, but Pa maintains it's good for business. He makes lots of useful contacts in the Party. Is there more tea?'

'The pot's full. Don't forget to put the cosy back on.'

He saluted. 'No, ma'am.'

When he came back, I was seated at my desk. He stood behind me, his arm resting lightly on my shoulder. 'This your report?'

'Uh-huh.' I pressed the mouse and the words rolled down the screen. I read them quickly. Despite night school and the subsequent A level in English, I worried that my terrible education might be obvious when I wrote at length. I hoped I hadn't split any infinitives or put an apostrophe in the wrong place.

'You've spelt "feasible" wrong,' James said. 'It's "-ible" not "-able".'

'I did that bit when I was tired. I probably wasn't thinking straight.' He'd gone to one of the best public schools in the country, followed by a good university.

'Shall we go somewhere special for lunch to celebrate? How about that new place in Formby?'

'Sorry, duty calls. Today I'm lunching with my parents.' I wished I had a more pleasant excuse.

'Of course, the last Sunday . . .' To my irritation, he knelt down and twisted the chair round until we were facing each other. 'When am I going to meet your folks?'

'What point is there in you meeting them?' I said coldly.

'You've met mine.'

'You invited me, I didn't ask.' I disliked going to see his family in the converted, centuries-old farmhouse in its own grounds three miles from Southport. I felt out of place, uncomfortably aware of the stark contrast between it and my own family's home on a council estate in Kirkby. His mother, with her expensive clothes and beautifully coiffured hair, was always patronising. His father was polite, but in the main ignored me. A business-man to the core, he spent most of the time on the phone or ensconced in his study plying fellow businessmen with drink. Phillip Atherton owned three garages on Merseyside, which sold high-class sports cars to 'fools who've got more money than sense', according to my own father. Atherton's rarely dealt in cars worth less than twenty thousand pounds. James was nominally in charge of the Southport garage, but his father kept a close eye on all three.

The phone went. James was still kneeling, his arms around my waist. After three rings, the answering-machine came on, with the sound still turned up. My mother again. 'Millicent. You've not been out all night, surely. Why don't you call back?'

James's eyes sparkled. 'Millicent! I thought it was Mildred.'

'I would have hated being Mildred even more.' I got up quickly to pick up the receiver. I didn't want him hearing any more of the whining voice with its strong, adenoidal Liverpool accent, one of the reasons I'd told my mother never to call me at the office. 'Hello, Mum.'

'There you are!' She sounded relieved. 'Can we expect to see you today?'

'Of course.'

'Sometimes I worry you'll forget.'

I rolled my eyes. 'As if!'

'Don't be sarcastic, Millicent. After all, it's only once a month you visit. You'd never think you only lived a few miles away in Blundellsands. Mrs Mole's Sybil comes every week from Manchester to see her mam.'

'Perhaps Mrs Mole's Sybil's got nothing else to do.'

'You might like to know she's got two kids and a husband.' There was a pause. 'You've become awfully hard, luv.'

'Don't be silly, Mum.' With an effort, I made my voice softer. Mum set great store by the regular family gatherings now that only Declan was left at home. 'What's the bad news?' I enquired.

'Eh? Oh, I nearly forgot. Your auntie Flo's dead. The poor old soul was knocked down by a car or something. But the thing is, luv,' her voice throbbed with indignation, 'she was already six feet under by the time some woman rang to let your gran know.'

'Why should Gran care? She had nothing to do with Flo.' Auntie Flo had, in fact, been a great-aunt, and the black sheep of the family, I had no idea why. Gran never mentioned her name. It was only when Auntie Sally had died ten years ago that I first set eyes on Flo, at the funeral. She was the youngest of the three Clancy sisters, then in her sixties, had never married, and seemed to me an exceptionally mild old woman.

'Blood's thicker than water,' my mother said meaninglessly.

'What did Auntie Flo do that was so awful?' I asked curiously.

'I think there was a row, but I've no idea what it was about. Your gran would never talk about it.'

I was about to ring off, when Mum said, 'Have you been to Mass?'

To save an argument, I told her I was going to the eleven o'clock. I had no intention of going to Mass.

I replaced the receiver and looked at James. There was a strange, intense expression in his light blue eyes, and I realised he'd been watching me like that throughout the entire conversation with my mother. 'You're very beautiful,' he said.

'You're not so bad yourself.' I tried to sound jokey. Something about his expression disturbed me.

'You know, marriage isn't such a bad thing.'

Alarm bells sounded in my head. Was this a roundabout way of proposing? 'That's not what you've said before.'

'I've changed my mind.'

'Well, I haven't.' He came towards me, but I avoided him by going on to the balcony. 'I've tried it before, remember?'

James was standing just inside the window. 'You didn't keep his name. Were things really so awful?'

'I didn't want his name once we were no longer a couple. And it wasn't awful with Gary, just deadly dull.'

'It wouldn't be dull with me.'

So it *was* a proposal. I stuffed my hands in my dressing-gown pockets to hide my agitation and sat down. Why did he have to spoil things? We'd made it plain to each other from the start that there was to be no commitment. I liked him – no, more than that, I was very fond of him. He was good to be with, extraordinarily handsome in a rugged open-air way. We got on famously, always had loads to talk about, and were great together in bed. But I didn't want to spend the rest of my life with him or with anybody else. I'd struggled hard to get where I was and wanted to get further, without having a husband questioning my every decision, interfering.

I remembered Gary's astonishment when I said I wanted to take an A level. We'd been married two years. 'What on earth d'you want that for?' I recalled his round pleasant face, his round moist eyes. We'd first gone out together at school and had married at eighteen. I'd realised, far too late, that he'd been my escape route from home.

Why did I want an A level? Perhaps to prove to myself that I wasn't as stupid as my teachers had claimed, for self-respect, to gain the enjoyment from books that I'd only briefly experienced before my father had put a brutal stop to it.

'I'd like to get a better job,' is what I said to Gary. I was bored rigid working at Peterssen's packing chocolates. 'I'd like to learn to type as well, use a computer.'

Gary had laughed. 'What good will all that stuff be when we have kids?'

We were living in Kirkby with his widowed mother, not far from my parents. Although we'd put our name down for a council house, one would not be forthcoming until we had a family – not just one child but two or three. I visualised the future, trailing to the shops with a baby, more kids hanging on to the pram, getting a part-time job in another factory because Gary's wages as a storeman would never be enough to live on. It was why we'd never even considered buying a place of our own.

Two years later we were divorced. A bewildered Gary wanted to know what he'd done wrong. 'Nothing,' I told him. I regretted hurting him, but he was devoid of ambition, content to spend the rest of his life in a dead-end job wondering where the next penny would come from.

My father was disgusted, my mother horrified: a Catholic, getting divorced! Even so, Mum did her utmost to persuade me to come back home. My younger sister, Trudy, had found her own escape route via Colin Daley and had also married at eighteen, though Colin had been a better bet than Gary. After ten years they were still happily together.

Wild horses couldn't have dragged me back to Kirkby and my family. Instead, I rented a bedsit. I had my English A level by then, and until I bought my flat, nothing in life had given me more pleasure than the certificate to say I'd achieved a grade C. Armed with a dictionary, I'd *made* myself read the books I'd been set, struggled for hours to understand them in the bedroom at my mother-in-law's, while downstairs Gary watched football and game-shows on television. It seemed no time before the words started to make sense, as if I'd always known them, as if they'd been stored in my head waiting to be used. I shall never forget the day I finished reading *Pride and Prejudice*. I'd understood it. I'd enjoyed it. It was like discovering you could sing or play the piano.

Once settled in the bedsit, I took courses in typing and computing at night school, left Peterssen's, and began to wonder if it had all been worth it as I drifted from one dead-end office job to another – until three years ago, when I became a receptionist/typist with Stock Masterton, an estate agent's in the city centre. Of course, I had to tell George Masterton I'd worked in a factory until I was twenty-four, but he had been impressed. 'Ah, a self-made woman. I like that.'

George and I hit it off immediately. I was promoted to 'property nego-tiator'. Me! Now George was contemplating opening a branch in Woolton, a relatively middle-class area of Liverpool, and I was determined to be appointed manager, which was why I was writing the report. I'd driven round Woolton, taking in the number of superior properties, the roads of substantial semi-detacheds, the terraced period cottages that could be hyped and sold for a bomb. I'd noted how often the buses ran to town, listed the schools, the supermarkets . . . The report would help George make up his mind and show him how keen I was to have the job.

It was through Stock Masterton that I'd found my flat. The builders had gone bankrupt and the units were being sold for a song, which was unfair on the people already there who'd paid thousands more but the bank wanted its money and wasn't prepared to wait.

'I've not done bad for someone not quite thirty,' I murmured to myself. 'I've got my own place, a job with prospects and a car. I earn twice as much as Gary.'

No, I'd not done badly at all.

Yet I wasn't happy.

I leaned on the iron rail and rested my chin on my arms. Somewhere deep within I felt a deadness, and I wondered if I would ever be happy. There were times when I felt like a skater going across the thinnest of ice. It was bound to crack some time, and I would disappear for ever into the freezing, murky water beneath. I shook myself. It was too lovely a morning for such morbid thoughts.

I'd forgotten about James. He appeared on the balcony tucking a black shirt into his jeans. Even in casual clothes, he always looked crisp, neat, tidy. I turned away when he fastened the buckle of his wide leather belt.

He frowned. 'What's the matter?'

'Nothing. Why?'

'You shuddered. Have you gone off me all of a sudden?'

'Don't be silly!' I laughed.

James sat in the other chair. I swung up my bare feet so they rested between his legs and wriggled my toes.

'Cor!' he gasped.

'Don't look like that. People will realise what I'm doing.'

'Would you like to do it inside where no one can see?'

'In a minute. I want to take a shower.'

He smacked his lips. 'I'll take it with you.'

'You've just got dressed!'

'I can get undressed pretty damn quick.' He looked at me quizzically. 'Does this mean I'm forgiven?'

'For what?' I was being deliberately vague.

'For proposing. I'd forgotten you modern women take an offer of marriage as an insult.' He took my feet in his hands. I was conscious of how large and warm and comforting they felt. 'As an alternative, how about if I moved in with you?'

I tried to pull away my feet, but he held them firmly. 'The flat's only small,' I muttered. 'There's only one bedroom.'

'I wasn't contemplating occupying the other if there were two.'

No! I valued my privacy as much as my independence. I didn't want someone suggesting it was time I went to bed or asking why I was late home – and did I really want the living room painted such a dark pink? I wished I could start the day again and stop him proposing. I had been quite enjoying things as they were.

James put my feet down carefully on the balcony floor. 'Between us we could get somewhere bigger.'

'You've changed the rules,' I said.

He sighed. 'I know, but it's not the rules that have changed, it's me. I think

I'm in love with you, Millie Cameron. In fact, I know I am.' He tried to catch my eyes. 'I take it the feeling isn't reciprocated?'

I bit my lip and shook my head. James turned away and I contemplated his perfect profile: straight nose, broad mouth, pale, stubby lashes. His hair lay in a flattering corn-coloured quiff on his broad, tanned forehead. He didn't look as if it was the end of the world that I'd turned him down. According to his mother, who never failed to mention it, there'd been an army of girls before me. How many had he fallen in love with? On reflection, I didn't know him all that well. True, we talked a lot, but never about anything serious; the conversation rarely strayed from films, plays, mutual acquaintances and clothes. Oh, and football. I sensed he was shallow and also rather weak, always anxious still to do his father's bidding, even though he, too, was twenty-nine. I felt irritated again that he'd spoiled things: I didn't want to give him up. Nor did I want to hurt him, but I couldn't be expected to fall in love with him just because he had decided he was in love with me.

'Perhaps we can talk about it some other time?' I ventured. In a year, two years, ten.

He closed his eyes briefly and gave a sigh of relief. 'I was worried you might dump me.'

'I wouldn't dream of it!' I jumped to my feet and ran inside. James followed. Outside the bathroom, I removed my dressing-gown and posed tauntingly before opening the door and going in. I stepped into the shower and turned on the water. It felt freezing . . . but it had warmed up nicely by the time James drew the curtain back and joined me.

2

'Hello, luv. You look pale.'

'Hi, Mum.' I made a kissing noise two inches from my mother's plump, sagging cheek. Whenever I turned up in Kirkby, she claimed I looked pale or tired or on the verge of coming down with something.

'Say hello to your dad. He's in the garden with his tomaters.'

My father – I couldn't even *think* of him as Dad – had always been a keen if unimaginative gardener. Dutifully, I opened the kitchen door and called, 'Hello.'

The greenhouse was just beyond the neat lawn, the door open. 'Hello there, luv.' My father was inside, a cigarette hanging from his bottom lip. His dark, sombre expression brightened at the sound of my voice. He threw away the cigarette, wiped his hands on the hips of his trousers and came inside. 'How's the estate-agency business?'

'Okay.' I managed to keep the loathing out of my voice. He told everyone I was a property negotiator. Nowadays he claimed to be proud of his girls. 'Where's Declan?'

'Gone to the pub.' Mum couldn't have looked more harassed if she had been preparing a meal for royalty. She took a casserole out of the oven, then put it back. 'What have I done with the spuds? Oh, I know, they're in the top oven. Declan's promised to be back by one.'

'Will the grub be ready on time, luv?'

'Yes, Norman. Oh, yes.' Mum jumped at her husband's apparently mild question, though it was years since he'd beaten her. 'It'll be ready the minute our Trudy and Declan come.'

'Good. I'll have another ciggie while I'm waiting.' He disappeared into the lounge.

'Why don't you have a talk with your dad and I'll get on with this?' Mum said, as she stirred something in a pan.

As if I would! She'd always tried to pretend we were a perfectly normal family. 'I'd sooner stay and talk to you.'

She flushed with pleasure. 'What have you been up to lately?'

I shrugged. 'Nothing much. Went to a club last night, the theatre on Wednesday. I'm going out to dinner tonight.'

'With that James chap?'

'Yes,' I said shortly. I regretted telling them about James. It was when Declan had jokingly remarked he was thinking of trading in his bike for a Ferrari that I'd told him about Atherton Cars where several could be had. The following Sunday, my father had driven over to Southport to take a look and I was terrified that one day he'd introduce himself to James.

Mum was poised anxiously over the ancient cooker, which had been there when we moved into the council house in 1969. I was three and Trudy just a baby; Declan and Alison had yet to arrive. These days, Mum wasn't just stout but shapelessly stout. Her shabby skirt, with no waist to fix on, was down at the front and up at the rear, revealing the backs of her surprisingly well-shaped but heavily veined legs. I always thought it would have been better if they had grown fat with the rest of her. As it was, she looked like some sort of strange insect: a huge, round body stuck on pins. Her worried, good-natured face was colourless, her skin the texture of putty. The once beautiful hair, the same ash-blonde as her children's, she cut herself with no regard for fashion. She wore no makeup, hadn't for years, as if she was going out of her way to make herself unattractive, or perhaps she just didn't care any more. She was fifty-five but looked ten years older.

Yet she'd been so lovely! I recalled the wedding photo on the mantelpiece in the lounge, the bride tall, willowy and girlish, the fitted lace dress clinging to her slim, perfect figure, though her face was wistful, rather sad, as if she'd been able to see into the future and knew what fate had in store for her. Her hair was long and straight, gleaming in the sunshine of her wedding day, turning under slightly at the ends as mine and Trudy's did. Declan and Alison had curly hair. None of us had taken after our father, with his swarthy good looks and bitter chocolate eyes. Perhaps that's why he'd never liked us much; four children and not one in his image.

The back door opened and my brother came in. 'Hi, Sis. Long time no see.' He aimed a pretend punch at my stomach and I aimed one back. 'That's a nice frock. Dark colours suit you.' He fingered the material. 'What would you call that green?'

Declan had always been interested in his sisters' clothes, which infuriated our father who called him a cissy, and had done his brutal best to make a man out of him.

'Olive, I think. It was terribly cheap.'

' "It was terribly cheap!" ' Declan repeated, with an impish grin. 'You don't half talk posh these days, Mill. I'd be ashamed to take you to the pub.'

A shout came from the lounge. 'Is that you, Declan?'

'Yes, Dad.'

'You're only just in time,' the voice said pointedly.

Declan winked at me. He was twenty, a tall, lanky boy with a sensitive face and an infectious smile, always cheerful. He was currently working as a labourer on a demolition site, which seemed an entirely unsuitable job for someone who looked as if a feather would knock him down. I often wondered why he still lived at home and assumed it was for Mum's sake. He shouted, 'Scotty met this smashing bitch. I had a job getting him home. I forgot to take his lead.'

'Where is Scotty?'

'In the garden.'

I went outside to say hello to the little black dog that vaguely resembled a Scotch terrier. 'You're an oversexed ruffian.' I laughed as the rough hairy body bounced up and down to greet me.

A car stopped outside, and seconds later two small children came hurtling down the side of the house. I picked up Scotty and held him like a shield as Melanie and Jake launched themselves at me.

'Leave your aunt Millie alone!' Trudy shouted. 'I've told you before, she doesn't like kids.' She beamed. 'Hi, Sis. I've painted you another bottle.'

'Hi, Trude. I'd love another bottle. Hello, Colin.'

Colin Daley was a stocky, quiet man, who worked long into the night six days a week in his one-man engineering company. He was doing well: he and Trudy had already sold their first house and bought a bigger one in Orrell Park. I sensed he didn't like me much. He'd got on well with Gary and perhaps he thought I neglected my family, left too much to Trudy. During the week, she often came over to Kirkby with the children. He nodded in my direction. 'Hello, there.'

'Do you really not like kids?' Jake enquired gravely. He was six, two years older than his sister, a happy little boy with Colin's blue eyes. Both Trudy's children were happy – she'd made sure of that.

'I like you two,' I lied. As kids went they weren't bad, but talking to them got on my nerves. I hugged Scotty, who was licking my ear. I would have had a dog of my own if I hadn't spent so much time at work.

Jake looked at me doubtfully. 'Honest?'

'Cross my heart.'

We all went indoors. Mum shrieked, 'C'mon, you little rascals, and give your gran a hug.' The children allowed themselves to be kissed, then they cried, 'Where's Grandad?'

'In the lounge.'

Mum looked wistful as Melanie and Jake whooped their way into the other room. She said, 'They've got a thing about their grandad.'

'I know.' It was strange that Trudy's children adored the man who'd once nearly killed their mother. She still bore a scar from his belt buckle above her left eyebrow.

When I went in Trudy was standing in the lounge, hovering near her children who were sitting on their grandad's knee. I noticed her eyes flicker to the big hands, one resting on each child's waist. We looked at each other in mutual understanding.

As usual, the meal was revolting. The mound of mashed potatoes, watery cabbage and stewing steak on my plate made me feel nauseous. 'I'll never eat all this, Mum,' I protested. 'I asked you not to give me much.'

'You look as if you need a decent meal, luv. There's a nice apple charlotte for afters.'

'It's a sin to waste good food,' my father said jovially.

I caught Trudy's eye and Declan hid a grin. The final Sunday of the month was a day for catching eyes and making faces. Odd phrases brought back bitter memories: 'It's a sin to waste good food,' was not said so lightly in those days.

On the surface, it was a civilised gathering, occasionally merry, a family united for Sunday lunch, except for Alison, of course. But I always felt on tenterhooks, as if I were watching someone blowing up a balloon, bigger and bigger until it was about to burst. Perhaps it was just me. Perhaps no one else remembered how Colin detested his father-in-law, how nervous Mum was, what Sunday dinner used to be like when we were little. Even now, I was still terrified that I would drop food on the tablecloth and that a nicotine-stained hand would reach across and slap my face, so hard that tears would come to my eyes, even though I'd sworn at an early age never to let him see me cry.

The conversation had turned to Auntie Flo. 'We were friendly for a while before I married your dad,' Mum said. 'I went to her flat in Toxteth a few times, though your gran never knew.' She turned to me. 'Actually, Millicent, that's where you come in.'

'What's Auntie Flo got to do with me?'

'Your gran wants her place cleared before the rent runs out, otherwise the landlord might chuck everything away.'

'Why ask me?' I could think of few less welcome things to do than clear out the belongings of an old lady I hadn't known. 'Why not you or Gran or Trudy? What about that woman you mentioned, the one who rang?'

Mum looked hurt. 'It's not much to ask, luv. I can't do it because . . .' she paused uncomfortably '. . . well, your dad's not very keen on the idea. Gran's too upset, she's taken Flo's death hard. Anyroad, she never goes out nowadays.'

'And Trudy's already got enough to do,' Colin growled.

'As for the woman who rang, she's just someone who lives upstairs. We don't want a stranger going through Auntie Flo's precious things, do we?'

'What precious things?' I noticed my father's fists clench. I reminded myself that he could do nothing to me now. I could say what I liked. 'I don't know what she did for a living, but I can't imagine Auntie Flo having acquired many precious things.'

'She worked in a launderette till she retired.' For a moment, Mum looked nonplussed. Then she went on eagerly, 'But there'll be papers, luv, letters perhaps, odds and ends of jewellery your gran would like. The clothes can go to one of those charity shops, Oxfam. I'm sure you'll find someone to take the furniture, and if there's anything nice, I wouldn't mind it meself. Declan knows a lad who has a van.'

I tried to think of a way of getting out of it. My mother was looking at me pleadingly, her pasty face slightly moist. *She* would probably thoroughly enjoy going through the flat, but Dad had put his foot down for some reason, not that he'd ever needed a reason in the past. The mere fact that Mum *wanted* to do something was enough. Maybe I could get it done in a few hours if I went armed with several cardboard boxes. I had one last try. 'I've always avoided Toxteth like the plague. It's full of drugs and crime. People get murdered there, shot.'

Mum looked concerned. 'Oh, well, if that's—' she began, but my father butted in, 'Your auntie Flo lived there for over fifty years without coming to any harm.'

It seemed I had no choice. 'Oh, all right,' I said reluctantly. 'When's the rent due?'

'I've no idea.' Mum looked relieved. 'The woman upstairs will know. Mrs Smith, her name is, Charmian Smith.'

'Don't forget to give me the address before I go.'

'I won't, luv. I'll ring and tell Gran later. She'll be pleased.'

After the meal was over and the dishes washed, Trudy produced the bottle she'd painted for me. It was exquisite, an empty wine bottle transformed into a work of art. The glass was covered with roses and dark green leaves edged with gold.

'It's beautiful!' I breathed, holding it up to the light. 'I'm not sure where to put it. The other one's in the bedroom.'

'I'll do you another,' Trudy offered. 'I'm running out of people to give them to.'

'I suggested she have a stall in a craft market,' Colin said proudly. 'I could look after the kids if it was a Sunday.'

I waved the bottle in support. 'That's a great idea, Trude. You'd pay ten pounds for this in a shop.'

'Millicent.' Mum came sidling up. 'Have you got much to do this afternoon?'

I was immediately wary. 'I'm in the middle of a report.'

'It's just I'd like to go and see Alison.'

'Can't you go yourself?' The only reason she'd learned to drive was so she could visit Alison in the home.

'There's something wrong with the car. Your dad promised to get it fixed but he never got round to it.'

He'd probably not got round to it deliberately. He would prefer to think his youngest child didn't exist. 'Sorry, Mum. As I said, I've got this report to write.'

'We'll take you, luv.' Colin must have overheard. 'It's a couple of weeks since we saw Alison.'

Mum looked grateful. 'That's nice of you, Colin, but there's nothing for Melanie and Jake to do. They get fed up within the first five minutes.'

'You can leave the kids here with me,' my father offered.

'No, thanks,' Trudy said, much too quickly.

'I'll take them for a walk once we get there, and you and Trudy can stay with Alison,' Colin said.

In the midst of this discussion, I went upstairs to the lavatory. The bathroom, like everywhere else in the house, reeked of poverty, the linoleum cracked and crumbling, the plastic curtains faded. I was well into my teens before I discovered we were relatively well-off – or should have been. My father's wages as a toolmaker were high, but the family saw little of the money. He'd been a betting man all his life and a consistent loser.

As usual, I couldn't wait to be back in my own place. I felt guilty for refusing to visit Alison, pity for my mother, angry that the pity made me turn up for the monthly get-togethers then guilty again, knowing that I would get out of coming if I could. When Stock Masterton had begun to open on Sundays, I'd hoped that would provide a good excuse, but George, a workaholic, insisted on looking after the office himself with the help of a part-timer.

After saying goodbye, I went outside to the car. Several boys were playing football in the road, and someone had written 'Fuck off' in black felt pen on the side of my yellow Polo. I was rubbing it off with my handkerchief when Trudy came out with the children. She ushered them into the back of the family's old Sierra and came over to me. 'Thank the Lord that's over for another month.'

'You can say that again!'

'I can't get me head round this kindly old grandfather shit.' Absent-mindedly she rubbed the scar over her left eyebrow.

'I suppose we should be thankful for small mercies.'

Trudy regarded me keenly. 'You okay, Sis? You look a bit pale.'

'Mum said that. I'm fine, been working hard, that's all.' I eyed the car. I'd got most of it off and what was left wasn't legible. 'Look, Sis, I'm sorry about Alison,' I said in a rush, 'but I really have got work to do.'

Trudy pressed my arm. She glanced at the house where we'd grown up. 'I feel as if I'd like to drive away and never have to see another member of me family again, but we're trapped, aren't we? I don't know if I could bear it without Colin.'

As I started the car, I noticed that the house opposite had been boarded up, although children had broken down the door and were playing in the hallway. There was a rusty car without wheels in the front garden. As I drove away, the sun seemed to darken, although there wasn't a cloud to be seen. Unexpectedly, I felt overwhelmed by a sense of alienation. Where do I belong? I wondered, frightened. Not here, please not here! Yet I'd been born in a tower block less than a mile from this spot, where nowadays Gran lived like a prisoner: Martha Colquitt rarely left home since she'd been mugged for her pension five years ago. My own flat in Blundellsands was a pretence, more like a stage set than a proper home, and I was a fake. I couldn't understand what James saw in me, or why George Masterton was my friend. I was putting on an act, I wasn't real.

And what would James think if he met my slovenly mother and chain-smoking father, and if I told him about my brutal childhood? What would he say if he knew I had a sister with severe learning difficulties who'd been in a home since she was three, safely out of my father's way? A scene flashed through my mind, of my father slapping Alison, knocking her pretty little face first one way then the other, trying to make her stop saying that same word over and over again. 'Slippers,' Alison would mutter, in her dull monotone. 'Slippers, slippers, slippers.' She said it still, when agitated, although she was seventeen now.

Even if I were in love with James, we could never marry, not with all the family baggage I had in tow. I reminded myself that I didn't want to get married again, that I wasn't capable of falling in love. I belonged nowhere and to nobody.

Nevertheless, I had an urgent desire to see James. He was calling for me at seven. I looked forward to losing myself in empty talk, good food, wine. He would bring me home and we would make love and all that business with my family would be forgotten, until the time came for me to go again. Except, that is, for the dreams, from which I would never escape.

3

It wasn't until Thursday that I managed to get to Toxteth. James had tickets for a jazz concert at the Philharmonic Hall on Monday night, which I had forgotten about. Tuesday, I'd promised to go to dinner with Diana Riddick, a colleague from the office whom I'd never particularly got on with, but then few people did. Diana was thirty-five, single, and lived with her elderly father, who was a 'pain', she claimed, particularly now that his health was failing. She was a small, slight woman, permanently discontented, with a garishly painted face, a degree in land and property management, and an eye on the position of manager of the Woolton office. She didn't realise that I nursed the same ambition and when we were alone together she openly discussed it. I'd suspected she had an ulterior motive in inviting me that evening and it turned out she wanted to pump me about George's plans.

'Has he ever talked to you about it?' she asked, over the Italian meal. There were red and white gingham cloths on the tables and candles in green bottles dripping wax. The walls were hung with plastic vines.

'Hardly ever,' I replied truthfully.

'I bet you anything he gives the job to Oliver.' She pouted. Oliver Brett, solid and dependable, was the assistant manager, in charge when George was away, which was rare.

'I doubt it. Oliver's nice, but he's proved more than once he couldn't handle the responsibility.' I sipped my wine. On nights like this, Kirkby seemed a million miles away. 'Remember last Christmas when he rang George in the Seychelles to ask his advice?'

'Hmm!' Diana looked dubious. 'Yes, but he's a man. The world is prejudiced in favour of men. I shall be very cross if it's Tweedledum or Tweedledee.'

'That's most unlikely.' I laughed. Apart from June, who'd taken my old job as receptionist, the only other permanent members of staff were two young men in their mid-twenties, Darren and Elliot, startlingly alike in looks and manner, which accounted for their nicknames. Both were too immature for promotion. 'George has never struck me as being prejudiced against women,' I added.

'I might do a survey of Woolton, see how the land lies.' Diana's rather heavy eyebrows drew together in a frown and the discontented lines between her eyes deepened further. 'I'll type up some notes for George.'

'What a good idea,' I murmured. I hadn't added to my own report since last week.

It was late on Wednesday when I returned to the office in Castle Street. I'd taken a couple, the Naughtons, to see a property in Lydiate. It was the sixth house they'd viewed. As usual, they walked round several times, wondering aloud whether their present furniture would fit, asking if I would measure the windows so they could check if the curtains they had now would do. George insisted that keys were returned, no matter how late, and it was almost eight when I hung them on the rack. George was still working in his glass-partitioned office and Oliver was about to go home. His good-natured face creased into a smile as he said, 'Goodnight.'

I was wondering if there was time to drive to Blundellsands, collect the cardboard boxes I'd acquired from a supermarket, return to town and start on Auntie Flo's flat. I couldn't bring the car to work with boxes on the back seat when I had to take clients to view.

Before I'd made up my mind George came out of his cubicle. 'Millie! Please say you're not doing anything special tonight. I'm longing for a drink and desperately in need of company.'

'I'm not, doing anything special that is.' I would have said the same whatever the case. At the moment it was essential to keep in George's good books.

We went to a wine bar, the one where I'd met James. George ordered a roast-beef sandwich and a bottle of Chablis. I refused anything to eat 'You should get some food down you.' He patted my hand in a fatherly way. 'You look pale.'

'That's what everyone keeps telling me. I'll wear blusher tomorrow.'

'You mean rouge. My old mother used to go to town with the rouge.' His mother had died only a year ago and he missed her badly, just as he missed the children his ex-wife and her new husband had taken to live in France. He was alone, hated it, and buried himself in work to compensate. George Masterton was fifty, tall and thin to the point of emaciation although he ate like a horse. He wore expensive suits that hung badly from his narrow, stooped shoulders. Despite this, he had an air of drooping elegance, enhanced by his deceptively laid-back, languid manner. Only those who knew him well were aware that behind the lazy charm George was an irascible, unpredictable man, who suffered from severe bouts of depression and panic attacks.

'Why the desperate need for company?' I asked lightly. I always felt at my oddest with George, as if one day he would see what a fake I was, and never speak to me again.

'Oh, I dunno.' He shrugged. 'It was Annabel's birthday on Monday. She was sixteen. Thought about whizzing over to France on Eurostar but told myself Stock Masterton would collapse without me. Really, I was scared I wouldn't be welcome. I'm supposed to be having her and Bill for Christmas, but I shan't be at all surprised if they don't come.'

It was my turn to pat his hand. 'I bet Annabel would have been thrilled to see you. As for Christmas, it's months off. Try not to start worrying yet.'

'Families, eh!' He chuckled. 'They're a pain in the arse when you've got them, and a pain when they're not there. Diana calls her old dad everything but now he's ill she's terrified he'll die. Poor chap, it sounds like cancer. Anyway, how's your lot over in Kirkby?'

'Same as usual.' I told him about Auntie Flo's flat, and he said to bring the boxes in tomorrow and put them in the stationery cupboard until I found time to go. He asked where the flat was.

'Toxteth, William Square. I don't know round there all that well.'

His sandwich arrived. Between mouthfuls, he explained that William Square had once been very beautiful. 'They're five-storeyed properties, including the basement where the skivvies used to work. Lovely stately houses, massive pillars, intricate wrought-iron balconies like bloody lace, bay windows at least twelve feet high. It's where the nobs used to live at the turn of the century, though it's gone seriously downhill since the war.' He paused over the last of the sandwich. 'Sure you'll be safe? Wasn't there a chap shot in that area a few weeks ago?'

'I'll go in daylight. Trouble is, finding the time. Things keep coming up.'

George grinned. 'Such as me demanding your company! Sorry about that. Look, take tomorrow afternoon off. I'd feel happier about you going then. Don't forget to take your mobile and you can call for help if you get in trouble.'

'For goodness sake, George, you'd think I was going to a war zone!'

'Toxteth's been compared to one before now. As far as I'm concerned, it's as bad as Bosnia used to be.'

At two o'clock on a brilliantly sunny afternoon, William Square still looked beautiful when I drove in. I found an empty parking space some distance past the house I wanted, number one, and sat in the car for several minutes, taking in the big, gracious houses on all four sides. On close inspection, they appeared anything but beautiful. The elaborate stucco decorating the fronts had dropped off leaving bare patches like sores. Most of the front doors were a mass of peeling paint, and some houses were without a knocker, the letterbox a gaping hole. Several windows were broken and had been repaired with cardboard.

The big oblong garden in the centre of the square was now, according to George, maintained by the council. Evergreen trees with thick rubbery leaves were clumped densely behind high black railings. I thought it gloomy, and the square depressed me.

With a sigh, I got out of the car, collected some boxes and trudged along to number one. Two small boys, playing cricket on the pavement, watched me curiously.

The house looked clean, but shabby. Someone had brushed the wide steps leading up to the front door recently. There was a row of four buzzers with a name beside each, so faded they were unreadable. I ignored these and used the knocker – Charmian Smith lived on the ground floor.

A few seconds later the door was opened by a statuesque black woman not much older than me, wearing a lime green T-shirt and a wrap-round skirt patterned with tropical fruit. Her midriff was bare, revealing satin smooth skin. She held a baby in one arm. Two small children, a boy and a girl, stood either side of her, clutching her skirt. They stared at me shyly, and the little girl began audibly to suck her thumb.

'Mrs Smith?'

'Yes?' The woman regarded me aggressively.

'I've come for the key to Flo Clancy's flat.'

Her expression changed. 'I thought you were selling something! I should have known from the boxes. Not only that, you're awful like Flo. Come in, luv, and I'll get the key.'

The magnificent hallway had a black-and-white mosaic tiled floor and a broad, sweeping staircase with an intricately carved balustrade. The ornate ceiling was at least fourteen feet high. But whatever grand effect the architect had planned was spoilt by crumbling plaster on the coving and cornices, hanging cobwebs and bare wooden stairs worn to a curve. Several sections of balustrade were missing.

I stayed in the hall when Charmian Smith went into the ground-floor room, the children still clinging to her skirt. Through the open door, I could see that her flat was comfortably furnished, the walls covered with maroon flock paper. Everywhere was very clean, even the massive bay window, which must have taken hours to polish.

'Here you are, girl.'

'Thanks.' I took the proffered key and wondered if the children stayed attached to their mother like that all day. 'Which floor is it?'

'Basement. Give us a shout if you need anything.'

'Thanks.' I returned outside. The basement was situated behind railings down a narrow well of steep concrete steps. Little light reached the small window. I struggled down with the boxes to a tiny area full of old chip papers and other debris. To my consternation, there were several used condoms. I wondered what on earth I'd let myself in for.

A plastic mac and an umbrella were hanging from a hook inside the tiny lobby, and a brass horseshoe was attached to the inner door, which opened when I turned the knob.

The first thing I noticed when I stepped inside was the smell of musty dampness, and the cold, which made me shiver. Although it was broad daylight, I could see nothing. I fumbled for a light switch just inside the door and turned it on. My heart sank. The room was crammed with furniture, and every surface was equally crammed with ornaments. There were two side-boards, one very old and huge, six feet high at least, with little cupboards in the upper half. The other was more modern, but still large. Beneath the window was a chest covered with a red fringed shawl and a pretty lace cloth. On top of that a vase stood filled with silk flowers; poppies. I touched them. The effect was striking, as if they'd been bought to echo the colour of the shawl. It was the sort of thing I might have done myself.

I walked slowly down the room, which ran the length of the house. Halfway along, two massive beams had been built into the walls to support an equally massive lintel, all painted black, and covered with little brass plaques. An elderly gas fire was fitted in the green-tiled fireplace, and on each side of it, more cupboards reached to the ceiling, one of which I opened. Every shelf was stuffed to capacity: clothes, crockery, books, bedding, more ornaments stored in boxes . . .

'I can't do this all on my own,' I said aloud. I had no idea where to start, and I would need more like a hundred cardboard boxes than ten.

A window at the far end overlooked a tiny yard, which was level with the rear of the flat. It contained a wooden bench, a table and plant-holders full of limp pansies. The wall had been painted almost the same pink as my lounge – another indication that Auntie Flo and I had shared similar taste. The woman upstairs had said I was like Flo, and I wondered if there was a photograph somewhere.

I turned and surveyed the room, and supposed that, in its way, it had charm. Very little matched, yet everything seemed to gel together nicely. There was a large brown plush settee and a matching chair with crocheted patchwork covers on the backs and arms. Obviously Flo hadn't believed in leaving an inch of space bare. There were numerous pictures and several tiny tables, all with bowls of silk flowers. Linoleum, with a pattern of blue and red tiles, covered the floor, and there was a handmade rag rug on the hearth. A large-screen television stood next to an up-to-date music centre, a record visible on the turntable beneath the smoky plastic lid.

If only it wasn't so cold! On the hearth next to the fire I saw a box of matches. I struck one, shoved it between the bars and turned the knob at the side. There was a mini explosion and the gas jets roared briefly before settling down into a steady flame.

I held out my hands to warm them and remembered I'd been looking for a photo of Flo. After a while, I got up and moved round the room again until I found some on a gate-leg table, which had been folded to its narrowest against the wall. The photos, about a dozen in all, were spread each side of a glass jar of anemones.

The first was a coloured snap of two women taken in what looked like a fairground. I recognised Flo from Auntie Sally's funeral. Despite her age, it was obvious that she'd once been pretty. She was smiling at the camera, a calm, sweet smile. Her companion wore a leopardskin coat and black leggings, and her hair was a violent unnatural red. I turned the photo over: 'Me and Bel at Blackpool Lights, October 1993'.

There was a picture of Auntie Sally's wartime wedding, which I'd seen before at Gran's. The bride, in her pin-striped suit and white felt hat, looked like a character out of *Guys and Dolls*. Another wedding photo, the couple in Army uniform. Despite the unflattering clothes, the woman was startlingly lovely. On the back was written, 'Bel & Bob's wedding, December, 1940'. Flo and Bel must have been friends all their lives.

I found two more photos of Bel getting married; 'Bel & Ivor's wedding, 1945,' in what looked like a foreign setting, and 'Bel & Edward's wedding, 1974' showed a glamorous Bel with a decrepit-looking old man.

At last I held a picture of a young Flo, a snapshot turning white at the edges. It was taken outside a ramshackle building with 'Fritz's Laundry' above the door. A man in a dark suit and wire-rimmed glasses – Fritz? – stood in the middle of six women all wearing aprons and turbans. Flo was recognisable immediately because she was so like me, except that she was smiling and I had never smiled like that in all my life. She looked about eighteen, and seemed to be bursting with happiness, you could see it in her eyes, her dimples, and the curve of her lovely wide mouth.

As I replaced the silver-framed photo on the table, I sighed. More than half a century spanned the images of my great-aunt, the one in Blackpool, the other outside Fritz's Laundry, yet little seemed to have happened over the years to make her expression change.

I was turning away with the intention of getting on with what I'd come for, when I noticed a studio portrait, in sepia tones, of a woman with a baby. There was something familiar about her grim yet good-looking face. I knew nothing about babies and couldn't tell the child's age – it was a boy in an old-fashioned romper suit with a sailor collar – but he was adorable. I looked at the back, and read, 'Elsa Cameron with Norman (Martha's godson), on his first birthday, May, 1939'.

The baby was my father! His mother had died long before I was born.

I slammed the photo face down on the table. I was shivering again. I was about to kneel in front of the fire once more, when I saw the sherry on the sideboard, the modern one. My jangling nerves needed calming. In the cupboard underneath, where I looked for a glass, I found five more bottles of sherry, and several glasses hanging by their stems from a circular wooden stand. I filled a glass, drank the sherry, filled it again, took it over to the settee, and sank into the cushions. My head was buzzing. How could such a beautiful child grow up to become such a *monster*?

The sherry took effect quickly and I began to relax. There seemed to be a sagging hole in the middle cushion of the settee into which my bottom fitted perfectly. Perhaps it was where Flo had always sat. Outside, cars drove past occasionally and I could hear children playing in the square. People walked by, heels clicking on the pavement, only their legs visible from the knees down through the small window by the door.

I put down the empty glass and promptly fell asleep.

When I woke up it was nearly half past five. There was a throbbing between my eyes, which I supposed was the result of the sherry, though it didn't feel particularly unpleasant. I would have given anything for a cup of tea or coffee and remembered I hadn't seen the kitchen yet, or the bedroom.

I got to my feet, and staggered towards the door at the back of the room, where I found myself in a little dark inner hall with a tiled floor and two more doors, left and right. The left led to a tiny Spartan kitchen with a deep porcelain sink, a cooker older than Mum's, a digitally operated microwave oven but no fridge. In the wall cupboard, behind several packets of biscuits, there was coffee and, to my relief, a jar of Coffeemate. I put a spoonful of each with water in a flowered mug and stuck it in the microwave to heat.

Whilst I was waiting, I went back to the inner hall, opened the other door, and switched on the light. The bedroom was mainly white, curtains, walls, bedspread. A pair of pink furry slippers were set neatly side by side under the bed. A large crucifix hung from the wall and there was a statue of Our Lord on the six-drawer chest, surrounded by smaller statues. The walls were covered with holy pictures: Our Lord again, Baby Jesus, the Virgin Mary, and an assortment of saints. Otherwise, the room was sparsely furnished: apart from the chest, there was only a matching wardrobe with a narrow, full-length mirror on the door, and a little cane bedside table, which held an old-fashioned alarm clock, a white-shaded lamp, and a Mills & Boon novel with an embroidered bookmark. An old brown foolscap envelope was propped against the lamp. I picked it up and put it in the pocket of my linen jacket. It might contain Flo's pension book, which would need to be cancelled.

I admired the wardrobe and the chest-of-drawers. They looked like stained oak and had been polished to satin smoothness. They'd look lovely in my flat, I thought. I wouldn't have minded the brass bedstead either. My own bedroom furniture had been bought in kits and had taken weeks to put together.

In the kitchen, the microwave beeped. I sat on the bed, which was like sitting on a cloud it felt so soft, and bounced up and down, but stopped when I caught sight of my reflection in the mirror. I saw a tall, graceful young woman who looked years younger than her age, dressed in white and pink, with long slim legs and hair that shone like silver under Auntie Flo's bedroom light. Her wide, generous mouth was turned up slightly – she'd been childishly enjoying bouncing on the bed. At school, she had been regarded as stuck up because of her straight, slightly patrician nose, but James's mother had said once, 'What fine bone structure you have, Millie. Some women would pay a plastic surgeon a fortune for cheekbones like that.'

The young woman had forgotten to use blusher and she *did* look pale, as everyone had been saying, but it was the deadness in the green eyes that shocked me.

I took the coffee and a packet of custard creams into the lounge, switched on the television and watched *Neighbours*, then an old cowboy film on BBC2.

Just as the film was finishing, I glimpsed through the window the majestic figure of Charmian Smith descending the concrete stairs. I kicked the boxes aside and opened the door, feeling slightly uncomfortable when she gave me a warm smile, as if we were the greatest friends.

'I'd forgotten all about you until our Minola, that's me daughter, collected her kids and said there was a light on in Flo's flat. Me feller's just got home and I wondered if you'd like a bite to eat with us.' She came into the room without waiting to be asked, as if it was something she was used to doing.

'What does your daughter do?' I was astonished to learn that Charmian was grandmother to the children I'd seen earlier.

'She's learning to use a computer. It was when Jay, that's me son, went to university last year, she decided it was time she used her brain.' Charmian's brown eyes danced. 'I told her she'd regret getting married at sixteen. I said, "There's more things to life than a husband and a family, luv," but kids never listen, do they? I didn't listen to me own mam when I got married at the same age.'

'I suppose not.'

'Are you married? Y'know, I don't know your name.'

'Millie Cameron, and no, I'm not married.' I wished the woman would leave so I could get down to work. It seemed imperative suddenly that I take at least half a dozen boxes of stuff to Oxfam tomorrow. To my dismay, she sank gracefully into the armchair, her long bead earrings swinging against her gleaming neck.

'I didn't know Flo had any relatives left after her sister Sally died,' she said, 'apart from Sally's daughter who went to live in Australia. It wasn't until Bel gave me a number to ring after the funeral that I knew there was another sister.'

Bel, the woman in the photographs. '*After* the funeral?'

'That's right, Martha Colquitt. Is she your gran?' I nodded. 'I felt terrible when the poor woman burst into tears, but Bel said that was the way Flo wanted it.' Charmian glanced sadly round the room. 'I can't get used to her not being here. I used to come and see her several times a day over the last year when she was stuck indoors with her terrible headaches.'

'That was very kind of you,' I said stiffly.

'Lord, girl, it was nothing to do with kindness. It was no more than she deserved. Flo was there for me when I needed her – she got me a job in the launderette when me kids were little. It changed me life.' She leaned against the crocheted cover and, for a moment, looked as if she might cry. Then, once again, her eyes swept the room. 'It's like a museum, isn't it? Such a shame everything's got to go. People always fetched her ornaments back from their holidays.' She indicated the brass plaques on the beams. 'We brought her the key and the little dog from Clacton. This was Flo's favourite, though – and mine.' She eased herself smoothly out of the chair and switched on the lamp on top of the television.

I had already noticed the cut-out parchment lamp with its wooden base and thought it tasteless. It reminded me of a cheap Christmas card: a line of laughing children dressed as they might have been in this very square a hundred years ago, fur hats, fur muffs, lace-up boots.

'I'll switch the main light off so you can see the effect once the bulb warms up,' Charmian said.

To my surprise, the shade slowly began to revolve. I hadn't realised there was another behind it that turned in the opposite direction. The children passed a toyshop, a sweetshop, a church, a Christmas tree decorated with coloured lights. Shadows flitted across the ceiling of the long, low room. Hazy, almost lifesize figures passed over my head.

'Tom brought her that from Austria of all places.'

I felt almost hypnotised by the moving lamp. 'Tom?'

'Flo's friend. She loved sitting watching her lamp and listening to her record. The lamp was still on when I came down the day they found her dead in the park. Did you know she got run over?'

'My mother said.'

'They never found who did it. Oh dear!' Now Charmian did begin to cry. 'I don't half miss her. I hate the thought of her dying all alone.'

'I'm terribly sorry.' I went over and awkwardly touched the woman's arm. I hadn't the faintest notion how you were supposed to comfort a stranger. Perhaps another person, someone who didn't have dead eyes, might have taken the weeping woman in their arms, but I could no more have done that than I could have sprouted wings and flown.

Charmian sniffed and wiped her eyes. 'Anyroad, I'd better go. Herbie's waiting for his tea – which reminds me, luv, would you care to join us?'

'Thanks all the same, but I'd better not. There's so much to do.' I gestured at the room, which was exactly the same as when I'd come six hours before.

Charmian squeezed my hand. 'Perhaps next time, eh? It'll take you weeks to sort this lot out. I'd offer to help, but I couldn't bear to see Flo's lovely stuff being packed away.'

I watched her climb the steps outside. I had meant to ask when the rent was due, so that I could pay a few weeks if necessary. I hadn't realised that dusk had fallen and it was rapidly growing dark. The streetlights were on, and it was time to draw the curtains. It was then that I noticed someone standing motionless outside. I pressed my face against the glass and peered upwards. It was a girl of about sixteen, wearing a tight red mini-dress that barely covered her behind and emphasised the curves of her slight body. There was something about her stance, the way she leaned against the railings, one foot slightly in front of the other, the way she held her cigarette, left hand supporting the right elbow, that made me guess immediately what she was. I pressed my face the other way, and saw two more girls outside the house next door.

'Oh, lord!' I felt scared. Perhaps I should let someone know where I was – James or my mother – but I couldn't recall seeing a phone in the flat and, despite what George had said, I'd left my mobile in the office. As soon as I'd had another cup of coffee, I'd go home and come back on Sunday to start packing.

The kitchen was like a fridge. No wonder Flo didn't have one – she didn't need it. I returned, shivering, to the settee, my hands wrapped round a mug of coffee. It was odd, but the room seemed even more cosy and charming now I knew about the girl outside. I no longer felt scared, but safe and secure, as if there was no chance of coming to any harm inside Auntie Flo's four walls.

I became aware of something stiff against my hip and remembered the envelope that I'd found in the bedroom. It didn't contain a pension book, but several newspaper cuttings, yellow and crisp with age, held together with a paper clip. They'd mainly been taken from the *Liverpool Daily Post* and the *Echo*. I looked at the top one for a date – Friday, 2 June 1939 – then skimmed through the words underneath.

THETIS TRAPPED UNDERWATER was the main headline, followed by a sub-heading. *Submarine Fails to Re-surface in Liverpool Bay – Admiralty Assures Relatives All Those On Board Will Be Rescued.*

I turned to the next cutting dated the following day. *Hope Fading For Men Trapped On The Thetis. Stunned Relatives Wait Outside Cammell Laird Offices in Birkenhead.* The news had been worse when the *Echo* came out that afternoon: *Hope Virtually Abandoned for 99 men on Thetis*, and by Sunday, *All Hope Abandoned* . . .

Why had Flo kept them?

On the television, the lamp swirled and the children did their Christmas shopping. I found myself waiting for a girl in a red coat and brown fur bonnet to come round. She was waving at someone, but the someone never appeared.

Flo had sat in this very spot hundreds, no, thousands of times, watching the girl in red, listening to her record. Curious, I went over to the record player and studied the controls. I pressed Play, and beneath the plastic lid, the arm lifted and swung across to the record.

There was crackling, then the strains of a vaguely familiar tune filled the room, silent until then except for the hiss of the gas fire. After a while, a man's voice, also vaguely familiar, began to sing. He'd been in a film on television recently – Bing Crosby. 'Dancing in the dark,' a voice like melting chocolate crooned.

What had Flo Clancy done to make her the black sheep of the family? Why had Gran refused to mention her name? Bel, Flo's old friend, had asked Charmian Smith to ring Gran *after* the funeral because 'that's the way Flo wanted it'. What had happened between the sisters to make them dislike each other so much? And why had Flo kept cuttings of a submarine disaster beside her bed?

I would almost certainly never know the truth about Auntie Flo, but what did it matter? As the lamp slowly turned and dark shadows swept the ceiling of the room and the music reached a crescendo, filling every nook and corner, I took a long, deep breath and allowed myself to be sucked into the enchantment of it all. A quite unexpected thing had happened, something quite wonderful. I had never felt so much at peace with myself before.

Flo

1

Flo Clancy opened her eyes, saw that the fingers on the brass alarm clock on the tallboy were pointing to half past seven, and nearly screamed. She'd be late for work! She was about to leap out of bed when she remembered it was Whit Monday and she could lie in.

Whew! She peeped over the covers at her sisters, both fast asleep in the double bed only a few feet away. Martha would have done her nut if she'd been woken early. Flo pursed her lips and blew gently at Sally who was sleeping on the outside, but Sal's brown eyelashes merely flickered before she turned over, dead to the world.

But Flo was wide awake and it was a sin to stay in bed on such a lovely morning. She sat up carefully – the springs of the single bed creaked like blazes – and stretched her arms. The sun streamed through the thin curtains making the roses on the floorcloth seem almost real. She poked her feet out and wriggled her white toes. As usual, the bedclothes were a mess – her sisters refused to sleep with her, claiming she fidgeted non-stop the whole night long.

Shall I get up and risk disturbing our Martha? Flo mused. She'd have to get dressed in the little space between the wardrobe and the tallboy. Since their dear dad, a railwayman, had died two years ago – struck by a train on the lines near Edge Hill station – and they'd had to take in a lodger, the girls could no longer wander round the little house in Burnett Street half dressed.

The frock Martha had worn last night when she'd gone with Albert Colquitt, their lodger, to see Bette Davis in *The Little Foxes* was hanging outside the wardrobe. Flo glared at it. What a miserable garment, dark grey with grey buttons, more suitable for a funeral than a night out with the man you hoped to marry. She transferred her gaze to her sister's head, which could just be seen above the green eiderdown. How on earth could she sleep with her hair screwed up in a million metal curlers? And did someone of only twenty-two *really* need to smear her face with layers of cold cream so she looked as if she'd been carved out of a block of lard?

Oh dear! She was having nasty thoughts about Martha again and she loved her just as much as she loved Mam and Sally and Mr Fritz who owned the laundry where she worked. But since dear Dad died, what with Mam not feeling too well, Martha seemed to think it was her job as the eldest to be In Charge and keep her sisters in line. Not that Dad had ever been strict – he'd been a soft ould thing. Flo's eyes prickled with tears. It was still hard to get used to him not being there.

She couldn't stand being in bed a minute longer. She eased herself out and got dressed quickly in her best pink frock with white piping on the collar and the cuffs of the short puffed sleeves. That afternoon, she and Sal were off to New Brighton on the ferry.

As she crept downstairs, she could hear Mam snoring in the front bedroom. There was no sound from the parlour. Mr Colquitt must have gone to work, poor man. Flo felt for him. As a ticket inspector on the trams, he had to work on days most people had off.

In the living room, she automatically kissed the feet of the porcelain figure of Christ on the crucifix over the mantelpiece, then skipped into the back kitchen where she washed her face and cleaned her teeth. She combed her silvery blonde hair before the mirror over the sink. As an experiment, she twisted it into two long plaits and pinned them together on top of her head with a slide. Irene Dunne had worn her hair like that in a picture she'd seen recently. Flo had been meaning to try it ever since. It looked dead elegant.

She made a face at herself and was about to burst into song, when she remembered the superstition, 'Sing before breakfast, cry before tea.' Anyroad, everyone upstairs was still asleep. She'd make a pot of tea and take them a cup when she heard them stir. Martha and Sally enjoyed sitting up in bed, pillows tucked behind them, gossiping, on days they didn't have to get up for work. Unlike Flo, they both had horrible jobs: Martha was a bottle topper in Goodlad's Brewery, and Sally worked behind the counter of the butcher's on the corner of Smithdown Road and Tunstall Street.

Oh, but it was difficult not to sing on such a glorious day. The sun must be splitting the flags outside, and the whitewashed walls in the backyard dazzled so brightly it hurt her eyes to look. Flo filled the kettle, put it on the hob over the fire in the living room, releasing the flue so the embers from the night before began to sizzle and glow, and decided to dance instead. She took a deep breath and was twirling across the room like a ballerina, when she came to a sudden halt in the arms of their lodger.

'Mr Colquitt! I thought you'd gone.' Flo felt as if she'd blushed right down to her toes. He was wearing his regulation navy blue uniform with red piping, and grinning from ear to ear.

'I'm glad I hadn't, else I'd have missed the sight of a fairy dancing towards me to wish me good morning.'

'Good morning, Mr Colquitt,' Flo stammered, conscious of his arms still around her waist.

'And the same to you, Flo. How many times have I told you to call me Albert?'

'I can't remember.' To her relief, he removed his hands, came into the room and sat in the easy chair that used to be Dad's. Flo didn't mind, because she liked Mr Colquitt – Albert – though couldn't for the life of her understand why Martha was so keen on capturing for a husband a widower more than twice her age. Since her best friend, Elsa, had married Eugene Cameron, Martha was terrified of being left on the shelf. Like Flo, she took after Mam's side of the family, with her slim figure, pale blonde hair and unusual green eyes, but had unfortunately inherited Dad's poor eyesight: she had worn glasses since she was nine and had never come to terms with it. She thought herself the unluckiest girl in the world, whose chances of finding a decent husband were doomed.

Martha had been setting her cap at Albert ever since he arrived on the scene. He was a tall, ungainly man with a round pot belly like a football. Although he was not handsome, his face was pleasant and his grey eyes shone with good humour. His wispy hair grew in sideboards to way below his ears, which Flo thought looked a bit daft. The main thing wrong with Albert, though, was that he didn't get his uniform cleaned often enough, so it ponged something dreadful, particularly in summer. It was ponging now, and she would have opened the window if it hadn't meant climbing on his knee.

'Would you like a bite to eat?' she enquired. Breakfast and an evening meal were supposed to be included in his rent, but he usually left too early for anyone to make breakfast, so compensated by eating a thundering great tea when he came home.

'I wouldn't say no to a couple of slices of toast, and is that water boiling for tea?'

'It is so.' Flo cut two slices of bread and managed to get both on the toasting fork. She knelt in front of the fire and toasted her arm at the same time.

'You've done your hair different,' Albert said suddenly. 'It's very nice. You look like a snow princess.'

'Ta.' Flo had never mentioned it to a living soul, but she sometimes wondered if he liked her better than he did Martha, though not in a romantic way, of course. She also thought that maybe he wasn't too keen to allow pretty, bespectacled Martha Clancy to get her claws into him. He might be twice her age and smell awful, but he didn't want to get married again. Flo hoped Martha wouldn't try too hard so that he'd feel obliged to leave. His thirty bob a week made all the difference to the housekeeping nowadays. It meant they could buy scented soap and decent cuts of meat, luxuries that they could never afford otherwise. Although there were three wages coming in, women earned much less than men.

He ate his toast, drank his tea, made several more flattering remarks about her appearance, then left for work. Flo returned to the living room, poured a cup of tea, and curled up in Dad's chair. She wanted to think about Tommy O'Mara before anyone got up. If Martha was in the room, it was impossible – her sister's mere presence made Flo feel guilty. For a second, a shadow fell over her face. Tommy was married to Nancy, but he'd explained the strange circumstances to Flo's satisfaction. Next year, sooner if possible, he and Flo would be married. Her face cleared. Until the magic day occurred, it was perfectly all right to meet Tommy O'Mara twice a week outside the Mystery.

Upstairs, Mam coughed and Flo held her breath until the house was quiet again. She'd met Tommy on the Tuesday after Easter when he'd come into the laundry by the side door. Customers were supposed to use the front, which led to the office where Mr Fritz was usually behind the counter. It was a dull day, slightly chilly, but the side door was left open, except in the iciest of weather, because when all the boilers, presses and irons were working at full pelt, the laundry got hotter than a Turkish bath.

Flo was pressing sheets in the giant new electric contraption Mr Fritz had only recently bought. She was nearest to the door, wreathed in steam, only vaguely aware of someone approaching through the mist until a voice with a strong Irish accent said, 'Do you do dry-cleaning, luv?'

'Sorry, no, just laundry.' As the steam cleared, she saw a young man with a brown suit over his arm. He wore a grey, collarless shirt and, despite the cold, the sleeves were rolled up to his armpits, showing off his strong, brown arms – there was a tattoo of a tiger on the right. A tweed cap was set jauntily on the back of his untidy brown curls. His waist was as slim as a girl's, something he must have been proud of as his baggy corduroy trousers were held up with a leather belt pulled as tight as it would go. A red hanky was tied carelessly around his neck, emphasising the devil-may-care expression on his handsome, sunburnt face.

'The nearest dry-cleaner's is Thompson's, that's along Gainsborough Road on the first corner,' she said. There was a peculiar feeling in the pit of her tummy as she watched him over the pressing machine. He was staring at her boldly, making no attempt to conceal the admiration in his dark eyes. She wanted to tear off her white turban and let him see she looked even prettier with her blonde hair loose.

'What's your name?' he asked.

Flo felt as flustered as if he'd asked to borrow a pound note. 'Flo Clancy,' she stammered.

'I'm Tommy O'Mara.'

'Are you now!' You'd think she was the only one there the way he kept his eyes locked on hers, and seemed unaware that the other five women had stopped work for a good look – Josie Driver was leering at him provocatively over the shirts she was supposed to be ironing.

'I suppose I'd better make me way round to Thompson's,' he said.

'I suppose you had.'

He winked. 'Tara, Flo.' With a swagger, he was gone.

'Tara,' Flo whispered. Her legs felt weak and her heart was thumping madly.

'Who was that?' Josie called eagerly. 'Jaysus, he could have me for six-pence!'

Before Flo could reply, Olive Knott shouted, 'His name's Tommy O'Mara. He lives in the next street to us, and before you young 'uns get too excited, you might like to know he's well and truly married.'

Flo's thumping heart sank to her boots. Married!

Mr Fritz came out of the office to ask what all the fuss was about.

'We've just had Franchot Tone, Clark Gable and Ronald Colman all rolled into one asking if we did dry-cleaning,' Olive said cuttingly.

'Why, Flo, you've gone all pink.' Mr Fritz beamed at her through his wire-rimmed spectacles. He was a plump, comfortable little man with a round face and lots of frizzy brown hair. He was wearing a brown coat overall, which meant he was about to go out in the van to deliver clean laundry and collect dirty items in return. Olive, who'd been there the longest and was vaguely considered next in command, would take over the office and answer the telephone.

'I didn't mean to,' Flo said stupidly.

'It must be nice to be young and impressionable.' He sighed gloomily, as if he already had one foot in the grave though he wasn't quite forty. For some reason, Mr Fritz was forever trying to make out he was dead miserable, when everyone knew he was the happiest man alive – and the nicest, kindest employer in the whole wide world. His surname was Austrian, a bit of a mouthful and difficult to spell, so everyone called him by his first name, Fritz, and referred to his equally plump little Irish wife, Stella, as Mrs Fritz, and their eight children – three girls and five boys – as the little Fritzes.

He departed, and the women returned to their work, happy in the knowledge that on Tuesdays he called at Sinclair's, the confectioner's, to collect the overalls and would bring them back a cream cake each.

Try as she might, Flo was unable to get Tommy O'Mara out of her mind. Twice before, she'd thought she was in love, the first time with Frank McGee, then Kevin Kelly – she'd actually let Kevin kiss her on the way home from the Rialto where they'd been to a St Patrick's Day dance – but the feelings she had for them paled to nothing when she thought about the man who'd looked at her so boldly. Was it possible she was properly in love with someone she'd exchanged scarcely more than half a dozen words with?

When they were having their tea that night Martha asked sharply, 'What's the matter with you?'

Flo emerged from the daydream in which an unmarried Tommy O'Mara had just proposed. 'Nowt!' she answered, just as sharply.

'I've asked three times if you want pudding. It's apple pie.'

'For goodness sake, Martha, leave the girl alone.' Mam was having one of her good days, which meant she resented Martha acting as if she owned the place. At other times she was too worn out and listless to open her mouth. More and more often, Flo found her in bed when she arrived home from work. Mam patted her youngest daughter's arm. 'She was in a lovely little world of her own, weren't you, luv? I could tell. Your eyes were sparkling as if you were thinking of something dead nice.'

'I was so.' Flo stuck out her tongue at Martha as she disappeared into the back kitchen.

'Can I borrow your pink frock tonight, Flo?' Sally enquired. 'I'm going to the Grand with Brian Maloney.'

'Isn't he a Protestant?' Martha shouted from the kitchen.

'I've no idea,' Sally yelled back.

Martha appeared, grim-faced, in the doorway. 'I'd sooner you didn't go out with Protestants, Sal.'

'It's none of your bloody business,' Flo said indignantly.

Mam shook her head. 'Don't swear, luv.'

Sally wriggled uncomfortably in the chair. 'We're only going to the pictures.'

'You can never tell how things develop with a feller. It's best not to get involved with a Protestant from the start.'

'I'll tell him I won't see him again after tonight.'

'In that case, you won't need our Flo's best frock. Go in something old. He might get ideas if you arrive all dolled up.'

Flo felt cross with both her sisters, one for being so bossy and the other for allowing herself to be bossed.

'What are you doing with yourself tonight, luv?' Mam asked.

'I thought I'd stay in and read a book – but I'll play cards with you if you like.' When Dad was alive, the two of them used to play cards for hours.

'No, ta, luv. I feel a bit tired. I might go to bed after I've had a cup of tea. I'll not bother with the apple pie, Martha.'

'I wish you'd go to the doctor's, Mam,' Flo said worriedly. Kate Clancy had never been a strong woman, and since the sudden, violent death of her beloved husband, she seemed to have lost the will to live, becoming thinner and more frail by the day.

'So do I.' Martha stroked Mam's hair, which had changed from ash-blonde to genuine silver almost overnight.

'Me, too,' echoed Sally.

But Mam screwed her thin face into the stubborn expression they'd seen many times before. 'Now, don't you girls start on that again,' she said tightly. 'I've told you, I'm not seeing a doctor. He might find something wrong with me, and there's no way I'm letting them cut me open. I'm just run down, that's all. I'll feel better when the warm weather comes.'

'Are you taking the bile beans I bought?' Martha demanded.

'They're beside me bed and I take them every morning.'

The girls glanced at each other with concern. If Mam died so soon after Dad, they didn't think they could bear it.

Mam went to bed and Sally got ready to meet Brian Maloney. Martha made her remove her earrings before she left, as if sixpenny pearl earrings from Woolworths would drive a man so wild with desire that he'd propose on the spot and Sally would feel obliged to accept!

It was Flo's turn to wash and dry the dishes. She cleared the table, shook the white cloth in the yard, straightened the green chenille cloth underneath and folded one leaf of the table down, before putting the white cloth on again for when their lodger came home. A meal fit for a giant was in the oven keeping warm. Flo set his place: knife, fork and spoon, condiments to the right, mustard to the left. As soon as she'd finished, she sank into the armchair with the novel she was halfway through, *Shattered Love, Shattered Dreams.*

Martha came in and adjusted everything on the table as if it had been crooked. 'You've always got your head buried in a book, Flo Clancy,' she remarked.

'You moan when I go out and you moan when I stay in.' Flo made a face at her sister. 'What do you expect me to do all night? Sit and twiddle me thumbs?'

'I wasn't moaning, I was merely stating a fact.' Martha gave the table a critical glance. 'Will you look after Albert when he comes?'

'Of course.' There was nothing to be done except move the plate from the oven to the table, which Albert could no doubt manage alone if no help was available.

'I'd stay meself, but I promised to go and see Elsa Cameron. That baby's getting her down something awful. I'm sure she smacks him, yet the little lad's not even twelve months old.'

'Norman? He's a lovely baby. I wouldn't mind having him meself.'

'Nor I.' Martha shoved a hatpin into a little veiled cocked hat, then sighed as she adjusted her glasses in the mirror. She was smartly dressed, although she was only going around the corner, in a long grey skirt with a cardigan to match. The whole outfit had cost ten bob in Paddy's Market. 'Trouble is, Flo, I'm beginning to think Elsa's not quite right in the head. She's been acting dead peculiar since Norman arrived. The other day when I turned up she was undoing her knitting, but when I asked why, she'd no idea. She mightn't be so bad if Eugene was there, but him being in the Merchant Navy, like, it means he's hardly ever home.'

'It's a terrible shame,' Flo said sincerely. Norman Cameron was Martha's godson and the most delightful baby she'd ever known. It was terrible to think he was getting his mam down. 'Can't Eugene get a different job?'

'Not with a million men already out of work,' Martha said. 'Mind you, that'll soon change if there's a war.'

'There won't be a war,' Flo said quickly. She looked at her sister, scared. 'Will there?'

'Oh, I don't know, luv. According to the papers, that Hitler's getting far too big for his boots.'

Like Mam dying, war was something best not thought about. After Martha left, Flo tried to bury herself in her book, but the man over whom the heroine was pining was a pale, insipid creature compared to Tommy O'Mara, and instead of words, she kept seeing *him* on the page: his dark, shameless eyes, his reckless face, the cheeky way he wore his cap. She reckoned it was a good job she wouldn't be seeing him again. If he'd been as knocked sideways by her as she'd been by him, he might ask her out, and although a good Catholic girl should never, never go out with a married man, Flo wasn't convinced she'd be capable of resisting Tommy O'Mara.

She *did* see him again, only two days later. He came into the laundry, this time bearing two white shirts that already looked perfectly clean. She looked up from the press and found him smiling at her intently as if she was the only woman in the world, never mind the laundry.

'I'd like these laundered, please.'

Flo had to swallow several times before she could answer. 'You need to take them round the front and Mr Fritz will give you a ticket,' she said, in a voice that sounded as if it belonged to someone else.

He frowned. 'Does that mean I won't see you when I collect them?'

'I'm afraid not,' she said, still in someone else's voice.

He flung the shirts over his shoulder, stuck his thumbs in his belt and rocked back on his heels. 'In that case, I'll not beat about the bush. Would you like to come for a walk with me one night, Flo? We can have a bevvy on the way – you're old enough to go in boozers, aren't you?'

'I'll be nineteen in May,' Flo said faintly. 'Though I've never been in a booz— a pub before.'

'Well, there's a first time for everything.' He winked. 'See you tomorrer night then, eight o'clock outside the Mystery gates, the Smithdown Road end.'

'Rightio.' She watched him leave, knowing that she'd done something terribly wrong. She felt very adult and worldly wise, as if she was much older than Sally and Martha. Tomorrow night she was going out with a married man and the thing was *she didn't care!*

'What did he want?' Olive Knott brought her down to earth with a sharp nudge in the ribs.

'He brought his shirts to the wrong place. I sent him round the front.'

Olive's brow creased worriedly. 'He didn't ask you out, did he?'

For the first time in her life Flo lied. 'No.'

'He's got his eye on you, that's plain to see. Oh, he has a way with him, there's no denying it, but it's best for nice girls like you to stay clear of men like Tommy O'Mara, Flo.'

But Flo was lost. She would have gone out with Tommy O'Mara if Olive had declared him to be the divil himself.

Friday was another dull day and there was drizzle on and off until early evening when a late sun appeared. It looked as soft as a jelly in the dusky blue sky, and its gentle rays filled the air with gold dust.

Flo felt very odd as she made her way to the Mystery. Every step that took her nearer seemed of momentous significance, as if she was walking towards her destiny, and that after tonight nothing would ever be the same again. She thought of the lie she'd told at home – that she was calling on Josie Driver who'd been off sick and Mr Fritz wanted to know how she was, which had been all she could think of when Martha demanded to know where she was going.

When she arrived Tommy was already there. He was standing outside the gates, whistling, wearing a dark blue suit that looked a bit too big, a white and blue striped shirt with a high stiff collar, and a grey tie. A slightly more respectable tweed cap was set at the same jaunty angle on the back of his curly head. The mere sight of the swaggering, audacious figure made Flo feel quite faint.

'There you are!' He smiled. 'You're late. I was worried you might have changed your mind.'

The thought had never entered her head. She smiled nervously and said, 'Hello.'

'You look nice,' he said appreciatively. 'Green suits you. It sets off your eyes. That was the first thing I noticed when I came into the laundry, those green eyes. I bet you have stacks of fellers chasing after you.'

'Not exactly,' Flo mumbled.

'In that case, the fellers round here must be mad!' When he linked her arm Flo could smell a mixture of strong tobacco and carbolic soap. She got the peculiar feeling in her tummy again as they began to stroll through the park, though the Mystery was more like a playing-field: a vast expanse of grass surrounded by trees. The Liverpool-to-London railway line ran along one side. The trees were bursting into life, ready for summer, and pale sunlight filtered through the branches, making dappled patterns on the green grass underneath.

Without any prompting, Tommy briefly told her the story of his life. He'd been born in Ireland, in the county of Limerick, and had come to Liverpool ten years ago when he was twenty. 'I've got fourteen brothers and sisters, half of 'em still at home. I send me mam a few bob when I've got it to spare.'

Flo said she thought that very generous. She asked where he worked.

'I'm a fitter at Cammell Laird's in Birkenhead,' he said boastfully. 'You should see this ship we're building at the moment. It's a T-class submarine, the *Thetis*. Guess how much it's costing?'

She confessed she had absolutely no idea.

'Three hundred thousand smackeroos!'

'Three hundred thousand!' Flo gasped. 'Is it made of gold or something?'

He laughed and squeezed her arm. 'No, but it's the very latest design. You should see the instruments in the conning tower! *And* it's got ten torpedo tubes. I don't envy any German ships that come near the *Thetis* if there's a war.'

'There won't be a war,' Flo said stubbornly.

'That's what women always say.' He chuckled.

She realised he'd omitted to tell her about one important aspect of his life – his wife. There was silence for a while, except for his whistling, as they strolled across the grass and the April sun began to disappear behind the trees.

Perhaps Tommy had read her thoughts, because he said suddenly, 'I should have told you this before, Flo. I'm married.'

'I know,' Flo said.

He raised his finely drawn eyebrows in surprise. 'Who told you?'

'A woman at work, Olive Knott. She lives in the next street to you.'

'Does she now.' He made a face. 'I'm surprised you came, knowing, like.'

Flo wasn't in the least surprised: she'd have come even if she'd been told he had ten wives.

They'd arrived at the other side of the Mystery and emerged into Gainsborough Road. Tommy steered her inside the first pub they came to. 'What would you like to drink?' he asked.

'I've no idea.' The only alcohol that ever crossed Flo's lips was a small glass of sherry at Christmas.

'I'll get you a port and lemon. That's what women usually like.'

The pub was crowded. Flo glanced round when Tommy went to be served, worried someone might recognise her, but there were no familiar faces. She noticed that quite a few women were eyeing Tommy up and down as he waited at the bar, legs crossed nonchalantly at the ankles. Without doubt he was the best-looking man there – and he was with *her!* Flo gasped at the sheer magic of it all, just as Tommy turned round and winked.

Her eyes flickered as she tried to wink back, but couldn't quite manage it. Tommy laughed at her efforts as he came over with the drinks. 'You know,' he whispered, 'you're the most beautiful girl here, Flo Clancy, perhaps the most beautiful in the whole of Liverpool. There's something special between us, isn't there? I recognised it the minute I set eyes on you. It's something that doesn't happen often between a man and a woman, but it's happened between you and me.'

Flo felt as if she wanted to cry. She also wanted to say something meaningful, but all she could think of was, 'I suppose it has.'

Tommy swallowed half his beer in one go, then returned the pint glass to the table with a thump. He took a tin of tobacco from his pocket and deftly rolled a ciggie out of the thick dark shreds that smelt of tar. He shoved the

737

tin in Flo's direction, but she shook her head. 'It's time I explained about Nancy,' he said grandly.

'Nancy?'

'Me wife. It's not a genuine marriage, Flo, not in any respects.' He looked at her knowingly. 'I met Nancy in Spain when I was fighting in the Civil War. She's a gypsy. I won't deny I fell for her hook, line and sinker. I would have married her proper, given the opportunity, but 'stead, I did it Nancy's way.' The way he told it it sounded like the most romantic novel ever written. He and Nancy had 'plighted their troth', as he put it, at a gypsy ceremony in a wood near Barcelona. 'It means nowt in the eyes of British law or the Roman Catholic Church,' he said contemptuously. He'd been meaning to leave for a long time, and as soon as Nancy got better he'd be off like a shot. 'Then I'll be free to marry an English girl, proper, like, this time.' He clasped Flo's hand and gazed deep into her eyes. 'And you know who that'll be, don't you?'

Flo felt the blood run hot through her body. She gulped. 'What's wrong with Nancy?'

Tommy sighed. 'It's a bit embarrassing to explain, luv. It's what's called a woman's complaint. She's been to Smithdown Road ozzie and the doctors said it'll all be cleared up in about six months. I don't like to leave till she gets better,' he added virtuously.

The guilt that had been lurking in a little corner of Flo's mind about going out with a married man disappeared, along with the suspicion that he'd only told her about Nancy in case someone else did. Why, he was almost single! It seemed wise, though, not to mention him and his peculiar circumstances to her family. Martha, in particular, would never understand. She'd say nothing until they got engaged.

'I trust you'll keep what I've just said under your hat for now, luv,' Tommy said conspiratorially. 'I don't want people knowing me private business, like, till the time comes to tell them.'

'I won't breathe a word,' Flo assured him. 'I'd already decided to keep you a secret.'

'A secret! I like the idea of being the secret man in Flo Clancy's life.' His brown eyes sparkled. 'How about another drink before we go?'

'No, ta.' The port and lemon had already gone to her head.

'I'll just have another quick pint, then we'll be off.'

It was dark when they went outside. The sky glowed hazy orange where the sun had set, but was otherwise dark blue, almost black. They wandered hand in hand through the Mystery, the noise of the traffic behind growing fainter, until nothing could be heard except their feet on the grass, the slight rustle of the trees, and Tommy's musical whistle.

'What's that tune?' Flo enquired. 'I can't quite place it.'

' "Dancing in the Dark." Have you never heard it before?'

'I couldn't remember what it was called.'

He began to sing. ' "Dancing in the dark . . ." C'mon, Flo.' He grabbed her by the waist and twirled her around. Flo threw back her head and laughed. ' "Dancing in the dark," ' they sang together.

They stopped when two men walked past and Flo shivered. 'I forgot to bring a cardy.'

Tommy put his arm around her shoulders. 'You don't feel cold.' He placed his hand on the back of her neck. 'You feel hot. Your neck's sweating.'

She wasn't sure if she was hot or cold. Her body felt as if it was on fire, yet she shivered again. Tommy's hand pressed harder on her neck as he began to lead her towards a tree not far away. He pushed her against the broad trunk and took her in his arms. 'I've been thinking of nothing else but this for days.'

A train roared past on the furthest side of the park, the engine puffing eerie clouds of smoke. Flo thought about Dad, who'd been knocked down on that very same railway line, but not for long: Tommy's lips were pressed against hers and she felt as if she was being sucked into a whirlpool. Her head spun and she seemed to be slipping down and down and down. She came to briefly and found herself lying on the damp grass with Tommy bent over her. He'd undone the front of her dress and his lips were seeking her breasts, his tongue tenderly touching her nipples. Flo arched her back and almost screamed because the sensation was so wonderful. She knew what was to come, she knew it was a bad thing, but she could no more have stopped him than she could have stopped the sun from rising the next morning.

Tommy was pushing up her skirt, pulling away her underthings. There was the sound of her stockings tearing and she felt his callused hand between her legs. He was groaning, murmuring over and over, 'I love you, Flo,' and she could hear other little breathless cries that she realised came from her own throat. All the while, she was running her fingers through his thick dark curls, kissing his ears, his neck . . .

He felt so *big* when he entered her, and it hurt, but the hurt soon faded and turned into something else, something that no words had been invented to describe.

It all ended in a wild, feverish explosion that left them shaken and exhausted, and with Flo convinced that the only reason she'd been born was to make love with Tommy O'Mara.

'Jaysus, Flo!' he said hoarsely. 'That was the best I've ever known.' After a while, he began to pull her clothes back on. 'Get dressed, luv, else you'll catch cold.'

Flo touched his sensually curved lips with her finger, feeling the love flow from her heart right down her arm. 'I love you, Tommy.'

'I love you, girl.'

There was the faint murmur of voices upstairs: Martha and Sally were awake. Flo leaped out of the chair to take them up a cup of tea. On the way to the back kitchen, she did a pirouette. She'd always been happy, but nowadays she was so happy she could burst – and it had all begun that night in the Mystery when she'd danced in the dark with Tommy.

She and Sally had a wonderful day in New Brighton. They went on every single ride in the fairground, even the children's ones. Sally complained afterwards she felt quite sick, though it was more likely caused by the fish and chips followed by a giant ice-cream cornet with strawberry topping. She recovered swiftly on the ferry back when they clicked with two sailors who invited them to the pictures. 'Why did you turn them down?' she grumbled, on the tram home to Wavertree.

'I didn't fancy that Peter,' Flo replied. In fact, both sailors had been quite nice, but she was meeting Tommy at eight o'clock. Even if she wasn't, she would have felt disloyal going out with another man.

'I quite fancied Jock.' Her sister sighed. Sally was neither plain nor pretty, a bit like Dad with her neat brown hair and hazel eyes. She hadn't had a date since the one with Brian Maloney, almost two months ago.

Flo felt bad about the sailors. If it hadn't been for Tommy she'd have gone like a shot. 'You gave Jock your address, Sal. He might write,' she said hopefully.

'And where are you off to?' Martha demanded that night when Flo came downstairs ready to go out.

'I'm going to see Josie.' Unknown to Josie Driver, she and Flo had become the greatest of friends since Tommy had appeared on the scene. She met Josie twice a week, Mondays and Fridays. Josie would have been surprised to learn she was thinking of becoming a nun and needed someone in whom she could confide her deepest, most intimate thoughts while coming to such a major decision.

Martha's eyes looked suspicious behind her thick glasses. 'Why do you need a red bow in your hair just to see Josie?'

'I bought the ribbon in New Brighton,' Flo replied haughtily.

'It looks very nice,' Albert Colquitt said, from the table where he was having his tea.

'I think so, too,' Mam concurred.

Martha gave up. 'Don't be too late.'

'Have a nice time,' Flo called, as she slammed the door. Albert had just bought a wireless and everyone was staying in to listen to a play, Mam armed with two bottles of Guinness to 'build her up', although she'd been feeling better since the weather had improved. Flo shuddered to think of her sisters sitting in the parlour on Albert's bed-settee. What a way for two young women to spend a bank-holiday evening!

'I like your bow,' said Tommy.

'I like your tie,' Flo sang.

'I like your face, your eyes, your lips. I like every single little thing about you!' He picked her up and spun her around until they both felt dizzy and fell, laughing, on to the grass, whereupon he began to kiss her passionately.

'It's still broad daylight,' Flo murmured.

'So it is.' He kissed her again and caressed her breasts.

'We might get arrested and it'd be in the *Echo*.'

'Would that matter?'

'Not to me it wouldn't,' Flo giggled, 'but me mam wouldn't be pleased and our Martha'd have a fit. Nancy wouldn't like it either.'

'Nancy would just have to lump it.' Nevertheless, he sat up and smoothed his unruly curls.

Flo had never told him she'd seen Nancy. One day when she knew he was at work she'd set out for Clement Street, off Smithdown Road. It was a respectable street of small two-up, two-down houses. The windows shone, the steps had been scrubbed that morning. Flo paused across the road opposite number eighteen.

So this was where he lived. Nancy must take pride in her house. The curtains were maroon cretonne, upstairs and down, and there were paper flowers in the parlour window. The front door and the window-sills were dark green, freshly painted. Flo's heart missed a beat – had *he* painted them? She'd never ask because she didn't want him to know she'd spied on his house.

She walked up and down the street several times, keeping a close eye on number eighteen in case Nancy came out to clean the windows or brush the step. After about half an hour, when she was about to give up, a woman carrying a shopping basket came towards her from the direction of Smith-down Road. Flo knew it was Nancy because she looked exactly like the gypsy Tommy had said she was. She was outstanding in her way, the sort of woman that would be described as handsome. Her skin was the colour of cinnamon, her eyes as black as night, and she had a big beaked nose and glossy black hair drawn back in a cushiony bun at the nape of her thin neck.

'Mercy me!' Flo muttered. She wasn't sure why, but something about the woman disturbed her. And what peculiar clothes she wore to go shopping! A flowing black skirt, red satin blouse and a brightly embroidered garment that wasn't quite a jacket and wasn't quite a shawl.

The two women passed. Flo had no idea if Nancy glanced in her direction because she kept her own eyes fixed firmly on the ground. After a few seconds, she turned and saw the colourful figure cross the road and go into number eighteen.

In the Mystery, Tommy got to his feet and reached down to pull her up. 'We'll come back later when it's dark. And then . . .' His dark eyes smouldered and Flo's tummy did a cartwheel.

'And then . . .' she whispered. Then they would come as close to heaven as it was possible to get on earth.

She told him about the sailors because she wanted to make him jealous and he duly was. 'You belong to me, Flo Clancy,' he said angrily. 'We belong to each other till the end of time.'

'I know, I know!' she cried. 'I wouldn't dream of going out with another man when I've got you.'

He looked sulky. 'I should hope not!'

In the pub, he informed her that the submarine he'd been working on, the *Thetis*, was taking its first diving exercise on Thursday. 'Some of the shipyard workers are sailing with it, but my name wasn't on the list. You get extra pay, at least ten bob.' He looked wistful. 'I would have gone for nothing.'

'Never mind.' Flo was keeping a close eye on the sky outside. She wasn't bothered about the *Thetis*. All her concentration was centred on how swiftly night would fall so they could go to the Mystery and make love.

2

The Fritz family had been to Anglesey for Whit, a regular haunt, and Mr Fritz didn't return to the laundry till Thursday when the children were due back at school. He'd bought a camera, there was one exposure left on the roll, and he wanted a snapshot taken of him with his girls. Later that morning, Mrs Fritz came bustling along to take it. It was the first of June and a perfect day for taking photographs. The weather had been brilliantly sunny all week.

The six women trooped outside, excited. 'You stand by me, Flo,' Mr Fritz hissed. 'It's an excuse to put my arm around you. I want a record of that smile. It's always been enough to dazzle the strongest eyes, but lately it's not just a smile, it's a miracle.'

Mrs Fritz stationed her plump body in the middle of the street. 'Try and get the sign in over the door, Stella,' her husband shouted, as everyone shuffled into position.

'Say cheese!' Mrs Fritz called.

'*Cheese!*'

There was a click. 'All done!'

'If it turns out all right, I'll order a copy each.' Mr Fritz squeezed Flo's waist and whispered, 'I enjoyed that.'

Flo knew he was only joking, because he adored his sweet little wife and eight children, but she hoped no one had noticed – Josie was always complaining that Flo was Mr Fritz's favourite.

The rest of the day passed in a dream, as the days did since she'd met Tommy. She lived for Monday, lived for Friday, then lived for Monday again. They would have met more often, but he didn't like to leave Nancy while she felt so poorly.

Six o'clock came and she made her way home, still immersed in her dream, and scarcely noticed the crowd that had gathered on the corner of the street next to hers until she reached it.

'What's up?' she asked.

A woman grabbed her arm. 'There's been a terrible accident, girl. Haven't you heard?'

'What sort of accident?'

'It's some ship, a submarine called the *Thetis* – it's trapped underwater in Liverpool Bay and they can't find its position. There's over a hundred men on board.'

'Holy Mary, Mother of God!' Flo crossed herself. At first she felt relieved that Tommy hadn't been on board, but concern followed quickly for the men who were. She could think of nothing more horrific than to be trapped beneath the sea in a vessel she imagined being shaped like a big black fish. 'They'll be rescued, won't they?' she said anxiously.

An elderly man butted in. 'Of course they will, luv. I'm an ould salt meself, so I know Liverpool Bay's no more than twenty-five fathoms deep. They'll have them men up in no time.'

When she got home Mam and her sisters had already heard the bad news.

Martha was wondering if they dared invade Albert's room and turn on the wireless.

'It's not been declared official yet,' Mam said. 'So far it's just rumour.'

'You mean it might not have happened?' Sally looked hopeful.

'Oh, it's happened all right.' Mam shook her head sadly. 'Mrs Cox's nephew works in Cammell Laird where everyone knows full well there's been an accident. Women have already started to collect outside to wait for news of their men. It's just that nothing's been confirmed, so the news won't have reached the wireless.'

It wasn't until ten o'clock that the plight of the *Thetis* was conveyed to the nation by the BBC. One hundred and three men were on board, fifty of them civilians. The Admiralty assured everyone concerned that rescue ships were on their way and there was every hope the men would be saved.

'I should think so!' Flo said indignantly. 'It's only twenty-five fathoms deep.'

'How much is that in feet?' Martha asked Albert, as if men automatically knew everything. Albert confessed he had no idea.

There was a search for Dad's dictionary, which had conversion tables at the back. Twenty-five fathoms was 150 feet.

In bed that night, Flo was unable to get the trapped men out of her mind. She tossed and turned restlessly.

'Are you awake, Flo?' Sally whispered.

'Yes. I can't stop thinking of those men in the *Thetis*.'

'Me neither.'

Martha's voice surprised them because she usually slept like a log, despite the metal curlers. 'Let's say a silent prayer. Remember that one we learned at school for shipwrecked mariners?'

Eventually the sisters fell asleep, the words of the prayer on their lips.

When they woke next morning the *Thetis* came straight to mind. The weather was lovely, gloriously sunny, and it seemed incongruous and unfair that those safe on land should be blessed with such a perfect day in view of the disaster unfolding beneath the sea.

Albert had given them permission to listen to his wireless, from which they learned there'd been no developments overnight. Ships and aircraft were still trying to pinpoint the position of the stricken submarine.

On her way to work, Flo passed several groups of people gravely discussing the tragedy, which had touched the hearts of everyone in Liverpool. Twice she was asked, 'Have you heard any fresh news, luv?' All she could do was shake her head.

She bought a *Daily Herald*. Everyone in the laundry had bought a paper and the *Thetis* was the main headline on them all, as well as the sole topic of conversation all morning. Betty Bryant knew a woman who knew a woman whose cousin's husband was on board.

'I know someone on board even better than that,' Olive Knott said smugly. 'In fact, we all do. Remember that feller who brought his suit in for dry-cleaning a couple of months ago, Tommy O'Mara? He's a fitter with Cammell Laird. His poor ould wife wasn't half making a scene last night! Running up and down the street she was, screaming her head off. It took half a dozen neighbours to calm her. Mind you, Nancy O'Mara's always had a couple of screws loose.'

'But he wasn't supposed to go!' Flo's horrified words were lost in the chorus of dismay.

'Such a dead handsome feller, what a shame!'

'He was a cheeky-looking bugger, but I liked him.' Josie Driver looked close to tears.

Olive made a sour face. 'I don't wish him any harm, but Nancy'll be better off without the bugger. He drove the poor woman doo-lally with his philandering. No woman, married or single, was safe near Tommy O'Mara.'

That's not true! Flo wanted to scream that Olive was talking nonsense. Tommy may have been a bit of a blade in the past – in fact, he'd hinted so more than once – but it was only because Nancy hadn't been a proper wife in a long time. Since he'd met Flo, he wouldn't have given another woman a second glance. Oh, if only she could tell them! But why on earth was she thinking like this when it didn't matter a jot what Olive thought? What mattered was that Tommy might die! If he did, Flo wanted to die, too.

In her agitation she nearly scorched a shirt. Then Betty made things worse by reading out something from the newspaper. There was only enough oxygen on board to last thirty-six hours. Once the supply dried up, the men would die from carbon-dioxide poisoning. 'It means there's not much time left.' Betty clasped her hands together as if she were praying. 'Holy Mary, Mother of God, please save those poor men!'

Then Mr Fritz came hurrying in, panting for breath. 'The *Thetis* has been spotted with its stern sticking out of the water fourteen miles from Great Ormes Head. It was on the wireless just before I left.'

'Thank the Lord!' Josie shouted. 'They're bound to save them now.'

Relief swept through Flo's body so forcefully that, for a moment, she felt sick. She swayed, and Mr Fritz snatched the gas iron from her hand. 'Are you all right, Flo?'

'I hardly slept last night. I feel a bit ragged, that's all.'

'You go home, girl, if you don't feel better soon,' he said concernedly. 'I don't want you on your feet all day if you've got problems.'

'Problems' meant he thought she had a period. Standing for ten hours in the equivalent of a steambath was hard on women who had trouble with their monthlies, and Mr Fritz was always sympathetic if someone needed a day off. Flo, however, had always sailed through hers without so much as a twinge. Apart from a week's holiday each year, she hadn't had a single day off since she'd started five years ago straight from school.

'I'll see how I feel,' she told him gratefully.

The feeling of sickness soon left her, but for the first time the noise in the laundry began to get on her nerves: the churning of the washing in the boilers, the clatter of the belt-driven wringers, the hiss of the irons. Flo knew she couldn't work all day with the sounds pressing against her brain while she remained ignorant of the fate of the *Thetis*.

At midday, she went into the office and told Mr Fritz she felt no better. 'I wouldn't mind going home, after all.' She felt slightly ashamed of how good she'd become at lying over the last two months.

He fussed around, patted her cheek, and said she didn't look anything like her usual glowing self. He even offered to take her to Burnett Street in the van.

'No, ta,' she said. 'I might walk around a bit to clear me head. I'll go to bed this avvy.'

'Good idea, Flo, I hope you feel better tomorrow.'

Several hundred men and women had congregated in front of the gates of Cammell Laird. Some of the women held babies in their arms with slightly older children clutching their skirts. Some faces were hopeful, others blank with despair. A woman she couldn't see was shouting for her man. Flo's heart sank. It would seem there hadn't been more good news.

A girl with a glorious head of red hair, about the same age as herself, was standing at the back. 'What's happening?' Flo asked.

'Four men got out through the escape hatches, otherwise nowt.' The girl's face was extraordinarily colourful: pink lips, rosy cheeks, black-lashed eyes the colour of violets, all framed in the cloud of red waves.

'But someone at work said the stern was sticking out the water,' Flo groaned. 'I'd have thought they'd have hauled it up by now.'

The girl shrugged. 'I'd have thought so, too, but they haven't.' She looked at Flo sympathetically. 'Have you got someone on board?'

Flo bit her lip. 'Me feller.'

'Aye, so's mine. Well, he's only a sort of feller.' She didn't look the least bit upset. 'I only came out of curiosity. I'm always looking for an excuse to get off work. I suppose it's about time I went – I called in and said I had to see the doctor.'

'I told a lie to get away meself,' Flo confessed.

The girl made a face as if implying they were partners in a crime. 'Are you from Liverpool or Birkenhead?' She spoke in a loud, musical voice that rose and fell as if she was singing.

'Liverpool. I came on the ferry.'

'Me, too. I'll catch the next one back. Are you coming?'

'I only just got here. I'd sooner stay and see if anything happens.' Flo wished the girl didn't have to go. She rather liked her friendly, down-to-earth manner.

'I might go to the pics tonight. It'll be all about the *Thetis* on the Pathé News. Tara, then.' She clattered away on her high heels.

'Tara.' Flo sighed. If the submarine hadn't been brought up by tonight, it would be cutting things fine for those on board.

She turned her attention to the crowd. 'What I'd like to know,' a man muttered aggressively, 'is why they don't bore a hole through the hull and get everyone out that way, or at least pass in a hose of oxygen.'

Somewhere a woman was still shouting: 'What have you done with my man?' Flo edged her way through the throng.

'There's no need for that carry-on,' an elderly woman remarked acidly. 'Most of us are feared for our lads, but we're not reduced to weeping and wailing like a bloody banshee. Just look at the way she's throwing herself about an' all!'

Flo didn't answer. She had almost reached the front when she froze. Nancy O'Mara was kneeling on the ground, her hands clasped imploringly towards the closed gates of the ship-builder's. Her crow-black eyes burned unnaturally bright, as if with fever. Long strands of hair had escaped from the big bun coiled on her neck, and writhed like little snakes as she rocked to and fro. She looked almost insane with grief. Every now and then she turned her tragic face towards the men and women standing silently each side of her. 'Why?' she pleaded. 'Why, oh, why?'

Nobody answered, the faces remained impassive. They had no idea why. At that moment, there wasn't a person on earth who knew why ninety-nine human beings still remained on the stricken vessel when it was surrounded by rescue ships and the stern was visible for all to see.

Flo stood stock-still as she watched Tommy's wife throw herself back and forth on the pavement. Nancy paused to seek succour from those around her yet again. 'Why?' Then she caught sight of Flo, who stood transfixed as the burning eyes bored into hers, so full of hate that she felt her blood turn to ice.

Nancy knew!

With a cry that almost choked her, Flo turned and pushed her way through the crowd. She ran, faster than she'd ever run before, past the docks, the half-built ships, the vessels waiting to be loaded or unloaded. She ran until she reached the ferry, where a seaman was just about to raise the gangplank, and launched herself on to the deck. 'Just made it, luv.' He grinned.

Flo hardly heard. She climbed the stairs until she reached the top deck where she leaned on the hand-rail and stared into the calm greeny-brown waters of the Mersey. A warm breeze fanned her face, and her mind was blank, devoid of emotion or thought.

'Hello, there,' said a familiar voice. 'I thought you were going to stay and see what happened?'

'I decided not to.' Flo turned. The red-haired girl was the only person she didn't mind seeing at the moment. 'I felt too upset.'

'You shouldn't get upset over a feller.' The girl leaned on the rail beside her. She wore a smart emerald-green frock that accentuated her vividly coloured face. At any other time Flo would have felt ashamed of the shabby blouse and skirt she wore for work. 'There's plenty more where he came from. Someone with your looks will soon get fixed up again.'

'I don't want to get fixed up again,' Flo whispered. 'I'll never go out with anyone else. Never!'

'Don't tell me you're in love?' The girl sounded faintly disgusted.

Flo nodded numbly. For the first time since she'd heard the news about Tommy, she began to cry. The tears flowed freely down her cheeks and fell silently on to the smooth waters below.

'Come on, girl.' Flo felt her shoulders being painfully squeezed. 'What's your name?'

'Flo Clancy.'

'I'm Isobel MacIntyre, but everyone calls me Bel.' She gave Flo a little shake. 'Look, the ferry's about to dock. Shall we find somewhere and have a cup of tea?'

'I'd love to, but what about your job?'

'Sod me job! I'll tell them the doctor said I was run down and I needed a day off to put me feet up. Anyroad, it says almost half past two on the Liver building clock, so it's not worth going in.'

Flo couldn't help but smile through her tears. 'You're the healthiest-looking person I've ever seen.'

There was a café a short way along Water Street, almost empty after the dinner-time rush. They were about to enter, when Flo remembered she had only enough money for her tram fare home.

'Don't worry,' Bel said, when she told her. 'I'm flush so it can be my treat.'

As they drank their tea and Flo nibbled at a sticky bun, Bel informed her that she worked as a waitress at La Porte Rouge, a restaurant in Bold Street. 'That's French for the Red Door. It's dead posh and I get good tips, particularly off the fellers. Last week, I got fifteen bob altogether.'

'Just in tips! Gosh, I don't get much more than that in wages.'

Bel asked where she worked and where she lived and all about her family. Flo could tell she was trying to keep her mind off the events taking place above and below the sea not too many miles away. She gladly told her all about Fritz's Laundry, about Mam and her sisters, and how they'd had to take in a lodger when Dad died. 'He's dead nice, Albert. The thing is, our Martha's determined to marry him. I can't think why, 'cos though he's nice, he's no oil painting, and he's forty-five. She wears glasses, though, and she thinks she'll never catch a feller. You should hear the way she bosses me and our Sal around, just 'cos she's the oldest,' Flo said indignantly.

'She couldn't be any worse than me auntie Mabel,' Bel said flatly. 'She's an ould cow if there ever was one.' She explained that her mam had died when she was only four and she'd been dumped on Auntie Mabel who lived in Everton Valley. 'Me dad's away at sea most of the time. I can't wait to get away meself. I'm eighteen, and the very second the war starts, I'm going to join the Army.'

'But the Army only take men!'

'Of course they don't, soft girl! They take women an' all. They're called the ATS, which stands for Auxiliary Territorial Service.'

Just then, two men came in, talking volubly, and sat at the next table. After they had given the waitress their order, they continued their conversation.

'It's bloody disgraceful!' one said angrily. 'If I had a son on board, I'd kick up a stink all the way to Parliament. Why was she allowed to dive with twice the normal complement on board? Why was the Navy so long finding her position? And I'll never understand why cutting gear hasn't been brought by now and a hole made in her stern. The men would be free if the powers-that-be had any sense of urgency.'

'If someone doesn't get their finger out pretty soon, it'll be too late,' the other man said.

'If it isn't already! That business about there being enough oxygen for thirty-six hours, I'd like to know if that takes account of the extra men as well as the crew.'

'Do you ever go dancing, Flo?' Bel asked brightly.

But Flo's mind had been distracted long enough. 'I wonder if anything's happened,' she whispered.

'Don't sound like it. But try not to lose heart, Flo. There's still hope.'

Flo gave a deep, shuddering sigh. It was strange, but she couldn't help thinking about Nancy.

'Your chap's married, isn't he?' Bel said knowingly.

'How did you guess?' Flo gasped.

'If he was a proper boyfriend, this Mr Fritz would have let you off like a shot. Instead, you had to tell a lie to get away.'

'So did you,' Flo pointed out. 'Your chap must be married, too.'

Bel made a face. 'It so happens he's not. Tuesday was only the second time I'd seen him. That's when he told me he was sailing with the *Thetis* because some other feller had been taken poorly. When I saw the headlines in this morning's papers, it seemed a good excuse for a ride on the ferry – I often go on me own. In fact, that's where I met my chap, on the Birkenhead ferry.' She pursed her red lips primly. 'I'm not the sort of girl who goes out with married men, thanks all the same. Mind you, Flo, you don't look the sort, either, particularly with you being a Catholic an' all, not like me.'

Flo felt it was important to explain the nature of her relationship with Tommy. 'My chap wasn't married proper. We were going to get married next year.' She paused, frowning. 'His wife – I mean, his sort-of-wife – was outside Cammell Laird's. You never heard such a carry-on.'

'Was she the one who was shouting?'

'That's right, Nancy. The thing is, I'm sure she recognised me.'

'Maybe she's been following you and your bloke around?'

Flo shuddered. 'Oh, don't! Tommy would have a fit at the very idea.'

'Who?'

'Tommy. Tommy O'Mara. What's your chap's name?'

Bel was scowling at the teapot as she poured more water in. Her cheeks were flaming. 'Er, Jack Smith,' she said shortly. Despite having refilled the pot, she leaped to her feet and paid the bill. Outside, she began to walk quickly, for no reason that a rather confused Flo could see, back towards the river.

They arrived at the Pier Head just as a ferry returning from New Brighton was docking. Children came running off the boat on to the landing-stage carrying buckets and spades, their hair full of sand, faces brown from the sun. Flo remembered going to New Brighton with Mam and Dad and her sisters. It seemed a hundred lifetimes ago. The area was unusually crowded for a weekday. People were staring out to sea, as if hoping to see signs of the attempts being made to rescue the ill-fated submarine. The girls wandered across to join them.

They stood for a long while in silence, until Flo said dully, 'I don't know what I'm going to do if Tommy's dead. I'll never love another man the way I loved him. If they don't fetch the *Thetis* up, me life's over.'

'I've never heard such nonsense!' Bel's expressive face conveyed a mixture of sympathy and impatience. 'No one's life's over when they're only nineteen. What about all the proper wives? Are their lives over, too? You're dead stupid you are, Flo Clancy, letting yourself get all worked up over a chap who's not worth twopence.'

The criticism was rather blunt and scathing coming from someone she'd only just met, but Flo was too upset to take offence. She began to cry again. 'How would you know what he's worth?' she sobbed. 'Tommy O'Mara's worth a million pounds to me.'

'I've never met a chap worth twopence meself,' Bel said brusquely. 'When I meet a threepenny one, I'll marry him like a shot. The trouble with you is you're dead soft. I'm as hard as nails, me. You'll never see me cry over a man, not even a threepenny one.' She seemed unable to grasp the extent of Flo's despair. 'C'mon, let's walk into town. It might take your mind off things, though we'd best steer clear of Bold Street case someone from work sees me.'

It wasn't until half past five that Flo and Bel parted. They exchanged addresses and promised to keep in touch. Flo wanted to arrive home as she usually did from work. She wouldn't tell anyone where she'd been that afternoon.

'Good heavens, Flo!' Mam remarked, when she went in. 'You're as white as a ghost and you're shivering. I hope you're not coming down with a cold. Summer colds are the worst to shake off.'

'Has anything happened?' Flo demanded abruptly.

Mam knew exactly what she meant. 'No, luv,' she said sadly. 'According to Mrs Cox, they managed to get a hawser to the hull, but it snapped and the ship sank underwater. I went to church today to say prayers with the Legion of Mary, but they don't seem to have done much good.'

Flo refused anything to eat. At Mam's insistence, she went to bed after a cup of tea. She felt uncomfortable when Martha came up later with a hot-water bottle and tucked her in. Martha wouldn't be so sympathetic if she knew the reason why her sister felt so out of sorts.

That night, she slept fitfully. Each time she woke, she was left with the memory of the same dream: she'd been wandering alone through the Mystery when an orchestra wearing full evening dress appeared before her, the sort she'd seen in films. But these were hollow, insubstantial figures – she could see right through them. They were playing 'Dancing in the Dark', and equally shadowy couples began to waltz in a circle around her. Instead of staring at each other, they gazed at Flo, unpleasant, gloating expressions on their faces. They were sneering because she was the only person without a partner. Her sense of isolation was so acute that she felt as if she was encased in a block of ice. Then the couples disappeared, the music stopped, and all that could be heard was the rustle of the trees. Flo was alone with only the moon for company.

Next morning, Mam came up with a cup of tea. 'To save you asking, I just listened to the BBC and there's no news, I'm afraid.'

Flo sat up. To her amazement there was no sign of Martha and Sally, and their bed was neatly made.

'They've gone to work,' Mam explained. 'We decided not to wake you. It wouldn't hurt to have the day off, it being Saturday, like, and you'd only be there till one. I'm sure Mr Fritz won't mind – you've never been off before.'

Flo was only too willing to comply. After Mam had gone, she pulled the bedclothes over her head and sobbed her heart out. She wasn't sure what time it was when she heard a knock on the front door, followed by Mr Fritz's voice asking how she was. 'We're all worried about her. It's not like Flo to be sick.' She hoped he wouldn't say she'd been off yesterday. It seemed he didn't, because Mam came up shortly afterwards and didn't mention it.

'He's a lovely man,' she said warmly. 'I'm very fond of him. You're ever so lucky, Flo, working in such a nice place.'

By late afternoon everyone was home, including Albert. Flo got up, and after tea they all trooped into the parlour to listen to the six o'clock news. In a chilling voice the announcer read a statement: 'The Admiralty regrets that hope of saving lives in the *Thetis* must be abandoned.'

Liverpool, the entire country, was stunned. A cablegram arrived from King George VI in Canada. His mother, Queen Mary, conveyed her sympathies to the grieving relatives, and Adolf Hitler sent condolences from the citizens of Germany. When this was announced in the cinema, the audience set up a chorus of boos. A fund was set up for relatives of the dead; within days it had reached thousands of pounds. The Clancy family clubbed together and managed to raise a pound between them. Albert Colquitt added another pound and promised to take it to the collection point in the town hall.

The following Tuesday was a day of mourning. Birkenhead Cenotaph was said to be a mass of wreaths. Fifteen thousand attended the service and five thousand workers marched in honour of the memory of those who had died.

While the country mourned and salvage work began on the *Thetis*, the press were asking questions. It was impossible to grasp that so many lives had been lost when only a few feet had separated the men from their rescuers. Why hadn't experienced divers been rushed to the scene? Where was the oxyacetyline gear? A tribunal was appointed to investigate.

It wasn't until November that the *Thetis* was salvaged and able to deliver her dead for proper burial. The ship was pronounced sound enough to return by sea to its place of birth in Birkenhead. At any other time, this would have been headline news, but by now the country was already in the grip of a tragedy that would result in far greater loss of life than on a single submarine. The unthinkable had happened: Great Britain was at war with Germany and immersed in the struggle to survive.

Flo Clancy drifted through the months after Tommy O'Mara died. Everyone wanted to know what had happened to her lovely smile. Mr Fritz gave her the lightest jobs, much to the chagrin of Josie Driver who turned quite nasty. Mam bought an iron tonic, which Flo took dutifully three times a day, though she knew it wouldn't do any good. Only Bel MacIntyre, whom she saw regularly, knew why Flo no longer smiled. But Bel knew only the half of it. Flo had more things than the loss of Tommy to worry about.

On the first Sunday in September, a day blessed with shimmering sunshine and an atmosphere as heady as wine, Flo sat in the parlour listening to Albert's wireless. She heard Neville Chamberlain, the Prime Minister, announce that the country was at war and wished it mattered as much to her as it did to the rest of her family. Sally had burst into tears. 'What's going to happen to Jock?' she wept.

Jock Wilson had been writing to Sally ever since Whit Monday when they'd met on the New Brighton ferry. He'd been back to Liverpool to see her whenever he could manage a few days' leave.

Albert turned off the wireless. He looked grim. Martha reached across and self-consciously took his hand. Poor Mam's face seemed to collapse before their eyes. 'Oh, I don't half wish your dad was here!' she cried.

But Flo was too concerned with her own luckless state to care. She'd scarcely noticed missing the first period, and it wasn't until July that she had become alarmed. By the time July had given way to August and there was still no sign, she realised, with increasing horror, that she was pregnant with Tommy O'Mara's child.

Millie

1

Sharp fingers of light strobed the dark ceiling of the nightclub, interlocking briefly; blue, red, green, then yellow, followed by blue again. The disc jockey's overwrought, grating voice announced a change of record, though his words could scarcely be heard above the music booming from the huge speakers on either side of him.

In the centre of the large room, which was mainly painted black, the dancers gyrated, faces blank. Only their bodies reacted to the pounding rhythm of Joey Negro's 'Can't Take It With You', the sound bouncing off the ceiling and the walls.

I could feel the noise vibrating through the plastic seat and the soles of my shoes. It throbbed through the table and up my arms. Although I hadn't danced so far, the heat felt tremendous and my neck was damp with perspiration.

Beside me, James didn't look bored exactly, but definitely fed up. He'd been like that since we met earlier, which wasn't a bit like him. I felt put out. After a stressful week, I'd been looking forward to Saturday and his relaxing company. The friends we'd come with, Julie and Gavin, had got up to dance about half an hour ago, though I could see no sign of them on the floor.

I put my mouth against James's ear and shouted, 'Enjoying yourself?'

'Oh, I'm having a wonderful time.' He spoke with a sarcasm I'd never heard before. 'Want another drink?'

I shook my head just as Julie and Gavin returned. Gavin was an old schoolfriend of James, a massively built yet graceful man who played amateur rugby. He surreptitiously removed a piece of folded paper from the breast pocket of his silk jacket and emptied the contents on to the table. Three pink tablets rolled out.

'Eleven quid each,' he shouted. He pushed one towards James. 'Have this on me.'

'Not tonight, thanks,' James said stiffly.

'Come on, James,' Julie coaxed. She was a pretty girl with a cascade of blonde curly hair. 'You look way down in the dumps. An E will put a different perspective on things.'

'I said no, thanks.'

Gavin shrugged. 'How about you, Millie? Does Miss Morality fancy changing the habit of a lifetime and popping a pill for once?'

I was tired of explaining that refusing Ecstasy had nothing to do with morality, but that the thought of not having full control of my faculties frightened me. Before I could refuse, James said angrily, 'No, she doesn't.' He looked at me, irritated at his own impatience, because he knew I would resent his answering on my behalf. 'Aw, shit!' He groaned. 'I can't stand it here. I'm going out for some fresh air.'

'He's not himself,' I said in excuse. I collected my coat and bag and James's jacket. 'We might see you later, but don't wait.'

I pushed my way through the crowded tables and found James outside in the car park. He was already shivering without his coat. October had brought an end to the beautiful Indian summer and the temperature must have dropped twenty degrees. I handed him the jacket. 'Put this on or you'll catch cold.'

'Yes, ma'am.' He forced a smile. 'Sorry about that, but I'm getting too old for clubbing.'

I linked his arm as we strolled through the car park towards the rear of the club. I had no idea where the place was situated; over the water, somewhere between Birkenhead and Rock Ferry. 'You'd think you were ready to collect your pension.'

'Seriously, Millie, once you reach a certain age, life has to have more to it than the non-stop pursuit of a so-called "good time". Life's got to mean something.' There was a tinge of desperation in his voice. 'Oh, hell! I'm no good at explaining. It's just that, at twenty-nine, I feel I should be doing something rather more worthwhile than prancing round a nightclub, taking happy pills.'

'Such as?' To my surprise, I found we'd reached a stretch of lumpy sand and the Mersey glinted blackly in the distance, reflecting a wobbly quarter-moon. We climbed the chain-link fence and walked towards the water.

'You'll be annoyed if I tell you.'

'I promise, on my heart, not to be.'

'I'd like us to get married and have kids,' James said flatly. 'And I'd prefer to do a job that made some sort of contribution towards society.'

Astonished, I came to a standstill on the sand. 'You'd give up the garage? What would your father have to say?' The business was to be his one day.

'Sod Pa, and sod the garage,' James said, even more astonishingly. 'I'm sick to death of selling poncy, overpowered cars to idiots like myself. The job's as worthless as my life. It's useless, *I'm* useless.' He kicked moodily at a stone. 'I took today off and went to Liverpool. There was a march, hundreds of dockers who've been turfed out by Mersey Docks and Harbour Board because they refused to sign contracts that meant worse conditions and less pay. They've been out of work a year. There were fathers and sons among them. Men like that are the salt of the earth. I feel so . . . so *inadequate* compared to them.'

We reached the water. James released my arm and stuffed his hands in his pockets. He stared into the black waves. 'I've led a charmed life, Millie. I've never had to struggle for anything. Everything I've wanted has just dropped into my lap without my needing to ask. We're very lucky, the pair of us.'

I wanted to laugh out loud and say, 'You speak for yourself! Nothing has ever dropped into *my* lap. I've worked very hard for what I've got.' But what did he know about it? I'd told him virtually nothing about myself. Instead, I muttered, almost inaudibly, 'Marriage may not be the answer, James. It sounds to me like you're going through some sort of crisis.'

'Oh, God, Millie!' He pulled me into his arms, so tightly I could hardly breathe. 'Then help me through, darling. I've been going out of my mind over the last week.'

Only a week, I thought wryly. It was only during the past two or three years that I'd vaguely begun to feel an acceptable member of the human race. I put my arms around his neck and laid my head on his shoulder, not sure what to say. A dredger, barely lit, was moving silently down the river. The music from the nightclub was a muted throb. A memory returned, as it so often did, of one of the worst beatings. Mam had been out, working evenings to make ends meet. I didn't hear him come in. I heard nothing until the slithering footsteps sounded on the stairs and my body froze with fear. *I was reading in bed with a torch!* I was six and had only just learned to read. The teacher was amazed at how quickly I'd taken to it, but books offered undreamed-of pleasures, as well as escape from grim reality. I read in the lavatory, at breaktimes, and in the canteen. I had no idea why my father should detest the idea of my reading. It was as if he couldn't stand his children, or his wife, getting enjoyment from something, being happy.

So I'd been ordered not to read in bed. At the sound of the footsteps, I fumbled frantically with the torch, but it wouldn't go off. My hands were clammy with terror and I dropped it on the floor. The book followed. Two little thuds that sounded like thunderclaps in the quiet house.

'I thought I told yer not ter read in bed.' His voice was low and quiet, full of menace. The words travelled the years, as if they'd been spoken only a few minutes ago.

'I'm sorry, Dad.' I quaked with fright. I could feel my insides tearing apart, the way the ground erupts in an earthquake.

'I'll give yer summat to be sorry for. Gerrout!'

But I was still frozen, terrified, under the covers. I couldn't move. He pulled them back, roughly dragged me on to the floor, and began to undo the buckle of his wide leather belt. 'Kneel down,' he ordered. 'Kneel down against the bed and pull yer nightie up.'

'I didn't mean it, Dad. I won't read again, I promise,' I wailed. This was before I vowed never to let him see me cry. In her bed on the other side of the room, our Trudy stirred. 'Whassa matter?'

'Get back ter sleep,' our father snarled.

With my face buried in the bedclothes, I began to whimper. 'I won't do it again, Dad, honest.'

'Yer can bet yer life on that, yer little bitch! Bend over further.'

My arms tightened around James's neck as I remembered and felt the blows rain down on my bare bottom for the millionth time. The hard leather cut into my soft, childish flesh and I felt blood trickle down my legs. I heard my screams of pain, my pleas for mercy. 'I won't read again, Dad, I promise.'

I never did, not for a long time. The teacher was mystified as to why words no longer meant anything to her best pupil. 'It must have been a flash in the pan,' she said.

Perhaps it was Trudy, sobbing hysterically, that made him stop or perhaps he was exhausted. I was never sure. My face was still pressed against the bed, when I heard him going downstairs, the most welcome sound on earth. 'Thank you, God!' I breathed.

I broke free of James's arms and began to walk along the sands. My heart was beating rapidly and my legs were shaking. The tide rippled in over my shoes, but I didn't notice.

James caught up and grabbed my arm. 'Darling, what's wrong? What did you just say? Thank you, God, for what?'

'Nothing.' I hadn't realised I'd spoken aloud.

'You're trembling. How can it be nothing?' He regarded me sadly. 'Why are you keeping things from me?'

'Because there are things I don't want you to know.'

'If we're to be married, we should know everything about each other.'

I put my hands over my ears to shut him – everything – out, I shouted, 'Who said we're to be married? *I* didn't. When you brought the subject up last Sunday I said I'd sooner talk about it some other time. I didn't mean a few days later.'

'Darling, your feet are getting soaked.' Before I knew what was happening, he'd picked me up in his arms and carried me back to where the sand was dry. He crouched down beside me and started to take off my wet shoes. 'We're a mixed-up pair, Millie,' he said.

'You were perfectly well adjusted when we met. If you're mixed up now, it must be my fault.'

He stroked my hair. 'That's probably true. You're driving me nuts, Millie Cameron.'

I relaxed against him. Perhaps marrying James wouldn't be such a bad thing, though I'd have to think long and hard before having children. He was so comfortable to be with, so nice. But, then, no one could have been nicer than Gary, who'd bored me silly, and presumably Dad had been as nice as pie when he was courting Mum.

He was hurt when I insisted that he leave immediately after lunch next day. 'I thought we'd be spending Sunday together,' he said forlornly.

But I was firm. 'I'm clearing out my auntie's flat. I told you about it, remember? This is my only free day.'

'Why can't I go with you?' he pleaded. 'I could help. I could carry stuff out to the car. Anyway, it isn't safe for a woman on her own round there. Isn't William Square a red-light area?'

'Don't be silly,' I said dismissively. I couldn't wait to get to Flo's flat and had no intention of taking anyone with me. Mum had telephoned on Friday night and offered to lend a hand after she'd finished in the newsagent's shop where she worked till noon. 'You could meet me off the bus in town and let me have the key – I'll leave it with the woman upstairs. As long as I'm home before your dad, he'd never know I'd been.'

'It's quite all right, Mum,' I assured her. 'I can manage on my own.' I felt as if the flat was mine.

'Are you sure, luv? Last Sunday I got the impression you didn't want to be bothered.'

'I don't know where you got that idea from,' I said innocently. 'I don't mind a bit.'

After James had gone, I dressed in jeans and sweatshirt, and was brushing my hair when the phone rang. I ignored it, and heard the answering-machine click on. It was Mum. I sat on the off-white settee with a sigh and listened to the whining voice.

'Millicent, it's Mam. Your dad and Declan are out. Are you there, luv? It's just that I got this letter yesterday from the charity that runs our Alison's home. They can only keep her till she's eighteen. Next April she'll be transferred to this adult place in Oxford. Is that far, luv? I daren't show the letter to your dad – you know how he feels about Alison – and I can't find the atlas anywhere . . .'

My mother rambled on, as if the answering-machine itself was enough to talk to. I felt tears prickle my eyes as I listened. Mum loved her youngest child to distraction. She spent any spare money saved from the housekeeping on little presents for Alison, and had never stopped pining for her lost daughter. I couldn't bear to think how she would feel if Alison was placed out of reach of her weekly visits.

Oh, if only I could get shot of my family as easily as I'd got shot of Gary! If only I could divorce them and never see them again! By now, tears were pouring down my cheeks and I couldn't stand my mother's pain another second. I stumbled across the room and picked up the receiver.

'Mam!' But she had hung up. I had neither the strength nor the courage to ring back.

I breathed a sigh of relief as I closed the door of Flo's flat behind me. It felt like coming home. There were letters on the mat. As I lit the fire I scanned through them quickly, then turned on the lamp and went into the kitchen to put the kettle on. Nothing important; circulars, a market-research survey, a reminder that the TV licence was due. I put them aside and made a cup of tea. This time, I'd brought teabags, fresh milk and sandwiches. Still dunking a teabag, I returned to the living room and sank into the middle of the settee.

After a few minutes, I got up and put on Flo's record. Listening to Bing Crosby's soothing voice, I relaxed even more. The newspaper cuttings about the lost submarine, the *Thetis*, were still on the coffee table. I'd meant to ask someone about it, but the only elderly person I knew was Gran.

For almost an hour, I breathed in the peaceful atmosphere of the room, and the tension flowed from my body. I would have been quite happy to stay there for ever, but after a while I got up and began to wander round, poking in cupboards and drawers. Flo had been only superficially tidy. One sideboard drawer was full of gloves, another full of scarves, all in a mess. Another contained balls of string, a tangle of old shoelaces, an assortment of electric plugs, and a wad of money-off coupons held together with a rusty paperclip, which were years out of date.

For some reason, I found it necessary to untangle the laces, and was concentrating hard on undoing knots and trying to find pairs when there was a knock at the door. It would be Charmian I thought, and went to answer it. An elderly woman, very thin, with a huge cloud of unnatural mahogany-coloured hair and a still lovely though deeply wrinkled face, was standing outside. She wore a fake leopardskin jacket over a purple mohair jumper and black leggings, and appeared to be in the middle of a conversation with someone.

'Can't you wear a jacket or something?' she demanded angrily. There was a mumbled reply I couldn't catch, then the woman said, 'You'll do even less business if you catch the flu.' She turned and smiled at me ruefully, revealing a set of over-large false teeth. 'That bloody Fiona! She's wearing a dress with no sleeves that barely covers her arse. She'll perish in this weather. Hello, luv.'

No one waited for an invitation into Flo's, it seemed: the woman bounced into the room with the vitality of a teenager, although she must have been well into her seventies, followed by a waft of expensive perfume. 'I'm Bel Eddison, Flo's friend,' she said loudly. 'I know who you are – Millicent Cameron. I asked Charmian to give me a ring next time you came. She was right. You're the spitting image of Flo, and it's even more obvious to me 'cos I knew her when she was a girl. It gave me quite a turn when you opened the door.'

I'd already recognised the woman from the snapshot taken in Blackpool. It felt strange shaking hands with Flo's best friend, as if I was stepping back into the past, yet Bel was very much part of the present. 'How do you do?' I murmured. 'Please call me Millie.' I don't think I had ever seen such lovely eyes before, genuine violet. They were heavily made up, though, far too much for someone so old. The purple shadow had seeped into the crêpy lids, giving the effect of cracked eggshells.

'I'm tip-top, luv. How are you?' Bel didn't wait for an answer. Instead, she put her hands on her hips and regarded the room with exaggerated surprise. 'You haven't touched a thing,' she remarked. 'I was expecting to see the place stripped bare by now.'

'I was working out a plan of action,' I said guiltily, pushing the laces back into the drawer and closing it. 'Would you like a cup of tea?' I asked, when the newcomer removed her coat and threw herself on to the settee as if she'd come to stay. The springs squeaked in protest.

'No, ta, but I wouldn't mind a glass of Flo's sherry,' she said. Not only did she speak loudly, but also very quickly, in a strong, melodic voice that gave no hint of her age. 'Me and Flo sat here getting pissed on sherry more times than you've had hot dinners.'

Flo pissed didn't quite fit the image I'd built up in my mind, and I said as much to Bel when I gave her a glass. I poured one for myself too.

'It was her only vice,' Bel said. 'That's if you could call sherry a vice. Otherwise she led the life of a saint. For a long while, she went on retreat once a month to some convent in Wales. What's these?' She picked up the newspaper cuttings. 'Oh, you found them.' She grimaced.

'They were by the bed. Why did she keep them?' I asked.

'Draw your own conclusions, luv. It should be obvious.'

'She was in love with someone and he died on the *Thetis*?' I did a quick calculation: Flo would have been nineteen at the time.

'I said, draw your own conclusions.' Bel pursed her lips. I got the impression she enjoyed being mysterious. 'I'm not confirming or denying anything. I'd be betraying Flo's memory if I told things she kept to herself all her life.' She regarded me with her bright violet eyes. 'So, you're Kate Colquitt's eldest girl?'

'You know my mother?' I said, surprised.

'I did once. She used to come and see Flo a long time ago, but not since she married your dad. She was a lovely girl, Kate Colquitt. How is she these days?'

'She's okay,' I said abruptly.

Bel wriggled contentedly on the settee. Her expressive face displayed even the most fleeting emotion. 'This is nice! I never thought I'd sup sherry in Flo's again – pass us the bottle, there's a good girl. Ta!' she said comfortably. 'I'll top your glass up, shall I? We used to do this regular every Sunday. Sometimes Charmian joined us. It's uncanny, what with Flo dead, but you looking so much like her. Actually,' she continued with a frown, 'I'm racking me brains trying to bring to mind your husband's name. Was it Harry? You'd only been married a couple of years when Sally died – can you remember me at the funeral? Sally was the only contact Flo had with your family. When she died, Flo had no way of knowing how you were all getting on.'

'I'm sorry I don't remember you. I looked out for Flo, wondering what she was like. She disappeared before anyone could speak to her.'

'And how's Harry getting on?' Bel probed.

'Actually, it was Gary. We're divorced.'

'Really!' Bel sipped her sherry, clearly interested. 'What's your position now?' She looked all set for a long jangle. I felt less annoyed than I'd expected that the afternoon I'd anticipated having to myself had been interrupted. In fact, I *wasn't* annoyed. I liked Bel: she was so cheerfully vivid and alive. I wondered if we could trade information. If I told her a few things about myself, would she provide some details about Flo?

'I've got a boyfriend,' I explained. 'His name's James Atherton and we've been going out for a year. He's twenty-nine, and his father owns three garages on Merseyside. James manages the Southport one.'

'Is it serious?' Bel enquired gravely.

'On his side, not mine.' I thought about what James had said last night on the sands outside the nightclub. 'He's been going through some sort of crisis for an entire week.'

'Poor bugger,' Bel said laconically. 'Fellers wouldn't recognise a crisis if it crept up behind and threw them to the ground.'

'It's all my fault.' I wrinkled my nose.

'It shouldn't do him any harm. Men generally have it too easy in relationships with women.'

'Where did you meet Flo?' It was time she answered a few questions.

'Birkenhead, luv, a few months before the war began. She was a year older than me. She lived in Wavertree in those days.'

'Did Flo join the forces like you?'

'How did you know . . . ?' Bel began, then nodded at the photographs on the table. 'Of course, the photo of yours truly getting hitched to dear ould Bob. That was me in the ATS. No, Flo stayed working in the laundry during the war. I was posted to Egypt and it was years before I saw her again.' She glanced sadly around the room. For the first time she looked her age as her face grew sober and her eyes darkened with sadness. She appeared to be slightly drunk. 'She was such a lovely girl. You should have seen her smile – it was like a ray of sunshine, yet she buried herself in this place for most of her life. It's a dead rotten shame.'

'Would you like more sherry?' I asked. I much preferred the cheerful Bel, even if it meant her getting even drunker.

'I wouldn't say no.' She perked up. 'The bottle's nearly gone, but there'll be more in the sideboard. Flo always had half a dozen in. She said it helped with her headaches. Is there anything to eat, luv? Me stomach's rumbling something awful. I would have had summat before I left, but I never thought I'd be out so long.'

In the kitchen, I found several tins of soup in a cupboard. I opened a tin of pea and ham, poured it into two mugs and put them in the microwave to heat, then unwrapped the ham sandwiches I'd brought with me. I didn't realise I was singing until Bel shouted, 'Someone sounds happy! You've been listening to Flo's record.'

It was totally different from how I'd spent Sunday afternoons before and I wasn't doing anything that could remotely be considered exciting, yet I felt contented as I watched the red figures count down on the microwave. I wondered if Flo had bought the microwave and other things like the record player and the television on hire purchase. During my rather pathetic forays into drawers and cupboards, I hadn't come across any papers. Flo must have a pension book somewhere, possibly an insurance policy, and there were bound to be other matters that had to be dealt with; electricity and gas bills, council tax, water rates. I was being negligent in dealing with her affairs. This was the second time I'd come and the flat was no different now than it was when Flo died, except that there was less sherry and less food. As soon as Bel went, I'd get down to work, clear a few drawers or something.

I searched for a tray and discovered one in the cupboard under the sink. There was salt and pepper in pretty porcelain containers – 'A Gift from Margate'. I put everything on the tray and took it into the living room where Bel was half asleep.

'Who paid for the funeral?' I asked.

Bel came awake with a furious blinking of her thickly mascaraed lashes and immediately attacked a sandwich. 'Both me and Flo took out special funeral policies. She showed me where hers was kept and I showed her where to find mine. We used to wonder which of us would go first. Flo swore it would be her. I never said anything but I thought the same.' She made one of her outrageous faces. 'I'll have to show someone else where me policy is, won't I?'

'Haven't you got any children?'

'No, luv.' For a moment, Bel looked desolate. 'I was in the club three times but never able to bring a baby to term. Nowadays, they can do something about it, but not then.'

'I'm sorry,' I said softly. In fact, I was so sorry that a lump came to my throat.

Unexpectedly Bel smiled. 'That's all right, luv. I used to joke with Flo sometimes that we were a barren pair of bitches but, as she'd say, kids don't automatically bring happiness. Some you'd be better off without.' She went on tactlessly, 'How's that sister of yours, the sick one? I can't remember her name.'

'Alison. She's not sick, she's autistic.' I shrugged. 'She's the same as ever.'

'And what about your other sister? And you've got a brother, haven't you?'

I was being cross-questioned again, I told her about Trudy. 'As for Declan, he just drifts from job to job. He's getting nowhere.'

Bel screwed up her face in an expression of disgust. 'There's not much hope for young people nowadays.' She sipped her soup for a while, then said casually, 'How's your gran?'

I had the definite feeling that Bel had been leading up to this question from the start. 'She's fine. She was eighty in June.'

'Is she still in the same place in Kirkby?'

'Yes.'

Bel stared at her ultra-fashionable boots: lace-ups with thick soles and heels, not quite Dr Marten's, but almost. 'I don't suppose,' she said wistfully, 'you know what that row was all about?'

'What row?'

'The one all them years ago between your gran and Flo.'

'I don't know anything about it,' I said. 'We were always led to believe Flo had done something terrible, and Gran never spoke to her again.'

Bel pulled one of her peculiar faces. 'I heard it the other way round, that it was Martha who'd done wrong and Flo who'd taken umbrage. More than once she said to me, 'Bel, under no circumstances must our Martha be told if I go to meet me Maker before she does – at least not till the funeral's over,' but she'd never tell me why, although she wasn't one to keep secrets from her best friend. We knew everything about each other except for that.'

At six o'clock, Bel announced that she was going home, but changed her mind when Charmian arrived with a plate of chicken legs and a wedge of home-made fruitcake. By then I was a bit drunk and gladly opened another bottle of sherry. At half past seven we watched *Coronation Street*. It was hours later that my visitors left, and I was sorry to see them go. Charmian was natural and outgoing, with a sharp wit, and I felt completely at ease, as if I'd known them both all my life. It was as though I had inherited two good friends from Flo.

'I've had a great time today,' Bel said, with a satisfied chuckle when she was leaving. 'It's almost as if Flo's still with us. We must do this again next Sunday. I don't live far away in Maynard Street.'

I was already looking forward to it, forgetting that I was there to sort out Flo's possessions, not enjoy myself.

Charmian said, 'Our Jay's twenty-one this week, Millie, and we're having a party on Saturday. You're invited if you're free – bring a boyfriend if you've got one.'

'Of course she's got a boyfriend, a lovely girl like her!' Bel exclaimed. 'A party might be just the thing to help your James through his crisis.'

Charmian rolled her eyes. 'It's a party, not a counselling session.'

'I'll ask him, but I'm sure he's already got something arranged.' I was convinced that James would hate the idea.

The flat felt unusually still and quiet without Bel and her loud voice, though it still smelt strongly of her perfume. A police car came screeching round the corner, the flashing blue light sweeping across the room through the thin curtains. It made me realise that I'd had more glasses of sherry than I could count. If I was stopped and breathalysed, I would lose my licence, and I couldn't afford that: a car was essential to my job. I'll have to stay here tonight, I thought.

The idea of sleeping in the soft, springy bed was appealing. I made coffee, put it in the microwave and went into the bedroom to take stock. There were nightdresses in the bottom drawer of the chest. I picked out a pretty blue cotton one with short puffed sleeves and white lace trimming on the hem. A dramatic quilted black dressing-gown, patterned with swirling pink roses, was hanging behind the door, and I remembered the pink furry slippers under the bed. I undressed quickly and put on the nightie. It felt crisp and cold, but the dressing-gown was lined with something fleecy and in no time I was warm. I shoved my cold feet into Flo's slippers. Everything smelt slightly of that lovely scent from the Body Shop, Dewberry! It seemed odd, because I kept thinking of Flo as belonging to another age, not someone who frequented the Body Shop.

It didn't seem the least bit odd or unpleasant to be wearing a dead woman's clothes. In fact, it seemed as if Flo had left everything in place especially for me.

There wouldn't be time in the morning to go home and change, and George disapproved of jeans in the office. A quick glance in the wardrobe showed it to be so tightly packed with clothes that I could barely get my fingers between them. There was bound to be something I could wear.

I collected the coffee, took it into the bedroom and climbed into bed. I switched on the bedside lamp and picked up the book Flo had been reading before she died, turning to the first page. I was deeply involved when my eyes started to close, although it wasn't yet ten o'clock, hours before I usually went to bed. I turned off the lamp, slid under the bedclothes and lay in the cool darkness, vaguely aware of the saints staring down at me from the walls, and the crucifix above my head.

There were shouts in the distance, followed by a crashing sound, as if someone had broken a window. A car's brakes shrieked, there were more shouts, but I scarcely noticed. I thought about James. Perhaps I was too hard on him. I resolved to be nicer in future. My thoughts drifted briefly to Bel, but she had scarcely occupied my mind for more than a few seconds before I fell into a deep, restful and dreamless sleep.

2

'That's a charming dress,' said George. 'You look exceptionally sweet and demure this morning.'

'So do you,' I replied tartly. I always resent men considering it their prerogative to make comments on a woman's appearance. 'The dress belonged to my aunt. I stayed the night in her flat.'

George looked at me askance. 'That's a bit risky, isn't it? I hope you weren't alone.'

'I was, but seem to have survived the experience.'

The extension rang on my desk and George disappeared into his office. It was James. 'Where on earth were you last night?' he demanded crossly. 'I rang and rang and left increasingly desperate messages on your answering-machine. Then I called early this morning and you still weren't there.'

I frowned in annoyance. What right had he to know my whereabouts for twenty-four hours a day? 'I had visitors at my aunt's flat and we drank a bottle of sherry between us. It didn't seem safe to drive.'

'If I'd known what number your aunt had lived at, I'd have come to William Square in search of you.'

'If you had, I'd have been very cross,' I said coldly.

James groaned. 'Darling, I've been out of my head with worry. I thought you might have come to some harm.'

I remembered that I'd vowed to be nicer to him, so bit back another sharp reply. 'I'm perfectly all right,' I said pleasantly. 'In fact, I had the best night's sleep in years.' Even Diana had remarked on how well I looked. 'Sparkling' was how she had put it. 'You never usually have much colour, but your cheeks today are a lovely pink.'

'Shall we meet tonight, catch a movie, have dinner? *Leaving Las Vegas* is on at the Odeon.'

'Not tonight, James. I really need to get on with some work at home. I haven't touched my report in ages.' George had muttered something earlier about having found an ideal site in Woolton for the new office. 'Perhaps Wednesday or Thursday.'

'Okay, darling.' He sighed. 'I'll call you tomorrow.'

I hadn't time to worry if I'd hurt him because the phone rang again immediately I put the receiver down. The Naughtons wished to view a house in Ormskirk; they'd received the details that morning. This time they'd make their own way there, and I arranged to meet them outside the property at two o'clock.

The phone scarcely stopped ringing for the rest of the morning. I ate lunch at my desk, and remembered my appointment with the Naughtons just in time to avoid being late. Snatching the keys off the wall, I told George I'd probably be gone for hours. 'They take for ever, wandering around dis-cussing curtains and stuff.'

'Humour them, Millie, even if it takes all day,' George said affably. He grinned. 'I must say you look a picture in that dress.'

I stuck out my tongue at him because I knew he was teasing. Flo's dress was a pale blue and pink check with a white Peter Pan collar, long sleeves and a wide, stiff belt. The material was a mixture of wool and cotton. It fitted perfectly and didn't look in the least old-fashioned. Neither did the short pink swagger coat that had been tucked at the back of the wardrobe, though I'd had an awful job pressing out the creases with a damp tea-towel. Even Flo's narrow, size seven shoes could have been bought with me in mind: the clumpy-heeled cream slingbacks went perfectly with everything.

Until I reached the countryside, I hadn't noticed how miserable the weather was. Mist hung over the fields, drifting in and out of the dank wet hedges. The sky was a dreary grey with blotches of black.

When I drew up outside the house the Naughtons were waiting in their car. It was a compact detached property on a small but very smart estate that had been built only five years ago.

I got out and shook hands with the rather homely middle-aged couple. Their children had left home and they were looking for something smaller and easier to clean. The trouble was, they were unwilling to give up a single item of furniture and seemed unable to visualise life without their present curtains. 'Let's hope this is it!' I smiled. They were registered with several other agents and had been viewing properties for months. 'The vendors are both at work, so we'll have the place to ourselves.'

The house was owned by schoolteachers who were moving south. It had been very untidy when I had called to take details a few days before, but I'd assumed they would tidy up when they knew prospective purchasers were coming – I'd never known a seller yet who hadn't. However, when we went in, the place was a tip. Heaps of clothes lay on the stairs to be taken up, the remains of breakfast was still on the kitchen table and there were years of ground-in dirt on the tiled floor.

'This is disgusting,' Mrs Naughton expostulated indignantly. Her husband nudged her, embarrassed, but she refused to be silenced. 'It smells!' she claimed.

After a brief glance in the lounge, which looked as if a hurricane had swept through it, Mrs Naughton refused to go upstairs. 'I dread to think what the bathroom must be like. I couldn't possibly live here.' She made for the door.

Seconds later, I found myself shaking hands again and apologising for the state of the house. They drove away, Mrs Naughton in high dudgeon, and I returned to my car. I had expected the view to take at least an hour but it had been over within a few minutes.

I drove out of the estate and was about to turn right towards Liverpool when I remembered that the St Osyth Trust, where Alison lived, was only about five miles away. On impulse, I turned left in the direction of Skelmersdale. I'd tell George the Naughtons had taken their usual lengthy time. 'I'm normally very conscientious,' I told myself virtuously. 'I rarely take time off. I'm never ill.'

It was months since I'd seen my sister. I preferred to go without Mum, who frequently made a big emotional scene, patting and kissing a mystified Alison who had no idea what all the fuss was about.

The sky was growing darker and it began to drizzle. I hated driving with the windscreen wipers on, and it was with relief that I turned off the narrow, isolated road into the circular drive of the gloomy red-brick mansion.

The big oak trees bordering the grounds at the front had shed their leaves and a gardener was leisurely raking them into little heaps on the lawn. Round the side of the house, a bonfire smouldered reluctantly. I parked in the area reserved for visitors. Perhaps because it was Monday, I appeared to be the only one there.

The heels of Flo's shoes clicked loudly on the polished wooden floor as I went over to Reception where a woman was typing. She looked up questioningly. 'Can I help you?'

'I've come to see Alison Cameron. I'm her sister.' I felt uncomfortable. The woman, Evelyn Porter, had worked there for as long as I could remember, yet she didn't recognise me because I came so rarely.

'Of course. I should have known. Alison's in the lounge. She's already got a visitor. You know the way, don't you?'

I nodded and turned to go, when Evelyn Porter said, 'I should warn you that Alison's a little upset today. We had to have the upstairs redecorated – it was in a terrible state, and the painters are in her room. Alison can't stand her precious things being disturbed and you'll find her rather agitated.'

The lounge was built on to the rear of the house, a sturdy conservatory that went its entire width, filled with brightly cushioned cane furniture. I paused before going in, praying it would be Trudy who was visiting, not Mum. Trudy's car hadn't been outside, though, and Mum couldn't fit in the bus journey to Skelmersdale between finishing work and being home in time to make my father's tea. During the week he monopolised the car – it would have been fixed quick enough when he needed it himself, assuming there'd been anything wrong in the first place.

To my pleased surprise, when I opened the door I found Declan, who was supposed to be at work, alone in the lounge with Alison. 'What on earth are you doing here?'

He stood up and hugged me. 'Hi, Sis. You're the last person I expected to see.'

We stayed in each other's arms for several seconds. It was only when I saw him that I remembered just how much I loved my little brother, though he was several inches taller than me now. 'Declan, love, you're thinner than ever,' I said. I could feel the bones protruding from his neck and shoulders, and I remembered the violence meted out to his puny body by our father. I gave him an affectionate push and turned to my sister. 'Hallo, Alison. It's Millie. I've come to see you.'

Over the last few years, Alison Cameron had grown into a beautiful young woman. She'd always been the prettiest of us three sisters, but now she was breathtaking. Her eyes were large and very green, like a luminous sea in sunlight, the lashes long and thick, several shades darker than her abundant ash-blonde hair, emphasising the creamy whiteness of her flawless skin. Her condition was only evident in the movements of her lovely body: stiff, clumsy, lacking grace.

'Hallo, hallo, hallo.' Alison flicked her long fingers in front of her eyes. 'You want to go upstairs.'

She meant, 'I'. 'I want to go upstairs.'

'Sorry, luv. You can't,' Declan said gently. 'Your room's being painted a nice new colour.'

I kissed the smooth, porcelain cheek, but Alison didn't seem aware of the gesture. 'It will look very pretty when it's done, darling. Then you can spread all your lovely things out again.' She kept her talcum powder, hairslides, toys and other odds and ends in neat rows on the bedside table and window-sill, and was always deeply distressed if anything was put in the wrong place.

'You want to go upstairs.'

'Later, darling, later.'

Alison looked at the floor, avoiding eye-contact. 'Come in thing with wheels?'

'I came in my car, yes.'

'You go in thing with wheels.'

'You've been in a car? Whose car, darling?'

'I think Trudy and Colin took her for a drive yesterday,' Declan whispered, when Alison shook herself irritably and began to flick her fingers again.

I had never been able to comprehend what went on in my sister's mind, although one of the doctors had once tried to explain it to Mum. It was something to do with mind blindness, the inability to perceive another person's emotions, which was why she sometimes laughed when our mother cried. Poor Mum was unable to accept that Alison wasn't laughing at *her*. My sister just wasn't aware of tears.

'Would you like to do a jigsaw puzzle, luv?' Declan suggested. 'The woman brought some in before,' he said. 'Thought they might calm her down, like.'

But Alison was looking out of the window, where a narrow line of smoke was drifting upwards from the bonfire. She had an uncanny, inexplicable ability to do the most complicated jigsaws in a fraction of the time it would have taken most people.

Declan and I looked at each other. As far as Alison was concerned, we might as well not be there.

'You know,' Declan said softly, 'I used to think me dad was responsible for the way Alison is. I thought he shook and slapped her so hard it damaged her brain. I envied her something rotten. I always hoped he'd do the same to me so I'd be sent here, too.'

'He did more than shake and slap you, Dec. He leathered the three of us regularly.'

'You had it the worst, Mill. You were the oldest, and he seemed to have it in for you more than the rest of us.'

I made a face. I seemed to have caught the habit from Bel. 'Maybe there was something about me that drove him over the edge,' I suggested lightly.

'Still, it didn't damage our brains. We all stayed quite normal.' Declan grinned. 'Least, relatively normal. Mind you,' the grin disappeared, 'there's still time for one of us to snap. I'll end up behind bars if I stay in that house much longer. I swear one day I'll kill the bastard because of the way he treats Mam. He hasn't given her any money in weeks. It used to be the horses, now it's that bloody lottery. Yet you should hear him moan if the food isn't up to scratch. He nearly hit the roof when we got a reminder for the electricity bill, as if she could pay everything out of the fifty quid a week she earns and what I hand over for me keep. He called her a lazy bitch and said it was about time she got a full-time job. If she did, there'd be hell to pay if his meals weren't ready on time.'

Declan's soft, rather feminine voice was rising, and I noticed that his hands, long and white like Alison's, were gripping the arms of the chair, the knuckles taut. His gentle face was drawn and tired. I leaned back in the chair and sighed. My brother's unhappiness was painful to watch and it was to avoid that pain that I kept as far away from my family as I could. I almost wished I hadn't come or that Declan hadn't been there. 'Why don't you leave, Dec?' I pleaded. Then there'd only be Mum for me to worry about.

'As if I could leave Mam on her own with that bastard.'

'You can't stay for ever, love.'

'I'll stay as long as I have to.'

I got up and walked down the long room to the coffee machine provided for visitors. The light was on, which meant the machine was working. 'Fancy a coffee, Dec?' I called. Alison remained fascinated by the smoke.

'Please.'

'What are you doing here, anyway?' I asked, when I returned with the drinks. 'You're supposed to be at work.'

Declan recovered his good humour swiftly. His knack of making a joke of things that would have driven another person to despair was impressive. Dad's belt had broken once in the middle of a thrashing. 'Never mind, Dad,' he had said chirpily. 'I'll get you another for Christmas.'

'I lost me job.' He smiled. 'I got the sack three weeks ago.'

'Mum never said!'

He shrugged his delicate shoulders. 'That's because she doesn't know. She gets dead upset every time I get the shove. No one knows except our Trudy. I've looked for other work, Millie, honest, but I can't get anything. I've got no references because I've never held a job down long enough. The thing is, all I know is labouring and I'm not up to it.'

'Oh, Dec! What do you do with yourself all day?' I felt hurt that he had confided in Trudy and not in me. I was his sister, too. I wanted, reluctantly, to help.

'I wander the streets, go to the Job Centre, call on Trudy, then go home for six o'clock so Mam thinks I've been to work. This is the third time I've come to see Alison, but it means hitching lifts and last time I had to walk all the way back.'

'You should have told me.' I would have given him the key to my flat, where he could watch TV and help himself to food.

'I didn't think you'd be interested,' Declan said, which hurt more.

'I'll have to go soon,' I said. 'They'll be expecting me at the office. We don't seem to be doing much good here.' I made a quick decision. 'Look, I'll take you into town and you can go to the cinema – *Leaving Las Vegas* is on at the Odeon. When I finish work, we'll go back to my place for a meal. I've got pizza in the freezer.'

Declan's big green eyes sparkled. 'Great idea, Sis. I'll ring Mam and tell her I'm working late or she'll want to know how I met you. The pictures are out 'cos I'm skint. I give Mam all I get off the social, but it'll be nice to look round the shops. I haven't been to town in ages.'

It was even worse than I'd thought. 'What have you been doing for money all this time?' I asked, dismayed.

'Trudy gives me the odd few quid, but she doesn't want Colin to know what's happened. She reckons he's had enough of the Camerons.'

Despite Declan's protests that he didn't want to scrounge, I insisted he take all the money I had with me, twenty pounds.

A woman in a white overall came in to ask how Alison was. 'She doesn't want to know us today, do you, Sis?' Declan chucked his beautiful sister under the chin, but she remained as unaware of the gesture as she'd been of my kiss. 'Slippers,' she muttered. 'Slippers, slippers, slippers.'

'The builders are just packing up for the day so we can put her things back in place. They've only got the ceiling to do tomorrow. Would you mind if I took her upstairs? I think she'll feel happier once she knows everything's back to normal. Next time you come she'll be fine.'

Well, as fine as she'll ever be, I thought sadly. I watched Alison being led away, oblivious to the presence of her brother and sister.

When it came down to it, I was no good at telling blatant lies. I couldn't bring myself to tell George that the Naughtons had taken ages viewing the house when it wasn't true. 'I hope you don't mind, but I went to see my sister. She only lives a few miles away. It was a spur-of-the-moment thing.'

'The one in the home?'

'That's right.' Sometimes I forgot George knew things about me that no one outside my family did.

'No problem,' George said easily.

'I should have let you know on the mobile.'

George laughed. 'I said, no problem. You could get away with murder in that dress, Ms Millicent Cameron. What prompted your folks to call you that, by the way?'

'It's after a singer my mother liked, Millicent Martin.'

'Oh, Lord!' he groaned. 'I liked her, too. Does that show my age?'

'Very much so, George,' I said gravely, getting my own back for his comments on Flo's frock.

We grinned at each other amiably, and George said, 'I was wondering where you were. Mrs Naughton telephoned to complain to a higher authority about the state of that house. I'll give the vendors a ring tonight, suggest they tidy up, but be prepared to warn people in future, just in case.'

I hung up the keys and went over to my desk, aware of how close I'd come to blotting my copybook with George.

It was my job to prepare a list of properties to advertise in the local press and I was gathering together details to feed into the computer when I became aware that Diana, whose desk was next to mine, was crying quietly. Tweedledum and Tweedledee were out, and Oliver Brett was in George's office. June, the receptionist, was on the phone, her back to us.

'What's the matter?' I asked. The woman's eyes were red with weeping.

'It's my father. I don't know if I told you he was ill. It's cancer of the stomach. A neighbour's just called to say she found him unconscious on the kitchen floor. He's been taken to hospital.'

'Then go and see him straight away. George won't mind.'

'Why should I?' Diana looked at me mutinously. 'I've got work to do – I'm just finishing off those notes on Woolton. It could affect my prospects of promotion.'

I said nothing, but wondered where my priorities would lie in the same situation.

'Parents are a pain,' Diana said, in a hard voice. 'When they grow old, it's worse than having children.' She blew her nose, wiped her eyes, and began to cry again. 'I don't know what I'll do if Daddy dies!'

'I think you should go to the hospital.'

Diana didn't reply. She typed furiously for a while, then said, 'No. I'm too busy. I wish that bloody neighbour hadn't phoned. There comes a time when you've got to put yourself first.'

'If you say so.' I tried to ignore her as I finished off the adverts then faxed them through to the press, by which time it had gone six o'clock. I was meeting Declan in a pub in Water Street close to where I'd parked the car. When I left Diana was still typing, her brow creased in concentration, her eyes still red. I stood for a moment, looking at her and wondering what to say. Eventually, all I could think of was, 'Goodnight, Diana.'

'Night,' Diana replied, in a clipped voice.

Declan had thoroughly enjoyed the film. 'Dad would be in his element in Las Vegas,' he said, chuckling, on the way to Blundellsands.

'Only if he had a few thousand pounds to play with,' I said drily, 'and he'd probably lose that within a day.' I patted his knee. 'Try to forget about him and enjoy yourself for a change. We can watch a video later, if you like.'

'That'd be the gear, Sis.' Declan sighed blissfully as I drove into the parking area at the side of my flat. 'I feel dead honoured. I've only been here once before.' His voice rose an octave and became a squeak. 'Jaysus, look at that car! It's only a Maserati!'

A low-slung black sports car was parked against the boundary wall. It wasn't possible to see through the dark-tinted windows who was inside it, but a terrible suspicion entered my mind.

'I'd sell me soul for a car like that!' Declan murmured reverently. He leaped out of the Polo as soon as it stopped and went over to the black car with the deference of a pilgrim approaching the Pope. My suspicions were confirmed when the car door opened and James climbed out. He frequently turned up in strange cars belonging to the garage.

'Millie?' His voice contained a great deal of anger and hurt. It even sounded slightly querulous. 'Millie?' he said again.

I realised he thought that Declan was a boyfriend. He'd asked me out that night and I'd refused, saying I had work to do. Instead I was seeing someone else. I felt irritated. Why shouldn't I go out with another man if I wanted? I was cross that James had turned up uninvited. Now I would have to introduce him to Declan, and I wanted the Camerons and the Athertons kept apart for as long as possible. For ever would be even better.

'This is my brother, Declan,' I said stiffly. 'Declan, this is James.'

James's broad shoulders sagged with relief. 'Declan!' he said jovially, as he shook hands. 'I've heard a lot about you.' He was being polite: he knew nothing about my brother other than that he existed.

'Is this your car?' Declan's jaw dropped in disbelief: he had a sister who had a boyfriend who drove a Maserati.

'No, I just borrowed it for tonight. My own car is an Aston Martin.'

'Jaysus! Can I look under the bonnet? Would you mind if I sat behind the wheel, only for a minute, like?'

James was happy to oblige. He got back into the car and pulled the lever to raise the bonnet. Seconds later the pair were bent over the engine and James was explaining how things worked. I trudged upstairs, dreading the evening ahead.

I put the kettle and the oven on, and began to prepare a salad. James would probably expect to stay to dinner and fortunately the pizza was a large one. I opened a bottle of wine and drank a glass to steady my nerves. By the time James and Declan arrived, almost half an hour later, I'd drunk half the bottle and had to open another to have with the meal. I blamed Flo. It wouldn't have crossed my mind to drink alone if I hadn't come face to face with all that sherry.

The two men were getting on famously. The conversation had turned to football. 'There's a match on TV later, Liverpool versus Newcastle.' James rubbed his hands. 'You don't mind if we watch it, do you, Millie?'

'Not at all.' By now, I was terrified Declan would say something, give the game away, and the whole respectable edifice I'd built around myself would come tumbling down.

It wasn't until they had finished their meal that he revealed the smallest of my secrets. 'That was great, Sis. I haven't had such decent grub in ages.' He turned to James. 'Our mam does her best, but everything comes with mashed spuds and cabbage.' He patted his stomach. 'I'm not half glad I went to see Alison in Skem, else I wouldn't have met our Millie.'

'I thought Alison lived in Kirkby with you,' James said, puzzled.

'Oh, no. Alison's autistic. She's in a home. Hasn't Millie told you?'

'Who'd like coffee?' I said brightly. I went into the kitchen, bringing that line of conversation to an abrupt end. When I returned with the coffee, Declan had just rung home. 'I forgot to tell Mam I'm supposed to be working late. I lost me job the other week,' he explained to James, 'and I still haven't got round to telling our mam and dad.'

James looked sympathetic. 'What sort of work do you do?'

I gritted my teeth as Declan replied, 'Only labouring. I was working on this demolition site, but it seemed to be me who got demolished more often than the building.'

'You're wasted as a labourer. Why don't you take a college course like Millie did?'

To my surprise, Declan's face turned bright red. He blinked his long lashes rapidly and said, 'It's never entered me head.'

Fortunately, it was time for the match to start. I switched on the television, then the computer. I wanted to finish my report, but my brain was incapable of competing with the sound of the television and James and Declan's bellows of support alternated with groans of despair whenever Newcastle went near the Liverpool goal. I tried to read a book, gave up, and went into the kitchen where I caught up with the ironing and prayed the match wouldn't go into extra time. The minute it was over, I'd take Declan home. It was imperative that my brother and my boyfriend were separated before any more of the Camerons' dirty linen was aired.

To my dismay, James had already offered Declan a lift. I thought of the burnt-out car abandoned opposite my parents' house – hopefully James wouldn't notice in the dark – of the lads who'd still be playing outside and might not feel too charitably towards the driver of a Maserati.

'Tara, Sis.' Declan punched me lightly on the shoulder. 'It's been a smashing evening.'

'We must do it again soon. Perhaps next time there's a match, eh?' James kissed me on the lips. 'I'll call later.'

'Oh, no, you won't,' I cried as soon as I'd closed the door. I took the phone off the hook, ran a bath, and finished off the wine while I soaked in the warm, scented water. The events of the day swirled through my mind: the Naughtons and that filthy house, Alison, Declan, Diana and her father, James.

James! What was Declan saying to him? It wasn't that I cared about him loving me less, I only cared about him – anybody – *knowing*. And when it came down to it, it was nothing to do with the house in Kirkby, or being poor, or Mum letting herself go, or Alison. It was the terror of my childhood that I wanted to keep to myself: the beatings, the fear, the sheer indignity of it all. I'd felt as if my body didn't belong to me, that it could be used by someone else whenever the whim took them. What I wanted more than anything was to put the past behind me so that the dreams would stop. I wanted to forget everything and become a person not a victim. But this would never happen while my family remained a haunting reminder, always there to ensure that the past was part of the present and, possibly, the future. The only solution would be to go far away, start a new life elsewhere – but although my mother set my teeth on edge, I loved her so much that it hurt. I could never desert her.

The water in the bath had gone cold. I climbed out, reached for a towel, and was almost dry when the doorbell rang.

'Blast!' I struggled into a bathrobe.

'I tried to call you on the car phone,' James said, as he came breezing in, 'but you seemed to be incommunicado.' He noticed the receiver was off the hook. 'Is this deliberate or accidental?'

'Deliberate,' I said irritably. 'I want some peace. I want to be left alone.' He tried to take me in his arms, but I pushed him away. 'Please, James.'

He threw himself on to the settee with a sigh. 'Why didn't you tell me all that stuff before?'

My heart missed a beat. 'What stuff?'

'You know what I mean. About Alison, and about Declan being gay.'

'Declan's not gay!' I gasped.

'Of course he is, Millie. It's obvious.'

'You're talking utter rubbish,' I said half-heartedly, remembering how Declan had blushed when James paid him a compliment. Then I remembered all sorts of other things about my brother. He was girlish, no doubt about it, but gay?

'Darling, I guessed straight away.'

I shook my reeling head. It was too much, coming after such an eventful day. 'What did you and Declan talk about on the way to Kirkby?'

'Cars, mainly, football a bit. Why?'

'I just wondered.'

'After I dropped him off, I gave some kids a ride around the block. They were very impressed with the Maserati.'

'That was nice of you.'

I made him a coffee, then insisted he went home. Before going to bed, I took three aspirins. Even so, unlike last night at Flo's, it was several hours before I eventually fell asleep, a restless, jerky sleep, full of unwelcome, unpleasant dreams.

Diana's father was kept in hospital overnight. The fall had nothing to do with his illness; he had had a dizzy spell. Next morning she said that a neighbour had offered to bring him home. 'I suppose you think I'm awful, not going myself,' she went on.

'Why should I?'

'Well, I think I'm awful. Daddy's being incredibly brave. At times, I wish he'd have a good old moan and I'd really have something to complain about. I'd feel less of a louse.' She wrinkled her nose. 'I'm all mixed up.'

'Who isn't?' I snorted.

3

James had been told bluntly that I needed time to myself, time to think. If he turned up uninvited again, I would be very cross. He agreed meekly that we wouldn't meet again until Saturday. 'Will you be very cross if I call you?' he asked, in a little-boy voice.

'Of course not, but if I'm not around I don't want anguished messages left on my answering-machine.'

'No, ma'am. Thank you very much, ma'am.'

I kissed his nose, because he was so patient and understanding. I couldn't imagine allowing a man to mess me about as much as I did him. Nor could I understand why he put up with it from someone like me.

Throughout the week, I did my utmost to get to the flat in William Square, but the estate-agency business, while not exactly booming, was picking up. On Wednesday and Thursday I was still hard at work in the office until well past seven o'clock.

On Friday night, I finished off the report and stapled together the eight pages. I decided to read through it again and give it to George on Monday: he'd begun negotiations for the empty shop, which he hoped to have open by Christmas. Even if Diana got her 'notes' in first, it would show that I was equally keen.

Afterwards, I phoned home, which I'd been meaning to do all week, and was relieved when Declan answered.

'Where's Mum?' I asked.

'Out. Dad went to the pub, so I gave her five quid of that twenty I got off you on condition she went to bingo.' He chuckled. 'She was dead chuffed.'

'Declan?'

'Yes, luv?'

'That suggestion James made, about you going to college, why don't you do it? You could learn car mechanics or something, get a job in a garage.' Unlike me, he had left school with two reasonable O levels.

'Oh, I dunno, Millie. Me dad would blow his top.'

'You're twenty, Declan. It's nothing to do with him what you do with your life.'

'That's easy for you to say. It's not you who'd face the consequences when he finds out I've given up work for college.' He sounded peevish, as if he thought I'd forgotten the way my father's powerful presence still dominated the house in Kirkby.

'You've already given up work, Declan – or, rather, work's given up on you.' He was too soft, too unselfish, not like me and Trudy, who couldn't wait to get away. He was also weak. In a strange way, the horror had made my sister and me stronger, but our father had beaten all of the stuffing out of his only son. Declan's sole ambition seemed to be to exist from day to day with as little effort as possible.

'I suppose it wouldn't hurt to make a few enquiries,' he said grudgingly. 'What I've always fancied is learning about fashion – y'know, designing dresses or material, that sort of thing.'

'In that case, go for it, Dec,' I urged, and tried to imagine what our father would say when told his son was training to be a dress designer. Even worse, how would he react if James was right and he, too, realised that Declan was gay? I would have liked to discuss it with Declan there and then, but it was up to him to out himself. Until he did, I would never breathe a word to a soul.

I had expected James to claim he'd missed me dreadfully, but when he picked me up on Saturday night he said 'I've had a great week. I've joined the SWP.'

'The what?' I felt a trifle put out, particularly when he didn't even notice my new outfit, a short black satin shift, nor that I'd parted my hair in the middle and smoothed it back behind my ears for a change.

'The Socialist Workers' Party.'

'Good heavens, James!' I gasped. 'Isn't that a bit over the top? What's wrong with the Labour Party?'

'Everything!' he said crisply. 'This chap, Ed, said that they're all a shower of wankers. This morning I helped collect money for those dockers I told you about. I nearly brought my placard into Stock Masterton to show you.'

'I'm glad you didn't!' I hid a smile. 'Does this mean you're over your crisis?'

'I'm not sure, but for the first time in my life, I feel as if I have some connection with the real world, real people. I've learned an awful lot this week. You wouldn't believe the tiny amount single mothers have to live on, and I never knew the National Health Service was in such a state.'

All the way into town, he reeled off statistics that most people, me included, already knew. Only a tiny percentage of the population owned a huge percentage of the country's wealth; revenue from North Sea oil had disappeared into thin air; privatisation had created hundreds of millionaires.

In the restaurant, a favourite one in the basement of a renovated warehouse, with bare brick walls and a Continental atmosphere, he didn't show his usual interest in the food. 'I went to Ed's place on Wednesday to watch a video. Did you know that in the Spanish Civil War the Communists fought on the side of the legally elected government? I'd always thought it was the other way round, that the Communists were the revolutionaries.'

I stared at him, aghast: he'd been to public school, followed by three years at university during which he'd studied history, for God's sake, and he hadn't known that! 'What does your father have to say about your miraculous conversion?' I asked. 'A couple of weeks ago, you were in the Young Conservatives.'

He frowned and looked annoyed. 'My folks think it jolly amusing. Pop said he's glad I've started to use my brain at last. My sister got involved with a group of anarchists at university, and he thinks I'll grow out of it, like Anna did.'

Anna was married with two children and lived in London. So far, we'd not met. I sipped my coffee thoughtfully. I wasn't sure if I wanted him to grow out of it. The trouble was, like his folks, I found the whole thing rather amusing. Although, no doubt, he felt sincerely about his newly found beliefs, he didn't sound sincere, more like a little boy who'd discovered a rare stamp for his collection.

'Where shall we go?' He looked at his watch. 'It's only half past ten.'

All I could think of was a club, but James reminded me he'd gone off them. 'I've just remembered,' I said, 'We're invited to a party in William Square.' It was Charmian's son's twenty-first.

'Great,' James said eagerly. 'Let's go.'

'But you'd hate it,' I laughed. 'They're not at all your sort of people.'

He looked hurt. 'What do you mean, not my sort of people? You'd think I came from a different planet. I quite fancy partying with a new crowd. Wherever we go it's always the same old faces.'

The same old middle-class professionals; bankers and farmers, stock-brokers and chaps who were something in insurance. Some of the women had careers, and those who'd given up their jobs to have children com-plained bitterly about the horrendous cost of employing cleaners and au pairs. I always felt out of place, just as I probably would at Charmian's. I wondered if there was anywhere I'd feel right.

'We'll go to the party if you like,' I said, but only to please James. After all, now he'd joined the SWP he'd have to get used to mixing with the hoi polloi.

Charmian looked exotic in a cerise robe with a turban wound round her majestic head. 'Lovely to see you, girl,' she murmured, and kissed me.

Rather to my own surprise, I kissed her back as I handed over the wine James had bought in the restaurant for a ludicrous price because he couldn't be bothered to search for an off-licence. I introduced him to Charmian, who seemed taken aback when he shook her hand and said, in his beautifully cultured voice, 'How lovely to meet you.'

The Smiths big living room was packed, though several couples in the middle were managing somehow to dance to the almost deafening sound of Take That's 'Relight My Fire'. I met Herbie, Charmian's husband, a mild, good-humoured man with greying hair who was circulating with a bottle of wine in each hand. 'Our Jay's around somewhere.' Charmian peered over the crowd. 'You must meet the birthday boy.' With that, she plunged into the fray.

I found a bedroom and left my coat. When I returned, there was no sign of James so I helped myself to a glass of wine and leaned against the wall, hoping Bel had been invited so that I would have someone to talk to.

A young man with a wild head of shaggy black curls and a fluffy beard came and stood beside me, his dark eyes smiling through heavy horn-rimmed glasses. 'You look like the proverbial wallflower.'

'I'm waiting for my boyfriend,' I explained.

'Fancy a dance in the meantime?'

'I wouldn't mind.' I felt rather conspicuous on my own.

He took my hand and led the way through to the dancers. There wasn't room to do anything other than shuffle round on the spot.

'Do you live round here?' I asked politely. I'd never been much good at small talk.

'Next door, basement flat. Do you still live in Kirkby?'

'You know me!' I never liked coming across people from the past.

'We were in the same class together at school. You're Millie Cameron, aren't you?'

I nodded. 'I'm at a disadvantage compared to you,' I said. 'I don't recall anyone in class with a beard.'

'I'm Peter Maxwell, in those days known as Weedy. You can't have forgotten me. I usually had a black eye, sometimes two, and an inordinate amount of cuts and bruises. The other lads used to wallop me because I was no good at games. Me mam wasn't slow at walloping me either but she didn't need a reason.'

'I remember.' He'd been a frail, pathetic little boy, the smallest in the class, smaller even than the girls. There never seemed to be a time when he wasn't crying. Rumour had it that his father had been killed during a fight outside a pub in Huyton. I envied his ability to talk about things so openly: there'd been no need for him to tell me who he was. Maybe he knew my own history. It had been no secret that Millie and Trudy Cameron's father hit his girls.

'How come you grew so big?' I asked. He was only as tall as I was, about five feet eight, but his shoulders were broad and I could sense the strength in his arms.

'Turned sixteen, left home, found work, spent all my spare time in a gym, where I grew massively, but mainly sideways.' He grinned engagingly. 'Having developed the brawn, it was time to develop the brain, so I went to university and got a degree in economics. I teach at a comprehensive a mile from here.'

'That's a tough job!' I admired him enormously, particularly his lack of hang-ups.

'It helps to have muscles like Arnold Schwarzenegger,' he conceded, 'particularly when dealing with bullies, but most kids want to learn, not cause trouble. Now, that's enough about me, Millie. What are you up to these days? If I remember rightly, you married Gary Bennett.'

'I did, yes, but we're divorced. I'm a property negotiator with Stock—'

Before I could say another word, a young woman in a red velvet trouser suit pushed through the dancers and seized his arm. 'There you are! I've been looking everywhere for you.' She dragged him away, and he turned to me, mouthing, 'Sorry.'

I was just as sorry to see him go – it had been interesting to talk to someone with a background similar to my own. I spotted James, deep in conversation with a middle-aged couple. He seemed to have forgotten about me. I felt a bit lost and made my way to the kitchen where I offered to help wash dishes. Herbie shooed me away with an indignant, 'You're here to enjoy yourself, girl.'

By now, the party had spilled out into the hall. I went out in the hope of finding Bel, but there was no sign of her so I sat on the stairs and was immediately drawn into an argument over the acting ability, or lack of it, of John Travolta.

'He was great in *Pulp Fiction*,' a woman maintained hotly.

'He stank in *Saturday Night Fever*,' someone else said.

'That was years ago.' The woman waved her arms in disgust. 'Anyroad, no one expected him to act in *Saturday Night Fever*. It was a musical and his dancing was superb.'

The front door opened and a man came in, a tall, slim man in his twenties with a pale, hard face and brown hair drawn back in a ponytail. He wore small gold gypsy earrings and was simply dressed in jeans, white T-shirt, and black leather jacket. There was something sensual about the way he moved, smoothly and effortlessly, like a panther, that made me shiver. At the same time, his lean body was taut, on edge. Despite his hard expression, his features were gentle: a thin nose, flaring wide at the nostrils, full lips, high, moulded cheekbones. I shivered again.

The man closed the door and leaned against it. His eyes flickered over the guests congregated in the hall. I held my breath when our eyes met and his widened slightly, as if he recognised me. Then he turned away, almost contemptuously, and went into the living room.

'What do you think? What did you say your name was?' The woman who had been defending John Travolta was speaking to me.

'Millie. What do I think about what?'

'Didn't you think he was fantastic in *Get Shorty*?'

'Amazing,' I agreed, still preoccupied with the man who'd just come in.

For the next hour I barely listened as the discussion moved on to other Hollywood stars. Someone brought me another glass of wine, then James appeared, gave a thumbs-up, and vanished again. I contemplated looking for the man with the ponytail to find out who he was – but I had left it too late: the front door opened and through the crowd I glimpsed him leaving.

At one o'clock, the party was still going strong. There were sounds of a fight from the living room, and Herbie emerged holding two young men by the scruff of the neck and flung them out of the door.

By now, I was tired of Hollywood and longed to go home. I searched for James and found him sitting on the floor with half a dozen people who were all bellowing at each other about politics. He'd removed his jacket and was drinking beer from a can. I didn't like to disturb him when he appeared to be enjoying himself so much. Nevertheless, I fancied some peace and quiet and knew exactly where I could find it.

William Square, bathed in the light of a brilliant full moon, was quiet when I went outside, though the silence was deceptive. Women, barely clothed, leaned idly against the railings, smoking and waiting for their next customer. A car crawled past, then stopped, and the driver rolled down the window. A girl in white shorts went over and spoke to him. She got in, the driver revved the engine and drove away. Two dogs roamed the pavements, casually sniffing each other. In the distance, the wail of a siren could be heard, and in the even further distance, someone screamed. A cat rubbed itself against my legs, but ran away when I bent to stroke it.

Suddenly, a police helicopter roared into the sky, like a monstrous, brilliantly lit bird. The noise was almost deafening. It really was a war zone, as George had said. I ran down the steps to Flo's flat. To my consternation, I saw that the curtains were drawn and the light was on, yet I could distinctly remember switching off the light and pulling back the curtains the last time I was there. Perhaps someone, Charmian or Bel, had decided it would be wise to make the place look lived in. But there was only one key, the one I held in my hand right now.

Cautiously I unlocked the door. It was unlikely I'd come to any harm with fifty or sixty people upstairs. I opened the inner door and gasped in surprise. The man with the ponytail was lounging on Flo's settee, his feet on the coffee table, watching the swirling lamp and listening to her record.

'Who are you? What are you doing here?' I snapped.

He turned and regarded me lazily, and I saw that his eyes were green, like mine. His face seemed softer than when I'd seen him upstairs, as if he, too, was under the spell of the blurred shadows flitting around the room and the enchanting music.

'I never thought I'd do this again,' he said. 'I came to leave me key on the mantelpiece and found Flo's place no different than it's always been.'

'Where did you get the key?'

'Off Flo, of course. Who else?' His voice was coarse, his Liverpool accent thick and nasal. He was the sort of man from whom I'd normally run a mile, and yet, and yet . . . I did my level best to hide another shiver.

'You still haven't told me who you are.'

'No, but I've told you why I'm here.' He swung his feet off the table with obvious reluctance, as if he wasn't used to being polite, and stood up. 'I was a friend of Flo's. Me name is Tom O'Mara.'

Flo

1

'Tommy O'Mara!' Martha's voice was raw with a mixture of hysteria and horror. 'You're having a baby by Tommy O'Mara! Didn't he go down on the *Thetis*?'

Flo didn't answer. Sally, sitting at the table, pale and shocked, muttered, 'That's right.'

'You mean you've been with a married man?' Martha screeched. Her face had gone puffy and her eyes were two beads of shock behind her round glasses. 'Have you no shame, girl? I'll never be able to hold up me head in Burnett Street again. We'll have to start using a different church. And they're bound to find out at work. Everybody will be laughing at me behind me back.'

'It's Flo who's having the baby, Martha, not you,' Sally said gently.

Flo was grateful that Sally appeared to be on her side or, at least, sympathetic to her plight. A few minutes ago when she had announced that she was pregnant, Martha had exploded but Mam had said quietly, 'I can't stand this,' and had gone straight upstairs, leaving Flo to Martha's rage and disgust. The statement had been made after tea deliberately, just before Albert Colquitt was due when Martha would feel bound to shut up. After Albert had been seen to, she might have calmed down a bit, but Flo knew that she would be at the receiving end of many more lashings from her sister's sharp tongue.

'It might be Flo having the baby, but it's the whole family that'll bear the shame,' Martha said cuttingly. She turned to her youngest sister, 'How could you, Flo?'

'I was in love with him,' Flo said simply. 'We were going to get wed when Nancy got better.'

'Nancy! Of course, he married that Nancy Evans, didn't he? Everyone used to call her the Welsh witch.' Martha scowled. 'What do you mean, you were going to get wed when she got better? She's never been sick, as far as I know. Anyroad, what's that got to do with it?'

As Martha was unlikely to know the intimate details of Nancy O'Mara's medical history, Flo ignored the comment, but she was disconcerted to learn that Nancy was Welsh when she was supposed to have been Spanish. In a faltering voice she said, 'He wasn't married proper to Nancy.' She didn't mention the gypsy ceremony in a wood near Barcelona because it sounded

777

ridiculous. In her heart of hearts, she'd never truly believed it. It was too far-fetched. She wondered bleakly if Tommy had ever been to Spain, and realised that everything of which Martha accused her was true: she was a fallen woman, lacking in morals, who'd brought disgrace upon her family.

It wasn't surprising to hear Martha say that there was no question of Tommy O'Mara not being married proper to Nancy Evans, because she had been in church when the banns were called. 'He used to lodge with the family of this girl I met at Sunday school,' she said, and added spitefully, 'She said her mam couldn't wait to get shot of him because she had a terrible job getting the money off him for his bed and board.'

Sally gasped. 'Shush, Martha. There's no need for that.'

'I'm sorry,' Flo said brokenly. 'I'm so sorry.'

'There, there, Sis.' Sally slipped off the chair and put her arms around her sister, but Martha wasn't to be swayed easily by expressions of regret.

'And so you should be sorry,' she blasted. 'You realise everyone will call the kid a bastard? No one will speak to it at school. It'll be spat upon and kicked wherever it goes.'

'Martha!' Mam said sharply, from the doorway. 'That's enough.'

Flo burst into tears and ran upstairs, just as the front door opened and Albert Colquitt arrived.

A few minutes later, Sally came in and sat on the bed where Flo was lying face down, sobbing.

'You should have taken precautions, luv,' she whispered. 'I know what it's like when you're in love. It's hard to stop if things get out of hand.'

'You mean, you and Jock . . .' Flo raised her head and looked tearfully at her sister. Jock Wilson continued to descend on Liverpool whenever he could wangle a few days' leave.

Sally nodded. 'Don't tell Martha, whatever you do.'

The idea was so preposterous, that Flo actually laughed. 'As if I would!'

'She doesn't mean everything she says, you know. I don't know why she's so bitter and twisted. You'd think she was jealous that you'd been with a man.' Sally sighed. 'Poor Martha. Lord knows what she'll say when she finds out me and Jock are getting married at Christmas, if he can get away. She'd have expected to go first, being the eldest, like.'

'Sally, Oh, Sal, I'm so pleased for you.' Flo forgot her own troubles and hugged her sister. Sally made her promise to keep the news to herself: she didn't want anyone to know until it was definite.

After a while, Sally went downstairs because it was her turn to do the dishes and she didn't want Martha getting in a further twist.

Flo sat up, leaned against the headboard, and rested her hands on her swelling tummy. She'd put off breaking the dreadful news for as long as possible, but it was October, she was four and a half months' pregnant, and it was beginning to show. One or two women in the laundry had been eyeing her suspiciously, and the other day when she'd been hanging out sheets in the drying room she'd turned to find Mrs Fritz at the door, watching keenly. Then Mrs Fritz had spent quite a long time in the office with Mr Fritz.

At first Flo had considered not telling a soul, running away and having the baby somewhere else. But she didn't want to stay away for ever and there'd be a baby to explain when she came back. Anyroad, where would she run to and how would she support herself? She had no money and wouldn't be able to get a job. She realised, sadly, that she would have to leave the laundry and it would be dreadful saying goodbye to Mr Fritz.

The door opened and Mam came in. 'I'm sorry I walked out, girl, but I couldn't stand our Martha's screaming. Perhaps it would have been best if you'd told your mam first and left me to deal with Martha.' She looked at her daughter reproachfully. 'How could you, Flo?'

'Please, Mam, don't go on at me.' Flo began to cry again at the sight of her mother's drawn face. Mam had seemed much better since the war began, as if she'd pulled herself together and was determined to see her family through the conflict to its bitter end. 'I'll leave home if you want. I never wanted to bring shame on me family.' Getting pregnant had been far from her mind when she'd lain under the trees in the Mystery with Tommy O'Mara.

'The man, this Tommy O'Mara, he should have known better. Martha says he was at least thirty. He was wrong to take advantage of a naïve young girl.' Mam pursed her lips disapprovingly.

'Oh, no, Mam,' Flo cried. 'He didn't take advantage. He loved me, and I loved him.' The lies he'd told meant nothing and neither did the promises. It was only because he was worried she might not go out with him that he'd said the things he had. 'If Tommy hadn't died, he'd have left Nancy by now and we'd be together.'

This was altogether too much for her mother. 'Don't be ridiculous, girl,' she said heatedly. 'You're talking like a scarlet woman.'

Perhaps she *was* a scarlet woman, because Flo had meant every word she said. Perhaps other couples didn't love each other as much as she and Tommy had. To appease her mother, she said meekly, 'I'm sorry.'

'Anyroad, that part's over and done with,' Mam sighed. 'What we have to deal with now are the consequences. I've had a word with Martha and Sal, and we think the best thing is for you to stay indoors until you've had the baby, then have it adopted. No one in the street will have known a thing. I'll go round and see Mr Fritz tomorrer and tell him you've been taken ill and won't be coming back. I hate to deceive him, he's such a nice feller, but what else can I do?'

'Nothing, Mam,' Flo said calmly. She was quite agreeable to the first part of the suggestion, that she stay indoors until the baby was born, but there was no way she intended giving up Tommy O'Mara's child, which was the next best thing to having Tommy himself. She wouldn't tell Mam that, otherwise there would be non-stop rows for months. Once it was born, she would move to another part of Liverpool, a place where no one knew her, but not too far for her family to come and visit. She'd say she was a widow who had lost her husband in the war, which meant there was no reason for anyone to call her child a bastard. She would support them both by taking in laundry and possibly a bit of mending – Mr Fritz often declared that no one else could darn a sheet as neatly as Flo.

War had made little impact so far on the country and people had begun to refer to it as 'phoney'. Lots of lads had been called up and ships were sunk frequently, with enormous loss of life, but it all seemed very far away. There was no sign of the dreaded air-raids and food was still plentiful.

779

Flo passed the days knitting clothes for the baby: lacy matinée coats and bonnets, unbelievably tiny booties and mittens, and dreaming about how things would be when her child was born. Occasionally, she could hear Mam and her sisters having whispered conversations in the kitchen, and the word adoption would be mentioned. It seemed that Martha already had the matter in hand. Flo didn't bother to disillusion them – anything for a quiet life. When she wasn't knitting, she read the books that Sally got her from the library. Once a month, she wrote to Bel MacIntyre, who'd joined the ATS and was stationed up in the wilds of Scotland where she was having a wonderful time. 'There's a girl for every fifteen men,' she wrote. 'But there's one chap in particular I really like. Remember I said once I'd never met a chap worth twopence? Well, I've come across one worth at least a hundred quid. His name is Bob Knox and he comes from Edinburgh like me dad.' Flo didn't mention the baby in her letters. Bel had thought her daft to become involved with a married man, and she didn't want her to know just how involved and completely daft she'd been.

Often, she wished she could go for a walk, particularly when it was sunny, and as the time crawled by, she ached to go out even in the pouring rain. The worst time was when visitors came or their lodger was at home and she had to spend hours shut in the bedroom. According to Martha, of all the people in the world, Albert Colquitt was the one who must remain most ignorant of Flo's dark secret. If he knew what sort of family he was living with he might leave, and that would be disastrous, 'seeing as you're no longer bringing in a wage.' She sniffed. Sally thought Martha was mainly worried that he wouldn't want to marry her, a goal she was still working towards with all her might.

'How do you explain that I'm never there?' asked Flo.

'He's been told you're run down, anaemic, and have to stay in bed and rest.'

'I've never felt so healthy in me life.'

She was blooming, her cheeks the colour and texture of peaches, her eyes bright, and her hair unusually thick and glossy. She wondered why she should look so well when she felt so miserable without Tommy, but perhaps it was because she couldn't wait to have the baby. Also, Mam had ordered extra milk especially for her, and Martha, for all her carping comments and sniffs of disapproval, often brought home a pound of apples and made sure there was cod-liver oil in the house, which was what Elsa Cameron had taken when she was pregnant. 'And look what a lovely baby Norman turned out to be.' Flo knew she was lucky: another family might have thrown her out on to the street.

It was on a black dreary morning in December that the Clancys' lodger discovered the secret he was never supposed to know. Mam had gone Christmas shopping and Flo was in the living room, knitting, when the key turned in the front door. It wasn't often anyone used the front door apart from Albert. She assumed Mam's shopping bags were too heavy to carry round the back, and hurried out to help. To her horror, she came face to face with Albert.

'I forgot me wallet,' he beamed, 'least I hope I did, and it's not lost. It's not just the ten-bob note I had, but there's me identity card, and some photos

I'd hate to lose, as well as . . .' His voice faded and his eyes widened in surprise as he took in Flo's condition. 'I didn't know, luv,' he whispered. 'Jaysus, I didn't know.'

Flo was stumbling up the stairs. Halfway, she turned, 'Don't tell our Martha you've seen me,' she implored. 'Please!'

'Of course not, luv.' He looked stunned. 'Flo!' he called, but by then Flo was in the bedroom and had slammed the door.

She heard him go into the parlour, and a few minutes later Mam returned from the shops. 'Are you all right, girl?' she called.

'I'm just having a little lie-down, Mam.'

'I'll bring a cup of tea up in a minute, then I'm going round to St Theresa's to do the flowers for Sunday.'

Mam was obviously unaware that Albert was in the parlour and remained unaware for the whole time she was at home. After she'd gone, Albert didn't stir or make even the smallest of sounds. Flo wondered if he was still searching for his wallet. Perhaps he was contemplating handing in a week's notice and finding somewhere more respectable to live.

Another half-hour passed, and still no sound. Then the parlour door opened and heavy footsteps could be heard coming upstairs. There was a tap on the door and a voice said hesitantly, 'Flo?'

'Yes?'

'Would you come downstairs a minute, luv? I'd like to talk to you.'

'What about?' Flo said warily.

'Come down and see.'

A few minutes later she and Albert were sitting stiffly in the living room. She felt over-conscious of her enormous stomach and hoped Albert wasn't intent on giving her a lecture, because she'd tell him it was none of his business. She felt deeply ashamed when, instead of a lecture, Albert mumbled, 'I've missed you, Flo. The house doesn't seem as bright and cheery without you.'

'I've been . . . upstairs,' she said lamely.

He shifted uncomfortably in the chair, then, without looking at her directly, said, 'I hope you don't mind me seeming personal, luv, but what's happened to the feller who . . . ?' Words failed him.

'He's dead,' said Flo.

'I thought he might be in the forces, like, and one day he'd turn up and you'd get married.'

'There's no chance of that, not when he's dead.'

'Of course not.' His face was cherry red, and she could see beads of perspiration glistening on his forehead. That he was sweating so profusely made his uniform pong even more strongly than it normally did. She wondered why on earth he was so embarrassed, when if anyone should be it was her. 'It'll be hard, bringing up a kiddie without a husband,' he said awkwardly.

'I'll manage. I'll have to, won't I?'

'It'll still be hard, and the thing is, I'd like to make it easier if you'll let me.' He paused and his face grew even redder before he plunged on. 'I'd like to marry you, Flo, and provide you and the little 'un with a home. I earn decent money as an inspector on the trams, and it's a good, secure job with prospects of promotion to depot superintendent. We could get a nice little house between us, and I've enough put away to buy the furniture we'd need. What do you say, luv?'

Flo hoped the distaste she felt didn't show on her face: the last thing in the world she wanted was to hurt him, but the idea of sharing a bed with a middle-aged man with a pot belly and a dreadful smell made her feel sick.

'It's kind of you, Albert—' she began, but he interrupted, as if he wanted to get everything off his chest.

'Of course, I wouldn't expect to be a proper husband, luv. We'd have separate rooms, and if you ever wanted to leave, it'd be up to you. There'd be no strings. To make it easier, we could get wed in one of those register-office places. I'd just be getting you out of a temporary hole, as it were. You'd have marriage lines, and if we did it quick enough, the baby'd have a dad, at least on paper.'

He was incredibly unselfish, and Flo was angry with herself for finding his proposal so disagreeable. But she'd once dreamed of sharing her life with Tommy O'Mara, beside whom Albert Colquitt was – well, there wasn't any comparison. On the other hand, she thought, as she leaned back in the chair and stared into the fire, would it really be so disagreeable? It would be getting her out of a hole, as he put it. No one would call the baby names if it had a father, and Flo wouldn't have to take in laundry but would have a nice, newly furnished house in which to live. She wouldn't be taking advantage of him, not in a mean way, because it was his idea. Of course, everyone would kick up hell at the idea of a Clancy getting married in a register office but, under the circumstances, Flo didn't care. And Martha would be livid, claiming Flo had stolen Albert from right under her nose.

She was still wondering how to respond when Albert said wistfully, 'Me wife died in childbirth, you know, along with the baby. It was a girl. We were going to call her Patricia, Patsy, if we had a girl. I've always wanted a kiddie of me own.'

If he hadn't said that she might have agreed to marry him, if only on a temporary basis – he'd made it clear that she could leave whenever she wanted. But she knew she could never be so cruel as to walk out once he'd grown to love the baby he'd always wanted. She would feel trapped. It would be like a second bereavement and he would lose another wife and child. No, best turn him down now.

So Flo told him, very nicely and very gently, that she couldn't possibly marry him but that she would never forget his kind gesture. She never dreamed that this decision would haunt her for the rest of her days.

Much to Martha's disappointment, Albert took himself off to stay with a cousin in Macclesfield over Christmas, though Flo was glad because it meant she could remain downstairs except when the occasional visitor came. She wondered if he'd gone for that very reason, and said a little prayer that he would enjoy himself in Macclesfield and that the scarf she'd knitted him would keep him warm – the weather throughout the country was freezing cold with snow several feet deep. Before Albert went, he gave the girls a present each: a gold-plated chain bracelet with a tiny charm. Martha's charm was a monkey, Sally's a key and Flo's a heart.

'I bet he meant to give me the heart,' Martha said.

'We'll swop if you like,' Flo offered.

'It doesn't matter now.'

On Christmas Eve, a package arrived from Bel containing a card and a pretty tapestry purse. When Flo opened the card, a photograph fell out. 'Bel's married!' she cried. 'She's married someone called Bob Knox, he's a Scot.'

'I only met her the once, but she seemed a nice young lady,' Mam said, pleased. 'You must pass on our congratulations, Flo, next time you write. Why not send her one of those Irish cotton doilies as a little present?'

'I wanted those doilies for me bottom drawer, Mam,' Martha pouted.

Flo shook her head. 'Thanks all the same, Mam, but she won't want a doily in the Army. She'd prefer a bottle of scent or a nice pair of stockings.'

'And have you got the wherewithal to buy scent and nice stockings?' Martha asked nastily.

'I'll get a present when I'm earning money of me own,' Flo snapped.

Their mother clapped her hands impatiently. 'Now, girls, stop bickering. It's Christmas, the season of goodwill.'

'Sorry, Flo.' Martha smiled for once. 'I love you, really.'

'I love you too, Sis.'

Later, Martha said to Flo, 'How old is Bel?'

'Eighteen.'

'Only eighteen!' Martha removed her glasses and polished them agitatedly. 'I'll be twenty-four next year.'

Flo wished with all her heart that she could buy a husband for her unhappy sister and hang him on the tree. It didn't help when, on Boxing Day, a telegram arrived for Sally. GOT LICENCE STOP GOT LEAVE STOP BOOK CHURCH MONDAY STOP JOCK.

'I'm getting married on Monday,' Sally sang, starry-eyed.

Flo whooped with joy, and Mam began to cry. 'Sally, luv! This is awful sudden.'

'It's wartime, Mam. It's the way things happen nowadays.'

'Does it mean you'll be leaving home, luv?' Mam sobbed.

'Jock doesn't have a regular port. I'll stay with me family till the war's over, then we'll get a house of our own.'

At this, Mam's tears stopped and she became practical. She'd call on Father Haughey that very day and book the church. Monday afternoon would be best, just in case Jock was late. Even trains had a job getting through the snow. At this, Sally blanched: she had forgotten that the entire country was snowbound. 'He's coming from Solway Firth. Is that far?' No one had the faintest idea so Dad's atlas was brought out and Solway Firth was discovered to be two counties away.

'I'll die if he doesn't get here!' Sally looked as if she might die there and then.

'Surely he'll be coming by ship.' Martha hadn't spoken until then. Her face was as white as the snow outside and her eyes were bleak. She was the eldest, she was being left behind, and she couldn't stand it.

'Of course!' Sally breathed a sigh of relief.

Mam continued to be practical. Did Sally want a white wedding? No?

Well, in that case, tomorrow she'd meet her outside the butcher's at dinner-time, and they'd tour the dress shops in Smithdown Road for a nice costume, her wedding present to her daughter. 'It's no use getting pots and pans yet. And we'll have to have a taxi on the day. It's impossible to set foot outside the house in ordinary shoes in this weather, and you can't very well get married in Wellies. As for the reception, I wonder if it's too late to book a room?'

'I don't want a reception, Mam. I'd prefer tea in a café afterwards. Jock's mate will be best man. All I want is me family, you, Martha and Flo.'

'Our Flo can't go,' Martha pointed out. 'Not in her condition.'

Everyone turned to look at Flo, who dropped her eyes, shame-faced. 'I hate the idea of missing your wedding, Sal,' she mumbled.

'I'll be thinking of you, Flo,' Sally said affectionately. 'You'll be there in spirit, if not in the flesh.'

Flo summoned up every charitable instinct in her body. 'Albert will be back from Macclesfield by then,' she said. 'Perhaps he could go instead of me. He'd be a partner for our Martha.'

Albert declared himself supremely honoured to be invited to the wedding. 'He likes to feel part of the family,' Sally said. 'I suspect he's lonely.'

On the day of her sister's wedding, Flo sat alone in the quiet house, thinking how much things had changed over the last twelve months. A year ago Mam was ill, and the sisters' lives had been jogging along uneventfully. Now, Mam had bucked up out of all recognition, Flo had found, and lost, Tommy O'Mara, and was carrying his child, and at this very minute Sally, wearing an ugly pinstriped costume and a white felt hat that made her look like an American gangster, was in the process of becoming Mrs Jock Wilson. Martha was the only one for whom everything was still the same.

She laid her hands contentedly on her stomach. It was odd, but nowadays she scarcely thought about Tommy O'Mara, as if all her love had been transferred to the baby, who chose that moment to give her a vicious kick. She felt a spark of fear. It wasn't due for another six weeks, on St Valentine's Day, exactly nine months and one week since the date of her last period – Mam had worked it out – but what if it arrived early while she was in the house by herself? Martha had booked a midwife under a 'vow of confidentiality', as she put it, who would deliver the baby when the time came. Flo couldn't wait for everything to be over, when her life would change even more.

Snow continued to fall throughout January, and February brought no respite from the Arctic weather. By now Flo was huge, although she remained nimble on her feet. As the days crept by, though, she lost her appetite and felt increasingly sick. Martha left instructions that she was to be fetched immediately if the baby started to arrive when she was at work.

'Surely it would be best to fetch the midwife first?' cried Mam. 'If you'll tell me where she lives, I'll get her.'

'I'd sooner get her meself,' Martha said testily. 'There'll be no need to panic. First babies take ages to arrive. Elsa Cameron was twenty-four hours in labour.'

'Jaysus!' Flo screamed. 'Twenty-four whole hours! Did it hurt much?'
Martha looked away. 'Only a bit.'

The phosphorous fingers on the alarm clock showed twenty past two as Flo
twisted restlessly in bed – it was such a palaver turning over. St Valentine's
Day had been and gone and still the baby showed no sign of arriving. She
lifted the curtain and looked outside. More snow, falling silently and
relentlessly in lumps as big as golf balls. The roads would be impassable
again tomorrow.

Suddenly, without warning, pain tore through her belly, so forcefully,
that she gasped aloud. The sound must have disturbed her sisters, because
Martha stopped snoring and Sally stirred.

Flo waited, her heart in her mouth, glad that the time had come but
praying that she wouldn't have a pain like that again. She screamed when
another pain, far worse, gripped her from head to toe.

'What's the matter?' Sally leaped out of bed, followed by Martha. 'Has it
started, luv?'

'Oh, Lord, yes!' Flo groaned. 'Fetch the midwife, Martha, quick.'

'Where does she live?' demanded Sally. 'I'll go.'

'There isn't time for a midwife,' Martha said shortly, 'not if the pains are
this strong. Wake Mam up, if she's not awake already, and put water on to
boil – two big pans and the kettle. Once you've done that, fetch those old
sheets off the top shelf of the airing cupboard.'

'I still think I should get the midwife, Martha. You and Mam can see to
Flo while I'm gone.'

'I said there isn't time!' Martha slapped her hand over Flo's mouth when
another pain began. 'Don't scream, Flo, we don't want the neighbours hearing.
It would happen the night Albert's not out fire-watching,' she added irritably.

'I can't help screaming,' Flo gasped, pushing Martha's hand away. 'I've got
to scream.'

Mam came into the room in her nightdress. 'Help me pull the bed round a
bit so's I can get on the other side,' she commanded. When it had been
moved, she knelt beside her daughter. 'I know it hurts, luv,' she whispered,
'but try and keep a bit quiet, like.'

'I'll try, Mam. Oh, God!' Flo flung her arms into the air and grasped the
wooden headboard.

'Keep her arms like that,' Martha instructed. 'I read a book about it in the
library.'

Sally brought the sheets, and Flo felt herself being lifted, her nightie pulled
up, and the old bedding was slipped beneath her.

'You didn't book a midwife, did you, our Martha?' Sally said in a low,
accusing voice. 'It was all a lie. God, you make me sick, you do. You're too
bloody respectable by a mile. You'd let our poor Flo suffer just to protect
your own miserable reputation. I don't give a sod if me sister has a baby out
of wedlock. You're not human, you.'

'Is it true about the midwife, Martha?' Mam said, in a shocked voice.

'Yes!' Martha spat. 'There's not a single one I'd trust to keep her lip
buttoned. It's all right for Sal, she's married. I bet Jock wouldn't have been so
keen if he'd known what her sister had been up to.'

MAUREEN LEE

'It so happens, Jock's known about Flo for months, but it was me he wanted to marry, not me family.'

'Stoppit!' Flo screamed. 'Stoppit!'

'Girls! Girls! This isn't the time to have a fight.' Mam stroked Flo's brow distractedly. 'Do try to keep quiet, there's a good girl.'

'I'm trying, Mam, honest, but it don't half hurt.'

'I know, luv, I know, but we've kept it to ourselves all these months, there's only a short while to go.'

'Can I go for a walk once it's over?'

'Yes, luv. As soon as you're fit, we'll go for a walk together.'

In her agony, Flo forgot that by the time she was fit again she would be gone from the house in Burnett Street. She would be living somewhere else with her baby.

Afterwards, she never thought to ask how long the torment lasted: one hour, two hours, three. All she could remember were the agonising spasms that seized her body regularly and which wouldn't have felt quite so bad if only she could have screamed. But every time she opened her mouth, Martha's hand would slam down on her face and Mam would shake her arm and whisper, 'Try not to make a noise, there's a good girl.'

She was only vaguely aware of the argument raging furiously over her head. 'This is cruel,' Sally hissed. 'You're both being dead cruel. It's only what I'd expect from our Martha, but I'm surprised at you, Mam.'

Then Mam replied, in a strange, cold voice, 'I'm sorry about the midwife, naturally, but one of these days, you'll leave this house, girl, all three of you will. I don't want to be known for the rest of me life as the woman who's daughter had an illegitimate baby, because that's how they'll think of me in the street and in the Legion of Mary, and I'd never be able to hold me head up in front of Father Haughey again.'

Later, Sally demanded, 'What happens if she tears? She'll need stitches. For Christ's sake, at least get the doctor to sew her up.'

'Women didn't have stitches in the past,' Martha said tersely. 'Flo's a healthy girl. She'll mend by herself.'

'I want to go to the lavatory,' Flo wailed. 'Fetch the chamber, quick, or I'll do it in the bed.'

'It's coming!' Mam said urgently.

'Push, Flo,' Martha hissed. 'Push hard.'

'I need the chamber!'

'No, you don't, Flo. It's the baby. *Push!*'

Flo felt sure her body was going to burst and the hurt was so tremendous that the room turned black and little stars appeared, dancing on the ceiling. ' "Dancing in the dark," ' she bellowed. ' "Dancing in the dark. Dancing . . ." '

'Oh, Lord!' Sally was almost sobbing. 'She's lost her mind. Now see what you've done!'

Which was the last thing Flo heard until she woke up with a peculiar taste in her mouth. She opened her eyes very, very slowly, because the lids felt too heavy to lift. It was broad daylight outside. Every ounce of strength had drained from her body, and she could barely raise her arms. Unbelievably, for several seconds she forgot about the baby. It wasn't until she noticed her

786

almost flat tummy that she remembered. Despite her all-out weariness, she was gripped by shivers of excitement. She forced herself on to her elbows and looked around the room, but the only strange thing there was a bottle of brandy on the dressing-table which accounted for the funny taste in her mouth, though she couldn't remember drinking it. There was no sign of a baby.

'Mam,' she called weakly. 'Martha, Sal.'

Mam came into the room looking exhausted, but relieved. 'How do you feel, luv?'

'Tired, that's all. Where's the baby?'

'Why, luv, he's gone. Martha took him round to the woman who arranged the adoption. Apparently a very nice couple have been waiting anxiously for him to arrive, not that they cared whether it was a boy or a girl, like. They'll have him by now. He'll be one of the best-loved babies in the whole world.'

It was a boy *and he'd been given away!* Flo's heart leaped to her throat and pounded as loudly as a drum. 'I want my baby,' she croaked. 'I want him this very minute.' She struggled out of bed, but her legs gave way and she fell to the floor. 'Tell me where Martha took him, and I'll fetch him back.'

'Flo, luv.' Mam came over and tried to help her to her feet, but Flo pushed her away and crawled towards the door. If necessary, she'd crawl in her nightdress through the snow to find her son, Tommy's lad, their baby.

'Oh, Flo, my dear, sweet girl,' Mam cried, 'can't you see this is the best possible way? It's what we decided ages ago. You're only nineteen, you've got your whole life ahead of you. You don't want to be burdened with a child at your age!'

'He's not a burden. I want him.' Flo collapsed, weeping, on to the floor. 'I want my baby.'

Martha came in. 'It's all over, Flo,' she said gently. 'Now's the time to put the whole thing behind you.'

Between them, they picked her up and helped her back to bed. 'C'mon, luv,' Martha said, 'Have another few spoons of brandy, it'll help you sleep and you need to get your strength back. You'll be pleased to know none of the neighbours have been round wanting to know what all the racket was last night, which means we got away with it, didn't we?'

Why, oh, why hadn't she just taken a chance, run away and hoped everything would turn out all right? Why hadn't she made it plain that she wanted to keep the baby? Why hadn't she married Albert Colquitt?

In the fevered, nightmarish days that followed, Flo remained in bed and tortured herself with the same questions over and over again. She cursed her lack of courage: she'd been too frightened to run away, preferring to remain in the comfort of her home with her family around her, letting them think she was agreeable to the adoption to avoid the inevitable rows. She cursed her ignorance in assuming that she'd have the baby, leap out of bed, and carry him off into the unknown. Finally, she cursed her soft heart for turning down Albert's proposal because she didn't want him hurt at some time in the far-distant future.

All the time, her arms ached to hold her little son. The unwanted milk dried up, her breasts turned to concrete, and her insides felt as if they were shrivelling to nothing. She didn't cry, she was beyond tears.

'What did he look like?' she asked Sally one day.

'He was a dear little thing. I'm sure Mam wished we could have kept him. She cried when Martha made her give him up.'

'At least Mam held him, which is more than I did,' Flo said bitterly. 'I never even saw him.'

'That's what happens when women give their babies up for adoption. They're not allowed to see them, let alone hold them, least so Martha says. It's what's called being cruel to be kind.' Sally's eyes were full of sympathy, but even she thought that what had happened was for the best.

'Our Martha seems to know everything.' Flo had refused to speak to Martha until she revealed the whereabouts of her son.

'That's something I'll just have to get used to,' Martha said blithely, 'I couldn't tell you even if I wanted to because the names of adoptive parents are kept confidential. All I've been told is the baby's got a mam and dad who love him. That should make you happy, not sad. They'll be able to give him all the things that you never could.'

Flo gripped her painful breasts and glared contemptuously at her sister. 'They can't give him his mother's milk, can they? There'll be no bond between him and some strange woman who didn't carry him in *her* belly for nine whole months.'

'Don't be silly, Flo.' For once, Martha was unable to meet her sister's eyes. She turned away, her face strangely flushed.

March came, and a few days later the weather changed dramatically. The snow that had lain on the ground for months melted swiftly as the temperature soared.

Spring had arrived!

Flo couldn't resist the bright yellow sunshine that poured into the bedroom, caressing her face with its gentle warmth. She threw back the bedclothes, and got up for the first time in a fortnight. Her legs were still weak, her stomach hurt, her head felt as if it had been stuffed with old rags, but she had to go for a walk.

She walked further every day. Gradually, her young body recovered its strength and vigour. When she met people she knew, they remarked on how fit and well she looked. 'You're a picture of health, Flo. No one would guess you'd been so ill.'

But Flo knew that, no matter how well she looked, she would never be the same person again. She would never stop mourning her lost baby, a month old by now. There was an ache in her chest, as if a little piece of her heart had been removed when her son was taken away.

2

Sally had left the butcher's to take up war work at Rootes Securities, an aircraft factory in Speke, for three times the wages. She was coping well in the machine shop in what used to be a man's job. Even Mam was talking about looking for part-time work. 'After all, there's a war on. We've all got to do our bit.' Albert was out most nights fire-watching, though so far there hadn't been a fire for him to watch.

Flo realised it was time she got back to work. Sally suggested she apply to Rootes Securities. 'If we got on the same shift we could go together on the bus. You'll find it peculiar, working nights, but it's the gear there, Sis. All we do the whole time is laugh.'

Laugh! Flo couldn't imagine smiling again, let alone laughing. Sally fetched an application form for her to fill in and took it back next morning. Later, as Flo roamed the streets of Liverpool, she thought wistfully of Fritz's Laundry. She'd sooner work there than in a factory, even if the pay was a pittance compared to what Sal earned.

Since emerging from her long confinement, she'd passed the laundry numerous times. The side door was always open, but she hadn't had the nerve to peek inside. She felt sure the women, including Mrs Fritz, had guessed the real reason why she'd left.

On her way home the same day, she passed the laundry again. Smoke was pouring from the chimneys, and a cloud of steam floated out the door.

'I'll pop in and say hello,' she decided. 'If they're rude, then I'll never go again. But I'd like to thank Mr Fritz for the lovely necklace he sent at Christmas.'

She crossed the street, wondering what sort of reception she would get. To her astonishment, when she presented herself at the door, the only person there was Mr Fritz, his shirtsleeves rolled up, working away furiously on the big pressing machine that Flo had come to regard as her own.

'Mr Fritz!'

'Flo!' He stopped work and came over to kiss her warmly on the cheek. 'Why, it's good to see you. It's as if the sun has come out twice today. What are you doing here?'

'I just came to say hello, like, and thank you for the necklace. Where is everyone?'

He spread his arms dramatically. 'Gone! Olive was the first, then Josie, then the others. Once they discovered they could earn twice as much in a factory they upped and went. Not that I blame them. I can't compete with those sort of wages, and why should they make sacrifices on behalf of Mr and Mrs Fritz and their eight children when they have families of their own?'

Mrs Fritz came hurrying out of the drying room with a pile of bedding. Her face hardened when she saw Flo. 'Hello,' she said shortly. She scooped clean washing out of a boiler and disappeared again.

Her husband wrinkled his stubby little nose in embarrassment. 'Don't take any notice of Stella. She's worn out. Her mother is over from Ireland to look after the children, as we work all the hours God sends, including weekends. You see, Flo,' he went on earnestly, 'lots of hotels and restaurants have lost staff to the war and they send us the washing they used to do themselves. Business has soared, and I hate to turn it away, so Stella and I are trying to cope on our own. I've hired a lad, Jimmy Cromer, to collect and deliver on a bike with a sidecart. He's a right scally, but very reliable for a fourteen-year-old.' He managed to chuckle and look gloomy at the same time. 'One of these days, Stella and I will find ourselves buried under a mountain of sheets and pillowcases, and no one will find us again.'

'Would you like a hand?' Flo blurted. 'Permanent, like.'

'Would I!' He beamed, then bit his lip and glanced uneasily towards the drying room. 'Just a minute, Flo.'

He was gone a long time. Flo couldn't hear what was said, but sensed from the sound of the muffled voices that he and Stella were arguing. She supposed she might as well get on with a bit of pressing rather than stand around doing nothing, so folded several tablecloths and was wreathed in a cloud of hissing steam when he returned.

'We'd love to have you, Flo,' he said, rubbing his hands together happily, though she guessed he was putting it on a bit. Mrs Fritz had probably agreed because they were desperate. As if to prove this, he went on, 'You'll have to make allowances for Stella. As I said, she's worn out. The children daren't look at her in case she snaps their heads off. As for me, I'm very much in her bad books. She regards me as personally responsible for the war and our present difficulties.'

As the profit from the laundry had provided the Fritz family with a high standard of living and a big house in William Square, one of the best addresses in Liverpool, Flo thought it unfair of Stella to complain. She said nothing, but offered to go home, change into old clothes and start work that afternoon.

Mr Fritz accepted her suggestion gratefully. 'But are you sure you're up to it, Flo? Your mother said you were very ill each time I called.' He looked into her eyes and she could tell he knew why she'd been 'ill' but, unlike his wife, he didn't care. 'There'll be three of us doing the work of six.'

'Does that mean the wages will be more?' She was glad to be coming back, but it seemed only fair that if she was doing the work of two women, she should get an increase in wages. He might not be able to compete with a factory, but if business was soaring he should be able to manage a few extra bob.

He blinked, as if the thought hadn't entered his head. Just in case it hadn't, Flo said, 'I've applied for a job in Rootes Securities where our Sally works. She's paid time and a half if she works Saturdays.'

Mr Fritz's shoulders shook with laughter. 'Don't worry, my dear. I promise your pocket won't suffer if you work for me. I'll pay you by the hour from now on, including time and a half on Saturdays.'

Flo blushed. 'I didn't mean to sound greedy, like.'

He pecked both her cheeks and chucked her under the chin. 'I haven't seen you smile yet. Come on, Flo, brighten up my day even further and give me one of your lovely smiles.'

And to Flo's never-ending astonishment, she managed to smile.

Stella Fritz had seemed such a sweet, uncomplaining person in the days when Flo hardly knew her, but after they'd worked side by side for a short while, she turned out to be a sour little woman who complained all the time. Perhaps she was worn out and missed being with her children, but there was no need to be quite so nasty to Mr Fritz, who was blamed for every single thing, from exceptionally dirty sheets that needed boiling twice to food rationing, which had just been introduced.

'Bloody hell! She was only a farm girl back in Ireland,' Martha said indignantly, when Flo brought up the subject at home – Flo's vow never to speak to her eldest sister had been forgotten. 'She's dead lucky to have hooked someone like Mr Fritz. Have you seen their house in William Square?'

'I hope she's not nasty to you,' Mam remarked. 'If she is I'll go round there and give her a piece of me mind.'

'Oh, she just ignores me, thank goodness.' It was a relief to be beneath the woman's contempt. It meant she could get on with things without expecting the wrath of Cain to fall on her because the chain in the lavatory had stopped working or the soap powder hadn't arrived.

Mr Fritz said privately that he'd never felt so pleased about anything in his life as he was to have Flo back. She told him he was exaggerating, but he maintained stoutly that he meant every word. 'I love my wife, Flo, but she was beginning to get me down. The atmosphere has improved enormously since you reappeared on the scene. Things don't seem so bad if you can make a joke of them. Until you came, it all seemed rather tragic.' Every time Stella went into the drying room, or outside for some fresh air, he would make a peculiar face and sing, 'The dragon lady's gone, oh, the dragon lady's gone. What shall we do now the dragon lady's gone?'

When the dragon lady returned, he would cry, 'Ah, there you are, my love!' Stella would throw him a murderous look and Flo would do her best to stifle a giggle. She thought Mr Fritz was incredibly patient. A less kind-hearted person might have dumped Stella in one of the boilers.

She scarcely noticed spring turn into summer because she was working so hard, sometimes till eight or nine o'clock at night, arriving home bone weary, with feet swollen to twice their normal size, ready to fall into bed where she went to sleep immediately. Sally was equally tired and Martha's brewery was short-staffed, which meant she often had to work late. In order to hang on to their remaining staff, the brewery increased the wages, or the pubs might run out of beer, a situation too horrendous even to contemplate. Mam got a part-time job in a greengrocer's in Park Road. The Clancy family had never been so wealthy, but there was nothing to spend the money on. Rationing meant food was strictly limited, and the girls hadn't time to wander round the shops looking at clothes. They all started post-office accounts, and began to save for the day when the war would be over, though that day seemed a long way off.

By now, the war could no longer be described as 'phoney'. Adolf Hitler had conquered most of Europe; in June, he took France, and although thousands of British and French soldiers were rescued in the great evacuation of Dunkirk, thousands more lost their lives or were taken prisoner. The British Isles was separated from the massed German troops by only a narrow strip of water. People shivered in their beds, because invasion seemed inevitable, although the government did all it could to make an invasion as hazardous as possible. Road signs and the names of stations were removed, barricades were erected, aliens were sent to detention camps all over the country, including nice Mr and Mrs Gabrielli who owned the fish-and-chip shop in Earl Road.

One Monday, Flo arrived at work to find Mrs Fritz all on her own, ironing a white shirt with unnecessary force. Her eyes were red, as if she had been weeping. The two women rarely spoke, but Flo felt bound to ask, 'What's the matter? Is Mr Fritz all right?'

'No, he isn't,' Stella said, in a thin voice. 'He's been rounded up like a common criminal and sent to a detention camp on the Isle of Man. Oh, I said he should have taken British nationality years ago but he was proud of being Austrian, the fool. Not only that, we've lost two of our biggest customers. It seems hotels would sooner have dirty sheets than have them washed in a laundry with a foreign name.' Her Irish accent, scarcely noticeable before, had returned in full force with the power of her anger.

'Oh, no!' Flo was sorry about the lost orders, naturally, but devastated at the thought of dear Mr Fritz, who wouldn't have hurt a fly and loathed Hitler every bit as much as she did, being confined behind bars or barbed wire, like a thief or a murderer. 'How long are they keeping him?' she asked.

'For the duration of the bloody war.'

'Oh, no,' Flo said again.

'I suppose I'll just have to close this place down,' Mrs Fritz said bleakly. 'I can't manage on me own. Anyroad, those cancellations could be the start of an avalanche. Soon, there mightn't be any customers left. I suppose we're lucky the building hasn't been attacked. The German pork butcher's in Lodge Lane had all its winders broken.'

'But you can't close down!' Flo cried. 'You've got to keep going for when Mr Fritz comes home. The laundry is his life. And his old customers won't desert him, not the ones who know him personally. We can cope, just the two of us, if there's going to be less work.'

Mrs Fritz attacked the shirt again and didn't answer. Flo took a load of washing into the drying room and was hanging it on the line when Stella Fritz appeared at the door.

'All right, we'll keep the laundry going between us,' she said, in a cold voice, 'but I'd like it made plain from the start, Flo Clancy, that I don't like you. I know full well what you've been up to, and just because I've agreed we should work together, it doesn't mean that I approve.'

Flo tried to look indifferent. 'I don't care if you approve or not. I'm only doing it for Mr Fritz.'

'As long as we know where we stand.'

'Rightio. There's just one thing. What about changing the name from Fritz's Laundry to something else?'

'Such as?'

'Oh, I dunno.' Flo pondered hard. 'What's your maiden name?'

'McGonegal.'

'McGonegal's Laundry is a bit of a mouthful. What about White? White's Laundry. It's got the same number of letters as Fritz, so it'll be easy to change the sign outside. Of course, it won't fool the old customers but it'll certainly fool the new.' It seemed rather traitorous because no one could have been more patriotic than dear Mr Fritz, but if his foreign name was a hindrance to his business, she felt sure he wouldn't mind it being changed.

After a few hiccups – another two big customers withdrew – by August,

White's Laundry was back on its feet. More large hotels sent enormous bundles of washing, including one who'd used the laundry before and seemed content to use it again now the name had been changed.

'That was a good idea you had,' Stella Fritz said grudgingly, the day she heard their old customer had returned.

'Ta,' Flo said.

'Though it means we'll be even more snowed under with work than ever,' she muttered, half to herself.

'Hmm,' Flo muttered back. The two women still rarely spoke. There wasn't the time and they had nothing to say to each other. Occasionally Flo asked if Stella had heard from her husband, and was told he'd written and sounded depressed. It was hard to make out whether Stella was upset or angry that Mr Fritz had gone.

Mam had been discussing with her friends at the Legion of Mary the long hours her youngest daughter worked. One night she said, 'There's these two spinsters in the Legion, twins, Jennifer and Joanna Holbrook. They're in their late seventies, but as spry and fit as women half their age. They want to know if you'd like a hand in the laundry.'

'We're desperate. Stella's tried, but there's better jobs around for women these days. I doubt if two old ladies in their seventies would be much good, though, Mam.'

'I told them to pop in sometime and have a word with Mrs Fritz, any-road.'

Two days later the Holbrook twins presented themselves to an astonished Stella Fritz. They were nearly six feet tall, stick thin, with narrow, animated faces, and identical to each other in every detail, right down to each item of their clothing. Papa had been in shipping, they explained between them, in their breathless, posh voices, and they'd never done a day's work in their lives, apart from in a voluntary capacity in the other great war.

'Of course, we've been knitting squares for the Red Cross . . .' said one – Flo was never able to recognise one twin from the other.

'. . . and rolling bandages . . .'

'. . . and collecting silver paper . . .'

'. . . but we'd far sooner go *out* to work . . .'

'. . . it would be almost as good as joining up.'

Mrs Fritz looked flummoxed. She glanced at Flo, who rolled her eyes helplessly.

'We wrote to the Army and offered our services . . .'

'. . . but they turned us down . . .'

'. . . even though we explained we could speak French and German fluently.'

'I don't know what to say.' Normally blunt, often rude, Mrs Fritz was stuck for words before the two women towering over her.

'What about a week's trial?' Flo suggested.

One twin clapped her hands and cried, 'That would be marvellous!'

'Absolutely wonderful!' cried the other.

'The money isn't important . . .'

'. . . we'd work for peanuts . . .'

'. . . and regard it as our contribution towards the war.'

Stella Fritz offered them peanuts and agreed that they should start tomorrow.

The twins turned up next day in uniforms that had once been worn by their maids: identical white ankle-length pinafores and gathered caps that covered their eyebrows. They were undoubtedly fit, but not quite as spry as Mam had claimed. Every now and then, they required a 'little sit-down', and would produce silver cigarette cases from the pockets of their pinnies and light each other's cigarette with a silver lighter. Then they would take long, deep puffs, as if they had been deprived for months.

'I needed that, Jen.'

'Same here, Jo.'

When their first week was up, there was no suggestion of them leaving, and once again the atmosphere in the laundry improved. Observing the Holbrook twins at close quarters was like having the front seat in a theatre, because they were as good as a top-class variety act. Even Stella Fritz seemed happier, particularly as they didn't have to work so hard and could leave at a civilised hour. It was nice to have a proper break at dinner-time instead of trying to eat a butty and iron a shirt at the same time. Flo didn't bother going home for dinner, and continued to take butties, which she sometimes ate as she wandered along Smithdown Road peering in shop windows. Once or twice, she ventured into the Mystery, but that part of her life no longer seemed real. It was impossible to believe that eighteen months ago she hadn't even met Tommy O'Mara. She felt like a very old woman trying to recall events that had happened more than half a century before. Flo had once had a lover, then she'd had a baby, but now both were gone, she was back at work in the laundry, and it was as if nothing had ever happened. Nothing at all.

Perhaps Hitler felt too daunted by the English Channel, because the threat of invasion faded, to be replaced by a more immediate terror: air raids. Liverpudlians dreaded the ominous wail of the siren warning them that enemy planes were on their way, while the sweetest sound on earth was the single-pitched tone of the all-clear to announce that the raid was over.

Over tea, Mrs Clancy would reel off the places that had been hit: the Customs House, the Dunlop rubber works, Tunnel Road picture house and Central Station. Edge Hill goods station, where Dad had worked, was seriously damaged. Then Albert Colquitt would come home and reel off a different list.

Sally came home from work one morning to report that Rootes Securities had been narrowly missed, and did Flo know that Josie Driver, who used to work in the laundry, had been killed last week when Ullet Road was bombed? 'I thought she'd gone in a convent.'

Flo was wandering along Smithdown Road in her dinner hour, thinking about last night's raid, when she saw the frock and the war was promptly forgotten.

'Oh, it's dead smart!' She stood in front of the window of Elaine's, Ladies' and Children's Fashions, eyeing the frock longingly. It was mauve, with long sleeves, a black velvet collar and velvet buttons down the front. 'It's dead smart, and only two pounds, nine and eleven. I could wear it for church, or to go dancing in. It's ages since I've been to a dance. And I've enough money saved.' She caught sight of her reflection in the window. She looked a fright. It was about time she smartened herself up, did something with her hair, started to wear powder and lipstick again. She couldn't mope for ever. 'If I bought that frock, perhaps Sally would come dancing with me. I bet Jock wouldn't mind.' It was no use asking Martha because she was convinced that no one would ask a girl with glasses to dance, even though Flo assured her there were plenty of men in glasses who didn't hesitate to ask girls up.

'I'll buy it – least, I'll try it on. If it fits, I'll ask them to put it on one side and come back tomorrer with the money.' Excited, she was about to enter the shop when she saw Nancy O'Mara coming towards her pushing a big black pram.

Nancy was dressed less flamboyantly than the last time Flo had seen her, outside the gates of Cammell Laird, in a plain brown coat that looked rather old. Her hair was in the same plump bun on the back of her thin yellow neck. Long earrings with amber-coloured stones dangled from her ears, dragging the lobes so that they looked elongated and deformed. She stopped at the butcher's shop next door, nudged the brake of the pram with her foot, and went inside.

Curious, Flo temporarily put aside her longing for the mauve frock, and walked along to the butcher's. Nancy had joined the small queue inside and her back was to the window. The hood of the pram was half up. Inside, a pretty baby, about seven or eight months old, with fair hair and a dead perfect little face, half sat, half lay against a frilly white pillow, playing sleepily with a rattle. She supposed it was a boy, because he wore blue: blue bonnet and matinée coat, both hand-knitted. Nancy must be minding him for someone. Flo thought of all the baby clothes she'd knitted which had been left behind when her son had been taken away. She'd asked Sally to hide them, because she hadn't wanted ever to see them again. For the first time, she wondered what her little boy had been wearing when Martha took him out into the snow to give to the couple who'd been so anxiously waiting for him to be born.

One of the baby's mittens had come off. 'You've lost a mitt, love,' she said softly.

At the sound of her voice, the baby turned his head. He smiled straight at her, shook the rattle, and uttered a contented little gurgle. As Flo stared into the two huge pools of green that were the baby's eyes, she felt a tingling creep down her spine, and knew that he was hers. *Martha had given her baby to Nancy O'Mara!*

'Aaah!' she breathed. Her arms reached down to pick her son out of the pram, when a scrawny yellow hand appeared from nowhere and gripped her right arm like a vice.

'Stay away from him!' Nancy O'Mara hissed. 'Don't think you'll ever get him back because I'll kill him first. He's mine. D'you hear?' Her voice rose hysterically and became a shriek. *'He's mine!'*

3

Flo's feet scarcely touched the pavement as she flew along the narrow streets, her mind in turmoil. It would always hurt, but she'd more or less got used to the idea that her baby was with someone else, but she would never get used to him being with Nancy O'Mara. She'd get him back, she'd claim him as her own.

Her face was on fire, and there were waves of pain like contractions in her belly. She had no idea where she was going, but when she found herself in Clement Street, where Nancy O'Mara lived, she realised she'd known all along. Without even thinking what she was going to say, she knocked at the house next door. A woman in a flowered overall answered almost immediately. She wore a scarf over a head crammed with metal curlers. A cigarette was poking out of the corner of her mouth.

The words, the lies, seem to come to Flo quite naturally. 'I'm looking for me friend, Nancy O'Mara, but she doesn't seem to be in. I haven't seen her in ages and thought I'd check if she still lived in the same place before I came all the way back.'

'She's out shopping with the baby, luv. I expect she'll be along any minute.'

Flo feigned surprise. 'Baby! I never knew she was expecting.'

The woman seemed amenable to an unexpected gossip on the doorstep. She folded her arms and leaned nonchalantly against the door frame. 'To tell you the truth, luv, it came as a shock to everyone. Did you know her feller died on the *Thetis*?'

'Yes. That was the last time I seen her. We went together on the ferry to Cammell Laird's. She didn't say she was in the club.'

'She wouldn't have known then, would she?' The woman took a puff of her cigarette and narrowed her eyes. 'Let's see, when was Hugh born? – February, Tommy'd been gone a few months before she told me that she'd copped one.'

Hugh! She'd called him Hugh! How can I ask if she actually saw Nancy pregnant? Flo was wondering desperately how she could frame such a question, when the woman gave a rather sardonic smile, 'It's funny,' she said, 'but Nancy O'Mara's always kept herself to herself. Hardly a soul knocks on that door, yet you're the second friend who's turned up out the blue. Actually, she looked a bit like you, 'cept she wore glasses. I don't suppose the two of you are sisters?'

'I haven't got a sister.'

'Mind you, she doesn't come so often since Hugh was born.'

'Doesn't she?' Flo said faintly.

'No. Y'see, Nancy was one of those women who hides out of sight when she's pregnant. I've a sister-in-law in Wallasey like that, me poor brother has to do all the shopping. Nancy not having a feller, like, this friend used to get her ladyship's groceries for her.'

'The friend with the glasses?'

'Sright, luv.'

'Did she have the baby at home or in the hospital?'

'No one's sure about that, luv. Typical of Nancy, she just appeared with him in a pram one day. Proud as punch she was, pushing him round in the snow.' She laughed coarsely. 'If she hadn't announced all those months ago that she was in the club, I'd have thought she'd pinched him.'

'You don't say.'

'Know Nancy well, do you, luv?' The woman looked quite prepared to talk all day.

'Not all that well. Me brother worked at Cammell Laird's and Nancy and Tommy came to his wedding,' Flo explained. 'I've only seen her a few times since.' She was wondering how to get away.

'Well, she certainly fell on her feet when Tommy kicked the bucket. A bob a week she used to pay in life insurance – I only know because me friend's husband's the collector and we used to joke she was planning on doing away with him one of these days, randy bugger that he was. Oh, look, here comes Nancy now.'

Nancy O'Mara had just turned the corner. She didn't notice Flo and the neighbour because all her attention was concentrated on the occupant of the pram. She was shaking her head, laughing and clucking. Then she stopped, tipped the pram towards her, and said something to the baby inside. She laughed again. Her face wore an expression Flo had rarely seen on anyone before: a radiance so intense that it was as if every wish she'd ever made had come true.

'She don't half dote on that baby,' the woman in the flowered overall murmured.

To the woman's astonishment, Flo turned on her heel and walked away.

When she returned to work more than half an hour late Stella Fritz threw her a questioning look, but Flo wasn't in the mood to make apologies or excuses. Throughout the afternoon, she worked like a madwoman, well making up for the time she'd been late. She swung wildly between sorrow, rage and loathing for the sister who had so comprehensively betrayed her. But the feeling that towered above all others was jealousy. She kept seeing Nancy's radiantly happy face; happiness caused solely by the fact that she'd been blessed with the gift of Flo's baby. For eight months, Tommy's wife had had him all to herself, nursed him, soothed him, watched him grow; unique, wonderful experiences that had been denied his real mother. There was the oddest feeling deep within Flo, almost akin to making love with Tommy, when she imagined holding her baby to her breast.

'I'll get him back,' she swore, but remembered Nancy's face again and felt uneasy. '*Don't think you'll ever get him back, because I'll kill him first. He's mine!*' the woman had said. The way she'd looked at the baby wasn't quite natural. She loved him too much. Tommy had always claimed she wasn't quite right in the head, and even Martha had called her funny, a Welsh witch, though it hadn't stopped her from handing over her sister's child, Flo thought bitterly. As the afternoon progressed, it became easy to visualise Nancy O'Mara suffocating the tiny boy with that frilly pillow before she'd let Flo have him.

Perhaps she could snatch him from his pram, take him to another town . . . but Flo knew there would never be an opportunity to steal him.

She'd like to bet a hundred pounds that the baby would never be left outside a shop again. Now Nancy knew that Flo had recognised him, she would hang on to him like grim death.

When her youngest sister came storming in Martha was setting the table. Flo thought she looked furtive and immediately guessed why: Nancy O'Mara had been waiting outside the brewery to relay what had happened that afternoon.

Now that the moment had come to pour out the rage that had been mounting ever since dinner-time, scream about the terrible injustice that had been done, Flo couldn't be bothered. What was the point?

Mam was humming to herself in the back kitchen. 'Is that you, Flo?' she called.

'Yes, Mam.'

'I was just telling our Martha, I ordered a chicken today for Christmas. I couldn't believe they were taking orders so early but, as the butcher said, it's only eleven weeks off.'

'That'll be nice, won't it, Flo?' Martha said brightly. 'Maybe Albert will stay with us this year. You know, Mam,' she called, 'it might be possible to put Albert's name down for a chicken as well.'

'I suppose it might. I didn't think o' that.'

'I won't be living here by Christmas,' Flo said. The words seemed just to come out without any previous thought.

Martha's jaw dropped and she looked frightened. 'Why not?'

'You know darn well why not. Because I can't bear to live in the same house as you another minute.'

Mam came bustling in with plates of stew. 'Sal!' she yelled. 'Dinner's on the table. It's blind scouse,' she explained. 'There wasn't a scrap of meat to be had in the butcher's.' She wiped her hands on her pinny. 'What was that I heard about someone not living here by Christmas?'

'Ask our Martha,' Flo said abruptly. 'I don't want any tea tonight, Mam. It's been an awful day and I feel like a lie-down.'

Sally burst into the room, full of beans because she'd had a letter from Jock that morning. She kissed her sister's cheek. 'Hello, Flo,' she sang.

Sally's evident happiness only emphasised Flo's all-embracing misery, but she gave her a long, warm hug before going upstairs. To her surprise, she only lay down for a few minutes before she fell asleep.

It was pitch dark when she woke up. Someone must have been in, because the curtains were drawn. She was collecting her thoughts, remembering the events of the day, when she became conscious of a movement in the room. As her eyes became used to the dimness, she saw that her mother was sitting on the edge of the double bed watching her sleep.

Mam must have sensed she was awake. 'I've been thinking about your uncle Seumus,' she said softly.

'I didn't know I had an uncle Seumus,' Flo said dully.

'He died long before you were born, shot by the English on the banks of the Liffey. He was smuggling arms for the IRA.'

'How old was he?' Another time Flo would have been interested to discover she'd had a romantic, if disreputable, uncle. Right now, she didn't care.

'Nineteen. I was only ten when he died, but I remember our Seumus as clearly as if he died yesterday. He was a grand lad, full of ideals, though not many people, particularly the English, would have agreed with them.' Mam sighed softly. 'I still miss him.'

'What made you think of him just now?'

'You remind me of him, that's why – hot-headed, never thinking before you act. Oh, Flo!' Mam's voice rose. 'Did it never enter your head the trouble it could cause by sleeping with a married man? God Almighty, girl, we were such a happy family before. Now everything's ruined.'

Flo didn't answer straight away. She recalled the first time she'd been on her way to meet Tommy O'Mara outside the Mystery, and the strange feeling she'd had, as if nothing would ever be the same again. It had turned out to be true, but not in the way she'd imagined. Mam was right. The Clancy family was about to break up. Flo could no longer live in the same house as Martha. 'I'm sorry, Mam,' she whispered. 'I'll leave home, like I said. Things'll be better if I'm not here.'

'Better!' Mam said hoarsely. 'Better! How will they be better without you, girl?' She reached out and stroked Flo's cheek. 'You're me daughter and I love you, no matter what you've done. I just wish I could feel so charitable about our Martha.'

'Did she tell you – about Nancy O'Mara?'

Mam nodded bleakly. 'That was a terrible thing to do. I wish to God I'd known what she was up to. The thing is, I've relied too much on Martha since your dad died. I thought she was strong, but she's the weakest of us all. The only way she can feel important is by meddling in other people's lives. If anyone's going to leave home, I'd rather it be Martha, but I suppose she needs me more than you and Sal ever will, particularly if she doesn't manage to catch poor Albert.'

'Oh, Mam!' Her mother seemed to accept that she was leaving, and Flo felt the future loom up before her, dark and uncertain.

'Come on, girl.' Mam stood up with a sigh. 'There's scouse left if you feel like it. Albert's fire-watching, Sal's at work, and Martha's gone to see Elsa Cameron – Norman's had another bad fall. The little lad's only two, and every time I see him he's covered in bruises.'

'Mam?'

'Yes, luv?' Her mother paused at the door.

'D'you think I could get him back – my baby?'

'No, luv. According to Martha, the birth certificate has Nancy down as the mother and Tommy O'Mara as the dad. Everyone in the street believed she was pregnant. Legally, he's hers, fair and square.'

'But you know that's a lie, Mam,' Flo cried. 'We could go to court and swear he's mine.'

Mam's entire demeanour changed. 'Court! Don't talk soft, Florence Clancy,' she said sharply. 'I've no intention of setting foot inside a court. For one thing, we haven't got the money, and second, there'd be a terrible scandal. It'd be in all the papers and I'd never be able to hold me head up in Liverpool again.'

The raid that night was short and not too heavy. The Clancys usually stayed in bed until the last minute, then when danger seemed imminent, they would go down and sit under the stairs. That night, the all-clear sounded before anyone had stirred, but Flo remained wide awake long afterwards. Where would she live? Would Mam let her have some sheets and blankets and a few dishes? They hadn't got a suitcase, so how would she carry her few belongings?

'Are you awake, Flo?' Martha whispered.

Flo made no sign she'd heard, but Martha persisted, 'I know you're awake because you're dead restless.'

'So what if I am?' Flo snapped.

'I thought we could talk.'

'I've nothing to say to you, Martha. You're nothing but a bloody liar. All that talk about me little boy going to a nice mam and dad!'

'Just listen to me a minute. What I did was only for the best.'

'You mean giving my baby to a Welsh witch was only for the best?' Flo laughed contemptuously.

'Nancy's always longed for a child, but the good Lord didn't see fit to answer her prayers. No one could love that baby more than she does.'

'*I* could! And the good Lord had nothing to do with it. It was because Tommy hadn't touched her that way in years. He told me.'

'I was only thinking of you, luv,' Martha said piteously. 'I wish you'd change your mind about leaving home. Mam's dead upset, and I feel as if it's my fault.'

'It *is* your fault,' Flo spat. It was all she could do not to leap out of bed and beat her sister to a pulp until every ounce of frustration and anger had been spent. 'And you weren't thinking of me, you were thinking of yourself, about your stupid reputation and what people would say.' Her voice rose shrilly. 'You couldn't even arrange the adoption properly, could you? I bet you enjoyed conspiring with Nancy, doing her shopping, being her best friend.' She imagined her sister bustling round to Clement Street, eyes gleaming behind her round glasses, sounding Nancy out, skirting round the matter of Flo's pregnancy until she had established that the woman would jump at the chance of having Tommy's child. Neither had dreamed Flo would recognise her own baby, because neither had given birth to a child of their own. Flo buried her face in her hands and began to rock to and fro. 'I wish I'd had the nerve to leave once I realised I was expecting, I wish I'd married Albert, I wish—'

Martha sat up. 'What was that about Albert?' she asked tersely.

Flo blinked. She hadn't meant to mention Albert. There was still time to pretend she'd meant something else or used the wrong name, but all of a sudden she saw an opportunity to hurt her sister, not nearly so badly as she'd been hurt herself but enough to wound. Still she hesitated, because she'd never intentionally hurt anyone in her life. A hard voice inside her insisted that Martha needed to be taught a lesson. '*She took your baby and gave him to Nancy O'Mara,*' the voice reminded her.

'I've never mentioned it before,' she said lightly, 'but Albert knew about the baby. He offered to marry me there and then. He told me about his wife dying in childbirth, and his little girl, Patsy, who died at the same time. He was going to use his savings to buy furniture for our house. In view of what's happened, I'm dead sorry I turned him down.'

'I don't believe you!'

'Ask him.' Flo yawned and slid under the bedclothes. She didn't sleep another wink that night as she lay listening to her sister's sobs, unsure whether to feel glad or ashamed.

She had less trouble than she had expected in finding somewhere to live. Next day, after asking the twins if they would keep their eyes open for a room to let, Stella Fritz sidled up. 'Why are you leaving home?'

Flo resisted telling her to mind her own business. The woman was her employer and they'd been getting on much better lately. 'I just want to, that's all,' she said.

'Is it, I mean, are you . . . ?' Stella's face grew red. It was obvious she thought Flo might be in the club again.

'I'm leaving because our Martha's driving me dotty. Now our Sal's married, there's only me left to boss around. I'll be twenty-one next year, and I thought it was time I lived on me own.'

'I see. You can have our cellar, if you want. It's never used.'

'Cellar!' Flo had visions of a little dark space full of coal. 'I'm not living in a cellar, thanks all the same.'

Stella shook her head impatiently. 'I call it the cellar, but it's really a basement. It's where the housekeeper used to live in the days when William Square was full of nobs. There's a few odds and ends of furniture, and I can let you have some stuff from upstairs. The walls will need a coat of distemper. Otherwise, it's very clean.'

William Square was becoming a bit seedy, Flo thought when she went to see the basement. There was nothing you could put a finger on, but the gracious houses weren't being maintained as they used to be.

The living room was very big, only partially furnished and rather dark, but there was a separate bedroom, a kitchen, and, wonder of wonders, a bathroom with a lavatory. There was even electric light. Everywhere smelt strongly of damp, but all in all, the place was much grander than anywhere Flo had hoped to find.

'Fritz had the gas fire installed. He used to turn it on now 'n' again during the winter, case the damp spread through the house.'

Flo gazed in awe at the efficient-looking fire. Imagine not having to fetch in coal every day! Imagine just pressing a switch for the light, and sitting on the lavatory indoors!

'I'm not sure if I can afford the rent for a place like this.'

'I haven't said what the rent will be, have I? You'd make your own meals and pay your own gas and electricity – there's separate meters down here.' Stella pursed her lips. 'Five bob a week'll do.'

'But you could get as much as seven and six!'

'I could ask ten bob in this part of town, but you'd be doing me a favour if you take it.'

'What sort of favour?'

Stella ignored her and went to stand at the rear window, which overlooked a rather grubby little yard. 'Just look at that!' she said tonelessly. 'Walls, bricks, dirt! Back in Ireland all we could see from our winders was green fields, trees and sky, with the lakes of Killarney sparkling in the distance. It's like living in a prison here.' She seemed to have forgotten that Flo was there. 'It was something Fritz could never understand, that there's some things more important than money, like good clean air and a sweet, blowing wind. All that concerned him was his bloody laundry.'

Flo twisted her hands together uncomfortably, not sure what to say. The Fritzes had always seemed such a happy couple.

'Oh, well.' Stella turned away. 'The palliasse for the bed's up in the loft, case it got damp. I'll fetch it down, as well as a mat for in front of the fire and a few other bits and pieces. Those chairs aren't too comfortable, but there's not much I can do about it – Fritz used to come down here sometimes for a bit of peace and quiet. Me mam'll give the place a good clean, though if you want it painting you'll have to do it yourself. There's some tins of distemper in the yard. It should be ready to move in by Monday.'

It was awful leaving Sally, but when it came to saying goodbye to her mother, Flo felt cold. Mam hadn't acted as badly as Martha, but Flo had never dreamed she could be so hard, preferring her daughter to go without her beloved baby rather than risk the faintest whiff of scandal.

When she made her departure directly after tea on Monday Albert Colquitt wasn't home. 'Give him my love, Mam,' she said. 'Tell him he's been the best lodger in the world and I'll never forget him.' She was aware of a white-faced Martha across the room. Her sister still looked stunned from their row the other night. Flo had ignored her ever since.

Mam was close to tears. 'For goodness sake, luv, you'd think you had no intention of setting foot in Burnett Street again. You can tell Albert that to his face next time you see him.'

'Tara, Mam. Tara, Sal.' Flo slung the pillowcase containing all her worldly possessions over her shoulder like a sailor. She tried to force her lips to say the words, but they refused to obey, so she left the house without speaking to Martha.

The first few months in William Square were thoroughly enjoyable. Perhaps the favour Stella had mentioned was having Flo look after the little Fritzes – not that the two eldest, Ben and Harry, were little any more. Aged thirteen and fourteen, they were almost as tall as Flo. They invaded the basement flat, all eight of them, on her first night there.

'Have you come to live with us?'

'Did you know our dad?'

'Will you read us a book, Flo?'

'Do you know how to play Strip Jack Naked?' Ben demanded.

'The answer to every question is yes,' Flo grinned. 'Yes, yes, yes, yes. Sit on me knee – what's your name? – and I'll read you the book.'

'I'm Aileen.'

'Come on, then, Aileen.'

From that night on, Flo scarcely had time to have her tea before the children would come pouring down the concrete steps. By then Stella's mother, Mrs McGonegal, had seen enough of her lively grandchildren. She was a withdrawn woman, shy, with a tight, unhappy face. According to Stella, she missed Ireland and its wide open spaces even more than her daughter and couldn't wait to get back. 'And she's petrified of the air raids. She won't come with us to the shelter but crawls under the bed and doesn't come out till the all-clear goes.'

On Sunday afternoons, Flo took the children for walks. They formed a crocodile all the way to the Pier Head and back again. Sometimes, she took the older ones to the pictures, where they saw Will Hay and Tommy Trinder and laughed till they cried. She suspected Harry had a crush on her, so treated him more tenderly than the others, which only made the crush worse.

A week after Flo moved, Sally came to see her and was startled to find the room full of little Fritzes. 'Have you started a school or something?'

'Aren't they lovely?' Flo said blissfully. 'I can't wait for Christmas. I thought I'd be spending it all by meself for the first time in me life, but Stella's invited me upstairs.' She still saw a trace of disapproval in the little Irishwoman's eyes whenever they spoke. 'I'm making decorations for the tree and it's lovely wandering round the shops at dinner-time looking for prezzies for the kids. I'm buying one a week.'

But by the time Christmas arrived, Stella Fritz, her mother, and her eight children had all gone.

After what everyone called 'the raid to end all raids' at the end of November, when for seven and a half long hours the city of Liverpool suffered a murderous attack from the air, a night when 180 people were killed in one single tragic incident, December brought blessed relief. 'I think Mr Hitler is going to let us spend the festive season in peace,' one of the twins remarked.

She spoke too soon. At twenty past six that night, all hell broke loose as wave after wave of enemy bombers unloaded their lethal cargo of incendiary and high-explosive bombs. The city was racked by explosions for nine and a half hours. Fires crackled furiously, the flames transforming the dark sky into an umbrella of crimson. Ambulances and fire engines screamed through the shattered streets.

Would the dreadful night ever end, Flo wondered, as she sat in the public shelter with the two smallest Fritzes on her knee. It hardly seemed possible that William Square could still be standing. As she tried to comfort the children, she was overcome with worry for her family and her little son.

At one point, Stella muttered, 'It's all right for Fritz, isn't it? He's safe and sound on the Isle of Man.'

At last the all-clear sounded at four o'clock in the morning; the long piercing whine had never been so welcome. Stella gathered the children together and made for home. William Square was just round the corner, and in the red glow the houses appeared miraculously intact. A small fire sizzled cheerfully in the central garden area where an incendiary bomb had fallen and several trees and bushes were alight.

'I'll help put the kids to bed,' Flo offered.

'It's all right,' Stella said tiredly, 'you see to yourself, Flo. Forget about opening up on time tomorrer. The twins have got a key – that's if they turn up themselves.' She sighed. 'I wonder how me mammy is?'

When Flo woke it was broad daylight. The birds were singing merrily. She jumped out of bed, intent on getting to work as quickly as possible – not because she was conscientious but she wanted to make sure that Clement and Burnett Streets hadn't been hit. After a cat's lick, she threw on the clothes she'd worn the day before.

Before leaving, she went upstairs to ask after Mrs McGonegal. To her astonishment, Stella Fritz opened the door wearing her best grey coat and an astrakhan hat with a matching grey bow. Her eyes were shining, and she looked happier than Flo had ever seen her, even in the days when she and Mr Fritz had seemed such an ideal married couple. 'I was about to come and see you,' she cried. 'Come in, Flo. We're off to Ireland this afternoon, to me uncle Kieran's farm in County Kerry. Me mam's over the moon. Oh, I know there's no gas or electricity, the privy's in the garden and you have to draw water from a well, but it's better than being blown to pieces in a raid.'

'I'll miss you.' Flo was devastated when she saw the row of suitcases in the hall. It was the little Fritzes she'd really miss. She looked forward to their regular invasion of her room, the walks, the visits to the pictures. Upstairs, she could hear their excited cries as they ran from room to room and supposed they were collecting their favourite possessions to take to Ireland.

'The children are dead upset you're being left behind,' Stella said, looking anything but upset herself, 'but I said to them, "Flo's going to take care of things back here. She'll look after the house." I'll leave you the keys, luv, and if you'd just take a look round once a week, like, make sure everything's all right.'

So, that was the favour. Flo had been installed downstairs so that Mrs Fritz could up and leave whenever she liked, safe in the knowledge that the house would be cared for in her absence. Flo wasn't too bothered that she'd been used. It still meant she'd got a lovely flat dead cheap. But now it appeared she'd have the flat for nothing in return for 'services'. Would she mind running the water in cold weather, save the pipes from icing up, lighting a fire now and then to keep the place aired, opening the windows occasionally so it wouldn't smell musty?

'What's happening to the laundry?' Flo asked, when Stella had finished reeling off instructions.

'You'll be in charge from now on, luv,' Stella said carelessly. 'Take on more women, if you can. I'll write and tell you how to put the money in the bank each week.'

'Right,' said Flo stoutly, as yet more responsibility was heaped on her young shoulders. 'I'll just go upstairs and say tara to the children.'

She was about to leave the room, when Stella came over and gripped her by the arms. Her good humour had evaporated and her face was hard. 'There's something I'd like cleared up before I go.'

'What's that?' Flo asked nervously.

'I know full well why you left the laundry that time. Tell me truthfully, was it my Fritz who fathered your child?'

The question was so outlandish that Flo laughed aloud. 'Of course not! What on earth gave you that idea?'

'I just wondered, that's all.' She smiled and squeezed Flo's arms. 'You're a grand girl, Flo. I'm sorry I was horrible in the past, but everything got on top of me. And I always had me suspicions about you and Fritz. Now, say tara to the kids, and tell them to come down and we'll be on our way.'

*

It didn't seem possible but the raid that night was even heavier than the one the night before. For more than ten hours, an endless stream of fire-bombs and explosives fell on Liverpool. Flo didn't bother with the shelter, but stayed in bed trying to read a novel she'd found upstairs. She did the same the following night when the raid was even longer. The house seemed no less safe than a brick shelter, and at least she was warm and comfortable and could make a cup of tea whenever she liked.

Each morning, she left promptly for work, although she hadn't had a wink of sleep, and on the way made sure that Clement Street and Burnett Street were still standing.

On Christmas Day she went early to Mass, then spent the morning tidying up after the Fritzes. In their excitement, the children had left clothes and toys everywhere, and there were dirty dishes in the back kitchen. Flo moved from room to room, feeling like a ghost in the big silent house, picking things up, putting them away, gathering together the dirty clothes to wash. She helped herself to a few items for downstairs; a tablecloth, a saucepan, a teapot, more books, and supposed she'd better use up the fresh food that had been left behind – the bacon looked like best back – and Mrs McGonegal had walked miles in search of dried fruit for that Christmas cake.

She went into the living room and sat in the huge bay window beside the tree that she'd helped to decorate. William Square was deserted, though there must be celebrations going on behind the blank windows. As if to confirm that this was so, a motor car drew up a few doors away and a couple with two children got out. The man opened the boot and handed the children several boxes wrapped in red paper. Flo remembered the presents she'd bought for the Fritzes, which were still hidden under her bed, away from their prying eyes. She'd take them to one of them rest centres that looked after people who'd lost everything in the blitz, let some other kids have the benefit.

The house was so quiet, you could almost sense the quietness ticking away like a bomb. They'd just be finishing dinner in Burnett Street and starting on the sherry. Sally had said that Albert would be there, and Jock. No one would be coming to see Flo because they thought she was spending Christmas with the Fritzes. Flo sniffed dejectedly. It would be easy to have a good ould cry, but the situation was entirely of her own making. If she'd turned down Tommy O'Mara when he'd asked her to go for a walk, she'd be part of the group sitting round the table in Burnett Street with Martha rationing out the sherry.

Sherry! There were half a dozen bottles on the top shelf of the larder. She went into the kitchen, collected a bottle, and was about to take everything downstairs when she noticed the wireless in an alcove beside the fireplace. Unlike Albert's battery set, this one had an electric plug. It was also far superior to Albert's. The Bakelite casing had a tortoiseshell pattern, the gold mesh shaped like a fan.

She spent the rest of the day drinking sherry, half reading a book, half listening to the wireless, and told herself she was having a good time. It wasn't until a man with a lovely deep voice began to sing 'Dancing in the Dark', that she had a good ould cry.

*

On Boxing Day Flo moved the furniture into the middle of the room and distempered the basement a nice fresh lemon. It needed two coats and she was exhausted by the time she had finished and stood admiring her handiwork. The room had brightened up considerably, but the blackout curtains looked dead miserable. She raided upstairs and found several sets of bronze cretonne curtains, which she hung over the blackout. The place was beginning to look like home.

Home! Flo sat on one of the lumpy chairs and put her finger thoughtfully to her chin. She had a home, yes, but she hadn't got a life. The idea of spending more nights alone listening to the wireless made her spirits wilt, and she didn't fancy going to dances or the pictures on her own. Having two sisters not much older than herself meant she'd never gone out of her way to make friends. Bel was the closest to a friend she'd ever had, but Bel wasn't much use up in Scotland. Of course, she could always change her job so that she worked with women of her own age, but she felt honour-bound to keep the business going for Mr Fritz.

'I'll take up voluntary work!' she said aloud. It would occupy the evenings, and she'd always wanted to do something towards the war effort. 'I'll join the Women's Voluntary Service, or help at a rest centre. And Albert said there's even women fire-fighters. I'll make up me mind what to do in the new year.'

Next day, Sally and Jock whizzed in and out, but Flo didn't mention that the Fritzes had gone because Sally might have felt obliged to stay – and you could tell that she and Jock couldn't wait to be by themselves. The day after, Mam came into the laundry to see how she was and Flo said she was fine. She didn't want Mam thinking she regretted leaving home, because she didn't. She might have experienced the most wretched Christmas imaginable, but she'd willingly go through the whole thing again rather than live in the same house as Martha. More than anything, she couldn't stand the idea of anyone feeling sorry for her, though by the time New Year's Eve arrived, Flo was feeling very sorry for herself.

A party was going on across the square, a pianist was thumping out all the latest tunes: 'We'll Meet Again', 'You Were Never Lovelier', 'When You Wish Upon a Star . . .' In Upper Parliament Street, people could be heard singing at the tops of their voices. There'd been little in the way of raids since Christmas, and no doubt everyone felt it was safe to roam the streets again. She switched on the wireless, but the disembodied voices emphasised rather than eased her sense of isolation. She contemplated going early to bed with a book and a glass of sherry – there were only two bottles left – but ever since she was a little girl she'd always been up and about when the clocks chimed in the New Year. She remembered sitting on Dad's knee, everybody kissing and hugging and wishing each other a happy new year, then singing 'Auld Lang Syne'.

I could gatecrash that party! She smiled at the thought, and a memory surfaced: Josie Driver, God rest her soul, had once mentioned ending up on St George's Plateau on New Year's Eve. 'Everyone was stewed to the eyeballs, but we had a dead good time.'

Flo threw on a coat. She'd go into town. At least there would be other human beings around, even if she didn't know them, and they could be as drunk as lords for all she cared. She hadn't been a hundred per cent sober herself since finding that sherry.

The sky was beautifully clear, lit by a half-moon and a million dazzling stars, so it was easy to see in the blackout. Music could be heard coming from the Rialto ballroom and from most of the pubs she passed. People seemed to be enjoying themselves more than ever this year, as if they had put the war to the back of their minds for this one special night.

When she arrived in the city centre it was far too early, and her heart sank when there wasn't a soul to be seen on St George's Plateau. What on earth shall I do with meself till midnight? she wondered. She began to walk slowly towards the Pier Head, aware that she was the only woman alone. The pubs were still open – they must have got an extension because it was New Year's Eve. She paused outside one. She could see nothing, because the windows had been painted black, and there was a curtain over the door, but inside a girl with a voice like an angel was singing, 'Yours Till the Stars Lose Their Glory', as it had never been sung before.

Flo stared into the black window, seeing Tommy O'Mara's reckless, impudent face gazing back at her, his cap perched on the back of his brown curly hair. Their eyes met and her insides glowed hot. She wanted him, oh, how she wanted him! 'Nobody understood how much we loved each other,' she whispered.

'D'you fancy a drink, luv?'

She turned, startled. A young soldier was standing beside her, twisting his cap nervously in his hands. Lord, he was no more than eighteen, and there was an expression on his fresh, childish face that reflected exactly how she felt herself: a look of aching, gut-wrenching loneliness. She'd like to bet he'd never tried to pick up a girl before, that this was his first time away from home, the first New Year's Eve he hadn't spent within the bosom of his family, and that he was desperate for company. She also saw fear in his eyes. Perhaps he was going overseas shortly and was afraid of being killed. Or perhaps he was just afraid she'd turn him down.

The girl inside the pub stopped singing, everyone thumped the tables, burst into enthusiastic applause, and Flo was hit with an idea that took her breath away. She knew exactly what she could do as her contribution towards the war.

'What a nice idea, luv!' she cried gaily. 'I'd love a drink. Shall we go in here?'

Millie

1

'Are you the Tom who gave her the lamp?' I'd always imagined Flo's friend being as old as Flo herself.

''Sright. I got it her in Austria.'

I sat in the armchair, resentful that Tom O'Mara was occupying my favourite spot on the settee, his feet back on the table. 'What were you doing in Austria?'

'Skiing,' he said abruptly.

He looked more the type to prefer a Spanish resort full of bars and fish-and-chip shops, I thought. I said, 'I've always wanted to ski.'

'I didn't know Flo had these.' He ignored my observation and picked up the newspaper cuttings. His fingers were long and slender and I imagined . . . Oh, God! I did my best to hide another shiver. 'That's how me grandad died,' he said, 'On the *Thetis*.'

'Do you know much about it?' I asked eagerly. 'I keep meaning to get a book from the library.'

'Me gran used to pin me ear back about the *Thetis*. She had a book. It's at home. You can have it, if you like. I'll send it round sometime.'

'Thanks,' I said. A pulse in my neck was beating crazily, and I covered it with my hand, worried he'd notice. What on earth was happening to me? Usually, I wouldn't give a man like Tom O'Mara the time of day. I glanced at him surreptitiously and saw that he was staring at the lamp, oblivious of me. I almost felt a nuisance for having interrupted his quiet sojourn in the flat. There was little sign that a party was going on upstairs, just a muffled thumping as people danced, and music that sounded as if it came from some distance away. 'How come you knew, Flo?' I asked.

'She was a friend of me dad's. I knew her all me life.'

'Would it be possible to meet your father? I'd love to talk to him about Flo.'

' "Would it be possible to meet your father?" ' he repeated after me, in such a false, exaggerated impersonation of my accent that I felt my face redden with anger and hurt. 'Christ, girl, you don't half talk posh, like you've got a plum in your gob or something. And you can't talk to me dad about anything. He died fourteen years ago.'

'Is there any need to be so rude?' I spluttered.

Our eyes met briefly. Despite my anger, I searched for a sign that he didn't despise me as much as he pretended, but there was none. He turned away contemptuously. 'People like you make me sick. You were born in Liverpool, yet you talk like the fucking Queen. I think it's called "denying your roots".'

'A day never goes by when I don't remember my roots,' I said shortly. 'And there are people around who could have a great deal of fun with the way you speak.' I stared at him coolly, though cool was the opposite of what I felt. 'I came down for some peace and quiet, not to be insulted. I'd be obliged if you'd go.'

Before he could reply, there was a knock on the window and James called, 'Are you there, Millie?' He must have been looking for me, and someone, Charmian or Herbie, had suggested where I might be.

'Coming!' I stood, aware that Tom O'Mara's eyes had flickered over my body, and felt exultant. My ego demanded that he found me as attractive as I found him, not that it mattered. He was an uncouth lout. Anyway, there was no likelihood of us meeting again. He could keep his book on the *Thetis*, I'd get one for myself. In my iciest voice, I said, 'I've got to go. Kindly put the key on the mantelpiece when you leave. Goodnight.'

For James's sake, I decided reluctantly to give Flo's flat a miss the next afternoon. I couldn't bring myself to ask him to leave after refusing to see him all the previous week. Bel and Charmian would be expecting me, I thought wistfully, though I really should get down to clearing things out – and I still hadn't found out about the rent. I was anxious to speak to the landlord and pay another month before the flat was let to someone else, if that hadn't happened already. One of these days I might turn up and find the place stripped bare. The rent book was bound to be among Flo's papers, but I hadn't even discovered where her papers were kept.

'This is nice.' James sighed blissfully as we lay in bed in each other's arms after making love for the third time. 'An unexpected treat. I thought I'd be sent on my way ages ago.' It was almost three o'clock.

'Mmm.' I was too exhausted to reply. I felt guilty and ashamed. James wouldn't feel quite so happy if he knew that every time I closed my eyes he turned into Tom O'Mara.

He nuzzled my breasts. 'This is heaven,' he breathed. 'Oh, darling, if only you knew how much I love you.'

I stroked his head and said dutifully, 'I think I do.'

'But you never tell me you love me back!' he said sulkily. He pulled away and threw himself on to the pillow.

'James, please,' I groaned, 'I'm not in the mood for this.'

'You're never in the mood.'

I leaped out of bed and grabbed my dressing gown. 'I wish to God you'd give me some space,' I snapped. 'Why do you keep nagging me to say things I don't want to say, to feel things I don't feel?'

'Will you ever say them? Will you ever feel them?' He stared at me forlornly.

I stormed out of the room, 'I can't stand any more. I'm going to have a shower and I'm locking the door. I expect you to be gone when I come out.'

When I emerged from the bathroom fifteen minutes later there was no sign of a contrite James begging forgiveness. No doubt he would telephone or come back later, in which case he wouldn't find me in. I got dressed quickly in jeans and an old sweatshirt and raced down to the car. It was already growing dark and I couldn't wait to be in Flo's flat where I knew I would find the tranquillity I craved.

It wasn't to be, but I didn't mind. I was unlocking the front door when Bel Eddison appeared in her leopardskin jacket. 'I thought I heard you. I've been helping Charmian clear up after the party. We were expecting you hours ago.'

'I was delayed. Come and have some sherry. Why weren't you at the party? I looked everywhere for you.'

'I had another engagement.' She smirked. 'I wouldn't say no to a glass of sherry, but me and Charmian have been finishing off the bottles left over from last night. I'm not exactly steady on me legs.' She staggered into the basement and made herself comfortable on the settee. 'Charmian can't come. Jay's going back to university in the morning and she's still sorting out his washing.'

I turned on the lamp and poured us both a drink. I noticed Tom O'Mara's key on the mantelpiece. As the lamp began slowly to revolve, I said, 'I met the man who gave her that last night.'

'Did you now.' Bel hiccuped.

'He told me how his grandad died, and you said Flo was in love with someone who was lost on the *Thetis*. I wondered if they were one and the same person.'

'I said no such thing, luv,' Bel remarked huffily. 'I said, "Draw your own conclusions," if I remember right.'

'Well, I've drawn them, and that's the conclusion I've reached.' I felt that I'd got one up on Bel for a change.

To my consternation, the old woman's face seemed to shrivel, her jaw sagged, and she whispered hoarsely, 'Flo said, "I don't know what I'm going to do if Tommy's dead. Me life's over. I'll never love another man the way I loved him." The thing is, he was a right scally, Tommy O'Mara, not fit to lick Flo's boots. It sticks in me craw to think she wasted her life on a chap like him.'

I hoped Bel wouldn't be angry, but I had to ask, 'Last night, Tom talked about his gran. Does that mean this Tommy was married when . . . ?'

Bel nodded vigorously. 'She was the last girl in the world to go out with a married man, but he spun her a tale. He was such a charmer. He told *me* he was single.'

'You mean, you went out with him, too?' I gasped.

'Yeh.' Bel grimaced. 'I never let on to Flo, it would have killed her, but I'd been out with him twice just before the *Thetis* went down. Some men aren't happy unless they've got a string of women hankering after them. Tom O'Mara's another one like that. He was a nice lad once, but he's grown up without his grandad's charm. A woman would be mad to have anything to do with him.'

'I agree about the lack of charm. I found him very rude.' I would have liked to know more about Tom O'Mara, but Bel might have thought I was interested when I definitely wasn't. Well, I told myself I wasn't. 'Would you like some tea or coffee to sober you up?' I asked instead.

'A cup of coffee would be nice, but only if it's the instant stuff. I can't stand them percolator things. Flo's got one somewhere.'

For the next few hours we chatted amiably. I told her about my job and my problems with James, and she told me about her three husbands, describing the second, Ivor, in hilarious detail. Before she left, I asked where Flo had kept her papers.

'In that pull-down section of the sideboard, the old one. Flo called it her bureau. You'll have your work cut out sorting through that lot. I think she kept every single letter she ever got.'

Bel was right. When I opened the bureau I found hundreds, possibly thousands, of pieces of paper and letters still in their envelopes, crammed in every pigeonhole and shelf. I felt tempted to close it again and snuggle on the sofa with sherry and a book, but I'd been irresponsible for far too long. I sighed and pulled out a thick wad of gas bills addressed to Miss Florence Clancy, which, to my astonishment, went back as far as 1941, when the quarterly bill was two and sevenpence.

I wondered what the flat had looked like then – and wasted ages envisaging a young Flo, living alone and pining after Tommy O'Mara. Perhaps that's what the row with Gran had been about, Flo going out with a married man. Gran was incredibly straitlaced, though it didn't seem serious enough to make them lifelong enemies.

The cardboard boxes I'd brought were in the bathroom so I fetched one and threw in the bills. Then I almost took them out again. Flo had kept them for more than half a century and it seemed a shame to chuck them away. I pulled myself together, and more than fifty years of electricity bills quickly joined them. I decided I deserved a break, made coffee and helped myself to a packet of Nice biscuits. On my way to the settee, I jumped when something clattered through the letterbox.

It was a book: *The Admiralty Regrets*. I opened the door, but whoever had delivered it had disappeared.

Fiona was leaning against the railings, smoking. 'Hi,' I said awkwardly.

She glared at me malevolently through the railings. 'Sod off,' she snarled.

Shaken, I closed the door, and put the book aside to read later. I returned to the bureau with my coffee and continued to throw out old papers. One thick wedge of receipts was intriguing. From a hotel in the Isle of Man, they were made out to a Mr and Mrs Hofmannsthal, who had stayed there for the weekend almost every month from 1949 until 1975. I decided to ask Bel about them, then changed my mind. Bel had mentioned that Flo went on retreat to a convent in Wales once a month. Perhaps Flo had kept a few secrets from her old friend and I certainly wasn't about to reveal them after all this time. I threw away the receipts with a sigh. How I'd love to know what lay behind them, and especially the identity of Mr Hofmannsthal.

The contents of the bureau were considerably diminished by the time the unimportant papers had been discarded. All that remained were letters, which I had no intention of throwing away until I'd read every one. Some looked official, big fat brown envelopes, the address typed, but most were handwritten. I tugged out a wad of letters held together with an elastic band. The top one bore a foreign stamp. It had been posted in 1942.

It dawned on me that I hadn't found the rent book that had prompted my search, or a pension book. Flo might have had them in her handbag, which, like Gran, she had kept hidden. After a fruitless search through all the cupboards, I found what I was looking for under the bed, where dust was already beginning to collect.

I took the black leather bag into the living room and emptied the contents on to the coffee table. A tapestry purse fell out, very worn and bulging with coins, followed by a set of keys on a Legs of Man keyring, a wallet, shop receipts, bus tickets, cheque book, metal compact, lipstick, comb . . . I removed a silver hair from the comb and ran it between my fingers. It was the most intimate thing belonging to Flo I'd ever touched, actually part of her. The room was very still, and I almost felt as if she was in the room with me. Yet I wasn't scared. Even when I opened the compact to compare the hair with mine in the mirror, half expecting to see Flo's face instead of my own, I didn't feel frightened, more a comfortable sensation of being watched by someone who cared about me. I knew I was being silly because Flo and I had only set eyes on each other once, and then briefly.

'One day my hair will turn that colour,' I murmured, and wondered where I would be and who I would be with, should I live to be as old as Flo. For the first time in my life, I thought it would be nice to have children, so that a strange woman I hardly knew wouldn't sort through my possessions when I died.

I came back to earth, told myself to be sensible. The cheque book meant that, like Gran since she'd been robbed, Flo's pension had probably been paid straight into the bank. I flicked through the stubs to see if cheques had been made out for rent, but most appeared to be for cash, which was no help. I would have asked Charmian for the landlord's address, but glancing at my watch, I saw it was past midnight.

Good! It was a perfect excuse to sleep in Flo's comfortable bed again.

One by one, I returned the things to the bag, glancing briefly in the wallet, which held only a bus pass, a cheque guarantee card, four five-pound notes, and a card listing a series of dental appointments two years ago. I was putting the bag away in the bureau when there was a knock on the door.

James! He'd been to my flat, waited, and when I didn't arrive he had guessed where I would be. I wouldn't let him in. If I did, he'd never keep away and this was the only place where no one could reach me. It was one of the reasons why I always seemed to forget to bring my mobile phone. I fumed at the idea of him invading what I'd come to regard as my sanctuary.

'Who is it?' I shouted.

'Tom O'Mara.'

I stood, transfixed, in the middle of the room, my stomach churning. I knew I should tell him what I'd intended to tell James, to go away, but common sense seemed to have deserted me, along with any will-power I might have had. Before I knew what I was doing, I'd opened the door.

Oh, Lord! I'd thought this only happened in books – turning weak at the knees at the sight of a man. The jacket of his black suit was hanging open, and the white collarless shirt, buttoned to the neck, gave him a priestlike air. Neither of us spoke as he followed me inside, with that sensually smooth walk I'd noticed the night before, bringing with him an atmosphere charged with electricity. I patted my hair nervously, aware that my hand was shaking.

He was carrying a plastic bag that smelt of food. My mouth watered and I realised I was starving.

He held it out. 'Chinese, from the takeaway round the corner. Joe said there was someone in when he came with the book so I thought I'd see if you were still here on me way home.'

'What's this in aid of?' I gulped.

'Peace-offering,' he said abruptly. 'Flo would have slagged me off for behaving the way I did last night. No one can help the way they speak, you and me included.'

'That's charitable of you, I must say.' I'd worked hard to get rid of my accent, and felt annoyed that Tom O'Mara seemed to regard the lack of one as an affliction.

'Shall we forget about last night and start again?' He bagged my favourite spot on the settee and began to unpack the cartons of food. 'You're Millie, I'm Tom, and we're about to have some nice Chinese nosh – I don't know if you want to use these plastic forks, Flo used to fetch proper ones, and she'd warm plates up in the microwave. She didn't like eating out of boxes.'

I hurried to do as I was told, sensing that he was accustomed to giving orders, when he shouted, 'Fetch a corkscrew and some glasses while you're at it. I've got wine.'

'It's red,' he said, when I obediently brought everything in. 'I'm an ignorant bugger and I don't know if that's what you have with this sort of food.'

'Neither do I.' James always knew what sort of wine to order but I'd never taken much notice.

'I thought you'd be one of those superior sort of people who know about such things.' He shared out the food on to the plates.

'And I thought we'd made a fresh start.'

'You're right. Sorry!' His smile took my breath away. His face softened and he looked charmingly boyish. I could understand what the nineteen-year-old Flo must have seen in his grandfather.

'Did you and Flo do this often?' I asked, when he handed me my plate.

'Once a week. Mondays, usually, when I finish work early.'

'Where do you work?'

'Minerva's. It's a club.'

I'd heard of Minerva's, but had never been there. It had a terrible reputation as a hang-out for gangsters and a source of hard drugs. Scarcely a week passed when there wasn't something in the *Echo* or on local TV about the police raiding it in search of a wanted criminal or because a fight had broken out. As I sipped the rich, musky wine, I wondered what Tom O'Mara did there.

'The wine's nice,' I said.

'So it should be. It's twenty-two quid a bottle at the club.'

'Wow!' I gasped. 'All that much to have with a takeaway!'

He dismissed this with a wave of the hand. 'It didn't cost me anything, I just helped meself.'

'You mean you stole it?'

He managed to look both amused and indignant. 'I'm past the stage of nicking things, thanks all the same. Minerva's belongs to me. I can take anything I like.'

I felt a chill run through my body. He was almost certainly a criminal – he might have been in prison for all I knew. If he owned Minerva's, it meant he was involved in the drugs trade and other activities that didn't bear thinking about. But the awful thing, the really appalling thing, was that he became even more desirable in my eyes. I was horrified. I'd never dreamed it was in me to be attracted to someone like Tom O'Mara. Perhaps it was something passed down in the blood: Flo had wasted her life on a scally who, according to Bel, wasn't fit to lick her boots, Mum had fallen for my loathsome father. Now I found myself weak at the knees over possibly the most unsuitable man in the whole of Liverpool. I thought about James, who loved me and was worth ten Tom O'Maras, and for a moment wished it really had been him at the door.

I put my plate on the table and Tom said, 'You haven't eaten much.'

'I've eaten half,' I said defensively. 'I haven't a very big appetite.' He'd already finished, the plate scraped clean.

'I tell you what, let's have some music.' He went over to the record player and lifted the lid.

'Flo's only got the one record.'

'She's got a whole pile in the sideboard. Neil Diamond and Tony Bennett were her favourites. I got her this last year when she started humming it non-stop. She'd play it over and over.' The strains of 'Dancing in the Dark' began to fill the room. 'She said something once, she was half asleep, about dancing in the dark with someone in the Mystery years ago.'

'The Mystery?' I wondered if it had ever crossed his mind that the 'someone' might well have been his grandad.

'Otherwise known as Wavertree playground. There's a sports stadium there now.' He removed his jacket, saying, 'It's hot in here,' and I felt my insides quiver at the sight of his long, lean body, his slim waist.

'You were very fond of Flo?'

'I wasn't just fond of her, I loved her,' he said simply. 'I dunno why 'cos she weren't a relative, but she was more like a gran than me real one. Christ knows what I'd have done without Flo when me dad died.'

Surely he couldn't be so bad if he'd thought so much of Flo. Bing Crosby was singing and I had no idea why I should have a feeling that history was repeating itself when Tom held out his hand and said with a grin, 'Wanna dance, girl?'

I knew I should refuse. I knew I should just laugh and shrug and say, 'No, thanks, I'm not in the mood,' because I also knew what would happen when he took me in his arms. And if it did, if it did, the day might come when I would regret it. The trouble was, I had never before wanted anything so much. My body was crying out for him to touch me.

The lamp continued its steady progress, round and round, casting its dark, blurred shadows on the low ceiling of the room, and I stared at the shifting patterns, looking for the girl in the red coat. Tom O'Mara came across the room, put his hands on my waist and lifted me out of the chair. For a moment I resisted, then threw all caution to the wind. I slid my arms around his neck and kissed him. I could feel him, like a rock, pressing against me. My veins seemed to melt when our exploring tongues met, while his hard, eager hands stroked my back, my waist, my hips, burning, as if his fingers were on fire.

Still kissing, swaying together almost imperceptibly to the music, we moved slowly towards the bedroom. Outside the door, in the little cold lobby, our lips parted, and Tom cupped my face in his hands. He stared deep into my eyes, and I knew that he wanted me every bit as much as I wanted him. Then he opened the door, where the bed with its snowy white cover was waiting, and led me inside. By now, I felt weak with longing, yet once again I hesitated. There was still time to back out, to say no. But Tom O'Mara was kissing me again, touching me with those hot fingers, and I couldn't have said no to save my life. He kicked the door shut behind us.

In the living room, 'Dancing in the Dark' played through to a glorious crescendo. When it finished, I imagined, in a little corner of my mind, the needle raising itself automatically and the arm returning to nestle in the metal groove. There was silence in Flo Clancy's flat, though I knew that the lamp continued to cast its restless shadows over the walls.

I was woken by Tom O'Mara stroking my hip. 'You should have eaten the rest of that meal,' he whispered. 'You could do with a bit more flesh on you.'

Turning languorously into his arms, I began to touch him, but he caught my hand. 'I've got to go.'

'Is there nothing I can do to keep you?' I said teasingly.

'Nothing.'

He got out of bed and began to get dressed. I could have kept James in bed if the building was on fire. I lay, admiring his will-power and his slim brown limbs. His skin was as slippery as polished marble, the hollow of his neck as smooth as an egg. There was a tattoo on his chest, a heart with an arrow through it, and a woman's name I couldn't make out. I'd always thought tattoos repulsive, though it was a bit late in the day to remember that. 'What's the hurry?' I enquired.

'It's nearly seven o'clock. Me wife doesn't mind me staying out all night, but she likes me home for breakfast.'

'Mightn't it have been a good idea to mention you had a wife last night?' I said mildly. I wasn't the least bit shocked because I didn't care. We had no future together.

He paused while pulling on his trousers. 'Would it have stopped you?'

'No, but it might have stopped some women.'

'Then those sort of women should ask before leaping into bed with a bloke they hardly know.'

I made one of Bel's faces. 'You sound as if you disapprove of women who sleep with strange men.'

'It so happens that I do.'

'But you don't disapprove of men who do the same?' I laughed, pretending outrage.

'Blokes take what's on offer.' He was buttoning his shirt.

I eased myself to a sitting position. 'Do you know?' I said thoughtfully, 'I truly can't remember offering myself last night.'

'You didn't, but it's different with me and you, isn't it?'

'Is it?'

He sat on the bed. 'You know it is.' He held my face in both hands and kissed me soundly on the lips. I put my arms around his neck and kissed him back, greedy for him, and determined to keep him if I could, even if it meant I'd be late for work.

'I said I've got to go.' His voice was steely. He removed my arms none too gently and went over to the door.

'Oh, well,' I sighed exaggeratedly, 'see you around sometime, Mr O'Mara.' I was still teasing, though my heart was in my mouth, dreading he might take me at my word and say, 'See you too, Millie.'

'What the hell do you mean by that?' I was taken aback by the anger in his green eyes. The muscles were taut in his slender neck. 'Is that all it was to you, a night's shag?'

'You know it wasn't.' I blushed, remembering the night, so different from any I'd ever known. I looked at him directly. 'It was magic.'

I could have sworn he breathed a sigh of relief. 'In that case, I'll be round tonight, about twelve.' He left abruptly. A few seconds later, the front door opened and he shouted, 'It was magic for me, too.'

I got out of bed, removed the crucifix, the statues, and holy pictures off the wall, and put them in the drawer of Flo's bedside cabinet.

'You've been raiding your aunt's wardrobe again,' George said, when I arrived at Stock Masterton. 'I can tell.'

'Is it so obvious?' I stared down at the long, straight black skirt and demure white blouse with a pointed collar.

'Only because you don't usually wear those sort of clothes. You look very appealing. I could eat you for lunch.'

I tried to think of a put-down remark in reply, but couldn't.

George went on, 'That young man of yours must have had the same idea. You've got a love bite on your neck.' He sighed dolefully. 'It's called a hicky in America. I can't remember when I last gave a girl one. I must have been in my teens. Those were the days, eh?' He hooted.

Embarrassed, I went over to my desk and switched on the computer. Diana had just arrived. 'How's your father?' I asked.

'He seemed much better over the weekend,' Diana replied. Her face had lost the tense lines of the previous week. 'In fact, we had a lovely time. He told me all about his experiences during the war. I knew he'd been in Egypt in military intelligence, but I never realised he'd been in so many dangerous scrapes. He was very much a James Bond in his day.' She took an envelope from her bag. 'I managed to finish those notes I mentioned. Did George tell you his offer for the shop in Woolton has been accepted? We could be open by the new year.'

My own report was at home but didn't seem all that important any more. Nevertheless, I had to go back to the flat to collect a few things if I was going to stay at Flo's so I'd pick it up then.

'I'll give this to George.' Diana winked conspiratorially and hurried into his office. She seemed rather pathetic, I thought, yet until recently I'd wanted the job in Woolton just as much, which meant I'd been just as pathetic myself. Now, I didn't care.

The realisation surprised me. I stared at my blurred reflection in the computer screen and wondered what had changed. Me, I decided, though I had no idea why. I felt confused but, then, I'd felt confused throughout my life. Perhaps it was Flo who'd made me see things differently. Perhaps. I wish I'd known her, I thought wistfully, remembering the warm, comfortable sensation I'd had in the flat last night, as if she had been there with me. I had a feeling I could have talked to her about stuff I wouldn't dream of telling anyone else.

And there was Tom O'Mara. I cupped my chin in my hands and my reflection did the same. I'd been a married woman for four years, and there'd been other men before James, yet it was as if I'd made love for the very first time. My body had never felt so alive, so *used* in the most gratifying way. I held my breath and felt my scalp prickle when I thought about the things that Tom O'Mara and I had done to each other.

'Millie! *Millie!*'

Darren thumped my desk, and I became aware that June was shouting, 'Wake up, sleepyhead. There's a call for you.'

It was the Naughtons again. They'd had details of another house, which sounded ideal, this time in Crosby. I arranged to meet them there at noon, though felt sure it would be another waste of time. Crosby was close to Blundellsands, which meant I could call at home afterwards.

It felt strange going into my flat, as if I'd been away for weeks not merely twenty-four hours. It smelt dusty and unused, long empty. I opened the windows of the balcony to air the place, and had a shower. There was a bruise beneath my breast and another on my thigh and I wondered if Tom O'Mara also bore scars of our night together. I covered the bite on my neck with makeup. The red light was flickering on the answering-machine.

My mother's tearful voice announced that Declan had lost his job. 'He was sacked ages ago. Your dad only found out by accident off some chap in the pub. Of course he's livid, called poor Declan all the names under the sun. And, Millicent, I'd like to talk to you about Alison . . . Oh, I'll have to ring off now, luv. Your dad's on his way in.'

I waited. There was no message from James. I was glad, but thought about calling him at work to make sure he was all right. In the end, I decided not to. It might encourage him to think I cared, which I did but not nearly enough to satisfy him. I reversed the tape, packed a few clothes and toiletries in a bag, along with the folder containing the report. As I'd gone to the trouble of writing it, it wouldn't hurt to let George take a look.

He was working alone in his glass cubicle when I got back, so I took the folder in. 'You'll never guess what that bloody woman's gone and done,' he barked immediately he saw me.

I pretended to back away, frightened. 'What woman?' I couldn't recall seeing George so angry before.

'That Diana bitch. She's only given me a list of reasons why I should open the new office! I couldn't believe my eyes when I read it. Does she seriously imagine I haven't thought the whole thing through myself? Jesus Christ, Millie, I've been in the estate-agency business for over thirty years. I know it back to front, yet an idiot woman with a stupid degree thinks she knows better than I do.'

'She was only being helpful, George.'

'More likely after the boss's job,' he sneered. 'As if I'd give it her, the pushy little cow. The job's Oliver's. He never makes a decision without referring to me first, which is the way I like it.' He grinned. 'I guess I must be a control freak.'

'Did you say anything to Diana?'

'I bawled her out and she left for lunch in tears.'

'Oh, George!' I shook my head. 'You'll feel sorry about that tomorrow.' A few weeks ago I would have been as pleased as punch at Diana's fall from grace, but now, for some strange reason, I felt nothing but pity for the woman.

'I know.' He sighed. 'I'm a disagreeable sod. I'll apologise later, though it was still a stupid, tactless thing for her to do.' He nodded at the folder in my hand. 'Is that for me?'

'No. I just came to tell you about the Naughtons. Apparently, the draining board was on the wrong side.'

Later that afternoon, I fed my report into the shredder. I'd never stood the remotest chance of getting the manager's job, and it made me feel acutely embarrassed to have thought that I had.

Tom O'Mara didn't arrive at midnight as he'd promised. An hour later he still wasn't there. I lay on the settee, half watching an old film, not sure what to think. Had I been stood up? Maybe he'd had second thoughts. Maybe he'd meant tomorrow night. I tried to work out how I'd feel if I never saw him again. Hurt, I decided, hurt, insulted and angry, but definitely not heartbroken, possibly a little bit relieved. However, right now relief wasn't uppermost in my mind. I wasn't in love with Tom and never would be, yet my body ached for him and I could have sworn he felt the same. It was easy to while away the time imagining his lips touching every part of me. My pulse began to race, and I felt hot at the thought. 'Please come, Tom,' I prayed. 'Please!'

At some time during the night I fell asleep, and was woken when it was barely daylight by a kiss and the touch of a hand stroking me beneath my dressing-gown.

'How did you get in?' I whispered.

'Took me key back off the mantelpiece, didn't I?'

'You're late,' I yawned. 'Hours late.' It was delicious just lying there, feeling sleepy, yet conscious of his exploring hands.

'There was trouble at the club, and I couldn't ring. Flo always flatly refused to have a phone. How do I undo this knot?'

'I'll do it.' I unfastened the belt and he pulled the robe away.

'Anyroad, I'm here now,' he said, 'and that's all that matters.'

He was kneeling beside me, his face hard with desire. He would never say soft, tender things as James did, yet this only made me want him more. I held out my arms. 'Yes, Tom, that's all that matters.'

2

Time seemed to stand still; it had lost its meaning, all because of Tom O'Mara. I returned to my flat on Sunday morning to collect more clothes and take a shower – bathing at Flo's was like bathing in the Arctic – and found an increasingly frantic series of messages from my mother on the answering-machine. It was the last Sunday in October and it had completely slipped my mind.

'Don't forget, luv, we're expecting you for dinner on Sunday.'

'Why don't you ever ring back, Millicent? I hate these damn machines. It's like talking to the wall.'

'Have you gone away, Millicent?' the voice wailed fretfully. 'You might have told me. I'd ring your office if I didn't think it would get you into trouble.'

As usual, I felt a mixture of guilt and annoyance. I phoned home immediately. 'I'm sorry, Mum,' I said penitently. 'You were right, I've been away.' I hated lying to my mother, but how could I possibly tell her the truth? 'I know I should have called, but it was a spur-of-the-moment thing, and I was so busy when I got there, I forgot about everything. I'm sorry,' I said again, assuming this would be enough to satisfy her, but apparently not.

'When you got where?' she demanded.

I said the first place I could think of. 'Birmingham.'

'What on earth were you doing there?'

'George sent me.'

'Really!' Mum sounded so impressed that I hated myself even more. 'He must think highly of you, sending you all the way to Birmingham.'

To please her, I took particular pains with my appearance. I wore a cherry red suit with a black T-shirt underneath. To assuage my guilt, and make amends for lying, I stopped on the way to Kirkby and bought a bunch of chrysanthemums and a box of Terry's All Gold.

'You shouldn't have, luv,' Mum protested, though she looked gratifyingly pleased.

When we sat down to lunch, Flo's flat immediately became the main topic of conversation.

'I thought you'd have it well sorted by now,' Mum remarked, when I claimed there were still loads of things to do.

'I only have Sundays free, don't I?' I said defensively. 'You wouldn't believe the amount of stuff Flo had. It's taking ages.'

'Your gran keeps asking about it. I said you'd call in and see her on your way home.'

I groaned. 'Oh, Mum, you didn't!'

'She is your gran, luv. She's desperate for a little keepsake, something to remind her of Flo. A piece of jewellery would be nice.'

Flo mightn't be too pleased at the idea of anything of hers going to someone she'd specifically not wanted at her funeral. As for jewellery, I hadn't come across any so far. Everything's becoming incredibly complicated, I thought worriedly.

Things became even more complicated when Declan asked, 'How's James?'

'He's fine,' I said automatically, only then realising it was a whole week since I'd seen him, and he hadn't called once. Perhaps he'd decided being chucked out was the last straw. I dismissed him from my mind – there was already enough to think about – and said to Declan, 'Have you done anything about college?'

My father choked on his steak and kidney pudding. 'College? Him? You must be joking.'

'I think it's a very good idea,' Colin said quietly. 'If he took an engineering course, he could come and work for me. I could do with another pair of hands.'

'He'd prefer something different, wouldn't you, Declan?' I was determined to air the matter of Declan's future because I had a feeling he would never have the courage to do it himself. 'Something artistic.' I thought it wise not to mention fashion design or my father might choke to death before our very eyes.

My mother regarded him warily. 'It wouldn't hurt, would it, Norman, for our Declan to go to college? After all, Millicent went to night school and look where it got her.'

While Trudy and Colin did the dishes, I wandered down to the bottom of the garden with Scotty. The little dog jumped up and down like a yo-yo in front of me. I eased myself through the gap in the hedge that separated the main garden from the compost heap, and sat down on an enormous hump of hard soil, cuddling Scotty. This was the only place we had been allowed to play when we were little: our father wouldn't allow us on the lawn. I remembered the day when five-year-old Trudy had broken a window in the greenhouse with a tennis ball. She'd been so petrified she was literally shaking with fright and couldn't stop crying. 'He'll kill me when he gets home,' she sobbed hysterically.

Then I'd had the brilliant idea of pretending someone from the houses behind had done it. We exchanged the ball, which our father would have recognised, for a stone, and claimed ignorance when the broken pane was discovered. It was one of the few crimes we ever got away with.

'Penny for them!' Trudy murmured, as she squeezed through the hedge and sat beside me. Scotty, fast asleep, stirred and licked my knee.

'I won't say what I was thinking about. It would only depress you.'

'It was me smashing that window, I bet. I always remember when I come down here. Even now I break out in a sweat.'

I put an arm around her shoulder. 'How's things, Sis?'

Trudy shrugged. 'Okay. I'm growing a hair on me chin. See?'

'You've always had that,' I said. 'It appeared when you were about fourteen.'

'Did it? I've never noticed before. It must be the glasses.'

'What glasses?'

'I need glasses for close work, reading and painting. I've had them for months. I thought you knew.'

'No,' I said sadly. 'There was a time when we knew every single little thing about each other, but now . . .' In the darkness of our room, when our father was out, we'd whisper our innermost secrets to each other.

'Sorry, Sis.'

'Don't be.' I squeezed Trudy's shoulder. 'I'm not complaining. There's all sorts of stuff you don't know about me.'

'Such as?'

'That would be telling.' I grinned enigmatically.

Trudy pulled a face. 'Actually, there's things I can't even talk about with Colin.'

'Would you like to talk about them now?'

'No, Sis. It would take much too long.'

I watched a bee, well past its prime, buzz weakly on a dandelion. I was conscious of feeling far less fraught than I usually did on these occasions. Today hadn't been nearly as bad as other Sundays. Instead of constant reminders of the way things used to be, I was preoccupied with how things were now.

Mum appeared in the gap in the hedge, looking flustered, though she rarely looked anything else. 'You'll get your lovely clothes all dirty sitting on that soil.' She pushed her bulky frame through the sharp twigs and, ignoring her own advice, plopped down heavily beside us. Immediately Scotty jumped off my knee and on to hers. 'I wanted to talk to you both about Alison.' She began to pull at a weed. 'I found Oxford on the atlas,' she said hesitantly. 'It's almost as far as London. I was scared enough driving to Skem so I'll never make it that far in the car – that's if your dad would let me have it – and I couldn't afford to go every week by train.'

'I'll pay your fare, Mum,' I offered at the same time as Trudy said, 'Colin and me will take you.'

'No.' She shook her head. 'I don't want to be dependent on other people. Alison's me daughter. I don't love her any better than I do you and our Declan, but she needs me more than you lot ever will.'

It seemed to me that Alison didn't need anyone in particular, but perhaps the faithful figure of her mother appearing every Sunday provided a sense of security, a vague feeling that she was special in at least one person's eyes. On the other hand, perhaps the need was the other way round, and it was Mum who'd miss Alison. One day, Declan was bound to leave home and Alison, detached and indifferent, would be the only one of her children left. But, somewhat cruelly, fate had decreed she'd be miles away in Oxford.

'I want her to stay with the St Osyth Trust,' Mum was saying. 'They know and understand her. I'd have her home like a shot, but that's out the question with your dad. He's ashamed of her, for one thing, and he's no patience with her funny little ways. So I've decided to move to Oxford.'

'What!' Trudy and I cried together. It was the last thing we'd expected to hear.

'Shush!' She glanced nervously through the hedge, but the garden was empty. Her husband was inside playing with his beloved grandchildren, and Colin was on guard.

'You mean you'd actually leave him?' I gasped. Why hadn't she thought of this years ago when we were all being beaten regularly for the least little thing, and sometimes for nothing at all?

Mum said huskily, 'I should have left him a long time ago, I know, but it never crossed me mind. I always thought that if I became a better wife he'd stop hitting us, but the harder I tried, the worse he got. In the end, perhaps I was punch-drunk or something, but it all seemed quite normal.' Her voice broke. Scotty opened his eyes and looked at her curiously. 'I could never imagine things being any other way. I'm sorry, but at least I got Alison out the road, didn't I?'

'Don't rake over the past, Mum,' Trudy said softly. 'About Oxford, I don't know what to say.'

'Nor me,' I said, and then, meaning it with all my heart, 'I'll miss you, Mum.'

She dug me in the ribs with her elbow. 'Don't talk daft, Millicent. I only see you once a month as it is, and you're never there when I phone. I talk to that silly machine more than I do you.'

'I'd miss your messages,' I cried. 'Honest, Mum, I really would.' Suddenly I felt that there would be a dreadful hole in my life.

'I could still ring and leave messages.' She chuckled.

'Yes, but it wouldn't be the same if you weren't around.'

Trudy was frowning, as if she, too, was trying to contemplate a future that had so unexpectedly changed. 'Melanie and Jake would be lost without their gran,' she said, close to tears.

'They'll still have their grandad,' Mum said comfortably. Behind her back, Trudy grimaced at the idea that she'd still bring her children to Kirkby if Mum wasn't there.

'I'll get meself a full-time job,' Mum was saying, 'and look for a bedsit close to the home so's I can see Alison every day.'

'It's a big step, Mum,' Trudy said. 'Getting a job won't be easy at your age, and bedsits might cost the earth in Oxford.'

'Then I'll go on social security or whatever it's called these days,' Mum said serenely. 'I've never claimed a penny in me life, yet I've always paid me stamps.' She beamed at us. 'I feel better now I've talked to you two. Not a word about this to your dad, mind.'

Trudy shuddered. 'I wouldn't like to be in your shoes when you tell him. Would you like me and Colin to be here, give you moral support, like?'

'I don't need moral support, luv. I'll tell him to his face, and if he doesn't like it, he can lump it. Anyroad, it's months off yet.'

'Grandma,' Melanie piped, from the other side of the hedge.

'I'm here, sweetheart.' Mum scrambled to her feet, dislodging an indignant Scotty.

'Grandad said he wants a cup of tea.'

'Tell Grandad to make his own tea,' Trudy said curtly.

'No, no, don't say that, Melanie, whatever you do.' A stubby branch caught her cheek, drawing blood, as she frantically pushed her way back through the hedge.

Trudy glanced at me meaningfully. 'I wonder if she'll do it?'

I remembered the photo of Flo taken in Blackpool, the still pretty face, the lovely smile, when Gran opened the door. Age hadn't been as kind to Martha Colquitt as it had to her sister. I could never remember her smiling much, or looking anything but old. Her face was creased into a permanent scowl, and behind the severe, black-framed spectacles with their thick lenses, her eyes were unfriendly, disapproving. Her best feature was her hair, thick and silvery, which she kept in neat waves under a fine, almost invisible net.

'Oh, it's you,' she said sourly. 'Come in. I might as well not have grand-children, I never see them.' I followed her into the spotlessly clean, over-furnished room, which stank of a mixture of cigarettes, disinfectant and the vile-smelling ointment she rubbed on her rheumatic shoulder.

'Well, I'm here now,' I said brightly. I would have come more often, or so I told myself, if the welcome was ever warm, but even my kindhearted mother found visiting Gran an ordeal, fetching her weekly shopping out of a sense of duty.

The television beside the fireplace was on without the sound. Gran turned it off. 'Nothing on nowadays but rubbish.'

I sat down in an overstuffed armchair. 'Mum said to remind you there's an old film on later that you might like. It's a musical with Beryl Grable.'

'Betty Grable,' Gran corrected irritably. Her faculties were sharper than those of most people half her age, her memory for names and faces prodigious. 'I might watch it, I'll see. It depends on how long you stay. Do you want a cup of tea?'

'Yes, please,' I said politely.

Gran disappeared into the kitchen and I went over to the window. I'd lived in this flat until I was three, and the view from the fifth floor was one of the few things I could remember clearly. It couldn't be called magnificent: a shopping precinct, the Protestant church, miles and miles of red-brick houses, with a glimpse of flat fields in the far distance, a few trees, but it seemed to change from day to day. The sky was never the same, and I always seemed to glimpse a tree or a building I hadn't noticed before. It was certainly better than no view at all, but Gran felt the need to block it out with thick lace curtains, although no one could see inside except from a passing helicopter.

The curtains had been drawn back a few inches, as if Gran had been looking out, which, apart from going to Mass on Sundays, was all she had to do: she looked out of the window, watched television and smoked – an ashtray on the sill was full of butts. Each day must seem endless.

I adjusted the curtain and returned to my seat. God, it was depressing. The room seemed much darker than Flo's basement.

'I can't remember if you take sugar.' Gran came in with tea in two fine china cups, a cigarette poking from her mouth. Because she'd been to Mass that morning she wore a neat brown woollen blouse and skirt, though Mum reported that she usually spent the day in her dressing-gown. She had no friends, no one called, so what was the point in getting dressed?

'I don't, thanks.'

'Your mam forgot to get me favourite fig biscuits. All I've got is digest-ives.' Poor Mum could never get the shopping right.

'I don't want a biscuit, thanks all the same.' I sipped the tea, doing my best to avoid the ash floating on the top.

The wall above the sideboard was full of photographs in identical cheap plastic frames: Grandad Colquitt, long dead, a genial-looking man with erratic facial hair, various weddings, including mine and Trudy's, lots of photos of the Cameron kids taken at school – the happy faces, grinning widely, telling a terrible lie.

'There's a photo in Flo's of my father as a baby with his mother – my other grandma,' I said. At home his parents were rarely mentioned. All I knew was that his father had been a sailor, and his mother had died when he was twenty.

'Is that so? Your other gran, Elsa, used to be me best friend.' The thin yellow lips trembled slightly. 'What's it like in Flo's place?'

'Nice.' I smiled. 'I found gas bills the other day going back to nineteen forty-one.' At least this showed I'd been making an effort to get things done.

'It was nineteen forty when she moved in,' Gran said. 'November.' Her voice was surprisingly soft, considering she was talking about her lifelong enemy. 'Just before Christmas. Mam didn't find out till later that Mrs Fritz had gone to Ireland, leaving her in that big house all by herself.'

The name seemed familiar. 'Fritz?'

'Mr Fritz owned the laundry where she worked. He was sent to an internment camp during the war.'

'There's a snap of Flo outside the laundry.' In a fit of generosity, I said, 'Would you like me to take you?' Flo might turn in her grave if she knew, but Gran looked so wretched.

'To the laundry!' The crumpled jaw fell open. 'They knocked it down years ago, girl.'

'I meant Flo's. I'm on my way there now to try to get a few more things done,' I said virtuously. 'I'll bring you home in the car.'

Gran shook her head adamantly. 'Toxteth's the last place on earth I'd go. A man was murdered there only last week, stabbed to death right on the pavement. Even the town centre isn't safe any more. A woman at church had her gold chain snatched from round her neck when she was walking through St John's precinct. She almost had a heart attack.' She looked at me with frightened eyes. 'It's a terrible world nowadays, Millicent.'

'Flo lived in Toxteth most of her life without coming to any harm.' I vaguely remembered my father saying the same thing a few weeks ago. 'And Bel lives not far away. She comes and goes all the time.'

'Bel?'

'Flo's friend.'

'I know who Bel is,' Gran said bitterly. 'I met her once when she was young. So, even she didn't bother to tell me when our Flo died!'

'Maybe she didn't know your address.'

'There aren't many Mrs M. Colquitts in the Liverpool phone book. And someone knew where to contact me, didn't they? But only when it was too late.'

'I'm sorry, Gran,' I said awkwardly. I put the cup and saucer down; the dregs were grey with ash. 'I'd better be going. Don't forget to watch that film.'

'I wish you hadn't come,' Gran said tonelessly. She fumbled in the packet for another cigarette. 'You've raked up things I'd considered long forgotten.'

'I'm sorry,' I said again. I'd only come because I'd been told she wanted to see me.

'I expect you can see yourself out.'

'Of course. 'Bye, Gran.'

There was no answer. I closed the door and flew down the stone staircase where the walls were scrawled with graffiti. As I drove towards Toxteth, it was difficult to rid myself of the memory of the stiff, unhappy woman smoking her endless cigarettes.

I parked in William Square, and as I walked back towards Flo's, Bel and Charmian must have seen me arrive for they were standing by the basement stairs. Charmian waved a bottle of wine, and my heart lifted.

'Hi!' I called, beginning to hurry. Gran was forgotten and I had the strangest feeling, as if I *was* Flo, coming home to my friends.

It would seem that the banging wasn't part of a dream. Beside me Tom O'Mara was dead to the world. I almost fell out of bed, pulled on Flo's dressing-gown and hurried towards the door before whoever was there demolished it. The noise was even louder in the living room. Any minute now Charmian or Herbie might appear, wanting to know what was going on.

'Who's there?' I shouted crossly. It must be a drunk who'd come to the wrong house. I looked blearily at my watch – ten past two – and wondered if I should have woken Tom.

The banging stopped. 'It's James. Let me in.'

James! I was wide awake in an instant, and leaned against the door. 'Go away, James, please.'

'I've no intention of going away.' He began to hammer on the door again. 'Let me in!'

'I don't want to see you,' I yelled, but he almost certainly couldn't hear me above the noise he was making. A police siren sounded in the distance, and just in case it had been alerted by a neighbour to investigate the disturbance in William Square, I opened the door.

'You're not . . .' I began, as a wild-eyed James, smelling strongly of alcohol, brushed past me into the room, '. . . coming in.' Too late. I switched on the main light. Flo's room looked so different with every corner brightly illuminated.

James stood in the middle of the room. I'd never thought him capable of such anger. I shrank before it, terrified, my heart racing. His face, his neck, his fists were swollen, as if at any minute he would explode. 'What the hell do you think you're playing at?' he demanded furiously.

'I don't know what you mean.' I kept my voice mild, stifling my own anger, not wanting to provoke him further.

He glared at me, as if I was the stupidest woman on earth. 'I've been outside your flat since five o'clock waiting for you,' he raged. 'When it got to midnight, I decided to come here, but I couldn't remember where the fucking place was. I drove round and round for ages before I found it.'

I didn't know what to say, so remained silent. Once again I thought about rousing Tom, but it seemed weak. I was determined to handle the situation on my own: with Tom there, things might turn ugly. James began to pace the floor, waving his arms, his face scarlet. 'Last week, after you threw me out, I thought, I'll give her till Sunday, then that's it. If she doesn't phone, it's over.' He thrust his red face into mine. 'You didn't phone, did you? You didn't give a fuck how I was.' He mimicked my voice, which seemed to be becoming a habit with all the men I knew. '"I'm taking a shower and I expect you to be gone when I come out." And I went, like the good little boy I am. Then I waited for you to get in touch, but apparently you were willing to let me just walk out of your life as if I'd never existed.'

'James.' I put my hands on his arms to try to calm him. The police car screamed along the main road, William Square obviously not its destination. 'You're not making sense. You said it would be over if I didn't phone. Perhaps that would be the best thing.'

'But I love you! Can't you get into your stupid head how much I love you?' His eyes narrowed. 'You know, all my life I've had girls throw themselves at me. I've never gone short, as they say. But you, an uppity little bitch from Kirkby, you're the one I fell in love with, wanted to marry. How *dare* you turn me down?'

This wasn't happening! I closed my eyes for a second, then said quietly, 'I don't love you, James.'

At this, his hands and arms began to twitch, his blue eyes glazed. He raised his huge fist, ready to strike.

I felt myself grow dizzy. I was a little girl again, wishing I were invisible, waiting, head bowed, for a blow to fall. It was no use trying to escape, because wherever I went, wherever I hid, my father would find me and then the punishment would be even worse. I wanted to weep because this was the story of my life.

The blow I was expecting never came. The dizziness faded, reality returned. That part of my life was over. I took a step back. James was still standing, arm raised. 'Christ! What's the matter with me?' he gasped, in a horrified voice.

'What the hell's going on in here?' Tom O'Mara came out of the bedroom fastening his trousers and bare to the waist.

James's face turned ashen, his shoulders slumped. 'How could you, Millie?' he whispered.

Tom wasn't quite as tall as James, or so broad, but before I knew what was happening, he had James's right arm bent behind him with one hand, the other on his collar, and was propelling him roughly towards the door. Despite the way James had just behaved, I was shocked at the sheer brutality of it. 'There's no need for that,' I cried.

The door slammed. After a while, I could hear James stumbling up the concrete steps. I switched on the lamp, turned off the central light, and sat in the middle of Flo's settee, trembling and hugging myself tightly with both arms.

'What was that all about?' asked Tom from behind.

'Can't you guess?'

'Hadn't you told him about me?'

'It was nothing to do with you until you appeared,' I sighed.

A few seconds later, Tom sat on the settee beside me and put a glass of sherry on the coffee table. 'Drink that!' he commanded. 'It'll do you good. Flo took sherry for her nerves.'

I was actually able to smile. 'I get the impression Flo took sherry for an awful lot of things.'

He put his arm around me companionably. It was the first time he'd touched me when I didn't automatically melt. 'So, what's the story with the bloke I just chucked out? Is he the one you were with at the party?'

'Yes, and there isn't a story. He loves me and I don't love him, that's all. He'll feel worse now he's seen you.' I swallowed half the sherry in one go. Thank goodness Tom had been there. Even if James had calmed down he would have been difficult to get rid of. I thought about him driving home, drunk as a lord. The whole thing was my fault. I should have made it plain the minute he said he loved me that I didn't love him. But I did! The trouble with James is that he's spoilt, too used to having girls throw themselves at him to grasp that this one wasn't blinded by his fatal attraction. I sipped more sherry, conscious of Tom's arm, heavy on my shoulders. I would have let him hit me! I just stood there. I'd never have dreamed James had such an ugly side. He was always so gentle. I watched the lamp, waiting for the girl in the red coat, hating James for bringing ugliness into the place I loved, where I'd always felt supremely safe. I'll never see him again, I vowed.

'Better?' Tom enquired. 'You've stopped trembling.'

'Much better.' I snuggled my head against his shoulder. 'Were you happy as a child?'

'That's a funny thing to ask.' He thought for a while. 'I suppose I was. Knowing Flo helped a lot.'

'What was your dad like?'

'Me dad? Oh, he was a soft ould thing. Everyone pissed him about something rotten – Gran, me mam and me, I suppose, as well as the firm he worked for.' His voice became hard. 'That's why I swore I'd be me own boss when I grew up.'

'Where's your mother?'

He shrugged carelessly. 'No idea. She did a runner when I was five. Went off with another bloke.'

I patted his knee. 'I'm sorry.'

'Don't be,' he said carelessly. 'It were good riddance as far as I was concerned.' He kissed my ear. 'What about you?'

'What about me?'

'Were you happy – how did you put it? – as a child?'

'Sometimes I wish I could be reborn and start all over.'

'Well, you can't. You're here and that's it, you can't change anything.'

'Are these your wife's initials?' I traced the heart on his chest with my finger.

'No. Clare's always trying to persuade me to get rid of it. You can get it done with a laser.'

'Have you any children?'

'Two girls, Emma and Susanna.' He raised his eyebrows, and I sensed he was annoyed. 'What's this? The third degree?'

'I wanted to know a few things about you, that's all.'

'What's the point?' he said coldly.

Just as coldly, I replied, 'I thought it would be nice to know a little about the man I've been sleeping with for the past week.' I looked at him. 'Is there nothing you'd like to know about me?'

'You're a great fuck, that's all I care.'

I stiffened and pulled away. 'Do you have to be so coarse?'

He dragged me back against him. 'The less we know about each other the better, don't you understand that?' he whispered urgently. 'I may be coarse, but I'm not thick. I've always taken me wedding vows seriously. I love me kids, and I don't want to spoil things between me and Clare.' He twisted me around, so that I was lying on his knee, and undid the belt on my dressing-gown. 'Let's keep things the way they are. Getting to know each other could be dangerous.'

His hands were setting my body on fire. I told myself that I had no intention of falling in love with someone like him. But he aroused feelings in me that no other man had. His lips came down on mine, and we rolled on to the floor. The pleasure we gave each other was sublime, and in the midst of everything, when I was almost out of my head with delight too exquisite to describe, I could have sworn I shouted, 'I love you.'

Or perhaps it was Tom.

At some time in the early hours of the morning, he carried me into the bedroom. I pretended to be asleep when he tucked the bedclothes around me, and remained like that while he got dressed. It wasn't until the front door clicked behind him that I sat up. 'Did you ever get yourself into a mess like this, Flo?' I asked. 'If your bureau is anything to go by, you led a very neat, ordered life.'

It was ages before I had to leave for work but I got up, ran a few inches of water in the bath and splashed myself awake. I made coffee in the microwave and carried it into the living room, where I tried, unsuccessfully, to empty my mind. But as soon as I got rid of Tom O'Mara, James would take his place, followed by Mum, Alison, Declan, Trudy – what were the things my sister couldn't talk about to Colin?

I was back to Tom again when I noticed that the rising sun was shining through the rear window and the walls of the little yard were glowing a rosy pink. I'd never been up this early before, and it looked so pretty.

So far, I hadn't ventured into the yard. I went outside, wondering if Flo had sat here in the summer with her first cup of tea of the day, as I did on my balcony. A black cat regarded me benignly from the wall and graciously allowed me to stroke its back. The wooden bench was full of mould and needed scrubbing, and the pansies in the plant-holders were dead now. I nearly jumped out of my skin when a head covered with untidy black curls appeared over the neighbouring wall.

'Hi,' Peter Maxwell grinned. 'Remember me? We met the other week at Charmian's party.'

'Of course! You said you lived next door. What are you doing up so early?' I could only see him from the shoulders up and he appeared to be wearing a sleeveless T-shirt.

He flexed a bulging muscle in his arm. 'I work out every morning. I'm off for a jog in a minute.' He winked. 'You can come with me, if you like.'

'You must be joking!'

He rested his arms on the wall and said conversationally, 'Are you all right?'

'Don't I look all right?'

'You look great, even without my glasses. It's just that I heard a commotion in your place last night. I contemplated coming round, but the sounds died down.'

'It was a drunk,' I said dismissively. 'I soon got rid of him.'

'By the way, I'd like to apologise for Sharon.'

'Who's Sharon?'

'Me girlfriend – ex-girlfriend. I tore her off a strip for dragging me away when I was dancing with you at the party. She was very rude.'

'I hardly noticed.'

He looked dismayed. 'And I was quite enjoying our little chat. I thought you were, too.'

'Well, yes, I was,' I conceded.

'It means I've got a spare ticket for the school concert in December. I wondered if you'd come.'

I pulled a face. 'I hate schools.'

'So did I, but they're different when you're an adult. No one will test your spelling or demand the date of the battle of Waterloo. Come on,' he coaxed, 'it's Charles Dickens's *A Christmas Carol*. I'd love you to be there.'

'Why?'

'Because you used to know me as Weedy and I want you to see me as Peter Maxwell, MA, economics teacher, and scriptwriter of genius – I wrote the script for *A Christmas Carol* and set it in the present day. Tell you what,' he said eagerly, 'if you come to the concert, I'll let you show me round a property and we can negotiate. Then we'll have both proved to each other that we've made it.'

I smiled. 'How could I possibly refuse?'

Still smiling, I went indoors. Peter Maxwell had cheered me up. We'd both been through the mill and emerged unscathed. I paused in the act of pulling down the front of Flo's bureau, which hadn't been touched since the night Tom had arrived with a Chinese takeaway.

Unscathed? Was that true? Until that moment, I'd never thought I'd ever get over the tragedy of my childhood. I'd thought that, along with Trudy and Declan, I'd been irreparably damaged. But maybe time was fading the shadow of my father, and perhaps one day it would go away altogether. One day, the three of us would emerge, truly unscathed.

I decided not to think about it any more on such a lovely morning. I fetched a chair up to the bureau and took out the bundle of letters held together with the elastic band. It was rotten, and snapped when I pulled it off.

William Square began to wake up to the new day: cars drove away, others came to take their place; feet hurried past the basement window; children shrieked on their way to school – a football came over the railings and landed with a loud clang on the dustbin. But I was only vaguely aware of these activities. I was too engrossed in Flo's letters. It wasn't until I returned the last letter to its envelope that I remembered where I was. The letter was one of several from the same person, a Gerard Davies from Swansea, in which he implored Flo yet again to marry him. 'I love you, Flo. I always will. There'll never be another girl like you.'

Which was more or less what every other letter had said. They were love letters from a score of different men, all to Flo, and from the tone of quite a few, the relationships hadn't been platonic.

And Bel had claimed that Flo had led the life of a saint!

I remembered the mysterious receipts from the hotel in the Isle of Man. 'Oh, I bet you were a divil in your day, Flo Clancy,' I whispered.

Flo

1

1941

'Oh, Flo, you'll never guess!' Sally threw herself on to the sofa. 'Our Martha's captured Albert Colquitt at long last. They're getting married on St Patrick's Day.'

'Only two weeks off!' Flo sank beside her sister and they collapsed into giggles. 'How on earth did she manage that?'

Sally dropped her voice, though the entire house, all five floors of it, was empty and no one could have overheard. 'I think she seduced him,' she whispered dramatically.

'She what!' screamed Flo, giggling even more. 'You're joking.'

'I'm not, Flo, honest,' Sally assured her, round-eyed. 'One night after we'd gone to bed our Martha got up again. I didn't say anything, and she must have thought I was asleep. I thought she was going to the lavvy, but she sat at the dressing-table and started combing her hair. The moon was shining through the winder, so I could see her as clearly as I can see you now.' Sally frowned thoughtfully. 'I wondered why she hadn't put her curlers in or smothered herself with cold cream. Not only that, she was wearing that pink nightdress – you know, the one Elsa Cameron bought her for her twenty-first. Are you with me so far, Flo?'

'Yes, yes, I'm with you.' Flo wanted to throttle her sister for stretching the tale out so long. 'What happened then?'

'She just disappeared.'

'What d'you mean she just disappeared? You mean she vanished before your very eyes?'

'Of course not, soft girl. She left the room and was gone for ages. I was asleep by the time she got back.'

'Is that all?' Flo said, disappointed. 'I don't know how you worked out she seduced Albert. She might have dozed off on the lavvy. I've nearly done it meself in the middle of the night.'

'Why didn't she put her curlers in, then? Why didn't she use her cream? And she was keeping that nightdress for her bottom drawer. Not only that,' Sally finished triumphantly, 'she wasn't wearing her glasses.'

That seemed to provide final proof of Sally's claim. It was no longer a laughing matter. 'If that's how she caught him, then she's been dead devious,' Flo said soberly. 'Not many men could resist if a girl got into bed with them. She's shamed him into getting married.'

Sally nodded knowingly, with the air of a woman of the world, well aware of men's lack of will-power when it came to sex. 'They're very weak,' she agreed. 'Anyroad, Martha and Albert are going to live at home till the war's over. Mam said she's expecting you at the wedding.'

'In that case, Mam's got another think coming.' Even if she wasn't dead set against her sister, she'd feel peculiar, knowing that Albert had asked her first and that Martha was his second choice – that's if he'd had a choice. She would, though, write him a little note. In the time she had remained in Burnett Street after his kind proposal, she'd always made sure they'd never been alone. He didn't know the truth of what had happened to her baby but it would have been a sore reminder that she shouldn't have turned him down. Last week, her son had had his first birthday. She'd sent a card, writing simply, 'To Hugh, from Flo'. But the card had come back by return of post.

Sally sighed. 'She must have been desperate. Poor Martha.'

'Poor Albert,' Flo said cynically.

The young sailor stood before her, agonisingly shy, his face red with embarrassment. She had noticed him watching her all night. 'Would you like to dance, miss?'

'Of course.' Flo lifted her arms and he clasped her awkwardly. It was the first time he'd ventured on to the floor.

'I'm not very good at this,' he stammered, when he stood on her toe.

'Then you must learn,' she chided him. 'All servicemen should learn to dance. This is a waltz, the easiest dance of all. You'll find yourself in all sorts of different towns and cities and it's the best way to meet girls.'

He swallowed, and said daringly, 'I won't meet many girls like you. I hope you don't mind me saying, but you're the prettiest one here.'

'Why on earth should I mind you saying a lovely thing like that? What's your name, luv?'

'Gerard Davies. I come from Swansea.'

'Pleased to meet you, Gerard. I'm Flo Clancy.'

'Pleased to meet you, Flo.'

It always started more or less the same. She only picked the shy ones, who were usually, though not always, very young. Gerard looked eighteen or nineteen, which meant he'd not long left home and would be missing his family.

When the waltz was over, she fanned herself with her hand and said, 'Phew! It's hot in here,' knowing that almost certainly he would offer to buy her a drink. He took the opportunity eagerly, and she chose the cheapest, a lemonade. They sat in a corner of the ballroom, and she asked him about his mum and dad, and what he'd done for a living before he was called up.

His dad ran a smallholding, he told her, and his mum worked in the shop where their vegetables were sold. He had two sisters, both older than him, and everyone had been very proud when he'd passed the scholarship and gone to grammar school. Less than three months ago, he'd gone straight from school into the Navy, and he had no idea what he wanted to do when the war was over. Flo noticed that he had the merest trace of a moustache on his upper lip, and his hands were soft and white. It was easy to believe that until recently he'd been just a schoolboy. His brown eyes were wide and guileless. He knew nothing about anything much, yet he was about to fight for his country in the worst war the world had ever known. Flo felt her heart contract at the thought.

The drink finished, they returned to the dance floor. Flo could tell that he was gaining confidence because he had a girl on his arm, and it grew as the night progressed.

At half past eleven, she said she had to be getting home. 'I have to be up for work at the crack of dawn.'

'In the laundry?'

'That's right, luv.' She'd told him quite a lot about herself. She gave a little shudder. 'I don't live far away, but I'm terrified of walking home in the blackout.'

'I'll take you home,' he said, with alacrity, which Flo had known he would. She wasn't a bit scared of the blackout.

Outside, she linked his arm in case they lost each other in the dark. 'Have you got long in Liverpool?'

'No, we're sailing tomorrow, I don't know where to. It's a secret.' She felt his thin, boyish arm tighten on her own, and reckoned he was frightened. Who wouldn't be, knowing about all the ships that had been sunk and the lives that had been lost, mainly of young men like him?

When they got to her flat she made him a cup of tea and something to eat – he appeared to be starving the way he downed the two thick cheese sarnies.

'I'd better be getting back to the ship.' He looked at her shyly. 'It's been a lovely evening, Flo. I've really enjoyed myself.'

'So've I, luv.'

By the door, he flushed scarlet and stammered, 'Can I kiss you, Flo?'

She didn't answer, just closed her eyes and willingly offered her lips. His mouth touched hers, softly, and his arms encircled her waist. She slid her own arms around his neck, and murmured, 'Oh, Gerard!' and he kissed her again, more firmly this time. She didn't demur when his hands fumbled awkwardly and hesitantly with her breasts. She had thought this might happen. It nearly always did.

It was another half-hour before Gerard Davies left Flo in her bed. 'Can I write to you?' he pleaded, as he got back into his uniform. 'It'd be nice to have a girl back home.'

'I'd like that very much, Gerard.'

'And can I see you if I'm in Liverpool again?'

'Of course, luv. But don't turn up unannounced, whatever you do.' She worried that more than one of her young lovers might turn up at the same time. 'Me landlady upstairs wouldn't like it a bit. I'll give you the phone number of the laundry so you can let me know beforehand, like.'

'Thanks, Flo.' Then he said, in an awestruck voice, 'This has been the most wonderful night of my life.'

Gerard Davies was the seventh young man she'd slept with. Flo told herself earnestly that it was her contribution towards the war. Tommy O'Mara had taught her that making love was the most glorious experience on earth, and she wanted to share this experience with a few bashful young men who were about to fight for their country. It made her heart swell to think that they would go into battle, perhaps even die, carrying with them the memory of the wonderful time they'd had with Flo, the pretty young woman from Liverpool, who'd made them feel so special.

It was important that she didn't get pregnant. She'd asked Sally, casual, like, what she and Jock used.

'It's something called a French letter, Flo. They're issued by the Navy. I think you can get them in the chemist's, but I'm not sure.' Sally grinned. 'Why on earth d'you want to know?'

'No reason, I just wondered.'

There was no way Flo would even consider entering a chemist's to ask for French letters, so she inserted a sponge soaked in vinegar which she'd once heard the women in the laundry say was the safest way. But Flo had the strongest feeling she would never have another baby. It was as if the productive part of her had withered away to nothing when her little boy was taken away.

Just after Martha's wedding, Bel wrote to say she was expecting. 'I'll be leaving the ATS, naturally. Bob's being posted to North Africa, so I'll be back in Liverpool soon, looking for somewhere to live. Perhaps I can help out in the laundry if there's a sitting-down job I could do.'

Flo wrote back immediately to say she'd love to have Bel stay until she found a place of her own and that, if necessary, she'd invent a sitting-down job in the laundry. She bought two ounces of white baby wool to knit a matinée jacket, but in April another letter arrived: Bel had had a miscarriage. 'You can't imagine what it's like to lose a baby, Flo. I'm staying in the ATS, though I was looking forward to living in William Square and working in this famous laundry.'

The knitting was put away, unfinished. She seemed to waste a lot of time making baby clothes that would never be worn, Flo thought sadly. She wrote to Bel. 'I wouldn't know, of course, but I can imagine how heartbreaking it must be to lose a baby.'

Flo was proud of the way she'd run the laundry since Stella Fritz had returned to Ireland four months ago. As well as the Holbrook twins, she now employed two young mothers, friends, who worked half a day each. Lottie would turn up at midday with several lusty toddlers in a big black pram, and Moira would take them home. There was also Peggy Lewis, a widow, only four and a half feet tall, who worked like a navvy. Peggy had to leave early to prepare a massive meal for her three lads who worked on the docks and arrived home famished and ready to eat the furniture if there was no food ready.

When the delivery-boy, Jimmy Cromer, a cheeky little bugger but reliable, gave in his notice, having been offered a job with a builder at five bob a week more, Flo immediately increased his wages by ten. Jimmy was thrilled. 'If I stay, can I paint "White's Laundry" on me sidecart?'

'Of course, luv. As long as you do it neat and spell it proper.'

Every Friday, Flo sat in the office working out the week's finances, putting the wages to one side, and taking the surplus to the bank. There were usually several cheques in settlement of their big customers' bills. She paid everything into the Fritzes' account, then made out a statement showing exactly what money had come in and what had gone out, to send to Stella Fritz in County Kerry. At the bottom, she usually added a little message: the laundry was doing fine, there were no problems with the house, the window-cleaner still came once a month and she assumed this was all right. She kept all her own personal bills, stamped 'paid' by the gas and electricity companies, just in case there was ever any argument.

Not once did Stella acknowledge the hard work Flo was putting in to keep the business going and looking after the house. I suppose she's too busy breathing in the good clean air and looking out the winder, Flo thought. In the absence of any authority to tell her otherwise, she promoted herself – she'd remembered a white overall in the office cupboard with Manageress embroidered in red on the breast pocket. It had been there for as long as she could remember, together with a few other odds and ends that customers had forgotten to collect.

'You look dead smart, luv,' Mam exclaimed. She often called in on her way to or from work. 'Manageress at twenty! Who'd have thought it, eh?' Flo did her utmost not to preen. 'Which reminds me,' Mam continued, 'we were talking about you the other night. It's only a fortnight off your twenty-first, May the eighth. Martha and Sal both had a party. We can't let yours go without a little celebration, drink your health an' all. What do you say, Flo?'

'Where would the party be?'

'At home, luv, where else?'

Flo shook her head stubbornly. 'I'm not coming home, Mam, not while our Martha's there.'

'Oh, luv!' Mam's face was a mixture of grief and vexation. 'How long are you going to keep up this feud with Martha? After all, the girl's expecting. I can't wait to have me first grandchild,' she added tactlessly, as if Hugh O'Mara had never existed.

'Sal told me about the baby, Mam, and it's not a feud with Martha. I'm not sure what it is.'

'You'll have to speak to her sometime.'

'No, I won't.' Flo thought about Hugh. Then she thought about Nancy O'Mara, and that no one would take Martha's baby away and give it to a Welsh witch. 'I don't have to speak to our Martha again as long as I live,' she said abruptly.

Mam gave up. 'What about your twenty-first then?'

'You and Sal can come to William Square. I'll ask the women from the laundry, get a bottle of sherry and make sarnies. You can drink me health there.'

Sally reported that Albert seemed relatively content now that he was a member of the family he'd grown so fond of. 'He's started calling Mam "Mother" and she's a bit put out – she's two years younger than him! He always asks about you, Flo. He can't understand why you never come to visit.'

'Tell him I can't stand his wife,' Flo suggested. 'How's her ladyship taken to married life, anyroad?'

'All she's ever wanted was a wedding ring and Mrs in front of her name. She goes round looking like the cat that ate the cream.'

Now that Albert was to become a father, his joy knew no bounds. Flo was pleased for him: he was a nice man who deserved happiness. But when it came to Martha, she felt only bitterness.

Frequently, in the dinner hour or on her way home, she walked down Clement Street, but she never set eyes on Nancy and there was never a pram outside number eighteen. Once, she thought she heard a baby cry as she passed, but that might have been her imagination.

Everyone in the laundry was pleased to be invited to Flo's twenty-first. 'It won't be much,' she warned. 'There won't be any fellers, for one thing.'

'We don't mind,' Jennifer and Joanna Holbrook said together.

'Me husband wouldn't let me go if there were,' remarked Moira.

Lottie's husband was away in the Army. Nevertheless, she would have felt disloyal going to a party where there were fellers.

'I'm not bothered,' Peggy said, from somewhere within a cloud of steam. 'Anyroad, I see enough of fellers at home. You could ask Jimmy Cromer if he'd like to provide some masculine company.'

'I'm not going to a party full of ould married women,' Jimmy said in a scandalised voice.

'I'm not old and I'm not married,' Flo reminded him.

Jimmy leered at her far too maturely for a fifteen-year-old. 'Will you come out with me, then?'

'I'll do no such thing!'

'In that case, I'm not coming to your party.'

The first week of May brought air raids worse than any the city had known before. For a week, it seemed as if the Luftwaffe's intention was to blast Liverpool out of existence. Flo was convinced that her party would never take place. By the eighth no one would be left alive and there wouldn't be a building still standing. At night she stayed indoors, worried that if she went dancing a raid might start and that she really would be too scared to come home alone. In bed, with her head under the covers, she listened to the house grinding on its foundations as the bombs whistled their way down to earth and the ground shook, though it was the parachute mines, drifting silently and menacingly, that caused the greatest carnage. Bells clanged wildly as fire engines raced to put out the hundreds of fires that crackled away, turning the sky blood red.

Next morning, exhausted but still in one piece, Flo would go to work. There was rarely any sign of public transport and she had to make her way carefully along pavements carpeted with splintered glass, passing the sad, broken remains of buildings that had been the landmarks of a lifetime, and the little streets with yawning gaps where houses had been only the day before. The air was full of floating scraps of charred paper, like black confetti at a funeral.

Everyone at the laundry was miraculously still there to exclaim in horror about the events of the previous night: the narrow escapes, the bomb that had dropped in the next street killing a girl they'd gone to school with, or a chap who'd nearly married their sister. Moira lost the godmother of her youngest child. Peggy's brother-in-law, an ARP warden, was killed outright when the building he was in got a direct hit. How long, everyone wondered, would the terror continue?

'It can't go on for ever,' Peggy maintained.

It was that thought that kept them going. It had to stop sometime.

Flo arrived on the Friday of the nightmarish week to find that during the night all the mains had been fractured. There seemed little point in a laundry without electricity, gas or water so she told everyone they might as well go home. 'You'll still get paid,' she promised, not caring if Stella would approve or not. 'It's not your fault you can't work. It's that bloody Hitler's.'

'What are you going to do?' one of the twins enquired.

'I'll stay, just in case things come on again.'

'We'll stay with you.'

'Same here,' echoed Peggy.

'Me, too,' said Moira.

The next few hours always remained one of Flo's most vivid memories, proof that the human spirit obstinately refused to give in, even in the face of the worst adversity. Peggy produced a pack of cards and they played Strip Jack Naked, Rummy and Snap, and shrieked with laughter for no reason at all, though anyone listening would have thought the laughter a mite hysterical and a bit too loud. Every now and then, they'd pause for a sing-song: 'We'll Meet Again', 'Little Sir Echo', 'Run Rabbit Run'. In their quavery soprano voices, the twins entertained them with a variety of old songs, 'If You Were the Only Girl in the World', and 'Only a Bird in a Gilded Cage'.

Mid-morning, when they would normally have stopped for a cup of tea, Moira said wistfully, 'I'd give anything for a cuppa.'

As if in answer to Moira's prayer, Mrs Clancy appeared suddenly at the side door carrying a teapot. 'I expect you're all parched for a drink,' she said cheerfully. 'I always run a bucket of water before I go to bed, just in case, like, and Mrs Plunkett next door's got one of them paraffin stoves.'

There was a mad dash for cups. As usual, the twins had brought milk because they never used all their ration.

'I've got Albert at home,' Mam said to Flo. 'He hurt his leg fire-watching. He's a terrible patient. All he does is complain about people getting away without paying their fares.'

'There's hardly any trams running.'

'That's what I keep telling him. There's lines up everywhere.' She patted Flo's hand. 'I'm off to work now, luv. I'll call in for the teapot on me way home.'

'It's all right, Mam, I'll bring it. I wouldn't mind having a word with Albert. What time will you be back?' She would take the opportunity of Martha's absence to reassure Albert, though not in words, that they would always be friends. She'd prefer him not to be alone, just in case there was a message in his eyes it would be wiser not to see.

'I'll be home about half two. Sal's on mornings, so she'll be back not long afterwards.'

Later that morning the gas supply was reconnected, and just after one o'clock water came gushing out of the tap in the lavatory, which had been left turned on. There was still no electricity, so the steam-presser remained out of use, but the boilers could be loaded with washing and the ironing done. Flo gave a sigh of relief as the laundry began to function almost normally, the women setting to work with a will. Normality seemed precious in an uncertain, dangerous world, though it didn't last for long.

Just as Flo was thinking that it was almost time to nip round to Burnett Street with the teapot, the air-raid siren began its sinister wail. She particularly hated daylight raids. They were rarely heavy and usually brief but, unlike the night raids, were impossible to ignore – or, at least, pretend to. The women groaned, but when Flo suggested they abandon work for the shelter on the corner, they flatly refused.

'The shelter's just as likely to get a direct hit as the laundry,' said Lottie, who'd recently changed shifts with Moira. 'I'd sooner stay.'

There seemed no argument to this, although the laundry was flimsy in comparison. Soon afterwards a solitary plane could be heard buzzing idly overhead. Everyone went outside to take a look. They could see the German crosses on the wings.

'Is that a Messerschmidt, Jo?'

'No, Jen. It's a Heinkel.'

Suddenly the plane went into a dive. It appeared to be coming straight for them. Peggy screamed and they ran inside and slammed the door. Almost immediately, there was a loud explosion, followed by another, then several more. The plane must have dropped a stick of bombs. From somewhere within the building, there was a thud and the crash of breaking glass.

'Jaysus! That was close!' someone gasped.

They stood still, scarcely breathing, as the plane's engine grew fainter. Then the sound disappeared and the all-clear went. The raid was over.

The laundry had suffered superficial damage. At least, Flo assumed that a shattered office window and the door blown off its hinges could be described as superficial. 'The thing is,' she said shakily, 'I'd forgotten today's the day I do the accounts, otherwise I'd have been in here sorting out the wages, or writing the statement for Mrs Fritz.' There was a small crater in the street outside, and the houses opposite had also lost their doors and windows, but thankfully, no one had been hurt.

The twins began calmly to sweep up the broken glass and restore the room to relative order. Flo decided to take the money home and leave the bank till Monday, but it was important that the women were paid. Using the presser as a desk, she counted out the money and wrote each name on a little brown envelope. She felt angry with herself because her hands were trembling and her writing was all over the place. She'd had a close shave, that was all. Some people suffered far worse without going to pieces. Her stomach was squirming. She felt uneasy, full of dread. 'Pull yourself together, Flo Clancy,' she urged.

'Flo, luv,' a voice said softly.

Flo looked up. Sally was standing at the side door and the feeling of dread grew until it almost choked her. She knew why Sally had come. 'Is it Mam?' she breathed.

Her sister nodded slowly. 'And Albert.'

Sally said, 'Promise you'll make things up with Martha.'

'Why should I?' demanded Flo.

It was almost midnight. The sisters were as yet too exhausted to grieve. They paid no heed to the raid going on outside, which was as bad as any experienced so far, decimating the beleaguered city even further. They were in William Square, the only place Sally had to go now that she'd lost her home in Burnett Street. The joint funeral would take place on Monday, the day after Flo's twenty-first birthday. There was room for Albert in his mother-in-law's grave, where she would join her beloved husband. The wreaths had been ordered, a Requiem Mass arranged, and a friend of Mam's had offered to provide refreshments after the service. Father Haughey was trying to track down Albert's cousin in Macclesfield. The address would have been in the parlour, but there was no longer a parlour, no longer a house, nothing left of the place to which Mr and Mrs Clancy had moved when they married, where they'd brought up their three girls. The bomb had gone through the roof and exploded in the living room, demolishing the houses on both sides. Martha had been safe at the brewery but Mam and Albert, sheltering under the stairs, had been killed instantly. Their shattered bodies lay in the mortuary, waiting for the funeral director to collect.

'Oh, Flo,' Sally moaned, 'how can you be so unChristian and unforgiving? Martha's pregnant and she's lost both her mam and her husband.'

Martha had been whisked from the brewery to Elsa Cameron's house. When Sally went to see her, she was fast asleep, the doctor had given her a sedative.

'I can't begin to imagine how I'd feel if I'd lost Jock and Mam at the same time,' Sally shuddered.

'But you're in love with Jock,' Flo pointed out. 'Martha was no more in love with Albert than I was – and all three of us loved Mam.'

'You're awful hard, Sis.'

'I'm only pointing out the obvious. What's hard about that?'

'Oh, I dunno. It's just that you always seemed such a soft ould thing. I never dreamed you could be so unsympathetic.'

'I feel sorry for our Martha,' Flo conceded. 'I just don't want anything more to do with her, that's all.' She felt irritated that Sally didn't seem to appreciate the enormity of what Martha had done. Maybe, because Flo's baby was a bastard, she wasn't supposed to love him the way a married mother would.

'Despite our Martha being an ould bossy-boots, she depended on Mam far more than we did.' Sally sighed. 'She'll miss her something awful. We loved Mam, but we didn't need her.' She turned to her sister and said, 'Don't think I've forgotten about Tommy O'Mara and the baby, Flo. But you're a strong person, a survivor. You've got yourself a nice little home, an important job. It's time to forgive and forget.'

'I'll never forgive Martha, and I'll never forget.' Flo's voice was like ice. 'I'll speak to her politely on Monday, but that's as far as I'm willing to go.'

But Martha was too ill to attend the funeral. And Sally had been right: Elsa

Cameron reported that it was her mother Martha kept calling for. There was no mention of Albert.

2

The momentous year had flown by. Suddenly, it was Christmas again and Liverpool, though battered and badly bruised after the week-long May blitz, had survived to fight another day. The raids continued fitfully, but it was rare that the siren went nowadays. Life went on, and mid-December, Martha Colquitt gave birth to a daughter, Kate, named after the grandmother she would never know.

'She's the prettiest thing you've ever seen,' Sally told Flo. 'Ever so placid and good-humoured.'

'That's nice.' Flo did her utmost to sound generous.

'But I wish Martha'd find somewhere else to live.' Sally's brow puckered worriedly. 'I wouldn't want that Elsa Cameron anywhere near a baby of mine. She treats Norman like a punch-bag, poor bugger. He's only four, and such a lovely little chap.'

'What's happened to her husband?'

'Eugene used to come home from sea every few months, but last time he told her she was crackers and he's never been back since. I reckon he's done a bunk, permanent, like.'

'Martha said once Elsa had a sort of illness,' Flo remarked. 'She said some women go that way when they have a baby. Afterwards they're never quite right in the head.'

Sally nodded. 'There's summat wrong with the woman. By rights, Norman should be taken off her. She's not fit to be a mother.'

It seemed grotesquely unfair that Elsa Cameron, unfit to have a child, and Nancy O'Mara, unable to have one, should both have become mothers, yet Flo was childless. She changed the subject before she said something she might later regret.

'What d'you think of me decorations?' she asked. The room was festooned with paper chains and tinsel. Clusters of imitation holly hung in both windows.

'It looks like a grotto. I tried everywhere for decorations, but there's none to be had in the shops.' After living for a few months with Flo, Sally had found herself a small flat not far from Rootes Securities in Speke, which meant that she and Jock could be alone together during the precious times he was on leave.

'I got them from upstairs,' Flo said smugly. 'There's plenty more, if you'd like some. It's like having a big shop up there all to meself.'

'I wouldn't mind a few. I'm expecting Jock any minute, and it'd be nice to have the place looking Christmassy. Don't forget you're invited to Christmas dinner, will you?'

'No. And don't you forget me party the Saturday before. I feel as if I owe the girls in the laundry a party. I never had the one that was planned for me twenty-first.'

Sally twisted her lips ruefully. 'Mam was really looking forward to that. She was trying to get the ingredients for a birthday cake.'

'Was she? You've never mentioned that before.'

'I'd forgotten all about it.'

The sisters were silent for a while, thinking about Mam and Albert and how much their little world had changed over the past few years.

'Oh, well.' Sally sighed. 'I'm on early shift tomorrer. I'd better be getting home.'

It was a sad Christmas, full of bitter-sweet memories of Christmases that had gone before, made even sadder when a letter arrived from Bel to say that Bob had been killed in North Africa. 'I only wish you two had met, Flo,' she wrote. 'He was the dearest husband a woman could have. We were only married two years, almost to the day, and weren't together for a lot of that time, but I'll never stop missing him. Never.'

On New Year's Eve, Flo slipped into the Utility frock that she'd bought especially for the Rialto dance, which would go on till past midnight. It was turquoise linen, made with the minimum amount of material, short sleeves and a narrow collar. She adjusted the mirror on the mantelpiece, took a sip of sherry, and began to curl her hair into a roll.

Would she meet anyone tonight? She was glad Christmas was over and it would soon be 1942. She and Sally had both agreed that they would put the past firmly behind them and start afresh. With a wry smile, Flo glanced at the fluffy blue bunny, still in its Cellophane wrapping on the sideboard. She'd bought it for Hugh, but hadn't had the nerve to take it round to Clement Street, knowing that it would be refused. Anyroad, Hugh would be two in February and had probably grown out of fluffy bunnies. She still looked for him, walking up and down Clement Street two or three times a week. Nancy must have deliberately done her shopping when she knew Flo would be at work because there was never any sign of her out with Hugh. For a while, Flo was worried that she'd moved, but Sally said that Martha had taken Kate to see her.

She sipped more sherry, already slightly drunk and the evening hadn't even started. *She didn't even know what her son looked like!* How could she ever put the past behind her when he would still be on her mind if she lived to be a hundred? She hummed 'Auld Lang Syne', and told herself she was strong, a survivor. She wondered why she wanted to weep when she was getting ready for a dance where she was bound to have a good time. 'Because it's not really what I want,' she told herself bleakly.

When someone knocked on the door she turned, startled. Sal was spending New Year's Eve at Elsa Cameron's with Martha. 'If she's come to persuade me to go with her, she's wasting her time.'

A middle-aged man, sunburned, with hollow eyes and hollow cheeks, was standing outside the door holding a suitcase. He wore an ill-fitting tweed suit, and the collar of his frayed shirt was far too big.

'Yes?' Flo said courteously. She didn't recognise him from Adam.

'Oh, Flo! Have I changed so much?' he said tragically.

'Mr Fritz! Oh, Mr Fritz!' She grabbed his arm and pulled him inside. 'Am I pleased to see you!'

'I'm glad someone is.' He looked ready to shed the tears she'd so recently wanted to shed herself. He came into the flat and she pushed him into a chair, then stared at him as if he were a long-lost, dearly loved relative. He was much thinner than she remembered, but despite his gaunt features and the lines of strain around his jaw, he looked fit and well, as if he'd spent a lot of time working outdoors. His once chubby hands were lean and callused, but without his wire-rimmed glasses he seemed much younger. The more she stared, the less he looked like the Mr Fritz she used to know.

'Are you home for good?' she demanded. She wanted to pat him all over, make sure he was real, and had to remind herself he was only her employer.

He said drily, 'After all this time the powers-that-be decided I wasn't a danger to my adopted country. Just before Christmas they let me go.' His brown eyes grew moist. 'I've been to Ireland, Flo. Stella wasn't pleased to see me, and made it obvious she didn't want me to stay. The younger children didn't know who I was. The others were polite, but they're having such a good time on the farm I think they were scared I'd insist they come home.' He sighed. 'They're known locally as the McGonegals. Stella is ashamed of her married name.'

Flo had no idea what to say. She frowned at her hands and mumbled, 'I always thought you and Mrs Fritz were very happy together.'

'So did I!' Mr Fritz looked puzzled. 'I'm not sure what happened, but as soon as the war started Stella became a different person, bad-tempered, blaming me for things I had no control over. I couldn't produce coal or sugar out of thin air as if I were a magician. I wasn't personally responsible for the air raids. When the women left the laundry for higher wages, that was the last straw as far as Stella was concerned. It was a shock, after so many years, to discover she could be so unpleasant.'

'Perhaps,' Flo said hesitantly, 'once the war's over . . .'

'No.' He shook his head wearily. 'No, it's too late, Flo. I spent eighteen months in the camp. The other married men had letters from their families. Some wives travelled hundreds of miles to see their husbands for just a few hours. I had a single letter from Stella the whole time I was there, and that was to tell me she was back in Ireland and she'd left you in charge of the laundry and William Square.' There was a lost expression on his face. Something had happened with which he would never come to terms. 'You can't be sure of anything in this life, I hadn't realised that,' he murmured. 'I never thought it possible to feel so very alone, as if I'd never had a family. I still feel like that – alone. Do I actually have a wife and eight children? It seems absurd. It's even worse since I went to Ireland. We were like strangers to each other.'

'Oh, Lord!' Flo was horrified. He was such a dear, sweet man, who wouldn't hurt a fly. She said in her kindest voice, which seemed rather thick and emotional all of a sudden, 'You don't seem like a stranger to me.'

For the first time he smiled. 'That means a lot, Flo. It really does.' He glanced around the room and she hoped he wouldn't recognise the decorations and all the other things she'd pinched from upstairs. 'You've made this place very cosy. It's a relief to have somewhere, someone, to come back to.' He smiled again. 'But you're obviously getting ready for a night out on the town. I expect you have a date with a young man. Don't let me keep you.'

'As if I'd let you spend New Year's Eve all on your own,' Flo cried. 'I was only going to the Rialto by meself.'

Despite his protestations, she refused to leave. 'I'll pretend I got all decked up because I was expecting you,' she said, in the hope that it would make him feel less alone, more welcome.

Apparently it did. By the time she'd made a cup of tea and something to eat, he looked almost cheerful. She poured them both a glass of sherry and told him all about the laundry. 'I hope you don't mind but we changed the name to White's after we lost a lot of business.'

He already knew. Stella had given him the statements Flo had sent. 'It's all I have left now, my laundry.' He sighed, but more like the gloomy Mr Fritz of old than the joyless person who'd just landed on her doorstep.

She described the staff. 'You'll love the twins. They can only manage one person's work between them, but they only get one person's wage, so it doesn't matter.' She told him about Peggy, who had to leave early for her lads' tea, and Lottie and Moira who worked half a day each. 'And, of course, you know Jimmy Cromer, he's a treasure.'

'Jimmy will have to go now I'm back,' Mr Fritz said.

'You can't sack him!' Flo gasped. 'He's a good worker, dead reliable.'

'But there'll be nothing for him to do.' He spread his hands, palms upwards, a gesture she remembered well. 'I'll be able to collect and deliver, won't I?'

'Even so, you can't sack Jimmy for no reason,' Flo said stubbornly.

'He'll be superfluous to requirements, Flo. What better reason is there?'

'It seems very cruel.'

'It's necessary to be cruel sometimes if you run a successful business. It's what capitalism is all about. You can't employ superfluous staff and make a profit.'

'And here's me thinking you wouldn't hurt a fly,' Flo said sarcastically. 'I suppose you'll be reducing the wages next, so you make an even bigger profit. Well, you needn't think I'm working me guts out if everyone leaves.'

His eyes twinkled. 'You've changed, Flo. You would never have spoken to me like that before.'

Flo tossed her head. 'I'm not sorry.'

'Why should you be sorry for expressing an opinion? I like you better this way. But let's have more sherry and save the arguments for tomorrow. It's New Year's Eve. We'll talk about only pleasant things. Tell me, how are your family?'

'I'm afraid there's nothing pleasant to tell.' She explained about Mam and Albert being killed in the same raid that had damaged the laundry.

'So many tragedies.' Mr Fritz looked dejected. 'Hitler has a great deal to answer for. I suppose I should consider myself lucky to be alive.'

As midnight approached, he noticed the wireless and suggested they listen to Big Ben chime in the New Year. 'Is that the set from upstairs?'

'I hope you don't mind. I borrowed it,' Flo said uncomfortably, 'You can have it back tomorrer.'

'Keep it, Flo,' he said warmly. 'It will give me a good excuse to come down and listen to the news.'

'You mean I can stay?' She felt relieved. 'I thought you might prefer to have the house all to yourself, like.'

'My dear Flo,' he laughed, 'would I be silly enough to put my one and only friend out on to the street? Of course you can stay. What's more, this furniture's seen better days. There's a nice little settee and chair in Stella's sitting room that you must have. She's not likely to use it again.'

'Shush!' Flo put her finger to her lips. 'It's about to be nineteen forty-two.'

As the great clock in London chimed in the New Year, they shook hands and Mr Fritz kissed her decorously on the cheek. 'I'd expected it would be dreadful, coming back to the house without Stella and the children, Flo, but it's not been nearly as bad as I'd thought.' He squeezed her hand. 'It really is good to be home.'

He was still the same Mr Fritz, after all, who couldn't hurt a fly. Once face to face with Jimmy Cromer, he couldn't bring himself to dismiss the lad. 'I'm a hopeless capitalist,' he confessed. Instead, he gave him a job in the laundry, which Jimmy said disgustedly was women's work and got bored within a week. As a fit, able sixteen-year-old, he had no problem finding employment in war time, and he left quickly of his own accord.

While she'd been in charge Flo had got used to doing things her way. She had quite a task convincing Mr Fritz that her way was best. He got tetchy when proved wrong, she sulked when he was right, but they were always the best of friends again before the day was over. He maintained that they provided a substitute family for each other.

'Mam would be pleased,' said Flo. 'She always liked you.'

Life assumed a pleasant pattern. On Sundays, he would come to dinner, armed with a bottle of wine. On Saturday afternoons, Flo had tea upstairs, eating the thick, clumsily made sandwiches with every appearance of enjoyment.

During the week, she continued to go dancing, occasionally bringing home a young serviceman. Upstairs would be in darkness, so Mr Fritz remained ignorant of that part of her life. Not that it was any of his business, she told herself, but it was something she'd sooner keep to herself.

In July, Bel came home on five days' leave prior to being posted to Egypt, and preferred to spend the time with her best friend, Flo, rather than with her horrible aunt Mabel.

Like virtually everyone else, Bel had changed. There was an added maturity to her lovely face, and her violet eyes were no longer quite so dazzling. Even so, she swept into the flat like a breath of fresh air, filling it with noise and laughter. She enthused over the brown plush settee and chair that had once belonged to Stella, the tall sideboard, which had so many useful drawers and cupboards, and was particularly taken with the brass bed from Mr Fritz's spare room. 'It's like a little palace, Flo, but I hate the idea of you living in a hole in the ground.'

'Don't be silly,' Flo said mildly. 'I love it.'

The two girls attracted a chorus of wolf-whistles, and many an admiring glance, as they strolled through the sunlit city streets of an evening in their summer frocks: Bel, the young widow, with her striking red hair and rosy cheeks, and green-eyed Flo, as pale and slender as a lily.

Bel and Mr Fritz took to each other straight away and pretended to flirt extravagantly. On the last night of Bel's leave, he took both girls out to dinner. 'I wonder what Stella would say if she could see me now.' He chuckled. 'Every man in this restaurant is eyeing me enviously, wondering how such an insignificant little chap managed to get the two most beautiful women in Liverpool to dine with him.'

'Insignificant!' Bel screamed. 'You're dead attractive, you. If I was on the look-out for a feller, I'd grab you like a shot.'

Flo smiled. In the past, no one would have dreamed of describing Mr Fritz as attractive, but since returning from the camp he had acquired a gaunt, melancholy charm. The twins claimed he made their old hearts flutter dangerously, and Peggy declared herself bowled over.

That night, Flo and Bel sat up in bed together drinking their final mug of cocoa. 'I won't half miss you.' Flo sighed. 'The place will seem dead quiet after you've gone.'

'I'm ever so glad I came. It's the first time I've enjoyed meself since Bob was killed.'

'Remember the day we met?' said Flo. 'You were dead impatient because I was upset over Tommy O'Mara. Now you know how I felt.'

'There's a big difference.' Bel's voice was unexpectedly tart. 'Bob was worth crying over, not like Tommy O'Mara!'

'Oh, Bel! How can you say that when you never met him?'

Bel didn't answer straight away. 'Sorry, Flo,' she said eventually. 'It was just the impression I got. But you're well over him now, aren't you?'

'I'm not sure if I ever will be. I've never met a man who comes anywhere near him.' Perhaps if Hugh hadn't always been on her mind to remind her of Tommy's existence, she might have put the memory away.

'It's about time you got yourself a proper feller, girl,' Bel snorted, 'and stopped moping over a man who died three years ago. You're twenty-two. You should be married by now, or at least courting.'

'You sound just like our Martha.' Flo laughed.

'Which reminds me,' Bel went on. 'Why haven't I been to see your Martha's little girl?'

'I thought you didn't like babies.'

'I didn't until I lost the one I was expecting.' Bel's lovely face became unbearably sad. 'You've no idea what it feels like, Flo, having this little person growing inside you. When I had the miscarriage, it was like losing part of meself. Still,' she brightened, 'that's all in the past, and as Bob said to me in his lovely Scots accent just before he was posted to North Africa and we knew he might be killed, "I know you won't forget me, girl, but don't let the memory weigh you down, like unwanted baggage. Go light into the future."' Bel sniffed briefly. 'He was ever so clever, my Bob.'

Flo envied her friend's resilience and ability to look ahead. She spent too much time looking back.

'Anyroad,' Bel persisted, 'what's your Martha's baby like?'

'I've no idea. I haven't seen her.'

Bel's reaction was entirely predictable. 'Why ever not?' she screeched.

'Because me and our Martha had a falling-out.'

'What over?'

'Mind your own business,' Flo said irritably, and although Bel pressed for ages to know why, she refused to say another word.

Next morning, the two girls left for Lime Street station, Bel trim and smart in her khaki uniform. Mr Fritz had insisted Flo see her on to the train, even though it meant she'd be hours late for work. He bade Bel a mournful farewell. 'Take care of yourself in Egypt, there's a good girl.' He put his hand over his heart. 'I think I can already feel it breaking.'

Bel flung her arms around his neck. '*You*'re the heartbreaker, Fritz, you ould rascal. Us poor girls aren't safe with chaps like you around. I'm surprised those poor women in the laundry get any work done at all.'

The station was packed with servicemen and women returning from leave or *en route* elsewhere in the British Isles. Bel found herself a seat on the London train and leaned out of the window. 'He's a lovely chap, that Fritz,' she said.

'I know.' Flo nodded.

'I think he fancies you.'

Flo was aghast. 'Don't talk daft, Bel Knox! We're friends, that's all. I'm very fond of him, but he's got a wife and eight children in Ireland.'

Bel winked. 'I think he'd sooner be more than friends. Anyroad, it's over between him and Stella. He told me.'

'Yes, but it still makes him a married man. And they'll never get divorced, they're Catholics.'

'For goodness' sake, Flo. There's a war on. Forget he's married and let yourself go for once.'

The guard blew his whistle, the carriage doors were slammed, and the train began slowly to puff out of the station, Bel still hanging out of the window. Flo walked quickly along beside her. 'One of the first things you said to me was that you didn't approve of going out with married men.'

'Under the circumstances I'd make an exception in the case of you and Mr Fritz,' Bel said. By now, the train was going too fast for Flo to keep up. Bel shouted, 'Think about it, Flo!'

'The thing is,' Flo said under her breath, waving to the red-headed figure until the face was just a blur, 'I'm not sure if I fancy *him*, not in the way Bel's on about. I'm not sure if I'll ever fancy anyone again.'

3

1945

She recognised him immediately, a thin child, delicately boned like Flo herself, hair the colour of wheat. His round, innocent eyes were a beautiful dark green flecked with gold. The other children, boys first, had come charging through the school gates whooping like savages. He came alone, separate from the rest. She could guess one reason why he wasn't part of the gang: the other lads wore shabby jerseys and baggy pants but this five-year-old was neatly dressed in grey shorts with a firmly pressed crease, pullover, flannel shirt. Hugh O'Mara was the only child wearing a blazer and tie. Nancy was a good mother, but not very sensitive. Flo would never have allowed her son to stand out in such a ridiculous get-up.

Flo watched as he approached, a sensation in her gut akin to the one she'd had the first time she was on her way to meet his father. She thought of all the times when she'd glimpsed a dark-haired woman with a pushchair on the far side of the Mystery, or crossing the street leading a small boy by the hand. Either it had been someone else, or the woman and child had disappeared when she had hurried to catch up.

Now he was here, and in a few seconds he would be close enough to touch. Not that she would dare. Not just yet.

'Hello,' she said.

He looked at her, and she searched in his eyes for recognition, as if it was inevitable he would sense she wasn't a stranger but his mam, his real flesh-and-blood mam. But there was nothing, just a shy glance.

'What's that you've got there?' she asked. Like all the other children, he was carrying a large brown envelope.

'A photo. It's of all the school taken together.'

'Can I see?'

He opened the envelope and took out the photo. 'The infants are at the front. That's me there.' He pointed to the end of the row, where he was sitting, knees crossed, looking serious. 'Mr Carey said I spoilt it 'cos I'm the only one not smiling.'

'Perhaps there wasn't much to smile about that day.' Flo turned the picture over. The photographer's name was stamped on the back, which meant she could buy a copy for herself.

'I didn't like having me photo taken much,' he said as they began to walk in the direction of Smithdown Road. 'Are you a friend of me mam's?'

'No, but I know some people she knows. I knew your dad quite well.'

His eyes lit up. 'Did ya? He died on a big ship under the sea, but the other boys won't believe me when I tell them.'

'I believe you,' Flo declared. 'I've got newspapers at home that tell all about it.'

'Can I come and see them?' he said eagerly. 'I can read a bit.'

There was nothing Flo would have liked more, but she said, 'I live too far away. Tell you what, though, I'll come next Friday and bring the papers with me. We can sit on the grass in the Mystery and I'll read them to you.'

'Can't you come before?' The crestfallen look on his thin face was almost too much to bear. Flo wanted to snatch him up and carry him away. He was much too serious for a five-year-old. She'd like to teach him to laugh and sing, be happy. But it would be cruel to take him from the woman he thought was his mother, the woman he loved more than he would ever love Flo.

She said, 'No, luv. I only get away from work on Fridays when I go to the bank. I should have been back ages ago. Me boss'll be wondering where I am.'

'Me mam works in a sweetshop.'

'I know. Someone told me.' Martha and Nancy O'Mara still saw each other occasionally. Through Sally, Flo had learned that Nancy served in the

847

shop till five o'clock, leaving ninety minutes during which Flo could see her son, although she could only be with him for a fraction of that time because of her own job. St Theresa's junior and infants' school was a few minutes away from the laundry.

'She brings me pear drops home sometimes, and dolly mixtures.' Unexpectedly, he reached up and put his small hand in hers. Flo could barely breathe as she touched her child for the first time. She stroked the back of his fingers with her thumb, wanting to cry as all sorts of emotions tumbled through her head. She said, knowing it sounded stupid, 'I'd like to be your friend.'

He looked at her gravely. 'Me mam doesn't like me having friends.'

'Why not?' she asked in surprise.

'She said they're a bad inf—' He stumbled over the word and rolled his eyes. 'A bad inflex, or something.'

'A bad influence?'

''S right,' he said.

'Perhaps I could be your secret friend.'

'Yes, please. I'd like that.'

They arrived at the laundry, where Mr Fritz was standing by the door looking concerned. He hurried towards them. 'We were worried there'd been a hold-up at the bank. Peggy thought you might have been shot.'

'Peggy's seen too many films.'

'And who's this?' He looked at Hugh benignly.

'This is my friend, Hugh O'Mara.' Flo pushed her son forward. 'Hugh, say hello to me boss, Mr Fritz.'

'Hello,' Hugh said politely.

'Pleased to meet you, Hugh, old chap,' Mr Fritz said jovially.

Flo knelt in front of the little boy and said, in a whisper, 'If ever you're in trouble, this is where you can find me. I'm here every day from eight till half past five, and till one on Sat'days.' She stroked his cheek. 'Remember that, won't you, luv?'

He nodded. 'But I don't know your name!'

'It's Flo Clancy.'

'All right, Flo.'

'Tara, now. I'll see you next Friday.'

He trotted off in his smart clothes, clutching the brown envelope. Flo watched till he turned the corner, and still watched even after he'd gone, imagining him passing the shops in Smithdown Road on his way to Clement Street, where he would remain in the house, alone and friendless, until Nancy came.

'What's the matter, Flo?' Mr Fritz said gently.

'Nothing.' Flo returned to work, and it wasn't until she was inside that she became aware of the tears that were streaming down her cheeks.

For years Gerard Davies had been imploring Flo to marry him. After they'd first met in the Rialto, he'd come to Liverpool whenever he could and he wrote to her regularly. As far as he was concerned, Flo was his girl, his sweetheart. 'We'll see once the war's over,' Flo would say, whenever the subject of marriage was raised.

The war had been over for three months, the lights were on again and the celebrations, the parties, the dancing in the streets were just memories. Gerard Davies had been demobbed and was back in Swansea. He wrote to demand that Flo keep her promise.

He wasn't the only one of her young men to propose – she could have had half a dozen husbands by now – but he was the most persistent. Flo turned down the proposals as tactfully as she could. She didn't want to hurt anyone's feelings. They would never know that things hadn't been quite so wonderful for her as they had been for them. She put the lovely letters away to keep for always.

To Gerard Davies she wrote that she'd only said, 'We'll see,' when the war was over. She hadn't promised anything. She said that she liked him very, very much, and felt honoured that he wanted her for his wife, but he deserved to marry a woman who loved him far more than she did.

Perhaps it was unfortunate that she found Gerard's letter waiting on the doormat when she arrived home the day she'd met Hugh outside school for the first time, otherwise she might have given more serious consideration to his proposal. It would be nice to have a husband, children, a proper house. Sally, who was expecting her first baby in January, had got a nice council house in Huyton with gardens front and back. Jock would complete his naval service in two years' time and they would settle down and raise their family. And Bel had got married again in Egypt to a chap called Ivor, who claimed to be descended from the Hungarian royal family. She enclosed a photo of herself dressed in a lavish lace outfit standing next to a haughty young man with an undeniably regal manner. 'Ivor lives in the land of make-believe,' Bel wrote. 'He's no more royal than my big toe, but he makes me laugh. I'll never love another man the way I loved Bob, but me and Ivor are good company for each other. I'll be back in Liverpool very soon and you can see him for yourself.' The letter was signed, 'Bel (Szerb!)' and there was a PS. 'By the way, I think I'm pregnant!'

Why can't *I* make do with second best? Flo asked herself. Why am I haunted by memories of making love with Tommy O'Mara in the Mystery all those years ago? And why am I obsessed with the son I can never have? She knew that if she married Gerard, she would be only half a wife to him and half a mother to their children. It wouldn't be fair on him or them. She stuck the stamp on the envelope containing the letter to him, thumping it angrily with her fist.

When Bel returned, it was with news of another miscarriage. 'The doctor said I'll never carry a baby to full term. I've got a weak cervix,' she said. Flo nodded sympathetically, as if she knew what it meant.

Bel was upset, but determined not to take the doctor's verdict as final. 'Me and Ivor intend to try again. At least the trying's fun.' She winked. 'It's about time you got married and tried it, Flo.'

'Perhaps, one day.'

'I take it nothing came of you and Mr Fritz?'

'You were imagining things. We're just friends.'

Flo couldn't take to Ivor, whose manner was as haughty as his appearance. He expected his wife to wait on him hand and foot. Bel had a third miscarriage, and went to work behind the handbag counter in Owen Owen's department store, while Ivor lolled around in their flat in Upper Parliament Street, refusing so much as to wash a dish.

'He won't get a job,' Bel raged. She came round to Flo's often to complain and calm her nerves with sherry. 'Whenever I point out a suitable vacancy in the *Echo*, he claims it's beneath him.'

'But it's not beneath him to live off his wife?'

'Apparently not.' Bel snorted so loudly that Flo half expected flames to shoot out of her nostrils. 'I think I'll kick him out, get a divorce.'

'You should never have married him,' Flo said, with the benefit of hindsight.

'I know.' Bel uttered an enormous sigh. 'I don't half envy your Sally. Her little girl's a proper bobby-dazzler, and that Jock seems a dead nice feller.'

'Sal's already in the club again. She's making up for lost time now that Jock'll soon be home for good.'

'Have you been seeing Hugh O'Mara, luv?' Sally asked, one stormy December Sunday when Flo went to see her in Huyton.

'How did you find out?' Flo stammered.

'Someone told Nancy and she told our Martha.' Sally's face was misty with happiness as she nursed nine-month-old Grace on her lap.

'I've been meeting him outside school every Friday for more than a year – I suppose you think I'm daft.'

'Oh, no, luv. I might have done once, but not now.' Sally glanced at her daughter. 'I can't imagine how I'd have felt if someone had taken her away before I'd even seen her, or the little one I've got in here.' She patted her bulging stomach. 'Everyone was dead cruel, Flo, me included. I thought keeping the baby would ruin your life.'

Instead, it was the other way round, Flo thought wryly. 'Is Nancy mad at me?'

'Martha couldn't make out if she was or not. She seemed more resigned than anything. I suppose she thinks it can't do much harm now.'

'I don't suppose it can,' said Flo. 'How is our Martha?' She only asked because it would please Sally, who was forever trying to reunite the sisters.

Sally grimaced and said, predictably, 'I wish you'd go and see her, Flo. She's dead miserable. Kate's starting school in January, and she'll be stuck in the house with Elsa Cameron who's completely off her rocker now. The last time I went she was singing hymns the whole time. By rights, Martha should find a place of her own, but although you'll say she only wants to interfere, Flo, she's not prepared to leave Elsa in sole charge of Norman or the woman's quite likely to kill the poor bugger. Anyroad, Norman would be lost without little Kate. They've been brought up together, and he worships the ground she walks on.'

Hugh O'Mara emerged from school wearing a woollen balaclava, a long fringed scarf, and the horrible navy-blue belted mackintosh that Flo thought made him look like a miniature gas man.

It was another terrible winter, bleaker and icier even than the notorious winter of 1940, and the fuel shortages and power cuts made it seem even worse. Food remained rationed, and in such an austere atmosphere it was hard to believe that Great Britain had won the war.

There was a little girl with Hugh, a pretty child, like a fairy, with long fair hair. She wore three-quarter-length socks and patent-leather shoes, and her winter coat was much too big. There was something familiar about her face, though Flo couldn't remember having seen her before.

'I've got another friend,' Hugh beamed happily at Flo. 'She only started last week, but I knew her before school. Me mam goes to their house sometimes. She's nearly two years younger than me, but that doesn't mean we can't be friends.'

'Of course it doesn't, luv.' He would be seven in a month's time and was shooting upwards like a vigorous sapling. Flo had already bought his present, a toy car. If you twisted the steering wheel, the four wheels turned. She was taking the risk that Nancy wouldn't object.

'Can she come with us to the Mystery?' Hugh said eagerly. 'Have you brought the ball?'

Flo was about to say the little girl should ask her mam first, when another boy came up, a dark, handsome lad of about ten, with an ugly purple and yellow bruise on his forehead. She'd noticed him before. He was a bully and most of the children kept well out of his way. He put a possessive hand on the little girl's shoulder. 'I've got to take her home,' he said, scowling. 'We live in the same house together.' He turned to Hugh and spat, 'You leave her alone, Hugh O'Mara.'

'Don't you dare speak to him like that,' Flo said angrily.

The boy ignored her and pulled the child away. 'C'mon, Kate.'

'Is that Kate Colquitt?' Flo enquired, when the children had gone.

'Yes. Do you know her?'

'I'm her auntie.'

'You never are!' Hugh's brow creased in disbelief. 'I don't understand.'

'Her mam and me are sisters,' Flo explained carefully. Then she said, 'The boy with Kate, is that Norman Cameron?'

'Yes.' Hugh wrinkled his thin shoulders. 'He's not very nice. I don't like him. No one does, not even his mam.'

'Perhaps he can't help not being very nice.' She recalled sadly what a beautiful baby Norman had been, so happy – there was a photo somewhere in the flat, taken on his first birthday, that Martha had given her at the time. She hadn't realised the three children would be at the same school – Hugh and Kate were cousins, not that they'd ever know.

Flo took a rubber ball out of her bag and began to bounce it. 'C'mon, I'll race you to the Mystery. Whoever's last has to climb to the top of the tallest tree and shout "Hallelujah" ten times.' She always won, but Hugh's legs were getting longer. As soon as he was likely to get there first, she'd have to think of a less demanding penalty.

1949

Mr Fritz was stepping out with Mrs Winters, a widow who had tightly permed black hair and wore smart, tailored suits with very short skirts, though her legs were much too thick for ankle-strap shoes – or so Bel claimed when she saw them together. 'I don't like the look of her, Flo. Once she's installed upstairs you'll be out on your arse.'

'Oh, don't!' said Flo. She felt hurt and a touch dismayed, as if Mr Fritz was letting her down. Somehow, unreasonably, she'd considered herself the only woman he wanted in his life, though their relationship had always been strictly platonic.

'It's a pity he and Stella can't get divorced,' Bel remarked. It had taken her several years to get rid of Ivor. 'Still, I suppose the poor chap's got to dip his wick somewhere. I'm glad I'm a woman and not panting for it all the time.'

Mrs Winters lasted only two months. 'I couldn't stand the way she stuck her little finger out like a flagpole when she drank her tea,' Mr Fritz confessed to Flo. 'I felt I wanted to hang something on it.' He stared at her gloomily. 'What happened to your chap from the income-tax office?'

'I gave him up. We didn't have much in common.' All Ray Meadows had wanted to talk about was figures. Bel had tried to insist that Flo encourage him. 'He's dead keen, I can tell, and a good prospect. You're not getting any younger – you'll be thirty next year.' But Flo had decided, once and for all, that she would sooner remain single than marry a man she didn't love wholeheartedly. Books and the cinema provided all the romance and excitement she needed, especially as things usually ended happily. She enjoyed the quiet of her flat, buried half under the ground, drinking sherry, and feeling pleasantly cut off from the real world. Her only regret was that she no longer had a family. She missed the love that Mam and Dad had bestowed on her, and since Sally's son, Ian, had developed muscular dystrophy at the age of two, poor little lad, Flo saw her sister rarely now. Whenever she went to Huyton, Sal and Jock seemed so wrapped up in anxiety for their son that Flo felt in the way. Of course, there was always Martha, but if it hadn't been for her, Flo would have had a son of her own for the past nine years.

'I've been invited to the Isle of Man for the weekend in July,' Mr Fritz said, with the air of a man who'd been asked to attend his own funeral. 'Some of the chaps from the camp are having a reunion. Trouble is, they're taking their wives. I've no one to take.'

By now, half of the little Fritzes were in their twenties. The previous year Mr Fritz had been invited to Ben's wedding but had refused to go. 'I'd feel most peculiar,' he said, 'like a stranger at the feast.' A few weeks ago, he'd received a card to say Ben's wife had given birth to a son. He was a grandfather, which made him feel even more peculiar, and also very old, though he was only fifty.

'I'm sure not every chap will be bringing a wife,' Flo said briskly. 'You'll probably have quite a nice time.'

Over the next few weeks, he continued to raise the subject of the reunion, saying miserably, 'I hate the idea of going by myself.' Or, 'It wouldn't have to be a wife. It would be enough to take a friend.'

'If that's the case, why not ask Mrs Winters?' Flo suggested. 'It's only a few days, and you could put up with her little finger for that long, surely.'

'No, no,' he said, distractedly. 'There's someone else I'd far sooner go with.'

Two days before he was due to leave, he came down to the basement, where he sat, sighing continuously and staring moodily into the gas fire, which wasn't even lit. After half an hour of this, Flo said, 'Bel will be round in a minute. We're going to see *The Keys of the Kingdom* at the Odeon. She's mad about Gregory Peck.'

'Gregory Peck's got everything,' he said despondently. 'I bet he wouldn't be stuck for someone to take with him to the Isle of Man.'

Flo burst out laughing. 'If you carry on like this much longer, I'll offer to go with you meself.'

To her astonishment, he jumped to his feet and caught both her hands in his. 'Oh, *would* you, Flo? I've been wanting to ask for weeks.' His brown eyes were shining in a face that had suddenly come alive. 'We'll have separate rooms, of course we will. My intentions are strictly honourable. And we'll have a lovely time. Joe Loss and his orchestra are playing at the Villa Marina. I haven't been dancing in years.'

'But . . .' Flo began.

'But what, my dear girl?' he cried.

Everyone she knew, apart from Bel, would disapprove, despite the separate bedrooms and Bel would ask loads of embarrassing questions. Even so, perhaps it was the same lack of caution that had led her to accept Tommy O'Mara's invitation a decade ago, because all Flo said was, 'Oh, all right. But I don't want Bel and the women in the laundry to know. They'll only get the wrong idea.'

He put a finger to his lips. 'You can count on me not to breathe a word to a soul.'

Flo sat on the edge of the double bed and stared out of the hotel window at the choppy, green-brown waves of the Irish Sea. A large black and white ship with a red funnel was approaching Douglas, spewing white foam in its wake. It was the ship on which they would return to Liverpool.

The sky was overcast, the clouds leaden, as if about to unleash another downpour, and the pavements were still wet from the rain that had fallen all night long and the whole of the previous day. Holidaymakers wandered past forlornly in their plastic raincoats, some of the children carrying buckets and spades.

In the *en suite* bathroom, Mr Fritz could be heard humming as he shaved. At the initial gathering of the ex-internees, a man had shouted, 'Fritz Hofmannsthal, you old rascal! How are you?' and she'd been amazed when Mr Fritz went over and shook his hand.

'I didn't realise that was your name,' she whispered.

'I told you it was a mouthful,' he whispered back.

After proudly introducing her all round as 'My dear friend, Miss Florence Clancy,' Mr Fritz seemed to forget he was supposed to be at a reunion. That night, when they should have been at a special dinner, but were tangoing to 'Jealousy' in the Villa Marina, he said, 'Who wants to celebrate a miserable experience like that? It's the sort of thing I'd sooner forget.'

The first night she'd spent alone in the single bedroom he'd booked for her on the floor above. Yesterday, Sunday, they breakfasted together at a table by the window in the dining room with its cream and maroon striped

Regency wallpaper. It was raining cats and dogs, and the sky was so dark that the red-shaded wall lamps had been switched on, making the large room cosy and intimate.

'This is nice,' said Mr Fritz. He touched her hand. 'This is lovely.'

They caught a taxi to Mass and back again, then read the newspapers and drank coffee in the hotel lounge until it was time for lunch. Afterwards, they battled their way through the wind and rain to an amusement arcade, then, in the afternoon, they went to the pictures to see *Notorious* with Cary Grant and Ingrid Bergman. 'I must confess,' Mr Fritz said at dinner, 'that I've always nursed a soft spot for Ingrid Bergman.'

They took their time over the meal and it was ten o'clock by the time the wine was finished. They transferred to the bar for a cocktail, and continued to talk about things of mutual interest: the laundry, the little Fritzes, Flo's family, the house in William Square.

It was an unremarkable few days, yet Flo had rarely enjoyed herself more. It was nice to be with someone she knew so much about. There were no awkward silences, no mad scrambling through her mind for what to say next. She'd known Mr Fritz for more than half her life and they were entirely comfortable with each other.

The clock was striking midnight when he offered to escort her upstairs to her room on the third floor. When they reached the second floor, he paused and looked grave. 'Flo, would you, could you . . .' He gestured along the corridor and stuttered, 'Would you consider doing me the honour of— of—'

After their lovely time together, Flo had anticipated that this might happen and was quite prepared. What harm would it do? None, she had decided. Furthermore, she had no intention of making herself out to be a shy virgin and pretending to be coy. If Stella had known she'd had a baby, then so must he. As he looked incapable of saying the words he wanted, she said them for him. 'Of sleeping with you tonight?'

He was an ardent, yet gentle lover. Flo experienced none of the passion there had been with Tommy O'Mara, but as she hadn't expected to she wasn't disappointed. When it was over, she felt cherished and satisfied. Afterwards they sat up in bed like an old married couple. 'We must do this again, Flo,' he said warmly. 'Perhaps next month, August.'

'I'd like that.' She laid her head affectionately on his shoulder.

'In that case, I'll book a double room in a different hotel, and we'll be Mr and Mrs Hofmannsthal.'

'But we'll still be Miss Clancy and Mr Fritz back in Liverpool?'

He looked at her quizzically. 'I think that would be wise, don't you? Friends at home, lovers in the Isle of Man. That way, you're less likely to tire of me. It can be our little monthly treat, our little adventure. You know,' he breathed happily, 'I've always been a tiny bit in love with you ever since the day you came to the laundry for an interview all those years ago.'

So Bel had been right, after all. Flo squeezed his arm. 'I've always been very fond of you.'

'Let's hope Stella didn't notice, eh?'

She couldn't be bothered telling him that Stella had, because it was too late to do anything about it.

'I suppose we should get some sleep,' he suggested. She slid under the covers and he bent and kissed her forehead. 'We have to be up early to catch the boat home.'

He had fallen asleep immediately, but Flo had lain wondering what she'd tell Bel when she went away again in four weeks' time. She wasn't sure why, but she preferred keeping her relationship with Mr Fritz a secret, even from her best friend. Right now, Bel thought she'd gone on retreat to a convent in Wales. *I'll say I'm going on another one. It fits in with the image she's got of me. Let her go on thinking I'm as dull as ditchwater . . .*

'The boat's just about to dock, Mr Fritz,' she called.

He came out of the bathroom smiling, a towel tucked under his chin, patting his cheeks. His kindly, good-natured face looked young this morning, almost boyish. 'I think we can dispense with the Mr, don't you, Flo?'

As she smiled back, she felt a surge of emotion, not real love but almost. 'I'd sooner not, if you don't mind. I'll always think of you as Mr Fritz.'

Millie

1

I'd been so engrossed in Flo's love letters that I'd forgotten about the time. I'd be late for work if I didn't hurry. I dragged on the red suit and T-shirt I'd worn the day before, and combed my hair in the car when I stopped at traffic lights. The car behind hooted angrily as I was putting on my lipstick.

Halfway through the morning I answered the phone for the umpteenth time, doing my utmost not to sound as harassed as I felt.

'It's me,' James said humbly.

If I followed my instincts and slammed down the receiver, he would only ring back. 'What do you want?' I snapped.

'To see you, to apologise.'

'I'll take the apology for granted. There's no need for us to see each other.'

'Millie, darling, I don't know what came over me. Let's have dinner tonight. Let me explain.' He sounded desperate, but I hadn't forgotten that he'd raised his fist to strike me. I wasn't interested in explanations or apologies. I could never forgive him.

'I'd sooner not.'

'Please, Millie.' He was almost sobbing. 'Please, darling, I have to see you.'

'Look, James, I'm very busy. I don't like to be rude, but I'm going to ring off. Goodbye.'

An hour later, a van drew up outside the office and a girl came in with a bouquet of red roses for Miss Millicent Cameron; two dozen, surrounded by fern, wrapped in gold paper and tied with copious amounts of scarlet ribbon. There was no card, but only one person could have sent them. I thought them ostentatious, but Diana was impressed. I dumped the flowers on her desk. 'In that case, they're yours. Your father might like them.'

'But they must cost the earth!' Diana protested.

'I don't care. I don't want them.' I changed the subject. 'How's your father?'

Diana's face brightened. 'Much improved. We think he might be in remission. It happens sometimes with cancer. Yesterday I took him to Otterspool, and we had a picnic in the car. I can't think why we've never done things like that before.'

'My mother was talking about moving away from Liverpool, and I suddenly realised how much I'd miss her.' I'd never mentioned anything about my family to Diana before, and felt that I'd made the first gesture towards friendship.

We came to the conclusion that most children took their parents too much for granted, and agreed to lunch together if we could get away at the same time. Diana hissed, 'Is George still cross with me over those notes? I suppose I've blown my chances with that job I was after.'

'The job's Oliver's. It always was. As for the notes, I bet George has forgotten all about them.'

'God, I hope so.' Diana pursed her lips. 'I made a terrible cock-up there. I envy you, Millie. You never do anything to rock the boat. You're always so meek and pliable. Men prefer women they think they can control. George doesn't like me because I'm too independent.' It might have been unintentional, but there was a strong note of spite in her voice. She touched a rose. 'No one's ever sent me flowers like this.'

Whether she meant it or not, I still felt affronted. Meek and pliable? Me? I bent my head over my work, and decided to be too busy when Diana suggested it was time for lunch.

After work, I drove to Blundellsands to do some washing and take a shower. There was a message from James on the answering-machine, which I refused to listen to. I switched off the machine and rang my mother. 'Is everything okay, Mum?'

'Everything's fine, luv. Why?'

'It's just that my answering-machine's broken, I'll be out most nights this week and I didn't want you to worry.' Nor did I want a repeat of the Birmingham episode. During the week ahead, a minor crisis of one sort or another was bound to occur in the Cameron household and Mum would need someone to talk to. 'Call me at the office if something important crops up,' I told her.

'As long as it won't get you into trouble, luv.'

It wouldn't, I assured her. 'What will you be up to the nights you're out?' she asked.

I imagined telling the truth: that I would be sleeping with the grandson of the man who'd broken Flo Clancy's heart almost sixty years ago. I said, 'I thought it was time I put in a few more hours at Auntie Flo's. I'm getting nowhere at this rate.'

'I'm sorry you were landed with it, Millicent. I never thought it'd turn out to be such a mammoth task.'

'I'm quite enjoying it.'

'Gran said you'd met Bel Szerb.'

'Bel who?'

'Szerb. At least, that's how I knew her. I think she got married again. She was a dead scream, Bel was.'

'She still is.' After impressing on her that she must nag Declan to apply for a college course, I rang off. The washing had finished its cycle so I hung it over the bath, packed a bag and made my way to William Square and Tom O'Mara.

When I got out of the car, Peter Maxwell was going down the steps to his flat with several files under his arm. He wore jeans, a thick check shirt and a donkey jacket. He grinned at me through the railings. 'Hi! Fancy a coffee and a chocolate bicky?'

'I wouldn't mind.' His laid-back, easy-going manner was welcome after James's histrionics.

His flat was completely different from next door: red-tiled floor, red curtains and white walls hung with abstract paintings. It was a man's room. Apart from the paintings and a single white-shaded lamp, there were no other ornaments and the furniture was minimal, mainly of natural wood. Two armchairs were upholstered in black and white check. The effect was cool and airy, tranquil, giving the impression that the occupant was at peace with himself, which I envied.

'This isn't a bit like Flo's,' I remarked. Another difference was that everywhere was warm due to the two large radiators, one at each end of the room.

'I know. I'll just put the kettle on.' He took off his coat, hung it behind the door and disappeared into the kitchen. When he came back, he said, 'I used to see your auntie at least once a week. It was my job to get rid of the bottles.'

'What bottles?'

He grinned. 'The sherry bottles. She didn't want Charmian, the binmen and that aged but gorgeous red-head to know how much she was drinking. Flo was knocking back more than a bottle a day over the last year. She was a nice old girl, though. I liked her.'

'I only saw her once, at another great-aunt's funeral.'

'I wish I'd known you two were related. Flo would have been tickled pink to know we'd been in the same class at school.' He disappeared into the kitchen again, returning with two mugs of coffee and a packet of Jaffa cakes. 'I'm a lousy house-husband. I'm afraid my cupboards are bare. I hope you've eaten.'

'I keep forgetting to eat.'

He ran his fingers through his beard, which already looked like an untidy bird's nest, and said thoughtfully, 'I'm sure there's a tin of corned beef and a packet of instant spuds out there. I'll knock you up a plate of corned-beef hash if you like?'

'No thanks.' I shuddered. 'That's one of my mother's favourite dishes. It would remind me too much of home.'

'I used to feel like that about *Coronation Street*,' he said. 'Me mam never missed a single episode, and the house had to be dead quiet. You daren't sneeze else you'd get a belt around the ear. For years afterwards if I passed a house and heard the music I got goosebumps.'

We stared at each other and laughed. 'Memories, eh!' he said wryly.

At the end of the room, I noticed there were French windows leading to the tiny yard.

'I had them put in last year.' He looked quite houseproud. 'It's nice to have them open in summer, brightens up the place no end. That's how I met Flo. We used to gab to each other over the garden wall.'

'Does that mean you actually own this flat? It's not rented?' I said, surprised.

'I own about a quarter, the building society has the rest.'

'I can't imagine anyone choosing to live round here if they didn't have to,' I said incredulously.

'How dare you criticise my place of abode, Miss Cameron?' he said mildly. 'I love Toxteth. I've been broken into twice, but that can happen anywhere.

The people round here are the salt of the earth, including the girls who hang around the square. Okay, so it's violent, but otherwise it's a good place to live, steeped in atmosphere and history. This is the closest to how Liverpool was when it was the greatest port in the world. And did you know that, centuries ago, Toxteth was a royal park where King John used to hunt deer and wild boar?'

'I'm afraid that piece of information has been denied me until now.'

'If you like, I'll take you on a tour one day, show you precisely where his hunting lodges were situated.'

'I *would* like – it sounds fascinating.'

He looked chuffed. 'Then it's a date.'

I stayed for another cup of coffee before going next door. A scantily clad Fiona was shivering against the railings. To my surprise, she deigned to speak. 'There's been someone looking for you. She said she'd come back another time. It wasn't Bel or Charmian. It was someone else.'

'Thanks for telling me.'

Fiona yawned. 'Any time.'

As usual the air in Flo's flat smelt damp, and it was freezing cold. I turned the fire on full blast and knelt before the hissing jets, shivering and rubbing my hands, thinking enviously of Peter Maxwell's central heating. When the heat became too much, I retreated to my favourite spot on the settee and promptly fell asleep. It was nearly midnight when I woke up and my legs were covered with red blotches from the fire. Everywhere was still and quiet outside and the flat felt as if it was in a time warp, engulfed in flickering shadows and divorced from anything real.

My life's becoming more and more surreal, I thought. I scarcely ate, slept at the most peculiar times, spent hardly any time at home, and had lost interest in my job, though I still worked hard and hoped George hadn't noticed. Worst of all, I was having an affair with a man who was the epitome of everything I normally loathed about men. Things that had once seemed important, no longer mattered.

I went into the bedroom and changed into a nightdress, Flo's quilted dressing-gown, and her pink slippers, then sprayed myself with perfume ready for Tom, who might arrive at any minute. Until he came, I'd sort out a few more of Flo's papers.

With a sense of anticipation usually reserved for the start of a film or a television programme I was looking forward to, I settled in front of the bureau. The first thing I picked up was a bundle of letters from Bel sent during the war. It didn't seem proper to read them so I put them to one side in case Bel would like them back.

Next, a large, very old brown envelope with 'Wythenshaw's Photographic Studios – Portraits a Speciality' printed on the top left-hand corner. Predictably, it contained a photograph and, as I pulled it out, I wondered why Flo hadn't put it on the table with the others. It was a school photo: five rows of children, the smallest ones sitting cross-legged at the front. A boy at the end of the front row, the only child not smiling, had been circled with pencil.

What on earth was Flo doing with a photo of our Declan? I looked at the back, but there was only a stamped date, September 1945, a third of a century before Declan was born. There was something else inside the envelope, a piece of yellowing paper folded into four. It was a crude, crayon drawing of a woman with sticks for limbs, yellow hair and gooseberry green eyes. Her mouth was a huge upwards red curve, and she wore a blue dress shaped like a triangle with three buttons as big as Smarties down the front. Underneath was printed, in a careful, childish hand, 'MY FREND FLO'. There was a name at the bottom written in pencil: Hugh O'Mara.

Tom's father must have done the drawing I held in my hand. Despite the stick limbs and the mouth that stretched from ear to ear, there was something undeniably real and alive about the woman, as though the youthful artist had done his utmost to convey the inward radiance of his friend Flo. That both items had been together in the envelope meant that the child in the photograph was almost certainly Hugh O'Mara. I would have loved to have shown it to Tom, but Flo must have had a reason for keeping the photo hidden, and it seemed only right to respect it.

Tom had arrived – I could hear his light footsteps, and forgot about photographs, forgot about everything, as I waited for the sound of his key in the door. He came prowling in, a graceful, charismatic figure, despite the tasteless electric blue suit and white frilly shirt. No words were spoken as we stared at each other across the room. Then I got up and walked into his arms and we began to kiss each other hungrily. It was less than twenty-four hours since we'd parted, yet we kissed as if the gap had been much, much longer.

Another bouquet arrived at the office next morning, this time pink and white carnations. I found a vase and put them in the reception area. 'Diana's late.' June remarked. 'I thought she would have called by now.'

When she still hadn't arrived by midday, George approached me. 'Should I ring to see if she's all right? I'm still annoyed with her, but I suppose she's had it rough lately, and it wouldn't hurt to let her know we're concerned.'

'Would you like me to do it?'

'I was hoping you'd take the hint.' He looked relieved.

When I dialled Diana's home there was no reply. 'Perhaps her father's been taken to hospital again,' I suggested.

George had already lost interest. 'Can I buy you lunch?' He jingled the coins in his pocket. 'I'm desperately in need of a shoulder to cry on. I had a letter from Bill this morning. He and Annabel will stay with me over Christmas but, reading between the lines, I could tell they'd sooner not. They're only coming because their mother's off somewhere exotic with her new husband – his name's Crispin, would you believe?'

'I'm sorry, George, but I'm lunching with my sister, and I've an appointment at the Old Roan with the Naughtons at half past two. Perhaps tonight, after work?'

'You're on,' George said glumly, as he mooched into his office. 'I think I'm about to have a panic attack.'

Trudy had phoned earlier. 'Mum said you'd gone to William Square last night, but you weren't there when I called. That girl draped around the railings, is she what I suspect she is?'

I confirmed that she definitely was.

'Will you be there tonight if I come at the same time? I need to talk to someone and there's only you.'

'I'm not sure when I'll get away,' I said quickly. It was selfish, but I didn't want my sister in Flo's flat, which I regarded as my own property until the place was ready for another tenant – which seemed further away than ever. 'Are you free for lunch?' I enquired. 'My treat.'

'I thought you always worked through lunch?'

'I won't today,' I promised.

We met in Central Precinct under the high domed glass roof, where a woman was playing old familiar tunes on a white grand piano, her fingers rippling languorously up and down the keys. Trudy was already seated at a wrought-iron table, looking very smart in a dark green jacket, long black skirt and lace-up boots. We made a pretty pair, the Cameron sisters, I thought wryly: elegant, with our nice clothes, discreetly made-up faces, and lovely ash blonde hair. No one glancing at us would have guessed at our wretched childhood, though Trudy's face was rather pinched and tight, I thought.

'I've never been here before,' she said, when I sat down. 'I love the pianist.'

'Have you noticed what she's playing?' The strains of 'Moon River' came from the piano. 'Mum's favourite.'

Trudy's laugh was rather strained as she rubbed the scar above her left eyebrow. 'There's no escape, is there?'

When I returned from the counter with prawn salads and two giant cream cakes, she said, 'I've just been thinking about the way Mum used to sing it when us kids had been knocked black and blue, and Dad had probably had a go at her.'

'It was her way of coping, I suppose.' I ate several prawns with my fingers – it was my first proper meal since Sunday. 'What did you want to talk about, Sis?' I was reluctant to rush her, but I had to meet the Naughtons in an hour's time.

Trudy was shoving her food around the plate with her fork. 'I don't know where to begin,' she muttered.

'The beginning?'

'That's too far.'

I raised my eyebrows. 'I don't understand.'

My sister threw her fork on to the plate with a sigh. 'It's Colin,' she said.

A knot of fear formed in my stomach. 'What's he done?'

'Nothing,' Trudy said simply. 'He's a good, decent man. I love him, and he loves me, and he adores Melanie and Jake. He works all the hours God sends for us.'

'Then what's the problem, Trude?'

'I don't trust him.' Trudy put her elbows on the table and regarded me with abject misery.

'You mean you think he's having an affair?'

'Of course not. He wouldn't dream of it.' Trudy shook her head impatiently. 'It's nothing to do with affairs. It's to do with the children. Oh, Lord!' She dabbed her eyes with the paper napkin. 'I'm going to cry. Have I smudged my mascara?'

'A bit.' I reached out and rubbed under her eyes. A woman at the next table was watching with interest, but turned away when she saw I'd noticed.

'It's my painting, you see.' Trudy sighed. 'There must be two hundred bottles, jars, decanters and demijohns in the shed, all finished. I've painted light-bulbs, plates, tumblers, brandy glasses – we get them from car-boot sales. The children think it's great, looking for glassware for Mum to paint. And I love doing it, Millie. I get quite carried away, thinking up new ideas, new patterns, and I can't wait to see how they'll turn out. But what am I supposed to do with the damn things?' she said plaintively.

'Sell them,' I said promptly. I still hadn't grasped what the problem was. 'Didn't Colin suggest you have a stall and he'll look after the kids?'

'Yes. But I don't trust him, Mill. I feel terrible about it, but I don't trust him with me children for an entire day. I'm scared he'll hit them, and if he did I'd have to leave.'

I was beginning to make sense of things. 'Has he ever done anything to make you think he would so much as lay a finger on them?' I asked.

'*No!*'

'In that case, don't you think you're being a bit paranoid?' I said. 'More than a bit, in fact. Over-the-top paranoid, if you ask me.'

'I know I am. But I still can't bring meself to leave them. Colin's nagging me soft to start a stall. There's a church hall in Walton where they have a craft fair every Sunday. He can't understand why I keep putting it off.'

'Neither can I. Our father wrecked our childhood, and now you're letting him wreck your marriage. You've got to trust Colin, Trude. You've *got* to.' Even as I spoke, I recalled James, his fist raised . . . 'I think all of us are capable of violence when the chips are down, but only a very perverted person would hit children the way our father hit us.'

Trudy gnawed her bottom lip. 'I must admit I've smacked Jake's bottom once or twice. He can be a little bugger when he's in the mood.'

'Was Colin there?'

'Yes. He was ever so cross and said I must never do it again.'

'But he didn't leave!' I cried. 'And knowing your history – that children who've been abused often abuse their own children – it's *him* who should be worried about leaving Melanie and Jake with *you*! Think how upset you'd be if you thought he suspected you'd hurt them! He's always trusted you, and he deserves your trust. Start the stall now in case he guesses why you're putting it off. He might never forgive you if he does.'

Trudy began to attack her salad. 'I'm glad I talked to you, Sis. I never looked at it like that before.' She paused, a forkful of prawns halfway to her mouth. 'I wonder if Dad was hit when he was little?'

'That's something we'll never know.'

I thought about it later on the way to the Old Roan. The only feelings I'd ever had for my father were fear as a child, and loathing as I grew older. But could there have been a reason for his behaviour? For the first time in my life, I wondered if a badly damaged human being could be lurking inside the monster I'd always known.

The Naughtons found the garden of the property in Old Roan much too big, and I drove back to work irritated by the waste of time.

When I went in, George announced 'Diana's father's dead. She called earlier. He passed away peacefully in his sleep during the night.'

'How did she sound?'

'As hard as nails,' George said indignantly. 'You'd think she was calling to say her car wouldn't start.'

'She's putting it on. I reckon she's devastated.'

'You're an exceedingly charitable person, Ms Millicent Cameron. Anyway, the funeral's Friday afternoon.' He drooped. 'I suppose I'd better put in an appearance, represent the firm, as it were.'

'Do you mind if I come with you?'

'Mind? Of course not. I've rarely had a more welcome offer.'

Later, I called my mother with the news – she was always ghoulishly interested in hearing about a death. 'How old was he?'

'A good eighty,' I replied. 'Diana's parents were middle-aged when she was born.' I decided to change the subject. 'I met our Trudy for lunch.'

'That's nice, luv,' Mum said. 'I like it when you two get together.'

'Perhaps the three of us could have lunch one day, you and me and Trude. You'd love the restaurant, Mum.'

'Oh, I dunno, luv,' she said, flustered. 'I'd never get back in time to do your dad's tea.'

I assured her she'd have bags of time and my father needn't know anything.

'I'll think about it,' she promised.

'You'll have to do more than think, Mum,' I said. 'I'm going to badger you rotten till you say yes.'

There was a pause. 'You sound happy, Millicent. Has something nice happened? Has James proposed?'

'James is history, Mum. Perhaps I'm happy because I've just had lunch with my sister.'

'Whatever it is, luv, I'm glad. You were getting very hard. Not long ago, you wouldn't have dreamed of asking your mam out to lunch. Now, what's all this about James being history?'

Apart from George and me, there were only five other mourners at the funeral: Diana, stiff and unemotional, two women neighbours, and two old men who'd been friends of Diana's father.

It was a bone-chilling November day and a wind flecked with ice blew through the cemetery, whisking in and out of the gravestones, stripping the last few leaves off the trees.

'I didn't think people got buried any more,' George muttered, through chattering teeth. 'I thought they popped 'em in an oven. At least it'd be warmer for the mourners.'

I watched the coffin being lowered into the grave, then the vicar said a few respectful words, and Diana came over and thanked us for coming. I took her hand as we walked towards the cars, George trailing behind.

'I'm sorry about your father. At least he didn't suffer much pain.'

'No, and as everyone keeps saying, he had a good innings.' Diana removed her hand. 'You get over these things. From now on, I'll be able to live my life as I please.'

'If you need someone to talk to,' I said gently, 'then don't hesitate to ring. If I'm not there, I'll be at number one William Square. There's no phone, so you'll just have to turn up.'

'Thank you, Millie, but I'm fine. I can't understand people who go to pieces when somebody dies.'

2

Church bells pealed, nearby and far away, high-pitched and rippling, deep-toned and sonorous. I opened my eyes: a cold sun shimmered through the white curtains, and Tom O'Mara was leaning over me. His brown hair was loose, framing his long face. If it hadn't been for the earrings and the tattoo, he would have resembled one of the saints in the pictures I'd taken down.

'I was just wondering,' he said, 'what is it between us two?'

'I don't know what you're talking about.'

'I mean, the truth is, you're an uppity bitch, full of airs and graces, and your accent gets on me wick.'

My lips quivered as I traced the outline of the heart on his chest. 'I've always steered clear of your sort, and the way you speak sets my teeth on edge.'

He pulled the bedclothes down to my waist and buried his head in my breasts. 'So, what is it between us two?' he asked again. His lips fastened on my left breast, and I squealed in delight when his tongue touched the nipple.

'I haven't a clue,' I gasped truthfully. The deep-down feeling of intimacy was frightening, because I couldn't visualise there ever being an end. The bells were still ringing as we made love, and it wasn't until it was over that I said, 'Why are you still here?' He'd usually gone before sunrise and Flo's alarm clock showed almost half past nine.

'Me wife's taken the girls to see her mam. I thought we'd spend the day together, or at least part of it. I've got to be at the club by five.'

I was thrilled at the notion of spending the day in bed with Tom O'Mara, but he had other ideas. 'C'mon, let's have summat to eat and we'll be off.'

'Off where?' I sat up and blew the hair out of my eyes. Tom was getting dressed.

'Southport.'

'Why Southport?'

'I'll tell you later, after we've had some grub.' He pulled on a blue polo-neck sweater, and went over to the mirror, where he combed his hair and scooped it back into a ponytail with an elastic band. I watched, entranced. It was such a feminine gesture coming from such an overwhelmingly masculine man. 'Me stomach thinks me throat's been cut,' he said. 'I'm starving.'

'There isn't any "grub", as you call it, except for a few old packets of biscuits.'

He groaned. 'In that case, I'll just have a cup of tea and we'll get something to eat on the way. The pubs'll be open by then.'

The sun was as bright as a lemon, and little white clouds were chasing each other across the pale blue sky. The wind was dry and crisp and very cold. I stuffed my hands in the pockets of my tan overcoat, glad that I was wearing boots – after the funeral yesterday I'd gone home for some warm clothes.

Tom's car, a silver-blue Mercedes, was parked round the corner, a suede coat on the back seat. I remarked that he was taking a risk, leaving an expensive coat in full view. 'Someone might steal it.'

'It would be more than their life was worth.' His lips curled. 'Everyone knows whose car this is. They wouldn't dare touch it.'

'You sound like a Mafia godfather!' The words were meant as an insult, but Tom's face was impassive as he replied, 'No one's going to rip me off and get away with it, and the same goes for me friends and family. That's why Flo was always safe in her place. People round here know what's good for them, and that means not mucking around with anything belonging to Tom O'Mara.'

'I see.' The ominous message that lay beyond his words was repellent, yet I didn't hesitate to get into the car with him. I felt very aware of his closeness, the way he held the steering wheel, his long brown hand touching the gear lever.

'What are you looking at?' he asked.

'You. I haven't seen you in daylight before.'

He slid a disc into the CD player and a man with a hard, angry voice began to sing 'The Wild Rover'. 'I love Irish music,' he said. Then he looked at me in a way that made me catch my breath. 'You look great in daylight.' He started up the engine and steered aggressively into the traffic. 'But you're doing me head in, girl. I wish I'd never met you.'

We stopped at a pub in Formby, the first customers of the day. Tom demolished a mixed grill, while I forced myself to eat a slice of toast. As soon as he'd finished, I poured us a second cup of coffee, and said, 'Now will you tell me why we're going to Southport?'

'I thought you'd like to meet me gran.'

I looked at him, startled. 'Your paternal grand-mother?'

'What the hell does that mean?' he almost snarled.

'Is it your father's mother?'

He banged the cup down on the saucer. 'Christ! You talk like a fuckin' encyclopaedia. It's me dad's mam, Nancy O'Mara, eighty-six years old, as fit as a fiddle, but completely gaga.'

The nursing-home was a large, detached house in a quiet road full of equally large houses, all set in spacious, well-tended grounds. The décor inside was subdued and expensive, the floors thickly carpeted in beige. The fees must have been horrendous, and I assumed it was Tom who paid.

The smiling woman in Reception toned perfectly with her surroundings: beige suit, beige shoes, beige hair. When she saw Tom, the smile became a simper. The barmaid in the pub had looked at him in the same way.

'How's me gran been?' he enquired abruptly.

'Just the same,' the woman gushed. 'Sometimes she seems very aware of what people say to her, but in the main she lives in a world of her own. We persuade her to do her exercises every day and she's in remarkably good shape for a woman of her age. She's in the garden, which is no place for an old lady on a day like today but there's no arguing with Nancy. We just wrap her up and let her go.'

Tom led the way through to the rear of the house where a door opened on to a vast lawn. On the far side, a woman was sitting ramrod stiff on a wooden bench. She looked tiny beneath the fir trees that towered over the garden on three sides, so thick that not even the faintest glimmer of sunlight could get through.

She watched our approach with interest, ebony eyes flashing brilliantly in her hawk-like, liver-spotted face. Snow-white hair, with streaks of black, was piled in a bun as big as a loaf at the nape of her stringy neck. She wore a crimson coat and fur-trimmed black boots. A black lace stole was draped around her shoulders.

'Have you come to read the meter?' she enquired, in a hoarse, deep voice, when Tom sat down beside her. He motioned to me to sit the other side.

'No, Gran. It's Tom, and I've brought a friend to see you. It's no good introducing you,' he whispered. 'She wouldn't take it in.'

'There's no need to introduce her,' Nancy said unexpectedly. 'I know who she is.' She fixed the glittering eyes in their dry brown sockets on me. 'Oh, yes! I know who she is.'

'Who am I, then?' I felt uncomfortable, slightly afraid, under the woman's piercing gaze.

Nancy cackled. 'That would be telling!' Her long face became fretful. 'The chap hasn't been to read the meter in ages. One of these days, they'll cut the 'leccy off.'

'Stop worrying about the meter, Gran. Everything's all right. It's all been seen to.' Tom's attitude to his grandmother was tolerantly offhand. He hadn't kissed her, and seemed to be there out of a sense of duty, rather than affection.

A woman in a grey cotton frock and a white apron was coming towards us with a tray of tea-things. Nancy grabbed it eagerly, apparently capable of pouring the tea, heaping sugar in all three cups. We were drinking it in silence when I noticed that one of her dangling jet earrings had caught in the stole. I leaned over to unhook it, but was shrugged away with a sharp, 'Don't touch me!'

I made a face at Tom. 'I don't think she likes me.' I was hoping we wouldn't stay long. The garden was a melancholy place, cheerless and dark, the only sound was the dew plopping from the trees on to the thick, wet grass. It was doubtful that the old woman appreciated visitors. I'd hoped to get from her a feeling of the past, of the woman who'd been married to Tommy O'Mara when he'd lost his life on the *Thetis* in 1939, but it was impossible to imagine Nancy being young.

Tom said, 'Gran's never liked anyone much. The only person she ever cared about was me dad.' He glanced at his watch. 'We'll go soon. I don't mind paying the bills, but visiting bores me rigid. I only come once a month to keep the nursing staff on their toes. I don't want them thinking they don't have to look after her proper.'

For the next quarter of an hour, I did my awkward best to engage Nancy in conversation. I admired her coat, asked who did her hair, remarked on the weather, enquired about the food. It was hard to make out whether the old woman was merely being cussed when she didn't answer, or genuinely didn't understand.

'You're wasting your time,' Tom said eventually. 'Sometimes she catches on if you talk about the things she used to know, like the war, or the shops in Smithdown Road.'

'I can't talk about either.' Of course there was the *Thetis*, but under the circumstances that mightn't be a good idea.

'C'mon let's go.' Tom squeezed Nancy's shoulder. 'Tara, Gran. See you next month.'

We were half-way across the lawn, when a hoarse voice called, 'Hey, you.' We turned to see her beckoning.

Tom gave me a little push. 'It's you she wants.'

'Are you sure? Why should she want me?' I went back reluctantly, and got a fright when a hand came out and grabbed me painfully by the arm, pulling me downwards until our faces were almost touching. I could smell the fetid breath. 'I know what you're up to, Flo Clancy,' she said, in a voice that sent shivers of ice down my spine. 'But it won't work. Your Martha gave him to me fair and square. He's mine. You'll not get him back, not ever. I've told you before, I'll kill him first.'

'She's making a hole for her own back,' said Bel.

'A rod,' corrected Charmian. 'She's making a rod for her own back, or she's digging herself into a hole. You've got your sayings mixed up.'

'Tch, tch!' Bel snorted loudly. 'She knows what I mean.'

'Would you mind not talking about me in the third person?' I said mildly. 'Furthermore, it's none of your business who I go out with. I can make a hole for my own back if I like.'

'Rod,' said Charmian

'Rod, hole, whatever.' I waved a dismissive hand. I supposed it was inevitable that Tom O'Mara's regular visits to the basement flat wouldn't go unnoticed. When he had dropped me off after we got back from Southport Bel had been watching from Charmian's window to witness my folly.

'Fiona said he'd been in and out, but I didn't believe her.' Bel made no secret of her disapproval. 'Young 'uns nowadays,' she said disgustedly, 'they hop in and out of bed with each other like rabbits. I've only slept with three men in me life, and I married 'em all first.'

'Yes, but times have changed, Bel,' Charmian reminded her. She gave me a wink as she refilled the glasses, though even Charmian looked worried. 'I hope you don't mind me saying this, Millie, but Tom O'Mara's got a terrible reputation. It's not just women but all sorts of other things – drugs, for one. I wouldn't go near that club of his. It worried me to death when our Jay invited him to his twenty-first. I don't think Flo could have known the things he was up to.'

As the evening wore on, my irritation with the pair diminished in proportion to how much I drank. By the time we'd finished a bottle of sherry and started on another, the last, I didn't give a damn what anybody thought. I lay on the rug in front of the fire staring up at the faces of my friends, feeling extraordinarily happy and without a care in the world. 'He's a scoundrel,' I agreed, 'a villain, a good-for-nothing rogue. But he's also drop-down-dead gorgeous.'

'What's happening with poor James?' Bel demanded.

I thought hard, but couldn't remember. Before I could say anything there was a knock at the door and I said, 'Perhaps that's him now.' I walked unsteadily to the door and for several seconds couldn't recognise either of the small, clearly distressed women standing outside.

'You said it was all right to come,' a familiar voice said.

'Of course.' I blinked, and the two women merged into one: Diana, a different Diana from the one I'd always known, with uncombed hair and no makeup, her face white and shrivelled, like melting wax. I asked her in, trying not to sound too drunkenly effusive, and introduced her to Bel and Charmian, adding, because it was obvious that she was in a terrible state. 'Diana's father died last week. He was only buried the day before yesterday.'

Bel, who was over-effusive even when she was sober, jumped to her feet and took the new arrival in her arms. 'You poor girl! Sit down, luv – here, have my place on the settee. Oh, I bet you're feeling dead awful. Charmian, fetch the girl summat to drink. Millie, plump that cushion up and stick it behind her.'

Diana burst into tears. 'I've felt so alone since he died. The house is like a morgue,' she cried. 'I wanted someone to talk to.'

She was eaten up with guilt and anxious to share it. The words came pouring out in a plaintive, childish voice, nothing like her usual terse, clipped tones.

She'd always blamed her father for the fact that she'd never married, she sobbed. 'He said he was sorry. He took the blame but it wasn't his fault at all. No one's ever asked me to marry them. I was using poor Daddy as an excuse for being single, for having to stay in night after night, when I only stayed in because I had nowhere else to go. I'm a total failure as a human being, and it's nobody's fault but my own.'

'Don't be silly, luv,' Bel soothed. 'You stayed with your dad, didn't you? That was very kind and unselfish.'

But Diana wailed, 'I think he wanted to be rid of me so he could have his friends round for bridge. When I came home from university, he offered to buy me a flat. I refused. I told myself it was my duty to stay but I was terrified of being on my own. Then I complained so much about his friends that he stopped asking them. It was me who ruined his life, not the other way round.'

'You're exaggerating,' I said, in what I hoped was a sober, sensible voice. 'I'm sure it wasn't as bad as that.'

'It was,' Diana insisted tearfully.

'In time, you'll see things more reasonably,' Charmian said gently. 'I felt dead guilty when me own mam died. I wished I'd been to see her more often, that I'd been a better daughter.'

Having exhausted the subject of her relationship with her father, Diana turned to her job. She was worried about losing it. George didn't like her, no one did. She'd never fitted in. 'Daddy's gone, and if my job goes, too, I think I'll kill myself.'

'George sometimes gives the impression of being an ogre, but he wouldn't dream of firing you,' I assured her, adding, though I wasn't convinced that it was true, 'He regards you as an asset to the firm.'

At ten o'clock, Herbie came down to demand the return of his wife, and

Charmian went reluctantly upstairs. Bel muttered that it was time she was making tracks.

'I suppose I'd better go, too,' Diana sighed, 'though I dread the thought of spending another night on my own.'

'Come home with me,' Bel said instantly. 'I've got a spare bedroom. I can make the bed up in a jiffy.'

'Can I? Oh, Bel! You're the nicest person I've ever known.' Diana threw her arms around Bel's neck and looked as if she might easily cry again.

Nancy had said, 'I know who she is. Oh, yes, I know who she is.' She had taken me for Flo. They must have known each other, all those years ago. Was Nancy aware that Flo had been in love with her husband? And what did she mean when she said, 'Your Martha gave him to me fair and square. You're not getting him back. I'll kill him first.'

It didn't make sense, but perhaps that wasn't surprising coming from an elderly woman who'd lost her mind. Even so, Nancy must have had a reason for saying it.

I took the newspaper cuttings describing the last days of the *Thetis* over to the bureau and placed them alongside the school photo with the child who looked so much like Declan. Beside the photo, I put Hugh O'Mara's drawing of 'MY FREND FLO'. I looked thoughtfully from the cuttings to the photo to the drawing, then back again. The *Thetis* had gone down in June 1939, the photo had been taken six years later and the little boy was in the bottom class, which meant he must have been five and born in 1940. 'Your Martha gave him to me fair and square.' Flo had left instructions that Gran wasn't to be invited to her funeral. What had she done to make Flo hate her so much?

'Your Martha gave him to me fair and square.'

I felt my heart begin to race as I peered closely at the face of the little boy. He was a Clancy, no doubt about it, the same pale hair, slim build, Declan's sensitive features.

Suddenly, everything fell into place. Tommy O'Mara had been the child's father, but his real mother had been Flo. Somehow, Gran had given the baby to Nancy, against Flo's wishes, or she wouldn't have wanted him back. 'I've told you before, I'll kill him first,' Nancy had said.

It meant that Tom O'Mara and I were distant cousins. Tom had the Clancys' green eyes.

Poor Flo! I glanced around the basement room, at its fussy ordinariness, the flowers, lace cloths, abundant ornaments. When I'd first come, it had seemed typical of a place where a pleasant, but rather dull, unmarried woman had lived out most of her life. But as I'd discovered more about Flo, the atmosphere in the room had changed. There was the Flo who'd received those passionate love letters during the war; the woman who'd stayed in the Isle of Man with a man with a foreign name. The flat no longer seemed ordinary, but touched with an aura of romance and a whiff of mystery. This was where a twenty-year-old Flo had come when she was already a mother, but a mother without a child. Now, tragedy was mingled with the romance.

Yet, despite everything, Flo might have been happy. I would never know.

There was a box of drawing-pins in the bureau. I shook some out and pinned the drawing to the wall over the mantelpiece. Flo might have wanted to put it there herself fifty years ago.

The following Tuesday was unusually quiet at Stock Masterton. George went out at midday and hadn't returned by six. Darren and Elliot took the opportunity to leave early, and shortly afterwards June went home. Only Oliver and I were left.

He stretched his arms and yawned. 'I suppose one of us had better stay till George comes back.'

'Where did he go?' I asked.

'He didn't say. He got a phone call and went rushing off.'

'I'll wait,' I offered. Oliver had a long journey home through the Mersey tunnel to a remote village on the Wirral.

'Thanks, Millie.' He gave me a warm, grateful smile. 'You're a chum.'

Oliver had only been gone a few minutes when the light on the switchboard flashed to indicate there was a call. I was astonished to discover an angry Bel at the other end of the line. 'Is that woman there?' she barked.

I assumed she meant Diana, who'd been staying with her since Sunday. 'No, she hasn't been in since her father died. I thought she was with you?'

'She was until this morning,' Bel said. 'She seemed much better when she got up. I went to get us a nice chicken for tea but when I got back she'd upped and gone. Not a word of thanks, no tara, nothing!' she finished, with a high-pitched flourish.

'Perhaps she's coming back,' I suggested. 'She's gone home to collect something.'

'In that case she should have left a note – and it doesn't take five hours to get to and from Hunts Cross.' A loud indignant snort echoed round the empty office. 'Honest, Millie, me ears are numb from listening to her go on and on about bloody Daddy. I'm an ould softheart, me, and I didn't mind a bit, but I'm dead annoyed to think she's just scarpered. She ate me out of house and home. Me freezer compartment's nearly empty!'

'I'm sorry, Bel. I don't know what to say.' If Diana had been there, I could have easily strangled her for treating Bel so rudely. 'Why not come round to Flo's tonight for dinner?' I offered in an attempt to soothe her feelings. 'It'll be a takeaway, mind, from that Chinese place round the corner.'

'Me favourite's sweet and sour pork, and I really go for those little pancakes with roots in.'

'By the way, I found a bundle of letters in the bureau from you to Flo. I thought you might like them to read.'

'No, ta, luv,' Bel said firmly. 'Flo offered them to me once, but I said no to her too. I'm happy now, but I was happier when I wrote them. I'd sooner not be reminded of the ould days. Just chuck 'em out. See you later, luv.'

It was nearly seven by the time George strode into the office. 'I'd like a word with you, Millie,' he snapped, as he passed my desk and went into his cubicle.

Somewhat bemused by his tone, I followed, and was even more bemused when he nodded towards a chair, 'Sit down.' It seemed very formal. People usually sat down without waiting for an invitation.

George placed his arms on the desk and clasped his hands together, his expression grave and accusing. 'I don't think much of the way you treated Diana when she came to you for help,' he said coldly.

I heard the creak of my dropping jaw. 'I haven't the faintest idea what you're talking about.'

'Apparently she called at William Square, as you had invited her to do, desperate for someone to talk to, urgently in need of a shoulder to cry on . . .'

'That's right.' My voice shook. I was at a loss to understand what was wrong.

'But instead of help,' George went on, 'all she found was you and two other women all pissed out of your minds. Not only that, you quickly got her in the same drunken state as yourselves. Even worse, the poor girl was virtually kidnapped by a ghastly old woman who wouldn't let her go. She's been stuck in this woman's dismal little house for days. She rang just before lunch and I was forced to go and rescue her. I found her shaking, crying, and in a terrible state.'

I burst out laughing. 'Rescue her! Don't be so bloody stupid, George. Bel's anything but ghastly. In fact, Diana said she was the nicest person she'd ever met. Also, she's about seventy-five – a bit old to kidnap someone less than half her age, wouldn't you say?' It wasn't worth adding that although I'd never been in Bel's house I imagined it would be anything but dismal.

But George's face grew colder, if that was possible, and he said, 'I've never pulled rank, Millie. I've always treated my employees as equals, friends. I do, however, own this firm, and take exception to being called stupid by someone whose wages I pay.'

But he *was* being stupid! Diana had fooled him completely, putting on an act so outrageous that I marvelled at her nerve. I said nothing, just sat there, stunned, contemplating her treachery. She'd used us – me, Bel, Charmian – to rid herself of the guilt she'd felt over her father's death. Then she'd probably felt ashamed of having told so much and turned against us, possibly worried I'd tell George or the others in the office the things she'd said when she bared her soul.

'Oh, and another thing, Millie, I'd prefer it if you didn't refer to me in public as an ogre.'

'But I didn't . . .' I began, then remembered that I had. 'I didn't mean it in an offensive way.' I wanted to explain why I'd used the word, but it would probably be a waste of time at the moment. Just now George's mind was made up. It would be sensible to wait until he was able to see sense again, then put him right. 'Where is Diana now?' I asked.

'My place,' he said briefly. 'The poor girl's still very tearful. She's been through a lot lately. Her father dying was bad enough, but you and your friends only made it worse.'

'That's not fair, George,' I felt bound to say. 'If you think about it hard enough, you'll know it's not fair. Diana's having you on.'

For the first time, he looked straight at me and there was a trace of comprehension in his eyes. Then he blinked furiously and said, 'I'd better be getting back. I've promised to take her out to dinner.'

He strode out of the office, a knight on a white charger returning to his damsel in distress. I understood what had happened. His wife and children no longer needed him, his mother was dead, he was a man with no call on his emotions. Diana had got through to the part of him that longed for someone to cherish and protect.

When I sat down at my desk my legs were shaking, my mind a whirl. It was all so unreasonable, so unjust. I picked up the telephone, badly in need of someone sympathetic to talk to. Colin answered when I called Trudy and said she was out. 'She's taken Melanie and Jake to see *101 Dalmatians*. By the way, her bottle stall will be up and running on Sunday. She was going to call you.'

'I'll be there,' I promised.

Then I rang Mum. I couldn't explain what had happened, it would only upset her, but at least she would be a friendly voice. To my dismay, when the receiver at the other end was picked up my father reeled off the number. He always sounded mild, rather genial, on the telephone and it was hard to connect the pleasant voice with the man I knew. I didn't waste time with small talk. 'Is Mum there?'

'She's in bed with a touch of flu.'

'Oh!' I was temporarily flummoxed. 'Oh, well, give her my love and say I'll come and see her tomorrow after work. I'd come tonight, but I've promised to meet someone at Flo's.'

'All right, luv. How's things with you?'

'Fine,' I said brusquely. ''Bye.'

Bel would be only too willing to provide sympathy in buckets, though I wouldn't mention anything about kidnapping, or she was quite likely to burst a blood vessel.

3

'It's only me, Mum,' I called, as I ran upstairs. I found her propped up against a heap of pillows looking sleepy, but pleased with herself.

'Hello, Millicent.' She smiled when I went in and planted a kiss on her plump, pasty cheek. 'I'm all on me own. Your dad's gone to the pub and Declan's round at a mate's house.'

'How do you feel? I've been worried about you all day.' Halfway through the morning, I had wondered suddenly if flu was the real reason for her being in bed. Maybe my father had been up to his old tricks again.

'There's no need to worry, luv.' The contented smile was still there, enough to convince me that my suspicions were unwarranted. 'I'm really enjoying lying here and being waited on. Our Declan's been looking after me, and Trudy came this afternoon with some grapes. Now you've brought a lovely bunch of carnations, me favourite.' She buried her nose in them. 'They smell dead gorgeous. It's nice to know me children care about their mam. I even got a get-well card from Alison, though I don't suppose it was her idea to send it. I had to ring up on Sunday and say I couldn't go. The bug had already caught up with me by then, and I didn't feel up to the drive.'

'You should have rung, Mum. I would have come before.'

'I didn't want to bother you, Millicent. I know you're always busy.'

'Oh, Mum!' I stroked her brow, which felt rather hot. 'You've got a temperature,' I said, with a frown

'The doctor's given me some tablets. Look what the women in the shop sent.' She pointed to a little wicker basket of dried flowers on the bedside table next to Alison's card. She seemed far less bothered about being ill than that everybody had been so kind. 'Mrs Bradley from next door keeps bringing bowls of home-made soup. The potato's nice and tasty, but Declan ate the onion.' She giggled girlishly. 'I might be sick more often if this is the sort of treatment I can expect. Your dad's even brought a cup of tea up twice. I think he's a reformed character.'

'Don't bank on it, Mum.'

'I won't, luv. Look!' She patted her stomach. 'I've lost weight. This nightie would hardly go round me before but now it's dead loose. I used to be slim as a girl, just like you.'

'I know. Your wedding photo's downstairs.'

'That's right. I'd like to be slim again by the time I move to Oxford.' She giggled again. 'Start a new life with a new figure.'

I stared at her anxiously. Her expression was as innocent as a baby's. She'd lived under the iron hand of her husband for thirty years and had no idea how to cope with the world outside – how to deal with landlords other than the council, for instance, and the social-security people could easily convince her she wasn't entitled to a penny. 'Are you still set on that idea, Mum?'

'Oh, yes, luv.' She smiled radiantly. 'I'm looking forward to it, not just seeing our Alison more often but living on me own. I thought I might go back to nursing. They say the National Health Service is understaffed.'

'Nursing!' I gasped. 'I never knew you'd been a nurse.'

'I was halfway through training to become state-registered when I married your dad.' She sighed. 'I was sorry to give it up.'

'You should have finished your training, then got married,' I said indignantly.

'Life doesn't always go the way you want it, Millicent.'

'I suppose not.'

There was a noise downstairs. 'Jaysus!' she gasped, terrified. 'I hope that's not your dad back! I hope he hasn't heard.'

But it was only Scotty, bored with being left alone and looking for company. He came bouncing up the stairs and leaped on to the bed, settling himself comfortably between Mum's legs. He pushed his nose between her knees and looked at her adoringly.

'How's Flo's place coming along?'

'I'm nearly there,' I lied.

Mum laughed. 'Oh, come off it, luv. I don't know what you're up to but I've been to Flo's, remember? You can't kid me it takes six or seven weeks to sort out a one-bedroom flat.'

'Oh, Mum!' I slipped off my shoes and sat in my father's place on the bed. It was time I told her the truth. I took my mother's white hand, threaded with startling blue veins. 'I love it there, and I'm having a great time. I've met all sorts of interesting people. You already know Bel, then there's Charmian and Herbie upstairs, a young man next door who comes from Kirkby and was in my class at school, and . . . well, this other guy who knew Flo.'

'Bel used to be very glamorous.'

'She still is.'

'So you haven't done a thing,' Mum said, smiling.

'We've drunk all Flo's sherry and I've cleared out her bureau – well, almost. Otherwise, the place is no different from the first day I went.'

'Have you been paying the rent?'

'No, Mum.' I'd remembered to ask Charmian when the rent collector called. He came monthly, she said, and had been twice since Flo died but had never mentioned the basement flat. Next time he came Charmian had promised to ask about it. 'Flo must have paid several months in advance,' I told Mum. 'So far, I haven't come across a rent book.'

'I'd love to see the place again,' she said wistfully. 'See if it's changed much.'

'Come next week, Mum.' I couldn't keep the flat to myself for ever. 'Come one evening when I can show you round. The weekend would be even better. There's a takeaway round the corner. I'll buy more sherry and we can have a feast. Bel would love to meet you again, and you'll like Charmian.'

Mum squeezed my hand. 'I'll come as soon as I'm better. Now, I'm in a lovely hazy daze, all them tablets. I hope you won't mind if I go to sleep in front of you.'

'I'll make myself a cup of tea when you do.'

We talked in a desultory way about Declan: he'd had a form from a college, had filled it in and sent it off. Wasn't it smashing Trudy having her own stall? 'I hope I'm well enough to go by Sunday,' Mum said sleepily.

When her head began to droop I released her hand. I stayed where I was for a while, glancing round the dismal room. Years ago, Mum had painted all the furniture cream to make it look like a matching set, but she hadn't rubbed the varnish off underneath and the paint had started to peel. Perhaps she'd like that lovely stuff in Flo's bedroom, which I coveted – except that she was moving to Oxford. Where on earth did she get the courage from even to think of changing the course of her life at fifty-five? I sighed, got off the bed, adjusted the pillows and drew the bedclothes up to her shoulders. There was no heating upstairs and the air smelt cold. Scotty, also asleep by now and snoring gently, gave a little grunt when the eiderdown beneath him was disturbed.

Downstairs, I put the kettle on and stood watching until it boiled. It felt strange being in this house, danger-free, able to do anything I wanted. Yet I still felt on edge, scared I might break something or put something down in the wrong place. I poured the water into the pot, stirred it to make the tea strong, then took a cup into the lounge. The fire was dying, the hearth full of ash. I threw on a few more coals and watched them slowly catch alight. On the right-hand side of the fireplace an owl made out of string was hanging from a nail that protruded crookedly from the wall. Dad's best belt had hung there once, the one he wore on Sundays: black leather, two inches wide, the heavy brass buckle with a deadly sharp prong. I touched the owl gingerly: such an innocuous thing to put in its place.

The back door opened and my father came in. I was still fingering the owl. 'This is where you used to keep your belt,' I reminded him.

His face flushed a deep, ugly scarlet, but he didn't speak. How did he feel, I wondered, now that his children had grown up and we could see him for what he was? Was he ashamed? Uncomfortable? Embarrassed? Or perhaps he didn't give a damn.

I looked at him, properly for once, and tried to relate the handsome, shambling, probably drunken figure to the photo of the bright-eyed baby at Flo's, but it was inconceivable to think that they were the same person. My gaze returned to the owl. 'You nearly blinded our Trudy with that belt.'

He'd been lashing out at Trudy, the skirt of her gymslip scrunched in a ball in his hand. When she tried to get away, he dragged her back so violently by the collar of her school blouse, that she'd choked and lost consciousness. He probably hadn't meant the buckle to hit her forehead, narrowly missing her eye, but Trudy had been left with a permanent reminder of the incident every time she glanced in the mirror.

My father looked at me, bleary-eyed and bewildered. He still didn't speak.

'Mum's asleep,' I said. 'Tell her goodbye from me.'

He spoke at last. 'Did she seem all right to you? I've been worried. She's had a terrible temperature.' His voice was gruff and querulous.

'I think she'll live.' Could it be that he actually *loved* my mother? That he loved us all? I took my cup into the back kitchen and washed it, then left by the back door without saying another word.

Mrs Bradley was leaning on next door's gate talking to another woman. 'How's your mam, luv?' she asked. She was smartly dressed in a sequinned frock and the gigantic fur coat that she wore when she went ballroom dancing with Mr Bradley.

'She seems much better.'

'That's good,' Mrs Bradley said comfortably. 'I was just saying to Norma here how much better everywhere looks without that wreck of a car littering the place.'

Not only had the burnt-out car gone, but the boarded-up house was occupied. There were lace curtains in the windows and a television was on in the lounge.

'We got a petition up and sent it to the Council, didn't we, Norma?' Norma nodded agreement. 'What right have some folks got, spoiling the street for the rest of us? It's a respectable place, Kirkby. I remember us moving from Scotland Road in nineteen fifty-eight. It was like a palace after our little two-up, two-down. Will was tickled pink to have a garden.'

I went over to my car, unlocked the door and paused for a moment. Mrs Bradley and Norma were still talking. Mr Bradley came out, a thick car coat over his old-fashioned evening suit. He waved and I waved back.

Still I waited by the car, the door half-open. For the first time, I noticed the pretty gardens. Some of the original front doors had been replaced with more ornate designs, heavily panelled with lots of brassware. There were coachlamps outside several houses. It dawned on me that there was nothing wrong with Kirkby! It was all in my head, all to do with my childhood, my father, school. I'd centred my loathing on the place when it was my life that was wrong!

'What's up with George?' June demanded, for the umpteenth time. 'He's been like a bear with a sore head this week.'

Elliot swung his well-shod feet on to the desk. 'Perhaps he's going through the male menopause.'

'I reckon he's missing Diana.' Darren grinned.

Everyone except me hooted with derision, and Oliver said miserably, 'She'll be back on Monday, spreading her usual discord and as moody as hell.'

'Actually,' June hissed, 'I didn't say anything before in case I was hearing things, but Diana rang George this morning and when I put her through I could have sworn he called her darling.'

There was a gasp of disbelief.

'Never!'

'I don't believe it!'

'You must have been hearing things, June.'

It figures, I thought. She's managed to wrap him round her little finger. I was glad no one seemed to have noticed that it was me, more than anyone, on whom George vented his bad temper. One day, I'd tried to explain that I'd done nothing wrong, but he was only interested in Diana's version of the story.

What on earth would it be like when she returned? Awful, I decided. She'd be lording it over everyone, particularly me. I wondered if I should look for another job, but my only qualification was a single A level, along with the time spent working at Stock Masterton. Would another estate agent take me on with such a paltry record? I tried to tell myself that it didn't matter, but in my heart of hearts I knew it did. The time I spent at Flo's, the nights with Tom O'Mara, were bound to end sometime, and I'd have to live in the real world again, where my job mattered very much. I had a mortgage, I had to eat. And if I left this job, I'd have to return the car.

Taking advantage of George's absence, Darren and Elliot went home early, followed shortly by June. I suggested that Oliver make himself scarce and I would stay until six in case there were any phone calls: the office closed an hour earlier on Saturday. Oliver accepted the offer thankfully. 'We're in the middle of decorating. I'd like to get it done by Christmas.'

The door had hardly closed when it opened again. I looked up, thinking Oliver had forgotten something.

'I've been waiting across the road for everyone to go,' said James. 'I was praying you'd be the last.'

Over the past few weeks I had almost forgotten James's existence, and was surprised at how glad I was to see the tall, familiar figure; so glad that, for the moment, I put to the back of my mind what had happened the last time we met. He wore a new suit, grey flannel, and a pale blue shirt, and was leaning against the door regarding me shyly.

'Hi,' I said.

'Phew!' He put his hand on his chest in a gesture of relief. 'I was expecting to have something thrown at me – a computer, a telephone, a notebook, at least.' He came down the room and perched on the edge of Diana's desk. 'How's life?'

'Ninety per cent fine, ten per cent lousy.'

'Tell me about the lousy ten per cent.'

I'd always been able to talk to him about humdrum, day-to-day matters.

We spent ages discussing the meaning of a film we'd just seen, what frock I should wear to a party, his job, mine. It would have been a waste of time trying to talk to Tom O'Mara about office politics or Mum being ill, Trudy having a bottle stall or Declan going to college. Perhaps that was why I was so pleased to see James – not as a lover but as a friend.

I told him all about the week's events, and about Diana's treachery. 'Now George is really cross with me and I think I've blown my job.'

'But that's totally unfair!' James expostulated angrily.

It was comforting to hear Diana being called a conniving bitch and that George was a fool to let himself be taken in. I felt better after listening to James's loudly expressed indignation and didn't demur when he offered to buy me dinner.

'Shall we go to the wine bar where we first met?'

'I'd prefer to try that new place by the Cavern.' I didn't want to go somewhere that evoked old memories in case he got the idea that everything was back to normal, which it wasn't. 'I'll just ring home, make sure my mother's all right.'

Declan answered and assured me that mum was fine.

'Say hello to Declan for me.' James mouthed.

'James says hello, Declan.'

'I thought mam said James was history?'

I laughed. 'Bye, love.' I took a mirror out of my handbag, powdered my nose, combed my hair, retouched my lipstick. When I looked up James was watching me with an expression on his rugged face that I remembered well. Our eyes met, he shook his head slightly, as if remonstrating with himself, then turned away. 'I'm sorry,' he said. 'I'm doing my best not to put a foot wrong. I promise not to say a word out of place until the time feels right.'

I began to regret accepting the dinner invitation because I knew I would never feel the same about James after what had happened, but I hadn't the heart to change my mind when he was being so nice.

The restaurant was filled with memorabilia of the Beatles' era. We ordered salad, baked potatoes and a bottle of wine. While we waited, I asked, 'How's the Socialist Workers' Party?'

He looked faintly embarrassed. 'I never went back – it's not really my scene. They were a decent crowd, but I only joined to please you.'

'To please me! I can't remember ever expressing left-wing opinions,' I exclaimed. 'I'm totally uninterested in politics.'

'So am I, though those dockers got a raw deal and I'm on their side. No, I joined because I got the impression you thought I was shallow. I was trying to prove I had some depth.' He glanced at me curiously. 'Did I succeed?'

'I don't know.' I shrugged. 'I never thought about it much.'

'I doubt if you ever thought about me much,' he said drily.

'You promised not to say things like that,' I admonished.

'I'm not criticising,' he assured me. 'I'm trying to be coolly matter-of-fact. I pressurised you too much. I fell in love with you, deeply, passionately, wholeheartedly, and expected you to love me back in exactly the same way at exactly the same time. I wasn't prepared to wait. I wouldn't let you breathe.' He made a face. 'I'm used to getting everything I want, you see.'

'Including girls throwing themselves at you since you were fifteen!' I reminded him.

'Aw, shit, Millie.' He cringed. 'I'd had too much to drink, and I'd been waiting all week for you to call. I couldn't believe it was over between us.'

I played with my food. 'You nearly hit me, James. You would have, if Tom hadn't appeared.'

His face flickered with pain. 'So that's his name.' He leaned across the table, put his hand on mine, then hastily removed it. 'I would never, never have hit you, darling.'

There, in such civilised surroundings, it was easy to believe that he was a decent, honourable man who'd been driven over the edge. If I could feel about him as he did about me, everything would be perfect. He began to eat, but only because the food was there. 'This Tom,' he said, in a strained voice, 'are you in love with him?'

'No.'

'Is he with you?'

'No.'

'Who is he? How did you meet?'

'He was a friend of Flo's.' I smiled. 'She had an affair with his grandfather.'

'So, history is repeating itself.'

'Something like that.' I sipped the wine, which seemed preferable to the food. 'Look, can we change the subject?' I felt uncomfortable discussing my current lover with my old one.

'Perhaps that wouldn't be a bad idea.' James sighed. 'I'm trying valiantly to be grown-up but I think I'm about to explode with jealousy.'

We left the restaurant, the meal hardly touched but the wine finished, and strolled down Water Street towards the Pier Head. After a while, I linked James's arm. 'I'd like us always to be friends,' I said.

'Only a woman would ask a man who was crazy about her to be her friend,' he said with a dry chuckle.

'What would a man do in the same situation?' I asked.

'Run a mile, change his phone number, move house if necessary. If some woman had been chasing me as vigilantly as I was chasing you, I would have done all three in order to get away. You were very patient, Millie.'

The nearer we got to the river, the colder and more sharply the November wind blew. With my free hand, I tried to turn up the collar of my coat. James stopped, released my arm, and did it for me. 'I was with you when you bought this coat. You couldn't make up your mind whether to buy this colour or black. I said I preferred black, so you bought the other.' Still holding the collar by its corners, he said softly, 'Is that really all that's left for us, Millie, to be friends?'

'James . . .'

He released my collar and tucked my arm back in his. 'Okay, friends it is. Am I allowed to ask if I can see you again within the relatively near future?'

'Perhaps one night next week?'

We dodged through the traffic towards the Pier Head, where we propped our arms on the rail and stared at the lights of Birkenhead, reflected, dazzling, misshapen blobs, in the choppy waters of the Mersey.

'You know,' James said softly, 'we see movies about great love affairs that make us conventional folk seem very run-of-the-mill. We never imagine ourselves having the same passionate feelings as the characters on the screen, yet over the last few weeks, no one could have felt more gutted than I have. I was convinced I'd rather die if I couldn't have you.'

I said nothing, but shuddered as the wind gusted up my skirt.

James stared intently at the lights, as if the words he wanted to say were written there, prompting him. 'I wished I were a philosopher, who could cope with things more . . .' he grinned, '. . . more philosophically. Or a spiritual person, who would look at it with an intellectual sort of fatalism. But I don't go to church, I'm not even sure if I believe in God.'

'Did you come to a conclusion?' I asked gently.

'Yes – that I didn't want to die after all. That life goes on, whatever horrendous things might happen.' He grinned again. 'And that I still love you as much as I ever did, but less frenetically. Even so,' he finished, on a mock-cheerful note, 'I could easily throttle this Tom character.'

It had started to rain, so we walked back quickly to where my car was parked. On the way, he asked what was wrong with my mother.

'Flu. She's almost better.'

'I was always kept well hidden from your family. I only met Declan by accident. Were you ashamed of me or something?'

'Of course not, silly. It's them I was—' I stopped. All of a sudden I didn't care if he knew every single thing there was to know about me. 'Actually, James, my sister's having a stall at a craft market tomorrow. Perhaps you'd like to come if you're free.'

I was back at Flo's, going through the remainder of her papers. For the first time, I felt the urge to hurry things along, to finish with the bureau, get started on the rest of the flat. I emptied out the contents of a large brown envelope. Guarantees, all of which had run out, for a variety of electrical goods. I stuffed them back into the envelope and threw it on the floor. The next item was a plastic folder containing bank statements. I leafed through them, hoping they would give a clue to how the rent was paid. If Flo had set up a standing order, it would explain why the collector hadn't called, and also why there'd been little in the post – no electricity or gas bills, no demand for council tax. I admonished myself for being so negligent. I should have done this long ago, got in touch with the bank, sorted out Flo's financial affairs.

To my surprise, the account was a business one, begun in 1976 according to the first statement. The current balance was – my eyes widened – *twenty-three thousand, seven hundred and fifty pounds, and elevenpence.*

'Flo Clancy!' I gasped. 'What the hell have you been up to?'

I grabbed the next envelope in the rapidly diminishing pile. It was long and narrow and bore the name of a solicitor in Castle Street, a few doors along from Stock Masterton. My hands were shaking as I pulled out the thick sheets of cream paper folded inside, the pages tied together with bright pink tape. It was a Deed of Property, dated March 1965, written in complicated legal jargon that was hard to understand. I had to read the first paragraph three times before it made sense.

Fritz Erik Hofmannsthal hereinafter referred to as the party of the first part of Number One William Square Liverpool hereby transfers the leasehold of the section of Number One William Square hitherto known as the basement to Miss Florence Clancy hereinafter referred to as the party of the second part currently resident in the section of the property which is to be transferred for a period of one hundred years . . .

.No wonder no one had called to collect the rent! Flo owned the leasehold of the flat in which she'd spent most of her life. My brain worked overtime. Fritz Erik Hofmannsthal! It was Fritz's laundry where Flo had worked; Mr and Mrs Hofmannsthal had spent a weekend on the Isle of Man every month for over twenty years.

'Oh, Flo!' I whispered. I went over and picked up the snapshot taken outside the laundry nearly sixty years before; Flo, with her wondrous smile, Mr Fritz's arm around her slim waist.

I had no idea why I should want to cry, but I was finding it hard to hold back the tears. I felt as if I knew everything there was to know about Flo Clancy: the lover lost on the *Thetis*, the baby who had gone to another woman, the servicemen she'd made love to in this very flat. Now Mr Fritz . . .

Yet the more I knew, the more mysterious Flo became. I wanted to get under her skin, know how she felt about all the tragedies and romances in her life, but it was too late, far too late. Not even Bel knew the things that I did about her lifelong friend. I'm glad it was me who went through her papers, I thought. I'll never tell another soul about all this.

Of course, I'd have to tell someone about the money and the property. It dawned on me that, under the circumstances, Flo would almost certainly have made a will.

Curious, I was about to go back to the bureau, when the front door opened and Tom O'Mara came in, his face, as usual, sombre and unsmiling, and looking like a dark, sinister angel in a long black mac.

I caught my breath, and half lifted my arms towards him as he stood staring at me from just inside the door. 'I'm neglecting the club because of you,' he said accusingly, 'neglecting me family. You're on me mind every minute of every day.' He removed his coat and threw it on the settee. 'You're driving me fucking crazy.'

'I'll be finished here soon, then I'll be back in Blundellsands. You won't want to come all that way to see me.'

'I'd come the length of the country to be with you.'

I wanted him to stop talking, to take me in his arms so that we could make love. I forgot about James, about Flo, Stock Masterton. All I wanted, more than anything on earth, was for Tom O'Mara to bury himself inside me.

Tom shook himself, gracefully, like a cat. 'I think I'm in love with you, but I don't want to be.' He wiped his wet brow with his hand. 'I feel as if I'm under a spell. I want to keep away from you, but I can't.'

'I know,' I murmured. I didn't like him, I couldn't talk to him, he was hard, unsympathetic, a crook. But I felt drawn to him as I'd been drawn to no man before.

We made love in a frenzy, without tenderness, but with a passion that left us both speechless and exhausted. When I woke up next morning, Tom was still asleep, his arm around my waist. I wanted to slip away, escape, because I was frightened. Instead, I turned over and stroked his face. His green eyes opened and stared into mine and he began to touch me. We were locked into each other. There was no escape.

Flo

1962

Sally and Jock's son, Ian, died as he had lived; quietly and bravely and without a fuss. He was sixteen. The funeral took place on a suffocatingly hot day in July and the crematorium chapel was packed. The mourners stood and knelt when they were told, their movements slow and lethargic, a sheen of perspiration on their faces, their clothes damp. There were flowers everywhere, their scent sweet and sickly, overpowering.

Flo was at the back, fanning herself with a hymn book. She hated funerals, but who in their right mind didn't? The last one she'd been to was for Joanna and Jennifer Holbrook. Joanna had passed away peacefully in her sleep, and the following night her sister had joined her. But at least the twins had managed more than four score years on this earth, whereas Ian . . . She averted her eyes from the coffin with its crucifix of red and white roses. The coffin was tiny, because he'd grown no bigger than a ten-year-old and every time she looked at it she wanted to burst into tears.

She wished she'd asked Mr Fritz or Bel to come with her. She knew hardly anyone except Sally and Jock. Grace, their daughter, was a cold, aloof girl, who'd always resented the care and attention bestowed upon her invalid brother. She was in the front pew next to her dad, looking bored and not the least upset. She wasn't even wearing dark clothes, but a pink summer frock with a drawstring neck.

The woman on Grace's other side, who was kneeling, her head buried in her hands, must be melting in that black, long-sleeved woollen frock, she thought. Then the woman lifted her head and whispered something to the girl.

Martha.

Oh, Lord! She looked like an ould woman, her face all wizened and sour. She might well have achieved the coveted title of Mrs before her name and a lovely daughter but, if her expression was anything to go by, it had done nothing to make her happy. Or the nice new flat in Kirkby that she'd moved into a few years ago when Elsa Cameron had stuck her head in the gas oven and ended her tragic life. Perhaps happiness was in the soul, part of you, and it didn't matter what events took place outside. Some people, Martha was one, were born to be miserable.

'I'm happy,' Flo told herself. 'At least on the surface. I make the best of things. I'm happy with Mr Fritz, and me and Bel still have a dead good time, even though we're both gone forty – but I don't half wish we were twenty years younger. I'd love to go to the Cavern, I really would, and see them Beatles lads in the flesh.'

She was vaguely aware of someone genuflecting at the end of the pew. Then the person knelt beside her and whispered, 'Hello, Flo.'

'Hugh!' She flushed with pleasure and patted his arm. He was twenty-three and, as far as Flo was concerned, the finest-looking young man on the planet: tall, slender, with a gentle face, gentle eyes and the sweetest smile she'd ever seen. His hair had grown darker and was now a dusky brown, only a shade lighter than his father's, though it wasn't curly like Tommy's. He was mad about music and haunted the Cavern; she always listened to the charts on the wireless so she could talk to him on equal terms.

'I thought you couldn't get off work?' she said softly. He'd served an apprenticeship as an electrician and worked for a small firm in Anfield.

'I told them it was a funeral. They couldn't very well refuse. Ian was me friend, he taught me to play chess. Anyroad, I promised Kate I'd come.' He nodded towards the front of the church, and a girl in the row behind Sally and Jock turned round as if she'd sensed someone was talking about her. She had the Clancys' green eyes and silvery hair, and Flo had the strangest feeling she was looking at her younger self in a mirror.

So, this was Kate Colquitt. She'd been at St Theresa's Junior and Infants' school when Flo last saw her, that hulking great lad, Norman Cameron, never far from her side. Sally was right to say she'd grown into a beautiful young woman. Kate twitched her lips at Hugh, almost, but not quite, in a smile, because this was, after all, a funeral. The man kneeling next to her must have noticed the movement. He twisted round and gave Hugh a look that made Flo's blood curdle, a look of hate, full of threats, as if he resented his companion even acknowledging another man's existence.

Norman Cameron, still watching over Kate like an evil guardian of the night.

Everyone stood to sing a hymn: 'Oh, Mary, we crown thee with blossoms today, Queen of the Angels and Queen of the May.' It wasn't May and wasn't appropriate, but it had been Ian's favourite.

Flo saw Norman Cameron find the page for Kate, as if she was incapable of finding it for herself. She felt concerned for the girl, although she hardly knew her. Sally said Norman wanted them to get married and Martha, anxious as ever to meddle in other people's lives, was all for it. Kate had managed so far to hold out. She was working at Walton hospital as an auxiliary and wanted to become a State Registered Nurse.

'Norman's had a terrible life,' Sally had said, only a few weeks ago. 'No one could have had a worse mam than Elsa, yet the poor lad was inconsolable when she topped herself. I feel dead sorry for him. But he makes me flesh creep, and he's so much in love with Kate it's unhealthy. You'd think he owned her or something.'

'She should find herself another boyfriend,' Flo said spiritedly. 'Try and break away.'

'I reckon Norman would kill any man who dared lay a finger on her.'

'Lord Almighty!' Flo gasped.

The hymn finished, the priest entered the pulpit and began to speak about Ian. He must have known him well because his words were full of feeling: a bright, happy lad who'd borne his illness with the patience of a saint and had almost made it to adulthood due to the selfless commitment of his parents. The world would be a sadder and emptier place without Ian Wilson. Heaven, though, would be enriched by the presence of such a pure, unsullied soul . . .

Flo switched off. Any minute now, he'd start telling Sally and Jock that they should feel privileged their child was dead and had gone to a better place, where he was, even now, safely in the arms of God.

The priest finished. Flo buried her head in her hands when it was time for them to pray. The soft whisper of the organ came from the grille in the wall, the sound gradually growing louder, but not enough to hide a slight whirring noise. Flo peeped through her fingers and saw the curtains behind the altar open slowly and the coffin slide out of sight. The curtains closed and there was an agonised gasp from Sally as her son disappeared for ever. Jock put an arm around her shoulders, and Flo imagined the little curling red and blue flames licking the coffin, spreading, meeting, then devouring it and its precious contents, until only the ashes remained.

'Don't cry, Flo.' Hugh offered her his hanky.

'I didn't realise I was.' She pushed the hanky away. 'You look as if you might need it yourself.'

The service over, they went outside, where the heat was almost as great as it had been in church. When everyone stood round the display of flowers, which were laid out on the parched grass, the blooms wilting rapidly in the hot sunshine, Flo kept to the back. She could see her own wreath, irises and white roses, and would have liked to look for the flowers that Bel and Mr Fritz had sent, but didn't want to come up against Martha, particularly not today.

Hugh was talking to the bereaved parents. He shook hands with Jock and kissed Sally's cheek, very grown-up, very gentlemanly. Nancy O'Mara had raised him well. If she'd been there, she would have felt as proud as Flo. He came over. 'I have to be getting back to work.'

'I'll be going meself in a minute, after I've had a word with our Sally.'

He looked surprised. 'I thought you'd be going back to the house.'

'You're not the only one who has to be at work.'

'In that case,' he said, trying to sound casual, 'I'll give you a lift part of the way.' He had a car, his pride and joy, a little blue Ford Popular.

'That'd be nice, luv. Ta.'

What was she supposed to say to Sally? 'I'm dead sorry, Sal. I feel terrible for you. He was a lovely lad. I don't know how you'll cope without him.' After a few stumbling phrases, she threw her arms around her sister. 'Oh, Lord, Sal, you know what I mean.'

'I know, girl.' Sally nodded bleakly, then grabbed Flo's arm. 'Sis, I want you to do something for me.'

'I'll do anything, Sal, you know that.'

'Make things up with our Martha.' She shook Flo's arm impatiently. 'There's enough misery in the world without adding to it when there's no need. Martha would be overjoyed if you two were friends again.'

Flo glanced at Martha, who was talking to her daughter, Norman Cameron a dark shadow by her side. They weren't exactly a happy family group, but the mother and daughter relationship was there for all to see. Then she looked at Hugh, waiting, hands in pockets, for his 'friend' Flo, and she felt a sense of loss as vivid and painful as the morning she'd woken up and discovered her son had been taken away. Martha hadn't just stolen her son, she'd stolen her life.

Very gently, she removed her sister's hand. 'Anything but that, Sal,' she said.

'I'll miss Ian,' Hugh said, when they were in the car. He smiled shyly. 'I'll miss Kate, too. She was often there when I went to see him. It was the only place she went without Norman Cameron in tow.'

'D'you fancy her, luv?' They would make a perfect couple, Flo thought excitedly. The Catholic Church forbade relationships between cousins, though marriage might be possible with a dispensation. But as neither Hugh nor Kate were aware that they were related, there would be no need for the Church to become involved.

His pale cheeks went pink. 'She's okay.' He'd had several girlfriends, all of whom Nancy had disliked on sight. 'You'd think I was royalty or something,' he'd grumbled to Flo. 'She doesn't think any girl I bring home is good enough for me.'

Flo was inclined to agree, though where Nancy was concerned she always kept her opinions to herself.

Hugh dropped her off in Lime Street. 'See you soon, Flo, perhaps tomorrer.'

It was too nice a day to sit on a bus and Flo decided to walk home. She was in no hurry. Although she'd told Hugh she should be at work, her shift didn't start until two. A few years ago, when launderettes had sprung up all over the place and White's Laundry saw their work trickle away to almost nothing, Mr Fritz had closed the place down. Then he had opened a chain of launderettes, six in all, and put Flo in charge of the biggest, an ex-chandler's shop in Smithdown Road, less than a mile from William Square.

'Hello, gorgeous!' A man, quite good-looking, was standing in front, blocking her way.

'Hello . . .' She stared at him, frowning, before realising that he was a stranger trying to pick her up. 'I thought I knew you,' she said, exasperated.

'You could, very easily. I'd certainly like to know you.'

'Get lost,' she said, but smiled as she dodged past. It was flattering to think that at forty-two she could still attract men. She caught a glimpse of her reflection in the windows as she walked up Mount Pleasant. She never wore black, apart from skirts, and Bel had loaned her a frock for the funeral; very fine cotton with short sleeves and a sunray-pleated skirt. The wide belt made her already slim waist look tiny. She hadn't put on an ounce of weight with age. When they went on their regular visits to the Isle of Man, Mr Fritz complained that she looked no more than thirty. People would think he was spending a dirty weekend with his secretary.

'We're not married, so it is a dirty weekend.' Flo giggled.

He looked horrified. 'Flo! Our weekends together have been the most beautiful times of my life. Nevertheless,' he grumbled, 'all the other guests probably think they're dirty.'

Flo offered to dye her hair grey and draw wrinkles on her face, but he said that wouldn't do either. 'I rather enjoy getting envious glances from other men.' There was no pleasing him, she said.

She passed the women's hospital where Nancy O'Mara had recently had a hysterectomy. Hugh, the dutiful son, had gone to see her after work every night. On the way home, he sometimes called in at the launderette. He usually popped in at least once a week.

'How's Mrs O'Mara?' she asked. It sounded silly, but she could never bring herself to refer to Nancy as his mam.

'Progressing normally, according to the doctor.'

During the time he'd been at secondary modern school, she'd thought she'd lost him. Until then, he'd got into the habit of sticking his head round the door of the laundry on his way home from St Theresa's, just to say hello. When he changed schools, she had the good sense not to wait for him outside when she went to the bank on Fridays, reckoning an eleven-going-on-twelve-year-old in long trousers wouldn't be seen dead playing ball in the Mystery with a woman almost twenty years his senior.

'Where's your little friend?' Mr Fritz asked, after Hugh hadn't shown his face in months.

'He's at a different school and comes home a different way,' Flo explained, doing her best not to appear as cut up as she felt about it.

'That's a shame. I'd grown quite fond of him.' He gave Flo a look full of sympathy and understanding, as if he'd guessed the truth a long time ago.

The months became years. She saw Hugh once when he was fourteen. He was on his way home with a crowd of lads who were kicking a tin can to each other on the other side of the road. She was glad his collar was undone, his tie crooked, that he looked an untidy mess. She was even glad about the tin can. Nancy might not like it, but he'd found his place, he'd made friends, he was one of the lads. She felt a tug at her heart as she melted into a shop doorway out of sight. If only he was coming home to me!

Although Flo had a great time in the launderette – the customers came in with so many funny stories that her sides still hurt with laughter when she went home – she could never get her son out of her mind. She heard through Sally that he'd left school and begun an apprenticeship as an electrician. It wasn't what she would have chosen for him: she would have liked him to become something grander, perhaps even go to university.

It wasn't until almost five years ago, Christmas 1957, that she had seen Hugh again. The launderette was festooned with decorations, drooping in the damp. All afternoon she'd been pressing home-made mince pies and sherry on her 'ladies', as she called them – a few had even returned with more washing they'd scraped together because they'd had such a good time. The bench was full of women waiting for the machines to finish, and Flo was slightly tipsy, having drunk too many people's health when she wished them merry Christmas. Mr Fritz usually toured his six establishments daily to ensure that the automatic machines were working properly and not in need of his expert attention, but always ended up at Flo's because it had the nicest atmosphere. His brown eyes twinkled as he accused her of being in charge of a launderette while under the influence of alcohol. Just then the door opened for the hundredth time that day and he said, 'Why, look who's here!'

Hugh! A shy, smiling Hugh, in an old army jacket with a small khaki haversack thrown over his shoulder.

My son has grown up! She wanted to weep for all the years she'd missed. She wanted to hug and kiss him, to ask why he'd deserted his mam for so long, but merely smiled back and said, 'Hello, luv.'

'You've grown some,' Mr Fritz said enviously. 'You must be six foot at least.'

'Six foot one,' Hugh said modestly.

He never explained why he hadn't come before, why he'd come now, and Flo never asked. She guessed it was something to do with age, that between eleven and seventeen, he hadn't felt it proper for her to be his friend, but as he'd grown older something had drawn him back. She didn't care what it was. It was enough that he'd come, and continued to come, to tell her about his job, his girlfriends, how he was saving up to buy a car. Once, a few months ago, he had said, 'I wish me mam was a bit more like you, Flo. She thinks I'm crackers to want a car, but you wouldn't mind, would you?'

'I should have caught the bus,' she muttered, halfway home, when the straps of her high-heeled sandals began to dig into her feet. It would be a relief to reach William Square, where she'd have a nice cool bath before she went to work.

Stella Fritz would have a fit if she could see the square now. There was scarcely a house left that hadn't been turned into flats or bedsits and they all looked run down, uncared-for. Even worse, one or two women – Flo refused to believe they were prostitutes – had begun to hang around at night, apparently waiting for men to pick them up. Twice, Flo had been prop-ositioned on her way home in the dark, and Bel had threatened that if anyone else asked how much she charged, she'd thump them. There were frequent fights, which led to the police arriving. Mr Fritz moaned that the place was becoming dead rowdy, and Flo, who loved the square and never wanted to live anywhere else, had to concede that it had deteriorated.

She felt better after the bath and when she had changed into a pale blue cotton frock and canvas shoes. All afternoon, she couldn't get Sally out of her mind. On numerous occasions her ladies wanted to know what was wrong. 'You look as if you've swallowed a quid and shat a sixpence. What's up, Flo?'

If she told them about Ian, she knew what would happen: their great, generous hearts would overflow with sympathy, which would be expressed in flowery, dramatic language a poet would envy. She would only cry, she might possibly howl. She told them she was feeling out of sorts, that the heat was getting her down

Flo loved her ladies. They were coarse, often dirt poor, but they struggled through life with a cheerfulness of spirit that never ceased to amaze her. Through the door they would burst in their shabby clothes, which were usually too big or too small, too long or too short, carrying immense bags of washing. There were black ladies and white ladies, quite often grossly overweight because they existed on a diet of chip butties, but always with a smile on their careworn, prematurely old faces, making a great joke of their bunions and varicose veins, the swollen joints that plagued them, the mysterious lumps that had suddenly appeared on their bodies that they intended to ignore. 'I couldn't go in the ozzie and let them take it away, could I? Not with five kids to look after, and me ould feller propped up in the boozer all day long.'

It could be seven kids, ten kids, twelve. Most of the husbands were unemployed, and more than a few of Flo's ladies went out cleaning early in the morning or late at night. It was their money that paid the rent and put food on the table, but that didn't stop some husbands taking out their frustration with the government and society in general on their wives. Flo often found herself bathing bruises or bandaging cuts, cursing the perpetrators to high heaven.

But the women refused to listen to a word of criticism of their men – 'He couldn't help it, luv. He was stewed rotten. He wouldn't dream of hitting me when he's sober,' which Flo found an unsatisfactory explanation for her ladies' sometimes appalling injuries. She cosseted them, made them tea, laughed at their jokes, admired them. The only thing she refused was to let them do their washing on tick, which Mr Fritz had strictly forbidden. 'Before you can say Jack Robinson, they'll have run up a huge bill and we'll never get paid. No, Flo. They put their own coins in the machine and that's final. And if I find you've been loaning your own money, I'll be very cross indeed. They're a canny lot, and pretty soon you'll be subsidising washing for the whole of Toxteth.'

The thought of Mr Fritz being cross wouldn't have caused a tremor in a rabbit, but Flo was careful to take heed of his advice.

At seven o'clock on the day of Ian's funeral, it was a relief when she could turn the Open sign to Closed. Mr Fritz came and went, promising to have some iced tea ready for when she came home – he was obsessed with his new refrigerator. It would be another hour before all the machines were finished and she could tidy up and leave. The place felt like an oven. Perhaps that was why she had remained so slim: since she was thirteen, she'd spent a high proportion of her waking hours in the equivalent of a Turkish bath.

Bel had been promoted to manageress of ladies' outerwear in Owen Owens: long coats, short coats, raincoats, furs. She was frequently wined and dined by representatives of clothing firms who wanted her to stock their products. Occasionally, when Flo had nothing better to do, she would go to Owen Owens and listen while Bel dealt with a customer.

'Modom, that coat looks simply divine on you. Of course, Modom has a perfect figure, and red is definitely your colour.' The accent, Bel's idea of 'posh', and the voice, haughty yet obsequious, was stomach-churning. When the customer wasn't looking, Bel would make a hideous face at Flo, and mouth, 'Sod off!'

On her way home from the launderette, Flo let herself into her friend's flat in Upper Parliament Street, where Bel was lying on her luridly patterned settee wearing black satin lounging pyjamas and reading She. She looked up and grinned widely, the deeply etched laughter lines around her eyes and mouth adding yet more character to her already animated face. 'You look as if you've just been for a turn in one of your machines,' she said.

'I feel as if I have.' Flo threw herself into an armchair with a sigh. Bel's flat wasn't relaxing, more like a fairground with its bright walls and ceilings, and curtains that could do serious damage to the eyes. Still, it was nice to sit in a comfortable chair at last. 'I want you to promise me something, Bel,' she said.

'What, luv?'

'If I die before you, make sure I'm buried, not cremated. I want a few bits of me left to rise to heaven when the Day of Judgement comes.'

'Rightio, Flo,' Bel said laconically. 'I don't give a stuff what they do with me. Once I'm dead, they can throw me in the Mersey for all I care, or feed me to the lions at Chester Zoo.'

'Another thing, Bel. I've taken out an insurance policy to cover the cost of me funeral. It's in the first-aid box in the cupboard by the fireplace, the right-hand side. I'd put it in the bureau with all me papers, but you'd never find it. I can never find anything meself.'

'That's because you keep every single bit of paper that drops through your letterbox,' Bel snorted.

'It's a legacy from Stella Fritz. I always kept me bills in case she accused me of not paying the 'leccy, or something. Now I can't get out of the habit. Anyroad, when I'm looking for something, it's nice reading through me old letters. I've still got the ones you sent during the war. You can have them back if you like.' She didn't say, because Bel would have been disgusted, that it was quite interesting to look at old bills, see how much prices had gone up.

Bel grimaced. 'Thanks, but no thanks.'

'One more thing. Under no circumstances must our Martha come to me funeral. I'm not having it, d'you hear?'

'I hear, Flo, but why all this morbid talk about death and funerals?'

'I took the policy out years ago. It was this morning at the crematorium that I decided I'd sooner be buried.'

'Flo!' Bel's face was a tragedy. 'I'd completely forgotten about Ian's funeral. Was it awful, luv? How's your Sally taking it? Did the dress fit all right?'

'The dress looked simply divine,' Flo said tiredly. The expression had become a joke between them. 'As for the other, it was awful, yes. Sally's taken it hard, and so's Jock.'

'Shall we do something exciting tomorrer night, Sat'day, like go somewhere dead extravagant for a meal? It might cheer you up.'

'Sorry, Bel, but I'm going on retreat in the morning.'

Bel groaned. 'You're a miserable bugger, Flo Clancy. What do you do on these retreats, anyroad?'

'Pray,' Flo said virtuously.

'They're a waste of time – a waste of life!'

'I don't see you doing anything earth-shattering.'

'I've got an important job.'

'So've I.'

'I get taken out to dinner.'

'Mr Fritz takes me out to dinner sometimes.'

'He takes us both, so that's not counted.' Bel sat on the edge of the settee and rested her chin in her hands. She said, thoughtfully, 'Actually, Flo, it's well past the time you and Fritz got something going together.'

Flo laughed. 'I'm happy as I am, thanks all the same. Anyroad, it's well past the time you found yourself another husband.'

Bel ignored this. 'These damn retreats, I can't think of anything more boring and miserable than praying non-stop for two whole days.'

'Oh, I dunno,' said Flo. 'The thing is, I always come back feeling spiritually uplifted and enriched.'

2

'I can't understand it,' Sally said distractedly. 'It's as if Ian was the glue that kept us together.' She ran her fingers through her short, greying hair. 'But when did me and Jock need anything to keep us together? I love him, and I know he loves me. Remember the day we met him and his mate, Flo, on the New Brighton ferry?'

'I'll never forget that day, luv.' It was the last time she had seen Tommy O'Mara.

Her sister's marriage was falling apart. Grace didn't help. She accused her mam and dad of always having cold-shouldered her, of making her feel second best. 'Then me and Jock have a go at each other,' Sally moaned. 'I tell him it's his fault Grace feels the way she does, and he says it's mine.'

The only good thing to come out of the whole sad business was that the two sisters had become close again. Sally frequently turned up at the launderette just as Flo was closing, and they would walk back to William Square, arm in arm. Jock went to a social club in Kirkby almost every night – 'As if all he wants is to have a good time with his mates. I think I remind him too much of what we went through with Ian. He won't come with me to church.'

'I don't know what advice to give, Sal,' Flo said truthfully. She thought her sister spent far too much time in church, but preferred not to say so. 'Perhaps it's just a stage he's going through. He needs to let off steam. Jock's a good man at heart.'

'It's not advice I need,' Sally sniffed, 'just someone to talk to. Our Martha's come up with enough advice to write a book, from giving our Grace a good hiding to wiping the floor with Jock.'

'Both of which would do more harm than good.'

'That's what I said. Mind you, her Kate's been a great help. She often comes round to see me.' Suddenly Sally seemed to find a mole on the back of her hand enormously interesting. Without meeting her sister's eyes, she mumbled, 'I can't understand how our Martha ended up with such a lovely daughter, and we were landed with Grace. Oh!' she cried tearfully. 'Forget I said that. I love my girl, but I don't half wish she were different.'

'I wish all sorts of things were different, Sal.' Flo sighed. 'You must bring Kate round to see me sometime. I'd like to get to know her.'

She had never intended it to be this way, but it had all started the day she first saw Tommy O'Mara through a mist of steam in Fritz's laundry: Flo's life seemed to be divided into little boxes, each one carefully marked 'Secret'.

Martha and Sally knew this about her, Mr Fritz knew that. Hugh O'Mara thought he was her friend. No one knew about the servicemen during the war. There were her bogus 'retreats'. Bel, who thought she knew everything there was to know, knew virtually nothing, only that for a short time before the war she'd gone out with Tommy O'Mara.

Flo often worried that one day something might be said that would lift the lid off a box, give away one of her secrets, expose one of her lies.

It nearly happened the day Sally came to the flat, bringing Kate Colquitt with her. Bel was there, and they'd just watched *Roman Holiday* on television – Bel still went weak at the knees over Gregory Peck.

'This is Kate Colquitt, our Martha's girl,' Sally said.

Flo could have sworn that Bel's ears twitched. She still longed to know why Flo and Martha never spoke. 'Martha's girl, eh! Pleased to meet you, Kate. How's your mam keeping these days?'

'Very well, thank you.' The girl had a sweet, high-pitched voice.

'Why didn't you bring her with you?' Bel enquired cunningly. Flo threw her a murderous glance. Bel caught the look and winked.

Kate merely replied, 'Me mam doesn't know I've come.' She turned to Flo, green eyes shining in her lovely fresh face. 'I've always wanted to meet you, Auntie Flo. I saw you at Ian's funeral. I was going to introduce meself, but when I looked for you you'd gone.'

'Please call me Flo. "Auntie" makes me feel a bit peculiar.'

'Okay.' She followed her aunt into the kitchen when Flo went to make a pot of tea, chatting volubly. 'I like your flat, it's the gear. I'd love a place of me own, but me mam's dead set against it. She says I'm too young. How old were you when you came here, Flo?'

'Twenty.'

'There! Next month I'll be twenty-two. So I'm not too young, am I?' She looked at Flo, wide-eyed and artless.

'I was a very old twenty,' Flo muttered. An incredibly old twenty compared to this girl, who was too innocent for this world. She looked as vulnerable and defenceless as a flower by the wayside.

'There are times,' Kate sighed, 'when I'd love to be by meself. Y'know, read a book and stuff, watch the telly.'

Flo imagined her mother, Martha the Manipulator, never allowing her daughter a minute's peace. 'Why do you need a red bow in your hair when you're only going to see Josie Driver?' 'I'd sooner you didn't go out with a Protestant, Sal.' 'You've always got your head buried in a book, Flo Clancy.' And then there was Norman, which meant that Kate had two overbearing people to cope with, wanting her to do things their way. Sally said that he had moved to Kirkby and he was round at the house almost every night.

'Are you having a party on your birthday?' Flo asked brightly, as she arranged the cups and saucers on a tray.

'Just a few friends. You can come if you like.'

'Ta, luv, but I don't think that's such a good idea.' She picked up the tray. 'D'you mind bringing that plate of biscuits with you, save me coming back?'

'What happened between you and me mam, Flo?' Kate enquired earnestly. 'Auntie Sally says I'm not to mention I've been to see you. It must be something awful bad.'

Flo chuckled. 'That's something you need to ask your mam, luv.' One thing she knew for certain was that the girl wouldn't get a truthful answer.

They went into the living room. 'You took your time,' Bel said. 'I'm parched for a cuppa.'

'I remember you used to wait for Hugh O'Mara outside St Theresa's,' Kate went on, 'though I didn't know you were me auntie then.'

Bel's head jerked upwards and she looked at Flo, her face full of questions.

The very second Sally and Kate left, Bel burst out, 'Hugh O'Mara! Who's Hugh O'Mara? Is he related to Tommy? I didn't know he had a kid.'

'Why should you?'

'I thought you'd have said.'

Flo explained that Hugh had been born after Tommy died. It was hateful giving credit to Nancy for something she'd done herself, but too much time had passed for Bel to know the truth. Flo couldn't have stood the gasps of incredulity, the astounded comments. Bel *would* have crawled through the snow to get back her baby. Bel would have stood on the rooftops screaming to the world that her baby had been stolen, then demolished Nancy's front door with a battering ram once she had discovered where he was. The realisation that another woman wouldn't have taken it as meekly as she had made Flo feel uneasy. It was a bit late to regret what a coward she'd been, too easily influenced by the wishes of her family.

'That's all very well,' Bel hooted, when Flo finished her careful explanation, 'but what the hell were you doing waiting for the lad outside St Theresa's?'

I should have been a spy, Flo thought. I would have been brilliant at lying meself out of the most dangerous situations. She said that a woman at the laundry had had a son in the same class as Hugh. 'They were friends. I used to go by St Theresa's on Fridays on me way from the bank. Peggy asked me to make sure Jimmy was going straight home. That's how I met Hugh. He was a nice lad, quite different from his dad. I still see him,' she added casually. 'If he's passing the launderette, he might drop in.'

'Why didn't you tell me this before?' Bel said, outraged out of all proportion.

'I didn't think you'd be interested.'

'Why, Flo Clancy, you know I'm interested in *everything!*'

'Well, you know now, don't you?' Flo snapped.

It was a whole year before Jock tired of the social club and Sally stopped going quite so often to church. The old harmony was restored. It helped when Grace got engaged to a nice young man called Keith, who worked in a bank, and became absorbed in plans for her wedding eighteen months off at Easter 1966. 'Jock's pulling out all the stops. It's going to be a grand affair,' Sally announced. 'He thinks if we spend all our savings she'll realise we love her just as much as we did Ian.'

Sally continued coming to William Square, sometimes bringing Kate Colquitt with her. Flo and Kate got on like a house on fire. 'You should have had kids, Flo,' said Bel, who usually managed to be there when visitors came. 'You would have made a wonderful mother.'

It was a bitterly cold January afternoon, a month after her twenty-third birthday, when Kate turned up alone at the launderette. 'I hope you don't mind. I finish work at four.' She made a nervous face. 'Norman's off with a terrible cold and he's moved in with us for a while so me mam can look after him. I don't feel like going home just yet. I can't stand it when both of them get on to me.'

'I don't mind a bit, luv.' Flo sat the girl in her cubby-hole and made her some tea. Once she'd warmed up, she'd let her loose among her ladies, who'd soon make her forget her troubles. 'What do they get on to you about?' she asked.

Kate raised her shoulders and heaved a great sigh. 'Norman wants us to get married and me mam thinks it's a grand idea. He's so sweet. I can't remember a time when he hasn't been around, yet . . . oh, I dunno. It's worse now Grace is engaged – she's four years younger than me. Mam keeps saying I'll be left on the shelf, but I'm not sure if I care. I've started training to be a State Registered Nurse, and I'd like to finish before I settle down. In fact, sometimes I think I wouldn't mind staying single like you, Flo.'

She made herself useful, helping to untangle washing that had knotted together in the spin-driers, and getting on famously with the customers. She was still there when Flo was about to turn the Open sign to Closed, and Hugh O'Mara came in wearing the leather coat that had taken three months to save for, and which Nancy strongly disapproved of him wearing for work.

'Hugh!' Kate cried, her face lighting up with pleasure. 'I haven't seen you in ages.'

He appeared equally pleased to find her there. They sat on a bench, heads together, engrossed in conversation, and when the time came for Flo to lock up, the pair wandered off happily, arm in arm. A few days later, Kate turned up again, then Hugh arrived as if it had been prearranged. The same thing happened the next week and the next, until Flo got used to Tuesday and Friday being the days when Kate came to help untangle the washing, was joined by Hugh, and they would go off together into the night. She watched, entranced, as the looks they gave each other became more and more intimate. She realised they were falling in love, and couldn't have approved more. Her son would never find a prettier, nicer, more suitable wife than Kate Colquitt. She felt sure that even Nancy would be pleased when she was told. So far, everyone except Flo was being kept in the dark.

As the months crept by they were still in the dark. It was obvious to everyone in the launderette, including Mr Fritz, that the young couple were mad about each other, but Kate was too scared to tell her mam. 'She never liked Hugh much. She said there was something not quite right about his background.' She asked Flo how people got married in Gretna Green.

'I've no idea, luv,' Flo confessed, exasperated. She badly wanted to interfere, to tell them to get a move on, but held her tongue.

'Martha suspects Kate's got a secret boyfriend,' Sally remarked one day. Apparently there were nights when Kate didn't get home till all hours and refused to say where she'd been. Poor Norman Cameron was doing his nut.

Flo wondered if Kate was more scared of Norman than of her mam. 'He'd kill any man who laid a finger on her,' Sally had said once. Perhaps she was scared for Hugh. Or maybe she was enjoying the clandestine nature of the affair, just as Flo had enjoyed her illicit meetings with Hugh's father all those years ago.

Secrecy must have run in both families, the O'Maras and the Clancys, because Kate and Hugh continued to see each other for over a year before everyone found out and all hell broke loose.

Flo had been out of bed barely five minutes when there was a pounding on the door. She opened it, still in her dressing-gown, and Sally came storming in, her normally placid face red with rage.

'Why aren't you at work?' Flo said, in surprise. Sally had been working full-time at Peterssen's the confectioner's to help with the wedding expenses, which were turning out to be horrendous. She wondered why her sister was so angry. Had Jock gone off the rails again? Grace was getting married on Saturday – perhaps she'd called it off or, even worse, perhaps Keith had.

Either Sally didn't hear the question or she ignored it. 'You knew, didn't you?' she said, loudly and accusingly.

'Knew what?' Flo stammered.

'About Kate and Hugh, soft girl. Nancy O'Mara passed the launderette on the bus last night and she saw them come out kissing and canoodling, so you must have known.'

'So what if I did?'

'You're a bloody idiot, Flo Clancy, you truly are. They're *cousins*!'

'I know darn well they're cousins. What's wrong with that?'

'They're *Catholic* cousins. The Church forbids that sort of thing between cousins.' Sally was staring at her sister belligerently, as if Flo had committed the worst possible crime. 'I hope they're not planning on getting married or anything daft like that.'

'They are, actually, once Kate plucks up the courage to tell her mam. It's not illegal. As they don't know they're related, under the circumstances it never entered me head that anyone would care.'

'Holy Mary, Mother of God.' Sally groaned. 'Not care! You never heard anything like the commotion that went on in our Martha's last night. 'Stead of going home, Nancy went straight to Kirkby, then Martha sent for me. We had to turn Norman Cameron away as we didn't want him listening to private family business. Me and Nancy had left before Kate came home. Christ knows what Martha said to the girl. And what's Nancy supposed to tell Hugh?' She groaned again. 'Why the hell didn't you do something to stop it, Flo?'

Flo gave a little sarcastic laugh. 'Such as?'

'I don't know, do I?'

'I suppose,' Flo said slowly, conscious of her own anger grating in her voice, 'I could have said "Sorry, Hugh, but you're not to have any romantic notions about Kate Colquitt, because the truth is, I'm your mam, not Nancy, which means you're cousins." That might have stopped it, and I'm sure everyone would have been dead pleased, particularly Martha and Nancy.'

Sally's rage subsided. 'I'm sorry, luv. Our Martha got me all worked up. I hardly slept a wink all night, but I shouldn't have blamed you.' She looked curiously at her sister. 'Did you ever think about telling him when he got older?'

Flo had thought about it a million times. 'Yes, but I decided it wouldn't be fair. It might do the poor lad's head in, knowing the truth after all this time. He'd feel betrayed. All the deceit, all the lies. He might never want to see either me or Nancy again, and he'd be the one who'd suffer most.'

Sally shivered suddenly. 'It's cold in here.'

'I'm used to it. I'll turn the fire on.'

'What are we going to do, Flo, about Kate and Hugh?'

'Leave them alone, do nothing. Let them get wed with everyone's blessing.'

'Come off it, Flo. You must be out of your mind,' Sally said resignedly.

'I've never felt saner.' Flo's voice was cold. 'You, Martha and Nancy are nothing but a bunch of hypocrites. You pride yourselves on being great Catholics, yet you're quite happy to let me son be lied to all his life. Martha and Nancy caused this mess and I don't see why Hugh and Kate should suffer. Anyroad, marriage isn't out of the question. Perhaps they can get a dispensation?' She couldn't understand the need some people had to interfere in other people's lives. The young couple had fallen in love in all innocence, and they were perfect for each other. She was desperate for them to be left alone, not be parted over some silly rule that couldn't even be explained to them. Kate was a nice girl, but she was weak. Once Martha got to work on her, Flo couldn't imagine her holding out.

'I suggested a dispensation,' Sally said tiredly, 'but Martha and Nancy nearly hit the roof. How would they explain the situation for one thing? It's not just the parish priest who gets involved, it can go up as far as the bishop. And it means Hugh and Kate would have to know the truth.'

'But, Sal,' Flo tried to convey her desperation to her sister, 'we're the only ones who know they're cousins. It's not against the law of the land. If all of us kept our traps shut, Hugh and Kate could get married tomorrer.'

To her relief, Sally looked more than half convinced. 'There might be something in what you say,' she conceded. 'I'll go straight to Kirkby and see our Martha.'

Over the next few days, Flo tried to ring Sally several times from the telephone in the launderette, but either there was no reply or Jock said she was out somewhere, busy with arrangements for Grace's wedding. There was no sign, either, of Hugh or Kate. She prayed that Hugh wouldn't be annoyed or get into trouble if she rang him at work, but when she did, she was told he hadn't been in all week. Desperation turned to frustration when she realised there was nothing she could do. She thought of going to Martha's, or to Clement Street to see Nancy, but she didn't trust herself not to blurt out the truth if there was a row.

She had bought a new outfit for Grace's wedding: a pale blue and pink check frock with a white Peter Pan collar, a white silk beret and gloves, and high-heeled linen shoes. On the day, she went through the motions, chatting to the guests, agreeing that the bride looked like a film star in her raw silk dress. She did her best to get Sally on one side and pump her for information, but found it impossible and came to the conclusion that her sister was avoiding her. She wanted to know why Martha wasn't there and what on earth had happened to Kate, who was supposed to be a bridesmaid.

The ceremony had been over for twenty-four hours, the newly wedded couple had already landed safely in Tenerife to start their fortnight's honeymoon when Sally came to William Square to tell Flo that, at the same time as Grace had been joined in holy matrimony to Keith, in another church in another part of Liverpool, Norman Cameron had taken Kate Colquitt to be his wife. It had been a hastily arranged ceremony, with an emergency licence, attended by only a few friends. The bride wore a borrowed dress. They were spending two days in Rhyl for their honeymoon.

'Martha made me promise not to tell you,' Sally said. 'She thought you might turn up and make a fuss.'

'Since when did I ever make a fuss?' Flo asked bitterly. 'I let her tread all over me. I let her ruin me life, just as she's ruined Kate's.' She thought of Hugh, who must have felt betrayed when he heard the news.

'You're exaggerating, Flo. Norman has loved Kate all his life. Now his dreams have come true and they're married. He'll make the best husband in the world.'

Perhaps Norman's dreams had been nightmares, because the stories that reached Flo in the months and years that followed scarcely told of a man who loved his wife.

Kate Colquitt, now Cameron, had become pregnant straight away. Late the following November she gave birth to a daughter, Millicent. Flo hadn't set eyes on Kate since the girl had walked out of the launderette on Hugh's arm just before Easter. She felt hurt at first, until a dismayed Sally informed her that Norman hardly let his new wife out of doors. 'She can go to the local shops and to church, but no further. I can't think why, but he doesn't trust her. Perhaps he knows about Hugh O'Mara, but Kate was single then so what does it matter?'

On impulse, Flo decided to go and see her niece at the maternity hospital. Afternoon visiting was from two till three so she arranged for the woman who did the morning shift at the launderette to hang on until she got back. 'I'm off to see me niece in hospital,' she said proudly. 'She's just had a baby, a little girl.'

'Would you like to see the baby first?' the nurse enquired, when Flo asked where she could find Mrs Kathleen Cameron.

'That'd be nice.'

The hospital bustled with visitors, mainly women at this time of day. 'That's her, second row back, second cot from the end.' The nurse's voice dropped to a whisper: 'I wouldn't want anyone else to hear, but she's one of the prettiest babies we've ever had.'

Flo was left alone to stare through the nursery window at the rows of babies. Some were howling furiously, their little faces red and screwed up in rage. A few were awake but quiet, their small bodies squirming against the tightly wrapped blankets. The rest, Millicent Cameron among them, were fast asleep.

'Aah!' Flo breathed. She was perfect, with long lashes quivering on her waxen cheeks, and a little pink rosebud mouth. Hugh had probably looked like that. She wondered if he'd also had such a head of hair: masses of little curls, like delicate ribbons. I never even knew how much he weighed, she thought. She pressed her forehead against the glass in order to see better. 'I wish you all the luck in the world, Millie Cameron,' she whispered. 'And I tell you this much, luv, I don't half wish you were mine.'

She left the nursery and went to the ward, but when she looked through the glass panel in the door, Martha was sitting beside Kate's bed. Flo sighed and turned away. On the way out, she took another long look at her new great-niece. She felt tears running warmly down her cheeks, sighed, wiped them away with her sleeve and went home.

Almost two decades passed before she saw Kate Cameron and her daughter again.

The girl came into the launderette and looked challengingly at Flo. She had jet black wavy hair, wide brown eyes, and enough makeup on her coarse, attractive face to last most women a week. She seemed to be wearing only half a skirt, and a sweater several sizes too small so it strained against her large, bouncing breasts. A cigarette protruded from the corner of her red, greasy mouth, and she spoke out of the other corner like Humphrey Bogart. 'Are you the one who's a friend of Hugh O'Mara?' she demanded in a deep, sultry voice.

Flo blinked. 'Yes.'

'He said I could leave a message with you. If he comes in, tell him I'll meet him outside Yates's Wine Lodge at half past eight.'

'Rightio. What name shall I say?'

'Carmel McNulty.' The girl turned, flicked ash on the floor, and strode out, hips swaying, long legs enticing in their black, fishnet tights.

Flo's ladies were all eyes and ears. 'Was that Carmel McNulty?' one enquired eagerly.

'Apparently so,' Flo conceded.

'I hope that nice Hugh chap isn't going out with her. She's no better than she ought to be, that girl.'

Everyone seemed to know or have heard of Carmel NcNulty.

'Didn't her last feller end up in Walton jail?'

'She was a hard-faced bitch even when she was a little 'un.'

'I'd give my lads the back of me hand if any of 'em dared to look twice at Carmel McNulty.'

Flo listened, appalled. In the year since Kate had got married, Hugh had never mentioned her name, or been seen with another girl. Surely he didn't have designs on Carmel McNulty. Maybe she had designs on him. Hugh was a catch – one of the best-looking men in all Liverpool, with his own car and a good, steady job. Perhaps she was prejudiced, but Flo couldn't understand why there wasn't a whole line of women queuing to snap him up.

Having demolished Carmel McNulty, Flo's ladies began to put her back together again. 'Mind you, Carmel's got her hands full with her mam. How many kids has Tossie got?'

'Twenty?' someone suggested.

'Twenty!' Flo squeaked.

'Nah, I think it was eighteen at the last count.'

'Carmel's the eldest and she's had a babby to look after ever since she wasn't much more than a babby herself.'

'She still looks after 'em. I saw her only the other Sunday pushing a pramload of kids down Brownlow Hill.'

'You can't blame her wanting a good time after all that. How old is she now?'

'Nineteen.'

Six weeks later Hugh O'Mara and Carmel McNulty were married. The bride held her bouquet over her already swelling stomach. Flo went to the church and watched through the railings. It was more like a school outing than a wedding, as hordes of large and small McNultys chased each other around the churchyard.

Nancy O'Mara hadn't changed much: she still wore her black hair in the same enormous bun and the same peculiar clothes, a long flowing red dress and a black velvet bolero. She looked as if at any minute she might produce castanets and start dancing, except that her face was set like yellow concrete in an expression of disgust. According to a rather sullen Hugh, she loathed Carmel and Carmel loathed her. Nancy had only come to the wedding because of what people would say if she didn't.

'It serves you right,' Flo murmured. 'If it weren't for you and our Martha, Hugh would be married to Kate by now and everyone would be happy, apart from Norman Cameron.' Instead, Kate was stuck with a man who kept her a prisoner, and Hugh was marrying a woman he didn't love. There was nothing wrong with Carmel: once she'd got to know her, Flo liked the girl. She was big-hearted, generous to a fault, and as tough as old boots. But she wasn't Hugh's type. Flo clutched the railings with both hands. Her son was doing his best to look as if he was enjoying his wedding day, but his mam could tell he was as miserable as sin.

Flo went through the backyard of the terraced house in Mulliner Street and let herself into the untidy kitchen. She shouted, 'Is he ready for his walk yet, Carmel?'

Carmel appeared in slacks and one of Hugh's old shirts, a cigarette between her lips. She looked exhausted. 'The little bugger kept us awake half the night laughing! I'll be glad to be shut of him for a few hours, I really will.'

A small boy burst into the kitchen and flung his arms around Flo's legs. 'Can we go to the Mystery? Can we play ball? Can I have a lolly? Can I walk and not sit in me pushchair?'

Smiling, Flo loosened the arms around her legs and picked the child up. 'You're a weight, young man!'

Tom O'Mara was over-active and inordinately precocious for a three-year-old. Even as a baby, he had hardly slept. He didn't cry, but demanded attention with loud noises, which got louder and louder if he was ignored. As he grew older, he would rattle the bars of his cot and fling the bedding on the floor. Lately, he'd begun to sit up in bed in the early hours of the morning chanting nursery rhymes or singing, and now, apparently, laughing. He could already read a little, count up to a hundred and tell the time. Carmel said she'd never come across a child quite like him. 'I feel like knocking bloody hell out of the little bugger, but you can't very well hit a kid for being happy!'

When relations between Carmel and her mother-in-law broke down completely and Nancy was barred from Mulliner Street, Flo grasped the opportunity and offered to take her grandson out in the mornings.

'Would you, Flo?' Carmel said gratefully. 'Honest, I don't know where Hugh found a friend like you. I wish you were me mother-in-law, I really do.'

It was June, not exactly hot, but quite warm. Flo played football with Tom until her limbs could no longer move. She lay on the grass and declared herself a goal post. 'You can kick the ball at me, but don't expect to have it kicked back. I'm worn out.'

Tom sat on her stomach. He was a handsome little chap with the same devil-may-care expression on his face as his grandad. 'Are you old?'

'Is fifty-one old? I'm not sure.'

'Dad's old.'

'No, he's not, luv. He's nineteen years younger than me.'

'Mam says he's old.'

Things were not well with the O'Maras. In the evenings, after being stuck in the house all day with a child who would crack the patience of a saint, Carmel was anxious for a break, a bit of excitement. Hugh, who worked hard and was rarely home before seven, preferred to stay in and watch television. Flo had offered to babysit and did occasionally at weekends, but in the main the couple stayed put, much to Carmel's chagrin. She declared loudly and aggressively that she was bored out of her skull and might as well be married to an old-age pensioner.

Flo couldn't help but sympathise. Hugh was growing old before his time. He already had a stoop, his hair was thinning, his gentle face was that of a man weighed down by the cares of the world. He was unhappy. Flo could see it in his dead, green eyes. He didn't seem to care when Carmel started going out alone. She was going clubbing, she announced. Hugh was welcome to come with her if he wanted, otherwise he would just have to like it or lump it.

After the launderette had closed, Flo often went to Mulliner Street to sit with her son. She had never thought she would have the freedom to be alone with Hugh, Nancy out of the picture. Even so, she would have preferred the circumstances to be different. They didn't talk much. He sat with his eyes fixed on the television, but she could tell he wasn't really watching.

'Do you see much of Kate nowadays?' he asked one night.

'No, luv. I haven't seen her in years.'

'I wonder how she is.'

She didn't dare repeat the things Sally told her – Hugh was miserable enough. 'She's had another baby, a little girl called Trudy,' was all she said.

Another night he said, 'Why did you wait for me outside St Theresa's that day, Flo? I've often wondered.'

'I wanted to meet you. I knew your dad, remember?'

'That's right. What was he like? Mam never talked about him much, except that he died on that submarine.'

'The *Thetis*. He was an ould divil, your dad. Full of himself, dead conceited. Women were after him like flies.' Perhaps she should have come up with a more positive, more flattering description, but at least she hadn't told him his dad had lied through his teeth.

Hugh allowed himself the glimmer of a smile. 'Not like me.'

'No, I'm pleased to say.' She didn't like the way he always talked about the past, as if he'd given up on the future. Usually, Tom could be heard upstairs, where he'd been put to bed hours ago, making aeroplane or car noises, but

Hugh seemed unaware of his delightful son and his attractive wife – who might be as common as muck but was basically a good girl, anxious to be a good wife. Carmel was only twenty-three: she needed a husband who did more than just bring home a regular wage. If only Hugh would take her out now and then, she'd be happy, but he didn't seem to care.

In the Mystery, Tom bounced several times on her stomach. 'Strewth, luv,' Flo gasped. 'Are you out to kill me?'

'Can we go to your house for a cuppa tea?'

'There isn't time, Tom. It'd make me late for work.' Sometimes when it was raining she took him to William Square and read him books, which he adored. 'I'll get you an ice lolly, then take you back to your mam.'

He gave her stomach a final, painful bounce. 'Rightio, Flo.'

When she returned the kitchen was still in a state. It was unlike Carmel not to tidy up – she usually kept the house spotless. Flo went into the living room and could hear voices upstairs, one a man's. 'Carmel,' she shouted.

It was several minutes before Carmel came running down. She'd changed into a mini-skirted Crimplene frock. Her lipstick was smudged.

Flo frowned. 'Is Hugh home?'

The girl looked at her boldly. 'No.'

'I see.'

'I doubt if you do, Flo. If you were married to that drip Hugh O'Mara you might see then.'

'It's none of me business, is it, girl?' Flo considered herself the last person on earth entitled to criticise another woman's morals, but her heart ached for her unhappy, lacklustre son.

Tom had turned five and been at school only a matter of weeks when Carmel walked out for good. 'She's gone to live in Brighton with some chap she met in a club,' Hugh said wearily. 'She said she would have taken Tom but her new feller doesn't want to be landed with a kid. "Flo will look after him," she said.'

'I'll be happy to.' It would never have come to this if I'd been allowed to keep me baby, Flo thought sadly.

'There won't be any need,' Hugh said, in his expressionless voice. 'I'm moving back in with me mam. She'll take care of Tom. She's not seen much of him 'cept when I took him round.'

Flo turned away, her lips twisted bitterly. She supposed that that was the last she would see of her grandson, but on the day that the family moved to Clement Street to live with Nancy, Tom O'Mara burst into the launderette after school. He was everything his father had never been: untidy, uninhibited, full of beans. 'Hiya, Flo,' he sang.

'What are you doing here?' she gasped. He'd come half a mile out of his way to get there. She noticed he had a skull and crossbones drawn upside down on both knees. 'Mrs O'Mara will be worried stiff wondering where you've got to.'

'You mean me gran? Don't like her. Me mam always said she was an ould cow. Can I have a cuppa tea, Flo?' He settled on a bench and allowed himself to be made a fuss of by Flo's ladies.

'How on earth could Carmel McNulty bring herself to walk out on such a little angel?'

'He's the spitting image of Hugh.'

'He's the spitting image of Carmel.'

From then on, Tom never failed to turn up for a cup of tea after school. Nancy couldn't control him and Flo didn't even try.

3

Mr Fritz was seventy-five, the same age as the century, and becoming frail. His limbs were swollen and twisted with arthritis, and it was heartbreaking to see him struggle up and down the basement steps with his stick. Even worse, more important parts of his body had ceased to work. He and Flo went to the Isle of Man rarely nowadays, and then only to lie in each other's arms.

'I'm sorry, Flo,' he would say mournfully, 'I'm like one of my old washing-machines. I need reconditioning. A new motor wouldn't do me any harm.'

'Don't be silly, luv. I'm not exactly in tip-top condition meself,' Flo would answer. In fact, she was as fit as a fiddle and missed making love.

Increasingly his family came over from Ireland to see him. Flo found it difficult to recognise the hard-eyed middle-aged men and women as the children she'd once played with, taken for walks and to the pictures. Their attitude towards her was unfriendly and suspicious. She sensed that they were worried she might have undue influence over the man with whom she'd shared a house for so long, a house that was now worth many thousands of pounds, added to which there were the six launderettes. All of a sudden, the little Fritzes seemed to regard their father's welfare of great importance.

'Harry would like me to live with him in Dublin,' Mr Fritz said, the night after Ben and Harry had been to stay for the weekend. 'And I had a letter from Aileen the other day. She never married, you know, and she wants me to live with her!' He chuckled happily. 'It's nice to know my children want to look after me in my old age, don't you think, Flo?'

'Yes, luv,' Flo said warmly. She felt frightened, convinced that it was their inheritance his children were concerned with.

'I told Harry that, if I went, I'd want nothing to do with Stella.' Flo went cold. He was actually considering Harry's offer. 'He said they hardly see her nowadays. She's still on the same farm and the toilet facilities are barely civilised, which is why none of them go to visit.'

It turned out he just wanted to spend a long holiday in Dublin, to get to know his children properly again. 'I would never leave you, Flo,' he said. 'Not for good.'

While he was away, the launderettes could virtually run themselves, but for the second time in her life, Flo was left in charge of Mr Fritz's business. This time though, an agent would collect the money each day and bank it. Flo would be sent a cheque to pay the staff, with the power to hire and fire should the need arise. Herbie Smith, a reliable plumber, had promised to be on call in case any of the machines broke down.

Harry came over from Ireland to fetch his father, and Flo longed to remind this cold, unpleasant man that he'd once had a crush on her. Mr Fritz made his painful way down the steps towards the taxi that would take them to the Irish boat. He gave Flo a chaste kiss on the cheek. 'I'll be back in three months. Keep an eye on upstairs for me.'

'Of course, luv. I've done it before, haven't I?' Flo had no idea why she should want to cry, but cry she did.

'So you have, my dear Flo.' There were tears in his own rheumy eyes. 'The day I came home from the camp and found you here will always remain one of my fondest memories, though not as precious as our weekends together.' He grasped both her hands in his. 'You'll write, won't you? Has Harry given you the address in Dublin?'

'I'll write every week,' Flo vowed. Harry was looking at them darkly, as if all the family's suspicions had been confirmed. 'C'mon, Dad,' he said, making no attempt to keep the impatience out of his voice. Flo felt even more frightened for Mr Fritz, the man she had loved since she was thirteen, not romantically, not passionately, but as the dearest of friends. 'I'll miss you,' she sobbed. 'The place won't seem the same.'

'It's not for long, Flo. The three months will go by in a flash.'

He'd been gone less than a fortnight when Flo heard noises coming from upstairs as if furniture was being moved around. She ran outside. The front door was open and two men were struggling down the steps with the big pine dresser from the kitchen. A removal van was parked further along the square.

'What's happening?' she cried.

'We're taking the good stuff to auction and leaving the rubbish behind,' she was told brusquely.

Flo returned to the basement, knowing that her worst fears had been realised. Mr Fritz would never again live in William Square.

Soon afterwards, a gang of workmen descended on the house. Each floor was being converted into a separate flat, and Flo feared for herself. She'd always insisted on paying rent, but it was a nominal sum. What if the little Fritzes put up the rent so that it was beyond her means? What if they threw her out? She couldn't imagine living anywhere else, where she might have to share a kitchen and lavatory with other tenants. Flo had grown used to her subterranean existence, where she happily ignored the real world. The years were marked for her not by the election of various governments, Labour or Conservatives, the Cuban crisis or the assassination of an American president, but by films and music, *Gone with the Wind*, *Singing in the Rain*, *The Sound of Music*: Paul Newman, Marlon Brando, the Beatles . . .

'Mr Fritz would never throw you out!' Bel scoffed.

'I'm not sure if he's got much say in things any more,' said Flo.

'You can always live with me.'

'That's very kind of you, Bel, but I couldn't stand you bellowing down me ear all day long. And it's not just the flat I'm worried about, what about me job?' Each week, she sent her rent, along with a little report: a woman had left and she'd had to take on someone new, a machine had needed servicing and she enclosed Herbie Smith's bill. The address Harry had given her turned out to be a firm of accountants, and although she frequently enclosed a letter for Mr Fritz, there'd been no reply so far, and she wondered if her letters were being passed on.

Four families moved in upstairs, but Flo heard nothing about her own situation. 'Perhaps the little Fritzes are playing games with me,' she said to Bel. 'Lulling me into a sense of false security, like.' She might come home one day to find the locks changed and her furniture dumped on the pavement.

Bel made one of her famous faces. 'Don't talk daft. Y'know, what you need is to get away for a while, leave all your troubles behind. I've been thinking, why don't we go on holiday? A woman at work is going to Spain for two whole weeks on a charter flight, I think it's called. It's ever so cheap and she said there's still a few places left.'

'Spain! I've never been abroad.'

'Neither have I since I left the forces, but that's no reason not to go now. We might cop a couple of fellers out there.'

The small swimming pool shone like a dazzling sapphire in the light of the huge amber moon, and the navy sky was powdered lavishly with glittering stars. Less than fifty feet away, the waters of the Mediterranean shimmered and rustled softly and couples were clearly visible lying clasped in each other's arms on the narrow strip of Costa Brava sand. Somewhere a guitarist was strumming a vaguely familiar tune, and people were still in the pool, although it was past midnight. There was laughter, voices, the clink of glasses from the outside bar.

Flo, on the balcony of their room on the second floor of the hotel, refilled her glass from the jug of sangria and wondered if you could buy it in Liverpool. Wine was so cheap that she and Bel were convinced they would never be sober if they lived in Spain.

They'd been lucky to get a room with a view like this. The guests on the other side of the building could see only more and more of the hotels that cluttered the entire length of coast.

Someone opened a door by the pool and a blast of music filled the air: The Who, singing, 'I Can See for Miles . . .' 'Miles and miles and miles,' Flo sang, until the door closed and all she could hear was the guitarist again. Every night at the Old Tyme Dance while she was being led sedately around the floor to the strains of 'When Irish Eyes Are Smiling', or 'Goodnight, Eileen', she thought enviously of the youngsters in the other ballroom leaping around madly to the sound of Dire Straits or ABBA.

Bel hadn't bothered to inform her that the group they were travelling with were old-age pensioners. Flo had been horrified when they got on the plane and she found herself surrounded by people with hearing aids and walking sticks and not a single head of hair in sight that wasn't grey.

To her further consternation, there were actually a few wolf-whistles – in this company, two women in their mid-fifties must seem like teenagers: Bel still managed to look incredibly glamorous, though her lovely red hair was in reality lovely grey hair that had required a tint for years.

There were still five more days of the holiday to go, and Flo supposed she'd had quite a good time. During the day, they wandered round Lloret de Mar, admiring the palm trees and the sparkling blue sea. They bought little trinkets in the gift shops. She got Bel a pretty mosaic bracelet, and Bel bought her a set of three little brass plaques that had taken Flo's fancy. Then they had found a bar that stocked every liqueur in existence and were sampling them one by one. Flo had sent cards to everyone she could think of, including Mr Fritz, though she had no faith that he would get it. Why had he never written as he'd promised? It was six months since he'd left William Square and she worried about him all the time. If she didn't hear soon, she resolved to go over to Ireland in search of him, even though she didn't have a proper address.

Evenings, they went dancing. Flo wrinkled her nose: she hated being taken in a pair of gnarled, sunburnt arms for the Gay Gordons or the Military Two-step or, somewhat daringly, a rumba, played to a slow, plodding beat in case it overtaxed a few dicky hearts. Mr Fritz was old, but in her eyes he had always remained the same lovely little man with brown fuzzy hair and twinkling eyes she'd first met in the laundry. The other night one sly old bugger in fancy shorts had had the nerve to get fresh during the last waltz.

'You're no spring chicken yourself,' Bel snorted, when Flo complained.

'I wouldn't mind dancing with fellers me own age,' Flo said haughtily. Bel had taken up with Eddie Eddison, a widower in his seventies, who came from Maynard Street, though it seemed daft to come all the way to Spain to click with a feller who lived only two streets away in Liverpool.

Most nights when Bel wasn't looking, Flo slipped away. She enjoyed sitting on the balcony, staring at the sky, listening to the sounds by the pool, drinking wine. When she got home, she might do something with her backyard, paint the walls a nice colour, buy some plants and a table and chairs, turn it into one of them patio things. It would be pleasant to sit outside in the good weather. The flat could get stuffy when it was hot.

That's if the flat remained hers. Oh, Lord, Bel would be cross if she knew she was worrying about the flat again. Flo rested her arms on the balcony and stared down at the pool. Even at this hour children were still up. Two little boys, one about Tom O'Mara's age, were splashing water at each other in the shallow end. If only she could have brought Tom with her. He would have had the time of his life. Instead of dancing with men old enough to be her father, or sitting alone on a balcony, she could have been down at the pool with Tom. It seemed a normal, everyday thing to do, to bring your grandson on holiday, but the things that normal, everyday people did seemed to have passed her by.

Flo sat back in her chair and sighed. Another few days and they could go home. She couldn't wait, though she wouldn't let Bel know she was homesick. She would laugh and smile, and look cheerful, pretend to be having a great time, make the best of things as she always had.

Out of the corner of her eye, she glimpsed a star shoot across the sky. It disappeared into the infinite darkness – or was it just her imagination that she could see the faintest, barely discernible burst of yellow, which meant that millions and millions of miles away there'd been an almighty explosion?

The idea made her shudder, and she remembered being told as a child that God had created the world in seven days. 'But did He create the universe as well, Dad? Did He create the sun and the moon and the stars at the same time?' She couldn't remember what his answer had been.

It was ages since she'd thought about Dad. Living in Burnett Street had been perfect when he was alive and Martha had yet to assume the role of Being In Charge. Flo had never planned on getting married, but had just known that one day she would and that she would have children, two at least. Then, as if the shooting star had struck its target, Flo felt as if every muscle in her body had instantly wasted, as if every bone had turned to jelly. All that was left was her heart, which pounded like a hammer in her cavernous chest.

She'd spent her entire adult life in the way she was spending this holiday! Making the best of things, pretending to enjoy herself. *Waiting for it to end!*

'Oh, Lord!' The awful feeling passed as quickly as it had come, but in the mad scramble of thoughts that followed she knew that she should have made the best of things in a more practical way, by marrying Gerard Davies, for instance, or almost any one of those other young servicemen. It was no use blaming Martha. It was Flo's own fault that she'd wasted her life.

The basement flat felt unusually chilly when she arrived home from Spain to find three letters waiting for her on the mat. She went through them on her way to the kitchen to put the kettle on, aching for a cup of tea made with ordinary leaves instead of those silly teabags. Two were bills, but she stopped in her tracks when she saw the name and address of a solicitor in Castle Street on the third. She'd never had a letter from a solicitor before, and her hands were trembling as she tore it open, convinced that the little Fritzes were demanding formally that she quit the flat.

The heading was enough to make her burst into tears. 'Re: Fritz Erik Hofmannsthal (deceased).'

He was dead! *Mr Fritz was dead* – and not one of his children had bothered to let her know. Flo forgot the tea and poured a glass of sherry instead. Her imagination ran riot as she thought of all the different ways he might have died, none of them pleasant. She'd like to bet he'd wanted to return to William Square and be with her, but his children hadn't let him. Lovely, long-cherished memories flicked through her brain: the laundry on Tuesdays when he'd brought cream cakes, the day Stella had taken the photograph of him and his girls outside – the family had just come back from Anglesey and seemed so happy. How strange and cruel life could be that it should all have turned so sour. She recalled their first weekend in the Isle of Man, two old friends comfortably together at last.

It was a long time before she could bring herself to read the letter, to learn that dear Mr Fritz had bequeathed her the leasehold of the basement flat, as well as the launderette in Smithdown Road. The letter finished, 'We would be obliged if you would telephone for an appointment so that arrangements can be made for various papers to be signed.'

'Mr Hofmannsthal's children are seeking to question the validity of his will,' the solicitor informed her. He was younger than expected, not the least bit pompous, and from his build and his broken nose, looked like a rugby player or a boxer. 'But as same was dictated in my presence ten years ago while my client was in full possession of his senses, there is no question of it not being valid.'

'I don't think the little Fritzes liked me very much,' Flo said, in a small voice. 'Least, not since they stopped being little.'

'They like you even less now, which isn't surprising. You're very much the fly in the ointment. They want the house in William Square put on the market, but it won't fetch anything like it would have done had the basement been included.' The solicitor smiled, as if this pleased him enormously.

'I'm sorry,' Flo said weakly.

'Good heavens, Miss Clancy!' he exploded. 'Sorry is the very last thing you should be. It's what my client, Fritz Hofmannsthal, wanted, and I'm sure he had the best reason in the world for doing so.'

Flo felt herself go pink, wondering what Mr Fritz might have told him. 'Do I still have to look after the other launderettes?' she enquired.

The solicitor was so outraged to discover that she'd been 'acting as manager', as he put it, for six whole months without even so much as a thank-you from the little Fritzes, that he suggested putting in a claim against the estate for 'services rendered'. 'We'll demand ten pounds a week for the period involved, and probably end up with five. Will that suit you?'

Flo was about to say she didn't want a penny, but changed her mind. Even if she gave away the money, it was better than the little Fritzes having it. 'Five pounds a week would be fine,' she said.

The whole thing went into another of Flo's invisible boxes marked 'Secret'. If people found out, they would wonder why Mr Fritz had remembered her so generously. She owned her own property. She owned her own business. But no one would ever know.

In his day Edward Eddison had been a professional magician and had appeared halfway down the bill in theatres all over the country. When he married Bel Szerb in a register office two months after their holiday in Spain, he produced two white doves from his sleeve, which fluttered around the room, much to the annoyance of the registrar who disapproved of confetti, let alone live birds.

Bel, gorgeous in lavender tulle and a feathered hat, screamed with laughter when a bird settled happily on her head.

Flo, still shaken by the strange, unsettling thoughts she'd had in Spain and the loss of Mr Fritz, felt depressed when the ceremony was over, and Bel and Eddie departed to Bournemouth on their honeymoon. The newly-weds intended to live in Eddie's house in Maynard Street, and Bel planned on doing the place up from top to bottom. Flo tried to cheer herself up by decorating her own flat. She painted the walls white and the big wooden beams across the middle of the room black. The plaques Bel had bought her in Spain went well against the glossy surface, and when she mentioned this to her ladies, they presented her with several more. She painted the little yard a pretty rose pink, bought garden furniture and plant-holders, but when it came to new furniture for inside, she couldn't bring herself to part with a thing. After all, Mr Fritz and Jimmy Cromer had struggled downstairs with the settee and chair out of Stella's sitting room, as well as the big sideboard, which was probably an antique – if the little Fritzes had known it would probably have gone for auction, along with the lovely oak wardrobe and chest-of-drawers in the bedroom. As for the brass bed, she'd no intention of changing it for one of those padded-base things like they'd had in Spain – it had been like sleeping on wooden planks. She even felt quite fond of the little rag rug in front of the fire, which had been there when she arrived. She made do with buying pictures for the walls and armfuls of silk flowers to arrange in vases, and a nest of round tables to put the vases on. The big table she folded against the wall because she rarely used it. Nowadays, she ate on the settee in front of the television. Last Christmas, Bel had bought her a coffee table for this very purpose, an ugly thing, Flo thought secretly, with legs like clumps of giant onions.

The only light that glimmered through this dark period was her grandson Tom, seven years old and a continual thorn in the side of Nancy O'Mara, just like his grandad. Tom came and went as he pleased, no matter what Nancy told him. Hugh, of whom Flo saw little these days, appeared to have given up on his son and took no interest. On Sundays, Flo would return from Mass to find Tom sitting on the steps outside her flat, ready to spend the day with her. She took him to matinée performances at the cinema. Once she got used to the idea that she was her own boss and could take time off whenever she pleased, she and Tom sometimes went to football matches to see Everton or Liverpool play.

Tom was at Flo's place too often to be kept hidden in one of her secret boxes, so Bel got used to finding him there, though she thought it most peculiar. 'You're obsessed with the O'Maras, Flo,' she hissed. 'Tommy, Hugh, now little Tom.'

Gradually the dark period passed. It was a relief when the unpleasant middle-aged couple on the ground floor moved out, and a beautiful black girl, still a teenager, with two small children, moved in. But Flo was shocked to the core when she discovered that Charmian was one of the women who took up position along the railings of the square each night. Even so, it was hard not to say, 'Good morning,' or 'Isn't it a lovely day?' or 'We could do with some rain, couldn't we?' when they came face to face. The two became rather wary friends, although Charmian continually felt the need to defend her doubtful and precarious lifestyle. 'Me husband walked out on me. No one'll give me a job with two kids under school age. How else am I supposed to feed 'em and pay the rent?' she demanded aggressively, the first time she came down to the basement flat.

'Don't go on at me, luv,' Flo said mildly. 'It's your life. I haven't uttered a word of criticism, have I?'

'I can see it in your eyes. You're disgusted.'

'No, I'm not, luv. The disgust is in your own eyes. I think you're ashamed, else you wouldn't go on about it so much.'

Charmian stormed out, but returned the following night to say, 'You're right, but I don't know another way to keep me head above water.'

Flo said nothing. As the months rolled by, she listened patiently while Charmian struggled loudly and vocally with her conscience. When the woman who worked the morning shift in the launderette gave in her notice, Flo casually mentioned it to her upstairs neighbour. 'There'll be a job going the Monday after next, eight till two. The pay isn't bad, enough for the rent and to keep two kids without too much of a struggle.'

Charmian glared at her. 'Is that a hint?'

'No, luv, it's an offer.' Flo shrugged. 'It's up to you if you take it.'

'What about the owner? He mightn't want an ex-pro working in his bloody launderette.'

The girl scowled, but she hated what she was doing and Flo could tell that she was tempted. 'The owner will go on my recommendation.'

'And you'd recommend me when you know . . .' Two large tears rolled down the satiny cheeks. 'Oh, Flo!'

4

Eddie Eddison didn't last long. He died a happy man in the arms of his glamorous wife only eighteen months after their wedding. Bel was left with a hefty weekly pension, a gold Cortina saloon, and immediately began to take driving lessons.

Charmian gave up her job when she married the emergency plumber, Herbie Smith, who moved into the ground-floor flat with his ready-made family. Unlike his dad, Tom O'Mara didn't desert his friend Flo when he started comprehensive school. He was a cocky little bugger, full of confidence and sure of his place in the world. It didn't bother him being seen going to the pictures on Sunday afternoons with a middle-aged woman, or two middle-aged women if Bel decided to come. Bel had transferred her affections from Gregory Peck to Sean Connery.

1983

When his dad died Tom was fifteen, and the cockiness, the confidence, turned out to be nothing but a sham.

The firm in Anfield swore that the accident had been caused by negligence on the part of their workman, Hugh O'Mara. The house he was rewiring was dripping with damp: he'd been a fool to try fitting a plug in a socket that was hanging off the wall, the existing wiring having been installed half a century before. Knowing O'Mara, he'd probably had only half his mind on the job. His heart hadn't been in it for years. He was usually in either a trance or a daydream, the boss was never sure. Anyroad, the stupid sod had been thrown across the room, killed instantly.

Flo didn't go to the funeral. She couldn't have stood it if Nancy, the Welsh witch, had behaved as she had outside the gates of Cammell Laird's, weeping and wailing and making an exhibition of herself. At least she'd had a claim on Tommy, but she'd none on Hugh.

It was as if Hugh had already been dead a long time, Flo thought, strangely unmoved, as if she had already mourned his loss. Tom, though, was distraught. He came into the launderette after the funeral, his face red and swollen as if he'd been crying for days. Flo took him into her cubicle out of the way of her ladies' curious eyes.

'No one wants me, Flo,' he wept. 'Me mam walked out, me dad went and died on me, and Gran doesn't like me.'

He was almost as tall as her. Flo's heart ached as she stroked his bleak, tear-stained face. If only her own history could have been rewritten, how would things have turned out then? 'I like you, luv,' she whispered.

'Promise not to die, Flo. Promise not to go away like everybody else.' He buried his face in her shoulder.

'We've all got to die sometime, luv. But I won't go away, I promise that much. I'll always be here for you.'

Tom took a long time to recover from the loss of his dad. When he did, there was a callousness about him that saddened Flo, a chill in his green eyes that hadn't been there before. He left school before he could sit his O levels and moved out of his gran's house to doss down in the homes of various friends, sleeping occasionally on Flo's settee if he was desperate. He got a job helping out at St John's market. 'I'm going to start a stall meself one day,' he boasted. 'There's no way I'm working for someone else all me life, not like me dad.'

He brought her presents sometimes: a portable wireless for the kitchen, expensive perfume, a lovely leather handbag. She accepted them with a show of gratitude, although she was worried sick that they were stolen. He even offered to get her a colour telly at half the list price.

'No ta, luv.' She would have loved a colour telly, but felt it might encourage the criminal tendencies she was convinced he had.

Bel was doing her utmost to persuade her friend to retire in May, when she turned sixty-five. 'You've worked non-stop since you were thirteen, Flo,' she said coaxingly. 'That's fifty-two long years now. It's time to put your feet up, like me.'

Tact had never been one of Bel's stronger virtues: the reason behind her solicitude for Flo's welfare was obvious. 'You only want me to retire so you'll have company during the day.'

'True,' Bel conceded. 'But that doesn't mean it's not a good idea.'

The launderette provided a good, steady income, and Flo had no intention of giving up, not while she remained fit and well, though she got tired if she was on her feet for too long. Her ladies had changed over the years, but they were still the irrepressible, good-humoured Scousers she loved. Nowadays not all were poor: they went on holiday to places like Majorca and Torremolinos and brought brasses back for Flo's walls.

When the letter came from the property firm in London offering to buy her out for twenty-five thousand pounds, her first instinct was to refuse. The firm was acting for a client who wished to turn the entire block into a supermarket. But the offer had come as a boon to Flo's neighbours. Hardly anyone ordered coal at a coal office, these days, when they could phone from home. Who'd buy wallpaper and paint from a little shop that had to charge the full price when it could be got for much less from a big do-it-yourself store? The watch-repairer, the picture-framer, the cobbler all reported that business was at an all-time low. Flo couldn't bring herself to turn down the offer and spoil things for those who were desperate to take it.

There were thousands of pounds in the bank now and not much to spend it on. Flo went to see the solicitor in Castle Street and made a will. She'd never thought she'd have property and money to leave behind, but she knew who she wanted to have it. She put the copy at the bottom of the papers in the bureau – one of these days, she must clear everything out. There was stuff in there she'd sooner people didn't know about when she died.

She bought the coveted colour television, a microwave oven, because they seemed useful, and a nice modern music centre, hoping that the man in Rushworth and Draper's didn't think a woman of her age foolish when she chose a dozen or so records: the Beatles, Neil Diamond, Tony Bennett. She didn't *feel* old, but later the same day, when she was wandering around Lewis's department store, she saw an elderly woman, who looked familiar with rather nice silver hair, coming towards her. As they got closer, she realised she was walking towards a mirror and that the woman was herself. She *was* old! What's more, she looked it.

When Bel was told she laughed. 'Of course you're old, girl. We all grow old if we don't die young. The thing is to get the best you can out of life till it's time to draw your last breath. Let's do something dead exciting this weekend, like drive to Blackpool. Or how about London for a change?' She was fearless in the car and would have driven as far as the moon if there'd been a road.

'Oh, Bel,' Flo said shakily, always grateful for her friend's unfailing cheerfulness and good humour. 'I'm ever so glad I went to Birkenhead that morning and met you.'

Bel squeezed her hand affectionately. 'Me too, girl. At least one good thing came out of that business with Tommy O'Mara, eh?'

'Where did we go wrong, Flo?' Sally cried. She asked Flo the same question every time they met.

Flo always gave the same reply. 'Don't ask me, luv.'

Ten years before, Grace, Keith and their two sons had upped roots and gone to live in Australia. Sally and Jock only occasionally received a letter from their daughter, and Grace ignored their pleas to come and visit. Jock was becoming surlier in his old age, Sally more and more unhappy. One of these days, she said bitterly, she was convinced she would die of a broken heart.

'I could easily have done the same when me little boy was taken,' Flo said. She thought of Bel with her three husbands and three lost babies. In her opinion, Sally was giving up far too easily. 'You and Jock have still got each other, as well as your health and strength. You should go out more, go on holiday. It's never too late to have a good time.'

'It is for some people. You're different, Flo. You're made of iron. You keep smiling no matter what.'

Flo couldn't remember when she'd last seen her sister smile. It was impossible to connect this listless, elderly woman with the happy, brown-haired girl from Burnett Street.

Sally went on, 'I remember when we were at school, everyone used to remark on me sister with the lovely smile.'

'Why don't you come to the pictures with me and Bel one night?' Flo urged. 'Or round to William Square one Sunday when Charmian usually pops down for a sherry and a natter.'

'What's the use?'

Grace didn't bother to cross the world to be with her father when her mother died. Sally's heart gave up one night when she was asleep in bed, but perhaps it really had broken.

Bel went with Flo to the funeral on a dreary day in March. It was windy, dry, sunless. Grey clouds chased each other across a paler grey sky. Jock held up remarkably well throughout the Requiem Mass. When Flo had gone to see him, he said that he intended moving to Aberdeen to live with his brother, and she could tell that he was looking forward to returning to the city of his birth. It was as if he and Sally had dragged each other down in their misery, frozen in their grief, unable to come to terms with the loss of Ian, and Grace's indifference. Flo had expected that Sally's death would be the last straw for Jock; instead, it seemed to have released him from a state of perpetual mourning.

It was obvious that Martha, stiff with self-importance, was relishing her role of Being in Charge. Jock, a bit put out, said that she'd taken over the funeral arrangements, had ordered the coffin, the flowers, seen the priest. In the cemetery, in the wind, beneath the racing clouds, Flo saw the gleam in her sister's eyes behind the thick-lensed glasses that she remembered well, as if this was a military operation and she'd like to tell everyone where to stand. When the coffin was lowered into the grave, Jock suddenly put up his hand to shield his eyes and Martha poked him sharply in the ribs. It wasn't done for a man to cry, not even at his wife's funeral. That gesture put paid to the vague thoughts Flo had had of exchanging a few polite words with her sister.

The Camerons were there, Norman handsome and scowling – but, oh, Kate had changed so much, her lovely hair chopped short, her once slim figure swollen and shapeless. There was a battered look on her anxious face, no bruises, bumps or scars, but the same look some of Flo's ladies had, which told of a hard life with many crosses to bear. Yet her eyes remained bright, as if she retained a hope that things would get better one day – or perhaps the light in her eyes was for her children, who would have made any mother proud. Millicent, whom Flo had last glimpsed in the hospital, only a few days' old, had grown into a graceful, slender young woman, with none of her mother's vulnerability apparent in her lovely, strong-willed face. She was with her husband, as was Trudy, whose wedding had been only a few weeks before. Trudy was pretty, but she lacked her sister's grace and air of determination. However, it was the son, Declan, who took Flo's breath away. A slight, delicate lad of ten, it could have been her own little boy she was staring at across the open grave. The Clancys might well be pale-skinned, pale-haired and thin-boned, but they had powerful genes that thrust their way forcefully through each generation. There was no sign of Albert Colquitt in Kate, no indication that Norman Cameron was the father of these three fragile, will o'-the-wisp children. There was another girl, Flo knew, Alison, who had something wrong with her and was in a home in Skem.

'Aren't we going for refreshments?' Bel was disappointed when the mourners turned to leave and Flo made her way towards the gold Cortina.

'I'm not prepared to eat a bite that's been prepared by our Martha,' Flo snapped. 'And don't look at me like that, Bel Eddison, because there's not a chance in hell I'll tell you why. If you're hungry, we'll stop at a pub. I wouldn't mind a good stiff drink meself.'

Sally had gone, to become a memory like Mam and Dad, Mr Fritz and Hugh. Each time someone close to her died, it was as if a chapter in her life had come to an end. One day, Flo too would die and the book would close for ever. She sighed. She definitely needed that drink.

September, 1996

Flo pressed her fingers against her throbbing temples, but the pressure seemed only to emphasise the nagging pain. She knew she should have been to the doctor long ago with these awful headaches but, as she said to Bel, 'If there's summat seriously wrong, I'd sooner not know.' There were times when the pain became unbearable, and all she wanted to do was scream: it felt as if an iron band was being screwed tighter and tighter around her scalp. A glass of sherry made it worse, two glasses made it better, and with three she felt so light-headed that the pain disappeared. Getting drunk seemed preferable to having her head cut open and someone poking around inside, turning her into a vegetable. Peter, the nice young lad from next door who reminded her so much of Mr Fritz, got rid of the bottles for her because she felt too embarrassed to put them out for the binmen.

A concerned Bel had persuaded her to have her eyes tested, but the optician said she had excellent sight for a woman of her age, though he prescribed glasses for reading.

Mam, Flo remembered, had been terrified of letting a doctor near her with a knife. The girls used to get upset, worried that she'd die. But Mam had only been in her forties. Flo was seventy-six, nobody's wife, nobody's daughter, with no children to care if she lived or died. Bel would miss her terribly, Charmian less so, what with a husband, two kids and three grandchildren to look after since Minola had gone back to school. Tom O'Mara didn't need her so much now that he was married with a family, two lovely little girls, though he still came to William Square regularly, at least once a week, often bearing food from the Chinese takeaway around the corner and a bottle of wine. She never asked how he made the money he was so obviously flush with. After years spent living on his wits, involved in ventures that were barely this side of legal, he was now something to do with a club that he adamantly refused to talk about. Flo suspected she was probably the only person on earth who knew the real Tom O'Mara, the man who loved and fussed over her tenderly, and brought her little presents. Outside the four walls of her flat, she'd like to bet that Tom was an entirely different person – even his wife and children might not know how soft and gentle he could be. Bel, who couldn't stand him, had to concede it was decent of him to put Nancy in a posh nursing-home in Southport when her mind went haywire and she could remember nothing since the war.

Music filled the basement flat, reaching every nook and corner, wrapping around her like a magic blanket woven from the dearest of memories. And shadows from the lamp Tom had brought from abroad passed slowly over the walls, the figures lifesize. When Flo felt especially dizzy, the figures seemed real, alive. He had brought the record, too, not long ago. 'Close your eyes,' he said teasingly, when he came in. 'I've got you a prezzie, a surprise.'

So Flo had closed her eyes, and suddenly the strains of 'Dancing in the

Dark' came from the speakers at each end of the room. Her eyes had snapped open and for several seconds she felt muddled. She'd told no one that this was the tune she and Tommy had danced to in the Mystery more than half a century ago. 'What made you buy that, luv?' she asked querulously.

'You've been humming it non-stop for months. I thought you'd like to hear it sung by an expert. That's Bing Crosby, that is, the one who sings "White Christmas."'

'I know who Bing Crosby is. It's lovely, Tom. Ta very much.'

At first she didn't play the record much, scared of raking up the painful past, but lately, as her head got worse and she couldn't read, not even with her new glasses, she played it more and more often. It was soothing, better than a book, to remember her own romantic affair, more passionate and tragic than anything she'd ever read. She saw herself dancing under the trees with her lost lover, making love, whispering what was to be their final goodbye.

Bel had told her she should exercise more, not sit like a lump in front of the telly getting sozzled every day. 'I ride for miles every morning on me bike in the bathroom,' she hooted loudly, through her ghastly new dentures, which were much too big and made her look like an elderly Esther Rantzen.

'I'm seventy-six, Bel,' Flo said indignantly. 'I'm entitled to be a sozzled lump at my age.' What would she have done without Bel? Without Charmian and Tom, Mr Fritz, Sally, even Hugh, her son, for a while? She'd been lucky to have so many people to love and love her back.

'What time is it?' She looked at the clock. Just gone six. But was that night or morning? What month was it? What year? It was frightening when she couldn't remember things, when she forgot to go to bed, forgot to eat, forgot to watch one of her favourite programmes on the telly. Once she'd nearly gone out in her nightie. One of these days she'd forget who she was. It wasn't that she was losing her mind like Nancy. She smiled. No, the trouble was, she was either in terrible pain or as drunk as a lord.

She went over to the window and lifted the curtain, but still couldn't tell if it was dawn or dusk. A thick mist hung in the air, suspended a few feet from the pavement. There were noises in the square, but there always were, no matter what the time; a car drove away, she could hear people talking, someone walked past and she could see less of them than usual because their knees were shrouded in mist. She heard the clink of milk bottles. It must be morning, which meant she'd been sitting up all night.

The record, which she'd played countless times, came to an end yet again. Oddly, the ensuing silence felt louder than the music. It was a buzz, as if she was surrounded by a million bees. As she listened to the silence, Flo's mind drained of everything and became completely blank. She sat on the chest in front of the window and wondered what was she doing in this strange room full of shadows. There was too much furniture, too many ornaments, too many flowers. She didn't like it. A memory returned, crawling like a worm into her head: she lived in Burnett Street with Mam and Dad.

'But what am I doing here?' she asked of the strange room and the shadowy figures passing overhead. There was no answer. Had she been visiting someone? Whose house was this?

'Is anyone there?' Still no answer. Flo pressed her hands together distractedly, trying to make up her mind what was the best thing to do. Get away from this place, obviously, go home. Even better, go into work early, get on with the pressing left over from yesterday. It would give Mr Fritz a nice surprise when he came in.

She saw a coat hanging behind the door that looked faintly familiar. She put it on and went outside. A man was running towards her dressed in a funny red outfit, just like Father Christmas. 'Mr Fritz!' She smiled.

The man reached her. 'It's Peter Maxwell, Flo, from next door. I've been for a run. But what are you doing out so early, luv? It's awful damp. You'll get a chill.'

'I've got to go somewhere,' she said vaguely.

'Would you like me to come with you?' The man was looking at her worriedly.

'No, ta,' she told him pleasantly.

She set off into the wet mist at a fast pace, along Upper Parliament Street and into Smithdown Road, passing closed shops and empty shops, new buildings and old, Clement Street and Mulliner Street, names that seemed familiar, though she couldn't remember why. She looked for the dress shop, which had that lovely lilac frock in the window – she'd seen it only yesterday and intended to buy it. Later, in the dinner hour, she might well come back and get it. But she couldn't see the shop anywhere. The fog didn't help – perhaps that was why no trams were running – she could scarcely see across the road. Worse, when she turned into Gainsborough Road, there was no sign of the laundry. A brick building stood in the place where the old wooden shed should be, a clinic, with notices in the window advertising a playgroup, ante-natal classes, a mother-and-toddler group.

'Oh, Lord!' Flo groaned. The fog seemed to have entered her head. It lifted briefly when she read the notices and wondered how she had got to Gainsborough Road. Why was her heart racing? Why did her legs feel so weak? She didn't realise she'd walked for miles with the energy of a young girl. The fog drifted in again, smothering the pain and everything that was real.

'I'll go and see Mam and Dad.' She made her way towards Burnett Street. The fog in her head cleared for a second when she stood outside the three terraced properties at the end of the street and remembered that they'd been built on the spot where the Clancys' and two neighbouring houses used to be. She stood for a moment, staring up at the tiled roofs, the small windows. The door of the middle house opened and a man in a donkey jacket and greasy overalls came out.

'Are you after something, missus?' he demanded irritably, when he found an elderly woman standing virtually on his doorstep.

'I used to live here,' said Flo.

'You couldn't have.' He scowled. 'Me and the missus were the first to move in when the place was built forty years ago.'

The fog had descended again, enveloping her brain. 'There used to be a bay window and steps up to the door.' She put a trembling hand to her forehead. 'Did it get bombed? Is that what happened?'

'Look, luv,' the man's gruff voice became kind, 'you seem a bit confused, like. Would you like to come inside and me missus'll make you a cup of tea, then take you home? You live round here, do you?'

'I thought I lived here.' Flo wanted to cry. She said fretfully, 'Is the Mystery still there?'

'Of course it is, luv, but this isn't a good time to go walking in the park.'

But Flo was already on her way, nineteen years old, with a red ribbon in her hair, about to meet Tommy O'Mara outside the gates for the first time. She felt as if she was walking towards her destiny, and that afterwards nothing would be the same again.

He wasn't there. He was probably inside waiting under one of the trees, which were shrouded in a veil of mist. The wet grass quickly soaked through her shoes as she made her way towards them. A whiff of reality returned when she noticed the road leading from gate to gate, and the sports arena glimmering palely through the haze, things that hadn't been there before.

It was 1996, not 1939. 'Flo Clancy,' she breathed, 'you're making a right fool of yourself this morning.' She'd better catch the bus home while she had the sense to do it. But she hadn't brought a handbag, she had no money. She wept aloud. 'I feel too weary to walk all that way back.'

She plodded back towards the gates. It wouldn't be a bad idea to take the red ribbon out of her hair. It must look dead stupid on an ould woman. She blinked when she found there was no ribbon there. Martha must have snatched it off before she left the house.

Poor Martha! Flo had never before had such a feeling of sympathy for the sister who'd never had much happiness in her life, if any. 'It's time to forgive and forget, luv.' Sally must have said that a hundred times over the years.

'I'll go and see her tomorrer,' Flo vowed. 'I'll take her a bunch of flowers.' At that moment, she couldn't precisely remember where Martha lived, but it would come. The fog inside her head kept lifting and falling, she kept drifting backwards and forwards in time, and the present was becoming confused with the past. She was leaving through the gates when she heard a shout. 'Flo!'

Flo turned. Her face melted into a smile, the dimples deepened in her wrinkled face, she could feel the brightness shining from her eyes as she watched Tommy O'Mara emerge from the white mist that swirled and floated in and around the Mystery and come towards her. She stood stock-still, waiting for him, waiting for him to take her in his arms.

She waved. Oh, he was a divil of a man, with his swaggering walk, a red hanky tied carelessly around his neck, an old tweed cap perched jauntily on the back of his brown curls. She had never stopped loving him. She never would.

'Flo, girl,' he called again.

'Tommy!' Flo held out her arms to welcome her handsome lover, who had never told a lie, had meant everything he'd said, who would have married her one day if he hadn't gone down with the *Thetis*. They would have lived happily ever after with their child. Then, from somewhere within the hazy clouds, she heard the orchestra of her dream a lifetime ago, playing 'Dancing in the Dark'. Her tired old body was swaying, this way and that, to the music that swelled and quivered in the smoky, dew-spangled morning.

She didn't hear the lorry backing slowly through the fog and the gates of the Mystery. It hit her full square, flinging her forward, and the phantom figure of Tommy O'Mara was the last thing Flo saw before she died.

The lorry drove away, the driver unaware that he'd hit anyone.

It was a young lad on his way home from his paper round who found the body. He stared at the old woman lying face down on the path. Was she dead, or had she just fainted?

He knelt down and gingerly turned the old girl over by the shoulder. She was dead all right, he could tell, but, Jaysus, never in all his life before had he seen such a brilliant smile.

Millie

1

The church hall was an Aladdin's cave of treasures; stalls with handmade jewellery, tie-dyed T-shirts, embroidered waistcoats, patchwork cushions, pottery, paintings, intricately moulded candles far too elegant to burn. But I'm sure I wasn't prejudiced in thinking our Trudy's stall was the most outstanding of all – and the cheapest.

Colin had added a shelf to the back of a pasting table so that the glassware could be exhibited on two levels. Nightlights flickered in painted wineglasses and tumblers that had been placed between the taller bottles so that the flames glittered through the jewel-coloured glass, the patterns outlined lavishly in gold or silver. The stall was alive with every imaginable hue – 'Like a rainbow on fire,' I said, and sighed with satisfaction when everything was done. I'd come early to help Trudy set up.

Trudy was shaking, as if she was about to take the starring role in her first play. 'What if I don't sell a single thing?'

'Don't be daft. I've got my eye on at least five bottles for Christmas presents.'

'I can't take money off me sister.'

'What nonsense! There's no room for sentiment now you're a business-woman, Trude.'

'Oh, Mill!' Trudy glanced left and right at the other stallholders, most of whom had finished setting up and were waiting impatiently for the doors to open at eleven o'clock. 'I feel dead conspicuous.'

'You look perfectly okay to me. Would you like a cup of tea?'

'I'd love one. But don't stay away long, Sis,' she called nervously, as I went towards the room behind the stage where tea and coffee were being served. 'I can't do this on me own.'

It turned out to be a day when the Camerons came of age, I thought afterwards, when we appeared to be just like any other family. James came at exactly half past eleven, as promised. Declan was already there, deeply interested in the process of tie-dying. Mum arrived at midday, her face red and bothered. Beads of perspiration glistened on her brow, although the November day was cold. I went to meet her. 'Your dad turned dead nasty when he realised I was going out,' she panted. 'He insisted I made his dinner first. I've put it in a low oven for when he comes home from the pub, but I daren't think what it'll be like by then.' She dropped her handbag, bent to retrieve it, then dropped the car keys and her gloves. 'How's our Trudy getting on?'

'Her bottles are selling like hot cakes. Half have already gone. She's not asking nearly enough.' Trudy hadn't even noticed I was no longer there. Flushed with confidence, she was coping with her busy stall on her own. I clutched my mother's arm. 'Mum, could you come back to Flo's with me when this is over? There's something I want to show you.'

'What on earth can that be, luv?'

'You won't know till you've seen it, will you?'

She shook her head. 'I couldn't possibly, Millicent. Your dad was in a terrible mood. It'd be best if I went straight home.'

'In that case I'll come over tonight and fetch you,' I said firmly. 'There's something you've got to see.'

James had already been introduced to Trudy. It was time he met my mother. How could I ever have felt ashamed, I wondered, with a lump in my throat, of this warm-hearted, kind woman, whose face shone with pleasure as she said, 'I'm ever so pleased to meet you, James, luv. Does your mam call you Jim or Jimmy?'

When Colin arrived with Melanie and Jake after dinner, Trudy's stall was almost empty. Starry-eyed and triumphant, she'd taken over two hundred pounds. 'I can't believe people are actually willing to pay for me bottles. Just imagine, they'll be on window-sills all over Liverpool.' She promised to paint more for me over the next few days. Mum was in her element. She wandered around, saying, 'I see you've bought one of me daughter's bottles. Aren't they lovely?' If people were inclined to stop and chat, she'd tell them about her other daughter. 'That's her over there,' I heard her say more than once. 'That's our Millicent. She works for an estate agent in Liverpool town centre. And that's me son, the lad in the brown jersey. He's going to college next year.'

To everyone's astonishment, Gran turned up and bought the last of Trudy's bottles. 'I couldn't very well not come, could I?' she grunted sourly. 'Someone gave me a lift. I hope our Kate came in the car so she can take me home.'

I studied my grandmother carefully. This was the woman who'd given Flo's baby to Nancy O'Mara. Oh, how I'd love to find out exactly what had happened. But this wasn't the right time – would there ever be a right time to raise such an emotive subject?

We all went into the room behind the stage for a cup of tea. Trudy folded up her stall and joined us, which meant that there were three Camerons, four Daleys, Martha Colquitt and James – who were, inexplicably, having an animated conversation about football. The only person missing was my father, which probably accounted for the jubilant atmosphere.

'I never thought I'd witness this,' Colin whispered to me.

'Witness what?'

'Well, it's almost a case of Happy Families, isn't it? It's the way you'd expect any normal family to behave. Everyone's had a great day, including the kids.'

When it was time to leave, I arranged to pick up Mum at seven o'clock and take her to Flo's flat. My father would have gone out again by then.

'I wish you'd tell me what it's all about,' she said.

'What is it all about?' James asked later. We'd driven into town in our separate cars and met up in a restaurant for a meal. 'I'd hoped we'd spend the rest of the day together.'

I ignored the last comment. 'It's something truly amazing and wonderful,' I said happily. 'Auntie Flo's left her flat and all her money, nearly twenty-four thousand pounds, to Mum. I only found a copy of the will last night. I want her to be at Flo's when she reads it for herself.'

When I drew up outside, the house in Kirkby was in darkness. Surprised, I went round to the back. The kitchen door was unlocked, which meant that someone must be in. 'Mum?' I shouted. 'Declan? Is anybody home? It's me.'

A faint noise came from upstairs, a whimper. Alarmed, I switched on the light on the stairs and went up. 'Mum?' I called.

'In here, luv.' The voice, little more than a whisper, came from the front bedroom. I pushed open the door and reached for the light switch.

'Don't turn the light on, Millicent.'

I ignored her. In the dim glow of the low wattage bulb, I saw my mother half sitting, half lying in bed. Her right eye was swollen, her lip split and bleeding. She had bruises on both arms. She looked utterly wretched, but despite everything, there was still that indefatigable look in her eyes, as though she was the most resilient victim in the world, who would survive whatever came her way. I was convinced that if a tank rolled over her, she would pick herself up and carry on as if nothing had happened.

'Mum! Oh, Mum, what's he done to you?' Rage enveloped me like a cloak and I could scarcely speak. If my father had been there, I think I could easily have killed him.

'Close the curtains, luv. I don't want people seeing in.'

I drew them with an angry flourish, and sat on the bed. Mum winced. 'It's not as bad as it looks,' she said. 'I tried to ring you, stop you coming, but all I got was your machine.'

'I've been in town with James.' I forced myself to speak calmly.

'Mrs Bradley dabbed some TCP on it, and she bathed me eye an' all. I'm just a tiny bit tipsy too. She gave me this great big glass of brandy. She wanted to call the police, but I wouldn't let her.' Over the years, Mrs Bradley had frequently threatened to report Norman Cameron, but Mum had always stopped her. 'I told her this was the first time he'd hit me in years, which is the God's honest truth.'

'What brought it on, Mum?'

She shrugged, then winced again. 'His dinner was ruined. I knew it would be, stuck in the oven all that time.'

'You mean this . . .' – I gestured towards the black eye, the split lip, the bruises – '. . . is solely due to a ruined dinner?'

'Only partly. I was out an awful long time, Millicent, nearly four hours. And, oh, it was a lovely afternoon.' Her eyes brightened when she thought about the day that had gone. 'I really enjoyed meself, what with our Trudy doing so well, Colin and the kids being there, your gran turning up, you and Declan. James is ever such a nice chap, I really liked him.' She managed a laugh. 'I even bought meself a pair of earrings to wear at your wedding – little red flowered ones to go with me best coat.'

'Oh, Mum!' I lightly touched her fading hair.

She sighed. 'He could never stand me being happy. I daren't ever come in with a smile on me face that I got from somewhere else, it always riled him. It makes him feel shut out, and he hates that. Today I just didn't think. I suppose I expected him to be pleased about Trudy and everything. 'Stead, he just lashed out at me. He'd been getting more and more worked up the longer I stayed out.'

'He's always been a miserable bugger,' I said acidly.

There was a long silence. Mum seemed to have drifted off into a world of her own. A motorbike growled to a halt outside. I got up and looked through the curtains. A girl from a house opposite came out, got on to the pillion, and the bike shot away. I stayed at the window, though there was no longer anything to see apart from the orange street lights, the still houses, the occasional car driving by. A group of boys wandered past, kicking a football to each other. Then my mother spoke in a soft, far-away voice: 'I remember once, I was only a titch, two or three. We'd been out for the day, your gran and me. It was late when we got back. Did I ever tell you we lived with Elsa Cameron for a long time? Anyroad, Elsa was out, and we heard noises coming from the cupboard under the stairs, terrible sobs. The poor little lad had been shut in there in the dark for hours. You never saw anything like his eyes, all feverish and bright, as if he'd have gone mad if he'd been left there much longer. He was only six.'

'Who are you talking about, Mum?' I asked perplexed.

'Why, your dad, luv. After that, your gran never left him alone with Elsa again. She had that illness, they call it purple depression or something now. She should never have been allowed to keep a child.'

I felt myself grow cold. I recalled the photo in Flo's flat of the grim-looking woman with the beautiful baby on her knee, the baby that had become my father. I tried to visualise the monster who had conducted a reign of terror throughout our childhood as a terrified little boy of six. It was hard. 'Why have you never told us this before, Mum?' I asked shakily.

'Your dad made me swear never to breathe a word to another soul. I suppose he felt ashamed. I'd be obliged if you didn't mention to him that I'd told you.'

'It might have helped us to understand.' It only might have.

'I suppose things would have been different if I hadn't let him down,' she said, half to herself.

'In what way, Mum?'

Her face went blank, as if she'd said too much. 'Oh, it doesn't matter, luv. It's a long time ago now. Do you fancy a cup of tea? I'm dying for one meself. I haven't had one since I came home.'

'I'll make one straight away. Where's Declan?'

'He's not back yet. He went off with the couple who made them funny-coloured T-shirts.'

While I made the tea my mind was in a whirl. I had no idea what to think. No matter what had happened to my father, it was impossible to excuse the things he'd done. It wasn't Mum's fault, or his children's, that his own mother had suffered from puerperal depression. Why take it out on us?

When I returned to the bedroom with the tea, Mum said, 'What's the big surprise for me at Flo's? Or are you still not prepared to tell me unless I'm actually there?'

'I'd forgotten all about it!' I took hold of both Mum's hands. 'Prepare yourself for a shock. Flo's left you her flat and all her worldly wealth. Twenty-three thousand, seven hundred and fifty-two pounds and eleven-pence to be precise.'

I didn't leave until my father came home. The back door opened, I kissed Mum goodbye, and went downstairs. He was coming through the kitchen, unsteady on his feet, eyes blurred.

'If you lay a finger on my mother again,' I said, in a grating voice that made my ears tingle, 'so help me, I'll kill you.' He looked at me vacantly, as if he wasn't sure where the strange voice had come from. 'Do you understand?' I persisted.

He nodded. I paused, my hand on the front door, feeling oddly perturbed by the look of naked misery on his face, which I probably wouldn't have noticed before. Then he said something that didn't make sense, but never-theless made my stomach curl.

'It's all your fault.'

I was scratching through my mind, trying to think of a response, when I realised he was drunk, talking rubbish. I shook myself and left.

I'd tried to talk Mum into leaving there and then. Flo's flat was ready to move into. Wasn't it fortunate I hadn't touched a thing? The place was exactly as Flo had left it.

'There's no hurry, luv,' she said. 'Your poor dad'll be feeling dead sorry about things for a week or two. I'd sooner tell him, face to face, when I'm ready to go. I owe him that much, and I won't be scared, not now I've got money and somewhere to live. It makes me feel strong.' She still looked stunned, as if she couldn't get over the news of her good fortune. 'I remember saying to Flo how much I liked her flat when I first went there. I can't believe it's mine,' had been her initial reaction.

'Don't tell Dad about the money yet,' I warned. 'If he got his hands on it, every penny would go in no time on the lottery and the horses.'

'I may look a fool, Millicent, I've probably been a fool for most of me life, but I'm not that stupid.'

'Come and have a proper look round in the morning,' I said excitedly. 'I'll take the day off work. I've still got two days' holiday left, I was leaving them till Christmas.' My mind was working overtime, sorting out my mother's life. 'You need only stay at Flo's for a few months, then you can sell it and buy a similar place in Oxford.'

'Mmm, I suppose I could,' Mum said, in a dreamy, rather vague way that made me wonder if she could ever bring herself to leave Kirkby when it came right down to it.

'Do you still love him?' I demanded sharply.

'No, Millicent. I never loved him. The trouble is, you might find this hard to believe, but he loves me, he always has. I'm not sure how he'll manage with me not here.' She laughed girlishly when she saw me frown. 'Don't worry, I'm going. I'd already planned to, hadn't I? It's thirty years last Easter since we were married, so I've done me stint. You and Trudy have got your own lives, Declan will be off soon. Now, Alison comes first.'

'And you? What about you?' I was doing my best to hide my impatience. 'Isn't it time you put yourself first?'

'I'll be doing that when there's just me and Alison.'

Later, when I parked the car in William Square, I thought sadly that this would be one of the last nights I would spend there. But the place was staying in the family, at least for a while. Even if that hadn't been the case, I could still come back to see Bel and Charmian. As I went down the steps to the basement room, I saw that the light was on and my heart lifted eagerly. I opened the door. Tom O'Mara was sitting on the settee watching television, his feet resting on the coffee table. Everything that had been good or bad about the day that would shortly end was forgotten.

'Hi,' he said. Our eyes met. 'You're late.'

'No, you're early.'

'Whatever.' He stood up and took me in his arms and we locked together in a long, lingering kiss. I couldn't wait for us to make love, I couldn't wait a minute longer. Neither could he. He picked me up and, still kissing, carried me into the bedroom.

Later, when it was over, Tom fell asleep, but I had never felt more wide awake, as if little electric currents were passing endlessly around my head. The affair had to end some time. He would never get divorced, and I didn't want him to. Perhaps, now that I was moving back to Blundellsands, it was time to call a halt. But could I bring myself to turn him away? Would he let me? Had I the will to resist if he flatly refused to be turned away?

My restless brain refused to stop working. Would Mum be safe in Toxteth, even if it wasn't going to be for ever? It hadn't crossed my mind till now. I thought of the few people I knew who already lived here: Charmian and Herbie and their children, Bel, Peter Maxwell, nice, respectable, honest people, like Flo. Anyway, Mum would be safer anywhere in the world, including Toxteth, than with her husband.

When I got up in the morning, I must clear the bureau of the things that gave away Flo's secrets. I'd keep the love letters, the photo of the little boy who looked so much like Declan, and the drawing he'd done of 'MY FREND FLO'. No wonder Tom had felt so drawn towards her. He was her grandson. I recalled how indifferent he'd been with Nancy.

'Don't worry, Flo,' I whispered. 'Everything's safe with me.'

At half past nine next morning, I asked Charmian if I could use her phone – I never remembered to bring my mobile to William Square – and called Stock Masterton to say I wasn't coming in. Oliver answered. 'Diana's back,' he hissed. 'She's ruling the roost already.'

I groaned. 'I'm not looking forward to tomorrow.'

Next, I called the solicitor in Castle Street who'd dealt with Flo's affairs and made an appointment for late that afternoon.

Downstairs again, the bureau looked pathetically empty, the papers I wanted to keep already stowed in the boot of the car, the rest thrown away. I dusted everywhere, swept the yard, pulled the last few dead leaves off the plants, had a word with the same black cat that had watched me before. Then

I cleaned the kitchen and the bathroom, although they'd scarcely been used, but I wanted everywhere to look perfect for when Mum came. The flat looked different today, not just cleaner but more impersonal. I didn't feel quite so much at home.

I'd barely finished when there was a knock on the door. It was too early for Mum. Perhaps it was Charmian inviting me upstairs for a coffee. I rather hoped so. Charmian had been thrilled to learn that my mother was moving in below. I was sure they'd get on well together.

'Gran!' I remarked in astonishment, when I opened the door. 'Come in.'

'Your mam phoned with the news this morning,' Martha Colquitt said grumpily, as she crunched into the living room in the crêpe-soled, fur-lined boots that were almost as old as I was. She wore a camel coat, and a jersey hat shaped like a turban with a pearl brooch in the middle. The room instantly began to reek of mothballs and liniment. 'I had an appointment at the women's hospital, so I thought I'd come and look the place over.'

'What's wrong? I mean, why did you have to go to hospital?' None of us Cameron children had much affection for our grandmother, but it was impossible to imagine life without her bad-tempered presence.

Gran was predictably bad-tempered with her reply. 'I dunno what's wrong, do I?' she barked. 'They took X-rays and did tests. I have to wait for the results till I know what's wrong.' Her voice softened. 'So this is where she lived, our Flo. I always wondered what it looked like.' She walked into the room. 'This is her all over. She liked things to be pretty.'

I watched her closely. I'd never seen her face so gentle, almost tender, as she surveyed her sister's room. 'Take your coat off, Gran,' I said. 'Would you like a coffee?'

'I never touch coffee, you should know that by now. I'll have tea. And I'll not take me coat off, thanks all the same. I'm not stopping long.'

'I'm afraid there's only powdered milk.'

Gran shrugged. 'I suppose that'll have to do, won't it?' Her head was cocked on one side, she was almost smiling as she watched Flo's lamp turn round. 'I'm dying for a ciggie and it tastes better with a cup of tea.'

When I came back, she was examining the drawing on the wall over the mantelpiece, which I'd meant to take down.

'What does this say?' She peered at it closely, her nose almost touching the wall. 'I can't see in these glasses, and I left me reading ones at home. I could never get along with them bi-focals.'

'It says, "MY FREND FLO". It was done by someone called Hugh O'Mara.'

Gran took a step back, but continued to stare at the drawing. I would have given anything to know what was going on inside her head. A faint hum came from upstairs, Charmian was vacuuming the carpets. One of Minola's children gave a little shriek. Gran was still looking at the drawing, as if she'd forgotten I was there. I licked my lips, which suddenly felt dry. I didn't want to upset her, but I *had* to know.

'He was Flo's son, wasn't he, Gran? She had him by a man called Tommy O'Mara who died on the *Thetis*. He probably never knew she was pregnant.' I licked my lips again before plunging on. 'You gave him away to Tommy's wife, Nancy.'

'What in God's name are you talking about, girl?' She spun round, wobbling slightly when her clumsy boots became tangled with each other. I felt myself shrivel before the angry eyes behind the thick lenses. 'What the hell do you know about it?'

'I know because Nancy told me.'

'Nancy!' The yellow lips split in a hoarse, unbelieving laugh. 'Don't talk rubbish, girl. Nancy's dead.'

'No, she isn't, Gran. I met her the other week. She's in a nursing-home in Southport. She said . . .' I screwed up my eyes and tried to remember word for word what Nancy had said. I visualised the old liver-spotted face, the hot dark eyes, the long fingers clawing at my arm. 'She said, "Your Martha gave him to me fair and square. You're not getting him back. I'll kill him first." Her's mind's gone,' I finished. 'She thought I was Flo.'

Gran's face crumpled and she started to cry, an alarming and uncomfortable sight. She stumbled back into a chair and lit a cigarette with shaking hands.

'Gran!' I put the tea down, ran across the room and knelt at her feet. 'I didn't mean to upset you.' I was angry with myself for being too curious, too uncaring, yet I knew I wouldn't have hesitated to do the same thing again.

'It's all right, Millicent. Where's that tea?' There was a loud sniff, a quick removal of spectacles to wipe her eyes, a conscious effort to pull herself together. She looked embarrassed, unused to revealing any emotion except anger. Her hands were still shaking as she took the tea, though she'd recovered enough to grimace disapprovingly at the mug. She said, 'I never regretted what I did. It's hard for you young 'uns to realise the disgrace it was in those days for a baby to be born on the wrong side of the blanket. The whole family would have suffered.' Her face was hard again, her tone fierce. This was the grandmother I had known all my life. 'Nancy kept her head down and Hugh well hidden for a good six months. We never dreamed Flo would recognise the baby after all that time.'

She wasn't sorry! Despite everything that had happened, losing her sister for a lifetime, she still wasn't sorry. Frowning, she jabbed the air with her cigarette. 'I can't understand this business with you and Nancy. Who told you about her? Who took you to see her in Southport?'

I sank back until I was sitting cross-legged on the floor, the heat from the gas-fire hot on my shoulders. 'Tom O'Mara did. He's Nancy's grandson – or Flo's grandson. I'm not sure how to describe him.'

'Tom O'Mara!' Gran's eyes narrowed. She stared, her gaze so penetrating, so intensely suspicious, that I knew straight away she'd guessed what was going on. I felt my cheeks burn.

At the same time, to my surprise, her face turned parchment white. Her bottom lip quivered. She looked a hundred years old. She put the half-full mug on the floor, the cigarette fell in, sizzled briefly and floated on the top, but she didn't seem to notice. She immediately lit another. 'I reckon there's a curse on the Clancys and the O'Maras,' she said. Her voice was dull, listless, almost funereal. It scared me.

'What do you mean?'

'Well, first there was Flo and Tommy.' She took a long, hard drag on the cigarette, and the end glowed bright red. 'Then our Kate and Hugh. Would you believe they actually wanted to get married?' She gave a little strained laugh, and nodded at me incredulously.

'Why couldn't they get married?' I ventured. *I'd nearly had Hugh O'Mara for a father!*

'Because they were cousins, of course,' Gran explained, as if to a child. 'It's not allowed – least, it wasn't then. Fortunately, Norman stepped in like the good lad he always was, even though he knew he was accepting soiled goods. Poor Norman . . . Until then, he'd worshipped the ground your mam walked on. He would have made the best husband in the world if she hadn't spoiled things.'

'I don't know what you're talking about, Gran.'

'I'm talking about your mam being up the stick when she married Norman Cameron.' She still spoke in the same flat, dull voice, which seemed at odds with the rather coarse expression. 'We told her Hugh O'Mara had done a bunk once he knew she was pregnant, else we'd never have got her up the aisle.'

'Who's we?' I said weakly.

'Me and Nancy. As if we could have asked for a dispensation, like our Sally suggested. Imagine telling the Church authorities about our Flo's dirty little secret.' She almost choked on the last words.

Upstairs the vacuuming had stopped. I heard the front door open and Charmian come out with the children. I felt totally mixed up. My brain, which had been working so well the night before, could no longer take anything in. What was this leading up to?

'If Mum was pregnant when she married my father,' I said slowly, 'then what happened to the baby?'

'I'm looking at her.'

'Me?'

'Yes, Millicent, you.' Gran's eyes had shrunk, skull-like, deep into their sockets. She took another long puff on her cigarette, and blew the smoke out in an equally long sigh. 'You know what that means, don't you?'

I felt myself tingle all over. 'Hugh O'Mara was my father?'

'That's right. It means something else an' all. Jesus, Mary and Joseph!' She groaned. 'It was bad enough with our Kate! I bet the devil's laughing up his sleeve at the moment.' She leaned forward, her eyes boring into mine. 'Think, Millicent, think what it means.'

So I thought very hard and eventually came up with the answer. 'It means that Tom is my brother, my half-brother,' I breathed.

2

'Millie,' Diana said importantly, 'Will you come here a minute, please?'

'Yes, miss.' I abandoned the photocopier and stood in front of Diana's desk, my hands clasped meekly behind my back. June grinned and Elliot stifled a giggle.

Diana looked at me suspiciously, not sure if she was being made fun of. She flourished a sheet of paper. 'This property you went to see last week, the one in Banks. On the particulars you describe the upstairs as having a recess with a window. You quite clearly don't know that this is what's called

925

an oriel window. Would you change it, please, before we run the details off?'

The first thing I'd done when I was promoted was buy a book on architecture so that I could accurately describe any unusual aspects of a building. 'I'm afraid you've got it wrong, Diana,' I said sweetly. 'An oriel is a recess in the projection of a building. There's no projection on the house in Banks, just a recess.'

Diana waved the paper again. 'I beg to differ. I think I know what an oriel window is by now.'

'Millie's right,' Oliver said, from across the room. 'I doubt if I could have described it better myself.' The man sitting next to him at the same desk, nodded. Barry Green had only started the day before. He was taking over as assistant manager when Oliver transferred to Woolton on 1 January. 'I second that,' Barry said, with a charming smile.

'Even I knew that,' June chortled.

'Oh!' Diana got up and flounced into George's office. She slammed the door, and everyone glanced at each other in patient resignation when we heard the sound of her raised, complaining voice.

'Actually,' June said, 'I've never heard of an oriel window. I just wanted to get up Madam's nose.'

'I must say,' Barry Green remarked, 'that I'm glad the horrendous Miss Riddick won't be here much longer. I don't know what's got into George but he's well and truly smitten.' Barry Green had given George his first job thirty years ago, and they had remained friends ever since. His vast experience as an estate agent hadn't prevented him from being made redundant when the chain he worked for had been taken over by a building society. He reminded me of actors in the old black-and-white British films I sometimes watched on television. In his sixties, with bountiful silver hair, perfectly coiffured, he wore a light grey suit with a slight sheen, and an eggshell blue bow-tie. His diction, like his hair, was perfect, as was his moustache, two neat, silvery fish. He looked the embodiment of a 1930s ladies' man, but appearances were deceptive. Barry had a wife, Tess, four children and eight grandchildren, whose various achievements he let slip into the conversation whenever he found the opportunity. One son was an architect, his two daughters had given up dazzling careers when they started their families, several grand-children were already at university, including the one who could walk at eight months and play the piano when she was three. He rarely mentioned his youngest son, who was abroad, but no one asked what he was up to in case Barry launched into another long, adulatory explanation.

There was nothing subtle about the change of atmosphere in Stock Masterton since Diana had returned yesterday. I wondered if it was just my imagination that I was being picked on more than the others. If I hadn't been so preoccupied with my own life, it might have mattered more. Diana wasn't rude, merely loudly and forcefully officious. She kept telling people what to do when they already knew, offering advice when it wasn't needed. She was having an affair with the boss and wanted everyone to know how much her stock had risen.

'What did you mean,' I said to Barry, 'about Diana not being here much longer?' Maybe she was leaving to marry George.

'Because she's coming to Woolton with me.' Oliver sighed. 'George only told me yesterday. She's got a title, assistant manager. I'm not sure if I can stand it.'

'Your bad luck is our good fortune,' I said cheerfully. With Diana out of the way, perhaps I could get back on good terms with George.

This seemed unlikely when Diana appeared, saying, 'George would like a word with you, Millie.'

'I'd be obliged,' George said coldly, when I went in, 'if in future you'd refrain from upsetting Diana in front of the entire office. Everyone makes mistakes from time to time. It doesn't help to have them exposed in public.'

I made one of the faces I'd caught off Bel. 'Isn't this all a bit juvenile, George, like telling tales at school?'

'It's not long since the poor girl's father died. She's feeling very vulnerable at the moment.'

'So am I,' I said curtly. I'd scarcely slept for two nights in a row and was already sick to death of the situation at work. I knew I was only sinking to Diana's level when I said, 'It was Diana who pointed out my mistake first – what she thought was a mistake. I put her right, that's all. As she did it in front of the entire office, Oliver and Barry merely backed me up.'

'Oh, is that what really happened?' George looked nonplussed.

'Yes, George, it is.'

'I'm sorry, I must have got the wrong end of the stick.' He became quite friendly and asked how I was getting on with the flat in William Square.

'It's a long story, George. Perhaps I could tell it to you one day over lunch?' I'd only tell him the least important bits.

'Great idea, Millie. We'll do that, eh?'

Diana was scowling at me through the glass partition. I resisted the urge to stick out my tongue, and reckoned there was no chance of having lunch with George once she got back to work on him. She seemed to be pursuing a private vendetta against me.

When I came out, June shouted, 'There's just been a phone call, Millie. Some woman particularly asked for you. She says her boss, a Mr Thomas, has a property to sell as soon as poss in Clement Street off Smithdown Road, number eighteen. It belonged to a relative. He wants a valuation. I looked in the diary and told her you'd be there at two o'clock.'

'I think I'll go,' Diana stretched her arms. 'I feel like some fresh air.'

'They asked for Millie,' June said pointedly.

'This is an estate agent's, not a hairdresser's,' Diana snapped. 'It doesn't matter who goes.'

Oliver said sweetly, 'Yes, it does, Diana. It might be a former client who would prefer Millie rather than another member of staff.' He winked at me. 'Will you be all right on your own? Take Darren, if you'd feel safer.'

'I doubt if I'll come to any harm in Clement Street, it's too built-up.' Female staff weren't usually sent to deal with properties if a man on his own was involved.

It felt odd to drive past William Square and think of Flo's flat, as familiar now as the back of my hand, waiting for my mother to move in on Friday. Yesterday, she'd astounded me by announcing that when the time came for

Alison to leave Skelmersdale, she'd have her in William Square instead of going to Oxford.

'Is that wise, Mum?' I said worriedly. 'You realise it's a red-light area. That girl outside is a prostitute. And it can be very violent.'

'I don't know what's wise or not, luv. Our Alison's always had plenty of care and attention, but she's never had much love. The change is bound to upset her, whether she goes to Oxford or comes to me, so I'd like to give it a chance.' Kate's eyes glistened. 'We'll sleep together in the same bed and I'll hold her in me arms if she'll let me. As to the prostitutes, they're only working girls who've fallen on hard times. They won't harm our Alison. The violence I'll just have to take a chance on. After all, I can always move, can't I?'

I regarded her doubtfully. 'I hope you're not making a terrible mistake. What will you live on?'

'I'll eke out the money Flo left so it lasts as long as possible. In a few years, I'll be due for me pension. I might get a carer's allowance for looking after Alison. Don't worry, luv,' she said serenely, 'I'll be all right. I haven't felt so happy in ages.'

Perhaps the last time she'd been happy was with Hugh O'Mara. Even now, the next day, I found it difficult to grasp what Gran had told me.

I turned into Clement Street, found a place to park, took a photograph of number eighteen, then knocked at the door. The street was comprised of small terraced properties, the front doors opening on to the pavement. The house in question had been relatively well maintained, though the down-stairs window-sill could have done with a fresh coat of paint. I noticed the step hadn't been cleaned in a while.

The door opened, 'Hello, Millie,' said Tom O'Mara.

Yesterday, I'd written to him, then fled back to Blundellsands when I came out of the solicitor's with my mother, so there would have been no one in when he turned up at Flo's last night. I'd thought long and hard about what to write. In the end, I'd merely stated the facts baldly, without embellishment or comment. I didn't put 'Dear Tom', or who the letter was from, just a few necessary words that explained everything. He would know who'd sent it. I'd posted it to the club because I didn't know his address.

Tom turned and went down the narrow hallway into a room at the rear of the house. He was dressed in all black: leather jacket, jeans, T-shirt. I took a deep breath and followed, closing the door behind me. The room was furnished sixties style, with a lime green carpet, orange curtains, a melamine table, two grey plastic easy chairs, one each side of the elaborate tiled fireplace, which had little insets for knick-knacks. Everything was shabby and well used, and there were no ornaments, or other signs that the place was inhabited.

'This is where me gran used to live,' Tom said. His jacket creaked silkily as he sat in one of the chairs and stretched out his long legs. He wore expensive boots with a zip in the side, and looked out of place in the small dark room with its cheap furniture. I sat in the other chair. 'I bought it years ago as an investment. I got tenants in when Nancy went to Southport. Now they've moved I thought I'd sell. They say the price of property has started to go up.'

'When did you decide to sell?'

'This morning, when I heard from you. It made a good excuse. I got a woman from the club to ring the place you work. I had to see you again.'

'Why?'

'I dunno.' He shrugged elegantly. 'To see what it felt like, maybe, knowing you were me sister, knowing it was over.' He looked at me curiously. 'Didn't you want to see me?'

'Oh, I don't know, Tom. I've no idea what to think.' I felt slightly uncomfortable, but not embarrassed or ashamed. I'd pooh-poohed Gran's gruesome claim that the family was cursed, that the devil was involved, and the world was about to end because a half-sister and brother who'd known nothing about their relationship had slept with each other. 'We didn't know, Gran. It wasn't our fault. If it hadn't been for all the secrets . . .' It was irritating to know that I was now accumulating secrets of my own, things I couldn't tell my mother or Trudy or Declan. 'Don't repeat a word of this to your mam,' Gran pleaded. 'I'd be obliged if you wouldn't mention to your dad that I told you,' Mum had said the other night, about something or other I couldn't remember right now.

'You can go back to that boyfriend of yours,' Tom remarked drily. 'What's his name?'

'James.'

He looked amused. 'James and Millie. They go well together. What's Millie short for, anyroad? I always meant to ask.'

'Millicent.'

There was silence. Then Tom said something that made my stomach lurch. 'Will you come upstairs with me?' He nodded at the door. 'There's a bed.'

'*No!*' Despite my vehemently expressed horror, somewhere within the furthest reaches of my mind, I remembered what we'd been to each other and did my best not to imagine what it would be like now.

'I just wondered,' Tom said lightly. 'It's not that I want to, bloody hell, no. The whole idea makes me feel dead peculiar. I'm just trying to get things sorted in me head.'

'It's all over, Tom.' I could hardly speak.

'Christ, Millie, I know that. I'm not suggesting otherwise.' He smiled. Over the short time I'd known him, he'd rarely smiled. Whenever he did, I'd always thought him even more extraordinarily attractive than he already was, more desirable. I had that same feeling again, and it made me slightly nauseous. He went on, 'I wish we'd found out we were related before we . . .' he stopped, unwilling to say the words. 'It would have been great, knowing I had a sister.'

'And knowing Flo was your gran.' And my gran, I realised with a shock.

'Aye.' He nodded. 'That would have been great an' all.'

I refused to meet his eyes, worried about what I might see there. It seemed sensible to get away as quickly as possible. I took my notebook out of my bag and said briskly, 'Is it really your intention to put the house on the market?'

'I'd like to get rid of it, yes.'

'Then I'd better take some details.' I stood, smoothed my skirt, conscious of Tom watching my every move. I didn't look at him. 'I'll start upstairs.'

Quickly, I measured the rooms, made a note of the cupboards, the state of decoration, the small modern bathroom at the rear. Downstairs again, I took a quick look in the lounge, which was the same size as the front bedroom and had a black iron fireplace with a flower-painted tile surround, which could be sold for a bomb if it was taken out. There was an ugly brocade three-piece with brass pillars supporting the arms – I must tell Tom to get rid of the furniture.

In the hall, I paused for a moment. Tommy O'Mara had lived here, walked in and out of the same rooms, up and down the same stairs, sat in the same spot where I'd sat only a few minutes ago when I talked to his grandson. One day, a long time ago, Martha Colquitt, my other gran, had probably come to this house bringing Flo's baby with her, the baby who'd turned out to be my father. I stood very still, and in my mind's eye, I could actually see the things happening like in an old, faded film, as if they were genuine memories, as if I'd lived through them, taken part. It was an eerie feeling, but not unpleasant.

When I went into the living room, Tom O'Mara had gone. He'd left the key to Flo's flat on top of my handbag. He must have slipped out of the back when I was upstairs, and I was glad that my main emotion was relief, mixed with all sorts of other feelings that I preferred not to delve into. A car started up some way down the street and I didn't even consider looking through the net curtains to see if it was him. In one sense, I felt numb. In another, I felt entirely the opposite. I knew I would never make love with another man the way I had with Tommy O'Mara – Tom! The thing that had drawn us together was a crime, yet it would be impossible to forget.

When I returned to the office, Diana was cock-a-hoop. She'd just shown the Naughtons round a property in Childwall, and they were anxious to buy.

'How many places did you show them, Millie – ten, a dozen? I only took them once and they fell in love with it straight away,' she crowed.

'I'm sure they were more influenced by the house than the agent,' I said mildly. Right now, I couldn't give a damn about the Naughtons, or Diana.

After my parents' thirty brutal, wretched years of marriage, I expected there would be something equally brutal about its end: a fight, a huge scene, lots of screaming and yelling. I even visualised my father physically refusing to let Mum go. In other words, I was dreading Friday. Several times during the week, I asked Mum, 'What time are you leaving?'

'For goodness sake, Millicent, I don't know. It's not high noon or anything. I'll pack me suitcase during the day, and once I've had me tea I'll tell him I'm off before he has time to brood over it.'

'It can't possibly be that simple, Mum.'

'He can't stop me, can he? He can't guard over me for ever.' She bit her lip thoughtfully. 'I'll leave him a casserole in the fridge for the weekend.' She smiled at me radiantly. Over the last few days, the anxious lines around her eyes and mouth had smoothed away. I had never known her look so happy.

'I'll come straight from work and give you a lift,' I offered.

'There's no need, Millicent. I'll catch the bus. I won't have much to carry – a suitcase, that's all.'

I didn't argue, but on Friday, as soon as I finished work, I drove straight to

Kirkby. Trudy had obviously had the same idea. When I drew up the Cortina was parked outside the house.

My mother was kneeling on the kitchen floor playing with Scotty, who was lying on his back, wriggling in ecstasy as his tummy was tickled. 'I'll really miss this little chap,' she said tearfully, when I went in. 'I'd take him with me if there was a garden. But never mind, he'll be company for your dad.'

'Where is he?' I asked.

'In the front room.'

'Does he know?'

'Yes. He's taken it hard, I knew he would. He pleaded with me to stay. He promised to turn over a new leaf.'

'Really!' I said sarcastically.

Mum laughed. 'Yes, really.'

'Do you believe him?'

'Not for a minute, luv. I don't think he could, no matter how much he might want to.'

Trudy came into the room with a plastic bag. 'You'd forgotten your toothbrush, Mum.' She grinned at me. 'Hi, Sis. She's hardly taking a thing, just a few clothes, that's all.'

'I don't want to leave your dad with the house all bare. It'll be nice to start afresh with Flo's stuff. I must say,' Mum nodded at the ancient stove, 'I'll be glad to see the back of that ould thing.'

'Flo's is even older,' I said.

'Yes, but she's got a microwave, hasn't she? I've always wanted a microwave. Now, Trudy,' she turned to my sister, 'I want you to promise that you'll bring Melanie and Jake to see their grandad from time to time. He loves them kids, and it would be cruel to deprive him of their company.'

Trudy rubbed the scar on her left eyebrow and muttered, 'I'm not promising anything, Mum. We'll just have to see.'

'Well,' Mum said cheerfully, 'it's time I was off.'

The moment had come. Trudy and I looked at each other, and I saw my own incredulous excitement reflected in her green eyes as we followed Mum into the hall, where she paused at the door of the lounge. The television was on, a travel programme showing an exotic location with palm trees, sun and sand. To my surprise, Declan was sitting on the settee reading a newspaper. My father – the man I'd always thought was my father – was smoking, apparently quite calm, but there was something tight about his shoulders, and he seemed to hold the smoke in for too long before he blew it out again.

'I'm going now, Norman,' Mum said. She spoke as casually as if she were going to the shops. I sensed a subtle shifting of power.

Her husband shrugged. 'Please yerself,' he said.

'Your clean shirts are in the airing cupboard, and there's a meat casserole in the fridge. It should last at least two days.'

Declan got up. 'I'll come out and say tara, Mam.'

'Heavens, lad! I'll be seeing you tomorrer. You promised to come to dinner, didn't you? There's no need for taras.'

'Yes, there is, Mam. Today's special.'

Trudy picked up the suitcase and we trooped outside. Dry-eyed and slightly breathless, Mum paused under the orange street lights, looking back, her brow furrowed in bewilderment, at the house of silent screams and hidden tears, as if either that, or the future she was about to embark on, was nothing but a dream. Trudy put the case into the boot of the Cortina, Mum gave a queenly wave, and the car drove away.

It was as easy as that.

Declan and I were left standing at the gate, with me feeling inordinately deflated by this turn of events. I'd expected to take my mother to William Square, help her settle in, show her where everything was, gradually hand the place over. But now I felt excluded, unnecessary. All of a sudden it hurt badly, imagining other people going through Flo's things, sitting in Flo's place, watching her lamp swirl round, playing her favourite record.

Scotty came out and licked my shoe. I picked him up and buried my face in his rough, curly coat to hide the tears that trickled down my cheeks. I'd never felt so much at home anywhere as I'd done at Flo's. From the very first time I'd gone there, the flat had seemed mine. I knew I was being stupid, but it was almost as if I'd entered my aunt's body, become Flo, experienced the various highs and lows of her life. I'd discovered something about myself during the short time I'd spent there, though I wasn't sure what it was. I only knew I felt differently about things, as if Flo had somehow got through to me that I would survive. Never once, in all the nights I'd slept there, had I dreamed the old dream, heard the slithering footsteps on the stairs, wished I were invisible.

I sighed. I could follow the Cortina, still help Mum settle in, but I knew I was being daft, feeling so possessive about a basement flat that had belonged to a woman I'd never even spoken to.

'What's the matter, Sis?' Declan said softly.

'I feel a bit sad, that's all.'

Declan misunderstood. 'Mam will be all right, you'll see.'

'I know she will, Dec.' I put Scotty down and gave his beard a final rub, wondering if I would ever see the little dog again. 'Will he be all right?'

'Scotty's the only member of the family Dad's never laid a finger on.' Declan grinned.

'And what about you? You can always sleep on the sofa in my place until you find somewhere of your own.' I'd welcome his company at the moment. The thought of returning, alone, to Blundellsands and the flat I'd been so proud of was infinitely depressing.

'Thanks, Millie, but I think I'll stay with me dad.'

I stared at him, open-mouthed. 'But I thought you couldn't wait to get away?'

'Yes, but he needs me, least he needs someone, and I suppose I'll do.'

'Oh, Dec!' I touched his thin face. My heart felt troubled at the idea of my gentle brother staying in Kirkby with Norman Cameron.

'He can't be all bad,' Declan said, with such kind reasonableness, considering all that had happened, that I felt even worse. 'I know he loves us. Something must have happened to make him the way he is.'

I thought of the little boy locked in a cupboard. 'Perhaps something did.' I watched Scotty sniffing the rose bushes in the front garden. One day, I might come back. Perhaps we could talk. Perhaps.

A taxi drew up outside the house next door and hooted its horn. The Bradleys came out, dressed in their ballroom-dancing gear.

'Has your mam gone?' Mrs Bradley shouted.

'A few minutes ago,' I replied.

'About time, too. I'm going to see her next week.' Mr Bradley helped to scoop the layers of net skirt into the taxi. As it drove away, I said, 'I suppose I'd better go, it's cold out here.' I kissed Declan's cheek. 'Take care, Dec. I won't stop worrying about you, I know I won't.'

'There's no need to worry, Mill. Nowadays, me and Dad understand each other in our own peculiar way. He accepts me for what I am.'

I paused in the act of unlocking the car. 'And what's that, Dec?'

Beneath the glare of the street lights, Declan flushed. 'I reckon you already know, Sis.' He closed the gate. 'Do you mind?'

'Christ Almighty, Dec!' I exploded. 'Of course I don't mind. It would only make me love you more, except I love you to death already.'

'Ta, Sis.' He picked Scotty up and waved a shaggy paw. 'See you, Mill.'

I started up the car and watched through the mirror as my brother, still hugging Scotty, went back into the house. A door had opened for my mother, at the same time as one had closed for Declan.

3

Every morning, I woke up with the feeling that I'd lost something infinitely precious. I had no idea what it was that I'd lost, only that it had left a chasm in my life that would never be refilled. There was an ache in my heart, and the sense of loss remained with me for hours.

My flat, my home, seemed unfamiliar, like that of a stranger. I stared, mystified, at various objects: the shell-shaped soap dish in the bathroom, a gaudy tea-towel, the yellow filing basket on the desk, and had no idea where they'd come from. Were they mine? I couldn't remember buying them. Nor could I remember where particular things were kept. It was as if I'd been away for years, having to open cupboards and drawers to search for the bread knife or a duster. There was food in the fridge that was weeks old: wilted lettuce, soggy apples, a carton of potato salad that I was scared to take the lid off. The cheese was covered in mould.

The only place where I felt comfortable and at ease was the balcony. Most nights I sat outside wearing my warmest coat, watching the branches of the bare trees as they waved, like the long nails of a witch, against the dark sky. I listened to the creatures of the night rustling in and out of the bushes below. There were hedgehogs, two, never seen during the day. The light from the living room was cast sharply across the untidy grass and straggly plants – no one tended the garden in winter – and under the light I read the book that Tom O'Mara had given me about the *Thetis*. I read about the bungling and ineptitude of those at the top, the heroism and desperation of the ordinary seamen as they tried to rescue the men who were trapped, so near and yet so far.

How would it have been, I wondered, if Tommy O'Mara hadn't died? How differently would things have turned out for Flo?

I felt very old, like someone who knew that the best years of their life were over and was patiently sitting out the rest. Having a birthday didn't help. I turned thirty, and became obsessed with wondering how the next ten years would turn out. What would I be doing when I was forty? Would I be married, have children? Where would I be living? Where would I be working? Would Mum still be living in William Square with Alison?

Which was stupid. I told myself how stupid I was being a hundred times a day, and made sure no one guessed how dispirited I felt. When I went with James to the theatre one night, I sat in the bar in the interval while he went to fetch the drinks. He came back, saying, 'Are you all right, darling? I looked across and your face was terribly sad.'

'I'm fine,' I said confidently.

'Are you sure? Is it over between you and that Tom chap? I've kept longing to ask. Is that why you're sad?'

'I said I wasn't sad, James, though it is over between me and Tom.'

He looked relieved. 'I'm glad there's no one else.'

'I never said that!' His face collapsed in hurt. I knew I was being horrid, but the last thing I wanted was to offer him encouragement. The strangest thing had happened with James, and I didn't know how to deal with it.

He'd promised not to pressurise me and he hadn't, but in the few times I'd seen him since we'd broken up, then come together again, he wanted to know every little thing about me, every detail. It was as if now that he could no longer have my body he was determined to possess my mind. Perhaps some people were willing to divulge their every thought, their every wish, but I wasn't one of them.

It was hard to escape from such overpowering, almost suffocating love, his tremendous need, which some women might have envied. It was also hard to reject, as if I was giving away something uniquely precious by refusing him. Such love might never come my way again. He appeared to worship the ground I walked on.

Where had I heard those words said before only recently? The bell rang once to indicate that the interval was nearly over and I finished off my drink. Back in the theatre I remembered. They were the words Gran had used to describe how Norman Cameron had felt about my mother . . .

The curtain rose, but as far as I was concerned the actors' efforts were wasted. I had no idea what had happened in the first act. Perhaps you could love someone too much, so much that you resented all the things they did without you, resented them even being happy if you weren't the reason why they smiled.

It wasn't strictly true to hint that there was someone else, but tomorrow night I was meeting Peter Maxwell. He was going to show me where the tall, wild forests had once been in Toxteth, which King John had turned into a royal park and where he had hunted deer and wild boar.

'It's incredible!' I breathed, the following evening, as we strolled through the icy drizzle along Upper Parliament Street and into Smithdown Road. I closed my eyes and tried to imagine I was stepping through a thick forest and the drizzle was the dew dripping from the trees at dawn.

'The area's mentioned in the Domesday Book,' he said proudly.

I forgot how cold the night was as he explained, with mounting enthusiasm, that Lodge Lane was called after one of the King's hunting lodges, that the ancient manor of Smethedon was where the name Smith-down came from. The descriptions, the words he used seemed incongruous, as we passed the narrow built-up streets and endless shops. Traffic fizzed by in the wet; cars, buses, lorries, headlights fixed on the noxious fumes spewing out from the vehicles in front, and reflected in the watery surface. We seemed to be walking through a toxic yellow fog, as Peter talked about Dingle Dell, Knot's Hole, sandstone-cliff creeks, glens, farms, a game reserve. He even quoted a poem – 'The Nymph of the Dingle'.

'It's fascinating, Peter,' I said, when he paused for breath. His black bushy hair and beard glistened in the damp, as if they'd been touched with frost.

'I've not nearly finished, but this isn't a good night. Perhaps we could come one Sunday. I can show you other places. Did you know that less than two centuries ago Bootle was a spa? There used to be watermills, springs, sandhills and fields of flowers?'

I confessed I'd had no idea. He asked if I'd like a drink, and when I said yes he steered me into the nearest pub. 'Will it be safe in here?' I asked nervously.

'I doubt it,' he said soberly, though I noticed his eyes were twinkling. 'We're probably taking our lives in our hands.'

The pub was old-fashioned, Victorian, with sparkling brasses and a gold-tinted mirror behind the bar. The few customers looked very ordinary and not in the least threatening.

'Well, we seemed to have survived so far,' Peter said, apparently amazed. 'What would you like to drink?'

I poked him in the ribs with my elbow. 'Stop making fun of me. I'd like half a cider, please.'

A few minutes later he returned with the drinks. 'Sorry I was so long, but the barman offered me five thousand quid to carry out a contract-killing. See those old girls over there?' He pointed to two elderly women sitting in a corner. 'One's a Mafia godfather in disguise, the other is the chief importer of heroin in the northwest. The cops have been after her for years. She's the one he wanted me to kill.' He took his donkey jacket off and threw it on a vacant chair. Underneath, he wore a polo-necked jersey, which had several loose threads. He regarded me solemnly. 'I refused, of course, so I doubt if we'll get out of here alive.'

By now, I was doubled up with laughter. 'I'm sorry, but I always feel a bit fearful around here.'

'It sounds priggish, but the worst thing to fear is fear itself. Taking the worst possible scenario, no one's safe anywhere.'

'I like being with you, it's rather soothing.' I smiled, feeling unusually contented.

He stroked his beard and looked thoughtful. 'To be "soothing" is not my ultimate aim when I'm with a beautiful young woman, but it'll do.'

I welcomed the fact that he was so easy to be with, relaxing, particularly after the intensity of James, and the total preoccupation Tom O'Mara and I had had with each other. There was a hint of flirtatiousness between us, which meant nothing. He reminded me about the Christmas concert at his school next week. 'You promised you'd come.'

'I hadn't forgotten.' It would soon be Christmas and I hadn't bought a single present. I must remind Trudy about the bottles she'd promised to paint, and remembered that one had been for Diana. After the way things had gone, I wasn't sure whether to give it to her or not.

For the next half-hour, we chatted about nothing in particular. We'd been in the same year at school, which meant that Peter had also recently had his thirtieth birthday, and we discussed how incredibly old we felt. 'It's quite different from turning twenty. Twenty's exciting, like the start of a big adventure. Come thirty, the excitement's over,' he remarked, with a grin.

'Don't say that. You make thirty sound very dull.'

'I didn't mean it to sound dull, just less exciting. By thirty you more or less know where you are. Would you like another drink?'

'No thanks. I thought I'd pop in and see my mother. I left my car in William Square.'

'I've already met your mum. She seems exceptionally nice.' He reached for his jacket. 'Come on. If we make a sudden rush for the exit, we might get out of here all in one piece.'

It was only natural that Mum should have the keys to Flo's flat. Even so, I felt slightly miffed at having to knock to be let in. Fiona, who was draped outside in her usual spot, condescended to give me a curt nod.

'Hello, luv!' Mum's face split into a delighted smile when she opened the door. 'You're out late. It's gone ten.'

Peter Maxwell leaned over the railings. 'Hi, there, Kate. 'Night, Millie. See you next week.'

'Goodnight, Peter.'

'Have you been out with him?' Mum sounded slightly shocked as she closed the door.

'He's very nice.'

'Oh, he's a lovely young feller. I knew his mam in Kirkby. She's a horrible woman, not a bit like Peter. No, I just thought you and James were back together for good, like.'

'We're back together. I doubt very much if it's for good.'

Mum shook her head in despair. 'I can't keep up with you, Millicent.' Then, eyes shining, she demanded, 'What do you think of me new carpet?'

In the two weeks since I had left and my mother had taken over, much in the flat had changed. Too much, I thought darkly, but kept my opinion to myself. It was none of my business, but as far as I was concerned Flo's flat had been perfect. I wouldn't have altered it one iota. But now the silk flowers had gone because they gathered dust, as well as the little round tables and the brasses on the beams. Colin had fitted deadlocks on the windows, a heater on the bathroom ceiling and, with Declan's help, was going to wallpaper the place throughout. 'Something fitting,' Mum announced excitedly, 'little rosebuds, violets, sprigs of flowers.' She would have liked a new three-piece, but needed to conserve the money and was buying stretch covers instead. 'I don't like that dark velour stuff. It's dead miserable.' Next week, British Telecom were coming to install a phone.

I regarded the maroon fitted carpet. 'It looks smart.' I far preferred the faded old linoleum. 'What's happened to the rag rug?'

'I chucked it, luv. It was only a homemade thing.'

Trudy came out of the bedroom, struggling with a cardboard box full of clothes. 'Hello, Sis. I didn't know you were here. I'm just sorting out the wardrobe. Phew!' She plonked the box down and wiped her forehead with the back of her hand. 'I'll take this lot to Oxfam tomorrow, Mum. Hey, Mill, what do you think of this? I thought I'd keep it. It's not at all old-fashioned.' She held up the pink and blue check frock with a Peter Pan collar. 'I'm sure it'll fit.'

'It's lovely, Trude.' It had fitted me perfectly. George had said it made me look sweet and demure.

'Help yourself to anything that takes your fancy, Millicent,' Mum said generously.

'There's nothing I want, Mum.' I felt all choked up. It was horrible to see Flo's things being thrown away, given to Oxfam. I didn't even want Trudy to have the check frock. Then I thought of something I did want – wanted desperately. 'Actually, Mum, I'd like that lamp, the swirly one.' I looked at the television, but the lamp wasn't there, and I felt a thrust of pure, cold anger. If it had been chucked away I'd track it down, buy it back from Oxfam . . .

'I'm afraid your gran's already nabbed it,' Mum said apologetically. 'I wish I'd known, luv. You should have said before.'

If I'd known she was going to tear the place apart, I would have. I knew I was being unreasonable, and felt even more unreasonable when I refused a cup of tea. 'I only came for a minute to say hello. I think I'll have an early night.'

I'd never felt less like an early night. Outside, I thought about calling on Charmian, but the ground-floor flat was in darkness – Herbie had to get up at the crack of dawn for work. Peter Maxwell's light was on, but did I know him well enough to call at this hour? He might think I was being presumptuous, a bit pushy.

Fiona, in a short fur coat, thigh-length boots, and no other visible sign of clothing, was staring at me suspiciously, as if I'd set myself up in competition. I got into the car and drove round to Maynard Street. It was weeks since I'd seen Bel, though she'd been to William Square to renew her acquaintance with Mum.

'She'll probably think me an idiot.' I didn't even switch the engine off when I parked as near as I could to Bel's house, but drove off immediately. On my way to Blundellsands, I slipped a tape into the deck and turned up Freddie Mercury's powerful voice as loud as it would go to drown my brain and stop me from thinking how much I would have liked someone to talk to. It didn't work, so I turned it down and talked to myself instead. 'I must pull myself together, keep telling myself there is Life After Flo. Tomorrow I'll take a proper lunch break, buy some Christmas presents. I'll get jewellery for Mum, gold earrings or a chain.' By the time I got home I was still musing on what to get Declan, feeling more cheerful. My flat was slowly beginning to feel my own again, though it still seemed oddly empty when I went in.

Mum's decorating splurge was catching. I didn't want to change the colour of my own living-room walls, but a wide frieze would look nice, or stencilled flowers. I decided I'd take a look at patterns at the weekend.

Next day after lunch, I was showing June the gold chain with a K for Kate that I'd bought for Mum, and the red-velvet knee-length dress with short sleeves I'd got as a Christmas present for myself, when George called, 'Can I have a word with you, Millie?'

'Sit down,' he said shortly, when I entered his office. This was always a bad sign, and I wondered what I'd done wrong now. He cleared his throat. 'I've been having a long talk with . . . with someone about your position in the firm. It was pointed out that you have no qualifications for the job you do. Darren and Elliot both have degrees, and even June has three A levels.' He regarded me sternly, as if all this was new to him and he'd been misled.

'You knew that when you took me on, George. You knew it when you promoted me.' I tried to keep my voice steady. 'I've always carried out my work satisfactorily. No one has ever complained.'

George acknowledged this with a cursory nod. 'That's true, Millie, but it was also pointed out that there are a lot of people around, highly qualified people, who might do the work even better. Yet by employing you, I am, in effect, denying one of these people a position with Stock Masterton.' He leaned forward, frowning earnestly. 'Look at that business with the Naughtons, for example. You must have shown them around a dozen properties, but Diana had only to take them once and a deal was clinched on the spot.'

I clenched my fists, feeling the nails digging painfully into my palms. My heart thumped crazily. 'Are you giving me the sack, George?' I'd never find another equivalent job if I was sacked.

He looked slightly uncomfortable. 'No, no, of course not. We, that is, I, thought it would be a good idea if you went to Woolton with Oliver and Diana.'

'I don't understand,' I stammered. 'If I'm useless here, I'll be just as useless in Woolton.'

'No one's said you're useless, Millie. Oh dear!' He put his hand to his chest. 'I feel a panic attack coming. Lately, I've been having them quite frequently. No, we . . . I think you should be our receptionist. After all, that's what you were originally taken on as.'

It was so unfair. I'd never asked to be promoted, it had been all his idea. I blinked back hot tears of anger. No way would I let him see me cry. I knew I'd be burning my boats, but didn't care. I said, 'I'm afraid that isn't acceptable, George. I'd sooner leave. I'll finish at the end of the month.'

It hadn't gone quite the way he wanted – the way he knew Diana wanted. He rubbed his chest, frowning. 'Then you'd be breaking your contract. One month's notice is required, dated the first of the month.'

'In that case,' I said coolly, though I felt anything but cool, 'I'll leave at the end of January.' I got up and went to the door. 'I'll let you have my resignation in writing this afternoon.'

It was worse, far more shocking, than having discovered all those closely kept family secrets. I'd been dumbfounded to learn that my father wasn't who I'd thought he was. But I'd rejected Norman Cameron a long time ago, and the news didn't matter now – in fact, it was welcome. As for Tom

O'Mara, I had thought I would never forget, but already it was hard to remember the way we'd felt about each other. There was just relief that it was all over, though I knew I would worry about him, watch for his name and any mention of Minerva's in the paper, hope that he wouldn't come to harm in the vicious world he lived in. After all, he was my brother.

But the business with my job – trivial in comparison to the rest – was different, directed against me personally. I felt as if someone had just delivered a mammoth blow, knocking all the stuffing out of me. I realised that my job had given me a sense of identity, a feeling of achievement, and without it I was nothing. I hadn't, after all, done better than the other girls in my class, the ones who'd seemed so much smarter than me. I was the backward child again, the girl who could hardly read, so hopeless that I hadn't been entered for a single O level.

Later, when I tried to type a letter of resignation, my fingers no longer seemed capable of accepting messages from my brain. I'd thought George was my friend. I'd tried to help Diana. Why had they turned against me? I felt betrayed.

In the window, through the glass around the boards showing the houses Stock Masterton had for sale, I watched the people passing, their bodies crouched protectively as they fought their way through the gale that howled up Castle Street from the Mersey. I longed to go down to the Pier Head, hold on to the railings, let the wind blow me any way it wanted.

There was a photo of Nancy's house on one of the boards in the window, between the house in Banks which didn't have an oriel window, and a manor house with ten acres of grounds priced at half a million, which George dealt with exclusively. I'd asked Oliver if he would please send someone else to Clement Street if a prospective purchaser wanted to view. 'I know the chap who's selling it slightly. I'd sooner not go,' I said. I still felt the same when the keys for the property arrived through the post, which meant that no one would be there. Unlike Flo's flat, Nancy's house, the place where she'd lived with Tommy O'Mara, where the father I'd never known had been raised, would go to strangers, who would know nothing about the drama that had taken place. People rarely thought about previous owners when they bought a house, no matter how old it was. As far as they were concerned, its history began when they themselves moved in.

Across the office, Darren and Elliot were having a deskbound lunch, eating sandwiches and giggling over something in *Viz*. I felt envious of their gloriously trouble-free lives. June was on the telephone, Barry's carefully combed silver head was bent over a heap of files. Oliver was out with a client. In his office, George, who usually made his presence loudly felt, was strangely quiet. At the next desk, Diana was singing a little tune as she typed into her computer. Was there a note of triumph in her voice? She must know why George had called me in, be aware of my humiliation. Was it worth making a fuss, I wondered, causing a row, telling Diana exactly what I thought in front of everyone? No, it wasn't, I decided. George seemed slightly ashamed of what he'd done. If I left quietly, at least I'd get a good reference, possibly a glowing one if he felt contrite enough.

Oliver returned, his face flushed by the wind. He hung up the keys. 'Whew!' he exclaimed. 'That was a proper shambles. Mum and Dad insisted on viewing the loft, so I went up with them, then one of the kids pushed the ladder up and the damn thing got stuck halfway. I thought I'd be there all afternoon. I managed to do a Tarzan and swing myself down.'

Diana said, 'I was beginning to wonder why you were taking so long.'

'Were you now! I didn't realise you kept an eye on my movements.' Oliver took his coat off, then put it on again. 'I think a beer and a snack in the Wig and Pen is called for after that misadventure. Come on, Millie, I'll treat you.'

I looked up, surprised. Oliver had never made such an offer before. 'I've already been to lunch.'

At the same time, Diana said quickly, 'She's already had lunch, Oliver.'

Oliver poked his head inside George's office. 'I'm off for a quick bevvy, George, and taking Millie with me. Okay?'

George didn't look up. 'Okay,' he mumbled.

'Okay, Diana?' Oliver raised his eyebrows questioningly.

'It's none of my business, is it?'

'Too right it isn't.'

'What was all that about?' I asked, when we were outside. The wind gripped me immediately, powerfully, blowing my hair up into a fan around my head. The air was sharp and clean and refreshingly salty. I twisted my face to and fro, trying to breathe in as much as I could, until I felt almost light-headed.

Oliver's usually good-natured face twisted into a scowl. 'I loathe that bloody woman. I can't abide the thought of working with her. I want her to know that when we move I'm the one in charge. She thinks I'm a wimp who can't take decisions, but she doesn't realise how much George regards Stock Masterton as his baby. Take a major decision over his head and he goes ballistic. She'll find that out for herself soon enough if she starts throwing her weight around.'

When we turned into Dale Street the wind lessened fractionally. Oliver's scowl disappeared and he said kindly, 'Enough of my hang-ups. It's you I'm worried about. You look as if you've been crying, which is why I asked you out.'

I clapped my hands to my cheeks, which felt both hot and cold. 'I haven't been crying, but I'm dead upset. Is it so obvious?'

'Yes. I don't want to pry. Don't tell me if it's something private.'

We arrived at the Wig and Pen, where the midday rush was over and only a few tables were occupied. Oliver brought me a whisky and a chicken sandwich, and I told him what had happened. 'I feel gutted,' I finished. I could have said more, much more, but kept myself to a few short words.

Oliver shook his head unbelievingly. 'Darren and Elliot may well have degrees, but neither has an ounce of charm. As for Diana, she positively alienates the clients. She's in completely the wrong profession, which George knows only too well. He's talked about letting her go more than once.' He shook his head again. 'I don't understand the sudden turnaround. Mind you, the poor man has been an emotional wreck since his wife walked out with the children. He's easy prey for any woman who sets her cap at him.'

'But why does Diana hate me so much?' I wailed.

'That's easy to explain.' Oliver smiled and patted my hand. 'George was smitten with you right from the start. I think I can safely say that your promotion had more to do with your legs than your capabilities, not that you didn't make a good fist of the job once you had it,' he added hastily, when he saw my dismayed expression. 'I wasn't the only one to notice, Diana did, too. She's jealous of you, Millie. She wants you out of George's way.'

'I knew George liked me, that's all,' I muttered. 'You see an awful lot, Oliver.' I felt a bit better. I'd been demoted because of another person's weakness, not my own, though it didn't change the fact I was about to give up my job.

On the way back to the office, Oliver said, 'By the way, you mentioned the Naughtons. Mr Naughton rang this morning to say they've withdrawn from the house in Childwall. They parked outside for several nights. Apparently, there's several teenagers next door, belting music out till all hours, which they find totally unacceptable – it would seem the neighbours they have now are darn near perfect.'

Despite everything, I couldn't help laughing. The talk with Oliver had done me good. I even felt a tiny bit flattered. Diana might well have had the upper hand at the moment but, incredibly, it was me who had the power. If I wanted I could ruin everything. I was no good at flirting, but I knew how it was done, I could learn. I didn't know I'd ever had George, but I could easily get him back. It was a challenge I might once have welcomed but, thinking about it now, it seemed rather demeaning.

'About the Naughtons,' I remarked, 'it's time someone suggested they stay put. They're already in their ideal house, and they'll never find another like it.'

'Someone already has – me. Mr Naughton said he'd never wanted to move, it was all his wife's idea. He's going to try to talk her out of it. If he's successful, every estate agent on Merseyside will breathe a big sigh of relief.'

4

There was no tortuous Christmas dinner in Kirkby this year to bring back memories of the bleak dinners that had gone before. Norman Cameron had always nursed a decidedly unfestive spirit throughout the holiday, grim and bitter, his dark eyes searching for any signs of unwelcome gaiety from his children, rationing our time spent in front of the television or with our presents. For the first time, with a glimmer of understanding, I wondered if his own childhood Christmases had been so dark that he could see no other way, though I wasn't convinced I would ever have the Christian charity to forgive.

This year, we had dinner at Flo's without Norman. The dining table was pulled out as far as it would go, so big that only a sheet would cover it. It was set for eight, and there was already a trifle laid out, mince pies, an iced cake from Charmian, the plates intertwined with tinsel. Night-lights in delicately painted wine glasses were waiting to be lit when the meal began. Mum asked Trudy if she would bring her cutlery because there wasn't enough, so Trudy bought her a set for Christmas. It wasn't an expensive set, the handles were bright red plastic, but they looked perfect on the table with the red paper napkins.

There was a real tree in the window, the coloured lights shaped like pears, and new decorations strung from wall to wall. The flat – no longer Flo's with its carpet, new curtains and pink-and-white-flowered wallpaper – was warm with the smell of roasting turkey and Christmas pudding. Melanie and Jake were persuaded that it was too cold to eat on the wooden table in the yard. 'You can have a drink out there afterwards,' Trudy told them, 'as long as you get well wrapped up first.'

Bel was there. She'd always had dinner with Flo on Christmas Day, ever since she'd come out of the forces, she'd hinted, and she wasn't looking forward to eating alone for the first time in her life. 'Mr Fritz always came. Later I used to bring Edward, and Charmian would come down with her little ones. When she married Herbie, me and Flo used to have our dinner upstairs.' She turned up on the day in her leopardskin fur coat, a silver lamé suit and high-heeled silver boots, her hair a magnificent halo of russet waves and curls, and her lovely old face as shrivelled as one of the nuts in the bowl on the sideboard. The first thing she did was grab my hand. 'I've not seen much of you lately, girl. I thought we were friends.'

'I nearly called one night, but it was awfully late,' I explained. 'I wanted someone to talk to, but I was worried you'd think I was stupid.'

'Jaysus, Millie. You're talking to the stupidest woman in the world. I always welcome company, no matter what the hour. What was it you wanted to talk about?'

'I can't remember now. I think I was missing Flo.'

'You never met her, but you miss her. Now, that really is stupid.' Bel's beautiful eyes were wise. 'Mind you, luv, I understand, I'll never stop missing Flo.' The violet eyes searched the room. 'Where's your gran, by the way? There's something I've always wanted to ask Martha Colquitt.'

'She's at an old-age pensioners' do in Kirkby.' Gran needed an operation, only minor, but her own prognosis was gloomy – she was convinced she'd die: 'Me mam swore she'd never let a surgeon near her with a knife,' she'd said. 'I don't trust them doctors.'

I gave Bel her present, an unusual oval-shaped bottle that Trudy had painted various shades of blue and green. Bel gave me an intricately patterned mosaic bracelet. 'It's not new, Flo bought it me in Spain. I thought you'd like it as a memento.'

'Oh, thank you,' I breathed. I fastened the bracelet on to my wrist. 'I'll treasure it all my life.'

Mum presided over the table. I could scarcely take my eyes off my new mother, and every now and then noticed the others glancing at her curiously, as if they, too, found it hard to believe that this Kate Cameron had been lurking behind the old one for so many years. She already looked thinner. Charmian had trimmed and silver-tinted her hair the day before, and the thick, straight fringe and feathery cut took years off her. For the first time in ages, she was wearing makeup, and had bought a new dress – the last new one had been for Trudy's wedding ten years ago. It was plain dark green, emphasising the colour of her sparkling eyes. She already had my present, the gold chain with K for Kate, around her neck. Mum was reborn, confident, relaxed, with her children all around her, except for Alison who was coming to tea that afternoon. 'As an experiment, like, to see how she gets on. See if she takes to the place.' It would be best if not too many people were around in case it frightened her. I was going to Southport to have tea with James's family, the Daleys to Colin's parents in Norris Green. Bel had been invited upstairs. Only Declan would be there to see if his sister felt at home in William Square.

Declan seemed perfectly content living in Kirkby with his father. They saw little of each other, Norman either at work or in the pub, and Declan deeply involved with helping the couple he'd met at the craft fair with their tie-dyed T-shirts. His own first attempts had been highly professional, and Melanie and Jake had been given one each as a present. Next September, he was starting a course in fabric design.

'What about that young feller from next door?' Bel said suddenly. 'Flo always had him in for a drink on Christmas Day.'

I offered to fetch Peter Maxwell. It was a still, windless day, without a patch of blue in the sombre grey sky. The leathery leaves on the trees in the central garden shone dully, still wet with dew. Cars lined the square, but otherwise it was empty, no sign of Fiona or the other girls, who must be having a rare day off. Gran had once mentioned that Flo had spent her first Christmas in the flat entirely alone: Mrs Fritz had gone to Ireland. I wondered what it had looked like then, with only a few cars and a single family living in each house.

Peter was getting ready to have Christmas dinner with a colleague from school. There was just time for a drink with the Camerons.

'Did you enjoy the play?' he asked, as he walked around the plain room with its clean-cut furniture, so different from next door, turning off lights and testing locks.

'It was very cleverly written and well acted,' I said tactfully. It had been awful and I hoped he hadn't any ambition to become a playwright. 'I found it hard to talk to the other teachers, though. I kept expecting to get marks out of ten whenever I answered a question.'

'They liked you. Quite a few said next day what a cracking girl you were.' He took his coat off the rack, and dark eyes glinted at me mischievously. 'They wanted to know when we were getting married.'

'What did you say?'

'What do you think I said?'

I stuck my finger under my chin and thought hard. 'Never?'

Peter laughed. 'Precisely! There's no spark, is there, Millie? I wish there were because I like you very much. We know things about each other that would be hard to tell other people.' He looked at me quizzically. 'Could you pretend I'm a woman so we could be best friends?'

'Oh, Peter!' He was right, there was no spark. If we went out together for long enough we might get married because it seemed the comfortable thing to do, but it wasn't what I wanted – and neither did he. 'You'd need to do something about your beard before I could remotely regard you as a woman, but there's nothing wrong with having a man for a best friend.'

He kissed my forehead, as if to seal our friendship. 'Friends it is, then. Now, where's that drink? Has your mum got beer? I'm not a wine person.'

I was convinced that nowhere on earth could a family have enjoyed their Christmas dinner more than the Camerons. It was nothing to do with the food, though for the first time in months I ate a proper, three-course meal, and the skirt of my red-velvet dress felt tight when I'd finished. It was to do with a shared sense that the nightmare had ended. It had already faded, a little, for Trudy and me, but now it was well and truly over for Mum. As for Declan, he was coping. The only awkward moment came when Melanie, pulling a cracker with her father, said in surprise, 'Where's Grandad?'

'He couldn't come, luv,' Mum said firmly. She looked anxiously at Declan 'He's all right, isn't he?'

'Fine, Mam. He'll have found a pub that's open all day. That's where he'd have been, anyroad.'

'I suppose so.' A shadow almost cast itself over Mum's face, but she blinked it away. 'I'll go round in a day or so, give the house a bit of a clean, like, take him some rations.'

Later, when Trudy and I were washing the dishes, Trudy said, a touch bitterly, 'What a pity she couldn't have brought herself to do this years ago. Think of all the misery it would have saved.'

'It was the money and the flat that gave her the courage, Trude.'

'I'd never have stood it for a minute. I'd have been off the first time he laid a finger on me, and once he'd touched me kids . . .' Trudy shook her head. It was beyond her comprehension.

I reached for a fresh tea-towel – the one I was using was sopping wet. 'We're a different generation, but there's an even newer generation of kids roaming the streets of London and other cities who've run away from violent homes. Why didn't we run away, Trude? He nearly killed you once, but you still stayed. You waited for Colin to rescue you, like I waited for Gary.'

Trudy stared at me blankly. 'I think I felt paralysed,' she whispered.

'Maybe Mum did, too.' One day soon, despite my promise, I resolved to tell Trudy and Declan about the little boy locked in the cupboard. They had a right to know, and could be left to make their own judgement.

Melanie and Jake were aching to sit in the yard. Colin put their coats on, Kate supplied a glass of lemonade and a plate of mince pies and, giggling, they perched themselves on the bench in front of the wooden table. I watched through the window, bemused. It seemed such an uncomfortable thing to do on a cold day in December, and I marvelled at the children's ability to turn it into a great adventure. Colin and Trudy came indoors, shivering. 'Perhaps we could get some garden furniture?' Trudy suggested. They began to discuss the best sort to buy, wood or plastic. They would have preferred wrought-iron, but it was too expensive.

It was just such mundane, ordinary decisions that made the world go round, I thought wryly. Freed from the tensions and the dreary atmosphere of our old house, I became aware of the easy-going intimacy between Colin and my sister, the way they smiled at each other for no reason in particular, as if they were passing on an unspoken message or reading one another's thoughts. I noticed the way they seemed to form a unit with their children, a little world of their own. I thought how satisfying it must be to have little human beings completely dependent upon you, loving you without question, the most important person in their lives. To my surprise, I felt envious of my sister.

Though I could have what she had, I thought later at the Athertons', I could have it easily, straight away. I could be a wife, possibly a mother, by next Christmas. All I had to do was say yes to James. I'd no longer have to worry about my job. I could share in some of this . . .

The difference between my mother's Christmas table and the Athertons' couldn't have been greater. Cut-glass decanters, crystal glasses, heavy silver cutlery with embossed handles, beautifully laundered napkins in silver rings were laid with geometrical precision on a vast expanse of rich, gleaming mahogany, with a rather formal display of upright chrysanthemums in the centre. The dining room was about half as big again as Flo's entire flat, with only a fraction of the furniture. The curtains were ivory satin, drawn carefully to hang in smooth, symmetrical folds.

Mrs Atherton had kissed me coolly on the cheek. 'It's ages since we've seen you, dear. What have you been doing to my son?'

'Nothing that I know of,' I replied, startled. Had James told her about our problems? Or Mrs Atherton might have guessed. After all, she was his mother.

Anna, James's sister, was up from London with her husband and two children. I'd never met her before and found it hard to believe that she'd been an anarchist at university. Her husband, Jonathan, was a dealer in the City, a hearty, fresh-faced man with neat brown hair and designer spectacles. The children, boys, were equally neat, in white shirts, grey pullovers and shorts. They were well behaved and said little, even when their parents encouraged them to talk. I found myself yearning for Melanie and Jake's bright faces, their inability to keep quiet no matter how many times they were told. I longed to discuss garden furniture and tie-dyed T-shirts. Instead, I was forced to listen to Jonathan's talk of bull markets and bear markets, shorts, longs and mediums, stocks and shares. He'd recently netted a cool hundred thou profit on a highly risky venture in Indonesia that everyone else had been too afraid to touch. Anna, blonde hair swinging, pretty face glowing with admiration, leaned over and stroked his chin. 'You're so clever, darling!' she cooed.

Throughout the meal, James kept his eyes glued on me so firmly that I felt uncomfortable. Afterwards we went into the vast, chintzy living room, where he sat on the arm of my chair, towering over me. I felt as if I'd been stamped with his personal seal of ownership.

Jonathan gave his rather unfortunate high-pitched giggle and said to James, 'Understand you've given up flirting with left-wing politics, brother-in-law. Are you still marching with those wretched dockers?'

'I haven't for some time,' James admitted.

So far, Mr Atherton hadn't opened his mouth except to eat; his eyes were always far away, thinking of other things, probably business. He spoke now, with contempt in his voice: 'Lazy buggers, don't know which side their bread's buttered. It's about time they got back to work.'

I had no idea if I was pro-establishment or anti, or if my politics were left or right, I only knew it made my blood boil to hear the dockers being called 'lazy buggers' by a man smoking a fat cigar who owned three garages. I wished I knew some hard facts and figures that I could quote in the dockers' defence, but I knew nothing about the dispute other than it was happening. I jumped up. 'Excuse me.'

In the eau-de-Nil tiled bathroom with its matching carpet and fittings, I stared unseeingly at my reflection in the mirror and realised, with a sense of overwhelming relief, that I was wasting James's time. I felt alien from his family. If I loved him, I would have taken them on and done my best, but I didn't love him and never would. 'I'm glad I came,' I whispered. 'It's helped me make up my mind once and for all.'

When I came out, James was hovering on the landing, and I felt a stab of anger. I wanted to say something coarse and brutal: 'Would you like to have come in to watch me pee?'

He stared at me and I felt repelled by the abject adoration in his eyes. 'You look lovely in that dress,' he said huskily. 'You suit red.' He tried to take me in his arms, nuzzle my hair, but I pushed him away. He patted his pocket, 'I've a present for you, a ring.'

'I don't want it!'

'But, Millie . . .' His lips twisted in an arc of misery. 'Is it this other chap you've been seeing?'

'I haven't been seeing another chap – least I have, but he's just a friend. There's no one, James. No one!' I emphasised the last word, my voice unnaturally shrill, to impress upon him that I was announcing I was free – and he was free to forget me and find someone else.

We began to argue. He refused to believe I meant what I said. Anna must have heard the raised voices. She came out into the hall downstairs. 'Are you two all right?' Her laugh tinkled up the stairs. 'Oh, you're just having a little domestic.' She made a show of pretending to creep back into the room.

James's eyes were glassy, his face was swollen, red. I didn't know this man. Falling in love with me had changed him for the worse. 'It can't be over,' he insisted doggedly.

'It is, James.' I was worried that he was about to hit me. His fists were clenching and unclenching, as if he was itching to use them and it could only be on me. Then I did something that surprised me later when I thought about it. I flung my arms around his neck and hugged him tightly. 'James, I'm bad for you,' I whispered urgently. 'Can't you see? There's something not quite right about the way you love me.' I stroked his neck. 'One of these days, you'll meet someone else who you'll love in a quite different way, and everything will be wonderful for you both.' I pulled away. 'Goodbye, darling,' I said softly.

He remained silent, his eyes no longer glassy, but full of misery and shock. I thought, I wasn't sure, that there was also a trace of comprehension that I could be right.

I flew down the stairs, opened the door of the living room, and said breathlessly, 'I'm awfully sorry, I have to go. Thank you so much for the meal. It was lovely. No, no, please don't get up,' I implored, when Mrs Atherton began to get to her feet. 'I'll see myself out.'

It was past nine when I got back to Blundellsands. The first thing I did was ring my mother. Alison had been very quiet but not too disturbed by the strange surroundings. 'She didn't flick her fingers, the way she does when she's upset,' Mum said gratefully.

Relieved, I hung up my red dress carefully and ran a bath. Afterwards I watched a Woody Allen film on television, then went to bed with a book and a glass of warm milk, feeling contented and relaxed.

Just after midnight the telephone rang. I prayed it wouldn't be James, pleading for a second chance or a third, or whatever it would be by now, but when I picked up the extension by the bed, Peter Maxwell said cheerfully, 'Hi! I've just got in and thought I'd give you a ring. Did you have a nice day?'

'Nice and not so nice. I finished with a boyfriend. It wasn't very pleasant.'

'The hunk from the party?'

'That's right.'

'I didn't realise you were still seeing him. He's definitely not your type.'

'Are you going to be the arbiter of who's my type from now on?' I smiled at the receiver.

'It's what friends are for. I shall always ask for your opinion on any future girlfriends.'

'It shall be given with pleasure,' I said graciously. We chatted idly, and he was about to ring off when I remembered something. 'By the way, knowing it won't be taken the wrong way and you'll think I'm after your body or your money, would you like to come to a drinks party tomorrow afternoon?'

'Sorry, but I'm taking a group of first-years to a pantomime. Will you be at Charmian's on New Year's Eve?'

I said I would, and we promised each other the first dance.

The drinks party was being held at Barry Green's. He had casually offered an invitation to the whole office. 'We've been having one on Boxing Day for more than thirty years. The world and his wife usually come. Any time between noon and four, you're all welcome.'

Elliot and Darren had wrinkled their noses: a drinks party sounded much too tame. June would be away. Oliver welcomed the idea of escaping from his kids for a few hours. 'I love them, but it's usually hell on earth at home over Christmas.' George, who always went anyway, would be there with Diana, bringing his children who were over from France. I had intended taking James, but now I would have to go alone.

The Greens' house in Waterloo, only a mile from my flat, was semi-detached and spacious, the furniture and carpets shabby and worn. The Christmas decorations looked well used, as if the same things were hung in the same place year after year. Everywhere had a comfortable, lived-in look, very different from the Athertons' Ideal Home. By the time I got there it was already crowded. Barry's wife, Tess, let me in. She was a pretty woman with a tumble of grey curls and a wide, smiling mouth, wearing an emerald-green jumpsuit. She took my coat and ordered me to mingle. 'I'll do the hostess bit later and we'll have a proper talk. Right now, I'm busy with the food.'

I found Oliver and his alarmingly aggressive wife, Jennifer, waved to George, who was standing in a corner with two rather sullen teenagers, clutching his chest as if in the throes of a panic attack. There was no sign of Diana. Barry came up with a tray of drinks. 'Food's in the kitchen, help yourselves, won't you?' He'd abandoned the usual bow-tie for a Paisley cravat under a canary-yellow pullover.

Over the holiday, Jennifer had been pressing Oliver remorselessly to start his own estate agency. 'Then he won't get pissed around rotten by whoever George happens to be screwing at the moment. I told him, "Millie will go in with you."' She gave me a painful but encouraging dig. 'You would, wouldn't you, Millie? You could be his assistant.'

'Willingly,' I said, with a smile. Oliver groaned.

Over the next few hours, I well and truly mingled. Several guests were estate agents, and we gravely discussed the state of the market. Was it up or down? One man gave me his card. 'If you should ever think of changing your job . . .' Barry introduced me to his children: Roger, the architect, an earnest man in jeans and an Arran sweater, Emma and Sadie, who would take the world by storm for a second time as soon as their children were old enough and they could resume their careers.

'Where's your other son?' I asked. 'Is he still abroad?'

Barry's perfectly groomed moustache quivered slightly. 'According to his mother, Sam won't be gracing us with his presence until New Year's Eve.'

Later, I forced myself to approach George. He eyed me appreciatively in my red dress before introducing me to his children, Annabel and Bill. 'Have you had a nice holiday?' I asked them.

They both shrugged. 'Okay.'

'I haven't a clue what teenagers get up to nowadays.' George sighed and looked harassed. 'I think they've been rather bored.' Bill rolled his eyes to confirm that this was definitely the case.

'Why don't you take them to the Cavern?' I suggested.

'Oh, Dad, would you?' Annabel pleaded. 'The girls at school will turn green if I tell them I've been to the Cavern.'

'Aren't I a bit old?' George said plaintively.

'You can just hover in the background,' I said. 'By the way, where's Diana? I thought she'd be here.'

George shrugged vaguely. 'She spent Christmas at her place. I haven't seen her in a few days.'

'Diana's horrible!' Bill burst out. 'You'll never guess what she did. She actually drew up a timetable of things for us to do – the pantomime, McDonald's, card games, charades, and idiotic films to watch on telly. She seemed to think we were children!'

Tactfully I wandered off. People had begun to leave. For the first time, I was aware of being the only youngish woman without a partner, and felt conspicuous as the crowd thinned, though I told myself I shouldn't care. I went upstairs to look for my coat. It was with a pile of others in what appeared to be Barry and Tess's untidy bedroom. I was putting it on when Tess came in, wearing her rather impish smile. 'Ah, there you are, Millie! I've been so rude. I always like to have a little chat with guests who've come for the first time, get to know them, as it were.' She sat on the bed and patted the space next to her. 'Sit down a minute.'

Under Tess's friendly questioning, I revealed all sorts of things about myself I wouldn't normally: about Diana, being demoted, James, and the awful tea at the Athertons' the day before.

'Never mind, love,' Tess said comfortingly. 'Things always turn out for the best in the long run, or so I've always found. Oh, well,' she levered herself off the bed, 'I'd better go downstairs and be the good hostess. I always feel a sense of relief when it's over, but sad too that it will be another year before I see some of our friends again. The children always found them a bit of a giggle, but they wouldn't miss their mum and dad's Boxing Day party.'

'Except Sam,' I reminded her.

'Ah, yes, Sam. He's in Mexico.' I was surprised when Tess looked at me rather speculatively, then said, 'Let me show you our Sam.' She opened the drawer in a bedside cupboard and took out a sheaf of newspaper cuttings. 'Barry doesn't know I've kept these. He's rather ashamed of Sam.' She handed me a cutting. 'That's him, in the *Daily Express*.'

A wiry young man with crew-cut hair was standing on a wall, baring his chest defiantly to the world. He held a banner aloft proclaiming, AXE THE TAX. Several policemen were reaching up in a vain attempt to grab his feet. 'He was sentenced to three months in prison or a thousand-pound fine for that,' Tess said proudly. 'Barry paid the fine and he was released, much to Sam's disgust. They rub one another up the wrong way, yet secretly they think the world of each other.'

There was a photo of Sam at the gates of Greenham Common with his then girlfriend, several of him protesting during the miners' strike. 'He hasn't been in court for years,' Tess said, slightly disappointed. 'Our three elder children are very conformist, but Sam takes after me. I used to go on CND marches when I was a girl – Barry disapproved of that, too.'

'What's he doing in Mexico? Has he gone to start a war?' I wasn't sure if I approved of Sam or not, but I admired his independent spirit.

'Oh, no. He's a record producer. He spends three or four months of the year travelling the world, taping folk songs, tribal music, that sort of thing. Then he comes home and turns them into proper recordings. He's got a studio in the attic. Much to his dad's amazement he's doing very well.' Suddenly she changed the subject, rather drastically, I thought. 'I expect your mum worries about you, still single at your age?'

'She does, yes.'

Tess hadn't changed the subject, after all. 'I worry terribly about Sam. He's thirty-three and I wish he'd establish some roots, start a family, have something more worthwhile to come home to than boring old Mum and Dad.'

A woman came in to collect her coat and Tess put the cuttings away. I thanked her for a lovely time and went home.

Over the final days of the year, I felt like two different people. There was only a skeleton staff at work and I had several half-days off, during which time I stencilled flowers on the corners of the living room and cleaned the flat from top to bottom, whistling tunelessly, happy. But when I stopped for a break, my mood would darken and I would feel restless, haunted by a sense of failure and hopelessness. There'd been a time, not long ago, when I'd considered myself the only Cameron with an aim in life and any hope of a bright, successful future, but now I was the one with nothing to look forward to. Empty years loomed ahead, a vast, yawning abyss.

Mum had got a job in an office and would start the following week. 'Only making the tea, running a few errands.' She'd giggled merrily. 'I'll be the office junior. It's just temporary, till Alison comes.'

Trudy was gearing up for when Melanie started school in January or painting bottles for the stall she intended having every week. Should I get a hobby? I wondered. I rang Declan several times, worried that Norman would answer and whether I should engage him in conversation if he did, but there was never any reply. I badly missed Flo's flat, where I'd been quite happy to do nothing but watch the swirling lamp and listen to music. For want of something to do, on Sunday morning, I went to Mass at the Cathedral with my mother. I felt no spiritual reawakening or miraculous re-conversion in the remarkable circular building with its brilliant blue stained-glass windows, but on the way back to Flo's, I thought I might go again. Then something happened that I'd always dreaded.

Two boys were coming towards us. I hardly took them in, aware only that they were about fourteen and relatively well dressed. As they passed, one leaped at Mum and snatched the chain with K for Kate from around her neck.

Mum screamed, the boys ran only a short distance, then turned. The one who'd snatched the chain dangled it at us tauntingly, before they skipped away, laughing, almost dancing in their triumph.

'It could have happened anywhere,' Mum said later, when we were back at Flo's and she'd calmed down after I'd made us tea. 'It's not just Liverpool. It could have happened anywhere in the world.'

Something funny was going on between George and Diana – or perhaps there was nothing going on at all. Everyone managed to glean little pieces of information and put them together to make a whole. It appeared that George had suggested Diana return home when it became obvious that she and the children weren't getting on, but had made no suggestion that she come back now that the children had gone. She'd spent Christmas alone in the house where she'd lived with her father. Even Oliver had to concede he felt sorry for the haggard little woman who stumbled round the office as if she were drunk, ignored by George. It wasn't that George was being deliberately cruel, he was taken up with the new office, which was opening in a few days' time. He appeared to have forgotten that Diana existed.

Like Oliver, I was sorry for Diana. If I'd been gutted by my demotion, she must have been feeling as if the bottom had dropped out of her world. But I was terrified that I was seeing myself in another five or ten years' time. Might I one day find myself waiting for a kind word from a man I'd been hoping would rescue me from a life of loneliness?

'Is this the girl who's just dumped a guy who runs an Aston Martin speaking?' Peter Maxwell chuckled when I phoned him. 'Men are terrified of loneliness, not just women. Sit back, have a good time, and see what happens. Don't wait for things, don't expect them, they won't come any sooner. It's like that song Flo used to play all the time. We're all dancing in the dark.'

'You're very clever,' I said admiringly. We rang off, deciding that if we were still single at forty we would live next door to each other.

I thought of James, who was going through the same experience as Diana, and wondered if I'd been too cruel, too abrupt. If he hadn't followed me to the bathroom, I would have told him tactfully in a more appropriate place. I recalled the way he'd been outside the nightclub – it seemed like years ago, but it was only a few months – when he'd said he was sick of selling cars to idiots like himself. He wanted to do something more worthwhile with his life. And the time by the Pier Head when he told me how much he loved me. He'd joined the Socialist Workers' Party to prove he wasn't shallow. We'd got on well until he decided he was in love with me; from then on, he began to fall apart. I felt sure that one day James would marry someone who didn't play such havoc with his emotions. They would have several children, and he would be back in the Conservative Party, still running his father's garage – perhaps all three – having forgotten he'd ever wanted to do anything else.

On New Year's Eve, I woke up with that aching feeling of loss again, a haunting sensation that something was missing from my life. I'd never been able to identify what it was, but in the darkness of my bedroom on the final day of the year, the knowledge came washing over me so forcefully that my body froze.

I was mourning the father I'd never known!

After a while, I made myself get up, convinced I might freeze altogether, die, if I stayed in bed any longer. I felt heavy and lethargic as I made myself a cup of tea. After I'd drunk it, I fetched the photo of my father, the one I'd found at Flo's, and stared at the sober little five-year-old, the only child not smiling. How would it have been if he'd married Mum? Would there have been a Trudy, a Declan, an Alison? If so, they would be different from the ones I knew now, and Tom O'Mara would never have existed. I remembered reading that if a time traveller went back to the beginning of time and destroyed a blade of grass, it could change the entire course of history.

It was all becoming too deep for me. Anyway, if I thought about it long enough it would be easy to cry and never stop. I took a long shower, made myself a decent breakfast for a change, then went to work, feeling only slightly better.

Stock Masterton was in turmoil. The Woolton office had been decorated and furnished; it was ready to move into the following day. To celebrate the opening, clients would be offered refreshments and a glass of wine. There were adverts in the local press, though no mention of the food and drink, otherwise there would be a deluge of people who had no intention of buying or selling a house.

Every file had been copied, duplicates made of the wall charts. The contents of Oliver and Diana's desks were transferred. People kept rushing in, collecting papers and rushing out again. I sat behind my desk, feeling dazed. I hadn't the faintest idea what was happening to me. Should I transfer my things to Woolton or not? George seemed to have forgotten that I was to have been the receptionist, just as he'd forgotten that Diana lived and breathed. I'd typed out my notice weeks ago and put it on his desk, but it had never been acknowledged. Yesterday he'd asked me to make an appointment early in January with a firm who were erecting a small estate in Seaforth and wanted Stock Masterton to handle the sales side.

'An appointment for you?' I enquired.

'No, for yourself, of course,' George replied testily. There was mention of someone called Sandra in the new office, but no one seemed sure what job she was to do.

Oliver was no help. He complained that he was being kept in the dark and was at loggerheads with George, though George hadn't noticed, and Jennifer, Oliver's wife, was touring commercial property agents, presenting him with sheafs of offices to rent when he got home. 'She's approached her father for a loan,' he said soon after I arrived. 'I told her that Diana's like a pricked balloon, but she said, "You never know, the whole thing might start up again." Would you come in with me, Millie?' he said plaintively. 'I don't think I could do it on my own.'

'I'd be glad to,' I told him, for the umpteenth time. Even if my job turned out to be safe, after all, I didn't think I could bring myself to trust George again.

To add further to my confusion Barry Green came up later in the morning and looked at me searchingly, as if he'd never seen me before, then gave a little 'Humph' of what sounded like approval. 'Tess has suggested I invite you round to dinner one night next week,' he said jovially. 'She said to please give her a ring if you'd like to come.'

I said I would, and meant it. I'd liked Tess enormously, and everything else about the Green household. I was thrilled to be asked to dinner.

Oliver took off again for Woolton. George was in his office, noisily slamming drawers and talking to himself. Everyone else was either at lunch or in Woolton, except for Darren, who had taken a client to view Nancy O'Mara's old house in Clement Street. I'd seriously thought of buying the place myself, cutting my mortgage by a third. After about half a minute, I realised it would be wrong, like going back instead of forward.

I leaned on my desk and thought about Flo, who would always remain a mystery, even though I knew so much about her. Had she been happy in the flat in William Square with her memories of Tommy O'Mara? Flo, with her secret lover, her secret child, the weekends spent with Mr Fritz on the Isle of Man.

George appeared, clutching his forehead dramatically, and announced that he was off to the Wig and Pen to have a pint and a panic attack. June had already left for lunch.

There'd been numerous times in the past when I'd been in the office alone, but when George slammed the door, it was like being shut in a place I'd never been before. I looked around uneasily, as if adjusting to strange new surroundings. There were decorations, very tasteful: a silver tree with 'presents' – a dozen empty boxes wrapped in red and green foil – and silver bells pinned to the walls. The fluorescent lights seemed to be humming much too loudly. Outside, people hurried past, loaded with carrier bags, and I remembered that the sales were on. The sound of the endless traffic was oddly muted, and I had a sensation of being in a different dimension, and while I could see the people, they couldn't see me. The light, bouncing off one of the silver bells on the wall behind, was reflected in turn on to the screen of the computer, and all I could see was the dark shadow of my head surrounded by a bright, blurred halo. I stared at the screen, hypnotised, and the shadows seemed to shift and change until I thought I could see a face, but it wasn't mine. The eyes were very old, set in deep, black hollows, the mouth was . . .

The phone on my desk rang stridently. I jumped and grabbed the receiver, glad to escape from the face on the screen. It was Declan.

'Could you come to Mam's early tonight?' he said eagerly. The Camerons and the Daleys had been invited to Charmian and Herbie's New Year's Eve party.

'Why?'

'You'll never guess what our Trudy's bought!' Declan paused for effect. 'Champagne! I've never had champagne before. We're going to drink to the future, before we go upstairs. Oh, and there'll be a special guest – Scotty!'

I laughed, delighted, and promised to be there by eight. When I rang off, there was no longer a face on the computer, merely the dazzling reflection of a silver bell, and the office appeared quite normal. A man tapped on the window and made the thumbs-up sign. He could see me, I was real. I smiled at him and he opened the door.

'You should bottle that smile and sell it, luv,' he said. 'You'd make a fortune.'

I knew then that I'd come through. My mind cleared, and I was myself again, but better than the self I'd been before. The future no longer seemed bleak and hopeless, but bright and full of promise. Never again would I dream about slithering footsteps on the stairs or wake up with a feeling that something was missing from my life. I stretched my arms as wide as they would go, scarcely able to contain the sensation of total happiness.

There was wine on Elliot's desk. I went over and poured myself a glass just as the door opened and a boy came in, not very tall, with an engaging face burned dark brown by the sun. He looked so ridiculous I had to smile. A long mac swirled around his muddy, wrinkled boots, but the comical thing about him was his hat: a brown felt beehive with a wide turned-up brim and a brightly patterned band.

'Hi!' He grinned, and lines of merriment crinkled beneath his eyes and around his mouth. I realised that this wasn't a boy but a man. I recognised the young rebel in the photographs Tess Green had showed me on Boxing Day, as well as her impish smile.

I returned to my desk. 'If you're looking for your father, I'm afraid he's out, I'm not sure where.'

'Shit,' he said amiably. 'Will he be long?'

'I'm not sure about that, either.'

'How come you know who I am?'

'Your mum showed me your photograph.'

He grinned again. 'Did she now?'

The atmosphere in the office had changed yet again. There was a tingling in the air, a crackle of excitement.

'So, you're just back from Mexico,' I said.

'That's right, early this morning. Dad had left for work by then, and Mum suggested I come and make my peace. I'd promised to be home for Christmas, you see, but got delayed. Dad gets worked up about these things, not like Mum. I had to borrow his matinée-idol mac. I mislaid my coat somewhere on the journey.' He gestured vaguely. 'He'll be annoyed.'

I could feel my lips twitching and longed to laugh. 'It's a pity you didn't mislay your hat instead.'

He removed the beehive and regarded it dispassionately. His hair was yellow, like wild straw. 'All the men wear them in Mexico.'

'This is Liverpool,' I reminded him.

'So it is.' He threw the hat to me like a frisbee. I caught it and put it on. 'It suits you. Keep it, not to wear, to hang on the wall.'

'Thanks. Help yourself to a drink while you're waiting.'

He poured a glass of wine and perched on the edge of his father's desk. I noticed his eyes were very blue, his face neither ugly nor handsome. It was an interesting face, open and expressive, and I could tell he had a great sense of humour. 'You obviously know loads about me,' he said, 'but I bet you'll be astounded to learn I also know a lot about you. You're Millie Cameron, you live in Blundellsands, have just dumped a boyfriend called James, and are in a bit of a tizzy over your job.'

'What on earth possessed your mum to tell you that?' I wasn't sure whether to be annoyed or not.

'Because – you'll be horrified to hear this – she really fancies you for a daughter-in-law. She started pinning my ear back about it the minute I arrived home. That's the real reason she asked me to come, not to see Dad but to see you.'

I released the laughter I'd been trying to contain ever since he came in. 'That's a mad idea.'

'I just thought I'd warn you, because I understand you've been invited to dinner next week, when Mum will really get to work on you.'

'Will you be there?'

'She'll handcuff me to the chair if I refuse. What about you? Will you come?'

'Under the circumstances,' I said gravely, 'I'll have to give the matter some thought.'

I removed the Mexican hat, which suddenly felt too heavy, and laid it carefully on the desk. The door opened and Oliver came in, followed by a sullen Diana.

'Do you fancy lunch?' Sam Green said. 'We can laugh ourselves silly over my mother.' Our eyes met fleetingly and I felt something pass between us. I had no idea if it meant something or not.

I reached for my bag. 'Why not?'

And why not go to dinner at the Greens next week. If the truth be known, I quite liked Sam Green, and fancied Tess for a mother-in-law. Nothing might come of it, but so what? As Peter Maxwell said, we were all dancing in the dark.